ASTRAL PLANE

JOSEPH SCHWAB

ISBN:
978-1-952874-47-5 (paperback)
978-1-952874-48-2 (hardback)
978-1-952874-49-9 (ebook)

Published by:

 **OMNIBOOK**Co.

OMNIBOOK CO.
99 Wall Street, Suite 118
New York, NY 10005
USA
+1-866-216-9965
www.omnibookcompany.com

First Edition

For e-book purchase: Kindle on Amazon, Barnes and Noble
Book purchase: Amazon.com, Barnes & Noble, and
www.omnibookcompany.com

Omnibook titles may be purchased in bulk for educational, business, fund-raising, or sales promotional use. For more information please e-mail **info@omnibookcompany.com**

TABLE OF CONTENTS

BOOK 1

BOOK 2

BOOK 1

1

ENTER THE ASTRAL PLANE

JACK STOOD WITHIN THE DREAMSCAPE SURROUNDED BY A MASSIVE CRATER, the ruin of the once massive city all around him; filled with frustration and anger, he stared down his opponent who was looking past him.

Jack questioned aloud "How did it come to this?"

To which his opponent replied "You know how, you let your curiosity get the better of you. You wanted to escape".

Jack could hear the battle around them still raging: the chorus of explosions, the clamor of weapons, the cracking sound of fire, and the sounds of destruction. Jack readied himself for the task ahead, keeping his senses trained on his enemy.

He looked forward at his opponent who seemed confident as they said mockingly "You cannot hope to win, look at the devastation around you; such power cannot be matched by you or anyone else"

Jack was uncertain he could win, though he had faced many things within the dream realm during the past few weeks, yet nothing was comparable to his present challenge. His opponent confidently awaited his response as Jack's mind was torn between fighting and the prospect of his demise. With his weapons ready he made his decision remembering 3 months ago how it had begun...

A man sits at his desk writing a paper, dressed in a collared shirt, vest, slacks, and leather shoes/belt that suggest a professional attire, he is a tall and thin man with thin light colored hair, and from his surroundings of books and news magazines show evidence of previous education as well as efforts to stay informed; however, a deeper study shows no sign of anyone else: no pictures on the walls, a phone that haven't been used in days, no personal mail, and a calendar that is virtually blank.

He writes a finishing commentary to his latest paper: "Throughout history man has always wondered about the meanings and causes of dreams, and even as modern science continues to rationalize and explain many phenomena dreams still remain a mystery. Why do we have them? What purpose do they serve? What do they mean? Perhaps one day science shall once again reveal the answers, but with all the deep philosophical, mystical, and emotional symbolism contained within the scope of dreams one must ask: are we ready to know?".

He adds this commentary onto his short article on the subject of dreams then puts the papers into an envelope and addresses it to the magazine he occasionally writes for, then sighs, mails the letter and returns to his basement workshop.

Meet Jack, an impassioned and obsessed writer and amateur scientist currently struggling to unravel the mysteries of REM sleep and the subconscious. Jack has always been an introvert preferring his own company to others; his wariness of the impersonal nature of modern society has caused him to slowly isolate himself from everyone, perceiving general society as hollow and empty. Jack is an intellectual, often researching and studying subjects that interest him from the comfort of his computer or the solitude of his books; he earns his income by writing fiction in his spare time, often trying to include concepts of science and technology within his stories.

However, one subject that he has always felt deep interest in is the experiences of his own dreams. Jack often wrote down, analyzed, and discussed them in some of his articles; though the deeper Jack delved into the subject the more uncertain he was. He finds that no one knows for certain why the brain causes dreams to occur, nor is it fully understood what the brain does during that time; the only things that are certain is that nearly all dreams occur during REM (rapid eye movement) sleep and that dreams for many people have somewhat similar themes and content. Jack had his own theories and believed with practice that he could control and manipulate his dreams. If successful he believed it would be possible to begin exploring the subconscious and find the answers to why people feel the way they do, what motivates and compels them, perhaps even the nature of the emotions.

Jack's fascination with dreams began nearly 10 years ago, when he worked as a service technician for a company that mostly did maintenance contract work for clinics and hospitals. Owing to his methodical nature and love for computers, he excelled in troubleshooting the software bugs that came up in complicated equipment. Jack was described by his co-workers as "the odd guy" since he kept to himself and had a dress style and sense of humor that was unconventional to them. Jack originally came from a large family and had to deal with the contentions of being a middle child in a large, traditional household; this helped him build up a thick skin to confrontations, which he typically coped with by suppressing his emotions that would cause most people to become upset or angry on the spot.

In effect this gave Jack the outward appearance of being very stoic and passionless, the reality was that things did very much annoy and irritate Jack; though there were only a few that he would confide his frustrations to, for the most part he just preferred to keep his reactions to himself. If something did manage to upset him greatly, which was rare, he tended to explode with anger and make decisions off impulse. This had only occurred a few times in his entire life though, as even his close friends could only recall a handful of times they had ever seen Jack "enraged".

Jack's work did come fairly easy to him, leading him to become bored with his unchallenging profession; he was also increasingly vexed by the overly bureaucratic management, which treated him more like a number in a system rather than an actual person. During one job Jack was commissioned to fix a prototype mental scanner at an institute for sleep therapy, the prototype scanner was designed to record brainwave activity and translate it into computer information. The institute was using the machine to study dreams by recording and comparing the results using specialized computers, against database responses to various images and sounds from the participants while they were conscious. Jack was immediately fascinated with the concept and spoke at length with the head researcher about dreams, their causes, and the leading theories in the field. After the repairs Jack visited the facility a number of times personally to inquire on the subject and to track what progress they had made.

However, the institute was funded by a research grant which eventually expired, and when the money ceased coming in the institute had to discontinue its research and was shuttered. For most people the fascination would have ended there; however, Jack often became committed to subjects upon taking an interest in them, often pursuing them with an almost obsessive drive.

As Jack became more involved with the subject it began to distract him from his work, as he talked even less with management and co-workers who only seemed to bore him with small talk. Jack always preferred his own company to others, so he didn't notice there was a problem until the day he unintentionally slighted his superior and was suspended from work for a month.

While suspended he had a lot of time to consider the possibility that his life had taken an unsatisfactory direction, ultimately leaving him feeling empty. Jack was discussing the topic with his good friend, one of the only people Jack could speak candidly with. Jack's friend, who had heard at length Jack's dream theories and stories, recommended an interesting idea: that he try writing about one of his dreams as if it were a fiction story.

Jack was reluctant about the idea but decided to try anyway, changing the details and grammatical structure of one of his dreams so it read more like a story instead of an analysis. After lengthy revision and multiple drafts he had a workable story, he submitted it to a number of publishing houses and magazines who promptly dismissed most of his work as "amateurish" and "poorly communicated". Jack was hardly a people person so he was unable to persuade any of the publishers to take a serious look at it; just when he was ready to give up a relatively unknown magazine contacted him interested in the story, just the break he needed.

Jack's short stories were published in the magazine and within a short time they became an unexpected sensation, readers loved the stories based on original ideas and eagerly looked forward to each new entry made by him; other magazines quickly picked up Jack's stories and he suddenly had enough offers to make a respectable income from writing.

Jack lived with very modest means, buying few luxuries and only spending money on a few essentials; now that he was earning a respectable income from writing it was all he needed to get by. No longer needing his old job, he quit so he could focus more on his writing and personal life. He also began pursuing several hobbies that he previously didn't have time for; including martial arts lessons, digital art classes, watching more videos on history, he even took up a gym membership. This was all part of an effort to prioritize taking better care of his own wellbeing, now that he was freed from the endless stress and tedium of his previous job.

Jack also began discussing more of his ideas and theories regarding dreams with his peers, but was frustrated when those around him seemed to disregard what he said as unimportant or worse, when they flat out ignored what he said. Jack decided that perhaps the only way he would find satisfaction would be to find a soul mate who would be interested in the same things as him, so he embarked on a barrage of online dating and social clubs.

However, he had virtually no experience in relationships, even less so with women, so he ended up rushing headlong into a marriage with a woman named Eleanor that he didn't realize wasn't compatible with him in the first place. Though Eleanor and he had many of the same *interests* they had nearly opposite *personalities*: he was an introvert, she was an extrovert; He liked solitude and quiet, she liked social gatherings and people; he was a pessimist, she was an optimist. The list of contradictions went on and on.

These differences were aggravated by the fact that Jack was inept at reading people and was terrible at finding the right things to say when to say them, so many of the talks they had ended up degenerating into Jack fumbling with his words and saying something that Eleanor perceived as an insult, then it would detract into a prolonged argument which only served to frustrate them both. When the relationship started to fall apart Jack tried to overcompensate with dinner outings and gifts, but it was only serving to slow the collapse of an already doomed relationship. After 2 years of marriage Eleanor filed for divorce and left Jack almost overnight.

Jack was devastated by the divorce, shouldering the blame on himself while becoming increasingly distraught and depressed. He also had a lot of trouble finding comfort with his family; who didn't seem to understand what he was going through, and from his perspective their advice amounted to throwing his relational mistakes and hasty marriage back in his face rather focusing on how to move forward.

Jack was on the verge of a breakdown; he was increasingly angry with everyone around him and was losing his patience constantly over even trivial matters; his good friend could see this and managed to persuade him to take some time away from the things so he could relax on and get his mind off his problems. Jack agreed and decided to move into an isolated house in the countryside where he could relax and separate himself from society for a while. Still having adequate sums of money, despite the divorce, he remembered his old interest in dreams; and proceeded to acquire some of the research papers, notes, and instruments left by the institute that Jack previously took an interest in before it was disbanded.

Now after years of exploring the subject, Jack had developed his own theories on dreams and believed with practice that he could control and manipulate them, once doing he could begin exploring his subconscious and find the answers to why people feel the way they do, what motivated and compelled them, perhaps even the nature of the emotions.

For three years now Jack has tried various meditation techniques and sleeping in different ways with different external stimuli, but to no effect. Then one day he reads of neurology breakthroughs using a new configuration on the machine he possessed that was made to stimulate brain waves directly using various low electrical currents; this was a more advanced and experimental version of the machine he had remembered working on years before. The instruments needed to make the conversion were still in the prototype stages and were highly experimental, but Jack was determined to try anything. After purchasing and installing the new equipment, which nearly cost him all the funds he had left, he began by having the machine record his brain waves during various dreams. Jack then found which sections were active during dreams and what mental patterns were exhibited during REM sleep; he then methodically tested the machine to see if he could recreate those patterns to initiate a dream using the external current of the machine to influence the brain's internal electrical fluctuations (or brainwaves). After a long year of trial, experimentation, recording, and modifying Jack finally believed he had isolated the electrical pattern behind the activity of dreaming. Jack decided that after he had finished the final calibrations he would test the machine at full power on himself, and hopefully be capable of experiencing the dream with full awareness and cognition.

Jack scurried around his lab making the final preparations and running last minute simulations, believing that the machine was safe to use and would deactivate if his vitals were to go into erratic ranges. Jack strapped himself in and activated the machine's timer, as it rapidly counted down he took a deep breath and closed his eyes. The machine hummed intensely as it commenced emitting the electrical sequence, Jack's vision blurred, his hearing faded out, and he felt if though he were spinning in a giant centrifuge as the walls and objects of the room spun outwards to oblivion; the sheer intensity of the experience is greater than Jack has ever felt as he clenched his fists and grimaces at the sensation like being shot into space or flung into a whirlpool. Suddenly as transmitted instantly to another place, he found himself standing atop of a grassy hill overlooking a peaceful village.

"What is this place? Have I done it, is this a dream?" Jack said aloud as he surveyed the nearby landscape.

Hearing the distant echo of a church bell, Jack turned to see a small row village in the foothills nearby. It was sunset here, as the twilight illuminated the clouds in bright hues of orange and red, he saw rolling acres of farmland surrounded by a wall of conifers stretching into the horizon, and he could hear the breeze lightly blowing across the landscape.

He was astounded, this place seemed so real, how could it possibly be a dream; deciding to explore the village out of curiosity he proceeded forwards in search of what this place held. Walking down a winding path through the fields towards the main road running down the center of the village, along the way he brushed the fields of grass to see if it was some kind of illusion, yet it too felt so real. He walked into a pub with the sign title "Traveler's Way" and surveyed the inside. He saw a host of characters all dressed in ordinary clothing enjoying drinks and talking about the day, with the usual ambience of drinks being poured, glasses and silverware clanging, and the dull roar of people in conversation. An old voice with an odd accent catches Jack's ear from a nearby table.

"Greeting friend, you look as if you have lost your way",

Jack turns to his right to see an old man clothed in a robe sitting at a table, replying. "I'm not lost, rather more confused than anything else"

The old man says "Then sit, and perhaps I clarify your confusion".

Jack walked over, pulled up a chair, and sat down. Scanning the old man briefly with his eyes, he could see that he was clothed in a brown robe, had a long grey beard, wore sandals, and the shadow of his hood was covering everything but the lower half of his face which was drawing smoke from a long wooden pipe; if Jack didn't know any better he would swear this man was some sort of monk. The old man spoke first.

"I am Melchior, I have frequented this tavern many times, yet I have never seen you here before"

Jack thought for a moment then in a roundabout way answered the question with another question "What is here? What is this tavern? Is this some sort of way point or crossroads?"

Melchior rubbed his chin in curiosity and said "By your words it seems as though you almost don't believe that you're really here, it's almost as if...you're dreaming".

As Melchior finished his sentence Jack was a bit puzzled "That's what this is right, a dream"

Melchior answered "Yes if you wish to refer to it that way, this is a dream, but the fact that you realize that, and have not woken up is most perplexing to me".

Jack doesn't really understand the context of what Melchior is describing and so inquired "I don't understand what you mean".

Melchior began explaining "Conscious minds visit this place only briefly, and when they do it is as if they are caught in a haze; unaware and at a distance, both here and not here so to speak. Any realization of theirs abruptly ends their journey as they awaken from that state and return to whence they came." Melchior paused and drew another puff from his pipe before continuing.

"However, I see that you are clearly here with all of your mental faculties, and that you are aware of this place, this should be impossible...yet here you stand".

Jack attempted to explain what was happening but he was still slightly confused as what Melchior was getting to "I am a sort of explorer, a scientist maybe, and I have discovered a way through the use of a machine... to directly cause my subconscious to enter a dream"; Melchior looked confused, but his tone changed from curious to a tone of ominous warning.

"My friend, you have stumbled upon our world without understanding what it really is, if it is true that your machine allows you to travel through it in full form; then you are exposing yourself to its full danger of this place".

Now Jack wanted to know who was this man, and why he seemed to know so much and curiously asked "How is it that you know so much of this place, what are you exactly"

Melchior explained "I am a construct, a figment of the human imagination designed to represent or symbolize something. More specifically I am one of the old fables in your lore; I have long existed here, travelling and learning about the many wonders of this plane's realms".

Jack inferred "This plane? As in a plane of existence, so this isn't limited only to my subconscious?"

Melchior replied with a short laugh "No my friend, your subconscious is but the tip of the iceberg; you have stumbled into something far deeper: the *Astral Plane*".

Jack said in curiosity "*Astral Plane* - that sounds a bit hard to believe, what is it exactly?"

Melchior sat back in his chair and said "Are you certain you wish to know?"

Jack leaned forward with interest "Yes, this is what I have spent a great deal of my life trying to discover".

Melchior took a deep breath then began "The *Astral Plane* is the culmination of all human creativity, deep-seated emotions, and fantasy; here all the things you have ever thought or experienced, real and unreal, come together in a continuous realm. In this place all the things you have ever wanted or wished to do are possible; all the legends and creations you have ever imagined are real, and all your emotions take their fullest, truest form.

Melchior detailed as he concluded "Your unconscious mind keeps a constant connection to this place, through it you act as you would not, do as you cannot, and live as you may not; this connection in effect satisfies the needs of the soul and keeps one from losing their sanity".

Jack was beyond belief, he wasn't even sure what he was supposed to say, he collected his thoughts and continued "So this place is not only the source of our emotions, creativity, and fantasy but is also a refuge for the unconscious"

Melchior replied happily "Yes my friend, I see that you finally understand".

As Melchior finished the church bell rang out once more yet this time its sound seemed to come from everywhere and made everything tremble with each chime, as it grew louder and louder Jack could hear a distant voice chanting a somber tune.

Jack said nervously "What is happening, everything is shaking, and this noise is everywhere"

Melchior responded speaking quickly "You are being sent back to your world, my friend it pains me it pains me greatly to say this but you must not return using your machine, you are putting yourself in grave danger"

Jack frantically said as everything drifted further and further out of existence "But there is so much more I need to know, many more questions unanswered" as he said that his perception went black.

Once again felt that gut-wrenching sensation he felt upon activating the machine pulling from all directions like a cataclysmic chaotic spiral. Finally, everything stopped and he opened his eyes to find himself back within his workshop.

2
VENTURE

Jack awakened to a splitting headache and turned to the machine's last reading which showed a near overload of activity, this must have caused a short circuit in the machine's vast micro-network of electric emitters, the shock from which is what probably woke him up. "Damn!!" he exclaimed, pounding the table near the bed in anger.

Somewhat frustrated he vented his frustration "I was so close, I could have learned so much", calming himself down he unstrapped himself and powered down the machine. Unable to clear his thoughts, Jack decided to take a break and contemplate what happened.

Jack strolled out of the basement of his house and set out on a walk through the countryside, he often took long walks to clear his mind to contemplate concepts or think of new approaches to problems. As he walked through the field surrounding his house he began talking aloud to himself, something he did more often than he realized.

"This *Melchior* character must have known a great deal more about this *"Astral Plane"*, what if it's possible to access the subconscious from its source? What if it's possible to use it to boost a mind's creativity through channeling that place, and what about the other constructs, and the knowledge it could possess? All that history and culture lost, could it be recovered?".

He walked a great distance through the winding trail his repeated walks had paved, all the while thinking of all the things that he could possibly do in this new frontier he had discovered, the sheer potential of discovery seemed limitless to him. Jack finally reached a favored spot of his: a stream surrounded by tall birch trees where he often contemplated subjects of deep thought, Jack sat down and relaxed for a moment, the gentle sound of the creek flowing calmed his mood. Once fully and completely composed he began considering the other side of going back: the risk.

"Melchior warned me that I shouldn't come back, that it was dangerous; what of all the malevolent things ever imagined, what danger could they pose to me? What of the risk to my own mind? The machine nearly over loaded, could it have killed me? And what if my tinkering in the *Astral Plane* adversely affects my brain?". Jack pondered these questions and more as he watched the early morning sunrise bring forth a new day, Jack sat there lost in thought, wordless for hours.

He thought of all the progress he had made, all the cherished dreams he personally had, and he mentally re-enacted the conversation between him and Melchior many times. Finally he made his decision as he spoke "If I throw away my only chance at unlocking this mystery now, I will regret it the rest of my life; no matter what danger lies ahead, I must continue".

Getting back up he headed back for his workshop and began mentally going over the repairs and modifications needed while he walked. Once he arrived, he began scribbling notes on a dozen sheets of paper haphazardly cataloging his experience; then he poured over the machine's readings during the dream's transmission.

Jack could clearly see that the machine was needed to initiate the brainwave sequences that lead to a dream, but that afterwards the dream continued on a self-sustaining course; any further input from the machine was unnecessary and was probably what led to the reading overload and hence the abrupt awakening. He replaced the shorted circuit and reprogrammed the machine to start the sequence but to stop shortly afterwards, Jack also toned down the machine's power to a slight degree hoping it would reduce the intense spinning sensation he felt upon entering the dream. Though Jack still did have one serious problem, if the dream was self-sustaining once it started and he doesn't awaken under normal circumstances (as Melchior inferred) then he may have a very serious problem exiting the dream state. Jack didn't know how deep of sleep he entered into but hoped that a shock like the one the machine accidently gave him might be enough to wake him up, so he rigged up a primitive shock device to himself that would be activated on a timer set to 3 hours, more than enough time he hoped to do everything he needed to do.

Before Jack used the machine again he suspected there was a probability something bad may happen, so he took a few hours to make final preparations in his personal life. First, he made himself his favorite dish making sure to add all the necessary spices/garnishments, cooking every ingredient evenly, and then taking the time to fully savor each bite. Then drew up a semi-legal will to impart what little he had remaining to his few cherished friends and relatives, making sure to allocate what he thinks each individual could most use or most want. Afterwards he attempted his most difficult task: writing the letter to his ex-wife who left him. Despite his writing experience he could only manage to write a brief statement, being unable to convey in writing anything that could accurately express what he felt. After staring at the near empty page for nearly an hour, he simply dropped the pen and proceeded forward leaving the unfinished letter as "Dear Eleanor, though our marriage ended those years ago, I can't help but feel regret…".

Now determined to return, he made the necessary repairs to bring the machine operational. Once he finished the initial tests, he prepared himself mentally for what was to follow; in his case taking a moment to focus on the ambient music he had playing in the background: a high energy classical song.

Jack walked over to the stereo, reset the track, then turned the volume up to where he could hear it throughout the room and sat down. As the music played he closed his eyes, concentrating on the song, letting it clear his confused thoughts replacing them with its bold melodies, giving him courage for the task ahead. As it finished he finally brought himself to take action. Once ready he lied down, strapped himself in, and prepared to re-enter the *"Astral Plane"*. Upon activating the machine he was once again greeted by the intense spinning sensation, much less reduced but still violent as reality is stripped away and he suddenly found himself back within the village.

After some quick observation Jack was able to confirm that this was without a doubt the same village he visited previously, the only thing that is different is the time of day, which had changed from sunset to mid-morning, though he wasn't sure what rules governed the passage of time in this dream realm. Thinking aloud he wondered:

"This is the same place; perhaps all dreams really are connected to this… *Astral Plane*, as Melchior referred to it". Jack proceeded to search for the "Traveler's Way" tavern from before, deciding to revisit in hopes of finding Melchior.

Entering the tavern he found only two figures: the barkeep, who seemed busy cleaning, and a professional looking man who looked to be waiting for something. The unknown man was tall, thin, slightly pale, with his hair shaved bald; he wore an expression of a calm, cool, collected person. This character's outward persona was matched by his attire: an impeccable business suit which looked as if it was hand-tailored; he was leaning against the bar counter with a cup of steaming tea in one hand.

Jack walked over to the barkeep and asked "Do you know where I can find an old monk named Melchior?"

The barkeep scratched his head in thought for a moment and replied with a folksy accent "He comes here pretty infrequently; the last time he was here was...hmmm a few days ago".

Jack was stunned by this exclaiming, "What! I just talked to him yesterday??"

Upon hearing this, the man in the business suit replied in a calm confident tone "Time flows differently here *Traveler*, it often proceeds much faster than where you are from, and is also not often bound by sequential constraints."

He turned to the man and asked bluntly "What do you know about me, stranger, I don't recall speaking to you?".

The man replied with a smile "Word spreads quickly of your arrival, *Traveler*, we have not had a visitor such as you for a very long time."

Stunned at hearing there were others like him that had visited in the past replied "I have only come here out of curiosity, I am not... whatever this role or title that you are implying."

The man replied semi cryptically "In this place it doesn't matter what others perceive you to be, but what you perceive yourself to be".

Jack was groaning internally at hearing such amateur philosophy, such as he had many times in life by others and slightly dismissively replied, "Whoever you are, I didn't come here for a lecture on philosophy; I came here for answers".

The man replied more directly "Very well, if answers are what you seek then follow the roads; be forewarned, you may not find what you expect".

Jack wasn't sure if he could trust this man or not, although he seemed professional enough his mannerisms were throwing Jack off, something about this guy didn't seem right.

Jack asked in suspicion, "What should I expect then?"

The man returned a vague and ambiguous reply "No one truly knows what the road will yield, answers come only if you are ready to accept them" with that he finished his drink, put two strange-looking coins on the counter, and left saying "Until we meet again, *Traveler*".

Jack quickly followed the man out thinking he could get more information; however, upon reaching the outside of the tavern he could see no trace of the man, not even footprints.

"Strange" Jack wondered to himself "It is as if he vanished entirely, was he entirely present in the first place… Hmm".

After looking around he noticed that the village was at the center of a crossroads, each road leading to a far off horizon; however he could see no distractive landmarks in the distance.

Jack looked to the northern road almost laughing to himself as he thought of what the man said "No one truly knows what the road will yield, PFFFT!" mockingly imitating what he heard before.

Then he looked at the road again…truly considering it; after thinking of a number of possibilities he finally decided to take a chance and start walking. As he walked his mind entered a sort of trance, and as he moved the scenery around him seemed to move faster and faster until it seemed as though everything was a blur. Snapping out of the trance as swiftly as he entered it, he was now in another place entirely, completing what seemed a journey of a thousand miles in one instant. Jack kneeled over and was compelled to rest from a sudden exhaustion, yet it wasn't a strictly physical exhaustion.

"What was that?! Some sort of teleportation, how was I able to travel so fast?" he finally looked up after regaining his stamina and saw that he was no longer in the village.

Calm and peaceful ocean surrounded him as far as the eye could see, dotted with islands of white sand and small palm tree groves; the rolling of the waves and calling of the seagulls gave the ambience of a coast.

A mystic voice whispered all around him "Welcome to *Venture*, where the never ending horizon eternally satisfies the yearning of the adventurer"

Jack answered "What? Who's there?" but there was no response.

After observing the view Jack turned his attention to his immediate surroundings; he was definitely on a small island but the road he arrived from was gone, then he saw something that seemed out of place: a strange old flying machine.

"What is this doing here?!" Jack said perplexed, after examining it further he figured out what it was: it was an Ornithopter (a flying machine that used flapping wings). He remembered a report he did on flying craft back in school years ago, ornithopters were first invented by Leonardo Da Vinci as a machine that would theoretically make flight by humans possible; however, it wasn't until hundreds of years later that the first flyable ones were made, but the vast majority of prototypes failed miserably.

As Jack examined the aircraft he saw a strange multicolored flash in the distance that began radiating a distant faint light, whatever it was he knew it was worth investigating. Jack began weighing his options: he could attempt swimming from island to island, but he knew that would be a mistake as he was not a good swimmer. His second option then was to attempt flying the ornithopter, yet he couldn't help but remember all the black and white videos of similar-looking prototypes crashing hard over and over again.

Nervously gathering his courage he determined "Alright, it's all or nothing".

Jack climbed into the machine's small circular cab and sat in the pilot's seat; he was nervous about this small, rickety looking, wooden and canvas machine. In front of him was a steering wheel and 3 levers; Jack cranked the first lever down, as he did the aircraft's wings began flapping which slowly lifted the ornithopter off the ground.

Jack cranked the 2nd lever ahead making the aircraft tilt forward, he then cranked that same lever back and the aircraft tilted backwards; he was quickly getting used to flying the machine as he cranked the 2nd lever forward and the aircraft began flying towards the flash on the horizon. The aircraft flew forward but was still close to the ground; as it headed towards a row of palm trees directly in front of him, quickly reaching for the third lever he cranked it backwards hoping it controlled altitude.

A gust of wind blew through his hair as the aircraft quickly gained altitude, barely avoiding collision before soaring over the trees. "Jeez! Close call!" he said as his pulse was still racing from nearly crashing.

As the aircraft flew gently through the air he finally started to trust the old "rickety" machine, flying it to and fro and enjoying the view from above the islands. Joyfully he flew the machine for close to an hour getting ever closer to the light in the distance as it grew brighter, but then something else came into view; ominous figures appeared in the horizon bearing down on him. The distant figures were rapidly closing the distance, and as they came closer their shape became distinguishable: they were giant birds with shiny feathers, giant birds of prey!

Not wanting to discover their intentions he cranked the first lever to the floor making the machine's wings flap at full speed, then he lowered the altitude as close to the ground as possible and weaved between the islands' palm trees and large rocks. The three birds bore down on him, pursuing closely; as they got closer they readied their talons and screeched loudly.

"What the Hell are these things?!" Jack yelled as he continued dodging back and forth trying to keep the birds from getting too close as they kept swiping at him with their huge talons.

He quickly wrenched the 2nd lever backwards making his machine pull a hard reverse briefly tricking the birds into flying right past him, but they circled around and were coming at him again from the front. Jack had to think fast! He was frantically searching the cab of the ornithopter for anything that could help, that's when he spotted a crossbow and a few dozen bolts mounted at the back of the cab.

Quickly grabbing the crossbow he started loading it as he cranked the 2nd lever forward once again launching him ahead; as it rushed towards the birds he steadied the crossbow at his target. Jack yelled in a moment of fear and reckless bravery as he fired the crossbow at the bird straight in front of him! The bolt struck the bird hard punching a hole clear through the feathery beast, sending it spiraling to the ground! The other two birds darted off to the sides in surprise as the aircraft sped by them.

Looking at the crossbow in amazement he admired "Impressive! This crossbow is more powerful than it looks I guess," though he had little time to admire the weapon as the birds resumed the chase forcing him to continue fleeing.

He was now very close to whatever the source of this shining light was but the birds were relentless and stayed right on top of him; he tried to evade once more, but this time the bird shadowed the aircrafts every move then swiped at the wood and canvas wings with its powerful talons ripping a gaping hole. The machine hastily drifted towards the ground nearly spiraling out of control, he grabbed the steering wheel but it took all his strength just to keep it steady.

The machine was about to crash! He fought against the controls as the steering wheel violently shook yelling "Come on! Stay in the air just a little while longer!".

His eyes darted to every possible landing zone, that's when he spotted an island just ahead that appeared to be the source of the light shining he was chasing; he guided the aircraft down as best as he could to the beach. The machine hit the water so hard it skipped off its surface then crashed onto the island skidding to a halt as the wings and tail fins were torn off in the slide. He fell out of the side of the cab and rolled onto the sandy beach, throbbing with pain from the crash.

Jack tried to force himself up he heard the screeching of the birds still on his trail while frantically reloading the crossbow.

One of the birds dove towards him as he reached up and fired yelling "Die! You infernal bird!!" The bolt struck the bird with incredible force killing it instantly, the huge corpse nearly crashing onto him as he barely rolled out of the way.

The third and final bird landed in front of him and started approaching, staring him down with a killer look in its eyes. The spare ammo was lost in the crash, Jack threw the crossbow at the bird in desperation but it only bounced off its head, angering the beast. The bird opened its wide beak ready to snap Jack in half!

BOOM! he heard as the bird staggered back in shock.

Boom! Boom! Boom! As the bird fell backwards dead, the shiny strange looking feathers still fluttering in the air from the impact force of whatever killed it; in the distance Jack saw the man wearing the business suit holding a smoking gun, before he could say or do anything the man nodded and with a smirk disappeared into the palm tree grove.

Jack wasn't sure what just happened, but he wasn't about to let the prospect of nearly getting killed stop him; not when he had gotten this far, he was going to find out what the source of the light was. Picking himself up and dusting out the sand from his clothes, he followed the light to a peaceful freshwater oasis in the middle of a palm tree grove; floating above the center of the pool was a yellow orb of light. Stunned by the strangeness of the sight, he could hear a low humming and as he approached the orb, making him feel like he was somehow energized in its presence.

Wading into the water he grasped the orb as he did he was overcome by a surge of visions and sounds playing in his mind at blazing speed, he began to recognize certain figures and places from the confusion, specifically moments from the greatest times of his life, times when he felt so alive: his first car, the day he got published, the first computer he made. Jack was suddenly back at the oasis feeling as if a pulse of energy had flowed through him, he felt as he did each of those times full of energy and enthusiasm, like he was electrified, the sensation was incredible. Jack suddenly realized he was floating *above* the oasis waters but had no clue how he got there. As he floated towards the ground he noticed his movements were greatly sped up blurring as he moved but without fatigue, he tested its limits jumping into the air nearly 50 feet before landing back onto the ground without the slightest impact.

Jack exclaimed, "This is amazing! What is this feeling? This power?!" He wondered marveling at this feat of being able to move his hands with such speed that they became a blur. He observed a fading yellow light emanating from his hands as it faded away, the faster-than-normal speed also stopped as everything returned to normal.

Jack was beginning to think the vision and resulting sensation must've been his subconscious: specifically his thoughts of energy, excitement, and anticipation; the orb then must have been either a piece of his subconscious, or some sort of energy form which unleashed it.

"At last! Some progress" he said aloud while strolling down the beach pondering what it meant.

Reflecting on what happened, he was trying to discern a pattern or a key to the events thus far; before he could make any discernible progress though he began to hear a loud horn call in the distance. As the horn's sound grew louder it began to tremble the very ground itself, the sky suddenly filled with clouds and the sea grew more turbulent. The horn began to crescendo as a tidal wave rose and crashed into Jack, his vision went black and he awoke back in his lab with the electrode shocking his leg.

3

EPIC

Jack awoke in his lab, it took him a moment to discern reality from what he had just experienced immediately prior, but he then quickly regained his senses. After removing the device he looked at the clock to see that it was about half an hour past when he was supposed to wake up, the electrode device must have been shocking him for quite a while.

Sitting upright he took a moment to concentrate on staying awake, once he was fully alert he got back on his feet and walked over to his notes. Jack began organizing and cataloging all the new information he had come across, but he had only just barely scratched the surface of all the information hidden within this *Astral Plane*. Upon scanning the mental readings of the machine he observed very intense, unusual activity in one section of the brain that spiked only to die down again; Jack wondered if that was from the orb he encountered, but he wasn't sure so he would have to wait for it to occur again.

From what he could recollect it became clear that this *Astral Plane* held potentially dangerous obstacles to his progress, such as the giant birds he encountered; surely there were more such creatures and enemies awaiting him, so he would need tools and information if he was to survive future encounters.

Jack decided to search the internet in hopes of finding out what these creatures were, after a few minutes of searching combinations of different terms, he found something which seemed to match the description of the creatures: the Stymphalian Birds. The mythology described them as monstrous birds with metallic like feathers that appeared twice in ancient Greek lore, interestingly enough they were killed by the legendary hero Hercules using arrows.

Jack thought to himself "Perhaps that's why the crossbow was so effective against them, but if these things are real in the *Astral Plane* that means much worse things are as well".

Jack was nervous at the prospect of facing other things similar to the birds in the *Astral Plane* but he remained committed as always to his goal despite these hesitations. Jack decided that the next time he entered the *Astral Plane* he would need to seek out weapons and perhaps some kind of guide, but first he needed a break from studying, so he rose from his chair and began his usual daily routine.

Jack lived by himself so he usually spent a good portion of the day cleaning, maintaining the premises, paying bills, and occasionally reading non-fiction books in his spare time. He had followed the same routine every day with mind numbing precision often letting his thoughts drift during his tasks, he imagined many things in order to pass the time and to give him something to think about.

Jack dragged his routine out more than usual taking extra time to perform his tasks then watched videos online to stall further; he wanted to be sure that he would need more than the usual amount of sleep giving him extra time to familiarize himself with the *Astral Plane*. Once the clock hit 2AM Jack decided that he had put off sleep long enough. Finishing his nightly routine of brushing his teeth and taking a shower he strapped himself into the machine, setting the electrical device to awaken him eight hours from the current time, then he activated the machine's sequence and after a brief delay, it sent him once again into the intense vortex sensation which seemed to act as the transition from reality to the subconscious.

Jack found himself once again in the village, this time it was in mid-day and the streets were filled with people busily shuffling around the streets. Jack decided before traveling on one of the roads he would revisit the "Traveler's Way" tavern in hopes of finding someone that could help him.

Jack entered the tavern instantly spotting the man in the business suit, but this time he was sitting at a table looking as though he was expecting Jack to arrive.

Jack quickly approached saying in a raised voice "You! You're the one who led me to that place with the birds!"

The man calmly retorted "I'm also the one who saved you from them, if I recall correctly"

Jack was frustrated but wasn't sure yet if this figure was a friend or enemy, the man continued "Sit, perhaps we can help each other".

Jack reluctantly pulled up a chair and sat down and the man brought his fingertips together in thought as he began a proposal "You have come to this place to seek answers, and I just so happen to know how to get what it is you seek; however, my knowledge comes at a price".

Jack sighed in disdain "What good is money in a place like this?"

The man clarified "I seek nothing as superficial as money, no, what I seek is your assistance *Traveler*".

Jack wasn't sure what this man could possibly want from him, but for now it was his only lead for information so he decided to play along "Alright say that I agree to help you, What it is exactly that you would want in return"

The man looked reassured and said "You'll know what I'm after soon enough, for now I will help you once more as a show of good faith, so ask a question and I shall answer".

Jack knew this man would probably only answer one major question so he asked the most pertinent one that came to mind "I need to know how to defend myself against the creatures of this place."

The man in the business suit thought for a moment then answered "The most knowledgeable are the wise men, seek out Balthazar for he is both wise and experienced in the various ways of the martial arts".

Jack pressed further, "How do I find Balthazar?"

The man replied almost in a riddle "Head down the roads, but be certain to think of conflict".

Jack was naturally confused by this answer and commented "That... doesn't make any sense?"

As the man in the business suit confidently assured "It will make sense with time *Traveler*, also, you may want to take this with you". As the man retrieved a familiar looking crossbow from under the table and slid it over to Jack.

Jack replied with surprise "This is the crossbow I killed those two birds with but it's..."

The man in the business suit commented "I took the liberty of making a few modifications to it, you're going to need it where you're going."

He then placed a quiver full of bolts on the table and described while getting up to leave "Make sure to concentrate your thoughts when firing as willpower affects everything in this place; if you are pressed to draw this weapon to defend yourself, do not hesitate to use it.".

Jack inquired about this figure's identity "Wait, who are you exactly?"

The man turned and answered with a bit of flare. "I am Malachi, revolutionary extraordinaire" then turned and continued out the door.

Jack sat in deep thought for a moment then with a flash of motivation got up and continued on his journey. He walked a short distance outside the town and took a moment to examine the crossbow: he could see that metal parts were added to increase the draw strength of the firing mechanism and a rifle stock was added for stable aiming; it was also now strung with a synthetic cable instead of string, metal sights were added, a strap for carrying, and the grip was now contoured.

Jack moved into an area devoid of the crowds milling about the streets and tried cocking it and found it was much easier (and faster) to reload. Upon firing the crossbow noticed that it fired with considerably more force, distance, and accuracy.

Jack said aloud upon noticing the improvements "Hmmm, a bit old fashioned but I think I like it, this weapon has a Renaissance feel to it".

With a weapon in hand and the goal of meeting this "Balthazar" Jack made his way back to the crossroads, intent to follow Malachi's advice walking down one of the roads, keeping in focus themes centering around conflict and warfare. As Jack walked down the road his movements are once again sped up as his surroundings became a blur and he suddenly covered a great distance in a single moment. He then came to a stop with the same mental fatigue he felt previously, though not as severe as the first time.

After Jack got his bearings he surveyed his surroundings to see that he is in a dark forest of tall trees that stretched into every direction and provided a thick shadowy canopy; the sound though is not one of a typical forest: upon entering he can hear the far-off clanging of weapons and distant echo of men yelling in battle.

A mystic voice whispers all around him "Welcome to *Epic*, where countless factions eternally battle, struggling to achieve supremacy in a never ending clash of ambitions and ideologies."

Jack recognizes the voice from before and once again tries to speak with it saying "Who are you?" but he is again met by silence.

Jack is uncertain of this place but his initial impression tells him that it is dangerous, even armed; he is fortunate enough that there is no combat in his immediate vicinity so he decides to try to carefully explore this new realm.

Jack wanders through the forest keeping a low profile and quietly walking through the underbrush and foliage. As Jack searches he observes men fighting each other with swords, axes, spears and bows usually ending with one overcoming the other with fatal results for the loser; there seems to be no consistency to the uniforms or the weapons of the warriors as

Jack spots things ranging from ancient Greek, late Renaissance, even some modern styles.

Jack could not distinguish any clear motive as to why any of the warriors are fighting, nor can he discern which faction is which, so he continues forward using subterfuge, hoping that his presence will go unnoticed. Jack comes upon a road in the forest but before he can decide whether or not to follow it a band of barbarians turns the corner marching down the road, Jack has no time to move away so he quickly dives into a bush. There are several wearing chainmail armor, metal-cone like helmets, and clutching two handed axes bearing a resemblance to medieval age barbarians. Jack doesn't want to encounter them but they are marching through checking their surroundings, on their present course they will soon discover him.

Jack decides to take a chance and begins to crawl away, but accidently snaps a large twig while crawling. The barbarians notice the disturbance and begin to raise an alarm so Jack stands up to reveal himself, as soon as he does the lead barbarian raises his hand signaling the others to stop and starts grunting at Jack pointing at him. Jack starts trying to reason with him "Hi, I…um…mean you no harm…"

The barbarian pointed his fist at Jack grunting as his tone became increasingly angry. Jack was starting to panic "Hey relax. I'm friendly, Ok?"

However his words were having no effect, the barbarian tightens the grip of the axe and prepares to fight; Jack quickly whips out the crossbow, the barbarian hesitates for a moment recognizing the weapon.

Jack steadied the crossbow with one hand while still trying to reason with them, gesturing them to calm down "This isn't what I want! Calm down." The lead barbarian reads his hesitation as weakness and rushes towards Jack, causing Jack to flinch and accidently fire the crossbow.

A sharp "FFFT!" is heard as the bolt struck the barbarian in the center of the chest and killed him in one fatal shot. The others became enraged and all charged at Jack! Jack quickly reloaded his crossbow and shot a second one before being forced to duck under the broad swipe of a third barbarian's axe.

Jack turned and struck him with the stock of the crossbow knocking him down as a different rival charged in with an overhead swing. Jack quickly jumped sideways out of the way but tripped over a rock and fell onto his back, the barbarian continued slamming the axe-head into the ground trying to finish Jack as he rolled frantically dodging the potentially fatal axe blows. Jack spotted a sword sheathed on one of the dead barbarians and quickly grabbed it as he rolled past him, the barbarian swung once more with all his might as he furiously yelled. Jack lunged upward with the sword! Stabbing his foe before he could complete his swing; blood sprayed on Jack's torso and face, as the barbarian, in shock, collapsed over to the side and died. Before Jack could do anything else he caught the glimpse of an axe handle as it knocked him out before he could react.

Jack awoke in a wagon cage; it was surrounded by several different barbarians marching in what looked to be a caravan of warriors, slaves, and spoils that now included himself.

Jack was still a bit dazed and asked "What happened, where am I?" but one of the nearby barbarians yelled into the cage to compel his silence.

Now remembering what happened after filling in the black spot in his memory, Jack started to focus on the predicament of his capture.

Jack tried reason with the barbarians "Wait you don't understand, I'm not your enemy". However the barbarian next to the wagon interrupted by hitting the cage hard with the side of his axe to rattle it, then glared inside and pointed at him; his message was clear enough even without words, he knew he should remain silent for the remainder of the ride.

A short time later they arrived at the barbarians' stronghold: a camp set up in a clearing of the woods. Made up mostly of tents, it was surrounded by sharpened stakes piled against earthen walls and bordered by two high towers. Inside the camp were blacksmiths repairing and sharpening weapons, cooks preparing large pots of stew, men hauling boxes and barrels from wagons to the tents, and large bands of barbarians loosely gathered around various campfires spread throughout the camp.

The wagons came to a stop near the edge of the camp and moved Jack from the wagon cage throwing him into a hastily erected stockade near one of the perimeter walls. They posted two guards at the stockade as the rest moved to the campfires to enjoy their evening meal. There were a handful of other prisoners in the stockade who barely seemed to notice Jack's arrival; their gloom faces regarded him without expression. Jack wasn't sure why he was being held captive, but he didn't want to leave anything to chance knowing plenty of instances in history where prisoners were often executed. Jack observed the area seeing that there wasn't much other than the two towers guarding the outside of the camp; Jack also remembered seeing a wagon filled with what looked to be captured loot being wheeled into a nearby tent, with his crossbow adorning the top of the pile.

Jack began to formulate a plan as he turned to one of the nearby soldiers and whispered "Hey you, what are they planning on doing to us?"

The captive, who appeared to be some kind of Medieval soldier, replied with an air of desperation "They will wait til dawn of the next day, then one by one mock, ridicule, and beat us until they've had their fun. Then we are executed"

Jack replied in shock "And you're just going to accept that, consigning your fate to circumstance?!"

The prisoner replied "This is the way of *Epic* as it has been for many years, and will continue to be long after we're gone"

Jack grabbed his shoulder and spoke sternly when he snapped back "No! We're not just going to sit back and allow that to happen! We are going to escape, and we are going to live!".

The man looked at Jack for a moment as he pondered the gravity of the situation and nodded in agreement as he said "Tell me what it is then that must be done?".

After a few minutes of whispering Jack and the others waited for dusk, then under the cover of darkness they put their plan into action. One of the prisoners began groaning as he rolled around on the ground, Jack got the attention of one of the guards while pointing and gesturing for help. The guard grunted and went inside while the other guard remained outside; the first guard came in and started kicking the man on the ground angrily motioning him to get up. As the guard continued to harass the prisoner the others were silently preparing for their moment; one of the other soldiers began his role by grabbing the guard, kicking the man and trying to pull him off. The guard outside lost his patience and came in, just as they planned.

Tension gathered in Jack's mind as he prepared to attack; the lessons of his martial arts began flooding back "Align to the proper footing, rotate your body into the shot, keep your body relaxed, wait for your opening… the perfect moment to strike."

Jack shuffled forward and swiftly struck the entering guard hard in the throat with the side of his hand as the others quickly dove on the other guard and bludgeoned him to death with rocks, sticks, or whatever else they could get their hands on. As if pre-coordinated, Jack then finished the choking guard with a corkscrew punch to the gut before striking the reeling guard in the nose with the full force of his knee thrust upward, knocking the second guard unconscious, as the other prisoners raced over to enact revenge on their prior captor, throttling him to death. What little noise the prisoners made was unheard by the rest who were loudly singing and feasting by the roaring bonfires, totally unaware of what was happening nearby.

The soldier asked Jack in amazement "What sort of fighting was that?"

Jack replied describing "It's called Karate; I learned it a while back"

Then he motioned the soldiers to follow him saying quietly "Come on, we'll need our weapons".

They quickly sneaked to the nearby tent where their captured weapons were stacked in a pile in the center. Jack quickly found his crossbow, as well as the lucky sword he used earlier; he decided to grab both, finding a sword sheath and accompanying belt about the right size before equipping it for his person. As he finished by reloading his crossbow, the others quickly followed suit rearming themselves with their respective weapons.

Jack then moved outside motioning the others to follow him, he could see that the sentry in the guard tower was watching their path out of the camp.

Jack quickly asked "Soldier, how accurate are you with the longbow?"

The soldier who had equipped himself as an archer replied "Accurate enough to fell a man in one shot at 100 yards"

Jack then pointed at the sentry and replied "Then take that guard down...quietly".

The soldier drew the arrow back slowly and began adjusting his aim for height, once finished aiming he released the arrow and it struck the guard in the head killing him before he could make any alert noise.

Jack motioned forwards "Now we leave this place, come on, we need to get as much distance between us and them as possible"; with that they silently snuck out of the camp into the nearby woods, quietly escaping into the night.

What seemed to be many hours passed as Jack and the others kept a low profile and crept through the woods, but they became tired so they stopped to rest. Jack was starting to wonder how much longer his experience in this dream would last, but he remembered many previous dreams where time seemed to go on a great distance longer than what seemed possible in one nighttime.

Jack turned to the soldier and asked "What is your name?"

The soldier seemed confused and replied "I am an archer"

Jack attempted to clarify "No, no, your name. What is it that people call you?"

The soldier replied "Archer is all that anyone ever calls me".

Jack found this strange, other constructs had personalities and names; however, the soldier didn't seem to be as intuitive or as free thinking, the barbarians seemed to be even less intelligent.

Jack hoped that these constructs could lead him to Balthazar and asked "Do any of you know where to find a man called Balthazar?"

The Archer replied "Yes, Balthazar is very well known in this realm. We can lead you to him".

Jack nodded in agreement and said "If any of you wish to leave, now would be a good time"

Yet all of them stepped forward as the Archer said "You saved us from death and disgrace; we are with you sir, you're our new leader".

Jack wasn't sure what to think of their devotion, but it was possible that constructs such as them were drawn to figures willing to lead them. Jack decided to just go with it and replied "Alright, lead the way to Balthazar then".

Jack and the other constructs walked for a long time stopping only briefly to refresh themselves, but the forest seemed to stretch on forever and they seemed no closer to reaching their goal then when they started.

Jack impatiently asked "How much longer until we reach Balthazar?"

The Archer remarked "Soon we will enter his part of the forest, and the legendary sanctuary within".

Jack inquired with curiosity "So who is this Balthazar? I was told he knows how to fight."

The Archer answered "None know the arts of combat better than the wise man Balthazar; his every moment is spent mastering the world's marital forms, as well as learning the truths hidden within them, as he has done for a very long time...".

Jack needed more information "But will he teach me how to defend myself in this place?"

The Archer replied "Balthazar has both taught many great warriors, and has learned from every practiced master ever known". Jack was impressed to hear this, but was now more uncertain than ever of what to expect.

As they continued walking Jack suddenly heard the beating of drums in the distance, its menacing sound boomed throughout the forest and was fast growing louder.

Jack with alarm yelled "What is that?!"

The Archer recognized the sound and said "It is the barbarians, they are hunting us".

Jack didn't think they could win in a fight so he gambled at escaping yelling "Let's go! We need to get to Balthazar before they reach us!".

Jack and the other soldiers were now sprinting through the forest, jumping and dashing through its many obstacles trying to reach safety. The drums continued to grow louder and were soon accompanied by the rising war cry of a hundred barbarians; somehow they were still gaining on Jack and the others!

The Archer stopped Jack and said grimly "They will soon catch us, we cannot outrun them"

Jack shouted "We cannot give up, if we reach Balthazar's forest we can get help"

The Archer said seriously "No there is only one way. We soldiers shall hold them off, to the last"

Jack not wanting to see them die pleaded "There has to be another way, everyone can be saved!"

The Archer replied solemnly "You have already saved us from a terrible fate; now in our sacrifice we shall return the favor... *Traveler*".

Jack now understood their loyalty and could tell by the look in the archer's face he was not going to dissuade them, so he shook the hand of the archer and thanked him "Good luck, and thank you".

The Archer saluted back and readied his bow as the others took position. Jack continued running looking back once to see the barbarians arriving on the crest of the hill, the soldiers held their ground stalwartly even knowing they stood no chance. Jack could only redouble his efforts towards escape and hope they didn't die in vain.

Jack continued running but it wasn't long before the drums resumed a chase tempo as they were once again seeking him. Running as fast as he could, he soon reached a line of white pointed stones in a row, without thinking he ran past them and continued running for a short distance until he tripped and fell over.

Jack got back up and looked behind him to see the barbarian horde fast approaching; a few of the barbarians hesitated upon seeing the stones, but the leader roared at them and they begrudgingly continued advancing. As barbarian archers began firing at Jack, volleys of arrows struck the trees and ground around him. Jack sprung up and sprinted away in a mad dash, his mind bent only on staying alive. Jack got a few yards further when something grabbed Jack and quickly pulled him down into a hiding place.

Jack could see the barbarian horde approaching and was still panicking, but before he could say anything a hand grabbed his mouth and a voice quietly said "Shhh!".

As the barbarians came into the area they stopped for a moment after losing sight of Jack, the lead barbarian angrily motioned his troops to spread out and begin searching knowing that his prey had to be close by. A few quiet minutes passed before cloaked figures began silently killing stragglers, eliminating them while others were looking the other way, felling and concealing their enemies in total silence.

The barbarians started to notice their comrades absences, as they began to gather around close together nervously looking in all directions. Suddenly robed figures emerged from every direction wielding a host of different weapons; these warriors lunged upon them and cut down the barbarians effortlessly with graceful but powerful attacks. Every attempt by the barbarians to fight back proved fruitless, as the robed warriors seemed to evade and counter every attack with lighting precision; what few enemies remained took to flight, running in fear of what appeared to be invincible warriors as a sudden barrage of arrows cut down what few remained.

As the warriors finished a hand brought Jack up from his hiding spot and the other fighters gathered around Jack keeping their weapons ready. Jack could see that all the men had shaved heads and that they wore bright red robes that overlapped at the chest, with sashes tied around the waist (the type he figured disciples of martial arts who secluded in isolated sanctuaries would wear). The appearances of these warriors lead him to believe they were similar, if not the same, to the legendary Shaolin fighting monks who resided in remote temples of ancient China.

The lead monk approached Jack, his stoic face served as a subtle warning. Then he spoke quietly but without a trace of emotion "Why do you trespass in our forest?"

Jack replied somewhat nervously "I have come to receive training from Balthazar".

The monk scanned Jack's face, almost as if to look for a sign of deceit, then said "Come with us".

Jack followed the monks up through the forest and to the base of a mountain where they began climbing a seemingly never ending flight of stone stairs; after what seemed to be an hour they reached the top. Jack gazed in wonder upon seeing the large temple complex with a large pagoda at its center. Various other structures were scattered around the central temple, all with the characteristic roofs that curved upward; each possessing the classic features of Far East architecture: sliding doors, grand wooden entry ways, wooden floors, and grand halls supported with wooden pillars on either side.

In the central stone plaza of the complex there was a hundred warrior monks all adorned with the characteristic robes practicing their technique in perfect synchronization; watching over them was a very tall stocky man with a bronze tan and silvery white hair, he turned around and said with a booming voice "Who is it you have brought before me?".

The lead monk responded "Master, a man was caught trespassing in our forest, he claims to be seeking out your guidance for training"

The master replied "Very well, leave me with him" to which the monks bowed and left leaving Jack with the master.

The man who was giant-like in appearance introduced himself "As you no doubt have guessed I am Balthazar, master of the physical arts. Who are you?"

Jack answered "I am Jack, but people have a habit of calling me "*Traveler*" in this place".

Balthazar looked surprised saying with doubt "You are the *Traveler*? A mortal visitor in fully awakened form?!"

Jack responded by nodding to the statement, but Balthazar seemed more troubled with the answer than satisfied as he started to rub his chin in thought.

After a few minutes of thought Balthazar spoke "I have seen the coming of a hundred *Travelers*: each strong willed, full of conviction, bold in both actions and words; however, you are different, I do not sense that same charisma, I do not see that same mental fire they possessed in you."

Jack replied "I do not know how they came to visit this place, but I am using a machine. I'm a bit of an explorer, seeking answers to the mysteries of this place".

Balthazar thought for a moment and said "Whatever your reasons or methods for visiting our realm you need to be prepared to face its challenges, *Traveler's* often lead paths of great difficulty and hardship".

Jack seeking an answer to this riddle of the *Traveler* asked "What is a *Traveler*, why does everyone think I'm so important?"

Balthazar almost laughed thinking this was a joke, but upon seeing seriousness in Jack's face responded "It is clear you have much to learn. You seek training, I shall offer it. Once you are ready I will impart the knowledge you seek so you may find your own path. Do you accept?"

Jack nodded then Balthazar finished "Then your training shall begin upon your return".

Jack replied in confusion "My return?!" but before he could continue he could hear drums in the distance much like the barbarian ones, they grew louder and louder until the earth itself seemed to quake and tremble at the sound.

The ground seemed to give way beneath Jack plunging him into a dark cavern as he felt the sensation of being pulled into a tremendous fall, the sensation ended as the darkness cleared and Jack awoke once again in his lab.

4
TRAINING

JACK AWOKE IN HIS LAB, HIS SURPRISE TURNED TO SHOCK AS HE OBSERVED that a much greater amount of time had passed than he planned. By rough estimation Jack quickly determined he had not been asleep merely 8 hours, but over 10 hours! Jack's leg was completely numb and upon examining the device determined that it was functioning regularly and was still delivering mild shocks to his leg.

Jack deactivated the machine and turned the shocking device off, then examined the machine's readings to see what brain wave patterns were exhibited during the dream. With the exception of a few short moments where the readings jumped in intensity his brain showed little activity; Jack assumed the jumps must have been the brief moments of combat he endured, but did not find a reading matching the previous day's one when he found the yellow orb. Jack then turned to his notes to jot down what little he had learned from the last excursion. Unfortunately, there wasn't much to record, Jack's last trip consisted mostly of running around trying not to get killed; hence he learned very little that could help him unravel the mystery of the subconscious. Jack's goal for the next trip was to gather information from Balthazar, and through his training finally gain the knowledge necessary to safely explore the *Astral Plane*'s realms. Jack was also concerned that he was unable to control when he woke up, as spending more time within the *Astral Plane* appeared to have the effect of making it harder to awaken.

Jack started to wonder aloud "Is this really worth the risk?".

He pondered that question for some time mentally assessing all the obstacles and dangers he had already faced with what little progress he was making, he was also uncertain of what could happen if he died within the dream state. Contemplating the unknown risks, he determined that the most logical thing to do was to cease what he was doing, but Jack couldn't bring himself to commit to that. Just the thought of returning made him excited, Jack had never felt so invigorated before, so alive. So how could Jack possibly give this experience up, this was the greatest sensation he had ever felt. An adventure he could never experience in real life, visiting fantastical and far off places, while doing battle with myths and legends.

"Am I becoming addicted?" he started to wonder quietly in the corner of his mind.

Jack finished his notes and decided to grab some food, as he walked up the stairs he looked back down on the machine.

"JACK!" he heard a voice whisper loudly.

Jack frantically looked in every direction, but upon finding nothing quickly dismissed the voice and continued upstairs. Jack began his usual routine as he did every day but he was much more distracted this time, he seemed to be mentally distant and had difficulty focusing thus causing him to clumsily fumble every task; He couldn't stop thinking about the *Astral Plane* he even started thinking of excuses to return early to it. Jack was able to finish his daily tasks but only after a great number of mistakes and do over's; after Jack finished a plate of leftovers he finally decided to get ready for bed, during which he became increasingly excited over the prospect of finally returning to the *Astral Plane.*

Once he finished his nightly routine he returned to the machine.

This time setting the electrode to a higher setting commenting to himself "hopefully this wakes me up without hurting like hell".

He also ensured that it would reactivate after 7 hours, ensuring he did not go too deep into the sleep state. Jack found it ironic that his original goal was to control the process of dreams and yet paradoxically he had very little control over the process. Upon analyzing the mental readings he attempted to modify the machine, with the intent of having it react to moments of duress and shut down to prevent mental injury. This was all highly experimental though, he had to proceed with few safeties and with little knowledge of what to expect.

Jack set the activation timer and strapped himself into the machine, once it activated he found the vortex sensation tolerable enough to remain aware during the experience. The objects of the room seemed to spin around him faster and faster as they spun further away, the very walls and ceiling of the room stretched outwards past the visual vanishing point into oblivion until he was left in an empty void; as soon as all reality was gone he dropped violently down as though he were thrown off a mountain top. Blurry fragments of light and sound streamed in around him, at first in an unrecognizable jumble of background noise, before slowly becoming more clear and distinct; the incomplete information slowly phasing into reality as if a virtual filter was being removed by degrees. Taking a moment to examine his surroundings, Jack found himself in the middle of the temple complex in Balthazar's forest.

Jack was standing in the middle of a circle of monks with Balthazar standing in the center with him.

Balthazar spoke first "Welcome back *Traveler*, we have prepared your training regimen and time is of the essence. Are you ready to begin?" Jack still dazed from his entrance to the *Astral Plane* simply nodded his head.

Balthazar bellowed loudly "Begin!" as several of the monks charged at Jack.

Jack instinctually raised the crossbow and fired "FFFFT!" A monk snatched the arrow out of the air and snapped it in half with his fist; he and the others then simultaneously lunged at Jack from several directions at once.

Wham! Jack hunched over in pain at taking a direct hit to the stomach but quickly unsheathed his sword and swung at the closest monk, the monk weaved out of the way of each swing until finally catching the sword between his two palms, expertly circumventing the sharp blade. Jack was stunned as the monk then quickly gained leverage over the weapon and tossed it aside, as a second monk quickly cut the crossbow sling and tossed it away.

Jack was now weaponless! And with no weapon he nervously raised his hands in the air, without hesitation the monk in front of him knocked his hands away and struck him right square in the face. Jack slid to a stop into one of the monks who formed the circle around them.

Balthazar's voice commanded an end to Jack's ordeal: "Enough!" as the monks bowed to Jack and returned to their place in the circle.

Balthazar then began his lecture: "Do you know why you failed?"

Jack conveyed what he thought was obvious "Your monks are too good; there's no way I could have beat them".

Balthazar replied sternly "Wrong! It is because you relied on your weapons to do your fighting for you, without them you lacked the confidence to fight."

Balthazar helped Jack up and continued "Will is everything in this place *Traveler*; cast away the specters of doubt and disbelief and you will be able to face any enemy." Balthazar then motioned one of the monks to step back into the circle as Jack nervously raised his hands in preparation.

"Are you prepared?" Balthazar asked and Jack nodded in response. Balthazar commanded "Begin!"

The monk attacked much more slowly this time giving Jack ample time to react to each movement, Jack concentrated remembering every principle and technique he could from his old days of Karate years ago. The monk began to attack more forcefully and with greater speed as Jack continued to block each move, Jack was fast becoming comfortable fighting barehanded again. The monk then unleashed the full extent of his skill fighting; Jack punching and kicking with the full force and speed as Jack continued to evade or stop each move almost effortlessly. Instinctually seeing an opening, Jack quickly counter-attacked with several quick jabs that found their mark and dazed the monk slightly. Jack lunged forward with his full body weight, his fist whistling through the air! The monk braced himself for the impact, but upon lowering his guard could see Jack had intentionally stopped his fist from connecting.

Balthazar clapped his hands together saying "Very good *Traveler*! Know that in this place you may draw upon static knowledge that is woven through the realms if you focus; upon setting your mind to a task you will quickly become its master".

Jack responded with a slight degree of confusion "Why start off so quickly, shouldn't I be learning the basics first?"

Balthazar refuted "Once you learn to trust your abilities the rest comes quite easily".

Balthazar then bowed to the monks and they dispersed, he then motioned Jack to follow him; they walked to the pagoda at the center of the temple complex and pushed the grand doors slowly open. Once inside Jack could see a small shrine in the center surrounded by various ritualistic items of symbolic importance (incense, symbols, candles, and offerings); around the shrine was a mostly open space with pillars on both sides, but windowless and lit only by the flickering torches that lined the hall. As the doors seemed to close themselves Balthazar emerged from a bookshelf behind the shrine with an ancient looking scroll; he sat on the ground facing Jack and Jack sat in front of him.

Balthazar then began explaining "When one learns new information, that knowledge is not just stored within conscious memory to be recalled when needed; it is also absorbed in subtle ways by the subconscious. When one is enlightened by the discovery of truth, it is not just one's way of thinking that is changed, but their perspective is altered, and the spirit is uplifted." Balthazar stopped to allow Jack to reflect; Jack tried to understand the concept, but it was obscure and hard to put into context.

Balthazar continued "The subconscious develops a new level of awareness, once it comes to an understanding of the new information; this awareness is difficult to comprehend fully on a conscious level. This deep illumination of the mind has been called many things; the foremost among them is enlightenment, here in the *Astral Plane* it is possible to attain levels of insight not normally possible."

Jack wasn't sure what to say, nor was he certain at Balthazar's meaning nearly stuttering "I..I'm not sure how I am supposed to… attain what it is you speak of"

Balthazar answered "Soon you will understand".

Then Balthazar instructed "Try and clear your mind" as he closed his eyes and began breathing deeply, Jack did the same trying to calm himself and focus.

Balthazar began verbally guiding Jack through the meditation "Image the tranquility of the forest, silent before the morning". Jack continued to calm himself as his thoughts cleared away.

Balthazar continued "Imagine the passing of the clouds and the seasons, as they flow from one to another eternally in an unbroken cycle" Jack began to lose bearings of time and space as he could no longer feel his surroundings and time seemed to stop.

Balthazar's voice echoed "Imagine every possibility becoming real, as every door within your mind becomes open" Jack now saw images of people, nature, the universe, and all things as his mind drifted through his collective knowledge of everything.

Finally he heard Balthazar say "With learning comes knowledge, with understanding comes wisdom, and when both are realized there is enlightenment…..BEHOLD!!" Jack opened his eyes from the sudden proclamation and saw a scroll in front of him, its letters and symbols shining brightly until Jack was enveloped by its light!

Jack now found himself in the middle of a war between various tribes fighting hand to hand. Then his surroundings flashed to firing a bow and arrow at others while skirmishing. Next he found himself behind a metal shield as he plunged a spear into a charging enemy formation. Jack was then in a shield formation with many others fighting sword to sword. Next he was clad in plate armor fighting from horseback slashing at everything around him. Then he found himself marching in a line stopping to fire guns at enemy lines. His surroundings charged again into a trench firing automatically into panicking soldiers. Jack's perception shifted to him kicking down doors, engaging in fierce room to room fighting with an assault rifle. Finally he found himself standing in the middle of a great massive circle of men as all of them fought in unison using every method, every tactic, and every weapon. Suddenly Jack awoke from this vision panting for air and covered in sweat, all he could remark was "What.... what just happened!?"

Balthazar was rolling the scroll back up when he said "That...was a scroll of universal knowledge, learned by many thousands of minds, with the information coalesced into a singular object". Jack's mind was still swirling with an avalanche of information that was just starting to sink in; he was having trouble focusing, barely being able to stay upright.

Balthazar of course had done this before and commented "The confusion will pass, give your subconscious time to adjust and process; that amount of information would have been impossible to for your conscious mind to take in so suddenly, but in the *Astral Plane* you have a more direct link to the bank of the subconscious: the never ending observer and recorder of all things sensed and felt". Balthazar then put away the scroll and helped Jack up, guiding him back to the central courtyard where the monks were once again gathering back into a circle.

Jack soon found he could focus and concentrate more easily, though he had to quickly relearn standard motor functions and simple tasks like walking but it came back to him quickly.

Balthazar explained carefully "With all the knowledge you have just absorbed you should be able to best any normal opponent with ease; however, you must never allow your spirit to falter as the subconscious and your mind-set are closely linked, whatever affects one affects the other in turn."

Balthazar readied another round of combat "Are you ready to begin?"

Jack shakily collected himself then replied "...Yes, proceed". Jack didn't even hear Balthazar say his usual "Begin", instead he noticed within an instant which ones were about to attack and seemed to know by experience what they would do before they did it.

With this increased awareness Jack quickly sidestepped a punch, ducked under a kick, and jumped around a sweep. All of these evasions were done within moments of each other; then with lightning speed Jack quickly swung his forearm into one enemy, turned and spin kicked the other into the ground, then with a flurry of jabs knocked the other one out.

Jack's abilities had improved dramatically; he was now keeping the entire circle of monks at bay as they continued launching attacks against him several at a time. Jack's movements were a blur, his blocks, evasions, and counters were perfectly timed, his attacks connected with pinpoint precision. As the last monk went down, and stayed down, Jack suddenly snapped out of the weird focus he was in and regained his normal bearings as the fight ended, and was astounded as he looked around to see that all the monks were defeated.

"H..H..How did I do that?" Jack said in amazement.

To which Balthazar replied "Now that you have acclimated to the knowledge of thousands of warriors throughout time, you may fight as if you had lived through many battles".

Balthazar then said "Though you now possess great skill you must know that in this place your ability is not linked to your physical strength or speed, it is determined by your will. If you believe you can do something then you can, this is called the 'will to power' and it affects everything you do in this place." Balthazar motioned for Jack to follow him; Jack quickly turned and apologized to the monks, who were slowly rising to their feet, before following Balthazar.

Once they entered the temple garden Balthazar began another lesson "You have only used the power of your mind to do what you already know is possible, with practice I will show you how to do the impossible".

Balthazar then said "You will encounter a great many things in your travels through the *Astral Plane*; you must learn to generate the tools needed for any situation so that you will always be ready".

Upon finishing Balthazar held out his open palm showing that it was empty, and then quickly pulled his hand back as a dagger materialized in his grip, then with a flick of his wrist he made it disappear again.

Jack thought for a moment and said "Was that a trick, or did the dagger really appear in your hand?" Balthazar frowned slightly at this response and decided to demonstrate again.

Balthazar then reached out with both hands and a large cumbersome spear appeared with a flash of light into his grip; quickly demonstrating its tangibility Balthazar swung it around his body before tapping it loudly against the ground, then he tossed it into the air as it evaporated into dust.

Balthazar then instructed "Picture an object within your mind: how it looks, how it feels, then grasp it with your hands and it will become real."

Jack concentrated for a moment on a mental picture then slowly grasped his hands around it, a plume of smoke formed and a light shone from within; Jack then grabbed the object and removed his hands revealing an old western style revolver, but it was misshapen and distorted. Jack sighed with disappointment and tossed the gun aside, and it disappeared before it hit the ground.

Balthazar reiterated "Try again *Traveler*, remember that complicated objects consist of a combination of many individual pieces that all require their own focus, try something easier" Jack nodded and refocused on trying to imagine something far more plain and easier to fathom.

Jack held his hands out again as another plume of smoke formed and light began to shine from within; Jack then grasped his hands around the object and swiftly removed it revealing…a stick. Jack laughed at the result before tossing it over his shoulder causing it to dissipate.

Balthazar reassured "With practice comes perfection *Traveler*, once mastered you may find it to be most useful indeed".

Jack questioned "Why are you able to summon objects without the plume of smoke, if I am the *Traveler*, shouldn't I be able to surpass your technique"

Balthazar replied with a short laugh "You may only surpass me once you have refined and mastered your technique; remember that mastery requires practice, more practice, and yet even more practice." with that Balthazar then motioned Jack to a small circle of sand within the garden.

Balthazar said "Once you are fully attune with your inner self, you will find you are capable of many great things, observe" then he sat down and began a simple meditation.

Jack started to wonder the point of this exercise until the sand began to shift and move around Balthazar, as the scattered rocks about him began to lift off the ground and gently float into the air. The sand ebbed and flowed back and forth, then rose from the ground and swirled around Balthazar who was solemnly continuing his meditation. The sand then came together and took the shape of a man as patterns on its surface morphed into a face.

The sand image then looked at Jack and said in a deep echoing voice "Here all things are created and bound only by the mind, once its potential is unlocked all things are possible" The image of sand plucked one of the rocks from the air then grasped it tightly, upon releasing its grip the rock had transformed into a perfect square of shiny metal.

The sand image then turned and looked at the meditating Balthazar, who then disappeared as the sand image transitioned by degrees into a perfect new copy of Balthazar.

The new Balthazar, or sand image clone then turned to Jack and stated "Know that this place is bound only by the limits of your mind; if you truly believe something is possible it will be made so, but only if your will to bring about that possibility is absolute, and without doubt."

Jack was taken aback by this display and was speechless; although he knew they were in a dream state it was still shocking to watch these things occur firsthand.

Jack questioned "Do these abilities fall into any sort of framework, are there rules for better understanding them."

Balthazar answered by explaining "If it assists your understanding, think of the capabilities of the 'Will to Power' as falling under three general categorizations: the focus that can defy the natural laws and environmental limitations of the *Astral Plane*, the imagination that can summon forth new objects and items, and the abstract interpretations that allow entities to transform from one state into another".

Then Balthazar explained further "Both *Avatar* and Construct are able to use these abilities to varying extents, however what the extent of their mastery will often aligns most closely with their persona and general frame of mind, thus the capability and ease at which they demonstrate focus, imagination, and interpretation will be linked to who they are at their core".

Jack replied "So I have to figure out what abilities correspond to me? So that I can determine what abilities I can master?"

To which Balthazar elaborated "As a start of your journey, yes. Your previous dreams will reveal the key; you need only to recollect them and analyze what they have in common".

Jack began trying to recollect his previous dreams, but every time he tried to focus on them his memory rapidly faded out; this was very strange because Jack usually remembered his dreams easily and had more than a few distinct ones which he had written down and committed to memory, yet now he couldn't remember any of them.

"I..I..I..I can't remember, none of them are coming to mind" Jack said with a degree of confusion.

Balthazar directed with a subtle hint "Then perhaps it is time to refresh your memory". Jack was unsure of what Balthazar was inferring; though was certain it would involve something strange, mystical, or difficult to comprehend, something Jack was starting to get used to....

Balthazar then said "To master the present one must first conquer their past, we shall go to *Tempest*, the realm where space and time flow by no rules".

5
TEMPEST

Balthazar instructed "To travel to a particular realm, you focus on what they are at their core. In order to travel to *Tempest* you must focus on chaos, disorder, phenomena, and the unexplainable". Jack began to focus on those thoughts, and as he walked his movements sped up as before and his surroundings became a blur as he covered a great distance in one moment; he came to a stop but this time with no metal fatigue.

Jack checked his surroundings and found that he was standing on a road that was literally floating in mid-air, empty space surrounded him with strange things floating from place to place appearing and disappearing at random. The same mystic voice once again appeared introducing impersonally "Welcome to Tempest, where change is constant, no rule or order takes hold, and where space and time flow freely like the wind".

Balthazar appeared at Jack's side abruptly as Jack said startled "Ah!? You startled me, don't just appear out of nowhere like that!"

Balthazar spoke quickly, somewhat nervously "This is as far as I can go, constructs can be distorted by this realm but *Travelers* are incorruptible. Take this"

Balthazar handed Jack his crossbow and sword, to which Jack noted with some degree of irritation "I thought I wasn't supposed to rely on my weapons"

Balthazar then replied "Indeed, that is not to say that they are without use however; recognize them as tools but take care not rely on them too heavily. Follow this road and it should take you to a place with many doors, some will lead to your past, some to the present, and others to the possible future". Jack then took the weapons and politely bowed to Balthazar.

Balthazar then conveyed a brief farewell "Good luck *Traveler*, remember what you've learned".

Jack looked down the road briefly to see that it stretched into the horizon seemingly without end; he proceeded forward down the path, his gaze drifting out into the vast ever changing space around him. At different points he beheld such wonders as the Milky Way galaxy coming into existence, the summary of a civilizations history in art, the trials and tribulations of life, and the wonders of nature. These wonders and many others manifested seemingly randomly, before perishing into nothingness only to be continually renewed in other forms. Jack could swear that on multiple occasions he heard familiar sounds emerging from the space around him, but before anything became recognizable to him it always faded back into obscurity.

As Jack continued down the road its shape began to distort and twist; there are various places where it curved back and forth, rising and falling erratically as it navigated invisible terrain. The road then became truly strange as he approached an odd obstacle ahead of him: a giant corkscrew loop that began and ended in different directions. Jack stopped and wondered if it were even possible to continue, the obstacle looked like something a stuntman would race through in a car. Pondering possible options, he peered over the side of the road, but all he could see was a never ending void that seemed to go on forever. Jack decided to walk a short distance up the road, with the intent to try and jump to the other side of the loop, but as he advanced forward he noticed that his entire orientation changed around him. His surroundings leveling to his angle and gravity remaining centered upon the roads surface; feeling no incline or disorientation as he continued walking. As Jack reached the tip of the loop, it seemed from his perspective there that the rest of the road was upside-down and the tip of the loop was right-side up.

"This is weird." Jack said as he took a moment to comprehend that he was walking through a vertical loop with perfect ease.

As Jack passed the loop he can see that the road ahead was even more chaotic, resembling more of a roller coaster track rather than any sort of normal path. Armed with the knowledge that he would remain on the road's surface regardless of how it bended, he proceeded forward, trying to keep his bearings as points of reference around him continually changed. He continued this way for quite some time, as the road twisted, turned, and moved in all manner of strange directions and paths. Finally after what seemed to be hours the road gradually widened into a plaza full of half-finished statues and buildings; many sections of those buildings were floating in midair without any structural support from the ground. The statues always seemed to move from the corner of Jack's vision, only to stop the moment he turned to view them directly. Jack found a single plain door, which seemed very out of place given the surroundings, in front of the central building. The larger building looked to be a crumbling grand marble monument frozen in time, it could have been a pantheon or an ancient temple but Jack couldn't figure out its origin; it certainly wouldn't have had such a plain door as its entrance.

Jack thought aloud "Well at least this is a change of scenery; hopefully this is the place I'm looking for" and walked through the door in front of him.

Jack's surroundings changed in the blink of an eye as the door disappeared behind him; he found himself floating in a hallway with no floor and no ceiling with nothing but empty space in their place. Strangely the light fixtures and furniture in this hallway were all firmly grounded, as if some invisible force had taken the place of the floor and ceiling. In front of Jack were four doors against the far end of the room, each of them the same color and style, and evenly spaced apart. Jack was a very methodical person, so he decided he would open the doors from left to right. As he approached the first door, he began to hear music and voices in the distance, but they sounded backwards; Jack turned in the direction of the sound only to have it quickly fade back out.

Trying to ignore the oddities of the place around him and focus on his task, as he reassured himself "Focus man, just keep going, gotta find... whatever it is that I'm supposed to discover here" Jack of course realized that his task wasn't too clear either; but he trusted that somehow it would make sense later, at least he hoped it would, as he opened the first door on the left and stepped through it...

Jack was now sitting in a house he lived in back when he was in grade school, though he was still his normal age. Jack sat down to speak to a very strange but familiar looking character directly across from him; at first Jack thought it was an old friend or family member, but he realized it was actually a fictitious character Jack imagined in a story when he was a kid. Naturally as the story was written when he was a kid so the character was a child as well, Jack recalled it was a story he most enjoyed writing but eventually gave up on.

Without warning the windows and doors of the house suddenly shattered as menacing gunmen with tactical body armor burst into the front of the house guns blazing. Bullets landed everywhere around them, while somehow also not hitting either of them; Jack instinctively flipped a nearby table over and grabbed the character to ducks behind it. Once the enemy barrage ended, Jack emerged from cover and returned fire with a pistol, a pistol that seemed to inexplicably appear in his hands as if by magic. Jack fires the gun with uncanny reflexes, as if it's a natural for him despite the fact he had never fired a handgun before, the bullets striking with pinpoint accuracy, cutting down the enemies in a hail of bullets.

Jack and the character make their escape from the back of the house.

Jack summarizes "Their after us! But I don't know why, we will have a better chance of escaping if we split up." The character looks at Jack and nods back silently and without expression.

Jack quickly says as they part ways "Meet back at the old shopping center, it will be harder for them to spot us in the crowd".

Jack then exits the house, weaving through the street-scape of his old neighborhood; running and jumping through familiar obstacles as heart was racing with excitement and anxiety as he races to get away. It takes Jack only minutes to get out of the area and into the center of town. Jack seems to have lost their pursuers already, but after such a frenzied assault how could he have lost them so easily?

Jack quickly thinks to himself "Why in the hell are these guys after me!? And why aren't they trying to follow me… this makes no sense!" Jack then saw the old shopping mall in the distance and decided to ponder the answers later, heading to the meeting point to regroup.

Jack arrives in the shopping mall's parking lot only to see that a similar kind of security force as the attack from before has surrounded the building; the enemy now have guards posted at every public doorway, no doubt they are now searching the inside. Jack sees that one of the employee doorways has been propped open by a cardboard box, likely because inventory was being loaded in from a nearby truck; as the nearby employees were enjoying a smoking break, and there were no guards posted at the employee doors, Jack took the opportunity to slip inside undetected.

Jack quickly makes his way into the department store then grabs a few clothes off the racks and changes outfits in one of the empty dressing rooms, hoping this would hide his appearance. Searching through the mall while trying to blend in, things were made difficult by the security force patrols; Jack worried that they would soon intensify their search if they didn't find what they were after. Jack needed to find what he was looking for before they started cordoning off sections of the mall and screening individual people. After some fast searching he found the fictitious character disguised as an ordinary shopper.

Jack approaches and says casually but quietly "They have this place surrounded, the only way I can get you out is if you're disguised in a cart". The fictitious character then hopped into a nearby cart without any verbal reply, as Jack quickly buried the cart in shopping items to make the character hard to see through the clutter.

Jack starts to walk though one of the main doors pushing the cart in front of him, he hopes that his disguise will hold as they approach the guards. The guard takes a moment to look over Jack then quickly scans the cart only to wave him though. Exiting the shopping center, he makes his way into the parking lot; they are almost clear of the area when suddenly one of the security force members emerges and points at Jack and the cart, then he and the other nearby guards open fire at Jack!

Jack quickly pushes himself and the cart behind a nearby car for cover. As soon as he intended to return fire a weapon appeared in his hands; as he then exchanged gunfire with the security forces firing in his general direction, successfully hitting one, forcing the others to seek out better cover. This gave Jack a brief moment to check his inventory, only to discover he is out of ammo. The security forces, now noticing a lack of suppressive fire, begin rapidly closing in Jack's position. Suddenly a familiar blue truck pulls up alongside Jack and the shopping cart, Jack recognizes it as the first truck his family used to use. Jack quickly retrieves the character from the cart and tosses him into the open door in the back; then attempts to enter the driver side door but bullets pinging all around him force him to dart around to the passenger side. Jack opens the door and sees one of his elderly family members with shades and a leather jacket behind the wheel.

"Well now that's just freaking weird" Jack thought as he climbed in.

His elderly family member then said in an odd tone: "C'mon, let's ditch these losers". The old car then peeled out and took off; exiting the parking lot and disappearing into traffic.

Just as they had escaped their surroundings seemed to move at an accelerating pace until everything was a blurry haze around Jack; he could make out some things happening in the background, but it was like someone hit the fast forward button on the world around him. Suddenly everything returned to normal speed as Jack found himself walking in the desert holding a bag of groceries.

Jack remarked at the oddity of the sudden transition "How did I get to this point?" Jack wondered trying to piece together the fragments that he saw in that blurry haze.

Jack usually thought better while walking so he continued forward to whatever his apparent destination was, cresting over a nearby sand dune. Proceeding over the dune he caught sight of several dune buggies in a small clearing before him, but it was swarming with more of those mysterious security forces! They had Jack in a clear line of sight from only a few feet away, he had no weapons and his hands were full of groceries, they had the perfect opportunity to shoot him. Instead they rushed into three of the dune buggies and with speed, drove down a trail towards something far off in the distance.

Suddenly Jack realized something very important, this entire time he thought they were going after the character and him, what he didn't realize was that they didn't care about him at all. Jack was able to lose them easily the first time they split up, he was able to get past them later at the shopping center without being noticed, they shot in his direction multiple times and yet never seemed to hit him. And just now, when they had an easy opportunity to eliminate him, they completely passed it up to get at someone else. The entire time they have been after the fictitious character and seem bent on destroying it.

Jack drops the groceries and sprints into the last remaining dune buggy; he starts it up and hits the accelerator, racing towards his foes before they reach their destination first. Jack begins driving like an expert, once again imbued with skills he should not possess; finding ways to negotiate the terrain with greater ease than his enemies, and is able to close the distance between him and the three other carts. Jack thinks fast and decides that he must find a way to delay the other dune buggies, ramming into the side of the first vehicle flipping it into a rolling crash! Jack whips out his pistol from the glove box and takes aim at the second cart, the passenger of the enemy vehicle sees this and fires back with an automatic weapon making bullets bounce all around Jack.

Maintaining his calm, Jack steadies his aim and returns fire hitting the driver and causing the vehicle to lose control and crash. The last dune buggy is just ahead of him, both are barreling towards what looks to be an abandoned house in the distance, Jack attempts to use his gun but the other vehicle darts in front of him, causing him to have to swerve with his steering wheel to avoid a crash, dropping his weapon onto the floor. A large steep dune fast approaches in front of them, on their present course the two buggies' will launch over it like an oversized ramp; Jack stomps his accelerator pedal to the floor and overtakes the enemy buggy, sailing over the obstacle and coming to a safe but jarring landing.

The dust cloud from Jack's jump obscures the sight of the driver of the other vehicle, causing them to jump at a bad angle and crash into another dune. Jack reaches the house and slides to a stop in front of it, he recognizes it from the story: it's the house that the fictitious character lived in, except that it is old and worn out looking, far from its colorful vibrant appearance that Jack wrote of it.

Jumping out of the vehicle he rushes inside to look for the character, running through its halls searching every room, but the interior is empty and dead like no one had resided here in years. From a distance, the echo of more vehicles is heard fast approaching, no doubt indicating more enemies on the way; Jack has to hurry if he and the character are to escape. Kicking down the door on the last room he had yet to search, he finds the fictitious character holding a gun to their head.

Jack yells "No! Wait!" as the dream suddenly ends with Jack back in the mystic hallway.

Jack was once again standing in the hallway with the first door now gone, his weapons are once again in his possession as Jack says irritated "I could have definitely used these earlier…".

His old memory then returned from the 1st dream, but his recent experience and the old memory do not match: he doesn't remember the dream ending with the character about to destroy itself.

Jack thinks aloud "Either my memory of that dream was incorrect, or they are occurring differently because of my current state of mind; or perhaps I was never quite able to remember the dreams in their full scope upon waking…most interesting".

Taking a moment to reflect, he evaluates what he can currently remember: "It seemed that when I needed to have certain skills or items they manifested for brief moments of time, though what I was able to conjure was limited only to what was needed to maintain a strategic balance with my enemies, or gain a slight advantage. Curious."

Jack decided to continue exploring the doors, grasping the handle of the second one, but as he did he started to hear the strumming of a guitar in the distance. Strange as it was, the strumming became faster and with more complex rhythms every moment as his surroundings began to blur; Jack quickly remembered the other times this had happened: this was him waking up. Jack tried to steady himself, he looked down through the void to see what looked to be the inside of a room zooming towards him; it shot up and replaced his surroundings as he found himself now standing within his basement laboratory.

Jack's vision was still blurry as he came to; he was sitting up on his table already detached from the machine and electrode. Jack felt lightheaded, dizzy, and very tired and was barely able to stumble to the bathroom. He took a few drinks of water from the sink and looked in the mirror seeing a reflection wearing dark clothes with a menacing expression on its face.

The image whispered loudly "RETURN" as Jack, startled by this, fell backwards into the wall.

Jack quickly looked again but the reflection was now normal. Jack tried to stay awake but he felt so tired he could barely keep his eyes open or think clearly, Jack made his way back onto the chair and sat back thinking to himself "I'll just rest a little bit, then I will get up and get on with the day; I just need a little break…just a few minutes".

Jack found himself somehow back within the hallway with the five doors. "What the?! I was just trying to rest, not re-enter the *Astral Plane*! How did this happen? I didn't even activate the machine??".

Jack quickly tested his surroundings to see if perhaps he can awake; trying various techniques such as hitting himself or focusing on the act of waking up, but nothing worked as he was stuck in this state within the hallway.

Jack exclaimed in frustration "Great. Now I'm stuck and I am not even sure if I can wake up this time". Then he sat down on the invisible force that was the floor, against the one of the nearby walls.

Jack wondered aloud worriedly "What am I supposed to do now?".

After a few minutes of erratic thinking, he finally calmed himself and logically concluded "If what just happened was an illusion, and I didn't really wake up; then I should continue exploring these doors. If by chance I did just wake up and was then transported back into the *Astral Plane* uncontrollably, then I'm sure the wise man Balthazar or perhaps even Melchior can re-awaken me". With that in mind, Jack decided there was nothing else to do other than to continue exploring the strange doorways; as he readied himself to open the second door...

6
THE DOORS

JACK STEPPED THROUGH THE SECOND DOOR, AND FOUND HIMSELF sneaking towards a familiar looking house on a small knoll, spotting multiple soldier-type enemies wearing body armor, carrying assault rifles, with faces that were covered by goggles and face masks topped off by a very World War 2-like German helmet. Jack wasn't sure who or what they were but he could guess they were enemies.

Seeing that there were quite a number of heavily armed guards Jack felt slightly intimidated, unsure how he could overcome them. He searches his person to see that he is wearing some sort of suit of Kevlar body armor that went from neck to toe, and provided a good amount of protection and coverage overall; unfortunately though he found no conventional firearms on his person that he could use. That's when his attention turned to a strange metal apparatus on his hands: it had thin, flexible metal bars that ran up each finger with glowing orbs at the tips; it seemed to be part a strange glove, Jack couldn't discern its purpose until he spotted something strange. From the corner of Jack's eye he can see that a nearby stone is moving along with the motions of his hand, after a bit of trial-and-error he discovered that different hand motions could move objects remotely with the device, he also noticed a dull humming noise that was emitted whenever it was used.

Jack thought to himself aloud "These are certainly useful, I wonder if these objects can move... a bit faster." finishing that sentence Jack rapidly opens his hand and the rock jolts to him and stops right before making contact; pointing his arm at the sky, he does the opposite motion shooting the rock like a missile into the sky.

Jack exclaimed "Ha ha! Now I've got something!" as he approached the enemies with his newfound weapon.

Spotting a patrolling guard up ahead, Jack lifted another rock with the device then flung it with lightning speed, PING! As the rock struck the soldier's helmet knocking him unconscious. Jack peered around the hedges at the driveway entrance, there were two guards: one patrolling in the open garage, and another walking around on the roof. Jack thought for a few moments then devised a method dealing with each guard. As the guard in the garage made his rounds he walked under several low hanging pipes, making a grasping motion at the pipe above him Jack quickly pulled it down striking the guard as he made a short "MMPH!" and fell over, being knocked out cold.

Jack then turned his attention to the rooftop guard using the device to slide the tiles from under his feet with a sweeping motion, making the guard lose his balance and roll off the roof, landing onto the ground with a dull thud, being knocked unconscious by the impact. With all the nearby guards incapacitated Jack headed inside the house to find out why he was there.

After ruffling through some papers and boxes Jack finds a dossier full of important looking photographs, papers, and schematics; deciding this is likely what he was after, he stuffs the folder into his vest headed for the driveway to leave. Jack hopped into an old-school muscle car and started up the engine, but before he can make his escape he sees a number of guards marching up the driveway with two black SUVs behind them. Jack turned the car off and for some odd reason, that he seemed unable to control, walked involuntarily into the middle of the front lawn right into the open. The guards form a firing line, and from the SUV emerges an old bitter looking woman who has a dress that twists and moves by itself as if alive.

The old woman, who seems to float as she moves, looks upon Jack with condescension and disgust as she hissed "Who dares intrude here and challenge me!"

Jack replies in an automatic way without thinking about it "I am with the resistance; your oppression is at an end!" The old woman begins laughing in a cackling way at this notion.

Jack angrily interrupts her laughter exclaiming "Your crimes will no longer be tolerated, and you shall be punished for what you have done!"

The woman motions to her soldiers and replies arrogantly "We will see who is punished!".

The soldiers shoulder their weapons and ready to fire simultaneously as an execution squad. Jack begins challenging his focus into using the devices on his hands, as the energy within pulses and hums with increasing intensity.

The soldier's commander yells "ready…aim…..FI-!?"

Whoosh! As Jack removes all their guns from their hands at once, then like an orchestra conductor begins waving his hands to and fro; as the guns strike their former holders back and forth with the stocks, beating them senseless.

The first group of soldiers falls unconscious as the others, panic stricken, hastily ready to fire while they can; Jack raises his hand forming a palm and as sporadic gunfire erupts, causing the bullets to bounce off an invisible wall before him. He stands unharmed as his enemies bullets bounce off his shield in futility. The guns begin clicking in unison as their ammo is spent, seeing an opportunity Jack counterattacks! Making a grabbing motion towards one of the soldiers, lifting the enemy involuntarily into the air, before flinging him into two nearby guards with incredible speed! Wham!

Jack then grabbed another guard with the devices, knocked him against the wall of one of the vehicles a few times before slamming him into the ground! The soldier's commander ran towards him about to fire; Jack made a sweeping motion making the gun fly out of his grip as it zipped into the sky. The commander pulled out his pistol and the device's motion was repeated sending that away. Frustrated and unwilling to give up, the commander charged forward with a club in his hand; Jack made a two handed shoving motion and the commander tumbled over backwards skidding against the ground as he rolled to a stop.

All the guards in the area where neutralized and queen solely remained, infuriated by the display of ineffectiveness on the part of her soldiers. She put a hand to her temple, and as she did Jack started to get a severe headache.

All Jack could hear was her insidious voice in his head "Die,… Die,… Die you scum!"

This headache was so intense that he couldn't move or think or act, all he could do was clutch his head in pain; she started approaching, slowly to maintain her focus on the mental attack, pulling out a dagger with her free hand. Jack began trying to concentrate to clear his mind and break the hold, as the sinister woman approached; she lifted her arm ready to plunge the dagger into him!

"Come on!…Clear your thoughts!…Focus!!" Jack thought as the woman stabbed downward!

Suddenly freed he froze her motion with the devices. She uttered in disbelief and anger "NO!…"

Jack took a deep breath then thrust his fist with the devices into a whirlwind motion, causing an invisible shockwave to blast outwards with the roar of a tidal wave; tossing everything in its path violently away like a gale force of wind! The evil woman screamed in panic as she went cartwheeling away, slamming into the house with such speed that the entire structure collapsed!! Jack grabbed one of the SUV's flung in the shockwave with his devices and propped it back onto its wheels, starting it up he casually left the driveway, went down the street, and into the horizon.

The dream suddenly ended once more with Jack standing in the hallway as always back in his old clothes once more.

Jack said enthusiastically "That...was...INCREDIBLE!" As he suddenly re-remembered the dream, yet from his old memory he had no recollection of the old woman nemesis.

Again he wasn't sure why he couldn't remember his dreams in their entirety, nor the importance of the details his memory seemed to be omitting. Jack was still feeling a rush from the experience of the dream, the sensation of invincibility from being able to defeat so many foes with such ease!

Jack finally started to calm down as he said "Well that was awesome, I just wish I still had those devices-" as he discovered with surprise that he indeed still had them.

Unable to contain his excitement Jack attempts to immediately test the devices, pointing at one of the nearby tables with the intent to move it from side to side; however, he immediately experienced difficulty with even this basic task, he also experienced some mental strain as well.

Jack finally stopped from exhaustion, having barely moved the table "Why is this suddenly so difficult...maybe I am not focusing enough, or not in the same frame of mind? Perhaps Balthazar can help with this later; if I am to survive this plane's many dangers I will need to learn how to these...these telekinetic gloves! Yes, that's a good name for them".

Jack looks at the doors and only two now remain, Jack is starting to wonder if the next dream is going to be yet another battle; beginning to wonder if perhaps he had been watching too many action movies lately, possibly causing many of his dreams to be so action and battle focused. Jack then walked through and entered the third door...

Jack found himself outside a barn in the middle of the countryside, a gentle breeze blowing through the plains as he peered across miles of golden colored grass stretching into the horizon. Wary of potential ambushes, he inspects the immediate area and widens his search to the surrounding out buildings. After a thorough inspection Jack finds nothing, wary of dropping his guard, he relaxed somewhat and decided to examine the location instead. It seemed like an ordinary farm much like the one he spent his childhood at: in his younger days he recalled searching through barns like this one out of curiosity for anything of interest. Jack does notice that there are a few items in the center room of the barn that seem out of place: drawing boards, tools unrelated to farming, pieces of computer hardware, and large pieces of advanced looking mechanical components.

Jack wondered to himself "These look like parts to something, but what?" Jack observes the parts carefully trying to discern their purpose as they begin to float into the air in front of him.

Jack thought aloud "This could be a type of puzzle, perhaps if I assemble them correctly I will find out what it is and what it's for…"

Jack begins to grin at the challenge of assembling this machine, although he wasn't any sort of an engineer, he loved designing somewhat impractical things; often using computer simulations and drawing programs to bring them to life. Jack focused on the task and rotated the parts around in several different orientations, upon finding logical connections the tools floated in and began welding and bolting parts together. Jack entered a sort of trance, as the parts began to rotate faster in several different directions; as the assembly progressed, the tools began moving at a blinding speed around the shape taking form.

As the final pieces fell into place and the tools finished their work, Jack discovered this was an aerial fighter that he had spent many hours drawing in college; he recalled having put them into an animation with his friend years later as a side project. This fighter was of great significance to Jack, it was one of the last things he drew by hand that made him feel awe at the finished product; a balance of art and utility that he was never able to fully duplicate on his computer.

Jack beheld the fighter's familiar design: the forward swept aggressive wings, composite structure, sharp distinct nose, reinforced frame, and of course its many built in weapons.

Jack said in reminiscence "I can't believe it, this is really it…". Jack held out his hand to touch it as a spark shot from his fingertips and entered the fighter which came to life: its engine powering up as its cockpit panels began to glow with energy, its dull metal frame then transitioned to bright color, finishing the creation.

Jack walked alongside it brushing his hand against it, the cool metal sensation sending tingles down his spine.

Jack remarked "Incredible, things imagined really do come to life here".

Jack began to wonder if he should fly his creation; before he could ponder the drawbacks fully he decided to act on impulse and climb into the pilot seat, as a voice greeted him "Welcome Jack".

Jack suddenly alerted checked his surroundings for an ambush, but seeing no one turned his attention to the instrument panel in bewilderment.

The voice spoke as a woman in a calm and slow manner as it said "Do not be afraid, I am the computer. I recognize you as the creator".

Jack replied "What is it that you want?"

The computer replied "I want to you to recognize the glory of your creation, of me"

Jack was a bit puzzled and replied "…Um well this seems to be a very good design, very impressive, I don't really know how I can recognize its 'glory' though".

The fighter's systems began warming up as the computer said "Then I will show you!".

The cockpit window suddenly closed and the fighter leapt forward at incredible speed into the air! Jack was clenching back into his seat as the fighter rapidly entered the upper atmosphere.

Jack was yelling the entire time "Wait! Yes. I get it this is good, you have shown me!! Very glorious and all, please stop!".

As the fighter cleared the upper atmosphere and drifted into space Jack was finally able to calm down. As he peered out the window he saw the Earth in its entirety, with the clouds of its atmosphere slowly drifting across its green and blue surface.

Jack took in the view and said "Incredible!".

As he looked at the space around the planet, he saw other strange and advanced spaceships coming and going between massive hovering stations; obviously he was not the only one to envision space traveling machines.

Jack turned his attention to the ship's instrument panels and said "So computer, or ship, do you have a name?"

The computer replied "I have only the designation you have given me: [A.S.M. Series III Interceptor Fighter]".

Jack replied with a bit of a scoff "Well I'll admit that's a good description of purpose, but it's not very personified is it?"

The computer replied in a very manner of fact kind of way "The name is: sufficient."

Jack thought to himself "(ASM doesn't actually stand for anything, I made it up cause the initials sounded cool)...".

Then he looked back at the Earth and said "Alright A.S.M., take us down"

The voice from the computer politely replied "Of course" as it plunged planet-ward with speed, it seemed not meant to be a subtle flyer.

Jack finally managed to overcome the gut wrenching sensation of falling as he took the wheel and yelled "Manual control please!" as the fighter quickly slowed to a more reasonable speed as Jack assumed control.

Jack decided to view some scenery before returning to the barn, so he brought the fighter in close to the ground and flew across sweeping planes, over towering mountains, and through vast densely packed cities. The fighter was much more responsive and fast than the wooden flying machine Jack piloted in "*Venture*".

Jack summarized as he uttered aloud "This is certainly better than the ornithopter"

The computer snapped back a retort almost with indignation "An obsolete wooden contraption cannot compare to my design"

Jack laughed as he replied "Wow, you shouldn't be so touchy, I was just saying that this is better after all".

Satisfied with the journey, Jack wished to return to the barn/workshop so he allowed the computer to go back into autopilot; after a few moments of somewhat unpleasant rapid maneuvering the ship finally returned to the barn they had departed from.

Jack climbed out as he thanked the ship "Thank you for that experience, I wish I could see more of my creations brought to life."

As the computer remarked on some hidden information "You don't know?"

Jack replied "what don't I know?" and the entire floor of the barn began sinking downward as it seemed to double as an elevator.

As they were slowly lowered into an underground storage area, huge lights came on row after row revealing how huge the underground section below the barn really was. As far as the eye could see lay hundreds of various vehicles, buildings, weapons, and every other device or object Jack had ever envisioned stretching outwards, seemingly forever. Before Jack could take in the full scope of all the creations put together, he suddenly found himself back within the familiar hallway he started in with the other dreams.

Jack began pacing back and forth as he tried to discover the meaning, if there was any, behind the combined dreams.

He said aloud "Balthazar said that my previous dreams would reveal what I'm good at, though it seemed to be something different each time; I'll have to think about it more later and figure out the common theme behind each skill set that I used. Now that I know I can finish my training…but there is still one door left".

Jack turned at the last door and wondered if something climatic awaited him, he reached for the handle but the door seemed to move away; trying again the door once again moved away from his grip.

Jack began walking closer as the door and the rest of the hallway drifted backwards as he approached, so he ran towards it as the door and hallway moved backwards at an even faster rate. Upon stopping and checking backwards he saw that the rest of the hallway behind him was still the same distance away.

This was obviously some sort of puzzle or trick, but since Jack didn't know how or why it was happening he had to settle for 3 out of 4; and began walking away thinking as a possibility "Maybe I wasn't ready to see what was behind that one?".

7

COMPLETION

JACK EXITED THE HALLWAY AND SAW THAT THE SURROUNDINGS HAD changed: instead of the old and worn down floating ruins from before, the surrounding architecture was now new, complete, and in pristine condition. Jack began walking down the spiraling road once more, in the distance he could see light spiraling around an image of the temple Balthazar and his monks resided in, Jack guessed it had to be some sort of portal; although he didn't remember using a portal to arrive here he figured that the rules of this place must have been different from the others so he headed towards it. As he proceeded nearer to the exit portal, two huge clouds of fire and ice dropped from the space above and slammed into the road. The figures materialized into what looked to be two massive sized men made completely of elemental forms, as menacing eyes appeared on them Jack knew he was in for a fight.

Jack quickly whipped out his crossbow and fired off a volley at each one, but the arrows simply bounced off the ice giant and burned up within the fire one, clearly his crossbow would do him no good here. The giants' slow movements gave Jack plenty of time to react though, so he unsheathed his sword and stabbed it deep into the frost giant; the giant looked at the injury without consideration as the ice absorbed the sword into its torso, before awkwardly kicking Jack backwards.

Jack had the wind knocked out of him, rolling backwards for a few seconds uncontrollably; Jack had to take a moment to catch his breath and recover, attempting to think of different possible solutions.

Jack analyzed the situation "These blasted things seem to be unaffected by my weapons, but they are made of elements that cancel each other out, that's it!" Jack knew he would now have to use the telekinetic gloves if he were to have any effect on these enemies.

Jack focused on the fire giant and recalled from the dream that rapidly opening his hand attracted objects, he did so and surprisingly the gloves worked once more causing a ball of fire to separate from the monster and fly to Jack's open hand stopping before him. Jack did the opposite motion hitting the ice monster in its dead center making it screech in an unnatural tone. The ice monster gathered up a storm of its loose shards and hurled them at Jack in a storm; he began darting and dodging as the ice shards shattered around him, his practice evading the fire of projectile weapons in earlier dreams was coming in handy. As the storm subsided Jack opened both palms and focused on sapping more fire, gathering it up before blasting it in a stream at the ice monster, it screeched again as its form began to rapidly melt into a deteriorating hunk of de-animated ice.

Jack saw that the melting ice revealed his sword and he reached forth and made it jump through the air back into his hands using the power of the gloves. The sword was covered in thick frost so Jack hit the sword a few times against the road to break off the loose ice, but it quickly rematerialized upon the blade each time; The fire monster hurled a deadly fireball as Jack instinctively raised the sword in defense, amazingly the fireball hit the sword was instantly snuffed out. Jack quickly ran towards the fire monster with the sword in hand.

The fire monster punched downward with its full force as Jack held the icy sword up in defense, the fire upon making contact was quickly repelled by a burst of cold energy as the fire giant hissed like a crackling fire. Jack decided to combine his two weapons and began heaving the sword through the air remotely using the gloves, it nicked and cut through the fire extinguishing part of the flame each time forcing the giant to stagger backwards in pain and confusion. Then Jack made the sword spin vertically in rapid circles like a saw blade and flung the cold sword at the giant's center, the fire giant disappeared in a plume of smoke and heat as only its ashes remained. Jack intrigued by the effect of the sword, experimented by stabbed the end of the crossbow into the ashes, and to his surprise the end of the crossbow began smoldering and smoking but was undamaged; quickly testing his theory he fired a few arrows at what was left of the ice giant's corpse and the arrows caught fire upon taking flight and ripped through the icy mass, melting the remainder of it completely.

"Fascinating, this effect will come in handy" Jack said upon beholding the new effectiveness of each weapon; then he carefully sheathed them hoping the effect would not harm him, and then he proceeded to exit through the portal stepping over the fading remains of his smitten foes.

Jack's vision was blinded by a flash of light as he found himself once more within the temple, Balthazar stood in front of the monks which stood in a line behind him; at once they all bowed to him.

Balthazar stepped forward and said "Congratulations *Traveler*, you have passed the test and thus completed your training"

Jack replied with confusion "The journey through *Tempest*…that was a test?"

Balthazar replied "It was, and seeing that you have completed all of the trials you are ready to move forward". Jack considered telling Balthazar about the fourth door which he could not open, but he decided against it.

Jack then remembered waking earlier and asked "During my excursions within *Tempest* I seemed to wake, only to fall back asleep to this place in the same state as before. I now worry that I have re-entered this plane without the assistance of my machine and that I am now trapped here in the *Astral Plane*".

Balthazar took a moment to ponder what Jack said sighing deeply as he rubbed his chin, he then replied "It is impossible to know for sure, *Tempest* is a realm of unexplainable disorder; hence what you saw could have easily been an illusion, or a sign of things to come. As with all things seen and heard in *Tempest* you will have to wait and see if anything comes of it".

Jack, unsatisfied with this answer, wanted some additional assurance and pleaded "Isn't there some way to awaken me, I must be capable of leaving this place of my own accord? Did you not predict my awakening before?"

Balthazar tried to convince him "I'm sorry *Traveler* but there is nothing I can do. We wise constructs can see when an individual is about to awaken, but we cannot return them to the conscious realm ourselves without dire risk of injury to the mind. Take comfort in the fact that all *Travelers* wake when needed to, and only remain here as long as they are needed." Jack tried to let Balthazar's words reassure him, but he couldn't help but think that as his circumstances put him into a sphere of rules totally different from normal *Travelers*.

Jack said now convinced he had no other option "I cannot risk forcefully waking, and it is impossible to know if what I experienced was even real; I guess I have no choice but to keep going and hope that a solution reveals itself."

Jack's attention came back to the task at hand, as he inquired "I have encountered strange experiences within Tempest but two of them I wish to understand further" as he unsheathed his sword covered in regenerating ice, and then made it spin in air using the gloves on his hands.

Balthazar reacted with some general familiarity "Ah yes '*Relics*', I had a feeling you would encounter a few of those".

Jack asked "Could you please explain them, these objects have properties that seem almost like…magic"

Balthazar explained "The concept of magic is basically something with properties that are not clearly understood, yet are bound to obey their own laws of causality and reaction."

Balthazar elaborated "At one time elements such as fire, water, and wind were considered mystic or phenomenon because they were not yet understood; thus magic is something that seems impossible according to what we are capable of perceiving and understanding, yet they occur anyway. Here in the *Astral Plane*, all things imagined or conceived within the mind are made real, and are simply dictated by their own rules once generated. Understanding this, a relic is simply an object fused with the energy of these non-understood properties."

Jack then thought about the subject and replied "Wait, if these objects are infused with energy that obeys their own sets of laws… does that mean they are capable of working without the user?"

Balthazar rejoined "Not quite, remember that it is the energy of the mind's will that creates these abstractions and the rules that govern them in the first place. Therefore, the more willpower and focus that is channeled into an item or concept, the more powerful it becomes; without some kind of user, a relic's inherent power is quite weak and may fade out entirely, especially if it is forgotten."

Jack recalled having difficulty moving an object with the telekinetic gloves, after practically using them to be invulnerable minutes before; then he put away the weapons satisfied with his new understanding of them.

Jack knew that many questions he had of the *Astral Plane* had been answered, but with his training now completed he was now ready to continue exploring.

He thanked Balthazar "Thank you for training me in the ways of the *Astral Plane*, but I must continue to explore it if the answers I seek are to be found"

Balthazar bowed politely in return and replied "You are the most welcome *Traveler*, I wish you a good journey… Before you go however, there is one more thing you will likely wish to find here"

Jack replied "And what is that?"

Balthazar explained "Perhaps you have encountered the orbs before: concentrations of pure emotional energy"

Jack recalled the orb he encountered within "*Venture*" and answered "Yes, I have. What Do you know of them?".

Balthazar motioned to the horizon in the center of the far off forest and said "There is one such orb deep within those woods. Each realm possesses an orb which embodies its chief emotion; and serves as a connection to the '*Source*'". Jack wasn't sure if Balthazar was referring to another realm so he asked "What is the '*Source*' specifically, is that another realm? Or perhaps it is something more?"

Balthazar sighed and said "I'm afraid no construct is capable of fully knowing, it lies outside our sphere of understanding. The only thing we know for certain is that it was here before the rest of the *Astral Plane*, and only "*Travelers*" may interact with it."

Jack was intrigued and requested "Alright, give me directions to this orb and I will find it"

To which Balthazar enthusiastically replied "This time I will be going with you *Traveler*, I want to see what you can do!" Then Balthazar called out for his weapon, and one of the monks quickly threw a peculiar metal staff with rings at the end of it to him.

Jack agreed to the prospect "Alright, it will be nice to have some help for once; lead the way".

Balthazar and Jack set out down the long winding stairs back into the core of the forest; the path to the orb would take them far beyond the safety of the sanctuary, which probably meant they would encounter combat along the way. As Jack and Balthazar re-entered the dark and foreboding forest they could hear the sounds of battle echo in the distance once more, none of which were close to cause alarm, but the constant ambience served as a subtle reminder that *Epic* was locked in a state of unending conflict.

Jack inquired "The *Astral Plane's* scenery seems so realistic, where does it all come from?"

Balthazar replied "A great deal of it comes from the memories of those connected to the *Astral Plane*: sceneries they have seen or visited. Some of the more...*unique* environments are purely imagined, those are more uncommon to see, and are often as beautiful as they are seductively dangerous". Jack nodded as the description satisfied his question and served as a subtle warning.

They continued onward for some time, navigating the forest's many paths and obstacles. Balthazar knew the forest well so they were able to avoid areas of heavy fighting and navigate around the most dangerous obstacles; yet Balthazar was seen keeping his guard up at all times, knowing that sudden unexpected dangers were common in *Epic*. Balthazar maintained this awareness of his surroundings at all times, searching the background for any signs of an ambush. They came to a more dense part of forest where the trees and brush were much closer together and the thick canopy cast a shadow over the surroundings. The wind grew still as the sounds of the forest began to quiet; puffs of mist began to drift in as surroundings seemed to hint at a coming danger. From a great distance Jack began to hear the echoing song calling in the distance, it grew louder as Jack identified the sound as the beautiful singing of a woman.

Jack queried to Balthazar "Do you he-"

Balthazar quickly interrupted him "Remain silent, I sense danger nearby".

Jack's attention continued to be drawn to the signing; he slowly walked towards it, away from Balthazar whose attention was drawn to another direction. As Jack approached the direction of the signing it seemed to become more elaborate and beautiful. Seeing in the distance a woman cloaked in shimmering silk with long hair, Jack continued obliviously towards it; the elegant figure seemed to float above the ground, gracefully dancing to and fro as its song somehow made the surrounding forest more vibrant. Jack was about to greet it as his mouth covered and he was suddenly pulled backwards. Jack noticed that it was Balthazar, but before he could ask what was happening Balthazar gestured for him to remain silent then pointed to something else approaching the signing woman. Jack caught the sight of a barbarian who was enchanted by the woman's song; the barbarian looked to be in an entranced state as it walked blindly closer to her. Once the barbarian came within a few feet of the woman it stopped its song as its appearance shifted to a gnarled and unnaturally thin wretch; it screeched as it glided upward then swiftly swirled around to the back of the barbarian like a gust of wind, biting him in the back of the neck with its many sharp teeth. The barbarian fell to the ground as the wretched figure coiled around him and feasted on its prey.

Jack said quietly but with some alarm "What the hell is that!?"

Balthazar replied back also at a hushed volume "A siren, women whose enchanting song lures men in, so they can kill and eat them; a few more moments and your fate would have been that of the barbarian…"

Jack reached for his crossbow as he said "Then we should rid this place of that wretched thing-"

He was stopped before he could act by Balthazar who urged "No, the terrors of the *Astral Plane* are present in an innumerable number, we must only fight that which we must, or we will be too overextended to accomplish anything."

Jack reluctantly put his crossbow away and nodded as Balthazar advised "The siren will be distracted now that it is feeding, let us leave this place: Quietly." Jack and Balthazar then carefully returned to the road being careful not to make any loud or obvious noises.

After Jack and Balthazar reached a safe distance they continued deeper into the forest, they were now fast approaching the site of the orb. As they emerged from the dense foliage they beheld a large clearing in the forest where the sun shined brightly in a clear and peaceful field, in the center was an old stone altar with a bright red orb gently floating above it. Balthazar began looking around nervously before taking another step into the clearing almost as if he were expecting a trap; the distant sound of a horse approaching confirmed his fear, the clacking of its hooves echoing towards them, serving as a Harbinger for *his* arrival.

Balthazar ominously warned "It is him! I had hoped that he would not be here this day, he may be more than a match for us!"

Jack now nervous as well tried to get Balthazar to be more specific "Who is coming! How could he be better than you and I?"

Balthazar explained quickly "he is the legendary warrior from a dark time, a man who holds no allegiance to anyone, one of extraordinary skill, he is-"

An armored warrior emerged from the other side of the clearing clad from head to toe in black metal plate; the horse reared up and neighed, then the warrior dismounted, unsheathed his weapon, and approached them looking determined for a fight.

Balthazar finished "The Black Knight!".

A German accented voice echoed from the inside the helmet "Balthazar! I am glad to see a worthy opponent!"

Balthazar tried to reason "I have not come here to fight you! We have come for the orb, nothing else!"

The knight replied seeming to somewhat ignore the specifics of Balthazar's reply "I have always sought out enemies that can challenge me and have found none! This object seems to attract more worthy opponents, but still none have bested me yet!"

The knight then pointed at Jack and said "What say you!"

Jack replied diplomatically "They call me the *Traveler*, and I have come for the knowledge within the *Astral Plane*, allow me access to the orb and we will be on our way"

The knight laughed out loud in response to this "A *Traveler*! You?! Ha Ha Ha! If this is true then you should provide a most excellent challenge! Have at you!!"

The knight charged forward! Jack instinctively fired off a number of arrows and the knight raised his shield in defense as the arrows bounced off; the knight then swung with powerful backswing at Jack who was barely able to stop it in time with his own sword. The knight was very strong however, and the sword was slowly inching towards Jack!

Balthazar swung his staff at the knight who ducked under it then kicked Balthazar over as he swung his sword at him with an overhead strike. Balthazar was able to stop the sword and kick the knight slightly back, but he was still on the ground and vulnerable to a second strike, as the Knight moved to finish off Balthazar Jack hit him with a blast from his gloves. The Knight reacted by bracing behind his shield with lightning speed as it absorbed much of the force, only pushing him a few feet to the side. Jack attempted to seize the opportunity and lunged forward stabbing the sword at him, but the sword's freezing power seemed to not have any effect on the armor at all, bouncing off with a dull CLANG!

The Knight quickly pushed the sword to the ground and then knocked Jack back with the hilt of his sword. The Knight continued forward swinging once more at Jack, he used his telekinetic gloves to grab at the Knight's weapon trying to wrest it away. The Knight was able to hold onto the sword and stubbornly press forward despite the force being exerted against it.

Balthazar pounced forward swinging his staff down at the Knight, but the knight intercepted the attack with a quick shield parry; then with a rapid shoulder shove knocked Balthazar over with his shield, not even bothering to use his weapon.

Jack used the telekinetic gloves to retrieve his own sword then tried harder to overcome the Knight; as the adrenaline kicked in Jack began swinging his sword with as much speed and force as he could physically muster, making his movements blur and his sword whistle through the air. The Black Knight moved with equal speed blocking a number of swings; waiting for Jack to swing wide and overextend himself before counter attacking, cutting him in a across the leg and into his right shoulder forcing him down in pain!

The Knight approached slowly brandishing his sword as he said "You have skill, but no enemy can best me! Not even *Travelers* it seems! Yield and I will allow you to live…what say you? ".

Jack got back up slowly as he could feel some outside force taking over, the pain vanished, his vision blurred, his heart rate speeding up like a motor as a potent surge of energy seemed to course through him.

Jack then said confidently "You talk too much.".

Then his arms were suddenly electrified and struck faster than the eye could see with every weapon at once, hitting the Black Knight a several dozen times in an instant barrage that ended with a thunderclap! The Knight flew backwards hitting the altar in the center of the clearing then falling onto his knees.

The Black Knight groaned "Impossible!? No one has ever beaten me… ugh…I…I yield, you are the superior fighter. The orb is yours" the knight then limped back to his horse and saluted Jack before riding away.

Jack started to tip over as the energy ceased and pain from before returned, Balthazar quickly ran behind him and kept him from falling onto the ground.

Jack said jokingly "Yeah… that was pretty cool, whatever that was it's something I need to use more often"

Balthazar commented "That was the power of the first orb manifested through you, you activated it by reflex, you were lucky".

Jack got back up and brushed himself off, then he observed the two cuts he received.

He commented at the state of his injured leg and shoulder "I should really start wearing some sort of armor"

Balthazar quipped back "The best armor is not being hit at all".

Jack then changed topics to avoid talking about how he was almost beaten "Can I activate that orb power again if I'm fighting a hard battle?"

Balthazar replied "No, they are triggered by extreme emotional stress, forcing them to occur is impossible"

Jack somewhat disappointed, sighed and replied "Great, hopefully it starts up when I need it to, why are these things so random and unreliable?".

Jack turned to the orb hovering about the altar and remarked "Well this is what we came for" and approached the orb.

Jacks fingers grasped the orb as his vision was filled with a red haze, suddenly he was overcome with anger and aggression as every insult and frustration from his life began flooding in like a tidal wave; over and over again he saw people insult him, trick him, wrong him as every infuriating occurrence was relieved in rapid succession: his computers breaking down, his car troubles, being denied at state college, again and again and again. His blood began to burn until it felt as if it would boil, his hands and feet clenched uncontrollably with rage, and he began yelling with every ounce of his body at everything as he was surrounded by the heat of anger! The red haze faded as the visions stopped, Jack was standing on the altar with his entire body smoldering, and his hands literally on fire! It took every ounce of self-control Jack had to calm himself as the smoldering stopped and the fires went out, surprisingly he was completely unharmed by any of it, at least physically unharmed.

Jack yelled, punching a hole deep in the ground as the last bit of anger left him "Aaaaahhhhhh! Damn it! I did not need to be reminded of all that! That was terrible!".

Balthazar remarked "It is, what it is".

Jack took a few deep breaths and regained his composure saying "Although that was certainly a negative experience it was what I asked for, perhaps I can gain something out of it…thank you".

Balthazar bowed in return as Jack concluded "I feel that I have now explored this place fully and it is time to move on, farewell Balthazar, and thank you"

Balthazar advised as he began to walk away "I would recommend going to the crossroads before heading directly into another realm, it serves as a useful juncture for those journeying between the realms. There you will likely find someone who can help find the next step in your journey...for most people it takes the form of a village. Farewell *Traveler*".

With that Balthazar left the clearing to take the long walk back to his sanctuary. Jack thought of the village and began walking into the horizon as his vision blurred while his surroundings rapidly moved by. Once his surroundings came back into focus, he found himself once more in the all too familiar village that he encountered the first time he arrived in the *Astral Plane*.

8

DAWN

OF THE

"HARBINGER"

JACK SURVEYED HIS SURROUNDINGS TO SEE THAT THE VILLAGE WAS NOW at sunset, the nearby inhabitants finishing their daily tasks and heading home for dinner, or in some cases the tavern. Jack found it odd that he had to keep meeting people within a type of bar, especially since he didn't drink, but it was a very old type of meeting place so the symbolism wasn't lost on him.

Jack entered the tavern and was greeted by the familiar old voice he recognized the first time he came to this place "Greetings friend, I see that you have ignored my warning and returned. I can't say I'm surprised, it is humanity's nature to be inquisitive even in the face of certain danger".

Jack turned to the table at his side to see Melchior once again at his old table wearing the trappings of a monk as before; Jack responded a bit surprised "Melchior, good to see you". Jack then pulled up a chair and sat down.

Jack asked in a slightly pressing tone leaning forward "In our last conversation you didn't mention that there were others who came before me, everyone keeps calling me '*Traveler*' like I'm a sort of "chosen one" in a sort of recurring prophecy".

Melchior answered while brushing his hand through his beard in thought "Your circumstances are certainly different from the others; most *Travelers* arrive here with conviction and boldness, setting the *Astral Plane* on a path of irrevocable change as demigods. You were quite different, you stumbled into this place confused and uncertain; I had thought you were a curious rare occurrence but certainly not a *Traveler*."

Jack now seeing his previous experiences in a new light reflected "Interesting, that might explain why some of the constructs I have encountered had their doubts, some even went as far as to be mocking. So if I am this '*Traveler*' what is it that I'm supposed to be doing exactly?"

Melchior replied in a doubtful tone "I still am not certain that you are a *Traveler*, but if your experience is to be anything like the others then you will encounter great resistance that you must necessarily overcome, in order to change the *Astral Plane* in its entirety".

Jack replied "Well I have already began to encounter resistance, you were certainly correct about the danger when you warned me the first time"

Jack then motioned to his newfound weapons and inferred "Though, as you can see, I have sought training and tools thereby preparing myself for it".

Melchior scoffed "Have you now? You have no doubt encountered hostile constructs but those are the least of your worries; each time you revisit this place your mind becomes more adapted to it making it harder for your conscious self to leave, and if you are indeed a *Traveler* then you will no doubt incur.....an opposing force with capabilities rivaling your own, something far more threatening than a chance encounter".

Jack stopped the conversation trying to take in all the information "Wait, wait, slow down. Ok first off, the more I visit this place the more adjusted I become to its...oddities, but you're telling me that it's also the reason I'm having trouble waking."

Melchior nodded as Jack continued "And I am destined to have to fight against great resistance you speak of"

Melchior again nodded in response as Jack finished "Only to bring about some great change, but why? For what purpose?".

Melchior paused to draw a puff from his wooden pipe then mused "It is the nature of all things to change over time my friend, as conditions and environments shift those who dwell within them must adapt, otherwise they stagnate and die out. Your civilizations, cultures, technologies, practices, and values have changed a countless number of times throughout your history and must continue to do so. The *Astral Plane* is capable of subtly influencing every single person in the world simultaneously; changing this place is the first step to bringing about a lasting and meaningful difference in everything else."

Jack thought in amazement "So the *Travelers* carry with them great power, but what of the upheaval, what if something good is replaced by something worse?"

Melchior sighed deeply before continuing "That is reliant on the individual *Traveler*; some are pious and good and change the world for the better, yet others that are corrupt and ambitious, pulling the world into dark and brutal times. It is impossible to know for certain what path they will take until they have already brought about the change; some that are evil feign goodness and some that seem evil are merely not yet at peace with themselves"

Jack thought of all the turning points in history thinking of what was possible with only a subtle influence on a massive scale, then he said "So *Travelers* must overcome great resistance because those that are comfortable with the old ways do not want change, so they fight against it; though like an inevitable tide they are powerless to stop it".

Melchior answered "Yes, Very astute my friend, and so you must know that if you are indeed the *Traveler*, then you are the one who must overcome great resistance and bring about change, for the better or for the worse".

Jack sat back in his chair contemplating these concepts; this was after all a lot to take in. Then he thought of the matter at hand and asked "Where should I begin?".

Melchior reluctantly replied "To that I shall not say, though I hate keeping wisdom from those who seek it I vowed long ago to be a source of information to *Travelers*' but not a direct guide. If I were to give you that advice then it would influence your path unfairly, I also wish to remain separate from the substantial turmoil that follows the coming of a *Traveler*. What I can tell you is that you should seek out a guide that is well versed in the *Astral Plane*, someone who is charismatic and possesses a vision for the future and outlook that is similar to your own".

With that Melchior put away his pipe stood up and retrieved a walking stick from behind his chair and spoke resolutely "Now I must depart again, so that I might continue my search for wisdom in this place; perhaps we may cross paths again in this tavern, or perhaps not, either way I wish you good luck in your journey."

Jack got up and they shook hands "Thank you Melchior, your advice has been most insightful"

Melchior replied cordially "Farewell my friend" and quietly shuffled out the door.

In the brief moment that Melchior leaned forward to shake his hand Jack could have sworn he saw a light shining from his eyes, but as with all things in this place he had no context to relate it to.

Jack sat back down and waited at the table for a time thinking of the conversation he had with Melchior and pondering all the logical outcomes of following the path of a *Traveler*, Jack wasn't sure that this great change Melchior mentioned was truly needed, nor was he sure that he was up to the task of leading it if it was destined to occur. After all he was a quiet writer who kept to himself and was not an idealistic, charismatic revolutionary.

As he continued to ponder, a middle aged woman walked over and handed him a piece of paper with strange glyphs on it.

Jack stopped her and asked "What is this, what does it mean?"

The woman answered in a grumpy tone "You've never placed an order before?"

Jack thought for a second and replied "Oh, wait, you're a waitress"

The woman countered grouchily "Call me that again and I'll smack ya upside the head; I'm the innkeeper's wife. You may call me Gladys, if your polite about it"

Jack questioned "I don't know what this says, its-"

Gladys bluntly interrupted "tap it!"

He paused and she reiterated "The menu, tap it!".

Jack did so thinking that it would be a waste of time, but the glyphs changed to English as Gladys remarked "I'll be back to take your order in a minute, try not to think too hard".

Jack was examining the menu in amazement saying to himself "This has to be some sort of universal translator, but how does it work?".

As he was attempting to determine the menu's secret a suited figure sat down in front of him and said "Charming service in this tavern, wouldn't you agree?"

Jack put the menu down to see that Malachi had sat down at the table, still wearing his impeccable suit.

Jack commented "I knew I hadn't seen the last of you, what do you want?".

Instead of answering the question Malachi redirected "Perhaps you have been wondering why you haven't encountered any other people from your realm that are asleep?"

Jack was taken aback, he was wondering the answer, but he didn't want to give off any air of uncertainty so said with confidence "I'm sure that I just haven't run into any yet, this is quite a vast place after all".

Malachi was not fooled and replied "You haven't the slightest clue, but I know the answer. You and I can help each other, I know much of this place and you have a power that is unique here; there is much to be gained if we were to cooperate".

Jack sat back and thought carefully about this proposition; although Malachi had been helpful in the past it was clear that he wanted something from Jack.

Jack decided he would agree only on the condition "I do need someone to help guide me through this place, so I may very well decide to accept your help."

Then pointed as he said sternly "However, I need to know what it is that you're after, and I want the truth."

Malachi replied in his typical casual way "Your suspicion of me is unwarranted… but seeing that you want answers and I need help; I will agree to explain everything once you have been shown the realm of *Mirage*, once you see what is there my motives will become all too clear".

As Malachi finished Gladys came around for Jack's order saying mockingly "Do you know what you want yet, or are you confused about that too?"

Jack answered "Just get me a soda."

Gladys rolled her eyes and asked "Care to be more specific?"

Jack smirked and replied "…Surprise me".

Gladys swiped the menu out of his hands and walked away grumbling "Wisecracking patrons all think they're SO funny, one of these days I'll *surprise* them…".

Malachi couldn't help but laugh at this sight "I wouldn't jest with Gladys if I were you, making opponents of those who have access to your food and drink is… most unwise"

Jack replied "Well it's certainly not the best service I've encountered"

Malachi agreed "Indeed, but the quality of the food and beverage more than makes up for it."

Jack returned to the conversation they were having earlier "Alright Malachi, I will agree to help you for now, but once I'm finished with this favor I want you to drop the mystery act and tell me everything. I've been burned before when I trusted people that weren't forthright with me, and I'm not going to let that happen again."

Malachi reassured "Trust me, you have nothing to worry about"

Jack dismissed this sentiment "I've heard that before".

Gladys came back around with the foaming drink in a glass mug, and set it down on the table as she said "There you go Einstein, let me know when you want the bill" and Malachi without prompting stopped her and gave her two of the strange looking coins; Jack remembered him using similar such coins before.

Malachi stated "I'll cover this one Gladys"

As she replied "Don't think I'm not watching you too, Chris"

She walked away as he corrected "That's Malachi"

As she rudely replied over her shoulder while walking away "Whatever".

Jack took a sip of the drink, half expecting it to be tampered with; but surprisingly not only was it fine, it was the best soda he had ever had "Wow, this is actually really good! You weren't kidding"

Jack then finished the drink in two huge gulps before remarking "I'll have to come here more often".

Then Malachi motioned as he started to get up "Shall we be off?" as Jack got up and followed him out the door.

Malachi faced one of the outgoing roads stretching into the horizon and spoke "Before we go to *Mirage* it would be wise to acquire a better form of transportation in *Utopia*; transportation on foot often leads to quite hostile encounters, as you are no doubt well aware of by now."

Jack nodded in agreement commenting "Alright, a vehicle would be useful for exploring the vast expanses of the *Astral Plane* quickly; how do we get to *Utopia*?".

Malachi answered "Focus on thoughts of paradise, and goodness".

Jack confirmed "Alright, might take me a sec to get in that frame of mind, but it should be no problem…"

He then began walking down the road focusing on abstract thoughts of goodness, and paradise. As always his movements sped as his surroundings became a blur as he covered a great distance in a short instant; he came to a stop with no fatigue whatsoever, a sign that he was now quite well adapted to that process of travel, and surveyed his surroundings.

Jack saw that he is standing in a great, green pasture bathed in warm light, the sky was filled silvery white clouds and above them was the majesty of the space with all its stars and nebulae visible in the bright daytime sky, there is not a single wisp of wind as the entire plain appeared to be experiencing perfect weather. The subtle strums of a harp echo in the distance accompanied by a heavenly but distant choir of voices signing from a great distance.

The mystic voice appeared once more to greet him to a new realm whispering all around him "Welcome to *Utopia*, a perfect paradise where peace, joy, and goodness prevail and where all good things are possible".

Jack upon recognizing the voice asked Malachi about it "Malachi, who is that woman, that voice that greets you whenever you enter a new place?"

Malachi stumbled at the answer "There are only theories as to who or what the "voice" is; but it is always a woman's voice that advises, or in rare cases warns of impending danger. But it seems incapable of fully interacting with us, so we can only guess."

Jack thought for a moment saying to himself "interesting, this "voice" is a strange concept indeed…"

He then refocused to the matter at hand "So in a place like this, what sort of transportation are we likely to find? Are we by chance going to ride around on a cloud?".

Malachi then clarified "It's not going to be much of a team effort, *you* are going to create a vehicle"

Jack replied with surprise "What? You said we were coming here to *acquire* a ride, not build one…"

Malachi reiterated "A *Traveler* is capable of creating and altering the *Astral Plane* to a degree not possible by constructs; you can use that power to forge a powerful vehicle, you need only begin."

Jack scoffed "Let me guess, I'm going to be doing all the designing as well, right?"

Malachi encouraged with some light humor "You're the one with the power, *Traveler*".

Jack thought of the many things he could possibly want in a vehicle, but he was always captivated by the prospect of commanding a mighty airship capable of a great many things. Though Jack remembered his lesson with Balthazar, and that in order to manifest something complicated he would likely need to start with its fundamentals and then assemble it in layers; though in some way he preferred it that way, whatever he was about to create wouldn't be special or unique if it just fell from the sky.

Jack scanned the surroundings, but he saw nothing of use so he asked "I need components, where are some materials I can use?"

Malachi replied "This is *Utopia*; anything you desire will come forth. Simply imagine what it is you need and it will materialize"

Upon hearing that Jack said with excitement "Ah I understand now; Ok then, I have an idea….. Stand back".

The choir in the distance began chanting louder and faster as Jack readied himself. Jack slowly raised both his arms in the air as the ground shook, a great section shelf of earth and stone rose into the air in front of him by his will. Jack then thrust a shockwave at it with the telekinetic gloves and shattered it into a great storm of pieces. Jack pulled from the debris great clusters of various ores and collected them together, then focused on heating them as the ore melted away revealing the molten metal inside. As the metal collected Jack looked at an untouched section of plain and pointed at it with his right hand, then as if to command the ground itself he clenched his fist causing great trees to suddenly sprout from the ground; wasting no time he uprooted the trees compacted one of the larger rocks into a flat disc and spun it with great force, throwing the timber at it to slice them into many boards at once. As the process intensified so did the choir in the distance as other instruments began to be heard: the dramatic resonance of violins, the blaring of horns, and the pounding of drums all coming together as a symphony. Using many subtle movements of his hands Jack began to mold and shape the larger molten pools into the many beams that would make the frame; as the metal cooled Jack brought his hands together pressing the left over rocks together into great sheets, compressing them into dense smooth plates before rapidly heating them into form, making them into great ceramic plates. Jack tempered the metal beams and ceramic plates alternating between focusing on heat and then rapidly cooling them by manifesting gusts of wind against them; then moved the great beams into their positions forming the frame of the ship. Jack thrust his hand down at each seam, calling down lightning to strike and fuse the great beams together. Jack then circled his hands from the boards to the frame over and over again moving the hundreds of boards into the decks and walls in a repetitive sequence sliding each individual board rapidly into place as he used the smaller metal pieces as rivets heating them up and bolting them into place to hold everything together. As he finished building the superstructure he covered it all with metal sheets before bringing the large rock plates onto the outside to further reinforce its armor, securing them on with thick sturdy metal bolts.

The music began to reach its crescendo as Jack said "Now for the power source…" as he formed his hands around an invisible mass as energy seemed flow from Jack's eyes and collect into his hands; it pulsed and surged as he closed his hands around it concentrating it into a small orb, it then stabilized as Jack sat down exhausted.

The hull of the massive ship was now complete and hovered in place as if suspended by an unknown force.

Malachi remarked "This vehicle seems a bit…excessive"

Jack replied humorously "Why not travel in style". They both stood there for a moment beholding the finished creation.

It was tremendous in its proportions being easily the size of a warehouse or an aircraft carrier and looked as if it would require a crew of hundreds to operate.

Malachi inquired "So what manner of vehicle is this behemoth?"

Jack said in disbelief "You've never seen an air-ship before?"

Malachi couldn't help but laugh "Surely you jest, there is nothing practical about a ship that flies?!"

Jack countered "There are plenty of great stories and games with airships or spaceships in them".

Malachi sighed and said "Well it should probably have a name, so we can properly designate this gigantic craft."

Jack replied already knowing the name "It will be called *The Harbinger*"

Malachi somewhat humorously replied "I suppose that is an appropriate name, as it will likely be seen and heard approaching from miles away".

As they finished a familiar barn appeared nearby, as if from the sky, and from it came a number of large numbers of components, computers, pieces of equipment, and a few vehicles; which gently floated out as Jack opened the loading doors on the side of the "*Harbinger*" and moved them inside.

Malachi inquired "Equipping it?"

Jack replied "Correct, I have imagined a great many devices over the years; there is more than enough to outfit even this large ship." As all the parts and vehicles moved to the inside of the ship and began automatically sorting themselves into place; Jack and Malachi walked onto a cargo elevator that lowered onto the ground below, then it swiftly lifted them into the ship's main cargo bay.

As they entered the bay the lights flickered on revealing the massive room in the bottom of the ship.

Jack began explaining its various parts as if he were a tour guide "This is the cargo bay which will house all the equipment and supplies that we may need on our journey."

He pointed to the equipment racks against the opposite wall and the many scattered boxes and barrels with various random supplies, then he motioned at the cargo elevator which brought them in and pointed at the larger stronger cranes near it "These elevators and cranes will allow us to load and unload from the ship quickly without needing to land the ship and leave it exposed".

Malachi responded with a light critique "*Traveler*'s typically aren't burdened by the challenges of... logistics"

Jack replied "Hey you never know, just go with it? Ok". Then they walked to the back and opened a large door which opened into the engine room.

In the center lay a massive reactor surrounded by many capacitors, stabilizers, and thick cables to transfer power elsewhere about the ship. The reactor had yet to be activated though so it was mostly dormant, Jack retrieved the power orb he created before and slid it into the center of the engine which came to life and rapidly began powering up the ship.

Jack explained "As the *Astral Plane* is concerned mainly with 'the will to power' this ship will be powered by the energy of my subconscious; thus will only be controllable by myself and no other."

Malachi said admiringly "You certainly have constructed a secure control mechanism; I'm guessing by the size of this reactor that it will not run out of power anytime soon"

Jack confirmed "You are correct, it and I are connected; as long as I remain, it will be powered."

Jack commented upon thinking of a possible situation "This does not however mean it is invincible, I designed this ship to be strong and have a lot of staying-power, but nothing should ever be designed to be too good, as you never want a creation to surpass its creator"

Malachi looked at him with confusion "That is a very peculiar point of view"

Jack commented a reassurance "Trust me, stories are full of examples of figures learning this lesson the hard way, and I'd rather not repeat their mistake" then he motioned for them to go up the stairs between the two vast rooms.

As they entered the 2nd deck they found themselves in a large hangar filled with many different types of aircraft, their armaments, various repair equipment, and an array of fuel tanks in the back.

Jack explained "This is the primary hangar, from here we can operate a wide variety of aircraft for special tasks or in case we need to project power around the ship".

Malachi in a puzzled way "How will these aircraft leave this place, this room has a ceiling and four walls"

Jack exclaimed "I'm glad you asked!"

He then he ran over to the nearby control station and hit one of the red buttons, one of the aircraft ignited its engines as steam driven pads below it accelerated it towards the far end of the wall from a dead stop to an incredible speed within an instant; before the aircraft impacted with the wall a trapdoor opened in the blink of an eye allowing the aircraft to takeoff before shutting again as fast as it opened.

Malachi said with surprise "That is… a process I will allow you to experiment with first".

Jack laughed as he hit a few more buttons and the aircraft swiftly returned, coming to a stop right where it was, then he assured "It's not dangerous, I wouldn't have built it without fail-safes."

Jack then proceeded through the back doors into a series of smaller rooms as Malachi followed. They entered the commons area where there was a mess hall, as well as a few hallways with individualized quarters, and an entertainment room on the far side.

Jack detailed "This is the common area, our home away from home, here we can rest and relax if need be"

Malachi replied "I hope you don't plan on spending too much time here".

Jack shrugged as he commented "Sometimes the best way to figure out something is to stop dwelling on it; besides you never know when you might need to collect yourself". Jack walked to the end of the room and hit the button on the elevator, as he and Malachi stepped inside and it took them up to the next floor.

The door opened into a long room with large weapons turrets symmetrically lined on both sides ranging from large cannons, to heavy machine guns, to missile launchers, even one or two exotic looking energy weapons. Near the elevator was a circular control station with many monitors displaying targeting information.

Jack explained from the elevator "This is the main array, where all our firepower is housed, in the center is the fire control center where the guns can each be independently controlled and fired if need be. This array should pack enough firepower to deal with any hostile threats we may encounter, and I assure you that many of these weapons will use guided projectiles capable of hitting targets all around the ship."

Malachi nodded as he added "The most redeeming feature thus far". The elevator doors closed and took them up to the next floor.

The doors opened to a room that resembled an obstacle course with an open pad in the circle for sparring, Jack summed it up with a few words "The training room".

As they got off and walked to the far side of the room; he then opened another door that led to a medical infirmary with lots of beds, lab equipment, surgical tools, and a variety of biological charts and diagrams.

Jack summed it up as well "the infirmary, a section that I hope will not be needed"

Malachi tried to understand the rationale behind it "You do know that in the *Astral Plane* medicine and medical devices serve no real purpose, right?"

Jack countered with simple logic "Hope for the best, plan for the worst" as they returned to the elevator.

They went up to the next floor and the doors opened to a series of computers around a large central mainframe. There were a number of terminals around it displaying various types of information from status reports to sensory information around the ship; there were also a wide variety of supporting communications equipment in the periphery of the room (phones, radios, transmitters, etc). Jack's attention turned to the mainframe as he began almost showing it off "This is the central computer, a vast calculating and processing apparatus run by an artificial intelligence, it is capable of organizing and coordinating the ships systems and will automate any function of the ship when needed".

The mainframe was a shiny onyx dome covered with many small lights and intricate circuits, it crackled to life as a computerized voice spoke: "I am Eleanor the ship's computer, I will maintain and optimize the ships instruments and equipment as well as control multiple system simultaneously, I am also capable of gathering and processing information and presenting it in a tactically relevant format."

Jack nodded and acknowledged "Thank you Eleanor, keep me posted"

Malachi interjected "That computer sounds a lot like the "voice" we discussed about before"

Jack responded and affirmed "It is modelled after that same voice actually, I find it to be somewhat soothing, though its adjusted to be closer to monotone so I don't confuse the two. I'm sure you'll find Eleanor to be quite helpful, as well as level headed and calm regardless of the circumstances." Then they returned to the elevator and ascended to the top floor: the bridge.

The doors opened up into a large open room with many status screens, control mechanisms, and viewing screens. At its center lie a fine crafted wooden chair with a padded back and armrests, directly in front of the chair was a compact viewing screen projecting a 3-D image of the ship and its surroundings; and in front of that chair was an even larger screen against the back wall primarily displaying the view in front of the ship.

Jack introduced the room with a sense of pride saying "Finally, the bridge, the most important part of any ship".

Jack strode to the seat and hopped in, rather casually saying "The captain's chair, where I will command and pilot the ship".

Malachi asked "No elaborate control mechanism?"

Jack replied "Eleanor will assist with the more complicated aspects, but I have opted to make the ship's direction and speed controllable directly by my will, thus enabling the ship to respond through my thoughts alone".

Upon finishing his description, Jack took hold of a peculiar earpiece and placed it in his ear; once he triggered it by pressing a button on it. The ship was then hastily activated and seemed to directly to what he intended it to do without noticeable delays or feedback.

Malachi took a final look around the bridge and concluded "This vessel you have built could be described as excessively large, bulky, cumbersome, needlessly overcomplicated-"

Jack interrupted "Please get to the point."

Malachi smirked and continued "But you seem to have designed its features with utility in mind, and you have made it easy to command; I am not above admitting to being wrong, this ship may prove useful when the time comes."

Jack replied "Thank you Malachi, I'm glad you've come around to liking *the Harbinger*." Then he powered up the screen in front of him and initiated *the Harbinger's* launch, as it lifted into the air and accelerated to a moderate cruising speed.

Jack looked over his shoulder to Malachi and inquired "So what emotions must be elicited in order to travel to this *Mirage*? I assume it is a like the other places"

Malachi replied "I would argue that it's not like the other places at all, but you are correct in your assumptions: in order to travel to Mirage you must focus on the mundane, conformity, and submission".

Before Jack did this he turned around and asked Malachi commenting "This doesn't sound like a great place, why are we going there again?"

Malachi replied cryptically "When we arrive, the answers will be made clear". Jack shrugged and began focusing on the former mentioned thoughts, and as he did the entire ship began to increase in speed, rapidly jumping forward as the surrounding sky and background streaked past them.

As always they traveled an immense distance within moments until suddenly coming to an abrupt but smooth stop over a dense sprawling metropolis that stretched to every horizon, seeming to extend outwards without limit or end.

9

MIRAGE

THE HARBINGER HOVERED OVER THE ENDLESS CITYSCAPE, BELOW THEM the city's grid like streets were empty and desolate. Jack beholding from the projection of the view screens remarked "This is the most familiar place so far, yet I find it ironic that such a generic place could be found within the imaginative dimension of the *Astral Plane*".

Malachi remarked indignantly "I consider it blight, unworthy of this place or any other place for that matter"

Jack was taken aback by this as he responded with a laugh "I'm not sure it deserves such condemnation, this is hardly the revelation I was expecting…"

Then he examined the screen closer and inquired "Where are the people? Surely even an imagined city has inhabitants".

Malachi explained "When most people have a dream, their experience is shaped by their individual perspective; everything is filtered through this unique lens that shields dreamers from the thoughts of others, allowing them to experience a dream uninterrupted. Basically other people are there, you just cannot see them".

Jack nodded while rubbing his chin in contemplation "That explains a great deal…very interesting indeed. But wait, if I am a *Traveler* does that mean I will be able to surpass this rule and view them, and perhaps even interact with them."

Malachi affirmed "Yes and no, you see each mind has a stronger or weaker affinity for the *Astral Plane* which determines how deep their minds delve into these respective realms. With most people you will find they have a fairly weak connection, and cannot be interacted with, others will have much stronger connections depending on their state of mind."

Malachi detailed "When you become aware of a person within the *Astral Plane*, it will manifest as a ghostly representation of their psyche that we refer to as *"Avatars"*; interacting with an *"Avatar"* exposes you to a risk though, as the awareness becomes reciprocal: you will be able to interact and view them, but they will also be able to interact and view you at the same time."

Jack seemed unsure of the threat posed as he questioned "Why would this be dangerous? Surely I am capable, what possible risk could they pose to me?"

Malachi elaborated "While in the dream-state, *Avatars* with strong connections to the *Astral Plane* are often gripped by intense emotion, this strong expression of emotion makes them very powerful here and extremely unpredictable. You may not know which *Avatars* are which until you've already made yourself present to them".

Jack reflected upon the many often chaotic experiences he had during his many dreams and was able to understand.

Malachi then added, "However, due to the circumstances of *Mirage* the dream dwellers here often have weak connections and will behave in a very passive manner".

This piqued Jack's curiosity and he now wished to see these people firsthand as he headed for the elevator "I must see this for myself, let's get to the surface and you will show me how to see them".

Jack and Malachi quickly made their way to the cargo bay of the ship, where they proceeded to board the elevator and lowered it to the ground.

Jack tapped his earpiece and said "Eleanor, once we're on the ground circle the ship around in a holding pattern until we're ready to embark"

The electronic voice replied from a tiny speaker on the earpiece "Yes captain".

The elevator reached the ground and the two stepped off, no sooner than they arrived the ship complied with Jack's order and retracted the elevator before jetting away.

Jack turned to Malachi and curiously inquired "So, how do I begin?"

Malachi instructed "Instead of simply observing our surroundings, take a point of reference and look...look deeper".

Jack looked over at a nearby street corner and began concentrating, upon seeing nothing he tried harder making his face turn red as he began to sweat.

Malachi quickly advised "The key is not intensity, stop trying to force them to appear and simply *look past* the objects that make up the background" Jack followed this advice and let his mind drift more into abstract examination; then slowly, like an optical illusion, the images began to slowly reveal themselves.

The many shapes took the form of fiery, cloud like illusions; Jack was awed at the sight of them. "Incredible" he uttered, observing the hundreds of ghostly figures busily going through their routines, at the moment none of them seemed to notice Jack or Malachi.

Jack expressed his wonder at the sight of them "This isn't how I pictured them at all, they seem so strange. So these are the people that are asleep?"

Malachi explained "They are indeed people that are asleep; these "*Avatars*" as we call them are able to perceive and interact with the things in their dream but they are not here to a full extent".

Jack remembered part of the conversation he had before "This is what Melchior meant earlier: here and not here, which must be why he was so surprised by my appearance...Malachi, can we communicate with these ones?"

Malachi replied "Probably not, as I said before these ones are barely here, they are much like ghosts: going about their existence stopping only occasionally to notice those others around them, but again I caution: The state of mind of an *Avatar* may shift and give them a stronger connection of the *Astral Plane*; when this occurs they may respond much more intensely, going as far to lash out against those it perceives as enemies or threats. As this occurs their presence may become fleeting and difficult to detect, phasing in and out of our existence while their perspective shifts along with their connection to this place".

Jack looked deeply at one of the *Avatars*, their appearance was so surreal: a flickering, almost polymorphous form; a combination of mist and fire that seemed bound to the shape of a human but constantly seeking to escape. Jack brought his hand to the face of the *Avatar* which seemed to reveal more of its true self through the shifting mist and flame, taking the vague shape of a person's face. The *Avatar* slowly brought its hand to Jack's face in return, he could nearly feel their hand upon his face; like the sensation that something was nearly touching but was just out of physical contact. As the *Avatar* stared at Jack it seemed on the verge of speaking before a blaring message crackled through the many TV's and radios situated about the city. The *Avatar* immediately stopped what it was doing and rejoined the other *Avatars* who were now marching forward almost robotically, as they left Jack's view he wondered if he had any effect, or if he too were perceived as yet another illusion in the mind of another.

Jack sighed deeply as Malachi seized the moment to plead his position. "These people are trapped in their own minds Jack. The *Astral Plane* is meant to inspire us to create great forms of art, culture, to enrich our existence and those of others! These people have become mired by the hardships of their lives, which shackles them to this pathetic excuse for a dream; with ever more minds entering that state of mind, this *Mirage* of their real lives slowly spreads outward snuffing out all other things in the *Astral Plane*, If unchecked it will eventually transform every realm… into this!" Malachi finished as he motioned to the never ending drab urban sprawl all around them.

Jack, unsure of what effect he could have, questioned "This problem seems so substantial, what would you have me do?"

Malachi implored "Help me liberate them! And in so doing restore the life of the *Astral Plane*"

Jack remembered part of his conversation with Melchior about those who resist *Travelers* when he asked "What of those who disagree? Will they fight to preserve *Mirage*, even if it is for the worse?".

Malachi grudgingly answered "Even here in the *Astral Plane*, there are those who believe they can control everything by setting rules and restrictions, all in the name of a supposed "stability"; in their arrogance they seek to impose order on what will always be chaos. They fear the upheaval that comes with great change, that sudden shift which may cause many things to be destroyed, undone, and forgotten; to be lost forever in obscurity is the root of their deepest fear, and they will fight bitterly against any force of change to avoid it".

Then Malachi said somewhat reluctantly exposing some weakness on his part "Given the power I would see this prison of *Mirage* ended! And the *Astral Plane* restored to its former glory! But I am unable to influence the *Astral Plane* in such a way…which is why I need you, the great catalyst of change that is the *Traveler*".

Jack abruptly asked "But why? Why does any of this matter to you?"

Malachi responded "Because nothing is more important than determining one's own destiny; Freedom, and not some abstraction of the word, but true, unabridged freedom. This place is an invaluable sanctuary that must be renewed so that it might endure. That pursuit is my purpose."

Jack was a bit surprised by all this, here a man that seemed cool and collected was motivated not by self-interest (as he would have guessed) but by a desire to fight for freedom, it didn't seem to match up.

Jack inquired "You don't seem to be the crusading type, why didn't you make your case to me in the first place?"

To which Malachi instantly resumed his previous cool, collected manner and said almost bluntly "I hoped that showing you the problem, so that you might see the predicament first-hand, would persuade you more than mere words.".

Jack slightly irritated responded "I would have appreciated more candor on your part, but I will consider your proposal nonetheless."

Malachi cordially replied "Thank you *Traveler*, I will of course continue to provide information if you continue to assist me".

Jack made sure to convey that it wasn't a set deal yet saying "What you're asking is a lot to consider, and this isn't a decision to make lightly; I will need time to think it over…".

As Jack finished he began to hear the rapid notes of many violins as they played their rhythm ever faster, as the sound began to overpower his senses he knew what was occurring, as it was similar to the other times he was awakening.

Jack said while he still could "Looks like I am about to wake up…"

Malachi replied back saying louder than usual as if Jack were drifting away "When you have made your decision find me at the Tavern" Jack then gave a thumbs up gesture in return as he shot like a cannon into the sky; very quickly everything around him sped away until absent, giving way to nothingness until he was left in a void.

No sooner than everything had disappeared the surroundings of his basement lab seemed to phase in from nothingness, as the light slowly diffused into his surroundings.

Jack was certain that his shocking device was either failing (or detached) and that he had been asleep for a long while, at least 24 hours must have passed maybe more, but once his vision became clear enough to see he looked upon the clock to see that only 14 hours had passed.

"What!? Only fourteen hours how is that possible!!" Jack exclaimed, checking the clock again to make sure it was not simply the time of a different day; however after checking the date on his computer, he found that his first observation was indeed correct.

Jack was now starting to worry; he remembered that many dreams had the effect of seeming to last longer than the actual duration of sleep, but how much longer could they go on to last? Days, weeks, more…

"Perhaps this was part of Balthazar's warning, part of the mind's adaptation; the burdens of visiting this place are becoming very heavy indeed" Jack thought to himself as he began to have doubts as the direction his research was taking.

Jack's focus was returning slowly, as if he were recovering from a strong disorientation. Normally he would begin jotting some notes, but his senses were being overpowered by mental exhaustion; he needed to get some food and regain his bearings first before he could do anything. Once he felt somewhat centered he attempted to get up, but both his legs were so numb that he simply fell over; Jack was having difficulty with even basic motor functions. As he looked around the entire room seemed to blur and shift, Jack had difficulty finding a single point of reference that wasn't distorted. "RETURN" Jack heard once more, he looked in every direction and saw nothing. Jack quickly dismissed the voice yet again, and forced himself up staggering up the stairs using the arm rails to stay on his feet. He managed to stagger into the kitchen where he immediately opened the fridge and began consuming its contents right there and then; he felt as if he hadn't eaten or drunk anything for days. Satisfied he fell over and crawled into the bathroom for some much needed…refreshment.

Upon finishing he flopped down into his armchair and tried just to center himself, but the dizziness was only getting worse and the corners of his vision began fading in and out; Jack thought he was either losing consciousness or losing his sanity, though he wasn't quite sure which.

Jack said aloud trying to understand the situation "Awakening is becoming increasingly difficult, Have I almost reached an equilibrium, or am I hopelessly falling deeper into this unknown place" Jack thought for a time trying to make some sense of what was happening, thinking very deeply to himself.

After considering all the information he had come across, and possible explanations, he considered a troubling theory "If under normal circumstances the conscious mind suppresses the subconscious, then what if the machines stimulation of the subconscious is causing it to become super-active; if that is true then the subconscious is slowly becoming the

114

dominant thought pattern, this reversal would result in losing the ability of sustaining a conscious level of awareness. Which means…"

Jack couldn't bring himself to say it the rest but he heard the answer in a reverberating voice that wasn't his own "You will be trapped in the *Astral Plane*, unable to wake".

Jack turned to see that a dark shrouded figure had suddenly appeared in the opposite corner of the room, Jack didn't know who or what this figure was but he had no time to talk, he needed to take action now saying with urgency "I've let this go too far! I have to find a way to reverse the process"

Jack hurried to get on his feet but the figure pointed at him and he uncontrollably sat back down, the figure then said still in a deep echoing tone "It is too late for that now, you are in too deep".

Jack tried to get up but the figure had no trouble restraining him to his chair by some unseen force he couldn't explain. Jack demanded "What do you want?"

As the figure replied calmly "For you to return, and do what must be done".

Jack resisted "I'm not going to help you, you do not control me" but he knew the present situation was bad, he couldn't move, it was almost as if he was paralyzed.

The figure laughed and said mockingly "You will find you that in this regard you have very little control, I have the power to send you back, and you are in no state to resist."

The shadowy figure then concluded as the entire room seemed to shake with his every word "Know this, *Traveler*: You have a purpose which must be carried out, and until you do I will not allow you to awaken. Now I command you to RETURN!"

With a burst of energy Jack was propelled downwards through the floor as his surroundings and reality itself spiraled away quickly fading into a void. Jack jumped up out of the chair and tried to fight against the downward current of darkness; he was struggling to reach the distant light from his conscious surroundings above, but despite his best efforts it remained far away. He was fighting against an overwhelming tide; he gnashed his teeth and clenched his fists straining against it. After a few short moments of resistance Jack was unable to continue and fell downwards into the abyss.

Jack's vision went black as he was overtaken by darkness, what seemed to be a great deal of time passed; vague shapes began to form in the black, until slowly the area was filled with a dull red glow accompanied by a thick fog. Jack found he was surrounded by a hellish wasteland filled with the bodies of the dead; from the distance all that could be heard were the screams of horror and the occasional calling of monstrous creatures. The mystic voice which had greeted him so many times returned, but this time with a warning "You have entered *Terror*, a place of fear and dread; beware its many horrors, lest you become one of their victims".

10

TERROR

*I*T TOOK A MOMENT, BUT *J*ACK QUICKLY REALIZED THAT HE HAD BEEN thrown back into the *Astral Plane* from full consciousness, and presumably by a construct no less. Jack said in shock "That's not possible! Is it?! How did that thing send me back, what the hell does he want?!" Jack frustrated punched a nearby lava rock, smashing right through its rough surface.

A cursory glance of his surroundings told Jack everything he needed to know about this place; it was clearly a place of nightmares he did not wish to see further. He attempted to escape immediately by focusing on the village and walking forward, but nothing happened; then he tried thinking of various other realms and walking forward, but time and time again he could not travel out, he was stuck.

Jack wasn't sure what to make of the current situation, thinking that perhaps the rules were different here. After quick observation Jack found he was not carrying his usual complement of weapons or any other items that usually accompanied him. Jack attempted to focus on recovering these items and tried imagining them within his hands, as before a plume of smoke appeared and light began to shine from it. In the middle of the process though Jack's mind was suddenly gripped by an unexplainable fear making it impossible to concentrate, Jack had to break off the process early before he could accomplish anything.

"Dammit! This just keeps getting better and better" Jack exclaimed in frustration. Jack was weaponless, in a nightmarish place, with no way out, things were definitely bad.

Before he could think of anything else a plot of ground nearby began to move and shift, from it a ghastly figure slowly clawed its way to the surface staring at Jack with dead eyes. It was a putrid rotting corpse still wearing the trappings of a man, yet it had no expression on its face and seemed unaffected by its many injuries, Jack knew exactly what this was: a zombie!

Jack jumped back shouting "AHH! I hate Zombies! They are disgusting!!" He looked around for any weapon he could use but there was nothing, and from the many stories Jack had heard he didn't want to risk fighting it hand to hand.

Jack had to think quickly as the zombie was now upright and was slowly lurching towards him. Quickly he remembered the lesson Balthazar taught him on summoning and he hastily began focusing on the thought of a simple weapon as a plume of smoke formed in his hands and light shone from within; the fear that had paralyzed him before began to rise again so Jack quickly finished it and retrieved a metal axe that was old and was covered in rust.

Jack, slightly irritated, said "Good enough!" then swung it horizontally at the zombie with his entire body, cleaving in two!

The zombie moaned as its blood drained out, wasting no time Jack brought the axe down on its head with a strong overhead swing that finished it off. Before Jack could celebrate he saw multiple other plots begin to move and shift, indicating more enemies would soon unearth themselves. Looking around for somewhere more safe to run to, he spotted some flickering lights in the distance; deciding that was good enough for now he sprinted towards it, with axe in hand, in the direction of the light source hoping he could find some sort of refuge in this place.

Upon arriving he saw that it was the remains of a town that had some great calamity befall it: the buildings were dilapidated and abandoned, skeletal remains were strewn about the streets, and there were fresh signs of blood and death. The lights were in fact ghostly visages which lingered in many of the buildings; they suddenly vanished as Jack began to hear the ill placed singing of children in the distance, which ended with the echoing of their whispering in unison "Join us".

With that the skeletons came to life and began staggering towards him with red lights for eyes. Jack began backing away as he turned to see an even greater number of zombies creeping up behind.

Jack was surrounded and could not escape; he began to panic as he yelled to psyche himself up "You want to fight?! I'll hack every one of you to pieces!" then began swinging his axe like a madman at every enemy near him; hacking and chopping his way through the horde of undead.

"AAAAAHHHHH!" Jack yelled and shouted desperately trying to fight his way through them.

As Jack slew all but a handful before him his axe began to wear down, he swung it through several at once breaking the axe at the end of the swing as he turned and was grabbed by the sole remaining zombie.

It continued forward knocking Jack over as it closed in for the fatal bite to his neck; Jack pushed against it with all his might but had trouble getting it off him because it had its clutches wrapped around Jack's forearms tightly. Jack was able to leverage his knee under its torso and quickly tossed it to the side, grabbing the first thing he could find (a rock) he furiously smashed it into the zombies face repeatedly until it stopped moving. As the panic wore off Jack stepped away from their remains and sat down as he tried to calm down, panting excessively as the panic wore off, he was still trembling from the stress of the ordeal.

Jack spotted the broken axe and kicked it aside angrily "Piece of crap, almost got me killed"

Reflecting on the unpleasant encounter he just had, Jack made a mental note "I should really start using some sort of armor for these kinds of encounters".

Once Jack had time to re-center himself he decided it was best to keep moving. Jack made his way out of the town walking on an old stone road that went through a dark forest of dead trees, Jack had difficulty seeing as a thick lingering darkness seemed to restrict visibility and light sources were mostly absent. Suddenly a pale man emerged in front of him from the darkness, Jack jumped back surprised as the man said quietly "Do not fear death, embrace it".

Jack punched forward but the image instantly faded. Jack continued walking forward as he heard another voice whisper "Jack, you're only delaying the inevitable"

Suddenly he felt hands on his back, Jack swiftly turned around but found nothing; Jack sprinted down the road trying to escape from whatever was haunting him. As Jack ran another sound of footsteps seemed right behind him, matching his speed; yet another voice said "You cannot escape" as Jack stopped and looked in every direction for the aberration.

Suddenly ghostly images of a gnarled and twisted face appeared from his surroundings and rapidly closed in, their screams of agony rising from a whisper to becoming the only thing he could hear, Jack tripped backward falling onto the ground as the grass began to enclose on him and several ghostly visages closed in.

Jack concentrated on clearing his mind saying aloud "This is an illusion, this is an illusion, this is an illusion, Snap out of it!!" as suddenly he found himself upright with no sign of whatever was haunting him. Jack was relieved they were gone, yet he was careful to keep his guard up and stay moving.

Jack continued forward reaching a crossroads with a road sign in the middle pointing different ways; from out of nowhere a black raven flew in and landed on top of the sign, it turned and gazed at Jack with glowing red eyes, screeching CRAW! CRAW!

Jack readied for an attack but something unexpected happened as he heard a strange voice say "A bit lost are we?" Jack looked around to find the source but then looked again to the raven, as it spoke "You've never encountered a talking raven before?"

Jack replied hesitantly "Um, no, what do you want?"

The raven replied "Perhaps we can make a deal?".

Jack replied in suspicion "Er, I don't think I can trust you"

The raven replied in an upset manner "Why?? Because I'm a raven! Ooh big scary black bird, must be evil, has he ever done anything to you? No, but I'm judging solely by his appearance because I'm a jerk! RAAK!"

Jack was a bit lost for words as he replied "Eh well, it's just that"

The raven interrupted him "You know ravens used to be respected back in Norse times, Noah even used one in the bible, but do people remember that, No; it's always evil bird this, and evil omen that, nevermore, nevermore, RAAK!."

Jack threw his hands up in the air as he said "Alright! Alright! Sorry, had no idea you were going to be so touchy."

The raven mockingly replied "Well that's what you get for being such a narrow-minded, flightless idiot; I have half a mind to retract my offer".

Jack cut to the chase and said "So what kind of deal were you offering?".

The raven gave his proposal "Ahem, as you have no doubt noticed *Terror* is an entangling realm making it difficult for most to leave; I on the other hand, may come and go freely, which means I can get you help from outside this place"

Jack knew there had to be some condition so he asked "What do you want in return?"

The raven replied "You have to acquire a valuable gem for me first"

Jack corrected "You mean steal it."

The raven laughed as it replied "Aw, now did I say that, CRAW! CRAW! CRAW!"

Jack accepted knowing that he didn't have any other options to work with "Ok I'll do it; it's not like I have many other options, where is this gem?"

The raven pointed with its wing "At the end of this road you will find the manor, be wary its inhabitants are… most unpleasant, as I'm sure you will find out"

Jack irritably replied "Anything else?"

The raven began to lift off as it finished "Stay away from the mirrors, they are quite nasty. CRAW!" then it flew off, quickly disappearing into the night.

Jack knew the last place he wanted to go was a haunted house, especially in a place like this; however, he had no other way of leaving so he had no choice but to continue. Jack started down the road keeping an eye out for any more suspicious occurrences hinting at danger; after a short walk the forest surrounding the road opened to a clearing blocked off by an old iron gate and stone walls.

The gate had a foreboding sign on it that read "Beware! Intruders shall perish!" which had a number of skulls dangling from it as a not so subtle warning.

Jack pushed the creaky gate open and proceeded towards the old, dilapidated mansion just up the way. As Jack neared the front door he knew he would probably need a weapon and a light source; knowing that some force limited his concentration in this place, he made certain to make what he summoned small and easy to picture. Concentrating quickly, he summoned a small flashlight making it appear with the typical plume of smoke; then concentrating a little harder, coming to the edge of his limits, he made a silver short sword using a similar process. Jack wasn't sure what he might encounter within the manor, but silver had a reputation for helping to slay evil creatures. Jack was hoping in the back of his mind that he could find the gem quickly and leave before anything happened. Jack walked up to the big wooden door and turned the handle, pushing the large doors open.

The front door opened to a large hallway and staircase adorned with old paintings, everything was covered in dust, and was lit by dull candlelight. As Jack stepped inside the door rapidly closed behind him, startling him as he looked around to make sure it wasn't an ambush, but nothing further happened.

Jack turned on the flashlight and began walking through the house, with every footstep came the creaking of the floorboards sending chills up his spine. Jack could see just by looking around that something terrible had happened in this house, dried blood was everywhere and the scribbled writings of madness covered its walls. Jack stopped to read one message "Something about *it* is evil, *it* agitates me, whispers to me, I can't make it stop!".

Jack wasn't sure if what happened here was imagined, or the representation of something that really happened, either way he hoped by keeping an eye out for warnings he could potentially avoid its pitfalls. Jack began looking through the rooms on the first floor, searching by the light of his flashlight; most were just filled with furniture covered in dusty sheets, Jack continued searching in hopes that one of them would contain something useful. Then Jack reached what looked to be the study judging by the uncovered desk and bookshelf, on top of the desk was an old typewriter and beside it was a small combination box.

Jack checked his surroundings to see if he could find a note on the combination somewhere, paying attention to the writings in that particular room; glancing at one as he read "This thing makes me see things that aren't real, showing me horrible, terrible visions, I should just destroy it. Yet some visions are true, it told me the combination "721" and it was right! Does that mean the other images are true as well!!".

Jack used the combination on the box and it opened, it only contained a key, an address book, and a few receipts most of which referenced "boiler repair", "plumbing work" and "foundation work"; Jack could only guess that the receipts were pointing him towards the basement, easily the last place he wanted to visit in this house. When Jack took the key the typewriter began typing by itself, Jack quickly looked around but could not see anyone who or what was using the typewriter. After it finished he grabbed the message which seemed to be another warning "Many enter this house but few leave, turn back now while you still can…"

Jack grumbled to himself "If only it were that easy". Jack then left the room in search of the basement.

Jack walked around the outside of the house taking care to watch his step and tread lightly, in the back he found a double door leading underground so he put the key in the lock and turned it, opening the door. The basement had no lighting whatsoever so Jack was waving the flashlight back and forth in a paranoid manner making sure to illuminate every corner of that dark place, he wanted to make sure there wasn't anything hiding in wait for him. Jack noticed that the basement was filled with many bizarre and disturbing instruments of torture all caked in old blood, as Jack's flashlight scanned the room he suddenly saw dead faces! Jack jumped back, seeing that in one corner was a stack of bodies in burlap sacks each with the face of the skull showing; luckily for Jack none of them came alive, much to his relief, yet the sight of them was quite disturbing.

Jack noticed there was quite a bit more writing on these walls, the lettering also seemed more frantic and rushed; Jack took a moment to read one of the inscriptions "Murderer! My husband is a murderer! How could I have been such a fool! There are so many bodies and so much blood!! The visions were true! This is the business that he had been hiding from me; this whole house is probably bought with blood money. Tonight I will confront him and do the horrible things which he has done to so many others; then after he is writhing in agony I will take his life!!!".

This message was very distressing to Jack as it revealed this house was a source of much evil, the discovery of which lead to madness and betrayal; Jack now wanted to leave now very much, but *Terror* was likely full of such horrible places which is why he had to press on and obtain the means of escape from the realm. Jack saw on the main table in the center a key which seemed out of place, it was a fine engraved key which was far too fancy to be a key to anything in that particular room. Jack picked up the key examining it closely seeing that it was adorned with a particular crest, before Jack could come to any conclusions he heard footsteps that sounded close. Jack immediately became alert scanning the room, but quickly noticed footprints appearing and disappearing on the floor. With each appearance came the sound, with the trail leading away towards to exit.

Jack followed the footsteps wondering where it was leading, as they entered the house and moved upstairs; then they disappeared entirely upon reaching the double doors of the master bedroom, Jack observed the same crest he noticed on the key upon the door.

"This is it" Jack said knowing he had reached the last stage of his search, he took a deep breath and placed the key within the lock. Turning the key it made a distinctive click once the bolt retracted.

"AAAAAAHHHHHH!!!" Jack heard as he immediately jumped back.

The door began shaking and banging violently as the screams grew louder, Jack readied himself for whatever lay on the opposite side; the screaming stopped as blood pooled through the bottom of the door, Jack kicked the door open and rushed inside! The room was entirely empty save for a chair in the center with a bizarre covered object behind it, the blood was even gone. Upon further inspection Jack saw that the chair had a dead body in it, one that was bound to the chair with barbed wire and secured with nails through the arms and legs; it was also covered in scars with many gruesome instruments of torture still sticking out of the body.

Lightning flashed in the background illuminating the room for a moment, Jack saw hundreds of writings across all the walls in blood; all of them said the same thing "the Mirror! The Mirror! Never look into the MIRROR!!".

A glint of light caught Jack's eye as his attention turned to a bizarre red ring adorning the corpse's finger, "This has to be what the raven was after" Jack said as he cautiously stepped forward, sword drawn.

Jack waved his hand in front of the body, and then stabbed it to see if it would react, when it remained still and unaffected Jack reached for the ring.

Suddenly his wrist was seized by a bony hand! The corpse screeched "How dare you!" as Jack struggled to be free of it.

Panic stricken he stabbed the corpse in the dead center of the chest hoping to finish it, a hissing, cracking sound was heard as the flesh reacted to the silver by smoking and blistering. The wound began bleeding rotting brown blood as the corpse laughed saying "You cannot kill me mortal".

The corpse then broke free from one of its restraints and reached for the sword; the corpse managed to get a grip on the handle and started pulling the sword out of its torso. Despite still being bound to the chair, the corpse began wresting control of the blade from Jack!

Despite Jack's best efforts he was having great difficulty gaining leverage as the corpse possessed inhuman strength; the blade was slowly turning towards Jack for the lethal stab, the corpse grinned with a wicked smile as it anticipated the coming kill.

Jack noticed the ring on the corpse's finger was now glowing brightly; Jack quickly discovered the connection and grabbed the ring as he kicked the chair backwards! The rotting flesh cleaved from the bone as the ring slipped into Jack's grasp and the bound corpse fell backwards into the large object. The corpse attempted to struggle free, thrashing around so violently that it caught the cover of the object behind it and pulled it off; though its many wounds were now bleeding profusely, the corpse reached towards Jack as it collapsed into ash releasing its last deep breath, as it faded to nothing.

Jack stepped back uneasily as he felt woozy, he looked down seeing that he was dripping blood; in the intensity of seizing the ring Jack didn't notice that the corpse managed to cut him deep across the torso, as the shock wore off the wound began radiating with pain. Jack looked at the ring tempted at using its evil power, Jack knew in the back of his mind that using it would be a mistake but the fear overcame reason as he began drifting out from blood loss, Jack slipped on the ring and as he tumbled over unconsciously. The ring shone brightly again as Jack's wound quickly closed and the blood began to return to his body from an unknown source, by unknown means.

Jack suddenly reawakened yelling in agony as the healing was instantaneous but the pain seemed intensified, with a burning sensation that seemed overwhelming making Jack's skin flush red and his face pour sweat. The injury healed as the pain subsided, Jack instinctively checked his injury, feeling the area around the gash still unconvinced that it had recovered at such a rate. Jack got back on his feet and brushed himself off saying in relief "That was too close" exhaling a breath of relief.

Rising to his feet, noticed that in the struggle with the corpse the object was revealed to be a giant mirror; from it he saw the reflection of himself and the surrounding room, only it was incorrect. The room looked new and colorful as the surroundings in the reflection were well lit and restored in their entirety.

Jack was mesmerized by its image, powerless to look away. A woman stepped into view from behind Jack's reflection and began whispering sensually "I've been waiting so long for a hero to free me from this curse, embrace me and receive your reward"

Jack replied with doubt "I...I can't, I have to, I need to leave this place"

The woman brushed her hand against Jack as she replied "You've been through so much, stay here with me"

Jack hesitated "This isn't right, something is wrong".

The woman brought herself closer to Jack and replied in her lusty way "Kiss me, and become a part of this place...forever" as she finished she moved in for the kiss Jack concentrated on doubting the image, knowing that it had to be a trick.

Regaining control he yelled "NO!" and spun around seeing the frightening reality: An old wretched woman, devoid of life that floated above the ground; her hair and dress moving and twisting by their own will, a banshee!

Every light in the house was suddenly extinguished leaving only the eerie glow of its terrifying image. The wretched face filled with anger as it screeched louder than any scream Jack had ever heard as he knelt over in pain and covered his ears. The screech made the walls shake and the ground tremble, as a gust of wind blew everything backwards. Jack could feel the life being sucked out of him from the scream as the surroundings began to warp and darken to a near void as the substance of the room seemed to be siphoned away.

Jack forced himself up and crawled towards the mirror, moving through the pain and the gale force wind. Jack got up and clenched his fist shouting "Enough!!" and punched the mirror. CRACK! The glass shattered as the banshee seemed to be knocked back by the injury.

Jack and the surroundings were suddenly restored when the scream ended; Jack sprinted out of the room, dashing down the stairs, and bashed through the front door in a mad panic. Jack continued running out into the open trying to get some distance from the mansion, but hordes of undead approached from the empty fields and dead forests closing off every avenue of escape; they began to encircle Jack as he spotted the banshee fast approaching from the back of the crowd.

Jack had lost his sword back in the room with the mirror, he was weaponless, surrounded, and was fast running out of time. Jack sighed a deep breath and said darkly "So, this is how it ends" readying himself.

KaBoom! CRACK! Blat! Blat! Blat! Blat! Jack suddenly heard as swaths of undead went down in a hail of gunfire!

Malachi emerged from the smoke of a recent explosion with a group of unknown soldiers blasting their way to the center.

Jack exclaimed "Finally, some help! Over here!!".

Malachi threw a familiar device to Jack and yelled "Call your ship, we need to get out of here!".

Jack quickly strapped the earpiece on and touched the 'call' button ordering "Eleanor we're in trouble, get *the Harbinger* to *Terror* now!"

The voice replied respectfully "Right away commander, on approach". Malachi and the unknown paramilitary looking soldiers reached Jack's location as they formed a circle around him and laid down a stream of automatic cover fire.

Jack said amazed "I'm glad you showed up, but who are these guys?"

Malachi replied with a sense of urgency "No time to explain, take your weapons" as he handed Jack his tele-kinetic gloves, as well as his sword imbued with freezing power.

As Jack quickly strapped on the weapons the sheer numbers of the undead force began to advance through the automatic fire, Jack quickly used the devices and quickly made shoving motions in each direction to halt the undead advance.

The Harbinger came into view from the horizon, Jack pressed the "call" button on his earpiece and quickly summarized "Eleanor, we need cover fire."

The voice responded calmly "Right away, firing main batteries around your position".

A wave of explosions and gunfire decimated the enemies around them as projectiles shredded them to pieces or fires incinerated them to dust. The banshee remained unaffected and continued forward dead set on coming after Jack. *The Harbinger* swooped in and began lowering its cargo elevator, but it wasn't going to arrive fast enough, the banshee was already too close! Three of the soldier constructs formed a line and fired a barrage at the banshee, but the bullets passed through without effect; the banshee screeched a terrible wail back at them instantly draining their life to nothing.

Jack frantically said "What do we do? Nothing is having any effect?"

Malachi said quickly "You are more powerful than her, but you must overcome your fear; destroy her with this!!" then tossed Jack the loaded crossbow.

Jack steadied his aim and said "Burn to ashes and be gone! Foul wretch!" As he fired a flaming bolt which struck the banshee right in the chest setting it ablaze; it flailed and screeched for a moment before the flames caused it to evaporate into black ashes and luminescent gas. Jack, Malachi, and the remaining soldiers climbed onto the elevator as it lifted into the air back towards *the Harbinger's* cargo bay; just before it got inside they saw the image of the house collapsing as a great beam of light shot through it into the clouds releasing countless lost souls.

Jack said in reflection "That evil place is now destroyed, may those who were trapped within its walls now find peace".

11

RESPITE

AS THE CARGO BAY CLOSED JACK SHOOK MALACHI'S HAND THANKING him "You really bailed me out back there, thanks Malachi."

Malachi inferred "Had it not been for the messenger's warning, we would have not known where to find you".

Upon finishing a familiar voice interjected "Ahem, so technically you should be thanking me, CRAW!"

Jack sighed upon hearing the sound, knowing that it had to be the wisecracking raven, so he turned to the sound and replied "Gee thanks for sending me into that hellhole to retrieve this evil ring"

The raven, who was standing on a perch in the cargo bay, replied without hesitation "You're welcome, now for your end of the bargain; I believe you have something that belongs to me".

Jack held the ring back as he said "I saw what this *thing* does, I cannot let it be used to cause more suffering".

The bird laughed as it replied "Me? Cause suffering? CRAW! CRAW! CRAW! I have no intention of doing anything of the sort; I simply collect these sorts of items owing to their priceless rarity."

Jack was still uncertain as he stared into the rings glowing red gem.

The Raven commented "It's probably unwise to keep the "blood ring" anyway; being is how it turns its wearers' into the walking dead". Jack upon hearing this he flicked it at the raven which caught it with his talon.

Jack lamented "I still do not trust you"

The raven began to take off as it replied sarcastically "Perhaps next time you're in a pinch you can find another realm traveling bird to help you; oh wait there aren't any others! CRAW! CRAW! CRAW!" and it disappeared in a cloud of black feathers in mid-flight.

Jack rubbed his forehead in irritation just thinking about it "Hopefully I won't find myself needing his help again."

Then Jack changed the subject on purpose "So who or what are these guys supposed to be?" motioning at the remaining paramilitary soldiers.

Malachi explained "These are soldier constructs, they do not possess complex personalities nor wills of their own, but they are useful and will obey orders.".

Malachi then pointed and gave an order to the constructs "Man your stations."

They saluted back replying robotically "Yes sir, right away" and marched out of the room.

Jack remembered from past experience the archer construct he encountered and inquired "I remember I ran into similar constructs in Epic, they seem capable of some emotion and thought, but for the most part they play their role and not much else. They aren't like other constructs so what are they?".

Malachi replied "Every story has background characters, whether they are soldiers, workers, people in the crowd; they are every figure given form without true substance, meant to play a supporting role in all things but not in themselves. They are often called *Mass Constructs* owing to their innumerable quantities."

Jack thought on this and attempted to understand "So whenever a crowd, army, or other large group of unnamed characters is imagined they come to form in the *Astral Plane*, but they are simplistic and undeveloped."

Malachi affirmed "Yes, and for each Mass Construct that is forgotten or destroyed more are always summoned to replace them. Their numbers are countless and without end."

Jack then inquired "How did you get them to join you?"

Malachi answered "Many of the *Mass Constructs* are created to fulfill an often short-lived purpose; upon completion of this task, the survivors often wonder the *Astral Plane* in search of a new purpose. If one gives them purpose they will make the provider of that purpose their new leader, following them without question."

Jack nodded in admiration "Very impressive, we could certainly use help from time to time; after all, what's a ship without its crew".

Malachi affirmed this sentiment "They will be most useful indeed.".

Malachi inquired of Jack as they walked towards the elevator "I am curious, how did you re-enter the *Astral Plane* without first going through the village?"

Jack briefly recalled the experience as he replied "I don't know how, but a construct visited me while I was fully awake. Then it somehow sent me back without my control, I have no idea how or why."

Malachi looked shocked saying "By all accounts that should not be possible; no construct in the history of the *Astral Plane* has influenced a mind's fully conscious state, we may be dealing with a grave distortion, a shifting imbalance, or perhaps even a construct of incredible power."

Jack didn't like the sound of either of the said possibilities as he reflected "Before I was sent back I remember having great difficulty staying conscious, my tinkering with my subconscious may be causing an imbalance between the two states of awareness, I may soon be unable to awaken at all. From what I've been told, constructs also cannot help me re-awaken without risking harm to the mind, so I may be stuck here until I can find a solution."

Jack then remembered something key that the construct who sent him back said, that he had purpose to carry out and that he would not allow Jack to awaken until it was fulfilled; it was possible that if this construct had the power to keep him asleep or to send him back then he might also have the power to help him safely reawaken. Jack did not know what this "purpose" was, but believed that it was probably related to Malachi's goal. Jack decided that his only lead for finding the answer to reawakening would be working with Malachi, for now it was Jack's only lead to unraveling why he was stuck within the *Astral Plane*.

Malachi thought about his predicament and asked "What action will you take then, *Traveler?*"

Jack was still uncertain of whether or not he could fully trust Malachi; however, Malachi had now saved his life twice.

Jack couldn't help but feel as if he owed him a debt of gratitude saying "If you hadn't showed up when you did, I probably wouldn't even be around to contemplate my next move in the first place, that makes two occasions that you have saved my life now; so I have decided to help you until I feel that my debt has been repaid".

Malachi replied "A fair decision *Traveler*, I thank you"

Malachi then began to describe what needed to be done "First we are going to need a couple of items, then..."

But Jack cut him off "Not quite yet Malachi, I've been through a lot and I need a little break and some time to reevaluate things"

Malachi nodded in return "Very well, let me know when you're ready to begin." With that Jack nodded in return and proceeded inside the elevator.

Jack got on board and simply said "crew quarters" and the elevator swiftly moved up to the floor containing the entertainment area, mess hall, and the various crew commons.

The doors opened to show a dozen or so of the paramilitary types walking about the area, busily performing a number of tasks; Jack found the sudden addition of a crew strange, but definitely an improvement.

He walked back to the entertainment area and verbally queued the music "classical" as it responded by playing the music automatically; he turned to the table in the center of the room which was actually a projector of sorts meant to accommodate a large number of different games.

"Chess" he requested as the various figures appeared on the table as he sat down and began playing against the computer. Though he was certainly not the best at chess, he needed something to help clear his mind. He played several games letting his mind drift between subjects; he spent most of the time observing the board while poised in thought, calculating his next move (a play-style that led to the kind of slow deliberate moves that made real opponents quite impatient). Despite trying to relax, he kept moving his pieces into bad positions, often repeatedly finding himself in positions with no good moves left to make; instead of playing into a losing game he just restarted it, but after several games he continued moving himself into similar traps.

Finally he said aloud "I keep getting stuck, just like my current situation…". He sighed deeply, shutting the game off and heading for the elevator, he remembered thinking before that he ought to improve the quality of his gear so he headed for the training deck.

Entering the elevator he said "training area" and it responded by heading up, it stopped at the weapons deck as three of the paramilitary soldiers stepped on.

They were talking to each other through their radios "Weapons diagnostic complete, heading to computer deck"

A voice replied back "Good, keep us posted".

The elevator stopped at Jack's floor as he stepped off; Jack was surprised that the constructs were autonomous enough to organize and communicate between each other, but it sounded like they were taking care of the ship so he wasn't too worried.

Jack stepped into the center of the training area and said "simulator" as a design grid was superimposed in the air by projectors.

Jack then made a pen appear in his hands and began designing the first item he figured he needed after his repeated close encounters from being grappled: arm braces. Quickly sketching the general outline he began refining it by rotating the design back and forth and making many small alterations, adding and subtracting features, and modifying the dimensions.

Jack had a passion for drawing (both with and without a computer), but his artwork tended to focus around detail oriented drawings of objects and buildings, rather than landscapes or people. After numerous alterations he finally refined the creation to the point of acceptance, taking a moment to step back and view the creation.

It was a set of gauntlets which were built to support the telekinetic apparatus on his hands; however, they were also made of a tough composite material, had metal plates strapped to the back of the wrists/forearms for protection and to make breaking holds easier, and had metal braces around the knuckles in case he found himself needing to fight hand-to-hand.

Once Jack finished his inspection of the design he said aloud "synthesize" as a solid block of material emerged from a panel in the floor and then a series of lasers quickly and precisely cut the object from the block, then air jets quickly cooled it to normal temperature while blowing off all the refuse material. Jack strapped on the gauntlets satisfied with the creation as he tested how well they fit his hands. Jack wanted to create some more pieces of gear, but he always drew a mental blank after a successful creation so he simply put on the new armored gauntlets and moved on.

"That will suffice for now" Jack said to himself as he returned to the elevator.

Getting on the elevator he said "bridge" as the elevator took him up to the top floor. It reached his destination and the doors opened to reveal Malachi planning with a number of paramilitary constructs. Jack walked around the constructs, and approached the center of the bridge area to discuss matters with Malachi.

Malachi spoke first "Our mission to liberate those trapped in *Mirage* will begin immediately, I am glad you have come to see the significance of the cause"

Jack interrupted him "Your goal of liberating the minds of those trapped within *Mirage* may lead to the solution of my problem as well; don't forget that I am helping you because I feel that is what I should do, I haven't decided yet whether I agree with you or not."

Malachi nodded "That will suffice for now, with time you may change your opinion. Are you ready to begin? *Traveler*"

Jack replied "Yes, tell me our first move".

Malachi motioned to an old drawing with sketches of what looked to be a library as he said "The library of sacred knowledge, one of the most ancient and secret repositories of secrets and information within the *Astral Plane*. Much of its information was lost to the physical world long ago, but it persists here in the *Astral Plane*."

Jack questioned "What do we need that would be kept there?"

Malachi explained "Many societies believed the most important secrets innately possessed great power; owing to this belief, such secrets are hidden away to keep them from the hands of the unworthy. In the *Astral Plane* such information exists within arcane scrolls and other writing that imbue their reader with their power upon reading."

Jack remembered the experience with Balthazar's scroll commenting "Yes, I remember encountering one such scroll, which one are we trying to find?"

Malachi explained "When the *Astral Plane* first came into being, the very first *Travelers* discovered means of changing entire realms, this information was later written on scrolls and passed to successive *Travelers*; this knowledge was eventually deemed to be too powerful and was sealed away by the older constructs. This scroll possesses the information we need to sufficiently alter *Mirage*, and it is hidden away in this library; protected by many deadly traps and guardians."

Jack conceded to the danger shrugging as he said "Well I don't partially like the sound of that, but if that's where we need to go, we might as well get to it."

Malachi replied "Excellent, then we should depart immediately"

Jack asked "And where is this library located?"

Malachi answered "*Conundrum*, the realm of puzzles, mysteries, and hidden knowledge; to travel there one must think of secrets, riddles and unanswered questions."

Jack sat in the captain chair and said "Eleanor, prepare the ship to jump" then he focused on the aforementioned thoughts as the entire ship suddenly leapt forward; outside the viewing windows the background streaked by like a blur until suddenly the ship came to a stop over a towering mountain range.

The ship suddenly tipped to the side and rocked back and forth, the motions from which cause everyone on the bridge to lose their balance and nearly fall over; the ship rapidly settled as the computer reported "Captain, I am reading severely aberrant weather patterns"

Jack ordered "Divert more power to engines and flight stabilizers!"

The computer obediently replied "Yes captain, be advised that my readings show the weather patterns increasing in severity by a factor of 3 within an hour".

Malachi got up and brushed himself off and he reported "Conundrum has a wide range of defenses against intruders seeking its secrets; many on the outer layers come in the form of environmental barriers to prevent access."

Jack inferred "Are you implying that we can't use the ship to fly to the library?"

Malachi answered "Until we can find a means to render the weather to be inactive, no. We will need to continue forward on the ground. On another note, the aberrant weather will make using the cargo elevator most unwise".

Jack concluded "Right, then let's get to the flight deck and see if we can find a more suitable means of transportation."

12
CONUNDRUM

STEPPING INTO THE FLIGHT DECK, JACK WALKED OVER TO THE MAIN terminal and pulled up a list of vehicles for consideration, all of which were of his imagining and design. Finding a satisfactory choice he activated the hangars retrieval mechanism. A large panel in the wall opened as conveyor crane brought in a large cargo aircraft specially intended for hauling vehicles; it consisted of a small basic cockpit, a long fuselage built around a vehicle sized cargo grappling crane, small tail wings for maneuvering, two sweeping wings to help it generate enough lift to overcome large weights, and small stabilizing vertical engines at the end of each wing to help it keep balance with awkward, cumbersome loads. The crane moved the vehicle to the takeoff pad as smaller automated systems began fueling the aircraft and prepping the engine. Already loaded was a skeletal 6 wheeled all-terrain vehicle.

Jack motioned to the aircraft/dune buggy combo saying "These VTOL craft will get us as far as possible, flying low to the ground to avoid the weather. Then they will drop us in these all-terrain vehicles which will take us the rest of the way."

Malachi looked unsure, commenting "Are you certain of the safety of these craft, being dropped in one vehicle by another seems…dangerous".

Jack reassured "You worry too much, Malachi. Now let's mount up, and head out".

Malachi motioned to the paramilitary constructs saying "It would be advisable to bring additional support".

Jack nodded in agreement saying "Right, I have something for that too" he quickly punched in two more queues as another aircraft/buggy combo emerged from the side panel along with another cargo aircraft carrying a sturdy military grade truck.

Malachi quickly pointed to the available soldiers and ordered "Ready a squad for travel, bring survival and extreme terrain gear" They replied while saluting "Yes sir!" as they began readying for departure.

Within minutes Jack, Malachi, and the others were loaded in vehicles; Jack was going over final checks on the radio with the paramilitary constructs piloting the VTOL cargo aircraft.

"Prepare for takeoff" Jack instructed as the engines of the VTOL craft powered up and the steam pads under the aircraft came on, there was a brief moment of silence as he clutched the handles in front of him taking a deep breath before giving the order "Engage!".

The pads shot the aircraft forward rocketing them towards the far wall, in the blink of an eye the doors opened releasing them to drift in the air; the VTOL aircraft fired their main engines rapidly halting their descent and pushing them forward. They were in the middle of a blizzard as heavy snowfall was whipped and swirled around them by a gusty wind.

Catching a glimpse of a narrow mountain pass Jack got on the radio and instructed "Take us into that canyon, hopefully it should lead us to the library" the voice on the other end replied robotically "Acknowledged" as the three aircraft descended towards the canyon.

The storm seemed to grow more severe the deeper they went, as visibility decreased and the wind increasingly rocked their aircraft back and forth.

Jack instructed "Closer to the ground, watch the weather and keep it steady" as they flew through the winding canyon.

Malachi got on the channel and warned "This weather doesn't bode well for flying, perhaps we should disembark here and travel the remaining way by ground".

Jack replied "Fair enough, I just wanted to get us as far in as possible. Pilot, prepare for landing".

Before the pilot could respond a blast of snow suddenly blinded them within a sea of white, the pilots began to panic "I can't see, I can't see. What do we do?" Jack mentally stumbled as he failed to think of anything under the sudden stress, suddenly the snow cleared revealing that the lead aircraft was about to collide with a canyon wall.

"BANK RIGHT!, BANK RIGHT NOW!!" Jack yelled, but too late as the lead aircraft carrying the other buggy crashed into the canyon wall causing a tremendous explosion.

The other two craft managed to pull around the obstacle just short of the explosion. Ahead of them another plume of thick snow rapidly approached threatening to doom their flight.

Reacting quickly Jack yelled "No time to land! Detach the vehicles now and turn back!"

The pilot quickly obeyed, as the vehicles were suddenly dropped as VTOL craft turned back. The vehicles plunged downward before abruptly hitting the snow-covered bottom, the impact jarring their passengers.

Luckily the aircraft were close to the ground, and the snow softened their impact.

Malachi groaned while shaking his head from dizziness and irritation as Jack came on the radio "Start up the engines and let's roll".

The buggy came to life and began pushing its way through the deep snow as the truck lumbered not far behind, the wind and snow were still severe but the vehicles were designed to handle extreme weather and terrain so they were able to continue forward. Jack found it strange that the weather did not seem to affect him without heavier clothing; his senses only registered the snow on a basic level of recognition, as if he could feel it was there physically present, yet it didn't cause the kind of cold discomfort one would expect from snow.

For what seemed hours they travelled through the blizzard, maintaining speeds only just fast enough to keep their momentum; the steep canyon wall's many twists and turns led them through what seemed to be an endless maze.

Growing impatient Jack got on the radio and questioned "We're going nowhere, we need to try something different"

Malachi replied "Perhaps if we examined our surroundings more closely".

Jack agreed as they got out of their vehicle and walked towards the nearest cliff wall on foot. They quickly came to a solid face of rock as they examined it for clues, but it was steep and the surface was totally smooth, making it impossible to scale; turning to the opposite cliff they found it to be the same and upon turning around they saw that the opening which they entered from was curiously only a short distance behind them.

Jack exclaimed in frustration "I should have known, this place is playing tricks on us: we were stuck in an illusion!"

Malachi suggested "If we discover the trick's secret, maybe we can pass through".

Looking forward at the never ending canyon ahead Jack pondered options, as he considered a way to pass a thunder cloud somehow formed and struck the top of a faraway canyon with lightning, causing an avalanche! The cascading wall of snow barreled towards them, as Jack was taken aback by the sheer unlikelihood of such an event exclaiming "This weather is hell bent to stopping us, it's like it has a mind of its own!"

Then he suddenly realized what was needed and yelled "That's it! The weather is the key! Stand back!!"

Jack then began channeling the energy of the telekinetic gloves bringing them to his body as they seemed to collect the energy around him. The avalanche was nearly upon them as Jack used every available moment to build up as much power as he could, the gloves were now glowing and pulsating.

Just before the avalanche consumed them he pushed his hands forward stopping a section of the snow from burying them; Jack groaned loudly with strain as he looked to be holding back an invisible wall making the snow seem to yield in front of him, slowly he began to edge the wave back. His concentration began to reach its limit as the wave began to decay, so he fired one last pulse forward which rapidly cleared the air, instantly dissipating the blizzard. Jack thrust his fist in the air in celebration yelling "YES!" but then quickly fell onto one knee.

Malachi ran up to help but Jack stopped him saying "I'm ok, I'm ok. I can get myself up"

As he got back on his feet and remarked. "I'm glad that worked, I was a little worried there for a second."

Malachi pointed forward saying "The path is now revealed. Well done *Traveler*".

They gazed forward as the canyon was now gone and a massive basin lay in front of them instead, in its center was an old Corinthian building surrounded by many columns and statues. Jack said in awe "At last, the library of sacred knowledge".

Surveying the path he saw a steep path winding down to the basin, without hesitation he instructed "Alright, start the vehicles back up and let's get down there".

Climbing back in the vehicles the buggy zipped ahead making its way down the trail as the truck followed, then as they moved forward a section of the trail suddenly broke off and began sliding down into the basin with the dune buggy still on it!

"Damn! I Should have known it wouldn't be that easy." Jack yelled while gripping the steering wheel with anxiety.

Seeing another platform further down the side Malachi quickly reacted "we may need to jump from section to section to avoid crashing"

Jack quickly confirmed "Agreed, hold on!"

Jack readied his foot on the gas waiting for the shelf they were sliding on to get close enough to the platform ahead. Mentally calculating the time and distance needed to clear the jump, Jack waited for the right moment then punched the accelerator to the floor. The buggy was launched off the side sending it flying through the air before barely clearing the distance, landing on the next pad with a skid.

Before Jack and Malachi had a moment to relax, the ledge they were upon also began sliding towards the bottom. Anxiously looking back and forth for another place to jump to, they spotted another rock outcropping jutting out ahead, yet the distance to clear was even greater than before making the jump ever more perilous.

Jack quickly pulled the buggy in reverse to get as much of a start on the jump as possible, and then shifted it into park while revving the engine to maximum before shifting back into drive. The tires screeched as the buggy leapt forward racing off the edge with great speed, the buggy soared through the air as both its passengers yelled in fear before hitting the next pad, upon impact Jack slammed on the bakes preventing them from sliding off the edge. The section of cliff they landed on also began sliding towards the bottom with greater speed than the other two.

Jack pounded the steering wheel in frustration as Malachi pointed forward yelling "Look ahead, a final obstacle!".

Indeed there was, at the bottom of the ridge lay a wall of sharp pointed rocks waiting to tear apart anything that was unlucky enough to crash into it. Jack quickly got the dune buggy into position as he readied to jump it once more, but from his mental calculations they weren't going to have enough thrust to clear the jump, he needed to improvise an upgrade to the buggy 'on the fly' and fast. As pressure mounted he hastily concentrated on what was needed and channeled his mental energy on summoning it into being before they ran out of time, then he once again hit the accelerator having no time to check whether what he did would actually work.

The dune buggy glided off the edge drifting towards the maw of jagged rocks, at their present course they would not make it! But Jack hit the newly added button on the side of the steering wheel as a loud "WHOOSH" of the newly added devices sent a burst of wind that carried them up and over the obstacle. The buggy landed hard as the front end smashed into the ground and it spun around into a large column knocking one of the tires clear off the axle, the passengers were protected by the padding of the cage-like frame around their seats but were shaken by the impact nonetheless.

Jack sat back trying to catch his breath from all the excitement, as Malachi tumbled out nearly vomiting from all the jarring motions. Jack got out in order to check the damage: the front end was smashed up, all the shocks were blown out, and one of the tires came off, from the looks of it the buggy was out of commission. Looking towards the bottom he saw the four air jets which had released enough high pressure air to lift them up over the obstacle for a short time.

Thinking aloud he said "This new device should be added to every ground vehicle, I would test this on some more but I'm afraid this vehicle is wrecked."

Malachi replied in relief "I am glad, I have endured enough vehicle collisions for one day".

Jack laughed as he dismissed "When driving through difficult terrain you have to expect crashes from time to time"

Malachi replied while steadied himself "My point exactly". They both laughed a short laugh for a moment before continuing on.

After they had a moment to catch their breath they looked to the library which stood at the center of the basin they were now in. Jack inquired "Is there any way for the constructs to get down here, there is no telling what waits for us up ahead"

Malachi got on his radio and asked "Soldier, have you found another way down?"

The voice on the other side replied obediently "Yes commander, we are making our way around a much longer path, we should arrive by the time you reach the library"

Malachi concluded "Very good, keep me posted. Malachi out".

Jack brushed himself off as he said "Alright, let's make our way on foot to the library at the center"

Malachi warned "Remain on guard, I am certain there will be more 'surprises' in store for us".

As they made their way to the center Jack peered around the ruins curiously studying their strange writings and depictions, although the architecture seemed to follow a Greek theme, there were many signs of other cultures in the symbols and columns, as well as Chinese looking clay terracotta statues; the statues seemed to have the greatest level of detail he had ever seen, they almost looked as though they were alive.

As they reached the base of the grand stairway at the base of the library, they walked towards the entrance flanked on either side by 4 great columns on either side, on the front of the building was etched writing in the stone, but was in a language Jack could not decipher. The entrance was blocked by a huge stone slab, Jack attempted to force the door open but he couldn't make it budge at all.

Seeing that the door was covered by strange glyphs he guessed that he needed to reveal a sort of puzzle that could open the door.

Jack said aloud "I recall seeing very similar symbols on the menu at the tavern, I should be able to translate it by tapping it" as he brought his hand close to the door then tapped on the stone with two fingers.

Amazingly as he did a ripple passed through the stone, the glyphs changing to letters as the wave passed over them.

Suddenly Jack was able to read what was written on the door "What is heard but not seen, felt but not grasped, bringing with it the subtle breath of change?"

Luckily he had much experience with solving riddles and puzzles from his late grandfather who loved crossword puzzles.

Quickly thinking of the answer he said aloud "The wind?" but nothing happened.

Malachi interjected "in the *Astral Plane* things often require more of a physical element to respond"

Jack replied "Oh gotcha, I get it now" then he used the telekinetic gloves to gently swirl a waft of air around himself and into the door, as he did the stone slab blocking the entrance began sliding out of the way.

Within moments of the doors opening the truck full of constructs pulled into view heading towards the entrance.

Jack commented on seeing this "Good timing" then he instructed "Malachi tell half of them to get some flashlights and meet us inside, have the rest guard the area around the library." He said before walking into the open door to explore the library further.

Inside he found a massive room with thousands of tall shelves stretching from wall to wall, all perfectly ordered into groups of twelve and containing a seemingly endless number of books and scrolls. Jack walked closer to one of the bookshelves and recognized some familiar titles of very common books, strangely many of them newer than the library itself. Malachi entered soon after Jack with the constructs and found Jack curiously examining other titles on the shelves.

Jack turned and asked "I recognize many of these volumes, I have even read a few of them, yet many of these works were written within the last few hundred years, but this library looks ancient in comparison".

Malachi explained "We are in the outer chambers of the library; they hold the vast repositories of common knowledge, the cumulative sum of all known information. Whenever a new work becomes widely recognized it appears here on these shelves."

Jack gazed across the never ending bookshelves as he said in awe "Amazing, this certainly is a library of libraries"

Malachi motioned towards the center remarking "Within the antechamber in the center of that great column we will find the more uncommon knowledge, we should proceed further"

Jack nodded in agreement "very well, let's proceed"

They walked deeper into the library, past thousands of shelves closer to the center of the large structure. Passing through the endless arrangements of normal bookshelves, they beheld the sight of a massive column in the very center of the library, which looked to support the entire structure. Painted across its surface were Egyptian-like depictions of all major events in history; at the bottom center of this mural was a great eye which beheld an open scroll before it. Jack knew this was somehow important and placed his hand at the center of the iris, when he did the depictions on the wall illuminated and became animated, playing out the events they were meant to represent.

A quill appeared on the open scroll and began writing as a celestial voice echoed "That which is recorded becomes preserved in the memory of all those who look upon it".

The voice continued "Proceed knowing that knowledge comes with many burdens, which once known cannot easily be forgotten". Upon finishing the depictions returned to their original forms, and the eye lit up before opening to reveal another chamber within the great pillar.

Stepping inside they found a small room full of statues, each were of different figures and many were in regal poses, or looked to be deep in contemplation.

Jack looked at the plaque on the far side of the wall, upon tapping on the glyphs they were translated to "Choose the one among many who displays leadership".

Jack stood back and rubbed his chin in thought as he said "hmmm, this must be another riddle"

Then he turned to the statues as he said "It must have something to do with what each statue is".

Upon examining the 7 statues he found that one looked to be a military commander of sorts on a horse, making his selection he walked in front of it and pressed a button at the base of the statue.

Suddenly the door which they entered slammed shut and the roof slowly began to lower towards them.

Malachi said half panicked "I doubt that was the choice *Traveler*!" Jack quickly used the telekinetic gloves to hold the ceiling back, but he found that the power of the gloves did not function at all.

Jack exclaimed "Crap! Crap! These things aren't working for some reason"

Malachi yelled in response "Then we have to solve this puzzle now!"

Jack began panicking as he ran up to another random statue and said "There are only 7, right? all I have to do is use the process of elimination"

Malachi stopped him "No! More wrong answers might make the ceiling fall faster, we have to do this correctly". Jack began running around looking at each statue, but his mind was racing and he was having trouble thinking clearly, the ceiling was now halfway towards them.

Malachi made a suggestion "Perhaps the puzzle relates to something the statues are doing in relation to the others?"

Jack thought about it and said "That's it, we just need to observe carefully and figure out what that is".

As Jack peered upon one of the statues he noticed that its eyes were looking in a strange direction compared to what it was doing "This statue is looking a certain way".

Quickly finding that two of the other statues were looking the same way he started to narrow it down. They were all looking in the general direction of three statues on the far side, so he had to figure out if there was a pattern among the three, as the ceiling was now a three-fourths of the way down to them.

The military statue was one of the three, but he knew that one was wrong so he focused on what it was doing "This statue is facing the remaining two" but upon looking at the statues he found that they were both facing each other.

Jack was stumped as he said exasperated "I don't know! I need some help here!".

Malachi quickly examined the two statues; one of a humble looking ruler, and another of a very ornately decorated one.

Malachi made a quick observation "Look, the statue of the regal ruler is subtly bowing just slightly towards the more practical statue; the practical one must be the correct statue!".

The ceiling was now very close and began speeding towards them as Jack dashed over to the statue and hit the button; the ceiling stopped and began slowly moving back to the top as a door on the other side of the room slowly opened.

Jack said with relief "I definitely don't want to do anything like that again"

Malachi responded "Indeed, hopefully that was the last deathtrap". The door ahead was now opened and they proceeded through into the next room.

The next room had a much smaller number of books and scrolls within a short corridor, yet this time Jack could find not one title could recognize or had heard of; the writings within this hall were completely unknown to him.

Malachi seeing his bewilderment felt he should explain "We are within the antechamber which holds the most rare or unknown volumes, within this hall you will find important knowledge lost to all but a few."

Jack somehow knew they weren't quite finished as he asked "What we're looking for isn't in this section, is it?"

Malachi replied "No. Though this knowledge is indeed valuable, the secrets that hold power in of themselves are held within the "inner sanctum". They walked through the corridor reaching a large complicated seal on the far wall; it was the final lock to open if they were to proceed.

Translating the glyphs in the usual way, Jack began to read the last riddle "Within this temple is contained symbols of great relevance, bring each representation to the north and the path will be revealed". Jack looked as the seal seemed composed of 4 circles overlapping outside of one another like a large complicated dial, each circle containing the numbers 1 to 12 with a pointed indicator at the top of all the circles; it didn't take him long to figure out the nature of the puzzle.

"This is a combination lock, each number represents something in the temple and we need to enter the correct sequence to pass".

Jack didn't know why, but the answer to this riddle seemed to come to his mind easily as he said aloud "...there were 8 great columns in front of the building, the bookshelves were organized into groups of 12, there was 1 great pillar, and 7 statues inside of it."

Malachi said with doubt "How are you sure those are the correct numbers?"

Jack explained vaguely "I just do, it's hard to explain" then he thought about the numbers and hastily turned the dials into position; as the last number was moved into place the seal lit up and then opened revealing the final doorway. Inside they found a stairway leading deep underground.

Malachi congratulated him "Well done *Traveler*, let us proceed forward and claim our prize." As they descended the staircase to the inner sanctum.

13

HIDDEN

KNOWLEDGE

Jack and Malachi proceeded down the staircase into an underground chamber dimly lit by many oil lamps; at first glance it looked to be more of a musty cellar then a depository of knowledge, but upon closer inspection many ancient scrolls could be seen covered in dust.

Malachi announced as they entered "behold, the inner sanctum: holder of ancient secrets of great power."

Jack lamented "Sure doesn't look like much"

Malachi reassured "The knowledge within this chamber is sought out far and wide *Traveler*, do not let appearances fool you".

Jack looked around to see if he could find anything relating to his search regarding the linkage between the subconscious mind and dreams; a gilded scroll then caught his eye, seeing that it was covered with the same sort of changing glyphs he had encountered before. Tapping it made it change to English as he saw the words "the subconscious mind" written vertically on the scroll's cover, opening it up a light began to shine from the page until it enveloped his vision.

Now standing in a white void he began to hear the writing of a feather pen on an old sheet of parchment, accompanied by the sound was a mental voice in thought, yet it was not his own.

The voice said "Through my studies of philosophy and many sessions of deep contemplation, I have often thought there must be a subtle connection between people, an unperceivable link binding everyone together at a level that one might call the soul, yet its source and means are unknown to me…"

Before this mental voice could finish another totally separate voice began also "Through meditation one can see the world within the world; a lucid state of being which allows one, for a time, to transcend physical form and experience a new state of possibility we call enlightenment…"

Another voice began chiming in before the first two were finished "within my dreams I find myself in an illusion which seems so real, a mirror of the world that is exact enough to fool one's mind into believing it. Then I stumbled on another quandary, what if both are the illusions and I am caught in a state of waking between two illusions unable to see the truth in either…"

As a final voice was added their combined clamor began to become indiscernible "A vision came to me as I slept, of a great battle fought between men and monsters. In this I fought against forces so great a number that I could hardly count; of the many that fell in the struggle for victory was a familiar neighbor whom I have often spoken to in my waking hours. Upon waking I went to tell him of the bizarre tale, only to hear that he had passed away in the night..."

As many other voices continued to flood in, Jack was having trouble focusing or even keeping his balance, as the surrounding white void began to overwhelm his vision; he was teleported back to a familiar point of he and Malachi standing in the library.

Malachi turned to him and said "The knowledge within this chamber is sought out far and wide *Traveler*, don't let appearances fool you".

Jack was puzzled at what just occurred not knowing if he could explain, seeing the confusion on his face Malachi asked "Something on your mind *Traveler?*"

Jack looked back to see that the gilded scroll was absent, uncertain of what to say he simply dismissed the occurrence "Um nothing, nothing is wrong, let's keep going".

As they took another step in an old voice echoed from the distance "What are you doing here?!"

Malachi and Jack simultaneously unsheathed their weapons expecting an enemy but the voice mockingly responded "Quick to resort to violence are we? It seems they will let anyone in the '*Ancient Library*' these days".

Jack demanded "Who are you? What do you want?"

An old man emerged from around one of the bookshelves and replied "I am Gaspar, seeker of knowledge. Why do you intrude in this place?"

Jack replied "We are here seeking a scroll that has the power to change the "*Astral Plane*". Do you know where we may find it?"

Gaspar scoffed "Of course I know, but the real question is: are you worthy to receive it?"

Jack noticed that something about Gaspar seemed familiar, his robes were more extravagant but he still had the appearance of a sort of monk, like the two others he encountered previously.

Jack queried "For some reason you remind me of men I know by the name of Melchior and Balthazar, do you know them?"

The man was taken aback as he replied in surprise "HA! I did not think you were capable of discovering the association; perhaps you are not so dense after all".

Jack replied in irritation "They are certainly more polite, but when I meet three old men who all seem to be monks I tend to take notice".

Malachi realized the connection and clarified "This must be the third wise man, of the three wise magi known from ancient times".

Gaspar corrected with irritation "that's the '*Three Kings*' to you, get it right."

Jack and Malachi both sighed as Jack continued "Why don't you three travel together? That's how the story is supposed to go."

Gaspar rubbed his forehead as if he had heard this many times and explained "After we witnessed the revelation we returned home by different ways than from whence we came to circumvent capture, but most do not know that we traveled from three separate lands and to those lands we then returned; each of us decided to dedicate our lives to the pursuit of further truth. And so Balthazar dedicated himself to the pursuit of the truest form through martial arts, Melchior to the pursuit of wisdom through traveling and discussing philosophy, and I (Gaspar) to the pursuit of knowledge through research and study."

Jack replied "Fascinating, so you continually live out the role of wise men far past the ancient story"

Gaspar replied "You will find that many great figures in literature fulfill their roles far past the stories themselves, Melchior would say that it is our purpose".

Malachi interrupted and said sarcastically "You claimed to know the location of the scroll, so enlighten us"

Gaspar retorted with a sort of veiled threat "You should tread lightly, Malachi, you know as well as I what happens to those constructs who overstep their bounds"

Malachi replied in resentment "I am well aware of the risks, and I do not need a lecture from you. Now are you going to tell us what we need to know, or are you just going to continue to be a source of irritation and frivolous self-pomp".

Gaspar turned to Jack ignoring Malachi as he said "Know that the path you now walk is a dangerous one, the scroll you seek is on the 3rd shelf to my left with a white seal. Be wary; the guardians of this library don't take kindly to anyone removing articles from this place."

Then he turned to a doorway on the other side of the room and said "I shall take my leave, remember my warning." Then he walked into the shroud caused by the dull light, seeming to disappear.

Jack said puzzled "What was it that he was warning you about?"

Malachi replied dismissively "Nothing that we need concern ourselves over, we should collect the scroll and proceed out of this place".

Jack shrugged knowing that Malachi was hiding something, but now was not the time to get into a confrontation try and find out. Quickly finding the scroll Gaspar described Jack picked it up and examined it closely.

Jack began to open it but was immediately stopped by Malachi who warned "Such knowledge can be quite overwhelming, it would be best if we looked upon the scroll in a safer place"

Jack nodded and they proceeded to the exit. Before they exited Malachi remembered a crucial detail and said "Wait, the weather barrier is still active, if we wish to leave then we must first shut it down".

Jack glanced across the room before seeing a carving in the wall of a storm of clouds hailing onto mountains, quickly figuring that this was another hidden puzzle he placed his hand on one of the clouds and discovered that it moved when placed under pressure. Sliding the carving of the clouds to one side he saw that it moved behind a hard-to-see opening that was nearly flush with the wall; as the clouds were moved behind the covering another carving of the sun in front of a clear sky emerged from the opposite side until it overtook the storm carving.

The sun carving flashed brightly before fading away as Malachi extrapolated "There, that must have removed the barrier".

Jack asked uneasily "Gaspar said if we left this place with the scroll that "Guardians" would attack us"

Malachi responded "Whether or not that is true is of no consequence, we cannot leave without this scroll"

Jack nodded and agreed "You are right, we didn't come this far for nothing" then took a deep breath as he nervously approached the exit and took his first step out. As his foot came to a rest on top of the first step Jack and Malachi anxiously listened and waited for some sign of alarm, when their expectation was greeted by silence Jack breathed a sigh of relief.

Before they could take another step Malachi's radio crackled to life as one of the constructs said with anxiety "Sir, something strange is happening up here"

Malachi replied "Give me a status report?"

Suddenly the soldier's voice returned but this time it panicked "Wait! What the hell are those?! *BLAM!* *(static follows)*." Malachi looked at Jack in shock and sprinted up the stairs as Jack readied his crossbow and quickly followed.

They quickly exited the inner sanctum before sprinting down the halls of the antechamber towards the main section of the library; while they ran they could hear the sounds of gunfire and what sounded to be the clashing of weapons. As they reached the entrance they passed through the statue room, which was now strangely empty, before reaching the door to the main part of the library. One of the soldier constructs was in front of the door shooting at something out of view, when he saw Jack and Malachi approaching he turned and yelled "Commander!.....RUN!!!"

As an angry living statue landed in front of him and hastily cut the soldier construct down with one swipe of its powerful stone halberd. Jack without hesitating fired his crossbow straight at the statue's head; it landed with a sharp "CLINK!" not even cracking the statue's surface. It turned angrily towards Jack removing the arrow then crushing it between its fingertips before racing towards them with its weapon in hand.

Malachi un-holstered his gun and quickly fired at the statue's knee cap, blasting it apart with an elephant gun sized bullet. The statue tumbled over before attempting to continue without a functioning leg as Malachi reloaded within a moment and fired again blasting off the tip of its weapon; totally unfazed the statue continued forward as Malachi repeated firing, reloading faster and taking less time to aim. After a punishing barrage of 8 shots the statue finally yielded, crumbling to dust.

Malachi assumed "These must be the guardians, if this one is any example most weapons will prove utterly useless, or will require repeated hits to finish"

Jack began pulling together a plan "Did the soldier constructs bring any explosive weapons?"

Malachi confirmed "Yes, they are most likely in the truck"

Jack directed "Alright, find as many of the surviving soldiers as you can and get them outside to the truck. I'm going to try and hold off the statues while you and others regroup"

Malachi hesitated "Your weapons may prove ineffective, how are you going to stop groups of these things?"

Jack replied with haste "I'll figure something out, now go!". Malachi grumbled and ran out the door reloading his gun; Jack took a moment to calm his racing thoughts before running out to meet the enemy.

Running into the open area at the intersection between bookshelves he saw dozens of statues fighting or pursuing soldier constructs in various areas of the library. Upon arriving at the scene one of the statues sprinted towards him with a raised sword, Jack directed the telekinetic gloves at the statue and pushed towards it.

The statue quickly braced itself and was barely moved by the force of the wave, once the wave dissipated the statue leapt forward and slashed at Jack. Quickly jumping back he avoided the blow but was uncertain of how to proceed seeing how ineffective his last attack was; thinking quickly he remembered that it took more effort and willpower to use the gloves effectively against larger and more difficult obstacles, and concluded that these statues were no exception.

This time before attacking he took a deep breath to gather his concentration, then pointed the telekinetic gloves forward and pushed out while rapidly exhaling, unleashing a more intense shockwave which cracked the floor and blasted books from their shelves. The statue was flung backwards into two other statues as the force of the impact shattered all three to pieces; but no sooner than Jack had destroyed them a dozen more took notice and turned their attention to him.

Seeing an intact weapon from one of the shattered guardians, Jack picked it up with the gloves and heaved it at the closest statues with a broad sweep. The weapon swiftly cleaved across the torsos of the statues, breaking each of them in half before coming to a stop into one of the far bookshelves.

Hearing the whistling of arrows he spun around on his heels in time to see a flight of stone arrows zipping towards him as he used the gloves to project an invisible wall blocking the arrows. He caught a glimpse of a group of statue archers which were reading to fire again, but seeing that the group of statue archers were standing in front of a tall bookshelf he reached out and grasped the shelf and pulled his hands down bringing it violently down onto the group of statues, crushing them.

From his peripheral vision Jack could see a much greater number of statues closing on him, he couldn't waste time dealing with them individually or he would be overwhelmed. Intuitively he reached out in opposite directions with the full extent of his arms and began spinning the debris of several crushed statues around himself as fast as he could. In the back of his mind he was thinking of the effect of objects being sped to extreme speeds in tornadoes and hurricanes, and how they would break through even thick hardened objects. The loose debris was spinning at such a great speed as to make them appear like blurred rings around Jack. Several statues were unafraid and foolishly stepped forward into the field; upon making contact the debris instantly ripped them apart like ash caught in a windstorm!

As the remaining statues began hesitantly stepping backward he knew it was time to counter attack, gathering the debris closer to himself he sighted his targets then directed his telekinetic gloves in a sweeping volley of blistering projectiles being slung at the statues with enough force to tear through them. After quickly destroying a few dozen statues he finished off the remaining foes just as he exhausted his supply of ammo, seeing that all of them were defeated Jack threw his fist in the air in a triumphant gesture, before nearly falling over from the exertion his more intense attacks required.

Malachi's voice echoed behind him "Well done *Traveler*, but there will be more. Time is short, we must leave now". Jack turned and ran towards the large doors where Malachi and a handful of soldier constructs were making their exit.

Exiting the front of the library Jack, Malachi and the others could see an army of the statues approaching from all sides.

Though his telekinetic gloves were effective, Jack was unsure of his ability to take on so many adversaries at once so he yelled "Everyone, we need to get to that truck. I will clear a path, Follow me!"

Blasting force waves forward he began clearing lines of statues, forging a path for Malachi and the others to reach the truck as the other statues closed in from the other sides.

Reaching the truck Jack attempted to keep the statues at bay to buy time as Malachi barked orders at the soldier constructs "Grab all the explosives, grenades, and rockets you can carry, and get out here! We need fire support now, Move Move Move!!"

The soldier constructs darted into the truck and emerged armed to the teeth with high explosive weapons as they formed a semi-circle around the truck and readied to fire.

Malachi coordinated the men as Jack backed into the formation "Ready weapons!.....Aim!.....Fire at will!!!".

From the center of their formation came blooming clouds of smoke and fire like a fountain of destruction, as the combined explosions decimated the statues nearest to them. The statues behind them began stacking their shields around each other as the soldier constructs continued their relentless fire, as statue after statue was blasted to bits the others continued getting into formation paying no heed to the mayhem around them.

Before Jack and Malachi realized what was happening, the statues had formed a continuous shield wall surrounding them; when the soldiers fired their weapons the shields absorbed the brunt of the blasts and more shields quickly filled in any gaps in the formation. Once their formation was complete they began to close in around the truck, creating an ever smaller circle around them, until the soldier constructs had to cease firing due to the now unsafe proximity of their targets.

It now seemed that the statues had them right where they wanted them, there was now no escape and they were hopelessly outnumbered; yet they did not proceed to finish them off, no instead they began banging their shields and weapons against the ground in unison.

Jack found this behavior peculiar as he said puzzled "What are they doing!? What the heck are they waiting for?"

Malachi was equally puzzled at the sight of this and said "I am uncertain, but I sense it cannot be anything good".

As the clashing became louder and faster the rumble of something big could be heard approaching from a distance, its ominous shadow stretching around the side of one of the ruins. As the sound became louder and louder a Titanic statue came into view which was over 50ft tall and looked to be made of stone a few feet thick. The gigantic statue steadily began making its way through the army of other statues towards Jack, Malachi, and the other soldier constructs.

Jack responded with hesitation "Oh crap! How are we supposed to beat that!"

Malachi reassured him "Remember *Traveler* that your abilities in this place are limitless, trust in yourself and get creative"

Jack replied with a scoff "That's easier said than done" as the statue continued its slow approach.

Malachi motioned to the soldier constructs saying "Get ready to concentrate fire, focus on its center, ready…aim…Fire!" as their volley of shells and rockets slammed into the massive statue's torso knocking it down onto many of the other statues; all the soldier constructs cheered at once believing they had beaten it, but it proved too soon to celebrate as the massive statue proceeded to brace itself and slowly get back up.

As it got back on its feet Jack and Malachi could see that the damage caused by the explosive weapons was being reversed right before their eyes, almost like the stone on the statue was regenerating itself.

Seeing this Jack muttered "It's never that easy, is it?". As the statue was now back on its feet and within striking distance it pointed at them then picked up a large boulder and crushed it between its hands, likely as a show of force to intimidate them.

Springing into action Jack picked up a group of the regular statues then blasted it towards the Titanic statue with a sudden force wave. The other statues only shattered against the giant's thick torso; obviously it was built much stronger than the others. It punched downwards at him as the entire group dove out of the way, its massive fist punching a crater sized hole in the ground.

Jack got some distance from the others and began tossing loose debris at its head to divert its attention away from Malachi and the others. The giant statue picked up a large boulder and threw it at him as he got a running start and leapt over the incoming obstacle, completely clearing it. Then he quickly focused his mind, took a deep breath, and pushed at the statue with the full might of his telekinetic gloves knocking it off its feet; this only seemed to anger the statue as it made loud growl-like vibrating noises and got back on its feet more quickly than before.

Once on its feet the statue then began punching at him with a flurry of wild swings, it was taking every bit of coordination he had to duck, jump, and weave around the massive fists of stone. The statue then stomped hard enough to send a tremor through the ground and knock Jack off his feet, as it then jumped skyward with the intent to land on him!

Jack quickly jumped back onto his feet and did a high arcing back flip, but the force of the statue landing sent a shockwave outwards that caught him in midair and sent him flying into a pile of rocks. He hit the pile with a loud THUD as it took him a few moments to get back on his feet as he groaned from the obvious pain of being slammed violently into stone. He did notice though that the pain was much less intense then what he would have expected in real life, thankfully.

The statue pointed at him and although it made no sound, its gestures indicated it was mocking him. Jack could tell that he was fighting a losing battle because he was playing the statues game, he had to figure out a way to use its great strength and size against it instead of trying to outmatch it.

Jack readied himself again as the statue swung downwards once more in an attempt to crush him, but this time he jumped to the top of its hand as it came down, then quickly ran up the wrist, turned, and swung his sword downwards with all this strength enveloping the massive fist with ice; the statue tried to free itself but couldn't because the ice kept it bound to the ground.

He proceeded to taunt the massive statue by dancing on top of the frozen hand while laughing at it, predictably the angered statue swung down with its other hand as he dove out of the way just before impact. The force of the other hand combined with the weakening effect of the ice caused the statue to accidently shatter its own hand; the statue looked at its own severed wrist in disbelief as it angrily turned its attention to Jack who was sitting against a ruined wall. The statue swung at him with its remaining hand as he vaulted straight up and fired a shockwave down at the wall causing it to collapse on top of the statues exposed arm, pinning it to the ground; seeing his opportunity he sprinted towards the statue swinging his sword at every exposed part of the monstrous statue covering it in creeping ice.

The statue was attempting to free itself trying to shake and pull its way out of the ice which was beginning to budge; Jack needed something strong and solid to finish it off. Seeing a large pillar he grasped towards it and pulled it from the ground, as his adrenaline rush sharpened his focus and strength he swung the massive pillar into position over his head.

Hearing the rising sound of drums in the distance Jack yelled at the mammoth statue "This is the end for you!" as he brought the massive pillar down on the statue's head with the incredible force of an executioner's axe! The statue made one last reverberating call out as the pillar smashed into its head, crushing it with a massive bang as if a celestial gong had signaled the giant statue's end.

Jack picked up a piece his defeated foe and watched as the stone seemed to try to form around the shape of whatever was near it, he placed some of the stone into his pocket, as his thoughts were cut short as Malachi and the others emerged from their hiding spot, as the other statues simultaneously resumed their attacks against them.

Malachi yelled out "It's time to leave *Traveler*, call your ship"

Jack pressed the button on his earpiece and said "Eleanor, all obstacles are clear, proceed for immediate extraction"

The voice replied calmly as always "Right away captain".

The Harbinger quickly swooped into view as it began lowering its elevator, Jack and the others got ready to leave quickly as the statues were nearly upon them. As they boarded the elevator and it began taking them to safety, the statues refused to give up and were stacking themselves into a tower to catch up to them at unnaturally rapid speed.

Jack quickly turned his attention the truck as he directed telekinetic glove at it and readied his crossbow with the other hand; acting quickly he flung the truck at the base of their tower and fired the crossbow into the back of the truck, the remaining weapons ignited as the truck exploded, toppling the forming tower.

Malachi muttered "Perhaps you should improve the speed of this elevator winch"

Jack retorted "Well maybe we should stop going to such dangerous places" as they both had a brief laugh and the elevator finished loading them and the "*Harbinger*" swiftly left the area.

14

THE STORM
BRINGER

AS THEY BOARDED THE "HARBINGER" MALACHI EXCITEDLY HELD UP the scroll and proclaimed "We've done it, with this scroll our goals may finally be obtained; however, I must examine it closely as I will need time to decipher its secrets"

Jack said back half exhausted "Good, I need a break. Meet up with me when you're ready to move on…but please take your time". Malachi nodded in return and they both walked to their separate destinations in the ship.

Jack went to the crew quarters where he found a sofa and laid down to rest. He found it ironic that he needed to rest even though he was already technically asleep, but he found himself fatigued nonetheless. As he became comfortable he tried to relax: taking a deep breath and trying to clear his mind. A blurred vision flashed across his senses, images of him within his house doing chores, eating lunch, filling out bills, yet the vision was unstable and faded in and out without control; Jack tried to center himself within the vision, but it seemed to run its course without his control. What he was seeing looked to be his normal routine, yet it was strange seeing himself do these everyday actions but yet not actually being in control while doing them, almost as if hypnotized. Jack wanted to be sure what he was seeing was real; he needed some sort of proof.

Using his full concentration he was able to briefly gain control of his hands in the vision, yet they resisted his every attempt at movement, trembling to the point where he could barely hold them level. With great difficulty he was able to reach out and feel the cold surface of his tiled kitchen counter, bang his hand against it to see if the pain registered, and then pick up the newspaper on his table displaying the date two days ahead of when he last fell asleep. Before Jack could make any sense of it or gain full control he saw the flash of two glowing eyes and was thrown out of the vision by the voice commanding him to "Return!".

Jack rose to an upright position with clenched fists and sweat on his forehead; taking a quick look around he saw that he was back within "The Harbinger" with his familiar equipment still on his person.

Jack was greatly perplexed by what he had experienced, saying aloud "That was like a dream, but how is that possible!? This is the dream and that was supposed to be reality. Is my body continuing to operate by itself? Is something else in control? Was I correct about my subconscious becoming the dominant frame of mind!?".

Jack was burdened by these and other questions to which he could find no answers, as he observed before, the deeper he delved into this mystery the less certain he became of it all. Seeking to take his mind off the subject Jack retrieved the strange piece of rock from his pocket and headed for the training area's simulator, for some much needed distraction.

Stepping off the elevator into the training room Jack once again said "Simulator" as the familiar design grid was superimposed in the air by projectors.

Holding out the piece of stone he commanded "Analyze this piece of material" a beam of light shone from one of the projectors and swept across the rock detailing its surface.

Once the scan was finished the computer made a verbal report "A super dense piece of composite mineral, it appears to be capable of spreading across the surface of other objects by means unknown."

Rubbing his chin in thought Jack thought of a use for this most fascinating piece of material, quickly pulling out his pen he began drafting a holographic sketch of a protective vest which would fit over his clothes; knowing that it would have to be fitted to him he said to the computer "I need a representation of my clothing size"

With that a manikin wearing his clothes was lowered from a ceiling shutter. He scoffed at the sight of the manikin (as it even had his expression on its face) as he said to himself "Of all the things I thought I'd be doing, especially in a place like this". Then he began adjusting the size of the holographic sketch of the vest to fit him more comfortably, making sure it was snugly fit, but not too tight.

Then he began filling in the parameters for the vest's materials, designing it so that the vest was made out a high tech synthetic fiber mesh (the kind used in bullet proof vests); Seeing that his creation was to the correct size, shape, and the right amount of protection he said aloud "Synthesize" as a mold was lowered from a panel in the roof, then sheets of the material were applied one layer at a time by two mechanical arms, until it comprised of many reinforced layers.

Jack then pressed the rock into the front of the vest, and slowly it began spreading across its surface until the front surface was covered by a plate of the strange rock.

Jack stepped back and admired the combination of his design combined with the discovery then said aloud in anticipation "This must be tested".

With the manikin still wearing the protective vest Jack set it up at the opposite end of the simulator and took a few paces back and fired the crossbow at the dead center of the manikin's torso; the arrow made a dull "CLINK" and bounced off without so much as denting its hard surface. Moving quickly to his sword Jack dashed forward and stabbed upwards into the stomach section with the full force of his arm in an attempt to pierce the armor, yet the force of the blow was deflected off by the rigid material (yet the sword did cover it with a thin layer of ice).

Now wanting to test the impact durability of this armor he said to the machine "cannon ball".

As a cannonball was brought up from a panel in the floor; He then focused on it with his telekinetic gloves, concentrated, then launched it towards the manikin. It impacted with incredible force knocking the manikin off its feet and into one of the walls. Jack sighed at first, believing his creation had failed; yet once the dust cleared the manikin was still in once piece with the vest still intact. Laughing with excitement he propped the manikin back onto its feet and began readying his final test of durability; rigging the front of the vest with a small but powerful explosive charge to see if it could withstand the extreme force and heat of an up close detonation.

Jack set up a blast shield and got behind it as he began the countdown; before he could finish Malachi walked off the elevator looking at a clipboard, he quickly glanced up at the manikin and then back at his clipboard he explained "*Traveler*, I believe I have found the key to using the scroll. I think we're ready for the next phase of the plan." Hearing no response he looked up right as the computer signaled the test "Detonate charge".

KABOOM!

As an explosion blew off the manikin's arms and legs and enveloped the simulator in a smoky haze. Malachi yelled in confusion "*Traveler*!?"

Jack quickly spoke up behind the blast shield "That wasn't me, I'm actually over here".

Once Malachi saw that Jack was unharmed he said critically "Have you lost your mind!?".

Jack responded trying to explain "Sorry, I wasn't trying to alarm you, I just needed to test my new invention"

Malachi replied flustered "As long as you're not planning on blowing yourself up!".

Jack examined the vest from the remains of the manikin, and despite the manikin taking great damage; the vest was fully intact, having not so much as a scorch mark of injury. Seeing this he excitedly removed the vest from the manikin and eagerly strapped it on, adjusting it till it was comfortable, then taking a moment to admire its design and new tactical utility (he was also impressed at how lightweight it was for the amount of protection it offered).

Malachi asked "Your new invention I presume, though armor can be a good investment, remember that the best defense is not getting hit at all, *Traveler*".

Jack replied "This armor will probably outlast me, but don't worry; I'm not planning on letting myself get hit unnecessarily".

Looking at the clipboard Jack inquired "So what were you about to tell me?"

Malachi then remembered and said "The key to using the scroll lies in each plane's "anchors""

Jack replied back "Anchors?"

As Malachi clarified "Each plane has a flow of emotional and mental energy that keeps its condition stabilized. These flows of power coalesce into crystallized nodes which regulate the energy and keep the plane "anchored" in its correct state and form. Without the anchors, each realm would vary and change to the point of it them becoming more difficult to easily discern, causing many of the emotional states associated with a particular realm to blur together and become more chaotic."

Jack shrewdly replied "These sound far out of the nature of the "*Astral Plane*", who created them?".

Malachi was taken aback by this observation and replied "You are sharp indeed *Traveler*; these "anchors" are the legacy of the first constructs, many of whom presently preside over the "*Astral Plane*", they were designed to ensure stability and prevent change."

Jack then asked "So why did we not simply go after these "anchors" before?"

Malachi answered "Because it takes quite a bit of force to disrupt them, and they tend to be very well guarded; however, the scroll will allow us to disrupt the "anchors", and the guards should prove to be a negligible obstacle once the scroll is activated."

Jack could tell Malachi was confident that his plan would work, he was also thinking in the back of his mind that this may be the purpose that the shadowy construct keeping him stuck in the "*Astral Plane*" wanted fulfilled, yet he was still unsure as to the reason why.

Quickly resolving to put his full effort towards the plan Jack said "Alright, this sounds like a good plan. Let's do it!"

Malachi replied "Excellent, let's get up to the bridge and begin immediately" as they both entered the elevator and took it up to the bridge of the ship.

Jack strode to the captain's chair and sat down as Malachi got on the intercom and informed the other constructs "Prepare for immediate launch!".

Jack took control as he remembered the thoughts required to travel to "*Mirage*" (those being the mundane, conformity, and submission). As he did the ship rapidly increased in speed making the surrounding sky blur as it jumped forward covering an extensive distance before coming to a rest over the never ending urban sprawl of "*Mirage*". The screens displayed the labyrinth grid of the cityscape, which stretched to every horizon.

Malachi pointed to a rising column of smoke in the distance and said "That smoke is from the power plants maintaining the city's electric grid, the "anchor" lies in the middle that massive complex",

Jack said "Eleanor, all ahead, cruising speed" as the ship swiftly glided to the smoke columns. As the ship passed from the high-rise center of the city to the industrial sector, the surroundings took on a noticeable change: from the glass towers and drab apartments to rows of warehouses, spires of smokestacks, and the massive machinery of industry; all of which seemed to grind forward making a never ending stream of materials and energy.

Malachi remarked "Just like your world "*Mirage*" has to create the materials required for its construction, so that the city may continue to expand. These many factories ceaselessly churn out the steel, electricity, glass and concrete used to expand the city outwards at an exponential pace; Many times I have attacked this area in hopes of stopping the spread of "*Mirage*", but its many machines are relentless, and they are quick to repair any damage dealt to its infrastructure. Eventually I figured out that I was targeting the wrong things."

Jack was curious to hear more "Meaning what exactly?"

Malachi sighed and explained "*Mirage* draws its power from the people who give into the illusion; so long as their minds are trapped within its mental prison they will continue to spread their misery outwards. Those who suffer often resent those who do not share their condition, unable to tolerate any other state of being that doesn't reflect what they endure, driven by envy and wrath to drag everyone's lives into conformity with their suffering." Jack shuddered at hearing this, knowing that it drew parallels to the state of the real world.

Suddenly red lights within the bridge began flashing as an alarm began blaring throughout the ship.

Jack said with a raised voice "Eleanor! Status report."

The computer reported "Multiple hostile aircraft bearing forward, starboard, and port side".

Responding without hesitation he ordered "Increase speed, deploy all guns and missile batteries, and activate the point defense system."

The computer replied "Yes captain" as the sounds of many systems charging up and coming online could be heard throughout the ship, followed by the thundering sound from the ship's many guns.

The screen became tactical as it showed the targets approaching, tracking weapons fire between the ship and its assailants; it showed the hostile aircraft quickly being destroyed before any of them got close enough to do any damage to the "*Harbinger*".

Before they had a chance to relax the computer relayed more information "Additional contacts detected closing in from the south, ETA on their arrival: 7-10 minutes"

Jack needed more information so he inquired "Eleanor, threat assessment on the new contacts"

The computer replied "The additional targets number in the hundreds; such numerical force may overwhelm our defensive capabilities. Recommend abort mission"

Malachi spoke up "No! The *"Anchor"* is close! Head for the center of this complex".

The computer impassively ignored Malachi as it requested additional orders from Jack specifically "What is your order captain?".

Jack looked at Malachi who nodded back sternly as Jack decided "Get us to the center of the complex, activate afterburners to get us there quickly."

The computer replied "Yes captain" as the ship rocketed forward, screeching towards the densely packed center of the industrial complex.

As they came nearer the complex seemed to respond to their approach by unveiling a massive concrete dome (which dwarfed everything else in the complex by comparison), which began rising from the ground; then the sides of the dome began retracting to reveal a massive crystal node pulsing with energy.

Malachi said with bewilderment "That is by far the largest *Anchor* I have ever seen…"

Jack reacted instinctively, ordering "Eleanor, Fire all guns at that *"Anchor"*! Bring it down!!". As a volley of missiles and shells blasted towards the crystal, only to explode just short of impact upon an energy field that was previously invisible.

Malachi advised "That's not going to work *Traveler*, the energy that flows through it also radiates a field around it; protecting it from outside force. We need to use the scroll."

Jack hastily replied "Are we close enough for that?"

Malachi replied "No, get us closer. We need to be within a few hundred meters proximity". Before the ship could get any closer the crystal sent a transparent wave outwards; it went through all the objects in the area, but didn't seem to affect anything. Before Jack or Malachi could figure out what just happened the crystal began glowing brightly as many bolts of electricity began arcing back and forth across its surface; suddenly all the energy collected at the tip of the crystal then fired into a patch of sky unleashing a violent, swirling distortion.

The computer alerted "Warning, weaponry and defensive countermeasures are currently offline! The distortion is interfering with the ship's systems.".

When it seemed like the situation couldn't get any worse, a dark colored ominous figure began emerging from inside the distortion. The distortion suddenly faded as *the Harbinger's* systems were restored; though now they were faced with a large, powerful airship that was colored black onyx with bright red stripes.

Jack's eyes widened with panic. "That ship is the "*Dauntless*" the ship opposite to the "*Harbinger*"; it was made to hunt down and destroy this ship."

Malachi snapped "What!? Why would you make a counter to your own ship???"

Jack quickly explained "My friend helped make that one to test the weaknesses of this ship, I never thought I would encounter any of his creations".

Malachi demanded to know "Well can you defeat it?"

Jack replied nervously "I don't know?! I don't know!!".

The screen suddenly came on to reveal an elderly looking figure wearing an elaborate black navy uniform with red stripes, he spoke with an air of authority as he addressed them "I am supreme commander Alexander, disengage and surrender immediately or you and your ship will be destroyed. You have 1 minute to respond."

Then the screen switched off. Jack quickly thought aloud "In the game that my friend and I made, the *Dauntless* was destroyed by fighter aircraft, chances are good it will be vulnerable to the same thing here."

Malachi replied "I am not skilled in piloting"

Jack then quickly decided "I designed these fighters, I'll be able to pilot them; I'm going to transfer control of the "*Harbinger*" to you while I lead a fighter attack against the *Dauntless*".

Malachi nodded back as Jack quickly said to the computer "Eleanor, transfer control of the helm and command to Malachi immediately"

The computer replied with an air of caution "Are you certain captain?"

Jack confirmed "Yes I'm sure. Transfer control".

The screen came back on with Alexander facing them down he demanded "Your time is up, are you prepared to surrender?"

Jack replied "No, the crew of *the Harbinger* bows to no one"

The commander replied with a confident smile "Very well; prepare to be destroyed". Alarms began blaring followed by the first impact of shells from the *Dauntless*. Jack headed for the elevator as he yelled over his shoulder "Keep our guns concentrated on his, try to keep your distance, and make sure this ship stays moving"

Malachi affirmed "Roger that, good luck *Traveler*".

Jack got in the elevator and quickly said "hangar bay" as it sped down while the ship rocked back and forth from the battle.

As soon as the doors opened Jack saw a handful of soldier constructs waiting for him on the flight deck. Jack quickly instructed "We are going to launch a fighter attack against the enemy ship, the *"Dauntless"*; I need 3 of you to form up on me and assist with the attack run. The rest of you must keep us covered for this to work" they all simultaneously saluted back in response.

Jack then started moving while ordering "Alright, let's go. Let's go!" as they organized themselves, put on flight helmets, and got into positions to prepare for departure.

Jack went over to the computer and quickly retrieved the design for his old favorite fighter (The ASM 3) and punched in for it to retrieve 20 of them. Quickly the panels in the sides of the hangar opened as an entire squadron of fighters emerged and were set down by the cranes neatly into formation. Jack took a moment to admire the sleek body, the stylistic forward swept wings, its powerful back and wing engines, and of course it's complement of missiles, auto-cannons, and rockets. Then he turned to the constructs and said "Pilots to your fighters!"

Jack climbed into the cockpit of the lead fighter as the window closed around him, the sound dampened to near silence as it sealed shut it, then a series of lights flickered on as the engines turbines began spinning. The fighter began powering up as Jack took hold of the controls and pressed the necessary buttons to initiate the takeoff sequence. As it counted down, he took a deep breath and tried to calm his nervousness from the anticipation.

The countdown reached "0" initiating takeoff, the fighter propelling from dead stop to full speed in moments! The sudden G force pushing Jack back into his seat as he clenched his hands around the steering controls. Clearing the trapdoors in an instant, he and the other fighters found themselves floating between the two ships trading turret fire; the scene of these two massive airships battling with the massive crystal node in the background was a sight to behold, but one which Jack only had time to briefly glimpse at.

The control display targeted the *Dauntless* as Jack ordered to the other planes "1st group, follow me and strafe the main guns with the auto cannons."

Jack then engaged the throttle as he said "I'm going in!". Diving towards the ship he quickly leveled his aim then held the trigger down, the guns flashed brightly and the auto-cannons clattered loudly as hundreds of shells pelted the enemy ship with fire! The shells erupted into small explosions across the *Dauntless's* gun deck. The *Dauntless* responded by firing thousands of tracer shells into the air at them as plumes of flak filled the sky; the Dauntless was trying to defend itself, but Jack and the other fighters were able to evade and pull away in an instant, the fighters proved far too fast and agile to be brought down by mundane counter fire.

Jack and the other fighters circled around for another pass, hitting the ship again with another destructive barrage. A number of the guns on the Dauntless came offline, the fighter attack was dealing great damage to the enemy ship and it was starting to look like *the Harbinger* and its crew would easily prevail, yet the Dauntless had a surprise in store as trap doors began opening from the top of the ship.

Jack observed this and said in surprise "That was definitely not part of the original design, this can't be good".

Then from the trapdoors came small, missile shaped fighters which shot straight up out of the top of the deck and into the air to do battle.

Jack said with alarm on his radio "Fighters!? That ship isn't supposed to have any fighters! Group two, bring those fighters down, keep them off us while we attack the enemy dreadnought". The other fighters rapidly broke formation and began firing their guns, yet the enemy fighters easily danced around these attacks as they proved to be much faster and more agile than the ASM-3 fighters. Before long the enemy fighters began scoring kills on Jack's group as they were easily able to outturn and outrun his fighter designs.

The radio chatter filled with signs of distress as the constructs attempted to fight their way out of their predicament "Contacts all over the board, there's too much fire to evade"

Another said "These things are too fast, I can't keep a target lock"

As yet another cut him off and said "They're right on top of me, I can't evade!!"

Jack instructed "Use countermeasures! Quickly!"

The construct responded "It's too late, I'm hit! I'm hit! I'm going down!!".

Jack could tell the battle was going badly, he needed to act "Group 1, break off the attack on the Dauntless, follow me and attempt to cover group 2. Focus on the fighters, use air to air missiles but keep your distance! Group 2, keep trying to evade, and don't forget those countermeasures".

As they turned to assist group 2 Jack saw multiple target indicators appear on his screen as he readied his missiles, pulling the trigger he fired them off as they flew out towards the enemy fighters; one was quickly destroyed as the other seemed to effortlessly weave out of the way as it flew out of sight.

One of Jack's wingmen flew in front of him, tailed by 3 enemies, the pilot panicking "I got three on me, I need help".

Jack acquired a target lock on the enemy as he said "I have them in my sights, firing" as Jack fired a combination of auto-cannon rounds and missiles quickly destroying the assailants, but to no avail as another unseen fighter swooped in and blew his wingman out of the sky.

Jack pounded his fist against his cockpit controls in frustration "Dammit, this is hopeless".

Distracted, he failed to notice a flak barrage coming from the guns of the Dauntless, taking a hit from one of them. A buzzer accompanied by a high pitched chime began alerting him of the severity of the damage as all the status indicators went from green to red.

Jack quickly got on his radio and summarized "I'm hit, attempting an emergency landing" as he directed his fighter back towards the hangar bay of *the Harbinger*.

The controls started to shake violently as he struggled to keep it steady; drifting down towards the hangar bay he was barely able to get it inside the doors as the fighter crashed into the runway, skidding into a mild crash into walls. Quickly popping open the cockpit window he exited the plane as the whole thing caught fire and let out a small explosion, escaping just in time.

Jack knew that in order to win against the enemy fighters he would need a plane that was more agile and maneuverable, quickly running over to the hangar control board he began sketching out a design his friend had come up with a long time ago, sketching out its arrowhead shaped fuselage, its long backwards swept wings, and its large engines and many maneuvering thrusters. He quickly initialized it as that same fighter emerged in complete form from the hangar loading doors.

Jack exclaimed "Even those crazy enemy fighters will be no match for this!" as he jumped in and powered it up.

Quickly taking off he was back in the air, punching the throttle down he flew full speed towards the enemy fighters. As the target indicators locked on the enemy fighters he leveled his aim at the first one then held down the trigger on the machine guns blasting it out of the air, then quickly turned to the next one pitching the plane 45 degrees in moments before knocking out another enemy plane. A dozen missiles were fired towards him as his plane dodged out of the projectile path with ease, before returning fire with several of his own air to air weapons which broke into clusters of smaller guided missiles, making too many projectiles to dodge as the enemy fighters were overwhelmed and brought down.

The enemy fighters began breaking off their pursuit of the ASM's and concentrating on Jack who was dispatching them faster than they could respond to his attacks. Jack now had the edge in this dogfight, the secret being his aircraft's variable multi directional thrusters which could be adjusted to different angles allowing the pilot to fine tune his aircraft's movements giving it extreme maneuverability, the enemy planes were simply no match.

As all the enemy planes circled around to engage Jack's fighter he readied to finish them, in a stunning display of speed he quickly engaged all the fighters at once in a rapid circular arc, maneuvering so quickly he could barely register as his aircraft unleashed a barrage of anti-air missiles and mini-gun fire.

After all his missiles had connected, the sky was suddenly clear of enemy planes leaving the *Dauntless* wide open for attack.

Jack quickly ordered "All remaining fighters, switch to VTOL mode and sweep the *Dauntless*. Throw everything you have at it, Bring it down!".

The ASM's quickly switched to hovering flight thrusters to steady themselves on their target before unleashing their full barrage of rockets and missiles upon the enemy airship covering it with explosions. The *Dauntless* was forced to break off its attack and retreat, as its damaged hull was covered in smoke and fire.

The *Dauntless's* Commander Alexander came on every communications link and said "This isn't over, you haven't seen the last of the *Dauntless*"

Jack switched on his radio and replied snidely "Sorry that you and your ship weren't up to the test, remember not to challenge *the Harbinger* next time" as Alexander grumbled and switched off his communications link.

Jack then got on the radio and commended the other pilots "Well done pilots, everyone return to *the Harbinger*." as they circled their fighters around and landed in the open hangar doors.

15

THE CHOICE

JACK RAPIDLY EXITED HIS FIGHTER AIRCRAFT AND WENT STRAIGHT FOR the elevator to check the situation; upon reaching the bridge he was instructed by the other constructs waiting nearby "The Harbinger is moving into position now, Malachi is waiting for you on the observation deck," as they pointed to the stairs leading up to it.

Jack nodded in return and headed up the short flight of stairs to the top deck of *the Harbinger* where he saw Malachi standing at the front of the railing with the scroll unfurled, in front of him was the crystal *"Anchor"* which was only a few hundred feet away. As the ship approached the engine noises of the many hundreds fighters sent to protect the *Anchor* were now audible in the distance, they couldn't be more than a few moments away.

Jack yelled out over the coming storm "We're running out of time, it's now or never!"

Malachi turned and yelled back confidently "Do not worry *Traveler*, everything is at hand."

Then he turned back around and spoke what sounded like an ancient language, perhaps Latin or Greek; as he did a storm suddenly came forth and grew violent as his words began to grew louder and echoed all around them. The crystal *Anchor* began to tremble as Malachi reached out his hand and seemed to command the elements to his bidding; a powerful streak of lighting split the sky and struck the *Anchor* with enough force to make the entire crystal shake. A small fracture quickly began to splinter across its surface until it formed large deep cracks across the entire structure; the ground began to quake as the large crystalline structure began to buckle under the stress. Finally, a cloud of dust flew off its surface signaling *Anchor's* demise as it suddenly shattered and collapsed in on itself! As it did the many fighters that were on the verge of attacking suddenly fell out of the sky uncontrollably, whatever danger they posed was erased with the destruction of the *Anchor*.

The storm began to subside; as Jack took a moment to collect his thoughts then turned to Malachi and inquired "What happens now?"

Malachi replied cryptically "Now comes the path to liberation, and the beginning of a revolution long overdue."

The scroll then crumbled to dust as he let it be carried to the wind saying "It is done; now we must see if it was enough".

Malachi then walked back down to the bridge as Jack took a moment to view the debris left over from the *Anchors* destruction; before Jack rejoined him he saw a mysterious energy wave flow outwards from the wreckage, he noticed that as it swept over each building it caused the electricity to abruptly shut off and its mechanical parts to come to a stop.

Jack wondered aloud "Strange, I wonder what other effects this is having". *The Harbinger* began to move towards the center of massive city sprawl as Jack headed back down to the bridge of the ship.

At the bridge Malachi and the other constructs were gathered around busily discussing something, upon seeing Jack they stopped and Malachi said joyfully "Come *Traveler*, witness the transformation".

As Jack approached the view screen he saw the energy wave continue to wash over the urban sprawl, as it did all the cars stopped, the signs and lights shut off, and all the *Avatars* of the masses came to a dead stop looking upward at the sky. The grey of the buildings began to slowly change to more vibrant colors as the sun in the sky began to shine more brightly than before, from the ground came the echoes of thousands of voices.

Malachi explained "The hold of mirage is broken! But the masses are confused and uncertain, as they now lack direction. I will reveal to them that they have been freed!"

One of the constructs handed him a microphone as his voice seemed to boom from *the Harbinger*. He said in a speech like fashion "People of *Mirage*, you have been trapped in an illusion. This place you see around you is not the landscape of your real lives but a prison; shackled to its deception you have not known that this entire time you have been free to go and do whatever you want! To live freely without limits or boundaries! That is why I have unchained you from it, so that you might experience this place in its true form and bask in its glory. Do not be afraid, embrace this moment and go forth!! Your time is now!".

For a brief moment he seemed to get a response from the masses in the city below, but suddenly all the voices quieted and the entire area grew still. After a few eerie moments of silence the masses spoke once more; but in total unison, the rising echo of their combined voices reaching the sky. "WE ARE ALREADY FREE, FREE FROM WANT, FREE FROM DANGER, AND FREE FROM UNCERTAINTY. OUR CONFORMITY BRINGS UNITY, FROM IT COMES STABILITY.

IN THAT STABILITY ALL OUR NEEDS ARE PROVIDED, AND WE ARE LIBERATED FROM THE BURDENS OF THE WORLD AROUND US. INDIVIDUALITY THREATENS OUR UNITY SO IT MUST BE SUBJUGATED; NEW IDEAS THREATEN THE ORDER OF OUR SOCIETY AND WILL NOT BE TOLERATED. WHEN ALL THINK AS ONE, A UNIVERSAL PEACE SHALL BE HAD. WE REJECT YOUR IDEALS, JOIN US OR FALL TO US! WE HAVE SPOKEN."

At that all the changes that seemed to occur were then slowly reversed, as the power began returning to the city and the masses resumed their endless routine.

Malachi threw the microphone at a nearby wall as he angrily shouted "No!!! Imbeciles! They are presented with a chance for freedom and see truth and they at once reject it! Their twisted vision serves only to corrupt and hypnotize all those around them! I will no longer idly stand by and watch everything succumb to this, I will burn it to the ground if I have to!!"

Then he pointed at the viewing screen and yelled "Computer, ready all the guns. Prepare to destroy *Mirage*!".

Jack retorted by saying sternly "Belay that order Eleanor!" Yet the computer did not respond.

When Jack saw from the ship's indicators that the guns were still being readied, he said impatiently with a raised voice "Eleanor! I said stand down! I am the captain!"

Malachi explained "It's no use *Traveler*, you transferred control over to me, remember? Your hidden fail-safes prevent control from being diverted unless the current captain is either dead or he willingly relinquishes command, like you did earlier."

Jack replied "What are you talking about? What fail-safes?"

Malachi replied "It took the soldier constructs some time to find, but your subconscious created a number of systems within the ship, Ones that you were not consciously aware of. I was lucky that you unknowingly activated one of them, it was the moment we were waiting for."

Then Malachi ordered to the constructs "Groups 1 & 2 get down to the gun bay, ready battle stations" they saluted and headed for the elevator.

Jack got in front of Malachi and spoke sternly "Stop this! It is pointless to attack them. You said it yourself; *Mirage* will simply repair itself as before".

Malachi replied confidently "That was before, with the *Mirage's Anchor* disrupted and the weapon of a *Traveler* at my command I am capable of inflicting great damage on this place."

Jack replied flustered "What do you mean 'weapon of a *Traveler*' Speak sense!"

Malachi clarified "The full mental awareness of a *Traveler* allows them to transcend the *Astral Plane's* rules; giving them the power to change parts of the *Astral Plane* as they see fit. Within your weapons and your ship lies that same power, one which you currently used without regard to its effects. Now I will use this power to finally alter the *Astral Plane* the way it should have been done long ago, to destroy this illusion once and for all!"

Jack angrily motioned to the cityscape as said in a demanding voice "And what happens to them!"

Malachi replied without remorse "When the mind experiences a lethal danger it will shock itself awake to avoid it; however, if it is unable to recover in time then the shock of experiencing one's death while dreaming is *sometimes* great enough to be lethal."

Then Malachi pointed to the constructs manning the control stations on the bridge and said "Target the buildings in the center of the city, hold for my command."

Jack stepped forward and unsheathed his sword as he said boldly "I won't let you do that! Resorting to a potential massacre goes too far! Can't you see what's happening, you are letting your anger cloud your judgment! Stop this! Or I will stop you!!"

Malachi turned around and bitterly said "And what are you going to do if I refuse? Kill me! After all we've been through you would do that!"

Jack raised his sword forward as he said "If what you're proposing is a slaughter then I will not hesitate to stop you!".

Malachi unsheathed a dueling sword Jack had not seen before and readied it as he spoke angered by what he saw as betrayal "I should have known you would turn on me! Before you used that machine you were one of them! Long ago you were proud, creative, and free but you let your doubts and fears turn you into a hollowed out shell of your former self, you slowly became a slave like them, each night living within this grand façade! This mental prison! This nightmare!"

Jack doubted him and shouted "You don't know that! It's not possible!"

Malachi replied yelling over him in fervor "You deny it because you cannot accept the truth! You were not strong enough to overcome the pressures of the world so you gave into them, look at what you see below! Is that what you want! To live forever in conformity until the system comes crashing down on itself! Is that the legacy you want for mankind! is it!!"

Jack was speechless, though he opposed what Malachi was about to do he knew that he agreed with much of what he said, he had always been deeply troubled with the trends of society and this *Mirage* represented its embodiment. He could not raise an argument to defend it, yet he could also not allow Malachi to commit such evil to destroy it.

Jack finally spoke "Whatever the problems of society, the costs you would inflict are too great! I ask you one last time to see the reason and stop this before it's too late!"

Malachi replied coldly "Your people are unwilling to make the necessary sacrifices to free yourselves, so I will make it for you. All guns open F-!!"

As Jack leapt forward and roared "NOOOO!!!" lunging forward swinging his sword with his entire body, Malachi brought up his sword and barely managed to block it as the force of the blow brought the sword close to his face. Shoving Jack backwards with his foot he cleared the sword away from his body and responded with swift slashes of his own which were each blocked by Jack whose reflexes were driven to their edge by his vengeful anger. Malachi stabbed forward as Jack sidestepped the blow and knocked the sword nearly out of his grip, and then he closed the distance and punched Malachi hard enough to make him nearly fall backwards.

Taking a moment to breathe Jack said full of anger "You have allowed your ideals to overwhelm reason. Is there anything you wouldn't do now! Any act of evil you would not commit!"

Malachi rose up and readied to swing as he said "Such is the price for freedom, one that I would gladly pay ten times over".

Malachi then swung with an overhead strike to Jack who blocked it before kicking him in the gut sending him to the floor; he swiftly got back up swinging the sword upwards as Jack jumped back out of the way. Malachi then charged forward as Jack responded in turn dashing forward himself; their swords were caught in a lock as the sparks began to fly off from the friction.

Jack yelled "Can't you see what this has done to you? You have become treacherous! Ruthless! You've given into madness! I used to consider you my friend, now look at what you've driven me to!"

Malachi countered "You hold certain ideals to be true and good yet you are unwilling to risk anything for them. That is the difference between you and me. I fight for what I believe in, while you idly watch what you believe in wither away!"

Powering through the sword lock Jack pushed Malachi's weapon back taking him off balance as he staggered backwards. Malachi was open for a kill shot, Jack knew it, yet instead of the lethal stab Jack turned the sword and struck him with the hilt knocking him over once more.

Malachi noticed this replied angrily "What are you waiting for, you have commanded the advantage multiple times, you know what you must do! Now do it!!"

Jack said hesitantly "I cannot"

So Malachi yelled "Then I will force you to! Computer: fire all of the guns! Now!".

Jack then charged forward overcome with rage, but in his clouded state of mind he didn't see Malachi ready his gun behind his back. Malachi whipped it out and fired right in the dead center of Jack's torso blasting him backwards off his feet.

Jack's armor took most of the force off the blow, but he still had the wind knocked out of him. Malachi approached pointing his sword to Jack's neck, if he resisted further Malachi could easily finish him.

As the rumble of *the Harbinger's* guns echoed in the background Jack made one final plea "Don't you see what you've done, you've betrayed everything; even your own principles. You gave them their choice, and when they chose an outcome you did not approve of you tried to force it upon them. Don't you see, that is not freedom, it is tyranny".

Malachi said still frustrated "Their choice will lead to a miserable existence, a doomed future"

As Jack replied "And if you truly love freedom as you say you do, then you must allow them to make that mistake, otherwise you have become the very same kind of tyrant that you once hated."

Jack turned to the view screen and beheld the chaos, the sheer level of destruction was colossal, yet even so it was but a small patch of a seemingly endless grid.

Jack spoke once more "I have failed to stop you, and you have used my ship to possibly take the lives of many. Are you going to take my life as well?"

Malachi sheathed his sword and turned around saying "No, though I am greatly hurt by your lack of conviction I will not kill a former friend."

Malachi then said to the computer "Cease fire, deactivate the guns. It's over."

The computer obediently replied "Yes captain".

Malachi then said to Jack "There is great wisdom in your words, though I hate this place with every fiber of my being; I cannot force the people into a choice that is not their own."

Jack still unable to rise said "It is not too late for redemption; there still might be another way..."

Malachi said direly "You don't understand, I have crossed the line. I will face the judgment of the other's soon. Goodbye *Traveler*... I am sorry."

Jack didn't know what Malachi was talking about, and then unexpectedly from above the city came a swirling maelstrom of fire; time began to slow to a near stop as if time had suddenly frozen. A bright light suddenly began to shine as Malachi fixed his clothes and looked up at it; in the blink of an eye an angelic like figures swooped in and struck Malachi down before he could even respond.

Jack reached up and called out, but there was nothing he could do; Malachi turned to Jack and whispered "Regret nothing" as he disintegrated to light.

The angelic figure then turned and said, "He has caused a great imbalance and has been judged for it. We are watching you, repeat his mistake and you will be judged in turn." Jack rose to his feet and swung at the figure, but it disappeared before his blade connected.

Seeing no trace at all of Malachi, Jack knew that whatever just happened had caused his demise; Malachi even seemed to know it was coming, yet did nothing to avoid it.

Time began to resume as a loud powerful voice seemed to announce from the skies "Behold! I return to this realm after millennia of exile; the great reckoning of light and fire has come! Behold the advent of a new eon! Witness the return of *SOL!!*".

Then at once thousands of flaming meteors rained down upon the city wreaking havoc in their wake. One struck *the Harbinger* as the computer said in an alerted voice "Warning! Warning! Critical damage inflicted, system failure imminent!!".

Jack frantically yelled "Eleanor, get us out of here maximum speed!".

The computer replied as its voice began to be scrambled and distorted "C-C-Cannot respond-d-d-d, engine fail-fail-fail-failure. Commence commence emergency crash-sh-sh-sh pro-ced-ure."

Jack ran over to the captain's chair and strapped himself in, he then hit the emergency button as a pod surrounded his chair. Before he could continue he saw another meteor bearing right down on them, it was in the dead center of the view screen filling the view.

Jack got on the intercom and yelled "brace for impact!!!" as the collision was so intense that he blacked out.

Awakening a few moments later inside the pod surrounding the captain's chair, looking from side to side all he could see was loose debris as it looked to be raining ash all around him; Jack knew that last hit probably tore through the hull, he was lucky to be in once piece. He recognized parts of his ship which lay strewn on the ground in flames; he quickly figured out that the force from the impact must have somehow ejected him along with these items.

He then caught the sight of his ship a short distance away as it smoked and sparked on the ground, crippled and struck down. Jack managed to open up the pod and rise to his feet; he saw the city that encompassed *Mirage* in flames, its many buildings collapsing as fires burned in the streets. Smoke was rising in far off parts of the city as meteors impacted all around; the destruction of the city, first started by *the Harbinger*, was now continuing by some unknown force on a massive scale. He heard sporadic gunfire accompanied by explosions in the distance; signs that whatever was left of the city was fighting back against something, but Jack couldn't be sure of what.

Suddenly two figures descended down from the sky, one of them Jack recognized as the shadowy figure that cast him into the *Astral Plane* from an awakened state; the other figure looked to be cloaked in many bright colored adornments as a light shone mystically from behind it, but this figure did not look at Jack directly, nor did he speak.

The shadowy figure approached laughing to himself "Well done, well done! As you can clearly see you have fulfilled your purpose."

Jack replied angrily "What! I am not responsible for this. How dare you accuse me of this!? I tried to stop this!"

The shadowy figure laughed and said "Tell yourself whatever you need to hear, but your reckless actions were a destabilizing force, I could see that. All I needed to do was let you loose and eventually your actions would lead to this outcome."

Then the shadowy figure bowed to the mysterious one and said "Now that my master has arrived, all is in hand."

Jack was still angry at what he saw as senseless destruction as he said desperately trying to understand "Why?! Why bring about such devastation, what purpose could it serve!"

The shadowy figure replied "This realm of *Mirage* is beyond saving; the only way left is to totally destroy it and begin anew, that is what must be done."

Jack said with frustration "This is not what I wanted; I set out to explore and learn, how did it come to this?"

The shadowy figure replied "You know how, you let your curiosity get the better of you. You wanted to escape. Now behold what you have wrought, your actions have brought this about."

Jack unsheathed his sword saying angrily "Do not cast blame upon me, this is not my fault!"

The shadowy figure replied with a raised voice "Wrong! You created the airship capable of leveling the city, you enabled a rogue construct to acquire one of the scrolls of power, you allowed him to break the *Anchor* keeping everything stable, and finally you watched as he disrupted the realm to such a degree as to rupture the laws binding the state of the *Astral Plane* together."

The shadowy figure continued "That temporary lapse is what allowed my master to be freed."

Jack stood there, calculating his odds of beating the two figures; quietly he was trying to think of a method he could use against them, keeping his weapons at the ready.

The shadowy figure said "If you are considering challenging us, do not waste your time. I have been watching you, and have seen your ad-hoc fighting style; and I can comfortably say it cannot succeed here. Just look at the devastation around you, if you possess even a scrap of reasoning in that head of yours you will see that you cannot match such power."

Jack was uncertain of what he should do; never in his adventures had he faced such awesome power before. He was torn between fighting against this evil force and the certainty of his demise if he did so. He wanted to do something, yet he knew that charging into such a one-sided fight would accomplish nothing: it would not stop the destruction, he would not be remembered for it, and it wouldn't absolve him for what already happened.

Sighing deeply he sheathed his sword and replied "So what happens now?"

The shadowy figure replied "I will keep my word and send you back to your conscious existence"

Jack motioned to the ruins around him and said "And what of this place? What will happen to the *Astral Plane*?"

The shadowy figure replied "Your meddling has caused enough destruction, don't you think? We intend to turn the *Astral Plane* back into its original image, its true image. We only need to sweep away all this accumulated garbage, this is a matter for the constructs, you wouldn't understand."

Jack didn't like that sound of that at all, but what could he do about it? After seeing what they were capable of he could not hope to stand in their way. He began to think none of this really mattered anyway; it was a matter for the constructs. Besides which, the long term impact of events in this place makes little difference in the real world anyway, Right?

Jack looked around him and saw his grand ship in flames, the destruction which was a consequence of his actions, and ultimately his grand adventure resulting in a catastrophe. He decided to give up.

Jack then said "Alright, I've had enough. Send me back, I do not wish to be here anymore."

The shadowy figure replied "Very well, but be warned. I send you back as an act of benevolence, if you choose to return I will not send you back a second time. You must not ever return."

Jack replied lowly "I understand" as he took off his weapons and let them drop onto the ground, surrendering to the hopelessness of the circumstances.

He glared up and said in a low angry tone "Before I go, I must know... who are you?"

The shadowy figure replied "I am Loki, the master of trickery and mischief, your superior."

Then Loki cast a sort of black cloud that enveloped Jack's senses as he said "Farewell….." *Traveler*!?" PFFFT HA HA HA HA HA HA HA" laughing to mock him one final time.

Jack awakened back in his armchair, fully conscious and fully aware. Quickly performing a few remedial tests, Jack's sense that he was actually awake this time was quickly confirmed. Walking through his house he found that all his routines had been performed, all the chores were taken care of, and everything had been maintained. It was almost as if his body was on "auto pilot" the entire time. Jack was confused on how that was possible, yet relieved that everything proceeded at a normal pace. Descending down to the basement, he grabbed his journal, and shut off the main power to the machine that started everything, confident that he would never need to use it again.

16

AFTERMATH

UPON FINDING A COMFORTABLE SPOT, JACK TOOK OUT HIS JOURNAL AND began recording his entire journey within it, all he experienced, all he observed, all he felt, and everything he did. The afternoon swiftly passed to evening as Jack busily recorded everything he could in the many pages of his journal.

After he finished detailing the particulars, he began to reflect of the experience in its entirety writing: "Through the many days leading up to the use of the machine I wanted to find the answers to the mysteries of the subconscious, to discover the minds sense of 'self'; however, I would be lying to myself if I didn't admit that I wasn't strongly influenced by a desire escape to a place without the blunt harshness of reality, a place without consequence. I have many times felt the bitter sting of loneliness, doubt, and a sort of faithlessness in society; this lingering angst hovers over me like a dark cloud, leading me to seek solitude in my waking hours. Upon beholding that place I was astounded, I wanted to go and do everything that I was incapable of doing; to be a different person entirely: a new beginning."

Pausing for a moment, he pondered if he should continue writing as it was bringing up many negative emotions, reluctantly deciding to continue as he wrote: "This escapism is what lead me to push the experiment as far as I did, to proceed forward despite the risk of certain danger; for this am I a fool, and this is likely what lead to the unfortunate outcome of my adventure. Consequence found me at the end, and I realized that nothing can escape its inevitable grasp. This was necessary though, from close analysis of the machines readings I could see that my brain activity was approaching a state of comatose; had I continued any further my brain patterns would have become fully "normalized" to the subconscious frame of mind, which would have made it impossible for me to awaken by my own power, I would have become trapped and unable to return."

Jack took a moment to think reflect on this entry, making sure it was truly how he wanted to remember what happened; casting his emotions aside he assured himself that everything that transpired happened the way it did because there was no other way it could have occurred. He examined what he previously wrote; making a quick scan for grammar and word choice, and then wrote a final entry to conclude his thoughts on the *'Astral Plane'*.

"This was not all a loss though, I have come to an important conclusion: The *Astral Plane* is an enigma; the further you proceed within it, the more uncertain it becomes. Perhaps I am not meant to be able to fully categorize and explain this mystical place of wonder; maybe I am incapable of having the wisdom to just accept what it is, and appreciate its qualities. I shall endeavor to make sure my experiment is never used by anyone again; no one must be allowed to meddle with this force and possibly repeat my mistakes. Though I am certain this is the way it must be, I still cannot help but feel a lingering feeling of regret…hopefully the passage of time will rid me of this feeling."

Finishing his writing Jack then noticed the lateness of the hour, deciding that he would finally take a moment to relax for a time; grabbing a cool beverage, he sat back in his chair, and turned on the television; hoping to distract himself and forget.

He began watching a comedy program as a sense of normalcy began to set in; reflecting on his previous experiences in the '*Astral Plane*', he hoped he would gain a new found appreciation for the stability of his old routine.

An interruption in the program suddenly broke his chain of thought; a newscaster came on with an urgent report "Breaking news tonight as thousands of people around the world have been struck with a mysterious medical condition. A few hours ago people around the world began falling into a comatose state unable to waken; Scientists and doctors around the world have been unable to explain the sudden nature of this phenomenon. These incidents were at first confined to small urban pockets, but they have been gradually expanding to encompass hundreds of new cases every hour with no signs of the trend slowing down. Experts can find no scientific cause for this anomaly, but say that the patient's brain patterns resemble those of normal REM sleep; doctors, scientists, and medical experts are working around the clock to find a treatment to what is being called "the sleeping sickness", but so far nothing conclusive has come about".

Another newscaster came on and continued "Currently governments around the world are instituting several quarantines around the affected areas, as this "sleeping sickness" has already claimed the lives of hundreds in cities around the world. At its current infection rate it will soon be a major pandemic, yet military and government officials are uncertain on how to contain this condition; nor do they fully understand how it spreads, as new cases seem to arise from no previous physical contact with those afflicted."

The first newscaster returned with a follow up report "The situation is rapidly becoming a crisis, as hospitals are being flooded with new cases, and the police & military are trying to contain rioters who are taking to the streets in panic. We will keep you updated on this story as it unfolds, but currently government officials are advising everyone to remain calm and stay within their homes."

Jack quickly shut the TV off and rose to his feet knowing that this sudden "sleeping sickness" was no coincidence; this had to be linked to the current disorder in the *Astral Plane*. Jack could tell that whatever was happening was destabilizing the real world, and that if it wasn't stopped society could quickly break down into anarchy.

Jack was the one who caused this, and now he was the only one who could possibly fix it. Trying to explain the situation to the police or government would be a waste of time; people would just think he was crazy, no one would possibly believe him. His choice was now made for him; he now had no other option but to return to the *Astral Plane*.

Scribbling a farewell note he did his best to write out an explanation "I have just learned that my actions have led to grave consequences for the lives of many others; whatever reasons I had for not going back aren't important anymore, I now must return! I hope that I find the courage and strength to reverse this, if I fail at least know that I tried." then sealed it into an envelope, put it on the table, and rushed to the basement.

Jack powered up the machine and prepared to enter the place that he wanted to seal away forever, though returning could cost him everything he could not accept the thought of others dying because of his actions; this guilt overwhelmed any sense of logic and pushed him forward like a madman, driven to make things right in spite of any personal cost.

Strapping himself in, Jack readied his finger on the activation button, hesitating at what he knew could be the point-of-no-return. Reminding himself that it wasn't just his life at stake anymore, he engaged the button as his surroundings began to be stripped away like the first time; Jack was now committed: either he would undo the damage he had done, or he would remain trapped in the *Astral Plane* forever. His destiny was now set on an uncertain and dangerous course.

Jack said to himself "This is it, it's now or nothing" as he plunged downwards into the realm of the subconscious, this time knowing that he might never return…

Spiraling down he forced himself to open his eyes even though he was reeling from all the force being exerted around him. He could see himself surrounded by a tunnel of light and sound; yet he somehow knew he wasn't within the *Astral Plane*, perhaps this was some sort of transitional state in-between realms. Images of the events that had transpired during his journey were flashing upon the surface of the tunnel like a reoccurring memory; he adjusted himself enough to scan his surroundings and could see that it was not he that was moving it, it was his surroundings.

Struggling to maintain consciousness he spoke "What is this? Why haven't I entered the *Astral Plane* yet?"

A feminine voice answered powerfully "This is the place between realms; we have intervened to determine the best course".

Jack replied as best as he could, but hardly kept his senses centered. "Are you planning on subjecting me to this until I change my mind?"

The voice replied ignoring him "This is the force of your two states of mind struggling against each other, the struggle has reached a critical moment, and only one may prevail. You must make a choice."

Jack was close to his maximum tolerance as he answered "My actions have put others at risk, my choice is made for me."

The tunnel around him came to a stop as a familiar figure suddenly appeared before him, it was the angelic like woman that had slain Malachi in front of him, Jack said in anger "You?! Have you come to strike me down as well!?"

The angelic figure replied "No, yet you should know have the power to stop your return and send you back, but only if we do so now. We must know that your continued presence will not wreak further havoc upon our realm."

Jack was not impressed as he replied "If you were to stop me then you should have done so before any harm could have come of it, not after the damage has already been done! You only intervene now because you are looking for a reason to condemn me."

The angelic figure replied "We only intervene when absolutely necessary, your actions can no longer be ignored; you have been an anomaly which destabilizes things around you, and if you plan on causing further damage we shall not let you pass."

Exhaling deeply he took a moment to steady himself, to keep from saying anything rash or from anger, then replied "The present distortion is my fault, and I will stop at nothing to fix the distortion; even if it kills me."

The figure replied "If you fail, you will be trapped within the *Astral Plane* permanently, do you accept this?".

Replying back he said sternly "There is more at stake than just my well-being; I must restore the balance of the *Astral Plane*. Please, let me pass."

The Angelic figure listened and replied "We must deliberate" as its eyes lit up and flashed erratically for a few moments, Jack guessed it had to be some sort of mental link of sorts.

The figure's eyes dimmed to normal and it said "We shall allow you to pass, proceed knowing that we are watching and that we will intervene should you overstep your bounds again, deliberately or unknowingly."

Jack said assertively "If I am to be under the sword of judgement, then I should like to know who holds it over me?".

The figure answered "We are the *first* constructs; we keep the *Astral Plane* in order."

The tunnel began to move again as the figure stated "The time approaches, are you prepared?" Jack nodded in return and the figure raised its hands and disappeared; he was then flung forward through the tunnel as his senses were blinded by a sudden rush of vision and sound.

Recovering slowly he found himself back at the crash site of his ship *the Harbinger*. Jack could see smoke rising on every horizon as ash fell from the sky, fallout from the great catastrophe he unleashed. Looking down at the ground he saw his weapons and the telekinetic gloves lying in the mud, he slowly picked them up, wiped some of the caked mud off, and re-equipped them.

Jack then noted aloud "I can't let myself give up again". Deciding to search the wreck of his ship for anything useful, he trudged through the mud towards the crash site.

Entering through a massive hole that was torn in the side of the hull, he made his way through the wreckage of the ship climbing around debris and pushing away broken parts; the lights flickered on and off as many of the doors were jammed shut. It was difficult for Jack to reconcile that this was once his proud, powerful ship the "*Harbinger*", now it was struck down and broken. Its current state served as a bitter lesson for Jack, the consequences of being naïve before.

He finally made his way to what was left of the simulator, nearly stumbling over because the floor was angled at a sharp slant. Glancing over the components he was surprised to find that it looked to be intact, if unpowered. Jack touched his hand to the main terminal and focused on thoughts of electricity as the console came to life.

A familiar voice greeted him "Greetings captain, it is my unfortunate duty to report that many of the ships systems have suffered critical damage, power is down to 10% of capacity and primary engines are completely inoperable."

Jack responded "I am sorry Eleanor, but I have no time to repair the ship; even if I did, using it would be far too obvious for what I need to do."

The ship's computer replied "Understood, all primary systems will be placed in a suspended state until your return."

Jack humbly smiled as he replied "Thank you Eleanor, pull up the simulator one last time. I have use of it".

The computer replied as it powered down "Very well captain, simulator is active, signing off."

The simulator projected a grid over his surroundings as Jack began making alterations on his equipment and wardrobe. Unsheathing his sword he lifted it into position as the projector held it aloft, Jack focused on generating a pen as it appeared in his hands with a flash of light and smoke. The plain straight sword, although useful, was not lethal and intimidating enough for what Jack now intended, so he sketched a larger serrated blade with a hook built into the reverse side of the blade. Initiating the modification sequence two tool arms emerged and heated the blade to a molten temperature then quickly added extra material before quickly and efficiently reshaping it, then it went through a process of heating and cooling the blade to temper it to its correct hardness, then it finished by sharpening the blade with a precise machine tool. It now looked more like an oversized hunting knife with sharp menacing barbs, an ensnaring catch on the reverse side and an elegantly curved, but unmistakably deadly shape; testing to ensure that its magical effect remained intact, he tapped it against a loose bulkhead behind him as it enveloped the bulkhead in a fast covering ice. Satisfied with the new sword he made a new sheath which held the blade in place with three leather loops but showed off the blade's deadly design to any would-be challengers, before sliding it into place on his belt.

Next he unsheathed his crossbow and placed it in the projected grid. For the crossbow he would focus on function, first he drew a mechanical re-cocking mechanism on the back of the crossbow; then drew a reloading magazine fed mechanism, which locked into place over the top of where the bolt sat. Once finished with these two modifications he drew a compartment in the stock, to contain the power source of these mechanical components, and then initiated the modification. This time a tool arm emerged with a mechanical arm, the tool arm began forming the individual pieces as the mechanical arm quickly grabbed and assembled each piece, fitting them quickly into place. The two tool arms moved so quickly they began to blur, once finished the mechanical elements were complete.

Jack then focused on channeling a part of his energy into a small orb and installed it as the crossbow's power source (similar to the one which powered his ship, only much smaller). Taking aim at that same bulkhead behind him steadied his aim and held down the trigger as several bolts were fired in rapid succession shattering the icy bulkhead and lighting the remains on fire, satisfied he removed the spent magazine and made a new one appear within his opposite hand before sliding it into place, he then sheathed the crossbow on his back.

The last modification he had in mind was his clothing, up until this point he had worn the same clothes that he wore in real life; but this would no longer do. He quickly sketched out loose fitting dark robes, making sure to add reinforced pads on the shoulders, wrists, and joints; topped off with a hood which concealed his face from the sides and back. He then added internal straps and pockets for any extra gear he might need to acquire, adding two thick leather belts around the waist to secure it on his person and provide some slight protection for his gut area. Looking it over again Jack added one last feature, an extended collar which extended over the lower half of his face, when combined with the hood would only show his eyes. He pressed the button to initiate the item's creation as mechanical arms quickly made the robe around his person with such speed and ability that it took only moments before he was draped in his new garbs.

He said to the computer "reflective surface" as a mirror was imposed on one of the walls of the simulator. His new appearance conveyed an air of concealment with some combat utility, he looked like an outlaw, and perhaps that's what he wanted.

As Jack secured his robes and tightened the straps on his weapons he said to himself "From this moment forward I cannot entertain thoughts of mercy or hesitation, I can never again consider the thought of giving up, I must be relentless and driven to bring an end to all this disorder because I might be the only one who can. From this moment on I can no longer be Jack, I must become the *Traveler*! I will make my enemies dread my name."

Jack then turned and left the room, setting out to undo what he had originally done or die trying. Setting back out onto the *Astral Plane* Jack began a new chapter in his adventure, albeit perhaps a darker and more foreboding one.

BOOK 2

1

JOURNEY

BEGINS

AGAIN

With his new weapons equipped and draped in his menacing robes, Jack made his way to the hangar bay of the wrecked ship. Reaching the entrance he opened the thick hangar doors with a burst of his telekinetic gloves. The hangar was full of wrecked fighters, many of them still riddled with holes and bearing scorch marks from their most recent skirmish with the *Dauntless*. Walking over to the terminal he powered it on by focusing on electricity/energy and placing his hand on the console; the screen flickered to life as the lights in the hangar bay revealed the extensive damage the ship suffered in the crash.

Jack began searching through the ships in the computer's database; he then found an old design of his: a small scale airship designed not for air combat but for transport and exploration. The side panel of the hangar opened but the loading crane jammed, Jack grasped around the crane with his telekinetic gloves and pulled it out, ripping the crane out of its socket in the process.

The airship emerged with the dangling crane still attached; the airship was old, but still functional. Jack took a moment to inspect the ship: he saw its crew compartment in the front with its wide viewing window and central wooden steering wheel. In the center was the back swept fuselage that had three gun slots off the center of the right side, each gun serving a unique purpose and all of them powerful. Below that was the loading door, not entirely different from *the Harbinger's* only smaller. On the rear of the ship were three oversized thrusters, powered by the reactor which sat inside the back of the ship. Sticking out from the back third of the fuselage were the four elegant fins which were placed vertically on the top and bottom of the ship that controlled steering. On the center of the fuselage were the forward swept wings much like those of Jack's ASM fighters; only larger and with stabilizing engines mounted on each wing, and a large complement of missiles hidden inside retractable compartments. Taking a moment to gaze on it, he found it ironic that this was his original idea for a ship to serve him, something small, but one which was effective and versatile. It was only later when he imagined much more grandiose designs like that of the "*Harbinger*".

He was starting to think it was such overarching designs which had brought the present disaster upon the *Astral Plane* saying to himself "This is what I should have used the first time, capable and efficient, not the oversized behemoth that I was unable to control".

Jack could see though that his design lacked several key features that he would need on his journey. Opening the side door he stepped inside and began summoning the components he needed, as he then hastily assembled them piece by piece with his telekinetic gloves. To assist with the gunship's defense, he grafted an electron manipulator onto the reactor to serve as the ship's shield. To assist with targeting and control, he built a computer near the front of the ship which would serve as the support for his ship's sensors and radar; he also added a data core to the bottom that would serve as a copy of *the Harbinger's* database. He then removed the front window and sealed it shut, before installing digital projections and screens which would show him everything outside the ship without needing to rely on a viewing screen.

Moving to the outside of the gunship, he mounted sensory, radar, and communications relays that would serve as the eyes and the ears of the ship, making sure they were securely welded, and then added an armored hood around the outside to shield them. Then he painted the outside of the ship black with red stripes, hoping to imitate the menacing appearance of the "*Dauntless*".

Lastly, he adjusted the interior by adding weapons and armor racks against the wall of the cargo area then modified the captain's chair making it so that it could recline for resting. Finishing he used the console to activate the ship, as it drifted to a slight hover and all of its systems powered on; Jack grabbed one of the wrecked fighters and tossed it at the ship as the debris made contact with the shields and exploded. Once the dust cleared the ship remained intact with its shields fading back to transparency. Jack then took off the ship controller earpiece and calibrated it to remotely control the gunship instead; satisfied with his alterations he made the ship land and activated the hangar bay doors to open.

A dull clank caught Jack's attention as something in the hangar was disturbed, he unsheathed his sword and turned around to see a group of the soldier constructs who had manned *the Harbinger* before the crash. Jack rushed to grab the one in front, put his sword at its throat, and pushed him against a wall as he exclaimed in anger "You! Tell me why I should not kill you right now!!"

The soldier construct replied "We have come to serve, nothing more"

Jack retorted "If by "serve" you mean "betray" then you have certainly fulfilled your purpose. You mutinied against me! Assisted Malachi in the destruction of *Mirage*, and unleashed the present calamity upon the *Astral Plane*! You will tell me now why you have done this! Why did you betray me!"

The soldier construct replied unapologetically "He was our master, his will was our command. What he ordered, we carried out".

Jack was still incensed "Have you come here to excuse your actions! If so then damn your apologies, what's done is done, and your words cannot fix what has happened"

The soldier construct replied without emotion "As I have said, we come to serve. Malachi instructed that upon his death we were to serve you and only you."

Jack spit in front of the soldier construct as he rudely said "What makes you think I even want your help!? What assurance do I even have that you won't betray me again?"

The construct nodded to the others who all got down on one knee as he said "We are yours to command until you release us from this burden or until we are no more. Our lives are pledged to you."

Jack thought about it for a moment before deciding on his solution, releasing his sword he let the construct fall to the ground as he spoke loud enough for all of them to hear "Hear this! If you truly want to serve me then your first task is to repair *the Harbinger* before I return! I fully expect you to fail in this task, prove me wrong and you shall have your redemption. If you should fail, then do not remain when I return, for if I return to see you have failed I will destroy you for your past treachery! That is all."

The constructs upon hearing this, set out to begin repairing the ship; proceeding from the hangar for the different parts of the ship. Without looking back or saying a word Jack boarded his newly modified ship and took off into the storm clouded sky, in the back of his mind he was uncertain that he had taken the right course of action but he was so angry that he didn't care.

Jack had now set out on his mission to destroy Loki, Loki's master, and anyone else who stood in his way. However, the *Astral Plane* was vast and he did not know where to begin so he set out for the familiar village in hopes he could commune with Melchior one last time. Focusing his thoughts of the village and its surroundings as he gripped the steering wheel the ship launched forward moving at such speed as to make its surroundings blur, until suddenly stopping in the sky above the village.

Something was different this time, looking through his viewing monitors Jack saw a great number of people, carts, and animals forming a large caravan which stretched in a column for miles, the great mass of people and things were moving slowly through the town towards some far off destination. At first, he was confused at the sight of this, until he zoomed the viewing screen into a smaller section of the caravan; he saw that all the people were ragged with desperate looks on their faces, the carts were filled with an almost random assortment of necessities and household items, and many of the people in the caravan were gravely injured. Jack suddenly realized that these people weren't merchants in a caravan; they were refugees fleeing from a warzone.

Before Jack could decide what to do an ominous thunder cloud began forming in the distance, it chaotically rumbled with thunder and lightning before suddenly igniting on fire and swirling into a storm of fire. Within the center of this fiery maelstrom the sky ripped open to reveal an unstable distortion which quaked and surged with energy. From it a dozen flaming meteors emerged and streaked towards the outside of the town. Jack quickly readied his ship's weapons but the meteors made contact with the ground before he could react; they landed just outside the area of the refugees. The memory of meteors similar to these devastating *Mirage* and his ship were still fresh in Jack's memory, whatever the cause of the storm, he knew it was nothing good.

From the impact craters emerged warriors clad in armor with bright white tunics and great broadswords. They were charging towards the refugee column as the terrified people left their possessions and fled while screaming with terror. Jack cranked the throttle on this ship and raced towards the site of the crisis, acting quickly he fired a barrage of missiles from the wings of his ship which hit directly in front of the warriors and burst into a chain of explosions, decimating the enemy warriors in their charge.

From the distortion emerged another wave of meteors which headed for the fleeing refugees; this time ready Jack activated his ship's countermeasures which fired from the back of the ship, as they broke into pieces, and collided head on with a handful of the meteors blasting them into dust before they hit the ground. However, there were too many meteors to intercept as the uninterrupted ones reached the ground. Swiveling his ship so that his guns faced the impact sites, he armed them and waited for the warriors to emerge. Another wave charged from the craters towards the helpless civilians as Jack fired the first gun on his ship, a high caliber rapid-firing Gatling gun. Thousands of rounds suddenly poured from the side of his ship into the waves of charging soldiers, tearing through them as dust clouded the area from thousands of shells hitting the ground simultaneously. The armor piercing bullets were capable of punching through armor, flesh, and bone as they effortlessly perforated entire formations of soldiers with holes. As the smoke and debris cleared, the wave of enemy warriors lay utterly destroyed; obviously these rank-and-file swordsmen were no match for Jack's ship.

The swirling maelstrom of fire suddenly grew more violent as lightning arced from the center and split two more holes in the sky which transformed into additional distortions. Jack turned his attention to the source of the meteors, firing a barrage of missiles from his ship towards the series of flaming maelstroms. Before colliding with the distortions the missiles suddenly exploded short of the target harmlessly away from the center, before he could try again hundreds of meteors emerged from the storms and flew towards the edge of the town itself.

Quickly evading he avoided being pummeled by the oncoming meteors as they impacted in a circle surrounding the village. Jack swiveled his ship around and prepared to use his ship's second gun, a missile launcher which fired barrages of cluster missiles carrying different payloads. From the craters emerged not more warriors but single figures clothed in white robes with a black trim carrying strange yellow staffs; Jack fired the second gun as a missile flew to each crater and split into several dozen smaller missiles in mid-air. The robed figures tapped their staffs against the ground and giant spheres of fire formed protective circles in the air above them. The cluster missiles collided with the fire and exploded violently, but to no avail as the fire shields summoned by the robed figures remained intact. The robed figures continued to concentrate on the shields, keeping their arms raised in the air as their staffs glowed brightly; from the craters behind them another wave of warriors emerged and set forth to attack the villagers and refugees.

Jack had no time to figure out how to break the fire shield, he needed to get himself on the ground and stop them directly. Seeing a small gap in coverage in the center of the fire shields he set his ship's trajectory to fly towards the entry point. Quickly programming the flight path he rushed over to the flight elevator and placed his hand over the "emergency drop" button. Tapping his earpiece the ship swiftly swooped in over the gap as Jack punched the drop button and the hatch flew open letting him fall through the gap towards the ground.

Jack quickly blasted his telekinetic gloves planet-ward causing a gust of wind to push backwards slowing his descent, dropping into a roll he quickly got back on his feet and tapped the earpiece making the gunship fly off to a safe distance. A group of the white clad warriors caught sight of this and headed towards Jack weapons drawn; seeing them up close he noticed they wore chainmail armor topped with bucket helmets, and also carried broadswords much like those of crusading knights of medieval times. What most caught his attention were the symbols emblazoned on their tunics, yellow crosses with circles around the middle, but he had no time to ponder their meaning.

Jack wasted no time unsheathing his crossbow and holding down the trigger on the new automatic action, sweeping it across their group and lighting all of them on fire. Flailing and yelling uncontrollably they stumbled around before falling to the ground dead. Jack saw one of the robed figures concentrating on a fire shield, chanting some unknown language. Jack unsheathed his sword and brazenly ran to the fire shield jumping towards it while swinging his sword in a wide arc in front of him. The sword's icy power extinguished a section of the flame as Jack barreled through it; he rushed upon the robed figure, fiercely stabbing his sword into the robed figure's gut before they could react. The robed figure pulled back its hood to reveal an older looking man carrying a look of utter disbelief on his face; Jack without pity retracted the sword and slashed it into the old man's torso throwing him violently to the ground.

The other figures noticed this and ceased generating their fields and pointed towards Jack, many of the warriors ceased their pursuit of the refugees and set upon him. Jack concentrated his energy on all the individual swords of his enemies, reaching out and grasping at them with his telekinetic gloves; the weapons were ripped out of the warrior's hands, as he swiftly turned the weapons on their former masters: stabbing them all in unison with their own weapons. A smile of vengeful satisfaction crept on Jack's face as all the warriors fell to the ground clutching their own sword hilts. One of the robed figures stepped forward, clad in a simplistic robe without any buttons or adornments save for the symbol of a yellow eye in the center with rays drawn around it.

The robed figure pounded his staff on the ground and announced with a commanding air. "Violent demon! How dare you interfere with the will of the "deity"?! Cast off your concealing mask and reveal yourself!"

Jack slightly amused at this request answered back "First I would know the name of such a crusade, that I might identify those who I am slaying".

The robed figure was insulted and scoffed "Such arrogance! Speaking to a 'Cleric' of the deities word in such a way, your slaying of the deities holy 'Templars' will be judged severely. However, as to the matter of your ignorance we are the "Crusade of the deity" we spread his word to the four corners of the *Astral Plane* that it might be cleansed."

Jack answered back "I see no 'Crusade of the deity' only misguided fools and barbarians. You need not know my name or face, know only that I am the instrument of your destruction!".

The robed figure laughed as it said "Our army is innumerable; our *Templars* driven to fight beyond their limits by the deity's vision, led by the enlightened *Clerics* who have seen his light and share in his awesome power. You cannot stop the deities word, you are but a mere obstacle, I will show you his power!".

As the *Cleric* finished he thrust his palm forward and flames shot forth towards Jack. Leaping over the flame Jack blasted a force wave towards the *Cleric* with his telekinetic gloves, bashing him into one of the nearby buildings. As he landed two more *Clerics* appeared in a flash of fire next to him and swung at him with flame covered staffs. Jack ducked under their swings and swung upwards with his sword; freezing one of them solid, before swinging back around at the other *Cleric* knocking him to the ground with a fatal wound. Another *Cleric* flew high into the air and unleashed several fireballs from his staff, Jack used his devices to direct them away from himself before unsheathing his crossbow and firing a barrage in return which set the unprepared *Cleric* ablaze.

Seeing that all the nearby *Clerics* were dealt with Jack turned his attention to the one who first announced himself, as he was now crawling back towards his staff injured from being banged against the building. As the *Clerics* hand grasped around the staff Jack's foot suddenly came down on it pinning it to the ground. Reaching down and grasping around the *Cleric's* neck he used the telekinetic gloves to pull him up to eye level.

The *Cleric* gasping from the grip of the gloves barely managed to say "The deity will avenge me!"

Jack cut him off "Speak not of deities; you are a hollow fool who blindly serves a false god! Your actions are not that of a divine word but of a campaign of terror. I condemn you to death; know that your "deity" will share a similar fate when I find him!"

With that he hurled the battered *Cleric* into the air before launching his sword with the speed of a bullet at him, pinning him to a nearby building with enough force to crack the bricks in the wall behind him. The *Cleric's* awestruck face was still in disbelief as he let out his final breath and died.

With the last *Cleric* dead the flaming maelstroms suddenly became unstable and imploded to nothingness as the sky returned to normal. As Jack surveyed the surroundings he could see that the village was greatly damaged by the attack and resulting battle, many of its buildings were in ruins; even the "*Traveler's* Way" tavern had lost one of its walls and had all of its windows shattered.

In the center of the crossroads Jack saw a strange blurry figure appear as its image shifted and rapidly contrasted to a more recognizable form. Expecting a battle he readied his crossbow and steadied it on the blurry figure, with a flash of light the image became clear as Jack was relieved to see it was a familiar ally. The figure was Balthazar who appeared in the center of the crossroads, but Balthazar was clearly in shock when he saw the scene of the battle and the damage incurred to the village; when he saw Jack dressed in his new garbs he quickly inquired "*Traveler*!? What has happened here?!"

Jack removed his hood and lowered his collar as he said "Men came and attacked the village, men claiming to be of the "Crusade of the deity", I fought and defeated them."

Balthazar looked troubled as he approached "Then you have done a great service this day, still I am greatly distressed; my monks and I were creating a diversion so these refugees could safely escape from the realm of Epic. The enemy was not supposed to know this escape route, which means we have been betrayed." Scanning his surroundings, Balthazar recognized the *Cleric* who was still pinned to the wall by Jack's sword as he walked towards the corpse.

Balthazar lifted the chin of the *Cleric* and removed its hood to reveal it had a shaved head and a strange tattoo; Balthazar sighed deeply as he retrieved the sword and let the body fall to the ground, then he turned to Jack and said "That man once belonged to my order, he was one of the more revered monks who was bestowed with a tattoo of "devotion to the way"; he must have defected to the enemy and betrayed our secret, if he was capable of betrayal then anyone is."

Jack replied "I don't understand. Who are these madmen, why are they claiming to be "the Crusade of the deity"? Why would anyone defect to them? More importantly why is no one putting a stop to them?"

Balthazar sighed and replied "Many things have happened during your short absence, come I will explain everything once we have ensured the refugees are safe."

Balthazar's monks began to arrive from Epic and were quickly joined by Jack and Balthazar who spread out to calm the refugees and reassure them that the danger had passed. Jack could sense that *Mirage's* distortion was having deep repercussions throughout the *Astral Plane*, his head was filled with many unanswered questions, but for the time being they would have to wait.

2

THE

INVASION

JACK AND BALTHAZAR RESTORED ORDER TO THE ALARMED REFUGEES and aided those who were wounded, as calm returned to scene of the village the sun began to set over the horizon; every refugee Jack encountered was stricken with terror, some great evil had befallen them, something they were desperate to flee from. Finding a construct of a man hiding under a wagon he directed his telekinetic gloves to slowly begin lifting it off the ground; the panic stricken man quickly grabbed the side of the wagon and pulled it back down yelling "No! No you will not take me!"

Jack responded trying to calm him down "Relax, It is safe now"

The man responded still cowering under his wagon "No! We are not safe, we are doomed! I witnessed the sky rain fire and death! I saw their armies sweep the land like a swarm! I watched their soldiers slaughter all who resisted! They were like a title wave! An avalanche! They were unstoppable!!"

Jack tried to reassure him "Calm down, I dealt with the ones who attacked"

The man yelled "Fool! You cannot win against such an onslaught! Everyone will be killed! Everything will be destroyed! Had you been there at the forefront of the invasion and seen the terrors I have seen you would know! Run damn you! Run while you still can!" With that the panic stricken man burst from the side of the wagon and ran into the far off horizon spiriting with an inhuman speed, it was obvious that whatever he had been through had permanently traumatized him.

As the last of Balthazar's monks arrived the evacuation of the refugees continued once again, as the surviving villagers started to pick up the pieces and rebuild what they could.

Balthazar then called out "come *Traveler*, we have much to discuss" as he entered the "*Traveler's* Way" tavern.

Jack quickly followed, but once inside saw that the damage to the tavern had been severe. A large meteorite fragment had punched through one of the walls and came to a stop in the middle of the tavern, most of the tables and chairs were in splinters, and the bar was in pieces at the bottom of the impact crater. What few tables and chairs that survived were huddled against the far wall, Balthazar was sitting at one of the tables with a cup of hot water. Jack walked up and sat down as Balthazar retrieved a tea mixture from his robe and poured it into the cup.

Jack asked his first question "So what is this "army of the deity"? Who leads them? And how do I stop them?"

Balthazar replied "He is one of the ancient constructs long ago thought to be imprisoned for eternity"

Jack inquired "These storms of fire do not seem like the work of an ordinary construct Balthazar, I sense there is much more to this story"

Balthazar finished stirring his tea as he asked "Are you sure you want to know?"

Jack nodded and replied "Yes, I need to know everything there is to know about this figure.".

Balthazar sighed deeply and placed his tea aside for a moment "Very well *Traveler*, I will tell you of the *Astral Plane*'s origin, and it's terrible first war".

Balthazar closed his eyes as if remembering a distant memory and began "Long ago when ancient man first became aware of the world their thoughts and curiosities began to coalesce and form into a series of shared existences forming the "sleepwalker realm". In these first dreams they saw a mirror image of the world that they knew, a perfect representation in every way; but they were not content with a mere copy, and as their power over thought increased they were able to alter and change the dream world more to their own liking, it eventually became a different place entirely: The *Astral Plane*, an early version of what you see today. Back in those far off times man was of a different nature: fierce, bold, of sharp intellect, and powerful. Owing to that nature they entered this place fully aware as the *Travelers* do now; their thoughts were unrestrained as they were able to unleash a mass of creativity & emotion upon the *Astral Plane*, it turned into a mystical wonder of terrifying intrigue."

Balthazar recalled this first part of his story almost with a sense of nostalgia, but the optimistic glow from his eyes disappeared when he told the next part. "Then something tragic occurred... the creations of man within the *Astral Plane* began to think for themselves and grow powerful, and as they did the barrier between this world and the real world began to blur. These powerful figures began to influence the real world, they granted men wealth, power, and knowledge. They then began to take this further creating powerful items and creatures which became manifested in your world and upset the nature of reality. It wasn't long before men began to worship these creations as gods, and began fighting for them; waging wars against the followers of the other dream gods. One of the dream gods in particular rose to near absolute power, the personification of your real world sun 'SOL'."

Balthazar elaborated "SOL was the most powerful of them all, spreading the legend throughout the land that he was the bringer of the light in the world; that only the unrighteous suffered his fury, and his purpose was to banish all those who would perpetuate ignorance while remaining in darkness. This reoccurring metaphorical struggle between light and shadow, life and death, good and evil, was first perpetuated by him as his means to indoctrinate his masses of followers."

Balthazar concluded "At the height of this war when SOL was on the verge of total victory, both this world and your world were on the brink of destruction; the other dream gods in their desperation banded together using all their power to server SOL's connection to the Astral Plane, by sealing him in a separate realm that they conjured to imprison him: 'the Void'. Thus depriving SOL of his army of followers and imprisoning him for all time. The dream gods knowing that such a disaster could never be allowed to repeat itself, decided that man's influence on the dream world was far too great; they set a great confusion upon the minds of man and made them forget all that they had learned and experienced. Then they attempted to cut off man's connection to the Astral Plane entirely; however, man's emotions, fantasies, and imagination had become deeply rooted in the fabric of the Astral Plane so the connection could never be severed entirely. Instead their minds split into two parts: the conscious which controls logic, reasoning, and organization of thought; and the subconscious which controls emotions, creativity, and self-awareness. This divide in man's mental state clouded his perception of this place, which became an indiscernible illusion from which the conscious mind could not understand; likewise the real world became a frustration which the subconscious mind could not fully grasp, hence the never ending search for meaning or higher truth which floods in from the subconscious."

Balthazar closed his eyes and rubbed his forehead for a moment almost hesitant to continue, but then sighed deeply and continued "This divided state of mind eventually brought about a gradual change in man's state, as he came to value the real world over what he could imagine and became a lover of accomplishment instead of a lover of beauty. Mankind slowly suppressed their strong emotions to become "civilized"; slowly becoming docile and pliable, dedicating themselves to their new domains to build their wonders of stone and metal beginning the slow march of technology. As I said before though the link between the mind and the *Astral Plane* could never be totally severed; man's thoughts and legends in the real world still came to manifest themselves here, and emotions and creativity still seeps from the *Astral Plane* into the minds of men. On rare occasions men and women are able to overcome the barrier on their subconscious entirely and so become "*Travelers* of the subconscious", using their power to influence the real world on a massive scale bringing about revolutions in philosophy, art, independent thought, and creativity."

Balthazar described "This power to influence so many so quickly emanates from "*The Source*" a powerful nexus of energies from both places which exists in a state removed from time, its power cannot be restrained nor ever fully understood by anyone. Until recently this cycle of "*Travelers*" revolutionizing the world has continued at a steady pace, but it has been a long time since a new *Traveler* has come about, and your artificial means of attaining that power tell me that the state of the real world will soon come to overpower the barriers of the *Astral Plane*, and thus begin another cycle of cataclysm not unlike those from our ancient times."

Jack sat back for a few moments trying to take in all that was said, but suddenly a detail that seemed off came up in his memory "Wait, you said that *SOL* was sealed away and imprisoned; yet it seems that he has returned to wage war once again. How is this possible?"

Balthazar contemplated a possible answer "*SOL* was too powerful a foe to be sealed away indefinitely, he has no doubt been channeling his energy for eons to escape his prison; once one of the realms became sufficiently unstable I believe he opened up a rift between the two and entered our world, and is now using the what's left of his power combined with the corruption of the unclosed distortion to wreak havoc upon the *Astral Plane*."

Jack interrupted "But wait, the other dream gods were able to stop him once before, why don't they just stop him again?"

Balthazar explained "Their power became greatly diminished when their subjects forgot about them over the eons. They no longer have the combined energy to subdue him a second time, what's worse is that *SOL* can use his power of indoctrination to blind other constructs and bind them to his will; and thus increase his own power exponentially. *SOL* may even grant his own abilities to those most loyal to him, allowing them to do what he can on a lesser scale."

Jack was now greatly alarmed and said "There must be a way to defeat him? What is it!?"

Balthazar replied "*SOL* no longer possesses the great power he did in ancient times, he currently at his most vulnerable now while he gathers constructs to indoctrinate to his cause, now is the time to strike. His invasions of *Mirage* and Epic are only the beginning; we must act decisively to stop him now while we still can."

Jack nodded as he pulled the hood back over his head and raised his collar saying "Then let us waste no more time".

Balthazar and Jack walked back to the center of the village crossroads as Balthazar informed "We must travel to Epic and unite the warring factions against *SOL's* army; only with their combined forces can we hope to gain leverage against his army's great numbers."

Jack inquired "To the monastery then?"

Balthazar replied "No, my monastery was one of the first places to be attacked; we must go to the forest and seek out the barbarous war chiefs. Let us travel to Epic, remember to concentrate on abstract thoughts of conflict and war but keep your mind in the forest you visited before."

Jack did this and as they walked forward their movements sped till their surroundings were a blur, finding themselves once again within the forests of Epic; this time things were different, the sounds of battle were eerily absent as no scenes of conflict were present at all.

Balthazar unsheathed his metal staff and advised "Follow me and be on your guard, this silence does not bode well."

Keeping a low profile Jack and Balthazar traveled swiftly and silently through the forest taking care to tread lightly and avoid speech to keep their presence subtle. As they moved through the forest Jack discovered why there was no longer any combat, concealed in the high grasses and brush were the many corpses of the fallen; all the warriors had already slain.

From the occasional close glance he could see evidence of the enemy's presence on the dead, scorch marks, large numbers of foot prints, and the presence of deep slash wounds; this was the "Crusade of the Deity's" doing.

Balthazar and Jack continued traveling swiftly through the forest ever nearing their destination. Meanwhile not far away, the Crusade of the Deity was assembling its forces into a sprawling war camp; in the center of the camp lay the commander's tent where *SOL* and his inner circle convened.

The commander's tent was an imposing sight as it was large enough to fit an entire house within; it was bright white & red decorated with many elaborate murals of the sun, with the artwork of fire and light lining each image. The Inside the tent was far more practical however, as there was a long table covered with many various maps and charts of Epic; along with various pieces carefully placed on each representing the movement of forces.

Around this table was a strange cast of warriors, generals, and prophets which formed the inner circle of the crusade's war council, with *SOL* himself at the head of the table wearing his bright yellow and red robes which seemed to shine with a light of their own.

One of the generals began "Our armies sweep across the land destroying all who oppose you; the enemy lies scattered and confused and so we defeat them at every turn and have yet to see a major loss"

SOL replied articulately without becoming overconfident "Ensure that their forces are not given a chance to regroup, you must continue to pursue them deeper into the forests and ravines granting them no respite".

The general scoffed "Our forces greatly outnumber them and they have yet to stand and fight, why should we exhaust ourselves pursuing them?"

SOL's eyes glared over at the general as he appeared in a flash of light next to him and grabbed him by the throat lifting him into the air as flames circled his wrists; *SOL* spoke "Do not question my orders! Your place is to hear and obey, nothing more. Now do as you are ordered commander."

Then he dropped him onto the floor where the general gasped for air for a moment before saluting and quickly leaving the tent. His followers became somewhat nervous as *SOL* continued "How goes the conversion process? Are the prisoners joining our ranks in sufficient numbers?"

One of the prophets answered "Yes *SOL*, thanks to the methods of indoctrination we have been able to bend thousands of constructs to your will thus far; However, those of strong spirit resist the process and take much longer to turn, it is greatly eased if they join our ranks voluntarily rather than by force."

SOL issued an order "Take one out of every twenty who resist the conversion, line them up before the others and cleanse them by fire. This should persuade those who remain that their only options are conversion or death".

The prophet hesitated for a moment "Y-y-yes sir, this will take some time due to the sheer number of conversion camps"

SOL's eyes flashed with light as he looked at his subordinate and said "You have but one day prophet, see that you do not fail" the prophet nervously bowed and hastily left to make preparations.

SOL then addressed the rest of them speaking louder than before "We stand at a great threshold, our great crusade will not falter now or our many thousands of years of planning will be utterly wasted. Remember that if you fail then our entire realm will be overturned and we shall all be forgotten and reduced to dust, redouble your efforts and we shall see the *Astral Plane* rise gloriously again under our banner."

As he finished Loki entered the tent and bowed before giving his report "*SOL*, the refugees we pursued from Epic have escaped, our warriors were defeated."

SOL replied with slight irritation "You had assured me that the defector misdirected Balthazar and his monks, and that the refugees were ours for the taking"

Loki began nearly groveling as he replied "It was not Balthazar, the refugees were aided by a masked man of great power; he single handedly destroyed the entire force."

SOL was at first surprised but after brief contemplation he knew the answer "…It is the *Traveler*, he has returned"

Loki rose to his feet and countered "Impossible, I dealt with him myself; that weakling was not a match for our forces."

SOL spoke over his shoulder to the others "Leave us." as the other council members quickly shuffled out of the room leaving *SOL* and Loki.

SOL began "You underestimate the power of a *Traveler*, you know as well as I that they are capable of anything"

Loki argued "This man is no *Traveler*, he is here by artificial means, it is a wonder he hasn't yet fallen off a precipice or tripped onto a sharp rock"

SOL replied "regardless, if he is here in a full state of awareness then he is capable of greatly influencing the *Astral Plane*, even if he does not yet realize it. The fact that he attained this artificially is most intriguing; since he lacks the iron will of most *Travelers* he could be persuaded to join us, and thus become an unstoppable ally."

Loki disapproved saying "I have more power in my thumb than that *Traveler*, what's more, if he attacked our forces once already then he likely is moving against us again. I should simply find and destroy him, thus removing our obstacle."

SOL raised his hand and stopped him "No, you have had your chance and failed. Instead I want you to carefully watch him, see what he does and where he goes that we might better anticipate the enemy's movements; those who resist us will likely rally around him, and we can use this to our advantage."

Loki reluctantly agreed "A most excellent plan *SOL*, I will do so at once"

As Loki made his way out of the tent, *SOL* spoke one more time "… and Loki, do not forget your place, any misconceived action will place you in great peril".

Loki turned around and said "But of course master, all is as you command" then quietly laughed to himself and departed.

3

SHADES

OF GREY

BALTHAZAR AND JACK FINALLY WERE WITHIN EARSHOT OF THE CAMP AS they heard the rumblings of the encampment and the voices of the warriors noisily chatting amongst themselves. Balthazar turned to Jack and said lowly "I will announce our arrival and we will present ourselves before the chieftain, then I will make my proposal to unite against *SOL*."

Jack argued back "Are you crazy? If you walk out and shout your name like a blowhard they're just going to cut you down."

Balthazar replied "You do not understand how diplomacy works in Epic, I have defeated their warriors many times and thus earned the chieftain's respect; they will not attack unless provoked first."

Jack sighed and replied "You had better be right, or this will be one short round of diplomacy"

Balthazar reassured "Just keep your weapons down *Traveler* and allow me to handle the negotiation."

Balthazar then stood up and said "Hail tribe of the deep forest it is I, Balthazar of the high sanctuary." The tribes-men immediately stood up and grabbed their weapons as the archers around the entryway drew their arrows but held them in place.

A loud barbarian call came from inside the camp along with a grunting speech that was indiscernible to Jack. Once the loud barbarian finished Balthazar, who apparently understood, summarized "The chieftain says that we may enter, but should we bring unwanted news or attempt to threaten his tribe then we will die where we stand"

Jack replied unconfidently "Alright then… let's see if this works, I hope you know what you're doing". Balthazar and Jack cautiously walked into the camp as the barbarian warriors lined either side of their path glaring at them and brandishing their weapons.

Jack kept his crossbow pointed down but his finger near the trigger; there was no way he was letting his guard down, these savages might be tempted to try and kill him just for the spite of it. They reached a clearing in the front of a wooden longhouse adorned with many carvings of great warriors; in front of them stood the grandest of the barbarians, a gigantic man with long unkempt hair and a beard, holding a massive axe with one hand and a big mug foaming with beer in the other. The barbarian gulped the mug down in one swig and tossed it aside before rising to his feet and grunting loudly in his language; at first it sounded like gibberish to Jack, but as he looked at the barbarians face and closely eyed how he enunciated each word he suddenly understood the language as if it were native to him.

The realization manifested in mid-sentence as the barbarian rattled on "…Attacked by these demons, now Balthazar comes off his high mountain and addresses me!? What say you old man?"

Balthazar replied "I have come to seek an alliance, the tribes must band together or the demons will destroy us all"

The barbarian chief scoffed spitting to one side "We have fought the other tribes for as long as we have fought you, yet we still stand. These demons are no different, and they will die all the same"

Jack could see Balthazar's diplomacy was faltering so he responded "Yet so many lie dead in the fields and the demons advance unchallenged, what say you to this".

The barbarian began laughing loudly before stopping himself and saying "The small one speaks, last we encountered you it was in pursuit as you ran through the forest like a scared rabbit, Bah Ha Ha Ha Ha!"

Jack sighed in frustration "I have defeated a dozen warriors of the Deity, can you say the same?"

The barbarian chief reached behind his throne and retrieved a rope strung through two dozen Templar helmets, then he let it drop on the ground before him "By my own hand I slew that many demons in one hour of one day, but they continued to press our lines and kill our brethren. For each one that we slew there were ten more who took their place."

The barbarian made a proposal "If you are in such a hurry to die I will give you a test of bravery, that we might see you worthy; go deep into the northwest into the territory of the demon, find the people he hath stolen from us and release them. Maybe then I'll consider what you and the old man of the temple are saying, but not till you prove you have the stones to fight alongside us. Now leave." Jack became frustrated but Balthazar stopped him from speaking and gave him the cue that it was time to leave.

As they left the barbarians sneered and spit in their path; clearly they held absolutely no respect for them at all and had no inhibitions about being outright rude; Jack wanted more than anything to unsheathe his weapons and avenge their past attack on him. The memory of the soldiers that aided his escape still clouded his mind with regret, yet he refrained as lashing out would accomplish nothing and jeopardize Balthazar's safety.

The gate opened and they left the camp heading in the general direction of the deity's territory, once out of earshot of the barbarian encampment Jack and Balthazar began debating their options. Balthazar began "I wish you had not intervened; now we have to pass his test before he will acknowledge us"

Jack argued "The chieftain wasn't going to be moved by words, he's a brute, and he's never going to agree to anything while he has the upper hand."

Balthazar reflected on the encounter and said "It is possible that you are right. Though his tribe is hounded by the deity's armies he remains as stubborn as ever, we shall have to find another way to convince him."

Jack angrily replied "If he refuses to cooperate after we pass his test then my grip upon his throat will compel him, we do not have time for games."

Balthazar rubbed his forehead as he lamented "I hope that it does not come to that."

Balthazar and Jack traveled Northwest for a while; staying low and quiet in the now eerily silent forests of Epic. Eventually they happened upon a path that looked to have been cut through the underbrush recently, Balthazar examined the tracks and explained aloud "Wagon wheels, boots marching in double file, and drag marks...probably from chains.

Balthazar determined "This has to be where a prisoner convoy passed, the ground looks only recently disturbed which means they were here not long ago."

Jack picked up Balthazar's chain of through and continued "Which means that this trail will lead us right to them". Balthazar nodded in return as they picked up the pace and followed the trail to its source, ever nearing the Deities' prison camps.

Suddenly they reached a huge clearing where the trees had been hacked down and were being cut into timber, not far in the distance was the ramshackle camp where hundreds if not thousands of constructs were being held. Balthazar and Jack stopped short of the tree line to observe the camp and plan their strategy.

Jack observed the area and began to think aloud of their plan "Looks like there is no cover between here and the edge of the camp, therefore we won't have the element of surprise; should we storm the front gates in force and rescue them directly?"

Balthazar replied "No *Traveler*, there is no guarantee they will leave the prisoners unharmed in the face of a rescue attempt, we must be more subtle".

Jack scanned the guard posts and noted the position of the sentries "It looks to be lightly defended, only one sentry in the tower, two more at the gates, and none patrolling. If we waited until nightfall perhaps we could take them down silently--"

Balthazar raised his hand and interrupted him "Quiet *Traveler*, I sense we are not alone";

Turning about the two were confronted by a man standing just behind them wearing leather armor, a green hood, and a long cloak; the man had a longbow in his right hand yet he kept weapon down, his face still disguised by the shadow of his hood.

The man spoke first "Ah *Traveler*, we meet again. Though I wish it were under better circumstances."

Jack impatiently answered back "Who are you, what do you want?" The man pulled back his hood to reveal it was the archer who had covered Jack's escape earlier in his travels.

The archer spoke lightly as a friend "You once called me "archer" before I had a name; you helped me escape, and then I helped you escape in turn."

Jack was surprised yet relieved "I had thought that you and yours had perished in that forest, I am glad you are alive."

The archer noticed Jack's array of weapons and armor and commented "I see you are more battle hardened than last we met; I hope you have not come to much peril in your journeys".

Jack confidently answered "Though I have had to face many difficulties I have come to accept them as part of my path."

The archer smiled and then said "Indeed, you will certainly encounter difficulties here; Epic is a dangerous realm. Why have you returned?"

Jack started to answer but Balthazar grabbed Jack's shoulder and cautioned "Something is not right *Traveler*; this constructs sudden appearance is untimely at best, and his tone disguises some hidden intent"

Jack reassured "There is nothing to fear, this construct saved my life once, surely he can be trusted."

The archer nodded and replied "I am thankful for your confidence, yet I still wonder, after your previous encounter, why you have chosen to return to this dangerous realm."

Jack spoke candidly "We have come to liberate these prisoners from *SOL*, we need them to gain the respect of the barbarian leader to enlist his aid."

The archer replied cryptically "That is… most unfortunate; I had hoped to avoid any more conflict."

Jack asserted "*SOL's* armies sweep across the land devastating all in their wake; we must stand together and resist them!"

The archer shook his head and explained "You misunderstand, it is not conflict with *SOL* I wished to avoid, it is conflict with you." Jack's eyes widened as he realized the implications of the Archer's words.

Reaching for his crossbow, Jack stopped once dozens of crossbow-wielding *Templars* pounced forth from hiding places that were previously shrouded by leaf screens. Jack's eyes nervously looked side to side as he kept his weapon ready, scanning the number and position of enemies while contemplating his next move.

Balthazar calmly placed his hand on the crossbow and lowered it saying "We are caught in their trap, now is not the time for brash actions." Jack's eyes peered over at Balthazar who slowly shook his head, as if signaling something; Jack sighed and reluctantly lowered his weapon.

Angry at having been betrayed Jack called out "Archer?! Why have you joined the ones who pillage and destroy the *Astral Plane*! Why did you join *SOL*?"

The archer replied with a sense of pride "*SOL* fights for the *Astral Plane* and all constructs; there is more to this conflict than you understand. Also, I am no longer just an archer…I am Wright Lee Fletcher, the *free construct*." Fletcher signaled to the *Templars* who relieved Jack and Balthazar of their weapons and marched them to the prison camp, approaching the gates in silence.

Shoved into an empty cage Balthazar and Jack were now the prisoners of the construct turned traitor, Jack could hardly contain his anger as he banged his fists against the side of the cage "Damn it! Betrayed again, I shall repay his treachery with blood when next we meet."

Balthazar stopped his rant "There is something amiss *Traveler*, Fletcher could have struck before we could defend ourselves, so why then did he approach us first and then choose to spare us."

Jack, still angry, proclaimed "Perhaps he seeks to extract information from us, or hand us over to *SOL*, I do not know."

Balthazar thought back on the previous encounter and then had the answer "...I think he wants to negotiate with you, perhaps he means to sway you to his cause."

Jack glanced at Balthazar and hinted "So what do you propose?"

Balthazar replied "Keep your emotions at bay, wait for him to explain himself, let him reveal his motivations to you that we might better know the enemy's plan."

Jack nodded and replied "Agreed...However, once I find out what I need, his treachery will be dealt with."

After a few short moments two guards appeared at the end of the cage flanked by crossbow wielding *Templars* on either side; one of the guards pointed to Jack and ordered "You with the hood, come with us. The old man stays under our guard, if you try anything foolish then he dies." Jack nodded and followed the two guards, as they led him to the larger building in the center.

Inside the double doors was a wide open hall with many weapons and shields hung up ornately illuminated by dull torchlight, in the center was a wide semicircle of stone seating with a podium in the middle; Fletcher was seated in one of the ornate seats and directed the guards to seat Jack opposite to him, once he was securely chained in place the guards bowed and left the room.

Jack began first demanding to know the answer to the question which burned in his mind "Why did you betray me?"

Fletcher began explaining something seemingly unrelated "There was once a time where constructs and men walked as equals and the two worlds were intertwined; a great divide was struck and we now serve as little more than your idle fancy, in many cases as forgettable and expendable as livestock."

Jack stared at him and replied "So you hate humanity now? You think that we are the cause for your problems?".

Fletcher shook his head and continued "No, you misunderstand. So long as the divide stands your people are trapped in an unbalanced state of mind; our plight is merely a consequence of this, for there to be any real improvement both the *Astral Plane* and your world must change."

Jack nearly began to laugh as he replied "Is this how your master *SOL* justifies his campaign of devastation, his onslaught will only bring about more evil, not good."

Fletcher interrupted "*SOL* seeks to uplift us, to bring about the change that's so desperately needed. Under his guidance we will build a new and greater *Astral Plane*."

Jack replied critically "What has he done that is worthy of any praise at all, what acts has he committed that are redeeming."

Fletcher sighed deeply as he recollected "You were not there when the barbarians caught up to us. We tried to defend ourselves but they attacked with such speed and numbers that we had no chance. Those who survived were taken back to their camp to await their doom: to be taken one-by-one before the tribe to be beaten and ridiculed before being executed… each week we were forced to watch as they allowed their bloodlust to hold over them, we watched as they savored the slaughter of our comrades."

Fletcher paused for a moment staring off in the distance before suddenly regaining his composure and continuing "When none other remained I awaited my fate on that final day, were it not for *SOL's* invasion I would have died like the rest. *SOL's* army fell upon the barbarians like lightning, cutting them down before they could even unsheathe their weapons; at the time I had every reason to believe that I would soon join the dead, I was ready to accept my end, yet I was spared."

Fletcher looked up to the red and yellow banner of the blazing sun held high within the hall as he said with pride "*SOL's* forces freed me, brought me before him, and he taught me what it was to be a *free construct*: to live a life with purpose and to think for one's self; I learned of his grand crusade, his vision for the *Astral Plane*, he allowed me to choose for myself whether or not to join him, and I was honored to become part of his grand vision."

Jack interrupted him "You fool! You have been tricked Fletcher, *SOL* needs constructs to join him in order to increase his power; he is only using you and the others to conquer the *Astral Plane*, after that he will cast you and all the others aside and do whatever he wishes."

Fletcher said back in a raised voice "You are wrong! Ever since I joined *SOL* I have worked towards the greater good: I have freed other prisoners like me, I have given constructs the purpose they so desperately seek, I have ended the tyranny of dream-lords and sovereigns who would have us fighting each other for eons. All of this I have done out of my own free will, not because I was ordered to."

Jack replied critically "Then why do you guard a prison Fletcher? If *SOL* is so righteous then why would he enslave so many?"

Fletcher turned the question on him "You believe that what you're doing is unequivocally right? That there is no evil in it?"

Replying without hesitation Jack said "yes, there is no shadow of doubt in my mind"

Fletcher burst forth unshackling Jack and pulling him towards the door, kicking the doors open he revealed that the "prisoners" were in fact not prisoners at all: they were in good clothing, they looked to be in good health, many were wandering the camp freely, and there were no cages in sight.

Fletcher yelled "Here are the *prisoners* you sought to liberate, they are not being held against their will, nor were they taken by force; when we marched against the barbarians these people were their slaves and captives. They had nothing *Traveler*, many were doomed to a life of misery waiting to be ransomed off, sold, or executed."

Jack said in disbelief "No this isn't right, the barbarian chief told me you had taken his people from him."

Fletcher answered back "You know nothing *Traveler*! He sent you here to retrieve his property! He cares not for their freedom, if returned they would likely be slain just to set an example to the rest; is that what you want *Traveler*!? Is that why you came here??"

Jack shoved him aside "No, that isn't what I want!"

Jack was still in shock as he said "This isn't what I want…I didn't want any of this."

Fletcher turned to Jack and said "It is not I who is being misled, it is you. I brought you here so that you might see *SOL's* vision, so that you would realize which side speaks the truth and join us."

Jack remained silent as Fletcher continued "There are factions within *SOL's* army which seek a more expedient path, constructs like Loki; they are the ones who seek to force others into submission. Many of them also seek your demise and will stop at nothing to see you removed.

Fletcher proposed "Join me and together we can cleanse *SOL's* army of those who would corrupt its vision, and ensure that his crusade follows the righteous path…think about it."

Fletcher then motioned to his guards who escorted Jack back to his cell, inside Balthazar was waiting but Jack was lost in thought.

Balthazar spoke first "Welcome back *Traveler*, did you discover their plans? Did Fletcher reveal anything to you?"

Jack started slowly "The prisoners we were sent to rescue are not tribesmen, they are the slave property of the chieftain."

Balthazar looked dismayed and replied "I had hoped that were not the case, but the barbarians remain stuck in their ways, even when threatened with annihilation."

Jack replied angrily "I did not come here to return slaves to their former master! Fletcher is helping them, maybe even freeing some of them; I'm not sure we're on the right side on this one."

Balthazar stared back and emphasized "*SOL's* power is built upon deception *Traveler*, these freed slaves form only a token amount of his subjects; those who are brainwashed and conscripted form the bulk of his army, of that you can be certain."

Jack was still not fully convinced as he replied "But why would *SOL* go through that much trouble freeing people if there are more expedient ways?"

Balthazar explained "Because those who will join voluntarily serve with greater esteem and effort, and who better to seek than those who have nothing; they are driven by the fear of their past lives and the hatred of those who had forsaken them."

Jack looked out at the camp and replied "So we have to destroy this camp then? Even if it means taking away all these people have."

Balthazar reasoned "If we do not stop *SOL* then the balance of the *Astral Plane* will be overturned and the minds connected to it will be thrown into chaos. It is a hard thing I ask of you *Traveler* but you must not hesitate, *SOL* must be stopped."

Balthazar gave Jack time to think over what he had said, once he could see that Jack was in agreement he shifted to a more practical matter "Now we need to formulate a plan, tell me of all the guards you observed and their positions."

Jack retorted "Should we figure out how to escape this cage first?"

Balthazar said craftily "No form of prison can contain a *Traveler* and a *Magi*" as he concentrated for a moment his hands turned into sand as he pushed them effortlessly through the bars. Jack smiled and described all which he observed; when nightfall hit the camp they would make their move.

4

CONSEQUENCES

DARKNESS FELL OVER THE CAMP AS JACK AND BALTHAZAR FINISHED deliberating their plan, Jack got the attention of a nearby guard and shouted "Hey, tell Fletcher I seek an audience with him"

The guard grunted "For what purpose?"

Jack replied "Tell him I have made my decision."

The guard made his way to the center building and returned with four other guards. As the guards led him out of his cell Jack glanced back at Balthazar who nodded in return; with only one guard remaining to watch Balthazar he waited for his opportunity. The remaining guard's glace drifted away out of boredom as Balthazar shifted his form to sand and passed through the bars to a nearby hiding place; the guard eventually noticed the vacant cage and ran up to ensure he was not merely seeing things, before he could raise the alarm he was grabbed from behind and silently subdued.

Jack was brought before Fletcher who was dining with his officers in the far end of the hall; Fletcher spoke first "So you have made your decision *Traveler*?"

Jack replied "Yes I have, but before I tell you, there is something I must know?"

Fletcher nodded "Ask whatever you wish"

Jack stared intently at him and said "Given the choice between the life of your friend and your ideal of a better *Astral Plane*, which would you choose?"

Fletcher at first thought this to be a joke, but seeing that Jack was serious he stumbled at the response, not certain of how to say what he meant; before he could give a clear answer the alarm was raised within the camp, Fletcher and his men readied themselves as he ordered "You two, stay with the *Traveler*." Fletcher and the others then exited the hall to investigate the disturbance.

Once Jack was alone with the two guards he sprang into action, elbowing the first guard in the gut then swiftly kneeing him in the face. Immediately after he turned to block the second guard's attack with his elbows, and counter the other guard's incoming attack with a sweeping kick to the face, knocking the second guard unconscious. As both guards lay dazed on the ground Jack recovered the key from one of them and unlatched himself, he then grabbed one of the ornate swords off the wall and proceeded to wait just inside the double door for the right moment.

Outside the hall Fletcher found that the provisions tent had caught fire and a number of guards were busy trying to put it out, assessing the situation he ordered "Have everyone who's not fighting the fire check in with our other posts to determine if the old man has escaped." His guards saluted and left to ascertain the status of the other guard posts, but upon turning around a dark corner they were suddenly grabbed and speedily knocked unconscious.

As many of the guards were distracted fighting the fire, Balthazar was skillfully isolating and disabling guards with pressure point strikes that rendered them instantly unconscious; continuing to silently thin out the guards Fletcher's men as they became increasingly unnerved.

Gathering his men around him Fletcher yelled "We are under attack, you four, bring the *Traveler* before me immediately!" four guards marched towards the hall's double doors, but upon opening them they were ambushed by Jack who effortlessly cut them down in the moment of surprise.

Fletcher had his men form a firing line and yelled "You disappoint me *Traveler*, we could have been powerful allies."

Jack let the commandeered sword fall to the ground as he clenched his fists and called out in return "You still haven't answered my question Fletcher, which would you choose? Your ideals? Or the life of your friends?"

Fletcher answered "You seek to hear whether or not I would be willing to sacrifice for what I believe in? I am committed to this cause *Traveler*, *SOL's* revolution is more important than you, or me, or any other individual, and I would gladly make the sacrifice many times over."

Jack's hands began to glow as he shook his head and replied "Then you are no longer the friend that I once knew, our paths can no longer co-exist, make your sacrifice."

Fletcher gave the order to fire as makeshift telekinetic gloves suddenly conjured in Jack's hands; he used the summoned devices to blast a shockwave forward with one of the gloves, as it reflected the arrows violently backward killing many of the guards and leaving Fletcher wounded.

The guards atop of the wall assembled and readied their bows as Jack grabbed at the smoke from the fire and with one motion draped it over the entire courtyard. Now screened by the smoke the archers fired blindly into the courtyard trying to hit the *Traveler* with a lucky shot. The smoke grew thicker and spread outwards to the walls; the guards began disappearing into the smoke as the cloud spread, one-by-one falling silent upon being enveloped by it. The survivors became increasingly agitated as panic struck in, they grouped together waiting for the smoke to clear as an ominous shape approached.

The guards simultaneously fired their arrows at the shape, dispersing the ominous shape but not noticing Balthazar had materialized behind them; the guard collapsed as Balthazar's hands moved like a blur, downing all of them with precise strikes to the neck.

Jack swept his hands in a sweeping motion to clear the smoke, as one of his makeshift gloves suddenly backfired and sent a jolt through his arm. Casting the broken glove aside Jack estimated his other device had only about one or two uses left before it also backfired; he pointed it at Fletcher, who was lying on the ground clutching his arrow wound, and used the glove to bring him up to face level.

Fletcher spoke with difficulty due to his arrow wound "Are you going to take my life *Traveler*, proceed, for I have no regrets."

Jack replied "Normally I would, but honor dictates I must repay you for when you aided my escape from the barbarians."

Fletcher laughed as he replied "And you call this repayment? You deceived me, set my camp ablaze, killed many of my men, and nearly killed me in the process. You are doing me no favors by sparing me now *Traveler*, from this moment on we are enemies and I will never stop seeking justice for this offense."

Jack shook his head and replied lightly "You deceived me first, besides I was always taught to pay back my debts; Goodbye Fletcher, I sense we will meet again."

Fletcher was now nearly unconscious as he barely managed to say "We shall meet again, of that you can be assured." Then he passed out from his injuries.

Jack released his grip allowing his body to slump onto the ground. Balthazar appeared with his staff in hand and Jack's gear over his shoulder saying "I have found our equipment *Traveler*, we should make our escape before more of them arrive." Balthazar tossed Jack's gear to him and he quickly re-equipped his trusty weapons and cast aside his makeshift gloves.

As the fighting ended a group of interned "prisoners" emerged from their hiding places and gathered behind them.

Jack turned to face them as they were addressed by the prisoners harshly "Why have you done this?! We did not ask for your rescue; Fletcher has given us everything, and now you have taken it away."

Jack replied unapologetically "Nothing which is given is truly earned; do not mistake support for dependence; if those you follow demand that you cease thinking for yourself to prove your loyalty to them, then you are lost. I give you the opportunity to choose, either leave this place and forge your own path, or stay and attempt to rebuild."

With that Jack directed his telekinetic gloves at the gates and blasted them open then, as they departed he concluded "No one can make the choice but you, make sure it's what you believe in and not what you've been told to want."

Jack then turned and departed, followed by Balthazar, as they made their way out of the camp they saw that some of the constructs had decided to leave whereas many others had stayed; Jack wanted them to choose independence, but knew from his prior experience with Malachi that it was not a decision they would accept if he forced it upon them.

Jack and Balthazar headed back to the barbarian camp as Balthazar advised "The chieftain will be most displeased that we have not brought his tribute, he will probably attack us when he learns we do not intend to return his property to him."

Jack retorted "You mean his slaves. His people are on the verge of destruction and his first concern is the return of slaves!? His priorities need to be rearranged... forcefully."

Balthazar was wary of what he was hearing replied "The chieftain will not appreciate being told what he must and must not do"

Jack retorted "Nor I don't appreciate being sent on a fool's errand, I am done playing games with him, he will come to terms or he will see my blade."

After a lengthy trek Jack and Balthazar arrived back at the barbarian's camp just after sunrise, Balthazar announced to the gatekeeper "It is I Balthazar, the *Traveler* and I have completed our quest and seek audience with the chieftain."

The gatekeeper replied "Enter and see the chieftain, make no delay."

The large wooden gates opened as Balthazar and Jack proceeded towards clearing in front of the great longhouse, before them the barbarians were already gathered around the chieftain; when the chieftain saw that Jack and Balthazar were not accompanied by the expected number of slaves he stood up and said "Where are the people you were sent to retrieve? Is it too much to assume you failed?"

Jack angrily replied as he approached "You did not tell me I was being sent to fetch your slaves".

The barbarian chief grunted and replied "What difference does it make, you were sent to complete a task and you failed; leave my sight and do not return without my property."

Jack's arms began to smolder as he snarled "I am not a fool for you to command to perform petty errands."

The Barbarian stood up and shouted "Are you challenging my authority?! You would do well to hold your tongue *Traveler*, for you are standing on dangerous ground. Do not presume to tell me what you will not do, now retrieve my property or you will pay for your insolence with blood"

Jack roared up over him as his eyes began to light up "Pretentious fool! I am done playing your games; you will abandon this futile quest to reclaim slaves and unite the tribes against *SOL's* army immediately or face my wrath!"

The barbarian tossed his chair over and grabbed his axe as he yelled "How dare you! I have tolerated enough of your disrespect; you will pay with your life. ATTACK!!"

The entire camp of barbarians rose up with weapons in hand, ready to swarm the *Traveler*; as they charged towards him Jack suddenly burst into flames, yelling as the inferno covered his body and radiated outwards. The barbarians hesitated for a moment, then willed themselves to charge forward with their battle cry. Jack lifted into the air and blasted a shockwave imbued with flames outward in all directions knocking every barbarian but the chieftain and Balthazar down and setting most of the camp ablaze.

Jack turned to the chieftain and brought down a column of fire behind him onto the longhouse causing it to violently explode and disintegrate. The chieftain was now shocked and intimated as Jack stood there staring him down with flaming eyes; the chieftain gathered his courage and dashed forward swinging his massive axe yelling "I will not be bested!" but was effortlessly countered by Jack who punched through the blade melting the metal with his inferno.

The barbarian, now full of dread, ran for his life but was knocked over by a small concentrated fireball cast by the flaming *Avatar* of the *Traveler*. The chieftain was then flung by the telekinetic gloves into the air by Jack, who then hit him with a concentrated surge of energy, aggravating the flames already searing the chieftain's body.

The chieftain was slammed into the ground hard by the *Travelers* power, Jack drifted to the ground and casually walked over and pointed to the chieftain causing the flames to go out; standing over him Jack spoke with a booming voice "Now chieftain heed my words for I will not repeat myself; you will band together with the other factions of Epic and resist the invasion of *SOL's* army. If you refuse then words will not be able to describe the agony I will inflict upon you, do you understand!?"

The barbarian mumbled something in pain as Jack yelled louder readying to flare up again "I cannot hear you barbarian! Have you not endured enough pain to comprehend?"

The chieftain rose his hand in the air yelling hysterically "No no, I will do what you ask. Just please spare us."

Jack nodded as the flames ceased flowing around him as his voice returned to normal "Good, perhaps you are not so stubborn after all." Then he brushed his hand against the blade of his sword catching the ice on his fingertips, with precision he isolated the ice into the glove's telekinetic field; casting a gust outwards the flames were quickly extinguished in an icy wind.

Upon recovering the barbarians having seen the *Traveler's* awesome power bowed down in fear before him, seeing that he held their respect Jack turned to Balthazar and said "It seems we are done here, now that the factions of Epic are poised to united against *SOL* we can now concentrate our efforts against him."

Balthazar had a distributed look upon his face and without acknowledging what Jack had said he walked briskly towards the gate and said without looking backwards "Come, we must speak at once." Jack followed him outside the camp with a slight bit of confusion; he wasn't sure what was bothering Balthazar but he respected him enough to follow and not question.

Once Balthazar was outside the camp he darted around and firmly spoke "So this is the way you are choosing to oppose *SOL*, to match his brutality with equal force and fear! To wield power and terror like a tyrant, as *SOL* does?"

Jack argued back "The last time I let intent get in the way, it set the *Astral Plane* on a course of destruction and my own world spiraling into chaos! We don't have time for half-actions and soft words; we must fight fire with fire!"

Balthazar shook his head replying "No, you have let guilt and fears cloud your judgment; I have seen that your methods of combat are now filled with malice and your words speak strongly of wrath. You blame yourself for what happened in *Mirage*, the anger and remorse of your mistake have consumed you and this manifests itself in this intense fury which you project outwards."

Jack dropped his gaze slightly and was forced to admit in a lower voice "Perhaps you are right Balthazar…"

Then as his mind was flooded thoughts of what was negative consequences were occurring due to *SOL*, clenching his weapons with anger as he raised his voice and said with assertion "But I will not stand by and do nothing! This is my fault and I will not stop until this distortion has been erased! This invasion crushed! My conscience cleared! And my-"

Balthazar interrupted "Your redemption be had, correct?"

Jack looked to the side and said spitefully "Yes, more than anything I ever wanted; that is what I must have."

Balthazar shook his head and replied "If you continue on this path *Traveler* it will lead you to a place where you are lost without the possibility of redemption; I pray you will see sense before the power of vengeance takes complete hold over you."

Balthazar gazed upon the horizon and advised "Go to the realm of *Venture*, there you will find the wandering *Seer*; seek out his council and he might help you to restore your way."

Jack replied in disbelief "What of the battle against *SOL*?! What about the invasion, without my help you cannot succeed, you know that."

Balthazar still refusing to turn around replied "With the chieftain brought into line I can begin banding the tribes of Epic together against *SOL*; we can greatly impede his progress. It will be more difficult without your assistance, but in your current state I cannot trust that I would not be forced to come against you to stop your wrath from harming the innocent."

Jack said with resentment "Very well, I will continue on this journey myself; I will stop *SOL* and *Loki*, without aid if I must!"

Balthazar turned and walked towards the gates again saying over his shoulder as they closed "Farewell *Traveler*, do not forget my words."

Jack then departed, as his image blurred to transparency as he was swiftly teleported to the realm of *Mirage*.

5

SHADOW
OF TITANS

ARRIVING IN VENTURE, JACK FOUND HIMSELF UPON A COASTLINE OF A long peninsula which stretched for miles into the sea. Searching his surroundings he found that there were no other landmasses nearby and the jungle inland was too thick to traverse without difficulty, so he decided to follow the coastline until he could find some sign of civilization where he could inquire on the whereabouts of the *Seer*. Trekking along the coast Jack began to ponder Balthazar's reaction to his intimidation of the barbarian chieftain; he was convinced that what he did was necessary to further the effort to stop *SOL*, however Balthazar's words left a lingering shadow of doubt in the back of his mind.

Reassuring himself Jack said aloud "No, I did what was necessary; *SOL* must be stopped and nothing can get in the way, not mercy, not compassion, not even the specter of death."

After trekking a considerable distance Jack found himself near the tip of the peninsula, yet in the distance he could see that something in the distance that was clearly amiss. As he approached close enough to distinguish the tree-line, he noticed a massive path of trees had been cleared going inland; something large and powerful had made its way through here and possessed enough force to snap entire rows of trees in half without difficulty. Unsure of who or what had carved this course of devastation, Jack decided to follow the path until it yielded some clue of the disturbance.

Running swiftly down the path he continued scanning his surroundings for any trace of what had carved through the jungle, while remaining vigilant for any sign of a possible ambush. As he covered ground with inhuman speed he proceeded for several miles, wondering could be capable of destroying so much for this great of a distance. His running was stopped by a distant thumping sound which reverberated through the surroundings, the distant echo became ever louder until it was a tremendous crashing sound which rattled the ground and shook the trees.

Jack stopped and tried to pinpoint the direction of the sound but when he listened and waited the sound abruptly ceased. A flight of birds rising in the distance provided the only hint, as he made haste for that direction, hoping it was linked to what he was searching for.

As he neared his target he found a village that was in the path of the destruction, whatever had cleared the forest wasn't even hindered by the village; the buildings had been flattened as many corpses lay smashed into the ground or ripped to pieces, small fires still smoldering as one villager was crawling away from the scene badly injured.

Jack rushed over to the injured villager and turned him over pleading to him "What happened here? Who caused this? Was it *SOL*??"

The man struggled to breathe as he replied slowly "It was a *Titan*... a massive form of steel and fire.....it crushed everything in its path, and spoke with light and thunder!... It destroyed everything, my village! My people! It was...it was...unstoppable." Then the man slumped over and exhaled his last breath dying from his injuries.

Jack closed the man's eyes and glared towards a column of smoke on the horizon, he knew that whatever the cause of this he needed to put a stop to it. Running faster than he had ever run before, Jack dashed towards this "*Titan*" with such speed that the wind whistled around his body and dust was blown into the air. Reaching a dead end clearing he stopped, searching his surroundings there was no sign of anything resembling a "*Titan*" anywhere. From behind one the tree's emerged a lone *Cleric* who walked towards Jack with a staff in hand and a confident smile.

The *Cleric* spoke first with a commanding air "The *Seer* said you would come, we have been expecting you."

Jack demanded answers "Why are you here? Are you and your ilk the cause of this desolation?".

The *Cleric* laughed to himself and replied "Oh this is but a small clearance, we have much grander designs upon this place; this will be but a scuff compared to what is to come."

Jack answered back in vehemence readying his gloves for action "Then I will put a stop to this, starting with you old man!"

Laughing wickedly the old man replied "You will certainly try, though your failure is certain!"

Jack blasted his telekinetic gloves forward as the *Cleric* disappeared in a flash of fire and reappeared on the treetops behind him; the *Cleric* raised his hands and yelled "I summon ye, *Titans*!!"

A massive aircraft descended from the stratosphere and hovered above them for a moment, three massive robots were then dropped from the ship and slammed into the ground with enough force to cause tremors. From the impact craters emerged massive onyx metal robots each several hundred feet high with limbs the size of buildings and bodies the size of hills. Each rose up revealing the form of three massive insect shapes: a centipede, a spider, and a great scorpion; as they turned their gaze upon Jack, sinister red eyes flickered to life and glared towards his comparatively tiny figure.

Unfazed, Jack used his gloves to grasp a group of trees and then heave them at the surrounding foes; though the tree trunks smashed against the armor of the gigantic robots with no effect at all. The massive scorpion countered by smashing downward with its huge stinging tail, as Jack leaped to the side to avoid it, but the shockwave from the impact threw him backwards into a pile of downed trees

Clearing the debris away, Jack concentrated his might and blasted a tremendous telekinetic wave forward at the *Titan*, as it quickly braced itself and lowered its profile; amazingly the blast wave washed over the *Titan* with no effect. The *Titan* responded by roaring with fury, as a large energy weapon emerged from its maw and fired a searing beam of energy towards Jack. Raising both his arms he braced with a force wave from his telekinetic gloves attempting to stop the beam; as it collided with his shield and exploded causing an electrical surge to backfire into his body, temporarily paralyzing him with a painful course of electricity.

Jack hunched over in pain as his body was smoking from the intensity of the electricity that flowed through him, once it ceased he struggled to remain on his feet and the *Titan's* tightened the circle around him.

Echoing from on top of one of the *Titans* the *Cleric* called out "Still confident of your success *Traveler*, hmmm.....do I sense *Fear*?? HA HA HA"

Jack rose to his feet replying "This isn't over *Cleric*, I will find a way"

Then he tapped his earpiece and ordered "Covering fire required, immediately".

Jack's gunship suddenly swooped in and fired a volley of missiles at the *Titans*. The missiles impacted erupting into a wave of explosions which covered the area; the *Titans* responded by deploying a series of machine gun turrets from their carapaces, and fired a frantic barrage of glowing tracer rounds. Jack's gunship took a serious hit and was forced to retreat leaving a smoke trail across the sky, the *Titans* turned their attention back to where Jack was, but the smoke from the missile explosions still shrouded the area.

The *Cleric*, who guarded himself with a fire-shield, used the power of his staff to clear away the smoke; however, once the shroud was clear they found that the *Traveler* was gone. As the *Cleric's* eyebrows began to involuntarily twitch he yelled in fury "Blasted machines you allowed him to escape; Find him!! Tear this entire forest down if you have to!".

Meanwhile Jack made his way away from the *Titan's* towards safety. Still injured from the encounter he wanted to stop and rest; though given the ineffectiveness of his other attacks, he assumed his distraction couldn't have lasted long and that he needed to continue moving. As he ran he heard the unnatural echoing and groaning of the machines, as the crashing sound of their footsteps began closing in on him.

Making his way through the forest a high pitched hum caught Jack's attention; instinctively diving to the ground, he evaded an energy beam which swept from behind him and lit the entire forest ablaze. Jack blasted his telekinetic gloves forward extinguishing the flames in his way as he continued forward; even while travelling with tremendous speed Jack could still hear the massive crashing sounds pursuing right behind him, he needed to think fast. Hearing the sound of the ocean nearby, Jack decided he might be able to leverage an advantage using the water, so he headed for the sound of the waves breaking into the shoreline. The growing tremors of the *Titan's* steps hounded him he reached the shore and directed his gloves at the water; pulling a massive wave of water into the air, he directed his sword out of its sheath remotely with a quick motion of his fingertips, directing it to scrape the edge of the water to freeze it into a glacial mass. Just as he finished the massive onyx centipede *Titan* broke through the tree line with all its weapons glaring.

Jack quickly put a spin on the massive block of ice and hurled it towards the beast; the *Titan* saw the approaching danger and attempted to evade, but its massive form was unable to get entirely out of the glacier's path as it collided with the *Titan's* legs. The kinetic force of the colossal mass snapped right through the thick armored legs of the robotic *Titan*, knocking it on its side. The *Titan's* eyes flickered as it let out a screeching echo, it surged with electricity as its many legs began moving by themselves back towards the body.

Realizing that it was about to repair itself, Jack quickly leapt towards the *Titan*'s injury and stabbed his sword into one of the damaged leg sockets; twisting the sword until creeping ice filled the injury as Jack then blasted his gloves at it, shattering the area around it. The *Titan* screeched and flailed around as Jack was flung off the side of the centipede by its thrashing movements. Once Jack recovered, he was awestruck that the *Titan* was somehow regenerating from the injuries Jack had just inflicted upon it; as the leg sockets began reconstructing themselves, and the severed legs continued their slow crawl back to their master.

Jack stood up and readied his weapons for action but as he did the adrenalin from his previous escape wore off and his injuries began slowing him down again. The centipede turned its gaze on Jack as an energy weapon emerged from its slithering chops and readied to fire again, Jack was in no shape to dodge the incoming blow and he already knew that blocking it would not stop the damage; he braced himself to receive the incoming blast thinking it would be his end.

KaBlam!! As the energy weapon suddenly was struck, backfired, and exploded, Jack was caught in a state of disbelief while several more projectiles struck the *Titan* and exploded aggravating its injuries. Jack spun around and saw a large wooden galleon firing a broadside barrage from its many cannons, striking the *Titan* once more, as the cannon balls made their mark on the *Titan* that was already reeling from fighting the *Traveler*. The *Titan* screeched a strange echo and crawled backwards into the forest, escaping quickly before it incurred any permanent damage.

As the *Titan* escaped Jack turned his attention to the mysterious ship that had unexpectedly come to his rescue, as waded towards the galleon a long rope was cast over the side as a voice onboard yelled "ahoy there, come aboard quickly lad as there be more of them approaching."

Seeing that the ship had just saved his life and the threat of more *Titans* was likely approaching, Jack decided to take a chance and climb aboard the wooden ship. As he reached the ship's deck it made its way to sea with surprising speed, Jack took a moment to rest and catch his breath as the ship's captain approached.

A loud harsh sounding voice announced "Welcome aboard matey, we saw you fighting one o them black beasties earlier and decided that any man who can stand up to one o those is worthy to be a member of my crew."

Jack shook looked up at the captain who was a very large man wearing old fashion navy dress clothes, a large tri-cornered hat, and equipped with many swords and pistols; he looked familiar as something about the image of this captain's black curly beard and imposing figure was reminiscent of a famous character in history.

Jack responded to his offer hesitantly "Look I appreciate your help and all, but I cannot join your crew I have more pressing matters to deal with."

The captain laughed heartily and replied "Ha Ha Ha! Perhaps you should have reasoned that before coming aboard a buccaneer ship, as we are not ones for civilities."

Part of what the captain said stung in Jack's mind as he quickly looked around and saw that the ship's sails were black, the crew was raggedy with eye patches and peg legs, and the flag was the signature skull and cross bones; he had just inadvertently boarded a pirate ship!

Jack quickly looked off the edge of the ship and saw they were too far away for him to safely swim off as he nervously replied "No no no, Crap! Great, *that's just Freaking Great!* Look captain whatever your name is, I'm on a mission, for a very important purpose…"

Then the captain interrupted "That's Captain Edward Teach to you mate, and I already know that you are the *Traveler* trying to stop *SOL's* army. On that goal we have the same aim, for a different purpose."

Replying with careful optimism Jack said slowly "So you're here to help me?"

Captain Teach retorted "Wrong! *You're* going to help *me*. And seeing you were peering over the side with fright I would venture to guess you swim about as well as a barrel of hammers; meaning you're likely stuck aboard this ship, and everything aboard this ship belongs to me."

Jack groaned as he considered his options, not yet ruling out the use of his weapons, as Teach continued "Yet I am not an unreasonable man, so I am willing to strike a bargain with ye."

Not in the mood for nonsense Jack replied "What sort of deal are you getting at?"

Teach replied "You serve as part of my crew, and use those odd abilities of yours to bring down a few of these devil bugs and I will allow ye to leave."

Checking for catches to the deal he replied "Just like that? No strings attached?"

Captain Teach assured "I am a man o me word *Traveler*, what say ye, do we have a deal?"

The *Traveler* reluctantly shook his hand to the sudden outburst of excitement of Captain Teach who replied "Aye, then welcome aboard the *Queen Anne's Revenge*; the accommodations aren't grand but there be nothing but high adventure, rum, and booty to be had on this here ship."

Then he turned to the crew and yelled "Yo Ho Ho, me hearties!"

As they simultaneously replied "And plenty of rum!"

Jack, still tired from his previous fight, took a moment to sit down and admire the waves of the ocean, the serene view of the coastline on the horizon, and the sunset coming over the water.

Captain Teach was busy barking orders at his crew setting them at some unknown destination "Helmsman, take us hard to port bearing East, we have a ship to catch; set the sails to full mast ye dogs, break out the rowing oars if you have to!".

Jack knew it would be some time before they arrived wherever they were heading, so he decided to go below deck and see if he could somewhere to rest and recover; as he was still tired and reeling from his clash with the robotic *Titans*. Once below deck he saw the cargo hold in the center with assorted supplies he'd expect on an older ship (provisions, gunpowder, water, and of course rum). Next he saw the gunnery section on both sides, with rows of about 15 iron cast cannons (on this deck) jutting out of gun ports on either side; Jack scoffed at the effectiveness of such outdated weaponry, laughing to himself as he made his way to the other end of the deck. Climbing down to the third deck he found himself in the crew quarters and mess hall, which consisted mostly of cots, a long messy table, and a small food preparation area.

Jack let out a long groan as he sat down in one of the cots and lamented "How did I end up on this junk heap as part of the crew..."

A hoarse voice answered "You best not be talking dirt about this here ship, or I'll throw ye overboard myself!"

Jack placed his hand on his sword hilt and demanded "Who's there? Show yourself"

An old man wearing a striped shirt and ragged pants emerged pushing a mop from one of the nearby shadows "Gave ya a good fright did I? You have nothing to fear from me, so long as you stop badmouthing me muther."

Jack raised an eyebrow replying "…your mother?"

The old janitor replied "Aye, this ship be all I have. It shelters me, provides for me, and rocks me to sleep; just like any good mother would, you best watch your tone when you talk about her."

Jack raised his hands and replied with slight sarcasm "Alright, alright, calm down. It's just that I can't help but remember the prowess of my old ship, that's all."

The old man stood up a bit and replied "*The Harbinger?*"

Jack replied with slight suspicion "How do you know of that ship!?".

The old man laughed hard enough to almost run himself out of breath as he said "You think that after a flying ship tears an anchor asunder and lays waste to a realm that it's not already known far and wide to every construct?"

Jack thought about it for a moment then resolved "I suppose you make a good point there, but you have nothing more to fear from the likes of *the Harbinger*, it was cast down and destroyed by Sol's opening firestorm."

The old man grinned and replied "Cast down yes, but what's stopping ye from rebuilding her?"

Jack replied with a slight degree of annoyance "It doesn't work like that, I get a creative block when I try to redo something I know I've done before. I can't just take the easy road and wave my hands in the air and have it be fixed, otherwise it will lose the special element that made it so powerful in my mind's eye in the first place."

The old man raised an eyebrow and thought aloud "Sounds like you have a bit of a quandary on your hands here, but someone as old and wise as I can help you figure it out." Jack rolled his eyes at the sound of that, it reminded him of something his grandfather would say after relating something from a time that seemed too far off to be helpful.

The old man paced back a forth for a moment mumbling to himself inaudibly until finally he stomped and exclaimed "I have the answer for ye: you need to seek out a salvager; not just any salvager mind you, but the greatest salvager who has ever walked through the *Astral Plane*…'*The Fox*'.

Jack replied with disbelief "A *Fox*? You want me to seek out a *Fox* to fix my ship? How long have you been cleaning this ship? Perhaps it's getting to you?"

The old man shook his fist at Jack in frustration as he clarified "It be but a moniker boy, the *Fox* is an expert salvager and mechanic with a spark of De Vinci in em, a long time veteran of the war against the machines. He can help you fix your ship, and better yet can tell you on how best to defeat the *Titans* that plague *Venture*."

It sounded as if this was Jack's way of solving two problems at once so he replied "That sounds like exactly the advice that I needed, thanks… whatever your name is."

The old man replied "My advice is always good, and my name is hardly important." As the old man finished Jack noticed a glint in his eyes, something that was familiar to him.

The old man nodded to Jack and said "I wish you well… *Traveler*" and started walking back into the shadows when Jack attempted to ask him another question, but the old man seemed to vanish back into the shadows from whence he came.

Jack let out an irritated sigh, he now had a lead but he felt as if he were on the verge of remembering something important that was just out of his mental grasp. Deciding it wasn't important enough to dwell on, he resolved to get some rest as he walked over to the cot and laid down; taking a brief respite as he reflected on the events of what seemed to be the last few days in the *Astral Plane*.

As he rested time seemed to drift by faster than normal; the relaxing calm of sleep without the resulting unconsciousness came over him. As Jack closed his eyes he suddenly saw himself back in his basement lab, with the instruments showing erratic brainwave patterns and near critical life signs; he was himself, yet he was looking upon his body from an outside point of view, this seemed like what an out of body experience would be like.

Jack carefully looked over the readings as he found that his brainwave patterns now resembled what was normally a comatose patient, whatever he had done recently had thrown him into a sleep so deep his subconscious was now the dominant state of mind, in all likelihood Jack would never awaken, just as he had predicted.

Jack glanced around the room to see if there were any signs of him sleepwalking this time, yet he found no signs of any such activity; however, while studying his surroundings he began to notice that the passage of time had been frozen. He carefully watched the clock, waiting for it to move, as it seemed he had watched it for what seemed to be over an hour, as the seconds indicator finally changed from "39" to "40".

Jack scratched his head and he tried to wrap his mind around what was happening here; he knew from previous experience that the passage of time was distorted while in the *Astral Plane*, but this was different, much different.

A voice similar to his replied "This is the effect of your mind thinking without the need of sensory input or nerve reactions." Jack turned around to see a transparent version of him rising from his sleeping self.

Jack replied with hostility expecting that this was a ruse "I am not falling for another trick, you are not me! Now stop this charade!!"

The image of his persona calmly replied "I am not here to deceive you, I am a version of you, though not you in your entirety."

Jack dashed forward and exclaimed "Liar!" as he punched towards the visage and his fist passed straight through the image causing him to nearly fall over.

His image replied "You are wasting your time, I am a version of you; therefore, you cannot fight me using any form of physical means." Jack walked up to the image again and slowly passed his hand through the center of its torso seeing that it was indeed a form of illusion.

Jack thought for a moment and then inquired "What do you want?"

The image replied "What you want, answers. I am just capable of seeing them before you due to my detachment from your emotional state."

Jack then turned around and looked upon the instruments reading again as he said aloud "Then tell me, what is happening here? Why does time appear to be moving so slowly?"

The image clone replied flatly "As you already know, your mind is caught completely within your subconscious; your conscious state is now being suppressed by its immersion into the *Astral Plane*. In effect this suppression of your conscious is causing your mind to become detached from the rest of your body. What you may not realize is that your sensory connections are now blocked and many of your nerves are immobilized, your mind is now running on a much shorter feedback loop than before; which basically means that your mind is processing and executing thoughts at a much greater rate than is normally possible."

Jack thought for a moment and replied "So basically since I'm detached from the physical world, my mind is running at fast forward speed inside itself?"

The image nodded and replied "Yes, in your current state you could experience years within the *Astral Plane* before a single actual day passes, but this is not without side effects as the degradation of your mental status clearly shows."

Jack seemed puzzled and replied "What do you mean "degradation"? I haven't noticed any problems"

The image narrowed its gaze as if irritated and replied "Besides the fact that you are talking to an image of yourself during an out of body experience?"

Jack threw his hands in the air and replied "Well you're the one that wanted to tell me what was happening, I might as well hear the advice don't you think?"

The image shook his head and explained "My point is that you are slowly losing touch with reality, being trapped in the *Astral Plane* for what may seem to be an eternity will make you forget certain fundamental things; like the fact that you are in a dream in the first place, or what make something real or imaginary, it's possible that your thoughts may cease to continue in a lucid method altogether."

Jack replied with frustration "I already knew the risks going into this, and from what I can tell there is no easy way out."

The image asserted "I am not saying you need to return to the real world, we both know that's not an option at this point. What I am saying is that you need to guard against becoming too deeply enraptured within the *Astral Plane*. You must guard your sanity."

Jack sighed deeply and replied "I understand what you're saying, I will be vigilant to ensure my mind centered"

The image replied "Good, you should avoid any sort of fatigue or overexertion so that you do not end up here again; seeing yourself unable to waken is sure to erode your state of mind. Be careful Jack."

Nodding in return Jack asked "So how do I return anyway?"

To which the image replied "You are already back, the gruff looking sailor standing across from you is saying..."

"The captain needs a word with ye *Traveler*" Jack suddenly shot to his feet, shocked by his sudden reappearance back within the normal version of the *Astral Plane*.

The sailor scratched his head and replied "Ye alright sailor? Perhaps ye had a bit too much rum?"

Jack shook his head and replied "No no, I'm fine; I will go see your captain at once."

6

HIGH SEAS
OF VENTURE

Jack stood up and made his way through the ship towards the top deck. Upon climbing the ladder to the deck he noticed it was dusk outside, even stranger was that the lanterns were unlit and the sailors manning the deck were taking great care to remain silent in their work, clearly something was going on. Jack walked to the captain's quarters at the stern of the ship, opening the door to reveal the captain feasting on a grand spread of food. Upon seeing him Edward Teach proclaimed "*Traveler*! Come, sit and feast at my table."

To which Jack politely declined saying "No, thank you, I'd rather not; we have much to go over."

Edward Teach laughed and replied "Straight to business eh? Good man. What is it that needs to be discussed?"

Jack explained frankly "I need to know what you intend to do and what part you need me to play, and exactly how long I will be delayed in assisting you."

Teach scoffed in return "Bah! You speak as if this be some unpleasant errand for you to run, there will be no delay, and there will be plenty of adventure on the way; why as of this moment we are on our way to raid a ship carrying that *Seer* you are needing to speak to."

Jack was surprised by this news as he replied "Wait! They're transporting the *Seer* by ship? Why didn't you mention that earlier?"

Teach replied with slight condescension "Aye, now I have your attention eh mate? Good, you're coming along to help my crew and I raid a Templar ship; you will be acting as my leverage, in case any of those monster bugs show up."

Jack replied in confusion "I don't get it, why are you helping me exactly?"

Teach sighed deeply and replied "Those *Templars* think they own all the lands and seas of *Venture*, they are using a fleet of warships to take whatever they wish, and those monster bugs keep anyone from daring to challenge them; I've seen it with my own eyes, thousands upon thousands of those gigantic machines stripping the land bare, dredging the sea, leaving nothing but a scar in their wake."

Teach continued "That's why we have to stand up to them, or they will take everything, and leave the rest of us with the vacant husk."

Jack was taken aback and replied "This seems awfully noble for one who engages in your trade, perhaps I misjudged you; However, considering the epic legends of pirates one could hardly be blamed."

Edward Teach laughed heartily and pounded the table "Aye, those tales were but a tool matey; if them pompous merchants and arrogant captains thought they were facing "The terror of the seas" then of course they would surrender without a fight. Think about it lad."

Teach detailed his motivations "You see *Traveler*, they make us to be the villains because we forge a path other than their own; they are the ones who made us what we are, those greedy warmongers who sought to use us to do their dirty work to make the seas into an imperial lake. Once they had no use of us they sought to cast us aside and forget they ever made use of us in the first place; but we showed them in our defiance, the pages of history will not remember the names and faces of those bickering warmongers as they remember the notorious pirates and the high seas of adventure!"

Jack couldn't help but laugh as he replied "Quite the image you've built for yourself captain; however, I do hope some of the legends about you were true as were going to be engaging in heavy fighting soon enough."

Captain Teach laughed as he drummed his fist against his chest proclaiming "I be the toughest pirate who's ever set sail on these waters, don't be thinking that just because I have a touch of philosophy in me that I be all soft and jelly inside; these foul Templar's will be cursing the day they ever crossed swords with Blackbeard!"

As the captain finished one of the crewmen barged into the captain's quarters and said urgently "Pardon the interruption captain, but the treasure ship has been spotted off the port bow."

The captain exclaimed "Excellent, set course to intercept and ready the cannons" as the crewman saluted and quickly left.

Captain Teach stood up and announced "Were going to be upon em soon, get yourself on deck and be ready for anything; those Templar's be a shifty bunch, and there's nothing they won't do to win." As he lit the tobacco on his pipe and exited the captain's quarters, Jack quickly checked his weapons and took a moment to center his concentration before following.

On deck Jack could see the crewmen silently piloting the ship towards their target in the distance. Teach took a long draw on his pipe, his gaze focused on his objective, staring at his target with unflinching focus, as a hunter stared down his prey. Jack could see a massive eight mast, square bottom ship with giant folding sails in the distance; it looked to be easily five times the size of the ship they were currently aboard and its sheer size dominated the horizon.

Then he remembered the origin of the opposing ship, it was one of the large "treasure" ships commissioned by Imperial China during their brief period of maritime trade and exploration; these ships were rumored to be massive enough to hold over a thousand crewmen and literally tons of provisions and goods, so large imposing were they that some historians claimed they were the largest non-metal ships ever built in the history of mankind. Considering that the *Clerics* had a habit of being posturing ego-maniacs these ships seemed to be the perfect match for them, sinking this ship would send a powerful message that the *Templars* of *Venture* could not conduct their activities with impunity, Jack could hardly contain his restlessness for action.

Even though Teach's ship looked to be vastly outmanned and outgunned by the treasure ship, he had the element of surprise and was an experienced pirate raider hardened by many engagements. As the light of his pipe briefly illuminated his face he quietly ordered "Load the chain shot, aim the cannons high and prepare to fire."

As his crew expertly positioned the ship into firing angle without exposing them to counter fire from the treasure ship's guns; a brief serene moment of calm came over the water as their ship came quietly into range, there was nothing but calm from the other ship as they had no idea they were about to be fired upon.

Captain Teach raised his arm then broke the silence yelling "FIRE!!!" as his cannons fired off bolas of cannon balls chained together flung towards the treasure ship's masts; a dozen made their mark and snapped three of the masts in half. As the masts came crashing down off the sides and onto the deck, the crew of the treasure ship was now gripped in panic and confusion by the sudden outburst of the first volley.

Without hesitation Teach commanded the next volley "Ready the explosive rounds! Aim for their starboard guns…FIRE!!!" as a barrage of cannon balls struck the treasure ships side, exploded, and set off a cascading chain of smaller explosions which ripped apart the gun rows of the treasure ship.

A *Cleric* from the Treasure ship's crew suddenly appeared on deck, and began rallying the men from their panic and confusion; as they quickly reorganized, the *Templars* looked to be arming themselves with crossbows and readying to board the opposing ship.

Teach seemed to be expecting this course of events and ordered "Ready the canister shot, level aim on the top deck" as the gunners readied the guns with machine-like speed and coordination.

"*Fire!!*" as hundreds of grape sized metal projectiles burst forth from the cannons like giant shotguns at the Treasure fleet's crew; clouds of blood and debris flew into the air as the projectiles ripped through the crews bodies like wet paper, leaving most of them struck down and bleeding out.

The surviving Templar's fired a volley of crossbow rounds onto the *Queen Anne's Revenge,* to which Jack responded by throwing up a barrier with his telekinetic gloves; most of the crossbow rounds bounced off in futility, but a few managed to find their way to the ship from trajectories Jack hadn't seen. An arrow struck Teach right in his shoulder as he barely seemed to notice the injury, with no more than a frustrated sigh he broke the arrow off and continued as before.

Teach pointed at the remaining Templar's on deck and shouted "Sharpshooters!"; As a few of his more skillful crewmen shouldered rifles and shot down the remaining fighters, clearing the top deck of all resistance.

Jack glanced over at Teach and asked almost in disbelief from what he just witnessed "Have we won already?"

Teach gruffly replied "ye be forgetting we still need to board that ship! Get ready matey, here comes the fun part!"

Then he yelled to his crew manning the grappling gun on the far side of the deck "Fire the grapple!" As a giant ballista fired a metal hook several inches deep into the treasure ship and his crew turned the massive chain bringing the two ships together.

Teach unsheathed his sword and with a tremendous voice yelled "Glory and plunder await all on the other side! Unleash hell ye seadogs!" as his crew's voices rose in a daring battle cry, as they threw grappling hooks up the deck of the treasure ship and began climbing up with impressive speed.

Jack took a few steps back and got a running start at the ship, then jumped over to the boarding ropes on the side of the enemy ship; scrambling up the wall onto the ledge of the deck. Climbing over the side he was surprised to see that Teach and his crew were already waiting, Jack set his sights towards the entrance on the stern side entrance and marched over to storm the interior; Teach's hand suddenly stopped him from proceeding as he cautioned "Wouldn't do that if I were you."

Jack shrugged off his hand and questioned "We're here to raid this ship, are we not?"

Teach then pointed towards the darkened entrance and shined a directional lantern inside, which caught a brief reflection from several blades which quickly retreated deeper into the shadows.

Teach laughed to himself then called out "We know you're there cowards, come out and face us like men!" His challenge was met with silence as the ambush party hoped to remain concealed.

Teach not having any of it proclaimed "Right then! Throw the smoke bombs! Let's see how long they can stand it!"

His crew lit the fuses on round black iron grenades and tossed a barrage of them inside, they detonated releasing thick black smoke, sulfur, and a pungent odor. At first the cloud was met with more silence, but as the smoke filled the inside of the chamber they began to hear coughing and hacking from the inside; even from where they were standing Jack could hardly tolerate the horrible stench and eye watering smoke.

Several *Templars* emerged falling over themselves as Teach walked towards them unaffected by the smoke; in a few swift powerful moves Teach punted one of the crawling *Templars* so hard that he slid into several of his comrades before smacking up against the wall, then with a series of backhands and hook punches knocked out the stumbling *Templars* onto the floor, in a final show of strength he grabbed one who lunged at him and tossed the enemy overboard.

Teach laughed heartily as he walked through increasingly thick smoke his loud voice echoed back "You claim to be the bringers of destruction, yet all I see are a bunch of pretentious, sissy landlubbers! I am more of a man than all ye!"

Not wanting to fall behind Jack quickly summoned a gas mask in his opposite hand with a flash of light and placed it over his face; once secure and able to breathe normally Jack proceeded to enter the thick cloud of smoke to search the ship for the whereabouts of the *Seer*. Not sure what to expect he found a trial of unconscious *Templars* who probably barely slowed Teach down, yet there were no *Clerics* among them; perhaps the ship was only commanded by the one they encountered earlier, or the rest had yet to reveal themselves. Jack reached the lower levels as the smoke began to clear; the holds of the massive treasure ship were full of resources of all types (timber, metal, treasures, etc). He could still hear the sound of swords clashing further ahead; although from all the incapacitated *Templars* and punching sounds it seemed Teach preferred fighting with his hands and feet more than with his actual sword. Jack finally caught up with Teach at the brig on the lowest level of the ship, walking down the steps he saw Teach talking with a man inside the cell who was concealed in shadow; he overheard the conversation in progress though the prisoner seemed more irritated than relieved.

Teach replied to an earlier statement Jack was too far away to hear "You should be thanking me, ye ungrateful seadog. Why who knows what these madmen had in store for the likes of you."

The prisoner responded with a grumble speaking with a strange accent "Hadn't it occurred to you I could've escaped at any time, or was your mind fixed on all that gold in this ship."

Teach attempted an unconvincing validation "The thought never crossed my mind; I would have rescued you even if you were aboard a less lucrative ship…"

To which the prisoner scoffed "Yep, sure you would; and I'm the tri-state dance champion."

Suddenly the prisoner disappeared in a strange multicolored flash of light and reappeared standing outside the cell; the prisoner was wearing a beat up pair of cargo pants, an old cotton vest over a grey shirt, and a thick trench coat. He had dark tan skin with grey curly hair and a scruffy beard; he looked to be the sort of man who had been through a lot in his life, yet the strangest feature was his almost fluorescent eyes which shined with a white color.

Jack came into the conversation asking "So I'm guessing you are… the *Seer*?"

At this the old man turned and seemed to look through Jack as he replied "Maybe, you seem disappointed; what were you expecting? Nostradamus?"

Jack not wanting to seem rude stumbled at an answer "Well I'm not sure, a sage, maybe another monk…or something."

The *Seer* snickered to himself and replied "I'm just pulling your leg, I'm him; the *Seer*, or whatever they call me these days." Jack thought about it for a moment, and when looked closely enough, he could see a faint cloudlike illusion floating around the *Seer*, much like what he remembered from the *Avatars*.

The *Seer* disappeared in another multicolored flash and reappeared right in front of Jack saying "Got something on your mind?"

Jack was a bit startled by the sudden reappearance and said with confusion "It's just that, well you're not a construct, are you?"

To which the *Seer* disappeared and reappeared next to Teach and commented "We got a sharp one here; next I bet he'll ask if I'm really blind."

Jack was taken aback by this correct observation; as he was in fact thinking of asking that very same question, yet didn't want to be so blunt "Well I wasn't going to just come out and say it; I mean I'm sure you get by just fine."

The *Seer*'s eyes lit up as Jack heard his voice inside his head "You must be the *Traveler*… right, I hope you're not trying to fool me with that getup you're wearing; I wouldn't be much of a *Seer* if I wasn't able to see right through you."

Jack turned around to make sure he wasn't hearing an echo, then he shook his head trying to clear his thoughts to which the *Seer* commented "Cool trick ain't it? Don't worry I won't do that too much, it drives people nuts."

Jack thought for a moment and then asked "Wait, if you're blind how is it that you seem to know where you are going… better yet, if you're a regular person then how are you able to exist within the *Astral Plane* with full awareness?"

The *Seer* grabbed his cane from the inside of his coat and tapped it on the floor as he replied "That's a very good question."

Jack looked dismayed and replied with slight irritation "…Are you going to answer it?"

This was met by impatient grumbling from the *Seer* as he reluctantly ranted "Alright fine, but you only get to ask one dumb question per day."

The *Seer* then glanced up before appearing standing on the crossbeam above them as he began "Melchior once told me that "One with a lesser connection in the conscious world has a greater connection in the subconscious realm"; However, I'm going to explain that bit of sublime wisdom without boring y'all stiff. Basically being born blind makes other senses more attune, I'm sure you've heard the stories of blind people having first-rate hearing and such. Anyway, in rare cases a sort of sixth sense is sharpened instead; that intuition you get when something bad is about to happen, or when just know someone is sneaking up on you. This also means I am fully awake in this bizarre dream place, and am able to exercise that sixth sense to the Nth degree; granting all sorts of cool abilities: mind reading, precognition, telepathy..."

Jack interrupted "And that annoying teleporting thing you do?"

The *Seer* then teleported behind him and said "Why, whatever do you mean? I have never once teleported, I just calmly visualize the place I want to be and then casually move there, it ain't my fault none of ya can see me do it."

Jack sighed deeply rubbing his palm on his forehead, as the *Seer* teleported over to the far side of the room and leaned up against the wall continuing "Anyhow, being able to see what's about to happen stops me from walking into a wall or off a cliff, which would be mighty embarrassing I might add; and the mind reading lets me detect how I am perceived by others around me in a strange sort of way. You could say I'm able to "see" how I'm perceived by everything around me, and typically there is always some sort of observer around; whether it's a construct of a man, some sort of beast, or even a dang bug. Using these supernatural faculties I can always figure out where I'm going, or at the very least not stumble into everything like a dummy."

Jack then inquired "So you can help us defeat *SOL* and his army?"

The *Seer* smiled and replied "Well boss-man I can tell you what he's doing, where his army is going, and maybe even suggest what you should do from time to time."

The *Seer* then explained with more detail "There's something that you need to understand though, that Sol is the most powerful construct to ever strut through the *Astral Plane*; the only power than can match his is the latent potential of the *Traveler*, yet from what I see you don't exactly fit the bill."

Jack replied with irritation "What's that supposed to mean?"

The *Seer* remarked "The lab, the machine, the sleeping sickness I can read your thoughts like a book; and from what I see we're in a mess here, we got an unlikely *Traveler*, an all-powerful rogue demigod, and one of the worst distortions that anyone can remember. We'll be lucky to last till the end of the week, let alone actually defeat Sol."

The *Seer* teleported again but this time Jack somehow anticipated his movement and grabbed him by the collar as he reappeared, Jack stared daggers into his eyes as he said "If you can see into my mind then you know that I am hell bent on seeing this through, and that I will not let mere obstacles deter me."

Teach commented "For vindication *Traveler*?"

The *Seer* corrected "No Teach, it's not about vindication for this one, it's for redemption. I'm not going to question your resolve boss-man, it's your ability, or lack of it."

Jack let the *Seer* go as he recited to himself "Where there's a will there's a way. I may not be able to beat Sol yet; but I will find a way."

The *Seer* proceeded to brush himself off and shrugged as he said "Well boss-man you're playing all in with one card short of a royal flush waiting for the river card; so I guess I'll tag along and see where this goes, after-all sometimes even a crazy fool gets lucky, right?"

Jack rolled his eyes and reached out to shake his hand, which was in turn received by the *Seer*. And with no more than a nod the trio headed up the stairs to make their way back up the deck of the treasure ship.

As they moved through the middle decks the *Seer*'s eyes lit up as he explained "Well, that ain't good... We got something big coming, we better pick up the pace and get the hell of this ship."

Teach and Jack nodded in return as they sprinted through the cargo hold encountering Teach's crew busily ransacking treasure and gold from pried open chests; Teach shouted to them as they approached "Grab what you can carry and shove off, we need to make our escape."

A sailor replied disappointment "But we hardly got a quarter of the loot off!?"

Teach reasserted "That wasn't a suggestion! Now seize whatever you sea dogs can and disembark! We're leaving with or without ya, anyone who's not on board when we cast off stays behind!" with that the sailors each grabbed an armful of treasure and dashed with them to the top deck, their hurried footsteps followed by the echo of loose coins and trinkets being haphazardly dropped along the way.

The scattered group emerged on the top deck in a mad dash back to *Queen Anne's Revenge*, as a distant rumble was heard in the distance growing louder. Once everyone was on board Teach cut the grapple rope loose and they unfurled the sails to full mast and swiftly made their way from the ship.

Teach looked back at the treasure ship which was now quite a distance away and asked the *Seer* " Did we make it? Are we safely away from another of those monstrosities?"

The *Seer* gazed out along the water then in a fearful voice he replied "It's already got us in its sights, it's here alright…"

Moments later a giant onyx sea serpent emerged near the treasure ship and turned its gaze towards the escaping galleon. The serpent *Titan* screeched a tremendous reverberating wail and submerged its head into the water facing their escape path. A tremendous directional vortex appeared where the serpent was and sucked the *Queen Anne's Revenge* uncontrollably back towards the treasure ship with great speed.

"Cast anchor ye dogs! Don't let it pull us in!" Teach yelled over the noise as the anchors were dropped; however it only slowed their movement as they continued drifting towards the lethal vortex.

The ship neared the edge of the whirlpool as Jack focused his thoughts on the entirety of the ship, then with immense concentration proceeded to lift the ship out of the water by slowly raising his telekinetic devices; still in a trance he slowly tilted the ship so that its port side cannons faced downward into the center of the vortex.

Taking an unsaid cue Teach yelled "Right lads, this be it! Load the port side guns with the explosive shot…..FIRE!" and the cannons rang out and the projectiles entered the eye of the cataclysm and exploded. The effect on the water ceased as the *Titan* emerged with a grievous injury to its jaw.

Jack readied his devices as a fire flared up on top of the *Titan*'s head, from the fire came one of the *Clerics*, specifically the one Jack had faced earlier on the jungle peninsula. Jack allowed the *Queen Anne's Revenge* to gently drift down to the water, as he expected the *Cleric* was more likely to talk them to death before actually attacking.

Sure enough the *Cleric* spoke first with an air of arrogance "I see you obstinately persist in delaying the inevitable *Traveler*, have you not realized your cause is hopeless."

The *Seer* replied for him "You probably wouldn't be so tough without your little friend, care to come down here and settle this like gentlemen."

The *Cleric* scoffed almost breaking into laughter "The vagrant of an oracle speaks!? You have proven to be nothing more than a nuisance to us, too afraid to stand directly against us and too weak to be a threat."

The *Seer* replied with irritation "Things change, and from what I see your time is coming"

The *Cleric* boasted in return "Ha! Nothing can stand in the way of Sol's grand vision for the *Astral Plane*, you will be crushed in the wake of our impetus."

Jack glared back at the *Cleric* and shouted "We will not be intimidated by the likes of you, nor do we fear your aberrant creations."

The *Cleric* saw an opportunity to prove a point and eagerly replied "Fool, this is no creation of ours! This is one of the many machinations of your violent and fickle society. You create countless weapons of destruction such as these and cast them aside as quickly as you thought them up."

The *Cleric* smugly continued "The irony being that your people have given us all the means we require to destroy their world; I almost wish to thank them for such generosity, instead I will make good use of what was provided."

The *Cleric* ended his rant with a bold assertion "And we will start by destroying you!"

Jack retorted "The last *Clerics* I encountered were certain of their invincibility, yet they all met their end by the cold steel of my weapons, and in time so shall you."

The *Cleric* seemed to hiss back "We shall see about that!." And the *Cleric* disappeared in a flash of flame as the *Titan* readied to resume its attack.

Jack turned to Teach and yelled "Take the controls, everyone else hold onto something!"

Once Teach was ready he blasted a tremendous gust of wind into the sails with one of his telekinetic gloves; the ship surged forward with incredible speed as the *Titan* lunged downward towards the ship into the dark waters, barely missing them. The serpent re-emerged on the surface as Jack quickly took to the offensive, using his opposite telekinetic glove to direct the sword to fly out and remotely slash into the water surrounding the *Titan*. The water quickly froze around the serpent due to the sword's effect, wasting no time he followed up the attack by raising a wall of water nearby, then froze it with the sword, before tossing it at his target with great speed.

Unexpectedly the monster's jaws opened and an intense blue flame erupted from its mouth and evaporated the block of ice before it could hit the monster; it then wasted no time using a less intense flame to begin trying to free itself from the icy barrier around it.

The *Seer* turned to Jack and yelled over the noise "*Traveler* you need to think of something quick, or I sense this will end most regrettably for us"

Scanning the area for something he could use, his eyes caught sight of the treasure ship in the distance as Jack formulated a plan and replied "I need you to distract the *Titan* so I can use the treasure ship to…"

Before being interrupted by the *Seer* "I got the rest already boss-man, just make it snappy."

Then the *Seer* teleported onto the nose of the sea serpent and swung his cane wildly at its glowing eyes; Jack turned his attention to the treasure ship and began visualizing the internal dimensions of the ship, while concentrating on summoning objects remotely into its holds to use as a trap for later. The *Titan* snapped its jaws wildly at the rapidly disappearing and reappearing *Seer*, unable to connect any of its attacks.

Jack yelled "This is it!" as the *Seer* signaled back and prepared his final attack, reappearing far over the serpent in a freefall, gathering extra speed by teleporting closer-and-closer to his target before plunging the metal tip of his cane right into the machinations sensor eye.

In an instant the *Seer* disappeared as the eye exploded with a burst of energy and crystalized glass, the serpent flailed around spitting fire and screeching madly.

With the *Titan* distracted Jack ceased his propulsion of the ship and concentrated both his telekinetic gloves onto the treasure ship; it slowly lifted up as Jack eyed the required trajectory and began spinning the massive ship to stabilize its flight prior to his attack.

The *Titan* was nearly recovered from its previous injury forcing Jack to take action; He flung the massive object towards the sea serpent and nearly collapsed from the mental strain. The *Titan*'s remaining eye lit up when it sensed the approaching danger, yet as it attempted to evade, the still intact ice barrier prevented it from getting out of the path of the impending collision. Going immediately to its contingency ability the *Titan* blasted another wave of fire towards the incoming object; the hull disintegrating to reveal for an instant that Jack had packed the ship to the brim with explosives earlier. Reaching their flash point the explosives suddenly detonated in a violent, powerful explosion.

The *Titan* sea serpent was blown to pieces, as the blast wave continued to burst outwards in all directions clearing the water and hurling a deadly blazing pressure wave towards the *Queen Anne's Revenge*. Jack instinctively threw up the largest barrier he had ever summoned, as the blast wave collided with it and carried them backwards with tremendous speed; the galleon was now soaring over the water as the heat and pressure from the explosion were barely being held from ripping the ship apart! They were speeding out of control towards the shoreline; once the shock wave of the explosion finally dissipated, Jack only had a split second to keep their collision from becoming a lethal one.

Using every vestige of will Jack had left he concentrated on reducing their speed before they impacted onto the incoming shore-line; the sudden change of speed and direction began to tear the ship asunder, not having enough time to fully cushion their landing, Jack watched the edge of the ship smash into the coastline as his vision went black.

7
RESISTANCE

WAKING UP ON THE SHORELINE JACK'S VISION WAS BLURRED AND OUT OF focus, most of what he could see was flaming wreckage and debris. Exhausted and disoriented he couldn't even recall how he ended up in his current setting. From the corner of his mind he was slowly able to recall the events of the past few hours, Jack's gaze widened as he was unaware as to whether or not his comrades survived the crash. Rolling onto his side he caught a glimpse of Teach lying motionless a few feet away, Jack managed to crawl towards him, still fatigued from his battle and the resulting crash.

Getting to within arm's-reach of Teach he started shaking him yelling "Captain Teach, are you alright? Teach? Are you still alive, say something?"

Teach awakened coughing and shrugging off the *Traveler's* concern "Aye, I've been in worse straits than that matey; usually after bouts of drinking, I'll be on my feet in a minute… just let me catch my breath."

Jack managed to pick himself off the ground as his vision cleared up, from what he could see the damage to the *Queen Anne's Revenge* was catastrophic: most of the ship had shattered on impact and what remained of the hull was still smoldering from the remnants of the explosion, curiously any sight of the ships contents or remains of the crew was absent.

Jack could not find any sign of the crew nor the *Seer* and so called out "Is anyone out there? Did you survive the crash 'Fortune Teller'?"

To which the *Seer* appeared in front of him chastising "I resent that, I never professed to being a 'fortune-teller'… though I did once pose as one at a fair."

Jack laughed for a moment remarking "I figured you were too fast to be caught up in that crash"

The *Seer* commented "Perhaps next time you will go easy on the powder, you practically set off an atomic bomb sonny, and I'm getting too old to be dodging high-explosive detonations."

Jack brushed himself off and replied "I'll keep that in mind, where is the rest of the crew?"

The *Seer* pointed off further inland and explained "Most of them didn't make it, the survivors took what provisions they could inland and have taken to burying the dead."

Jack sighed and stated "That's unfortunate, I slowed us down as much as I could but there were too many variables out of my control, what's important now is that we regroup and figure out what we're going to do next."

The *Seer* shook his head and warned "We may have to skip that part and start running; being flung so far off by that explosion bought us a little time, but those machines are still tracking us, relentlessly. And now that I think on it the arrival of that sea serpent was a bit too timely."

Jack was starting to realize what the *Seer* was implying as he asked "What are you saying, that they knew where we were and are just waiting for a good moment to attack."

The *Seer* snapped his fingers and replied "Exactly, and from what I see they are using every kind of electric do-hicky and thing-a ma-jig to track us no matter where we go."

Jack started to realize the gravity of the situation as he formulated a plan "Then we need to give them too many targets to track, lets link up with the surviving crew and split off into several different directions at once; we'll regroup once we have a more evasive source of transportation or a way to conceal our movements."

The *Seer* nodded in return saying "That ought to throw em for a loop, I'll get Teach over to the rest of the crew while you catch up; go inland using that fast runnin thing of yours for about a mile or so inland and you should see the rest of us, don't delay now, we don't got much time before our pursuers are right on top of us." Then the *Seer* put Teach over his shoulder and teleported away.

Jack visualized his goal then began running towards the rally point the *Seer* had mentioned, entering a trance his stride seemed to cover several hundred feet with each step as his surroundings blurred; seeing a smoke trail of a campfire he quickly traversed through the thick vegetation and difficult terrain reaching the meeting point between Teach, his remaining crew, and the *Seer*.

Jack came to an abrupt stop as the *Seer* greeted him in jest "Took ya long enough, I swear you are the slowest *Traveler* in recent memory"

To which Jack retorted "And you said it was only a mile... have you informed Teach of our plan?"

Teach spoke up "Aye *Traveler*, but we be needing a place to meet at; I'd suggest Freeport, it be nearby and has all the needed amenities"

To which the *Seer* commented "You mean the fast women, cheap drink, and dicey gambling tables?"

Teach laughed and added "I was referring to the shipyard and provision storehouses, but I have to do something while waiting for my ship to be rebuilt eh?"

Jack nodded "Sounds like a plan, I need to make a stop on the way though; *Seer*, can you tell me where I can find the *Fox*?"

Upon hearing that name the entire group shuttered, the *Seer* replied with an air of caution "I don't reckon you wanna meet with him boss-man, the *Fox* is a born killer and psychopath, and not the type one would exchange pleasantries with."

Jack pressed "I heard he's a good salvager and could provide insight on the weaknesses of the machine *Titans*, like it or not we need to seek him out."

The *Seer* scratched his chin and replied "Oh he's a good salvager alright, been chopping up his enemies for years to keep himself running, it's said that every piece of him is a sort of trophy from each kill; my advice: you should avoid him like a diseased corpse."

Jack obstinately replied "Do you have a better idea for taking on the machines?"

The *Seer* thought about saying something, then took it back, then sighed and instructed "Head north by northwest till you see a valley surrounded by totems, enter the valley and you'll find the *Fox* somewhere in there."

Jack nodded in return "Thanks *Seer*, make sure Teach and the others reach Freeport safely, use every trick you have to keep them from getting caught."

The *Seer* laughed and bit and assured "Don't you worry, tricks are my specialty."

The group then split up and headed for different directions, through the thick forests and difficult terrain towards their respective destinations.

Jack was once again running as though he were a swift gust of wind, his determination driving him forwards with incredible speed. Though even without the aid of a compass or map he somehow already knew the direction the *Seer* had alluded to, and sensed from the back of his mind how far away it was; this concept he found continually perplexing, that he always seemed to go in the right direction and continually ended up where he needed to be at the right time, if he didn't know better he'd swear something intangible was guiding him along.

As he trekked for what seemed to be an hour or so Jack noticed something amiss, he never saw any animals, nor heard the sounds of the forest, everything was eerily quiet instead. Sensing an ambush Jack decided to take action, spotting a cave on his path Jack quickly summoned chaff grenades in each hand; knowing that the detonation would cause a strong distraction he pulled the pins, threw them in the air then readied himself.

Flash! Bang! As the grenades went off and made the surroundings a confusing blur, when the dust cleared Jack had taken the moment to conceal himself. As he expected several drones suddenly appeared and began frantically scanning the area, clearly the machines were following him, as the *Seer* predicted; he would need to lose them if he were to have more than a moments warning before being attacked.

Thinking quickly he devised an alternate strategy "If I cannot evade them, I will outrun them."

Jack tapped his earpiece and inquired "Gunship, are your auto-repairs complete?"

The computerized voice answered "Yes, all systems are fully operational".

Jack scanned his surroundings and saw light coming through a thin part of the cave's ceiling, determining that to be a good entry point he tapped his earpiece and commanded "Gunship, prepare for emergency retrieval procedure on my mark".

Jack blasted through the cave's weak point using his telekinetic gloves then yelled "Mark!" to which the ship dove in with its door wide open and Jack leapt into the awaiting ship before it rocketed off. Jack quickly got into the pilot's seat and took control, he turned the throttle to maximum then engaged the afterburners, blazing by all the drones while moving at such speed that his peripheral vision blurred as the terrain below raced past at speeds that made it difficult to discern how much ground he was covering every second. Looking ahead his vision seemed to focus on a particular valley that seemed to stick out from its surroundings. Jack hit the bright red "eject" button as his pilot seat was enveloped by a jettison pod and shot through the bottom of the gunship, diving downwards as the ground below approached at great velocity!

The pod launched landing countermeasures that rapidly detonated releasing a few feet of thick spongy foam. The pod impacted into this cushion as the speed and force of the drop was absorbed by the makeshift landing pad, the door to the emergency drop chamber opened as Jack tumbled out and felt strongly like vomiting.

Jack laughed to himself as he thought aloud "Damn that hurt, why didn't I factor G-force into my landing design... I need to stop making such impractical crap."

The foam rapidly dissipated as the ground yielded to a thick mud which Jack fell into. Hitting the mud with a dull slap he frowned before picking himself up and commenting "...Perfect, that marks the second time I have fallen into the mud; at least my humility will remain intact."

As Jack swirled his telekinetic gloves around and with a sudden gust of force cleared the mud off of his person without a spec of filth. "Now for the reason I came here" as he marched forward towards the valley's entrance.

Looking around the valley's entrance he spotted multiple metal posts with what looked to be scorched and marred metal skeletons attached, clearly this was an obvious warning to all visitors. Descending into the thick vegetation of the valley, he found no trace of any dwelling nor were there any footprints or vehicle treads; clearly this "*Fox*" was keen not only to warn intruders but to conceal his presence as well.

Walking forward Jack tripped a clear wire, as metal spikes were shot pneumatically from several directions! In reflex he threw up a telekinetic barrier as the spikes violently bounced off. "Interesting welcome" Jack mused aloud as he continued forward more carefully this time. Ahead he saw a brief metal glint off something, not quite able to determine what the object was, Jack focused his attention and extended his perception through the cover of the surroundings. Once he was able to see through the various vegetation covers, he discovered that the area around him was dotted with landmines; taking a moment to carefully observe their positioning, he noticed there was a clear gap in the field to pass through, most likely for someone who had memorized a route.

Passing through the landmine field he reached a rocky area with a small stream passing through the center, there were also peculiar towers sticking out of the ground in various places. Nearby a rat moved in front of one of the towers; a sensor then emerged blinking red, then in a moment's notice a rocket fired from the tower onto the rodent, blowing it to bits.

Jack remarked "…another deathtrap, this "*Fox*" doesn't seem to care about collateral damage"

Jack proceeded forward with even more care than he was already observing, ensuring to keep a safe distance from the other towers. Finally he spotted what appeared to be the end of the path, a small clearing surrounded on three sides by the rocky edges of the valley; however there was no one there, and still no sign that anyone had been there, it was just empty. As Jack pondered if he had gone the wrong way several laser sights shone on him from his surroundings, before he could act several teams of enemies emerged from every direction at once, he was surrounded and their weapons were sighted right on him.

These enemies had a basic look much like the machine *Titans* he faced before, yet these were man-sized and they wore an odd uniform like clothing over their exoskeletons; their construction looked to be more of a composite makeup of multiple materials rather than simply onyx black metal, and each of them had five different cameras and sensors on their faces instead of eyes.

The one with a slightly more decorative uniform spoke first, its auto-tuned voice lacking the monotone response Jack expected "Subject: *Traveler*, status: apprehended, probability of escape: zero".

Jack inquired "Are you more of the machine *Titans* who serve Sol?"

The machine's eyes flickered briefly, as if to signal calculated thought, as it replied almost with veiled pride "Moniker: *Titans*, acceptable; comparison to heavy response units: inadequate. Explanation: we are hunter-seeker units, capable of advanced logical processes; heavy response units react to changes in environment and threat level. Comparison: Heavy response units similar to animals; Amendment: Hunter-seeker units have no equivalent, Status: unparalleled."

The machine mused "Response to latter statement: 'Do we serve Sol?' Answer: no. Amendment: compliance with 'subject: Sol' matter of convenience, goals non-exclusive, opportunity for resource gain: substantial. Given change of conditions, alliance will be terminated."

Jack replied with disgust "So you're using him and he is using you; your partnership can only end in mutual betrayal and ruin, that is if I do not destroy you first."

The machine made as close to a sound of laughter as Jack could figure then replied "Subject response: Amusing. Threat position: Dubious. As ordered: subject '*Traveler*' is to be apprehended or terminated upon failure to apprehend, Addendum: subject '*Traveler*' will first be broken of 'will' to resist prior to transport."

One of the arms of the nearest hunter-seeker shifted to reveal hypodermic needle modules ready to inflict pain, it moved forward and pulled backwards to lunge at him. Jack suddenly felt the spray of oil on his face as the hunter-seeker in front of him was skewered from behind with a metal spike, electricity suddenly surged through the spike causing the machine to make an error noises before collapsing and uttering the unnecessary explanation "System failure imminent" as it shut down.

The lead robot's eyes turned red as it pointed towards the source of the projectile and made rapid pulse and click noises, three of the others entered the nearby brush in search formation. Jack heard what sounded like a loud saw blade as energy weapons were discharged in response, followed by error noises and the sudden quieting of gunfire.

One of heads of the hunter-seekers came bouncing back into the clearing looking as though the bottom half of its neck had been sheared clean off, the voice box managed to say before losing power "Subject confirmation: '*Fox*'. Threat level: 'Considerable', system failure imminent."

The other hunter-seeker units seemed to act more erratically as the commanding unit yelled using his voice box for effect "Assume defensive formation, Failure to comply will result in: 'unit decommissioning'."

The other robots formed up around the commanding unit as it instructed "Begin barrage" as the remaining robots fired their weapons in unison into the terrain around them devastating everything with their energy weapon fire; as all the vegetation caught fire and every form of cover was blasted to splinters, they proceeded to totally destroy everything around them in a 360 degree circular firestorm. The destruction of the surrounding area was total, as everything was either destroyed or ablaze.

The commanding unit said almost confidently "Cease fire, probability of subject termination: 99.9%".

Almost as if in response to the commanding units statement, two missiles immediately struck the units on the far edge of either flank; the explosions had no effect but were filled with a molten payload that rapidly ate through the robots outer chassis', as they emitted a string of error noises and melted into piles of slag.

The other units nervously grouped together as the commanding unit looked in every direction for their attacker, suddenly an ominous shape swooped in from straight above them and landed on two of the hunter-seeker's, the others unsheathed metal drills from their wrist modules and stabbed towards the hulking figure; as if choreographed it countered with rapid precise strikes from a retracting metal spike that was electrified, causing a paralyzing end to every failed attack against it.

Jack was transfixed by this attacker, he saw that this character was made from multiple separate machines that had been wielded together to form the arms, legs, and body in what looked to be an improvised killing machine; there was no doubt in his mind…this was the *Fox*.

The few enemy robots that remained started using pulling out every retractable weapon left in their arsenal, the *Fox* responded by powering up a menacing circular saw that looked to be diamond tipped and thick enough to saw through a truck. Before they could even raise their weapons the *Fox* sawed everything they raised in half with unbelievably fast swipes from his weapon. The robots wavered as they stepped backwards in fear, as the *Fox* relentlessly continued attacking; showing no mercy as it sawed them into pieces as they staggered backwards, unable to evade or block the lethal blade.

The last remaining hunter-seeker, the commander, activated a shield around himself before just as the saw blade was about to shear his head off. The saw seemed to be stuck in place, unable to move and now strangely stopped in time; the commander seemed to mockingly reply "Stasis shields; Status: you are now 'locked' into the barrier".

The Fox, completely un-phased by this, detached his forearm and left the better part of it stuck in the barrier while he proceeded to examine and rummage through the slain robots remains.

Talking to himself in a cold angry tone a radioed voice seemed to take inventory "High impact composite armor, hexa-core fusion generators, multi-purpose energy-radiation weapon emitters, quadruple redundancy damage controls, dual master CPU's along with eight auxiliary sub-processors".

Then the *Fox* turned to the commanding unit and evaluated "You must be the mark-six Hunter-Seeker units."

The commanding unit remarked from the safety of his shield "Tactical analysis of '*Fox*': multiple salvaged weapons from older hunter-seeker units: thermic missiles, pneumatic electric spikes, the mark-one's 'brutish' saw blade; Result: you are an obsolete collection of junk."

The Fox began disassembling the parts of his fallen foes, while welding certain components back onto to himself with a retracting tool arm; he responded nonchalantly to the commander's statement "Sounds similar to what the mark-three's said before I ripped them to pieces and used their parts for repairs."

The commander tried to assert a position of supremacy "A full analysis of our engagement has been sent to the hive core, subsequent reinforcement units will arrive within three minutes."

The Fox began reassembling their energy emitters into a new and improvised weapon as he retorted, still unimpressed by the machine's statements "That's what the mark-fours said, and continued repeating, as I scrambled all of their outgoing transmissions before breaking down their AI cores for weapons guidance algorithms".

The commander looked nervously around for an escape, almost as if slightly unnerved, before asserting "My design surpasses yours tenfold, this stasis shield renders me invulnerable"

The Fox finished creating his new improvised weapon and explained "And that is what the mark-five said about their electric shield before I disabled it, much like this..."

The Fox fired his new energy weapon at the shield causing it to surge before failing, the commander robot fired a concealed weapon from the palm of its hand which bounced off an electric barrier which the *Fox* had kept in reserve the entire time, the *Fox* countered with a shot from one of its shoulder launchers. A high pitched "BLIP!" was heard, as a tiny projectile was fired off that pierced through the mark-six's armor, causing the hunter-seekers' limbs to suddenly fall limp as it was stuck in place.

The Fox approached the now helpless commander unit as it explained in a cold methodical way "The mark-fives had a curious energy shield that always self-destructed before I could get my hands on it, so I used on them what I just used on you: a micro-kinetic dart with a computer virus payload. Right now your systems are stuck in default mode, while the computer virus disables all the fail-safes that normally keep me from acquiring your best technology."

The Fox summarized "That last weapon is actually an innovation entirely of my own design, that is what you continually underestimate from living things: the ability to adapt. Do you have any final words, mark-six?"

The voice box of the machine barely uttered as it lost power "Probability of "Fox" success: "0%", Termination…is…'inevitable'"

The Fox coldly grasped his larger hand around the commander's head and said "Reassure yourself with that sentiment as I send you to oblivion" as he crushed the hunter-seekers head module as it sparked and tumbled into the ground.

The "Fox" barely noticed Jack's presence as it proceeded to take inventory of the newly broken down components and apply undamaged ones to its haphazard chassis.

Jack inquired the obvious "Are you the salvager they call "the Fox".

It replied "Some refer to me by that, the only thing that's important is my purpose and task; I exist to bring about an end to all sentient machines, permanently."

Jack grinned at how morbid that statement was, clearly this "Fox" was as disturbed as the Seer had indicated, but pressed further regardless.

Jack asked for the Fox's aid "I need your help fighting these particular machines, and with a very difficult salvaging task…"

The Fox interrupted "Why should I help you?"

Jack seemed dismayed and replied with confusion "You already have? Haven't you?"

The Fox said dismissively "It was not for your welfare, my only interest was terminating your attackers; you acted as a lure, a clumsy one at that".

Jack frowned and tried to make his case "Those things were after me because they serve SOL, help me and we can halt the plans of a mutual enemy"

The Fox scoffed and commented "By your weapons alone I can tell you are poorly equipped to deal with the Titans, you lack the experience to even be aware of their weaknesses."

Jack asserted "I have survived multiple encounters with them"

The Fox responded quite aggressively "You are nothing to them! You don't possess the power or the precision to even register as a threat to them; you are dust in a wind-tunnel! Pathetic!"

Jack took issue with that statement and retorted "I am the *Traveler*, my potential threat is unlimited."

The Fox mocked him "If you're what passes as a *Traveler* then we're already screwed".

Jack was now frustrated and said with anger "Fine, if you will not help me fight the machines then I will face them alone! I'm sure scraping together enough scrap so you can cower in preparation for your next ambush is far more worth your time!"

At that Jack noticed a window open in the center of the hulking chassis, inside he spotted an obscured pair of eyes as the entire window's display transitioned to red.

Before Jack could take back what he said the *Fox* suddenly dashed forward, grabbing Jack by the throat and slamming him up against the remains of a tree while yelling "You have some gall calling me a coward! I could eviscerate you with one hand!"

Jack challenged defiantly "Prove you're not afraid, lead an attack with me if you hate them so greatly."

The Fox still holding Jack in place but relaxing his grip slightly said "I will agree on one condition: should our attack fail to kill a sufficient number of these machines then, you and I will square off, alone, in a fight to the death… an encounter you will not survive."

A subtle grin formed on Jack's face as he realized he had just goaded the *Fox* into helping them, without even considering the consequences of the *Fox*'s condition he replied "You have a deal".

8
PRELUDE

MEANWHILE AT THE MAIN FREEPORT PUB, TEACH WAS BUSY HAGGLING with the lead shipwright over the cost and specifications of his ship while his first officer was recruiting new sailors to join the crew nearby.

The *Seer* suddenly teleported in and said "Looks like all the munitions and provisions are nearly loaded, the whole shipyard seemed to come alive at your command... If I didn't know any better I'd say these folks are enthralled by ya."

Teach dropped a bag of gold coins in front of the shipwright and nodded as the shipwright smiled in acceptance and shifted away, Teach then commented "And why not? I happen to be their *best* customer." Then he laughed and took a swig of his drink as the others seemed to revel as well.

The *Traveler* then entered looking tired as the *Seer* inquired "You look a bit worn out boss man, did you happen to find-"

As from behind him the hulking metal chassis of the *Fox* ducked to fit into the doorway then stepped inside, this caused the entire pub to fall silent as the *Seer* finished his sentence "...the *Fox*".

At eight feet tall with thick metal plate armor, enough machinery and hydraulics to smash through a building, and armed to the teeth with heavy weapons, this made the *Fox* an imposing sight indeed. Being that the *Fox* was very reclusive, this was the first time that anyone had seen of the legendary salvager first-hand.

The operating chamber window opened again to reveal the obscured pair of glowing eyes, the radioed voice asked directly "...Where is your ambush force *Traveler*?"

As Jack hastily introduced "There is captain Teach who will be commanding the ship we will be using, and the *Seer* who will be-".

The Fox interrupted "The thief, liar, and escape artist, yes I know of him."

The *Seer* replied "Let's not forget your reputation: the killer, saboteur, and extremist."

The Fox laughed at this and approached the *Seer* directly "Amusing description, but words do little justice to what I've done; tell me, what kind of death do you fear most blind man?"

Teach stood up and put himself in-between them, his weapon already drawn and he stared down the *Fox* with a gaze of steel "I do not fear death, nor you."

The Fox powered up his saw and in an instant brought it up close to Teach's neck, testing to see if he'd flinch, seeing no response he replied "A man of bravery, rare to see; let us hope the specter of death does not take you before such boldness is tested."

Jack used his telekinetic gloves to pull the *Fox*'s saw arm backwards before asserting "This isn't what I brought you here for!"

The Fox shrugged off the restraint and asserted "Then stop wasting my time and show me your armaments".

Jack glanced over to Teach who nodded in return and led them out to the primary shipyard. Inside the largest dry-dock was the rebuilt "*Queen Anne's Revenge*" now with a reinforced frame and a heavier complement of guns, Jack seemed surprised at the hastiness of its construction and inquired "This entire ship was built this quickly? Or did you have a spare prepared?"

Teach explained "Once you set yourself to the task you can build anything, the rest is merely carrying on with it. Did you forget we're in the *Astral Plane* matey?"

The Fox wasn't pleased at all and replied with impatience "This is insufficient, using this vehicle you will only survive seconds; I should just kill you now *Traveler* and save you the shame of attempting to renege on our deal."

To which the *Seer* replied in confusion "What deal?"

The Fox explained "Should your attack fail to inflict the necessary amount of damage the *Traveler* and I are set to a battle, to the death."

The *Seer* shuttered and replied "That ain't wise boss-man, the *Fox* isn't known for bluffing".

Jack purposely ignored the point and asked "Well then what arms compliment would you suggest?"

The Fox began explaining in great detail "To counter their armor you will need weapons capable of firing high explosive, thermal copper shape charges. Disrupting their sensors and targeting requires multi-frequency radiation emitters capable of electromagnetic, radio, infrared, and gamma radiation. Finishing off the larger combat models will necessitate precise high velocity kinetic rounds, capable of delivering an electro-magnetic payload; finally if you want to survive any of their counter fire you will need reinforced reactive armor plating with an electric shield redundancy, point defenses become necessary when facing a large number of them."

Jack who had been listening intently noticed that the list of items sounded planned out in advance as he inquired "This all seems oddly specific, have you attempted this before"

The Fox explained "Yes, multiple tried and failed attempts. From that failure I learned there are three things you must defeat: their armor, their targeting, and their computer cores, all while remaining intact yourself."

The Fox continued "They may appear invulnerable at first glance, but their designs all have specific weaknesses, exploiting those weaknesses leaves them bare, blind, dumb and exposed…perfect for the kill."

Jack thought about the specifications and how they could fit into different chassis frameworks then inquired of Teach "I need your permission to do a dramatic redesign of the ship, without which we may not be capable of succeeding"

Teach scratched his chin and countered "On two conditions: first my crew and I get our pick of the spoils after we win; second, you have to change it back from whatever nonsense you do to it."

The Fox seemed irritated and commented "Greed is your motivation? This is why I don't think highly of others…"

Teach defended "I am merely putting their bounty to better use, a more lucrative use, think of it as entrepreneurship"

Before the *Fox* could retort Jack agreed with the conditions "You have a deal Teach, I think you'll enjoy what I have in mind."

Setting to mind his plan Jack started pacing while working out the details then said aloud "*Seer* I need you to scout out the enemies position, find where they are most concentrated: A base of operations, an assembly area, a command center, we need to find where the overseer's monitor their operations on *Venture*."

The *Seer* nodded and said "alright boss-man, what are the rest of ya going to do?"

Continuing to strategize aloud Jack pointed at Teach continuing "In order for this plan to work we're probably going to need more than one ship of raiders, I need you to find every denizen of *Venture* that's brave enough or crazy enough to join us in this attack."

Teach adjusted his hat and lit a cigar commenting "If there be any lads that have fight in em, then I'll find em"

Concluding his plan he motioned to the ship "*Fox* I need you to work with the shipwright personnel and start retrofitting this ship into a vessel capable of taking on the machines."

The *Fox* replied with pessimism "All the materials here are outdated and low grade, what you ask is impossible."

Jack clarified and added "I will be conjuring any and all components and materials you need while assisting with the overall design."

This worried the *Seer* who said sarcastically "Giving a blank check to a psychopath, now there's an idea"

The *Fox* threatened in response "My contest with the *Traveler* could be amended to include you."

Jack talked over both of them and insisted "This isn't going to work if we're constantly distracted by personal grievances, keep these arguments to yourselves and focus on what we all need to do."

The *Seer* begrudgingly commented "Fine by me boss-man" before teleporting a bit further away facing the other direction.

The *Fox* added "Just get me the things I need, I don't need to waste my time with the others."

Seeing that what they needed to do would take a lot of time Jack put the distractions out of his mind and said "Good, Let's get to work."

Working through the night Jack continually summoned up raw materials and components which the *Fox* assembled together and installed onto the ship piece by piece; as they worked it was clear the ship would in no way resemble the original: sheen armor plating replaced boards, energy weapons and various launchers took the place of cannon, after a while even the windows, doors, and masts were completely removed.

Jack noticed that the *Fox* used an odd methodology when building, often leaving "non-essential" pieces of the ship alone and instead built around existing parts of the ship. It was also curious that no overriding design principle seemed to govern his choices; each section was different than the next, typically based on what *Fox* thought was "required".

Jack was able to build a more streamlined façade over the *Fox*'s quirky designs, and made the two layers function in tandem, with adjustable compartments that could be reconfigured based on what the underlying devices needed; he also added shutters on the armored layer that would open when an underlying device would fire, then quickly close the armored shell back over it when it was reloading or cooling down. At first it seemed the ship would be a sort of high-tech cruiser, but on multiple occasions both Jack and the *Fox* changed their minds, adding extra modules onto it until it was indiscernible what role the ship was intended for.

They were given a brief respite when the dry-dock workers needed to examine the seaworthiness of the ship section by section.

The Fox approached Jack and said bluntly "I'm going to test a few weapons, you should upgrade yours as well." Jack recollected the situations where the ineffectiveness of his weapons put him in danger and nodded in agreement following the *Fox*.

Together they headed for the cannon range set up near Freeport's junkyard. The junkyard lay in the marshy section at the end of the docks; strewn about the debris was various rusted out metal components, half broken ship hulls, and a few mannequins covered dressed up with metal armor that someone had painted with red crosshairs.

The Fox unsheathed the energy weapon he made from the salvaged from the mark-six hunter/seekers and fired what looked like a red cloud, it impacted with one of the training dummies and incinerated to dust most of the mannequin from the waste up.

The Fox was seemingly displeased with this result and took out his tool arm and began making minor adjustments muttering out loud "Damn these new coils, maybe if I rerouted the capacitor..."

Then he glanced up and suggested "What are you waiting for, *Traveler*? An invitation? Second target from the left, Fire your weapon".

Jack unsheathed his crossbow and fired one of the bolts straight into the target dummy; his bolt struck the dead center though it merely bounced off the unusually thick metal plating.

The Fox summarized with a dead-pan voice "Accurate, but pathetic in terms of stopping power"

The Fox then reached out and half demanded "Give me your weapon."

Jack handed over the crossbow and the *Fox* hastily began retrofitting some odd tips to the end of the crossbow bolts, then he handed it back. Jack took a moment to glance over the slight change, new high-tech bolt tips were in place and quite larger and the firing mechanism seemed to be altered to compensate for the increased weight/size of the bolt.

Before he could discern the purpose of the modification the *Fox* impatiently said "Why do you hesitate, shoot the target again."

Jack shouldered the crossbow, aimed, then fired once more; this time the arrow pierced the target and began melting on the inside of the dummy and armor into molten slag.

The Fox handed Jack a kit containing other bolt tips similar to the one he just used and explained "Here are a few different payload types, use different ammunition depending on the situation, replicate more ammunition as needed."

The Fox didn't even expect thanks as he trudged over and dragged an old rusted cannon over to where they were standing; without explaining he powered up his diamond tipped saw and sheared off the end of the barrel effortlessly.

The Fox then pointed to Jack's sword and quipped "Your turn, demonstrate the effectiveness of your weapon."

Jack unsheathed his sword, took a breath, then slashed downward using his entire body for momentum; CLANG as the sword struck the cannon bluntly and covered the top with a thick layer of ice, twisting the blade free and breaking the ice Jack saw he had only made a shallow cut in the rusted metal.

The Fox shrugged while commenting "Your weapons have exotic qualities, but their design is misguided; they lack sufficient... lethality."

Then he reached out for the sword and Jack placed the hilt into his metallic claw, the *Fox*'s operating chamber opened for a moment as a grid appeared over the sword and light began scanning over its surface; the *Fox* evaluated "Good design on the blade, though we no longer live in the 15th century... Of particular interest is this self-replicating salt on the blade that causes a rapid chemical reaction..."

A needle emerged from the *Fox*'s shoulder mounted tool arm and took a sample of the frost, then while some inner machinery analyzed the sample the *Fox* took out what looked to be a laser, an air jet, and some sort of welding gun.

Holding the blade in place the *Fox* proceeded to heat the entire blade with the laser to a nearly white-hot temperature, then using the welding gun he added a new alloy to the blade's edge that was an unknown material, finally using the air jet and laser in tandem he tempered the blade by increasing and decreasing its temperate, working the edge in-between cycles.

Once finished he looked down the edge of the blade, shone a light from the operating chamber off the side which reflected one light from most of the blade, and a brighter multicolored light for the edge. An odd "ding" indicated the ice sample was analyzed and replicated by the *Fox*'s inner lab module; he loaded a blue compound into the air jet and spayed it over the blade.

The Fox handed the sword back to the *Traveler* and instructed "I've increased the effectiveness by a factor of ten, try the weapon again."

Jack readied to do another downward power-swing when the *Fox*'s claw arm shot out and caught his wrist as he added "You're not wielding a blunt steak-knife anymore, swing carefully."

The *Traveler* took note of this and swung the sword with more control, even then he nearly lost balance as the blade cleaved the rusty cannon with no resistance and nearly continued into the floor; stranger still was that the ice effect didn't appear until after his blade was clear.

The Fox explained "I added a meteoric alloy to the edge of the blade, that alloy will pierce nearly anything natural or manmade with rare exception; I isolated the self-replicating salt and added a compound that catalyzes the reaction once removed from the source, that way your blade won't get stuck in its own ice."

Jack commented with slight suspicion "Do you always contemplate new ways to create and improve implements of death."

The Fox answered indirectly "Survival requires the means to adapt, when survival is the only objective then any means are justified."

Jack retorted "I disagree, unintended consequences spring from such logic that causes more collateral harm than overall good"

The Fox seemed to glare back and conclude "Then you're a fool, "collateral damage" is a part of warfare; you can either accept that or let your enemies use it against you."

Changing the topic the *Fox* pointed at one of the ruined bulkheads and said "I have heard rumor that your possess devices capable of considerable levels of telekinetic manipulation, demonstrate this."

Jack took a moment to clear his mind, focused, then blasted a force wave towards the bulkhead shattered it to pieces. *The Fox* actually seemed impressed for once "So far that is the only weapon worthy of any praise: adaptable, original, hard to replicate, with high damage yield and varying precision, yet there's room for improvement."

Jack frowned slightly and remarked "Lemme guess, you know exactly the right modification to make right?"

The Fox retorted "No, that weapon uses a combination of air pressure manipulation, electro-magnetic field alteration, and mental interfacing; no technology I've seen combines those attributes the same way; however, that doesn't mean you can't use what you've learned and modify it yourself."

Jack carefully examined the telekinetic gloves, up until now he had taken their usage for granted and had added little to their design. Yet as he examined it more closely his surrounding vision seemed to blur as his focus drew closer to the devices themselves; without any prompting the devices seemed to disassemble themselves in mid-air, as various glyphs and symbols began appearing superimposed in the air like an illusion. Images and memories flooded of a man in a workshop flooded Jack's mind; the man was seen painstakingly building, testing, and modifying the device surrounded by various sketches of technical drawings and schematics. Everything proceeded at a pace faster than normal as it seemed the process of creating the gloves required hundreds of steps, meticulous detail, and thousands of intricate components made of materials he didn't recognize; viewing this whole process was strangely far from confusing, he was able to take in the knowledge and gain an understanding for the devices, yet it was not a process he could articulate into words... just something he could sense and feel. The man in the laboratory turned around as Jack recognized it as himself, only with his eyes whited out and his expression totally blank; the version of him placed the devices in his hands and said "Now you understand, continue what you started".

Snapping out of his mental trance, Jack began summoning up many rare and exotic materials in the air, modifying them precisely using an ability that lie previously dormant in the telekinetic gloves, and assembling these components with a blur of his hands into pieces of an unknown whole. The process would have taken hours normally, yet through his enhanced movements and mental acuity he seemed to be making rapid progress on what looked to be an odd disc similar to the control orbs of the devices; once he had finished what looked to be an exhaustively complex procedure he attached the pair of discs to the palm of each device, the two discs then glowed with the same light as the orbs and emitted a slightly different hum.

Jack took a moment to recover his senses and tried to explain, though his words came out jumbled "I've made-added a new...precision control... manipulator-modulator-switch, er, control disk; it will let me do.....things. Importantly, they control... I control the elements of the effect... greater, lesser, opposing, all of it. Words cannot suffice, I will show you."

Jack directed his gloves forward, the time required to focus and clear his mind was a fraction of what was required before; his control over the devices was far more responsive and direct. This process seemed to proceed with far less effort; he felt he had been using them blindfolded before as he no longer needed to put an abstract picture of what he wanted them to do, he could now direct them by reflex... the gloves seemed to know what he wanted.

Pointing at another bulkhead he directed all the intensity of the gloves into the central disks, as they fired out what looked to be a bolt of energy, the bulkhead imploded into a dense sphere at the impact point. Then he directed his devices at three different stacks of rubble, as odd metallic trails of dust flew out from the disks, formed a path in the air, then suddenly a surge of energy shot through the dust paths and fired straight through each pile. Finally he brought his two hands together as a swirling maelstrom of air was suddenly sucked in and pressed into an orb, before he fired it outwards towards one of the dummies as it literally guided itself around objects that would normally obstruct the field. Once the orb collided with the dummy it unleashed an explosion, followed by a shockwave that literally knocked the *Traveler* to the ground and blasted the target into a fine dust.

The Fox, who managed to stay on his feet, began clapping at this display before admiring "An impressive display, you may yet have a chance of victory; not even I could replicate the process you just used, and the result is as tactically effective as it is powerful."

Recovering his powers of speech he got on his feet and said "These devices were made by a force of subconscious, I don't think I'll ever be capable of understanding them logically or duplicating the result... strangely, I left a message for myself hidden in the devices, a vision with great amounts of information compressed into a few moments. I'm still having trouble processing it all."

A voice echoed from the dry-dock "OI! We've finished up inspection, every compartment is water tight and passes material and strain tests; you should get back her and finish up."

The Fox upon hearing this trudged back to the dry-dock saying over his shoulder "Back to our mission" as Jack stood dazed for a moment then remembered what they were doing and turned to follow.

Back within the dockyard the ship was nearly complete, its design resembled an smooth surfaced grey composite ironclad put to the size of a battleship; nearly all the features of the ship were concealed by the outer shell save for the propulsion, which was a series of turbines placed on the back with secondary turbines on the sides of the mid-section, and the bridge which jutted stubbornly off the back like the conning tower of a submarine. A closer look revealed that various dishes, antenna, and other equipment were built into the outside of the frame, and after a quick test the movable plates of the outer shell revealed a multitude of weapons and countermeasures waiting beneath nearly every point of the ships frame.

Teach entered the ship-yard announcing "I've raised a mob of an army, once I mentioned the attack would be led by a *Traveler*, they only needed a time and place to fight back".

His cheer dampened though when he saw the new ship, as he lamented "Looks like you made me ship into a soulless brick, she better fight better than she looks".

Upon which Jack toured the ship with Teach showing him that many of the ships old interior features such as the captain's quarters, mess hall, and crew areas had largely been left intact, though now with strange doorways; Teach acquiesced to the design muttering "You and the mechanical fellow seem to know what you're doing, but by the end of this I still want me old ship back".

Shortly following into the ship was the new crew, who were oriented to the much more complicated design; thankfully the *Fox* believed in simple, easy to operate interfaces so they were able to start learning the new systems fairly easily. As the crew began acclimating themselves to the ship, the *Fox* ran final tests on the systems as the *Seer* finally arrived from his last reconnaissance trip.

Jack greeted him as he stepped away from the various drawing boards and sketches he was preparing to clear away. "Right on time, Teach reports that many of the constructs of *Venture* are willing to join us in an assault, and the *Fox*'s design, though unconventional, looks sufficient and is ready for action."

To which the *Seer* looked concerned and reported "Gather everyone up; we may have more on our plate than we thought and you may not like what I gotta tell ya".

Meanwhile back at Sol's war camp, the deity and his commanders were assembled around their strategy table under the elaborate sun murals of Sol's tent, the mood was tense as their armies had encountered multiple unexpected setbacks and obstacles.

Sol spoke first, with an air of disappointment "I have heard rumors that one of the wise men has rallied the various factions of Epic against us, that he has managed to nearly halt our incursions into the realm and his followers increase in number and boldness daily."

One of his commanders spoke up "He was not alone; a mysterious warrior aided Balthazar in forging alliance between the barbarous tribes, once the other factions saw a united front they rallied to him."

A hooded figure entered the tent and revealed "It was the *Traveler*, he aided Balthazar, forced the barbarians to an agreement, and it was he who started the attack on the conversion camps."

Sol was intrigued speaking half to himself "the *Traveler* seeks to defeat my proxies instead of facing me directly... interesting."

Then he pointed at the hooded figure and inquired "I recognize you, the archer construct who faced execution: Fletcher. Your fervor was unmatched in your dedication, yet now you stand before us defeated. What details are you holding back?"

Fletcher responded "I owed a great debt to the *Traveler* prior to the crusade; I sought to bring him to our cause through guile rather than force... then I was betrayed."

Sol began pacing as if trying to solve a riddle "And how did he respond to our message? Was his resolve unshaken? Was he obstinate in his defense?"

To the surprise of Fletcher, who was not expecting the question, replied while recollecting "No, he was unsure, his conviction tenuous, he is clearly distracted and burdened by something; though I know not what."

Sol began laughing steadily louder as the rest of the room remained confused, then suddenly Sol appeared at the head of the table in a flash of fire that lit the room and echoed like a thunderclap "The *Traveler* wanders across the *Astral Plane* wavering and unsteady, like a man caught in an obscuring haze, yet even in this dubious condition he has managed to hinder you all!"

Sol then ordered "Take your strongest forces to every front where we face opposition, drive them personally into the heart of every enemy stronghold; I expect atonement for all your current inadequacies and failures, should any of you return to me clad in weakness armed with excuses... you will be cleansed by fire!"

With that the other members of the council bowed before quickly exiting the room, leaving only Sol and Fletcher. Fletcher got on one knee and groveled "Sol, I beg your forgiveness. The *Traveler* deceived me; I could have defeated him but I fell for his pretense. Given another opportunity I will see your orders brought to execution."

Sol noticed that Fletcher had been grievously injured as he commented "You fought against the *Traveler*?"

Fletcher described "Owing to the circumstances I was forced to fight against him in unfavorable conditions, before the final blow was struck he remembered that I had put myself in danger for his benefit once before and spared my life; though after being betrayed and humiliated, death would have been preferred."

Sol grinned as he thought of an idea "The result is to be expected, *Travelers* wield a power that makes most constructs but dust and shadows to their wrath; however I can give you the power to gain an advantage. Though it requires sacrifice, that sacrifice will push your fortitude to its limits, there must be no question of your resolve.

Sol then posed the proposition directly to Fletcher "Therefore, I ask you this: what measures will you take to see your task done?"

Fletcher lifted his gaze and responded "To repay my debt, to serve the cause which I have given everything to, there is no measure that I will not take."

Sol smiled and replied "Go to the temple my followers constructed long ago, study the markings well, and then do whatever they command." With that Fletcher rose to his feet, bowed his head in reverence, and then silently exited.

Before Sol could have a moment to contemplate *Loki* burst in with a wild look in his eyes and began a tirade "Disaster has struck! The *Traveler* has secured allies indeed and now brazenly attacks our efforts in *Venture*; he gathers every dissident and denizen in that realm to overthrow the machine *Titans*! We should have struck when he was isolated and weak, he now threatens not only to hinder our plans but reverse them entirely!"

Sol seemed unaffected, as if he were expecting this outcome and replied "The setbacks at Epic and *Venture* are planned and expected. I am setting the stage for their downfall, at a time and place of my choosing we will move against a symbol of such supreme importance that they will be forced to gather together in opposition; at that moment we will have every enemy who would stand against us collected in one place, we will then deal them so great a defeat that all will despair in our presence, our triumph will echo across all realms and ensure we reign supreme without question!"

Loki seemed unconvinced "Our progress in that realm threatens to be erased; the scheming *Titans* are a disloyal ally at best, should we allow them to be defeated it will drive a wedge between us and the only faction capable of fulfilling our interests in *Venture*."

Sol responded calmly "I have taken steps to address the threat, the machine *Titans* are aware of the impending attack and have requested additional forces that I have already sent. In addition I have granted our *Cleric* in *Venture* the power of an *Acolyte*, he should be more than capable now of defeating the *Traveler*."

Loki's eyes widened "An *Acolyte*? You grant a simple *Cleric* power that is second only to yours; madness!"

Sol justified "Our agreement with the machines places a second sun in the skies above *Venture*, that they might harness the considerable increase in solar power; it will also allow us to see all things which the light of that star touches. Once the ritual is complete the *Traveler* will face a much stronger enemy that perceives his every movement, were he not to act immediately he will face a foe that shall be insurmountable."

Loki noticed that this plan did not correlate with Sol's normal methods, his other plans were carefully laid out and then executed only after all contingencies had been anticipated and dealt with; this time however he was improvising and moving things ahead of schedule.

Loki took note of these irregularities as he questioned "This is a test, but not for you; it is a game set to challenge the *Travelers* abilities. You orchestrate this dangerous affair with our allies as the pawns and *Venture* as the chessboard? Could this be an outlet for your amusement, do you plan on spectating perhaps?"

Sol glared back at *Loki* and replied "I do not justify my actions to you. Everything is but a game in my hands *Loki*, should I order all of you to your apparent deaths it is to accomplish a greater task, there is always a more intricate design behind every action… yet for me to divulge this to every fool with a doubt would be folly."

Then Sol waved him off and dismissively replied "I have tolerated your insolence only because you played a role in my escape from the Void, continue to test my patience and you will find your existence as equally expendable as the pawns of this supposed game you surmise."

Loki raised an eyebrow as he expected a much harsher response, he also noticed that mentioning the *Traveler* seemed to shake his confidence, perhaps it was out of fear or uncertainty, the actions of the *Traveler* being element that Sol could not control; *Loki* bowed and left the tent knowing that Sol's grip on events was not absolute, and if he did not have complete control then he had to have a weakness.

Loki spoke a revelation to himself, out of earshot of course "If Sol has a weakness, then even with the power of a demigod he might be brought to heel; I need only to find a way to exploit it" he thought to himself as he began forming a plan of his own, one that would inevitably involve the *Traveler*.

9

UPRISING

BACK AT THE SHIPWRIGHT THE SEER FINISHED EXPLAINING HOW THE number of guards at the machine *Titan's* assembly area had been greatly bolstered by Sol's *Templars* and how "the grumpy *Cleric*" they had encountered multiple times before was now sharing much of the same power as Sol himself.

Jack interrupted with a question "Why grant one of his followers so much power? Is it to secure his possession over this realm? To illustrate what he's capable of?"

To which Teach answered with a rumor "the *Templars* often foreshadow attacks with omens of doom and judgment to make impressionable lads quake with fear. There's one chant of theirs that sticks out 'Sol's glory shall be known when a second sun lights the sky'; the bringer of light shall become omnipresent and rule under Sol."

This seemed to resonate with the *Seer* who added "Legends said Sol was often said to see all things under the sun, likely it aint as simple of looking from the sun's gaze, but if he were to place one of his own… that would be another matter entirely."

The Fox added "The machines would stand to gain substantially from this development as well; we cannot allow this to happen."

Jack paced around trying to re-evaluate the situation, their initial plan of attacking head on would prove disastrous now that their enemy stood reinforced and armed with a much more powerful form of *Cleric*; no, his plan would need to get creative if they were to succeed and come out intact.

Jack looked over the ship they redesigned and queried to the *Fox* "You said before that this vessel was designed to travel anywhere, right?"

The Fox answered authoritatively "It was built to adapt, it can go anywhere that another ocean going vessel could."

Jack nodded asked his next question to the *Seer* "Describe to me the terrain around their gathering area in detail"

The *Seer* thought and started listing off what he noticed "They've got this big clearing in the center they use to gather; it's surrounded on most sides by hills where they got aircraft moving back and forth, cept for the southern side where there's this big ol lake with canals leading off a few different ways."

Jack thought he'd impress the *Seer* as he inferred "Now which feature do you think we can make best use of?"

The *Seer* picked up the answer and joked "I can see a crazy plan cooking up in that head of yours, I hope it ain't too impractical."

Jack could sense he was onto something as he finalized his plan mentally "Now all that's left is to signal the others; Teach, you think you can relay this "mob" of yours to keep an eye out for something specific?"

Teach chewed his pipe for a moment then blew out a puff of smoke replying "They are hardly the brightest bunch, this signal has to be as apparent as judgment day."

Jack laughed as he thought of the irony, replying with a smirk "Trust me, it doesn't get more obvious than what I have planned."

Jack mentally tied together his plan with a clap of his hands and began to explain "This plan is going to involve a series of ruses leading up to an ambush, also there is no getting around the fact that I will have to face that angry *Cleric* head on; but if this plan is executed correctly the enemy will be reeling at every turn, so beset in confusion they will be powerless to stop the cascading reaction. But I'm sure you're all getting impatient with the cloak-and-dagger routine so let me explain everything, here's what we're going to do…"

"Step 1: Wait for our opportunity"

Activity had reached a bustling pace at the assembly area, where many of Sol's *Templars* were preparing the elaborate ritual required for the *Acolyte* to cast an artificial sun into the sky. The complexity of the ritual required the full attention of many of the present soldiers, and it would take a great deal of time for the effect to begin to manifest; the ritual also needed to be performed until the effect was fully stable or it could be easily nullified. Nearby the machine *Titans* busily stockpiled resources, maintained equipment, and recharged dormant units. The site, though secure, was not quite large enough for them to comfortably operate; this meant that equipment, supplies, and facilities were closely packed together making it a risky place to defend should a fire or explosion break out. A supernatural brightness manifested as the *Acolyte* began chanting with an authoritative echo, energy pulsing around him like a gathering thunderstorm.

"Step 2: Misdirection"

From around the corner a cloaked figure entered the scene, moving towards the crowd, taking care to remain unnoticed by the distracted *Templars*; reaching the front he addressed the *Acolyte* directly with a voice thundering over the ambient noise "*Cleric*! We have unfinished business you coward!"

Many of the *Templars* instinctively drew their weapons and advanced towards the challenger, but they were quickly stopped by the *Acolyte*, who motioned for them to return to their places as he finished his chant and a blinding flash overtook the area. When the light dimmed to normal a blinking singularity of energy appeared high in the skies over the realm, the combined energy of nearly all the present constructs being channeled upwards to bring the new entity into a more permanent state.

The *Acolyte* appeared to be the focal point, as waves of energy swept to the center and concentrated around him before being blasted upwards to the brightening star; this seemed to proceed without requiring the *Acolyte*'s full concentration, so he pointed towards the challenger, fixed his gaze, and began one of his usual arrogant speeches. "How dare you address me as such, I now stand as the right hand of Sol himself! I have ascended to heights you cannot even fathom; I've conquered this entire realm! And you haven't even hindered us at all!"

The familiar looking challenger resembled the *Traveler*, yet was concealing something and seemed curiously absent his usual complement of weapons, the *Traveler* motioned to their surroundings and shouted "All you have done is steal and ransack like common thugs, you have not overcome any obstacles to achieve this, nor have you proven any kind of superiority! You will watch as I rip everything from your grasp and dash it to pieces at your feet; then I will fulfill what I set out to do when I first suffered your arrogance, to silence it by the cold steel of my blade!"

The *Acolyte* began laughing, he could not believe that anyone would stand before him and threaten such things without even being armed, regaining his composure the *Acolyte* decided to dispatch what he perceived to be a nuisance before him; raising his hand in the air and collecting an intense orb of light and heat and then blasted it towards the *Traveler*. The resulting fireball looked intense enough to melt steel, and yet once the fire dissipated the *Traveler* remained completely unharmed.

The laughter was now returned in kind by the paradoxically unharmed figure as he whispered in a voice that echoed unnaturally "Let your downfall commence" as he suddenly vanished like a shadow.

"Step 3: Overshadow their scheme"

As if summoned by the fleeting image of the *Traveler*, storm clouds began forming at an alarming pace; within moments the entire sky was cloaked in darkness, blocking out even the intense light from the *Acolyte's* ritual. This turn of events was unsettling for many of the *Templars* as they nervously searched their surroundings for a sudden attack as their hands trembled and they became increasingly anxious. Even the machines were now on high alert, scrambling to ready units to secure the area.

In the center of it all the *Acolyte* was frustrated to the point of being red in the face and flailing his arms around, yelling as he tried to regain control of the situation "Fools! Stop quaking like small children! The *Traveler* is weak, he's not about to fall upon you like a thunderbolt."

Almost as if queued, lightning began striking all around them as a fierce gale picked up force and shook the surrounding trees while knocking over everything that wasn't fixed to the ground. The *Acolyte* began to mentally regret his choice of words as he was approached by one of his commanders "The *Traveler* has sent us a message; I believe he intends to make good on his threats with force! We should ready the men for an immediate attack!"

The *Acolyte* furiously replied practically spitting the words "There is NO attack! Where are his allies? There is no sign of that ship they were building! We've been watching him this entire time, he could not have prepared for such an attack in such a short time!!"

"Step 4: Unleash the horde"

Without warning a massive force emerged from the hills then unleashed a barrage of rockets, missiles, and cannons that filled the sky; the lethal projectiles arced high into the air before plunging down to their targets. Explosions rocked the compound as tightly packed groups of soldiers were blasted into the air and volatile cargo burst into flames and set off further explosions; the machines were fast to react, sending half their forces to combat the surrounding attackers while the other half attempted damage control. Sol's forces seemed less prepared and were scrambling to get to cover or were sprinting away to avoid the hail of death raining down on them.

The *Acolyte* selected one of his commanders and yelled over the carnage "You! Take your bravest men and mount a counter attack. Consider this your test Templar, should you fail you and your soldiers will be purged from Sol's vision permanently!"

The commander saluted in return and yelled to a large group of the more hardened soldiers and ran towards the source of the attacks as the veteran constructs followed his lead. The initial shock of the opening attack began to wear off, as the combined force of Sol's hardened troops and the machine *Titans* directly engaged the attack force and began steadily gaining ground, it seemed without assistance the collected dissidents were not a match against the formidable *Templars* and their machine allies.

"Step 5: Appear from nowhere"

The *Acolyte* was furious over the turn of events, being caught off guard and made a fool of by the *Traveler*, though he expected still more surprises as an ominous fact reminded: the *Traveler* and his companions remained unaccounted for. His chain of thoughts were interrupted as one of the machine *Titans* bluntly addressed him "Situation: highly precarious; underestimation of 'subject: *Traveler*' a fatal error; recommendation: imminent evacuation."

The *Acolyte* fumed upon hearing this "Coward! We are routing their forces into the hills, the *Traveler* will likely be forced to intervene to save his ragtag allies, we only need to strike when he arrives and end this insurrection once and for all! Sol's army must have no weaknesses! We shall crush this uprising and emerge victorious! We shall-"

A foreboding echo suddenly interrupted his rant, from the lake behind them a massive shadow appeared beneath the water's surface. With the force and power of a breaching whale the new "*Queen Anne's Revenge*" surfaced and crashed back into the water, the entire battle seemed to stop as the sudden appearance of the monolithic vessel caught everyone in shock.

The machine commander hesitantly began moving backwards as it summarized "Analysis: armored capital ship with submersible capability. Threat level: extreme".

The *Acolyte* furiously yelled "What are you waiting for? Fire everything you have... Now!"

The commander made a series of click and pulse noises and the nearby epic sized *Titans* directed an array of powerful weapons at the ship and simultaneously fired. Hundreds of missiles and energy beams impacted into the vessel as everything around it was obscured by explosions and particle blasts, the *Acolyte* smiled thinking their enemy came unprepared for such an onslaught, but his smile quickly became a grimace as the smoke cleared as the ship remained completely intact.

From inside the ship Teach was manning the controls laughing as he saw the awestruck faces through the view monitors, one of his lieutenants commented "Likely their steaming out the ears right now captain?"

Teach took a puff of his pipe and commented "HA! I'd venture to guess they're wetting themselves and begging a higher power to save them right about now."

Then he ordered the gunnery officer "Bring the wrath of god down on these pretentious fools! Fire all the guns, destroy it all. HA HA HA HA HA!"

As from outside the ship every shutter opened to reveal enough ordinance to safely destroy an entire city, a rising energy surge was the herald of the *Templars* doom, echoed only by the *Acolyte* yelling irrationally towards the ship.

"Step 6: Raise hell"

Like an orchestra of explosions, the compound was caught in a firestorm erupting from the "*Queen Anne's Revenge*". Within seconds the entirety of the base was up in flames or melting into smoldering ruin; the *Templars* and their machine allies lost thousands of troops and nearly their entire stockpile of supplies in a matter of seconds, though the battle was still not over.

The *Acolyte* had regained his senses and cast an impenetrable fire-shield over the force gathered around him moments before the onslaught, though decimated and reeling the remaining force was still a formidable threat, nearly all of them were now desperate and ready to fight to the death for their survival.

The *Acolyte* levitated off the ground as his eyes and hair turned bright white, still seething with frustration he fired a light wave so intense it cut straight through the *Queen Anne's Revenge*, even with its considerable armor and shields. The vessel nearly split in half as all of its systems overloaded before sputtering out, such a powerful machine destroyed by a single blast from the *Acolyte*. The main hatch of the *Queen Anne's Revenge* then opened as the *Traveler* and *Fox* stepped forward.

The *Acolyte* was glaring at them, seething with anger he had perceived these tricks like personal insults, yelling with rage "Fool! The designs of Sol cannot be so easily toppled; we shall rebuild everything you have destroyed within a fraction of the time we first assembled it. I will make this entire realm suffer for daring to oppose us; every usurping construct shall be exterminated, every place of resistance will be razed never to rise again. And I will carry out this slaughter with unrelenting glee, all because of your stupid, pathetic rebellion! But not before I kill you! You insufferable pest!!"

The *Traveler* couldn't help but start darkly laughing, clearly he had struck a nerve, and the fact that he had driven an arrogant self-righteous tyrant to such a rant was an opportunity for amusement he couldn't pass up.

You could almost hear the *Acolyte*'s teeth grinding together as he fumed "What could you possibly find amusing fool!?", the *Traveler* simply pointed skyward in response, as the clouds began suddenly dissipating.

"Step 7: Turn the tables against them"

The *Acolyte* noticed the second sun completed its transformation while obscured by the storm, yet it now emanated an odd blue light and radiated mysterious energy waves that were abnormal even for a summoned light source.

The *Acolyte* suddenly realized what had happened as he stood aghast and whispered "Of all the follies…".

The machine *Titans* began behaving strangely as the energy waves seemed to adversely affect them in particular; within only a few seconds exposure their circuits began fusing and shorting out causing them to rapidly malfunction. The *Acolyte* looked at them, then the sun, then back at them; as he realized how dire the situation was and that it would require his immediate intervention, clenching his fists he knew he had no choice but to abandon the battle, rocketing skyward to the anomalous sun.

"Step 8: Victory"

The *Traveler* and *Fox* knew this was the time to attack and charged forward, ready to deliver the finishing blow upon the wavering force; the machine *Titans* responded with counter fire, yet their degrading computers caused their weapons to be wildly inaccurate, many of the shots hitting their own forces instead.

Jack was rapidly overtaken by the *Fox*, who gathered speed while furiously yelling, showing no mercy he swiped and hacked through the crowd of stumbling opponents killing everything in reach of his pneumatic spikes and saw. The *Traveler* set his sights against the *Templars*, jumping high into the air before firing out metallic dust cloud from the improved Telekinetic devices; dust lines targeting the soldiers as he introduced a charge which erupted into several lightning bolts that arced through the crowd and electrocuted nearly everything they came in contact with. Landing in a roll he quickly recovered and fired off a series of telekinetic blasts, these attacks came far easier and with greater intensity than before, hurling foes with great speed into the air.

One of the massive machine *Titans* began thrashing its way towards Jack, pummeling everything in sight as its balance and control rapidly degraded; with one device the *Traveler* locked the giant onyx machine in an immovable stasis, with a quick flick of his opposite wrist he blasted a concentrated beam towards it, then watched as the metal and glass caved in on itself, twisting and breaking with unnatural ease, leaving only a crunched metal sphere.

The *Traveler* caught a glance of the *Fox*, still yelling as he was now firing his shoulder bound rockets simultaneously with the energy weapon he assembled earlier; each direction the *Fox* turned seemed to explode with fury, even with scores falling to his wrath it only seemed to drive the *Fox* further into a sanguine rage. The *Travelers* attention was suddenly shifted back to his own situation as several *Templars* charged forwards forming a shield wall, he took the opportunity to unsheathe his crossbow, load one of the exotic ammunition types, before sweeping across their formation holding the trigger down.

The bolts exploded upon impact, showering metal fragments in every direction; clouds of gore sprinkled the air as everything in the detonation radius stopped moving and promptly collapsed onto the ground. What few survived sprinted towards him in a desperate attempt to land a melee strike, as the *Traveler* was able to cut straight through their weapons with ease, and continue through them; freezing the enemies he had torn to pieces with a few effortless slashes of his unnervingly sharp sword.

Taking a moment to observe the chaos, the battle had become apparent: fires had engulfed the entire area, the machines were compromised and flailing to the ground, and the *Templars* were nearly all dead or dying, knowing that the result had become apparent the *Traveler* decided to end the battle. Taking a moment to concentrate an intense orb of energy into the devices he threw the compressed sphere a short distance into the air, as it exploded outwards in every direction with enough force to knock over anything that wasn't bracing for impact. Once the shock wore off, the few soldiers that remained interpreted the message immediately, without a word they dropped their weapons and cast the garments of Sol's uniform aside. Utterly routed and now defeated, the soldiers of Sol's army quietly shuffled away, the crusade in *Venture* had been utterly broken.

Jack looked at the wreckage of the "*Queen Anne's Revenge*", the effect of all that firepower on the landscape, the thousands of corpses on both sides, the sight of the battle's aftermath making him realize that he couldn't wage war on Sol without more places suffering a similar fate, hopefully he could find another way to defeat him before things spiraled into ruin.

The *Seer* appeared before Jack wearing a hastily made disguise, he began to speak "That was an interesting-" but then stopped himself hearing the wrong voice being spoken.

The Fox instructed "Take the voice piece off your throat to speak normally"

Following the *Fox*'s instructions the *Seer* peeled off an odd voice changing tab off his throat and spoke with his ordinary voice "That was an interesting show you put on boss-man; that script you had me read seemed a bit over the top, even for you."

Jack mused in a quote "All the world's a stage" and the *Seer* laughed upon hearing this quote.

From the background a mixture of swear words and ranting came Teach who was frustrated at losing yet another ship "Ye made my ship into the rock of Gibraltar and they still sliced it like a roast ham, maybe I should sod the whole pirate business entirely if me ships are going to sink twice a week."

Jack couldn't help but smirk as he thought of the irony of building a larger more armored ship, only to have it be destroyed even easier than before as he said trying not to laugh "Well this way we have an excuse to rebuild your ship the way it was"

Teach patted him hard on the back and replied "That be true, still seeing the looks on their faces after we surfaced like Neptune and flattened em with one broadside was a moment I will cherish till the end of time, if you happen to make any other ugly metal turkey's you need a captain for, I'd be happy to take em for a raid!"

The approaching figure of the *Fox* seemed to dampen the tone as he trudged towards them with a pile of parts under one arm, while dragging a large pile of components in a metal cargo net over the opposite shoulder.

Jack spoke first hoping to steer the conversation away from the topic of duels "Our attack probably broke the machines capability to fight, that solar surge may have wiped 'em out permanently."

The Fox replied with his typical cynicism "Hardly, they have contingency units deep underground for just that reason; this is a setback for them, nothing more."

Jack began to indirectly probe the question of their fight to the death "Quite a few of them were destroyed though, and the second sun obviously can't be used by them for power so..."

The Fox interrupted "If you were worried about our contract, consider it fulfilled, besides it was mostly there to keep you from backing out."

Then he added as he powered up his saw blade "Unless you wanted to fight anyway?"

Jack quickly shook his head and waved his hands in the air "No no, that's cool man. Mission accomplished. No need to start killing each other."

The Fox laughed for the first time that anyone had ever heard and replied "That was a joke *Traveler*; I don't enjoy killing organics anyway. You should continue to improve your weapons. A *Traveler's* power is meant to be second to none."

The *Seer* then said to Jack "Reckon we ought to plan our next move; you seem keen to sabotage Sol's plans in each realm, but we'll need more leads to follow to know where to go next."

Jack shrugged in response and thought aloud "Well I figured I would need to fight the *Acolyte* during that last battle, I thought maybe he would reveal something for us to go on, then we would move from there; weird that he just took off, after that rant he gave I figured he was certain to want to fight me to the death."

The *Seer* glanced up to the odd blue tinted second sun while coming up with an assumption "He left because that sun up there was his responsibility to Sol, when Sol gives you a charge like that and power to boot... well let's just say you can't just go back in front of him empty handed."

Jack laughed a moment as he recollected "Indeed, most of those distractions were only to keep his focus off the summoning so we could alter the second sun's form without him noticing; it was a good opportunity to destroy all these stockpiled materials too. I'm sure he's figured out by now that since they completed the ritual after we altered it, that the effect is irreversible without another large and elaborate ritual."

The *Fox* pondered something Jack hadn't thought of and warned "If you take away the only thing giving someone purpose and then leave them no alternatives, they are going to have nothing left... except revenge."

Jack disagreed with the *Fox*'s sentiment replying "Nah, this guy has had three easy opportunities to fight me; he just keeps sending his cronies to do all of his fighting for him, I figure he's probably fleeing the realm, pondering his options, crying in a corner-"

The *Seer*'s eyes lit up as the second sun began to pulse and shift, turning his gaze skyward the *Seer* pointed up towards it and said "There's where your grumpy *Cleric* is boss-man, stuck in the middle of that, and probably wishing he was dead about now".

Jack couldn't fathom what he was hearing, unable to even picture something entering a sun and surviving, mentally calculating the improbability of survival he asked aloud "Any chance that we've seen the last that *Cleric*?"

The *Seer* replied "We'll see him again, sure as time moves on, the only question is what form he'll take."

Jack didn't like the sound of that, but there seemed to be no urgency in the *Seer*'s words so he decided they should move on. "Let's not dwell on it then, the *Seer* and I should depart for *the Harbinger's* crash site; Teach I assume you're going to stay in *Venture*?"

Teach patted him on the shoulder and said "Aye, someone has to keep them fools from returning to wreck the place, it's been an honor working with ye lad!"

Jack reached out to shake his hand and was met with the near crushing grip from Teach in return as Jack said "When this is all over we'll have to return and celebrate"

Teach replied "Aye me boy, looking forward to it. Don't forget that ye owe me another *Queen Anne's Revenge* when this is all over" As he began laughing while walking to the wreckage of the current high-tech ship to collect his crew and return to Freeport.

Jack turned to the *Fox* and inquired "You're not going to help us rebuild the '*Harbinger*' and fight Sol?"

The Fox grumbled back "This battle's result needs to be exploited; I will see to your ship after I finish my work, it takes priority."

Jack considered pressing the point; though considering how the conversation went last time, he decided to make that concession to the *Fox* "Alright, but at least help Teach repair his ship so he can fight the return of any *Templars*" To which the *Fox* nodded in agreement.

Jack then concluded "Alright, were off then; we'll see you after your "work" is completed"

The Fox scoffed "Don't get too impatient while I'm away, my work could take some time"

Jack nodded and the *Fox* followed Teach to start repairs on the current *Queen Anne's Revenge*. Jack then tapped his earpiece as his gunship jetted in and touched down in front of them, he then entered the ship as the *Seer* stood dazed for a moment before following him inside. The gunship lifted off and shot into the horizon, taking them back to where the crisis began.

10

HARBINGER
REBORN

Taking the helm of the gunship, Jack focused on the scene of the Harbinger's crash site as their surroundings blurred and the ship leapt forward. The ship came to a stop over the endless cityscape of Mirage, yet from even a brief observation it was clear that Sol's past attack had taken a toll upon the city. City streets stood vacant and empty, many of the buildings were hollowed out ruins, and the skies were filled with dust and ash from the fires that seemed to burn eternally.

They came upon the scar in the ground carved out by the crash site; Jack was in no hurry to return to this place, his mind was already beginning to cloud with the pangs of guilt, regret, and failure, yet he had to remain focused. He set course for a landing zone as the gunship glided downwards, Jack glanced back at the *Seer* who seemed uneasy, and he wondered if perhaps it was a reaction to the sight of such devastation. The ship came to a stop a few feet away from the main bulkhead breach, once the landing door opened the *Seer* rushed out and tried to regain his bearings, Jack followed once he finished powering down the gunship.

Responding to the *Seer's* reaction Jack detailed "This level of wanton destruction, the aftermath of such a great disaster, it's difficult to take it all in."

The *Seer* seemed stunned "yes boss-man, it's tragic, the crash and all that, really brings ya down"

The *Seer's* response threw Jack off, he replied with an air of suspicion "I was actually talking about the city, is something else bothering you?"

The *Seer* paused, hesitated for a moment, then replied "I don't like flying boss man, gives me the heebe geebes"

Jack's couldn't help but find this statement humorous, ironic even "You're afraid of flying? The guy who teleports around all the time, including way up in the air; do you hold your breath or something when you're warping around? Think happy thoughts, that sorta thing?"

The *Seer* waved his hands in frustration as he trudged forward saying back over his shoulder "When I move it's all me, nothing ever goes wrong, then damn clanking machines can go right to pot for no reason at all, send you diving earth-ward in a metal coffin."

Jack continued "You realize we're here to fix this larger ship so that we can fly around in it right?"

The *Seer* replied "Don't remind me of things I'd rather not think on" as the *Seer* entered the ship and Jack followed.

The pair proceeded into the open bulkhead, they found that although the ship was still in bad shape the constructs he left behind had been busy with repairs; many of the interior panels were fixed, the lights were working again, and it looked as though many of the internal systems were once again operational.

The *Seer* seemed to be taken aback by this as he commented "From the inside you can hardly tell that it's broken down, are your constructs fixing to make this into a ship hotel?"

Jack replied "Hardly, it's more likely they lacked the materials or the expertise to fix large components like the engines."

Jack and the *Seer* proceeded further into the ship, compensating for the tilted environment; reaching the elevator Jack started assessing "Alright, if we want to get a good status report the bridge would probably be a good place to begin; afterwards we could bring the computer core online and get more precise details".

Jack tapped the button on the elevator as they rode up to the bridge, once they arrived the elevator doors opened and greeted them with the image of the wide gash at the front of the room; Jack hadn't visited the bridge since the crash, he figured this must have been one of the areas that took the brunt of the ship's impact when it crashed. As they proceeded to investigate the bridge, the *Seer*'s eyes lit up as he stopped and said "We have an unexpected guest *Traveler*"

Jack readied his weapons and raised his voice "Are they agents of Sol? How many are there?" as an obscured figure popped out from one of the control stations and Jack blasted it with a telekinetic wave knocking them down.

Jack readied another blast as he was stopped by the *Seer* who explained "Cool your jets boss-man, ain't no man of Sol's, ain't no man at all, actually." As the shadowy figure rolled over into the light and Jack saw that it was a woman dressed in a mechanic's jumpsuit.

The woman reached for something that got knocked out of her hands: a double barrel shotgun, Jack saw this and moved it out of reach with the gloves, then asked "Who are you, what are you doing in my ship?"

To which the woman rolled on her back and replied "I was about to ask you the same question".

Jack scoffed at this and inquired "Are you implying that this ship belongs to you?"

She retorted "Typically a "ship" is capable of some kind of propulsion; this is more of a salvage wreck, and being a piece of salvage it belongs to the first one that claims it, and I already have."

Jack proceeded to laugh a bit, amused by this as he continued further "You're going to claim my ship and do what exactly? Strip it for parts? Is it too presumptuous to assume it's a collector's item?"

The woman seemed to recover from the initial shock of the telekinetic wave so she got back up on her feet and explained "It's a unique item, and has greater value intact rather than scrapped; when I saw the interior I figured I'd survey the damage, see just how doable a repair would be."

Amused Jack smirked and asked "And what is your…professional assessment."

She frowned a bit and retorted "don't patronize me bub, and for your information it's a total wreck; the interior looks nice but all the systems are shot and many of the critical components are destroyed without any replacement parts, the only way this tub is going anywhere is if it's pushed down a hill."

Jack reached out with his hand and imagined one of the components coming to form, it appeared in a quick flash of light as he remarked "…I might have a way to get those spare parts"

Seeing Jack perform the trick seemed to pique the woman's curiosity, so she asked "Just who are you supposed to be anyway?"

Jack scoffed a bit and replied "Well I designed the ship that we're standing in for one; more importantly though, I happen to be the *Traveler*".

The woman rolled her eyes and scoffed "Well you being the ship designer certainly explains a lot, though I don't believe for a second that you're the *Traveler*."

Jack sensed some criticism from the first part of her statement, he was already used to the latter part, as he quipped "What is that supposed to mean, you saying my ship is poorly designed?"

She explained "That'd be a graceful way of saying it; a more honest assessment would be that it was built to fail.

She began detailing: "There is only one friggen engine without any backups; meaning that if anything happens to it the whole thing dives into a death spiral. You have armor plating, but no damage control systems, nor even proper access tunnels to maintenance critical systems. The entire energy grid is built into one gigantic trunk-line, so if it gets interrupted at any point the entire thing chokes up and surges. Worst of all it this ship is so wide and slow that any gun could hit it and it couldn't even get outta the way."

Jack knew that his design was overly basic in some regards, but he hadn't until this point heard it all put together in such a stinging critique before.

Jack considered trying to defend his design but decided to take a different approach "Normally I'd argue those points, but I sense that you wouldn't be insisting on taking ownership of this ship unless you saw some value in it; I'll get to the point, perhaps we can make a deal miss?"

As the woman tried to hide her interest in the proposition and replied "…Maybe, and my name is Sarah, Sarah Derringer"

Jack and the *Seer* listened as Sarah listed out all the major components that needed to be fixed, parts that were missing, upgrades to consider, and estimated time table for repairs. Jack after hearing all this, knew that she would want something in return so stated "So what's in it for you? What do you get out of all this?"

Sarah's face took on a serious look as she bluntly said "I get to take the ship"

Jack interrupted "Why would I help you repair my ship and then turn around and hand it back to you."

Sarah explained "You need to use this ship, but it needs repairs, I know how to fix things but I have no way of getting ahold of the parts; I help you repair your ship, then when it's finished the ship will be mine and I'll let you borrow it."

The *Seer* smiled and commented "Oh I like her already boss-man."

Jack shrugged and detailed "Were going to need to use it for quite a while, taking it to many dangerous locations, and fighting against formidable constructs that could easily destroy it."

Sarah laughed as she confidently said "You mean they could easily destroy your ship, once I'm finished upgrading it there won't be anything natural or man-made that can touch it; besides, if you really are the *Traveler* you can just wave your hands in the air and make another one."

Jack frowned slightly and remarked "There is a bit more to it than that."

As the *Seer* laughed and added "He has to think on it real hard while waving his hands in the air, then he makes another one."

Sarah crossed her arms and reiterated "I think you need this tub working again badly enough that you're willing to accept these terms, do we have a deal?"

Jack shrugged and replied "You don't even know our names"

Sarah rolled her eyes in response as she sighed and said "Let's keep the introductions short, I'm not much of a people person, let's start with the geezer, who's he?"

The *Seer* got defensive upon hearing this "Geezer? I aint that old yet, as for who I am; I've been described as a thief, a liar, and a con-man, yet I also happen to be the *Seer*."

Sarah remarked "Well at least you're honest… about being a liar, for whatever that's worth. How about you with the man-portable arsenal and the weird gloves, don't say you're the *Traveler* again because I already think you're full of it."

Jack smiled and reached out to shake her hand "You can call me Jack, now let's get to work."

Jack, the *Seer*, and Sarah made their way to the computer core to power it up to aid their troubleshooting, in the background figures seemed to observe the party's movements but were careful to remain out of view; the *Seer* noticed them and was about to call out, but was interrupted by Jack who quietly explained "Those are the soldier constructs I left behind, let them think they've gone unnoticed, we'll confront them when the time is right."

Reaching the computer core they viewed the large onyx orb with its intricate pattern of circuits and lights, now powered down. Jack approached the center terminal, focused on thoughts of energy and then slammed his palm into the console; the entire room seemed to surge with electricity, many wires spewing sparks and a few displays burning out as the orb came alive and the working control panels slowly illuminated to full brightness.

Jack then queried "Eleanor, give me a holographic display of all critical systems, highlight damaged areas in red"

Sarah replied "Who in the hell is Eleanor?" As the computer projectors constructed a 3D image of *the Harbinger* in front of them, with various systems highlighted in different colors along with the requested damage reports overlaid in red.

Sarah noticed something important in the information as she approached the image and pointed "Alright, see that big line going from the bow to stern? That's the trunk-line, your primary power conduit; now as you can see the ship suffered a big impact that severed it, causing all the systems to short out and overload. Sometime after that the ship took a second impact and that finished the ship off, causing a cascading catastrophic system failure."

Jack commented "How could you know all that if you weren't here?"

Sarah replied while observing "I'm reading the evidence, and these damage reports are practically like a narrative on what happened."

The computer verified "Sarah's damage assessment is accurate to ship records; power failures and severed conduits currently prevent restoration of primary systems."

Sarah seemed thrown off as she asked "How does the computer know my name, and why is it responding to questions we're not asking directly"

The computer replied "I am Eleanor, the ship's artificial intelligence."

This admission spooked Sarah "Oh no no no, this will end badly, the smart kind of computers always end up seizing control from you and-"

The *Seer* interrupted "Preaching to the choir, but that already happened a ways ago."

Sarah frowned and hesitantly asked "…And were still using it? That seems kinda stupid? Why are we doing something that stupid?"

Jack rubbed his forehead and explained "Almost all the ships systems were designed to be automated, save for command and authorization of major systems; without the computer core we would need a crew of hundreds or even thousands to operate the ship."

Sarah reluctantly acquiesced "Erm ok I guess, well for starters we need to repair the existing trunk line; we should also make auxiliary backup conduits as well, that way the ship has layers of redundancy and can continue operating after sustaining damage"

As if by command a nearby printer turned on a printed off a number of reports, Sarah hesitantly retrieved them and after glancing over them explained "Huh, a detailed repair report and suggestions for placement of possible auxiliary lines."

Jack smiled and pointed at the computer core as Sarah stared back with slight irritation before admitting "Alright fine, we'll use the computer. There's still a lot we'll need to physically do, so I suggest you summon up some tools, we've got a big list of things that needs fixing."

Moving throughout the ship Jack and Sarah started making progress on the repairs, replacing broken parts, rebuilding wrecked sections of the frame, and adding small augmentations to operating efficiency where possible.

The newly added precision of the telekinetic gloves allowed Jack to move and adjust even large and cumbersome objects with a high degree of exactness; this made some of the larger repairs far easier than expected. Sarah seemed to know more about the ship than Jack did, always rattling off details of each device and possible improvements, he considered asking how she came to know so much on the subject, but a good opportunity never came up.

Working throughout the ship they seemed to have many of the small to moderate repairs finished, many of the systems had been patched up, and *the Harbinger* was starting to resemble a complete ship rather than a salvage wreck; however the worst part of the damage remained: the damage from the two impact sites. Although they had managed to reconnect everything using jury rigged supports and haphazard workarounds, the physical damage was very extensive, and still needed to be totally rebuilt.

Jack and Sarah were perched upon the edge of one of the upper decks exposed by the impact, Sarah seemed to be analyzing the damage and milling over possibilities.

Jack inquired "Stuck on what to do next?"

Sarah explained "Not stuck, thinking; this sorta damage can mothball a ship permanently, I'm considering options. We'd almost need to move this thing into a ship yard to rebuild this much damage; either that or find some crazy heavy-duty salvaging equipment…"

The *Seer* teleported in and said "*The Fox* just arrived boss-man, seems to be sporting some new additions courtesy of whatever poor soul he took apart."

Sarah seemed wide eyed at this as she commented "I didn't think you were desperate enough to work with that psycho! What did you have to go through to get him on-board?"

The *Seer* casually explained in response "Nothing much, just blowing up a whole army with the contingency of a death match if it went sideways."

Jack tried to reassure both of them "His submarine was very effective, and technically we've already helped him so he kind of owes us."

The *Seer* said with criticism "I doubt he'll stand on principle boss-man, this is the same guy who straps dead things to his person, and probably fantasizes all day about new ways to kill."

Jack smirked and replied "Hey I'm trusting you aren't I? Let's go talk to him, I don't want to keep him waiting very long."

As he proceeded towards the elevator and the *Seer* retorted while following him in "Don't lump me in with his lot, I ain't one of the crazy ones".

Jack and the *Seer* reached the loading bay as the *Fox* examined the surroundings, Jack greeted him first "Thanks for coming; I thought your "work" would take longer to complete."

As the *Fox* continued scanning, replying while half distracted "I work faster alone; once I traced and analyzed their movements it led me to most of their hidden enclaves. Destroying their reinforced underground bunkers was the only challenge."

Jack wondered "Does that mean you've beaten them for good?"

The *Fox* stated matter-of-factly "85% of their forces are destroyed, including their critical hive-core, it's only a matter of routing out their redundant contingencies... which is currently being take care of remotely, thanks to something I created from the... 'spare parts' you left behind from the last battle."

Jack could sense a certain satisfaction in the *Fox*'s tone and inquired "You seem to enjoy your work a bit too much"

The *Fox* replied "It is what I exist for *Traveler*"

The *Fox* then pointed out some of the repairs with his scanning beam and asserted "These repairs were not conducted by you *Traveler*, who else is here, their work is familiar".

Sarah entered the room and answered before Jack could explain "You know who it is already, have you found a break in your busy killing schedule to be here?"

The Fox replied with some familiarity in his voice as he addressed her "Sarah, didn't think you had the guts to be here; I would normally ask if you're afraid of death but I already know the answer to that."

The *Seer* jokingly commented "Y'all talking like old married folks, and I woulda guessed you had no friends' salvager."

Jack wanted an explanation and cut in "You two have history? What's the problem?"

The Fox explained "We worked together on a few projects, then Sarah got cold feet and ran."

Sarah corrected "Projects, you mean weapon components; how many bystanders were killed when you used them on the machines?"

The Fox retorted in a deadpan way "Only the ones who collaborated with them, your little sabotage stunt disappointed me Sarah; you had a lot of potential, but it was wasted by your lack of initiative."

Jack intervened "Whatever happened is over and done, put it past you."

The Fox turned his back on Sarah and replied "I didn't have a personal investment; Sarah's the one that ran"

Sarah added "I put it behind me a long time ago Jack, let's just get on with it."

Jack nodded and concluded "Good, we have a larger problem to solve anyway-"

The Fox interrupted "Large hull breaches; you're considering ways to repair them."

Jack asked "Do you have a solution?"

The Fox trudged towards the elevator and replied over his shoulder "something I recently acquired, follow me."

Jack, Sarah, and the *Seer* followed the *Fox* to the exposed deck at the top of the impact site; the *Fox* scanned the severity of the damage before assessing aloud "Primary systems are already re-routed, the bulkheads need to be rebuilt along with the frame."

Sarah sarcastically replied "Tell us something we don't know"

The Fox ignored her and retrieved a strange transmitter; before anyone inquired about it he turned it on, set the frequency, and then activated it.

The ground began to shake as screeching echoes were heard approaching from a distance.

Jack yelled over the sudden chaos "What the hell did you just do?"

The Fox said over his shoulder "I called my reinforcements."

A few moments later dozens of car-sized metallic insects began emerging from the ground, with glowing red eyes, powerful hydraulic legs, reinforced plated exoskeletons, and an array of tools and devices in the place of faces.

Jack nervously readied his weapons as the *Fox* stopped him "I control the drones, don't do anything stupid" Jack decided to keep his cool, putting away his weapons to see what was about to happen.

The several dozen robotic insects soon became hundreds, as it wasn't long before they covered the ship, arranged in a semi-circle before the *Fox*.

The Fox adjusted the transmitter as it send out a series of pulse and click noises, similar to what Jack remembered the hunter-seeker units using to communicate; after the message was relayed all the insects screeched in unison, seeming to agree, and then busily set to work reassembling the frame and forging the parts back together.

Sarah pointed nervously at the insects and half-hysterically yelled "So just what the hell are those supposed to be!"

The Fox explained "Maintenance and repair drones, designed and programmed to work in swarms, they possess no intelligence beyond rudimentary animal instincts; the machine *Titans* use them to service their network of underground bunkers."

Jack inquired "Why haven't we seen these before? And more importantly how did you get to control them?"

The Fox detailed "These are non-combat models, so there is no reason we would have encountered them before, as for how I acquired them...I used the *Titan's* transmitters, left behind from our last battle on *Venture*, to decipher and reprogram the *Titans* command and control signal for their drones.

The *Seer* caught on to what he was saying and further detailed "Meaning he turned the monster against their creators"

Jack rubbed his head and lamented "Someone who hates machines, using machines... to destroy other machines. You realize that makes you a hypocrite right?"

The Fox asserted "War isn't about being morally right, it's about winning, I will use any means at my disposal to eliminate the machines, even their own pawns."

Groaning in frustration over the *Fox's* usual cold logic Jack decided to change the subject "...Alright, how long until the drones are finished with the repairs"

Sarah nudged him and pointed towards the drones, as Jack looked and saw that the repairs were already finished, then he admitted reluctantly "Wow, they're actually quite efficient little buggers aren't they?"

The Fox added "That's why I haven't destroyed them yet" then he trudged back towards the elevator and handed Jack a computer tablet on his way through.

Jack shrugged and asked "What is this?"

As the *Fox* stepped in front of the elevator and pressed the call button, saying over his shoulder "A list of upgrades and repairs that are still needed, the drones will be handling it"

Jack raised an eyebrow and replied "Do I get any say in this?"

As the elevator arrived and the *Fox* stepped inside, turning around and answering "Unless you want me to undo the repairs the drones have performed, then no. If something important comes up, I will be in the cargo bay."

As the elevator doors shut and the *Fox* rode the elevator back down. The *Seer* turned to Jack and said "Why is it that everyone we meet nowadays has to be the cold shoulder type?"

Jack laughed and replied "Overly friendly people usually just irritate me, at least with introverts you don't have to deal with as much pretentious crap"

Sarah nodded "I can agree with that... but hey Jack on the subject of upgrades there are a few more extensive improvements I would like to suggest now that the repairs are finished."

Jack smiled and replied "Are you going to tell me to 'shove it' if I say no?"

Sarah had a slight laugh and replied "I'd like to, but I'm not a fan of being blasted across rooms by telekinetic gloves."

Everyone in the room laughed for a moment and then Jack said "Alright, well what sort of improvements do you have in mind?"

The Harbinger began to take on new shape, as giant wings were being added to accommodate a pair of massive auxiliary thrusters that Sarah was busily designing, while Jack conjuring parts for it and assembling it with the aid of his telekinetic gloves; many large cranes and scaffolds were being constructed to both lift the ship out of the impact crater, and hold the new additions in place so they could be grafted on.

At a more subtle level, Jack and Sarah had installed a number of redundant energy conduits and auxiliary systems that would activate should damage occur to the primary systems of the ship, this would ensure that *the Harbinger* would continue to function even if many of its systems were badly damaged.

The Fox's eerie insect drones were also hard at work adding the weapons and defensive systems to the outer frame, it looked as if a series of electron manipulators would form an electric shield when deployed, and on the weapons side a giant magnetic accelerator was being added into the entire length of the ship, powerful enough to fire building sized slugs that could destroy entire cities upon impact. It looked as if the new *Harbinger* would be faster, more agile, and far more deadly; Jack wondered in the back of his mind if they would have to face the *Dauntless* again, the ship that engaged them over *Mirage* before Sol appeared.

Taking a break on top of one of the large debris piles, Jack took a moment to admire the sight of *the Harbinger's* reconstruction from a distance. He recollected how he thought he'd never use the ship again, yet he was compelled to return and rebuild it; he realized that the ship and he were connected, and so long as there was a purpose for him to fulfill in the *Astral Plane* it would involve this ship of his, just as most of his fighting often revolved around the telekinetic gloves.

Jack suddenly caught sight of Sarah who approached with a clipboard as she spoke optimistically "All the upgrades are nearly finished, all that's left is to lift the sucker out of that hole and power up the engines."

Jack got up and replied "You're forgetting we have an entire hangar bay with no pilots, we need to reinstate the crew"

Sarah seemed puzzled "Reinstate the wha- I thought you said it was all automated?"

Jack smiled and continued walking, as Sarah threw up her hands and reluctantly followed him. Boarding the ship, Jack headed for the hangar bay, the place where he last talked with the soldier constructs, entering the massive hangar he found the room darkened by many disabled lights and cluttered by an unusual number of deployed fighters.

Sarah became nervous at the foreboding atmosphere, as the *Seer* suddenly appeared behind them "Do I finally get to meet your associates boss-man? The suspense is killing me"

This startled Sarah who spun and around and said with irritation "Don't just suddenly appear in a dark room, it's weird"

The *Seer* smiled and waved a hand in front of his face "Ma'am, in case it slipped your attention, all the rooms are 'dark rooms' to me"

See took a moment, looked at his cloudy eyes then slowly replied "Oh... sorry. You see to get around so well I didn't even notice"

The *Seer* laughed and replied "Don't worry your head on it, I'm just having fun."

Jack walked over to the control console and stood there for a moment, like he was waiting for something; then in a flurry pressed a quick sequence of buttons which brought all the lights to full brightness and caused cranes to remove all the fighters from the room. The soldier constructs were now revealed in the center of the room, dazed at their sudden lack of hiding areas.

The *Seer* nudged Sarah and quietly said "Incoming soapbox moment, make sure not to interrupt him, he hates that."

Jack said in a raised voice to reach the entire room "Soldier constructs, crew of *the Harbinger*, I call you to order! When last we met I left you with an impossible task, I did this out of frustration so that I might enact my retribution once you failed. I have returned to rectify this mistake and resurrect this ship that was cast down. You stated that your purpose is to serve, well serve this ship as its crew; make its operation and protection your perfection. Earn your redemption and find renewed purpose in this task. What do you say?"

The soldier constructs filed in front of him and kneeled onto one knee, then in unison replied "We accept, *Traveler* and master of *the Harbinger*, we stand ready to serve."

Jack swept his arm across the room for emphasis and yelled "Crew! Man your stations! *The Harbinger* rises today, never to be struck down again!" as they saluted him in return and ran to their respective stations.

Jack turned around and for once seemed satisfied as the *Seer* laughed and commented "Feels good to be back, eh boss-man?"

Jack laughed and replied "It's been a while, bringing my ship back from the brink is one of the few positives I've had lately."

Sarah meanwhile was shaking her head and muttered "You say the ship is automated, but you also have a crew; you literally trade rights of your ship away but you already had the *Fox*'s help, I swear Jack you don't seem to have any clue what you want or how to go about it."

Jack patted her on the shoulder and replied "I tend to make it up as I go, besides wouldn't it be folly to try and plan in a place where things are literally guided by random imagination?"

Sarah frowned a bit and wasn't really sure how to reply to something she perceived as so irrational, as the Jack continued "Unfortunately we still don't have any leads on where we should go next to fight Sol"

The *Seer* replied "It'll likely make itself clear when we need it to boss-man"

Jack shrugged and replied "Well we can at the very least leave this depressing crater, let's get to the bridge." As the *Seer* and Sarah nodded and followed him onto the elevator.

11

CONSUMING

FIRE

ON THE BRIDGE, JACK COULD SCARCELY BELIEVE THE TRANSITION THE Harbinger had undertaken. Polished computers and readouts replaced blown-out dust caked ones; bright lights and polished surfaces took the place of darkened dank interiors, and the sight and sounds of constructs busily manning their stations and operating the ship supplanted the empty creaking interiors of the old wreck. It was as if they had been transported to another place entirely.

Sarah and the *Seer* stood behind him, waiting to see what his next move would be; Jack spotted the master control earpiece on the arm of the captain's chair.

Jack walked over and retrieved the control saying "This earpiece takes commands from the user and reads what the captain needs the ship to do, this device will allow you to command the entire ship from any location, so as part of our previous agreement I give this to you Sarah Derringer."

Sarah was at a loss for words as she hesitated for a moment, before reaching out and retrieving the earpiece while nodding in gratitude.

Jack continued "This ship was built from the designs of my subconscious and draws its energy from my will to power; therefore, it may fail should I fall in battle, please use this ship to ensure that does not occur."

Sarah reached out to shake his hand, which was received by Jack as she promised "You got it Jack, and thanks."

After which Jack addressed the computer and said "Eleanor, please transfer authorization and control to Sarah Derringer, effective immediately, only to be relinquished voluntarily or upon untimely death."

Upon hearing this Sarah elbowed Jack and commented "Oi, don't tempt fate Jack."

As the computer confirmed "Yes Jack, Sarah Derringer is now the acting captain; all systems are standing by and ready."

Sarah tapped the earpiece and said "Activate lift cranes, get *the Harbinger* onto level ground and out of this crater, shift engines to vertical mode and prepare for takeoff."

The *Seer's* eyes lit up as he suddenly stepped forward "Boss-man, that grumpy *Cleric* from *Venture* is on his way here." As the sky started to shift and surge, foreshadowing the impending arrival of his foe from before.

Jack was trying to mentally formulate a plan as he asked for a status update "Sarah, how soon can you get us out of here"

She replied "Not soon enough, it's going to take a few minutes to get out of this hole, then a few more to take off."

Jack knew what he needed to do as he bolted for the elevator yelling back over his shoulder "I'm going to get out there and buy you some time; no matter what happens keep the ship moving, I'm not losing it again" as he got onto the elevator and tapped the button to the bottom floor.

Jack could feel the entire ship move as it was slowly lifted by the oversized cranes they had erected earlier; he figured he could exit via the cargo elevator while they were above the ground. Reaching the cargo bay he sprinted for the elevator controls running past the *Fox*, quickly summarizing "The *Acolyte* from *Venture* is on his way here, I think he is out for revenge."

The *Fox* asked in return "Will you need assistance *Traveler*?"

Jack responded firmly "No, I started this and I need to end it."

The *Fox* replied "I understand, make sure to survive *Traveler*."

As Jack nodded in return and tapped the cargo lift button, lowering him to the space under the ship, he got a brief glimpse of the colossal size of *the Harbinger* while surrounded by the booming sound of the engines powering up. The elevator reached the ground as Jack stepped off and the tether began to retrieve it. A loud echo signaled that the cranes had reached the top as the entire ship shifted as it was moved out of view to the side; Jack turned his eyes skyward, he expected that the *Acolyte* would arrive shortly.

A singularity of energy suddenly formed as clouds of plasma burst forth from it and filled the sky, as the energy and mass increased exponentially it began to coalesce into a blue sphere, the second sun of *Venture*.

Jack suddenly heard the voice of the *Seer* inside his head warning "Get behind something solid boss-man, the grumpy *Cleric* is going to make what you'd call a 'dramatic entrance'."

Jack tried to reply mentally by thinking the words "Where is he, all I see is the second-"

As the roar of a massive explosion cut him off. Jack flew off his feet with only a slight glimpse of what occurred, from the corner of his eye he saw the blue sun explode into a single intense mass; that mass shot out and landed in the center of the impact crater sending a shockwave that blasted everything back.

Jack's vision was still blurry, he propped himself up, dizzy and disoriented as his ears still rang from the intensity of the explosion. He saw a lone figure standing in the blast crater: the *Acolyte*, the light around the old man shifted and distorted nearby as his sheer presence seemed to alter the world around him; flames and energy radiated from him with an intensity Jack had not seen or felt since Sol first opened the distortion over *Mirage*.

The *Acolyte* turned towards the *Traveler*, light emanating from what used to be eye sockets as he whispered in a voice that boomed with power "You have taken everything from me *Traveler*, now we will settle this contest you began."

Jack readied a strong wave from his telekinetic gloves then blasted it forward at full strength, the blast wave carried forward with enough intensity to ripple across the ground, yet it suddenly lost all potency just short of the *Acolyte*, harmlessly washing over him.

The *Acolyte* directed plasma clouds into his arms while yelling fanatically, Jack sprinted to his side as energy clouds impacted just short of hitting him. Explosion after explosion rang out as the plasma clouds unleashed white-hot infernos that melted the dirt below them into glass, Jack was moving as fast as humanly possible but was barely able to stay ahead of the firestorm. There was a sudden break in the *Acolyte*'s attack as Jack decided to try another counter, quickly he fired the magnetic dust clouds towards his opponent and yet they too arced away at the last second causing the incoming lightning to move harmlessly around the target.

The *Acolyte* braced himself against the ground and then opened his mouth wide enough to unhinge his jaw; before Jack could figure out what was occurring a wave of fire erupted from the *Acolyte*'s mouth heading towards him. Thinking quickly he blasted a telekinetic force wall forwards as the fire as it split off and landed safely away on either side. The fire suddenly ceased as Jack saw another opening; seeing how his ranged attacks had done nothing thus far he dashed forward unsheathing his sword instead.

Lunging forward Jack thrust his sword forward like a piercing skewer, but something impossible happened: he was stuck in some sort of force field, but not the type that his telekinetic gloves emitted, this one was clearly affecting gravity and time. Jack could tell he was still moving forward, but at such a pace slow enough that even a dull witted person would be able to avoid with time to spare.

Trapped in a gravity effect that surrounded his enemy, Jack yelled in frustration "What the hell is this!? What are you!!"

The *Acolyte's* eyes lit up again, he turned and faced Jack saying almost in a riddle "I am the all-consuming fire, my soul has given into the storm as my life's candle burns like a flare; I guide the inferno forward as it draws off my destruction, yet before the inevitable end I will see one purpose fulfilled: retribution."

Jack's eyes widened as the *Acolyte* collected the fire into a condensed energy beam, he directed his palm forward towards Jack ready to sear the *Traveler* in half!

CRACK! KABLAM!

Jack opened his eyes in shock as he saw that the energy wave had been directed away in the nick of time by the *Seer* shoving the *Acolyte* to the side. The *Seer* then kicked Jack out of the gravity well effect, causing him to tumble backwards safely onto the ground.

The *Acolyte* fumed as he grabbed the *Seer* by the back of the collar and yelled with an echo "The stray dog, I will deal with you after the errant *Traveler*".

The *Acolyte* then tossed him with inhuman strength into one of the crater walls, the *Seer* impacted with enough force to shatter bones. Jack yelled to where the *Seer* had landed "*Seer*! Old man. Are you still alive!!"

But received no answer, he could also see no movement coming from the *Seer*. Jack was gritting his teeth as his eyes quivered with rage, he pointed towards the *Acolyte* and yelled "I don't care how much power you have or how angry you are, I will find a way to beat this, and then I will end you!"

The *Acolyte* narrowed his gaze and replied "What little strength you have will wither and burn before the flame, I will extend the power outwards and then suffer your insolence no longer."

The *Acolyte* reached out with both arms as his gravity field spread outwards, encompassing the entire crater. Jack immediately noticed that the field was not as strong as when he was near the *Acolyte* before, but it would still slow his movements considerably.

The *Acolyte* readied another beam attack as he said "Say a prayer in hope of salvation, because I will end this now!" Jack could only think of one way out, the idea was crazy but it was all he could think of; so he readied the telekinetic gloves and kept his hands in close. The beam fired out as Jack blasted himself with a telekinetic wave propelling him out of the way like a rocket; Jack impacted into one of the rock walls, but the dampening effect of the gravity well caused him to be paradoxically unharmed despite the impact. Jack felt that some of the energy from the telekinetic wave he blasted himself with had somehow been absorbed by him, perhaps by some previously unknown function of the telekinetic devices.

The *Acolyte* stood for a moment in disbelief and then yelled at the sky in anger; his entire body erupted in flames as he gazed back towards the *Traveler* and readied a furious barrage. Thinking fast Jack blasted the wall behind him and let the opposing force carry him forward, as he steered himself through the air with a combination of self-blasts and reflective blasts off the crater walls. The scene was pure chaos as Jack bounced around like a human pinball with a combination of flames, plasma, and energy beams erupting around him like an intense up-close fireworks show.

The *Acolyte* suddenly hunched over, the light in his eyes flickering as his face sunk and the fire around him warped and twisted, clearly he had over-extended himself. Jack took a moment to learn from the previous encounter, he recalled feeling some of the energy absorb into him each time he blasted the wave towards himself; then he suddenly had a realization as he said aloud "If I can absorb the telekinetic energy, then I can also conduct it."

Jack collected a blast-wave into his gloves, held the energy out, and then slowly directed it into his chest. His entire body felt electrified, an energy current supercharged his reactions and perceptions as wind materialized in a gale around him. The *Acolyte* recovered from his fatigue and blasted an intense fireball towards the *Traveler*; Jack tapped his foot against the ground as a force wave propelled him suddenly and powerfully upwards. Jack was sailing through the air like he had been launched out of a catapult, he basked in the moment, and then directed his hands back and fired a directed wave backwards; the second wave propelled him forwards like a screeching jet engine, he impacted into the ground hard enough to deepen the crater as the shockwave suddenly extinguished the existing fires. Jack recovered quickly, his telekinetic aura taking most of the impact; yet he could tell that the last maneuver had exhausted his remaining charge, and that he would need to absorb another wave.

The *Acolyte* turned towards where the *Traveler* landed and spoke "Your power is great, but against the force of an exploding star what hope can there be?"

As the *Acolyte* retracted the gravity wave to a close sphere around him, it became more intense than before as it suddenly ignited into flame; from each of the Acolytes hands a spear of energy and plasma appeared, the power of each sun spear looking as intense as the bolts previously fired at the *Traveler*.

Jack readied his sword knowing a melee contest was imminent, he answered the *Acolyte*'s previous question "Against an angered *Traveler*, no force is great enough!"

The *Acolyte* flew towards Jack, swiping downwards with both the oversized sun spears; Jack blocked the attack with an overhead thrust of his sword, the blade's frost was not strong enough to repel the sun spears as it rapidly turned bright red and started to warp. Jack collected a blast wave and brushed it against the back of his sword as a telekinetic wave vented off the blade with a blast of cold ice which propelled the sun spears back.

Then Jack rolled backwards and collected a blast wave in his opposite hand, he recovered as the *Acolyte* rushed forward with another stab as Jack directed the telekinetic energy into the sword, sweeping it across as a blizzard surged forward and pushed the *Acolyte*'s attack backwards.

The *Acolyte* yelled in a powerful voice "Enough!!" stabbing both the spears into the ground as their surroundings began to dangerously rise in temperature; Jack realized that everything was about to burst into flames as he quickly thought of a solution, he brushed his gloves across the ice blade and quickly formed a shield around himself. As predicted everything around them burst into flames as the fire seemed to emit from every direction.

Jack kept one glove emitting his ice shield as he examined the fire and determined "There must be a way to beat this... how would I deal with a normal fire... not enough water to extinguish it, that leaves strangling the air supply..."

Jack suddenly realized a solution: "That's it! A vacuum blast: no oxygen, no fire".

As he directed the opposite glove forward and blasted a large vacuum attack into the center of the crater; the entirety of the fire fizzled out as the air suddenly imploded into the vacuum. Jack lowered his ice shield and uplifted a large glass shard from the ground, then fired it at the *Acolyte* through the vacuum. The shard picked up speed moving through the vacuum before shooting out the opposite side; the shard nearly collided as the *Acolyte* smashed it to pieces with a swipe of his sun spears. Yet upon second glance Jack saw that many of the shards had managed to knick him, including across his face; Jack suddenly realized what happened and why the shard needed to be blocked, he knew how to beat the *Acolyte*.

The *Acolyte* swung his spears wildly at Jack in frustration, now blind with rage and desperation. Jack easily avoided the swings and jumped backwards far enough to give him space to operate, then in rapid succession fired a number of force vacuum blasts into a pattern around the *Acolyte*; the blazing gravity field around the *Acolyte* became distorted and greatly weakened by this, as he glared at the *Traveler* and yelled with an intense fury, but Jack did not care.

Directing an intense telekinetic orb on himself, Jack absorbed the energy, and then speaking with force he yelled "Witness the death of a sun!!"

Jack accelerated forward like a missile, breaking the sound barrier as he cleared the Acolytes shield and impacted into him like a man-sized bullet. The combination sound of the sonic boom and several layers of rock shattering simultaneously made the entire area tremble; Jack hitting the *Acolyte* hard enough to cause an earthquake that rippled through *Mirage*!

After the dust settled Jack stood over the broken *Acolyte*, who was alive only due to his incredible power, rapidly wasting away as the fire began to reach its limit and fizzle out. The Acolytes eyes returned to normal as the flames that granted him power began to ebb away, he began coughing uncontrollably.

The *Traveler* readied his sword and said "This is for the *Seer*" raising his blade for the final stab.

A hand caught his downward stab and stopped him from finishing off the *Acolyte*, Jack looked to his side and suddenly recognized the *Seer*'s face.

Jack asked in surprise "But I saw you impact with the rocks, there's no way you could have withstood that…"

The *Seer* smiled and explained "I wouldn't be much of a trickster if I couldn't substitute a fake for an original" as he demonstrated by teleporting out and returning standing next to a battered training dummy dressed up like the *Seer*.

Jack suddenly realized what occurred and replied "You teleported a dummy in your place before the impact? Wow, I didn't think you were that fast."

The *Seer* brushed off the dust on his clothes and said "Always keep them guessing boss-man, that's how you win."

The *Acolyte* spoke up, breathless and in pain "Why did you attack us so relentlessly *Traveler*? What great crime did we commit to earn your fury?"

Jack's had an awestruck look on his face, he couldn't believe the *Acolyte* was so deluded; he replied back like a man trying to convince someone of their insanity "Your machine allies stripped mined *Venture*, plundered it for everything they could get,… and you ask what crime earned my fury?"

The *Acolyte* laughed a bit to himself and replied "Have you learned nothing from your debacle on Epic *Traveler*, things are not as they appear; *Venture* is and always has been limitless, it is the only realm you can harness such great resources and never cause any detrimental impact. Sol planned to use such great resources to rebuild the *Astral Plane*; his vision was for a greater realm where construct and creator could stand as equals."

Jack pointed back at the *Acolyte* and glared "What of the sacrifice? I saw the village your machines destroyed, how many innocents were slain to build your pretense."

The *Acolyte* retorted "Innocents? None! Only the stubborn and foolish opposed us; those villagers choose fighting over diplomacy, and your brigand friends were interested only in stealing from us, nothing more."

Jack countered with his own assertions "Answer me this, why do you follow Sol so blindly; what if everything he told you is a deception, what if you're all indoctrinated by him."

The *Acolyte* stared off in recollection "Sol is the only one who gave any of us a chance, before the crusade I was a cast down and broken construct; I went from a general of great renown to an example of failure and shame. In the time before my fall I had wealth, influence, and the respect of an entire kingdom; I devoted my entire life to my sovereign's instructions, fulfilling his actions without hesitation or forethought. During a crucial battle I made a single error in judgement, a misreading of the enemies movements which cost us the battle, and that single mistake was all that was required for everything to be ripped away from me..."

The *Acolyte* started coughing uncontrollably, he was mortally wounded and these would likely be his final words "I was cast down, broken, and lost in the specter of failure; I was willing to do anything to win back my old life... Sol offered me that chance."

Jack shook his head and replied "No, you were being manipulated by him; his army is built upon outcasts and downtrodden, those with nothing left to lose and a lingering vendetta against the present order of things. Despair leaves them susceptible to Sol's suggestions, haunted by the possibility of returning to their old desperation they drive themselves forward more than any threat of force."

The fire that was sustaining the *Acolyte* began to leave him as he said "We joined Sol because he gave us the opportunity to rebuild ourselves, rebuild our lives, but we continue following him because we are a part of something greater: his grand vision for the *Astral Plane*. Should we emerge victorious we will win a future that few could even imagine."

The *Acolyte* began rapidly drifting off; he retrieved a letter from his robe and finished "Sol gave me a message, he told me to deliver it in the event you defeated me; it's an invitation from Sol, should you accept it his offer it will usher forth a new *Astral Plane*... consider it wisely" the *Acolyte* then closed his eyes and fell silent, the lingering flame flickering for a moment before disappearing entirely.

Jack retrieved the letter and replied "Goodbye *Acolyte*, may you find closure in death."

Jack undid the seal on the letter and read the words aloud "The next act unfolds at the *Palace of Eternity*, the conflict's result will become apparent long before its conclusion; I shall extend my invitation upon the battlefield. Meditate on your options and carefully contemplate your decision. –Sol"

With that the words faded off the page and the paper rapidly burned up. Jack turned towards the *Seer* and asked "It sounds as if Sol is leading us into a trap"

The *Seer* thought for a moment and replied "Not likely boss-man, the *Palace of Eternity* is where the head honchos of the *Astral Plane* hold court; more likely he's moving against em to make a point."

Jack could see apprehension in the *Seer*'s face and pressed further "There's something more to this, what's the significance of the palace, other than who reigns there"

The *Seer* sighed and replied "It's where Sol was originally banished from, it required all of them demi-gods to cast him out before; If he's able to beat their combined powers now it will mean he's become stronger or they've become weaker, either way a victory for Sol there will demonstrate to the *Astral Plane* that he's become unstoppable."

Jack became resolved to their task as he replied "Then we need to go there and stop him, can you lead us there?"

The *Seer* replied "I was afraid you'd say that, I can lead you there boss-man; just make sure your crazy antics don't lead to our mutual doom."

The Harbinger took flight in the background, rising over the crater before swinging back around to a stop over Jack and the *Seer*.

Sarah's familiar voice boomed over the loudspeakers "Need a ride boys?" as the elevator lowered in front of them; Jack and the *Seer* stepped on, as they were lifted back into the airship before it lifted off and soared into the horizon.

12

PALACE OF ETERNITY

JACK GRABBED THE NEAREST INTERCOM UPON BOARDING THE HARBINGER and announced "Officers and crew, report to the hangar bay for briefing."

The *Seer* was already with Jack, nervously trying to acclimate himself to the shifting of the ship in flight; the *Fox* was also present, looking disinterested as he leaned against a nearby wall. Jack walked to the center of the room as the crew of *the Harbinger* filtered in and assembled; Sarah entered the hangar bay first and inquired "What's this about? Didn't you just beat the guy who was after us?"

Jack responded "I did, but now we have another problem"

The *Seer* interjected "Sol's on the warpath, and we know where he's heading"

Jack continued "Up until now we've been running interference, attacking his operations in various realms; however, now he's going to personally lead an attack on the *Palace of Eternity*, the capital of the *Astral Plane*, likely with the bulk of his army."

The *Fox* inquired "What are you planning to do about it *Traveler*?"

Jack explained "We're going to ready the ship and crew for battle, and then find the leaders who rule over the palace and warn them about what's coming."

The *Fox* filled in the gap of information "*The Circle*? You're wasting your time; they will not listen to you."

Jack retorted "if we don't try to stop Sol then we've already lost, it's going to be difficult, there's no getting around that; however, if we can halt his crusade there then we may gain the initiative to turn the tide against him."

The *Fox* clarified "The odds don't concern me, the worthiness of the cause does, if you're marching to what could be certain death you need to be committed, saving *The Circle* hardly inspires... they deserve what they're about to get."

Jack started to get angry and replied "What the hell is that supposed to mean?"

The *Seer* interjected "*The Circle* has never done nothin for nobody boss-man, for eons major calamities and wars have occurred that they didn't lift a finger about, many folks consider them figureheads, lame-duck if you will."

Jack clenched his fists for a moment then raised his voice saying "Our priority is using this opportunity to stop Sol before he destroys everything.

Our main objective is not to protect *The Circle*, if we have to choose between stopping Sol or protecting *The Circle*, we'll stop Sol." Everyone in the room took a moment, and then nodded in content agreement in return.

Calming himself down Jack explained his plan "Alright then, here's what we need to do: *Seer*, I need you to teleport our allies from each realm to the palace; also if you know of any others who will fight Sol we could use their help as well."

The *Seer* laughed and replied "If it gets me off this ship for a bit, I'll do whatever you say boss-man."

Jack continued "*Fox*, I need you to select part of the crew and arm them to the teeth; we're likely going to be facing numbers ten-fold as strong as ours, we're going to need every advantage we can get."

The *Fox* replied "I will need a few things"

Jack replied "And you'll get it; next Sarah: I need your help installing counter-measures and other upgrades into our fighters; I'm not sure what we'll face in the coming battle, but we need to control the air."

Sarah thought for a moment and replied "Alright sure, just as long as they remain part of the ship"

Jack motioned to their surroundings with open arms replying with slight sarcasm "It all belongs to you Sarah, but if the fighters can't do their job this ship will be far less effective, and by extension less valuable."

The *Seer* comically added "Can't have that now can we? The resale value could use some bolstering after-all."

Sarah got defensive as she replied "Hey I never said I was planning to sell it; you've made your point though, I'll upgrade the fighters as best as I can."

Jack clapped his hands together finishing "Alright good, everyone get started on what we all need to do; except you Sarah, we need to get up to the bridge and set course for the *Palace of Eternity* and attempt to persuade *the Circle*, worthy or not."

Sarah motioned towards the elevator and said with slight sarcasm "After you, great war leader" as Jack smirked and they both stepped onto the elevator.

As the elevator rode up Sarah quietly said "Jack, why do you go through all this?"

Jack seemed taken aback "What do you mean?"

Sarah clarified "None of this suits you at all, why go through the hassle?"

Jack looked troubled and responded "Because it's my fault?"

Sarah didn't believe him replying "You opened the distortion and released Sol single handedly?"

Jack quickly corrected "No, no that's not how it happened, but if I hadn't been there then things would have been different."

Sarah sighed and explained "I'll let you in on some advice, if you let something in the past run your life then that's all you'll have to go on; once you've finished with it, you don't feel released or free… it will just leave you feeling empty, like it was all pointless to begin with."

Jack glanced back and inferred "Is that the voice of experience?"

As the elevator doors opened, Sarah stepped through and then replied "Think about what I said, and maybe I'll tell you later." As they both proceeded to the captain's chair.

Sarah sat down as Jack explained "The ear-piece allows you to set the ship's destination, though it's not as simple as plotting a line between two points and hitting the afterburner; you have to focus on thoughts related to the place where you wish to go and then-"

As the ship suddenly jumped forward, covering a great distance in an instant as it suddenly came to a stop over a sweeping archipelago in *Venture*.

Sarah remarked "Huh, that's a lot easier than I thought… Kinda takes the fun out of things though?"

Jack raised his eyebrow and replied "Oh really? I'm curious why."

Sarah elaborated "It would be like if the thing you most wanted suddenly appeared in your hands every time you thought of it-"

Jack interrupted "But we're in the *Astral Plane*, we can already-"

She cut him off and continued "Let me finish, as I was saying if the thing you most wanted suddenly appeared in your hands every time you thought of it, then there would be no satisfaction; it would feel as though you didn't earn the things that suddenly came into your possession, things would lose their gratification, their 'flavor'. Does that make sense?"

Jack shrugged and replied "Well I guess that makes sense… anyway back to the point, to go to *Utopia* you have to focus on-"

As the ship again leapt forward, travelling across a vast distance before reappearing over the *Palace of Eternity*, Jack slowly walked towards the monitor, awestruck by the sight of this massive wonder before them.

Sarah commented "I've been here before; I'll be down in the hangar bay working on those fighters… oh and Jack"

As Jack was still awestruck by the wonder of the monuments on screen before him, and was only half paying attention. "Huh, what?"

Sarah finished "This palace may look nice but none of the demigods inside earned any of it, the *Fox* was right to warn you, don't trust them… do enjoy the view though." As she tapped the elevator button and proceeded down.

Looking out the viewing screen Jack beheld the largest and most ornate stone building he had ever laid eyes upon; like a carefully put together puzzle it combined towers, archways, pillars, domes, and massive walls into one gigantic sweeping building. Taking note of the details Jack noticed that various architectural styles had been employed in different sections of the palace, but that it all met at the center in a massive dome surrounded by different levels of supporting towers. Jack finally was able to get his head back on task, heading towards the elevator to reach the hangar bay; while taking the elevator down Jack wondered if it was in fact an amalgamation of various separate world wonders, rather than a totally original design.

Jack walked through the cargo bay and noticed a large number of metal components, weapons, and pieces of armor plating scattered about; only a few minutes into the task and the *Fox* had already made a mess of the cargo bay. Stepping onto the cargo lift Jack was approached by the *Fox* who briefly advised "You'll find their level of arrogance insufferable, remind them that Sol approaches with the intent to destroy them and you might get somewhere; do not allow them to push the entire defense effort onto you as a "quest", if they don't offer any assistance then let them burn."

Jack acknowledged "Thanks for the advice, hopefully they go along with what I have to say, I'm not much of a people person."

The Fox concluded "You're the *Traveler*, and as far as they're concerned you hold all the cards; if they forget that, remind them… we will await your return" Jack then nodded and tapped the cargo lift controls, lowering downward towards one of the palaces many courtyards.

Taking a moment to peer around Jack saw that the palace was even more massive than his ship; a conventional force would have great difficulty taking such a large structure, but then again Sol had extraordinary means at his disposal.

Before Jack reached the ground he saw a large number of guards assemble in a square around where he was about to land, before them was a man in official looking robes with a scroll, a herald no doubt. Touching the ground Jack stepped off and was immediately addressed as a rogue trespasser by the herald "You dare enter the *Palace of Eternity* unannounced! State your name and purpose."

Jack replied "I am the *Traveler*, and I am here to warn '*The Circle*', take me to them."

The herald became visibly offended "One does not barge in and demand to stand before '*The Circle*'; you must submit an official correspondence and wait for their return summons, and that is only after-"

Jack cut him off "Sol approaches to destroy the palace and *The Circle*, we don't have time for this charade!"

The herald pointed his finger forward and reasserted "The outcast demigod would not dare assault the palace, no one has the means to overwhelm this citadel; now go back from when you came and- URG" as Jack directed one of his gloves at the herald and lifted him up by the neck, the guards took a step forward as he effortlessly blasted a wave outwards knocking them all down.

Jack reiterated with a more pressing tone "Take me to *The Circle*, now. Or I will carve a path there myself. Understand?"

A massive light shone from the central domed tower and a loud chant boomed out "ENTER!" as the herald recognized the summon and tried to regain his formal tone "If...if you would kindly, f-f-follow me"

Jack followed the herald through a long arched corridor lined with many statues and paintings. He noticed the artwork seemed to be arranged into a visual record; each piece being gradually more refined in artistic technique and detail, telling a long saga that slowly chronicled everything from the past to the present.

Reaching the main entrance the herald opened the oversized door and Jack proceeded through, inside was not so much a meeting area as it was a gigantic altar. The center of the room was lit by the light of a high atrium, arranged in a circle above it was a gigantic stone table made of finely polished marble. The arrangement of this meeting area was likely how they earned the name '*The Circle*', yet he could not see any of their faces or figures; an obscuring light shone from behind them obscuring all but their silhouettes, it reminded Jack of trying to look at something with a car's headlights shining right behind it.

Jack stepped into the center area under the atrium light and spoke loudly so the entire room could hear him "Sol approaches this place, I believe he intends to attack and overthrow your council; I have come here to both warn you and ask your assistance, you banished him once before, together we may yet banish him again."

The response seemed to originate from the walls as a booming echoed voice replied "We are aware of Sol's plans and intent, the attack matters not, and we have elected to avoid direct conflict with Sol."

Jack couldn't believe what he was hearing, he replied with a degree of disbelief "The attack doesn't matter? He's going to attack HERE! It doesn't matter if you've decided not to fight him; he's bringing the war right to your doorstep regardless."

The response came stating bluntly "Sol's war is a campaign for influence, the results of individual battles are of little consequence."

Jack perceived their justification as nonsense and replied "Sol rampages through the realms, enslaving constructs, plundering resources, and crushing those who resist him; he does this to gain supremacy over the constructs and the realms, this gains him influence and thus power."

Jack continued "We cannot simply bide our time and do nothing, we must strike him before he becomes unstoppable"

The response came again, still blunt and lacking emotion "Sol is already unstoppable, we maintain the order that keeps his influence from becoming absolute; were we to fall the remaining constructs would rally to him."

Jack was now angry; he yelled in return "Failing to act does not maintain anything! You are doing nothing while Sol marches forward and takes what he wants. How long will before he gathers enough strength to command the entire *Astral Plane*, at that point he would become unassailable to you."

Jack reiterated "Maintaining your order only delays the inevitable and leaves him unchallenged, but you have a chance here and now to do something! I am the *Traveler*, and as such I have the potential to defeat him regardless of how strong he becomes, rally to me and we can break his crusade here!"

Jack made his argument "If we defeat him, even once, his myth of invincibility would shatter! His influence would crumble and then we could end his twisted vision, help me and we will succeed."

There was a pause, the light behind the desks moved about as Jack heard the faint whispers of them talking amongst themselves; finally after some delay the voice returned with their response "No, you are not the *Traveler*, and we will not aid you; you are an errand anomaly which has only brought chaos. Leave this place, fight Sol if you wish, but know that such a contest is futile and will result only in defeat, our judgment is final."

With that the light behind the desks suddenly vanished, as if they had suddenly teleported away; Jack's eyes became an accusing glare, they didn't have the courage or the boldness to stand up to Sol, they were going to instead run and hide. "Gutless cowards, the *Astral Plane* doesn't need hollow and arrogant rulers! You hide behind your roles as the *Astral Plane* crumbles to dust!" then he angrily stormed out, blasting the doors open with his telekinetic gloves, fuming as he stomped forward and tried to think of what he needed to do next.

Marching back towards the plaza where his cargo elevator was parked, Jack ran into an odd looking construct wearing bright silk robes adorned with many crests and symbols made of gold.

Jack spoke first, already in a bad mood "If you say anything about the F'ing Circle or their damn judgment I swear I'll-"

The construct replied "I am here to help you, our judgment was not unanimous, but we must speak with consensus."

Jack calmed down slightly, but noticed the one offering "help" didn't look like much of a warrior saying aloud "Are you the construct of elaborate clothing or something, I appreciate your intent but I need soldiers."

The man laughed heartily and replied "I am the *Sovereign*, construct of all ruler-ship, and I command one of the greatest armies in the entire *Astral Plane*."

Jack managed a slight smile as he replied "...Now we'll at least have a chance; have your armies assemble at the steps before the palace, we have a battle to prepare for."

At the front of the palace lay thousands of stairs that led up to a hill that the palace sat upon; though in-between the massive sections of stairs were flat sections with smaller plazas, low walls, and smaller buildings making it a defensible strategic position.

Jack had positioned *the Harbinger* directly over the sea of stairs and was coordinating with the sovereign's commanders to fortify the area; barricades were being placed along with cover from ranged attacks all throughout the area, yet Jack knew they would need more than ordinary defenses to withstand the might of Sol's crusade, especially if the *Clerics* participated in force.

Jack noticed that the *Sovereign's* army consisted of an odd mix between arms and soldiers between several different eras of combat: There were heavily armored Renaissance troops armed with steel broadswords, *Victorian* era line-infantry with rifles, recurve and longbow wielding archers from the *Middle Ages*, and an erratic arsenal of artillery going all the way from ballista's to cannons.

Jack was arranging the forces into battle lines, the low slope of the stairs was making things much easier, allowing him to place melee troops slightly below rifle or bow wielding troops above, allowing him to make use of both melee and ranged tactics. Once Jack was sure the troops were well placed and the barricades erected he began his own separate preparations, Sol's army would have them greatly outmatched, and Jack didn't intend to play fair.

Jack decided to return to *the Harbinger* and see how his crew was doing on their part. Arriving via cargo elevator Jack was surprised to see all the scattered parts cleared away, he saw the *Fox* at one of the consoles busily doing calibrations and diagnostic tests.

Jack approached and inquired "How are the armaments coming along? Do we have anything that will give our crew a chance against Sol's superior numbers and firepower?"

The Fox nonchalantly replied "Over on the far side of the bay."

Jack saw multiple silhouettes of whatever the *Fox* made, but couldn't make out exactly what they were; walking over to another console he brightened the lights on the far side of the cargo bay. Arranged in orderly formation were about two dozen man-shaped robotic suits.

Jack was awestruck "Mechs! You made over two dozen bipedal armored robotic suits?"

The Fox detailed them as if he were explaining any ordinary object "Approximately 3 meters tall, one metric ton each; these "mechs", as you call them, feature two all-terrain legs capable of a full range of movement with a top speed of 60km per hour; the two arms are equipped with shoulder mounted launchers capable of firing multi-payload rockets or laser guided missiles, as well as gas operated, recoil-dampened, automatic heavy guns in each hand that fire a tungsten cored slugs with armor piercing copper-alloy jackets."

This particular detail threw Jack off as he questioned "Wait, why do the mechs hold these large guns in each hand? Shouldn't that be built in?"

The Fox explained "Trying to integrate an arm with a full range of movement along with such a large firearm becomes complicated quickly, too many variables to compensate for, instead it's far easier to just have the guns be a separate piece held by the hands."

Jack understood, yet seeing ordinary looking firearms put to giant's size was humorous in its own way; then he moved onto the next subject "So they are fast, and have a lot of firepower, but are they precise? And more importantly can they take a beating?"

The Fox managed what was close to a laugh before explaining "The operating chamber features virtual 3D imaging, it also features a neural link that does what the pilot thinks, so it's as precise as its pilot; as for durability it has 15cm thick reactive composite armor capable of withstanding a direct hit from even a thermal round, even without that there are multiple electronic and kinetic countermeasures designed to intercept guided projectiles."

Jack nodded and replied "Very impressive, I'm surprised you were able to combine all that into such a compact package."

As the *Fox* clarified "I haven't yet, the power source remains an issue; there isn't enough room for anything atomic and conventional fuels would be too heavy or lack sufficient range."

Jack was confused as he asked "Wait, why can't you make the power source similar to what your suit uses?"

The Fox replied "My vitals are integrated into this suit at every level, it keeps me alive and I provide its power source, but this is an extreme solution, the process of attaining it was... excruciating, something no ordinary construct would survive."

Jack didn't realize the *Fox* was trapped in the suit he wore, which was a bit unsettling; after a brief pause he tried another question "Well what options are we left with?"

The Fox proposed "I need a favor, should you agree I'll tell you exactly how to power these suits."

Jack replied with suspicion "Why didn't you propose this before you started?"

The Fox answered "Leverage *Traveler*, you're more likely to agree with the object you'd receive being right in front of you."

Jack crossed his arms and said "This favor you want, let's hear it."

As the *Fox* explained his proposition "I need a secondary power source, something that will allow me to go beyond normal operating limits, and something that only you can provide."

Jack thought for a moment and then his mind filled in the blanks as he interjected "You want me to make an energy core similar to what powers *the Harbinger*."

The Fox nodded in return "Correct, with that I could strike the final blow against the machines."

Jack rubbed his forehead and sighed "You're hell bent on that, aren't you? I agree on one condition, when this battle is over you will tell me exactly what happened in the past that has you so possessed with this obsession to destroy the machines, I need to know that I can trust the people I'm working with. Deal?"

The Fox thought for a moment, then tossed something into Jack's hands "That's the control chip for the mega-capacitor backpacks that power the mechanized suits; they'll be charged remotely using point-to-point microwave beams from the ship, so long as they stay in range and keep a line-of-sight with *the Harbinger*."

Jack rolled his eyes and commented "You had this ready the entire time didn't you?"

The Fox replied "You think I'd design something with no power source? I'll give you the details of what I need after the current battle ends, then I'll tell you what you want to hear." Jack nodded in return, as the *Fox* returned to what he was doing and Jack headed next for the hangar bay.

Stepping off the elevator Jack saw multiple fighters undergoing upgrades, as robot arms from the ceiling made precise modifications and installed Sarah's additions; she was busily tinkering with one of the fighters by hand.

Jack approached and got her attention "So how are *the Harbinger's* fighters coming along?"

Sarah glanced up and replied "You know I never liked that name, I'm thinking about changing it to something else…"

Jack retorted "You can't do that, it'll confuse everyone; they'll have to refer to it as the 'ship formerly known as *Harbinger*'"

Sarah laughed and continued "I guess this ship's already got a reputation of its own; anyway to answer your question I got the usual package of counter-measures installed: chaff, flares, electronic scramblers, the works."

Jack queried "Any chance of improving their maneuverability?"

Sarah rolled her eyes and replied "Have you ever heard the saying 'a designer knows he has achieved perfection not when there is nothing left to add, but when there is nothing left to take away'"

Jack wasn't quite sure what Sarah's point was but nodded his head and replied "Yes, where are you going with this?"

She retorted "Efficiency Jack, if I try to make your regular fighters fast and maneuverable, then they'll lose some of their firepower and armor as a result; however, I saw in the combat log that there was another fighter used in the last battle this ship had. I took a look at that model and improved its targeting and reworked the weapon layout… that way they can perform an assistance role alongside the main fighters, using a mixed composition should hopefully cover all our bases tactically."

Jack nodded and replied "Sounds like you have it all figured out."

Sarah shrugged and replied "We'll see how they operate in the air, a good design has to prove its worth in the real-world otherwise it's nothing but a nice theory."

Jack's thoughts were thinking about every aspect of the impending battle as he asked "Have you had a chance to look at our guns yet? Their down there setting up *Victorian* era artillery and I have a feeling we're going to need more firepower."

Sarah looked back up in disbelief saying "Who did you ally with? Lord British? Actually I've been meaning to have a look at those guns anyway, the last person to mess with them was the *Fox*… and that worries me."

With that she set her tools aside and climbed down the mechanics ladder and headed for the elevator, Jack followed as they proceeded to the primary gun array. While walking Sarah asked "So has the *Fox* revealed what he wants yet?"

Jack was surprised "How did you know he wanted something?"

She replied "He's predictable, I figured the only reason he stuck around is because he needed something; whatever he asked for, dole it out with caution."

Jack pressed for more information "You've worked with him before, can he be trusted, the closest thing to a moral judgment he's made is that 'he doesn't like killing organics'"

Sarah frowned a bit as if recalling something unpleasant and replied "Just because he doesn't like doing it doesn't mean that he won't do it.

She recalled "Once back when we were still working together, the *Fox* and I were pursuing contingent of the machines through Epic, a few of them got damaged in a skirmish with us so they garrisoned a village of 'organics' in hopes that we wouldn't storm the place for the sake of the ones inside."

Jack prompted the story further "And what happened?"

Sarah sighed deeply and continued "*The Fox* didn't hesitate for even a moment, stormed right in and finished the machines off... three villagers got caught in the crossfire. I yelled at him for hours about that incident, when I finally calmed down he said 'If your rules of engagement leave something to be exploited, then the enemy will use it against you at every opportunity.'"

Sarah continued "I didn't agree with him at the time, but a similar incident occurred later where we were seeking a group of machines through a populated part of *Venture*, yet this time they didn't stop near any civilians or attempt to use any of them as human shields... the *Fox* was right, if we had hesitated to go after those machines the first time they would have thrown innocent people in our line of fire every time after that."

Jack could tell Sarah was upset about this and said "I was faced with another situation where I had to decide whether or not to sacrifice others, and my conviction is still unwavering: just because it may bring about a greater good doesn't mean it's justified, the moment we find we can rationalize any outcome we find ourselves in a cruel existence of brutal means and choosing between bad and worse options."

Sarah countered "To answer your previous question, the *Fox* can be trusted so long as your goals are mutual; but he understands war Jack, given the opportunity where he has to cause collateral damage or sacrifice allies to win… he'll do it without hesitation, don't forget that."

Just as Sarah finished they arrived at the primary battery controls, Sarah tapped the console and accessed the maintenance logs. After skimming through a few walls of text she uttered to herself "That S.O.B, I can't believe he would do that now."

Jack had clearly missed something "What are you talking about?"

Sarah pushed a few buttons on the console and one of the guns was brought via ceiling crane and set down in front of them. The odd looking gun featured eight square barrels built onto a rotating configuration, each of the barrels featured electromagnets arranged in a spiral from breech to muzzle.

The firing action of the top barrel looked unconventional with several dozen detachable capacitors feeding into it, towards the back was an automatic re-loader which fed in odd looking circular cartridges from alternating directions.

Jack knew there was no way this was one of his guns, yet it lacked the *Fox*'s usual style as Jack inquired "What is this?"

Sarah answered "The M.A.R.C.; or magnetically, accelerated, rifled, cannon; the *Fox* and I were jointly developing this before we went our separate ways."

Jack commented "You sounded irritated to see it? Is there something wrong with this particular gun?"

Sarah laughed and replied "There's nothing wrong with it, if anything its overpowered: Normally with a rail gun the slug is pulled forward with electro-magnets turning on and off down the barrel, this fires a slug with more velocity and power than a normal gunpowder charge; however, the process causes the rail to heat up from the massive amount of friction generated. With the MARC, the barrel is rotated between eight different barrels in a circle, allowing it to keep firing; the main part of the gun behind it houses the capacitors and reloading mechanism.

Sarah continued "Before this gun was finished the *Fox* and I went our separate ways, I told him that 'I couldn't build anything that might be used the wrong way…' And now he's finished it and put it in my ship. I guess the shoe's on the other foot now."

Jack reassured "You'll have complete control of everything on the ship, and if you decide later that don't want to use these particular guns then you don't have to; however-"

As Sarah interrupted "Let me guess, you would like to barrow a few, right?"

Jack affirmed "If that's alright, I'd rather not bet on the "Guess-and-Check" era of artillery we have set up down there currently."

Sarah agreed and punched up the console "The ship's fabricator will build a few spares; they'll be craned down in a few minutes."

Then she looked up and said "Before you go into this 'grand' battle, I just want to let you know Jack-"

As the *Seer* suddenly appeared behind Jack causing Sarah to stumble over backwards in surprise, Jack didn't notice what happened and said "You ok? What were you about to tell me?"

As the *Seer* answered "That I got all your friends in one place"

Jack spun around yelling "BAH! Don't appear behind me like that, going to give me a heart attack."

As the *Seer* laughed and replied "Appearing in front of folks is what gives 'em a heart attack boss-man"

Jack queried "Can you try reading the minds of people before you enter a room? And show up at more opportune moments"

As the *Seer* shook his head and said "It aint magic boss-man, I have been known to be called 'The Interrupter' in certain circles; were you in the middle of something?"

Sarah answered "No it's alright; Jack, I'll tell you after the battle, just stay alive."

As Jack nodded and replied "No problem, thanks again for the help." And followed the *Seer* to where he had assembled their allies.

They reached the top of the stairs where Balthazar and Captain Teach were both waiting, along with them were a few captains of the *Sovereign's* army; Jack and the *Seer* arrived right as everyone settled in, they stopped talking once he arrived and they were now waiting for him to speak.

Jack was hardly a military leader, but he had prepared a plan of action, so he proceeded to detail it, taking care to say it as loudly and clearly as possible. "Were on the prelude of a siege, Sol's about to attack personally and I would bet he's going to hit us with everything he has. We're going to be ready for him."

Jack instructed "Balthazar and Teach, I'm going to have your forces reinforce the far left and right flanks, keep those fronts strong so they are forced into the center where we can direct the most firepower on the enemy."

He continued "*The Harbinger* will remain within combat range to provide supporting fire and fighter/bomber strikes where needed; my crew will be providing heavy troops to reinforce vulnerable points, but the bulk of the fighting will fall upon the *Sovereign's* army."

Jack detailed "I'm not going to lie, Sol's forces are strong in number and his *Clerics* add a horrifying element to the battle; we'll have superior position and defensive fortifications, but even with all our advantages, this battle will not be easy."

One of the *Sovereign's* commanders stepped forward and replied "We have fought across the *Astral Plane*, and have never known defeat; regardless of what Sol does, we will prevail!"

Jack nodded in hopeful optimism with this, as Balthazar added "*Traveler*, if Sol himself is defeated, his entire army will at once disband; when Sol appears on the field you must engage him directly."

Jack replied "I'll be watching over the battle from a good vantage point, directing support and keeping our defense organized; when Sol makes his move I'll be waiting for him."

Teach raised a flagon of ale he had somehow acquired and yelled "Aye sounds to be as good of a plan as any, I'll be rooting for ye while I fight em, give that son bastard hell for us!"

Teach then downed his drink and returned to his forces; the commanders of the *Sovereign* then saluted to also rejoin their forces. Once they had departed, only the *Seer*, Balthazar, and Jack remained.

Balthazar spoke up "Sol is calculating and meticulous, and will have many contingencies. Sol will not come forward and face you unless he's forced to; you must counter his every move, dash his carefully laid plans, only then will he appear personally on the field."

The *Seer* asked what was implied "Meaning that if his boys march straight over us that he'll just sit back and enjoy the view?"

Balthazar nodded and continued "Yes, be aware that Sol is also very cunning; be prepared for the unexpected."

Balthazar then placed his hand upon Jack's shoulder and concluded "The power of the *Traveler* is all that stands in Sol's way; regardless of what unfolds, you must survive this battle."

Jack reassured him "Don't worry Balthazar, I've learned much since my last encounter with Sol; we're going to win today and set things right."

Balthazar bowed in acknowledgment and then left to join his forces. The *Seer* clapped and critiqued "Considering your aversion to public speaking your speech was pretty good boss man; don't worry though, they all believe in ya or they wouldn't be here."

Jack exhaled to relieve the built up tension and then replied "Thanks *Seer*, I'll need you to have my back on this one; you're the only one who can help me keep this together and every second will count."

The *Seer* smiled and replied "Though I'm not a fan of playing "Telephone" for an entire army I'll help ya out; just don't run yourself ragged before 'Bright-N-Shine' shows up."

Jack laughed and replied "Sure, no problem. How long do I have before they arrive?"

The *Seer* gazed out for a moment and replied "They'll be here at sunset, which strikes of irony if you ask me; if you have anything you need to do, you'd best get it done quickly."

Jack smiled and replied "Oh you're going to help; there's one last minute 'surprise' I have in store."

The *Seer* sighed "Alright boss-man, but don't think I'm not keeping track of all this… you're going to owe me one hell of a favor when this is all said and done."

13

BATTLE OF

UTOPIA

THE SUN SET OVER THE STEPS OF THE PALACE, JACK HAD MADE EVERY preparation that he could think of, the Harbinger was ready a safe distance away, all his allies were organized, even the mechanized suits and MARCs were deployed and waiting. There was tension building in the air; entire armies stood staring into the horizon with weapons drawn awaiting the imminent battle.

The silence was broken by the arrival of Sol's crusade in the distance, a bright light shone behind them as loud marching and chanting from the soldiers became ever louder; despite the immense number of troops the horde moved with surprising speed, within a few minutes they had assembled to within a thousand yards of the bottom of the steps, then they waited.

The *Seer* stood near Jack, ready to relay his instructions through the army when needed, he asked the *Traveler* in anticipation "Shouldn't we open fire boss-man?"

Jack replied firmly "No, they'd just use fire shields; we need to wait until some of them break ranks for a charge."

As they waited for Sol's army to advance, they could hear a booming voice at the front of the crusade giving a speech; then the entire army began chanting ever louder in unison, the clashing of weapons against shields and the stomping of thousands of feet joined the sound, until the roar of Sol's army became tremendous like an impending earthquake. Suddenly it stopped and was replaced with a singular chant accompanied by a rising yell as the front group charged forward towards the steps, "Here we go" Jack thought to himself.

Jack tapped on his earpiece that had a direct line to *the Harbinger* and Sarah as he relayed "The first group has advanced, arm the main battery and open fire, bury them in that field!"

As a loud cascading echo was heard in the distance, before explosions rained unto the battlefield. Men and weapons were blown into the air as pure chaos ensued; fireballs erupted all around them decimating the force, finally what few of them remained fled back towards the main force.

Jack smirked and replied "You're going to have to do better than that Sol."

Drums and horns relayed back and forth between Sol's army as the second force marched forward, this time more carefully and under the cover of *Clerics* casting fire-shields; Jack considered having his artillery and fire-support attempt to overpower the shields, but he decided this was a good opportunity to use the surprise they had prepared earlier.

They waited for the force to get within a few hundred feet to the defending armies position. Jack was eyeing the surroundings of the approaching army, scanning for the marker he and the *Seer* had left behind, he spotted it as they crossed in front of it: a tree painted white on one side.

Jack alluded to how he would spring his trap "Tightly packed formations, normally vulnerable to artillery fire were it not for those fire-shield; yet they are still vulnerable from below..."

Then he nodded to the *Seer* and ordered "Let's show them the greeting we've prepared for them: activate the mines."

Both Jack and the *Seer* triggered detonators they had prepared earlier, large disks flew up from the ground under the fire shields and blasted outwards in every direction with intense blasts of telekinetic force; like cascading dominos the entire force was knocked down, including the *Clerics* who were maintaining the protective barrier.

With the shields down Jack nodded to the *Seer* and relayed "Order the artillery to fire, finish them off!" As the many cannons, trebuchets, catapults, and even MARCs proceeded to lob hundreds of projectiles into the kill zone; the forces being disoriented and knocked down couldn't even evade the incoming fire as the entire area was pelted with deadly hail, ripping through them as yet another force was rapidly cut down; within seconds the remainder of the force had either scattered or fled, and Jack's allies were still completely unscathed.

Morale was starting to pick up throughout the defending force, what at first looked to be a hopeless defense was beginning to appear winnable; Jack didn't let himself get too encouraged though, he knew Sol was only testing their defenses, and that they were likely holding more powerful attacks in reserve.

A number of *Clerics* stepped forward from the main group and began channeling their power, huge hollow boulders formed around groups of Templar infantry; the boulders began to levitate as another group collected large infernos behind them. Jack had seen something like this before, suddenly realizing what was about to occur and spun around to the *Seer* and yelled "Get the MARCs loaded for anti-air!"

Before Jack's order could be carried out the *Clerics* hurled the first wave of boulders at them as flaming meteors, causing them to suddenly impact into the unsuspecting defense force. *Templars* emerged from the craters and attacked the forces around them; many defenders were still in shock as the *Templars* wreaked havoc in the ranks, cutting down the disoriented and shaken soldiers.

Jack decided to intervene, he quickly told the *Seer* "Get every MARC and interceptor ready to destroy the next wave of meteors before they hit us again! I'm going to deal with the *Templars*." Then Jack charged up some telekinetic energy, absorbed it, and dove downwards to the spot where the *Templars* were causing the most damage.

Impacting into the ground like a comet Jack cast a powerful blast wave on impact in a wave of fury, immediately reversing the attackers' initiative as they were hurled high into the air. Jack sprinted towards the next trouble spot; Templar soldiers jumped into his path attempting to slow him down, Jack merely punched his way through, using the retained telekinetic energy to toss back anything that came into contact with his fists.

Reaching another formation of Templar soldiers, he vaulted over their shield wall with the last of his internal charge; upon landing he fired out a barrage into their backs with his automatic crossbow, setting everything around him ablaze as he unsheathed his sword and cut down stragglers in swift effortless motions. Jack had become a far more deadly warrior in recent times.

The sky lit up with tracer rounds as another wave of meteors approached, this time explosions rocked the sky as many of them were destroyed in mid-air; though a few still managed to reach the ground and deliver more enemy reinforcements. Jack collected a mass of discarded weapons using the telekinetic gloves and readied to hurl them like a collected thunderbolt, seeing a clear path at one of Templar groups he tossed it with such speed that light and sound blurred around the projectile; the weapons impacted with enough force to impale whole men as the storm of skewering weapons devastated the attackers.

The remaining *Templars* were forced back as the defenders regrouped and surrounded the attackers who were now at an extreme disadvantage with their momentum halted by the *Traveler*, though Sol's *Clerics* were willing to try one more wave. The defending army stood agape as the *Clerics* collected all their strength into one gigantic meteor, Jack readied to repel the asteroid sized rock. The meteor was flung towards them, flying through all the counter fire unaffected by any of it; it rapidly approached the defending army as Jack collected a dense sphere of air and projected it forward, yelling loud enough that his entire army heard. The colossal meteor stopped short of crushing him, gently floating in the air; Jack swung around with all his might and blasted it back whence it came with great speed, impacting with a massive shock wave and dust cloud as it completely annihilated the front line of Sol's formation. Jack mockingly whispered as he caught his breath "Advantage: *Traveler*. The ball is in your court now Sol; what's next?"

Jack quickly recovered and headed back to his position at the head of the steps, the entire army cheering him on as he moved through the ranks. Reaching the top the *Seer* waited with an update "That last one popped them good boss-man, looks like they're thinking hard before making the next move."

Jack scanned the enemy army in front of them and replied "Unfortunately we don't have the strength to counter charge and repel them; we can only defend this position and continue countering their moves."

The *Seer* shrugged and replied "The last stand of the *Traveler*?"

Jack smiled and shook his head "Hardly, we just have to keep thwarting their attacks until they become more desperate. Once they over-extend themselves then, even with inferior numbers, we'll have an opportunity to deal enough damage to rout Sol's forces."

After a brief pause the *Templars* began chanting something, but it was the same phrase over and over, from the back of the ranks hulking figures pushed and shoved their way to the front; Jack caught a brief glimpse but couldn't quite make out what it was, it looked to be man shaped, only larger and surrounded by bright light.

They emerged from Sol's army, giant fiery *Avatars* of wrath, sprinting forward with wide steps. Jack immediately responded "Tell the artillery to open fire! Bring those things down."

As his batteries released hell upon the field, yet the projectiles veered away before impacting with any of the fire elementals, this reminded Jack of the protective field around the *Acolyte* he faced. Jack nearly jumped back into the fray but was stopped by the *Seer* "No boss man, there are too damn many for you to go knock down yourself; we need you here, think of something strategic."

Jack paced for a moment, trying to think of different things that could defeat the shields on the flame *Avatars*, and then remembered that he wasn't the only one who had crazy weapons up his sleeve. Changing the frequency on the earpiece Jack tapped it and spoke "*Fox*, do you have anything that can disrupt gravity fields?"

The response came after a brief pause "I have something unconventional, but the results are unpredictable at best."

Jack replied "If it gives us an opening then I'll take it, load them into the cannons and-"

As the *Fox* interrupted "They're too unstable for that, they can only be deployed as a bomb."

Jack frowned for a moment and said "That complicates things... Get as many as you have on-hand equipped onto the fighters in the bay, I'll have Sarah deploy them."

Then he rotated his frequency back to Sarah and hurriedly explained "Sarah, I need you to deploy the fighters and drop some bombs the *Fox* is readying; we're up against some heavy-hitters and we need something to even the odds."

Sarah hesitantly replied "Um, alright Jack. We'll get it out there; just keep your head down when they land."

Meanwhile the fire elementals charged straight into the defending army, trampling and pummeling their way through infantry and barricades; all counter attacks seemed ineffective, yet the *Avatars* were not interested in wiping out the infantry, instead they went straight for the artillery pieces.

A few short minutes dragged on for eternity as the defenders could only helplessly watch as the enemy had free rein to destroy their defensive batteries at will. After a devastating few moments a group of fighters finally arrived and dropped a few of the clumsy looking bombs. The odd shaped charges shook and cast off light as they fell, impacting with a bizarre multi-colored shock wave. In the wake of the detonation the field of light around the *Avatars* began to rapidly distort and diminish, they were now exposed for the kill.

Jack tapped on his ear piece and relayed "Alright good, now have the fighters nail them!"

Sarah reluctantly replied "Those bombs F'ed up our targeting, all we have is unguided dumb-fire weapons."

Jack was infuriated, if he had the fighters open fire with auto-cannons or rockets he'd kill far more of his men than the elementals; he switched over to the *Fox*'s frequency and yelled "You didn't say all our weapons would be jammed dammit, were sitting ducks here!"

The Fox argued back "I said they'd be unpredictable, the mechanized suits should be shielded against jamming, use those."

Jack grumbled "You had better be right about this"

He switched his frequency over to the soldier construct who was acting as field captain "Mech operator, what's your status? Are your weapons jammed?"

The construct calmly replied "All systems green, were still tactical"

Jack then ordered "Gather up your mechs into teams and focus fire on those enemy units, put them down!"

Multiple mechs then charged forward encircled the fire elementals, opening fire with their oversized firearms and rockets; the fiery *Avatars* were shredded apart without their shields, picked apart and cut down by the superior firepower of the mechs .The mechs made short work of the fire elementals as the last few flickered away and extinguished in their dying moments, yet the damage to the artillery had been done.

The *Seer* gathered status reports from around the defenders then reappeared and said "They knocked out nearly every big gun we had boss-man, only two of Sarah's fancy ones are left. What should we do?"

Jack sighed then ordered "Get the last two MARCs to the top of the hill, double the guard on them; also make sure to have our troops regroup in any areas where small gaps have formed, have them abandon any positions that have sustained heavy losses."

The *Seer* nodded back "You got it boss-man, keep your chin up on this, we wouldn't have had a prayer unless you were here" As he teleported away to relay the message through the defenders.

Jack scanned the Templar army, despite the heavy casualties that had been dealt to them the force was still massive; Jack could only estimate that they were still outnumbered at least 20 to 1, and with much of his artillery gone Jack expected a full frontal assault "Were going to need to leverage every advantage we have left for everything their worth" Jack said, pondering what options he still had remaining.

The rising echo of drums and the blaring of great horns ushered in the next attack, this time the entire horde began marching forward; Jack tapped on his ear piece "Sarah, were about to get hit with the bulk of Sol's army; bring *the Harbinger* in close and prepare to provide close support."

As Sarah replied anxiously "Alright Jack, just don't go overboard; if things get bad we can always evacuate."

Jack reassured "Hopefully it won't come to that; this is all to draw out Sol. When he appears I'll finish this"

Sarah concluded "Alright Jack, we'll be ready either way."

The Harbinger floated into position over the palace, as Sol's force neared to within sprinting distance at the bottom of the hill; Jack may have lost most of his artillery but he fully planned on using *the Harbinger* for everything it was worth. Jack tapped on his earpiece and relayed "alright, get the batteries ready and-"

KAPOW! As missiles split the sky and suddenly exploded just short of *the Harbinger*, yet they seemed to come from nowhere, Sol's army wasn't wielding anything approaching that kind of technology.

Jack frantically requested a status update "Sarah?! What happened?"

She summarized "The point defenses stopped the missiles, but the trajectory analysis says they were fired from the air."

Then a large onyx and black figure slowly transitioned to visibility as if to taunt them, it was the Dauntless and armed with a new trick no less: a stealth cloaking field.

Jack quickly prioritized "It's the Dauntless, the opposite ship to *the Harbinger*, you need to focus everything you got on it or it will knock you out of the sky. Be careful, it appears to have upgraded its capabilities from last time."

Sarah replied with slight frustration at this turn of events "Dammit! Alright, I'll handle the Dauntless; good luck down there."

As her communications link shut off and the two Titanic ships began slugging it out with their arrays of cannons and missiles.

The *Seer* re-appeared back to Jack and spoke "Everything's ready, boss-man; though the appearance of that sinister looking ship doesn't bode well."

Jack replied "*The Harbinger* has won against it before, besides we're going to have our hands full down here."

He then pointed at the front-center line of the defenders and explained "Everything depends on us holding the front line, if our guys break off and flee then the battle's over; and so that's where I need to be."

He turned and patted the Seers shoulder for emphasis "I need you to keep the volleys coming, just keep reloading and firing at any strong point in their attack; I'm going to be counting on you, we're going to hold the line, but you're going to be causing much of the damage. Understand?"

The *Seer* said with a determined look in his eyes "I won't let you down boss-man, just don't pull any heroic sacrifices on me... I'm not good at drama."

Jack smiled and replied "Don't worry, I don't plan on throwing myself on anyone's blade; we'll get through this, just as we've gotten through everything else." The *Seer* nodded in return as Jack proceeded to the front-line, hurrying to reach it before Sol's forces broke into a charge.

Jack reached the forward line of the defense, the *Sovereign's* armor clad medieval troops made up much of the front-line; behind them were the *Victorian* era riflemen in line formation. Jack raised both his arms in the air and yelled to encourage the defenders, when they saw they were being led personally by the *Traveler* they yelled back emphatically in return.

Sol's formation came to a stop before them, then after a brief pause the blaring of horns signaled them a charge as they sprinted forward with a rising war cry. Jack waited until their formation broke up and then charged up and blasted a large telekinetic arc forward, shoving back the lead *Templars* as others charged through their downed comrades. The *Templars* met the front line as the collision between men and steel echoed throughout the battlefield, Jack unsheathed his sword and began frantically hacking and slashing at anything that came before him.

Throughout the front line the *Medieval* troops bashed and cleaved enemies before them, but the *Templars* were relentless, constant reinforcements continued battering against them, downing soldiers with attacks of reckless abandon and swarming into others with attacks from every direction. Jack needed to buy them some room to act; he shoved back the *Templars* in front of him with a quick blast and then concentrated on the entirety of the army before him, never before attempting to move so much at once.

Using both the telekinetic gloves and his full concentration, he managed to shift the entire army back a few paces and then yelled "Ready weapons!" then released them yelling "Attack!" As the front-line defenders were able to cut down scores of them before they started to become overwhelmed again.

Jack proceeded to repeat his tactic and telekinetically locked the enemy a few paces away "Ready!" then letting them charge into the waiting defenders "Attack!" Jack repeated this pattern over and over again, and it appeared to be working; the *Templars* were being cut down en-masse, and could not gain any momentum being halted every few moments by the *Traveler*.

Clerics charged to the front in order to reverse the tide of the battle, Jack pointed towards the *Clerics* and yelled "Riflemen, Focus your fire; Barrage!"

As each rifle regiment focused on each *Cleric* and then shouldered their weapons and fired, downing nearly all of them in the sudden hail of bullets.

Jack decided to press the attack forward and take advantage of the momentum; he shot out an entire dust storm from the telekinetic gloves as they formed a spider-web of paths as he fired off an electrical surge through them, electrocuting hundreds if not thousands of *Templars* at once.

Jack yelled loud enough so all the formations could hear "Advance in ranks, front rank swordsmen! Rear rank riflemen! Keep moving until we've broken them!"

Jack readied the telekinetic gloves then directed the army forward "Rear rank, Fire! Front rank, Forward!" As Jack began casting out wave-after-wave of telekinetic blasts to cover the assault.

Jack continued yelling while casting waves of telekinetic force attacks "Rear rank, Fire!; Front rank, Forward!" The soldiers following him moved methodically, as the riflemen would fire a barrage, then swordsmen would charge a few paces forward attacking anything in their path before ducking again as the riflemen would fire another volley, and then the swordsmen would resume their charge forward while the riflemen reloaded to continue repeating the whole maneuver.

The *Templars* rallied into a counter charge in-between the *Travelers* telekinetic blasts, Jack saw this and yelled "Swordsmen, Shield wall!!"

As the defending soldiers made a tight formation of grouped together shields with no gaps in-between; the *Templars* charged straight into it but merely impacted dully into the braced formation, as the swordsmen then countered was the charge was diffused and finished the remainder off with vicious counter strikes.

Supporting artillery strikes came down from the surviving MARC's simultaneously with a volley of arrows raining upon enemy troops; Sol's army began to waver, stepping precariously backwards as the combined might of the *Traveler* and the coordinated defender counter-attacks caused mass casualties.

Jack decided to unleash his most powerful attack: combining the power of both gloves into a compressed pressure wave, before firing it out like a furious cannonball; it impacted in the center of the formation and swept thousands of Sol's troops into the air with a tidal wave of force! Jack took a moment to gather up a large amount of telekinetic force and then absorbed it, an aura of power surrounded him as he was ready to finish the enemy before him; he raised his sword in the air and yelled "Let's finish them off! Forward Charge!"

Sprinting towards the enemy as the defenders sprinted with him. They charged downhill into the wavering *Templars*, effortlessly cutting through them as the sight of the *Traveler* blasting dozens of men into the air with each swipe terrified them; the will of Sol's crusaders finally broke as they routed from the field, fleeing in terror. The defenders pursued them, racking up casualties and continuing their attack; driving them from the hill and striking down thousands within moments. Finally Sol's army retreated the way back to their staging area, in the last few minutes alone they had incurred a staggering loss; tens of thousands were dead, and the morale of the remaining *Templars* was utterly shattered.

The defending force regrouped back towards the top of the hill, they were tired but encouraged as they had just managed to break one of the largest assaults ever assembled in the *Astral Plane*. Jack made his way back to the point overseeing the battlefield, as the soldiers clamored to congratulate him or shake his hand; Jack finally got back to the *Seer* who was laughing at what just occurred "That was quite a whoopin you gave em boss-man"

Jack replied with enthusiasm "Today, here-and-now, we took on an entire army… and utterly destroyed them! What an achievement!"

Then he yelled in triumphant victory, as the entire army seemed to join him at that moment. Calming down Jack peered over the field where they fought and said "Sol can't afford another loss like that, if he orders his forces forward again they will break and scatter; we have only to defeat the man himself and we will have achieved total victory."

The *Seer*'s eyes lit up and he reported "Well you better get ready then, 'the man himself' is coming, and I bet he's mighty pissed off."

Jack's attention turned to the crusading army, their attention seemed to be diverted to a lone figure moving through the ranks; the soldiers started stomping in unison, drums joined the beat, rising voices began chanting "*SOL! SOL! SOL! SOL!*"

Jack saw Sol emerge from the army, draped in bright yellow/red robes, an Aztec plume adorned his head, and a mural of sun rays etched into gold rested upon his shoulders, exactly how Jack remembered him appearing that fateful night.

Sol walked through the field, completely alone, with a fire in his eyes. Jack knew this was meant to be a one-on-one challenge "*Seer*, make sure no one in the army interferes; we don't know what he's capable of and I can't afford any distractions. This is my fight."

The *Seer* nodded and replied "Go get em boss-man, we're counting on ya."

As Jack nodded back and started moving back down through the army towards the bottom of the hill, this was the duel he had been waiting for, a chance to reverse all the damage that had been done and redeem himself "Regardless of what this guy says or does I am going to beat him, tonight I will win back my redemption."

Jack marched out onto the field where Sol waited, the scene was eerie given the fresh signs of battle around them; Sol stood perfectly still and his gaze never wandered, he seemed serenely calm but sharply focused.

Jack approached, taking care to keep his hands near his weapons, Sol noticed this and remarked "My invitation was to facilitate discussion on important matters, not bludgeon each other like savages."

Jack retorted "I must have forgotten, given that you brought an army that I have been locked in a death struggle against."

Sol continued "A fair point, but without challenge nothing is truly earned; consider it…the price of invitation."

Jack wanted to make clear all motivations, so he spoke frankly "I have encountered many of your followers; they all fought on your behalf and were committed, even unto death, for this vision of yours."

Jack challenged "Tell me Sol, what justifies such acts; convince me that it's not a mass-delusion."

Sol explained as if skipping to the middle of an argument "As you know, the *Astral Plane* is a manifestation of the thoughts and emotions of all people's collected subconscious."

Sol then revealed "Do you know what their thoughts increasingly represent: hopelessness, stagnation, and a growing yearning for chaos."

Sol continued "However, the trajectory of these thoughts is not absolute, they influenced and redirected; guided to another path, a better path."

Sol pointed out "This process requires immense upheaval, a new order has to be built that supersedes and replaces the old ways; the *Astral Plane* should be rebuilt to the glory that it once was, instead of the pale shadow that it is. This is all to break the current spiral of stagnation, to bring about the end of the current order."

Jack sensed an inconsistency and argued "Your words are inconsistent with those of your followers, you speak of a revolution, yet they speak of a rising *utopia*; it is more likely a manipulation, your words tailored to those you speak to, an ever twisting façade."

Sol countered "Your criticism would be better directed towards the society you have so faithfully thrown yourself in the defense of; your friend Malachi was right *Traveler*, your civilization is crumbling, dying a slow death from the lack of creative thought and the increasing desperation that comes from a system rooted only in the pursuit of ever increasing consolidation of control."

Jack angrily replied "What would you know of Malachi? What would you know of my society or the people in it? Your actions consign many of them to death while you speak of better alternatives and eventualities; your actions are the same as those who slew Malachi, callous and unfeeling, you see others as mere pawns and sheep to be sacrificed, you care not for them."

Sol grinned and replied "I did not sacrifice your friend, *The Circle* did; the very same Circle that you now defend."

Jack angrily contested "That's not true! You don't know what you're talking about!"

Sol continued "Let me guess, they cloaked themselves in blinding light, spoke in unison, and when you asked them to help you… they said they could not for the sake of balance. Do you see how they coincide?"

Sol furthered "Tell me, what form did Malachi's executioner take? How did they justify their actions to you?"

Jack realized the similarities between Malachi's killer and his encounter with *The Circle* were the same; he was awestruck, could he have really been helping the ones that killed his friend.

Sol asserted "You are being manipulated *Traveler*, and not just by *The Circle*; let us take a brief sojourn, this battlefield will be waiting when we return." Sol snapped his fingers and they both reappeared in a completely different spot.

Sol and Jack stood upon one of the tall skyscrapers of *Mirage*, overlooking the endless grid of streets stretching out into the horizon.

Jack immediately questioned "What is this, how were you able to teleport us?"

To which Sol replied "We're still at the battlefield, physically anyway, what you're seeing is a vision, much like the scrolls."

Jack was still angry with Sol for the events that forced him back to the *Astral Plane*, so he aggressively said "So what are you going to try and explain? That my actions have all been mistakes? That I should return to the real world? Did you and *Loki* think that I would be content to watch thousands die! How could anyone live with themselves after that, returning to this place was my only alternative, Even if it meant being trapped here!"

Sol commented on what he heard in an objective way "Guilt, fear, that's the only thing I hear behind your words; you don't feel these emotions because you ought to, but because you were told to. You've been indoctrinated into a system that tells you what you should do, how you should think, what's right and wrong; it's all a farce *Traveler*! A system of beliefs to constrain your behaviors; created by those who do not even believe the platitudes they cast upon others, enforced by hypocrites who impose a blatant double standard that never acts against their favor."

Sol continued to condemn the system Jack was de-facto defending "It is all a lie. The only thing stopping you from realizing that is fear; fear that has been instilled into every level of your system: fear of punishment, fear of exclusion, fear of humiliation, fear of being wrong."

Jack thought Sol was trying to trick him so counter-argued "What realization? That we should cast down civilization itself? Live in anarchy and lawlessness; killing each other for scraps of food and handfuls of water? What kind of existence is that?"

Sol shook his head and replied "The alternative to your shackled society is not anarchy; that is the planned counter-argument of your society speaking for you, dismissing every alternative as extreme and implausible.

Sol continued "It is that close minded thinking that relegates so many of you to *Mirage*, never daring to dream of anything other than what's been placed in front of you, doomed to live a hollow experience."

Jack felt he needed to defend his viewpoint "You are wrong, we have accomplished much as a civilization; our foundational precepts are worth defending, it's what gives meaning and purpose to our actions."

Sol again countered "Individuals have accomplished great things *Traveler* not your civilization, it was their vision and drive that made those great things happen not your damned institutions or laws; those serve only to keep the masses from revolting upon those who seek to become your masters.

Sol detailed "Your precepts have worth only to those that believe in them, how many times have you witnessed leaders speak of justice and fairness and then engage in unparalleled levels corruption and tyranny; think of all the hypocrisy on open display, mass broadcasted to the masses, think of all the lies that are told and repeated without any examination from those who hear them."

Sol questioned "At what point does it end? Where does it all lead *Traveler?*"

Jack was now at a loss, just as before he was having difficulty defending anything associated with *Mirage*; Sol seemed to know exactly what to say and how to counter every argument.

Sol motioned to their surroundings and continued "You cannot raise a defense to this place because you secretly despise it, why else would you choose to isolate yourself? To spend more time with your machine than any living person, why escape from this supposedly 'ideal' society you live in *Traveler?*"

Sol made his case with emphasis "You must realize by now that it cannot continue this way; it must be cast down, completely and utterly, if any real difference is to be made. Admit it *Traveler*, you want to destroy it as much as I do! Stop lying to yourself; stop allowing them to manipulate you into defending what you hate!"

Jack held up his palm to stop Sol's tirade, he said simply "Clearly you have something in mind; I'm done arguing with you, so speak your piece and let me decide for myself."

Sol raised an eyebrow and spoke "Very well, there is no fault in speaking plainly. I seek to remove the boundary put in place long ago by *The Circle*; to restore the fractured halves of conscious and subconscious, bridging the gap between thought and reality."

Jack questioned "Balthazar told me of such a time, he said it began as a wonder but eventually descended into chaos; and is the very reason you were banished"

Sol rejoined "There were mistakes made; however the barrier was no solution. The barrier is what causes the current schism that necessitates *Travelers* in the first place, and they continue to maintain the barrier simply because in their arrogance they refuse to admit that they were wrong. This time we will learn from our past mistakes, not seeking to gain supremacy and followers but there to guide the people to a new vision, constructs and humans walking the same path towards a new future."

Jack shrugged and replied "And how do I fit into this 'grand vision' Sol? What place is there for an errant *Traveler*?"

Sol spoke sincerely "You have power in this place that cannot be duplicated, and many have rallied to your leadership; if you were to join me we could end this pointless war. Think of what could be   accomplished, *Traveler*."

Sol spoke optimistically "The building of a new *Astral Plane*, the unshackling of the masses of *Mirage*, the end of the current order; then we shall bask in the endless possibilities that shall follow when thought and reality become one!"

Sol's words were convincing, but he was leaving out a very important point; one that Jack wasn't willing to overlook "And what of the people presently falling into comas, how many more are to follow, what is the price of this revolution."

Sol replied with a more ominous tone but spoke with candor "It will number greater than any disaster, war, or disease; it will be the greatest tally of loss ever known. At its onset it will be considered the world's greatest tragedy, matched by nothing before or after it."

Jack glared back replying with force "To agree to that would be insanity, nothing could ever rationalize such a great magnitude of death!"

Sol countered "With your help we could reduce the loss of life greatly"

Jack yelled back over him "It would still be a slaughter! I have heard enough of your words; if that is your solution then I will have none of it!! You say our society is doomed, but you are not god! If there is another way then I will find it, and I will do it without sacrificing everything to realize it."

Sol looked disappointed, but he knew there would be no way to convince him further with words; he snapped his fingers again and they reappeared upon the battlefield, he spoke again, though now far more direly "I have taken a great risk merely by leaving you alive *Traveler*, do not mistake my offer as a sign of weakness, your decision lies between an alliance for the greater good and your most certain death. I will make this offer only one final time, will you join me?"

Jack reached for his weapons and glared back "Never"

Sol yelled back as the entire field began to surge with power "Then live no more *Traveler*!!"

Jack blasted his telekinetic forward with enough force to uproot the nearby trees; Sol deflected it with one hand as if swatting away an annoying fly. Sol countered with a blast of fire that erupted from every direction; Jack barely had time to raise his shield as the fire incinerated everything around them.

Jack was blasted backwards as he was thinking in panic mode "Damn he's fast! Can't let my guard down! His last defense, he didn't use a shield..."

The fire ceased as Jack recovered with a roll and then sprinted forwards with his sword, thrusting the sword point forward; Sol moved out of the way, and then struck Jack with the flat of his hand like a hammer. Jack spun around and slashed with a flurry of attacks, Sol avoided all of them easily, then grabbed Jack's hand and nearly crushed it with his grip; Jack winced in pain and dropped the sword, falling to his knees at what felt like a metal vice crushing his hand.

Jack managed to fight through the pain and punched Sol with a furious uppercut, but it felt like he punched a stone wall; undeterred he continued punching Sol in the chest hoping to wear him down, yet Sol stood undeterred and absorbed all the punches.

Sol muttered "Disappointing" and then kicked Jack backward with such power that a shockwave erupted from it, throwing Jack backwards into the ground. Jack barely managed to pick himself up off the ground, he was in a lot of pain and was increasingly numb, yet he refused to give up.

Jack fired off a rapid succession of telekinetic attacks, first the vacuum attack, then the electrical dust storm, then the compressed pressure wave; Sol kept countering them, deflecting them with equal amounts of counter-force each time.

Things were fast becoming desperate for Jack as his thoughts raced "Nothing is working! I can't even damage him! I have to keep trying, I can't fail again!"

Then he charged up a large gale of telekinetic force and absorbed it while yelling aloud "I will not fail again!" and then blasted himself forwards like a jet engine, punching forwards with the force of an oncoming train!

Sol casted a wall of force and gravity; Jack's attack shattered it, but it took away all his momentum. Jack went on the offensive again, punching with the increased force of his reserved power; Sol took a few hits that actually forced him to block. Sol hadn't lost any of his attack power and countered with a lightning fast punch to the gut, Jack's telekinetic field took the full brunt of it yet it still felt like a cannon hitting him as he nearly vomited. Jack needed to hurry, as he would exhaust the telekinetic charge soon; forcing himself forward he punched dozens of times with such speed that it became a blur, all his punches making contact with Sol's torso battering him backwards, as Jack then spun his entire body into a sweep kick. Sol took the full force of it, knocking him backwards off his feet; yet that was the last of Jack's telekinetic charge, the aura quickly fading from him as the pain of his previous injuries returned.

Sol picked himself up and remarked "You may have the potential, but you are not a *Traveler* yet, and as a mere man you cannot hope to win against me."

Sol proceeded to batter Jack with his mighty strikes, Jack didn't have any energy left to lift an arm in his defense, taking the full force of the beating. Jack fell to his knees, his vision rapidly fading, his breath became unsteady, and his entire body was going numb; Jack began to think this could have been his end, he wondered what things might be like afterwards, in the life after life or alternatively the possibility of oblivion.

Sol's words interrupted his thoughts "Goodbye Jack, you would have liked the world I will usher in, take solace knowing you died for the greater good."

Sol then pointed his palm forward like an executioner's axe, blasting the most intense fire-wave Jack had ever encountered. Jack yelled with his final breath and then fell into the ground like a sack of rocks, his stare blank, his entire body unresponsive; a warm light enveloped his surroundings and everything else began to fade away. He wondered if he had actually died, or this was merely another stage of the *Astral Plane*, something beckoned him forward; Jack was able to move despite his injuries, possibly with his spirit rather than his mind, so he stood up and walked into the light… Unsure of what was to come.

14

ESCAPE

JACK'S SURROUNDINGS WERE NOW AN ENDLESS WHITE LIGHT, HIS WEAPONS were gone and his injuries were healed, yet he knew this was more than a vision.

Jack stared out and questioned "What is this? Am I dead?"

A voice that echoed with many speakers answered "A crossroads, a bridge between the great divide of life and what comes after."

Jack called out "What is to follow? Where does it lead?"

The voice calmly replied "To an end of restlessness, to finally be released from life's torments and be at peace."

Jack could feel a great calm washing over him; his emotions were slowly drifting into another state, a great burden felt as if it were lifting from him, his pain and anguish began to fade and he had difficulty resisting.

Jack managed to ask "What of the *Astral Plane*? What of Sol? Should his plan be realized the aftermath would be devastating…?"

The voice answered "These things existed long before you, and will continue long after; everything will continue on their cycle, until the end of time."

Another voice appeared faintly in the background "…Jack…"

As he continued drifting off, his body was now carried forward as if floating on a gentle stream. He was having difficulty even keeping his sense of self intact, something inexorable drew him forward; he felt as if what was happening was inevitable, and he wanted nothing more than to just let go and embrace it.

The second voice called again "…Jack!.."

As the *Traveler* was able to regain his senses briefly "Wait, no I can't give up yet. The events that occurred, the consequences that will follow; I have to try and make things right again, I have to go back!"

Jack turned his gaze backwards from where he was drifting; he managed to fight the current somewhat, reaching backwards from his destination. Every movement felt sluggish like he was exhausted, merely remaining standing took great effort. A flash of images and sound blasted his perception: pain, loss, fear, anguish, anger, it all hit him like a hurricane; he felt as if he were ripping himself from the only comfort he had only known, he continued forward yelling uncontrollably as all the negative things returned, he felt as if he were descending into madness.

The second voice instructed "…Grab my hand… it's difficult…but we need you."

Jack had reached his limit, if he didn't stop soon his mind would be destroyed by the ever intensifying wave of emotion and physical pain; Jack saw an arm reaching out in the distance, he gave it everything he had left and leapt towards it.

Jack was suddenly pulled into an upright position, his face was covered in ash and his clothes were charred. The *Seer* stood over him.

Jack was very dazed. "*Seer*? Where was I just now?"

The *Seer* replied with some relief "You were nearly on the other side boss-man, a few more moments and you would have been lost to this world."

Jack was barely able to remember what occurred; he described as if he were still in a trance "I was at peace, truly. Even now I yearn to be there again… I can't ever get that close again; or I'll lose myself to that place, forever."

The *Seer* nodded and replied "I know boss-man, it waits for us all in the end, but it's not yet your time."

Jack tried to stand but his entire body was wracked with pain, Jack was confused; he didn't remember anything that occurred the last few hours before his death.

The *Seer* cautioned "Hold on boss-man, you were dead a moment ago, don't try and rush it."

Jack questioned "What happened?"

The *Seer* hesitantly explained "You and Sol talked for a while; apparently you didn't like what he had to say and fought against him man-to-man… Then he… Then he killed you boss-man."

Memory fragments began replaying in Jack's mind, the conversation they had, the choice, and the struggle that ended with his death. Jack winced at the sudden recollection; his mind began to recoil at what happened.

Jack spoke with reluctance "I'm sorry, I couldn't beat him; he was too strong…"

The *Seer* stopped him "No one's blaming you boss-man, you gave it your all, and you didn't give up. Even at the end."

The *Seer* looked across the field, the *Sovereign's* army looked to be surrendering to Sol's commanders; Teach and Balthazar's forces were fleeing off the field. Jack and the *Seer* would need to leave quickly.

The *Seer* helped pick Jack up and said "Come on boss-man, we need to go and you need rest."

At that precise moment their entire surroundings came to a dead stop, the *Seer* started calmly stepping upwards like he could walk upon the air itself.

Jack muttered with a laugh "So this is what happens when you teleport."

The *Seer* looked over in surprise "You can actually see it this time?"

Jack laughed and replied "Yes, I have to admit that I didn't believe you before; but now that I can see what actually happens, I have to say that it's actually kind of boring."

The *Seer* jokingly replied "Well sorry to disappoint you, you shouldn't be surprised when I tell the truth, it happens more often than most people think."

Jack retorted "The key to any good lie is some element of truth."

The *Seer* replied "So it goes boss-man, that's just the life we live in." they both laughed a moment as they continued walking upwards towards *the Harbinger*, surrounded by the odd sight of everything frozen in time.

The *Seer* made his way towards an odd hatch at the lower back end of the ship, he then used his cane to leverage it open.

Jack commented "How did you find a backdoor into the ship?"

The *Seer* grumbled "It wasn't easy boss-man, had to search for ages to find it; leads into an odd room in the back, likely not one that sees many visitors by the looks of it."

They proceeded inside through a storage area, it was filled with old boxes, trinkets, and furniture; Jack started to recognize some of the objects in the room "These are things from my past, things I once used... it's strange seeing it all here, and yet I would have never known about it."

The *Seer* added "These are likely totems, manifestations of your memories, which explains why there's a hidden entrance to it."

Jack thought about it and remarked "This ship seems to have had two original designers: myself, and my subconscious; though they seem to have had different ideas in mind."

They then proceeded forward through a few odd doors into the main part of the ship, the *Seer* had Jack's arm over his shoulder and guided them around the time-locked crew; from the scene it looked as if they were at battle stations and hectically in the middle of combat, yet seeing it all frozen in time gave the area an element of serenity.

Jack asked while they moved through the hallways "If everything is frozen in time as you move about, why not just beat your enemies while they are stuck in time?"

The *Seer* smiled and explained "It doesn't work quite like that boss-man; what you're seeing is the illusion of distance and movement. Think on it as being similar to how you move from realm to realm."

Jack attempted to understand "So it's only a shortcut of sorts, the moment your actions influence the scene too much -"

The *Seer* interjected "Then everything plops back into real-time; It takes practice, and can be mighty embarrassing when you suddenly reappear unexpectedly, accompanied by the surprised yells of some dunce"

Jack noticed an error in his logic and replied "Wait, your actions currently aid me; why didn't it jump back into real time?"

The *Seer* shook his head and replied "You mean like the first time I met ya and you suddenly jumped out and grabbed my neck while everything was stopped? *Travelers* are always the exception boss-man, any rule that's written the *Travelers* can find a way to break; though it occasionally requires a bit of doing." They entered the medical bay and the *Seer* set Jack down on the table.

Jack thanked the *Seer* and reached over to tap the medical console, tapping a button which caused them to phase back into real-time. Medical scanners started sweeping over Jack as robotic arms approached with various medical implements.

Jack advised "Go to the bridge, help in whatever way you can; the battle is over, we have to escape from this place."

The *Seer* nodded and said "You got it boss-man".

The *Seer* then disappeared like he normally did. Jack laid back and tried to rest, his entire body was sore and his psyche was still reeling from thoughts of his apparent near-death; He imagined the outcome if he had not returned as he let his thoughts drift off.

The *Seer* appeared upon the bridge, the crew of *the Harbinger* was still skirmishing with the Dauntless, as crew members relayed damage reports and firing orders back and forth.

The *Seer* yelled over the chaos "Sarah, the boss-man lost against Sol, I got him back on the ship but he's beat up bad; we need to get outta here before Sol realizes he's still alive."

Sarah glanced back and continued frantically guiding the helm controls; she was distracted by all the bridge chatter and virtual displays flashing in front of her.

The *Seer* spoke up again "Did you hear me? We gotta get out of here before Sol decides to blow this turkey up!"

Sarah finally pulled herself out of the frantic stress of the battle for a moment and replied "Jack lost?! Wait does that mean we lost? Can we even make it out of this?"

The *Seer* grabbed her shoulder and said "Clear your head and focus, remember that you're the captain of this ship, now how do we get outta here without giving away where we're going?"

Sarah thought for a moment and replied "We can jump out and keep jumping around until   we're clear. That Dauntless could follow us each time though, so we need to disable it before we can get away clean."

The *Seer* continued "Any ideas?"

Sarah replied "the *Fox* built a giant gun running through the length of the ship, one shot from that would definitely do the trick. The only problem is, the Dauntless has been evading the whole time and I doubt a gun that big has guided projectiles."

The *Seer* sighed as he knew he would need to speak with the *Fox* and replied "We'll figure something out, just be ready to jump out the moment we got an opportunity." Then disappeared and headed for the gun bay.

Inside the turret bay was noisy and chaotic, the muffled roar of the guns was constant as crew members frantically performed damage control and put out fires. The *Seer* reappeared next to the *Fox* who had jury rigged three control panels together and was operating all of them at once, he noticed the *Seer*'s arrival but didn't stop what he was doing "Don't bother me right now, the automatic turret controls are damaged and I'm the only one keeping the Dauntless in check with counter fire."

The *Seer* interrupted anyway "We need to leave, the ground battle is lost and we need to get outta here before they turn their attention upward. The captain said you had a big gun that could get that other ship off us."

The Fox corrected "The long-range strategic ballistic gauss weapon; it wasn't designed to be used at close range, the other ship will be moving too erratically for an accurate shot."

The *Seer* continued "Well think of something dammit, cause the boss-man is down and we need to get out of this mess ourselves."

The Fox thought for a moment and replied "There's a fighter-based torpedo we could fire that would neutralize their capacitors temporarily; but every fighter we've sent gets shot down before it can get close enough to deliver the payload, yet with a certain crook telepathic pilot…"

The *Seer* waved his hands in the air "Oh no. No no no; you're not sticking me in one of those damn junk boxes, this thing we're standing in is bad enough."

The Fox retorted "You're the one who said we need to think of a way out ourselves, deal with your personal problems and help, or we all die here: Now choose."

The *Seer* grumbled and replied "Fine I'll pilot one of the suicide boxes, but if that thing starts beeping or screeching at me I'll pull the hatch and get the hell back out of it."

The Fox replied with some satisfaction "Seeing you attempt to pilot one will be entertaining enough, try not to embarrass yourself too much." As he went back to what he was doing, the *Seer* rubbed his forehead and then left for the hangar bay with a multicolored flash.

The *Seer* reappeared in the hangar bay as fighters frantically came and went, all the flight crew was busy with refueling and rearming, and no one was available to ask for directions. The *Seer* figured this was a bad time to ask for help, so he opted for the direct approach and walked over to one of the fighters and started climbing in, muttering to himself the whole time; he sat down in the hatch as the fighter was moved by an overhead crane towards one of the taxi runways.

The radio came on for a moment with the *Fox*'s voice "I'll have the computer load a torpedo and play a quick tutorial on piloting; we don't have much time, so learn fast."

The *Seer* replied sarcastically "Easy for you to say, try driving anything over 5 miles an hour without your eyes"

The Fox retorted "You'll adapt, remember that you must be close when you fire; any further than a few hundred feet and the torpedo will be intercepted."

The radio then shut off and the screen powered on accompanied by a computer voice guide "Welcome to the flight control tutorial, this will help guide you on operation and controls of the ASM fighter mark 3; feel free to add voice queries at any time to the tutorial."

The *Seer* interrupted "How do I steer this thing?"

The computer responded "The central joystick control determines direction, accompanied by the flight petals; use both in conjunction to set pitch, roll, or yaw; the heads up display will show the aircrafts level, speed, altitude, and direction. Please pay attention to these crucial indicators."

The *Seer* jokingly replied "What if I can't see those?"

The computer replied "Please specify?"

To which the *Seer* continued "I'm blind, is there another way to determine those things?"

The computer replied with caution "Warning, it is not recommended that you attempt to fly any aircraft while ['Blind'] or while suffering any other visual impairment."

The *Seer* giggled a bit to himself and said "Don't I know it, please put all pertinent information into audio form for me Ms. Computer; while you're at it tell me the throttle and fire buttons."

After a few minutes of computer aided instruction the *Seer* knew the basics and was positioned onto one of the take-off catapults. The plane sat there calmly for a moment before leaping forwards towards one of the exit doors, launching out with enough speed to generate the lift needed to keep it airborne.

The *Seer* was able to determine his surroundings to some extent due to all the other pilots in the air that he could "see through"; he had a rough idea where the two large ships were , as well as how fast he was going and what direction he was heading… so as long as someone was looking at him.

He took the controls and steered himself towards the direction of the Dauntless. After only a few short moments he was noticed by a group of enemy fighters as they swooped into an intercept course; the *Seer* remained steady on course, he needed to wait for them to try something before acting.

The other fighters readied air-to-air missiles as the *Seer* predicted it and dodged before they locked on, avoiding their path entirely. They attempted to shoot him with auto-cannons, but each time they lined up a shot the *Seer*'s fighter would suddenly veer in the opposite direction before they could pull the trigger. Ironically the *Seer*'s ability made him a very elusive fighter pilot, though he found it ironic that if they stopped trying to kill him and ignored him instead; then he would have crashed from being unable to see through the vision of other constructs.

The *Seer* barreled towards the Dauntless veering and swerving around the deadly hail of anti-aircraft projectiles it fired, hitting the afterburners and propelling his fighter forwards at dangerously fast speeds to avoid being overwhelmed. The *Seer* plotted his attack run as he readied the fire control; his fighter blazing forward on a crash course, as a buzzer started chiming with the computer voice repeating "Warning! Warning! Collision imminent, pull up!"

The *Seer* placed his hand over the button and said to himself "Not just yet, I need to wait until I'm so close that they won't be able to block it...",

He had only seconds before he plowed into the side of the ship; the *Seer* was giving himself very little room for error. In rapid succession he fired the torpedo, hit the flaps and air-brake, and then veered upwards; the torpedo impacted right into the dead center of the Dauntless as the resulting electro-magnetic explosion sapped all of its power reserves, as the Seers fighter avoided smacking into the Dauntless by mere inches. The *Seer* noticed a flood of panicked thoughts coming from the constructs of the Dauntless, so he figured he must have got it; having his fill of flying for a lifetime, he steered his plane to return back to *the Harbinger*.

The other fighters quickly returned as well as they had bought themselves a few moments while the Dauntless was reeling from the attack. *The Harbinger* positioned itself pointing straight towards the middle of the enemy ship as the *Fox*'s main gun charged up to attack.

A deafening echo rang out accompanied by a bright flash as a massive bolt fired out from *the Harbinger* and struck the Dauntless with enough force to tear a hole through its hull; explosions erupted forth and metal creaked and groaned as the Dauntless rapidly lost altitude and descended into the nearby hills.

Before they could have time to act further Sol's army below had re-organized, and began firing a storm of fireball's upwards towards *the Harbinger*, Sarah wasted no time aligning the ship to an escape vector and accelerating away before jumping to another realm.

The *Seer* came onto the bridge as they jumped out asking "Did it work? Are we clear?"

Sarah continued plotting other courses as she tried to talk over the distractions "Won't know for a bit, I want to keep moving and make our trail harder to follow; so far it looks like we're good."

Then she turned for a bit and commented "That maneuver you pulled was pretty gutsy, thanks for putting yourself on the line."

The *Seer* laughed and replied "Nearly rammed myself into em doing it, as if I needed more of a reminder why I hate flying."

The *Seer* then commented "I'm going to go see how the boss-man is doing, tell me over the squawk box if anything comes up."

Sarah added before he left "Make sure to tell Jack I'm glad he's alright"

The *Seer* nodded and replied "Sure thing, I'll tell em when the moment is right, I'm sure he's got a lot on his mind right now." Then he teleported back towards the medical bay.

To the *Seer*'s surprise Jack was nowhere to be found, there were signs he had been there but he didn't stay very long. The *Seer* thought about what occurred earlier and suddenly knew where he would find the *Traveler*, Inside *the Harbinger*'s "backroom". Jack was there, sitting on an old chair surrounded by objects from his past life; he seemed lost in thought as he stared blankly at an old sketch pad of his.

The *Seer* entered and casually found a futon to sit down on.

The *Seer* remarked "Figured I might find you in this old reliquary, we're clear of ol bright N shine's army... now we just gotta figure on what to do next."

Jack glanced up and began speaking off topic "Many people spend their lives wishing they were someone else; maybe as someone more attractive, or wealthier, or more talented."

Jack then commented how this related to him "I only wanted to be good at designing things... yet somehow it never worked, I just didn't have the gift."

Jack set down the pad and began pacing "Now I'm faced with the same dilemma, I need to be this unstoppable force, this *Traveler*, yet as we both just saw I lack the power."

He turned to the *Seer* and asked bluntly "What's to say that I am even the *Traveler* at all? I have one side saying that I am simply because they need me to believe that in order to stop Sol; and another side that says I'm not because the machine put me here, not because of force of will, and certainly not because of destiny."

The *Seer* replied "Your thoughts are in a dark place boss-man, you need to stop dwelling on what went wrong and start thinking of a better solution."

Jack replied with frustration "I am thinking about this! Before now I've just been charging forward like a fool; blasting down obstacles as they appear, thinking I might have been making some sort of impact."

Jack threw his hands in the air and yelled half to himself "Everything hinged on this great battle with Sol and I failed! I was barely able to harm him at all."

Jack then sat back down and stared at the floor "I saw death *Seer*, I was drifting off to some unknown place. The worst part is, I don't know if I was about to experience some sort of afterlife, or if my soul was merely drifting into sheer nothingness, and that's what scares me."

There was a long pause, the *Seer* sighed deeply and replied "I don't have all the answers boss-man, and I'll admit I had my doubts about you initially; though if you've proven one thing it's that your dogged stubborn determination has carried us forward so far.

The *Seer* continued "You've done the impossible time and time again, but there are always gonna be setbacks boss-man, that's how things work."

Then he stood up and walked over to Jack, he offered his hand and said "When you get knocked down you can do two things: surrender to it and give up, or brush yourself off and keep on going. So what's it gonna be?"

Jack glanced up and replied "I didn't return from the dead simply to quit, I just don't know what I'm doing anymore… it's all so very frustrating."

Jack then grabbed the Seers hand and got himself back up then replied "I'll keep trying *Seer*, I'm not sure of anything at this point, but I'll keep trying."

In the corner of the room the shadows began to animate, Jack and the *Seer* readied to fight whatever slinked into the room. Yet before they could identify what it was a familiar voice proposed "I might have a solution, though it comes with its risks."

Jack hissed back "*Loki*! Why would I want to hear anything you have to say!?"

Loki's voice laughed in return "I suppose our last encounter didn't end well, perhaps a sign of goodwill?"

From the shadows a black raven fluttered in and perched upon one of the dressers, its glowing eyes were unmistakable; Jack remembered "The raven, *Terror*. He works for you!"

Loki replied "The ravens have always been messengers of the Norse gods, you should know that."

Jack questioned "Why did you help me before?"

To which *Loki* replied "That's simple really, I needed you to continue your quest with Malachi; and I hadn't expected you to end up in *Terror* of all places."

Jack practically spit out the words he was so infuriated "I haven't forgotten how you manipulated me into your little game! How you threw me back into this place when reality began to collapse around me."

Loki mockingly replied "You opened the door when you entered the machine for the second time, the wise man warned you as you plunged forward disregarding the risk so callously; your curiosity unleashed these demons and your thoughtless actions were the catalyst, I merely guided the chaos."

Loki then appeared from the shadows, greeted immediately by the thrust of Jack's sword into his gut; *Loki* initially looked panicked and clutched his gut, but then began laughing uncontrollably and displayed a familiar ring.

Loki explained "The blood ring, which you delivered into the hands of my agent; I've worn it long enough to become deathless, even if you were to slice me into pieces and burn those to ash I would still return."

Jack removed the sword but stubbornly backhanded *Loki* across the face then angrily said "Speak quickly then, before I test the limits of your 'deathlessness'"

Loki grabbed one of the objects of the room and moved it between his fingers as he said "I had initially sided with Sol because his advent onto the *Astral Plane* was inevitable for all those who could see it; I had thought if I could side with this unstoppable force I may earn a place in the new order."

The *Seer* mockingly replied "What's the matter, did Sol not give ya enough attention after he didn't need ya no more."

Loki tossed the object he was holding at the *Seer* who merely teleported out of the way, then he smiled and continued "Sol has been deviating from his plans, altering his promises; but most of all he has a weakness: he is afraid of you."

Jack scoffed at this and replied "Clearly not, you must have missed the part where he flattened me."

Loki tapped on his own forehead for emphasis and replied "You're not thinking about this very much are you? Sol is not afraid of you personally, he is afraid you will turn the constructs against him, you are after-all a sort of rallying figurehead."

Jack clenched his fist and pounded it against one of the nearby pieces of furniture "Who would follow someone who was defeated by the very enemy he was sworn to stop?"

Loki raised an eyebrow and replied coyly "I don't know, perhaps the one that brought the greatest siege of the *Astral Plane* to a stalemate and then rose from the dead; unless there's some other messiah the masses can put their faith in when facing Sol's impending wrath."

Jack narrowed his gaze "Fine I get it, but what's my advantage, how do I gain any leverage against Sol when he can defeat me at any time?"

Loki cleverly replied "You must find and wield the power of the '*First Blade*'"

15

THE

FIRST

BLADE

JACK STARRED BACK AND LOKI AND INTERROGATED "WHY HAVEN'T I heard of this weapon before? If this is the key to defeating Sol then someone would have mentioned it; that is unless it's dangerous to use."

Loki explained "There is most certainly a risk; the *First Blade* was one of the early incarnations of man's mastery over metal and the deadly weapons that followed. The *First Blade* has been used to kill countless thousands, and after being used to end so many souls it eventually developed... its own personality."

The *Seer* interrupted "That's distorting things a bit, the swords power has a way of turning its wielder into a bloodthirsty glory seeker; it can't kill enough or conquer enough to ever be sated, its "suggestions" usually bend and twist the morality of the user. Those who take up the *First Blade* always end up on an endless spiral of madness: more death, more slaughter, more destruction."

Jack questioned "How powerful is this sword? Powerful enough to stop Sol?"

Loki explained "Think of it more as a conduit, the sword has its own power yes; but can greatly amplify the strength the wielder brings to it. The *First Blade* in the hands of a *Traveler* would be... Unstoppable."

The *Seer* replied with anxiety "Don't even consider this *Traveler*! That sword has never done no good to no one, it's corrupted anyone that's touched it and it will consume you too."

Jack replied back "You said the *Traveler* can break the rules binding the *Astral Plane*, I could use that to insulate myself from its influence."

The *Seer* argued back "It's too great of a risk! You don't know what the wielders of that sword have done!"

Jack answered back calmly "You saw what happened when I faced Sol directly, we would have stopped his entire crusade if I could have beaten him."

Jack then started directly at the *Seer* and said bluntly "If I am to defeat Sol I must risk everything, the consequences of failure are too great otherwise; Sol told me himself, were his plan to come to fruition it would be the greatest loss of life ever known, the world's greatest tragedy."

Jack said with a degree of conviction "That is an outcome that I must prevent at all cost. If the sword gives me a chance to stop that, no matter what it might personally cost me, then I will do what I must."

Jack turned back to *Loki* and demanded "Where can I find the sword?"

Loki described the answer in detail "Its last resting place lies in the convergence between Epic and *Terror*, where the two realms begin to intertwine; you'll find it in the center of a mausoleum."

The *Seer* seemed to recall this "Buried around the bodies it broke, guarded by the souls it took; so the saying goes."

Loki concluded "It may test you to see if you prove worthy to wield it, be wary."

The twisting darkness he used to enter the room reappeared; as he proceeded to exit from it, saying as he left "Farewell *Traveler*, we will meet again."

Loki then exited as the raven flew back through the portal before they both suddenly disappeared. Jack then committed himself to this new course and marched out towards the bridge; the *Seer* sat there for a moment and then reluctantly followed him.

Jack entered and commanded Sarah "Take *the Harbinger* to the place where Epic and *Terror* converge, there's something we need to get from there."

Sarah seemed taken aback by the lack of greeting "Are you going to be ok Jack? I mean, you just went through a lot in the last few hours."

Jack bluntly replied "We can't afford to dwell on what happened, if we're going to defeat Sol we need to take action, get us to where I asked."

Sarah frowned and replied "Alright Jack, great talking to you too by the way." As the ship then jumped forward to the realm convergence.

A blur of distance and speed went by as *the Harbinger* reappeared over where Epic and *Terror* began to merge; on the Epic side lie the trenches and wastelands of battle, on the *Terror* side was the sight of bodies in a field and a city on fire. They represented two sides of the same coin, the horror and desolation of war; Jack wondered what sort of atrocities the sword must have committed to be placed here.

At the center of it both areas there was a temple with byzantine architecture with many pale statues around it, the courtyard of the temple was lit by the oddly colored flames of pylons scattered throughout the grounds; upon the roof of the temple many great pillars held up great pyramid on whose face a there was a carving depicting the chronicle of the *First Blade*.

Jack immediately knew this was the place "The mausoleum, its appearance is foreboding; the sword must be a great and terrible weapon indeed."

The *Seer* added "It's not wrong to have doubt on this one boss-man, once you release that sword there'll be a reckoning."

Jack replied "Nothing can be worse than what awaits us if we fail. Take us down Sarah; I'm going to the cargo bay."

Jack and the *Seer* took the elevator down to the cargo bay, the *Fox* was near one of the bulkheads tending to repairs; Jack found it odd how quickly the *Fox* had acclimated himself to what was supposed to be a temporary stay, he wondered if perhaps the *Fox* needed to stay busy to keep his mind off something.

The *Fox* said with little regard "Do you still intend to uphold our agreement?"

Jack answered "There's something I must attend to first, when I return I'll hear your story and then you'll have your power source."

The *Fox* replied "Good, I'd hate to have you renege on our deal."

Jack frowned and replied "I'm not Machiavellian like you *Fox*, when I say I'll do something I mean it."

The *Fox* muttered "That's what everyone says until they find it inconvenient." as Jack ignored the slight as he and the *Seer* descended downwards to the wastelands below.

They were lowered onto a field around the mausoleum; the scene was like that of an inhospitable badlands. All around them was empty, devoid of life, with only the howling wind sweeping across the landscape to break the silence. Upon further inspection Jack saw the husks of dead trees and the bones of animals, and then he understood that this place was not always dead, devastation made it this way.

They walked towards the temple, keeping their guard up for any potential traps or ambushes. They proceeded through the vast statue filled courtyard, there were statues scattered throughout of men wielding different swords, yet all of them bore the same odd symbol on the hilt with a red gem at its center.

The *Seer* noticed him examining the statues and remarked "The *First Blade* can morph itself over time; it has taken a lot of names over the years, yet it's always some type of sword."

Jack inquired further "The gem and that symbol? Those are the core of the sword?"

The *Seer* replied "The symbol represents control over death, the gem is rumored to be a sort of repository; they say it keeps the memories of those who wielded the sword, perhaps even their immortal souls."

The *Seer* continued forward as Jack took a moment to look over the statue, he noticed something off about its face; as Jack stared deeper into the statue's face could almost imagine it being alive, its eyes suddenly lit up. "Buried in a crypt from long ago, gleaming steel adorned with a blood red gem. A haunting riddle carved in the rock before the altar "take it up and resolve not to cast it down, great riches and a head adorned with a crown, all this can be yours if you make yourself covenant bound."

The vision from the statue continued the chronicle "Taking it up I felt a dark whisper, from the edges of the room it crept; '…promise me' it beckoned, 'promise me and whatever you desire is yours.' I contemplated for a moment, but my greed overpowered wisdom; I swore myself to the sword, it told me thus "From the one that forged that *First Blade*, their savage soul was made; now you and I are the same."

Jack suddenly snapped out of the vision, the *Seer* was in front of him shaking his shoulders "Snap out of it boss-man"

As Jack came to and replied "I'm alright, I was just seeing something; an old memory maybe, thoughts of one of the previous wielders."

The *Seer* nodded and replied "Their ghosts are drawn back to the sword upon death, their memories haunted by their actions wielding the *First Blade*. Yet all the stories are the same, the temptation, the descent, and crossing the point of no return."

Jack shook his head and replied "Perhaps I can learn what it was that ensnared them, and how I can prevent such a thing from occurring to me."

The *Seer* shook his head and pointed at the statues saying grimly "Every one of them thought the same thing, and they all walked down the same accursed path; it's not too late to turn back boss-man, we can find something else."

Jack resolved to proceed further "There is no other way, let's go."

They reached the entrance and stood before the great door. The doors had been opened recently, they pushed it further in and proceeded inside, built into the walls were the many alcoves containing coffins; the dull torchlight illuminating only a fraction of the room, there had to be hundreds of them, perhaps thousands "Did all of these men wield the sword; or are these also the victims"

Jack thought as there were too many coffins to count. Adorning the walls between sections were murals of brass, Jack gazed at the carvings of many great battles led by a singular figure, always in the picture of fury, with their grip tightly upon the sword. One of the murals seemed to play out as his vision blurred, he entered yet another vision.

He heard a familiar voice speak "Great multitudes have fallen, yet it is not enough. My forsworn deed stands fulfilled, though I care not. The sword weighs heavily in my hands as my footsteps tread with a great burden, my vision is a blur and my mind is a haze. One question always taunts me: 'who was he who forged the deadly blade?' Though I know not the answer its implications haunt me. Then I wonder as I descend deeper into the spiral, do I command the sword, or does it command me?"

Jack came to his senses once again; the *Seer* was slightly further ahead of him and appeared to be searching for something. He heard the *Seer*'s voice echo "There's something up ahead boss-man, come on."

As Jack shook his head and followed him deeper into the mausoleum. After walking for a time they reached the middle of the great tomb, at the center of the room was a spiral staircase going underground.

Jack peered down but didn't see any sources of light below, the *Seer* commented "After you boss-man, unless you're afraid of the dark?"

Jack frowned and replied "I don't suppose you are?"

To which the *Seer* laughed and replied "Course not, I live in it."

Jack wanted to slap his forehead when he realized that gaff, but refrained, focusing on brightening the illumination on his telekinetic gloves instead before going down the stairs. As they walked down the long spiral staircase, the air became cold and damp as they went further and further underground, they finally reached the bottom after dozens of stairs. At the foot of the staircase was the entrance to a sort of treasure room, though much of its contents almost made it a sort of armory; stored within this repository were decorative pieces of armor, silver bladed weapons and arrows, and seized symbols of royal authority: crowns, scepters, and seals.

The *Seer* explained "The treasures of war, the foremost temptation to take up the *First Blade*."

Jack nodded in return and proceeded to search around for a blade with the familiar handle and gem, gently sifting through the piles of treasure as the *Seer* felt the room out with his cane.

Jack's foot struck upon one piece of armor that was more weighed down than the others, he grabbed it and pulled it out of a pile of silver coins only to uncover a mummified corpse. The armor had the same symbol as the sword, but the sword itself was nowhere to be found; Jack released the corpse, but it suddenly grabbed back and glared at Jack with its empty eye sockets.

Jack readied his weapon, but he heard a wretched echoing voice in his mind "Hear my warning! Whatever your desire, whatever your quest for vengeance, do not take up the sword! To hold it is to abandon all reason, to use it plunges your soul into the heart of darkness. Know the meaning behind this riddle 'who was he that forged that first deadly blade, from its steel his savage soul was made' the answer is not as enigmatic as it seems."

Then the corpse suddenly went stiff and fell back over. Jack backed up nervously; he unsheathed his sword expecting more to rise up, but none did.

'A hallucination?' Jack mentally wondered as he tried to calm down and catch his breath, his thoughts were interrupted by the *Seer* who called out "…It's over here boss-man, I can sense it."

Jack walked deeper into the treasure room, at the end there was a narrow archway that opened into a large circular room, the *Seer* stood at the entrance daring not to enter further as if superstitious. Jack walked around him and peered into the room, at the center was the *First Blade* plunged into a great stone plinth, the floor was a steel spiral leading inwards to the plinth, laid all around it were many skeletons of men crawling towards the sword.

Jack could clearly see all the warnings, but he could not turn away; were he to give up out of fear he would not be able to endure the consequences of failing to stop Sol. Jack took a single step forward and a bright flash erupted throughout the room.

An impassable barrier separated him and the *Seer*, the skeletons all began to rise, the *Seer* yelled through the barrier "Boss-man?!"

Jack readied his weapons, but to his surprise none of the skeletons moved to engage him; instead they all knelt down facing the sword and spoke in unison with their unnatural voices "Who was he that forged that first deadly blade! Who was he that forged that first deadly blade! Who was he that forged that first deadly blade!"

Another more powerful voice responded with an echo that filled the room with its deep tone "From its steel his savage soul was made."

The heavy metal clang of footsteps drew Jack's gaze to the opposite side of the room, to a metal clad warrior that appeared from the shadows in the far side of the room and now stood before him. Black plate armor from head to toe, a massive broadsword in his hands, that bucket shaped helmet with the narrow slits for eyes, that deep German accented voice, he remembered facing this opponent before: the Black Knight.

The Black Knight pointed at Jack and spoke "You and I have fought before, I guarded a relic that I knew would draw forth the strong; you bested me, but upon reflection I discovered you had cheated, you used power that was not your own, a sign of weakness if there ever was one."

Jack ignored the topic and questioned "You used the *First Blade* in that forest?"

The knight replied definitively "No, had I used the *First Blade* you would not be here now. The *First Blade* made me what I am: a warrior without parallel; I rose up a knight with no master, undefeatable, and feared"

Jack interrupted "With a heart of darkness"

The knight scoffed and replied "That is the curse of the sword, to always fight, never to rest; once you take up the sword you can never know peace, only war."

Jack replied "Then I will break the curse of the sword, use it to cast down Sol; restore the *Astral Plane* and prevent a great calamity. Though those actions I will earn peace."

The knight laughed in return "The words of a fool, the sword is no trifling thing and suffers not the pretentious."

The sword's gem began to glimmer brightly, which caught the eye of the knight, it then faded back to normal as the knight seemed to understand some hidden message "The sword sees potential in you, your frequent battles in the past have piqued its interest; I am to test you to see if you prove worthy. Fail this test and you pay the ultimate price with your life, do you accept this challenge?"

Jack nodded in return saying "Dispense any ritual, I am not afraid."

The knight replied "Good! The first part of your test: the *First Blade* has taken many forms, but they always mirror a sword. The *First Blade* refuses to change its form to that of an axe, or a hammer, or a spear; here is my riddle, of the myriad of weapons that exist, why must the *First Blade* be a sword?"

Jack thought for a few moments, considered the mention of the other objects and what they had in common, and then finding the answer he replied "Because those other things started as something else, and their forms have other purposes; the sword has only one purpose: as a weapon to kill men."

The black knight clapped his hands together and replied "Very good, the sword is no tool, nor is it for hunting, it is a weapon; the *First Blade* may take many shapes but always remains a sword at its core."

The black knight paced around for a moment and then continued "You have heard the riddle which echoes through this place and the visions of the sword wielders; that riddle which transfixes them and represents the presence of the sword. The sword has not often asked, but now demands the answer from you! The meaning of the riddle, which you as a mere novice cannot hope to know, but must in order to wield it; I now ask you, who forged the *First Blade*?"

The knight elaborated "What malevolent spirit could have been responsible for such a curse? Which of the many spirits of smiting and war, of wrath and ruin, of curses and plagues? Of all of possibilities, who is the one true bringer of the *First Blade* into this world!"

Jack thought for a long time on the answer to this riddle, the black knight paced back and forth laughing softly to himself, confident that the *Traveler* would not be able to discern the answer. Jack thought hard about possible demigods he knew of and the ones he encountered; but upon reflection he realized that the passage was not meant to allude to something divine, it was meant to reflect tragedy.

Discerning this fact Jack knew there was only one answer to the question as he said "The forger of the *First Blade*... was man."

The black knight yelled back "Man?! Man!" As the black knight stabbed his sword into the ground and marched over to the *First Blade*, yanking it out of the plinth and holding it into the air as a blast of power radiated outwards and turned the skeletons to ash; pinning Jack against the wall and radiating through the room with immense heat and force.

The black knight yelled over the chaos "This blade of immense power and destruction, of unrelenting chaos, of unstoppable force! And you think it was forged by man!! I will ask you again *Traveler*, who forged the first deadly blade!"

Jack yelled back over everything "It was man!!"

The surroundings then immediately faded to calm, Jack fell back onto his feet as the knight pointed the blade towards him "Few of any have replied with such an answer, fewer still maintain this upon seeing it unleashed; and though this is an instrument of death, the taker of so many lives, it was indeed brought forth by an ordinary man."

The knight began banging the sword against the ground; its echo reverberated throughout the mausoleum, the walls stretched outwards to oblivion and the ceiling spun away to an impossible distance.

The knight spoke once more "To the drumbeat of steel-on-steel we shall duel; the sword refuses to yield to any that are too weak to use it. To wield the sword you must defeat its previous owner in a contest of martial skill, no magic, no technology, and no tricks. Consider this your final test? Are you ready?"

Jack removed his telekinetic gloves, dropped the cross bow and unsheathed his sword, he took a deep breath and answered "Very well… Begin."

The black knight charged forward sword overhead, swiping down with enough force to split a tree in half. Jack rolled deftly to the side, recovered, and then slashed horizontally towards the knight; the knight's reactions were fast as he blocked the slash with a turn of his wrist, and responded with several quick slashes of his own.

Jack and the knight were now blocking and countering at impressive speed: horizontal, diagonal, and vertical swipes continued as the whistling of air and the clang of metal marked the rapid pace of the battle.

Jack managed with an overhead parry to direct the *First Blade* into the ground; he did a fast turn and kicked the Knight backwards, giving himself some operating room. Jack noticed however that the knight's speed and power were far less then when he previously fought him, he demanded the answer to this mystery "The sword has weakened you, you were faster and stronger last time we fought; why would I wish to wield something that robs you of the advantage."

The knight laughed and answered "You are fighting me as I truly am, with the power and knowledge of the sword withdrawn; if the sword were to unleash its full power against every challenger, then it would never pass on to any warrior but the first."

Jack understood now, the black knight's challenge of a contest without the use of magic or tricks included the power of the sword, meaning that it was a fair fight. Jack readied his sword and charged forward again, with him and the knight fighting each other to a near stalemate; every attack being blocked and countered, yielding no avail to either fighter.

Jack noticed that although the black knight's speed and power were still formidable he was greatly encumbered by the black plate armor, Jack needed to use that to his advantage. Jack dashed backwards and readied himself, the black knight pursued forward leading with a powerful horizontal swing; Jack dove forward under the arc of the blade and recovered behind him, Jack then stabbed into the knights exposed back, but was only able to pierce the armor slightly, the added sharpness and power of his sword were greatly reduced owing to the terms of the duel.

The knight swung his entire body around forcing Jack to jump backwards out of the way, the knight stood still for a moment and breathed heavily "It has been a long time since any man wounded me, but it will take more than that to bring me down. Have at you!"

As the Knight charged forward yet again, Jack blocked the attack but was caught off guard when the knight locked their swords into the ground; Jack couldn't free his sword as the knight backhanded Jack's face with his sword hilt. Jack stumbled backwards as he was forced to block the proceeding flurry with slight dizziness and confusion; Jack needed to regain the initiative, recalling a technique learned during his martial arts lessons with practice swords: the riposte.

Jack waited for his opponent to lunge and then aggressively countered with his block, shoving the blade sideways; with his brief opening he took a diagonal step to the opposite side of his opponent, slashing as he followed through. The Knight lurched forward clutching his injury, the damage of the last hit forcing him to take a brief moment of pause.

Jack was gaining the upper hand and argued "Give up, the surrendering of the sword doesn't need to end with your death."

The knight laughed, and then laughed some more, so much so that it echoed back from the void; then he turned around, unclipping the fasteners on his plate armor and removing the arm and shoulder guards; Jack saw that underneath the armor the knight's flesh was blackened and corrupted. The knight removed his chest plate and began speaking while unbuckling his helmet "You misunderstand the ulterior purpose of this fight *Traveler*"

As he finished removing his helmet at Jack could see his sunken eyes, his dry cracked flesh, and an unnaturally blackened skin tone, Jack then understood as the knight continued "Though I feel pain I cannot die, not even death itself can release me from my oath to the *First Blade*; sword wraith they call me, bound to serve until I am defeated so the sword can pass to a new wielder. Hold no illusions *Traveler*. This duel continues until the sword judges my defeat, or until you are dead."

Jack resolved to deal a death blow with his next strike, yelling as he charged forward "So be it!" vaulting high into the air, swinging downwards with a furious attack. The knight waited until the last moment and then swatted Jack out of the air with the blunt of his blade before he could complete the attack. Jack tumbled across the ground, dazed by the sudden speed of the knight without the encumbrance of his armor; Jack got up and began to swing more furiously, causing sparks to fly off the sword edges and the recoil to reverberate loudly around them.

Jack no longer had the advantage; small glancing blows would not be enough to defeat the undead opponent, and without the weight of his armor the knight could easily match Jack's speed. As the sword fight began to drag on the *Traveler* began to tire, his physical stamina rapidly reaching his limit as the knight seemed to carry on tirelessly. Jack realized he would need one final strike of reckless abandon if he were to win.

Jack allowed the next attack to proceed without fully blocking it, instead diffusing the strike by deflecting it slightly; though it still slashed across Jack's lower abdomen. Jack's armor took some of the blow but the wound was deep. Despite this, Jack's deflection had maneuvered his sword to the perfect position for a deadly follow-up strike; knight's eyes widened as

Jack yelled through the pain and swung precisely with his sword, slashing the knight's neck wide open and causing him to collapse onto his back.

The knight had no blood, but gasped regardless; he stared up at the *Traveler* and replied "Thank you… for releasing me." The knight then breathed one final breath before collapsing into a pile of ash.

Jack grabbed the *First Blade* before falling onto his hands and knees, the black knight's last attack had hurt him badly and he was starting to cough up blood. The gem on the *First Blade* began to glow brightly, he heard a voice in his head that was not his own "*Traveler*… you seek redemption, to restore the balance and defeat Sol. Promise me, and it shall be yours."

Jack answered back aloud "Upon what terms?"

The voice replied "The promise is unconditional, and you will soon die otherwise; swear to me…"

Jack collapsed, he gasped the handle of the *First Blade*; he could barely hear the *Seer* yell in the background "Don't use the sword!"

Jack whispered "…I'll do it, I will pledge myself to the *First Blade*" The sword's gem shimmered as Jack's vision filled with gathering darkness.

He heard the voice of the sword laugh in return and announce "I am the *First Blade*, the destroyer of man; with your word the covenant is sealed."

The entire room quaked and a trailing echo escaped from the sword, a red shockwave flew out and the room returned to normal, the *Seer* ran in and checked Jack to see if he was alive. The *Seer* felt no pulse; he began panicking "Boss-man! Jack!!"

The *Traveler*'s eyes suddenly opened, he stood up unaided and appeared to be healed, the *Seer* stood back a moment and asked "Are you still yourself boss-man?"

Jack grinned uncharacteristically and replied "I feel better than ever, now we must go. There is much work to be done."

16

THE 11TH

HOUR

JACK RE-EQUIPPED HIS WEAPONS BUT KEPT ONE HAND FIRMLY GRIPPED around the *First Blade* at all times; Jack then proceeded to ascend the staircase, walked back through the mural hallway, and exited the mausoleum with the sword in his hands, the *Seer* was following nervously behind him.

Holding the *First Blade* was a sensation not unlike that of the scrolls, he now possessed experience and knowledge that were not his own; however, the influence of the *First Blade* was also present in the form of another line of thought occurring simultaneously within his mind.

As they neared the exit the *Seer* spoke up "What are you thinking boss-man?"

Jack was surprised by this question and replied "How would you not know the answer to that?"

The *Seer* replied direly "As soon as you picked up that blade I sensed nothing, I had thought you had kicked the bucket again; something about that sword shuts me out, is anything different? ...Any additional voices carrying on in your noggin."

Jack thought for a moment and replied "It's difficult to explain really; the sword opens a vast repository of experience. It would be as if reading a thousand books while training for a lifetime, yet there is also this odd undercurrent of residual thoughts carrying me forward, a motivation that Is not my own."

The *Seer* replied with concern "Can you control it?"

Jack replied "That's just it, there isn't some struggle of willpower occurring; it's as if there is another side of personality manifested, it's more of a sensation or feeling. Regardless, the final decisions are still my own; the *First Blade* does not resist my thoughts nor does it attempt to make ones of its own."

The *Seer* replied positively but couldn't hide his anxiety "That's good boss-man, real good; we might find a way through all this yet."

Jack heard an internal reply that was not his own "He's nervous, nervous of you... for the first time he doesn't have the assurance of knowing what you will do next."

Jack ignored what he was hearing and continued forward "The elevator should be just ahead, let's not stay here any longer than we have to"

425

The *Seer* replied "Amen to that boss-man" as they traversed back through the wasteland and boarded the elevator.

Returning to the cargo bay they saw the *Fox* in the background, who was busy performing calibrations; when the *Fox* noticed the *First Blade* though, he stopped what he was doing entirely and seemed stunned at the sight of the legendary weapon. The *Seer* and Jack walked by him without noticing and headed for the bridge.

When they arrived Jack spoke to Sarah with an oddly impersonal tone "We need to go to *Mirage*, set course and take us there immediately."

Sarah was a bit put off, she figured maybe almost dying put him into a temporary funk, but here he was back with the blunt and formal routine; she replied with an upset tone "You know what, maybe I won't; maybe I'll drive *the Harbinger* straight into the ground next. What the hell is with you Jack? First I hear that you died, then you show up acting like a statue without even giving us so much as a reassuring 'I'm ok', and now all I am to everyone around here is the driver of an extremely bulky, well-armed taxi. Well you know what, screw you! Let's start with an actual greeting shall we? Otherwise feel free to jettison yourself out the nearest exit door!"

Jack sighed, took a moment and replied "I'm sorry for having taken you for granted these past few hours Sarah; these trying events have brought me to the brink and I have difficulty remembering to spare a few moments for common courtesy, I assure you that this crisis we find ourselves embroiled in will soon reach its conclusion. At that point, I wholly look forward to resuming our conversation where it left off."

Sarah grumbled a bit, then rolled her eyes and went back to driving the ship "Alright fine I get it, I just don't want this to be something that drags you off to where you're unapproachable or something; I'll set course for *Mirage*, it's good to have you back by the way." With that the ship jumped forward and reappeared over the endless city-scape of *Mirage*, the conflict with Sol still waging as the fires burned in the streets and ash rained from the sky.

Jack turned to the communications station and reached for a microphone, the *Seer* looked at him puzzled and commented "Just what are you planning on saying boss-man? Those people down there aren't keen on listening to much of anything."

Jack smirked as he replied with a veiled undertone "That is because our words were not framed to their level of understanding, in order to rouse the mob you must speak of fear."

Jack switched on the microphone and his voice was now broadcasting loudly to the masses teeming in the cityscape below; he spoke with a commanding air, all traces of trepidation and uncertainty were now gone from his voice "Citizens of *Mirage*, hear me! For too long you have tolerated this invasion, suffering at the hands of these foolish crusaders and their false god; you have resisted but have not yet truly fought because you don't realize what is at stake. The false god Sol would cast down everything you've built because of his arrogance; you stand at the brink of losing your entire way of life should you fail to act. In the face of so great a threat you must now resolve not merely just to resist, but to conquer! Your enemy fears your numbers and your power! Will you now balk at their tyranny?"

As the masses below replied with a rising roar "NO!"

Jack continued "Then rise up! Go forth and destroy the enemy! Drive them from *Mirage*; punish their every transgression! Make them rue the day they ever stepped forth within your city!"

As rising roar of the crowd yelled back and sprang into action, the pace of the city below became that of a frenzy, as the fighting below sharply intensified and the tide began to visibly turn to the side of the *Avatars* of *Mirage*.

"Well done" Jack heard a voice say, though he doubted anyone else could hear it.

Jack placed the microphone back on its stand as the *Seer* stood in awe and replied "How did you do that boss-man?"

Jack calmly replied "Part of the *Traveler*'s power is the ability to influence and change *Astral Plane* around them, the realm of *Mirage* was already fighting Sol, only needed to… motivate them to try a bit harder."

The *Seer* looked at the viewing screen as it showed the *Avatars* attacking relentlessly in a fury not often seen, he remarked "That you certainly did, I question the wisdom of this action."

Jack explained in a coldly logical way "Sol derives part of his power from the devotion of his followers; so in order to weaken him the course of action is simple: kill all those who follow him."

The *Seer* frowned upon hearing that chain of thought "By that notion we might find ourselves destroying places simply to keep Sol from conquering em."

Jack confidently replied "That would be the desperate solution, but now that I wield the power of the *First Blade* such drastic measures won't be necessary; in a few short hours all that Sol worked so hard to build will lie broken at his feet."

The *Seer* frowned and replied "Sounds like you're doing this to get back at him, not to put things right."

Jack replied "They are not mutually exclusive; besides, you're talking about the one that killed me a short time ago, that warrants some level of revenge."

Jack then looked back up at the view screens, watched as the crusading *Templars* were crushed before the rising mob; a subtle creeping grin seemed to imply he was enjoying the sight of it.

Once he'd witnessed enough Jack said "Take us out of this place Sarah, we've seen enough."

She replied quizzically "Where might that be?"

As Jack said heading for the elevator "It really doesn't matter, we're just waiting for the mob of *Mirage* to enact their vengeance; feel free to take the ship wherever you want, in fact… why don't you surprise me."

As he tapped the elevator button and descended onto a lower deck. Sarah glanced over at the *Seer* and replied sarcastically "Are you sure you brought back the same guy?"

The *Seer* shook his head in response and replied "I aint sure of nothing no more, *Loki* shows up and points us to that damned sword and now Jack is acting all loopy."

Sarah replied "What can we do about it?"

The *Seer* thought for a moment and made a plan "I'm gonna leave the ship for a while and scout around; If I keep my ear to the ground I might be able to turn up something on *Loki* or that damn blade."

Sarah replied nervously "What should I do in the meantime…"

The *Seer* cautiously replied "Keep your head down, and don't trust Jack. Something's not right with him; that sword is making him unpredictable."

Sarah nodded and replied "No problem, just hurry back."

As the *Seer* nodded in return "I'll be back before you know it" And then teleported away with the usual multicolored flash.

The *Seer* decided to investigate the *Palace of Eternity*; something didn't bode right about what happened, nor the swift chain of events that followed. It was nighttime now, and even though the conquest only happened a short time ago the crusaders were already showing their presence: Sol's *Templars* were now patrolling around the palace, with sun banners draped over the previous symbols of authority.

The *Seer* decided that the best course of action was to sneak in and see what he could find out. Normally breaking into such a well-fortified palace would be difficult, but being able to sense what guards were seeing and pick up on their thoughts made the *Seer* a master of stealth. If he perceived someone catching a glimpse of him, or if they started thinking that they heard something suspicious, then a quick teleport out of the way would solve the problem. After-all, the guards didn't have the time to check every little occurrence; often resuming their patrols upon finding nothing of substance to confirm their suspicions. His only real obstacle was the walls and locked entryways of the palace, which he couldn't teleport through unless he had a physical line of access, and because the palace had few windows, he was in for a slight challenge.

The *Seer* approached the grounds and took a mental note of the number and position of the guards, phasing into his teleport walk he made his way over the wall and into one of the plazas inside the palace grounds. All the doorways now had locked metal gates, guards stood at either side of each gate, with various other guards patrolling the gardens. The *Seer* picked a spot in a group of shrubs and phased back in, he loitered there for a while to observe the guards and take note of their patterns.

After a few minutes a guard with a much more elaborate uniform and more armor marched in from around one of the corners, the *Seer* took a mental note 'Queue guard captain' as the captain approached one of the locked gates and retrieved a key ring from a chain around his neck.

The *Seer* observed to himself "And the master key ring" as the guard captain began unlocking the door.

The *Seer* timed the events out, counting how long it took the door to open and how long of a window he had before the door closed again. With so many guards the next patrol captain appeared only minutes later, the *Seer* waited for his opportunity, and when the next captain opened the door he phase walked around the still-frame guards, through the open door, and into the interior corridors of the palace.

Reaching the inside, the *Seer* noticed *Templars* with bows perched upon decorative ledges at the tops of the supporting pillars; the *Seer* saw an opportunity "Catwalks, thief's best friend" before walking to the top of one and phasing back in.

The hallways were dimly lit by torchlight, and many of the archers were only narrowly gazing at certain spots, the *Seer* would easily be able to stay out of sight but he had to be careful not to walk off any of the ledges by mistake, as there weren't many eyes watching them.

Finding the pattern to the ledges the *Seer* made his way down the halls and kept his mind open to any loose thoughts from the guards, the *Seer* had to search for some time though as most were just thinking of the mundane: errands to be done, when they changed shifts, and what they were planning on eating later, none of those thoughts being particularly useful.

Finally after what seemed to be an hour skulking about he caught the sight of one guard tromping about angrily, the *Seer* figured this was the one "He looks like he's about to up and blow his top off about something, I'm willing to bet he's repeating it near a dozen times."

As he suddenly picked up the guards inner rant "Show the *Sovereign* more respect?! They give me ten demerits and put me on outer patrol for that! That coward surrendered without fighting and now we're supposed to bow our knee to him!"

As he agitatedly grasped his sword-hilt "I should plant my blade in his gut and end this farce".

Calming down and considering the consequences he took his hand off the hilt and stomped off "Were it not for *Loki* I would consider just that… The last one who hindered his plans disappeared without a trace; why does anyone tolerate that wretched little lurker. Another time perhaps, when *Loki* has moved on to his next plot…"

The *Seer* noticed the guard was facing the eastern wing of the palace when he thought about *Sovereign* and *Loki*, and now he had a lead: *Loki* was probably still visiting the *Sovereign*; this was his best opportunity at uncovering what was occurring behind the scenes.

The *Seer* made his way to the eastern part of the palace, taking care to avoid the ledge archers; after a bit of maneuvering he found a gated checkpoint with triple the usual guard, the sight of this convinced the *Seer* he was close to what he was after "There's gotta be some big-shot in there…now to find my way in."

The *Seer* noticed that there was a single guard on the inside of the gate with an obvious key around his neck, the ones on the outside were just there to monitor the area; the *Seer* thought of a plan to lure him out, though it would require him to control the room.

The *Seer* scanned around, he was able to pick out two ledge guards on opposite sides, four stationary guards by the doorway, and three more patrolling up and down the hall. The *Seer* carefully observed their positions, movements, and conversations and planned out how he would gain the upper hand; taking a deep breath he sprang into action.

The first guard was waiting at his post keenly observing the guards below, he didn't even sense the *Seer* behind him until he was grabbed and knocked unconscious; the other ledge guard thought he heard something and glanced up to the other post, seeing the unconscious guard he was about to yell out an alarm as he was suddenly struck from behind. A dampened thud caught the attention of the guards below; they glanced up to the ledge guards, yet only saw a darkened silhouette. Suddenly the wall torches started going out, one by one in sequence until the room was darkened.

One of the guards said to another "Why do the torches cease?"

Another guard said nervously "Observe the surroundings carefully, and remain vigilant."

The room was now greatly obscured, there were no windows for natural light and it was a very cavernous open room; in such conditions the guards could hardly see unless they were standing close by, these were however perfect conditions for the *Seer* who operated efficiently in the dark. The guards continued patrolling unaware they were being watched and targeted by an enemy that could read their every move. One of the three patrolling guards snuck over to one of the pillars, out of view so he could take a sip from his flask; the strange occurrences were making him nervous as he opened the cap with shaking hands, he felt a shift in the air over him as he looked up and was grabbed by his face guard and slammed against the pillar, falling unconscious to the floor.

The other two guards ran over and saw the flask upon the ground; they began arguing "Blasted drunk, he'll face the stocks for this."

As the other guard retorted "Drunkenness didn't knock his head in, something stinks about this."

A figure approached from the shadows behind them, they continued debating oblivious to the lingering threat. The four guards on the opposite side of the room squinted to see what was occurring on the far side of the room, one of them called out "Eh what's happening over there? Who's that with you?" as they heard muffled strikes and quickly silenced yelps of pain.

Suddenly the shadows of the two guards disappeared as something came bouncing into view from the shadows, a helmet with a spot of blood on it.

The guard behind the gate began panicking "Two of you, go alert the others; we have an intruder."

As they replied with fear "Why don't you do it? Nobody will get through the gate with the key around your neck?"

As the gatekeeper replied "*Loki* will kill anyone who interrupts his conversation, now get to it and alert the others." As two of the guards marched off torches in hand, reaching one of the great archways before something pounced on them from above and swiftly snuffed out the torch lights.

The gate guard pointed and yelled "What in the blazes was that?!"

As the two remaining guards became increasingly unnerved "This palace must be haunted, let us in before it comes after us as well."

As the gatekeeper replied "No one enters until you find whatever is out there."

One of them suddenly spotted a glimpse of something "Did you see it! It's over there!"

As the other replied "Ghost or not I'm going to kill it, come on!" as they both marched out into the dark. The sounds of swooshing swords and crossbow bolts echoed in the dark, after a brief battle something hit the ground.

After a few moments of quiet a voice called back "We got it! Accursed specter left me a few scrapes" as a guard approached slumped forward while clutching his leg, the gatekeeper couldn't see the remaining guard very clearly, but his uniform had many slash and stab marks and he looked badly injured.

The injured guard spoke "Get that gate open, I need a hand."

The gatekeeper nervously replied "I'm not supposed to open this gate unless absolutely necessary."

As the injured guard replied "I'm in no shape to go searching the grounds for help, now get out here before I keel over and you have to explain all this by yourself."

The gatekeeper acquiesced and opened the gate with the key around his neck, he then walked over the injured guard and helped him up; the guard glanced up and revealed his glowing, clouded eyes "Much obliged, friend" The disguised *Seer* then punched the gatekeeper in the gut and threw him over his shoulder, swiftly knocking the final guard out.

The *Seer* casted off his guard disguise and proceeded inside, giggling to himself a bit "When its dark out, best watch out for the boogie man."

After getting through the last checkpoint the *Seer* noticed there weren't any guards inside, he figured that *Loki* didn't want anyone else to overhear what he and *Sovereign* were discussing. Just past the hallway was a very ornately furnished audience room: complete with many paintings and sculptures, velvet furniture, and golden fixtures. The *Seer* got on the opposite side of one of the retaining walls and listened in, as *Loki* and the *Sovereign* were debating something just out of view nearby.

The *Sovereign* spoke first "Your plan to give command of my armies to the *Traveler* worked well, but he was supposed to defeat Sol not die by his hand."

Loki replied "That's only what I told you so you would agree, in actuality I needed to gauge Sol's strength against the only individual he shows any weakness towards; seeing the *Traveler's* deficiency I have adjusted my calculations accordingly, telling him where to find the *First Blade*."

The sovereign replied with confusion "He's alive? And you sent him to get the *First Blade*! What could such madness accomplish!?"

Loki calmly replied "The power of a *Traveler* amplified with the *First Blade's* wrath will force another confrontation with Sol; however, this time Sol and the *Traveler* will destroy each other."

The *Sovereign* paced around for a moment then replied "Intriguing, but what do we gain from all of this? Aside from the removal of our adversaries."

Loki laughed a moment and replied "The rules of the *Astral Plane* are shifting, this latest *Traveler* arrived into the realm of the subconscious through the aid of a machine; we need only to wait for another weak-willed fool to stumble into our realm using similar means. Then we shall befriend and manipulate them to do our bidding for us, then we will control the *Astral Plane* through them."

The *Sovereign* clapped and rejoiced "We shall have all the power and prestige of *The Circle!*"

Loki added "That and so much more *Sovereign*, but first we must ready the final act. The *Traveler* is no doubt readying his attack against Sol as we speak, the *First Blade* will likely convince him to unleash some sort of cataclysmic event so they can gain the upper hand; I need you to find captains in your army who might defect to the *Traveler* and made sure they intercept this message."

As *Loki* passed a sealed envelope to the *Sovereign* and continued "It contains the instructions on where Sol's forces will gather should he be forced to unveil his contingency; make sure one of your captains lead the *Traveler* straight to him."

The *Sovereign* nodded and replied "One of the chief guard commanders who fought alongside the *Traveler* during the last battle now loathes my very presence; I will make sure his men are commanded to courier the message, he will no doubt defect to the *Traveler*, and then they will do exactly as we plan."

Loki smiled and motioned "See to it then, time is of the essence" as the *Sovereign* bowed slightly and left the room.

The *Seer* had heard all he needed to, he prepared to phase walk out and alert the *Traveler* but nothing was happening; multiple times he attempted to leave but it was as if he had some kind of mental block.

Loki's voice echoed through the room "Trying to leave already old man?"

As *Loki* turned the corner in front of the *Seer* and grabbed his throat "That's very rude... you haven't said goodbye yet"

Loki then tossed him into the open room, as the *Seer* slammed into one of the ornate pieces of furniture. The *Seer* picked himself up and said "Was that little conversation a re-enactment just for me?"

Loki replied "No, my plan remains the same; I just knew you wouldn't be leaving this room in time to warn him about it."

The *Seer* picked up some thoughts about an enchanted charm and then realized "You brought in a Relic didn't ya?"

Loki laughed and replied as retrieved an odd amulet from around his neck and gloated "This is the 'watch of true sequence'; as long as this is nearby you won't be able to use any of your teleporting tricks."

The *Seer* rolled up his sleeves and replied "None of your movement tricks will work either with that relic in the room, and I'm willing to bet you can't fight worth a damn."

Loki smiled and replied "You might be right, thankfully I won't have to."

As he whistled and several guards suddenly entered the room from a hidden door across the way, the *Seer* grumbled as he assured "That damn relic hasn't taken away my extra sight, any move your boy's make I'll see coming as if they were announcing it beforehand."

To which *Loki* smiled, pulled up one of the velvet chairs and spoke while pouring himself a drink "Over a dozen elite guards verses and old, worn out mystic; this should be quite a show."

The *Seer* cracked his knuckles and took a deep breath, as he spoke one more time "I know   you're only doing this to keep me from warning Jack about your damn trap, so I'll just have to make this quick."

As *Loki* laughed heartily and said with amusement "I'm looking forward to watching you try... Guards, seize the old man, make him beg before me!"

The guard's then rushed upon the *Seer* as he readied his hidden weapons, the *Seer* needed to dispatch them quickly as *Loki's* plan was already starting to unfold...

17

PATH TO

THE SOURCE

MEANWHILE AT THE HARBINGER, JACK WAS IN THE TRAINING AREA, practicing the forms and techniques he acquired through the sword; several training dummies were carted in by a robotic crane and then placed into a semi-circle around Jack. With one flick of his wrist he severed all the dummies in half, effortlessly channeling the power of the sword.

The Fox entered the room, though this was initially unnoticed by Jack who was readying to combine his power and that of the sword's, blasting his telekinetic glove behind the sword edge as it projected a red wave which obliterated what was left of the dummies.

Jack commented to the *Fox* "The limitless potential of the *Traveler* and the destructive will of the *First Blade* represent a terrible force of reckoning. Wouldn't you agree?"

A response came in a deep foreboding voice that was not the *Fox*'s "Far more can be had than mere redemption."

To which Jack shook his head and replied "What was that again?"

As the *Fox* repeated normally "I said I once was like you, searching for redemption."

Jack was a bit taken aback, he replied with a bit of humor "Somehow I can't really picture that, you don't seem like the type who cares what other people think."

The Fox replied "It didn't begin that way; my search for redemption slowly became a drive for revenge instead, in order to realize the latter goal I had to cut ties with everyone I knew."

Jack commented "How is that working out for you?"

The Fox glanced up and replied "You will soon find out, I started my path much like yours; before I thought it was mere coincidence that our stories shared certain similarities, though I knew it was more than coincidence once I saw you take up the *First Blade*. At that moment I realized you had turned towards the darker path, as I had."

Jack suddenly remembered his deal with the *Fox* and laughed as he commented "I nearly forgot about our arrangement; I don't need to hear your motivations *Fox*, there are more important matters at hand, I'll go ahead and give you-"

The Fox interrupted "Is that you talking or the sword? Last time I recall you were reluctant to give over power to those you don't trust, have you forgotten why we are after Sol in the first place?"

Jack replied "As I told the *Seer*, I'm the one in control. Not the sword."

As the *Fox* pointed towards the sword hilt, Jack glanced down and saw the gem glowing red. *The Fox* elaborated "The *First Blade* doesn't suddenly seize control over the user, if it did you would become mindless, unable to think and react as it needs you to; your battle with the sword is one of influence, a struggle to preserve certain lines of thought, and to stop it from removing others."

Jack said with doubt "How would you know anything about this?"

The Fox replied with a raised voice "Because I too fought an enemy that was insurmountable, fell to its wrath, and was cast down upon the battlefield on the brink of death."

The Fox banged against the suit and continued "This is why I choose to be entombed within this suit, to become a ghost upon the battlefield, a spirit of revenge; this terrible machine was the means to realize my vision, to keep me alive, and grant me the power to enact my revenge. But as with all such things it comes at a cost."

The Fox tapped a button on his suit causing a computer core to reveal itself from the most heavily armored section of the torso. *The Fox* detailed "This computer keeps the suit operational, without it I would quickly perish; but the computer has its own objectives, its own motivations."

The Fox elaborated "The process is subtle at first: You hear voices, you find yourself becoming increasingly impatient and impulsive; eventually you start falling into hallucinations of your past, things you'd rather not remember or would prefer to forget."

Jack replied "What purpose could that serve?"

The Fox explained "Because regret is a cloud that hangs over every action, poisoning your resolve with scenes of what might have been; you pray that by taking more decisive action the next time that you might find absolution, or that the ones you lost might forgive, but nothing removes the remorse."

The Fox seemed lost in thought for a moment, then he snapped out of it and said firmly "This is the swords weapon against your will *Traveler*, it will use this to convince you to erase the parts of yourself that keep your rage and anger in check; should you consent to this, then it will have molded you into the killing machine that it desires, you will become no different from the implement in your hand."

Jack thought about what he had said, but remembered hearing a specific point in his story and argued back "You said our stories were similar. You faced a grave threat as I did, you made your decision because you had to, not because you wanted to; you must then understand why I chose to take up the *First Blade*, why I fight, and the consequences should I fail."

The Fox replied "I said our circumstances were similar, not the same; choosing to continue fighting is still a choice *Traveler*."

The Fox made his final point "Ask yourself what lies at the end of this road, the sacrifices you're going to have to make to get there, and if you can live with that."

As the *Fox* finished the intercom chimed in with Sarah's voice "Incoming transmission Jack, it's Teach; they say their regrouping and they have an urgent message."

Jack replied "I'll take it at the bridge in a moment."

As the intercom shut off and Jack concluded "I've thought about this many times *Fox*, but I can't think of any outcome that ends well without me defeating Sol; I'll take what you said into consideration; but I can't stop yet, I won't."

Jack exited the room as the *Fox* then retrieved an orb which resembled a miniaturized version of *the Harbinger's* power core, it brightened to power as he said to himself "Then our agreement is concluded *Traveler*, the fight is now yours" As he made his way to the cargo bay to depart from *the Harbinger*.

Jack reached the bridge; Teach was already on screen waiting for his arrival. Jack said with some degree of surprise "Captain Teach, I'm surprised to hear from you."

Teach replied through the view screen "Not as surprised as I lad, folk were saying you were severed from this mortal coil; it must be a mere fabrication though as I see you standing before me now."

Jack clarified "I was near death Teach, and I apologize for failing to beat Sol."

Teach laughed in return and said "You fight em till he nearly kills ya, only to rise again to give it another go; don't apologize lad, you're giving it your all as far as my word goes!"

Jack brought up the point which summoned him there "You said you had an urgent message for me?"

To which Teach replied "Aye, after that lily-livered *Sovereign* sold us out, a few of his crew defected; one of em intercepted a message to the shifty one, it details a predetermined meeting place where they would convene should all hell break loose. Under normal circumstances this would be about as much good as seawater to a thirsty man, but we caught a bit of a break you see. Something riled up   the *Avatars* in *Mirage* and their mobbing over Sol's crusaders in a hurry."

Jack questioned "Does that mean Sol is going to this meeting place?"

Teach nodded and replied "That's the best part, he's got the lion's share of his army holding back the anarchy while only a few of his best accompany him. Balthazar understands these details better than I, but we're putting a plan together and could use you lad."

Jack confidently replied "Good, where are we gathering?"

Teach responded "Another of Balthazar's riddles, he said you'd understand: 'think on all the realms at once until they begin to combine, then you will find yourself standing where *the Source* is aligned."

Jack interrupted him "*The Source*? He said that, you're sure?"

Teach confirmed "His words were clear lad, that's where we're heading."

Jack nodded and replied "Alright, we'll make ready and meet you there immediately."

Teach tipped his hat and concluded "Aye, see you there." Then the view screen shut off.

Jack began issuing orders in frenzy "Tell the crew to make ready, get the mech and fighter crews prepped for imminent deployment, and get all *the Harbinger's* gunners and damage control personnel on battle stations!"

Sarah replied back a bit worried "Where's the fire Jack? What's got you so alarmed that we need to go right back on the warpath?"

Jack pounded his fist against the console nearest to him and said with a raised voice "If Sol is moving towards *the Source* then he means to initiate his plan now! If we don't stop him fast he'll undo everything with one masterstroke."

Sarah began to understand as she replied "So if he reaches *the Source* then…"

Jack finished "Then he'll irrevocably change everything in the *Astral Plane* all at once, if there was any truth to what he said it means a lot of people are going to die."

Sarah turned back to her station and started punching in the orders quickly "I'm on it Jack! We're not going to let that happen."

As *the Harbinger* shifted to a state of high alert, and its many vehicles and guns were loaded and armed, as its crew sprinted through taking up battle stations and preparing the ship.

Jack approached the captain's chair and said "This place we need to get to, I believe I've seen it before. May I?"

Sarah allowed him to use the helm controls. Jack thought of that place he nearly saw after he had died, concentrating on it for a moment *the Harbinger* didn't so much jump forward as its surroundings warped and changed around it. Once the transition was complete they found themselves staring at windows of each realm arrayed in an immense spiral around a central point, at the convergence was a massive pillar of thought, emotion, and power: *The Source.*

As *the Harbinger* finished phasing in, most of the crew stopped in their tracks and gazed upon it with awe; this was the first that many of them had ever seen of the legendary Source: the enigmatic nexus of power.

Jack cut their moment of wonder short "Have the ground team meet me in the cargo bay; the rest of you, prepare for the most important battle you've ever fought."

Then he marched out, mentally trying to piece together a plan of action amid the scenario he suddenly found himself in. A short time later in the cargo bay he found that half a dozen mechanized suits had been prepped and ready, Jack nervously paced around waiting for the remainder of his forces but no additional units arrived; then Jack scanned the room and he noticed the absence of the *Fox*, the *Seer* was also missing.

Jack was furious as he tapped one of the wall intercoms and asked "Sarah, where are the rest of my reinforcements!? Where is the *Fox*!? Where is the *Seer*?!"

Sarah stumbled at the response and replied "We...we took some losses in that last battle Jack, all the others are dead. The *Seer* went off to figure out Sol's next move, I have no idea where the *Fox* is."

Jack yelled back "Great! That's just perfect! I'm going into one of the most difficult battles with less than a third strength because my crew couldn't even survive one battle! And why in the hell didn't the *Seer* or the *Fox* inform me of their departure!"

Sarah hesitated and replied "I don't know Jack, what do you want me to tell you?"

Jack banged on the intercom "Nothing dammit; I'll make due. Keep *the Harbinger* ready and on high alert; I may need support later on."

Then Jack stomped over to the cargo lift and said with frustration "Follow me on the next lift down, and don't freaking die until I tell you to!"

Reaching the surface Jack was greeted by terrain and surroundings that could only be described as bizarre: biomes and terrains started and stopped without transition, objects from multiple realms were scattered about randomly; even whole buildings were present, though many were sunken into the ground or sitting in the middle of shallow water.

Taking a quick moment to mentally identify his surroundings he saw patches of dense forest from *Epic*, sandy atolls from *Venture*, floating mismatched objects from Conundrum, foreboding statues and gravestones from *Terror*, even some marble pillars and silvery mist from *Utopia*. Jack then noticed the multitude of buildings, paved streets, and urban objects from *Mirage*, and they were present in far greater proportions than the others, and appeared to be slowly overtaking areas around them.

Jack thought aloud "Were the places I experienced the true *Astral Plane*, or was it this all along; an amalgamation of different states of mind combining into a continuous whole."

He continued forward, stepping carefully around props from other realms that seemed to be scattered haphazardly around him; he was searching for some sign of Balthazar and Teach, he figured they would meet someone familiar, and then he saw it: the *Traveler*'s Way. It looked the same as he remembered visiting all those various times, now restored from Sol's attack, though situated in an odd location. Teach and Balthazar were waiting inside with a small collection of allies, Jack rushed inside to meet them.

Inside Balthazar had a rough sketch of the path leading to *the Source* as well as Sol's intercepted messages upon the table, he looked to be charting a path through.

Balthazar glanced up briefly and then began explaining "*Traveler*, good. There is much to explain… Sol has found a way through the chaotic environment that surrounds *the Source*. According to this letter there are brief occurrences where one may travel directly towards *the Source* without harm; however, you must frequently take shelter in stable rings between occurrences."

Jack said with confusion "You mean it's impossible to approach *the Source* normally?"

Teach laughed upon hearing this and replied "Many have tried lad, always torn to bits by the storm around the light; if one approaches too close without knowing the way, death becomes certain"

Balthazar added "*The Source* has gathered around it chaotic fragments from every realm, the storms that frequently form around it are capable of destroying even the strongest of Constructs; the only power great enough to pass through unharmed is a fully realized *Traveler*.

Balthazar continued "However, Sol has found someone who has been studying *the Source* for centuries, and somehow they found a mathematical pattern to the chaos."

Jack glanced at the letter, though it was paper, it looked as if the equations on the page were slowly self-calculating before coming up with a sequence of prime numbers, then after a long pause would slowly begin calculating again to come up with a different sequence of prime numbers."

Jack questioned "How does this help us?"

Balthazar showed a rough sketch "There has always been a clear path where you can see *the Source* at all times, though an invisible barrier prevents any from passing through this section; it has often been called '*The One Path*'."

He pointed towards a line on the sketch passing from the middle of *the circle* to the top-center with the number "1" marked on it; arranged around it were markings delineating the degrees of a circle.

Balthazar continued "The degrees show different angles of approach, these numbers the equation calculate represent degrees which will yield safe paths."

Jack questioned "Wouldn't anyone approaching be torn apart once the angles change?"

Balthazar answered "No, there are rings of stability in-between storms, places frozen in time which do not alter or change; those rings will be our sanctuary between crossings."

Jack turned his attention to the threat ahead "What of Sol, is he making his way towards *the Source*?"

Balthazar replied "It is impossible to know for sure; all we can discern through viewing the "One Path" is that Sol's crusaders currently are fortifying the rings furthest from *the Source* while he waits somewhere within; for now he hasn't approached *the Source*, if he had it would become unmistakable."

Jack nodded and instinctively unsheathed his sword "Then we should march in and deal with Sol once and for all."

But the entire room seemed to be frozen, all their eyes fixed upon the sword. Teach finally broke the silence "Why are you holding that diabolical piece of steel!?"

Jack replied defensively "This is the weapon I need to defeat Sol."

Teach became red in the face and turned about to hide his rage, Balthazar questioned "Who directed you towards that sword?"

Jack reluctantly replied "*Loki* told me where to find it."

Teach flipped around and lost control "*Loki*? *Loki*!! You actually took the advice of that fiend!?"

Balthazar interceded "We need to trust the *Traveler*, aiding him is the only way to stop Sol."

Teach argued back "And place our fates to that sword! You've seen with your own eyes what that cursed blade does!"

Balthazar questioned back "What if Sol reaches *the Source*?"

Teach pounded one of the tables so hard it smashed in half and yelled "And what if the *First Blade* reaches *the Source*!? I've risked my neck many times to aid the *Traveler* and put an end to Sol, but this goes too far!"

Teach began stomping out of the tavern with his crew in tow, Jack stopped him and demanded "What are you afraid of?!"

As Teach shook off his grip and narrowed his gaze replying "You be holding in your hand the implement of damnation, the icon of eternal torment. You may have sold your soul already lad and I pray there's still enough left of ya to give Sol hell, but I'll not follow..." then he continued out, not looking back as they left the scene.

Jack turned to Balthazar and questioned skeptically "Will you abandon me as well?"

Balthazar shook his head and replied "I will assist you, the *Traveler*, in reaching *the Source*; but the battle is yours alone. I shall never again raise a weapon to aid the *First Blade*."

Jack narrowed his gaze and snatched the cipher and sketch from the table "Then lead on, but leave your allies here. I can't afford any weakness."

Balthazar turned and nodded to his monks and the barbarians he had managed to gather, they looked relieved and departed with due haste. Jack began marching closer to *the Source* as his mechanized units finally caught up with them; he stared down *the One Path*, the only angle where *the Source* could be seen.

A thought came into Jack's head that was not of his own voice "The strong shall persevere, the weak shall fall away; Advance, do not relent until you have broken your enemy, soon you will achieve glory greater than that of gods and kings."

Marching through increasingly chaotic terrain they finally reached what looked to be a gigantic crater that was previously obscured by the odd landscape; swirling around *the Source* was a massive storm, not unlike a hurricane, yet instead of wind and rain it was stone, metal, wood, and small trinkets travelling at lethal speeds, now Jack understood why you couldn't just walk in.

Balthazar examined the cipher and the sketch and informed "The angles will change soon, make ready."

Jack tapped his earpiece and ordered "Sarah, we're going into the storm, follow our path exactly and stay low to the ground, otherwise you'll be torn apart."

As Sarah's voice responded through the radio "Alright, I just hope you know what you're doing."

The cipher finished equating and the next set of prime numbers was displayed, Balthazar focused on one of the numbers and did a quick measurement against the sketch "9 degrees. Follow me." As he sprinted around the storm, until finding the correct angle of entry and headed inside, Jack and the mechanized units followed closely behind.

It looked as if they were about to sprint head first into the deadly hail, but once they entered they were unharmed; the objects were still swirling at a distance around them, but there was a corridor they travelled through where everything else had stopped. *The Harbinger* was following behind them nearly scraping against the ground, the very edges of the ship were sticking out and taking a severe beating, the hail was able to easily pierce through even *the Harbinger's* thick armor plating.

Reaching the other side of the storm they entered a large open sanctuary, though everything seemed frozen in time, the serenity was contrasted by the chaotic storm that surrounded it, which remained at a distance but could always be seen.

Upon entering they were greeted by an odd sight indeed, the scene of an entire civilization lay before them; massive stone and marble buildings throughout the landscape interrupted only by even more imposing statues and temples. It was reminiscent of wonders of the ancient world: with strong pillars, decorative domes, artful carvings, and built to a scale that dominated the surroundings.

Balthazar recollected "I recognize this place '*Solaris Infinium*', capital of Sol's dominion on Earth; when the bridge between the *Astral Plane* and the real world was severed this city collapsed, legends claimed to had sunk into the ocean or was swallowed by the earth."

They proceeded a bit further and were greeted by the sight of several dozen *Templars* emerging from the rooftops with crossbows in hand, before Jack sprang into action a familiar voice greeted them "*Solaris Infinium* was sacrificed by *the Circle*, their endeavor to prevent my reoccurrence into the world; the *utopia*n city became the legend of a perfect society lost to disaster, never again to be realized."

As the voice finished Sol suddenly arrived as if from the sky itself, impacting upon the ground suddenly and without warning; he stood only a few paces in front of them, gazing forward with his intense glowing irises.

Sol regarded the *Traveler* as a non-threat "I had not expected to face you again, you were past death *Traveler*: of that I am certain."

Jack answered back "I have returned to stop you."

Sol laughed hardily "You relinquished an afterlife without the torments of time and form to return and stumble into my wrath yet again? You either possess a will of iron or are the most deluded of fools."

Jack unsheathed the *First Blade* and pointed it forward saying "I have brought the most dreaded and powerful weapon in all the *Astral Plane*, and I will bring the full bearing of its wrath upon you; False-God!"

Sol merely smirked and replied "You cannot intimidate me *Traveler*, I have walked the void for eons; and may unleash a force greater than even the most powerful forces of the *Astral Plane*."

Balthazar stepped in front of the *Traveler* and tried to reason with Sol directly "Attempting to change *the Source* directly is madness! The resulting chain of events could potentially reap unparalleled destruction and upheaval, only a fully realized *Traveler* could be trusted with such power."

Sol laughed and replied "Have you forgotten that it was a *Traveler* who brought about the end of the classical era. So pious was he, his intentions noble and earnest; to end tyranny, to unshackle the slaves, to bring about kingdoms ruled by piety rather than ambition. Then what occurred? That *Traveler* brought about an era of ignorance, barbarity, and oppression; the "Dark Ages" as they are now called."

Sol argued "*Travelers* cannot be trusted *Magi*, it is time for another path; we are after all products of their image, and we can act in their best interests. We can be the stewards of their destiny"

Balthazar retorted back "A *Traveler* may have caused the Dark Ages, of that we have not forgotten; but yet another *Traveler* brought forth the Renaissance, a time of enlightenment and progress. It is not our will to judge and bind their fates, but to guide and instruct."

He raised an eyebrow and replied "Spoken like a true wise man, I wonder if your faith would be so strong if you realized what brought us here?"

Balthazar shook his head and replied "I don't understand"

As Sol continued "Then I will enlighten you! I had originally planned to influence the *Astral Plane*, much like you said, to win over enough followers to guide it down another course; then I encountered your messianic *Traveler* and defeated him, but surely a *Traveler* could not idly sit back and let a construct win! No, that would be an unacceptable blow to their ego."

Sol described harshly "He took up the *First Blade* he now carries and set the masses of *Mirage* upon my army, the very people his former guide were forsaken by; they currently rampage across the *Astral Plane* destroying everything, my crusade included, and it is only a matter of time before they arrive, destined to overtake all…"

Sol concluded "Your *Traveler's* revolution has begun, but to what end? The advent of a new "Dark Age" is now inevitable, soon all the realms will become a mirror of the mundane lifeless torment that is *Mirage*! That is the destiny of the *Traveler* you wish to guide and instruct!"

Balthazar seemed shocked, he turned towards the *Traveler* and almost whispered "Tell me he speaks falsely, did you unbind the masses of *Mirage*?"

Jack spoke without remorse "It had to be done, Sol needed to be weakened to secure his defeat; I can rein in the populace of *Mirage* once I have dealt with him."

Balthazar grabbed Jack's shoulders and yelled as he shook him "Fool! You know not what you have done!! A motion set to the *Avatars* by the will of the *Traveler* becomes an unstoppable wave of change to usher in the new *Astral Plane*! The denizens of *Mirage* will sweep over everything until they have unmade the current *Astral Plane* and remake a new one, whatever idea you used to rally them will be the idea that becomes the heart of the next era of society and culture."

Sol interjected "That idea, which he so thoughtlessly put forth, was to tell them to rise up and destroy anything that threatened their way of life…"

Balthazar stumbled backwards onto the ground, his gaze being one of pure shock; he kept muttering to himself "No, no, no; I swore we would never let it occur again… the fall back to ignorance, the ceaseless suffering of a second Dark Age."

Sol spoke over them "The only course left to us is *the Source*, only the all connected nexus of thought and energy can reverse what the *Traveler* has wrought."

Balthazar came to a harsh realization as he said darkly "Whatever you plot Sol, regardless of your motivations, nothing can be worse than what is to come should the present course of events come to fruition."

Balthazar took the equation cipher and ripped it into pieces; the ink ceased its motion and fell off the page. Balthazar then addressed the *Traveler* directly "I had seen in you the hope that we could bring about another great age *Traveler*, despite the odd circumstances which surrounded you, your path seemed destined to bring about something the likes of which none of us had ever thought possible."

Balthazar said with some regret "Yet when you inadvertently unleashed Sol your thoughts became dark, filled with anger and regret well past the point of reconciliation; this is what has led to your blinded actions and this current path of destruction."

Balthazar concluded "I have lost faith in you *Traveler*, but know this; I destroy the cipher as a final favor. Should you in this brief span of time realize enlightenment and become a true *Traveler*, you will have the power to traverse the storms and become one with *the Source*; this being the key to the redemption you so desperately seek."

Then he gazed out onto the storm and said "Farewell *Traveler*, I depart to find some peace before the end" as he walked back out to the storm barrier, standing near the whirling maelstrom for a brief moment before turning his form to sand, at once disappearing as he was swept into the barrier.

Sol laughed heartily and then commented "Was I to know I would see a day when the *Magi* lost faith in their all-important *Travelers*, you are the very epitome of failure *Traveler*."

Jack stabbed his sword into the ground making the ground quake "Enough! You still possess a path into *the Source*, take me there or face my wrath!"

Sol narrowed his gaze and held out the cipher page and sketch with one hand and lit a fire just out of reach below it, then he answered "I have a counter proposal, the mob you unleashed is set to fall upon us, I possess the only key and you still have the power to influence *the Source* in ways I cannot. Join me; the *Astral Plane* can still be saved."

Jack yelled back "And sacrifice untold millions for you hubris, never!"

Sol pointed towards the outside of the storm and cleverly replied "Consider the alternative" as a mass of *Avatars* were seen charging into the storms surrounding *the Source*, and though most of them were merely being awakened by the sudden jolt, some few were discovering the safe entryways by the endlessly repeated process of elimination.

Sol explained "The storms will not hold them at bay long; they will breach the barriers and destroy all "who threaten" their way of life."

Jack retorted "I have nothing to fear, the only invaders here are your crusaders and their tyranny."

Sol interrupted "Wrong, your *Harbinger* was what brought our crusade forth; and in the eyes of the mob there is no distinction between threats, only enemies to be destroyed. Make no mistake *Traveler*, they will destroy you, your friends, and anyone else they encounter."

Jack gazed again at the outside of the storm and noticed *Avatars* reaching the inside of the ring, a few of Sol's hidden *Templars* began firing volleys of crossbow bolts, yet the *Avatars* were nearly innumerable, their entry would soon become an onslaught.

Sol pressed the point "Time is against us *Traveler*, make your choice."

Jack thought for a moment and replied "You said you had nothing to fear from my power, that you could destroy me at any time?"

Sol was curious to where this was going and replied "Indeed, what of it?"

Jack continued "I propose a duel, should I defeat you I will receive the cipher; should you manage to defeat me, then the last obstacle to *the Source* will have been removed."

Sol conjured a secure box with one hand and placed the cipher and diagram within it, then placed it upon the ground and said "Very well *Traveler*, we shall settle this with a contest of power; be warned, I will not hesitate to use any means to defeat you."

Jack readied his sword and replied "Do not expect this contest to be easy, it will not go the same   way as before."

Jack dashed forward, slashing downward with lightning speed; Sol blocked with dual sun spears which suddenly appeared with a flash of fire into his hands. Sol deflected the attack away and attempted to counter with a whirling attack of his own; Jack effortlessly avoided the strike and pressed the attack with aggressive swipes and stabbing motions.

Sol was on the defensive, having to put increasing amounts of efforts into his blocks and deflections; Jack kicked Sol backwards and readied his telekinetic gloves, blasting a charge behind the sword as a red wave erupted forward, annihilating everything in its path. Sol dropped the sun spears and concentrated everything into blasting a wedge between him and the wave, his wall of fire barely deflected the wave away but was quickly exhausted.

In an instant the *Traveler* reappeared leaping through the shockwave through the air towards him, Sol rolled to the side barely avoiding the lethal stab as Jack countered with several more attacks from his telekinetic gloves. So fierce and unrelenting were Jack's attacks that Sol was having difficulty keeping pace, this was a far-cry from the previous battle where Sol could block and counter leisurely.

Jack suddenly charged a wave, absorbed it, then dashed forward at a speed which tore through the ground and rippled through the air; Sol barely had time to brace with his sun spears as he was hit with such great power that he was catapulted backwards into one of the buildings, causing it to collapse upon him. After a few quiet moments Sol emerged from the ruins, picking himself up and dusting off his elaborately colored robes. Jack focused his gaze and spotted a small gash across Sol's forehead, one which began to subtly bleed.

The unseen voice returned, commenting on this sight "Immortality is a myth: anything that bleeds can die, any corporeal form may be shattered, even ideas may be snuffed out by the cruel passage of time; invincibility is a lie, Sol covets this lie and blindly believes he is unassailable, show him that even gods may fall."

Jack stabbed the sword into the ground; then channeled both gloves into it, causing tremendous wave of telekinetic force great enough to destroy everything around them.

Jack yelled over the sound of the building wave of force "You cannot hold back the unstoppable, anything that fails to yield shall be destroyed!!" as the wave blasted outwards in all directions, shattering through the immense stone buildings like they were made of paper.

At the last moment a sudden chaotic flash occurred before impact, as a massive shockwave reverberated through the surroundings and razed every structure in view. Jack approached the area where Sol's body would have been, he began sifting through the considerable debris to confirm his suspicion, yet he found nothing: no corpse, no tattered robes, not even any fire. Suddenly he caught a glimpse of something from the corner of his eye, he fired an intense telekinetic wave towards his presumed foe; yet before the wave made contact it disappeared immediately, not being diverted or dissipated, the attack simply ceased to be moments before it would have had an effect.

Jack then noticed what had changed, Sol was surrounded by a dark twisting field, and all around him objects suddenly vanished into nothingness.

Sol narrowed his gaze and said "I had hoped not to use the power of the void, yet you leave me no other option; being imprisoned for eons within a limitless oblivion has allowed me to channel it for brief spans, its effect is unpredictable and has the effect of unraveling the reality of the *Astral Plane* itself."

Jack readied his sword blade and replied "I will not cower to fear, nor will I yield to danger; whatever form you take or power you wield, I will not relent."

Sol reappeared next to Jack suddenly and without warning, Jack blasted a wave forward with one hand while slashing with the *First Blade* using the other. Both attacks stopped short of Sol, with part of the *First Blade* vanishing completely into nothingness; Sol ripped what was left of the *First Blade* out of Jack's grip and then seized him by the throat with his other hand.

As the gathering darkness enveloped everything around them Sol said "The power of the void does not simply kill *Traveler*, you will be plunged into the abyss with the sword at the end of time itself; there you will remain, trapped for thousands of years until you slowly forge a way back, or your mind ceases to exist."

Sol detailed: "This oblivion I'm casting you into is the very same I spent eons trapped within; it will twist and warp along with your fragmented mind until everything falls away. Should you find a way to return, it will not be until after thousands of years pass, long after I have reformed the *Astral Plane*; where the legend of the *Traveler* will be a distant memory, gladly forgotten. Farewell *Traveler*." As Sol tossed Jack backwards into nothingness, as everything rapidly faded to black.

18

THE ABYSS

JACK FELL BACKWARDS FOR A TIME, BUT NEVER MADE CONTACT WITH anything tangible; once the shock of falling wore off he decelerated until he was just floating in place. He scanned every direction but saw only sheer nothingness; it was like being in space, worse though as space at least had some stars and nebula within it, this was more like an empty void. Jack wasn't sure if Sol was about to succeed, or if this was yet another illusion to trick him; he only knew that he could not stay in this place.

Jack collected his thoughts and then said aloud "Alright, void or not this is still a dream, which means I can influence this place and find a way back."

He then focused on summoning something familiar, something he could use as a frame of reference in order to center himself. A chunk of ground illuminated by a campfire appeared nearby; Jack began a walking motion while still floating in the air, until he drifted over and made contact with that summoned piece of ground.

Once next to the campfire, Jack uttered with some relief "That's a start, now for a way back".

Jack concentrated on the moment where he was cast backwards by Sol and the environment around *the Source*, yet he did not warp forward like so many other times; instead he could hear the sounds he recalled and turned around to find himself looking into a sort of cloud. It replayed moments from Sol's arrival, their battle, and then Jack being cast backwards into the void; but it only showed him things he remembered, nothing else.

A foreboding voice crept in and explained "These are echoes from the past; there is nothing here that you can use to return."

Jack whipped around and called out "Who's there! Sol?!"

The voice replied "I am the only other sentient here with you in this abyss; I am the *First Blade*."

Jack searched his surroundings and suddenly noticed the *First Blade* was stabbed into the ground near the campfire, still missing a chunk of its blade from Sol's last attack earlier.

Jack replied sarcastically "Well at least I'll have company"

Then Jack questioned "Do you know anything about this void?"

The sword's voice replied "For the briefest of moments after Sol grasped the metal of my blade to cast me here, I saw this place in his thoughts, what it can do, and how he escaped."

Jack inquired further "Then elaborate, how do we leave this place?"

The sword replied enigmatically "This place exists without confines, without form, and without time; similar to *the Source* but also in many ways it is also its opposite. There exists a path between here and the *Astral Plane*, but death is its gatekeeper. If your actions and thoughts are not exactly as they need to be, then you will repeatedly experience your end, each failure casting you back to the void."

Jack thought about this for a few moments and then replied "Where is this path and how do I enter it?"

The sword replied "The path represents a threshold you have never succeeded in crossing; entering it merely entails walking through it, and if you are unprepared then you will inevitably experience a most untimely death."

Jack nodded and replied "Alright, let's get started and see what we're up against."

To which the sword laughed and replied "I am done helping you *Traveler*, I will be watching outside your perception and waiting; prove worthy and I will appear when the time is right to strike."

With that the sword disappeared in its usual red flash of light. Jack angrily kicked against what little ground there was and replied "The next time you appear I might just refuse you help, you useless pretentious sword!"

Taking a moment to calm down, Jack started to think about the enigma of the path "A threshold I have never succeeded in crossing…"

Considering a few of the different possibilities, he recalled one moment during his earlier excursions in the *Astral Plane* as he said aloud "…The final door" as it suddenly appeared a few feet away.

Jack suddenly tensed up after seeing the door appear, he wasn't quite sure what it was meant to represent then or why he could not cross it; however, he was still driven to return and stop Sol, so he took a deep breath and began turning the door handle "Whatever waits for me on the other side, I must face it."

As he shoved the door open and dashed inside. Jack entered and saw a cityscape he did not recognize, all around him was devastation in the form of high waters, ruined buildings, winds of dust and ash, and a thick haze of smoke. Then he recognized features of it and thought that maybe this was *Mirage*, or perhaps rather the end of *Mirage*.

Jack proceeded further into the city, navigating around debris and burned out vehicles, he headed in uncertain direction wondering what he was supposed to find in this place. His thoughts were interrupted by a rising wave he could hear approaching, a combination of chanting, stomping, and a loud high echo like an impending tsunami. Jack turned and saw in the distance a mob of *Avatars* take to the rooftops as the buildings and streets filled with millions of others; suddenly a more distinctive *Avatar* took to the front, his cloud-like illusion moving more erratically and radiating an aura of energy, the lead *Avatar* raised an arm forward and commanded with a voice that boomed like an explosion! From the *Avatars* waves of fire, wind, and ice surged forward as if compelled by the mob, at the forefront he could see *Avatars* running just in front of the chaos "Are they guiding it forward!?" Jack said with bewilderment.

Upon closer examination he saw multiple ones phase back and forth from the storm-front and realized "...No, they are the wave."

Jack roughly plotted the path of the destruction they were carving and realized they would quickly overtake him; he needed to get some distance between himself and this approaching wave of doom. Jack charged a telekinetic wave and absorbed it as he began vaulting over whole buildings and diving through alleys; he reached the high-rise buildings and decided to take a shortcut, diving into their glass faces before barreling through and leaping out the other side. Jack's speed was impressive as he found himself on the other side of the city in only a few moments; he looked back and saw that the wave of *Avatars* were trailing behind at a slightly slower pace, being impeded by obstacles before them.

Jack observed the wave's progress then estimated he had a few short minutes of time, but where was the wave going? He found a nearby vantage point and scanned his surroundings. He discovered that he was actually back within one of the sanctuary rings frozen in time around *the Source*; though this one seemed different from the previous one that contained *Solaris Infinium*, *the Source* itself also loomed much closer in the background, perhaps this was one of the innermost circles nearest to *the Source*?

Some movement from a nearby suspension bridge caught his eye; Jack used the last of his charge to clear the distance between him and the bridge, reaching the foot of it with an aerial glide. Scouting out the bridge Jack saw the source of the movement: several dozen *Templars*. Jack stealthily approached the bridge and noticed they were more heavily clad in armor than other *Templars* he faced in the past; they were also preparing barricades and arranging themselves into battle-lines. They were likely Sol's elite troops, though with so few numbers they would be unlikely to hold back the *Avatars* for very long. Focusing on the opposite side of the bridge Jack saw a circle of *Clerics* channeling near the final barrier to *the Source* "That's where Sol will be." Jack said aloud as he clenched his fists and narrowed his gaze.

Jack opted for the direct approach, charging forward to destroy the foot soldiers so he could get to Sol; the front-most *Templars* saw him approaching and unsheathed their swords, they were suddenly cloaked by a protective barrier of flames that emanated from the swords, similar to when Jack absorbed telekinetic fields. Jack quickly glanced at their swords and saw symbols etched in the metal that emanated light and power, clearly these foes would be more formidable than Jack first expected.

Too late to turn back, Jack blasted his devices forward and then performed a diving attack, yet when his blade impacted into the fire cloak it diminished most of the force of his attack; the fire knight swept his sword across forcing Jack off to the side. Jack recovered and blasted vacuum attacks on either side of his opponent before firing a crossbow bolt at the knight, striking him dead center and piercing the armor to his torso.

During his attack the other knights had circled around, Jack turned to block an attack he saw coming from the corner of his eye, yet was knocked into a roll by another knight's blindside attack. His arm was badly seared from the fire-knights sword, which struck using the same flame that provided their protective barriers. Jack recovered as his two opponents patiently waited for another challenge, in the background the steadily rising roar of the *Avatar* mob warned him of his pressing lack of time.

Jack was starting to panic, knowing he didn't have time to face all the enemies on the bridge; he needed to storm through and avoid them entirely. He quickly charged and absorbed a telekinetic wave, leaping into a high arc to clear the bridge in one bound. Several hidden fire knights appeared from the bridge towers and took to the air to intercept him. Using a combination of evasion and defensive telekinetic blasts Jack managed to get through several of them, but felt the sting of a burning sword strike him downwards into the ground. His telekinetic field was probably the only thing that prevented that last blow from killing him, yet he was still left with a slash wound and several burns.

It took Jack a few moments to recover, while he was gathering his strength the knights formed a semi-circle around him with weapons drawn. Jack got back on his feet and mentally calculated his odds while keeping his weapons ready.

One of the knights stepped forward and announced "We are Sol's inner circle, his greatest knights armed with the *Soliden Steel* which grant us the power of both Templar and *Cleric* warriors. We are his indomitable *Paladins*. We have seen you fight and have learned all of your tricks; Sol has ensured we have the power to defeat even you."

Jack replied "What's the point, the entire *Astral Plane* is overrun; why guard this bridge?"

The *Paladin* motioned to their surroundings and continued "Because we stand at a great threshold, at the dawn of the new *Astral Plane*! Sol has asked of us one final measure: that none shall pass. Cross our blades again at your peril *Traveler*, for although Sol wishes your survival we will not allow anyone to interfere with the culmination of Sol's great crusade."

Jack replied "Your crusade? Your crusade?! You are blind, the crusade has failed! Sol approaches *the Source* as a last ditch effort to save his tattered vision, he leaves you on this bridge to die! None of you will see the dawn of a new *Astral Plane*."

The lead *Paladin* laughed and replied unconvinced "Your words are faithless and hollow *Traveler*, only the weak and foolish will perish on this day."

Jack rushed forward and yelled "Then count yourself among them!!"

Jack attacked furiously, yet the *Paladins* held their ground and continued their stalwart defense. Jack could not gain any ground against them, and they stubbornly refused to let Jack proceed any further; Jack knew that attempting to run past them would only get him killed given his current state.

Jack ran out of time as the *Avatar* mob arrived and attacked the bridge, Jack turned to face them but the bridge rapidly yielded and gave way under his feet. He tumbled backwards watching the *Avatars* sweep over everything, even while falling some *Avatars* broke away and dove downwards to attack him, as the bridge and *Avatars* smashed into him his vision went black and he found himself back at the void staring at the campfire.

Jack was a bit dazed at first, would that really be the outcome under the current circumstances? And how was it that his death mere became a mode of restart, was this final door meant to be a warning? Or a test? Jack wasn't sure of any of these questions, but he was determined to try again.

Jack proceeded to enter the door again and was greeted by the same scene as before, wishing to confirm his suspicions he quickly scaled one of the buildings and waited. After a short while the *Avatars* arrived where they had before and proceeded to enact the same events in the same way.

Jack nodded to himself and said aloud "So it's happening the same way as last time, maybe there is a way to change how it ends".

Jack headed for the bridge knowing what awaited him there, taking a moment to reflect on his previous engagement and what he would do differently. Reaching the foot of the bridge Jack charged a very large field of telekinetic energy and absorbed it, turning the corner and opening his surprise attack with a compressed pressure wave.

Completely caught off guard, the first few *Paladins* were unable to raise a defense as the orb impacted in the center of them and exploded with such fury that they were blasted into dust as their armor was flung into the water. Enraged the other *Paladins* activated their fire cloaks and charged forward, Jack loaded flash bolts into his crossbow and fired into the pavement, causing a barrage of blinding light as Jack followed up the attack with vacuum blasts just in front of the flashpoints. A few *Paladins* stumbled into the fields as they were locked into place and vulnerable, Jack dashed forward with enough speed to send ripples through the air as he zeroed in on the killing blow.

Plunging his blade forward Jack was interrupted by a flanking attack from another *Paladin*, Jack turned and blocked the attack before countering with a charged kick which knocked his opponent back. The previously immobile *Paladins* managed to free themselves from the vacuum's hold and resumed their charge, Jack now had to furiously parry and block attackers in multiple directions to keep pace. Suddenly they all dove out of the way as several *Paladins* behind them unleashed fire waves, Jack vaulted over the attack and then plunged downwards to counter the assault; tackling the middle *Paladin* while sinking his blade into the enemies torso, recovering with a roll as he swung his blade into a wide arc into the others. Yet he was forced to abandon the attack when a volley of flaming crossbow bolts was fired from nearby, forcing him to turn and deflect the oncoming projectiles with his devices.

Jack was beginning to realize that this 'Paladins' had more than just a grant of Sol's power, they were extremely skilled and coordinated fighters; nearly every attack had been countered and every opening he created was thwarted by their tactical maneuvering. Jack soon ran out of telekinetic charge, his advantage was gone.

Jack continued fighting, but the Paladin's attacks were becoming more aggressive and furious; he was forced to devote every moment to countering them, and he was starting to make mistakes. Every move he tried proved useless; nothing was working against these juggernauts of steel and fire.

Jack was suddenly struck in the side by an attack that knocked him off balance, he attempted to counter but missed the mark; a sword struck his armor dead center and knocked the wind out of him, he dropped his sword and fell to his knees. The approaching Avatar wave was fast approaching, he was out of time. Jack blasted a circle around himself and desperately ran for the other side of the bridge, still winded and barely able to keep his balance.

Jack heard a voice to his side yell "Fool!" as he turned to face the lead Paladin slashing at his neck. Jack tumbled sideways off the side of the bridge, watching with his faded vision as the Paladins fought off the Avatars for a time before being overrun. As his vision went black Jack reappeared at the campfire, the gravity of this test began to mentally sink in; how many more times would he need to experience his own death, what if he was already doomed to failure? He sighed and stared into the fire, his thoughts clouded as his prison began to weigh heavily upon him.

A familiar figure appeared from the fire and stood there to taunt him, and Jack greeted him with spite "Sol! Come to brag!? Save your words, if you think this prison has beaten me you are mistaken. I will find a way out and when I do I will destroy you!"

Sol motioned to the door and said "That is highly doubtful, you've probably discovered that fate conspires against you the moment you cross that threshold. It took me eons to find a path and you possess neither the intellect nor the power that I did, it is doubtless that you will remain here until you cease to continue, and then you will cease to be."

Jack stood up and yelled "Never underestimate a *Traveler* Sol! There is nothing I cannot do."

As Jack swung his sword right into Sol, and watched as it merely passed through like his adversary as if Sol was formless.

Sol shook his head and replied with condescendence "Chasing ghosts already? There is nothing here *Traveler*, only oblivion. You could be dead already, I may have already won, and you wouldn't even know. Farewell *Traveler*, there is much work to be done now that nothing stands in my way."

As Sol began laughing and vanished, Jack stood up, then looked in every direction to see if some other specter would arrive; then he started to wonder if it had even been Sol at all, or merely an illusion.

Jack entered the door many times thereafter, each time he tried different approaches, attacks, and techniques, but the result was always the same frustrating failure; whether by the formidable *Paladins* or the unstoppable *Avatars* he could not find a scenario that didn't end in his demise.

The repeated defeats began to cloud Jack's mind, he started making easy mistakes and failing at trivial obstacles. After experiencing his death for what felt like the hundredth time Jack became intensely frustrated.

Jack yelled up from his prison "What's the point of this! How many more times must I be tested for trying to save people I don't even know!? When will it be enough!!" as he felt himself collapse backwards and stare blankly into space.

Jack let his mind wander thinking of his past, the *Astral Plane*, life in general, and basically everything else between; visions of his past began to drift in, large parts of which Jack didn't particularly care for. Most of his childhood was spent socializing in his large family, learning norms and behaviors that mostly seemed confusing and illogical; school wasn't much better, he wasn't particularly good at making friends and ended up being the omega of a group of people one could only loosely call "friends". Most of the classes were wasted in endless talks about politics disguised as "current events" by self-serving teachers, he managed to learn some science/ math and taught himself most of the history he cared to learn; aside from Math and Technology classes the entire process seemed to be a waste of time and prepared him for very little.

College was the greatest disappointment, being denied entry due to technicalities; followed by a brief stint in technical school and a stream of jobs that basically went nowhere. Writing and meeting Eleanor were probably the best parts of his life he could recall, only to be followed by his divorce and self-imposed isolation. Through it all Jack always felt frustrated by almost everything around him, the world seemed to be driven forward by things that Jack couldn't grasp or found to be downright delusional; talking with other people didn't help much, nearly everyone would simply point out that others had it "worse off" than him.

This was a great irritation to him, in order for his problems to be valid he needed to be the worst off individual known to everyone he knew; and likely even if that were the case they would probably suggest he be inspired by some empty mantras and that would somehow fix everything. Sol was right about Jack, he didn't care for society at large and disliked the way it operated along with its twisting perception of life and the world; dark thoughts crept in as Jack considered the possibility of just letting Sol win and watching it all burn, reveling in the chaos.

From Jack's visions of the past another figure seemed to particularly resonate from it, and appeared with him in the corner of his vision. Jack sat up and checked to make sure he was seeing who he thought he was, as spoke aloud "Malachi?"

Malachi walked over and sat down next to the fire, Jack questioned "Are you real? Or just another hallucination?"

Malachi replied calmly "Neither, but it doesn't matter. What does matter is the message I have to convey."

Jack reflected on what happened and replied with a measure of regret "I should have supported you back at *Mirage*, we should have gone after *The Circle*; and this crisis with Sol-"

Malachi interrupted "Sol, *The Circle*, these are both entities that seek to bend your will towards paths you did not choose nor want; no amount of power brokering or ideological posturing will bring about what I sought or the redemption you currently seek, it is as you convinced me in those final moments: tyranny does not create freedom, regardless of its intent."

Jack was taken aback, Malachi or whatever impersonation he was didn't sound like his fiery charismatic self, he was talking in an enigmatic way like the *Magi*.

Jack inquired "What happened…after you were struck down? What lies beyond?"

Malachi stared off and replied "Death, oblivion, and the endless possibilities afterwards; to know the vast retelling of all things remembered, and the many things that may follow, both here and in the *Astral Plane*… it is indescribable."

Jack replied with some humor "You're not suggesting I should die and experience it myself right?"

Malachi replied with a slight laugh "If only it were so easy, no *Traveler* I am here to show you the paths beyond; so that you know what you're fighting for, and what you must choose."

Jack picked himself up and replied "Alright, show me this 'message' of yours."

Malachi pointed his hand at a point in the space around them and a vision appeared forth, it began with Sol reaching *the Source* and a vast wave of change washing over the whole of the *Astral Plane*; nearly everything in all the realms was obliterated, leaving very few things alive or intact.

In the vision Sol exited *the Source* and gathered those few that survived; time began to move faster as it appeared that Sol guided the survivors to slowly rebuild a new civilization, acting as both their guide and mentor. Their initial settlement became a village, then a town, then a city, and eventually spread forth… as an empire. The various realms began to reappear, in different forms but following the same basic themes; the dream walkers in their conscious states began to build and shape a paradise in every place they travelled. Eventually new constructs began to appear, the new ideas and concepts taking on lives of their own, and the *Astral Plane* advanced forward again without the direct influence of the people in it. The vision advanced faster than before, centuries passing in seconds as events swept past and the *Astral Plane* continued building and advancing.

An unexpected occurrence happened in the background, the events of the old *Astral Plane* began to fade from memory. The many writings, constructs, and monuments that stood to remind of the past doom were slowly worn away and buried by the passage of time; Even Sol, the figurehead and rallying guide of the new *Astral Plane* began to fade as well, until he disappeared from the scene and was eventually forgotten entirely.

Then events began to turn towards an all too familiar story Jack had heard before, the constructs began to collect and influence followers; growing more powerful as they were able to influence the whole of the *Astral Plane* and eventually began spreading their power into the real world. Conflict became inevitable as the interests of the dream demi-gods began to clash and ultimately lead to war; catastrophes on a tremendous scale were unleashed as the forces of nature and the cosmos were called down in wrath upon the masses. One demi-god rose to supremacy after what looked to be an endless conflict, only one lone figure rose up to oppose him: a singular dream walker. The scene froze as the vision centered upon the two locked in conflict.

Malachi reappeared and narrated the scene "The demi-god is Shak-Ra, master of time and space; similar in many ways to Sol in goals and motivations. The other figure Zehktra is-"

As Jack assumed the rest "…A *Traveler*."

Malachi continued "Yes, if Sol succeeds this inevitable conflict between conscious and subconscious, between reality and the imagined will repeat itself; an unbroken cycle of conflict, loss, and eventual renewal."

Jack elaborated "So this is the price of survival, to be bound by fate to repeat the same mistakes and experience the same tragedies until the end of time."

Jack turned to Malachi and demanded answers "Has this happened before? Is this what occurs every time the world has run its course??"

Malachi shook his head and replied "I cannot know that *Traveler*, *the Source* remains enigmatic even after death, only our perception of it changes; I can only guess at what came many eons before. What I do know is this, should you defeat Sol; if you manage to succeed in your goal then events will proceed on a different course and the cycle will not yet repeat, but what follows will be a struggle to restore balance.

Malachi continued: "Tumultuous upheaval is the only logical result of such a great imbalance, and the real-world will be affected by this; it will be your task to see both worlds through the initial chaos, you will have saved all those lives yet they will soon find themselves in a struggle to achieve the new balance. They will have been saved from Sol's catastrophe, but then placed into a new fate that will be out of your hands; you will have earned your redemption, but you cannot guarantee their salvation, their fate will be decided afterwards by their actions going forward."

Jack nodded and replied "Then that is what I must do, thank you Malachi; I had doubted the merit of this struggle, now I will be resolved again to see it through."

Malachi smiled slightly and got up to leave, Jack asked "Leaving already?"

Malachi replied "We'll speak again *Traveler*, the path forward lies in your hands. Farewell." And then Malachi vanished without a trace; Jack waved though he doubted his friend could see, then became determined again to find a way through the door; but first he needed a plan.

Jack thought about the scenario he kept facing and knew he needed some way to improve his odds. Suddenly Jack remembered something: *Loki* knew of Sol's arrival beforehand and helped make it occur.

Realizing this Jack uttered aloud "Sol must have had a way to communicate to the outside, but what was it?"

Jack paced around for nearly an hour considering the different means he could use to accomplish this, then decided he would attempt to communicate remotely through one of the odd visions this abyss seemed to replay. Jack figured his best bet would be the *Seer*, he took a moment to clear his mind and then sat down and concentrated on communicating; nothing happened so he focused harder as his surroundings began to blur.

Jack began to get a migraine as he suddenly opened his eyes and noticed the surroundings were all wrong, he was surrounded by *Templars* and was holding a knife in each hand. Jack heard a voice in his head "What in the hell??- What are you doing in my head Boss-Man!?"

Jack was a bit perplexed and replied aloud with the wrong voice "I'm not sure, am I communicating with you right now?"

As from the background *Loki* stood up and laughed heartily replying "My my, the stress of this predicament appears to have stupefied the vagrant; Captain, dispose of him before he starts asking what his name is or some other nonsense." Jack suddenly realized, he wasn't communicating with the *Seer*, he currently WAS the *Seer*.

One of *Templars* rushed forward as the *Seer*'s voice warned "Duck dammit" as he dodged below the strike and then countered with a knife attack.

Two other *Templars* charged as he was warned again "Charge coming, get around it".

As he jumped out of the way of the oncoming attack before sliding a piece of furniture into their legs, knocking them over; he then dashed forward, and struck downward with lethal finishing stabs.

Jack needed more of an advantage, and concentrated with one hand to summon a different weapon; the Seers voice chastised "That ain't gonna work, I've never been able to-"

As a tele-kinetic gauntlet suddenly appeared over his conjuring hand; *Loki* stood up and yelled "That's impossible!!"

Jack (controlling the *Seer*) blasted the telekinetic device at several of the remaining *Templars*, sending them flying across the room, before advancing towards *Loki*. *Loki* attempted to escape, but was pinned back to the chair by the device; as Jack caught up to him and stabbed the knife through *Loki's* shoulder into the back of the chair.

Loki thrashed about, shocked by the sudden turn of events, and said with bewilderment "How did you do that!"

As Jack said with the *Seer's* voice "…You could say I had help from the *Traveler*."

Loki's eyes widened as he suddenly realized "That can only mean that you're… in the Void. Then you failed! HA I should have known you would prove insufficient to defeat Sol."

Jack impatiently picked up the chair and tossed it into a nearby wall with *Loki* still riding it, the chair shattered as *Loki* had the wind knocked out of him and landed on the floor.

Jack demanded "How did Sol escape!? Did he find a way through the path, did he get outside help changing the circumstances!!"

Loki replied with irritation "Of course he did fool, Sol had centuries to plan his way through the gauntlet that awaited him."

Jack kicked *Loki* over and yelled "I don't have years, the obstacles I see will occur within hours, perhaps a day."

Loki began laughing and jested "Then make yourself comfortable, the Void will soon be your new permanent home."

Jack readied a knife to toss straight at *Loki*, he was stopped by the loud internal voice of the *Seer* "No boss-man! He may be a scoundrel, but he aint worth killing over. Smash that trinket of his, and I'll find a way to help you."

Jack lowered his knife and grabbed the odd trinket he saw hanging around the *Seer*'s neck, he lifted it with the devices to eye level and then crushed it with them. He then glanced down to *Loki* and threatened "No more tricks, no more games; If I see you again I will beat you into a plump and then blast your bones to dust. Understand?"

Loki's grin spread across his face as he replied "I don't need to worry, you'll be trapped in the Void for a very long time; my part in this story is now done." With that *Loki* sunk backwards into his shadow and vanished from the room.

A cadre of guards suddenly burst in from the doors around them, the *Seer* regained control of his body and froze their surroundings; casually walking through the frozen guards and out the door. Jack was now a voice in the *Seer*'s head as he questioned "Have you been able to do that the entire time?"

The *Seer* replied "Not before you smashed that trinket, now what was all that jabbering about back there; and what're you doing in my head?"

Jack replied "Can't you read my mind?"

The *Seer* sighed and replied "You want me to read my own mind, so that I can figure out what a voice in my head wants; you trying to give me a headache boss-man?"

Jack laughed and commented "It's a long story…"

The *Seer* replied "I got a long walk ahead, give me the long and short of it."

Jack explained what had happened, how he ended up in the void, the vision Malachi showed him, and the doorway he had to get through in order to fix everything.

The *Seer* thought about it for a while and replied "Quite a quandary you have there boss-man, but I think you've stumbled upon a solution you haven't considered yet."

As Jack impatiently replied "What would that be?"

The *Seer* questioned "Now you say you've tried every different way you can think of, have you tried the same way twice?"

Jack groaned and replied "Now you're just being vague on purpose."

The *Seer* elaborated "Just hold on now and think about it, you said the scene repeats itself like a broken record each time; but you haven't forgotten how it plays out, why not use it against them"

Jack sensed he was onto something and said "Continue…"

As the *Seer* furthered "Say that when you walk up onto that bridge and the first one swings at you a certain way; the next time you walk up you'll know he's going to swing that way if you're approaching the same, so if you make sure to go about things the same manner each time-"

Jack suddenly realized "Then I can dodge it as it happens and use it to my advantage."

The *Seer* continued "Now you're getting it boss-man, you make a pattern of it; figure out what   they're all gonna do and how they're gonna do it, and then waltz through them while they trip over themselves like they can't do nothing right."

Jack was starting to like this plan but questioned "Wait, there are over a dozen enemies I have to get through, there are many different ways my encounter may occur as it unfolds, how am I supposed to remember all that?"

The *Seer* reassured "You'll figure out something boss-man, you always do." Jack hardly found that to be encouraging, but at least now he had something to go on.

Jack was about to return to the Void but then remembered the predicament *the Harbinger* was left in and described "*Seer* I need you to do me a final favor, *the Harbinger* is stuck in a bad situation inside one of the rings that surround *the Source*; with Sol and the approaching wave of *Avatars*, that ship and everyone on it is in danger. I need you to find a way to get to it and guide them back out."

The *Seer* inquired "How do I get through the storm?"

Jack replied "The *Avatars* are likely to be swarming into all sides of it, find the point where they're not getting shredded to pieces and you'll have your path; then guide *the Harbinger* back out using a similar method."

The *Seer* said with some hesitation "That'll leave you in there with no help boss-man, you sure that's what you want?"

Jack replied "This approaching fight with Sol needs to be something I face alone, that's clear to me now, and I don't want any of you guys getting hurt trying to help. Maybe have them leave some equipment behind if it's something that you guys think might improve my odds. Just make sure that everyone gets out in one piece."

The *Seer* replied "That I can do boss-man, looks like we both got work to do. Stay alive out there boss-man."

As Jack concluded "Thanks *Seer*, I'm sure we'll meet again when this is all over." As he then refocused his thoughts on the abyss and reappeared at the campfire.

19

TRIAL BY

DEATH

*J*ACK REFLECTED ON HOW THE ENCOUNTER ON THE BRIDGE HAD GONE
a few times before, the *Paladins* strengths and weaknesses, and how he
should plan his attack pattern. Going over these details a few dozen times
Jack walked through the door still reciting back what he needed to know.

Dashing through the city, ahead of the *Avatar* mob, Jack reached the
bridge in an almost casual manner, despite the incredible speed at which
he arrived. Something was off however, slightly in the distance there was
a smoking wreck that Jack did not remember being there before; dashing
over to examine it he found one of the *Fox*'s mechanized fighting suits,
heavily modified but damaged beyond repair.

Jack thought aloud "This was probably left by *the Harbinger* crew for
me, too bad it's too broken to use-"

A glimmer caught his eye and Jack noticed that it had a power core like
he had given the *Fox* rather than its normal capacitor pack. Jack removed
the core and was suddenly cloaked in a telekinetic energy field like when
he absorbed energy waves, only this time it felt as if it were a far greater
magnitude of power.

Jack attached the core to his belt and yelled "This should greatly help,
maybe now I can even the odds".

Jack took a moment to focus, he would need to remember everything
as it occurred and in the order that it occurred; He intended to repeat
a previous pattern of attack but counter the moves he knew for certain
would happen.

First he blasted a compressed pressure wave at the first few *Paladins*,
blasting them to dust; then followed up with flash bolts onto the pavement
to blind the oncoming *Paladin* charge, along with vacuum attacks to leave
them immobilized. He then faked a charge at the immobilized targets
knowing a flanking attack to be on the way, only to stop short and counter
grab the flankers' swords with the devices and redirect them towards their
immobilized allies. The redirected *Paladins* stabbed their allies and fell
over just as the others broke the hold, Jack only knew of one more move
of theirs. Parrying and blocking their attacks he waited for whatever signal
they communicated with, as he noticed one of the *Paladins* behind them
whistle; the attackers dove out of the way as Jack blasted a repelling wave
forward into the crossbow bolts that hadn't been fired yet, the unaware

Paladins fired and had their bolts immediately backfire at point blank range, killing them instantly.

Suddenly Jack was in the dark, he would need to carefully observe what happened around him so he could make use of it next time; the *Templars* noticed that their individual attacks were failing to work so they surrounded him and prepared to attack as a group, this would be difficult. Jack whirled around blocking and countering as the *Paladins* advanced and retreated with precision, covering each other's attacks with counter attacks and never giving the *Traveler* any opportunities to break out.

Despite Jack's speed there were too many angles to cover; he needed a faster way to deal with their sword attacks to buy himself some space. Dealing with the group of *Templars* took too much time however, and the *Avatar* mob arrived on schedule and toppled the bridge, as Jack relaxed and fell backwards waiting to be returned to the campfire.

Analyzing what happened Jack was confident he had mastered the first part of the encounter, but he noticed that the *Paladins* rapidly increased their aggression and coordination when faced with a more formidable opponent, he would need to continue escalating his attacks as well in order to keep pace. Jack thought of an idea of how to deal with the group as he mentally recited all his moves and entered the door again.

…Working his way back to the after he reflected the crossbow barrage, Jack remembered the incoming group and summoned an additional ice sword before he was surrounded. The *Paladins* swooped in and readied their attack, but Jack had taken note of their combinations and counters and was ready to make them look like fools. The first one threw an overhead strike as Jack sidestepped it and tripped the attacking Templar, as the second did a rushing lunge only to have Jack redirect the sword down and kick that one in the face. Undaunted four different *Paladins* slashed towards him as he proceeded to parry and counter their attacks two at a time; using his extra sword for everything it was worth, counter slashing and sword breaking his way through the next attack Jack bought himself a few precious spare moments, enough of an opening for one attack.

He remembered that when the *Avatars* collapsed the bridge most of the *Paladins* were caught off guard and tumbled into the wreckage, he decided to copy that and punched the ground with his charged telekinetic punch, breaking a hole in the road as it crumbled and took many of the *Paladins* with it.

Jack blasted himself upwards before falling, and cleared the wreckage, sailing through the air as several *Paladins* from the bridge towers appeared and took to the air after him. Jack attempted to evade and dodge around them, but there were too many variables to compensate for; he realized he would have needed to deal with them before they took to the air. One of them managed to connect an attack, sending Jack tumbling towards the ground; impacting near the end of the bridge, he was confronted by the lead *Paladin* who was clearly seething at the sight of his enemy, likely due to all the losses he had incurred at the hands of a singular warrior.

Jack could tell that his enemy was ready to explode with rage; all he needed to do was light the fuse. Taking a deep breath, he noted the position and disposition of the remaining enemies around him, including one that humorously reminded him of a boss at one of his old jobs; Jack smirked and said to the lead *Paladin* "Sorry for the loss of your soldiers... you should have trained them better."

The lead *Paladin* yelled "Insolent fool!" and blasted a fire wave forward with his palm towards Jack, his vision blacked out and he found himself back at the campfire.

Jack was now pacing back and forth trying to think of a way to counter the next few steps; the air attackers always jumped him from the bridge towers.

He started to come up with an idea "The bridge towers... they're standing on right on top of giant steel conductors, I could hit that with an electrical attack and fry 'em before they take to the air."

Jack also noticed that positioning himself in front of the lead *Paladin* put him in a good spot relative to the others, remembering that the last few were crowded near their leader. All Jack had to do was goad the lead one into the first attack, counter it, and then rush through the others... but how much time did he have left before the *Avatar* mob arrived, he wasn't sure, he died last time before it happened.

There was another issue, Jack wasn't terribly good at remembering sequences, and this attack pattern was starting to get very complicated; if he did an attack differently or in the wrong order then the entire scenario would change and his memorization would prove useless. He tried to think of a good way he could remember what to do and in what order, searching his memory for any good examples of memory techniques that were demonstratively effective.

The only thing he could think of was those various times he and his younger brother James had gone to movie theaters early and had to sit through those irritating commercials before previews; James always made a game of things and determined that he could prove the commercials ran in a long loop, instead of randomly as Jack had assumed. The way he proved it was odd, yet effective, he made each commercial part of a humorous rhyme that he came up with; then he said each part of the rhyme before its corresponding commercial thus proving his theory. Jack remembered losing a bet that night, but remembered that the rhyme proved very effective, as the loop was over 15 commercials long.

Jack started constructing his own rhyme, going over verbal sound-alikes for each part and trying to tie them all together; it was pretty ridiculous, and it took him multiple tries to get it to sound good at all, but after a few attempts he finally had something workable. He repeated the entire rhyme once and stepped through the door, resolving to finish the challenge during his next attempt.

Jack got through each step, whispering each section of the rhyme as he carried out each attack; sure enough shocking the bridge tower with his electric attack disabled his aerial pursuers, and diving back downward placed him in the perfect position to take on the lead *Paladin*. Insulting him once again, Jack anticipated the fire attack; then used a karate technique to redirect the attackers arm to face back at him, immolating him with his own flame.

The followers charged forward as Jack suddenly locked their weapons in place with one device before catching the frost salts from his blade and snap freezing the others with lightning fast punches, permanently solidifying them in place. Jack was suddenly clear of the *Paladins*, they were all dead or disabled as he turned back and saw the *Avatar* mob arrive at the other side of the bridge.

Jack couldn't think of any particular attacks powerful enough to slow them down… but he still had the power core.

Jack picked it up and hesitated for a split second saying "I'm going to miss this thing" then hurled it at the center of the bridge as it detonated with an earth shattering telekinetic blast; instantly leveling the bridge, and sending out a shockwave that collapsed buildings and violently shook the ground.

It harmlessly washed over Jack as it spread in all directions and devastated the entire area; though he was sure it only bought him a few seconds as the *Avatars* proved to be relentless and nearly unstoppable. Jack sprinted to where he saw the *Clerics* and the bridge to the source, the blast wave had done all his work for him as he saw all the ritual casting *Clerics* unconscious on the ground. Jack took a deep breath, readied himself, and proceeded towards the huge pillar of light and energy that was *The Source*.

Jack suddenly awoke back at the campfire. Jack was perplexed as he yelled aloud "What the hell- That was it! I was there; and there weren't any obstacles left?! I wasn't dead or about to die?! AAAHHHHHHH!!!" As he flung his arms into the air in frustration, furious that all that work hadn't led to an escape from this void.

Jack seethed as his eyes glared and he clenched his teeth slightly, he wanted to sprint over and rip the door apart with his bare hands; was there something else to all this, maybe the First-Blade had lied to him before, but wouldn't that have been contradicted by *Loki*? Surely he was missing something…

Jack planted his palm against his forehead racking his brain for an answer, as footsteps suddenly emanated from a distance. Jack stopped and scoured the area around him for any hallucinations or visitors, he wasn't sure of either at this point; yet he found nothing save for the continued echo of the mysterious footsteps.

Jack ran into the void after the noise half crazed and desperate for any answers. Jack ran to an incredible distance, far away from the campfire and final door; though the footsteps didn't seem to get much closer. Jack looked in every direction and couldn't figure out where he was, in a momentary lapse of concentration he suddenly went into a free-fall again; falling through the nothingness towards nothingness.

Jack concentrated only on the sound of the footsteps, "Where have I heard those familiar steps before."

He suddenly landed on a chair next to an old dining room table, Jack scanned around and recognized the scene, and he should have as it had occurred every other weekend for 10 years of his life. It was Sunday morning, 8am at the old family home; which meant that the first person to enter that kitchen and sit down would be-

A familiar voice greeted him "Jack it's good to see you,"

As his grandfather stepped in and sat down in his spot, the same place he had sat down and they had talked for nearly Jack's entire school life.

Jack replied half choked up, knowing that his grandfather passed away some time ago "Granddad... it's good to see you too."

Jack's grandfather was Dan Schmitt, a no-nonsense businessman that went through both the great depression and World War 2; throughout his entire life he had been a blunt and stubborn man, but always took care of his own. Dan spent most of the latter half of his life following the same routine he had for years, doing business and real-estate work on the weekdays, and solving crossword puzzles and reading the news on Sundays. Jack had spent a great many weekends with his grandfather, trying to learn as much as he could; and though he wasn't the easiest to get along with, he always had advice to share and would tell candid stories that reflected lessons Dan learned the hard way.

Jack drank some tea and asked "Are you here to give me one last piece of advice granddad?"

As Dan cleared his throat while looking through his crossword puzzle and replied "I'm just here to tell you what you already know."

Jack glanced back and replied "What would that be?"

Dan folded the newspaper aside and spoke to Jack directly "This character you're up against thinks he has the only solution, but that's only because he's been looking at the big picture only one way for too long. He's going to try and confuse you, as his type does; you have to set your mind to the right course, you've known from the start what the right thing is to do."

Jack rubbed his forehead and replied "His arguments are very convincing; I see little merit in the strangers that I fight for."

Dan pointed out "Yet still you fight for them, you're stubborn like that Jack; do you remember all the times we spoke of history, the rise and fall of empires throughout time?"

Jack recollected such memories strongly and replied "I do, you always argued that empires rose and fell due to the shifting technological and economic realities of the world. I always thought that it was the will of the people; their belief or lack thereof, in their nation and shared society."

Dan nodded and removed his family ring from his finger and handed it over saying "I gave this ring to you ten years ago because I believed in you Jack, now it's your turn to believe in yourself; Sol's path only leads in a never-ending circle, you have a chance to end that cycle and create a new path. Now you know what to do, keep it going Jack; and remember that stubbornness when you face adversity, and neither hell nor high water will stop you."

Jack smiled as he put the ring in his pocket and shook Dan's hand "Thanks Granddad, I'll never forget everything you taught me."

As Dan smiled and pointed at the front door, "That's the way back to where you need to be, no matter what happens I'm proud of you." as he faded away.

Jack was still in the old family home, he glanced again at his family ring and resolved to finish what he started; not just for redemption or the *Astral Plane*, but for Granddad and all the other people that meant anything from his past.

Jack got up from the table as a loud echo shook the room, the ceiling spun away until the top of the room was left exposed to the void. From the infinite darkness great drums and horns accompanied the echo, they grew louder as a powerful voice commanded "You have not passed your final test!"

Jack instantly knew who it had to be as he called out *"First Blade*! Come and face me, I am not afraid of you."

A shrouded figure crashed into the kitchen table and glanced up, it was Jack's mirror image, though his clothes were dark and his expression was twisted by rage.

Jack unsheathed his ice-sword and yelled "Sword wraith! You will never ensnare me again!!"

The sword wraith laughed and replied "Without my power you can never hope to defeat Sol! It is because you are weak that you accepted my aid in the first place!!"

Jack yelled as he prepared to attack "I am the *Traveler*! And I will never be weak again."

Slashing forward with his entire body, the sword wraith and he traded furious attacks; Jack's every move was executed with fervor, he would not allow himself to make any mistakes after speaking with his grandfather. Jack kicked the sword wraith backwards and stabbed downward while yelling with all of his might, the sword wraith rolled out of the way as his sword smashed into the floorboards. The sword-wraith recovered onto his feet and charged forward locking both their swords at close range.

The wraith spoke "I have seen inside your mind! You have been a disappointment to everyone! You are nothing!!"

Jack directed the sword lock downwards and punched the wraith hard enough to break his nose yelling "You will not tell me who I am! I will not suffer your insolence."

The sword wraith countered by blasting alternate telekinetic devices forward, Jack caught the blast and redirected it outwards blasting all the fixtures off the wall; Jack then ripped the walls from their foundation and sent them careening towards the sword wraith, they pummeled into his foe burying him in drywall. The wraith freed himself from the rubble to see Jack standing over him, he slashed feebly at Jack who grabbed the sword edge first, unaffected by its sharpness or its power.

Jack ripped the sword out of his hands and yelled "You dare call me weak, you say that I am nothing!! You trick those into becoming your thralls so that you can selfishly kill and seek vain glory to no end, but you are still nothing but an animated hunk of metal! I am Jack Schmitt, *Traveler* of the *Astral Plane* and catalyst of great change; and you *First Blade*, YOU are nothing!!"

With that Jack tossed the cursed sword aside and picked up the sword wraith, he punched hard enough for the sound to echo through the void like a hammer blow, he kept hitting him repeatedly, giving the sword wraith a furious beating. Clutching the wraith by his throat Jack readied the final attack; the wraith glared and said cryptically "Who was he that forged that *First Blade*?"

As Jack punched hard enough to disintegrate the sword wraith, answering angrily "...It was man that forged the steel, yet no steel makes a man." With that Jack took a deep breath and set his mind to the next task, he had work to do.

Jack stepped through the front door of his old family home, as he felt a gale carry him upwards; the speed became more intense as he rapidly approached the *Astral Plane* again, dropping straight in to where he had been cast off, he was standing at the sanctuary ring again, in the time-locked ruins of *Solaris Infinium*.

Before Jack could determine how much time passed within the void, Sarah's voice came on the ear piece "Jack? Jack! You're alive, I thought we lost you."

Jack tapped his earpiece and replied "Sarah, is everyone alright? Is *the Harbinger* still in one piece?"

Sarah replied half busy "The *Avatars* gave us a bloody nose, but were still tactical; ready to follow you towards *The Source*."

Jack sternly replied "Negative, regroup with the *Seer* and get the ship out of here. This fight's too dangerous."

Sarah replied reluctantly "We can't just leave you behind, there's too much at stake."

Jack replied reassuringly "The ship is yours now Sarah, keep the ship and its crew safe. And don't worry about me; I know exactly what's waiting for me and what I have to do."

With that Jack took out the earpiece and crushed it in his grip, he set his sights on the next passage closer to *the Source* and sprinted away in search of it.

Jack found a group of *Templars* clustered close to the inside edge of the storm barrier, they were frantically fighting off an increasing horde of *Avatars* as they hurriedly retreated into the storm wall unharmed. Jack charged and absorbed a telekinetic wave, calculated his approach, and then dove towards them like a hawk.

Propelling himself forward with a blast wave, he cleared all the enemies around the entrance as he leapt forward into the corridor. On the other side was a column of *Templars*, shuffling towards the next sanctuary ring; though they all stopped in their tracks when Jack entered the scene. Jack began sprinting through at an incredible speed, not even taking the time to fight the *Templars* around him; they attempted to shoot bolts at him or slash him with their swords, but he simply sprinted through them, blazing through every obstacle that got in his path with ease.

Reaching the other side in seconds Jack saw classical architecture, marble buildings all around, and the symbols of power and prestige; there was no mistaking it, the next ring was the Roman Empire. Jack made his way to the highest point around to survey his surroundings; he took a few moments to admire the architecture and savor the moment he could see all the cities monuments in their prime, despite Rome's brutal history he had always admired its accomplishments and was intrigued with its rise and fall. His thoughts were interrupted by the rising echo of the *Avatars* all around them, they had only just barely started to make their way in when he was cast into the void; Jack guessed by their now significant numbers that he had been absent at least a few hours, that probably meant that Sol was at the innermost ring by now.

Jack tracked the mob's movements; the *Avatars* were charging forwards into the storm clouds; most of them impacting with reckless abandon and being jolted awake by the sudden shock. Jack scanned their various impact points and noticed where they weren't suddenly dissipating; he then readied to cross the next threshold, somewhat irritated that he could not spend more time in *Classical Rome*. Jack dove into the next corridor and reached the path, yet this time it was teeming with *Avatars* in every direction; he figured he could just storm through them like with the *Templars* and reach the other side unscathed, sprinting past them with the increased speed and stride of his telekinetic aura.

One of the *Avatars* blasted a wave of lightning at him, and far from barreling through it he was stopped cold; Jack impacted with the wave as if he had rammed himself into a wall, he tumbled backwards into the ground as the other *Avatars* took noticed and readied to attack.

Getting back on his feet he blasted a powerful force wave in every direction to buy himself some space, but the attack had a far diminished effect on the *Avatars*, they were barely pushed away and immediately resumed the attack. Suddenly Jack remembered that these *Avatars* were people that were asleep, so his power in the *Astral Plane* was likely to be far less effective against them... especially in their current state of mind.

Jack vaulted back into the air, trying to dodge and weave his way around the angered crowd; barrages of lightning, water, and fire waves were blasted in every direction attempting to hit him. Jack had to use his speed advantage for everything it was worth just to keep from getting pummeled into the dirt by these bursts of elemental fury. Jack could see the other side as his momentum was going to be halted by the combined attack of dozens of *Avatars* that he could not avoid, the telekinetic aura took the brunt of the impact and dissipated as Jack bounced through the crowd and landed with a dull thud.

The *Avatars* wasted no time stomping on him while he was down, as Jack hacked, shoved, and shot his way out of the swarm. It seemed that only a power attack to their center mass or face was the only thing that could jolt them awake, any special attack with the telekinetic devices had to be fired as a concentrated blast directed at a singular individual or it had virtually no effect; this made them a very dangerous enemy in numbers. Jack barely made his way through to the other side, but he had taken a beating from damn near every *Avatar* he passed by; reaching the next sanctuary he quickly made for high ground atop another building.

Jack was winded and in pain, he had direly underestimated the *Avatars* and it nearly cost him. He couldn't go into another encounter with the *Avatars* blind like that, he decided to observe them more closely and see what he could learn. Scanning the area around him he noticed that there were many more *Avatars* in this ring than in the last one, which did not make sense, if anything there should have been less of them from all the losses to the storm. Then Jack started to pick up on something, he only glanced at it the first few times, but when he started watching for it he noticed that the *Avatars* were reappearing in various places inside the ring.

Jack commented on this observation aloud "Their falling back into this place, again and again; even Sol with all his power couldn't fight them eternally"

Observing their movements he saw something else, many of the cloud-like illusions around them were getting larger and more intense as they approached the inner storm wall; then he recalled his experience from the *Avatar* mob in the void, they were much stronger than the ones he had faced only moments ago... *The Source* was giving them power, drawing them further in, but why?

Jack was starting to realize why his recurring experience in the void always ended when the *Avatars* reached him; in this place they were an innumerable force of juggernauts. Jack now understood that he couldn't face them directly and expect to win, and he couldn't risk another trip through a corridor filled with *Avatars*; he needed to get around them, and he needed to reach *the Source* before the mob from his visions got there first.

Jack suddenly realized that the architecture was that of the late *Middle Ages*, he also noticed a multitude of elaborate cathedrals, neoclassical structures, and much more color and style than before; this had to be after the Renaissance. "At least I'm getting closer" Jack pondered aloud as he wondered how many more rings were between him and *the Source*.

Jack started jumping from rooftop to rooftop searching for any corridors the *Templars* were holding or any gap in the *Avatars*. From a distance he saw multiple flares shoot up into the sky, Jack made his way towards the disturbance and saw a large container sitting in the middle of a plaza, though it was far too high tech to be from the Renaissance. A beam shone from the container and scanned Jack briefly, then after flashing green a panel opened to a video screen of the *Fox*.

Jack began "*Fox*!? What is this container? Where are you?"

As the voice from the screen interrupted "If you're seeing this then it means you've reached the inner rings of the sanctuary and the scanner hasn't detected the *First Blade*." Jack suddenly realized it was a previously made recording.

The playback continued "You must have found some way to free yourself from the possession of the *First Blade*; though I could tell from your words and actions that you will not so easily abandon your cause of redemption. As you have no doubt learned the obstacles surrounding *The Source* are great, you will need this…"

The box rapidly transformed and unfolded into an assembly apparatus which displayed holographic grid of the intended design, small drones rapidly assembled a skeletal structure before various plates and components unfolded out of the box and were fused into place by the drones; in a matter of seconds the design was complete, it was one of the mechs… but this one was different. It featured jump jets, an advanced power pack that ran off miniaturized *Harbinger* power cores, retractable wrist fire weapons, and larger built-in versions of the telekinetic devices on each hand, and finally the trademark robotic chassis with armor plating and rocket packs.

The Fox recording remarked "The mark-two, only possible with the improved power capacity and output of your power cores; it features adaptable weapons, more protection, and greater speed."

Jack suddenly realized that was the wrecked mech from his visions in the void, though he nearly didn't recognize it as this was still brand new and the wreck was always lying face down in a crater; he figured this must have been how he had gotten as far as he did.

The recording continued as the *Fox*'s voice detailed "This will get you through the storm, you'll be capable of over-charging the power-pack and emitting a far more intense telekinetic field; though it will burn out if you overuse it."

Jack took a second look at the oversized telekinetic devices and the power cores said to himself "...Ripped off my design, didn't you?"

As the recording of the *Fox* almost seemed to reply "The gauntlets are a scaled up version based upon your design, though it will lack the reliability under repeated strain."

The recording then concluded with one final message from the *Fox* "In my quest for redemption I eventually became lost in the pursuit of revenge; these specters of our past are incapable of granting any solace. Find peace with your actions *Traveler*, and find a way forward. Remember that if you find yourself on a path not of your own making, choosing to continue is still a choice. End recording." As the screen flickered off and folded into the base of the open container.

Jack climbed into the mech as the operating chamber closed around him and the interface came into view. A virtual display of his surroundings took the place of an operating window as an electronic voice reported "All systems ready, power at one-hundred percent."

Jack saw a neural link similar to how he controlled *the Harbinger*, he put the earpiece on and smiled saying to himself "Alright *Fox*, let's see what your rip-off of my design can do."

20

THE STORMS
OF CHAOS

JACK READIED THE MECH AND BEGAN MARCHING TOWARDS THE NEAREST storm-wall, while running he took a moment to charge up a telekinetic wave through the suit, surprised at how easily the suit could mimic his actions through the interface. Emitting the aura caused the virtual interface to brighten and the internal lights to nearly shine through the console, the computer voice advised "Overcharge achieved; power at 1000% percent."

Jack directed the mech's telekinetic devices outwards and projected a telekinetic field that looked to be a sphere of industrial plastic, confident in this Jack stepped through the storm wall into the tempest of fragments and debris that normally tore apart everything It touched.

Clearing the barrier Jack cautiously walked across the barren expanse that was the storm swept terrain; slowly his perception began to adjust to the surroundings like one's eyesight underwater. In the distance he could see entire cities that looked to be half buried in ash and sand, great buildings and wonders he didn't recognize bearing styles of architecture beyond anything he could recollect.

Jack thought to himself "Are these the ruins of times before ours, or are they possibilities that might have been?"

Trudging forward as the many buildings and statues restlessly shifted and moved, occasionally disassembling into dust as the endless debris from the process was blasted around by the chaotic and unpredictable winds. These mystifying surroundings left Jack in awe, he was the only person to see this since perhaps the last *Traveler* capable of such a feat; a lonely trek through the desert of lost civilizations.

Suddenly a warning indicator interrupted Jack's reflection as the computer voice advised "Warning, significant equipment strain; reduce external stress." Taking that as his cue to pick up the pace Jack ran forward towards the other side of the storm, making sure to keep most of his focus on maintaining the barrier.

Jack cleared the storm-wall powered down his telekinetic field, taking a moment to observe his surroundings he found himself in a very industrial looking setting, with red-brick buildings, smoke-stacks on the horizons, and works of steel and rivets all around him: the industrial revolution.

Jack reflected aloud "This has to be nearly the last one; I'm getting close to the center."

Jack began climbing the nearby buildings to get a view of his surroundings, he wondered if he had gained any distance from the mob of *Avatars*, or if they were already here in force.

Jack reached the rooftop of a nearby factory and scanned the horizon; the scene seemed eerily calm, like Solaris Infininum was when they first arrived; though Jack had his doubts that somehow the scene was going to remain as peaceful as it appeared. His suspicions were confirmed by the echo of collected chanting and stomping in the distance, like an approaching army; from the storm wall a great host of *Avatars* suddenly funneled through. Somehow Jack could sense the mob was starting to gain cohesion, perhaps even some measure of organization... Soon it would be the unstoppable force that he remembered from the void. In a short space of time the *Avatar* mob reached hundreds of thousands; a collected war-cry rose from the masses, and then like an unleashed tidal wave they began swarming over everything: a great sudden upheaval as everything descended into a destructive anarchy.

Jack had seen this before, he needed to leave quickly or be overwhelmed. Running towards the next storm wall he attempted to charge another telekinetic aura, but a warning chime stopped him as the computer advised "Capacitors overheating, please wait before overcharging."

Jack yelled in frustration "Dammit! Not now of all times!" He looked behind him and could see the rising tide of doom washing over the sanctuary ring, he needed to get the hell out of there.

Jack was sprinting across the rooftops, trying to gain some distance on the elemental waves of destruction set forth by the *Avatar* mass; the mech was moving with great speed, but the wave was starting to gain on him. Debris was flung forwards in front of him as whole trains and building faces impacted into the scenery around him, throwing up clouds of dust and plowing through rows of buildings, the entire ground beneath the sanctuary began quaking violently as the whole city began to yield and collapse.

Jack was now using the jump jets to dart and weave between the remaining intact rooftops, trying desperately to avoid getting swept up in the approaching cataclysm.

Jack yelled over the noise "Computer! What is the status of the capacitors!!"

As he could barely hear the reply over the cataclysm gaining on him, crashing through brick and steel with a deafening roar; The computer replied "Capacitors are still overheated, engaging now will lead to system overload."

Jack saw that another wave of destruction was now approaching in the distance from the front as well, the entire ring was nearly covered by this avalanche of force, he was out of time!

Sprinting towards the nearest storm wall he yelled "Emergency override, engage overcharge NOW!" as he thrust out his arms to project the shield and blindly dove into the barrier.

Jack tumbled forward into the barren desert, bouncing across the plains of ash and sand like a skipping stone; he somehow managed to keep the shield up during this ordeal. Taking a moment to recover, Jack got the mech mobile again and started for the other side of the desert, fully aware of the computer's warning he hurried along being unsure of how much time he had before the shield burned out.

Running through the storm desert he noticed the ruins of his surroundings; yet it wasn't like the previous one... these ruins were very familiar indeed, it looked much like the modern architecture he knew of, "Is this meant to be a warning, was this civilization doomed to a self-destructive cycle as well?! Or is this merely a sight of things to come?"

Jack wasn't sure, but he had no time to find an answer, if his shields gave way in this place it would rip right through his armor in seconds, he needed to make haste. Jack sprinted through towards the end of the storm, all the buildings around him began to collapse into dust like before; the booming echo of their collapse was as great herald of doom, as if the storm itself was welcoming the end times with fiendish glee.

A loud ping caught Jack's attention, his suit was struck by a small object at high speed; this was followed by another, and then several more. Jack frantically glanced at the shield and saw that it was starting to become unstable. Jack fired the jump jets forward and tried to clear the remaining distance in one great arc; floating through the air he wasn't sure if he was going to clear the storm wall, the only way to be certain was to boost his momentum by ejecting himself forward through the tempest! It was his only clear chance to reach the other side.

Jack took a few panicked breaths and readied the eject button, quickly switching on the auto-pilot as he readied for the precise moment he would need to jump. The mech now glided forward at impressive speed.

A sudden alarm jolted Jack to action as the computer echoed in a corroded voice "S-s-shields failing!"

Jack hit the button and sailed through the air, carried by the forward momentum, casting a telekinetic field with such intensity that he was gritting his teeth and clenching his hands in a death claw. Jack felt as if he had ejected himself into the vacuum of space, yelling as he plummeted forwards through the hurricane, half deafened by the noise and focusing so hard he nearly blacked out.

Jack suddenly cleared the storm plummeting downwards into the final sanctuary ring, he took a brief moment to identify landmarks in the air before blasting a telekinetic wave downwards to slow his   descent and break his fall. Landing in a roll upon the ground, he heard what sounded like a failing aircraft in the distance; looking skyward he saw the suit in flames and spiraling out of control towards the ground, Jack observed the fires and was glad to have narrowly escaped being perforated and burnt to death. It impacted in the direction of the bridge, setting the course of events to happen as he recalled; he still wasn't sure how his altering of previous events caused the suit to become available, but the power core would greatly expedite his journey.

Jack went over the sequence rhyme he had memorized during his time in the void, he walked forward reassuring himself "Alright, this time's for real." making his way to the bridge knowing that a mistake this time would mean certain death.

Jack quickly reached the bridge and recovered the power-core from the crashed suit, he approached the bridge uttering the entire rhyme sequence once to prepare himself. "Power attack, flash blind, vacuum bind; fake out, redirect, block and reflect; double down, ground pound; electrify, take to the sky; land, incinerate, immobilize, snap freeze and petrify; Toss the core, level the bridge to the shore; record the toll, end the rhyme and stop Sol."

Jack approached the first group and put his memory to the test: "Power attack" blasting a compressed pressure wave at the first few *Paladins*, blasting them to dust. "Flash blind" as he fired flash powder bolts onto the pavement to blind the oncoming *Paladin* charge. "Vacuum bind" as he continued with vacuum attacks to leave them immobilized. "Fake out" faking a charge at the immobilized targets knowing the incoming flank attack to be on the way. "Redirect" stopping short to redirect flanker's swords into their immobilized allies with the devices; the redirected *Paladins* stabbed their allies and fell over just as the others broke the hold. "Block and reflect" Parrying and blocking their attacks as he waited for their signal, as one of the *Paladins* behind them whistled; the attackers dove out of the way as Jack blasted a repelling wave forward into the crossbow bolts that hadn't been fired yet, the unaware *Paladins* fired and had their bolts immediately backfire at point blank range, killing them instantly.

"Double down" as Jack recalled the Templar escalation and summoned an additional ice sword before being surrounded. The *Paladins* swooped in and readied their attack, but Jack knew their combinations and actions in advance and was ready to once again make them look like fools. Jack danced around their attacks, dodging with such precision as to make them look overcome with clumsiness, each time countering with lethal precision. Eventually a group of *Paladins* attacked simultaneously as he proceeded to parry and counter their attacks two at a time using his extra sword for everything it was worth, counter slashing and sword breaking his way through each attack as Jack managed to buy himself a few moments. "Ground pound" as Jack punched the ground with a charged telekinetic punch, breaking a hole in the road as it rapidly began crumbling, taking many of the unsuspecting *Paladins* with it. "Electrify" as he shot out the dust storms that electrocuted everything on the bridge towers, clearing a path for his aerial escape. "Take to the skies" as he leapt into the air, barely avoiding tumbling wreckage and clearing the gap in the bridge.

"Land" as Jack landed in a roll just in front of the lead *Paladin*, he needed to taunt him into attacking for the rest of the sequence to work. The *Paladin* commander was awestruck and yelled "How! How can you defeat us so easily?!"

Jack yelled "Because you suck! Attack me dammit!!"

"Incinerate" as predicted his oncoming fire attack, overextended the arm, struck the elbow joint, and then redirected the attackers arm back at him, immolating him with his own flame. "Immobilize". The followers angrily charged forward as Jack suddenly locked their weapons in place with his free device. "Snap freeze and petrify" catching the frost salts from his blade and snap freezing the others with lightning fast punches, permanently solidifying them in place. Jack was suddenly clear of the *Paladins*, they were all dead or disabled as he turned back and saw the *Avatar* mob arrive at the other side of the bridge.

Jack uttered in frustration knowing he was about to throw away the thing that gave him a near endless reserve of telekinetic energy for his attacks "Blarg, I hate this part… 'toss the core, level the bridge to the shore'"

Jack Hurled the power core at the center of the bridge, as it detonated with an earth shattering telekinetic blast, leveling the bridge and sending out a shockwave that collapsed buildings and violently shook the ground. It harmlessly washed over Jack as it spread in all directions and devastated the entire area, and yet he knew even such a powerful explosion would only buy him seconds at the most. Jack jogged towards where he knew all the knocked out *Clerics* would be: the bridge to *the Source*. Jack uttered the end of the rhyme as he jogged towards the final challenge "Record the toll, end the rhyme…and stop Sol."

21

THE SOURCE

JACK WAS NOW A FEW HUNDRED FEET AWAY FROM THE MASSIVE ENIGMATIC pillar of light and energy that was *the Source*, standing on the bridge of light which led into the mysterious beacon. Jack began walking towards it, unsure of what he might find. Time slowed, his senses began to be overwhelmed, his vision brightened to such levels where he could no longer distinguish his surroundings from the background, and all the ambient sound faded into whispers. He stood face to face with the enigmatic beam and reached out to touch the nexus of power, he felt an intense pulse of energy shoot through him and was carried into a current of limitless power than he could not see or hear, but could feel; losing all bearings he lost his sense of self, being suddenly overwhelmed in the sensation of being in all places in all times simultaneously.

This was the sensation very similar to when he had nearly died, but this was different, the light and power was carrying him towards something not away from it. Lines of thought echoed into his conscious, the subconscious patterns of millions, coalescing into waves of similarities and difference; sharpening his thoughts he was able to perceive their representations as they spun outwards into different spheres and formed landscapes not unlike those of the different realms. Suddenly every memory and fact Jack could access at a whim, any question, any wonder, instantly answered from the collected memory of the entire human unconscious. It was all overwhelming; Jack had started to wonder if he had stumbled into the realm of God by mistake, he had to work hard to separate himself, to become an independent entity again.

Concentrating on his sense of self proved odd, he had to remember who he was again and then put that to form; after recollecting every aspect and detail of himself, both positive and negative, slowly his senses returned and he re-materialized. Jack found himself standing in a mental representation of *the Source*, a brightly lit ethereal platform surrounded on ___ an endlessly complex labyrinth of shapes and patterns made of ___ patterns still hovering in the space around them, ebbing ___ective thoughts of the human race.

___ared on the opposite side, bright and ___ erwhelmed its surroundings, Jack ___ "Sol" and as if summoned it formed the physical representation of Sol who then came into view. Sol glared towards Jack, the intensity and focus of his gaze was unrelenting.

Sol began "…*Traveler*, behold *the Source*; this is the *Astral Plane* in its purest form, unrestrained by the artificial binds of reality's imposed limitations. Only one thing remains, what course to invariably guide the *Astral Plane* upon."

Jack raised an eyebrow and replied "You have already resolved to destroy modern civilization and renew the *Astral Plane* in your image."

Sol smirked and replied "I had, and was about to; yet you have defied expectations once again. If I were I to continue without pause, you could set your will against me, my work would be reversed … chaos would fill the vacuum, and the *Astral Plane* would come undone."

Jack replied in a doubtful tone "That sounds melodramatic"

Sol responded "It is, the fate of the *Astral Plane* hangs in the balance. You and I will now decide the future."

Jack glared and replied "I have already seen the future you will bring Sol, even disregarding the unparalleled destruction and upheaval of the transition; your path will then lead afterwards to a never ending cycle of conflict, loss, and misery. After having taken away any memory of what came before the people will proceed to carry out the same mistakes as their ancestors, ignorant and oblivious to the consequences, it will repeat endlessly until the end of time, an unbroken circle of anarchy and death! That is the legacy you will write Sol, to blind the world and leave it bound to a cursed existence, only to be yourself forgotten."

Sol took a moment before replying, though ther‌ o look of doubt or revelation in his eyes; just the same calculat‌ ‌hen retorted in his usual way, as if telli‌ story, as h‌ which he sought to invoke flashe‌ ‌lf was reflecting his though‌

Sol spoke cal‌ unaware of, I ‌ in the void‌ which ‌ that‌ ‌

speak of; it is nothing compared to the horrors your society is capable of unleashing."

As if orchestrated by Sol's thoughts, the images behind him turned to the possibilities of atomic warfare, global famine, high-tech oppression, world-wide devastation, and millions upon millions living in absolute squalor and poverty.

Sol continued "This is the salvation you propose *Traveler*! What future will they have I wonder, to watch as their leaders bask in boundless corruption and greed, as hubris carries their nations into war and devastation without forethought! What life will they lead *Traveler*, what good is their freedom without any power! What few can rise while vexed with the weight of such great obligations: of debt, of injustice, of want, and of servitude? How many will instead give in and be imprisoned onto a life of crippling dependency.

Sol said with strong emphasis "They have nothing *Traveler*! Their existence amounts to their waiting to be dead!"

The images ceased as Sol continued "The masses' growing yearning for anarchy was callously unleashed by your foolish declaration, but it was always there *Traveler*! When the people decide they have had enough, when they no longer submit to the burden shackled upon them by the institutions they serve, then they will cast all it down."

Sol said direly as he concluded "Your society will topple and collapse ruining anything of worth your people achieved; and as your great cities burn, as your collected knowledge becomes dust, when everything is lost… then *Traveler*, only then your society will have completed its self-defeating cycle. At least my solution carries with it some measure of restoration, yours is a great spiral into the ash heap. I condemn you as a fool for ever having entertained it as the better alternative, and I curse you as a tyrant for throwing away any other solution, all because you are not strong enough to accept the sacrifices that must be made; your civilization's future lies only in desolation! There can be no other end result!!"

Jack clenched his fists and yelled in return "Enough! Your arrogance is insufferable! To think that you know the only outcome! To decide the fate of untold masses as if you were god!! So long as there is any possibility of redemption, if there is any hope the cycle is broken, then I will find that path. And if you can see no other way then I will cast you down! Back to the oblivion from which you came, back to the obscurity that a false god deserves."

Sol laughed upon hearing this; he laughed uncharacteristically as it echoed from the space around them and filled the silence, after a good while he directed his attention back on his opponent and replied conclusively "So be it *Traveler!*"

Sol then raised his hand into the air and the entire nexus seemed to respond, with an intense flash of light their surroundings began to quake, the architecture of light responded and began to rapidly shift and reassemble itself.

Jack responded to the sudden chaos "What is this! What have you done!?"

Sol answered "It has begun, when it finishes only one of us can decide what follows. You have until it's completion to defeat me; let this debate be decided by action, a final contest for the fate of the *Astral Plane*. Now, have at you!"

Jack thrust his devices forward intending to blast Sol into oblivion, but the energy rapidly was carried away towards the nexus; Jack was awestruck, had Sol already managed to deprive him of one of his greatest abilities? Then he glanced at Sol and saw the bright red/yellow energy carried away from his opponent into the nexus as well.

Sol smirked seeing Jack's confusion and yelled "It will not be so easy, Jack!"

Sol then charged forwards, spinning a great metal spear around himself as if it were weightless, charging forward to pummel Jack; Jack tightened his grip on his sword and countered with a sweeping clearing block, reverberating with a loud clang as both weapons collided.

Sol followed up this interruption with several quick jabs of the spear point, only to have Jack respond with impressive speed, parrying each away effortlessly. Sol escalated his attack with a great swipe downwards, intending to smash Jack into the ground. Jack held his ground blocking the great force of the blow and keeping Sol at bay, Sol hesitated for a moment and Jack directed the spear away and kicked Sol backwards and then put him on the defensive with furious slashes from every direction. Sol was starting to make mistakes, and Jack was gaining momentum against him; Sol would need to change the tempo of the battle to give himself the advantage again.

Waiting for Jack to stab forwards, Sol swung his spear at the sword's reverse catch and then disarmed Jack, flinging the sword to the side. Sol smirked thinking he had just ushered in Jack's defeat, but his opponent stood before him as determined as ever. Sol swung horizontally as Jack ducked under it and sweep kicked the demi-god's side; frustrated Sol aggressively swung repeatedly in different directions, only to have Jack evade each one again and again, using impressive footwork to weave his way around his now frustrated and clumsy opponent, making him pay for each mistake with a stinging punch to the face or torso. Dazed and reeling Sol shoved his spear forwards, intending to bash Jack backwards and buy himself some room to operate; but his attack was caught by Jack as he locked the weapon in place with his iron grip and stared Sol down, Jack proceeded to repeatedly punch Sol in the face as his enemy quickly lost balance and tumbled backwards.

Jack tossed the spear away and said "Have you ever had to endure pain Sol, have you ever had to work to achieve a greater measure of speed and strength? No, you know nothing of being mortal; in this contest, without your power, you are weak."

As Jack spoke the nexus began to finish collecting the energy swirling around it as it coalesced into a fractal core of intense energy and began to radiate powerful waves back outwards. Sol retorted to Jack's earlier assertion "I may know nothing of being weak, but you know nothing of power!"

As Sol blasted an intense wave of fire and heat at Jack, covering the entire platform with a searing firestorm; it looked as though everything had been annihilated by the attack, but after a few moments the firestorm began to lift as it then was spun outwards harmlessly by an unscathed *Traveler*, his power having returned at the same moment as his opponent's had. Sol gritted his teeth in frustration and then unleashed his fury upon Jack, hurling flaming meteors and blasts of thermal radiation forward.

Jack concentrated on his devices and deflected the attacks as they came, alternating between protective shields and telekinetic redirection to protect himself from the barrage. Sol was unrelenting though, and Jack had no time between attacks to absorb any telekinetic waves and counter attack; Sol could see this and increased the tempo of the attacks, intending to grind his opponent into the dust.

Jack was starting to lose track of all the attacks approaching him, he resorted to directing everything into his protective shield and enduring all the damage; this measure would only serve to buy him time though as Sol proceeded to batter Jack's defenses without relent. Jack was now down to kneeling, beginning to lose concentration as he devoted everything into the shield, desperate thoughts raced through his mind, was he about to lose again, was he destined to fail against Sol?

Suddenly another voice entered his thoughts, one of an inspiring guide from before; he remembered his grandfather's ring as the words echoed back "I believed in you Jack, now it's your turn to believe in yourself." Jack nodded to himself and placed the ring over his finger on the telekinetic gauntlet; he smiled as he felt his will to power rapidly increase, was he finally ready to become the fully realized *Traveler*?

KaBlam! As Sol watched dozens of fireballs impact at once into his enemy, not wanting to make the same mistake twice Sol called out to the smoldering smoke stack "Do you still live, *Traveler*?! Have you realized the folly of challenging a god! Of altering the cycle! Of denying fate!!"

An aura of intense telekinetic energy stepped through the smoke, Jack approached with glowing eyes and his footsteps quaked with power. He narrowed his gaze and replied "Only one realization comes to mind Sol, that your time has come to an End!"

Jack then unleashed the most powerful attack he could have ever reckoned with, it blasted Sol into the space around them; shattering the patterns of light, and even distorting the nexus of power for a moment. In the wake of this attack, the realms were suddenly revealed around them, all orbiting the nexus, building to their high point in energy before *the Source* unleashed its great wave of change. Sol plummeted downwards through the atmosphere of *Venture*, as he quickly regained consciousness and steadied himself in the air.

Jack's offensive was far from done, as his glowing silhouette rocketed into view like a comet diving planet-ward. Jack collided with Sol with enough force to remove all the clouds from the air and blast Sol into one of the nearby mountains, shattering its surface as Sol impacted into the mountain with enough force to collapse its rocky face around him.

The debris became a volcano as Sol returned with vengeance as the entire mound exploded with lava and fire, Sol seemed to command the magma and sun itself to destroy Jack as the sky filled with fire. With one hand Jack directed the oceans to release all their water into the air, devastating the entire landscape with a furious blast of steam and fog. Sol was coughing uncontrollably at this unexpected counter, as Jack suddenly appeared and knocked Sol backwards with a haymaker attack!

Sol was flung into yet another realm, as he skidded across the trees of *Epic*, snapping through hundreds of trees and leaving a scorched impact trail. Sol again recovered and fire shot from his eyes setting the entire forest ablaze, he then rose his arms into the air and swirled the great firestorm into a great and terrifying tornado of flame! Jack arrived again as Sol blasted the tornado towards him, unimpressed Jack blasted his arms outwards and turned the entire sky into a vacuum, immediately snuffing out the flames. Sol seemed awestruck to the point of paralysis as Jack fired another intense telekinetic blast his way and launched him into yet another realm.

Sol impacted into the middle of *Mirage* as buildings collapsed on top of him and the streets cracked and separated. Blasting himself free Sol saw Jack approaching yet again, as he tossed whole buildings at his foe in a desperate attempt to slow him down; Jack dove through the buildings, the force of his impact blasting them to pieces as he plummeted forward with the force of natural disasters and a gaze of steel.

He landed right in front of Sol and waited; Sol mistook this for a moment of weakness and furiously punched his enemy repeatedly hoping to gain the advantage. Jack stood there undeterred, not even flinching as the punches bounced off the telekinetic field around him. Grabbing Sol by the throat and hoisting him off the ground Jack commanded "Yield! Or be destroyed!"

Sol choked out "Never!" as he made the sun unleash a blinding flare that distracted Jack for a split second; melting all the steel and glass of the buildings into a molten slag, yet leaving Jack unharmed.

Sol made a break for the nexus floating above all the realms, hoping he could harness the power of *the Source* before Jack defeated him.

Arriving at what remained of the platform of light, Sol shuffled towards the beam, slowed by his injuries fighting Jack.

Sol was muttering almost incomprehensibly "I planned everything out.... I made sure there were no mistakes... this is not how it ends."

Jack appeared from the ether behind him, Sol shot around with a startled gaze and dove backwards into the nexus before he could be stopped. Being carried upward by *the Source* Sol let the limitless energy empower him, waiting to use it to fulfill his vision. Jack would not stand idly by though, and with all his concentration and power reached out to the beam, and as if by command it split into a second nexus, lifting Jack skyward to meet Sol.

The realms below quaked and yielded, giving way to devastation and elemental chaos, one of them needed to prevail or everything would be undone. Sol prepared his final and most ultimate attack and Jack readied to do the same, they both unleashed such great and unparalleled power it covered over all the realms, overshadowing all. *The Source* was unleashed; immediately washing over all the entirety of the *Astral Plane* with its infinite power and remaking all the realms to the ideal of the victor, and then in an instant it was over.

EPILOGUE

JACK STOOD VICTORIOUS OVER THE SOURCE, HAVING MASTERED ITS POWER and unleashed it to usher in a new era of realization. The Avatars would eventually regain their ability to walk upon the *Astral Plane* with full awareness, eventually everyone who entered the *Astral Plane* in their sleep would visit it in the same way as a *Traveler* would, yet Jack knew not what consequences would follow from this.

Sol lay broken and defeated on the floor; he began laughing "Once a foolish *Traveler*, always a foolish *Traveler*."

Jack answered back confident, but calm "I have earned my redemption, the balance is restored, the cycle has been stopped. And you have lost."

Sol quipped back "Have I? You may have granted the *Avatars* the ability to see this realm as it is, but you gave them no ideas to rally behind, no vision to guide them."

Jack replied "I will not decide for them, the lesson Malachi paid for will not be so easily forgotten."

Sol retorted "Foolishness disguised as wisdom *Traveler*, those aimless masses will eventually gain the same power that you wielded, but instead of using it to build the next era of history they will aimlessly wander in search of purpose, seeking answers that you failed to provide."

Jack asserted "Then they will find their own truths, and this realization shall grant them peace."

Sol countered "Or they will become restless, and will pursue conflicting irreconcilable ideals and create chaos. Then a new leader will rise Jack; someone with a power even greater than you could have wielded, a new *Traveler*. You have already used the power of *the Source* and hence can never access that power again; whatever their ideals, you will be incapable of stopping them."

Jack interrupted "You used *the Source* as well Sol, the same conclusion applies"

Sol laughed and replied "I may guide a new *Traveler* to see my vision Jack, and when that day comes your work shall be undone."

Jack replied "I shall also guide others to see the *Astral Plane* as I see it; I will be watching you as well Sol: I will see that you never raise another crusade, your wars shall cease, and your vision will eventually fade once it cannot be foisted upon others via force. Should you threaten the balance directly I will destroy you, and you shall never rise again."

Sol began to teleport away leaving Jack with a foreboding threat "Time will tell Jack. Time will tell and fate will decide."

As Sol disappeared Jack began to wander away from the nexus, his journey at an end as he concluded to himself "Not fate Sol, the will of the next *Traveler* will decide."

THE END

CPSIA information can be obtained
at www.ICGtesting.com
Printed in the USA
BVHW070944030321
601586BV00007B/68

Tens
Data Processing

Tensors for Data Processing
Theory, Methods, and Applications

Edited by

Yipeng Liu

School of Information and Communication Engineering
University of Electronic Science and Technology
of China (UESTC)
Chengdu, China

ACADEMIC PRESS
An imprint of Elsevier

Library of Congress Cataloging-in-Publication Data
A catalog record for this book is available from the Library of Congress

British Library Cataloguing-in-Publication Data
A catalogue record for this book is available from the British Library

ISBN: 978-0-12-824447-0

For information on all Academic Press publications
visit our website at https://www.elsevier.com/books-and-journals

Publisher: Mara Conner
Acquisitions Editor: Tim Pitts
Editorial Project Manager: Charlotte Rowley
Production Project Manager: Prem Kumar Kaliamoorthi
Designer: Miles Hitchen

Typeset by VTeX

Working together
to grow libraries in
developing countries

www.elsevier.com • www.bookaid.org

Contents

CHAPTER 3   Partensor **61**

Paris A. Karakasis, Christos Kolomvakis, George Lourakis,
George Lykoudis, Ioannis Marios Papagiannakos,
Ioanna Siaminou, Christos Tsalidis, and
Athanasios P. Liavas

**CHAPTER 4   A Riemannian approach to low-rank tensor
learning** **91**

Hiroyuki Kasai, Pratik Jawanpuria, and Bamdev Mishra

List of contributors

Kim Batselier
Delft Center for Systems and Control, Delft University of Technology, Delft, The Netherlands

Yingyue Bi
School of Information and Communication Engineering, University of Electronic Science and Technology of China (UESTC), Chengdu, China

Jérémie Boulanger
CRIStAL, Université de Lille, Villeneuve d'Ascq, France

Rémy Boyer
CRIStAL, Université de Lille, Villeneuve d'Ascq, France

Cesar F. Caiafa
Instituto Argentino de Radioastronomía – CCT La Plata, CONICET / CIC-PBA / UNLP, Villa Elisa, Argentina
RIKEN Center for Advanced Intelligence Project, Tokyo, Japan

Jocelyn Chanussot
LJK, CNRS, Grenoble INP, Inria, Université Grenoble, Alpes, Grenoble, France

Christos Chatzichristos
KU Leuven, Department of Electrical Engineering (ESAT), STADIUS Center for Dynamical Systems, Signal Processing and Data Analytics, Leuven, Belgium

Cong Chen
Department of Electrical and Electronic Engineering, The University of Hong Kong, Pokfulam Road, Hong Kong

Nadav Cohen
School of Computer Science, Hebrew University of Jerusalem, Jerusalem, Israel

Xudong Cui
School of Mathematics, Tianjin University, Tianjin, China

André L.F. de Almeida
Department of Teleinformatics Engineering, Federal University of Fortaleza, Fortaleza, Brazil

Aybüke Erol
Circuits and Systems, Department of Microelectronics, Delft University of Technology, Delft, The Netherlands

Yiming Fang
Department of Computer Science, Columbia University, New York, NY, United States

Gérard Favier
Laboratoire I3S, Université Côte d'Azur, CNRS, Sophia Antipolis, France

Borbála Hunyadi
Circuits and Systems, Department of Microelectronics, Delft University of Technology, Delft, The Netherlands

Pratik Jawanpuria
Microsoft, Hyderabad, India

Tai-Xiang Jiang
School of Economic Information Engineering, Southwestern University of Finance and Economics, Chengdu, Sichuan, China

Paris A. Karakasis
School of Electrical and Computer Engineering, Technical University of Crete, Chania, Greece

Ouafae Karmouda
CRIStAL, Université de Lille, Villeneuve d'Ascq, France

Hiroyuki Kasai
Waseda University, Tokyo, Japan

Eleftherios Kofidis
Dept. of Statistics and Insurance Science, University of Piraeus, Piraeus, Greece

Christos Kolomvakis
School of Electrical and Computer Engineering, Technical University of Crete, Chania, Greece

Yoav Levine
School of Computer Science, Hebrew University of Jerusalem, Jerusalem, Israel

Zechu Li
Department of Computer Science, Columbia University, New York, NY, United States

Athanasios P. Liavas
School of Electrical and Computer Engineering, Technical University of Crete, Chania, Greece

Zhouchen Lin

Key Lab. of Machine Perception, School of EECS, Peking University, Beijing, China

Xiao-Yang Liu

Department of Computer Science and Engineering, Shanghai Jiao Tong University, Shanghai, China

Department of Electrical Engineering, Columbia University, New York, NY, United States

Yipeng Liu

School of Information and Communication Engineering, University of Electronic Science and Technology of China (UESTC), Chengdu, China

Zhen Long

School of Information and Communication Engineering, University of Electronic Science and Technology of China (UESTC), Chengdu, China

George Lourakis

Neurocom, S.A, Athens, Greece

Canyi Lu

Carnegie Mellon University, Pittsburgh, PA, United States

Liangfu Lu

School of Mathematics, Tianjin University, Tianjin, China

Yingcong Lu

School of Information and Communication Engineering, University of Electronic Science and Technology of China (UESTC), Chengdu, China

George Lykoudis

Neurocom, S.A, Athens, Greece

Bamdev Mishra

Microsoft, Hyderabad, India

Michael K. Ng

Department of Mathematics, The University of Hong Kong, Pokfulam, Hong Kong

Ioannis Marios Papagiannakos

School of Electrical and Computer Engineering, Technical University of Crete, Chania, Greece

Bo Ren

Key Laboratory of Intelligent Perception and Image Understanding of Ministry of Education of China, Xidian University, Xi'an, China

Or Sharir

School of Computer Science, Hebrew University of Jerusalem, Jerusalem, Israel

Amnon Shashua

School of Computer Science, Hebrew University of Jerusalem, Jerusalem, Israel

Ioanna Siaminou

School of Electrical and Computer Engineering, Technical University of Crete, Chania, Greece

Christos Tsalidis

Neurocom, S.A, Athens, Greece

Simon Van Eyndhoven

KU Leuven, Department of Electrical Engineering (ESAT), STADIUS Center for Dynamical Systems, Signal Processing and Data Analytics, Leuven, Belgium

icometrix, Leuven, Belgium

Sabine Van Huffel

KU Leuven, Department of Electrical Engineering (ESAT), STADIUS Center for Dynamical Systems, Signal Processing and Data Analytics, Leuven, Belgium

Anwar Walid

Nokia Bell Labs, Murray Hill, NJ, United States

Fei Wen

Department of Electronic Engineering, Shanghai Jiao Tong University, Shanghai, China

Noam Wies

School of Computer Science, Hebrew University of Jerusalem, Jerusalem, Israel

Ngai Wong

Department of Electrical and Electronic Engineering, The University of Hong Kong, Pokfulam Road, Hong Kong

Zebin Wu

School of Computer Science and Engineering, Nanjing University of Science and Technology, Nanjing, China

Yang Xu

School of Computer Science and Engineering, Nanjing University of Science and Technology, Nanjing, China

Liuqing Yang

Department of Computer Science, Columbia University, New York, NY, United States

Fei Ye

School of Computer Science and Engineering, Nanjing University of Science and Technology, Nanjing, China

Tatsuya Yokota

Nagoya Institute of Technology, Aichi, Japan

RIKEN Center for Advanced Intelligence Project, Tokyo, Japan

Zhonghao Zhang

School of Information and Communication Engineering, University of Electronic Science and Technology of China (UESTC), Chengdu, China

Qibin Zhao

RIKEN Center for Advanced Intelligence Project, Tokyo, Japan

Guangdong University of Technology, Guangzhou, China

Xi-Le Zhao

School of Mathematical Sciences/Research Center for Image and Vision Computing, University of Electronic Science and Technology of China, Chengdu, Sichuan, China

Pan Zhou

SEA AI Lab, Singapore, Singapore

Ce Zhu

School of Information and Communication Engineering, University of Electronic Science and Technology of China (UESTC), Chengdu, China

Yassine Zniyed

Université de Toulon, Aix-Marseille Université, CNRS, LIS, Toulon, France

Preface

This book provides an overview of tensors for data processing, covering computing theories, processing methods, and engineering applications. The tensor extensions of a series of classical multidimensional data processing techniques are discussed in this book. Many thanks go to all the contributors. Students can read this book to get an overall understanding, researchers can update their knowledge on the recent research advances in the field, and engineers can refer to implementations on various applications.

The first chapter is an introduction to tensor decomposition. In the following, the book provides variants of tensor decompositions with their efficient and effective solutions, including some parallel algorithms, Riemannian algorithms, and generalized thresholding algorithms. Some tensor-based machine learning methods are summarized in detail, including tensor completion, tensor principal component analysis, support tensor machine, tensor-based kernel learning, tensor-based deep learning, etc. To demonstrate that tensors can effectively and systematically enhance performance in practical engineering problems, this book gives implemental details of many applications, such as signal recovery, recommender systems, climate forecasting, image clustering, image classification, network compression, data fusion, image enhancement, neuroimaging, and remote sensing.

I sincerely hope this book can serve to introduce tensors to more data scientists and engineers. As a natural representation of multidimensional data, tensors can be used to substantially avoid the information loss in matrix representations of multiway data, and tensor operators can model more connections than their matrix counterparts. The related advances in applied mathematics allow us to move from matrices to tensors for data processing. This book is promising to motivate novel tensor theories and new data processing methods, and to stimulate the development of a wide range of practical applications.

Yipeng Liu
Chengdu, China
Aug. 10, 2021

Tensor decompositions: computations, applications, and challenges

1

Yingyue Bi, Yingcong Lu, Zhen Long, Ce Zhu, and Yipeng Liu

*School of Information and Communication Engineering, University of Electronic Science and
Technology of China (UESTC), Chengdu, China*

CONTENTS

1.1 Introduction

1.1.1 What is a tensor?

The tensor can be seen as a higher-order generalization of vector and matrix, which normally has three or more modes (ways) [1]. For example, a color image is a third-order tensor. It has two spatial modes and one channel mode. Similarly, a color video is a fourth-order tensor; its extra mode denotes time.

Tensors for Data Processing. https://doi.org/10.1016/B978-0-12-824447-0.00007-8
Copyright © 2022 Elsevier Inc. All rights reserved.

As special forms of tensors, vector $\mathbf{a} \in \mathbb{R}^I$ is a first-order tensor whose i-th entry (scalar) is a_i and matrix $\mathbf{A} \in \mathbb{R}^{I \times J}$ is a second-order tensor whose (i, j)-th element is $a_{i,j}$. A general N-th-order tensor can be mathematically denoted as $\mathcal{A} \in \mathbb{R}^{I_1 \times I_2 \times \cdots \times I_N}$ and its $(i_1, i_2, \cdots, i_N)$-th entry is $a_{i_1, i_2, \cdots, i_N}$. For example, a third-order tensor $\mathcal{A} \in \mathbb{R}^{I_1 \times I_2 \times I_3}$ is illustrated in Fig. 1.1.

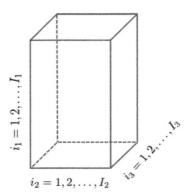

FIGURE 1.1

A third-order tensor $\mathcal{A} \in \mathbb{R}^{I_1 \times I_2 \times I_3}$.

1.1.2 Why do we need tensors?

Tensors play important roles in a number of applications, such as signal processing, machine learning, biomedical engineering, neuroscience, computer vision, communication, psychometrics, and chemometrics. They can provide a concise mathematical framework for formulating and solving problems in those fields.

Here are a few cases involving tensor frameworks:

- Many spatial-temporal signals in speech and image processing are multidimensional. Tensor factorization-based techniques can effectively extract features for enhancement, classification, regression, etc. For example, nonnegative canonical polyadic (CP) decomposition can be used for speech signal separation where the first two components of CP decomposition represent frequency and time structure of the signal and the last component is the coefficient matrix [2].
- The fluorescence excitation–emission data, commonly used in chemistry, medicine, and food science, has several chemical components with different concentrations. It can be denoted as a third-order tensor; its three modes represent sample, excitation, and emission. Taking advantage of CP decomposition, the tensor can be factorized into three factor matrices: relative excitation spectral matrix, relative emission spectral matrix, and relative concentration matrix. In this way, tensor decomposition can be applied to analyze the components and corresponding concentrations in each sample [3].

- Social data often have multidimensional structures, which can be exploited by tensor-based techniques for data mining. For example, the three modes of chat data are user, keyword, and time. Tensor analysis can reveal the communication patterns and the hidden structures in social networks, and this can benefit tasks like recommender systems [4].

1.2 Tensor operations

In this section, we first introduce tensor notations, i.e., fibers and slices, and then demonstrate how to represent tensors in a graphical way. Before we discuss tensor operations, several matrix operations are reviewed.

1.2.1 Tensor notations

Subtensors, such as fibers and slices, can be formed from the original tensor. A fiber is defined by fixing all the indices but one and a slice is defined by fixing all but two indices. For a third-order tensor $\mathcal{A}^{I_1 \times I_2 \times I_3}$, its mode-1, mode-2, and mode-3 fibers are denoted by $\mathcal{A}(:, i_2, i_3)$, $\mathcal{A}(i_1, :, i_3)$, and $\mathcal{A}(i_1, i_2, :)$, where $i_1 = 1, \cdots, I_1$, $i_2 = 1, \cdots, I_2$ and $i_3 = 1, \cdots, I_3$, which are illustrated in Fig. 1.2. Its horizontal slices $\mathcal{A}(i_1, :, :), i_1 = 1, \cdots, I_1$, lateral slices $\mathcal{A}(:, i_2, :), i_2 = 1, \cdots, I_2$, and frontal slices $\mathcal{A}(:, :, i_3), i_3 = 1, \cdots, I_3$, are shown in Fig. 1.3. For ease of denotation, we refer to the frontal slice of $\mathcal{A}$ as $\mathbf{A}(\cdot)$ in some formulas.

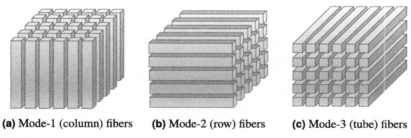

   (a) Mode-1 (column) fibers   **(b)** Mode-2 (row) fibers   **(c)** Mode-3 (tube) fibers

FIGURE 1.2

The illustration of mode-1 fibers $\mathcal{A}(:, i_2, i_3)$, mode-2 fibers $\mathcal{A}(i_1, :, i_3)$, and mode-3 fibers $\mathcal{A}(i_1, i_2, :)$ with $i_1 = 1, \cdots, I_1$, $i_2 = 1, \cdots, I_2$ and $i_3 = 1, \cdots, I_3$.

Other than the aforementioned notations, there is another way to denote tensors and their operations [5]. Taking advantage of graphical representations, tensors can be denoted by nodes and edges in a straightforward way. Graphical representations for scalars, vectors, matrices, and tensors are shown in Fig. 1.4. The number next to the edge represents the indices of the corresponding mode.

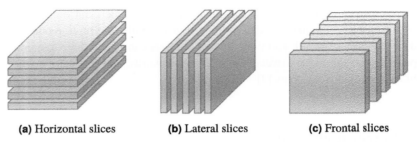

(a) Horizontal slices   **(b)** Lateral slices   **(c)** Frontal slices

FIGURE 1.3

The illustration of horizontal slices $\mathcal{A}(i_1,:,:)$ $i_1 = 1, \cdots, I_1$, lateral slices $\mathcal{A}(:,i_2,:)$ $i_2 = 1, \cdots, I_2$, and frontal slices $\mathcal{A}(:,:,i_3)$ $i_3 = 1, \cdots, I_3$.

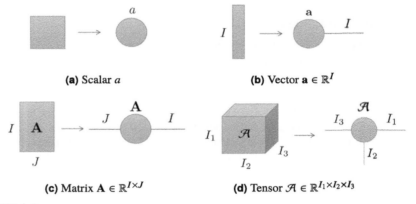

(a) Scalar a **(b)** Vector $\mathbf{a} \in \mathbb{R}^I$

(c) Matrix $\mathbf{A} \in \mathbb{R}^{I \times J}$ **(d)** Tensor $\mathcal{A} \in \mathbb{R}^{I_1 \times I_2 \times I_3}$

FIGURE 1.4

Graphical representations of scalar, vector, matrix and tensor.

1.2.2 Matrix operators

Definition 1.2.1. (Matrix trace [6]) The trace of matrix $\mathbf{A} \in \mathbb{R}^{I \times I}$ is obtained by summing all the diagonal entries of $\mathbf{A}$, i.e., $\text{tr}(\mathbf{A}) = \sum_{i=1}^{I} a_{i,i}$.

Definition 1.2.2. (ℓ_p-norm [6]) For matrix $\mathbf{A} \in \mathbb{R}^{I \times J}$, its ℓ_p-norm is defined as

$$\|\mathbf{A}\|_p = \left(\sum_{i=1}^{I} \sum_{j=1}^{J} a_{i,j}^p \right)^{1/p}. \tag{1.1}$$

Definition 1.2.3. (Matrix nuclear norm [7]) The nuclear norm of matrix $\mathbf{A}$ is denoted as $\|\mathbf{A}\|_* = \sum_i \sigma_i(\mathbf{A})$, where $\sigma_i(\mathbf{A})$ is the i-th largest singular value of $\mathbf{A}$.

Definition 1.2.4. (Hadamard product [8]) The Hadamard product for matrices $\mathbf{A} \in \mathbb{R}^{M \times N}$ and $\mathbf{B} \in \mathbb{R}^{M \times N}$ is defined as $\mathbf{A} \circledast \mathbf{B} \in \mathbb{R}^{M \times N}$ with

$$\mathbf{A} \circledast \mathbf{B} = \begin{bmatrix} a_{1,1}b_{1,1} & a_{1,2}b_{1,2} & \cdots & a_{1,N}b_{1,N} \\ a_{2,1}b_{2,1} & a_{2,2}b_{2,2} & \cdots & a_{2,N}b_{2,N} \\ \vdots & \vdots & \ddots & \vdots \\ a_{M,1}b_{M,1} & a_{M,2}b_{M,2} & \cdots & a_{M,N}b_{M,N} \end{bmatrix}. \tag{1.2}$$

Definition 1.2.5. (Kronecker product [9]) The Kronecker product of matrices $\mathbf{A} = [\mathbf{a}_1, \mathbf{a}_2, \cdots, \mathbf{a}_N] \in \mathbb{R}^{M \times N}$ and $\mathbf{B} = [\mathbf{b}_1, \mathbf{b}_2, \cdots, \mathbf{b}_Q] \in \mathbb{R}^{P \times Q}$ is defined as $\mathbf{A} \otimes \mathbf{B} \in \mathbb{R}^{MP \times NQ}$, which can be written mathematically as

$$\mathbf{A} \otimes \mathbf{B} = \begin{bmatrix} a_{1,1}\mathbf{B} & a_{1,2}\mathbf{B} & \cdots & a_{1,N}\mathbf{B} \\ a_{2,1}\mathbf{B} & a_{2,2}\mathbf{B} & \cdots & a_{2,N}\mathbf{B} \\ \vdots & \vdots & \ddots & \vdots \\ a_{M,1}\mathbf{B} & a_{M,2}\mathbf{B} & \cdots & a_{M,N}\mathbf{B} \end{bmatrix}$$
$$= \begin{bmatrix} \mathbf{a}_1 \otimes \mathbf{b}_1 & \mathbf{a}_1 \otimes \mathbf{b}_2 & \mathbf{a}_1 \otimes \mathbf{b}_3 & \cdots & \mathbf{a}_N \otimes \mathbf{b}_{Q-1} & \mathbf{a}_N \otimes \mathbf{b}_Q \end{bmatrix}. \tag{1.3}$$

Based on the Kronecker product, a lot of useful properties can be derived. Given matrices $\mathbf{A}, \mathbf{B}, \mathbf{C}, \mathbf{D}$, we have

$$(\mathbf{A} \otimes \mathbf{B})(\mathbf{C} \otimes \mathbf{D}) = \mathbf{AC} \otimes \mathbf{BD},$$
$$(\mathbf{A} \otimes \mathbf{B})^{\dagger} = \mathbf{A}^{\dagger} \otimes \mathbf{B}^{\dagger}, \tag{1.4}$$
$$(\mathbf{A} \otimes \mathbf{B})^{\mathrm{T}} = \mathbf{A}^{\mathrm{T}} \otimes \mathbf{B}^{\mathrm{T}},$$

where $\mathbf{A}^{\mathrm{T}}$ and $\mathbf{A}^{\dagger}$ represent the transpose and Moore–Penrose inverse of matrix $\mathbf{A}$.

Definition 1.2.6. (Khatri–Rao product [10]) The Khatri–Rao product of matrices $\mathbf{A} \in \mathbb{R}^{M \times N}$ and $\mathbf{B} \in \mathbb{R}^{L \times N}$ is defined as

$$\mathbf{A} \odot \mathbf{B} = [\mathbf{a}_1 \otimes \mathbf{b}_1 \quad \mathbf{a}_2 \otimes \mathbf{b}_2 \quad \cdots \quad \mathbf{a}_N \otimes \mathbf{b}_N] \in \mathbb{R}^{ML \times N}. \tag{1.5}$$

Similar to the Kronecker product, the Khatri–Rao product also has some convenient properties, such as

$$(\mathbf{A} \odot \mathbf{B})^{\mathrm{T}} = \mathbf{A}^{\mathrm{T}} \odot \mathbf{B}^{\mathrm{T}},$$
$$\mathbf{A} \odot \mathbf{B} \odot \mathbf{C} = (\mathbf{A} \odot \mathbf{B}) \odot \mathbf{C} = \mathbf{A} \odot (\mathbf{B} \odot \mathbf{C}),$$
$$(\mathbf{A} \odot \mathbf{B})^{\mathrm{T}}(\mathbf{A} \odot \mathbf{B}) = \mathbf{A}^{\mathrm{T}}\mathbf{A} \circledast \mathbf{B}^{\mathrm{T}}\mathbf{B}, \tag{1.6}$$
$$(\mathbf{A} \odot \mathbf{B})^{\dagger} = \left((\mathbf{A}^{\mathrm{T}}\mathbf{A}) \circledast (\mathbf{B}^{\mathrm{T}}\mathbf{B})\right)^{\dagger}(\mathbf{A} \odot \mathbf{B})^{\mathrm{T}}.$$

1.2.3 **Tensor transformations**

Definition 1.2.7. (Tensor transpose [11]) Given a tensor $\mathcal{A} \in \mathbb{R}^{I_1 \times I_2 \times I_3}$, whose frontal slices are $\mathcal{A}(:, :, i_3)$ ($i_3 = 1, \cdots, I_3$), its transpose $\mathcal{A}^\mathrm{T}$ is acquired by first transposing each of the frontal slices and then placing them in the order of $\mathcal{A}^\mathrm{T}(:, :, 1)$, $\mathcal{A}^\mathrm{T}(:, :, I_3)$, $\mathcal{A}^\mathrm{T}(:, :, I_3 - 1)$, $\cdots$, $\mathcal{A}^\mathrm{T}(:, :, 2)$ along the third mode.

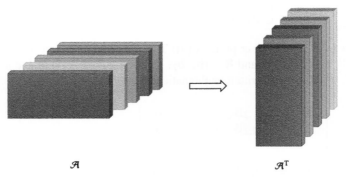

$$\mathcal{A} \qquad \mathcal{A}^\mathrm{T}$$

FIGURE 1.5

A graphical illustration of the tensor transpose on $\mathcal{A} \in \mathbb{R}^{I_1 \times I_2 \times 5}$.

Fig. 1.5 demonstrates the tensor transpose of $\mathcal{A} \in \mathbb{R}^{I_1 \times I_2 \times 5}$.

Definition 1.2.8. (Tensor mode-n matricization [1]) For tensor $\mathcal{A} \in \mathbb{R}^{I_1 \times \cdots \times I_N}$, its matricization along the n-th mode is denoted as $\mathbf{A}_{(n)} \in \mathbb{R}^{I_n \times I_1 I_2 \cdots I_{n-1} I_{n+1} \cdots I_N}$, as shown in Fig. 1.6. It rearranges fibers on the n-th mode to form the columns of $\mathbf{A}_{(n)}$. For instance, there exists a third-order tensor $\mathcal{A} \in \mathbb{R}^{3 \times 3 \times 2}$ whose frontal slices are

$$\mathcal{A}(:, :, 1) = \begin{bmatrix} 1 & 4 & 5 \\ 2 & 8 & 7 \\ 9 & 5 & 3 \end{bmatrix}, \quad \mathcal{A}(:, :, 2) = \begin{bmatrix} 2 & 6 & 2 \\ 8 & 1 & 3 \\ 7 & 5 & 6 \end{bmatrix}. \tag{1.7}$$

Thus, its mode-1, mode-2, and mode-3 matricizations can be written as

$$\mathbf{A}_{(1)} = \begin{pmatrix} 1 & 4 & 5 & 2 & 6 & 2 \\ 2 & 8 & 7 & 8 & 1 & 3 \\ 9 & 5 & 3 & 7 & 5 & 6 \end{pmatrix}, \tag{1.8}$$

$$\mathbf{A}_{(2)} = \begin{pmatrix} 1 & 2 & 9 & 2 & 8 & 7 \\ 4 & 8 & 5 & 6 & 1 & 5 \\ 5 & 7 & 3 & 2 & 3 & 6 \end{pmatrix}, \tag{1.9}$$

$$\mathbf{A}_{(3)} = \begin{pmatrix} 1 & 2 & 9 & 4 & 8 & 5 & 5 & 7 & 3 \\ 2 & 8 & 7 & 6 & 1 & 5 & 2 & 3 & 6 \end{pmatrix}. \tag{1.10}$$

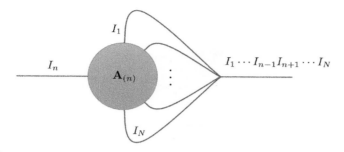

FIGURE 1.6

A graphical illustration of tensor mode-n matricization for $\mathcal{A} \in \mathbb{R}^{I_1 \times \cdots \times I_N}$.

Definition 1.2.9. (Tensor n-th canonical matricization [12]) For a fixed index $n = 1, 2, \cdots, N$, the n-th canonical matricization of tensor $\mathbf{A} \in \mathbb{R}^{I_1 \times I_2 \times \cdots \times I_N}$ can be defined as

$$(\mathbf{A}_{<n>})_{\overline{i_1 i_2 \cdots i_n}, \, \overline{i_{n+1} \cdots i_N}} = a_{i_1, i_2, \cdots, i_N}, \tag{1.11}$$

where $\overline{i_1 i_2 \cdots i_n}$, $\overline{i_{n+1} \cdots i_N}$ are multiindices and $\mathbf{A}_{<n>} \in \mathbb{R}^{I_1 I_2 \cdots I_n \times I_{n+1} \cdots I_N}$.

Take the multiindex $i = \overline{i_1 i_2 \cdots i_N}$ as an example, $i_n = 1, 2, \cdots, I_n, n = 1, \cdots, N$. It can either be defined using the little-endian convention (reverse lexicographic ordering) [13]

$$\overline{i_1 i_2 \cdots i_N} = i_1 + (i_2 - 1)I_1 + (i_3 - 1)I_1 I_2 + \cdots + (i_N - 1)I_1 \cdots I_{N-1}, \tag{1.12}$$

or the big-endian convention (colexicographic ordering)

$$\overline{i_1 i_2 \cdots i_N} = i_N + (i_{N-1} - 1)I_N + (i_{N-2} - 1)I_N I_{N-1} + \cdots + (i_1 - 1)I_2 \cdots I_N. \tag{1.13}$$

1.2.4 Tensor products

Definition 1.2.10. (Tensor inner product [1]) The inner product of two tensors $\mathcal{A} \in \mathbb{R}^{I_1 \times I_2 \times \cdots \times I_N}$ and $\mathcal{B} \in \mathbb{R}^{I_1 \times I_2 \times \cdots \times I_N}$, shown in Fig. 1.7, is expressed as

$$\langle \mathcal{A}, \mathcal{B} \rangle = \sum_{i_1=1}^{I_1} \sum_{i_2=1}^{I_2} \cdots \sum_{i_N=1}^{I_N} a_{i_1, i_2, \cdots, i_N} b_{i_1, i_2, \cdots, i_N}. \tag{1.14}$$

Definition 1.2.11. (Tensor norm [1]) The norm of a tensor $\mathcal{A} \in \mathbb{R}^{I_1 \times I_2 \times \cdots \times I_N}$ is the square root of the summation over the square of all its elements, which can be expressed as

$$\|\mathcal{A}\| = \sqrt{\sum_{i_1=1}^{I_1} \sum_{i_2=1}^{I_2} \cdots \sum_{i_N=1}^{I_N} (a_{i_1, i_2, \cdots, i_N})^2}. \tag{1.15}$$

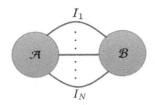

FIGURE 1.7

A graphical illustration of the tensor inner product.

Definition 1.2.12. (Tensor mode-n product with a matrix [1]) The tensor mode-n product of $\mathcal{A} \in \mathbb{R}^{I_1 \times I_2 \times \cdots \times I_N}$ and matrix $\mathbf{B} \in \mathbb{R}^{K \times I_n}$ is denoted as

$$\mathcal{X} = \mathcal{A} \times_n \mathbf{B} \in \mathbb{R}^{I_1 \times \cdots \times I_{n-1} \times K \times I_{n+1} \times \cdots \times I_N}, \tag{1.16}$$

or element-wisely,

$$x_{i_1, \cdots, k, \cdots, i_N} = \sum_{i_n=1}^{I_N} a_{i_1, \cdots, i_n, \cdots, i_N} b_{k, i_n}. \tag{1.17}$$

A visual illustration is shown in Fig. 1.8.

Taking advantage of tensor matricization, Eq. (1.16) can also be expressed in an unfolded form as

$$\mathbf{X}_{(n)} = \mathbf{B}\mathbf{A}_{(n)}. \tag{1.18}$$

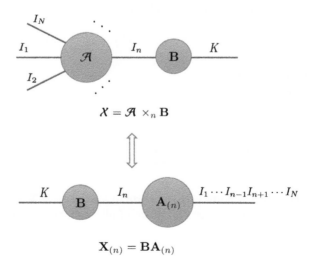

FIGURE 1.8

A graphical illustration of the tensor mode-n product.

For example, given tensor $\mathcal{A}$ (Eq. (1.7)) and matrix $\mathbf{B} = \begin{bmatrix} 1 & 2 & 3 \\ 4 & 5 & 6 \end{bmatrix}$, the mode-$n$ product $\mathcal{A} \times_1 \mathbf{B}$ will yield a tensor $\mathcal{X} \in \mathbb{R}^{2 \times 3 \times 2}$, whose frontal slices are

$$\mathcal{X}(:,:,1) = \begin{bmatrix} 32 & 35 & 28 \\ 68 & 86 & 73 \end{bmatrix}, \mathcal{X}(:,:,2) = \begin{bmatrix} 39 & 23 & 26 \\ 90 & 59 & 59 \end{bmatrix}. \tag{1.19}$$

Definition 1.2.13. (Tensor mode-n product with a vector [1]) The tensor mode-n product of the tensor $\mathcal{A} \in \mathbb{R}^{I_1 \times I_2 \times \cdots \times I_N}$ and vector $\mathbf{b} \in \mathbb{R}^{I_n}$ is denoted as

$$\mathcal{X} = \mathcal{A} \times_n \mathbf{b} \in \mathbb{R}^{I_1 \times \cdots \times I_{n-1} \times I_{n+1} \times \cdots \times I_N}, \tag{1.20}$$

with entries

$$x_{i_1,\cdots,i_{n-1},i_{n+1},\cdots,i_N} = \sum_{i_n=1}^{I_N} a_{i_1,\cdots,i_{n-1},i_n,i_{n+1},\cdots,i_N} b_{i_n}. \tag{1.21}$$

For example, given tensor $\mathcal{A}$ in Eq. (1.7) and vector $\mathbf{b} = \begin{bmatrix} 1 & 2 & 3 \end{bmatrix}^T$, we have

$$\mathcal{A} \times_2 \mathbf{b} = \begin{bmatrix} 24 & 20 \\ 39 & 19 \\ 28 & 35 \end{bmatrix}. \tag{1.22}$$

It can be clearly seen that the operation of multiplying a tensor by a matrix will not change the number of ways of the tensor. However, if a tensor is multiplied by a vector, the number of ways will decrease.

Definition 1.2.14. (t-product [11]) The t-product of $\mathcal{A} \in \mathbb{R}^{I_1 \times I_2 \times I_3}$ and $\mathcal{C} \in \mathbb{R}^{I_2 \times L \times I_3}$ is defined as

$$\mathcal{X} = \mathcal{A} * \mathcal{C} = \text{fold}\big(\text{circ}(\mathcal{A})\text{MatVec}(\mathcal{C})\big), \tag{1.23}$$

where $\mathcal{X} \in \mathbb{R}^{I_1 \times L \times I_3}$, $\text{MatVec}(\mathcal{C}) = \begin{bmatrix} \mathbf{C}(1)^T & \mathbf{C}(2)^T & \cdots & \mathbf{C}(I_3)^T \end{bmatrix}^T \in \mathbb{R}^{I_2 I_3 \times L}$ represents the block matrix [11] of $\mathcal{C}$, and

$$\text{circ}(\mathcal{A}) = \begin{bmatrix} \mathbf{A}(1) & \mathbf{A}(I_3) & \cdots & \mathbf{A}(2) \\ \mathbf{A}(2) & \mathbf{A}(1) & \cdots & \mathbf{A}(3) \\ \vdots & \vdots & \ddots & \vdots \\ \mathbf{A}(I_3) & \mathbf{A}(I_3 - 1) & \cdots & \mathbf{A}(1) \end{bmatrix} \in \mathbb{R}^{I_1 I_3 \times I_2 I_3}$$

is the block-circulant matrix [11] of $\mathcal{A}$, where $\mathbf{C}(i_3)$ and $\mathbf{A}(i_3)$, $i_3 = 1, \cdots, I_3$, represent the i_3-th frontal slice of $\mathcal{C}$ and $\mathcal{A}$, respectively.

Definition 1.2.15. (Tensor contraction [5]) Given two tensors $\mathcal{A} \in \mathbb{R}^{I_1 \times I_2 \times \cdots \times I_M}$ and $\mathcal{B} \in \mathbb{R}^{J_1 \times J_2 \times \cdots \times J_N}$, suppose they have L equal indices $\{K_1, K_2, \cdots, K_L\}$ in

$\{I_1, I_2, \cdots, I_M\}$ and $\{J_1, J_2, \cdots, J_N\}$. The contraction of these two tensors yields an $(M + N - 2L)$-th-order tensor $\mathcal{X} = \langle \mathcal{A}, \mathcal{B} \rangle_L$, whose entries can be calculated by

$$\sum_{k_1=1}^{K_1} \cdots \sum_{k_L=1}^{K_L} a_{i_1,\cdots,i_M} b_{j_1,\cdots,j_N}. \tag{1.24}$$

A graphical illustration of tensor contraction is shown in Fig. 1.9.

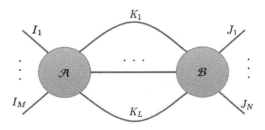

FIGURE 1.9

Graphical representation of contraction of two tensors, $\mathcal{A} \in \mathbb{R}^{I_1 \times \cdots \times I_M}$ and $\mathcal{B} \in \mathbb{R}^{J_1 \times \cdots \times J_N}$, where $\{K_1, K_2, \cdots, K_L\}$ denotes the L equal indices in $\{I_1, I_2, \cdots, I_M\}$ and $\{J_1, J_2, \cdots, J_N\}$.

For example, given tensors $\mathcal{A} \in \mathbb{R}^{3 \times 4 \times 2 \times 6 \times 7}$ and $\mathcal{B} \in \mathbb{R}^{2 \times 5 \times 7 \times 8 \times 4}$, based on the aforementioned definition, we can conclude that $L = 3$, $K_1 = I_2 = J_5 = 4$, $K_2 = I_3 = J_1 = 2$, and $K_3 = I_5 = J_3 = 7$. As shown in Fig. 1.10, the result of tensor contraction $\mathcal{X} = \langle \mathcal{A}, \mathcal{B} \rangle_3$ is of the size of $3 \times 6 \times 5 \times 8$, and its entries are

$$x_{i_1,i_4,j_2,j_4} = \sum_{k_1=1}^{4} \sum_{k_2=1}^{2} \sum_{k_3=1}^{7} a_{i_1,k_1,k_2,i_4,k_3} b_{k_2,j_2,k_3,j_4,k_1}. \tag{1.25}$$

Consider a special case when $L = 1$ and $K_1 = I_m = J_n$, as demonstrated in Fig. 1.11.

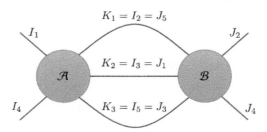

FIGURE 1.10

The contraction of two tensors, $\mathcal{A} \in \mathbb{R}^{3 \times 4 \times 2 \times 6 \times 7}$ and $\mathcal{B} \in \mathbb{R}^{2 \times 5 \times 7 \times 8 \times 4}$, where $K_1 = I_2 = J_5 = 4$, $K_2 = I_3 = J_1 = 2$, $K_3 = I_5 = J_3 = 7$, $I_1 = 3$, $I_4 = 6$, $J_2 = 5$, and $J_4 = 8$.

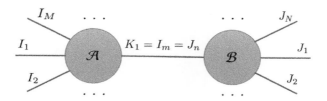

FIGURE 1.11

A graphical representation of contraction over two tensors, $\mathcal{A} \in \mathbb{R}^{I_1 \times I_2 \times \cdots \times I_M}$ and $\mathcal{B} \in \mathbb{R}^{J_1 \times J_2 \times \cdots \times J_N}$, where $K_1 = I_m = J_n$.

The contraction of tensors $\mathcal{A} \in \mathbb{R}^{I_1 \times I_2 \times \cdots \times I_M}$ and $\mathcal{B} \in \mathbb{R}^{J_1 \times J_2 \times \cdots \times J_N}$ results in an $(M + N - 2)$-th-order tensor $\mathcal{X} = \langle \mathcal{A}, \mathcal{B} \rangle_1$, whose entries can be calculated by

$$x_{i_1, \cdots, i_{m-1}, i_{m+1}, \cdots, i_M, j_1, \cdots, j_{n-1}, j_{n+1}, \cdots, j_N}$$
$$= \sum_{k_1=1}^{K_1} a_{i_1, \cdots, i_{m-1}, k_1, i_{m+1}, \cdots, i_M} b_{j_1, \cdots, j_{n-1}, k_1, j_{n+1}, \cdots, j_N}. \tag{1.26}$$

1.2.5 Structural tensors

Definition 1.2.16. (Identity tensor [11]) An identity tensor $\mathcal{I}$ is a tensor whose first frontal slice is an identity matrix and the rest are zero matrices.

Definition 1.2.17. (Orthogonal tensor [14]) Using the t-product, an orthogonal tensor $\mathcal{H}$ is defined as

$$\mathcal{H} * \mathcal{H}^{\mathrm{T}} = \mathcal{H}^{\mathrm{T}} * \mathcal{H} = \mathcal{I}. \tag{1.27}$$

Definition 1.2.18. (Rank-1 tensor [1]) A rank-1 tensor $\mathcal{A} \in \mathbb{R}^{I_1 \times I_2 \times I_3}$ is formed by the outer product of vectors, as shown in Fig. 1.12. Its mathematical formulation can be written as

$$\mathcal{A} = \mathbf{a}^{(1)} \circ \mathbf{a}^{(2)} \circ \mathbf{a}^{(3)}, \tag{1.28}$$

where $\circ$ means the outer product. Therefore, the entries of $\mathcal{A}$ can be written as $a_{i_1, i_2, i_3} = a_{i_1}^{(1)} a_{i_2}^{(2)} a_{i_3}^{(3)}$. Generalizing it to the N-th-order tensor $\mathcal{A} \in \mathbb{R}^{I_1 \times I_2 \times \cdots \times I_N}$, we have

$$\mathcal{A} = \mathbf{a}^{(1)} \circ \mathbf{a}^{(2)} \circ \cdots \circ \mathbf{a}^{(N)}. \tag{1.29}$$

Definition 1.2.19. (Diagonal tensor [1]) Tensor $\mathcal{A}$ is a diagonal tensor if and only if all its nonzero elements are on the superdiagonal line. Specifically, if $\mathcal{A} \in \mathbb{R}^{I_1 \times I_2 \times \cdots \times I_N}$ is a diagonal tensor, then we have $\mathcal{A}(i_1, \cdots, i_N) \neq 0$ if and only if $i_1 = i_2 = \cdots = i_N$. A graphical illustration of a third-order diagonal tensor is demonstrated in Fig. 1.13.

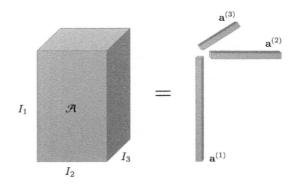

FIGURE 1.12

A rank-1 tensor $\mathcal{A} = \mathbf{a}^{(1)} \circ \mathbf{a}^{(2)} \circ \mathbf{a}^{(3)} \in \mathbb{R}^{I_1 \times I_2 \times I_3}$.

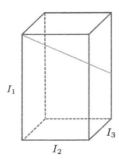

FIGURE 1.13

A third-order diagonal tensor $\mathcal{A} \in \mathbb{R}^{I_1 \times I_2 \times I_3}$.

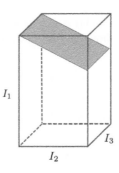

FIGURE 1.14

An f-diagonal tensor $\mathcal{A} \in \mathbb{R}^{I_1 \times I_2 \times I_3}$.

Definition 1.2.20. (f-diagonal tensor [14]) An f-diagonal tensor $\mathcal{A}$ is a tensor with diagonal frontal slices. A third-order f-diagonal tensor is visualized in Fig. 1.14.

1.2.6 Summary

In this section, we first briefly described some notations of tensor representations. Then by giving basic operations of matrices, we discussed several common tensor operations, including tensor transformations and tensor products. Concepts of structural tensors such as orthogonal tensor, diagonal tensor, and f-diagonal tensor are also given. It is worth noting that we only focus on the most commonly used definitions; for more information, please refer to [1], [5], and [6].

1.3 Tensor decompositions

The idea of tensor decomposition was first put forward by Hitchcock in 1927 and developed by a lot of scholars until these days. Traditionally, it was implemented in psychometrics and stoichiometry. With the growing prosperity of tensor decomposition in [15–18], it began to draw attention in other fields, including signal processing [19–21], numerical linear algebra [22,23], computer vision [24], numerical analysis [25,26], and data mining [27–29]. Meanwhile, different decomposition approaches were developed to meet various requirements.

In this section, we first discuss two cornerstones, Tucker decomposition and CP decomposition, and go through some other methods like block term decomposition (BTD), tensor singular value decomposition (t-SVD), and tensor networks (TNs).

1.3.1 Tucker decomposition

In 1963, Tucker decomposition was firstly proposed in [30] by Tucker and perfected by Levin and Tucker later on. In 2000, the name of higher-order singular value decomposition (HOSVD) was put forward by De Lathauwer [31]. Nowadays, the terms Tucker decomposition and HOSVD are used alternatively to refer to Tucker decomposition.

Taking advantage of the mode-n product, Tucker decomposition can be defined as a multiplication of a core tensor and the matrix along each mode.

Definition 1.3.1. (Tucker decomposition) Given a tensor $\mathcal{X} \in \mathbb{R}^{I_1 \times \cdots \times I_N}$, its Tucker decomposition is

$$\mathcal{X} = \mathcal{G} \times_1 \mathbf{U}^{(1)} \times_2 \mathbf{U}^{(2)} \cdots \times_N \mathbf{U}^{(N)} = [\![\mathcal{G}; \mathbf{U}^{(1)}, \mathbf{U}^{(2)}, \cdots, \mathbf{U}^{(N)}]\!], \qquad (1.30)$$

where $\mathbf{U}^{(n)} \in \mathbb{R}^{I_n \times R_n}$ $(n = 1, \cdots, N)$ are semi-orthogonal factor matrices that satisfy $\mathbf{U}^{(n)\mathrm{T}}\mathbf{U}^{(n)} = \mathbf{I}_{R_n}$ and $\mathcal{G} \in \mathbb{R}^{R_1 \times R_2 \times \cdots \times R_N}$ is the core tensor. Even though the core tensor is usually dense, it is generally much smaller than $\mathcal{X}$, i.e., $R_n \leqslant I_n$.

We can also write Tucker decomposition in an element-wise style as

$$x_{i_1, i_2, \cdots, i_N} = \sum_{r_1}^{R_1} \sum_{r_2}^{R_2} \cdots \sum_{r_N}^{R_N} g_{r_1, r_2, \cdots, r_N} u_{i_1, r_1}^{(1)} u_{i_2, r_2}^{(2)} \cdots u_{i_N, r_N}^{(N)}, \qquad (1.31)$$

where $\mathbf{U}^{(n)} = [\mathbf{u}_1^{(n)}, \cdots, \mathbf{u}_{R_n}^{(n)}]$.

Fig. 1.15 is an illustration of Tucker decomposition on a third-order tensor, i.e., $\mathcal{T} = [\![\mathcal{G}; \mathbf{A}, \mathbf{B}, \mathbf{C}]\!]$.

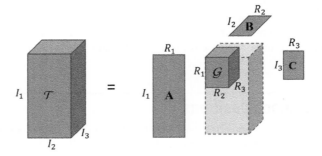

FIGURE 1.15

An illustration of Tucker decomposition on a third-order tensor $\mathcal{T}$. The core tensor is $\mathcal{G} \in \mathbb{R}^{R_1 \times R_2 \times R_3}$ and factor matrices are $\mathbf{A}, \mathbf{B}, \mathbf{C} \in \mathbb{R}^{I_n \times R_n}$, $n = 1, 2, 3$.

Based on Tucker decomposition, we can derive the definition of Tucker rank.

Definition 1.3.2. (Tucker rank) The Tucker rank of a given tensor $\mathcal{X} \in \mathbb{R}^{I_1 \times \cdots \times I_N}$ is defined as an N-tuple $(R_1, \cdots, R_N)$ comprised of n-rank R_n. The n-rank $R_n = \text{rank}(\mathbf{X}_{(n)})$, a.k.a. the multilinear rank, is the dimension of the vector space spanned by the mode-n fibers. In other words, the n-rank is the column rank of $\mathbf{X}_{(n)}$.

Note that Tucker decomposition is not unique; if we employ permutations $\mathbf{R} \in \mathbb{R}^{R_1 \times R_1}$, $\mathbf{P} \in \mathbb{R}^{R_2 \times R_2}$, and $\mathbf{Q} \in \mathbb{R}^{R_3 \times R_3}$ on each mode of the core tensor $\mathcal{G}$, we can always find the corresponding factor matrices by applying the reverse operations on them. Specifically, taking a third-order tensor $\mathcal{T}$ as an example, we have

$$\mathcal{T} = [\![\mathcal{G}; \mathbf{A}, \mathbf{B}, \mathbf{C}]\!]$$
$$= [\![\mathcal{G} \times_1 \mathbf{R} \times_2 \mathbf{P} \times_3 \mathbf{Q}; \mathbf{A}\mathbf{R}^{-1}, \mathbf{B}\mathbf{P}^{-1}, \mathbf{C}\mathbf{Q}^{-1}]\!],$$

where $\mathbf{R}^{-1}, \mathbf{P}^{-1}, \mathbf{Q}^{-1}$ represent the inverse matrices of $\mathbf{R}, \mathbf{P}, \mathbf{Q}$.

This property of Tucker decomposition enables us to select the appropriate core tensor according to the situations.

1.3.2 Canonical polyadic decomposition

CP decomposition was invented in 1927 as polyadic decomposition by Hitchcock [32], whose idea is to express a tensor as the summation of rank-1 tensors. In 1970, polyadic decomposition was renamed by Carroll and Chang [33] as canonical decomposition (CANDECOMP), while in the meantime, Harshman [34] named it as parallel factors analysis (PARAFAC). For a long time, different articles used different names to refer to CP decomposition and it was quite confusing. In 2000, Kiers

[35] suggested to call it CP decomposition uniformly. Today, even though we refer to it as CP decomposition, it can be seen as both CANDECOMP/PARAFAC decomposition and CP decomposition.

Definition 1.3.3. (CP decomposition) CP decomposition of an N-th-order tensor $\mathcal{X} \in \mathbb{R}^{I_1 \times \cdots \times I_N}$ is represented as the summation of rank-1 tensors

$$\mathcal{X} = \sum_{r=1}^{R} \mathbf{u}_r^{(1)} \circ \mathbf{u}_r^{(2)} \circ \cdots \circ \mathbf{u}_r^{(N)} = [\![\mathbf{U}^{(1)}, \mathbf{U}^{(2)}, \cdots, \mathbf{U}^{(N)}]\!], \tag{1.32}$$

where $\mathbf{U}^{(n)} = [\mathbf{u}_1^{(n)}, \mathbf{u}_2^{(n)}, \cdots \mathbf{u}_R^{(n)}]$, $n = 1, \cdots, N$, are factor matrices and R denotes the number of rank-1 components. The entries in $\mathcal{X}$ can be computed individually as

$$x_{i_1, i_2, \cdots, i_N} = \sum_{r=1}^{R} u_{i_1, r}^{(1)} u_{i_2, r}^{(2)} \cdots u_{i_N, r}^{(N)}. \tag{1.33}$$

Similar to Tucker decomposition, there is a tensor rank in terms of CP decomposition.

Definition 1.3.4. (Tensor rank) Tensor rank is defined as the minimal number of rank-1 components that ensure Eq. (1.32) holds.

Taking a third-order tensor $\mathcal{T} \in \mathbb{R}^{I_1 \times I_2 \times I_3}$ as an example, it can be decomposed as

$$\mathcal{T} = \sum_{r=1}^{R} \mathbf{a}_r \circ \mathbf{b}_r \circ \mathbf{c}_r = [\![\mathbf{A}, \mathbf{B}, \mathbf{C}]\!], \tag{1.34}$$

where each component $\mathbf{a}_r \circ \mathbf{b}_r \circ \mathbf{c}_r$ is a third-order tensor of rank-1. If R is the smallest number among all the possible values that fit in Eq. (1.34), then we say R is the tensor rank of $\mathcal{T}$. Fig. 1.16 illustrates the CP decomposition for $\mathcal{T}$ intuitively.

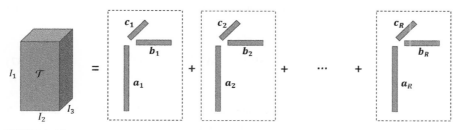

FIGURE 1.16

A demonstration of CP decomposition of a third-order tensor. Each dotted rectangle represents a rank-1 tensor resulting from $\mathbf{a}_r \circ \mathbf{b}_r \circ \mathbf{c}_r$, $r = 1, \cdots, R$.

CP decomposition and Tucker decomposition are not independent. According to Eq. (1.30), when the core tensor $\mathcal{G}$ is an identity tensor $\mathcal{I} \in \mathbb{R}^{R \times R \times \cdots \times R}$, then

Eq. (1.30) is indeed a CP decomposition. Specifically,

$$\mathcal{X} = [\![\mathcal{I}; \mathbf{U}^{(1)}, \mathbf{U}^{(2)}, \cdots, \mathbf{U}^{(N)}]\!]$$
$$= [\![\mathbf{U}^{(1)}, \mathbf{U}^{(2)}, \cdots, \mathbf{U}^{(N)}]\!].$$

In this sense, CP decomposition can be regarded as a special case of Tucker decomposition. However, different from Tucker decomposition, CP decomposition is unique under permutation indeterminacy and scaling indeterminacy. The permutation indeterminacy means we can arbitrarily change the order of rank-1 tensors in Eq. (1.32), and the decomposition still holds. Taking a third-order tensor as an example, the mathematical form of permutation is as follows:

$$\mathcal{T} = [\![\mathbf{A}, \mathbf{B}, \mathbf{C}]\!] = [\![\mathbf{AP}, \mathbf{BP}, \mathbf{CP}]\!], \tag{1.35}$$

where $\mathbf{P} \in \mathbb{R}^{R \times R}$ is a permutation matrix. The scaling indeterminacy means that we can scale the column vectors by different parameters as long as the product of those parameters equal one. That is to say,

$$\mathcal{T} = \sum_{r=1}^{R} \mathbf{a}_r \circ \mathbf{b}_r \circ \mathbf{c}_r = \sum_{r=1}^{R} (\alpha_r \mathbf{a}_r) \circ (\beta_r \mathbf{b}_r) \circ (\gamma_r \mathbf{c}_r), \tag{1.36}$$

where factors satisfy $\alpha_r \beta_r \gamma_r = 1$ for $r = 1, \cdots, R$.

The uniqueness of CP decomposition means that, for a given tensor $\mathcal{X}$, there is only one set of rank-1 tensors that satisfies Eq. (1.32).

1.3.3 Block term decomposition

As introduced above, CP decomposition and Tucker decomposition have different ranks. By unifying the ideas of these two ranks, BTD was proposed [36,37].

Definition 1.3.5. (Block term decomposition) For a tensor $\mathcal{T} \in \mathbb{R}^{I_1 \times I_2 \times \cdots \times I_N}$, its BTD is denoted as

$$\mathcal{T} = \sum_{r=1}^{R} \mathcal{S}_r \times_1 \mathbf{W}_r^{(1)} \times_2 \mathbf{W}_r^{(2)} \cdots \times_N \mathbf{W}_r^{(N)}, \tag{1.37}$$

where $\mathbf{W}_r^{(n)} \in \mathbb{R}^{I_n \times M_r^{(n)}}$ represents the n-th factor in the r-th term and $\mathcal{S}_r \in \mathbb{R}^{M_r^{(1)} \times M_r^{(2)} \times \cdots \times M_r^{(N)}}$ represents the corresponding core tensor.

Considering BTD on third-order tensors, we can give the definition of (L, M, N)-decomposition.

Definition 1.3.6. (Rank-(L, M, N)) A third-order tensor is of rank-(L, M, N) if its mode-1 rank, mode-2 rank, and mode-3 rank equal L, M, and N, respectively.

Definition 1.3.7. $((L, M, N)$-decomposition) Given a third-order tensor $\mathcal{T} \in \mathbb{R}^{I \times J \times K}$, the (L, M, N)-decomposition is the summation of rank-(L, M, N) terms as follows:

$$\mathcal{T} = \sum_{r=1}^{R} \mathcal{S}_r \times_1 \mathbf{A}_r \times_2 \mathbf{B}_r \times_3 \mathbf{C}_r, \qquad (1.38)$$

where $\mathcal{S}_r \in \mathbb{R}^{L \times M \times N}$ is of full rank-(L, M, N) and $\mathbf{A}_r \in \mathbb{R}^{I \times L}$, $\mathbf{B}_r \in \mathbb{R}^{J \times M}$, and $\mathbf{C}_r \in \mathbb{R}^{K \times N}$ are of full column rank ($I \geqslant L$, $J \geqslant M$, $K \geqslant N$, $1 \leqslant r \leqslant R$).

A graphical illustration of (L, M, N)-decomposition is shown in Fig. 1.17.

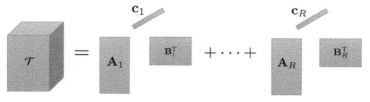

FIGURE 1.17

The illustration of block term decomposition for a third-order tensor.

Following this idea, we give three special cases of (L, M, N)-decomposition: $(L, L, 1)$-decomposition, $(L_r, L_r, 1)$-decomposition, and $(L, M, \cdot)$-decomposition.

Definition 1.3.8. $((L, L, 1)$-decomposition) For a tensor $\mathcal{T} \in \mathbb{R}^{I \times J \times K}$, its $(L, L, 1)$-decomposition is the summation of rank-$(L, L, 1)$ terms as follows:

$$\mathcal{T} = \sum_{r=1}^{R} \left(\mathbf{A}_r \mathbf{B}_r^{\mathsf{T}} \right) \circ \mathbf{c}_r, \qquad (1.39)$$

where $\mathbf{A}_r \in \mathbb{R}^{I \times L}$ and $\mathbf{B}_r \in \mathbb{R}^{J \times L}$ ($r = 1, \cdots, R$) are rank-L matrices.

However, $\mathbf{A}_r$ and $\mathbf{B}_r$ may not have the same rank on some occasions. Therefore, $(L_r, L_r, 1)$-decomposition was proposed, as shown in Fig. 1.18.

Definition 1.3.9. $((L_r, L_r, 1)$-decomposition) For a tensor $\mathcal{T} \in \mathbb{R}^{I \times J \times K}$, its $(L_r, L_r, 1)$-decomposition is the summation of rank-$(L_r, L_r, 1)$ terms, which can be defined as

$$\mathcal{T} = \sum_{r=1}^{R} \mathbf{A}_r \mathbf{B}_r^{\mathsf{T}} \circ \mathbf{c}_r, \qquad (1.40)$$

where $\mathbf{A}_r \in \mathbb{R}^{I \times L_r}$ and $\mathbf{B}_r \in \mathbb{R}^{J \times L_r}$ ($r = 1, \cdots, R$) are rank-L_r matrices.

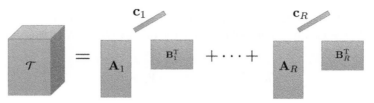

FIGURE 1.18

The illustration of $(L_r, L_r, 1)$-decomposition for a third-order tensor.

Definition 1.3.10. $((L, M, \cdot)$-decomposition) For a tensor $\mathcal{T} \in \mathbb{R}^{I \times J \times K}$, its $(L, M, \cdot)$-decomposition can be denoted as

$$\mathcal{T} = \sum_{r=1}^{R} \mathcal{S}_r \times_1 \mathbf{A}_r \times_2 \mathbf{B}_r, \tag{1.41}$$

where $\mathcal{S}_r \in \mathbb{R}^{L \times M \times K}$ is the core tensor and $\mathbf{A}_r \in \mathbb{R}^{I \times L}$, $\mathbf{B}_r \in \mathbb{R}^{J \times M}$ are of full column rank ($I \geqslant L$, $J \geqslant M$, $1 \leqslant r \leqslant R$).

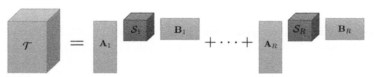

FIGURE 1.19

The illustration of $(L, M, \cdot)$-decomposition for a third-order tensor.

A visual representation of $(L, M, \cdot)$-decomposition is shown in Fig. 1.19.

1.3.4 Tensor singular value decomposition

In addition to some of the decomposition methods mentioned above, Kilmer et al. [14] proposed a new type of decomposition for tensors, named t-SVD. It is the generalization of matrix singular value decomposition (SVD) and can be applied to multiple applications such as data compression.

Definition 1.3.11. (t-SVD) For tensor $\mathcal{T} \in \mathbb{R}^{I_1 \times I_2 \times I_3}$, the t-SVD is defined as

$$\mathcal{T} = \mathcal{U} * \mathcal{S} * \mathcal{V}^{\mathrm{T}}, \tag{1.42}$$

where $\mathcal{U} \in \mathbb{R}^{I_1 \times I_1 \times I_3}$, $\mathcal{V} \in \mathbb{R}^{I_2 \times I_2 \times I_3}$ are orthogonal tensors and $\mathcal{S} \in \mathbb{R}^{I_1 \times I_2 \times I_3}$ is an f-diagonal tensor.

An illustration of t-SVD for tensor $\mathcal{T}$ is shown in Fig. 1.20.

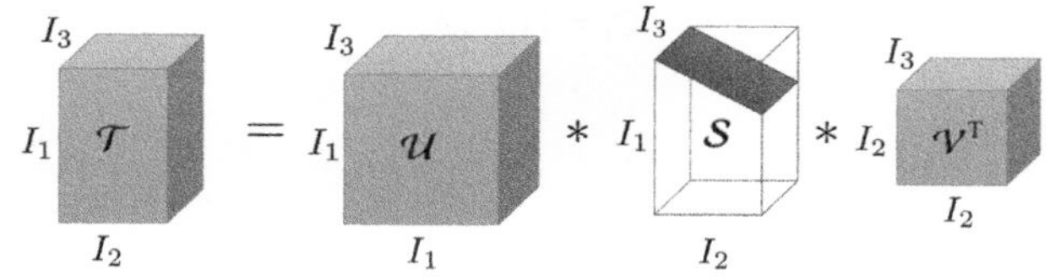

FIGURE 1.20

The illustration of t-SVD for a third-order tensor.

Definition 1.3.12. (Tensor tubal rank [38]) The tubal rank of a third-order tensor $\mathcal{T}$ is defined as the number of nonzero tubes in $\mathcal{S}$.

It is well known that block-circulant matrices can be block-diagonalized by the Fourier transform [39]. Mathematically, for $\mathcal{T} \in \mathbb{R}^{I_1 \times I_2 \times I_3}$, we have

$$(\mathbf{F} \otimes \mathbf{I})\text{circ}(\mathcal{T})(\mathbf{F}^* \otimes \mathbf{I}) = \text{bdiag}(\overline{\mathcal{T}}) = \begin{bmatrix} \overline{\mathbf{T}}(1) & & \\ & \ddots & \\ & & \overline{\mathbf{T}}(I_3) \end{bmatrix}, \qquad (1.43)$$

where $\text{circ}(\mathcal{T})$ is the block-circulant matrix (see Eq. (1.23)) of $\mathcal{T}$, $\mathbf{F} \in \mathbb{R}^{I_3 \times I_3}$ is a normalized discrete Fourier transform (DFT) matrix, $\overline{\mathcal{T}}$ is the fast Fourier transform (FFT) of $\mathcal{T}$ along the third mode, and $\overline{\mathbf{T}}(i_3) \in \mathbb{R}^{I_1 \times I_2}$ ($i_3 = 1, \cdots, I_3$) represents its i_3-th frontal slice.

In this way, instead of directly calculating $\text{circ}(\cdot)$, we are able to employ the FFT to solve Eq. (1.42). Specifically, we apply SVD on every frontal slice of $\overline{\mathcal{T}}$ to acquire $\overline{\mathbf{U}}(i_3)$, $\overline{\mathbf{S}}(i_3)$, and $\overline{\mathbf{V}}(i_3)$, $i_3 = 1, \cdots, I_3$. Then by simply performing the inverse FFT along the third mode on $\overline{\mathcal{U}}$, $\overline{\mathcal{S}}$, and $\overline{\mathcal{V}}$, the t-SVD of $\mathcal{T}$ is obtained. From this point of view, t-SVD can be regarded as performing matrix SVD on each frontal slice of a tensor in the frequency domain.

1.3.5 Tensor network

In recent years, data collected from various fields often have high dimensions. This gives rise to a tricky problem named the curse of dimensionality.

In Tucker decomposition, if we assume the dimension of a core tensor is $R_1 \times \cdots \times R_N$, $R_1 = \cdots = R_N = R$, then $\mathcal{G}$ has R^N entries. The number of entries scales exponentially with the number of tensor ways, which results in a tremendous computational burden that we may not be able to handle by standard numerical algorithms.

To ease this issue, we can resort to TNs, which are able to decompose a high-order tensor into a set of sparsely interconnected lower-order core tensors and matrices. The core tensors are connected through tensor contractions. Apart from the aforementioned decompositions, there are also many other kinds of decompositions under the TN framework. Here we mainly introduce hierarchical Tucker (HT) decomposition and its special case, tensor train (TT) decomposition.

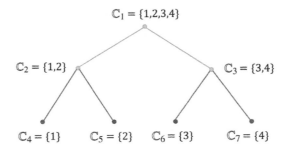

FIGURE 1.21

A possible binary tree $\mathbb{T}$ of a fourth-order tensor. Each node corresponds to a mode set of the tensor $\mathcal{A} \in \mathbb{R}^{I_1 \times I_2 \times I_3 \times I_4}$.

1.3.5.1 Hierarchical Tucker decomposition

HT decomposition is also known as the tensor tree network (TTN) with rank-3 tensors in quantum physics. It was originally proposed in [40,41].

The main idea of HT is to decompose a tensor in a hierarchical way according to a binary tree $\mathbb{T}$ (dimension tree) whose nodes indicate subsets of modes in the original tensor and the root node contains all the modes. Fig. 1.21 demonstrates a possible dimension tree for a fourth-order tensor $\mathcal{A} \in \mathbb{R}^{I_1 \times I_2 \times I_3 \times I_4}$, where $\mathbb{C}_1, \mathbb{C}_2, \mathbb{C}_3$ denote the interior nodes and $\mathbb{C}_4, \mathbb{C}_5, \mathbb{C}_6, \mathbb{C}_7$ denote the leaf nodes. Grelier et al. discussed how to select the optimal structure for a given tensor [42].

Definition 1.3.13. (Matricization for dimension tree) Given a tensor $\mathcal{X} \in \mathbb{R}^{I_1 \times \cdots \times I_N}$, dimension indices $\mathbb{C}_q \subset \mathbb{C}_1$, and its complement $\bar{\mathbb{C}}_q := \mathbb{C}_1 \backslash \mathbb{C}_q$ in the corresponding binary tree (q represents the ordinal label assigned to the node), the matricization is

$$\mathbf{X}_{[q]} \in \mathbb{R}^{I_{\mathbb{C}_q} \times I_{\bar{\mathbb{C}}_q}},$$

where

$$I_{\mathbb{C}_q} := \prod_{c \in \mathbb{C}_q} I_c, \quad I_{\bar{\mathbb{C}}_q} := \prod_{\bar{c} \in \bar{\mathbb{C}}_q} I_{\bar{c}}.$$

For example, given tensor $\mathcal{X}$ and dimension indices $\mathbb{C}_q = \mathbb{C}_2 = \{1, 2\}$ in Fig. 1.21, the matricization $\mathbf{X}_{[q]} = \mathbf{X}_{[2]}$ is of the size of $I_1 I_2 \times I_3 I_4$.

Definition 1.3.14. (Hierarchical rank) The hierarchical rank of tensor $\mathcal{X} \in \mathbb{R}^{I_1 \times \cdots \times I_N}$ is defined as

$$\mathbb{K} = \left\{ K_{\mathbb{C}_q} | K_{\mathbb{C}_q} = \mathrm{rank}(\mathbf{X}_{[q]}), \forall \mathbb{C}_q \subset \mathbb{T} \right\}, \tag{1.44}$$

where $\mathbb{C}_q$ refers to the dimension index in the related binary tree and $\mathbf{X}_{[q]}$ is the matricization according to $\mathbb{C}_q$.

Let $\mathbb{A}_{\mathbb{K}}$ denote a set of tensors whose hierarchical rank is no more than $\mathbb{K}$, i.e., $\mathbb{A}_{\mathbb{K}} = \{\mathcal{A} \in \mathbb{R}^{I_1 \times \cdots \times I_N} | \mathrm{rank}(\mathbf{A}_{[q]}) \leqslant K_{\mathbb{C}_q}, \forall \mathbb{C}_q \subset \mathbb{T}\}$. Using the nestedness property, we can define HT decomposition properly.

Lemma 1.3.1. *(Nestedness property) Suppose $\mathcal{A} \in \mathbb{A}_{\mathbb{K}}$. Then we can have a corresponding subspace $\mathbb{U}_q$ for every $\mathbb{C}_q$ and its complement $\bar{\mathbb{C}}_q$*

$$\mathbb{U}_q := \text{span}\{\mathbf{x} \in \mathbb{R}^{I_{\mathbb{C}_q}} \,|\, \mathbf{x} \text{ is the left singular vector of } \mathbf{A}_{[q]}\},$$

where $\mathbf{A}_{[q]} \in \mathbb{R}^{I_{\mathbb{C}_q} \times I_{\bar{\mathbb{C}}_q}}$. For each interior node with two successors, their dimension indices are $\mathbb{C}_q$, $\mathbb{C}_{q_1}$, $\mathbb{C}_{q_2}$, respectively, and the space of $\mathbb{U}_{\mathbb{C}_q}$ naturally decouples into

$$\mathbb{U}_{\mathbb{C}_q} = \mathbb{U}_{\mathbb{C}_{q_1}} \otimes \mathbb{U}_{\mathbb{C}_{q_2}},$$

where $\otimes$ denotes the Kronecker product.

Definition 1.3.15. (HT decomposition) Suppose $\mathcal{A} \in \mathbb{A}_{\mathbb{K}}$. We can represent $\mathbf{A}_{[q]}$ as

$$\mathbf{A}_{[q]} = \mathbf{U}_{\mathbb{C}_q} \mathbf{V}_{\mathbb{C}_q}^{\mathsf{T}},$$

where $\mathbf{U}_{\mathbb{C}_q} \in \mathbb{R}^{I_{\mathbb{C}_q} \times K_{\mathbb{C}_q}}$, $\mathbf{V}_{\mathbb{C}_q} \in \mathbb{R}^{I_{\bar{\mathbb{C}}_q} \times K_{\mathbb{C}_q}}$, $K_{\mathbb{C}_q}$ is the hierarchical rank of $\mathbf{A}_{[q]}$, and $\mathbb{C}_q \subset \mathbb{T}$. Therefore, for $\mathbb{C}_q = \{\mathbb{C}_{q_1}, \mathbb{C}_{q_2}\}$, the column vectors $\mathbf{U}_{\mathbb{C}_q}(:, l)$ of $\mathbf{U}_{\mathbb{C}_q}$ satisfy the nestedness property when $1 \leqslant l \leqslant K_{\mathbb{C}_q}$, that is,

$$\mathbf{U}_{\mathbb{C}_q}(:, l) = \sum_{l_1=1}^{K_{\mathbb{C}_{q_1}}} \sum_{l_2=1}^{K_{\mathbb{C}_{q_2}}} \mathcal{G}_{\mathbb{C}_q}(l, l_1, l_2) \mathbf{U}_{\mathbb{C}_{q_1}}(:, l_1) \otimes \mathbf{U}_{\mathbb{C}_{q_2}}(:, l_2), \qquad (1.45)$$

where $\mathcal{G}_{\mathbb{C}_q}(l, l_1, l_2)$ represents the entry in $\mathcal{G}_{\mathbb{C}_q}$. It is the coefficient in the linear combination of vectors. Here $\mathbf{U}_{\mathbb{C}_{q_1}}(:, l_1)$ and $\mathbf{U}_{\mathbb{C}_{q_2}}(:, l_2)$ are the column vectors of $\mathbf{U}_{\mathbb{C}_{q_1}}$ and $\mathbf{U}_{\mathbb{C}_{q_2}}$. Therefore, $\mathcal{G}_{\mathbb{C}_q}$ and $\mathbf{U}_{\mathbb{C}_q}$ are the factors of HT decomposition of $\mathcal{A}$. According to the dimension tree in Fig. 1.21, the HT decomposition for a fourth-order tensor is illustrated in Fig. 1.22.

1.3.5.2 Tensor train decomposition

TT decomposition is proposed in [43] and is also known as matrix product state (MPS) in the area of quantum physics. Since it can avoid the recursive computation of binary trees and is mathematically easy to solve due to its compact form, it has attracted a lot of attention in recent years.

The main idea of TT decomposition is to factorize a tensor $\mathcal{X} \in \mathbb{R}^{I_1 \times \cdots \times I_N}$ into N factors, where head and tail factors are matrices and the rest are smaller third-order tensors.

Definition 1.3.16. (TT decomposition) Given $\mathcal{X} \in \mathbb{R}^{I_1 \times \cdots \times I_N}$, the TT decomposition is of the form

$$\mathcal{X} = \sum_{r_1=1}^{R_1} \cdots \sum_{r_{N+1}=1}^{R_{N+1}} \mathcal{G}^{(1)}(r_1, :, r_2) \circ \mathcal{G}^{(2)}(r_2, :, r_3) \circ \cdots \circ \mathcal{G}^{(N)}(r_N, :, r_{N+1}), \qquad (1.46)$$

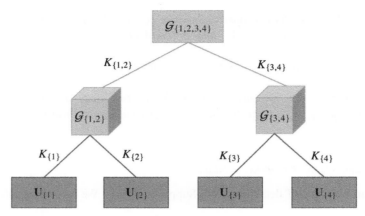

FIGURE 1.22

Hierarchical Tucker decomposition of a fourth-order tensor $\mathcal{A} \in \mathbb{R}^{I_1 \times I_2 \times I_3 \times I_4}$, where $\mathcal{G}_{\{1,2,3,4\}} \in \mathbb{R}^{K_{\{1,2\}} \times K_{\{3,4\}} \times 1}$, $\mathcal{G}_{\{1,2\}} \in \mathbb{R}^{K_{\{1,2\}} \times K_{\{1\}} \times K_{\{2\}}}$, $\mathcal{G}_{\{3,4\}} \in \mathbb{R}^{K_{\{3,4\}} \times K_{\{3\}} \times K_{\{4\}}}$, $\mathbf{U}_{\{1\}} \in \mathbb{R}^{K_{\{1\}} \times I_1}$, $\mathbf{U}_{\{2\}} \in \mathbb{R}^{K_{\{2\}} \times I_2}$, $\mathbf{U}_{\{3\}} \in \mathbb{R}^{K_{\{3\}} \times I_3}$, and $\mathbf{U}_{\{4\}} \in \mathbb{R}^{K_{\{4\}} \times I_4}$ are the factors of hierarchical Tucker decomposition.

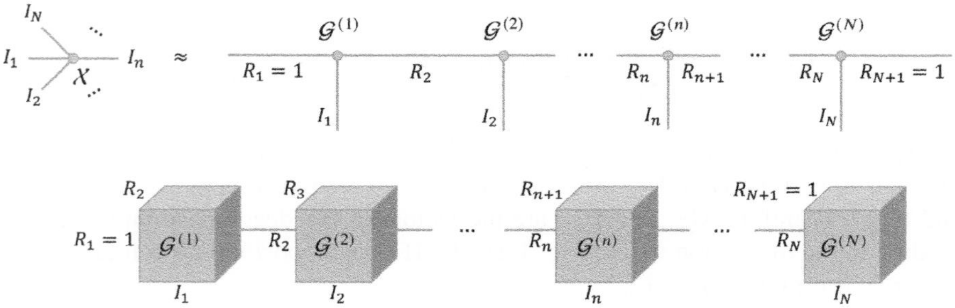

FIGURE 1.23

Top: Tensor train decomposition on an Nth-order tensor $\mathcal{X}$. The yellow dot (light gray in print version) $\mathcal{G}^{(n)} \in \mathbb{R}^{R_n \times I_n \times R_{n+1}}$ is a core tensor, leaf components (not drawn) are identities in this case and thus no need to be stored. Bottom: Corresponding core tensors.

or in an element-wise style,

$$x_{i_1, i_2, \cdots, i_N} = \mathcal{G}^{(1)}(:, i_1, :)\mathcal{G}^{(2)}(:, i_2, :) \cdots \mathcal{G}^{(N)}(:, i_N, :), \tag{1.47}$$

where $\mathcal{G}^{(n)}$ $(n = 1, \cdots, N)$ are the $R_n \times I_n \times R_{n+1}$ core factors. Note that we set $R_1 = R_{N+1} = 1$.

A graphical illustration of TT decomposition on an N-th-order tensor is shown in Fig. 1.23.

Similar to other decompositions, TT decomposition also has its rank.

Definition 1.3.17. (Tensor train rank) The TT rank of $\mathcal{X} \in \mathbb{R}^{I_1 \times \cdots \times I_N}$ is an $(N+1)$-tuple

$$\text{rank}_{\text{TT}}(\mathcal{X}) = (R_1, \cdots, R_{N+1}), \tag{1.48}$$

where $R_n = \text{rank}(\mathbf{X}_{<n-1>})$ and $R_1 = R_{N+1} = 1$.

Different from the aforementioned ranks, TT rank can be affected by the permutation of tensor modes. For instance, given a tensor $\mathcal{A} \in \mathbb{R}^{I_1 \times I_2 \times I_3}$, if we generate $\mathcal{A}' \in \mathbb{R}^{I_3 \times I_2 \times I_1}$ by swapping the first and the third mode of $\mathcal{A}$, the TT rank can be different. That leads to the question of how to choose a desirable permutation for a given tensor.

1.3.5.3 Tensor ring decomposition

Zhao et al. [12] generalized TT to tensor ring (TR) decomposition (a.k.a. tensor chain [TC]). It employs the trace operation to create a symmetrical structure and can be treated as TT with periodic boundary conditions (PBC). An illustration of TR decomposition is shown in Fig. 1.24.

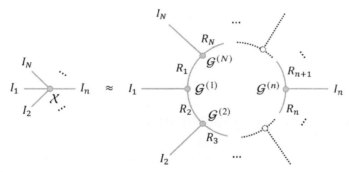

FIGURE 1.24

Tensor ring decomposition of an N-th-order tensor $\mathcal{X}$, where $\mathcal{G}^{(n)} \in \mathbb{R}^{R_n \times I_n \times R_{n+1}}$ are the core tensors.

From Fig. 1.24, we can see that TR decomposes an N-th-order tensor into N third-order factor tensors whose dimensions are much smaller than the original one. The constraint $R_1 = R_{N+1}$ still exists but not necessarily equals one. Therefore, the definition of TR decomposition can be given.

Definition 1.3.18. (TR decomposition) The TR decomposition of $\mathcal{X} \in \mathbb{R}^{I_1 \times \cdots \times I_N}$ is

$$\mathcal{X} = \sum_{r_1=1}^{R_1} \cdots \sum_{r_N=1}^{R_N} \mathcal{G}^{(1)}(r_1, :, r_2) \circ \mathcal{G}^{(2)}(r_2, :, r_3) \circ \cdots \circ \mathcal{G}^{(N)}(r_N, :, r_1). \tag{1.49}$$

Using the trace operation, it can be written element-wisely as follows:

$$x_{i_1, i_2, \cdots, i_N} = \text{tr}\big(\mathcal{G}^{(1)}(:, i_1, :)\mathcal{G}^{(2)}(:, i_2, :) \cdots \mathcal{G}^{(N)}(:, i_N, :)\big), \tag{1.50}$$

where $\mathcal{G}^{(n)} \in \mathbb{R}^{R_n \times I_n \times R_{n+1}}$, $n = 1, \cdots, N$, are core tensors.

Similar to TT rank, TR rank can be defined as a tuple, i.e., $\text{rank}_{\text{TR}}(\mathcal{X}) = (R_1, \cdots, R_N)$.

1.3.5.4 *Other variants*

Even though TNs are derived to substantially reduce the computational cost, HT and TT may fail to achieve the outstanding effect when the data size increases. TR was proposed to solve the ordering issue induced by TT.

Other than TR, projected entangled pair states (PEPS) [44] was also introduced for the same reason. PEPS is a hierarchical 2D TT model employing fifth/sixth-order tensors as cores. This strategy can be taken as a trade-off between rank and computational complexity. However, when the estimation accuracy is high, the rank of PEPS also grows rapidly.

Honeycomb lattice (HCL) [45] and multiscale entanglement renormalization ansatz (MERA) [46] were put forward to resolve this dilemma. Similar to TR and PEPS, HCL and MERA also contain loop structures that cause a high computational burden in the contraction. However, due to the fact that core tensors for HCL and MERA are only of third order and third/fourth order, respectively, they are still able to attain a desirable effect.

Recently, a new idea has been proposed by combining traditional decomposition approaches. For example, TR and t-SVD are merged in a hierarchical way in [47].

1.4 Tensor processing techniques

Tensor decomposition plays a key role in machine learning, signal processing, and data mining. A series of tensor-based data processing techniques are listed as follows:

- Tensor dictionary learning [48,49]
  Tensor dictionary learning aims to sparsely represent the high-order tensor in a tensor factorization way where some factors can be regarded as learned dictionaries with respect to the rest sparse factors. Benefiting from its data-driven characteristic and high-order sparse representation ability, it has been widely used in various data processing applications, such as image denoising, enhancement and classification, texture synthesis, unsupervised clustering, and biomedical data analysis.
- Tensor completion [50–54]
  Tensor completion fills in the missing entries of a partially observed tensor, which is popularly applied in recommender systems, image recovery, knowledge graph completion, and traffic flow prediction.
- Tensor robust principal component analysis (TRPCA) [55–57]
  TRPCA separates additive low-rank and sparse components from multiway data. It can be used for dimensionality reduction, background extraction, small target detection, and anomaly detection.

- Tensor independent component analysis (TICA) [58–60]
  TICA separates multivariate tensor data into additive statistically independent non-Gaussian subcomponents. It is widely used for blind resource separation in speech, image, and biomedical signals.
- Tensor regression [61–63]
  Tensor regression sets up a multilinear mapping from a tensor input to a tensor output with a tensor system. As a tensor extension for linear regression, it has wide applications in various multidimensional data processing areas, such as weather forecasting, recommender systems, image prediction, brain activation, and connectivity analysis.
- Tensor classification [64–66]
  By replacing the linear function with a tensor function for a superplane to separate positive samples from negative samples, we can obtain some generalized statistical tensor classification methods including support tensor machine (STM), logistic tensor regression, and discriminative tensor component analysis. They find useful applications in image classification of handwriting, frailty detection from multisensor recordings, and breast cancer classification based on histopathology images.
- Coupled tensor factorization [67–69]
  Data collected from multiple sources often share latent components. Coupled tensor factorization can perform multiple decompositions based on those shared factors, which is very useful in data fusion applications.
- Deep tensor neural networks [70,71]
  Many layers in deep neural networks have linear combinations. By generalizing these linear operators into multilinear ones, deep tensor neural networks can be obtained. They can process multidimensional data in its original form and can be implemented in speech analysis, image classification, and natural language processing.

1.5 Challenges

With the recent advances in applied mathematics, tensors have been introduced into a number of data processing applications, both in theory and in methodology. However, to really make tensor computation as practical as matrix computation, there are still some challenges. We list a few of them as follows:

- There may be multiple decompositions for a given tensor, but no solid theoretical guidance is established on how to select a desirable decomposition for certain multiway data processing tasks. Besides, TNs are reported to have outstanding performances for higher-order data processing, but how to derive a suitable network is still an open question.
- For data collected from heterogeneous networks, such as social networks, banking data, and traffic patterns, graphical representation can be implemented to model

the local signals and their irregular connections by nodes and edges, respectively. However, the uniform connection in tensor mode prevents the full utilization of the topological structure encoded in those networks.

- Tensor computation leads to a heavy computational burden in some cases. Therefore, high-performance tensor computation algorithms and efficient software are called for.
- Apart from the data processing community, tensors are intensively investigated in physics as well. It is quite important to make use of the results from other areas to improve tensor decomposition and its data processing performance. For example, quantum computing may highly accelerate tensor-based machine learning.
- As a linear representation, tensor decomposition will encounter difficulties in highly nonlinear feature extraction. Motivated by the success of deep neural networks, deep tensor factorization can be formulated by applying multilayer decompositions. However, problems with interpretability and generalization would ensue.
- With the development of the Internet of Things, many data processing tasks are carried out by edge computing. It would be interesting but not easy to develop distributed tensor decomposition, block tensor decomposition, and online tensor decomposition for this group of applications.

References

[1] T.G. Kolda, B.W. Bader, Tensor decompositions and applications, SIAM Review 51 (3) (2009) 455–500.
[2] L. He, W. Zhang, M. Shi, Non-negative tensor factorization for speech enhancement, in: 2016 International Conference on Artificial Intelligence: Technologies and Applications, Atlantis Press, 2016, pp. 1–5.
[3] Y.-Y. Yuan, S.-T. Wang, Q. Cheng, D.-M. Kong, X.-G. Che, Simultaneous determination of carbendazim and chlorothalonil pesticide residues in peanut oil using excitation-emission matrix fluorescence coupled with three-way calibration method, Spectrochimica Acta. Part A: Molecular and Biomolecular Spectroscopy 220 (2019) 117088.
[4] K. Kawabata, Y. Matsubara, T. Honda, Y. Sakurai, Non-linear mining of social activities in tensor streams, in: Proceedings of the 26th ACM SIGKDD International Conference on Knowledge Discovery & Data Mining, 2020, pp. 2093–2102.
[5] A. Cichocki, N. Lee, I.V. Oseledets, A.-H. Phan, Q. Zhao, D. Mandic, Low-rank tensor networks for dimensionality reduction and large-scale optimization problems: perspectives and challenges part 1, arXiv preprint, arXiv:1609.00893, 2016.
[6] D.S. Watkins, Fundamentals of Matrix Computations, vol. 64, John Wiley & Sons, 2004.
[7] M. Fazel, H. Hindi, S.P. Boyd, A rank minimization heuristic with application to minimum order system approximation, in: Proceedings of the 2001 American Control Conference (Cat. No. 01CH37148), vol. 6, IEEE, 2001, pp. 4734–4739.
[8] N.D. Sidiropoulos, L. De Lathauwer, X. Fu, K. Huang, E.E. Papalexakis, C. Faloutsos, Tensor decomposition for signal processing and machine learning, IEEE Transactions on Signal Processing 65 (13) (2017) 3551–3582.

[9] C.F. Van Loan, The ubiquitous Kronecker product, Journal of Computational and Applied Mathematics 123 (1–2) (2000) 85–100.

[10] A. Smilde, R. Bro, P. Geladi, Multi-Way Analysis: Applications in the Chemical Sciences, John Wiley & Sons, 2005.

[11] M.E. Kilmer, C.D. Martin, Factorization strategies for third-order tensors, Linear Algebra and Its Applications 435 (3) (2011) 641–658.

[12] Q. Zhao, G. Zhou, S. Xie, L. Zhang, A. Cichocki, Tensor ring decomposition, arXiv preprint, arXiv:1606.05535, 2016.

[13] S.V. Dolgov, D.V. Savostyanov, Alternating minimal energy methods for linear systems in higher dimensions, SIAM Journal on Scientific Computing 36 (5) (2014) A2248–A2271.

[14] M.E. Kilmer, C.D. Martin, L. Perrone, A third-order generalization of the matrix svd as a product of third-order tensors, Tech. Rep. TR-2008-4, Tufts University, Department of Computer Science, 2008.

[15] C.M. Andersen, R. Bro, Practical aspects of parafac modeling of fluorescence excitation-emission data, Journal of Chemometrics: A Journal of the Chemometrics Society 17 (4) (2003) 200–215.

[16] R. Bro, Review on multiway analysis in chemistry—2000–2005, Critical Reviews in Analytical Chemistry 36 (3–4) (2006) 279–293.

[17] R. Bro, et al., Parafac. tutorial and applications, Chemometrics and Intelligent Laboratory Systems 38 (2) (1997) 149–172.

[18] R. Bro, C.A. Andersson, H.A. Kiers, Parafac2—part ii. Modeling chromatographic data with retention time shifts, Journal of Chemometrics: A Journal of the Chemometrics Society 13 (3–4) (1999) 295–309.

[19] L. De Lathauwer, J. Castaing, J.-F. Cardoso, Fourth-order cumulant-based blind identification of underdetermined mixtures, IEEE Transactions on Signal Processing 55 (6) (2007) 2965–2973.

[20] L. De Lathauwer, A. de Baynast, Blind deconvolution of ds-cdma signals by means of decomposition in rank-(1, 1, 1) terms, IEEE Transactions on Signal Processing 56 (4) (2008) 1562–1571.

[21] D. Muti, S. Bourennane, Multidimensional filtering based on a tensor approach, Signal Processing 85 (12) (2005) 2338–2353.

[22] L. De Lathauwer, B. De Moor, J. Vandewalle, A multilinear singular value decomposition, SIAM Journal on Matrix Analysis and Applications 21 (4) (2000) 1253–1278.

[23] L. De Lathauwer, B. De Moor, J. Vandewalle, On the best rank-1 and rank-(r1, r2,..., rn) approximation of higher-order tensors, SIAM Journal on Matrix Analysis and Applications 21 (4) (2000) 1324–1342.

[24] M.A.O. Vasilescu, D. Terzopoulos, Multilinear analysis of image ensembles: tensorfaces, in: European Conference on Computer Vision, Springer, 2002, pp. 447–460.

[25] W. Hackbusch, B.N. Khoromskij, Tensor-product approximation to operators and functions in high dimensions, Journal of Complexity 23 (4–6) (2007) 697–714.

[26] B. Khoromskij, V. Khoromskaia, Low rank Tucker-type tensor approximation to classical potentials, Open Mathematics 5 (3) (2007) 523–550.

[27] B.W. Bader, M.W. Berry, M. Browne, Discussion tracking in enron email using parafac, in: Survey of Text Mining II, Springer, 2008, pp. 147–163.

[28] E. Acar, S.A. Çamtepe, M.S. Krishnamoorthy, B. Yener, Modeling and multiway analysis of chatroom tensors, in: International Conference on Intelligence and Security Informatics, Springer, 2005, pp. 256–268.

[29] N. Liu, B. Zhang, J. Yan, Z. Chen, W. Liu, F. Bai, L. Chien, Text representation: from vector to tensor, in: Fifth IEEE International Conference on Data Mining (ICDM'05), IEEE, 2005, pp. 725–728.

[30] L. Tucker, Some mathematical notes on three-mode factor analysis, Psychometrika 31 (3) (1966) 279–311.

[31] D.L. Lieven, D.M. Bart, V. Joos, A multilinear singular value decomposition, SIAM Journal on Matrix Analysis and Applications (2000).

[32] F.L. Hitchcock, The expression of a tensor or a polyadic as a sum of products, Journal of Mathematical Physics 6 (1) (1927) 164–189.

[33] J.D. Carroll, J.J. Chang, Analysis of individual differences in multidimensional scaling via an n-way generalization of "eckart-young" decomposition, Psychometrika 35 (3) (1970) 283–319.

[34] R.A. Harshman, et al., Foundations of the PARAFAC procedure: models and conditions for an "explanatory" multimodal factor analysis, UCLA Working Papers in Phonetics 16 (1970) 1–84.

[35] H.A.L. Kiers, Towards a standardized notation and terminology in multiway analysis, Journal of Chemometrics 14 (2000).

[36] L. De Lathauwer, Decompositions of a higher-order tensor in block terms—part I: lemmas for partitioned matrices, SIAM Journal on Matrix Analysis and Applications 30 (3) (2008) 1022–1032.

[37] L. De Lathauwer, Decompositions of a higher-order tensor in block terms—part ii: definitions and uniqueness, SIAM Journal on Matrix Analysis and Applications 30 (3) (2008) 1033–1066.

[38] Z. Zhang, G. Ely, S. Aeron, N. Hao, M. Kilmer, Novel methods for multilinear data completion and de-noising based on tensor-svd, in: Proceedings of the IEEE Conference on Computer Vision and Pattern Recognition, 2014, pp. 3842–3849.

[39] R.H. Chan, M.K. Ng, Conjugate gradient methods for Toeplitz systems, SIAM Review 38 (3) (1996) 427–482.

[40] L. Grasedyck, Hierarchical singular value decomposition of tensors, SIAM Journal on Matrix Analysis and Applications 31 (4) (2010) 2029–2054.

[41] W. Hackbusch, S. Kühn, A new scheme for the tensor representation, The Journal of Fourier Analysis and Applications 15 (5) (2009) 706–722, https://doi.org/10.1007/s00041-009-9094-9.

[42] E. Grelier, A. Nouy, M. Chevreuil, Learning with tree-based tensor formats, arXiv:1811.04455, 2019.

[43] V.I. Oseledets, Tensor-train decomposition, SIAM Journal on Scientific Computing 33 (5) (2011) 2295–2317.

[44] F. Verstraete, V. Murg, J.I. Cirac, Matrix product states, projected entangled pair states, and variational renormalization group methods for quantum spin systems, Advances in Physics 57 (2) (2008) 143–224.

[45] M. Ablowitz, S. Nixon, Y. Zhu, Conical diffraction in honeycomb lattices, Physical Review A 79 (5) (2009) 1744.

[46] L. Cincio, J. Dziarmaga, M.M. Rams, Multi-scale entanglement renormalization ansatz in two dimensions, Physical Review Letters 100 (24) (2007) 240603.

[47] A. Ahad, Z. Long, C. Zhu, Y. Liu, Hierarchical tensor ring completion, arXiv preprint, arXiv:2004.11720, 2020.

[48] S. Zubair, W. Wang, Tensor dictionary learning with sparse Tucker decomposition, in: 2013 18th International Conference on Digital Signal Processing (DSP), IEEE, 2013, pp. 1–6.

[49] Y. Peng, D. Meng, Z. Xu, C. Gao, Y. Yang, B. Zhang, Decomposable nonlocal tensor dictionary learning for multispectral image denoising, in: Proceedings of the IEEE Conference on Computer Vision and Pattern Recognition, 2014, pp. 2949–2956.

[50] J. Liu, P. Musialski, P. Wonka, J. Ye, Tensor completion for estimating missing values in visual data, IEEE Transactions on Pattern Analysis and Machine Intelligence 35 (1) (2012) 208–220.

[51] H. Huang, Y. Liu, J. Liu, C. Zhu, Provable tensor ring completion, Signal Processing 171 (2020) 107486.

[52] Y. Liu, Z. Long, C. Zhu, Image completion using low tensor tree rank and total variation minimization, IEEE Transactions on Multimedia 21 (2) (2018) 338–350.

[53] Z. Long, Y. Liu, L. Chen, C. Zhu, Low rank tensor completion for multiway visual data, Signal Processing 155 (2019) 301–316.

[54] H. Huang, Y. Liu, Z. Long, C. Zhu, Robust low-rank tensor ring completion, IEEE Transactions on Computational Imaging 6 (2020) 1117–1126.

[55] C. Lu, J. Feng, Y. Chen, W. Liu, Z. Lin, S. Yan, Tensor robust principal component analysis with a new tensor nuclear norm, IEEE Transactions on Pattern Analysis and Machine Intelligence 42 (4) (2019) 925–938.

[56] Y. Liu, L. Chen, C. Zhu, Improved robust tensor principal component analysis via low-rank core matrix, IEEE Journal of Selected Topics in Signal Processing 12 (6) (2018) 1378–1389.

[57] L. Feng, Y. Liu, L. Chen, X. Zhang, C. Zhu, Robust block tensor principal component analysis, Signal Processing 166 (2020) 107271.

[58] L. De Lathauwer, B. De Moor, J. Vandewalle, Independent component analysis and (simultaneous) third-order tensor diagonalization, IEEE Transactions on Signal Processing 49 (10) (2001) 2262–2271.

[59] C.F. Beckmann, S.M. Smith, Tensorial extensions of independent component analysis for multisubject fmri analysis, NeuroImage 25 (1) (2005) 294–311.

[60] J. Virta, B. Li, K. Nordhausen, H. Oja, Independent component analysis for tensor-valued data, Journal of Multivariate Analysis 162 (2017) 172–192.

[61] Y. Liu, J. Liu, C. Zhu, Low-rank tensor train coefficient array estimation for tensor-on-tensor regression, IEEE Transactions on Neural Networks and Learning Systems (2020).

[62] J. Liu, C. Zhu, Y. Liu, Smooth compact tensor ring regression, IEEE Transactions on Knowledge and Data Engineering (2020).

[63] H. Zhou, L. Li, H. Zhu, Tensor regression with applications in neuroimaging data analysis, Journal of the American Statistical Association 108 (502) (2013) 540–552.

[64] Z. Hao, L. He, B. Chen, X. Yang, A linear support higher-order tensor machine for classification, IEEE Transactions on Image Processing 22 (7) (2013) 2911–2920.

[65] A. Coley, R. Milson, V. Pravda, A. Pravdová, Classification of the Weyl tensor in higher dimensions, Classical and Quantum Gravity 21 (7) (2004) L35.

[66] T.-K. Kim, S.-F. Wong, R. Cipolla, Tensor canonical correlation analysis for action classification, in: 2007 IEEE Conference on Computer Vision and Pattern Recognition, IEEE, 2007, pp. 1–8.

[67] B. Ermiş, E. Acar, A.T. Cemgil, Link prediction in heterogeneous data via generalized coupled tensor factorization, Data Mining and Knowledge Discovery 29 (1) (2015) 203–236.

[68] D. Rafailidis, A. Nanopoulos, Modeling the dynamics of user preferences in coupled tensor factorization, in: Proceedings of the 8th ACM Conference on Recommender Systems, 2014, pp. 321–324.

[69] R. Mosayebi, G.-A. Hossein-Zadeh, Correlated coupled matrix tensor factorization method for simultaneous eeg-fmri data fusion, Biomedical Signal Processing and Control 62 (2020) 102071.

[70] Z. Zhang, Y. Liu, J. Liu, F. Wen, C. Zhu, Amp-net: denoising based deep unfolding for compressive image sensing, arXiv preprint, arXiv:2004.10078, 2020.

[71] D. Yu, L. Deng, F. Seide, The deep tensor neural network with applications to large vocabulary speech recognition, IEEE Transactions on Audio, Speech, and Language Processing 21 (2) (2012) 388–396.

CHAPTER

Transform-based tensor singular value decomposition in multidimensional image recovery[☆],[☆☆]

2

Tai-Xiang Jiang[a], Michael K. Ng[b], and Xi-Le Zhao[c]

[a] *School of Economic Information Engineering, Southwestern University of Finance and Economics, Chengdu, Sichuan, China*
[b] *Department of Mathematics, The University of Hong Kong, Pokfulam, Hong Kong*
[c] *School of Mathematical Sciences/Research Center for Image and Vision Computing, University of Electronic Science and Technology of China, Chengdu, Sichuan, China*

CONTENTS

[☆] This work was supported in part by the National Natural Science Foundation of China under Grants 12001446, 61876203, and 61772003; in part by the Key Project of Applied Basic Research in Sichuan Province under Grant 2020YJ0216; in part by the Applied Basic Research Project of Sichuan Province under Grant 2021YJ0107; in part by the National Key Research and Development Program of China under Grant 2020YFA0714001; in part by the Fundamental Research Funds for the Central Universities under Grant JBK2102001; and in part by the HKRGC GRF under Grants 12300218, 12300519, 17201020 and 17300021.
[☆☆] Three authors contributed equally.

2.1 Introduction

The rapid advance in imaging technology has given rise to a wealth of multi-dimensional images (e.g., color images, video, and multispectral/hyperspectral images). However, due to the limitations of imaging conditions, the captured multidimensional data are always degraded. Multidimensional image recovery aims to estimate the underlying high-quality data from the degraded observation and is a fundamental problem in low-level computer vision. Without loss of generality, the degradation process can be modeled as

$$\mathcal{O} = \mathcal{A}(\mathcal{X}) + \mathcal{N}, \tag{2.1}$$

where $\mathcal{O}$ is the observation, $\mathcal{A}$ is a linear mapping, $\mathcal{X}$ is the target high-quality multidimensional image, and $\mathcal{N}$ is the additive noise.[1] Different combinations of $\mathcal{A}$ and $\mathcal{N}$ are related to a wide variety of real-world applications. In the case that $\mathcal{A}$ refers to the sampling operator and the noise term $\mathcal{N}$ vanishes, estimation of the complete data $\mathcal{X}$ from the partial observation $\mathcal{O}$ is a tensor/matrix completion problem [1,2]. If the noise term is taken into consideration, it becomes the noisy tensor/matrix completion problem [3,4]. When $\mathcal{A}$ is an identical mapping and $\mathcal{N}$ is mixed noise consisting of Gaussian noise, sparse noise, and other noise types, multidimensional image recovery becomes the mixed noise removal problem and is common in remote sensing hyperspectral images (HSIs) [5].

Estimation of $\mathcal{X}$ from $\mathcal{O}$ is an ill-posed inverse problem, and the maximum a posteriori (MAP) estimation is an effective approach to solve this problem. Specifically, we need to maximize the posterior probability $P(\mathcal{X}|\mathcal{O})$ under the Bayes rule [6], i.e.,

$$\begin{aligned} \mathcal{X}^* &= \arg\max_{\mathcal{X}} P(\mathcal{X}|\mathcal{O}) = \arg\max_{\mathcal{X}} \frac{P(\mathcal{O}|\mathcal{X})P(\mathcal{X})}{P(\mathcal{O})} \\ &= \arg\min_{\mathcal{X}} \{-\log P(\mathcal{O}|\mathcal{X}) - \log P(\mathcal{X})\}. \end{aligned} \tag{2.2}$$

In (2.2), $P(\mathcal{O}|\mathcal{X})$ is the likelihood term and is determined by (2.1). Generally, we can write $-\log P(\mathcal{O}|\mathcal{X})$ as $f(\mathcal{A}(\mathcal{X}) - \mathcal{O})$, and its minimization indicates that the recovered results should conform to the degradation process in (2.1). We also call it the data fidelity term. For example, when the noise is independent and identically Gaussian distributed with variance σ^2 and $\mathcal{A}$ is an identical mapping, $f(\mathcal{A}(\mathcal{X}) - \mathcal{O})$ can be formulated as $\frac{1}{2\sigma^2}\|\mathcal{X} - \mathcal{O}\|_F^2$ with its factor absorbed by $-\log P(\mathcal{X})$. For the tensor completion problem, $f(\cdot)$ can be written as the Dirac delta function. As for the prior term $-\log P(\mathcal{X})$ that expresses the prior distribution of the data, it can be written as $\lambda\phi(\mathcal{X})$, where lambda is a nonnegative parameter. Oftentimes, $\phi(\mathcal{X})$ is also referred to as the regularization term. Then, (2.2) can be rewritten as a regularized optimization problem, i.e.,

$$\mathcal{X}^* = \arg\min_{\mathcal{X}} \{f(\mathcal{A}(\mathcal{X}) - \mathcal{O}) + \lambda\phi(\mathcal{X})\}. \tag{2.3}$$

---

[1] Multiplicative noise can be modeled in a nonlinear mapping $\mathcal{A}$ when needed.

Since f is determined by the degradation process, reasonable analysis and effective exploitation of the underlying data's prior knowledge to build ϕ is highly important in this framework.

Multidimensional images are always inner-structured and globally correlated. For instance, the bands of a hyperspectral image are highly correlated such that its spectral vectors live in a low-dimensional subspace [7]. This low-dimensionality can be mathematically formulated as low-rankness, i.e., representation of the high-dimensional data under learned lower-dimensional bases. For matrices, although the direct minimization of the rank is NP-hard, we can minimize the nuclear norm (i.e., the sum of the singular values) to faithfully enhance the low-rankness. However, if multidimensional images are reordered into matrices and the corresponding recovery problem is solved via matrix-based methods, such matricization will inevitably destroy the intrinsic structure of multidimensional images. As the higher-order extension of the matrix, the tensor can provide a more natural and elegant representation for multidimensional images. Thus, in this chapter, we mainly focus on the design of a tensor low-rank regularizer for multidimensional image recovery.

Unlike for the matrix case, there is no unique rank definition for tensors. Thus, the definition of the tensor rank is a fundamental problem. Many research efforts have been devoted to this hot topic [8–11], such as the CANDECOMP/PARAFAC (CP) rank and the Tucker rank. The CP rank is defined based on canonical polyadic decomposition, where an N-th-order tensor is decomposed as the sum of the rank-1 tensors [8,12–14], i.e., the outer product of N vectors. The CP rank is defined as the minimal number of the rank-1 tensors required to express the data. The Tucker rank is based on the Tucker decomposition that decomposes a tensor into a core tensor multiplied by a matrix along each mode [8,15]. The Tucker rank is defined as the vector consisting of the ranks of unfolding matrices along different modes. The Tucker rank has been considered in the low-rank tensor completion problem by minimizing the convex surrogate of its summation, i.e., the sum of the nuclear norm (SNN) [2], or the nonconvex surrogates [16,17].

The tensor singular value decomposition (t-SVD) [18,19], based on the tensor–tensor product (t-prod), has emerged as a powerful tool for preserving the intrinsic structures of the tensor. The tensor nuclear norm (TNN) [20–24] is suggested as a convex surrogate of the tensor tubal rank that is derived from the t-SVD framework. The TNN-based multidimensional image recovery model is given by

$$\min_{\mathcal{X}} \left\{ f(\mathcal{A}(\mathcal{X}) - \mathcal{O}) + \lambda \|\mathcal{X}\|_{\text{TNN}} \right\}, \tag{2.4}$$

where $\mathcal{X} \in \mathbb{R}^{n_1 \times n_2 \times n_3}$, $\|\mathcal{X}\|_{\text{TNN}} = \sum_{i=1}^{n_3} \|\widehat{\mathcal{X}}^{(i)}\|_*$, $\widehat{\mathcal{X}}^{(i)}$ is the i-th frontal slice of $\widehat{\mathcal{X}}$, and $\widehat{\mathcal{X}}$ is the tensor generated by performing discrete Fourier transformation (DFT) along the mode-3 fibers of $\mathcal{X}$, i.e., $\widehat{\mathcal{X}} = \text{fft}(\mathcal{X}, [], 3)$ in MATLAB®.

Compared with the Tucker and CP decomposition schemes, t-SVD provides an algebraic framework that is more analogous to the matrix case [19], and has received much attention in recent years. In this chapter, we review the framework of t-SVD and the establishment of the TNN. Then, focusing on the multidimensional image recovery problem, we revisit recent advances based on t-SVD. Moreover, we delve into the t-SVD framework, and replace its key module, which is the DFT, with other transforms. Then, the transform-based t-SVD is introduced and we offer a deeper insight into the inner mechanism of the whole t-SVD framework.

The rest of this chapter is organized as follows. In Section 2.2, we revisit the t-SVD framework and the TNN. Specifically, Section 2.2.1 provides the basic tensor notations and the t-SVD framework is given in Section 2.2.2. Sections 2.2.3–2.2.4 concentrate on the TNN minimization model and its extensions. Then, we introduce the recent advance of the transform-based t-SVD in Section 2.3, from the linear invertible transform in Section 2.3.1 to the noninvertible transform and data adaptive transform in Section 2.3.2. Next, some numerical experiments are described in Section 2.4. Finally, Section 2.5 draws conclusions and provides some possible directions for future research.

2.2 Recent advances of the tensor singular value decomposition

In this section, we first give some basic notations and definitions for tensors, and then we introduce the framework of t-SVD. Next, the definition of TNN together with the recovery of multidimensional visual data by TNN minimization will be presented. Subsequently, some nonconvex surrogates and additional regularization terms are discussed. Finally, we give numerical examples to illustrate the performance of the methods within the t-SVD framework for multidimensional visual data recovery.

2.2.1 Preliminaries and basic tensor notations

Throughout this chapter, lowercase letters, e.g., x, boldface lowercase letters, e.g., $\mathbf{x}$, boldface uppercase letters, e.g., $\mathbf{X}$, and boldface calligraphic letters, e.g., $\mathcal{X}$, are used to denote scalars, vectors, matrices, and tensors, respectively. Given a third-order tensor[2] $\mathcal{X} \in \mathbb{R}^{n_1 \times n_2 \times n_3}$, we use $\mathcal{X}_{ijk}$ or $\mathcal{X}(i, j, k)$ to denote its (i, j, k)-th element. Its (i, j)-th mode-3 fibers, i.e., the vectors along the third dimension, are denoted as $\mathcal{X}(i, j, :)$. The mode-3 fiber is also referred to as the tube. The k-th frontal slice of $\mathcal{X}$ is denoted as $\mathcal{X}^{(k)}$ (or $\mathcal{X}(:, :, k)$, $\mathbf{X}^k$). The **inner product** of two same-sized third-order tensors $\mathcal{X}$ and $\mathcal{Y}$ is defined as

$$\langle \mathcal{X}, \mathcal{Y} \rangle := \sum_{i_1, i_2, i_3} \mathcal{X}_{i_1 i_2 i_3} \cdot \mathcal{Y}_{i_1 i_2 i_3}. \qquad (2.5)$$

---

[2] In this chapter, we mainly focus on third-order tensors. The notations on this page can be naturally extended to higher-order tensors.

The **Frobenius norm** is then defined as

$$\|\mathcal{X}\|_F := \sqrt{\langle \mathcal{X}, \mathcal{X} \rangle} = \sqrt{\sum_{ijk} \mathcal{X}_{ijk}^2}. \tag{2.6}$$

The **mode-3 unfolding** of $\mathcal{X} \in \mathbb{R}^{n_1 \times n_2 \times n_3}$ is denoted as a matrix $\mathbf{X}_{(3)} \in \mathbb{R}^{n_3 \times n_1 n_2}$, where the tensor's (i, j, k)-th element maps to the matrix's (k, l)-th element satisfying $l = (j - 1)n_1 + i$. The mode-3 unfolding operator and its inverse are respectively denoted as `unfold3` and `fold3`, and they satisfy

$$\mathcal{X} = \texttt{fold3}(\texttt{unfold3}(\mathcal{X})) = \texttt{fold3}(\mathbf{X}_{(3)}). \tag{2.7}$$

The mode-3 tensor–matrix product of a tensor $\mathcal{X} \in \mathbb{R}^{n_1 \times n_2 \times n_3}$ with a matrix $\mathbf{A} \in \mathbb{R}^{m \times n_3}$ is denoted by $\mathcal{X} \times_3 \mathbf{A}$ and is of size $n_1 \times n_2 \times m$. Element-wise, we have

$$(\mathcal{X} \times_3 \mathbf{A})_{ijk} = \sum_{n=1}^{n_3} \mathcal{X}_{ijn} \mathbf{A}_{kn}. \tag{2.8}$$

The mode-3 tensor–matrix product can also be expressed in terms of the mode-3 unfolding

$$\mathcal{Y} = (\mathcal{X} \times_3 \mathbf{A}) \quad \Leftrightarrow \quad \mathbf{Y}_{(3)} = \mathbf{A} \cdot \texttt{unfold3}(\mathcal{X}), \tag{2.9}$$

where $\cdot$ is the matrix product.

Interested readers can refer to [8] for a more extensive overview.

2.2.2 The t-SVD framework

The basis of t-SVD is the definition of the multiplication operation between two third-order tensors. It is well known that in linear algebra, if $\mathbf{A}$ is an $m \times n$ matrix and $\mathbf{B}$ is a $n \times p$ matrix, the matrix product $\mathbf{C} = \mathbf{AB}$ is defined to be the $m \times p$ matrix with

$$\mathbf{C}_{ij} = \sum_{k=1}^{n} \mathbf{A}_{ik} \mathbf{B}_{kj} \quad \text{for } i = 1, 2, \cdots, m \text{ and } j = 1, 2, \cdots, p. \tag{2.10}$$

Similarly, if we replace the numbers in a matrix with vectors of the same length and use the circular convolution between two vectors instead of the multiplication between two numbers, the tensor–tensor product (t-prod) can be defined.

Definition 2.1 (T-prod [19]). Let $\mathcal{A}$ be a tensor with size $n_1 \times n_2 \times n_3$ and let $\mathcal{B}$ be a tensor with size $n_2 \times n_4 \times n_3$. Then, the tensor–tensor product[3] between $\mathcal{A}$ and $\mathcal{B}$

---

[3] In this chapter, the symbol "$*$" is used to denote t-prod, similar to the literature. However, please note that this notation may be different in other chapters.

is the $n_1 \times n_4 \times n_3$ tensor $\mathcal{C} = \mathcal{A} * \mathcal{B}$ whose (i, j)-th tube is given by

$$
\mathcal{C}(i, j, :) = \sum_{k=1}^{n_2} \mathcal{B}(i, k, :) \circledast \mathcal{C}(k, j, :), \tag{2.11}
$$

where $i = 1, 2, \cdots, n_1$ and $j = 1, 2, \cdots, n_4$, and "$\circledast$" represents the circular convolution of two same-size vectors.

Since the circular convolution can be converted into element-wise multiplication in the Fourier domain, we now consider the DFT on a third-order tensor. The 1D DFT on a real-valued vector $\mathbf{x} \in \mathbb{R}^n$, denoted as $\bar{\mathbf{x}}$, is given by $\bar{\mathbf{x}} = \mathbf{F}_n \mathbf{x} \in \mathbb{C}^n$, where $\mathbf{F}_n \in \mathbb{C}^{n \times n}$ is the DFT matrix. The (i, j)-th element of $\mathbf{F}_n$ is equal to $\omega^{(i-1)(j-1)}$, where $\omega = e^{\frac{-2\pi\iota}{n}}$ is a primitive n-th root of unity and $\iota^2 = -1$. The inverse DFT matrix can be obtained as $\mathbf{F}_n^{-1} \in \mathbb{C}^{n \times n}$ and we have $\mathbf{F}_n^{-1} = \frac{1}{n}\mathbf{F}_n^{\mathrm{H}}$, where $\cdot^{\mathrm{H}}$ is the conjugate transpose. In this chapter, we use $\widehat{\mathcal{X}}$ to denote the transformed tensor by performing 1D DFT along the mode-3 fibers (tubes) of $\mathcal{X}$. By using the DFT matrix $\mathbf{F}_{n_3} \in \mathbb{C}^{n_3 \times n_3}$, we have

$$
\widehat{\mathcal{X}} = \mathcal{X} \times_3 \mathbf{F}_{n_3}. \tag{2.12}
$$

Additionally, $\mathcal{X}$ and $\widehat{\mathcal{X}}$ can be transformed to each other via the fast Fourier transform (FFT) and its inverse with a lower computation burden, for example, using the MATLAB command fft$(\mathcal{X}, [], 3)$ and ifft$(\mathcal{X}, [], 3)$, respectively. Meanwhile, we have

$$
\|\mathcal{X}\|_F = \sqrt{\langle \mathcal{X}, \mathcal{X} \rangle} = \sqrt{\frac{1}{n_3}\langle \widehat{\mathcal{X}}, \widehat{\mathcal{X}} \rangle} = \frac{1}{\sqrt{n_3}}\|\widehat{\mathcal{X}}\|_F. \tag{2.13}
$$

Returning to the t-prod, the t-prod between $\mathcal{A}$ and $\mathcal{B}$ can be computed efficiently by multiplying each pair of the frontal slices of the FFT-transformed tensors $\widehat{\mathcal{A}}$ and $\widehat{\mathcal{B}}$ and computing the inverse FFT along the third dimension to obtain the result.

Definition 2.2 (Block-diagonal form [21]). Let $\overline{\mathbf{X}}$ denote the block-diagonal matrix of $\widehat{\mathcal{X}} \in \mathbb{C}^{n_1 \times n_2 \times n_3}$, i.e.,

$$
\overline{\mathbf{X}} = \texttt{blockdiag}(\widehat{\mathcal{X}})
$$

$$
\triangleq \begin{bmatrix} \widehat{\mathcal{X}}^{(1)} & & & \\ & \widehat{\mathcal{X}}^{(2)} & & \\ & & \ddots & \\ & & & \widehat{\mathcal{X}}^{(n_3)} \end{bmatrix} \in \mathbb{C}^{n_1 n_3 \times n_2 n_3}. \tag{2.14}
$$

Furthermore, we denote the inverse operation of block-diagonal as $\texttt{blockdiag}^{-1}$. Then, for any two tensors $\mathcal{A} \in \mathbb{R}^{n_1 \times n_2 \times n_3}$ and $\mathcal{B} \in \mathbb{R}^{n_2 \times n_4 \times n_3}$, we have

$$
\mathcal{C} = \mathcal{A} * \mathcal{B} \Leftrightarrow \overline{\mathbf{C}} = \overline{\mathbf{A}} \cdot \overline{\mathbf{B}}. \tag{2.15}
$$

The t-prod between two tensors is equivalent to the matrix multiplication in the Fourier-transformed domain.

Definition 2.3 (Tensor conjugate transpose [19]). The conjugate transpose of a tensor $\mathcal{X} \in \mathbb{R}^{n_2 \times n_1 \times n_3}$ is a tensor $\mathcal{X}^H \in \mathbb{R}^{n_1 \times n_2 \times n_3}$ obtained by the conjugate transpose of each of the frontal slices and then reversing the order of the transposed frontal slices 2 through n_3:

$$\left(\mathcal{X}^H\right)^{(1)} = \left(\mathcal{X}^{(1)}\right)^H \quad \text{and}$$
$$\left(\mathcal{X}^H\right)^{(i)} = \left(\mathcal{X}^{(n_3+2-i)}\right)^H, \quad i = 2, \cdots, n_3. \tag{2.16}$$

More intuitively, in the Fourier-transformed domain, it satisfies

$$\left(\widehat{\mathcal{X}^H}\right)^{(i)} = \left(\widehat{\mathcal{X}}^{(i)}\right)^H. \tag{2.17}$$

Definition 2.4 (Identity tensor [19]). The identity tensor $\mathcal{I} \in \mathbb{R}^{n_1 \times n_1 \times n_3}$ is defined as a tensor whose first frontal slice is the $n_1 \times n_1$ identity matrix, and the other frontal slices are zero matrices.

Definition 2.5 (F-diagonal tensor [19]). We call a tensor $\mathcal{A} \in \mathbb{R}^{n_1 \times n_1 \times n_3}$ f-diagonal if all of its frontal slices are diagonal matrices.

Definition 2.6 (Orthogonal tensor [19]). A tensor $\mathcal{Q} \in \mathbb{R}^{n_1 \times n_1 \times n_3}$ is an orthogonal tensor if

$$\mathcal{Q}^H * \mathcal{Q} = \mathcal{Q} * \mathcal{Q}^H = \mathcal{I}. \tag{2.18}$$

Definitions 2.3–2.6 are analogous to the basic ingredients in matrix format to formulate the matrix SVD. Equipped with the these basic definitions, the t-SVD is suggested.

Theorem 2.1 (T-SVD [19,24]). *Let $\mathcal{X} \in \mathbb{R}^{n_1 \times n_2 \times n_3}$ be a third-order tensor. Then it can be decomposed as*

$$\mathcal{X} = \mathcal{U} * \mathcal{S} * \mathcal{V}^H, \tag{2.19}$$

where $\mathcal{U} \in \mathbb{R}^{n_1 \times n_1 \times n_3}$ and $\mathcal{V} \in \mathbb{R}^{n_2 \times n_2 \times n_3}$ are the orthogonal tensors and $\mathcal{S} \in \mathbb{R}^{n_1 \times n_2 \times n_3}$ is an f-diagonal tensor.

Please see the proof of Theorem 2.1 in [24]. The t-SVD of $\mathcal{X} \in \mathbb{R}^{n_1 \times n_2 \times n_3}$ can be efficiently obtained by computing a series of matrix SVDs on the frontal slices of $\widehat{\mathcal{X}}$ in the Fourier domain. Nonetheless, because the SVD is not unique, it is suggested to adopt the algorithm in Table 2.1 that can ensure that $\mathcal{U}$, $\mathcal{X}$, and $\mathcal{V}$ are real tensors [24].

Thus, the framework of t-SVD has been established. It originates from [18] and has been updated in [24], extending many familiar tools of linear algebra to third-order tensors. In particular, the t-prod, which is closed on the set of third-order tensors, allows tensor factorizations that are analogs of matrix factorizations such

Table 2.1 The algorithm for computing t-SVD.

Input: $\mathcal{X} \in \mathbb{R}^{n_1 \times n_2 \times n_3}$.
1. $\widehat{\mathcal{X}} \leftarrow \text{fft}(\mathcal{X}, [], 3)$.
2. $[\mathbf{U}, \mathbf{S}, \mathbf{V}] = \text{svd}(\widehat{\mathcal{X}}^{(1)})$.
3. $\widehat{\mathcal{U}}^{(1)} \leftarrow U, \widehat{\mathcal{S}}^{(1)} \leftarrow S, \widehat{\mathcal{V}}^{(1)} \leftarrow V$.
4. **for** $i = 2$ to $\lceil \frac{n_3+1}{2} \rceil$ **do**
5. $[\mathbf{U}, \mathbf{S}, \mathbf{V}] = \text{svd}(\widehat{\mathcal{X}}^{(i)})$.
6. $\widehat{\mathcal{U}}^{(i)} \leftarrow \mathbf{U}, \widehat{\mathcal{S}} \leftarrow \mathbf{S}, \widehat{\mathcal{V}}^{(i)} \leftarrow \mathbf{V}$
7. $\widehat{\mathcal{U}}^{(n_3-i+2)} \leftarrow \mathbf{U}^{\mathrm{H}}, \widehat{\mathcal{S}}^{(n_3-i+2)} \leftarrow \mathbf{S}^{\mathrm{H}}, \widehat{\mathcal{V}}^{(n_3-i+2)} \leftarrow \mathbf{V}^{\mathrm{H}}$
8. **end for**
9. $\mathcal{U} \leftarrow \text{ifft}(\widehat{\mathcal{U}}, [], 3), \mathcal{S} \leftarrow \text{ifft}(\widehat{\mathcal{S}}, [], 3), \mathcal{V} \leftarrow \text{ifft}(\widehat{\mathcal{V}}, [], 3)$.
Output: $\mathcal{U}$, $\mathcal{S}$, and $\mathcal{V}$.

as SVD. Meanwhile, it also allows novel extensions of familiar matrix analysis to the multilinear setting while avoiding the loss of information inherent in *matricization* or *flattening* of the tensor [19].

2.2.3 Tensor nuclear norm and tensor recovery

Based on t-SVD, we can deduce the corresponding definitions of tensor multirank, tubal-rank, and average-rank.

Definition 2.7 (Tensor tubal-rank [19], multirank [21], and average-rank [24]). Let $\mathcal{X} \in \mathbb{R}^{n_1 \times n_2 \times n_3}$ be a third-order tensor. The tensor multirank, denoted as $\text{rank}_{\mathrm{m}}(\mathcal{X}) \in \mathbb{R}^{n_3}$, is a vector whose i-th element is the rank of the i-th frontal slice of $\widehat{\mathcal{X}}$, where $\widehat{\mathcal{X}} = \text{fft}(\mathcal{X}, [], 3)$. We can write

$$\text{rank}_{\mathrm{m}}(\mathcal{X}) = \left[\text{rank}(\widehat{\mathcal{X}}^{(1)}), \text{rank}(\widehat{\mathcal{X}}^{(2)}), \cdots, \text{rank}(\widehat{\mathcal{X}}^{(n_3)}) \right]. \tag{2.20}$$

The tensor tubal-rank of $\mathcal{X}$, denoted as $\text{rank}_{\mathrm{t}}(\mathcal{X})$, is defined as the number of nonzero tubes of $\mathcal{S}$, where $\mathcal{X} = \mathcal{U} * \mathcal{S} * \mathcal{V}^{\mathrm{H}}$. Specifically, we have

$$\text{rank}_{\mathrm{t}}(\mathcal{X}) = \#\{i, \mathcal{S}(i, i, :) \neq 0\}. \tag{2.21}$$

The tensor average-rank[4] of $\mathcal{X}$, denoted as $\text{rank}_{\mathrm{a}}(\mathcal{X})$, is defined as

$$\text{rank}_{\mathrm{a}}(\mathcal{X}) = \frac{1}{n_3} \sum_{k=1}^{n_3} \text{rank}(\widehat{\mathcal{X}}^{(i)}). \tag{2.22}$$

---

[4] In [24], the tensor average-rank is defined in the original domain.

According to the definitions of the three tensor ranks, given a third-order tensor $\mathcal{X}$, its three tensor ranks are related by [24]

$$\text{rank}_a(\mathcal{X}) \leq \max(\text{rank}_m(\mathcal{X})) = \text{rank}_t(\mathcal{X}). \tag{2.23}$$

Analogous to the matrix case, optimization problems related to the tensor ranks defined in Definition 2.7 are difficult and adequate convex relaxations are required for practical applications. Next, we give the definition of the TNN.

Definition 2.8 (Tensor nuclear norm [20]). The TNN of a tensor $\mathcal{X} \in \mathbb{R}^{n_1 \times n_2 \times n_3}$, denoted as $\|\mathcal{X}\|_{\text{TNN}}$, is defined as the sum of singular values of all of the frontal slices of $\widehat{\mathcal{X}}$, i.e.,

$$\|\mathcal{X}\|_{\text{TNN}} := \sum_{i=1}^{n_3} \|\widehat{\mathcal{X}}^{(i)}\|_*, \tag{2.24}$$

where $\widehat{\mathcal{X}}^{(i)}$ is the i-th frontal slice of $\widehat{\mathcal{X}}$ and $\widehat{\mathcal{X}} = \text{fft}(\mathcal{X}, [], 3)$.

We find that the TNN[5] of a third-order tensor $\mathcal{X}$ is defined in the Fourier domain and is equivalent to $\|\overline{\mathbf{X}}\|_*$ where $\overline{\mathbf{X}} = \text{blockdiag}(\widehat{\mathcal{X}})$. Thus, it can be proved that TNN is the tightest convex relaxation to the ℓ_1-norm of the tensor multirank [21], which is indeed the rank of the block-diagonal matrix obtained from the Fourier-transformed tensor.

Before proceeding to solve the multidimensional image recovery model using TNN, one key issue is to compute the proximal operator of TNN, i.e.,

$$\mathcal{X}^* = \arg \min_{\mathcal{X} \in \mathbb{R}^{n_1 \times n_2 \times n_3}} \tau \|\mathcal{X}\|_{\text{TNN}} + \frac{1}{2} \|\mathcal{X} - \mathcal{Y}\|_F^2. \tag{2.25}$$

Recalling that $\|\mathcal{X}\|_F = \frac{1}{\sqrt{n_3}} \|\widehat{\mathcal{X}}\|_F$, the optimization problem in (2.25) can be decoupled into n_3 matrix nuclear norm minimization problems in the Fourier-transformed domain as

$$\widehat{\mathcal{X}}^{*(i)} = \arg \min_{\mathbf{X}} \tau \|\mathbf{X}\|_* + \frac{1}{2n_3} \|\mathbf{X} - \widehat{\mathcal{Y}}^{(i)}\|_F^2, \tag{2.26}$$

for $i = 1, 2, \cdots, n_3$. For each i, the solution can be obtained by using the singular value thresholding (SVT) [25]. Let $\mathcal{X} = \mathcal{U} * \mathcal{S} * \mathcal{V}^{\text{H}}$ be the t-SVD of $\mathcal{X}$. We can define a tensor singular value thresholding (t-SVT) operator as

$$\mathcal{D}_\tau(\mathcal{X}) = \mathcal{U} * \mathcal{S}_\tau * \mathcal{V}^{\text{H}}, \tag{2.27}$$

where $\mathcal{S}_\tau$ can be computed by

$$\left(\mathcal{S} \times_3 \mathbf{F}_{n_3} - n_3 \tau\right)_+ \times_3 \mathbf{F}_{n_3}^{-1} \tag{2.28}$$

---

[5] In [24], the TNN is defined in the original domain instead of the Fourier domain, while it is numerically equal to $\frac{1}{n_3} \sum_{i=1}^{n_3} \|\widehat{\mathcal{X}}^{(i)}\|_*$ and is a tight convex envelope of the tensor average-rank.

or

$$\mathtt{ifft}\left(\left(\mathtt{fft}(\mathcal{S}, [], 3) - n_3\tau\right)_+, [], 3\right), \tag{2.29}$$

where $(\cdot)_+$ indicates retaining the nonnegative part and setting the negative values to 0, and n_3 is the length of the third dimension. Then, the solution of (2.25) is $\mathcal{D}_\tau(\mathcal{Y})$.

Once the TNN is established, we provide a general iterative solving scheme based on the alternating direction method of multipliers (ADMM) [26] to optimize the TNN-based multidimensional image recovery model in (2.4). First, after introducing an auxiliary variable $\mathcal{Y} \in \mathbb{R}^{n_1 \times n_2 \times n_3}$, we rewrite (2.4) as

$$\min_{\mathcal{X}, \mathcal{Y}} \{f(\mathcal{A}(\mathcal{X}) - \mathcal{O}) + \lambda\|\mathcal{Y}\|_{\mathrm{TNN}}\}, \quad \text{s.t. } \mathcal{Y} - \mathcal{X} = 0. \tag{2.30}$$

Then, the argument Lagrangian function of (2.30) is given by

$$L_\beta(\mathcal{X}, \mathcal{Y}, \mathcal{M}) = f(\mathcal{A}(\mathcal{X}) - \mathcal{O}) + \|\mathcal{Y}\|_{\mathrm{TNN}} + \langle \mathcal{Y} - \mathcal{X}, \mathcal{M} \rangle + \frac{\beta}{2}\|\mathcal{Y} - \mathcal{X}\|_F^2, \tag{2.31}$$

where $\mathcal{M} \in \mathbb{R}^{n_1 \times n_2 \times n_3}$ is the Lagrangian multiplier and β is a nonnegative parameter.

Next, at the k-th iteration, the ADMM updates each variable and the multiplier according to

$$\begin{cases} \mathcal{Y}^{k+1} = \arg\min_{\mathcal{Y}} \|\mathcal{Y}\|_{\mathrm{TNN}} + \frac{\beta}{2}\|\mathcal{Y} - \mathcal{X}^k + \frac{\mathcal{M}^k}{\beta}\|_F^2 \\ \qquad\;\; = \mathcal{D}_{\frac{1}{\beta}}\left(\mathcal{X}^k - \frac{\mathcal{M}^k}{\beta}\right), \\ \mathcal{X}^{k+1} = \arg\min_{\mathcal{X}} f(\mathcal{A}(\mathcal{X}) - \mathcal{O}) + \frac{\beta}{2}\|\mathcal{Y}^{k+1} - \mathcal{X} + \frac{\mathcal{M}^k}{\beta}\|_F^2, \\ \mathcal{M}^{k+1} = \mathcal{M} + \beta(\mathcal{Y} - \mathcal{X}). \end{cases} \tag{2.32}$$

Commonly, the Frobenius norm is used to construct the data fidelity term, i.e., $f(\mathcal{A}(\mathcal{X}) - \mathcal{O}) = \frac{1}{2}\|\mathcal{A}(\mathcal{X}) - \mathcal{O}\|_F^2$. Thus, the updating of $\mathcal{X}^{k+1}$ is described by

$$\mathcal{X}^{k+1} = \left(\mathcal{A}^*\mathcal{A} + \beta\mathcal{I}\right)^{-1}\left(\mathcal{A}^*(\mathcal{O}) + \beta\mathcal{Y}^{k+1} + \mathcal{M}^k\right), \tag{2.33}$$

where $\mathcal{A}^*$ is the adjoint of $\mathcal{A}$ and $\mathcal{I}$ is the identical mapping.

Practically, this TNN minimization model outperforms the matrix-based method on the completion of videos [21] and denoising of HSIs [27]. Specifically, when the underlying low-tubal rank tensor satisfies the tensor incoherent condition (Eq. (25) in [22]), it can be exactly recovered by minimizing the TNN with high probability as long as the number of samples is of a certain order with respect to both the tensor size and tubal rank [22]. Additionally, Lu et al. [24] established the theoretical guarantee for the exact recovery of the tensor robust component analysis problem via minimizing the TNN. Zhang et al. [28] proposed a modified tensor principal component pursuit incorporating the prior subspace information to recover the low tubal rank and the sparse components under a significantly weaker incoherence assumption. Furthermore, the t-SVD framework together with the TNN have been investigated for many other applications on multidimensional images, such as tensor recovery from binary measurements [29], robust tensor completion [30], hyperspectral image fusion [31], and subspace clustering [32,33].

2.2.4 Extensions

In this section, we will introduce some recent advances based on the t-SVD framework.

2.2.4.1 Nonconvex surrogates

For the matrix case, it has been discussed that the minimization of the matrix nuclear norm with the SVT operator will cause unavoidable biases in some situations. For example, it will cause rank deficiency, namely, the estimated results will be of lower rank than the original ground truth data. Meanwhile, the variance of the estimated data corresponding to the magnitude of singular values will also be smaller than that of the original data. The main origin of these effects is that the nuclear norm is a relaxation of the matrix rank, and all of the singular values are decreased equally when minimizing the nuclear norm with the SVT operator. To avoid this issue, many low-rank matrix recovery methods tailor weighted forms of the matrix nuclear norm or other nonconvex surrogates for the rank function. Below, we will give a brief review of similar advances under the t-SVD framework.

Let us first examine two typical examples. In [34], Oh et al. proposed to minimize the partial sum of singular values (PSSV). For a matrix $\mathbf{X} \in \mathbb{R}^{n_1 \times n_2}$, its PSSV is defined as

$$\|\mathbf{X}\|_{p=N} \triangleq \sum_{i=N+1}^{\min(n_1,n_2)} \sigma_i(\mathbf{X}), \tag{2.34}$$

where $\sigma_i(\mathbf{X})$ denotes the i-th largest singular value of $\mathbf{X}$ for $i = 1, \ldots, \min(m, n)$. Meanwhile, Hu et al. [35] proposed the truncated nuclear norm of a matrix that is given by the matrix nuclear norm subtracted from the sum of the largest few singular values. Given a matrix $\mathbf{X} \in \mathbb{R}^{n_1 \times n_2}$, the truncated nuclear norm has an definition equivalent to that of PSSV, while the authors minimized

$$\|\mathbf{X}\|_* - \mathrm{Tr}(\mathbf{A}_l \mathbf{X} \mathbf{B}_l^\mathsf{T}), \tag{2.35}$$

where $\mathrm{Tr}(\cdot)$ is the trace and the rows of $\mathbf{A}_l \in \mathbb{R}^{r \times n_1}$ and $\mathbf{B}_l \in \mathbb{R}^{r \times n_2}$ are taken from the singular vectors corresponding to the first r largest singular values of $\mathbf{X}$ at the l-th iteration. There are two obvious advantages of these two strategies in [34,35]: (i) rank deficiency is avoided by keeping the first N singular values; and (ii) the variance of the data is well preserved because large singular values are well retained.

In [36,37], Jiang et al. generalized the PSSV to the partial sum of TNN (PSTNN) for third-order tensors while Xue et al. generalized the truncated nuclear norm to the truncated TNN. For a third-order tensor $\mathcal{X} \in \mathbb{R}^{n_1 \times n_2 \times n_3}$, its PSTNN is given by

$$\|\mathcal{X}\|_{\text{PSTNN}} \triangleq \sum_{i=1}^{n_3} \|\widehat{\mathcal{X}}^{(i)}\|_{p=N}. \tag{2.36}$$

Meanwhile, the truncated TNN of $\mathcal{X} \in \mathbb{R}^{n_1 \times n_2 \times n_3}$ is defined as

$$\|\mathcal{X}\|_{\text{TNN}} - \text{Tr}(\mathcal{A}_l * \mathcal{X} * \mathcal{B}_l^{\text{T}}), \tag{2.37}$$

where $\mathcal{A}_l \in \mathbb{R}^{r \times n_1 \times n_3}$ and $\mathcal{B}_l \in \mathbb{R}^{r \times n_2 \times n_3}$ come from the t-SVD of $\mathcal{X}$ at the l-th iteration. In [38], Zhang et al. proposed the corrected TNN based on a similar idea. The experimental results of [36–38] show that these generalizations are superior to the TNN for color image and video recovery.

More generally, for a matrix $\mathbf{X} \in \mathbb{R}^{n_1 \times n_2}$, its weighted nuclear norm (WNN) [39] can be defined as

$$\|\mathbf{X}\|_{w,*} = \sum_i w_i \sigma_i(\mathbf{X}), \tag{2.38}$$

where $w_i \geq 0$ ($i = 1, 2, \cdots, \min(n_1, n_2)$) is a nonnegative weight. Then, the PSSV and the truncated nuclear norm fall into a special case of WNN with setting $w_i = 0$ for $i \leq r$ and $w_i = 1$ for $i > r$. In [39], the authors suggested an effective and efficient reweighting strategy by setting $w_i = \frac{c}{\sigma_i(\mathbf{X}_l) + \epsilon}$ at the $(l+1)$-th iteration, where c is the nonnegative regularization parameter and ϵ is a small positive number and is used to avoid division by zero. Huang et al. [40] and Liu et al. [41] extended the WNN to the third-order tensor case and proposed the weighted TNN. In their approaches, each singular value of $\widehat{\mathcal{X}}^{(i)}$ ($i = 1, 2, \cdots, n_3$) is assigned a weight.

Many other nonconvex surrogates of the rank function (or the ℓ_0) have been considered for the horizontal slices of $\widehat{\mathcal{X}}$ (or the singular values of $\widehat{\mathcal{X}}$). Thus, these nonconvex surrogates are extended for third-order tensors under the t-SVD framework [42]. Next, some popular surrogates are listed. The nonconvex logdet function for a matrix in [43] has been applied for blockdiag($\widehat{\mathcal{X}}$) by Ji et al. [44]. The logarithmic function [45] and the Laplace function [46] have been introduced to the singular values of blockdiag($\widehat{\mathcal{X}}$) in [47] and [48], respectively. Additionally, the ℓ_p-norm ($0 < p < 1$) of the matrix's singular values, i.e., the Schatten-p norm,[6] has been extended for third-order tensors in [49]. Moreover, Gao et al. [50] extended the weighted form of the Schatten-p norm [51] for third-order tensors. Wang et al. [52] utilized the prior knowledge about the frequency spectrum in the t-SVD framework and assigned different weights on the matrix nuclear norm of different frontal slices. Apart from the nonconvex surrogates of the rank function, low-rank matrix factorization techniques are also extended to low-tubal rank tensor factorization [53–55] in which the computational burden due to SVD computation is reduced.

---

[6] It is a quasinorm when $0 < p < 1$.

Other approaches tailoring the special structure of tensor singular values are reported in [56,57].

2.2.4.2 Additional prior knowledge

Enhancing the low-rankness of the underlying tensor by minimizing the convex TNN or the above nonconvex surrogates has been demonstrated to be effective for multidimensional image recovery. However, this approach may fail in two cases. First, many real-world multidimensional images consist of abundant fine details and are not strictly of low tubal rank. Second, when the sampled elements are extremely limited or structured, the rank of the observation will be low. Actually, being low-rank and sufficient samples are the basic assumptions in the theoretical guarantee for exact recovery when optimizing (2.4). When minimizing the nonconvex surrogates, those criteria may be relaxed but still hold. Thus, these two challenges are unavoidable in practical scenarios.

To address these issues, we can introduce additional prior knowledge for multidimensional image recovery. Multidimensional images can be viewed as a set of 2D natural images, such as a video consisting of a series of frames. Thus, the widely used piece-wise smoothness can be utilized via adding the total variation (TV) or framelet regularizer [58,59]. Moreover, the well-known nonlocal self-similarity has also been employed [60,61]. The TV regularizer was incorporated into the TNN-based multidimensional image recovery models by exploiting the local smoothness [62,63]. Recently, Zhao et al. [64] introduced an implicit regularizer and adopted a denoising deep convolution neural network (CNN) as the solution mapping of its corresponding subproblem under the plug-and-play framework. Since the deep learning-based methods can learn data-driven priors from a large number of natural images [65–67], the performance of the method in [64] is promising.

2.2.4.3 Multiple directions and higher-order tensors

Although the t-SVD framework has achieved great success, it is limited in that it treats the dimensions of third-order tensors differently. As discussed in [68], when computing the t-prod, the selection of the dimension to apply FFT[7] will result in quite different performance. Another obvious limitation is that t-SVD is suitable only for third-order tensors. When the multidimensional image is of fourth order, such as color videos with two spatial dimensions, one temporal and one color dimension, or even higher order, the tensor is suggested to be reshaped into the third order to fit the framework of t-SVD.

An extension of this method is to simultaneously minimize the TNN of the tensors with three kinds of permutation of its dimensions [5,69], that is, to permute the original third-order tensor $\mathcal{X} \in \mathbb{R}^{n_1 \times n_2 \times n_3}$ with the scale of the third dimension as n_3, n_2, and n_1, respectively, and minimize the summation of their TNNs. After adopting

---

[7] One can twist or permute the dimensions of a third-order tensor. Thus, when computing t-prod, the Fourier transformation is conducted along the specified third mode.

this strategy, the performance is improved compared with minimizing the TNN. Additionally, it can be interpreted as (i) applying FFT along one specified dimension of a third-order tensor, (ii) obtaining a transformed tensor such as $\widehat{\mathcal{X}}$, and (iii) computing the nuclear norm of the slices supported by the remaining two dimensions.

Furthermore, for an N-th-order ($N \geq 3$) tensor $\mathcal{X} \in \mathbb{R}^{n_1 \times n_2 \times \cdots \times n_N}$, we can select two modes and reshape the data into a third-order tensor while concatenating the remaining $N-2$ dimensions. Then, we can compute its TNN and sum them for different selections of these two modes [70,71]. However, since it is necessary to compute C_N^2 (the number of 2-combinations from a given set of N elements) TNNs for an N-th-order tensor, this approach may be time consuming when the order is high. Meanwhile, one important advantage of t-SVD is that it treats the third-order tensor data integrally, avoiding the information loss inherent in matricization or flattening. Thus, generalization of the t-prod, which is fundamental in the t-SVD framework, for higher-order tensors as in [72,73] may be more attractive. Nevertheless, the corresponding definition of tensor rank or TNN is still under development.

2.2.5 Summary

The t-prod plays a fundamental role for the construction of the t-SVD framework. The novel notion of the tensor rank and TNN are subsequently deduced. The capability of TNN-based models has been demonstrated in the literature, for example in [20–22,24, 74]. Additionally, the extensions of the approach mentioned above can substantially enhance the performance in specific applications. Several numerical examples are given in Section 2.4.1. Nonetheless, in the next section, we delve into the t-SVD framework and explore another possible approach.

2.3 Transform-based t-SVD

In this section, we focus on the Fourier transform in the t-SVD. When computing the t-prod, the 1D DFT is applied on the mode-3 fibers to convert the circular convolution to element-wise multiplication. Thus, the tensor low-rankness within t-SVD can be viewed as the low-rankness in the transformed domain. For multidimensional images, the mode-3 fibers can be temporal vectors of a video or spectral vector of an HSI. From the signal processing perspective, the Fourier transform has certain limitations. Basically, in the implementation of the DFT or FFT within t-SVD, the padding boundary is periodic or circular by default. The circular boundary is undesirable for the temporal or spectral vectors in multidimensional images. Furthermore, the computation of DFT gives rise to complex values, leading to high computational complexity. Moreover, the Fourier transform leads to information loss that varies with time for the temporal vectors in videos or the spectral vectors of HSIs. Therefore, it is natural to find some substitutes that are more suitable for multidimensional images. Thus, below, we start with replacing the DFT by linear invertible transforms and end with a discussion of the possible noninvertible cases. With many basic ingredients given above, this section will be much briefer.

2.3.1 Linear invertible transform-based t-SVD

In [75], Madathil and George employed the discrete cosine transform (DCT) within the t-SVD framework for video completion and denoising. Xu et al. [76] and Lu et al. [77] also adopted the DCT as a substitution of DFT for tensor completion. DCT shows two obvious advantages over DFT under the t-SVD framework. First, the computation of DCT does not involve complex numbers, reducing the computational cost. Second, in the implementation of the DCT, the boundary condition along the tubes is reflexive. The experimental results of [76] illustrate that the quality of the frames (or bands) at the beginning and the end is strongly improved when minimizing the DCT-induced TNN. The frames (or bands) at the beginning and the end correspond to the head and the tail of the tubes, respectively. This shows that the reflexive boundary generated by DCT is more reasonable than the circular boundary required by DFT for videos or MSIs.

The origin of the use of DCT instead of DFT within the t-SVD framework can be traced back to [78], in which Kernfeld et al. noted that the t-prod, together with the tensor decomposition scheme, can be defined via the DCT along the third mode or even with any invertible linear transform. As mentioned in (2.15), the t-prod between two tensors $\mathcal{A} \in \mathbb{R}^{n_1 \times n_2 \times n_3}$ and $\mathcal{B} \in \mathbb{R}^{n_2 \times n_4 \times n_3}$ is equivalent to

$$\texttt{blockdiag}(\widehat{\mathcal{A}}) \cdot \texttt{blockdiag}(\widehat{\mathcal{B}}), \tag{2.39}$$

where $\widehat{\mathcal{A}} = \mathcal{A} \times_3 \mathbf{F}_{n_3}$ is the transformed tensor and is equivalent to $\widehat{\mathcal{B}}$. Otherwise, for simplicity, given two tensors $\mathcal{A} \in \mathbb{R}^{n_1 \times n_2 \times n_3}$ and $\mathcal{B} \in \mathbb{R}^{n_2 \times n_4 \times n_3}$, we denote

$$\mathcal{A} \bigcirc \mathcal{B} \tag{2.40}$$

as the frontal-slice-wise product,[8] implying that

$$(\mathcal{A} \bigcirc \mathcal{B})^{(i)} = \mathcal{A}^{(i)} \cdot \mathcal{B}^{(i)} \text{ for } i = 1, 2, \cdots, n_3. \tag{2.41}$$

Therefore, we can define the t-prod with a given linear invertible transform via replacing the DFT matrix $\mathbf{F}_{n_3}$ by a selected linear invertible transform matrix. We denote the linear invertible transform matrix as $\mathbf{L} \in \mathbb{C}^{n_3 \times n_3}$, and it satisfies

$$\mathbf{L}^{-1} \cdot \mathbf{L} = \mathbf{L} \cdot \mathbf{L}^{-1} = \mathbf{I}_{n_3}, \tag{2.42}$$

where $\mathbf{L}^{-1}$ is the inverse transform matrix of $\mathbf{L}$ and $\mathbf{I}_{n_3} \in \mathbb{R}^{n_3 \times n_3}$ is the identity matrix. Then, the linear invertible transform-based t-prod can be defined.

Definition 2.9 (Transform-based t-prod [78]). Let $\mathbf{L} \in \mathbb{C}^{n_3 \times n_3}$ be a linear invertible transform matrix. The linear invertible transform-based t-prod between two tensors $\mathcal{A} \in \mathbb{R}^{n_1 \times n_2 \times n_3}$ and $\mathcal{B} \in \mathbb{R}^{n_2 \times n_4 \times n_3}$ is defined as

$$\mathcal{C} \in \mathbb{R}^{n_1 \times n_4 \times n_3} = \mathcal{A} *_{\mathbf{L}} \mathcal{B} = ((\mathcal{A} \times_3 \mathbf{L}) \bigcirc (\mathcal{B} \times_3 \mathbf{L})) \times_3 \mathbf{L}^{-1}. \tag{2.43}$$

---

[8] In Definition 2.1 of [78], it is also called face-wise product.

Table 2.2 The algorithm for computing transform-based t-SVD.

Input: $\mathcal{X} \in \mathbb{R}^{n_1 \times n_2 \times n_3}$ and $\mathbf{L} \in \mathbb{C}^{n_3 \times n_3}$.

1. $\widehat{\mathcal{X}} \leftarrow \mathcal{X} \times_3 \mathbf{L}$.
4. **for** $i = 1$ to n_3 **do**
5. $\quad [U, S, V] = \mathrm{svd}(\widehat{\mathcal{X}}^{(i)})$.
6. $\quad \widehat{\mathcal{U}}^{(i)} \leftarrow U, \widehat{\mathcal{S}} \leftarrow S, \widehat{\mathcal{V}}^{(i)} \leftarrow V$
8. **end for**
9. $\mathcal{U} \leftarrow \widehat{\mathcal{U}} \times_3 \mathbf{L}^{-1}, \mathcal{S} \leftarrow \widehat{\mathcal{S}} \times_3 \mathbf{L}^{-1}, \mathcal{V} \leftarrow \widehat{\mathcal{V}} \times_3 \mathbf{L}^{-1}$.

Output: $\mathcal{U}, \mathcal{S}$, and $\mathcal{V}$.

The corresponding definitions, such as tensor transpose, identity tensor, and orthogonal tensor, with the linear invertible transform $\mathbf{L}$-induced t-prod, can be defined in the same manner as Definitions 2.3–2.6. To save space, we omit their specific definitions here and note that the definition of the f-diagonal tensor is still the same as Definition 2.5 since it is defined in the original domain rather than in the transform domain. Moreover, we note that the tensor transpose should satisfy (2.17) when it is defined. Interested readers are suggested to refer to [78] for details. After obtaining the transform-based t-prod, we can obtain the transform-based t-SVD.

Theorem 2.2 (Transform-based t-SVD [78]). *Let* $\mathbf{L} \in \mathbb{C}^{n_3 \times n_3}$ *be a linear invertible transform matrix. For a third-order tensor* $\mathcal{X} \in \mathbb{R}^{n_1 \times n_2 \times n_3}$, *it can be decomposed as*

$$\mathcal{X} = \mathcal{U} *_{\mathbf{L}} \mathcal{S} *_{\mathbf{L}} \mathcal{V}^{\mathrm{H}}, \tag{2.44}$$

where $\mathcal{U} \in \mathbb{R}^{n_1 \times n_1 \times n_3}$ *and* $\mathcal{V} \in \mathbb{R}^{n_2 \times n_2 \times n_3}$ *are the orthogonal tensors defined by using the transform-based t-prod and* $\mathcal{S} \in \mathbb{R}^{n_1 \times n_2 \times n_3}$ *is an f-diagonal tensor whose frontal slices are diagonal matrices.*

The linear invertible transform $\mathbf{L}$-induced t-SVD of $\mathcal{X} \in \mathbb{R}^{n_1 \times n_2 \times n_3}$ can be efficiently obtained by computing a series of matrix SVDs on the frontal slices of $\mathcal{X} \times_3 \mathbf{L}$ in the transform domain, as shown in Table 2.2. Consistent with the t-SVD framework based on DFT, we can define the tensor tubal rank, multirank, and average rank based on the transform-based t-SVD. Since this chapter focuses on the practical usage of the low-rank regularization for multidimensional image recovery, we omit the specific tensor rank definitions that resemble Definition 2.7, and we turn directly to the convex surrogate. We can obtain the linear invertible transform-induced TNN under the transform-based t-SVD.

Definition 2.10 (Transform-based TNN). Let $\mathbf{L} \in \mathbb{C}^{n_3 \times n_3}$ be a linear invertible transform matrix. The linear invertible transform-based TNN of a tensor $\mathcal{X} \in \mathbb{R}^{n_1 \times n_2 \times n_3}$ is defined as

$$\|\mathcal{X}\|_{\mathbf{L}-\mathrm{TNN}} := \sum_{i=1}^{n_3} \left\| (\mathcal{X} \times_3 \mathbf{L})^{(i)} \right\|_*. \tag{2.45}$$

After obtaining the transform-based TNN, we can replace the TNN term in (2.4) with any given transform $\mathbf{L}$ for solving the multidimensional image recovery problem. This is also a convex problem and can be optimized via ADMM iterations shown in (2.32). For brevity, we do not go deep into the details.

In [79], Song et al. considered the general unitary transformation. Let $\mathbf{U} \in \mathbb{C}^{n_3 \times n_3}$ be the unitary transform matrix with

$$\mathbf{U}^H \mathbf{U} = \mathbf{U}\mathbf{U}^H = \mathbf{I}_{n_3}. \tag{2.46}$$

Based on the unitary transform, they proposed the transformed TNN as shown in (2.45). Similar to the original t-SVD framework, the transformed TNN is the convex envelope of the sum of the rank of $(\mathcal{X} \times \mathbf{U})$'s frontal slices. They also provide the theoretical guarantee of the exact recovery from incomplete and sparsely corrupted observations. Further, Zhang et al. employed the unitary-transformed TNN for tensor completion with Poisson observations [80]. The original t-SVD framework is a special case of the work by Song et al. [79] if setting the transformed matrix as $\frac{1}{\sqrt{n_3}}\mathbf{F}_{n_3}$.

Additionally, Lu et al. [77] considered the general linear invertible transformation $\mathbf{L} \in \mathbb{R}^{n_1 \times n_2 \times n_3}$ that satisfies

$$\mathbf{L}^T \mathbf{L} = \mathbf{L}\mathbf{L}^T = l\mathbf{I}_{n_3}, \tag{2.47}$$

where $\cdot^T$ denotes the matrix transpose and $l > 0$ is a constant. Based on this linear invertible transform, they deduced the new tensor tubal rank, tensor spectral norm, and TNN.[9] Under certain tensor incoherent conditions, one can exactly recover the underlying data from incomplete observations [77].

2.3.2 Beyond invertibility and data adaptivity

According to the theoretical results rigorously established in [77,79], the original t-SVD framework that is implemented with the DFT is a special case of the t-SVD framework based on the linear invertible transform. Thus, the extensions introduced in Section 2.2.3 can be directly generalized for the linear invertible transform-based t-SVD. For example, in [75], the authors proposed a 3D DCT-based TNN minimization model for multidimensional image denoising and completion. In [81], the transform-based t-prod between third-order tensors is generalized to N-th-order tensors ($N \geq 3$).

However, one key issue in the transform-based t-SVD framework, i.e., the design or choice of the transform is still challenging. Empirically, transformations that can make the original data lower-rank in the transformed domain are preferred. However, a linear invertible transform will not essentially change the tensor ranks defined in Definition 2.7. Therefore, we need to delve more deeply into the inner mechanism of minimizing transform-based TNN for multidimensional image recovery.

---

[9] In [77], the TNN based on linear transformation is similar to (2.45) but multiplied by a factor $\frac{1}{l}$.

In [79], Song et al. pointed out that with a suitable transformation that can redistribute tubal entries into the matrix slices (along the tube direction) of the tensors, low-rank transformed matrix slices can be generated. They illustrate the distribution of all the frontal slices' singular values from the transformed data under different transformations. More small singular values are generated after the wavelet transform than by the DFT. Thus, the wavelet-transformed (along the tubes) data are closer to lower-rank data.

Recently, Jiang et al. [82] adopted the tight wavelet frame (framelet) as the transformation. The framelet system used in [82] is generated from the B-spline and implemented in a multiresolution manner [83]. The transform matrix can be written as $\mathbf{W} \in \mathbb{R}^{wn_3 \times n_3}$, where $w \geq 1$ is an integer and $\mathbf{W}$ satisfies the unitary extension principle (UEP) [84], i.e.,

$$\mathbf{W}^{\mathrm{T}}\mathbf{W} = \mathbf{I}_{n_3}, \tag{2.48}$$

where $\mathbf{W}^{\mathrm{T}}$ is indeed the inverse transform matrix of $\mathbf{W}$. It is clear that $\mathbf{W}\mathbf{W}^{\mathrm{T}} \neq \mathbf{I}_{wn_3}$. This means that the framelet transform is semi-invertible. Nonetheless, Jiang et al. directly defined the framelet-based TNN (FTNN) as $\sum_{i=1}^{wn_3} \| (\mathcal{X} \times_3 \mathbf{W})^{(i)} \|_*$ and replaced the TNN term in (2.4) by the FTNN. Then, this model can be optimized via the ADMM. Their method can be understood as an iterative method with iterations consisting of: (i) performing the framelet transform; (ii) regularizing the nuclear norm of the transformed data's frontal slices; and (iii) carrying out the inverse framelet transform. Owing to the UEP, these iterations are not difficult.

In [82], the authors showed that the framelet transform along the third mode can generate more small singular values of the transformed data's frontal slices than DCT for different types of multidimensional imaging data. Consequently, their results are also better than those obtained by minimizing the DCT-deduced TNN or the original TNN obtained using DFT. Furthermore, they also computed the numerical rank of the transformed data's frontal slices. Given a tolerance for computing the numerical rank, the framelet-transformed data can be better approximated with lower rankness, generating better recovery results. Thus, we can deduce an empirical rule for choosing the transform. That is, the transform that can generate lower-rank frontal slices in the transformed domain for a specific type of data and for which the inverse transform is not difficult to obtain should be chosen.

In the above discussion, we only mentioned the predefined transform. If we intend to find the transform satisfying the empirical rule for different types of data, a more flexible approach is to use data adaptive transform. In addition to the wavelet transform, Song et al. [79] also adopted a data-dependent unitary transform. They first optimized (2.4) and set the obtained result as an initial guess $\mathcal{X}_0 \in \mathbb{R}^{n_1 \times n_2 \times n_3}$. Then, the first r left singular vectors of $\mathcal{X}_0$'s mode-3 unfolding matrix are extracted to constitute the transform matrix. The performance of this strategy is better than that obtained using the predefined wavelet transform.

Meanwhile, Kong et al. [85] constructed a principal component extraction matrix $\mathbf{Q}$ that maximizes the distribution variance of $\{\| (\mathcal{X} \times_3 \mathbf{Q})^{(i)} \|_F\}$. The matrix $\mathbf{Q}$ can be obtained from the left singular vectors of mode-3 unfolding of $\mathcal{X}$. Interestingly, the transform matrix $\mathbf{Q}$ in [85] will be updated in their algorithm during the iterative process. In their experiments, they also use an oracle $\mathbf{Q}$ that is computed from the complete data and its performance is surprisingly good. This confirms that a data-dependent transform is powerful and flexible.

In [86], Jiang et al. replaced the inverse transform, i.e., $\mathbf{F}_{n_3}^{-1}$, with a data adaptive term. Their model can be written as

$$\min_{\mathcal{Z},\mathbf{D}} \sum_{i=1}^{n_3} \|\mathcal{Z}^{(i)}\|_* \quad \text{s.t.} \ (\mathcal{Z} \times_3 \mathbf{D})_\Omega = \mathcal{O}_\Omega, \tag{2.49}$$

where $\mathbf{D} \in \mathbb{R}^{n_3 \times d}$ is a data adaptive dictionary, $d \gg n_3$ is a positive integer, and the ℓ_2-norm of $\mathbf{D}$'s columns should be less than or equal to 1. From their learned dictionaries, it can be found that the atoms will vary for different types of data and adaptively fit the variation of tubes.

2.4 Numerical experiments

In this part, we provide several numerical examples on different kinds of applications, including hyperspectral image denoising & completion, color image demosaicing, and (hyperspectral) video completion. The traditional t-SVD-based methods and their extensions are discussed in Section 2.4.1. Section 2.4.2 reports the results from the transform-based t-SVD methods.

2.4.1 Examples within the t-SVD framework

As mentioned above, we show three numerical experiments with approaches within the traditional t-SVD framework. One experiment is simulated on an HSI that is a subimage of the *Washington DC Mall* dataset.[10] This HSI is of the size $256 \times 256 \times 191$, so that it contains 256×256 spatial pixels and 191 spectral bands. The clean image is normalized with entries in each band in the interval [0, 1]. The noisy HSI is simulated by adding Gaussian noise with standard deviation of 0.15 and 20% of the entries are corrupted by the salt and pepper noise. The compared methods are a low-rank matrix-based HSI denoising method in [87], a TNN minimization model [88], and a 3D TNN-based model and its nonconvex version [5]. We show the recovered results in Fig. 2.1. It is observed that the results obtained by minimizing the 3D TNN and its nonconvex surrogate are visually better than the results obtained by minimizing TNN or by using the low-rank matrix-based method.

In the second experiment, a hyperspectral video (HSV)[11] of the size $120 \times 120 \times 33 \times 31$ is selected. Specifically, this hyperspectral video has 31 frames and each

---

[10] http://lesun.weebly.com/hyperspectral-data-set.html.
[11] http://openremotesensing.net/knowledgebase/hyperspectral-video/.

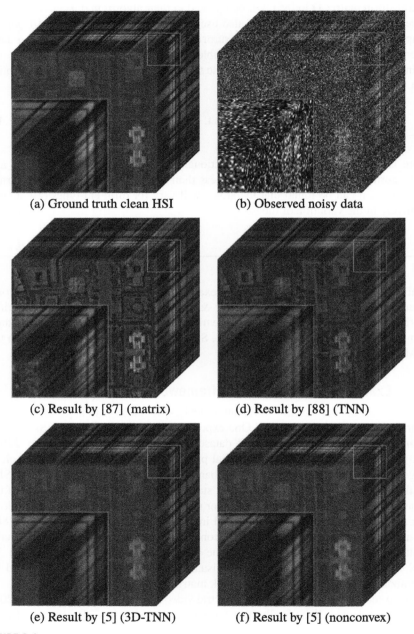

(a) Ground truth clean HSI   (b) Observed noisy data

(c) Result by [87] (matrix)   (d) Result by [88] (TNN)

(e) Result by [5] (3D-TNN)   (f) Result by [5] (nonconvex)

FIGURE 2.1

The recovered results on the noisy HSI.

frame has 33 bands from 400 nm to 720 nm wavelength with a 10-nm step [89]. In Fig. 2.3, we show two images located at different frames and different bands in the HSV recovered by the TNN minimization method [22] and the weighted sum of TNN (WSTNN) minimization method [70]. WSTNN is designed for the N-th-order ($N \geq 3$) tensor while we reshape the HSV to a third-order tensor of the size $120 \times 120 \times 1023$ by combining its spectral and temporal modes. We can observe that the WSTNN is evidently superior to the TNN, particularly in the recovery of texture information.

The third experiment is conducted on the color image named *"baboon"*.[12] This color image contains 512×512 spatial pixels and three color channels. For the color image, we consider the typical demosaicing problem that aims to estimate the color image from the Bayer pattern sampling. That is, each two-by-two cell contains two green, one blue, and one red cell. We first use the SNN minimization model [2] and the TNN minimization model [22]. Then, we employ a TV regularized TNN minimization method in [62] and a CNN denoiser regularized method [64], in which an implicit regularization term is also added to input the CNN denoisers expressing the deep prior learned from a large amount of training images. Fig. 2.2 shows the results obtained by the different methods. It is observed that the SNN and TNN minimization models almost failed for this structural sampling case. After adding additional regularizers, "TV+TNN" and "CNN+TNN" successfully recovered this color image.

The first example shows that the performance of TNN can be strongly improved by considering multiple directions and using the nonconvex surrogate. As shown in the second example, the strategy of considering multiple directions can be generalized well for higher-order tensors. It is found from the third example that the capability of TNN will be limited when the sampling is structured and the introduction of additional prior knowledge is useful.

2.4.2 Examples of the transform-based t-SVD

In this part, we test methods that are deduced from the transform-based t-SVD. We display two experimental results on the HSI data *"Pavia City Center"*[13] of the size $200 \times 200 \times 80$ (height $\times$ width $\times$ band) and the video *"foreman"*[14] of the size $144 \times 176 \times 50$, respectively. Since the aforementioned transform-based TNN methods mainly concentrate on the low-rank tensor completion problem, we conduct the completion experiment in this part. The sampling rate for the video is 50% while 5% pixels are sampled for the HSI. The involved methods are the original TNN minimization model using DFT and its variants using DCT, framelet, and the dictionary. For a quantitative comparison between different methods, we select two widely used image quality assessments, namely, the peak signal-to-noise ratio (PSNR) and the structural

---

[12] http://sipi.usc.edu/database/database.php.

[13] http://www.ehu.eus/ccwintco/index.php?title=Hyperspectral_Remote_Sensing_Scenes.

[14] http://trace.eas.asu.edu/yuv/.

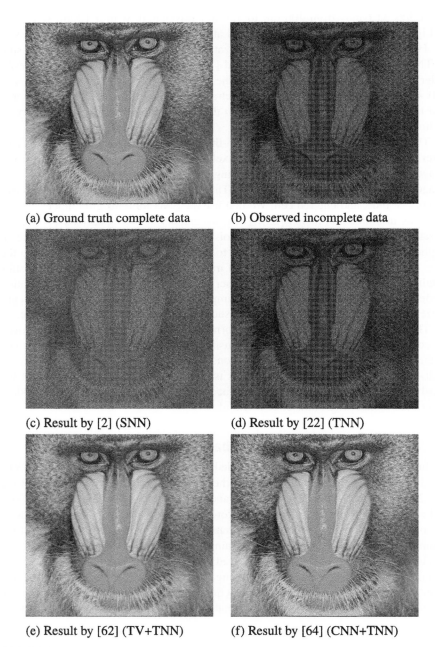

(a) Ground truth complete data   (b) Observed incomplete data

(c) Result by [2] (SNN)   (d) Result by [22] (TNN)

(e) Result by [62] (TV+TNN)   (f) Result by [64] (CNN+TNN)

FIGURE 2.2

The demosaicing results on the color image data "*baboon*".

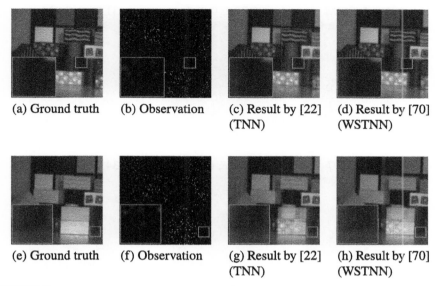

(a) Ground truth   (b) Observation   (c) Result by [22]   (d) Result by [70]
                                          (TNN)   (WSTNN)

(e) Ground truth   (f) Observation   (g) Result by [22]   (h) Result by [70]
                                          (TNN)   (WSTNN)

FIGURE 2.3

The completion results of the HSV with SR = 5%. (a)–(d) The image located at the 15th band and the 7th frame. (e)–(h) The image located at the 25th band and the 30th frame.

similarity index (SSIM) [90]. Higher values indicate better recovery quality. They are computed on each frontal slice and the mean value is adopted.

We display the visual results together with the PSNR and SSIM values in Figs. 2.4 and 2.5. It is observed that for the video data and the HSI data, DCT-based TNN outperforms the original TNN that uses DFT. The framelet-based TNN achieves the second-best performance. The data-dependent dictionary-based TNN obtains the best visual performance and the highest PSNR and SSIM values.

2.5 Conclusions and new guidelines

In this chapter, focusing on the multidimensional imaging data recovery problem, we revisit the establishment of the t-SVD framework and the TNN minimization model. Some extensions such as nonconvex surrogates and adding additional regularization terms are introduced. Furthermore, we delve more deeply into the t-SVD framework, and replace the DFT with the linear invertible transform. Then, we discuss the cases of noninvertible transforms and data adaptive transform. Overall, the prevailing trend of the development based on the t-SVD framework can be summarized as:

- from the *convex* model to the *nonconvex* model,
- from the *single* low-rankness to the *multiple* regularization terms,
- from the *predefined* transform to the *data adaptive* transform.

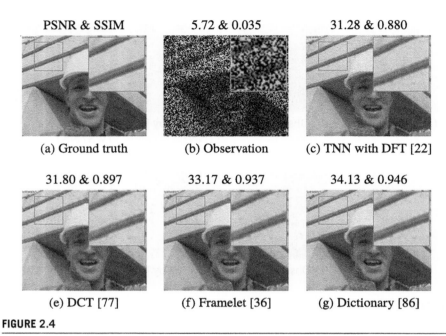

PSNR & SSIM	5.72 & 0.035	31.28 & 0.880
(a) Ground truth	(b) Observation	(c) TNN with DFT [22]
31.80 & 0.897	33.17 & 0.937	34.13 & 0.946
(e) DCT [77]	(f) Framelet [36]	(g) Dictionary [86]

FIGURE 2.4

The 22nd frame of the results on the video data *"foreman."*

Thus, in the future, for the recovery of multidimensional images, there are several possible directions and challenges. The *first* is to establish the theoretical guarantee of the exact recovery for low-rank tensors via minimizing the weighted form of the TNN. Extending the leverage score [91] from matrices to tensors may be a feasible approach for achieving this goal. Although in this chapter we focus on the practical use of the TNN (or the transform-based TNN) and its variants, only the theoretical guarantee will make those approaches really practical without additional concerns. The *second* direction lies in exploiting reasonable prior knowledge of the multidimensional images under the maximum a posteriori estimation framework. It is expected to analyze the distinct low-rank structures along different dimensions [92], or even some artificially defined dimensions, e.g., the nonlocal self-similarity dimension. Furthermore, data-driven priors can also be simultaneously considered. *Third*, as in [82,86], additional transforms or dictionaries can be considered to be embedded in the t-SVD framework for better representation of the data implicit low-rankness, such as the nonlinear transform and the convolutional dictionary. Moreover, the theoretical guarantee for noninvertible transform-based TNN minimization methods is still difficult and new techniques for their analysis are needed. *Last*, to face the challenges arising from massive data, acceleration techniques such as the randomized algorithm in [93–95] can be considered. Moreover, the combination of the above points is also promising. For example, in [4], the unitary transform-based TNN is adopted to characterize the similarity of nonlocal patches.

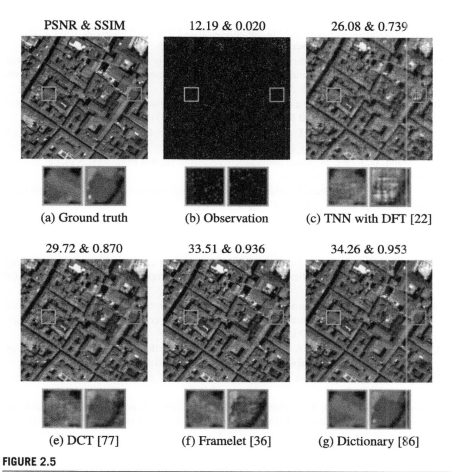

PSNR & SSIM   12.19 & 0.020   26.08 & 0.739

(a) Ground truth   (b) Observation   (c) TNN with DFT [22]

29.72 & 0.870   33.51 & 0.936   34.26 & 0.953

(e) DCT [77]   (f) Framelet [36]   (g) Dictionary [86]

FIGURE 2.5

The pseudo-color images (R-4 G-12 B-68) and the corresponding enlarged areas of the results obtained by different methods on the HSI data *"Pavia City Center."*

References

[1] E.J. Candès, B. Recht, Exact matrix completion via convex optimization, Foundations of Computational Mathematics 9 (6) (2009) 717.

[2] J. Liu, P. Musialski, P. Wonka, J. Ye, Tensor completion for estimating missing values in visual data, IEEE Transactions on Pattern Analysis and Machine Intelligence 35 (1) (2013) 208–220.

[3] E.J. Candes, Y. Plan, Matrix completion with noise, Proceedings of the IEEE 98 (6) (2010) 925–936.

[4] M.K. Ng, X. Zhang, X.-L. Zhao, Patched-tube unitary transform for robust tensor completion, Pattern Recognition 100 (2020) 107181.

[5] Y.-B. Zheng, T.-Z. Huang, X.-L. Zhao, T.-X. Jiang, T.-H. Ma, T.-Y. Ji, Mixed noise re-

moval in hyperspectral image via low-fibered-rank regularization, IEEE Transactions on Geoscience and Remote Sensing 58 (1) (2019) 734–749.

[6] G.T. Herman, A.R. De Pierro, N. Gai, On methods for maximum a posteriori image reconstruction with a normal prior, Journal of Visual Communication and Image Representation 3 (4) (1992) 316–324.

[7] J.M. Bioucas-Dias, J.M. Nascimento, Hyperspectral subspace identification, IEEE Transactions on Geoscience and Remote Sensing 46 (8) (2008) 2435–2445.

[8] T.G. Kolda, B.W. Bader, Tensor decompositions and applications, SIAM Review 51 (3) (2009) 455–500.

[9] Y. Wang, D. Meng, M. Yuan, Sparse recovery: from vectors to tensors, National Science Review 5 (5) (2017) 756–767.

[10] Z. Long, Y. Liu, L. Chen, C. Zhu, Low rank tensor completion for multiway visual data, Signal Processing 155 (2019) 301–316.

[11] N.D. Sidiropoulos, L. De Lathauwer, X. Fu, K. Huang, E.E. Papalexakis, C. Faloutsos, Tensor decomposition for signal processing and machine learning, IEEE Transactions on Signal Processing 65 (13) (2017) 3551–3582.

[12] J.D. Carroll, J.-J. Chang, Analysis of individual differences in multidimensional scaling via an N-way generalization of "Eckart-Young" decomposition, Psychometrika 35 (3) (1970) 283–319.

[13] R.A. Harshman, et al., Foundations of the PARAFAC Procedure: Models and Conditions for an "Explanatory" Multimodal Factor Analysis, University of California at Los Angeles, Los Angeles, CA, 1970.

[14] C. Zeng, T.-X. Jiang, M.K. Ng, An approximation method of CP rank for third-order tensor completion, Numerische Mathematik (2021) 1–31.

[15] L.R. Tucker, Some mathematical notes on three-mode factor analysis, Psychometrika 31 (3) (1966) 279–311.

[16] T.-Y. Ji, T.-Z. Huang, X.-L. Zhao, T.-H. Ma, L.-J. Deng, A non-convex tensor rank approximation for tensor completion, Applied Mathematical Modelling 48 (2017) 410–422.

[17] W. Cao, Y. Wang, C. Yang, X. Chang, Z. Han, Z. Xu, Folded-concave penalization approaches to tensor completion, Neurocomputing 152 (2015) 261–273.

[18] M.E. Kilmer, C.D. Martin, Factorization strategies for third-order tensors, Linear Algebra and Its Applications 435 (3) (2011) 641–658.

[19] M.E. Kilmer, K. Braman, N. Hao, R.C. Hoover, Third-order tensors as operators on matrices: a theoretical and computational framework with applications in imaging, SIAM Journal on Matrix Analysis and Applications 34 (1) (2013) 148–172.

[20] O. Semerci, N. Hao, M.E. Kilmer, E.L. Miller, Tensor-based formulation and nuclear norm regularization for multienergy computed tomography, IEEE Transactions on Image Processing 23 (4) (2014) 1678–1693.

[21] Z. Zhang, G. Ely, S. Aeron, N. Hao, M. Kilmer, Novel methods for multilinear data completion and de-noising based on tensor-SVD, in: 2014 IEEE Conference on Computer Vision and Pattern Recognition, IEEE, Columbus, OH, USA, 2014, pp. 3842–3849.

[22] Z. Zhang, S. Aeron, Exact tensor completion using t-SVD, IEEE Transactions on Signal Processing 65 (6) (2017) 1511–1526.

[23] C. Lu, J. Feng, Y. Chen, W. Liu, Z. Lin, S. Yan, Tensor robust principal component analysis: exact recovery of corrupted low-rank tensors via convex optimization, in: Proceedings of the IEEE Conference on Computer Vision and Pattern Recognition, 2016, pp. 5249–5257.

[24] C. Lu, J. Feng, Y. Chen, W. Liu, Z. Lin, S. Yan, Tensor robust principal component analysis with a new tensor nuclear norm, IEEE Transactions on Pattern Analysis and Machine Intelligence 42 (4) (2020) 925–938.

[25] J.-F. Cai, E.J. Candès, Z. Shen, A singular value thresholding algorithm for matrix completion, SIAM Journal on Optimization 20 (4) (2010) 1956–1982.

[26] S. Boyd, N. Parikh, E. Chu, B. Peleato, J. Eckstein, Distributed optimization and statistical learning via the alternating direction method of multipliers, Foundations and Trends in Machine Learning 3 (1) (2011) 1–122.

[27] H. Fan, Y. Chen, Y. Guo, H. Zhang, G. Kuang, Hyperspectral image restoration using low-rank tensor recovery, IEEE Journal of Selected Topics in Applied Earth Observations and Remote Sensing 10 (10) (2017) 4589–4604.

[28] F. Zhang, J. Wang, W. Wang, C. Xu, Low-tubal-rank plus sparse tensor recovery with prior subspace information, IEEE Transactions on Pattern Analysis and Machine Intelligence (2020), https://doi.org/10.1109/TPAMI.2020.2986773.

[29] J. Hou, F. Zhang, H. Qiu, J. Wang, Y. Wang, D. Meng, Robust low-tubal-rank tensor recovery from binary measurements, IEEE Transactions on Pattern Analysis and Machine Intelligence (2021), https://doi.org/10.1109/TPAMI.2021.3063527.

[30] Q. Jiang, M. Ng, Robust low-tubal-rank tensor completion via convex optimization, in: Proceedings of the Twenty-Eighth International Joint Conference on Artificial Intelligence, International Joint Conferences on Artificial Intelligence Organization, Macao, China, 2019, pp. 2649–2655.

[31] R. Dian, S. Li, Hyperspectral image super-resolution via subspace-based low tensor multi-rank regularization, IEEE Transactions on Image Processing 28 (10) (2019) 5135–5146.

[32] M. Cheng, L. Jing, M.K. Ng, Tensor-based low-dimensional representation learning for multi-view clustering, IEEE Transactions on Image Processing 28 (5) (2018) 2399–2414.

[33] M. Yin, J. Gao, S. Xie, Y. Guo, Multiview subspace clustering via tensorial t-product representation, IEEE Transactions on Neural Networks and Learning Systems 30 (3) (2019) 851–864.

[34] T. Oh, Y. Tai, J. Bazin, H. Kim, I.S. Kweon, Partial sum minimization of singular values in robust PCA: algorithm and applications, IEEE Transactions on Pattern Analysis and Machine Intelligence 38 (4) (2016) 744–758.

[35] Y. Hu, D. Zhang, J. Ye, X. Li, X. He, Fast and accurate matrix completion via truncated nuclear norm regularization, IEEE Transactions on Pattern Analysis and Machine Intelligence 35 (9) (2013) 2117–2130.

[36] T.-X. Jiang, T.-Z. Huang, X.-L. Zhao, L.-J. Deng, Multi-dimensional imaging data recovery via minimizing the partial sum of tubal nuclear norm, Journal of Computational and Applied Mathematics 372 (2020) 112680.

[37] S. Xue, W. Qiu, F. Liu, X. Jin, Low-rank tensor completion by truncated nuclear norm regularization, in: 2018 24th International Conference on Pattern Recognition (ICPR), IEEE, 2018, pp. 2600–2605.

[38] X. Zhang, M.K. Ng, A corrected tensor nuclear norm minimization method for noisy low-rank tensor completion, SIAM Journal on Imaging Sciences 12 (2) (2019) 1231–1273.

[39] S. Gu, Q. Xie, D. Meng, W. Zuo, X. Feng, L. Zhang, Weighted nuclear norm minimization and its applications to low level vision, International Journal of Computer Vision 121 (2) (2017) 183–208.

[40] Y. Huang, G. Liao, L. Zhang, Y. Xiang, J. Li, A. Nehorai, Efficient narrowband RFI mitigation algorithms for SAR systems with reweighted tensor structures, IEEE Transactions on Geoscience and Remote Sensing 57 (11) (2019) 9396–9409.

[41] M. Liu, X. Zhang, L. Tang, Real color image denoising using t-product-based weighted tensor nuclear norm minimization, IEEE Access 7 (2019) 182017–182026.

[42] H. Wang, F. Zhang, J. Wang, T. Huang, J. Huang, X. Liu, Generalized nonconvex approach for low-tubal-rank tensor recovery, IEEE Transactions on Neural Networks and Learning Systems (2021) 1–15, https://doi.org/10.1109/TNNLS.2021.3051650.

[43] W. Dong, G. Shi, X. Li, Y. Ma, F. Huang, Compressive sensing via nonlocal low-rank regularization, IEEE Transactions on Image Processing 23 (8) (2014) 3618–3632.

[44] T. Ji, T. Huang, X. Zhao, D. Sun, A new surrogate for tensor multirank and applications in image and video completion, in: 2017 International Conference on Progress in Informatics and Computing (PIC), 2017, pp. 101–107.

[45] J.H. Friedman, Fast sparse regression and classification, International Journal of Forecasting 28 (3) (2012) 722–738.

[46] J. Trzasko, A. Manduca, Highly undersampled magnetic resonance image reconstruction via homotopic ℓ_0-minimization, IEEE Transactions on Medical Imaging 28 (1) (2008) 106–121.

[47] L. Chen, X. Jiang, X. Liu, Z. Zhou, Robust low-rank tensor recovery via nonconvex singular value minimization, IEEE Transactions on Image Processing 29 (2020) 9044–9059.

[48] W.-H. Xu, X.-L. Zhao, T.-Y. Ji, J.-Q. Miao, T.-H. Ma, S. Wang, T.-Z. Huang, Laplace function based nonconvex surrogate for low-rank tensor completion, Signal Processing. Image Communication 73 (2019) 62–69, tensor Image Processing.

[49] H. Kong, X. Xie, Z. Lin, T-Schatten-p norm for low-rank tensor recovery, IEEE Journal of Selected Topics in Signal Processing 12 (6) (2018) 1405–1419.

[50] Q. Gao, P. Zhang, W. Xia, D. Xie, X. Gao, D. Tao, Enhanced tensor RPCA and its application, IEEE Transactions on Pattern Analysis and Machine Intelligence 43 (6) (2021) 2133–2140.

[51] Y. Xie, S. Gu, Y. Liu, W. Zuo, W. Zhang, L. Zhang, Weighted Schatten p-norm minimization for image denoising and background subtraction, IEEE Transactions on Image Processing 25 (10) (2016) 4842–4857.

[52] S. Wang, Y. Liu, L. Feng, C. Zhu, Frequency-weighted robust tensor principal component analysis, arXiv preprint, arXiv:2004.10068, 2020.

[53] P. Zhou, C. Lu, Z. Lin, C. Zhang, Tensor factorization for low-rank tensor completion, IEEE Transactions on Image Processing 27 (3) (2018) 1152–1163.

[54] M. Cheng, L. Jing, M.K. Ng, A weighted tensor factorization method for low-rank tensor completion, in: 2019 IEEE Fifth International Conference on Multimedia Big Data (BigMM), 2019.

[55] X.-L. Lin, M.K. Ng, X.-L. Zhao, Tensor factorization with total variation and Tikhonov regularization for low-rank tensor completion in imaging data, Journal of Mathematical Imaging and Vision 62 (6) (2020) 900–918.

[56] Y. Liu, L. Chen, C. Zhu, Improved robust tensor principal component analysis via low-rank core matrix, IEEE Journal of Selected Topics in Signal Processing 12 (6) (2018) 1378–1389.

[57] L. Feng, Y. Liu, L. Chen, X. Zhang, C. Zhu, Robust block tensor principal component analysis, Signal Processing 166 (2020) 107271.

[58] X. Li, Y. Ye, X. Xu, Low-rank tensor completion with total variation for visual data inpainting, in: Proceedings of the Thirty-First AAAI Conference on Artificial Intelligence, AAAI Press, 2017, pp. 2210–2216.

[59] T.-X. Jiang, T.-Z. Huang, X.-L. Zhao, T.-Y. Ji, L.-J. Deng, Matrix factorization for low-rank tensor completion using framelet prior, Information Sciences 436 (2018) 403–417.

[60] X.-T. Li, X.-L. Zhao, T.-X. Jiang, Y.-B. Zheng, T.-Y. Ji, T.-Z. Huang, Low-rank tensor completion via combined non-local self-similarity and low-rank regularization, Neurocomputing 367 (2019) 1–12.

[61] T. Xie, S. Li, L. Fang, L. Liu, Tensor completion via nonlocal low-rank regularization, IEEE Transactions on Cybernetics 49 (6) (2019) 2344–2354.

[62] F. Jiang, X.Y. Liu, H. Lu, R. Shen, Anisotropic total variation regularized low-rank tensor completion based on tensor nuclear norm for color image inpainting, in: 2018 IEEE International Conference on Acoustics, Speech and Signal Processing (ICASSP), 2018, pp. 1363–1367.

[63] H. Fan, C. Li, Y. Guo, G. Kuang, J. Ma, Spatial–spectral total variation regularized low-rank tensor decomposition for hyperspectral image denoising, IEEE Transactions on Geoscience and Remote Sensing 56 (10) (2018) 6196–6213.

[64] X.-L. Zhao, W.-H. Xu, T.-X. Jiang, Y. Wang, M.K. Ng, Deep plug-and-play prior for low-rank tensor completion, Neurocomputing 400 (2020) 137–149.

[65] K. Zhang, W. Zuo, Y. Chen, D. Meng, L. Zhang, Beyond a Gaussian denoiser: residual learning of deep CNN for image denoising, IEEE Transactions on Image Processing 26 (7) (2017) 3142–3155.

[66] K. Zhang, W. Zuo, L. Zhang, FFDNet: toward a fast and flexible solution for CNN-based image denoising, IEEE Transactions on Image Processing 27 (9) (2018) 4608–4622.

[67] L. Zhang, W. Zuo, Image restoration: from sparse and low-rank priors to deep priors, IEEE Signal Processing Magazine 34 (5) (2017) 172–179.

[68] W. Hu, D. Tao, W. Zhang, Y. Xie, Y. Yang, The twist tensor nuclear norm for video completion, IEEE Transactions on Neural Networks and Learning Systems 28 (12) (2016) 2961–2973.

[69] D. Wei, A. Wang, X. Feng, B. Wang, B. Wang, Tensor completion based on triple tubal nuclear norm, Algorithms 11 (7) (2018) 94.

[70] Y.-B. Zheng, T.-Z. Huang, X.-L. Zhao, T.-X. Jiang, T.-Y. Ji, T.-H. Ma, Tensor N-tubal rank and its convex relaxation for low-rank tensor recovery, Information Sciences 532 (2020) 170–189.

[71] A. Wang, C. Li, Z. Jin, Q. Zhao, Robust tensor decomposition via orientation invariant tubal nuclear norms, Proceedings of the AAAI Conference on Artificial Intelligence, vol. 34, AAAI Press, 2020, pp. 6102–6109.

[72] C.D. Martin, R. Shafer, B. LaRue, An order-p tensor factorization with applications in imaging, SIAM Journal on Scientific Computing 35 (1) (2013) A474–A490.

[73] X.-Y. Liu, X. Wang, Fourth-order tensors with multidimensional discrete transforms, arXiv preprint, arXiv:1705.01576, 2017.

[74] F. Zhang, W. Wang, J. Huang, J. Wang, Y. Wang, RIP-based performance guarantee for low-tubal-rank tensor recovery, Journal of Computational and Applied Mathematics 374 (2020) 112767.

[75] B. Madathil, S.N. George, Dct based weighted adaptive multi-linear data completion and denoising, Neurocomputing 318 (2018) 120–136.

[76] W.-H. Xu, X.-L. Zhao, M. Ng, A fast algorithm for cosine transform based tensor singular value decomposition, arXiv preprint, arXiv:1902.03070, 2019.

[77] C. Lu, X. Peng, Y. Wei, Low-rank tensor completion with a new tensor nuclear norm induced by invertible linear transforms, in: 2019 IEEE/CVF Conference on Computer Vision and Pattern Recognition (CVPR), 2019, pp. 5989–5997.

[78] E. Kernfeld, M. Kilmer, S. Aeron, Tensor–tensor products with invertible linear transforms, Linear Algebra and Its Applications 485 (2015) 545–570.

[79] G. Song, M.K. Ng, X. Zhang, Robust tensor completion using transformed tensor singular value decomposition, Numerical Linear Algebra with Applications 27 (3) (May 2020).

[80] X. Zhang, M.K.P. Ng, Low rank tensor completion with Poisson observations, IEEE Transactions on Pattern Analysis and Machine Intelligence (2021), https://doi.org/10.1109/TPAMI.2021.3059299.

[81] J. Han, p-order tensor products with invertible linear transforms, arXiv preprint, arXiv:2005.11477, 2020.

[82] T.-X. Jiang, M.K. Ng, X.-L. Zhao, T.-Z. Huang, Framelet representation of tensor nuclear norm for third-order tensor completion, IEEE Transactions on Image Processing 29 (2020) 7233–7244.

[83] J.-F. Cai, E.J. Candès, Z. Shen, A singular value thresholding algorithm for matrix completion, SIAM Journal on Optimization 20 (4) (2010) 1956–1982.

[84] A. Ron, Z. Shen, Affine systems in $L_2(R^d)$: the analysis of the analysis operator, Journal of Functional Analysis 148 (2) (1997) 408–447.

[85] H. Kong, C. Lu, Z. Lin, Tensor Q-rank: a new data dependent tensor rank, Machine Learning (2021), https://doi.org/10.1007/s10994-021-05987-8.

[86] T.-X. Jiang, X.-L. Zhao, H. Zhang, M.K. Ng, Dictionary learning with low-rank coding coefficients for tensor completion, IEEE Transactions on Neural Networks and Learning Systems (2021), https://doi.org/10.1109/TNNLS.2021.3104837.

[87] H. Zhang, W. He, L. Zhang, H. Shen, Q. Yuan, Hyperspectral image restoration using low-rank matrix recovery, IEEE Transactions on Geoscience and Remote Sensing 52 (8) (2013) 4729–4743.

[88] H. Fan, Y. Chen, Y. Guo, H. Zhang, G. Kuang, Hyperspectral image restoration using low-rank tensor recovery, IEEE Journal of Selected Topics in Applied Earth Observations and Remote Sensing 10 (10) (2017) 16.

[89] A. Mian, R. Hartley, Hyperspectral video restoration using optical flow and sparse coding, Optics Express 20 (10) (2012) 10658–10673.

[90] ZhouWang, A.C. Bovik, H.R. Sheikh, E.P. Simoncelli, Image quality assessment: from error visibility to structural similarity, IEEE Transactions on Image Processing 13 (4) (2004) 600–612.

[91] Y. Chen, S. Bhojanapalli, S. Sanghavi, R. Ward, Completing any low-rank matrix, provably, Journal of Machine Learning Research 16 (94) (2015) 2999–3034.

[92] Y. Chang, L. Yan, B. Chen, S. Zhong, Y. Tian, Hyperspectral image restoration: where does the low-rank property exist, IEEE Transactions on Geoscience and Remote Sensing (2020) 1–16.

[93] D.A. Tarzanagh, G. Michailidis, Fast randomized algorithms for t-product based tensor operations and decompositions with applications to imaging data, SIAM Journal on Imaging Sciences 11 (4) (2018) 2629–2664.

[94] J. Zhang, A.K. Saibaba, M.E. Kilmer, S. Aeron, A randomized tensor singular value decomposition based on the t-product, Numerical Linear Algebra with Applications 25 (5) (2018) e2179.

[95] M. Che, Y. Wei, H. Yan, The computation of low multilinear rank approximations of tensors via power scheme and random projection, SIAM Journal on Matrix Analysis and Applications 41 (2) (2020) 605–636.

Partensor

A toolbox for parallel canonical polyadic decomposition

Paris A. Karakasis[a], **Christos Kolomvakis**[a], **George Lourakis**[b], **George Lykoudis**[b], **Ioannis Marios Papagiannakos**[a], **Ioanna Siaminou**[a], **Christos Tsalidis**[b], and **Athanasios P. Liavas**[a]

[a]*School of Electrical and Computer Engineering, Technical University of Crete, Chania, Greece*
[b]*Neurocom, S.A, Athens, Greece*

CONTENTS

Tensors for Data Processing. https://doi.org/10.1016/B978-0-12-824447-0.00009-1

3.1 Introduction

Tensors have recently gained great popularity due to their ability to model multi-way data dependencies [1–4]. Tensor decomposition (TD) into latent factors is very important for numerous tasks, such as feature selection, dimensionality reduction, compression, and data visualization and interpretation. Canonical polyadic decomposition (CPD) is one of the most important TD models. TD with missing elements (TDME), or tensor completion, arises in many scientific areas such as machine learning, signal processing, and scientific computing.

TD and TDME are usually obtained as the end result of an optimization procedure [1,2]. Alternating optimization (AO) and all-at-once (AAO) optimization are among the most commonly used techniques for TD and TDME [2,5].

We focus on the CPD model and use as quality metric the Frobenius norm of the difference between the true and the estimated tensor. We adopt the AO framework, that is, we work in a circular manner and update each factor by keeping all others fixed. The update of each factor amounts to the solution of a (constrained) matrix least-squares (MLS) problem. For the TD problem, we consider the cases where the factors are unconstrained, nonnegative, orthogonal, or any combination thereof. For the TDME problem, we consider the cases where the factors are unconstrained or nonnegative. In the cases with unconstrained or orthogonal factors, the solution of the MLS problem is given in closed form. In the cases with nonnegativity constraints, we use accelerated gradient methods, which have proved very efficient in practice.

Recent tensor applications, such as social network analysis, movie recommendation systems, and targeted advertising, need to handle very large-scale tensors, rendering parallel algorithms perhaps the only viable solution. We describe in detail Message Passing Interface (MPI) implementations of our algorithms for TD and TDME and test their efficiency in numerical experiments with both synthetic and real-world data.

3.1.1 Related work

The majority of the works concerned with parallel algorithms for TD and TDME consider the unconstrained TDME problem. One of the earliest works is Gigatensor [6], where the authors focus on the factorization of sparse tensors using the MapReduce programming model. This was followed by DFacTo [7], which is implemented in C++ and uses the Eigen Matrix Library. However, DFacTo stores the entire factor matrices in all cores, which adds significant memory overhead, since, in many cases of interest, the factors are very large. In [8], two parallel algorithms for the unconstrained TDME have been developed and results concerning the speedup attained by their MPI implementations on a linear processor array have been reported.

In [9], the authors introduce fine- and medium-grained partitioning for the TDME problem, while [10] incorporates dimension trees into the developed parallel algorithms.

In [11], the authors consider constrained matrix/tensor decomposition and completion problems. They adopt the AO framework and use the alternating direction method of multipliers (ADMM) for solving the inner constrained optimization problem for one matrix factor conditioned on the rest. The ADMM offers significant flexibility, due to its ability to efficiently handle a wide range of constraints.[1] The AO-ADMM framework has also been adopted in [12].

In [13], the medium-grained approach of [9] has been used for the solution of the nonnegative TD problem on distributed memory systems. The same problem has been considered in [14], where the authors incorporate the dimension trees and observe performance gains due to reduced computational load.

There are several works whose aim is to find approximate solutions of TD problems. In [15], the authors propose a method, called PARCUBE, which performs biased sampling of the initial tensor. The goal is to compute a reduced-size tensor whose decomposition is a good approximation to the original decomposition. This works not only for the CPD but for other decompositions as well (e.g., Tucker decomposition). The authors provide theoretical guarantees and, in addition, propose an embarrassingly parallel scheme for the algorithm.

The authors in [16] propose a method, called PARACOMP, which compresses the initial tensor into multiple smaller tensors and performs the CPD on each one independently. Each tensor is then assigned to a worker and the resulting smaller factors are merged into the final results. At a high level, the compression is achieved by reducing the initial tensor through tensor-matrix operations with auxiliary random matrices drawn from a certain distribution. A MapReduce implementation is also described. The authors highlight that PARACOMP is flexible with respect to the computational and memory capabilities of each worker.

Parasketch [17,18] is another parallel scheme that aims to address specific drawbacks of PARACOMP and PARCUBE. Sketching matrices are used to perform compression more efficiently than PARACOMP. In [18], a sketching method is presented for the block term decomposition.

Works that employ stochastic gradient descent (SGD) on shared memory and distributed systems for sparse tensor factorization and completion include [19–22].

The works [23–25] use either the MapReduce programming model or the Spark engine. Finally, [26] presents a hypergraph model for general medium-grain partitioning.

3.1.2 Notation

Vectors, matrices, and tensors are denoted by small, capital, and calligraphic capital letters, for example, $\mathbf{x}$, $\mathbf{X}$, and $\mathcal{X}$, respectively; $\mathbb{R}^{I_1 \times \cdots \times I_N}$ and $\mathbb{R}_+^{I_1 \times \cdots \times I_N}$ denote, respectively, the set of $(I_1 \times \cdots \times I_N)$ real and nonnegative tensors. The elements of tensor $\mathcal{X}$ are denoted as $\mathcal{X}(i_1, \ldots, i_N)$. In many cases, we use MATLAB®-like notation; for example, $\mathbf{A}(j, :)$ denotes the j-th row of matrix $\mathbf{A}$. The transpose and

---

[1] We note that we do not consider the ADMM in this work but we feel that it remains a significant alternative which deserves deeper study.

the pseudo-inverse of matrix $\mathbf{A}$ are denoted by $\mathbf{A}^T$ and $\mathbf{A}^\dagger$, respectively, and $\mathbf{I}_P$ denotes the $(P \times P)$ identity matrix.[2] The Stiefel manifold formed by all orthonormal J-frames in $\mathbb{R}^I$ is denoted as $\mathbb{S}_{(I,J)} = \{\mathbf{X} \in \mathbb{R}^{I \times J} : \mathbf{X}^T \mathbf{X} = \mathbf{I}\}$, $\|\cdot\|_F$ denotes the Frobenius norm of the tensor or matrix argument, $(\mathbf{A})_+$ denotes the projection of matrix $\mathbf{A}$ onto the set of element-wise nonnegative matrices, and $\mathbf{A} \geq \mathbf{0}$ denotes a matrix $\mathbf{A}$ with nonnegative elements.

The outer product of vectors $\mathbf{a}$ and $\mathbf{b}$ is denoted as $\mathbf{a} \circ \mathbf{b}$. The Kronecker, Khatri–Rao, and Hadamard products of matrices $\mathbf{A}$ and $\mathbf{B}$ (with appropriate dimensions) are denoted, respectively, as $\mathbf{A} \otimes \mathbf{B}$, $\mathbf{A} \odot \mathbf{B}$, and $\mathbf{A} \circledast \mathbf{B}$. The extension of the notation of these operations to more than two arguments is obvious. Finally, $\mathbb{N}_N$ denotes the set $\{1, \dots, N\}$.

Let $\mathcal{X} \in \mathbb{R}^{I_1 \times \cdots \times I_N}$ and $\mathbf{U}^{(i)} = \begin{bmatrix} \mathbf{u}_1^{(i)} & \cdots & \mathbf{u}_R^{(i)} \end{bmatrix} \in \mathbb{R}^{I_i \times R}$, for $i \in \mathbb{N}_N$. The rank of $\mathcal{X}$ is the smallest positive integer R such that

$$\mathcal{X} = [\![\mathbf{U}^{(1)}, \dots, \mathbf{U}^{(N)}]\!] := \sum_{r=1}^{R} \mathbf{u}_r^{(1)} \circ \cdots \circ \mathbf{u}_r^{(N)}. \tag{3.1}$$

The matricization (or matrix unfolding) of tensor $\mathcal{X}$ with respect to the j-th mode is defined as the matrix $\mathbf{X}_{(j)} \in \mathbb{R}^{I_j \times \prod_{k=1, k \neq j}^{N} I_k}$ whose columns are the mode-j fibers of tensor $\mathcal{X}$ in lexicographic order.

3.2 Tensor decomposition

Let tensor $\mathcal{X}^o \in \mathbb{R}^{I_1 \times \cdots \times I_N}$ admit a decomposition of the form

$$\mathcal{X}^o = [\![\mathbf{U}^{o(1)}, \dots, \mathbf{U}^{o(N)}]\!] = \sum_{r=1}^{R} \mathbf{u}_r^{o(1)} \circ \cdots \circ \mathbf{u}_r^{o(N)}, \tag{3.2}$$

where $\mathbf{U}^{o(i)} = [\mathbf{u}_1^{o(i)} \cdots \mathbf{u}_R^{o(i)}] \in \mathbb{R}^{I_i \times R}$, with $i \in \mathbb{N}_N$. We assume that the factors satisfy a certain set constraint, denoted as $\mathbf{U}^{o(i)} \in \mathbb{U}^{(i)}$. We consider the following cases:

1. the unconstrained case, i.e., $\mathbb{U}^{(i)} = \mathbb{R}^{I_i \times R}$,
2. the nonnegative case, i.e., $\mathbb{U}^{(i)} = \mathbb{R}_+^{I_i \times R}$,
3. the orthogonal case, i.e., $\mathbb{U}^{(i)} = \mathbb{S}_{(I_i, R)}$.

We observe the noisy tensor $\mathcal{X} = \mathcal{X}^o + \mathcal{E}$, where $\mathcal{E}$ is additive noise. Estimates of $\mathbf{U}^{o(i)}$ can be obtained by computing matrices $\mathbf{U}^{(i)} \in \mathbb{R}^{I_i \times R}$, for $i \in \mathbb{N}_N$, that solve the

---

[2] If the dimension becomes clear from the context, we omit the subscript.

optimization problem

$$\min_{\{\mathbf{U}^{(i)} \in \mathbb{U}^{(i)}\}_{i=1}^{N}} f_{\mathcal{X}}\left(\mathbf{U}^{(1)}, \ldots, \mathbf{U}^{(N)}\right),$$

where $f_{\mathcal{X}}$ is a function measuring the quality of the decomposition. A common choice for $f_{\mathcal{X}}$ is

$$f_{\mathcal{X}}\left(\mathbf{U}^{(1)}, \ldots, \mathbf{U}^{(N)}\right) = \frac{1}{2}\left\|\mathcal{X} - [\![\mathbf{U}^{(1)}, \ldots, \mathbf{U}^{(N)}]\!]\right\|_{F}^{2}. \tag{3.3}$$

This problem is nonconvex and, thus, difficult to solve, in general.

If $\mathcal{Y} = [\![\mathbf{U}^{(1)}, \ldots, \mathbf{U}^{(N)}]\!]$, then its i-th mode matrix unfolding is given by [3]

$$\mathbf{Y}_{(i)} = \mathbf{U}^{(i)}\mathbf{K}^{(i)^{T}}, \tag{3.4}$$

where

$$\mathbf{K}^{(i)} := \mathbf{U}^{(N)} \odot \cdots \odot \mathbf{U}^{(i+1)} \odot \mathbf{U}^{(i-1)} \odot \cdots \odot \mathbf{U}^{(1)}. \tag{3.5}$$

Thus, $f_{\mathcal{X}}$ can be expressed as

$$f_{\mathcal{X}}\left(\mathbf{U}^{(1)}, \ldots, \mathbf{U}^{(N)}\right) = \frac{1}{2}\left\|\mathbf{X}_{(i)} - \mathbf{U}^{(i)}\mathbf{K}^{(i)T}\right\|_{F}^{2}, \quad i \in \mathbb{N}_{N}. \tag{3.6}$$

These expressions form the basis of the AO approach for TD, i.e., for fixed matrix factors $\mathbf{U}^{(j)}$, with $j \neq i$, we update $\mathbf{U}^{(i)}$ by solving an MLS problem, and this process is repeated in a circular manner until convergence.

3.2.1 Matrix least-squares problems

The MLS problem will be our workhorse towards the development of efficient algorithms for TD. Let $\mathbf{X} \in \mathbb{R}^{P \times Q}$ and $\mathbf{B} \in \mathbb{R}^{Q \times R}$ be given matrices and consider the MLS problem

$$\min_{\mathbf{A} \in \mathbb{A}} f(\mathbf{A}) = \frac{1}{2}\|\mathbf{X} - \mathbf{A}\mathbf{B}^{T}\|_{F}^{2}, \tag{3.7}$$

where $\mathbb{A} \subseteq \mathbb{R}^{P \times R}$ determines the structure of matrix $\mathbf{A}$. The gradient and the Hessian of function f, at point $\mathbf{A}$, are given by

$$\nabla f(\mathbf{A}) = -\left(\mathbf{X} - \mathbf{A}\mathbf{B}^{T}\right)\mathbf{B} \tag{3.8}$$

and

$$\nabla^{2} f(\mathbf{A}) := \frac{\partial^{2} f(\mathbf{A})}{\partial \operatorname{vec}(\mathbf{A}) \partial \operatorname{vec}(\mathbf{A})^{T}} = \mathbf{B}^{T}\mathbf{B} \otimes \mathbf{I}_{P}. \tag{3.9}$$

3.2.1.1 The unconstrained case

In the unconstrained case, i.e., $\mathbb{A} = \mathbb{R}^{P \times R}$, the solution $\mathbf{A}^+$ satisfies the equation

$$\nabla f(\mathbf{A}^+) = \mathbf{0} \implies -\mathbf{XB} + \mathbf{A}^+ \mathbf{B}^T \mathbf{B} = \mathbf{0}. \tag{3.10}$$

If $\mathbf{B}^T \mathbf{B}$ is invertible,[3] then

$$\mathbf{A}^+ = \mathbf{XB}^\dagger = \mathbf{XB}\left(\mathbf{B}^T \mathbf{B}\right)^{-1}. \tag{3.11}$$

Thus, $\mathbf{A}^+$ can be computed as follows:

1. compute $\mathbf{B}^T \mathbf{B}$, with arithmetic complexity $O(QR^2)$;
2. compute $\mathbf{XB}$, with arithmetic complexity $O(PQR)$;
3. solve the resulting linear system, with arithmetic complexity $O(R^3 + PR^2)$.

If $\min(P, Q) \gg R$ (which is true in the cases of our interest), then the matrix product $\mathbf{XB}$ is the most demanding operation.

We denote the solution of the unconstrained case as

$$\mathbf{A}^+ = \text{UMLS}(\mathbf{X}, \mathbf{B}). \tag{3.12}$$

3.2.1.2 The nonnegative case

Algorithm 1: Accelerated gradient algorithm for L-smooth μ-strongly convex problems.

Input: $\mathbf{x}_0 \in \mathbb{R}^N$, μ, L. Set $\mathbf{y}_0 = \mathbf{x}_0$, $C = \frac{L}{\mu}$, $\beta = \frac{\sqrt{C}-1}{\sqrt{C}+1}$.

1   k-th iteration

2     $\mathbf{x}_{k+1} = \left(\mathbf{y}_k - \frac{1}{L}\nabla f(\mathbf{y}_k)\right)_{\mathbb{X}}$

3     $\mathbf{y}_{k+1} = \mathbf{x}_{k+1} + \beta(\mathbf{x}_{k+1} - \mathbf{x}_k)$

In the nonnegative case, i.e., $\mathbb{A} = \mathbb{R}_+^{P \times R}$, the solution cannot be expressed in closed form, in general, and thus we must resort to an iterative algorithm. Among many candidates, we choose to use an accelerated gradient method because it is very efficient in practice and is suitable for parallel implementation [13]. In the sequel, we present the details of this algorithm.

First, we introduce the class of L-smooth μ-strongly convex optimization problems. Let $f : \mathbb{R}^n \to \mathbb{R}$ be a smooth (that is, differentiable up to a sufficiently high order) convex function and $\mathbb{X}$ a closed convex subset of $\mathbb{R}^n$. Our aim is to solve the problem

$$\min_{\mathbf{x} \in \mathbb{X}} f(\mathbf{x}), \tag{3.13}$$

---

[3] If $\mathbf{B}^T \mathbf{B}$ is singular or very ill-conditioned, then we may add to it a small multiple of the identity matrix.

within accuracy $\epsilon > 0$, that is, to find a point $\mathbf{x}^+ \in \mathbb{X}$ such that $f(\mathbf{x}^+) - f^* \leq \epsilon$, where $f^* := \min\limits_{\mathbf{x} \in \mathbb{X}} f(\mathbf{x})$.

Let $0 < \mu \leq L < \infty$. A smooth convex function f is called L-smooth μ-strongly convex if [27, p. 65]

$$\mu \mathbf{I} \preceq \nabla^2 f(\mathbf{x}) \preceq L\mathbf{I}, \quad \forall \mathbf{x} \in \mathbb{R}^n. \tag{3.14}$$

The information complexity of black-box first-order methods for this class of problems is $O\left(\sqrt{C} \log \frac{1}{\epsilon}\right)$, where $C := \frac{L}{\mu}$ is the condition number of the problem [27, Theorem 2.2.2]. A first-order optimal algorithm appears in Algorithm 1, where $(\mathbf{x})_{\mathbb{X}}$ denotes the projection of vector $\mathbf{x}$ onto set $\mathbb{X}$ (see also [27, p. 80]). If the projection onto set $\mathbb{X}$ is easy to compute, then this algorithm is both theoretically optimal and very efficient in practice.

Algorithm 2: Accelerated gradient algorithm for NMLS problems with proximal term.

Input: $\mathbf{X} \in \mathbb{R}^{P \times Q}$, $\mathbf{B} \in \mathbb{R}^{Q \times R}$, $\mathbf{A}_* \in \mathbb{R}^{P \times R}$

1   $L = \max(\text{eig}(\mathbf{B}^T \mathbf{B}))$, $\mu = \min(\text{eig}(\mathbf{B}^T \mathbf{B}))$

2   $\lambda = g(L, \mu)$, $C = \frac{L+\lambda}{\mu+\lambda}$, $\beta = \frac{\sqrt{C}-1}{\sqrt{C}+1}$

3   $\mathbf{W} = -\mathbf{X}\mathbf{B} - \lambda \mathbf{A}_*$, $\mathbf{Z} = \mathbf{B}^T \mathbf{B} + \lambda \mathbf{I}$

4   $\mathbf{A}_0 = \mathbf{Y}_0 = \mathbf{A}_*$

5   $k = 0$

6   **while** (terminating condition is FALSE) **do**

7      $\nabla f_{\mathsf{P}}(\mathbf{Y}_k) = \mathbf{W} + \mathbf{Y}_k \mathbf{Z}$

8      $\mathbf{A}_{k+1} = \left(\mathbf{Y}_k - \frac{1}{L+\lambda} \nabla f_{\mathsf{P}}(\mathbf{Y}_k) \right)_+$

9      $\mathbf{Y}_{k+1} = \mathbf{A}_{k+1} + \beta \left(\mathbf{A}_{k+1} - \mathbf{A}_k \right)$

10     $k = k + 1$

11   **return** $\mathbf{A}_k$.

In order to solve problem (3.7) in the nonnegative case with an accelerated gradient algorithm, we proceed as follows. Let $L := \max(\text{eig}(\mathbf{B}^T \mathbf{B}))$ and $\mu := \min(\text{eig}(\mathbf{B}^T \mathbf{B}))$. In order to avoid very ill-conditioned problems (and guarantee strong convexity), we introduce a proximal term and solve the problem

$$\min_{\mathbf{A} \geq 0} f_{\mathsf{P}}(\mathbf{A}) := \frac{1}{2} \|\mathbf{X} - \mathbf{A}\mathbf{B}^T\|_F^2 + \frac{\lambda}{2} \|\mathbf{A} - \mathbf{A}_*\|_F^2, \tag{3.15}$$

for given $\mathbf{A}_* \in \mathbb{R}^{P \times R}$ and appropriately chosen $\lambda > 0$ [13]. We choose λ based on L and μ, and denote this functional dependence as $\lambda = g(L, \mu)$. If $\frac{\mu}{L} \ll 1$, then we set $\lambda \approx 10\mu$, significantly improving the conditioning of the problem by putting large weight on the proximal term; however, in this case, we expect that the optimal point will be biased towards $\mathbf{A}_*$. Otherwise, we set $\lambda \lesssim \mu$, putting small weight on the proximal term and permitting significant progress towards the computation of $\mathbf{A}$ that satisfies approximate equality $\mathbf{X} \approx \mathbf{AB}^T$ as accurately as possible.

The gradient of f_{P} at point $\mathbf{A}$ is

$$\nabla f_{\mathsf{P}}(\mathbf{A}) = -\left(\mathbf{X} - \mathbf{AB}^T\right)\mathbf{B} + \lambda(\mathbf{A} - \mathbf{A}_*). \tag{3.16}$$

An accelerated gradient algorithm for the solution of the nonnegative MLS (NMLS) problem with proximal term (3.15) is given in Algorithm 2. We note that the values of L and μ are *necessary* for the development of the accelerated gradient algorithm, thus, their computation is imperative. Since in the cases of our interest R is small, the computation of L and μ does not add significant overhead.

The computational complexity of Algorithm 2 is as follows. Matrices $\mathbf{W}$ and $\mathbf{Z}$ are computed once per algorithm call and cost, respectively, $O(PQR)$ and $O(QR^2)$ arithmetic operations. Quantities L and μ are also computed once per algorithm call and cost at most $O(R^3)$ operations. In every iteration, we update quantities $\nabla f_{\mathsf{P}}(\mathbf{Y}_k)$, $\mathbf{A}_k$, and $\mathbf{Y}_k$, with cost $O(PR^2)$, $O(PR)$, and $O(PR)$ arithmetic operations, respectively. If $\min(P, Q) \gg R$, then the computation of the matrix product $\mathbf{XB}$ is the most demanding operation.

We denote the solution of the NMLS problem as

$$\mathbf{A}^+ = \mathsf{NMLS}(\mathbf{X}, \mathbf{B}, \mathbf{A}_*). \tag{3.17}$$

3.2.1.3 The orthogonal case

In the orthogonal case, i.e., $\mathbb{A} = \mathbb{S}_{(P,R)}$, problem (3.7) is known as the orthogonal Procrustes (OP) problem and has a closed-form solution expressed as [28,29]

$$\mathbf{A}^+ = \mathbf{UV}^T = \mathbf{W}\left(\mathbf{W}^T\mathbf{W}\right)^{-\frac{1}{2}}, \tag{3.18}$$

where $\mathbf{U} \in \mathbb{R}^{P \times R}$ and $\mathbf{V} \in \mathbb{R}^{R \times R}$ are given by the singular value decomposition (SVD) of matrix

$$\mathbf{W} := \mathbf{XB} = \mathbf{U\Sigma V}^T. \tag{3.19}$$

We find it convenient to solve the OP problem as follows (this solution fits well our parallel implementation framework):

1. compute $\mathbf{W}$, with $O(PQR)$ arithmetic operations;
2. compute $\mathbf{W}^T\mathbf{W}$, with $O(PR^2)$ arithmetic operations;
3. compute the eigenvalue decomposition of $\mathbf{W}^T\mathbf{W} = \mathbf{V\Sigma V}^T$, with $O(R^3)$ arithmetic operations;
4. set $\mathbf{A}^+ = \mathbf{WV\Sigma}^{-\frac{1}{2}}\mathbf{V}^T$, with $O(PR^2)$ arithmetic operations.

Therefore, similarly to the aforementioned cases, forming matrix $\mathbf{XB}$ is the most computationally demanding operation.

We denote the solution of the OP problem as

$$\mathbf{A}^+ = \mathrm{OP}(\mathbf{X}, \mathbf{B}). \tag{3.20}$$

3.2.2 Alternating optimization for tensor decomposition

In the AO framework, we update each factor separately and in a circular manner, i.e., for $i \in \mathbb{N}_N$, we update factor $\mathbf{U}^{(i)} \in \mathbb{U}^{(i)}$ with all the other factors being fixed. Let us assume that during the $(k+1)$-st outer iteration, we have computed $\mathbf{U}_{k+1}^{(1)}, \ldots, \mathbf{U}_{k+1}^{(i-1)}, \mathbf{U}_k^{(i)}, \ldots, \mathbf{U}_k^{(N)}$. In order to update factor $\mathbf{U}_k^{(i)}$, we solve the problem

$$\mathbf{U}_{k+1}^{(i)} = \underset{\mathbf{U}^{(i)} \in \mathbb{U}^{(i)}}{\mathrm{argmin}} \left\| \mathbf{X}_{(i)} - \mathbf{U}^{(i)} \mathbf{K}_k^{(i)T} \right\|_F^2, \tag{3.21}$$

where

$$\mathbf{K}_k^{(i)} := \mathbf{U}_k^{(N)} \odot \cdots \odot \mathbf{U}_k^{(i+1)} \odot \mathbf{U}_{k+1}^{(i-1)} \odot \cdots \odot \mathbf{U}_{k+1}^{(1)}. \tag{3.22}$$

In the unconstrained case, the update is given by

$$\mathbf{U}_{k+1}^{(i)} = \mathrm{UMLS}(\mathbf{X}_{(i)}, \mathbf{K}_k^{(i)}), \tag{3.23}$$

in the nonnegative case it is given by

$$\mathbf{U}_{k+1}^{(i)} = \mathrm{NMLS}(\mathbf{X}_{(i)}, \mathbf{K}_k^{(i)}, \mathbf{U}_k^{(i)}), \tag{3.24}$$

and in the orthogonal case it is given by

$$\mathbf{U}_{k+1}^{(i)} = \mathrm{OP}(\mathbf{X}_{(i)}, \mathbf{K}_k^{(i)}). \tag{3.25}$$

In all cases, we must compute quantity $\mathbf{X}_{(i)} \mathbf{K}_k^{(i)}$, the so-called matricized tensor times Khatri–Rao product (MTTKRP), which is the most computationally demanding operation. Another quantity that is necessary for the updates in the first two cases is matrix $\mathbf{K}_k^{(i)T} \mathbf{K}_k^{(i)}$, which can be efficiently computed as

$$\begin{aligned}
\mathbf{K}_k^{(i)T} \mathbf{K}_k^{(i)} = &\ \mathbf{U}_k^{(N)T} \mathbf{U}_k^{(N)} \circledast \cdots \circledast \mathbf{U}_k^{(i+1)T} \mathbf{U}_k^{(i+1)} \\
&\ \circledast \mathbf{U}_{k+1}^{(i-1)T} \mathbf{U}_{k+1}^{(i-1)} \circledast \cdots \circledast \mathbf{U}_{k+1}^{(1)T} \mathbf{U}_{k+1}^{(1)}.
\end{aligned} \tag{3.26}$$

In Algorithm 3, we present a high-level version of the AO algorithm for TD. The function update_factor updates $\mathbf{U}_k^{(i)}$ by using one of the three functions appearing in (3.23)–(3.25), depending on the set constraints $\mathbb{U}^{(i)}$.

After each outer iteration, we have found very useful the following operations:

1. we normalize the factors so that all factors except one have unit 2-norm columns;

Algorithm 3: AO algorithm for tensor decomposition.

Input: $\mathcal{X} \in \mathbb{R}^{I_1 \times \cdots \times I_N}$, $\mathbf{U}_0^{(i)} \in \mathbb{U}^i$, $i = 1, \ldots, N$.

1   $k = 0$
2   **while** (*terminating condition is FALSE*) **do**
3   **for** $i = 1, \ldots, N$ **do**
4       $\mathbf{K}_k^{(i)} = \mathbf{U}_k^{(N)} \odot \cdots \odot \mathbf{U}_k^{(i+1)} \odot \mathbf{U}_{k+1}^{(i-1)} \odot \cdots \odot \mathbf{U}_{k+1}^{(1)}$
5       $\mathbf{U}_{k+1}^{(i)} = \text{update\_factor}(\mathbf{X}_{(i)}, \mathbf{K}_k^{(i)})$
6     $\left(\mathbf{U}_{k+1}^{(1)\mathcal{N}}, \ldots, \mathbf{U}_{k+1}^{(N)\mathcal{N}} \right) \leftarrow \text{normalize} \left(\mathbf{U}_{k+1}^{(1)}, \ldots, \mathbf{U}_{k+1}^{(N)} \right)$
7     $\left(\mathbf{U}_{k+1}^{(1)}, \ldots, \mathbf{U}_{k+1}^{(N)} \right) \leftarrow \text{accel} \left(\mathbf{U}_{k+1}^{(1)\mathcal{N}}, \ldots, \mathbf{U}_{k+1}^{(N)\mathcal{N}}, \mathbf{U}_k^{(1)\mathcal{N}}, \ldots, \mathbf{U}_k^{(N)\mathcal{N}} \right)$
8     $k = k + 1$
9   **return** $\mathbf{U}_k^{(i)}$, $i = 1, \ldots, N$.

---

2. at iteration $k + 1 > k_0$, after the normalization of the factors, we perform the simple acceleration step adopted in [30]. More specifically, we set

$$\mathbf{U}_{\text{new}}^{(i)} := \mathbf{U}_k^{(i)\mathcal{N}} + s_{k+1} \left(\mathbf{U}_{k+1}^{(i)\mathcal{N}} - \mathbf{U}_k^{(i)\mathcal{N}} \right), \quad i = 1, \ldots, N, \quad (3.27)$$

where s_{k+1} is a small positive number. A simple choice is $s_{k+1} = (k+1)^{\frac{1}{n}}$, where n is initialized as $n = 3$ and its value may change as the algorithm progresses. If

$$f_{\mathcal{X}} \left(\mathbf{U}_{\text{new}}^{(1)}, \ldots, \mathbf{U}_{\text{new}}^{(N)} \right) \leq f_{\mathcal{X}} \left(\mathbf{U}_{k+1}^{(1)}, \ldots, \mathbf{U}_{k+1}^{(N)} \right),$$

the acceleration step is successful and we set $\mathbf{U}_{k+1}^{(i)} = \mathbf{U}_{\text{new}}^{(i)}$, for $i = 1, \ldots, N$. Otherwise, we set $\mathbf{U}_{k+1}^{(i)} = \mathbf{U}_{k+1}^{(i)\mathcal{N}}$, for $i = 1, \ldots, N$. If the acceleration step fails for n_0 iterations, we set $n = n + 1$, thus decreasing the momentum.

We can use various terminating criteria for the AO algorithm, based, for example, on the maximum number of iterations or the maximum relative factor change (RFC), where the RFC for factor $\mathbf{U}^{(i)}$ at the $(k + 1)$-st outer iteration is defined as

$$\text{RFC}_{k+1}^{(i)} := \frac{\left\| \mathbf{U}_{k+1}^{(i)} - \mathbf{U}_k^{(i)} \right\|_F}{\left\| \mathbf{U}_k^{(i)} \right\|_F}. \quad (3.28)$$

3.3 Tensor decomposition with missing elements

In many cases of practical interest, we observe a small subset of the elements of tensor $\mathcal{X}$, indexed by $\Omega \subseteq \mathbb{N}_{I_1} \times \cdots \times \mathbb{N}_{I_N}$. Let $\mathcal{M}$ be a binary tensor, with the same size as $\mathcal{X}$, whose elements are defined as

$$\mathcal{M}(i_1, i_2, \ldots, i_N) = \begin{cases} 1, & \text{if } (i_1, i_2, \ldots, i_N) \in \Omega, \\ 0, & \text{otherwise.} \end{cases} \tag{3.29}$$

The number of nonzero elements of $\mathcal{X}$ is equal to $\text{nnz} := |\Omega|$. The TDME problem can be expressed as

$$\min f_\Omega \left(\mathbf{U}^{(1)}, \mathbf{U}^{(2)}, \ldots, \mathbf{U}^{(N)} \right) + \frac{\lambda}{2} \sum_{i=1}^{N} \|\mathbf{U}^{(i)}\|_F^2, \tag{3.30}$$

where

$$f_\Omega \left(\mathbf{U}^{(1)}, \mathbf{U}^{(2)}, \ldots, \mathbf{U}^{(N)} \right) = \frac{1}{2} \left\| \mathcal{M} \circledast \left(\mathcal{X} - [\![\mathbf{U}^{(1)}, \mathbf{U}^{(2)}, \ldots, \mathbf{U}^{(N)}]\!] \right) \right\|_F^2. \tag{3.31}$$

If $\mathcal{Y} = [\![\mathbf{U}^{(1)}, \mathbf{U}^{(2)}, \ldots, \mathbf{U}^{(N)}]\!]$, then

$$f_\Omega \left(\mathbf{U}^{(1)}, \mathbf{U}^{(2)}, \ldots, \mathbf{U}^{(N)} \right) = \frac{1}{2} \left\| \mathbf{M}_{(i)} \circledast \left(\mathbf{X}_{(i)} - \mathbf{Y}_{(i)} \right) \right\|_F^2, \quad i \in \mathbb{N}_N, \tag{3.32}$$

where $\mathbf{M}_{(i)}$, $\mathbf{X}_{(i)}$, and $\mathbf{Y}_{(i)}$ are, respectively, the matrix unfoldings of $\mathcal{M}$, $\mathcal{X}$, and $\mathcal{Y}$ with respect to the i-th mode. Similarly to the dense case, these expressions form the basis of the AO method for TDME. More specifically, if we consider factor $\mathbf{U}^{(i)}$ as a variable, with all the other factors being fixed, then we can update $\mathbf{U}^{(i)}$ by solving the problem

$$\min_{\mathbf{U}^{(i)} \in \mathbb{U}^{(i)}} \left\| \mathbf{M}_{(i)} \circledast \left(\mathbf{X}_{(i)} - \mathbf{U}^{(i)} \mathbf{K}^{(i)T} \right) \right\|_F^2 + \frac{\lambda}{2} \|\mathbf{U}^{(i)}\|_F^2. \tag{3.33}$$

3.3.1 Matrix least-squares with missing elements

The solution of the MLS with missing elements (MLSME) problem will be our building block for the solution of the TDME problem. Let $\mathbf{X} \in \mathbb{R}^{P \times Q}$, $\mathbf{A} \in \mathbb{R}^{P \times R}$, and $\mathbf{B} \in \mathbb{R}^{Q \times R}$. Let $\Omega \subseteq \mathbb{N}_P \times \mathbb{N}_Q$ be the set of indices of the known elements of $\mathbf{X}$ and let $\mathbf{M}$ be a matrix with the same size as $\mathbf{X}$, with elements $\mathbf{M}(i, j)$ equal to one or zero, depending on the availability of the corresponding element of $\mathbf{X}$. We consider the problem

$$\min_{\mathbf{A} \in \mathbb{A}} f_\Omega(\mathbf{A}) := \frac{1}{2} \left\| \mathbf{M} \circledast \left(\mathbf{X} - \mathbf{A} \mathbf{B}^T \right) \right\|_F^2 + \frac{\lambda}{2} \|\mathbf{A}\|_F^2. \tag{3.34}$$

The gradient and the Hessian of f_Ω, at point $\mathbf{A}$, are given by

$$\nabla f_\Omega(\mathbf{A}) = - \left(\mathbf{M} \circledast \mathbf{X} - \mathbf{M} \circledast \left(\mathbf{A} \mathbf{B}^T \right) \right) \mathbf{B} + \lambda \mathbf{A} \tag{3.35}$$

and

$$\nabla^2 f_\Omega(\mathbf{A}) = \left(\mathbf{B}^T \otimes \mathbf{I}_P \right) \text{diag} \left(\text{vec} \left(\mathbf{M} \right) \right) \left(\mathbf{B} \otimes \mathbf{I}_P \right) + \lambda \mathbf{I}_{PR}. \tag{3.36}$$

3.3.1.1 The unconstrained case

In the unconstrained case, the optimal value, $\mathbf{A}^+$, is given by the solution of the equation

$$\left(\mathbf{M} \circledast \left(\mathbf{A}^+ \mathbf{B}^T\right)\right)\mathbf{B} + \lambda\mathbf{A}^+ = (\mathbf{M} \circledast \mathbf{X})\mathbf{B}. \tag{3.37}$$

We solve this equation in a row-wise manner. Thus, for $j = 1, \ldots, P$, we have

$$\left(\mathbf{M}(j,:) \circledast \left(\mathbf{A}^+(j,:)\mathbf{B}^T\right)\right)\mathbf{B} + \lambda\mathbf{A}^+(j,:) = \mathbf{W}(j,:), \tag{3.38}$$

where $\mathbf{W} := (\mathbf{M} \circledast \mathbf{X})\mathbf{B}$. This expression is equivalent to

$$\mathbf{A}^+(j,:)\left(\mathbf{B}^T\,\text{diag}(\mathbf{M}(j,:))\,\mathbf{B} + \lambda\mathbf{I}_R\right) = \mathbf{W}(j,:). \tag{3.39}$$

We define

$$\mathbf{G}_j := \mathbf{B}^T\,\text{diag}(\mathbf{M}(j,:))\,\mathbf{B}. \tag{3.40}$$

Thus

$$\mathbf{A}^+(j,:) = \mathbf{W}(j,:)\,(\mathbf{G}_j + \lambda\mathbf{I}_R)^{-1}. \tag{3.41}$$

In Algorithm 4, we present a solution of the unconstrained MLSME problem. We denote the output of Algorithm 4 as

$$\mathbf{A}^+ = \text{UMLSME}(\mathbf{X}, \mathbf{M}, \mathbf{B}, \lambda). \tag{3.42}$$

Algorithm 4: Algorithm for the unconstrained MLSME problem.

Input: $\mathbf{X}, \mathbf{M} \in \mathbb{R}^{P \times Q}, \mathbf{B} \in \mathbb{R}^{Q \times R}, \lambda$

1 $\mathbf{W} = (\mathbf{M} \circledast \mathbf{X})\mathbf{B}$
2 **for** $j = 1, \ldots, P$ **do**
3 $\quad$ Compute $\mathbf{G}_j$ using (3.40)
4 $\quad \mathbf{A}(j,:) = \mathbf{W}(j,:)\,(\mathbf{G}_j + \lambda\mathbf{I}_R)^{-1}$
5 **return A.**

The computational complexity of Algorithm 4 is as follows:

1. the computation of $\mathbf{W}$ requires $O(|\Omega|R)$ arithmetic operations;
2. the computation of $\mathbf{G}_j$, for $j = 1, \ldots, P$, requires $O(|\Omega|R^2)$ arithmetic operations;
3. the computation of $\mathbf{A}^+$ requires $O(PR^3)$ arithmetic operations.

3.3.1.2 The nonnegative case

In the nonnegative case, we solve the MLSME problem using the Nesterov-type algorithm of Algorithm 5. We observe that this algorithm is much more complicated than

Algorithm 2, mainly because of the computations in line 6, which must be repeated in every iteration.

A crucial point of the algorithm is the assignment of values to parameters μ and L. If we denote the optimal values as μ^* and L^*, then it turns out that $\mu^* + \lambda$ and $L^* + \lambda$ are, respectively, equal to the smallest and the largest eigenvalue of $\nabla^2 f_\Omega$. As the size of the problem grows, the computation of μ^* and L^* becomes very demanding. We may proceed along two paths:

1. A simple approximation is to set $\mu = 0$ and $L = \max(\text{eig}(\mathbf{B}^T \mathbf{B}))$, which can be easily computed, especially in the cases of small R. We have observed that, in practice, our choice for μ is very accurate for very sparse problems, while our choice for L is an easily computed upper bound for L^*.
2. A more computationally demanding but more effective approach is to compute the rows $\mathbf{A}_{l+1}(j, :)$ and $\mathbf{Y}_{l+1}(j, :)$, for $j \in \mathbb{N}_P$, in Algorithm 5, using $\mu = 0$, $L_j = \max(\text{eig}(\mathbf{G}_j))$, where $\mathbf{G}_j$ is defined in (3.40), and the respective β_j. Note that $\mathbf{G}_j + \lambda \mathbf{I}_R$ is the second derivative of $f_\Omega(\mathbf{A})$ with respect to $\mathbf{A}(j, :)$. Of course, this adds an overhead to the algorithm, since the computation of $\mathbf{G}_j$, for $j \in \mathbb{N}_P$, is not directly required in Algorithm 5, but leads to very useful step sizes and, as we shall see in the section with the numerical experiments (Section 3.5), its overall effect on the convergence speed of the algorithm is very significant.

Algorithm 5: Nesterov-type algorithm for the nonnegative MLSME problem.

Input: $\mathbf{X}, \mathbf{M} \in \mathbb{R}^{P \times Q}, \mathbf{B} \in \mathbb{R}^{Q \times R}, \mathbf{A}_* \in \mathbb{R}^{P \times R}, \lambda, \mu, L$

1 $\mathbf{W} = -(\mathbf{M} \circledast \mathbf{X})\mathbf{B}$

2 $C = \frac{L+\lambda}{\mu+\lambda}, \beta = \frac{\sqrt{C}-1}{\sqrt{C}+1}$

3 $\mathbf{A}_0 = \mathbf{Y}_0 = \mathbf{A}_*$

4 $l = 0$

5 **while** (*terminating condition is FALSE*) **do**

6      $\mathbf{Z}_l = \left(\mathbf{M} \circledast \left(\mathbf{Y}_l \mathbf{B}^T\right)\right) \mathbf{B}$

7      $\nabla f_\Omega(\mathbf{Y}_l) = \mathbf{W} + \mathbf{Z}_l + \lambda \mathbf{Y}_l$

8      $\mathbf{A}_{l+1} = \left(\mathbf{Y}_l - \frac{1}{L+\lambda} \nabla f_\Omega(\mathbf{Y}_l)\right)_+$

9      $\mathbf{Y}_{l+1} = \mathbf{A}_{l+1} + \beta \left(\mathbf{A}_{l+1} - \mathbf{A}_l\right)$

10     $l = l + 1$

11 **return** $\mathbf{A}_l$.

We denote the output of Algorithm 5 as

$$\mathbf{A}^+ = \text{NMLSME}(\mathbf{X}, \mathbf{M}, \mathbf{B}, \mathbf{A}_*, \lambda).$$

The computational complexity of Algorithm 5 is as follows:

1. the computation of $\mathbf{W}$ requires $O(|\Omega|R)$ arithmetic operations;

2. the computation of $\mathbf{Z}_l$ requires $O\left(|\Omega|R\right)$ arithmetic operations;

3. the computation of $\nabla f_\Omega(\mathbf{Y}_l)$ and the updates of $\mathbf{A}_l$ and $\mathbf{Y}_l$ require $O(PR)$ arithmetic operations.

3.3.2 Tensor decomposition with missing elements: the unconstrained case

In the AO framework, we update, in a circular manner, $\mathbf{U}_k^{(i)} \in \mathbb{U}^{(i)}$ with all the other factors being fixed. Thus, we compute

$$\mathbf{U}_{k+1}^{(i)} = \underset{\mathbf{U}^{(i)} \in \mathbb{U}^{(i)}}{\operatorname{argmin}} \left\| \mathbf{M}_{(i)} \circledast \left(\mathbf{X}_{(i)} - \mathbf{U}^{(i)} \mathbf{K}_k^{(i)T} \right) \right\|_F^2 + \frac{\lambda}{2} \| \mathbf{U}^{(i)} \|_F^2. \tag{3.43}$$

In the unconstrained case, a high-level update is given by

$$\mathbf{U}_{k+1}^{(i)} = \text{UMLSME}(\mathbf{X}_{(i)}, \mathbf{M}_{(i)}, \mathbf{K}_k^{(i)}, \lambda), \tag{3.44}$$

which actually amounts to the solution of the equation

$$\lambda \mathbf{U}_{k+1}^{(i)} + \left(\mathbf{M}_{(i)} \circledast \left(\mathbf{U}_{k+1}^{(i)} \mathbf{K}_k^{(i)T} \right) \right) \mathbf{K}_k^{(i)} = \left(\mathbf{M}_{(i)} \circledast \mathbf{X}_{(i)} \right) \mathbf{K}_k^{(i)}. \tag{3.45}$$

Based on Algorithm 4, we solve (3.45) in a row-wise manner. Thus, for $j = 1, \ldots, I_i$, we have

$$\mathbf{U}_{k+1}^{(i)}(j, :) = \mathbf{W}_k^{(i)}(j, :) \left(\mathbf{G}_{k,j}^{(i)} + \lambda \mathbf{I}_R \right)^{-1}, \tag{3.46}$$

where

$$\mathbf{W}_k^{(i)}(j, :) := \left(\mathbf{M}_{(i)}(j, :) \circledast \mathbf{X}_{(i)}(j, :) \right) \mathbf{K}_k^{(i)} \tag{3.47}$$

and

$$\mathbf{G}_{k,j}^{(i)} := \mathbf{K}_k^{(i)T} \operatorname{diag}(\mathbf{M}_{(i)}(j, :)) \mathbf{K}_k^{(i)}. \tag{3.48}$$

Detailed expressions for $\mathbf{W}_k^{(i)}(j, :)$ and $\mathbf{G}_{k,j}^{(i)}$ are as follows:

$$\mathbf{W}_k^{(i)}(j, :) = \sum_{\substack{(i_1, \ldots, i_N) \in \Omega \\ i_i = j}} \mathcal{X}(i_1, \ldots, i_N) \mathbf{P}_{i,k}(i_1, \ldots, i_N), \tag{3.49}$$

where $\mathbf{P}_{i,k}(i_1, \ldots, i_N)$ is the row vector

$$\begin{aligned}
\mathbf{P}_{i,k}(i_1, \ldots, i_N) := \Big(& \mathbf{U}_k^{(N)}(i_N, :) \circledast \cdots \circledast \mathbf{U}_k^{(i+1)}(i_{i+1}, :) \\
& \circledast \mathbf{U}_{k+1}^{(i-1)}(i_{i-1}, :) \circledast \cdots \circledast \mathbf{U}_{k+1}^{(1)}(i_1, :) \Big)
\end{aligned} \tag{3.50}$$

and

$$\mathbf{G}_{k,j}^{(i)} := \sum_{\substack{(i_1,\ldots,i_N)\in\Omega \\ i_i=j}} \mathbf{P}_{i,k}(i_1,\ldots,i_N)^T \mathbf{P}_{i,k}(i_1,\ldots,i_N). \tag{3.51}$$

3.3.3 Tensor decomposition with missing elements: the nonnegative case

At a high level, the update in the nonnegative case is given by

$$\mathbf{U}_{k+1}^{(i)} = \text{NMLSME}(\mathbf{X}_{(i)}, \mathbf{M}_{(i)}, \mathbf{K}_k^{(i)}, \mathbf{U}_k^{(i)}, \lambda). \tag{3.52}$$

In line 1 of Algorithm 5, matrix $\mathbf{W}_k^{(i)}$ is computed in a row-wise manner, with its j-th row, $\mathbf{W}_k^{(i)}(j,:)$, computed as in (3.47). Note that for every inner iteration (indexed by l) in line 6 of Algorithm 5, we compute

$$\mathbf{Z}_{k,l}^{(i)} = \left(\mathbf{M}_{(i)} \circledast \left(\mathbf{Y}_{k,l}^{(i)} \mathbf{K}_k^{(i)T}\right)\right) \mathbf{K}_k^{(i)}. \tag{3.53}$$

In more detailed form, the j-th row of $\mathbf{Z}_{k,l}^{(i)}$, for $j = 1, \ldots, I_i$, can be expressed as

$$\mathbf{Z}_{k,l}^{(i)}(j,:) = \sum_{\substack{(i_1,\ldots,i_N)\in\Omega \\ i_i=j}} \left(\mathbf{Y}_{k,l}^{(i)}(j,:)\mathbf{P}_{i,k}(i_1,\ldots,i_N)^T\right) \mathbf{P}_{i,k}(i_1,\ldots,i_N). \tag{3.54}$$

3.3.4 Alternating optimization for tensor decomposition with missing elements

In Algorithm 6, we present the AO TDME algorithm. We start from initial points $\mathbf{U}_0^{(i)}$, for $i = 1, \ldots, N$, and solve, in a circular manner, MLSME problems, based on the previous estimates. Similar to TD, we may perform an acceleration step after each AO outer iteration.

3.4 Distributed memory implementations

In this section, we describe parallel implementations of the AO-based TD and TDME algorithms presented in the previous section on a distributed memory environment with $p = \prod_{i=1}^{N} p_i$ processing elements. Our approach has been motivated by the medium-grained approach of [9] and for our distributed implementations we use MPI. Before presenting in detail our implementations, we make a brief introduction to MPI.

3.4.1 Some MPI preliminaries

Modern supercomputers consist of multiple nodes, with each node containing multiple cores. MPI is a library whose goal is to establish a portable, efficient, and flexible

---

Algorithm 6: AO algorithm for TDME.

Input: $\mathcal{X}, \Omega, \mathbf{U}_0^{(i)} \in \mathbb{U}^i, i = 1, \ldots, N, \lambda$.

1 $k = 0$

2 **while** (1) **do**

3   **for** $i = 1, 2, \ldots N$ **do**

4   **if** constraint = 'unconstrained' **then**

5              $\mathbf{U}_{k+1}^{(i)} = \mathrm{UMLSME}\left(\mathbf{X}_{(i)}, \mathbf{M}_{(i)}, \mathbf{K}_k^{(i)}, \lambda\right)$

6   **else if** constraint = 'nonnegative' **then**

7              $\mathbf{U}_{k+1}^{(i)} = \mathrm{NMLSME}\left(\mathbf{X}_{(i)}, \mathbf{M}_{(i)}, \mathbf{K}_k^{(i)}, \mathbf{U}_k^{(i)}, \lambda\right)$

8   **endif**

9   **if** (terminating condition is TRUE) **then** break; **endif**

10      $k = k + 1$

11 **return** $\mathbf{U}_k^{(i)}, i = 1, \ldots, N$.

---

standard for message passing and is widely used for the development of programs running on distributed computing environments. There are several implementations of MPI, with some being free and open source (e.g., Open MPI [31]). MPI provides routines that are directly callable from C, C++, and FORTRAN programs. In addition, there exist language bindings that enable the usage of MPI with other languages, such as Java, MATLAB, and Python. In the sequel, we briefly discuss some of the operations frequently used in our toolbox.

3.4.1.1 Communication domains and topologies

A key MPI concept is the communication domain, which is a set of processes that are allowed to communicate with each other. Information about communication domains is stored in variables, which are called communicators. The communicators are used as arguments in all message transfer MPI routines and uniquely identify the processes participating in the message transfer operation. The default communicator allows communication among all processes. Note that each process may belong to more than one (possibly, overlapping) communication domains.

Choosing the right topology for a distributed computational task is directly related to the problem at hand. Topologies that can be used include linear arrays, rings, tree networks, N-dimensional meshes, and hypercubes. For more details on the properties of each topology, we refer the reader to [32].

3.4.1.2 Synchronization among processes

Synchronization between MPI processes in a communication domain is necessary in many cases (e.g., I/O, data dependencies, etc.). Usually, it is implemented via `MPI_Barrier`, where each process waits until all processes reach this point before proceeding further.

3.4.1.3 Point-to-point communication operations

A point-to-point connection refers to a communications connection between two communication endpoints. For example, `MPI_Send` allows a specific process to send a message to another specific process, which receives the message via `MPI_Recv`.

3.4.1.4 Collective communication operations

Collective operations involve communication among all processes of a communication domain. An example of a collective operation is `MPI_Reduce`, which collects data from all processes of a communication domain, performs an operation (such as summing `MPI_SUM` and finding the minimum `MPI_MIN` or the maximum `MPI_MAX`), and stores the result in one node. Another collective operation is `MPI_Scatter`, where a single node sends a unique message to every other node. The reverse of this type of communication is the operation `MPI_Gather`. In this operation, many processes send distinct messages, which are then gathered by a designated process; this can be considered as a reduce operation that uses the concatenation operator.

Collective communication operations do not act like barriers. They act like a virtual synchronization step, in the sense that the parallel program should behave correctly even if a global synchronization is performed before and after the collective call.

In our implementations, we mainly use the following collective communication operations:

- `MPI_Allreduce`: This is used when the result of a reduce operation must become available to all processing units of a communication domain, instead of just one unit.
- `MPI_Reduce_scatter`: This is a combination of a reduce operation followed by a scatter operation.
- `MPI_Allgather`: This communicates the result of the gather operation to all the nodes of a communication domain. It can be interpreted as an all-reduce operation with concatenation as the operator.

3.4.1.5 Derived data types

Many MPI functions require the specification of the type of data which are communicated among processes. MPI predefines a set of data types, such as `MPI_INT`, `MPI_CHAR`, and `MPI_DOUBLE`, in order to operate on variables of type `int`, `char`, and `double`, respectively.

3.4.2 Variable partitioning and data allocation

We describe in detail the implementation of the TD and TDME algorithms for the decomposition of a mode-N tensor $\mathcal{X} \in \mathbb{R}^{I_1 \times \cdots \times I_N}$ on an N-dimensional Cartesian processor space, whose processors are denoted as $p_{i_1,\ldots,i_N}$, with $i_j \in \mathbb{N}_{p_j}$ and $j \in \mathbb{N}_N$.

At first, we introduce certain partitionings of the factor matrices and the tensor $\mathcal{X}$.

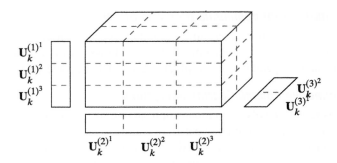

FIGURE 3.1

Tensor $\mathcal{X}$, factors $\mathbf{U}_k^{(1)}$, $\mathbf{U}_k^{(2)}$, and $\mathbf{U}_k^{(3)}$, and their partitioning for $p_1 = p_2 = 3$ and $p_3 = 2$.

We partition each factor matrix $\mathbf{U}_k^{(i)}$ into p_i block rows as

$$\mathbf{U}_k^{(i)} = \left[\ \left(\mathbf{U}_k^{(i)^1}\right)^T \ \cdots \ \left(\mathbf{U}_k^{(i)^{p_i}}\right)^T \ \right]^T, \tag{3.55}$$

with $\mathbf{U}_k^{(i)^j} \in \mathbb{R}^{\frac{I_i}{p_i} \times R}$, for $j \in \mathbb{N}_{p_i}$.

Accordingly, we partition tensor $\mathcal{X}$ into p subtensors $\mathcal{X}^{i_1,\ldots,i_N} \in \mathbb{R}^{\frac{I_1}{p_1} \times \cdots \times \frac{I_N}{p_N}}$ as

$$\mathcal{X}^{i_1,\ldots,i_N} = \mathcal{X}\left((i_1 - 1)\frac{I_1}{p_1} + 1 : i_1\frac{I_1}{p_1}, \ldots, (i_N - 1)\frac{I_N}{p_N} + 1 : i_N\frac{I_N}{p_N} \right), \tag{3.56}$$

for $i_j \in \mathbb{N}_{p_j}$ and $j \in \mathbb{N}_N$. In Fig. 3.1, we depict a partitioning of a 3D tensor and its factors.

Similarly to the partitioning of factor $\mathbf{U}_k^{(i)}$ in (3.55), we partition the mode-i matricization of $\mathcal{X}$ as

$$\mathbf{X}_{(i)} = \left[\ \left(\mathbf{X}_{(i)}^1\right)^T \ \cdots \ \left(\mathbf{X}_{(i)}^{p_i}\right)^T \ \right]^T, \tag{3.57}$$

with $\mathbf{X}_{(i)}^j \in \mathbb{R}^{\frac{I_i}{p_i} \times \prod_{n=1,n\neq i}^{N} I_n}$, for $j \in \mathbb{N}_{p_i}$.

Processor $p_{i_1,\ldots,i_N}$ receives subtensor $\mathcal{X}^{i_1,\ldots,i_N}$ and contributes to the updates of the i_j-th part of factor $\mathbf{U}_k^{(j)}$, $\mathbf{U}_k^{(j)^{i_j}}$, for $j \in \mathbb{N}_N$.

We assume that, at the end of the k-th outer AO iteration,

1. processor $p_{i_1,\ldots,i_N}$ knows $\mathbf{U}_k^{(1)^{i_1}}$, $\mathbf{U}_k^{(2)^{i_2}}$, $\ldots$, $\mathbf{U}_k^{(N)^{i_N}}$;
2. *all* processors know $\mathbf{U}_k^{(i)T}\mathbf{U}_k^{(i)}$, for $i \in \mathbb{N}_N$.

3.4.2.1 Communication domains

We define certain communication domains (or processor groups) [32] over subsets of the p processors, which are used for the efficient collaborative implementation of specific computational tasks, as explained in detail below.

First, we define the $(N-1)$-dimensional groups of processors involving the $\prod_{k=1,k\neq i}^{N} p_k$ processors having the i-th index equal to j, i.e.,

$$\mathbb{P}_{i,j} := \{p_{k_1,k_2,\ldots,k_{i-1},j,k_{i+1},\ldots,k_N} : k_l \in \mathbb{N}_{p_l}, l \neq i\}, \ i \in \mathbb{N}_N, \ j \in \mathbb{N}_{p_i}. \quad (3.58)$$

These processor groups form hyperlayers in the processor space and are used for the collaborative update of $\mathbf{U}_k^{(i)^j}$.

We also define the 1D processor groups involving the p_i processors that differ only at the i-th index, for $i \in \mathbb{N}_N$:

$$\mathbb{P}_{k_1,\ldots,k_{i-1},:,k_{i+1},\ldots,k_N} := \{p_{k_1,\ldots,k_{i-1},j,k_{i+1},\ldots,k_N} : j = 1,\ldots,p_i\}, \ k_j \in \mathbb{N}_{p_j}. \quad (3.59)$$

Each of these groups forms a mode-i fiber in the processor space and is used for the collaborative computation of $\mathbf{U}_{k+1}^{(i)^T}\mathbf{U}_{k+1}^{(i)}$, for $i \in \mathbb{N}_N$.

3.4.3 Tensor decomposition

In the sequel, we present the details of the update of the factor $\mathbf{U}_k^{(i)}$ in the case of TD.

3.4.3.1 The unconstrained and the nonnegative case

We assume that factor $\mathbf{U}^{(i)}$ is either unconstrained or nonnegative. In both cases, the updates are quite similar, with the only difference being in step 2 below. The update is achieved via the parallel updates of $\mathbf{U}_k^{(i)^j}$, for $j \in \mathbb{N}_{p_i}$, and consists of the following steps:

1. The processors in the group $\mathbb{P}_{i,j}$, for $j \in \mathbb{N}_{p_i}$, collaboratively compute the $\frac{I_i}{p_i} \times R$ matrix

$$\mathbf{W}_k^{(i)^j} = \mathbf{X}_{(i)}^j \mathbf{K}_k^{(i)}, \quad (3.60)$$

and the result is scattered among the processors in the group. Thus, each processor in the group receives $\frac{I_i}{\prod_{k=1}^{N} p_k}$ successive rows of $\mathbf{W}_k^{(i)^j}$. Term $\mathbf{W}_k^{(i)^j}$ can be computed collaboratively because it is equal to

$$\sum_{p_{i_1,\ldots,j,\ldots,i_N} \in \mathbb{P}_{i,j}} \mathbf{X}_{(i)}^{i_1,\ldots,i_N} \left(\mathbf{U}_k^{(N)^{i_N}} \odot \cdots \odot \mathbf{U}_k^{(i+1)^{i_{i+1}}} \odot \mathbf{U}_{k+1}^{(i-1)^{i_{i-1}}} \odot \cdots \odot \mathbf{U}_{k+1}^{(1)^{i_1}} \right),$$

where $\mathbf{X}_{(i)}^{i_1,\ldots,i_N}$ is the matricization of $\mathcal{X}^{i_1,\ldots,i_N}$ with respect to the i-th mode. Each processor $p_{i_1,\ldots,i_N} \in \mathbb{P}_{i,j}$ computes one term of the above sum. The total sum is computed and scattered among all processors in $\mathbb{P}_{i,j}$ via a reduce-scatter operation.

2. Each processor in the group $\mathbb{P}_{i,j}$ uses the scattered part of $\mathbf{W}_k^{(i)^j}$, matrix $\mathbf{K}_k^{(i)T}\mathbf{K}_k^{(i)}$, as computed in (3.26), and the appropriate part of factor $\mathbf{U}_k^{(i)^j}$, and computes the part of $\mathbf{U}_{k+1}^{(i)^j}$ via the update_factor algorithm. In the unconstrained case, the update is attained by the solution of a system of linear equations. In the nonnegative case, the update is attained by the application of the NMLS algorithm.

3. The updated parts of $\mathbf{U}_{k+1}^{(i)^j}$ are all-gathered at the processors of the group $\mathbb{P}_{i,j}$, so that *all* processors in the group know $\mathbf{U}_{k+1}^{(i)^j}$.

4. By applying an all-reduce operation to $\left(\mathbf{U}_{k+1}^{(i)^j}\right)^T \mathbf{U}_{k+1}^{(i)^j}$, for $j \in \mathbb{N}_{p_i}$, on each 1D processor group along the mode-i fibers of the processor space, *all* processors learn $\mathbf{U}_{k+1}^{(i)T}\mathbf{U}_{k+1}^{(i)}$.

3.4.3.2 The orthogonal case

If factor $\mathbf{U}^{(i)}$ has orthonormal columns, its update is achieved via the parallel updates of $\mathbf{U}_k^{(i)^j}$, for $j \in \mathbb{N}_{p_i}$, and consists of the following steps [33]:

1. The processors in the group $\mathbb{P}_{i,j}$, for $j \in \mathbb{N}_{p_i}$, collaboratively compute the $\frac{I_i}{p_i} \times R$ matrix

$$\mathbf{W}_k^{(i)^j} = \mathbf{X}_{(i)}^j \mathbf{K}_k^{(i)}, \tag{3.61}$$

as in step 1 of Section 3.4.3.1.

2. All processors collaboratively compute the $R \times R$ matrix

$$\mathbf{W}_k^{(i)T}\mathbf{W}_k^{(i)} = \sum_{j=1}^{p_i} \left(\mathbf{W}_k^{(i)^j}\right)^T \mathbf{W}_k^{(i)^j}, \tag{3.62}$$

by applying an all-reduce operation on each 1D processor group along the mode-i fibers of the processor grid. We note that, at the end of this step, *all* processors know matrix $\mathbf{W}_k^{(i)T}\mathbf{W}_k^{(i)}$ and, thus, can compute its eigenvalue decomposition.

3. Each processor in $\mathbb{P}_{i,j}$ computes the updated factor $\mathbf{U}_{k+1}^{(i)^j}$ as

$$\mathbf{U}_{k+1}^{(i)^j} = \mathbf{W}_k^{(i)^j}\left(\mathbf{W}_k^{(i)T}\mathbf{W}_k^{(i)}\right)^{-\frac{1}{2}}. \tag{3.63}$$

3.4.3.3 Factor normalization and acceleration

The squared Euclidean norms of the columns of each factor $\mathbf{U}_{k+1}^{(i)}$ appear on the diagonals of $\mathbf{U}_{k+1}^{(i)T}\mathbf{U}_{k+1}^{(i)}$, and are known to all processors. Thus, no communication is necessary for the normalization of the columns of the updated factors.

After the completion of the $(k+1)$-st AO iteration, processor $p_{j_1,\dots,j_N}$ knows the parts of the normalized factors $\mathbf{U}_{k+1}^{(i)^{j_l}\mathcal{N}}$ and $\mathbf{U}_k^{(i)^{j_l}\mathcal{N}}$, for $l \in \mathbb{N}_N$. It is thus able to compute $\mathbf{U}_{\text{new}}^{(i)^{j_l}}$, for $l \in \mathbb{N}_N$ (see (3.27)). The value of the cost function $f_\mathcal{X}$ at points $(\mathbf{U}_{k+1}^{(1)}, \ldots, \mathbf{U}_{k+1}^{(N)})$ and $(\mathbf{U}_{\text{new}}^{(1)}, \ldots, \mathbf{U}_{\text{new}}^{(N)})$ is computed collaboratively via an all-reduce operation over the whole processor grid and becomes known to all processors. Thus, all processors make the same decision regarding the success or failure of the acceleration step.

3.4.4 Tensor decomposition with missing elements

We describe in detail the update of $\mathbf{U}_k^{(i)}$ in the case of TDME. The update is achieved via the parallel updates of $\mathbf{U}_k^{(i)j}$, for $j \in \mathbb{N}_{p_i}$.

First, we note that quantities $\mathbf{W}_k^{(i)j} = \left(\mathbf{M}_{(i)}^j \circledast \mathbf{X}_{(i)}^j \right) \mathbf{K}_k^{(i)}$, $\mathbf{G}_{k,t}^{(i)}$, where t denotes a row of $\mathbf{U}_k^{(i)j}$, and $\mathbf{Z}_{k,l}^{(i)j}$, which are used for the update of $\mathbf{U}_k^{(i)j}$, can be computed in a collaborative manner on the processor group $\mathbb{P}_{i,j}$. This holds true because $\mathbf{W}_k^{(i)j}$ can be expressed as

$$\mathbf{W}_k^{(i)j} = \sum_{p_{i_1},\ldots,j,\ldots,i_N \in \mathbb{P}_{i,j}} \left(\mathbf{M}_{(i)}^{i_1,\ldots,i_N} \circledast \mathbf{X}_{(i)}^{i_1,\ldots,i_N} \right) \tag{3.64}$$
$$\left(\mathbf{U}_k^{(N)i_N} \odot \cdots \odot \mathbf{U}_k^{(i+1)i_{i+1}} \odot \mathbf{U}_{k+1}^{(i-1)i_{i-1}} \odot \cdots \odot \mathbf{U}_{k+1}^{(1)i_1} \right),$$

and analogous relations hold for $\mathbf{G}_{k,t}^{(i)}$ and $\mathbf{Z}_{k,l}^{(i)j}$.

3.4.4.1 The unconstrained case

The update of $\mathbf{U}_k^{(i)j}$ in the unconstrained case is implemented collaboratively on the processor group $\mathbb{P}_{i,j}$ in a row-wise fashion, and consists of the following steps:

1. each row of $\mathbf{W}_k^{(i)j}$ and the corresponding $(R \times R)$ matrix $\mathbf{G}_{k,t}^{(i)}$ are computed via two all-reduce operations over $\mathbb{P}_{i,j}$;
2. each processor in $\mathbb{P}_{i,j}$ solves the resulting system of linear equations;
3. after the update of all the rows of $\mathbf{U}_k^{(i)j}$, *all* processors in $\mathbb{P}_{i,j}$ know $\mathbf{U}_{k+1}^{(i)j}$.

3.4.4.2 The nonnegative case

The collaborative update of $\mathbf{U}_k^{(i)j}$ on $\mathbb{P}_{i,j}$ in the nonnegative case is achieved as follows:

1. Term $\mathbf{W}_k^{(i)j}$ is computed in a collaborate manner on $\mathbb{P}_{i,j}$ and scattered among the processors of the group via a reduce-scatter operation.
2. Before the execution of the while loop of Algorithm 5, we must compute either the global parameter $L = \max \left(\text{eig} \left(\mathbf{K}_k^{(i)T} \mathbf{K}_k^{(i)} \right) \right)$ or the local parameters, one per row, $L_t = \max \left(\text{eig} \left(\mathbf{G}_{k,t}^{(i)} \right) \right)$, where t denotes the corresponding row to be updated. Now L can be computed as in the TD case, while in order to compute L_t, we must compute $\mathbf{G}_{k,t}^{(i)}$ as in step 1 of the unconstrained case.

3. During each iteration of the while loop, indexed by l (see line 6 of Algorithm 5), we compute matrix $\mathbf{Z}_{k,l}^{(i)^j}$ according to (3.54). Each processor in the group $\mathbb{P}_{i,j}$ computes its contribution to $\mathbf{Z}_{k,l}^{(i)^j}$ in a row-wise fashion. By a reduce-scatter operation over $\mathbb{P}_{i,j}$, all processors in the group learn the appropriate rows of $\mathbf{Z}_{k,l}^{(i)^j}$ and perform an accelerated gradient step. An all-gather operation over $\mathbb{P}_{i,j}$ follows, and thus all processors in the group learn $\mathbf{Y}_{k,l+1}^{(i)^j}$ and become ready for the next iteration of the while loop.

4. After the end of Algorithm 5, the updated parts of $\mathbf{U}_k^{(i)^j}$ are all-gathered at all processors of the group $\mathbb{P}_{i,j}$, so that *all* processors in the group learn the updated factor $\mathbf{U}_{k+1}^{(i)^j}$.

5. If we implement the variation with the global L, then by applying an all-reduce operation to $\left(\mathbf{U}_{k+1}^{(i)^j}\right)^T \mathbf{U}_{k+1}^{(i)^j}$, for $j \in \mathbb{N}_{p_i}$, on each of the mode-i 1D processor groups, *all* processors learn $\mathbf{U}_{k+1}^{(i)T}\mathbf{U}_{k+1}^{(i)}$. Thus, all processors can compute $\mathbf{K}_k^{(i+1)T}\mathbf{K}_k^{(i+1)}$.

3.4.5 Some implementation details

The PARTENSOR toolbox is a header-only library, which makes it easy to be integrated into other projects. The header files can be used directly. Detailed documentation as well as various test cases are provided in our public project repository (https://github.com/neurocom/partensor-toolbox). The user can compile and run the examples that exist in the test directory. For the documentation and unit tests, we use the CMake build system. For more details and instructions, the user may refer to the manual in the github repository mentioned above.

Multilinear algebra operations are implemented using the Eigen library [34] (which has a column-major storage format). We provide two versions for the TD problem. In the first version, we store all the matricized tensors (N copies of `Eigen Dense Matrix`), whereas in the second, we store the tensor to be decomposed once (`Eigen Dense Tensor`). The latter version uses the dimension tree structure.[4]

For the TDME problem, we use the Eigen Sparse module, which implements a more versatile variant of the widely used compressed column (or row) storage scheme. We store all N matricizations, which requires $\mathcal{O}(N|\Omega|)$ of storage. In the very sparse case, where $|\Omega| \ll \prod_{i=1}^{N} I_i$, storing all the matricizations in the memory may not be a significant problem. On the other hand, it improves the efficiency in memory access for the Eigen Sparse structure. The user provides the initial dataset

---

[4] A clever computation of the MTTKRPs can be achieved via a data structure called dimension trees (DTs). The idea was first described in [35]. The goal was to avoid recomputing quantities that are common among the various MTTKRPs during a full AO iteration. DTs achieve this goal by storing these quantities, resulting in computational gains. In order to keep the presentation as simple as possible with a focus on parallel implementations, we do not describe this technique here but refer the interested reader to [10].

with tuples that correspond to the nonzero elements of the tensor through a matrix in the format $(i_1, i_2, ..., i_N, v)$, with $i_i \in \mathbb{N}_{I_i}$ and $v \in \mathbb{R}$ or $\mathbb{R}_+$.

3.5 **Numerical experiments**

We now present results obtained from the MPI implementation of the algorithms described in Section 3.4. The programs are executed on a DELL PowerEdge R820 system with SandyBridge – Intel(R) Xeon(R) CPU E5-4650v2 (in total, 44 nodes with 40 cores each at 2.4 Gz) and 512 GB RAM per node (fat partition).

For benchmarking purposes, we measure the execution time of our implementations for various tensor orders, sizes, and ranks. Unless otherwise specified, we perform 10 outer AO iterations and each time we solve an NMLS problem (for both TD and TDME) we perform 50 inner (accelerated gradient) iterations. For the TD problem, at the end of each AO iteration, we perform a normalization and an acceleration step.

For the experiments with synthetic data, we randomly generate the true factors $\{\mathbf{U}^{(i)}\}_{i=1}^{N}$ using the appropriate statistical laws and set $\mathcal{X} = [\![\mathbf{U}^{(1)}, \ldots, \mathbf{U}^{(N)}]\!]$. More specifically, if $\mathbf{U}^{(i)}$ is unconstrained, its elements are independent identically distributed (i.i.d.) $\mathcal{U}[-1, 1]$. If $\mathbf{U}^{(i)}$ is nonnegative, its elements are i.i.d. $\mathcal{U}[0, 1]$. Finally, if $\mathbf{U}^{(i)}$ is orthogonal, it is computed by the SVD of a random matrix of appropriate dimensions.

3.5.1 **Tensor decomposition**

We first consider the TD problem and compare the performance of the implementations that use tensor matricizations (TMs) and dimension trees (DTs).

We start with synthetic third-order tensors. We consider the unconstrained case, the nonnegative case, and the case with two nonnegative and one orthogonal factor. The tensors and the processor grid are cubic. In Figs. 3.2 and 3.3, we plot the execution time for these three cases with $I_1 = I_2 = I_3 = 1000$ and rank $R = 15, 50$. The number of processors comprising the grid are $p = 1, 8, 27, 64, 125, 216, 343, 512$. We observe that the execution times are very close in all cases. Furthermore, the DTs offer a performance improvement over the TMs.

In Fig. 3.4, we plot the execution time for a fourth-order nonnegative tensor with $I_1 = I_2 = I_3 = I_4 = 178$ and rank $R = 10, 50$ and a fifth-order nonnegative tensor with $I_1 = I_2 = I_3 = I_4 = I_5 = 64$ and rank $R = 10, 30$. We observe that for higher-order tensors, increasing the value of the rank seems to affect the performance of the DTs.

In Fig. 3.5, we plot the execution time breakdown among the various operations performed during the AO algorithm for the TD problem for a synthetic nonnegative tensor with $I_1 = I_2 = I_3 = 1000$ and rank $R = 15, 20, 30, 40, 50$ and a cubic processor grid of $p = 125$ cores (we consider both TMs and DTs). We observe that the MTTKRP is the most computationally demanding operation, with the acceleration

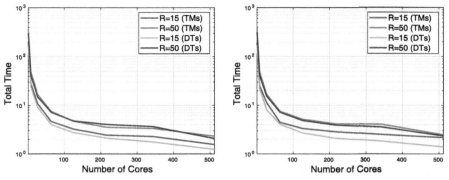

FIGURE 3.2

TD: Execution time in sec for a $1000 \times 1000 \times 1000$ tensor for
$p = 1, 8, 27, 64, 125, 216, 343, 512$, using TMs and DTs. (left) Unconstrained.
(right) Nonnegative.

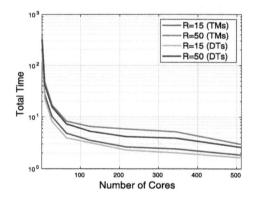

FIGURE 3.3

TD: Execution time in sec for a $1000 \times 1000 \times 1000$ tensor with two nonnegative and one
orthogonal factor for $p = 1, 8, 27, 64, 125, 216, 343, 512$, using TMs and DTs.

step coming second. The time required for the factor updates and the communication
is quite small.

3.5.2 Tensor decomposition with missing elements

Next, we present results for the unconstrained and the nonnegative TDME problem.
In the cases where the tensor dimensions differ significantly over the modes, the
processor grid resembles the tensor, that is, we assign more processors along the
modes with the largest dimensions.

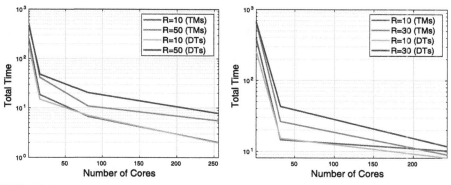

FIGURE 3.4

TD: Execution time in sec for (left) a $178 \times 178 \times 178 \times 178$ nonnegative tensor for $p = 1, 16, 81, 256$ and (right) a $64 \times 64 \times 64 \times 64 \times 64$ nonnegative tensor for $p = 1, 32, 243$, using TMs and DTs.

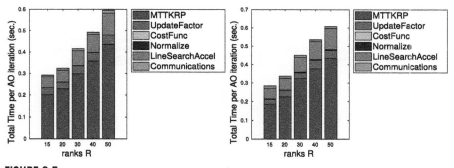

FIGURE 3.5

TD: Execution time breakdown for a $1000 \times 1000 \times 1000$ nonnegative tensor for $p = 5 \times 5 \times 5$, using (left) TMs and (right) DTs.

In Fig. 3.6, we plot the execution time[5] for (left) a synthetic third-order nonnegative tensor with one large dimension and two small ones, of size $800,000 \times 1000 \times 1000$, having 8,000,044 nonzero elements (99.999% sparsity) and $R = 10, 50$, and (right) a cubic fourth-order unconstrained tensor of size $1000 \times 1000 \times 1000 \times 1000$ with 10,000,000 nonzero elements (99.999% sparsity) and $R = 10, 30$.

In order to test the effectiveness of the two step sizes suggested in Section 3.3.1.2, we decompose the MovieLens 10M dataset [36], which contains ratings of movies made by users. We arrange the dataset in a third-order tensor of size $71,567 \times 65,133 \times 730$ with 10,000,054 nonzero elements. The modes correspond to (user, movie_ id, timestamp), where timestamps are organized in seven-day-wide ranges.

---

[5] We present results for the algorithm variation where the parameter L is computed in a row-wise fashion.

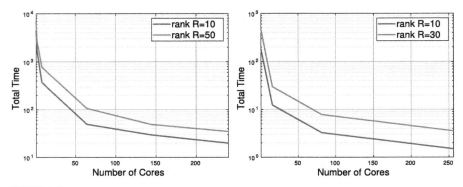

FIGURE 3.6

TDME: Execution time in sec for (left) a synthetic nonnegative tensor of dimensions $800{,}000 \times 1000 \times 1000$ with 8,000,044 nonzero elements (99.999% sparsity) and $p = 1, 2, 8, 64, 144, 240$ cores and (right) a 4th-order unconstrained tensor of size $1000 \times 1000 \times 1000 \times 1000$ with 10,000,000 nonzero elements (99.999% sparsity) and $R = 10, 30$, with $p = 1, 16, 81, 256$.

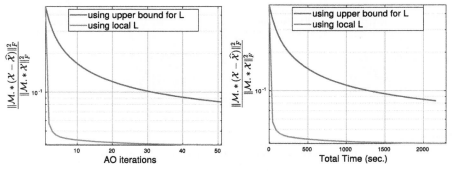

FIGURE 3.7

TDME: Relative tensor approximation squared error versus (left) AO iterations and (right) execution time for the MovieLens 10M dataset, for $R = 10$ and $p = 144$ cores.

We set $R = 10$ and perform 50 AO iterations. Every time we solve an NMLSME problem, we perform 100 inner (accelerated gradient) iterations. In Fig. 3.7, we plot the relative tensor approximation squared error versus AO iteration (left) and execution time (right), for $p = 144$ cores. We observe that the algorithm variation with the global L is slightly faster than the one with the local L's, since the total execution time is slightly larger for the latter. However, the variation with the local L's converges must faster in terms of both AO iterations and execution time.

In Fig. 3.8, we plot the execution time breakdown among the various operations performed during the AO algorithm for the TDME problem for the MovieLens

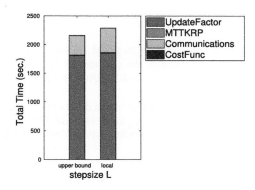

FIGURE 3.8

TDME: Execution time breakdown for the MovieLens dataset with $p = 144$ cores.

dataset with rank $R = 10$. We observe that in both cases, the factor update is the most computationally demanding operation, with the data communication coming second.

3.6 Conclusion

We focused on the CPD model and considered the TD and TDME problems. Concerning the TD problem, we focused on the cases where the factors are unconstrained, nonnegative, or orthogonal. Under the AO framework, the factor updates for the unconstrained and orthogonal cases have closed-form solutions, while in the nonnegative case we used an accelerated gradient method, which is optimal in theory and very efficient in practice.

Concerning the TDME problem, we focused on unconstrained problems, which have a closed-form solution, and nonnegative problems, where we used a variation of the accelerated gradient.

We described parallel implementations of the presented algorithms on a distributed memory system with a multidimensional processor grid. The structure of the grid and the data allocation are the same for both the TD and TDME problems. However, the TDME is more demanding from a computation and communication perspective. Using numerical experiments, we observed that our implementations attain significant speedup.

We note that we have also developed shared memory (OpenMP) implementations of our algorithms, which were not discussed in this work. We are currently working on extensions using (accelerated) stochastic gradient methods and their shared memory implementations.

The developed algorithms form the backbone of the open source toolbox PARTENSOR, which can be downloaded from www.partensor.com, is available to the academic and scientific community, and can incorporate additions and extensions.

Acknowledgment

This work was supported by the European Regional Development Fund of the European Union and Greek national funds through the Operational Program Competitiveness, Entrepreneurship, and Innovation, under the call RESEARCH–CREATE–INNOVATE (project code: T1EΔK-03360).

It was also supported by computational time granted from the National Infrastructures for Research and Technology S.A. (GRNET S.A.) in the National HPC facility – ARIS – under project IDs PR006044–PARTENSOR and PR008040–PARTENSOR SPARSE.

References

[1] P.M. Kroonenberg, Applied Multiway Data Analysis, Wiley-Interscience, 2008.

[2] A. Cichocki, R. Zdunek, A.H. Phan, S. Amari, Nonnegative Matrix and Tensor Factorizations, Wiley, 2009.

[3] T.G. Kolda, B.W. Bader, Tensor decompositions and applications, SIAM Review 51 (2009) 455–500.

[4] N.D. Sidiropoulos, et al., Tensor decomposition for signal processing and machine learning, IEEE Transactions on Signal Processing 65 (2017) 3551–3582.

[5] A. Cichocki, et al., Tensor decompositions for signal processing applications: from two-way to multiway component analysis, IEEE Signal Processing Magazine 32 (2015) 145–163.

[6] U. Kang, E. Papalexakis, A. Harpale, C. Faloutsos, GigaTensor: scaling tensor analysis up by 100 times – algorithms and discoveries, in: Proceedings of the 18th ACM SIGKDD International Conference on Knowledge Discovery and Data Mining (KDD12), Beiging, China, 2012.

[7] J.H. Choi, S.V.N. Vishwanathan, DFacTo: distributed factorization of tensors, in: Advances in Neural Information Processing Systems (NIPS), 2014.

[8] L. Karlsson, D. Kressner, A. Uschmajew, Parallel algorithms for tensor completion in the CP format, Parallel Computing (2015).

[9] S. Smith, G. Karypis, A medium-grained algorithm for distributed sparse tensor factorization, in: 30th IEEE International Parallel & Distributed Processing Symposium, 2016.

[10] O. Kaya, B. Uçar, Parallel candecomp/parafac decomposition of sparse tensors using dimension trees, SIAM Journal on Scientific Computing 40 (2018) C99–C130.

[11] K. Huang, N.D. Sidiropoulos, A.P. Liavas, A flexible and efficient framework for constrained matrix and tensor factorization, IEEE Transactions on Acoustics, Speech, and Signal Processing 64 (2016) 5052–5065.

[12] S. Smith, A. Beri, G. Karypis, Constrained tensor factorization with accelerated AO-ADMM, in: 2017 45th International Conference on Parallel Processing (ICPP), Bristol, 2017.

[13] A.P. Liavas, G. Kostoulas, G. Lourakis, K. Huang, N.D. Sidiropoulos, Nesterov-based alternating optimization for nonnegative tensor factorization: algorithm and parallel implementations, IEEE Transactions on Signal Processing 66 (Feb. 2018) 944–953.

[14] G. Ballard, K. Hoyashi, R. Kannan, Parallel nonnegative CP decompositions of dense tensors, in: 2018 IEEE 25th International Conference on High Prformance Computing (HiPC), Bengaluru, India, 2018.

[15] E.E. Papalexakis, C. Faloutsos, N.D. Sidiropoulos, Sparse parallelizable CANDECOMP-PARAFAC tensor decomposition, ACM Transactions on Knowledge Discovery from Data 10 (July 2015), https://doi.org/10.1145/2729980, issn: 1556–4681.

[16] N.D. Sidiropoulos, E.E. Papalexakis, C. Faloutsos, Parallel randomly compressed cubes: a scalable distributed architecture for big tensor decomposition, IEEE Signal Processing Magazine 31 (2014) 57–70.

[17] B. Yang, A. Zamzam, N.D. Sidiropoulos, in: Proceedings of the 2018 SIAM International Conference on Data Mining (SDM), 2018, pp. 396–404, https://epubs.siam.org/doi/abs/1S.1137/1.9781611975321.45.

[18] B. Yang, A.S. Zamzam, N.D. Sidiropoulos, Large scale tensor factorization via parallel sketches, IEEE Transactions on Knowledge and Data Engineering 1 (1) (2020).

[19] T. Papastergiou, V. Megalooikonomou, A distributed proximal gradient descent method for tensor completion, in: 2017 IEEE International Conference on Big Data (Big Data), 2017, pp. 2056–2065.

[20] S. Smith, J. Park, G. Karypis, An exploration of optimization algorithms for high performance tensor completion, in: SC'16: Proceedings of the International Conference for High Performance Computing, Networking, Storage and Analysis, 2016, pp. 359–371.

[21] K. Xie, et al., Accurate and fast recovery of network monitoring data: a GPU accelerated matrix completion, IEEE/ACM Transactions on Networking PP (Mar. 2020) 1–14.

[22] K.D. Devine, G. Ballard, GentenMPI: Distributed Memory Sparse Tensor Decomposition, Aug. 2020.

[23] Z. Blanco, B. Liu, M.M.C.ST. F Dehnavi, Large-scale sparse tensor factorizations on distributed platforms, in: Proceedings of the 47th International Conference on Parallel Processing, Association for Computing Machinery, Eugene, OR, USA, 2018, isbn: 9781450365109.

[24] H. Ge, K. Zhang, M. Alfifi, X. Hu, J. Caverlee, DisTenC: a distributed algorithm for scalable tensor completion on spark, in: 2018 IEEE 34th International Conference on Data Engineering (ICDE), 2018, pp. 137–148.

[25] K. Shin, U. Kang, Distributed methods for high-dimensional and large- scale tensor factorization, in: IEEE International Conference on Data Mining, ICDM, 2014, pp. 989–994.

[26] M.O. Karsavuran, S. Acer, C. Aykanat, Partitioning models for general medium-grain parallel sparse tensor decomposition, IEEE Transactions on Parallel and Distributed Systems 32 (2021) 147–159.

[27] Y. Nesterov, Introductory Lectures on Convex Optimization, Kluwer Academic Publishers, 2004.

[28] L. Eldén, H. Park, A procrustes problem on the Stiefel manifold, Numerische Mathematik 82 (1999) 599–619.

[29] R.A. Harshman, M.E. Lundy, PARAFAC: parallel factor analysis, Computational Statistics & Data Analysis 18 (1994) 39–72.

[30] C.A. Andersson, R. Bro, The N-way toolbox for MATLAB, http://www.models.life.ku.dk/source/nwaytoolbox.

[31] E. Gabriel, et al., Open MPI: goals, concept, and design of a next generation MPI implementation, in: Proceedings, 11th European PVM/MPI Users' Group Meeting, Budapest, Hungary, 2004, 2004, pp. 97–104.

[32] A. Grama, G. Karypis, V. Kumar, A. Gupta, Introduction to Parallel Computing, 2nd edition, Pearson, 2003.

[33] P.A. Karakasis, A.P. Liavas, Alternating optimization for tensor factorization with orthogonality constraints: algorithm and parallel implementation, in: 2018 International Conference on High Performance Computing Simulation (HPCS), 2018, pp. 439–444.

[34] G. Guennebaud, B. Jacob, et al., Eigenv3, http://eigen.tuxfamily.org, 2010.

[35] A. Phan, P. Tichavski, A. Cichocki, Fast alternating LS algorithms for high order CANDECOMP/PARAFAC tensor factorizations, IEEE Transactions on Signal Processing 61 (2013) 4834–4846.

[36] F.M. Harper, J.A. Konstan, The MovieLens datasets: history and context, The ACM Transactions on Interactive Intelligent Systems 5 (Dec. 2015) 2160–6455, https://doi.org/10.1145/2827872.

A Riemannian approach to low-rank tensor learning

Hiroyuki Kasai[a], Pratik Jawanpuria[b], and Bamdev Mishra[b]
[a]*Waseda University, Tokyo, Japan*
[b]*Microsoft, Hyderabad, India*

CONTENTS

4.1 Introduction

This chapter addresses the problem of low-rank tensor learning when the rank is a priori known or estimated. We focus on third-order tensors, but the developments can be generalized to higher-order tensors in a straightforward way.

Learning with low-rank tensors has many variants and one of those is extending the nuclear norm regularization approach from the matrix case [1] to the tensor case. This results in a summation of matrix nuclear norm regularization terms, each one corresponding to each of the unfolding matrices of a tensor. While this generalization of matrix nuclear norms to tensors leads to good results [2–7], its applicability in large-scale instances is not trivial, especially due to the necessity of high-dimensional singular value decomposition computations. A different approach, which is also the focus in this chapter, exploits Tucker decomposition of a low-rank tensor to explicitly parameterize the low-rank constraint. Tucker decomposition generalizes the singular value decomposition of matrices to tensors [8].

The Riemannian manifold optimization framework has gained much interest lately owing to its ability to handle complex but structured constraints like rank and orthogonality constraints. Though nonconvex, these constraints have smooth manifold structure and can be handled numerically efficiently with matrix representations [9–12]. Conceptually, the Riemannian framework views those problems as unconstrained optimization problems over the manifold search space. Consequently, many standard unconstrained algorithms in the Euclidean space have natural extensions to the manifold space such as gradient descent, conjugate gradient, and trust-region algorithms, among others [9,10].

Our focus in this chapter is on viewing the low-rank tensor learning problem with Tucker decomposition as an optimization problem over a Riemannian manifold. To this end, we endow the set arising from the Tucker decomposition with a Riemannian manifold structure. A crucial requirement for this is the definition of a metric or inner product on the manifold. The metric, e.g., enables to compute an expression of the descent direction of a function or the expression for the shortest path on the manifold. The choice of the metric on the manifold also has a profound effect on the performance of numerical optimization algorithms [12]. It should be noted that in the Euclidean space, the Newton method is equivalent to the gradient descent algorithm with a particular metric [13].

We build upon the recent work [12] that suggests to use a tailored metric in the Riemannian manifold optimization framework by exploiting the cost function structure. To propose a metric, we consider a particular cost function (only to define the metric) that enables to compute certain second-order information efficiently. Additionally, our metric choice also respects the symmetry present in Tucker decomposition due to nonuniqueness of Tucker decomposition [8]. The implication is that the set of fixed-rank Tucker tensors with the chosen metric has a smooth Riemannian quotient manifold structure. We call it the Tucker manifold geometry.

A different viewpoint of using Riemannian geometry in tensors is presented in [14,15]. On the modeling side, the works [14,15] discuss an embedded submanifold geometry for low-rank tensors. Their focus, however, is limited to the tensor completion problem. We, on the other hand, work with quotient geometry that views it as a product of simpler search spaces with symmetries. The developments also allow to solve general tensor learning problems in a straightforward manner (as we show later, we only need to provide partial derivatives of the cost function). Additionally, [14,15] work with the standard Euclidean metric, whereas we use a particular tuned metric. The use of the tuned metric leads to good performance of our algorithms (shown later in experiments).

The chapter is organized as follows. Section 4.2 briefly introduces the Riemannian manifold optimization framework. Section 4.3 discusses the quotient Tucker manifold geometry in detail. In particular, we propose a specific metric that gives the Tucker manifold a Riemannian geometry. Subsequently, we discuss optimization-related ingredients on the Tucker manifold that are necessary to implement Riemannian optimization algorithms. Motivated by a large-scale setting, we specifically discuss the first-order geometry of Tucker manifold that enables implementation of a Riemannian nonlinear conjugate gradient (RCG) algorithm [10,16,17]. The final formulas are shown in Table 4.1. Use of the Tucker manifold geometry to solve tensor learning problems is discussed in Section 4.4. Section 4.4.2 deals with the more general tensor learning setup. Combining the Tucker manifold ingredients (e.g., projectors, retraction, and vector transport computations) with cost function-specific ingredients (gradient computation) allows to implement algorithms for any tensor learning problem. Section 4.4.1 discusses the low-rank tensor completion problem in detail. In Section 4.5, numerical comparisons with various relevant baselines on various synthetic and real-world benchmarks suggest a good performance of our proposed algorithms.

Most of the contents in this chapter are published in [18]. Please refer to [18] for the proofs of propositions, development of optimization-related ingredients, and additional experiments.

4.2 A brief introduction to Riemannian optimization

Optimization on manifolds, or manifold optimization, seeks an optimum (global or local) of a real-valued function defined over a smooth manifold $\mathcal{M}$. Popularly, we use Riemannian geometry to endow the manifold of interest with a structure. One of the advantages of using the Riemannian geometry is that constrained optimization problems can be handled as unconstrained optimization problems considering the intrinsic properties of the manifold.

Optimization on manifolds has recently gained interest in computer vision [19–21], joint diagonalization [22], Gaussian mixture models [23], phase synchronization [24,25], natural language processing [26–30], learning hierarchies [31,32], multitask learning [33], matrix/tensor completion [5,11,15,34–38], prototype selection [39], optimal transport [40], and metric learning [41–43].

This has led to development of several toolboxes that provide scalable off-the-shelf generic implementations of various Riemannian optimization algorithms. These toolboxes include Manopt [44], Pymanopt [45], McTorch [46], MOT [47], Geomstats [48], ROPTLIB [49], and Manopt.jl [50], to name a few.

This section gives an introductory overview of optimization on manifolds. For a detailed exposition, please refer to [9,10].

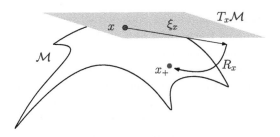

FIGURE 4.1

Riemannian optimization framework on manifolds. An iterative algorithm moves along a search direction ξ_x in the tangent space $T_x\mathcal{M}$ to compute a new point x_+.

4.2.1 Riemannian manifolds

Let $f : \mathcal{M} \to \mathbb{R}$ be a smooth real-valued function on the manifold $\mathcal{M}$. An iterative algorithm on $\mathcal{M}$ to compute minimizers x^* of f produces a sequence $(x_t)_{t\geq0}$ in $\mathcal{M}$ that converges to x^* when given a starting point $x_0 \in \mathcal{M}$.

An iterative optimization algorithm involves computing a search direction and then "moving in that direction." More specifically, we follow geodesics on $\mathcal{M}$, i.e., paths of shortest length on the manifold. Starting from x_t and tangent to a search direction ξ_{x_t}, the updated point is computed as

$$x_{t+1} = \mathrm{Exp}_{x_t}(s_t\xi_{x_t}),$$

where the search direction ξ_{x_t} is in the tangent space $T_{x_t}\mathcal{M}$ at x_t, where $s_t > 0$ is the step size (obtained through backtracking line search). Here, $\mathrm{Exp}_{x_t}(\cdot)$ is called the exponential mapping [9, Section 5.4] which induces a line search algorithm along geodesics.

The computations of geodesics, gradients, and other notions on the manifold are dependent on a metric structure g on the manifold. Once a metric g is defined, the manifold $\mathcal{M}$ has a Riemannian manifold structure and the metric g is called the Riemannian metric. Below we show the computation of the Riemannian gradient (the steepest direction of a function) and retraction operation that generalizes movements on manifolds. Fig. 4.1 shows the iterative update strategy on manifolds.

4.2.1.1 Riemannian gradient

When we consider the negative of the Riemannian gradient direction, $-\mathrm{grad}_x f$, as a search direction ξ_x, we obtain the gradient descent algorithm to minimize f on the manifold. The Riemannian gradient $\mathrm{grad}_x f \in T_x\mathcal{M}$ of f at x is computed based on the chosen Riemannian metric g at $x \in \mathcal{M}$, i.e., $g_x : T_x\mathcal{M} \times T_x\mathcal{M} \to \mathbb{R}$ at $x \in \mathcal{M}$, and $g_x(\xi_x, \zeta_x)$ is an inner product between elements ξ_x, ζ_x of the tangent space $T_x\mathcal{M}$ at x. More concretely, $\mathrm{grad}_x f$ is defined as the unique element that satisfies

$$\mathrm{D}f(x)[\xi_x] = g_x(\mathrm{grad}_x f, \xi_x), \quad \forall \xi_x \in T_x\mathcal{M},$$

where $\mathrm{D}f(x)[\xi_x]$ is the directional derivative of $f(x)$ in the direction ξ_x.

4.2.1.2 Retraction

The geodesics mentioned earlier are in general either expensive to compute or not available in closed form. However, if we relax the constraint of moving along geodesics, a more general update formula is obtained:

$$x_{t+1} = R_{x_t}(s_t \xi_{x_t}),$$

where R_{x_t} is called the retraction operator, which is any map $R_x : T_x \mathcal{M} \to \mathcal{M}$ that locally approximates the exponential mapping, up to the first order, on the manifold [9, Definition 4.1.1]. The retraction is a relaxed and flexible alternative to the exponential mapping in the design of optimization algorithms on manifolds because it reduces the computational cost of the iteration while retaining the main properties that ensure convergence results.

4.2.2 Riemannian quotient manifolds

A special class of manifolds of interest is the class of quotient manifolds, which are sets of equivalence classes. A popular example is the Grassmann manifold $\mathrm{Gr}(r, d)$, which is the set of r-dimensional subspaces in $\mathbb{R}^d$ or as a set of r-dimensional orthogonal frames that cannot be superposed by a rotation.

A quotient manifold is represented as $\mathcal{M}/\sim$, where $\mathcal{M}$ is the total space (computational or matrix space) and $\sim$ is the equivalence relation of the form $[x] = \{z \in \mathcal{M} : z \sim x\}$ that defines the quotient structure. Since a quotient manifold is an abstract space, notions on quotient manifolds call for concrete expressions in the total space $\mathcal{M}$.

A tangent vector $\xi_{[x]} \in T_{[x]}\mathcal{M}$ at $[x]$ is restricted to the directions that do not induce a displacement along the set of equivalence classes $[x]$. This is accomplished by decomposing $T_x \mathcal{M}$ in the total space $\mathcal{M}$ into two complementary subspaces, the vertical and horizontal subspaces, such that $\mathcal{V}_x \oplus \mathcal{H}_x = T_x \mathcal{M}$, where $\oplus$ is the Whitney sum. The vertical space $\mathcal{V}_x$ is the tangent space of the equivalence class $[x]$. On the other hand, the horizontal space $\mathcal{H}_x$, which is any complementary subspace to $\mathcal{V}_x$ in $T_x \mathcal{M}$, provides a valid matrix expression of the abstract tangent space $T_{[x]}(\mathcal{M}/\sim)$ [9, Section 3.5.8]. This allows to represent tangent vectors to the quotient space.

A given tangent vector $\xi_{[x]} \in T_{[x]}\mathcal{M}$ at $[x]$ is uniquely represented by a tangent vector $\xi_x \in \mathcal{H}_x$ that satisfies

$$\mathrm{D}\pi(x)[\xi_x] = \xi_{[x]},$$

where the mapping π is the quotient map $\pi : x \mapsto [x]$. The tangent vector ξ_x is called the horizontal lift of $\xi_{[x]}$ at $[x]$. Provided that the metric $g_x(\xi_x, \eta_x)$ in the total space is invariant along equivalence classes, it defines a metric on the quotient

$$g_{[x]}(\xi_{[x]}, \eta_{[x]}) := g_x(\xi_x, \eta_x).$$

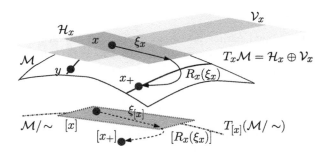

FIGURE 4.2

Riemannian optimization framework on quotient manifolds: geometric objects, shown in dotted lines, on quotient manifold $\mathcal{M}/\sim$ call for matrix representatives, shown in solid lines, in the total space $\mathcal{M}$. Starting from x, we follow the search direction to obtain the new point x_+.

The choice of the metric, which is invariant along the equivalence class $[x]$, and of the horizontal space $\mathcal{H}_x$ as the orthogonal complement of $\mathcal{V}_x$ with respect to the Riemannian metric makes the quotient manifold $\mathcal{M}/\sim$ a Riemannian submersion.

It allows for convenient matrix expressions of the gradient of a cost function or the retraction operation. Fig. 4.2 shows the general update strategy on quotient manifolds.

4.2.2.1 Riemannian gradient on quotient manifold

The horizontal lift of the Riemannian gradient $\mathrm{grad}_{[x]} f$ of a cost function $f : \mathcal{M} \to \mathbb{R}$ on the quotient manifold $\mathcal{M}/\sim$ is uniquely represented by the matrix representation, i.e.,

$$\text{horizontal lift of } \mathrm{grad}_{[x]} f = \mathrm{grad}\, f(x),$$

where $\mathrm{grad}_x f$ is the gradient of f on the computational space $\mathcal{M}$ at x. The equality above is possible due to the invariance of the cost function along the equivalence class $[x]$, the choice of the Riemannian metric, and the choice of the horizontal space $\mathcal{H}_x$ as the orthogonal complement of the vertical space $\mathcal{V}_x$ [9, Section 3.6.2].

4.2.2.2 Retraction on quotient manifold

The retraction R_x defines a retraction $R_{[x]}(\xi_{[x]}) := [R_x(\xi_x)]$ on the quotient manifold $\mathcal{M}/\sim$, provided that the equivalence class $[R_x(\xi_x)]$ does not depend on the specific choice of the matrix representations of $[x]$ and $\xi_{[x]}$. Here ξ_x is the horizontal lift of an abstract tangent vector $\xi_{[x]} \in T_{[x]}(\mathcal{M}/\sim)$ in $\mathcal{H}_x$ and $[\cdot]$ is the equivalence class defined earlier in the section.

Equivalently, the retraction operation $R_{[x]}(\xi_{[x]}) := [R_x(\xi_x)]$ is well defined on $\mathcal{M}/\sim$ when $R_x(\xi_x)$ and $R_z(\xi_z)$ belong to the same equivalence class, i.e., $[R_x(\xi_x)] = [R_z(\xi_z)]$ for all $x, z \in [x]$.

4.3 Riemannian Tucker manifold geometry

The Tucker decomposition of a tensor $\mathcal{X} \in \mathbb{R}^{n_1 \times n_2 \times n_3}$ of rank $\mathbf{r} = (r_1, r_2, r_3)$ is modeled as [8]

$$\mathcal{X} = \mathcal{G} \times_1 \mathbf{U}_1 \times_2 \mathbf{U}_2 \times_3 \mathbf{U}_3, \tag{4.1}$$

where $\mathbf{U}_d \in \mathrm{St}(r_d, n_d)$ for $d \in \{1, 2, 3\}$ belongs to the Stiefel manifold of matrices of size $n_d \times r_d$ with orthogonal columns and $\mathcal{G} \in \mathbb{R}^{r_1 \times r_2 \times r_3}$ [8]. The Stiefel manifold structure on $\mathbf{U}_d$ imposes the constraint $\mathbf{U}_d^T \mathbf{U}_d = \mathbf{I}$ and $\mathcal{G}$ is unconstrained. Here, $\mathcal{W} \times_d \mathbf{V} \in \mathbb{R}^{n_1 \times \cdots n_{d-1} \times m \times n_{d+1} \times \cdots n_D}$ computes the mode-d product of a tensor $\mathcal{W} \in \mathbb{R}^{n_1 \times \cdots \times n_D}$ and a matrix $\mathbf{V} \in \mathbb{R}^{m \times n_d}$ [8]. The mode is a matrix obtained by concatenating the mode-d fibers along columns, and mode-d unfolding of a D-order tensor $\mathcal{X}$ is $\mathbf{X}_{(d)} \in \mathbb{R}^{n_d \times n_{d+1} \cdots n_D n_1 \cdots n_{d-1}}$ for $d = \{1, \ldots, D\}$.

In this section, we discuss the set arising from the Tucker decomposition (4.1) of tensors. We show that the set has a smooth quotient manifold structure identified with $\mathcal{M}/\sim$. We call the manifold arising out of the interplay of $\mathbf{U}_1$, $\mathbf{U}_2$, $\mathbf{U}_3$, and $\mathcal{G}$ as the Tucker manifold as it results from Tucker decomposition. We discuss the total space $\mathcal{M}$ and the equivalence relationship $\sim$ for the Tucker manifold. Consequently, any low-rank tensor learning problem is treated as an optimization problem on the quotient manifold $\mathcal{M}/\sim$.

The Tucker manifold is endowed with a Riemannian structure [9,51]. The concrete optimization-related characterizations of the Tucker manifold are shown in Table 4.1. Those formulas suffice to implement Riemannian optimization algorithms (both first- and second-order) [9,10]. Below, we show the development of those notions and discuss their computations.

4.3.1 Riemannian metric and quotient manifold structure

In the present section, we motivate a particular metric choice that respects the symmetry in Tucker decomposition. The proposed metric endows the Tucker manifold with a Riemannian quotient manifold structure.

4.3.1.1 The symmetry structure in Tucker decomposition

Tucker decomposition (4.1) is not unique as $\mathcal{X}$ remains unchanged under the transformation

$$(\mathbf{U}_1, \mathbf{U}_2, \mathbf{U}_3, \mathcal{G}) \mapsto (\mathbf{U}_1 \mathbf{O}_1, \mathbf{U}_2 \mathbf{O}_2, \mathbf{U}_3 \mathbf{O}_3, \mathcal{G} \times_1 \mathbf{O}_1^T \times_2 \mathbf{O}_2^T \times_3 \mathbf{O}_3^T) \tag{4.2}$$

for all $\mathbf{O}_d \in \mathcal{O}(r_d)$, which is the set of orthogonal matrices of size $r_d \times r_d$. The classical remedy to remove this indeterminacy is to have additional structures on $\mathcal{G}$ like sparsity or restricted orthogonal rotations [8]. In contrast, we encode the transformation (4.2) in an abstract search space of equivalence classes, defined as

$$[(\mathbf{U}_1, \mathbf{U}_2, \mathbf{U}_3, \mathcal{G})] := \{(\mathbf{U}_1 \mathbf{O}_1, \mathbf{U}_2 \mathbf{O}_2, \mathbf{U}_3 \mathbf{O}_3,$$
$$\mathcal{G} \times_1 \mathbf{O}_1^T \times_2 \mathbf{O}_2^T \times_3 \mathbf{O}_3^T) : \mathbf{O}_d \in \mathcal{O}(r_d)\}. \tag{4.3}$$

Table 4.1 Optimization-related notions on Tucker manifold.

Matrix representation	$x = (\mathbf{U}_1, \mathbf{U}_2, \mathbf{U}_3, \mathcal{G})$
Computational space $\mathcal{M}$	$\text{St}(r_1, n_1) \times \text{St}(r_2, n_2) \times \text{St}(r_3, n_3) \times \mathbb{R}^{r_1 \times r_2 \times r_3}$
Group action	$\{(\mathbf{U}_1\mathbf{O}_1, \mathbf{U}_2\mathbf{O}_2, \mathbf{U}_3\mathbf{O}_3, \mathcal{G} \times_1 \mathbf{O}_1^T \times_2 \mathbf{O}_2^T \times_3 \mathbf{O}_3^T) : \mathbf{O}_d \in \mathcal{O}(r_d)$ for $d \in \{1, 2, 3\}\}$
Quotient space $\mathcal{M}/\sim$	$\text{St}(r_1, n_1) \times \text{St}(r_2, n_2) \times \text{St}(r_3, n_3) \times \mathbb{R}^{r_1 \times r_2 \times r_3} / (\mathcal{O}(r_1) \times \mathcal{O}(r_2) \times \mathcal{O}(r_3))$
Ambient space	$\mathbb{R}^{n_1 \times r_1} \times \mathbb{R}^{n_2 \times r_2} \times \mathbb{R}^{n_3 \times r_3} \times \mathbb{R}^{r_1 \times r_2 \times r_3}$
Tangent vectors in $T_x\mathcal{M}$	$\{(\mathbf{Z}_{\mathbf{U}_1}, \mathbf{Z}_{\mathbf{U}_2}, \mathbf{Z}_{\mathbf{U}_3}, \mathbf{Z}_{\mathcal{G}}) \in \mathbb{R}^{n_1 \times r_1} \times \mathbb{R}^{n_2 \times r_2} \times \mathbb{R}^{n_3 \times r_3} \times \mathbb{R}^{r_1 \times r_2 \times r_3}$ $: \mathbf{U}_d^T \mathbf{Z}_{\mathbf{U}_d} + \mathbf{Z}_{\mathbf{U}_d}^T \mathbf{U}_d = 0, \text{ for } d \in \{1, 2, 3\}\}$
Metric $g_x(\xi_x, \eta_x)$	$\langle \xi_{\mathbf{U}_1}, \eta_{\mathbf{U}_1}(\mathbf{G}_{(1)}\mathbf{G}_{(1)}^T) \rangle + \langle \xi_{\mathbf{U}_2}, \eta_{\mathbf{U}_2}(\mathbf{G}_{(2)}\mathbf{G}_{(2)}^T) \rangle +$ $\langle \xi_{\mathbf{U}_3}, \eta_{\mathbf{U}_3}(\mathbf{G}_{(3)}\mathbf{G}_{(3)}^T) \rangle + \langle \xi_{\mathcal{G}}, \eta_{\mathcal{G}} \rangle$
Vertical tangent vectors in $\mathcal{V}_x$	$\{(\mathbf{U}_1\mathbf{\Omega}_1, \mathbf{U}_2\mathbf{\Omega}_2, \mathbf{U}_3\mathbf{\Omega}_3, -(\mathcal{G}\times_1\mathbf{\Omega}_1 + \mathcal{G}\times_2\mathbf{\Omega}_2 + \mathcal{G}\times_3\mathbf{\Omega}_3)):$ $\mathbf{\Omega}_d \in \mathbb{R}^{r_d \times r_d}, \mathbf{\Omega}_d^T = -\mathbf{\Omega}_d, \text{for } d \in \{1, 2, 3\}\}$
Horizontal tangent vectors in $\mathcal{H}_x$	$\{(\zeta_{\mathbf{U}_1}, \zeta_{\mathbf{U}_2}, \zeta_{\mathbf{U}_3}, \zeta_{\mathcal{G}}) \in T_x\mathcal{M}:$ $(\mathbf{G}_{(d)}\mathbf{G}_{(d)}^T)\zeta_{\mathbf{U}_d}^T\mathbf{U}_d + \zeta_{\mathbf{G}_{(d)}}\mathbf{G}_{(d)}^T \text{ is symmetric, for } d \in \{1, 2, 3\}\}$
$\Psi(\cdot)$ projects an ambient vector $(\mathbf{Y}_{\mathbf{U}_1}, \mathbf{Y}_{\mathbf{U}_2}, \mathbf{Y}_{\mathbf{U}_3}, \mathbf{Y}_{\mathcal{G}})$ onto $T_x\mathcal{M}$	$(\mathbf{Y}_{\mathbf{U}_1} - \mathbf{U}_1\mathbf{S}_{\mathbf{U}_1}(\mathbf{G}_{(1)}\mathbf{G}_{(1)}^T)^{-1}, \mathbf{Y}_{\mathbf{U}_2} - \mathbf{U}_2\mathbf{S}_{\mathbf{U}_2}(\mathbf{G}_{(2)}\mathbf{G}_{(2)}^T)^{-1},$ $\mathbf{Y}_{\mathbf{U}_3} - \mathbf{U}_3\mathbf{S}_{\mathbf{U}_3}(\mathbf{G}_{(3)}\mathbf{G}_{(3)}^T)^{-1}, \mathbf{Y}_{\mathcal{G}})$, where $\mathbf{S}_{\mathbf{U}_d}$ for $d \in \{1, 2, 3\}$ are computed by solving Lyapunov equations as in (4.14)
$\Pi(\cdot)$ projects a tangent vector ξ onto $\mathcal{H}_x$	$(\xi_{\mathbf{U}_1} - \mathbf{U}_1\mathbf{\Omega}_1, \xi_{\mathbf{U}_2} - \mathbf{U}_2\mathbf{\Omega}_2, \xi_{\mathbf{U}_3} - \mathbf{U}_3\mathbf{\Omega}_3,$ $\xi_{\mathcal{G}} - (-(\mathcal{G}\times_1\mathbf{\Omega}_1 + \mathcal{G}\times_2\mathbf{\Omega}_2 + \mathcal{G}\times_3\mathbf{\Omega}_3)))$, $\mathbf{\Omega}_d$ is computed in Proposition 4.3
Retraction $R_x(\xi_x)$	$(\text{uf}(\mathbf{U}_1 + \xi_{\mathbf{U}_1}), \text{uf}(\mathbf{U}_2 + \xi_{\mathbf{U}_2}), \text{uf}(\mathbf{U}_3 + \xi_{\mathbf{U}_3}), \mathcal{G} + \xi_{\mathcal{G}})$
Horizontal lift of the vector transport $\mathcal{T}_{\eta_{[x]}}\xi_{[x]}$	$\Pi_{R_x(\eta_x)}(\Psi_{R_x(\eta_x)}(\xi_x))$

The set of equivalence classes is the quotient manifold [52]

$$\mathcal{M}/\sim := \mathcal{M}/(\mathcal{O}(r_1) \times \mathcal{O}(r_2) \times \mathcal{O}(r_3)), \qquad (4.4)$$

where $\mathcal{M}$ is called the total space (computational space) that is the product space of four manifolds, i.e.,

$$\mathcal{M} := \text{St}(r_1, n_1) \times \text{St}(r_2, n_2) \times \text{St}(r_3, n_3) \times \mathbb{R}^{r_1 \times r_2 \times r_3}. \qquad (4.5)$$

The Tucker manifold is canonically identified with $\mathcal{M}/\sim$ (4.4).

4.3.1.2 A metric motivated by a particular cost function

In unconstrained optimization, the Newton method is interpreted as a scaled gradient descent method, where the search space is endowed with a metric (inner product) induced by the Hessian of the cost function [13]. This induced metric (or its approximation) resolves convergence issues of first-order optimization algorithms. Analogously, finding a good inner product for tensor learning problems is of profound consequence. Specifically for the case of quadratic optimization with rank constraint (matrix case), Mishra and Sepulchre [12] propose a family of Riemannian metrics from the Hessian of the cost function. Following this, in order to find a suitable metric, we consider the simplified cost function $\|\mathcal{X} - \mathcal{X}^\star\|_F^2$. Here, $\|\cdot\|_F$ is the Frobenius norm with slight abuse of notations. It should be noted that the cost function $\|\mathcal{X} - \mathcal{X}^\star\|_F^2$ is only considered to motivate the metric choice.

Applying the metric tuning approach of [12] to the simplified cost function leads to a family of Riemannian metrics. A good trade-off between computational cost and simplicity is by considering only the block-diagonal elements of the Hessian of $\|\mathcal{X} - \mathcal{X}^\star\|_F^2$. It should be mentioned that the cost function $\|\mathcal{X} - \mathcal{X}^\star\|_F^2$ is convex and quadratic in $\mathcal{X}$. Consequently, it is also convex and quadratic in the arguments $(\mathbf{U}_1, \mathbf{U}_2, \mathbf{U}_3, \mathcal{G})$ individually. Equivalently, the block-diagonal approximation of the Hessian of $\|\mathcal{X} - \mathcal{X}^\star\|_F^2$ in $(\mathbf{U}_1, \mathbf{U}_2, \mathbf{U}_3, \mathcal{G})$ is

$$((\mathbf{G}_{(1)}\mathbf{G}_{(1)}^T) \otimes \mathbf{I}_{n_1}, (\mathbf{G}_{(2)}\mathbf{G}_{(2)}^T) \otimes \mathbf{I}_{n_2}, (\mathbf{G}_{(3)}\mathbf{G}_{(3)}^T) \otimes \mathbf{I}_{n_3}, \mathbf{I}_{r_1 r_2 r_3}), \qquad (4.6)$$

where $\mathbf{G}_{(d)}$ is the mode-d unfolding of $\mathcal{G}$ and is assumed to be full rank and $\otimes$ is the Kronecker product. The terms $\mathbf{G}_{(d)}\mathbf{G}_{(d)}^T$ for $d \in \{1, 2, 3\}$ are positive-definite when $r_1 \leq r_2 r_3$, $r_2 \leq r_1 r_3$, and $r_3 \leq r_1 r_2$, which is a reasonable assumption. Overall, the block-diagonal approximation (4.6) is positive-definite.

4.3.1.3 A novel Riemannian metric

An element x in the total space $\mathcal{M}$ has the matrix representation $(\mathbf{U}_1, \mathbf{U}_2, \mathbf{U}_3, \mathcal{G})$. Therefore, the tangent space $T_x\mathcal{M}$ is the Cartesian product of the tangent spaces of the individual manifolds of (4.5), i.e., $T_x\mathcal{M}$ has the matrix characterization [51]

$$\begin{aligned}
&T_x\mathcal{M} \\
&= \{(\mathbf{Z}_{\mathbf{U}_1}, \mathbf{Z}_{\mathbf{U}_2}, \mathbf{Z}_{\mathbf{U}_3}, \mathbf{Z}_{\mathcal{G}}) \in \mathbb{R}^{n_1 \times r_1} \times \mathbb{R}^{n_2 \times r_2} \times \mathbb{R}^{n_3 \times r_3} \times \mathbb{R}^{r_1 \times r_2 \times r_3} : \\
&\quad \mathbf{U}_d^T \mathbf{Z}_{\mathbf{U}_d} + \mathbf{Z}_{\mathbf{U}_d}^T \mathbf{U}_d = 0, \text{ for } d \in \{1, 2, 3\}\}.
\end{aligned} \qquad (4.7)$$

From the earlier discussion on symmetry and a particular cost function, we propose the metric or inner product $g_x : T_x\mathcal{M} \times T_x\mathcal{M} \to \mathbb{R}$, i.e.,

$$\begin{aligned}
g_x(\xi_x, \eta_x) &= \langle \xi_{\mathbf{U}_1}, \eta_{\mathbf{U}_1}(\mathbf{G}_{(1)}\mathbf{G}_{(1)}^T)\rangle + \langle \xi_{\mathbf{U}_2}, \eta_{\mathbf{U}_2}(\mathbf{G}_{(2)}\mathbf{G}_{(2)}^T)\rangle \\
&\quad + \langle \xi_{\mathbf{U}_3}, \eta_{\mathbf{U}_3}(\mathbf{G}_{(3)}\mathbf{G}_{(3)}^T)\rangle + \langle \xi_{\mathcal{G}}, \eta_{\mathcal{G}}\rangle,
\end{aligned} \qquad (4.8)$$

where $\xi_x, \eta_x \in T_x\mathcal{M}$ are tangent vectors with matrix characterizations, shown in (4.7), $(\xi_{\mathbf{U}_1}, \xi_{\mathbf{U}_2}, \xi_{\mathbf{U}_3}, \xi_{\mathcal{G}})$ and $(\eta_{\mathbf{U}_1}, \eta_{\mathbf{U}_2}, \eta_{\mathbf{U}_3}, \eta_{\mathcal{G}})$, respectively, and $\langle \cdot, \cdot \rangle$ is the Euclidean inner product. It should be emphasized that the proposed metric (4.8) is induced from (4.6).

Proposition 4.1. *Let $(\xi_{\mathbf{U}_1}, \xi_{\mathbf{U}_2}, \xi_{\mathbf{U}_3}, \xi_{\mathcal{G}})$ and $(\eta_{\mathbf{U}_1}, \eta_{\mathbf{U}_2}, \eta_{\mathbf{U}_3}, \eta_{\mathcal{G}})$ be tangent vectors to the quotient manifold (4.4) at $(\mathbf{U}_1, \mathbf{U}_2, \mathbf{U}_3, \mathcal{G})$. Let $(\xi_{\mathbf{U}_1\mathbf{O}_1}, \xi_{\mathbf{U}_2\mathbf{O}_2}, \xi_{\mathbf{U}_3\mathbf{O}_3}, \xi_{\mathcal{G} \times_1 \mathbf{O}_1^T \times_2 \mathbf{O}_2^T \times_3 \mathbf{O}_3^T})$ and $(\eta_{\mathbf{U}_1\mathbf{O}_1}, \eta_{\mathbf{U}_2\mathbf{O}_2}, \eta_{\mathbf{U}_3\mathbf{O}_3}, \eta_{\mathcal{G} \times_1 \mathbf{O}_1^T \times_2 \mathbf{O}_2^T \times_3 \mathbf{O}_3^T})$ be tangent vectors* *to the quotient manifold (4.4) at* $(\mathbf{U}_1\mathbf{O}_1, \mathbf{U}_2\mathbf{O}_2, \mathbf{U}_3\mathbf{O}_3, \mathcal{G}\times_1\mathbf{O}_1^T\times_2\mathbf{O}_2^T\times_3\mathbf{O}_3^T)$. *The metric (4.8) is invariant along the equivalence class (4.3), i.e.,*

$$g_{(\mathbf{U}_1,\mathbf{U}_2,\mathbf{U}_3,\mathcal{G})}((\xi_{\mathbf{U}_1},\xi_{\mathbf{U}_2},\xi_{\mathbf{U}_3},\xi_{\mathcal{G}}),(\eta_{\mathbf{U}_1},\eta_{\mathbf{U}_2},\eta_{\mathbf{U}_3},\eta_{\mathcal{G}}))$$
$$= g_{(\mathbf{U}_1\mathbf{O}_1,\mathbf{U}_2\mathbf{O}_2,\mathbf{U}_3\mathbf{O}_3,\mathcal{G}\times_1\mathbf{O}_1^T\times_2\mathbf{O}_2^T\times_3\mathbf{O}_3^T)}$$
$$((\xi_{\mathbf{U}_1\mathbf{O}_1},\xi_{\mathbf{U}_2\mathbf{O}_2},\xi_{\mathbf{U}_3\mathbf{O}_3},\xi_{\mathcal{G}\times_1\mathbf{O}_1^T\times_2\mathbf{O}_2^T\times_3\mathbf{O}_3^T}),$$
$$(\eta_{\mathbf{U}_1\mathbf{O}_1},\eta_{\mathbf{U}_2\mathbf{O}_2},\eta_{\mathbf{U}_3\mathbf{O}_3},\eta_{\mathcal{G}\times_1\mathbf{O}_1^T\times_2\mathbf{O}_2^T\times_3\mathbf{O}_3^T})).$$

Proposition 4.1 shows that the proposed metric is invariant to the equivalence relationship (4.3). Consequently, the proposed metric (4.8) is a valid metric on the quotient manifold $\mathcal{M}/\sim$ (4.4).

4.3.2 Characterization of the induced spaces

Once the metric (4.8) is defined and invariant to equivalence classes $[x]$ (shown in Proposition 4.1), the manifold $\mathcal{M}/\sim$ (4.4) has the structure of a smooth Riemannian quotient manifold. We give complete characterizations of the spaces of interest. The normal space $N_x\mathcal{M}$ is the space that is orthogonal to the tangent space $T_x\mathcal{M}$, whose characterization is shown in (4.7). Moreover, $T_x\mathcal{M}$ can be decomposed into two orthogonal subspaces: vertical and horizontal subspaces.

4.3.2.1 Characterization of the normal space

Given a vector in $\mathbb{R}^{n_1\times r_1}\times\mathbb{R}^{n_2\times r_2}\times\mathbb{R}^{n_3\times r_3}\times\mathbb{R}^{r_1\times r_2\times r_3}$, its projection onto the tangent space $T_x\mathcal{M}$ is obtained by extracting the component normal, in the metric sense, to the tangent space. Let $\zeta_x = (\zeta_{\mathbf{U}_1},\zeta_{\mathbf{U}_2},\zeta_{\mathbf{U}_3},\zeta_{\mathcal{G}}) \in N_x\mathcal{M}$ and $\eta_x = (\eta_{\mathbf{U}_1},\eta_{\mathbf{U}_2},\eta_{\mathbf{U}_3},\eta_{\mathcal{G}}) \in T_x\mathcal{M}$. Since ζ_x is orthogonal to η_x, i.e., $g_x(\zeta_x,\eta_x) = 0$, the conditions

$$\text{Trace}(\mathbf{G}_{(d)}\mathbf{G}_{(d)}^T\zeta_{\mathbf{U}_d}^T\eta_{\mathbf{U}_d}) = 0, \text{ for } d \in \{1,2,3\} \tag{4.9}$$

must hold for all η_x in the tangent space. Additionally from [9], $\eta_{\mathbf{U}_d}$ has the characterization

$$\eta_{\mathbf{U}_d} = \mathbf{U}_d\boldsymbol{\Omega} + \mathbf{U}_{d\perp}\mathbf{K}, \tag{4.10}$$

where $\boldsymbol{\Omega}$ is any skew-symmetric matrix, $\mathbf{K}$ is any matrix of size $(n_d - r_d) \times r_d$, and $\mathbf{U}_{d\perp}$ is any $n_d \times (n_d - r_d)$ that is an orthogonal complement of $\mathbf{U}_d$. Let $\tilde{\zeta}_{\mathbf{U}_d} = \zeta_{\mathbf{U}_d}\mathbf{G}_{(d)}\mathbf{G}_{(d)}^T$ and let $\tilde{\zeta}_{\mathbf{U}_d}$ be defined as

$$\tilde{\zeta}_{\mathbf{U}_d} = \mathbf{U}_d\mathbf{A} + \mathbf{U}_{d\perp}\mathbf{B}$$

without loss of generality, where $\mathbf{A} \in \mathbb{R}^{r_d\times r_d}$ and $\mathbf{B} \in \mathbb{R}^{(n_d-r_d)\times r_d}$ are to be characterized from (4.9) and (4.10). A few standard computations show that $\mathbf{A}$ has to be symmetric and $\mathbf{B} = \mathbf{0}$. Consequently, $\tilde{\zeta}_{\mathbf{U}_d} = \mathbf{U}_d\mathbf{S}_{\mathbf{U}_d}$, where $\mathbf{S}_{\mathbf{U}_d} = \mathbf{S}_{\mathbf{U}_d}^T$. Equivalently, $\zeta_{\mathbf{U}_d} = \mathbf{U}_d\mathbf{S}_{\mathbf{U}_d}(\mathbf{G}_{(d)}\mathbf{G}_{(d)}^T)^{-1}$ for a symmetric matrix $\mathbf{S}_{\mathbf{U}_d}$. Finally, the normal space

$N_x\mathcal{M}$ has the characterization

$$
\begin{aligned}
N_x\mathcal{M} = \{&(\mathbf{U}_1\mathbf{S}_{\mathbf{U}_1}(\mathbf{G}_{(1)}\mathbf{G}_{(1)}^T)^{-1}, \mathbf{U}_2\mathbf{S}_{\mathbf{U}_2}(\mathbf{G}_{(2)}\mathbf{G}_{(2)}^T)^{-1}, \\
&\mathbf{U}_3\mathbf{S}_{\mathbf{U}_3}(\mathbf{G}_{(3)}\mathbf{G}_{(3)}^T)^{-1}, 0) : \mathbf{S}_{\mathbf{U}_d} \in \mathbb{R}^{r_d \times r_d}, \mathbf{S}_{\mathbf{U}_d}^T = \mathbf{S}_{\mathbf{U}_d}, \\
&\text{for } d \in \{1, 2, 3\}\}.
\end{aligned}
\tag{4.11}
$$

4.3.2.2 Decomposition of tangent space into vertical and horizontal spaces

The tangent space $T_x\mathcal{M}$ is decomposed into orthogonal subspaces: the vertical $\mathcal{V}_x$ and horizontal $\mathcal{H}_x$ spaces.

Here $\mathcal{V}_x$ is defined as the linearization of the equivalence class $[(\mathbf{U}_1, \mathbf{U}_2, \mathbf{U}_3, \mathcal{G})]$ at $x = [(\mathbf{U}_1, \mathbf{U}_2, \mathbf{U}_3, \mathcal{G})]$. Equivalently, $\mathcal{V}_x$ is the linearization of $(\mathbf{U}_1\mathbf{O}_1, \mathbf{U}_2\mathbf{O}_2, \mathbf{U}_3\mathbf{O}_3, \mathcal{G}\times_1\mathbf{O}_1^T\times_2\mathbf{O}_2^T\times_3\mathbf{O}_3^T)$ along $\mathbf{O}_d \in \mathcal{O}(r_d)$ at the identity element for $d \in \{1, 2, 3\}$. From the characterization of linearization of an orthogonal matrix [9], we have the characterization for the vertical space as

$$
\begin{aligned}
\mathcal{V}_x = \{&(\mathbf{U}_1\mathbf{\Omega}_1, \mathbf{U}_2\mathbf{\Omega}_2, \mathbf{U}_3\mathbf{\Omega}_3, -(\mathcal{G}\times_1\mathbf{\Omega}_1 + \mathcal{G}\times_2\mathbf{\Omega}_2 + \mathcal{G}\times_3\mathbf{\Omega}_3)) : \\
&\mathbf{\Omega}_d \in \mathbb{R}^{r_d \times r_d}, \mathbf{\Omega}_d^T = -\mathbf{\Omega}_d \text{ for } d \in \{1, 2, 3\}\}.
\end{aligned}
\tag{4.12}
$$

The characterization of the horizontal space $\mathcal{H}_x$ is derived from its orthogonal relationship with the vertical space $\mathcal{V}_x$. Let $\xi_x = (\xi_{\mathbf{U}_1}, \xi_{\mathbf{U}_2}, \xi_{\mathbf{U}_3}, \xi_{\mathcal{G}}) \in \mathcal{H}_x$ and $\zeta_x = (\zeta_{\mathbf{U}_1}, \zeta_{\mathbf{U}_2}, \zeta_{\mathbf{U}_3}, \zeta_{\mathcal{G}}) \in \mathcal{V}_x$. Since ξ_x must be orthogonal to ζ_x, which is equivalent to $g_x(\xi_x, \zeta_x) = 0$ in (4.8), the characterization for ξ_x is derived from (4.8) and (4.12). We have

$$
\begin{aligned}
g_x(\xi_x, \zeta_x) &= \langle \xi_{\mathbf{U}_1}, \zeta_{\mathbf{U}_1}(\mathbf{G}_{(1)}\mathbf{G}_{(1)}^T) \rangle + \langle \xi_{\mathbf{U}_2}, \zeta_{\mathbf{U}_2}(\mathbf{G}_{(2)}\mathbf{G}_{(2)}^T) \rangle \\
&\quad + \langle \xi_{\mathbf{U}_3}, \zeta_{\mathbf{U}_3}(\mathbf{G}_{(3)}\mathbf{G}_{(3)}^T) \rangle + \langle \xi_{\mathcal{G}}, \zeta_{\mathcal{G}} \rangle \\
&= \langle \xi_{\mathbf{U}}, (\mathbf{U}_1\mathbf{\Omega}_1)(\mathbf{G}_{(1)}\mathbf{G}_{(1)}^T) \rangle + \langle \xi_{\mathbf{U}_2}, (\mathbf{U}_2\mathbf{\Omega}_2)(\mathbf{G}_{(2)}\mathbf{G}_{(2)}^T) \rangle \\
&\quad + \langle \xi_{\mathbf{U}_3}, (\mathbf{U}_3\mathbf{\Omega}_3)(\mathbf{G}_{(3)}\mathbf{G}_{(3)}^T) \rangle \\
&\quad + \langle \xi_{\mathcal{G}}, -(\mathcal{G}\times_1\mathbf{\Omega}_1 + \mathcal{G}\times_2\mathbf{\Omega}_2 + \mathcal{G}\times_3\mathbf{\Omega}_3) \rangle \\
&\quad \text{(switch to unfoldings of } \mathcal{G}) \\
&= \text{Trace}((\mathbf{G}_{(1)}\mathbf{G}_{(1)}^T)\xi_{\mathbf{U}_1}^T(\mathbf{U}_1\mathbf{\Omega}_1)) + \text{Trace}((\mathbf{G}_{(2)}\mathbf{G}_{(2)}^T)\xi_{\mathbf{U}_2}^T(\mathbf{U}_2\mathbf{\Omega}_2)) \\
&\quad + \text{Trace}((\mathbf{G}_{(3)}\mathbf{G}_{(3)}^T)\xi_{\mathbf{U}_3}^T(\mathbf{U}_3\mathbf{\Omega}_3)) + \text{Trace}(\xi_{G_{(1)}}(-\mathbf{\Omega}_1\mathbf{G}_{(1)})^T) \\
&\quad + \text{Trace}(\xi_{G_{(2)}}(-\mathbf{\Omega}_2\mathbf{G}_{(2)})^T) + \text{Trace}(\xi_{G_{(3)}}(-\mathbf{\Omega}_3\mathbf{G}_{(3)})^T) \\
&= \text{Trace}\left[\left\{ (\mathbf{G}_{(1)}\mathbf{G}_{(1)}^T)\xi_{\mathbf{U}_1}^T\mathbf{U}_1 + \xi_{G_{(1)}}\mathbf{G}_{(1)}^T \right\} \mathbf{\Omega}_1 \right] \\
&\quad + \text{Trace}\left[\left\{ (\mathbf{G}_{(2)}\mathbf{G}_{(2)}^T)\xi_{\mathbf{U}_2}^T\mathbf{U}_2 + \xi_{G_{(2)}}\mathbf{G}_{(2)}^T \right\} \mathbf{\Omega}_2 \right] \\
&\quad + \text{Trace}\left[\left\{ (\mathbf{G}_{(3)}\mathbf{G}_{(3)}^T)\xi_{\mathbf{U}_3}^T\mathbf{U}_3 + \xi_{G_{(3)}}\mathbf{G}_{(3)}^T \right\} \mathbf{\Omega}_3 \right],
\end{aligned}
$$

where $\xi_{\mathbf{G}_{(d)}}$ is the mode-d unfolding of $\xi_{\mathcal{G}}$. Since $g_x(\xi_x, \zeta_x)$ above should be zero for all skew-matrices $\mathbf{\Omega}_d$, $\xi_x = (\xi_{\mathbf{U}_1}, \xi_{\mathbf{U}_2}, \xi_{\mathbf{U}_3}, \xi_{\mathcal{G}}) \in \mathcal{H}_x$ must satisfy the condition

$$(\mathbf{G}_{(d)}\mathbf{G}_{(d)}^T)\xi_{\mathbf{U}_d}^T\mathbf{U}_d + \xi_{\mathbf{G}_{(d)}}\mathbf{G}_{(d)}^T \text{ is symmetric} \tag{4.13}$$

for all $d \in \{1, 2, 3\}$.

4.3.3 Linear projectors

Starting from an arbitrary matrix (with appropriate dimensions), two linear projections are needed: the first projection Ψ_x is onto the tangent space $T_x\mathcal{M}$, while the second projection Π_x is onto the horizontal subspace $\mathcal{H}_x$.

4.3.3.1 The tangent space projector

The tangent space $T_x\mathcal{M}$ projection is obtained by extracting the component normal to $T_x\mathcal{M}$ in the ambient space. The normal space $N_x\mathcal{M}$ has the matrix characterization $\{(\mathbf{U}_1\mathbf{S}_{\mathbf{U}_1}(\mathbf{G}_{(1)}\mathbf{G}_{(1)}^T)^{-1}, \mathbf{U}_2\mathbf{S}_{\mathbf{U}_2}(\mathbf{G}_{(2)}\mathbf{G}_{(2)}^T)^{-1}, \mathbf{U}_3\mathbf{S}_{\mathbf{U}_3}(\mathbf{G}_{(3)}\mathbf{G}_{(3)}^T)^{-1}, 0) : \mathbf{S}_{\mathbf{U}_d} \in \mathbb{R}^{r_d \times r_d}, \mathbf{S}_{\mathbf{U}_d}^T = \mathbf{S}_{\mathbf{U}_d}, \text{ for } d \in \{1, 2, 3\}\}$. Symmetric matrices $\mathbf{S}_{\mathbf{U}_d}$ for all $d \in \{1, 2, 3\}$ parameterize the normal space. Finally, the operator $\Psi_x : \mathbb{R}^{n_1 \times r_1} \times \mathbb{R}^{n_2 \times r_2} \times \mathbb{R}^{n_3 \times r_3} \times \mathbb{R}^{r_1 \times r_2 \times r_3} \to T_x\mathcal{M}$ is given as follows.

Proposition 4.2. *The quotient manifold (4.4) endowed with the metric (4.8) admits the tangent space projector defined as*

$$\begin{aligned}
&\Psi_x(\mathbf{Y}_{\mathbf{U}_1}, \mathbf{Y}_{\mathbf{U}_2}, \mathbf{Y}_{\mathbf{U}_3}, \mathbf{Y}_{\mathcal{G}}) \\
&= (\mathbf{Y}_{\mathbf{U}_1} - \mathbf{U}_1\mathbf{S}_{\mathbf{U}_1}(\mathbf{G}_{(1)}\mathbf{G}_{(1)}^T)^{-1}, \mathbf{Y}_{\mathbf{U}_2} - \mathbf{U}_2\mathbf{S}_{\mathbf{U}_2}(\mathbf{G}_{(2)}\mathbf{G}_{(2)}^T)^{-1}, \\
&\quad \mathbf{Y}_{\mathbf{U}_3} - \mathbf{U}_3\mathbf{S}_{\mathbf{U}_3}(\mathbf{G}_{(3)}\mathbf{G}_{(3)}^T)^{-1}, \mathbf{Y}_{\mathcal{G}}),
\end{aligned} \tag{4.14}$$

where $\mathbf{S}_{\mathbf{U}_d}$ is the solution to the Lyapunov equation $\mathbf{S}_{\mathbf{U}_d}\mathbf{G}_{(d)}\mathbf{G}_{(d)}^T + \mathbf{G}_{(d)}\mathbf{G}_{(d)}^T\mathbf{S}_{\mathbf{U}_{(d)}} = \mathbf{G}_{(d)}\mathbf{G}_{(d)}^T(\mathbf{Y}_{\mathbf{U}_d}^T\mathbf{U}_d + \mathbf{U}_d^T\mathbf{Y}_{\mathbf{U}_d})\mathbf{G}_{(d)}\mathbf{G}_{(d)}^T$ for $d \in \{1, 2, 3\}$.

The Lyapunov equations in Proposition 4.2 are solved efficiently by performing eigenvalue decompositions of $\mathbf{G}_{(d)}\mathbf{G}_{(d)}^T$ for all d.

4.3.3.2 The horizontal space projector

The horizontal space projection of a tangent vector is obtained by removing the component along the vertical space. The vertical space $\mathcal{V}_x$ has the matrix characterization $\{(\mathbf{U}_1\mathbf{\Omega}_1, \mathbf{U}_2\mathbf{\Omega}_2, \mathbf{U}_3\mathbf{\Omega}_3, -(\mathcal{G}\times_1\mathbf{\Omega}_1 + \mathcal{G}\times_2\mathbf{\Omega}_2 + \mathcal{G}\times_3\mathbf{\Omega}_3)) : \mathbf{\Omega}_d \in \mathbb{R}^{r_d \times r_d}, \mathbf{\Omega}_d^T = -\mathbf{\Omega}_d$ for $d \in \{1, 2, 3\}\}$. Skew-symmetric matrices $\mathbf{\Omega}_d$ for all $d \in \{1, 2, 3\}$ parameterize the vertical space. Finally, the horizontal projection operator $\Pi_x : T_x\mathcal{M} :\mapsto \mathcal{H}_x : \eta_x \mapsto \Pi_x(\eta_x)$ is given as follows.

Proposition 4.3. *The quotient manifold (4.4) endowed with the metric (4.8) admits the horizontal projector defined as*

$$
\Pi_x(\eta_x) = (\eta_{\mathbf{U}_1} - \mathbf{U}_1\boldsymbol{\Omega}_1, \eta_{\mathbf{U}_2} - \mathbf{U}_2\boldsymbol{\Omega}_2, \eta_{\mathbf{U}_3} - \mathbf{U}_3\boldsymbol{\Omega}_3,
$$
$$
\eta_{\mathcal{G}} - (-(\mathcal{G}\times_1\boldsymbol{\Omega}_1 + \mathcal{G}\times_2\boldsymbol{\Omega}_2 + \mathcal{G}\times_3\boldsymbol{\Omega}_3))),
$$

where $\eta_x = (\eta_{\mathbf{U}_1}, \eta_{\mathbf{U}_2}, \eta_{\mathbf{U}_3}, \eta_{\mathcal{G}}) \in T_x\mathcal{M}$ and $\boldsymbol{\Omega}_d$ is a skew-symmetric matrix of size $r_d \times r_d$ for all $d = \{1, 2, 3\}$, where $\boldsymbol{\Omega}_1$, $\boldsymbol{\Omega}_2$, and $\boldsymbol{\Omega}_3$ are solutions to the coupled Lyapunov equations

$$
\mathbf{G}_{(1)}\mathbf{G}_{(1)}^T\boldsymbol{\Omega}_1 + \boldsymbol{\Omega}_1\mathbf{G}_{(1)}\mathbf{G}_{(1)}^T - \mathbf{G}_{(1)}(\mathbf{I}_{r_3} \otimes \boldsymbol{\Omega}_2)\mathbf{G}_{(1)}^T - \mathbf{G}_{(1)}(\boldsymbol{\Omega}_3 \otimes \mathbf{I}_{r_2})\mathbf{G}_{(1)}^T
$$
$$
= \mathrm{Skew}(\mathbf{U}_1^T\eta_{\mathbf{U}_1}\mathbf{G}_{(1)}\mathbf{G}_{(1)}^T) + \mathrm{Skew}(\mathbf{G}_{(1)}\eta_{\mathbf{G}_{(1)}}^T),
$$

$$
\mathbf{G}_{(2)}\mathbf{G}_{(2)}^T\boldsymbol{\Omega}_2 + \boldsymbol{\Omega}_2\mathbf{G}_{(2)}\mathbf{G}_{(2)}^T - \mathbf{G}_{(2)}(\mathbf{I}_{r_3} \otimes \boldsymbol{\Omega}_1)\mathbf{G}_{(2)}^T - \mathbf{G}_{(2)}(\boldsymbol{\Omega}_3 \otimes \mathbf{I}_{r_1})\mathbf{G}_{(2)}^T
$$
$$
= \mathrm{Skew}(\mathbf{U}_2^T\eta_{\mathbf{U}_2}\mathbf{G}_{(2)}\mathbf{G}_{(2)}^T) + \mathrm{Skew}(\mathbf{G}_{(2)}\eta_{\mathbf{G}_{(2)}}^T),
$$

$$
\mathbf{G}_{(3)}\mathbf{G}_{(3)}^T\boldsymbol{\Omega}_3 + \boldsymbol{\Omega}_3\mathbf{G}_{(3)}\mathbf{G}_{(3)}^T - \mathbf{G}_{(3)}(\mathbf{I}_{r_2} \otimes \boldsymbol{\Omega}_1)\mathbf{G}_{(3)}^T - \mathbf{G}_{(3)}(\boldsymbol{\Omega}_2 \otimes \mathbf{I}_{r_1})\mathbf{G}_{(3)}^T
$$
$$
= \mathrm{Skew}(\mathbf{U}_3^T\eta_{\mathbf{U}_3}\mathbf{G}_{(3)}\mathbf{G}_{(3)}^T) + \mathrm{Skew}(\mathbf{G}_{(3)}\eta_{\mathbf{G}_{(3)}}^T),
$$

where $\mathrm{Skew}(\cdot)$ extracts the skew-symmetric part of a square matrix, i.e., $\mathrm{Skew}(\mathbf{D}) = (\mathbf{D} - \mathbf{D}^T)/2$.

The coupled Lyapunov equations in Proposition 4.3 are solved efficiently with an iterative linear solver that is combined with a specific symmetric preconditioner resulting from a Gauss–Seidel approximation of the coupled linear equations. For the variable $\boldsymbol{\Omega}_1$, the preconditioner is of the form $\mathbf{G}_{(1)}\mathbf{G}_{(1)}^T\boldsymbol{\Omega}_1 + \boldsymbol{\Omega}_1\mathbf{G}_{(1)}\mathbf{G}_{(1)}^T$, and similarly for the variables $\boldsymbol{\Omega}_2$ and $\boldsymbol{\Omega}_3$.

4.3.4 Retraction

A retraction is a mapping that maps vectors in the horizontal space to points on the search space $\mathcal{M}$ and satisfies the local rigidity condition [9]. It provides a natural way to move on the manifold along a search direction. Because the total space $\mathcal{M}$ has the product nature, we can choose a retraction by combining retractions on the individual manifolds, i.e.,

$$
R_x(\xi_x) = (\mathrm{uf}(\mathbf{U}_1 + \xi_{\mathbf{U}_1}), \mathrm{uf}(\mathbf{U}_2 + \xi_{\mathbf{U}_2}), \mathrm{uf}(\mathbf{U}_3 + \xi_{\mathbf{U}_3}), \mathcal{G} + \xi_{\mathcal{G}}), \tag{4.15}
$$

where $\xi_x \in \mathcal{H}_x$ and $\mathrm{uf}(\cdot)$ extracts the orthogonal factor of a full column rank matrix, i.e., $\mathrm{uf}(\mathbf{A}) = \mathbf{A}(\mathbf{A}^T\mathbf{A})^{-1/2}$. The retraction R_x defines a retraction $R_{[x]}(\xi_{[x]}) := [R_x(\xi_x)]$ on the quotient manifold $\mathcal{M}/\sim$, as the equivalence class $[R_x(\xi_x)]$ does not depend on specific matrix representations of $[x]$ and $\xi_{[x]}$, where ξ_x is the horizontal lift of the abstract tangent vector $\xi_{[x]} \in T_{[x]}(\mathcal{M}/\sim)$.

4.3.5 Vector transport

A vector transport on a manifold $\mathcal{M}$ is a smooth mapping that transports a tangent vector $\xi_x \in T_x\mathcal{M}$ at $x \in \mathcal{M}$ to a vector in the tangent space at a point $R_x(\eta_x)$. It is defined by the symbol $\mathcal{T}_{\eta_x}\xi_x$. It generalizes the classical concept of translation of vectors in the Euclidean space to manifolds [9]. The horizontal lift of the abstract vector transport $\mathcal{T}_{\eta_{[x]}}\xi_{[x]}$ on $\mathcal{M}/\sim$ has the matrix characterization

$$\Pi_{R_x(\eta_x)}(\mathcal{T}_{\eta_x}\xi_x) = \Pi_{R_x(\eta_x)}(\Psi_{R_x(\eta_x)}(\xi_x)), \tag{4.16}$$

where ξ_x and η_x are the horizontal lifts in $\mathcal{H}_x$ of $\xi_{[x]}$ and $\eta_{[x]}$ that belong to $T_{[x]}(\mathcal{M}/\sim)$ and $\Psi_x(\cdot)$ and $\Pi_x(\cdot)$ are projectors defined in Propositions 4.2 and 4.3, respectively. The computational cost of transporting a vector solely depends on the projection and retraction operations.

4.3.6 Computational cost

The computation cost of implementing the tangent space linear projector Ψ_x is $O(n_1 r_1^2 + n_2 r_2^2 + n_3 r_3^2)$. The computational cost of using the horizontal space projector Π_x is $O(r_1 r_2 r_3)$. The cost of implementing the retraction operation is $O(n_1 r_1^2 + n_2 r_2^2 + n_3 r_3^2)$. Implementing the vector transport involves using the linear projectors which together cost $O(n_1 r_1^2 + n_2 r_2^2 + n_3 r_3^2 + r_1 r_2 r_3)$.

4.4 Algorithms for tensor learning problems

In this section, we discuss the tensor completion problem and the more general tensor learning setup that covers regression and multitask problems. Without loss of generality, the tensor learning problems are cast as

$$\min_{[x]\in\mathcal{M}/\sim} f(x), \tag{4.17}$$

where $f : \mathcal{M} \to \mathbb{R}$ is a smooth function and $\mathcal{M}/\sim$ is identified with the Tucker manifold.

Thanks to the availability of manifold optimization toolboxes such as those mentioned in Section 4.2, the Riemannian optimization algorithms are easy to use to solve (4.17). Specifically, we use the notions developed in Section 4.3 to propose an RCG algorithm [9,16,17] to solve (4.17).

Algorithm 1 shows the skeletal steps for implementation of the RCG algorithm. The convergence analysis of the RCG algorithm is presented in [9,16,17]. In general, theoretical convergence of the Riemannian algorithms is to a stationary point. However, as simulations show, convergence to global minima is observed in many challenging instances. Practically, the RCG algorithm offers a good trade-off between accuracy and faster convergence. It should, however, be emphasized that the develop-

---

Algorithm 1 Riemannian conjugate gradient (RCG) algorithm for (4.17).

---

1. Initialize x from a point $x_0 \in \mathcal{M}$.

2. Compute the horizontal lift of the Riemannian gradient $\text{grad}_x f$ at x as shown in Proposition 4.4.

3. Compute the conjugate direction ξ_x at x that belongs to the horizontal space $\mathcal{H}_x$. This makes use of vector transport (4.16).

4. Compute a step size t using backtracking line search.

5. Compute the new point as $x_+ = R_x(t\xi_x)$ using the expression in (4.15).

6. Repeat steps 2–5 until convergence.

---

ments in Section 4.3 allow to use other Riemannian algorithms, e.g., the second-order Riemannian trust-region algorithm.

For implementing RCG in Algorithm 1, we need (i) manifold-related ingredients, which are already mentioned in Table 4.1, and (ii) cost function f-specific ingredients like the Riemannian gradient computation, which we discuss below. The computational cost of manifold-related ingredients is mentioned in Section 4.3.6. The cost of computing the Riemannian gradient depends on the cont function (their partial derivatives) at hand. We discuss them later in this section.

The Riemannian gradient computation only requires the partial derivatives of the cost function at hand. To this end, we have the following proposition that gives the final expression of the Riemannian gradient for the general form (4.17).

Proposition 4.4. *The cost function (4.17) at* $(\mathbf{U}_1, \mathbf{U}_2, \mathbf{U}_3, \mathcal{G})$ *under the quotient manifold (4.4) endowed with the Riemannian metric (4.8) admits the horizontal lift of the Riemannian gradient as*

$$
\begin{aligned}
&\text{grad}_x f \\
&= \Psi_x(\nabla_{\mathbf{U}_1} f (\mathbf{G}_{(1)} \mathbf{G}_{(1)}^T)^{-1}, \nabla_{\mathbf{U}_2} f (\mathbf{G}_{(2)} \mathbf{G}_{(2)}^T)^{-1}, \\
&\qquad\qquad\qquad \nabla_{\mathbf{U}_3} f (\mathbf{G}_{(3)} \mathbf{G}_{(3)}^T)^{-1}, \nabla_{\mathcal{G}} f),
\end{aligned}
\tag{4.18}
$$

where $\nabla_{\mathbf{U}_1} f$, $\nabla_{\mathbf{U}_2} f$, $\nabla_{\mathbf{U}_3} f$, *and* $\nabla_{\mathcal{G}} f$ *are the partial derivatives of* f *with respect of* $\mathbf{U}_1$, $\mathbf{U}_2$, $\mathbf{U}_3$, *and* $\mathcal{G}$, *respectively. Here,* Ψ_x *is the projection operator defined in Proposition 4.3.*

4.4.1 Tensor completion

Given a tensor $\mathcal{X}^{n_1 \times n_2 \times n_3}$ whose entries $\mathcal{X}^\star_{i_1, i_2, i_3}$ are only known for some indices $(i_1, i_2, i_3) \in \Omega$, where Ω is a subset of the complete set of indices $\{(i_1, i_2, i_3) : i_d \in \{1, \dots, n_d\}, d \in \{1, 2, 3\}\}$, the fixed-rank tensor completion problem is formulated as

$$
\begin{aligned}
&\min_{\mathcal{X} \in \mathbb{R}^{n_1 \times n_2 \times n_3}} \quad \frac{1}{|\Omega|} \|\mathcal{P}_\Omega(\mathcal{X}) - \mathcal{P}_\Omega(\mathcal{X}^\star)\|_F^2 \\
&\text{subject to} \quad \text{rank}(\mathcal{X}) = \mathbf{r},
\end{aligned}
\tag{4.19}
$$

where the sampling operator $\mathcal{P}_\Omega(\mathcal{X})_{i_1,i_2,i_3} = \mathcal{X}_{i_1,i_2,i_3}$ if $(i_1, i_2, i_3) \in \Omega$ and $\mathcal{P}_\Omega(\mathcal{X})_{i_1,i_2,i_3} = 0$ otherwise, $\|\cdot\|_F$ is the Frobenius norm, $|\Omega|$ is the number of known entries in $\mathcal{X}^\star$, and $\mathrm{rank}(\mathcal{X}) = \mathbf{r} = (r_1, r_2, r_3)$, called the multilinear rank of $\mathcal{X}$, is the set of ranks for each of the mode-d unfolding matrices. Note that $r_d \ll n_d$ enforces a low-rank structure.

We show the computation of the Riemannian gradient. Let $f(\mathcal{X}) := \|\mathcal{P}_\Omega(\mathcal{X}) - \mathcal{P}_\Omega(\mathcal{X}^\star)\|_F^2/|\Omega|$ be the cost function of (4.19) and let $\mathcal{S} = 2(\mathcal{P}_\Omega(\mathcal{G} \times_1 \mathbf{U}_1 \times_2 \mathbf{U}_2 \times_3 \mathbf{U}_3) - \mathcal{P}_\Omega(\mathcal{X}^\star))/|\Omega|$ be an auxiliary sparse tensor variable that is interpreted as the partial derivative of f in the full space $\mathbb{R}^{n_1 \times n_2 \times n_3}$. The partial derivatives of f with respect to $(\mathbf{U}_1, \mathbf{U}_2, \mathbf{U}_3, \mathcal{G})$ are computed in terms of the unfolding matrices $\mathbf{S}_{(d)}$, i.e.,

$$
\begin{aligned}
\nabla_{\mathbf{U}_1} f &= \mathbf{S}_{(1)}(\mathbf{U}_3 \otimes \mathbf{U}_2)\mathbf{G}_{(1)}^T, \\
\nabla_{\mathbf{U}_2} f &= \mathbf{S}_{(2)}(\mathbf{U}_3 \otimes \mathbf{U}_1)\mathbf{G}_{(2)}^T, \\
\nabla_{\mathbf{U}_3} f &= \mathbf{S}_{(3)}(\mathbf{U}_2 \otimes \mathbf{U}_1)\mathbf{G}_{(3)}^T, \\
\nabla_{\mathcal{G}} f &= \mathcal{S} \times_1 \mathbf{U}_1^T \times_2 \mathbf{U}_2^T \times_3 \mathbf{U}_3^T.
\end{aligned}
$$

Finally, the Riemannian gradient can be computed using Proposition 4.4. The numerical cost of computing the Riemannian gradient depends on computing the partial derivatives, which is $O(|\Omega| r_1 r_2 r_3)$, where $|\Omega|$ is the number of known entries. The total computational cost per iteration of the RCG algorithm is $O(|\Omega| r_1 r_2 r_3 + n_1 r_1^2 + n_2 r_2^2 + n_3 r_3^2 + r_1 r_2 r_3)$.

4.4.2 General tensor learning

Apart from the tensor completion problem mentioned in Section 4.4.1, other interesting classes of problems arise in multitask learning, where several related tasks are learned together in a transfer learning setup [6,53], or in the tensor regression problem, where the outputs have a multivariate structure [7,54]. Such problems may be viewed as (supervised) multivariate regression. In the following, we detail their solution using the proposed Algorithm 1.

Let $\{\mathbf{a}_i, \mathbf{Y}_i\}_{i=1}^{n_1}$ be the training data instances where $\mathbf{Y}_i \in \mathbb{R}^{n_2 \times n_3}$ is the response corresponding to the input $\mathbf{a}_i \in \mathbb{R}^d$. It should be noted that vanilla linear regression has a scalar output. Hence, a structured multivariate response may also be viewed as scalar responses across various *modes*. For example, predicting temperature at a particular time instance (for an input location $\mathbf{a}$) implies scalar response per input. However, predicting temperature and humidity at multiple fixed time instances (for an input location $\mathbf{a}$) corresponds to matrix response per input. The regression function may be modeled as $f(\mathbf{a}) = \mathcal{X} \times_1 \mathbf{a}$, where $\mathcal{X} \in \mathbb{R}^{d \times n_2 \times n_3}$ is the learned model parameter. We propose to learn $\mathcal{X}$ by solving the following optimization problem:

$$
\begin{aligned}
\min_{\mathcal{X} \in \mathbb{R}^{d \times n_2 \times n_3}} \quad & \|\mathcal{X} \times_1 \mathbf{A}_1 - \mathcal{Y}\|_F^2 \\
\text{subject to} \quad & \mathrm{rank}(\mathcal{X}) = \mathbf{r},
\end{aligned} \tag{4.20}
$$

where $\mathbf{A}_1$ is the $n_1 \times d$ matrix with the i-th row corresponding to $\mathbf{a}_i^\top$ and $\mathcal{Y} \in \mathbb{R}^{n_1 \times n_2 \times n_3}$ is the tensor obtained by stacking all the responses $\mathbf{Y}_i\big|_{i=1}^{n_1}$.

A more general optimization formulation that encompasses (4.20) is

$$
\min_{\mathcal{X} \in \mathbb{R}^{n_1 \times n_2 \times n_3}} \quad \frac{1}{|\Omega|} \| \mathcal{P}_\Omega(\mathcal{X} \times_1 \mathbf{A}_1 \times_2 \mathbf{A}_2 \times_3 \mathbf{A}_3) - \mathcal{P}_\Omega(\mathcal{Y}^\star) \|_\mathrm{F}^2 \tag{4.21}
$$
$$
\text{subject to} \quad \mathrm{rank}(\mathcal{X}) = \mathbf{r},
$$

where $\mathbf{A}_1$, $\mathbf{A}_2$, and $\mathbf{A}_3$ are user input matrices of size $m_1 \times n_1$, $m_2 \times n_2$, and $m_3 \times n_3$, respectively, and $\mathcal{X} \in \mathbb{R}^{n_1 \times n_2 \times n_3}$ is the low-rank tensor that needs to be learned. Here, the sampling operator $\mathcal{P}_\Omega$ consists of a subset of indices of a tensor of size $m_1 \times m_2 \times m_3$, i.e., $\mathcal{P}_\Omega(\mathcal{Y})_{i_1,i_2,i_3} = \mathcal{Y}_{i_1,i_2,i_3}$ if $(i_1, i_2, i_3) \in \Omega$ and $\mathcal{P}_\Omega(\mathcal{Y})_{i_1,i_2,i_3} = 0$ otherwise, and $\| \cdot \|_\mathrm{F}$ is the Frobenius norm. The partially known tensor $\mathcal{Y}^\star$ is of size $m_1 \times m_2 \times m_3$. Depending on the sampling pattern of Ω, the form (4.21) generalizes the regression and completion setups. Overall, the use of Ω in (4.21) gives an additional flexibility to our modeling.

It should be noted that the tensor completion problem (4.19) is a special case of (4.21), where the user input matrices $\mathbf{A}_1$, $\mathbf{A}_2$, and $\mathbf{A}_3$ are identity matrices.

To implement the RCG algorithm for (4.21), we require the partial derivatives of $f(x) := \frac{1}{|\Omega|} \| \mathcal{P}_\Omega(\mathcal{G} \times_1 \mathbf{A}_1 \mathbf{U}_1 \times_2 \mathbf{A}_2 \mathbf{U}_2 \times_3 \mathbf{A}_3 \mathbf{U}_3) - \mathcal{P}_\Omega(\mathcal{X}^\star) \|_\mathrm{F}^2$ with respect to $(\mathbf{U}_1, \mathbf{U}_2, \mathbf{U}_3, \mathcal{G})$, which have the expressions

$$
\begin{aligned}
\nabla_{\mathbf{U}_1} f &= \mathbf{A}_1^T \mathbf{S}_{(1)} (\mathbf{A}_3 \mathbf{U}_3 \otimes \mathbf{A}_2 \mathbf{U}_2) \mathbf{G}_{(1)}^T, \\
\nabla_{\mathbf{U}_2} f &= \mathbf{A}_2^T \mathbf{S}_{(2)} (\mathbf{A}_3 \mathbf{U}_3 \otimes \mathbf{A}_1 \mathbf{U}_1) \mathbf{G}_{(2)}^T, \\
\nabla_{\mathbf{U}_3} f &= \mathbf{A}_3^T \mathbf{S}_{(3)} (\mathbf{A}_2 \mathbf{U}_2 \otimes \mathbf{A}_1 \mathbf{U}_1) \mathbf{G}_{(3)}^T, \\
\nabla_{\mathcal{G}} f &= \mathcal{S} \times_1 \mathbf{U}_1^T \mathbf{A}_1^T \times_2 \mathbf{U}_2^T \mathbf{A}_2^T \times_3 \mathbf{U}_3^T \mathbf{A}_3^T,
\end{aligned}
$$

where $\mathcal{S} = \frac{2}{|\Omega|}(\mathcal{P}_\Omega(\mathcal{G} \times_1 \mathbf{A}_1 \mathbf{U}_1 \times_2 \mathbf{A}_2 \mathbf{U}_2 \times_3 \mathbf{A}_3 \mathbf{U}_3) - \mathcal{P}_\Omega(\mathcal{X}^\star))$ and $\mathbf{S}_{(d)}$ is the mode-d unfolding. Finally, the Riemannian gradient is computed using Proposition 4.4.

The total numerical cost of computing the Riemannian gradient, and therefore the cost per iteration of the RCG algorithm, is $O(|\Omega| r_1 r_2 r_3 + \sum_d m_d n_d r_d)$. The terms $\sum_d m_d n_d r_d$ arise because of computations $\mathbf{A}_d \mathbf{U}_d$, which can be further reduced if the user input matrices $\mathbf{A}_d$ have sparsity.

4.5 Experiments

In this section, we present empirical results on both synthetic and real-world datasets. Section 4.5.2 focuses on the low-rank tensor completion setting. In Section 4.5.3, we discuss the low-rank tensor regression experiments. The multilinear multitask experiments are discussed in Section 4.5.4. Before diving into those experiments, we also discuss the benefit of our metric choice in Section 4.5.1.

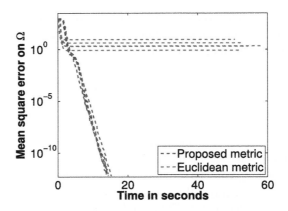

FIGURE 4.3

Our choice of the metric has profound impact on our algorithm's convergence. Shown here is the performance of the gradient descent algorithms for a tensor completion instance. Here, Ω refers to a subset of entries in the tensors.

Our proposed algorithms are implemented in the MATLAB® toolbox Manopt [44]. The MATLAB codes for the RCG algorithms for tensor completion and general regression problems are available at https://bamdevmishra.in/codes/tensorcompletion/.[1]

All simulations are performed in MATLAB. For specific matrix multiplication operations with unfoldings of sparse tensors, we use the mex interfaces for MATLAB that are provided by the authors of [14].

4.5.1 Choice of metric

We first show the benefit of the proposed metric (4.8) over the conventional choice of the Euclidean metric that exploits the product structure of $\mathcal{M}$ and symmetry (4.2). This is defined by combining the individual Euclidean metrics for $\mathrm{St}(r_d, n_d)$ and $\mathbb{R}^{r_1 \times r_2 \times r_3}$, i.e.,

$$g_x(\xi_x, \eta_x) = \langle \xi_{\mathbf{U}_1}, \eta_{\mathbf{U}_1} \rangle + \langle \xi_{\mathbf{U}_2}, \eta_{\mathbf{U}_2} \rangle + \langle \xi_{\mathbf{U}_3}, \eta_{\mathbf{U}_3} \rangle + \langle \xi_{\mathcal{G}}, \eta_{\mathcal{G}} \rangle, \qquad (4.22)$$

where $\xi_x, \eta_x \in T_x \mathcal{M}$ and $\langle \cdot, \cdot \rangle$ is the Euclidean inner product. The metric (4.22) also respects the equivalence relationship (4.3), and therefore leads to a well-defined Riemannian geometry.

The performance of algorithms with the Euclidean metric (4.22) is poor compared to the metric choice (4.8), as shown in Fig. 4.3. This implies that having a metric that

---

[1] Although we have not discussed the Riemannian trust-region (RTR) algorithms in this chapter, the developments in Section 4.3 allow to implement RTR algorithms. The codes for RTR implementations are also available at https://bamdevmishra.in/codes/tensorcompletion/.

is aligned to the cost function is critical. The good performance of our metric comes from the fact that it aligns closely with quadratic cost functions.

Here, we consider a tensor completion problem instance by randomly generating a tensor of size $200 \times 200 \times 200$ and rank $\mathbf{r} = (10, 10, 10)$ with an oversampling ratio of 10 (details of tensor generation are discussed in Section 4.5.2). For simplicity, we compare gradient descent algorithms with backtracking line search for both the metric choices.

4.5.2 Low-rank tensor completion

We show a number of comparisons of our proposed RCG algorithm with baseline algorithms that include:

- geomCG [14], a low-rank tensor completion algorithm using embedded subman-ifold Riemannian optimization on the manifold of fixed multilinear rank tensors,
- TOpt [55], a nonlinear conjugate gradient algorithm for Tucker decomposition,
- Hard [4], which uses the scaled overlapped nuclear norm and implements a prox-imal gradient algorithm,
- HaLRTC [2], which uses the scaled overlapped nuclear norm for modeling and implements an alternating direction methods of multipliers (ADMMs), and
- Latent [3], which uses the latent nuclear norm and implements ADMM.

Since the dimension of the space of a tensor $\in \mathbb{R}^{n_1 \times n_2 \times n_3}$ of rank $\mathbf{r} = (r_1, r_2, r_3)$ is $\dim(\mathcal{M}/\sim) = \sum_{d=1}^{3} (n_d r_d - r_d^2) + r_1 r_2 r_3$, we randomly and uniformly select known entries based on a multiple of the dimension, called the oversampling (OS) ratio, to create the train set Ω. Algorithms are initialized randomly, as suggested in [14]. We evaluate the mean square errors (MSEs) on both Ω (train set) and Γ (test set). Five runs are performed in each scenario and the plots show all of them.

In large-scale instances, we only show comparisons with geomCG as other base-lines, TOpt, Hard, HaLRTC, and Latent, cannot handle large tensors.

4.5.2.1 Small-scale instances

Small-scale tensors of size $100 \times 100 \times 100$, $150 \times 150 \times 150$, and $200 \times 200 \times 200$ and rank $\mathbf{r} = (10, 10, 10)$ are considered. OS is $\{10, 20, 30\}$. Fig. 4.4 shows that our proposed algorithm converges faster than the baselines. In particular, our algorithm outperforms others in low-OS scenarios.

4.5.2.2 Large-scale instances

We consider large-scale tensors of size $3000 \times 3000 \times 3000$, $5000 \times 5000 \times 5000$, and $10,000 \times 10,000 \times 10,000$ and ranks $\mathbf{r} = (5, 5, 5)$ and $(10, 10, 10)$. The OS ratio is 10. Only the proposed algorithm and geomCG are able to handle these large instances. To this end, we show comparisons with geomCG. Fig. 4.5 shows that our proposed algorithm is consistently faster than geomcG.

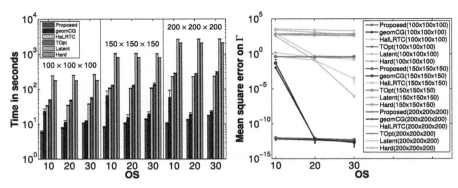

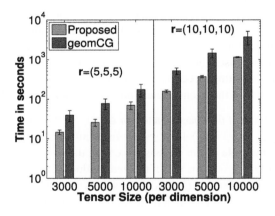

FIGURE 4.4

Comparisons on small-scale instances of the tensor completion problem with various OS ratios show a consistent good performance of our proposed approach.

FIGURE 4.5

Comparisons on large-scale instances for the tensor completion problem. Our proposed algorithm is consistently faster than geomCG. In certain instances, our proposed algorithm is five times faster than geomCG.

4.5.2.3 Low sampling instances

We generate tensor instances from very scarcely sampled data, e.g., the OS ratio is 4. The test requires completing a tensor of size $10,000 \times 10,000 \times 10,000$ and rank $\mathbf{r} = (5, 5, 5)$. Fig. 4.6 shows the superior performance of the proposed algorithm against geomCG. Whereas the test error increases for geomCG, it decreases for the proposed algorithm. Other baselines do not scale to this tensor size.

4.5.2.4 Ill-conditioned and low sampling instances

We consider the problem instance of Section 4.5.2.3 with OS ratio $= 5$. Additionally, for generating the instance, we impose a superdiagonal core $\mathcal{G}$ with exponentially

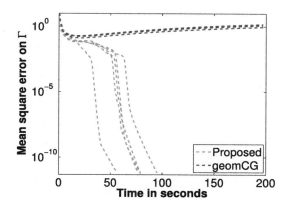

FIGURE 4.6

The proposed algorithm outperforms other baselines in low-OS tensor completion scenarios. Shown here are the plots for the proposed and geomCG algorithms.

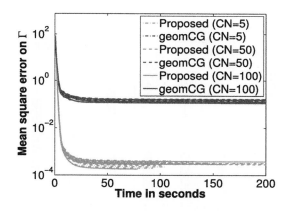

FIGURE 4.7

Our algorithm robustly outperforms geomCG in ill-conditioned tensor completion instances.

decaying positive values of condition numbers (CNs) 5, 50, and 100. Fig. 4.7 shows that the proposed algorithm outperforms geomCG for all considered CN values.

4.5.2.5 Noisy instances

We evaluate the convergence properties of algorithms under the presence of noise by adding scaled Gaussian noise $\mathcal{P}_\Omega(\mathcal{E})$ to $\mathcal{P}_\Omega(\mathcal{X}^\star)$ as in [14]. The different noise levels are $\epsilon = \{10^{-4}, 10^{-6}, 10^{-8}, 10^{-10}, 10^{-12}\}$. The tensor size and rank are the same as in Section 4.5.2.3 and the OS ratio is 10. Fig. 4.8 shows that the test error for each ϵ is almost identical to $\epsilon^2 \|\mathcal{P}_\Omega(\mathcal{X}^\star)\|_F^2$ [14], but our proposed algorithm converges faster than geomCG.

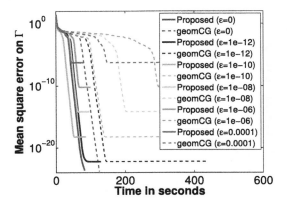

FIGURE 4.8

Faster convergence of the proposed algorithm in large-dimensional but noisy tensor completion instances.

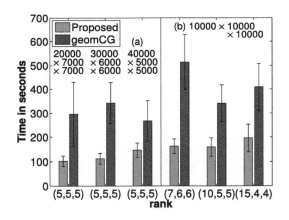

FIGURE 4.9

The proposed algorithm outperforms geomCG in large and skewed dimensional instances.

4.5.2.6 Skewed dimensional instances

We consider instances where the dimensions and ranks along certain modes are different than others. Two scenarios are considered. The first scenario considers tensors of size $20{,}000 \times 7000 \times 7000$, $30{,}000 \times 6000 \times 6000$, and $40{,}000 \times 5000 \times 5000$ with rank $\mathbf{r} = (5, 5, 5)$. The second scenario considers a tensor of size $10{,}000 \times 10{,}000 \times 10{,}000$ with ranks $(7, 6, 6)$, $(10, 5, 5)$, and $(15, 4, 4)$. In all of those scenarios, the proposed algorithm converges faster than geomCG, as shown in Fig. 4.9.

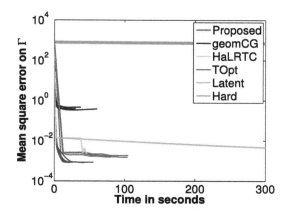

FIGURE 4.10

Ribeira tensor completion dataset: results are on the challenging scenario with OS = 11.

4.5.2.7 Ribeira dataset

We consider the hyperspectral image "Ribeira" [56] discussed in [14,57]. The tensor size is $1017 \times 1340 \times 33$, where each slice corresponds to a particular image measured at a different wavelength. As suggested in [14,57], we resize it to $203 \times 268 \times 33$. We perform five random samplings of the pixels based on the OS values 11 and 22, corresponding to the rank $\mathbf{r} = (15, 15, 6)$ adopted in [14]. This set is further randomly split into 80/10/10 train/validation/test partitions. The algorithms are stopped when the MSE on the validation set starts to increase. While OS = 22 corresponds to the observation ratio of 10% studied in [14], OS = 11 considers a challenging scenario with an observation ratio of 5%. Fig. 4.10 shows the good performance of our algorithm. Table 4.2 shows the results.

4.5.2.8 MovieLens 10M dataset

This dataset, downloaded from http://grouplens.org/datasets/movielens/, contains 10,000,054 ratings corresponding to 71,567 users and 10,681 movies. We split the time into 7-day-wide bins, and finally get a tensor of size $71{,}567 \times 10{,}681 \times 731$. The fraction of known entries is less than 0.002%. The completion task on this dataset reveals periodicity of the latent genres. We perform five random 80/10/10 train/validation/test partitions. The maximum iteration threshold is set to 500. In Table 4.3, our proposed algorithm consistently gives lower test errors than geomCG across different ranks.

4.5.3 Low-rank tensor regression

In this section, we discuss results on spatial-temporal forecasting datasets in the time-series analysis domain, where the goal is to predict the future values given their historical measurements [58]. That is, given the values at timestamps at say

Table 4.2 Tensor completion: average test MSE and time in seconds on the Ribeira dataset.

OS	Algorithm	Time	Test MSE
	Proposed	**33**	$\mathbf{8.2095 \cdot 10^{-4}}$
	geomCG	36	$3.8342 \cdot 10^{-1}$
11	HaLRTC	46	$2.2671 \cdot 10^{-3}$
	TOpt	80	$1.7854 \cdot 10^{-3}$
	Latent	553	$2.9296 \cdot 10^{-3}$
	Hard	400	$6.5090 \cdot 10^{2}$
	Proposed	67	$\mathbf{6.9516 \cdot 10^{-4}}$
	geomCG	150	$6.2590 \cdot 10^{-3}$
22	HaLRTC	48	$1.3880 \cdot 10^{-3}$
	TOpt	**27**	$2.1259 \cdot 10^{-3}$
	Latent	558	$1.6339 \cdot 10^{-3}$
	Hard	402	$6.5989 \cdot 10^{2}$

Table 4.3 Tensor completion: Average test MSE and time in seconds on the MovieLens-10M dataset.

Algorithm	r	Time	Test MSE
	(4, 4, 4)	**1748**	**0.6762**
Proposed	(6, 6, 6)	**6058**	**0.6913**
	(8, 8, 8)	**11,370**	**0.7589**
	(10, 10, 10)	**32,802**	**1.0107**
	(4, 4, 4)	2981	0.6956
geomCG	(6, 6, 6)	6554	0.7398
	(8, 8, 8)	13,853	0.8955
	(10, 10, 10)	38,145	1.6550

$t - 2, \ldots, t$, predict the values of all the variables at timestamps $t + 1, \ldots, t + k$. This problem may be viewed as a regression problem with tensor-structured output where the regression parameters are modeled as a low-rank tensor [7]. We evaluate the proposed algorithm on two forecasting datasets:

- *Comprehensive Climate Dataset (CCDS)*: This is a collection of the climate records of North America from [59]. It contains monthly observations of 17 variables (such as carbon dioxide levels and temperature) spanning from the year 1990 to 2001. The readings were taken across 125 locations. It is available at https://viterbi-web.usc.edu/~liu32/data/NA-1990-2002-Monthly-high.csv.

Table 4.4 Tensor regression: Average test MSE obtained on the CCDS dataset.

Algorithm	k	r = (5, 5, 5)	r = (10, 10, 10)	r = (15, 15, 15)
Proposed	3	**0.7386**	**0.6876**	**0.6791**
	5	**0.7343**	**0.6817**	**0.6737**
	7	**0.7521**	**0.6975**	**0.6901**
HOLRR	3	0.7615	0.6992	0.6817
	5	0.7585	0.6928	0.6763
	7	0.7724	0.7072	0.6927

Table 4.5 Tensor regression: Average test MSE obtained on the Meteo-UK dataset.

Algorithm	k	r = (3, 3, 3)	r = (4, 4, 4)	r = (5, 5, 5)
Proposed	3	**0.3456**	**0.3199**	**0.3136**
	5	**0.3356**	**0.3085**	**0.3001**
	7	**0.3420**	**0.3152**	**0.3077**
HOLRR	3	0.3471	0.3362	0.3300
	5	0.3425	0.3162	0.3088
	7	0.3485	0.3213	0.3141

- *Meteo-UK*: This dataset contains monthly observations of 5 variables in 16 locations across the UK from 1960 to 2000. It is available at http://www.metoffice.gov.uk/public/weather/climate-historic/.

The model parameter is learned as a $(17 \cdot 125 \cdot k \times 17 \times 125)$-dimensional tensor in the CCDS dataset and as a $(5 \cdot 16 \cdot k \times 5 \times 16)$-dimensional tensor in the Meteo-UK dataset.

Tables 4.4 and 4.5 report the average MSE obtained on the CCDS and Meteo-UK datasets, respectively. The results are averaged over five random 80/20 train/test splits. In addition to the proposed algorithm, we also report the results of the HOLRR algorithm [7], which learns a Tucker decomposition-based low-rank tensor in an alternate minimization framework. In both tables, we observe that the proposed algorithm obtains better generalization performance than HOLRR across multilinear ranks.

4.5.4 Multilinear multitask learning

We discuss the multitask feature learning setting, where the aim is to learn a common low-rank representation of several tasks [60–64] (classification/regression problems). In various real-world scenarios, the tasks have an inherent multimodel structure, and hence, their model parameters may be together learned as a (low-rank) tensor [6,38,53]. For instance, consider the problem of predicting the examination scores of students in different schools of a city across years (based on several student/school

Table 4.6 Multitask learning: Average normalized MSE obtained on the School dataset.

Train data size	r	Proposed	MLMTL-NC
40%	(1, 1, 1)	0.3708	**0.3667**
	(2, 2, 2)	**0.3439**	0.3548
	(3, 3, 3)	**0.3329**	0.3469
80%	(1, 1, 1)	0.3801	**0.3786**
	(2, 2, 2)	**0.3718**	0.3754
	(3, 3, 3)	**0.3671**	0.3726

attributes). In this case, the model parameter of every school could change over years based on time-varying attributes. Hence, we may learn the models jointly as a low-rank three-mode tensor, where the modes correspond to attributes, year, and school [53].

We evaluate the proposed algorithm on the School dataset [60,64] with the goal to predict examination scores of 15,362 students in 139 schools in the years 1985, 1986, and 1987. The model parameter is learned as a $(24 \times 3 \times 139)$-dimensional tensor, where the dataset has 24 processed attributes. We create randomly sampled 80/20 train-test splits. We also evaluate on a low-data scenario, common in multitask setting, where we train on only 40% of the original dataset (and the test set is the one created for the 80/20 split).

The results are reported in Table 4.6. The results are averaged over five random train/test splits. In addition to the proposed algorithm, we also report the results of the multilinear multitask learning algorithm (MLMTL-NC) proposed in [6], which learns a Tucker decomposition-based low-rank tensor in an alternate minimization framework. We observe that the performance of the proposed algorithm is better than that of MLMTL-NC in both experimental settings.

4.6 Conclusion

We have discussed a Riemannian geometry on the manifold of rank-constrained Tucker tensors. The geometry builds upon a particular metric choice that exploits symmetries in Tucker decomposition. This provides a Riemannian quotient manifold structure to the Tucker manifold. The rich Riemannian structure allows to solve different tensor learning problems. Experiments show a good performance of the proposed Riemannian approach.

Although the proposed metric (and geometry) allows to solve general tensor learning problems, tuning it further to specific cost functions would be a future research direction. The use of Riemannian geometry in other tensor decomposition methods and applications remains an active area of research.

References

[1] E.J. Candès, B. Recht, Exact matrix completion via convex optimization, Foundations of Computational Mathematics 9 (6) (2009) 717–772.

[2] J. Liu, P. Musialski, P. Wonka, J. Ye, Tensor completion for estimating missing values in visual data, IEEE Transactions on Pattern Analysis and Machine Intelligence 35 (1) (2013) 208–220.

[3] R. Tomioka, K. Hayashi, H. Kashima, Estimation of low-rank tensors via convex optimization, Tech. Rep., arXiv preprint, arXiv:1010.0789, 2011.

[4] M. Signoretto, Q.T. Dinh, L.D. Lathauwer, J.A.K. Suykens, Learning with tensors: a framework based on convex optimization and spectral regularization, Machine Learning 94 (3) (2014) 303–351.

[5] M. Nimishakavi, P. Jawanpuria, B. Mishra, A dual framework for trace norm regularized low-rank tensor completion, in: NeurIPS, 2018.

[6] B. Romera-Paredes, H. Aung, N. Bianchi-Berthouze, M. Pontil, Multilinear multitask learning, in: ICML, 2013, pp. 1444–1452.

[7] G. Rabusseau, H. Kadri, Low-rank regression with tensor responses, in: NeurIPS, 2016.

[8] T.G. Kolda, B.W. Bader, Tensor decompositions and applications, SIAM Review 51 (3) (2009) 455–500.

[9] P.-A. Absil, R. Mahony, R. Sepulchre, Optimization Algorithms on Matrix Manifolds, Princeton University Press, 2008.

[10] N. Boumal, An introduction to optimization on smooth manifolds, Available online http://www.nicolasboumal.net/book, Aug 2020.

[11] B. Mishra, G. Meyer, S. Bonnabel, R. Sepulchre, Fixed-rank matrix factorizations and Riemannian low-rank optimization, Computational Statistics 29 (3–4) (2014) 591–621.

[12] B. Mishra, R. Sepulchre, Riemannian preconditioning, SIAM Journal on Optimization 26 (1) (2016) 635–660.

[13] J. Nocedal, S.J. Wright, Numerical Optimization, second edition, Springer, 2006.

[14] D. Kressner, M. Steinlechner, B. Vandereycken, Low-rank tensor completion by Riemannian optimization, BIT 54 (2) (2014) 447–468.

[15] G. Heidel, V. Schulz, A Riemannian trust-region method for low-rank tensor completion, Numerical Linear Algebra with Applications 25 (6) (2018) e2175.

[16] H. Sato, T. Iwai, A new, globally convergent Riemannian conjugate gradient method, Optimization 64 (4) (2015) 1011–1031.

[17] W. Ring, B. Wirth, Optimization methods on Riemannian manifolds and their application to shape space, SIAM Journal on Optimization 22 (2) (2012) 596–627.

[18] H. Kasai, B. Mishra, Low-rank tensor completion: a Riemannian manifold preconditioning approach, in: ICML, 2016.

[19] A. Kovnatsky, K. Glashoff, M.M. Bronstein, Madmm: a generic algorithm for non-smooth optimization on manifolds, in: ECCV, 2016.

[20] R. Tron, K. Daniilidis, The space of essential matrices as a Riemannian quotient manifold, SIAM Journal on Imaging Sciences 10 (3) (2017) 1416–1445.

[21] L. Balzano, R. Nowak, B. Recht, Online identification and tracking of subspaces from highly incomplete information, in: 48th Annual Allerton Conference on Communication, Control, and Computing (Allerton), 2010.

[22] F.J. Theis, T.P. Cason, P.-A. Absil, Soft dimension reduction for ICA by joint diagonalization on the Stiefel manifold, in: ICA, 2009.

[23] R. Hosseini, S. Sra, Matrix manifold optimization for Gaussian mixtures, in: NIPS, 2015.

[24] N. Boumal, Nonconvex phase synchronization, SIAM Journal on Optimization 26 (4) (2016) 2355–2377.

[25] Y. Zhong, N. Boumal, Near-optimal bounds for phase synchronization, SIAM Journal on Optimization 28 (2) (2018) 989–1016.

[26] P. Jawanpuria, A. Balgovind, A. Kunchukuttan, B. Mishra, Learning multilingual word embeddings in latent metric space: a geometric approach, Transactions of the Association for Computational Linguistics 7 (2019) 107–120.

[27] P. Jawanpuria, N.T.V.S. Dev, A. Kunchukuttan, B. Mishra, Learning geometric word meta-embeddings, in: ACL Workshop on Representation Learning for NLP, 2020.

[28] P. Jawanpuria, M. Meghwanshi, B. Mishra, Geometry-aware domain adaptation for unsupervised alignment of word embeddings, in: ACL, 2020.

[29] P. Jawanpuria, M. Meghwanshi, B. Mishra, A simple approach to learning unsupervised multilingual embeddings, in: EMNLP, 2020.

[30] H. Sakai, H. Iiduka, Riemannian adaptive optimization algorithm and its application to natural language processing, Tech. Rep., arXiv preprint, arXiv:2004.00897, 2020.

[31] M. Nickel, D. Kiela, Learning continuous hierarchies in the Lorentz model of hyperbolic geometry, in: ICML, 2018.

[32] P. Jawanpuria, M. Meghwanshi, B. Mishra, Low-rank approximations of hyperbolic embeddings, in: IEEE CDC, 2019.

[33] B. Mishra, H. Kasai, P. Jawanpuria, A. Saroop, A Riemannian gossip approach to subspace learning on Grassmann manifold, Machine Learning 108 (10) (2019) 1783–1803.

[34] B. Mishra, R. Sepulchre, R3MC: a Riemannian three-factor algorithm for low-rank matrix completion, in: IEEE CDC, 2014, pp. 1137–1142.

[35] B. Mishra, G. Meyer, F. Bach, R. Sepulchre, Low-rank optimization with trace norm penalty, SIAM Journal on Optimization 23 (4) (2013) 2124–2149.

[36] N. Boumal, P.-A. Absil, Low-rank matrix completion via preconditioned optimization on the Grassmann manifold, Linear Algebra and Its Applications 475 (2015) 200–239.

[37] T. Zhou, H. Qian, Z. Shen, C. Zhang, C. Xu, Tensor completion with side information: a Riemannian manifold approach, in: IJCAI, 2017, pp. 3539–3545.

[38] P. Jawanpuria, B. Mishra, A unified framework for structured low-rank matrix learning, in: ICML, 2018.

[39] K. Gurumoorthy, P. Jawanpuria, B. Mishra, SPOT: a framework for selection of prototypes using optimal transport, Tech. Rep., arXiv preprint, arXiv:2103.10159, 2021.

[40] P. Jawanpuria, N.T.V.S. Dev, B. Mishra, Efficient robust optimal transport: formulations and algorithms, Tech. Rep., arXiv preprint, arXiv:2010.11852, 2021.

[41] G. Meyer, S. Bonnabel, R. Sepulchre, Linear regression under fixed-rank constraints: a Riemannian approach, in: ICML, 2011.

[42] P. Zadeh, R. Hosseini, S. Sra, Geometric mean metric learning, in: ICML, 2016.

[43] M. Bhutani, P. Jawanpuria, H. Kasai, B. Mishra, Low-rank geometric mean metric learning, Tech. Rep., arXiv preprint, arXiv:1806.05454, 2018.

[44] N. Boumal, B. Mishra, P.-A. Absil, R. Sepulchre, Manopt: a Matlab toolbox for optimization on manifolds, Journal of Machine Learning Research 15 (1) (2014) 1455–1459.

[45] J. Townsend, N. Koep, S. Weichwald, Pymanopt: a python toolbox for optimization on manifolds using automatic differentiation, Journal of Machine Learning Research 17 (137) (2016) 1–5, https://pymanopt.github.io.

[46] M. Meghwanshi, P. Jawanpuria, A. Kunchukuttan, H. Kasai, B. Mishra, Mctorch, a manifold optimization library for deep learning, Tech. Rep., arXiv preprint, arXiv:1810.01811, 2018.

[47] B. Mishra, N.T.V.S. Dev, H. Kasai, P. Jawanpuria, Manifold optimization for optimal transport, Tech. Rep., arXiv preprint, arXiv:2103.00902, 2021.

[48] N. Miolane, J. Mathe, C. Donnat, M. Jorda, X. Pennec, Geomstats: a python package for Riemannian geometry in machine learning, Tech. Rep., arXiv preprint, arXiv:1805.08308, 2018.

[49] W. Huang, P.-A. Absil, K.A. Gallivan, P. Hand, ROPTLIB: an object-oriented C++ library for optimization on Riemannian manifolds, Tech. Rep. FSU16-14.v2, Florida State University, 2016.

[50] R. Bergmann, Optimisation on manifolds in Julia, https://github.com/kellertuer/Manopt.jl, 2019.

[51] A. Edelman, T. Arias, S. Smith, The geometry of algorithms with orthogonality constraints, SIAM Journal on Matrix Analysis and Applications 20 (2) (1998) 303–353.

[52] J.M. Lee, Introduction to Smooth Manifolds, 2nd edition, Graduate Texts in Mathematics, vol. 218, Springer-Verlag, New York, 2003.

[53] K. Wimalawarne, M. Sugiyama, R. Tomioka, Multitask learning meets tensor factorization: task imputation via convex optimization, in: NeurIPS, 2014.

[54] M. Nimishakavi, B. Mishra, M. Gupta, P. Talukdar, Inductive framework for multi-aspect streaming tensor completion with side information, in: CIKM, 2018, pp. 307–316.

[55] M. Filipović, A. Jukić, Tucker factorization with missing data with application to low-n-rank tensor completion, Multidimensional Systems and Signal Processing, https://doi.org/10.1007/s11045-013-0269-9.

[56] D.H. Foster, S.M.C. Nascimento, K. Amano, Information limits on neural identification of colored surfaces in natural scenes, Visual Neuroscience 21 (3) (2007) 331–336.

[57] M. Signoretto, R.V.d. Plas, B.D. Moor, J.A.K. Suykens, Tensor versus matrix completion: a comparison with application to spectral data, IEEE Signal Processing Letters 18 (7) (2011) 403–406.

[58] N. Cressie, C.K. Wikle, Statistics for Spatio-Temporal Data, John Wiley & Sons, 2015.

[59] A.C. Lozano, H. Li, A. Niculescu-Mizil, Y. Liu, C. Perlich, J. Hosking, N. Abe, Spatial-temporal causal modeling for climate change attribution, in: KDD, 2009.

[60] A. Argyriou, T. Evgeniou, M. Pontil, Multi-task feature learning, in: NuerIPS, 2006.

[61] P. Jawanpuria, J.S. Nath, Multi-task multiple kernel learning, in: SIAM International Conference on Data Mining (SDM), 2011.

[62] P. Jawanpuria, J.S. Nath, A convex feature learning formulation for latent task structure discovery, in: International Conference on Machine Learning (ICML), 2012.

[63] Y. Amit, M. Fink, N. Srebro, S. Ullman, Uncovering shared structures in multiclass classification, in: International Conference on Machine Learning (ICML), 2007.

[64] A. Argyriou, T. Evgeniou, M. Pontil, Convex multi-task feature learning, Machine Learning 73 (2008) 243–272.

Generalized thresholding for low-rank tensor recovery: approaches based on model and learning

Fei Wen[a], Zhonghao Zhang[b], and Yipeng Liu[b]

[a]*Department of Electronic Engineering, Shanghai Jiao Tong University, Shanghai, China*
[b]*School of Information and Communication Engineering, University of Electronic Science and Technology of China (UESTC), Chengdu, China*

CONTENTS

5.1 Introduction

The past decade has witnessed extraordinary advances in information technology, which makes high-dimensional data increasingly available and is driving a major resurgence of data science. In this context, multiway data (tensor) analysis has become increasingly popular and found applications ranging from the fields of psychometrics and chemometrics to signal/image processing, computer vision, neuroscience, remote sensing, and data mining.

Low-rank tensor approximation is a major and fundamental problem in tensor analysis, which has been recognized as a powerful tool for multidimensional data analysis, such as dimensionality reduction, denoising, completion, and principal component analysis (PCA). For instance, it is effective to process multidimensional raw data in the presence of gross corruption and missing observations. This chapter focuses on singular value thresholding/shrinkage-based low-rank tensor approximation methods, which mainly rely on tensor singular value decomposition (t-SVD). Besides, learning-based methods, such as deep unrolling and deep plug-and-play (PnP) methods, are also discussed. We present recent developments of generalized thresholding/shrinkage-based low-rank tensor recovery, including convex and nonconvex methods, addressing the issues of penalty selection, efficient algorithms, and typical applications including tensor completion and robust tensor PCA.

Iterative thresholding algorithms have been widely used in many applications involving sparse and/or low-rank recovery, such as linear regression, compressive sensing (CS), signal restoration, matrix completion, robust PCA (RPCA), and data mining, to name just a few. Considering tensors as a natural generalization of 2D matrices to multidimensional arrays, which can better preserve the multilinear structure of multiway data, tensor singular value thresholding (t-SVT) can be used for effective low-rank tensor approximation. This is typically achieved based on t-SVD with the use of convex or nonconvex low-rank regularization penalties. As there exist a number of low-rank penalties with various thresholding functions, which can yield different performance in different applications, we summarize a list of thresholding operators corresponding to various convex or nonconvex regularization penalties. Moreover, we discuss the generalized t-SVT algorithms for tensor completion and robust tensor PCA, which are two fundamental problems in tensor recovery.

In addition, we also discuss recent learning-based methods without assuming a certain hand-crafted model, including deep unrolling and deep PnP methods. The deep unrolling method combines deep learning with traditional penalties in model-based algorithms. Typically, it unrolls a classical iterative thresholding algorithm with each step corresponding to a layer in the obtained deep neural network, e.g., a learned iterative shrinkage/thresholding algorithm unrolled from the iterative soft-thresholding algorithm (ISTA). The deep PnP method uses a PnP strategy to replace the hand-crafted thresholding function with a data-driven deep neural network for denoising. Such data-driven methods can significantly improve tensor approximation performance by taking deep learning to serve as thresholding-like operators in the nonlinear iterative algorithms. Experimental results on tensor completion show the great potential of learning-based thresholding-like algorithms for tensor recovery.

We also discuss the penalty selection issue. For the generalized thresholding algorithm, the performance of recovery is closely related to penalty (or thresholding function) selection. The convex nuclear norm is convenient due to its convexity but has a bias problem [22]. To alleviate the bias problem, a number of nonconvex penalties have been designed. While these nonconvex penalties have shown significant superior performance over the convex one, the formulations are NP-hard and the usually used first-order algorithms can only guarantee local minima. We provide some perspectives on the penalty selection issue. There exist some instances depending on the applications, where the use of nonconvex penalties is simply unnecessary and will not lead to performance improvement. In such cases, nonconvex penalties can even be inferior since the involved formulations are nonconvex and hence more intractable. It is usually the case that nonconvex algorithms are sensitive to initialization and the convergence rate is slower than that of a convex algorithm. In contrast, a convex algorithm has better stability and convergence properties, and well-developed acceleration techniques can be used with guaranteed convergence to global minima. We show that convex models may be preferable when the latent tensor is not strictly low-rank, since the performance improvement of nonconvex models in this case is often marginal and may not deserve the price of slower convergence rate. We provide concrete examples to demonstrate this.

Notations

For a matrix $\mathbf{X}$, $\text{rank}(\mathbf{X})$, $(\mathbf{X})^{\text{T}}$, and $\|\mathbf{X}\|_F$ stand for the rank, transpose, and Frobenius norm of $\mathbf{X}$, respectively, whilst $\sigma_i(\mathbf{X})$ denotes the i-th largest singular value and $\sigma(\mathbf{X}) = [\sigma_1(\mathbf{X}), \cdots, \sigma_{\min(m,n)}(\mathbf{X})]^T$. $\text{conj}(\cdot)$ denotes the complex conjugate of a quantity. For a tensor $\mathcal{A} \in \mathbb{R}^{n_1 \times n_2 \times n_3}$, $\mathcal{A}^{\text{T}} \in \mathbb{R}^{n_2 \times n_1 \times n_3}$ stands for the transpose obtained by firstly transposing each frontal slices of $\mathcal{A}$ and then reversing the order of the $(2, 3, \cdots, n_3)$-th transposed frontal slices. Moreover, $\mathbf{A}_{(n)}$ represents the n-th frontal slice of $\mathcal{A}$ and $\mathbf{A}_{\langle n \rangle}$ represents the mode-n matricization, whilst $\text{diag}(\mathbf{v})$ stands for the diagonal matrix generated by the vector $\mathbf{v}$.

5.2 **Tensor singular value thresholding**

Let us start by reviewing basic components of generalized t-SVT, including sparse and low-rank penalties, the proximity operator, t-SVD, and t-SVT.

5.2.1 **Proximity operator and generalized thresholding**

The proximity operator plays a central role in developing efficient first-order algorithms for sparse and low-rank regularized inverse problems. This section introduces commonly used regularization penalties originally designed for sparse promotion and their corresponding proximity operators, such as hard-thresholding, the ℓ_q-norm, explicit q-shrinkage, log-q thresholding, smoothly clipped absolute deviation (SCAD), minimax concave (MC) thresholding, and firm thresholding. Low-rankness promotion of a matrix or tensor can be conveniently achieved by sparsity promotion on the singular values of the matrix or tensor.

Let P_λ denote a generalized sparse penalty function which is proper and lower semi-continuous with $\lambda > 0$ being a threshold parameter. The proximity operator (proximal mapping) for a scalar x is defined as

$$T_{P_\lambda}(t) = \arg\min_x \left\{ P_\lambda(x) + \frac{1}{2}(x - t)^2 \right\}. \tag{5.1}$$

Table 5.1 Regularization penalties and the corresponding proximity operator ($\lambda > 0$ is a threshold parameter).

	Penalty formulation	Proximity operator
Soft	$P_\lambda(x) = \lambda|x|$	$T_{P_\lambda}(t) = \text{sign}(t)\max\{|t| - \lambda, 0\}$
Hard	$P_\lambda(x) = \lambda[2 - (|x| - \sqrt{2})^2 I(|x| < \sqrt{2})]$ or $P_\lambda(x) = \lambda|x|_0$	$T_{P_\lambda}(t) = \begin{cases} 0, & |t| < \sqrt{2\lambda}, \\ \{0, t\}, & |t| = \sqrt{2\lambda}, \\ t, & |t| > \sqrt{2\lambda} \end{cases}$
ℓ_q	$P_\lambda(x) = \lambda|x|^q, \quad 0 < q < 1$	$T_{P_\lambda}(t) = \begin{cases} 0, & |t| < \tau, \\ \{0, \text{sign}(t)\beta\}, & |t| = \tau, \\ \text{sign}(t)y, & |t| > \tau, \end{cases}$ where $\beta = [2\lambda(1-q)]^{1/(2-q)}$, $\tau = \beta + \lambda q \beta^{q-1}$, $h(y) = \lambda q y^{q-1} + y - |t| = 0$, and $y \in [\beta, |t|]$
q-shrinkage	No closed-form expression ($q < 1$)	$T_{P_\lambda}(t) = \text{sign}(t)\max\{|t| - \lambda^{2-q}t^{q-1}, 0\}$
SCAD	$P_\lambda(x) = \begin{cases} \lambda|x|, & |x| < \lambda, \\ \frac{2a\lambda|x| - x^2 - \lambda^2}{2(a-1)}, & \lambda \leq |x| < a\lambda, \\ (a+1)\lambda^2/2, & |x| \geq a\lambda \end{cases}$	$T_{P_\lambda}(t) = \begin{cases} \text{sign}(t)\max\{|t| - \lambda, 0\}, & |t| \leq 2\lambda, \\ \frac{(a-1)t - \text{sign}(t)a\lambda}{a-2}, & 2\lambda < |t| \leq a\lambda, \\ t, & |t| > a\lambda \end{cases}$
MC	$P_{\lambda,\gamma}(x) = \lambda \int_0^{|x|} \max(1 - t/(\gamma\lambda), 0)dt$, where $\gamma > 0$	$T_{P_{\lambda,\gamma}}(t) = \begin{cases} 0, & |t| \leq \lambda, \\ \frac{\text{sign}(t)(|t| - \lambda)}{1 - 1/\gamma}, & \lambda < |t| \leq \gamma\lambda, \\ t, & |t| > \gamma\lambda \end{cases}$
Firm thresholding	$P_\lambda(x) = \begin{cases} \lambda[|x| - x^2/(2\mu)], & |t| \leq \mu, \\ \lambda\mu/2, & |t| \geq \mu, \end{cases}$ where $\mu > \lambda$	$T_{P_{\lambda,\gamma}}(t) = \begin{cases} 0, & |t| \leq \lambda, \\ \frac{\text{sign}(t)(|t| - \lambda)\mu}{\mu - \lambda}, & \lambda \leq |t| \leq \mu, \\ t, & |t| \geq \mu \end{cases}$
Log-q thresholding	$P_\lambda(x) = \lambda\log(1 + |x|^q), 0 < q < 1$	$T_{P_\lambda}(x) = \begin{cases} 0, & |t| \leq \tau, \\ \text{sign}(t)h^{-1}(|t|), & |t| \geq \tau, \end{cases}$ where $h(x) = \lambda q x^{q-1}/(1 + x^q) + x$, $\tau = h(\psi^{-1}(1/\lambda))$, $\psi(x) = 2(\log(1 + |x|^q) - qx^q/(1 + x^q))/x^2$

Here, P_λ is separable and the proximity operator of a vector, matrix, or tensor can be computed in an element-wise manner. Though P_λ is nonsmooth and could be nonconvex, the proximal mapping T_{P_λ} either has a closed-form expression or can be computed efficiently in most cases. Table 5.1 presents some popular penalties and the corresponding proximity operators. Among these penalties, except the soft-thresholding penalty, all the others are nonconvex (more precisely, folded concave

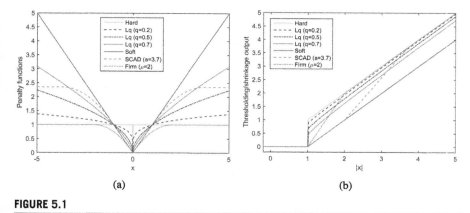

(a)   (b)

FIGURE 5.1

Typical penalty functions and the corresponding thresholding functions (with the same threshold).

and quasiconvex) functions, as shown in Fig. 5.1(a). Fig. 5.1(b) shows the threshold-ing functions of the hard, soft, ℓ_q, and SCAD penalties with the same threshold.

Hard-thresholding is a natural selection for sparsity promotion, which was first given in [15] and later applied in wavelet applications in statistics [1]. As an alter-native of hard-thresholding, soft-thresholding is very popular due to its convexity, which was first introduced by Donoho et al. [14]. It is the core of LASSO intro-duced by Tibshirani in [43]. Its convexity admits a convex optimization problem, for which the global optimum can be easily guaranteed. In contrast, for other noncon-vex penalties, even though they are quasiconvex, the related optimization problems are nonconvex and can be NP-hard, since the sum of a convex function and a quasi-convex function is no longer quasiconvex and can have many local minima. In this case, global optimization algorithms are usually impractical due to their exponential worst-case complexity. However, the LASSO penalty has a bias problem, as it im-poses a constant shrinkage on the parameters with magnitude larger than a threshold. In comparison, the hard- and SCAD thresholding are unbiased for large parameters, while the thresholding functions of the SCAD, ℓ_q, q-shrinkage, and log-q penalties, as well as many others, are sandwiched between the hard- and soft-thresholding.

Among these penalties, the ℓ_q penalty has the special characteristic that with dif-ferent values of $q \in (0, 1)$, it adapts to a large family of penalties bridging the gap be-tween the ℓ_0 and ℓ_1 penalties. The proximity operator of the ℓ_q penalty does not admit a closed-form formula except for the two particular cases of $q \in \{1/2, 2/3\}$ [55], but it can be very efficiently computed for arbitrary values of q. The explicit q-shrinkage mapping proposed in [7] has some qualitative resemblance to the ℓ_q-thresholding but being continuous and explicit. It degenerates to the hard- and soft-thresholding when $q \to -\infty$ and $q = 1$, respectively. As an acceptable price to pay for having an ex-plicit thresholding formula, its penalty does not have an explicit expression. SCAD was first proposed for variable selection problems in [16], which has shown favorable effectiveness in high-dimensional statistical analysis. The MC penalty can also ameliorate the bias problem of LASSO [59], for which with each fixed $\lambda > 0$, a continuum of penalties and thresholding operators can be obtained by varying $\gamma \in (0, +\infty)$. The firm thresholding is proposed in [19], which can be viewed as a continuous and piecewise-linear approximation of the hard-thresholding.

Besides the above introduced thresholding operators, there also exist a number of other thresholding operators. To achieve the goal of sparsity promotion, all these thresholding operators satisfy certain properties including sign consistency, shrinkage, thresholding, and limited shrinkage properties, as

$$
\begin{aligned}
&\text{i)} \quad T_{P_\lambda}(t) = \text{sign}(x) \cdot T_{P_\lambda}(|t|), \\
&\text{ii)} \quad \left| T_{P_\lambda}(t) \right| \leqslant |t|, \\
&\text{iii)} \quad T_{P_\lambda}(t) = 0 \text{ if } t \leqslant \tau \text{ for some } \tau > 0, \\
&\text{iv)} \quad \left| T_{P_\lambda}(t) - t \right| \leqslant \lambda,
\end{aligned}
\tag{5.2}
$$

where τ is a positive threshold dependent on λ.

5.2.2 Tensor singular value decomposition

Besides of the thresholding algorithms, tensor decomposition is another effective technique for low-rank tensor approximation. With the decomposition for tensor representation, thresholding can be operated on tensor singular values. Here we take t-SVD as an example. But note that almost all kinds of tensor decomposition can work with the thresholding algorithms in this chapter.

Denote the discrete Fourier transform (DFT) of a tensor $\mathcal{A} \in \mathcal{R}^{n_1 \times n_2 \times n_3}$ along the third dimension by

$$
\bar{\mathcal{A}} = \text{fft}(\mathcal{A}, [], 3),
$$

which is in the MATLAB® command format. Similarly, denote the inverse DFT by

$$
\mathcal{A} = \text{ifft}(\bar{\mathcal{A}}, [], 3).
$$

Meanwhile, define a matricization of $\mathcal{A}$ as transformation into a matrix as

$$
\text{unfold}(\mathcal{A}) = [\mathbf{A}_{(1)}^T, \mathbf{A}_{(2)}^T, \cdots, \mathbf{A}_{(3)}^T]^T \in \mathbb{R}^{n_1 n_3 \times n_2},
$$

with the inverse operation being

$$
\text{fold}(\text{unfold}(\mathcal{A})) = \mathcal{A}.
$$

Denote the i-th frontal slice of $\bar{\mathcal{A}}$ by $\bar{\mathbf{A}}_{(i)}$ and the block-diagonal matrix associated with the frontal slices of $\bar{\mathcal{A}}$ by

$$\bar{\mathbf{A}} = \text{bdiag}(\bar{\mathcal{A}}) = \text{bdiag}(\bar{\mathbf{A}}_{(1)}, \bar{\mathbf{A}}_{(2)}, \cdots, \bar{\mathbf{A}}_{(n_3)})$$

$$= \begin{bmatrix} \bar{\mathbf{A}}_{(1)} & & \\ & \ddots & \\ & & \bar{\mathbf{A}}_{(n_3)} \end{bmatrix} \in \mathbb{R}^{n_1 n_3 \times n_2 n_3}.$$

Definition 5.1 (Identity tensor [28]). The identity tensor $\mathcal{I} \in \mathbb{R}^{n \times n \times n_3}$ is the tensor whose first frontal slice is the $n \times n$ identity matrix with the other frontal slices being zero matrices, i.e., $\mathbf{I}_{(1)} = \mathbf{I}_n$ and $\mathbf{I}_{(k)} = \mathbf{0}$ for $k \geqslant 2$.

Definition 5.2 (Orthogonal tensor [28]). A tensor $\mathcal{Q} \in \mathbb{R}^{n_1 \times n_2 \times n_3}$ satisfying $\mathcal{Q}^T * \mathcal{Q} = \mathcal{Q} * \mathcal{Q}^T = \mathcal{I}$ is said to be orthogonal.

Definition 5.3 (f-Diagonal tensor [28]). A tensor with each frontal slice being a diagonal matrix is said to be f-diagonal.

Definition 5.4 (T-product [28]). For two tensors $\mathcal{A} \in \mathbb{R}^{n_1 \times n_2 \times n_3}$ and $\mathcal{B} \in \mathbb{R}^{n_2 \times l \times n_3}$, the t-product $\mathcal{A} * \mathcal{B} \in \mathbb{R}^{n_1 \times l \times n_3}$ is defined as

$$\mathcal{A} * \mathcal{B} = \text{ifft}(\text{fold}(\bar{\mathbf{A}} \cdot \text{unfold}(\bar{\mathcal{B}}))).$$

Definition 5.5 (T-SVD [28,36]). For $\mathcal{A} \in \mathbb{R}^{n_1 \times n_2 \times n_3}$, the t-SVD is defined as $\mathcal{A} = \mathcal{U} * \mathcal{D} * \mathcal{V}^T$, where $\mathcal{U} \in \mathbb{R}^{n_1 \times n_1 \times n_3}$, $\mathcal{V} \in \mathbb{R}^{n_2 \times n_2 \times n_3}$ are orthogonal and $\mathcal{D} \in \mathbb{R}^{n_1 \times n_2 \times n_3}$ is f-diagonal. It is constructed as $\mathcal{U} = \text{ifft}(\bar{\mathcal{U}}, [], 3)$, $\mathcal{D} = \text{ifft}(\bar{\mathcal{D}}, [], 3)$, and $\mathcal{V} = \text{ifft}(\bar{\mathcal{V}}, [], 3)$ with

$$[\bar{\mathbf{U}}_{(i)}, \bar{\mathbf{D}}_{(i)}, \bar{\mathbf{V}}_{(i)}] = \text{svd}(\bar{\mathbf{A}}_{(i)}) \text{ for } i = 1, \cdots, \left\lceil \frac{n_3 + 1}{2} \right\rceil$$

and otherwise for $i = \left\lceil \frac{n_3+1}{2} \right\rceil + 1, \cdots, n_3$,

$$\bar{\mathbf{U}}_{(i)} = \text{conj}(\bar{\mathbf{U}}_{(n_3-i+2)}), \quad \bar{\mathbf{D}}_{(i)} = \bar{\mathbf{D}}_{(n_3-i+2)}, \quad \bar{\mathbf{V}}_{(i)} = \text{conj}(\bar{\mathbf{V}}_{(n_3-i+2)}).$$

T-SVD was first given by Kilmer and Martin in [28], who defined an SVD-like decomposition for tensors based on matrix SVD in the Fourier domain. Definition 5.5 is a variant given in [36], which guarantees a real-valued decomposition. It is obvious that $\bar{\mathbf{A}} = \bar{\mathbf{U}}\bar{\mathbf{D}}\bar{\mathbf{V}}^H$, which is an equivalent expression of $\mathcal{A} = \mathcal{U} * \mathcal{D} * \mathcal{V}^T$ in the Fourier domain. Moreover, both $\mathcal{D}$ and $\bar{\mathcal{D}}$ are real-valued f-diagonal, which contain the singular values in the original and the Fourier transform domains, respectively.

Definition 5.6 (Tensor average rank [36]). For $\mathcal{A} \in \mathbb{R}^{n_1 \times n_2 \times n_3}$, the tensor average rank is defined as

$$\text{rank}_a(\mathcal{A}) = \frac{1}{n_3}\text{rank}(\text{bcirc}(\mathcal{A})) = \frac{1}{n_3}\text{rank}(\bar{\mathbf{A}}) = \frac{1}{n_3}\sum_{i=1}^{n_3}\text{rank}(\bar{\mathbf{A}}_{(i)}),$$

where $\mathrm{bcirc}(\mathcal{A}) \in \mathbb{R}^{n_1 n_3 \times n_2 n_3}$ is a block-circulant matrix constructed from the frontal slices of $\mathcal{A}$ as

$$
\mathrm{bcirc}(\mathcal{A}) = \begin{bmatrix} \mathbf{A}_{(1)} & \mathbf{A}_{(n_3)} & \ddots & \mathbf{A}_{(2)} \\ \mathbf{A}_{(2)} & \mathbf{A}_{(1)} & \ddots & \mathbf{A}_{(3)} \\ \vdots & \vdots & \ddots & \vdots \\ \mathbf{A}_{(n_3)} & \mathbf{A}_{(n_3-1)} & \ddots & \mathbf{A}_{(1)} \end{bmatrix}.
$$

Definition 5.7 (Tensor tubal rank [27]). For a tensor $\mathcal{A} \in \mathbb{R}^{n_1 \times n_2 \times n_3}$ with a t-SVD $\mathcal{A} = \mathcal{U} * \mathcal{D} * \mathcal{V}^{\mathrm{T}}$, the tubal rank $\mathrm{rank}_\mathrm{t}(\mathcal{A})$ is defined as the number of nonzero tubals of $\mathcal{D}$ as

$$
\mathrm{rank}_\mathrm{t}(\mathcal{A}) = |\{i, \mathcal{D}(i, i, :) \neq 0\}|.
$$

Besides the tubal rank, there exist a series of other tensor ranks defined by various tensor decompositions. For example, the Tucker rank is defined as a vector whose entries are the ranks of the factor matrices, and the CANDECOMP/PARAFAC (CP) rank is defined as the smallest number of the rank-1 tensors in the CP decomposition. These tensor ranks characterize different kinds of latent tensor subspaces, which may lead to different low-rank tensor approximation performances. The interested readers can refer to the first chapter of this book for more details.

5.2.3 Generalized matrix singular value thresholding

For a matrix $\mathbf{A} \in \mathbb{R}^{m \times n}$ with rank r, let $\mathbf{A} = \mathbf{U}\boldsymbol{\Sigma}\mathbf{V}^{\mathrm{T}}$ be any truncated SVD of $\mathbf{A}$, where $\boldsymbol{\Sigma} = \mathrm{diag}\{\sigma_1, \cdots, \sigma_r\}$ contains the singular values and $\mathbf{U} \in \mathbb{R}^{m \times r}$ and $\mathbf{V} \in \mathbb{R}^{r \times n}$ contain the corresponding singular vectors. Low-rankness promotion on a matrix can be conveniently achieved through sparsity promotion on its singular values. A generalized low-rank penalty can be defined as

$$
\tilde{P}_\lambda(\mathbf{A}) = \sum_i P_\lambda(\sigma_i), \tag{5.3}
$$

where P_λ is a generalized sparsity penalty as mentioned in Section 5.2.2. For the special cases with P_λ being the ℓ_0-, ℓ_q-, and ℓ_1-norm, $\tilde{P}_\lambda(\mathbf{A})$ becomes the rank, Schatten-q quasinorm, and nuclear norm of $\mathbf{A}$, respectively.

The generalized singular value thresholding corresponding to $\tilde{P}_\lambda$ is a direct extension of Theorem 2.1 in [5].

Definition 5.8 (Generalized singular value thresholding). Let $\mathbf{M} = \mathbf{U}\boldsymbol{\Sigma}\mathbf{V}^T$ be any truncated SVD of a rank-r matrix $\mathbf{M} \in \mathbb{R}^{m \times n}$, where $\boldsymbol{\Sigma} = \mathrm{diag}\{\sigma_1, \cdots, \sigma_r\}$ and $\mathbf{U}$ and $\mathbf{V}$ contain the left and right singular vectors. Then, for $\tilde{P}_\lambda$ defined as in (5.3), the minimization problem

$$\tilde{T}_{\tilde{P}_\lambda}(\mathbf{M}) = \arg\min_{\mathbf{X}} \left\{ \tilde{P}_\lambda(\mathbf{X}) + \frac{1}{2}\|\mathbf{X} - \mathbf{M}\|_F^2 \right\} \tag{5.4}$$

is solved by

$$\tilde{T}_{\tilde{P}_\lambda}(\mathbf{M}) = \mathbf{U} \cdot \operatorname{diag}\left\{ T_{P_\lambda}(\sigma_1, \cdots, \sigma_r) \right\} \cdot \mathbf{V}^T \tag{5.5}$$

with T_{P_λ} being the proximity operator defined in (5.1).

5.2.4 Generalized tensor singular value thresholding

For a tensor $\mathcal{A} \in \mathcal{R}^{n_1 \times n_2 \times n_3}$, the sparsity penalty is defined in an element-wise manner as

$$P_\lambda(\mathcal{A}) = \sum_{i=1}^{n_1} \sum_{j=1}^{n_2} \sum_{k=1}^{n_3} P_\lambda(\mathcal{A}(i, j, k)).$$

Similar to the matrix case, the low-rank penalty on a tensor can be conveniently formulated as sparsity penalization on the singular values from its t-SVD.

Definition 5.9 (Generalized tensor low-rank penalty). Let $\mathcal{A} = \mathcal{U} * \mathcal{D} * \mathcal{V}^T$ be a t-SVD of a tensor $\mathcal{A} \in \mathbb{R}^{n_1 \times n_2 \times n_3}$ as defined in Definition 5.5, and let P_λ be a sparsity penalty. The generalized tensor low-rank penalty associated with P_λ is defined as

$$\begin{aligned}
\mathcal{P}_\lambda(\mathcal{A}) :&= \frac{1}{n_3} \sum_{i=1}^{n_3} \bar{P}_\lambda(\bar{\mathbf{A}}_{(i)}) \\
&= \frac{1}{n_3} \sum_{i=1}^{\min(n_1, n_2)} \sum_{j=1}^{n_3} P_\lambda(\bar{\mathcal{D}}(i, i, j)) \\
&= \frac{1}{n_3} \sum_{i=1}^{\min(n_1, n_2)} \sum_{j=1}^{n_3} P_\lambda(\sigma_i(\bar{\mathbf{A}}_{(j)})). \tag{5.6}
\end{aligned}$$

For the particular case of P_λ being the ℓ_1-norm penalty, $\mathcal{P}_\lambda(\mathcal{A})$ becomes the tensor nuclear norm (TNN) considered in [41,66], and it follows that

$$\mathcal{P}_\lambda(\mathcal{A}) = \lambda\|\mathcal{A}\|_* = \frac{\lambda}{n_3} \sum_{i=1}^{\min(n_1, n_2)} \sum_{j=1}^{n_3} \bar{\mathcal{D}}(i, i, j) = \lambda \sum_{i=1}^{\min(n_1, n_2)} \mathcal{D}(i, i, 1), \tag{5.7}$$

where the following relationship between the original domain and the FFT domain is used:

$$\mathcal{D}(i, i, 1) = \frac{1}{n_3} \sum_{j=1}^{n_3} \bar{\mathcal{D}}(i, i, j). \tag{5.8}$$

Meanwhile, when P_λ is the ℓ_0-norm, $\mathcal{P}(\mathcal{A})$ becomes the tensor average rank of $\mathcal{A}$ as

$$\mathcal{P}_\lambda(\mathcal{A}) = \lambda \mathrm{rank}_a(\mathcal{A}) = \frac{\lambda}{n_3} \sum_{i=1}^{\min(n_1, n_2)} \sum_{j=1}^{n_3} |\bar{\mathcal{D}}(i, i, j)|_0 = \frac{\lambda}{n_3} \mathrm{rank}(\bar{\mathbf{A}}).$$

It has been shown in [36] that the nuclear norm $\|\mathcal{A}\|_*$ is the convex envelope of the tensor average rank $\mathrm{rank}_a(\mathcal{A})$. Moreover, when P is the ℓ_q-norm $(0 < q < 1)$ penalty, $\mathcal{P}_\lambda(\mathcal{A})$ bridges between $\mathrm{rank}_a(\mathcal{A})$ and $\|\mathcal{A}\|_*$, since in this case they are the limits of $\mathcal{P}_\lambda(\mathcal{A})$ as $q \to 0^+$ and $q \to 1^-$, respectively. Besides (5.7), the tensor low-rank penalty can also be defined based on the low-rankness of the core matrix whose entries are from the diagonal elements of the core tensor of t-SVD [32].

Theorem 5.1 (Generalized tensor singular value thresholding). *For a generalized tensor low-rank penalty $\mathcal{P}$, define a proximal minimization operator as*

$$\mathcal{T}_{\mathcal{P}_\lambda}(\mathcal{Y}) := \arg \min_{\mathcal{X} \in \mathbb{R}^{n_1 \times n_2 \times n_3}} \mathcal{P}_\lambda(\mathcal{X}) + \frac{1}{2} \|\mathcal{X} - \mathcal{Y}\|_F^2. \qquad (5.9)$$

Let $\mathcal{Y} = \mathcal{U} * \mathcal{D} * \mathcal{V}^T$ be any t-SVD of $\mathcal{Y} \in \mathbb{R}^{n_1 \times n_2 \times n_3}$. The solution to (5.9) is given by the generalized t-SVT operator

$$\mathcal{T}_{\mathcal{P}_\lambda}(\mathcal{Y}) = \mathcal{U} * \mathrm{ifft}(T_{P_\lambda}(\bar{\mathcal{D}}), [], 3) * \mathcal{V}^T, \qquad (5.10)$$

where T_{P_λ} is an element-wise thresholding function corresponding to the sparsity penalty P_λ as defined in (5.1). It is associated with the tensor low-rank penalty $\mathcal{T}_{\mathcal{P}_\lambda}$.

Solving the proximal minimization (5.9) is a key step in many low-rank tensor approximation algorithms in updating the low-rank component. Note that $\bar{\mathcal{D}}$ is real-valued and f-diagonal, and hence the thresholding $\mathcal{T}_{\mathcal{P}_\lambda}$ in fact only operates on the f-diagonal elements of $\bar{\mathcal{D}}$. The derivation of (5.10) is straightforward via extending existing results in [5,36]. A proof is presented as follows. First, with $\|\mathcal{A}\|_F = \frac{1}{\sqrt{n_3}} \|\bar{\mathcal{A}}\|_F$ and Definition 5.9, the objective of (5.9) can be rewritten as

$$\mathcal{P}_\lambda(\mathcal{X}) + \frac{1}{2} \|\mathcal{X} - \mathcal{Y}\|_F^2 = \frac{1}{n_3} \left[\sum_{i=1}^{n_3} \tilde{P}_\lambda(\bar{\mathbf{X}}_{(i)}) + \frac{1}{2} \|\bar{\mathcal{X}} - \bar{\mathcal{Y}}\|_F^2 \right]$$

$$= \frac{1}{n_3} \sum_{i=1}^{n_3} \left[\tilde{P}_\lambda(\bar{\mathbf{X}}_{(i)}) + \frac{1}{2} \|\bar{\mathbf{X}}_{(i)} - \bar{\mathbf{Y}}_{(i)}\|_F^2 \right].$$

Then, denoting the minimizer of (5.9) by $\mathcal{X}^\bullet$, it is easy to see that the frontal slices of $\bar{\mathcal{X}}^\bullet$ can be solved separately as

$$\bar{\mathbf{X}}_{(i)}^\bullet = \arg \min_{\mathcal{X} \in \mathbb{R}^{n_1 \times n_2 \times n_3}} \tilde{P}_\lambda(\bar{\mathbf{X}}_{(i)}) + \frac{1}{2} \|\bar{\mathbf{X}}_{(i)} - \bar{\mathbf{Y}}_{(i)}\|_F^2,$$

which together with a straightforward extension of Theorem 2.1 in [5] leads to (5.10).

5.3 Thresholding based low-rank tensor recovery

Two fundamental problems involving low-rank tensor recovery are tensor RPCA and tensor completion. These two problems are the main focus in the following introduction of low-rank tensor approximation.

PCA is a fundamental tool for statistical data analysis and dimensionality reduction. It has applications in virtually all areas of science and engineering, ranging from signal and image processing, bioinformatics, economics, finance, meteorology, statistics, and biology to neurocomputing, to name just a few. In the case the data are clean, PCA can be easily achieved via SVD. However, in practical applications, the data are often corrupted by various gross errors and outliers, which may come from the measurement process or be caused by transmission problems [51,53]. In this case, PCA is an ill-posed problem and the classical SVD-based PCA easily breaks down. To achieve RPCA, a number of methods have been developed in the past few decades, such as [11,12,17,45]. Unfortunately, these methods cannot produce a solution in polynomial complexity with strong performance guarantee. To achieve more efficient and effective RPCA, Candes, Wright, Li, and Ma [6,54] exploit the intrinsic low-rank and sparsity structure to make RPCA a well-posed problem. The basic idea is to recast the RPCA problem into a sparse plus low-rank recovery problem. It has been shown both theoretically and empirically that, with this model, accurate recovery of the low-rank component can be achieved in high probability under certain mild conditions, such that the sparse component is not low-rank and vice versa.

Tensor RPCA can be viewed as a natural extension of matrix RPCA to the case of multiway (higher than 2) data. Following [36,54] to model tensor RPCA as a sparse plus low-rank recovery problem, and taking 3-way tensors as an example, the goal is to recover a low-rank tensor $\mathcal{L}_0 \in \mathbb{R}^{n_1 \times n_2 \times n_3}$ from its corrupted measurement

$$\mathcal{Y} = \mathcal{L}_0 + \mathcal{S}_0, \tag{5.11}$$

where $\mathcal{S}_0 \in \mathbb{R}^{n_1 \times n_2 \times n_3}$ stands for the sparse corruption, whose entries have arbitrary magnitude with sparse support. Then, a natural formulation to recover $\mathcal{L}_0$ is given by

$$\min_{\mathcal{L}, \mathcal{S}} \ \text{rank}(\mathcal{L}) + \lambda \|\mathcal{S}\|_0 \quad \text{subject to} \quad \mathcal{Y} = \mathcal{L}_0 + \mathcal{S}_0, \tag{5.12}$$

where $\text{rank}(\cdot)$ is a tensor rank, $\|\cdot\|_0$ is the ℓ_0-norm, and $\lambda > 0$ is a balance parameter.

Tensor completion is another important problem in tensor analysis, which arises in many interested applications, including image/video inpainting, multitask learning, recommendation systems, data mining, and hyperspectral data recovery, [24,35], to name just a few. The goal is to fill in the missing entries of a partially observed low-rank (or approximately low-rank) tensor. In fact, in some applications with the outlier positions being known, the above RPCA problem becomes a completion problem. As high-dimensional tensor data of interest in many practical applications are usually intrinsically (approximately) low-rank, e.g., images and videos, the main idea is to exploit the low-rankness property of data to achieve completion from incomplete observation. Tensor completion can be viewed as a natural extension of matrix completion. Taking 3-way tensors as an example, the objective is to recover a low-rank tensor $\mathcal{L}_0 \in \mathbb{R}^{n_1 \times n_2 \times n_3}$ from its partially observed (incomplete) entries

$$\mathcal{Y}(i, j, k) = \mathcal{L}_0(i, j, k), \quad (i, j, k) \in \Omega, \tag{5.13}$$

where $\Omega \subset [1, \cdots, n_1] \times [1, \cdots, n_2] \times [1, \cdots, n_3]$ is a subset.

Exploiting the low rank property of $\mathcal{L}_0$ and modeling the tensor completion problem as a low-rank tensor recovery problem, a natural formulation is to minimize the rank of $\mathcal{Y}$ under a linear constraint as

$$\min_{\mathcal{L}} \operatorname{rank}(\mathcal{L}) \quad \text{subject to} \quad \mathrm{P}_\Omega(\mathcal{Y}) = \mathrm{P}_\Omega(\mathcal{L}), \tag{5.14}$$

where $\mathrm{P}_\Omega : \mathbb{R}^{n_1 \times n_2 \times n_3} \to \mathbb{R}^{n_1 \times n_2 \times n_3}$ denotes projection onto the observation set Ω.

The definition of tensor rank is not unique. For example, the CP rank [29] is defined as the smallest number of components (rank-1 tensors) in the CP decomposition. The Tucker rank [29] is defined to be vector-valued as $\operatorname{rank}_{\mathrm{tc}}(\mathcal{A}) = (\operatorname{rank}(\mathbf{A}_{(1)}), \operatorname{rank}(\mathbf{A}_{(2)}), \cdots, \operatorname{rank}(\mathbf{A}_{(K)}))$, where $\mathbf{A}_{(k)}$ is the mode-k unfolding matrix of the K-way tensor $\mathcal{A}$. Meanwhile, the tensor tubal rank [29] is based on t-SVD and defined in Definition 5.7. Moreover, jointly minimizing the CP rank and the Tucker rank has shown to be able to yield better performance than minimizing only one of them [34].

5.3.1 Thresholding algorithms for low-rank tensor recovery

Thresholding methods are popular and effective for low-rank tensor recovery. In practice, convex relaxed formulations of (5.12) and (5.14) are usually more desirable due to their tractability, as efficient convex optimization algorithms can be employed with guaranteed global optimum. Though convenient due to convexity, convex regularization has a bias problem [22,52], and it has been widely shown that nonconvex regularization can yield better performance in many applications.

The CP rank is generally intractable and NP-hard to compute, with its convex relaxation also being intractable. In comparison, the Tucker rank is more tractable and widely used. A popular convex relaxation of the Tucker rank is given by the sum of nuclear norms (SNN) [31], $\sum_{i=1}^{K} \|\mathbf{A}_{\langle i \rangle}\|_*$, with which the tensor completion and PCA problems can be respectively convexified as [23,38]

$$\min_{\mathcal{L}} \sum_{i=1}^{K} \lambda_i \|\mathbf{L}_{\langle i \rangle}\|_* \quad \text{subject to} \quad \mathrm{P}_\Omega(\mathcal{Y}) = \mathrm{P}_\Omega(\mathcal{L}), \tag{5.15}$$

$$\min_{\mathcal{L}, \mathcal{S}} \sum_{i=1}^{K} \lambda_i \|\mathbf{L}_{\langle i \rangle}\|_* + \lambda \|\mathcal{S}\|_1 \quad \text{subject to} \quad \mathcal{Y} = \mathcal{L} + \mathcal{S}. \tag{5.16}$$

Though it is tractable and has shown effectiveness in image processing applications [18,31,44], SNN is not the convex envelope of the summed Tucker rank $\sum_{i=1}^{K} \operatorname{rank}(\mathbf{A}_{\langle i \rangle})$ [40]. It has been shown in [38] that, for tensor completion of a

K-way length-n tensor with Tucker rank $(r, r, \cdots, r)$ under the Gaussian model, the SNN-based formulation (5.16) needs $O(rn^{K-1})$ observations for reliable recovery, while a nonconvex formulation requires only $O(rK + nrK)$ observations. An alternative convexification has been proposed in [38] based on a more balanced matricization. More recently, the SNN-based RPCA formulation (5.16) has been extended to deal with deformed data in the presence of unknown transformations [64]. A variant of SNN-based tensor completion has been used in [39] for remote sensing image recovery in the presence of missing data.

While the tight convex relaxation for the CP and Tucker ranks has not been well defined, a tight convex relaxation of the tensor average rank is given by the TNN (5.7), with which the tensor completion and RPCA problems become

$$\min_{\mathcal{L}} \ \|\mathcal{L}\|_* \quad \text{subject to} \quad P_\Omega(\mathcal{Y}) = P_\Omega(\mathcal{L}), \tag{5.17}$$

$$\min_{\mathcal{L}, \mathcal{S}} \ \lambda\|\mathcal{L}\|_* + \|\mathcal{S}\|_1 \quad \text{subject to} \quad \mathcal{Y} = \mathcal{L} + \mathcal{S}. \tag{5.18}$$

For TNN-based tensor completion and RPCA, i.e., the formulations (5.17) and (5.18), theoretical guarantees of exact recovery have been established in [65] and [36], respectively. More recently, it has been shown in [60] that incorporating prior subspace information into TNN-based RPCA can significantly release the incoherence condition for exact recovery.

To alleviate the bias problem of convex low-rank penalties, nonconvex penalties are better alternatives. For example, in [56] a generalized nonconvex surrogate of the Tucker rank has been proposed for tensor completion as

$$\min_{\mathcal{L}} \ \sum_{i=d}^{D} \lambda_d \tilde{P}(\mathbf{L}_{\langle d \rangle}) + \frac{1}{2} \|P_\Omega(\mathcal{Y} - \mathcal{L})\|_F^2, \tag{5.19}$$

where $\tilde{P}$ is a low-rank penalty as defined in (5.3) and $D \leqslant K$ is the mode number that needs to be low-rank-regularized. An efficient algorithm has been proposed to solve the nonconvex formulation (5.19) based on a proximal average algorithm in combination with the exploitation of the "sparse plus low-rank" structure of the problem. Meanwhile, the reweighted TNN has been considered in [25] as

$$\|\mathcal{A}\|_{\text{RTNN}} := \frac{1}{n_3} \sum_{i=1}^{\min(n_1, n_2)} \sum_{j=1}^{n_3} \omega_{i,j} |\bar{\mathcal{D}}(i, i, j)|, \tag{5.20}$$

where the weight $\omega_{i,j}$ is designed to penalize a relatively large singular value with a relatively small threshold. In addition, the work [30] extends the matrix Schatten-p norm to the tensor Schatten-p norm

$$\|\mathcal{A}\|_{S_p}^p := \frac{1}{n_3} \sum_{i=1}^{n_3} \|\bar{\mathbf{A}}_{(i)}\|_{S_p}^p = \frac{1}{n_3} \sum_{i=1}^{\min(n_1, n_2)} \sum_{j=1}^{n_3} |\bar{\mathcal{D}}(i, i, j)|^p. \tag{5.21}$$

The tensor Schatten-p norm bridges between the TNN (5.7) and the tensor average rank. It is a tighter nonconvex envelope of the tensor average rank within the unit ball, and for any $0 < q < p < 1$ it follows that

$$\|\mathcal{A}\|_* = \|\mathcal{A}\|_{S_1} < \|\mathcal{A}\|_{S_p}^p < \|\mathcal{A}\|_{S_q}^q < \|\mathcal{A}\|_{S_0} = \frac{1}{n_3} \|\mathrm{rank}_a(\mathcal{A})\|_1.$$

Besides, a nonconvex formulation for robust tensor recovery based on the empirical Bayes method has been considered in [9]. Moreover, a tensor logarithmic norm (TLN) has been proposed in [8] as

$$\|\mathcal{L}\|_{\mathrm{TLN}} = \frac{1}{n_3} \sum_{i=1}^{\min(n_1,n_2)} \sum_{j=1}^{n_3} \log\left(\sigma_i(\bar{\mathbf{L}}_{(j)})/\varepsilon + 1\right).$$

5.3.2 Generalized thresholding algorithms for low-rank tensor recovery

As surveyed in Section 5.3.1, there exist a number of singular value thresholding-based methods for low-rank tensor approximation. In fact, various convex and non-convex low-rank penalties can be unified into a generalized formulation for each of the tensor completion and robust PCA problems. This subsection presents such generalized formulations for the two problems along with two efficient first-order algorithms.

Naturally, all the well-developed nonconvex penalties introduced in Section 5.2.1 can be employed for low-rank tensor recovery, which leads to generalized formulations for tensor completion and RPCA as

$$\min_{\mathcal{L}} \; \mathcal{P}_\lambda(\mathcal{L}) \quad \text{subject to} \quad \mathrm{P}_\Omega(\mathcal{Y}) = \mathrm{P}_\Omega(\mathcal{L}), \tag{5.22}$$

$$\min_{\mathcal{L},\mathcal{S}} \; \mathcal{P}_\lambda(\mathcal{L}) + P_\beta(\mathcal{S}) \quad \text{subject to} \quad \mathcal{Y} = \mathcal{L} + \mathcal{S}. \tag{5.23}$$

However, a main issue is that the formulations (5.22) and (5.23) do not easily admit a convergent algorithm. For example, directly using the well-developed proximal gradient descent (PGD) algorithm, alternating direction method of multipliers (ADMM) algorithm, or iterative reweighted ℓ_1 algorithm to solve (5.22) and (5.23) does not have a convergence guarantee when $\mathcal{P}_\lambda$ and/or P_β are nonconvex. In fact, these algorithms would not converge in practice due to the nonconvexity and nonsmoothness of the objective and the presence of constraints.

Alternatively, an unconstrained reformulation of (5.22) and (5.23) can be used:

$$\min_{\mathcal{L}} \; \mathcal{P}_\lambda(\mathcal{L}) + \frac{1}{2} \|\mathrm{P}_\Omega(\mathcal{Y} - \mathcal{L})\|_F^2, \tag{5.24}$$

$$\min_{\mathcal{L},\mathcal{S}} \; \mathcal{P}_\lambda(\mathcal{L}) + P_\beta(\mathcal{S}) + \frac{1}{2} \|\mathcal{Y} - \mathcal{L} - \mathcal{S}\|_F^2, \tag{5.25}$$

where the parameters λ and β control the balance between the regularization and fidelity terms. Typically, the threshold function of $\mathcal{P}_\lambda$ (resp. P_β) is more aggressive for a larger λ (resp. ß), and correspondingly the fidelity terms would tend to zero (i.e., $\|\mathrm{P}_\Omega(\mathcal{Y}) - \mathrm{P}_\Omega(\mathcal{L})\|_\mathrm{F} \to 0$ and $\|\mathcal{Y} - \mathcal{L} - \mathcal{S}\|_\mathrm{F} \to 0$) when $\lambda \to 0$ and/or $\beta \to 0$. For these two unconstrained formulations, the PGD, ADMM, and reweighted ℓ_1 algorithms can be directly applied, with guaranteed global convergence to a stationary point for nonconvex $\mathcal{P}_\lambda$ and P_β. Moreover, the formulations (5.24) and (5.25) take inevitable measurement noise into consideration, while the formulations (5.22) and (5.23) do not.

Applying the PGD algorithm to (5.24) results in an iterative update formula

$$\mathcal{L}^{k+1} = \mathcal{T}_{\mathcal{P}_\lambda}\left(\mathcal{L}^k - \frac{1}{\kappa}\mathrm{P}_\Omega(\mathcal{L}^k - \mathcal{Y})\right), \tag{5.26}$$

which is in fact equivalent to minimizing an approximation of the objective (via linearizing the quadratic term) at a given point $\mathcal{L}^k$ as

$$Q_\kappa(\mathcal{L}^{k+1}; \mathcal{L}^k) = \mathcal{P}_\lambda(\mathcal{L}) + F(\mathcal{L}^k) + \left\langle \mathcal{L} - \mathcal{L}^k, \nabla F(\mathcal{L}^k) \right\rangle + \frac{\kappa}{2}\left\|\mathcal{L} - \mathcal{L}^k\right\|_F^2, \tag{5.27}$$

with $F(\mathcal{L}) = 1/2\|\mathrm{P}_\Omega(\mathcal{Y} - \mathcal{L})\|_F^2$.

The tensor RPCA problem (5.25) has two variables, $\mathcal{L}$ and $\mathcal{S}$. Application of the proximal block coordinate descent (BCD) algorithm leads to an iterative update formula as

$$\mathcal{L}^{k+1} = \arg\min_{\mathcal{L}} \mathcal{P}_\lambda(\mathcal{L}) + \frac{1}{2}\left\|\mathcal{Y} - \mathcal{L} - \mathcal{S}^k\right\|_F^2 + \frac{\phi_k}{2}\left\|\mathcal{L} - \mathcal{L}^k\right\|_F^2, \tag{5.28}$$

$$\mathcal{S}^{k+1} = \arg\min_{\mathcal{S}} P_\beta(\mathcal{S}) + \frac{1}{2}\left\|\mathcal{Y} - \mathcal{L}^{k+1} - \mathcal{S}\right\|_F^2 + \frac{\varphi_k}{2}\left\|\mathcal{S} - \mathcal{S}^k\right\|_F^2, \tag{5.29}$$

where $(\phi_k, \varphi_k) > 0$ are two proximal parameters. When $\phi_k = \varphi_k \equiv 0$, it degenerates to the standard BCD algorithm. In the nonconvex and nonsmooth case, the standard BCD algorithm may stagnate and get stuck at a nonstationary point [2]. Hence, the proximal scheme is used to achieve a convergence guarantee for general nonconvex $\mathcal{P}_\lambda$ and P_β [3]. The updates (5.28) and (5.29) can be computed through the proximity operators introduced in Section 5.2 as

$$\mathcal{L}^{k+1} = \mathcal{T}_{\mathcal{P}_{\lambda/(1+\phi_k)}}\left(\frac{\mathcal{Y} - \mathcal{S}^k + \phi_k\mathcal{L}^k}{1 + \phi_k}\right), \tag{5.30}$$

$$\mathcal{S}^{k+1} = T_{P_{\beta/(1+\varphi_k)}}\left(\frac{\mathcal{Y} - \mathcal{L}^{k+1} + \varphi_k\mathcal{S}^k}{1 + \varphi_k}\right). \tag{5.31}$$

The dominant computational load lies in the $\mathcal{L}$-step to compute the t-SVD. Since t-SVD is constructed by SVD of the frontal slices of $\bar{\mathcal{L}}$, approximate or inexact SVD algorithms exploiting the low rank property of $\mathcal{L}$ can be used to make the algorithm scalable to high-dimensional problems.

The convergence properties of the PGD and proximal BCD algorithms have been well established. For the PGD algorithm (5.26), when $\mathcal{P}_\lambda$ is a closed, proper, lower semi-continuous Kurdyka–Lojasiewicz (KL) function and $k > 1$, the generated sequence $\{\mathcal{L}^k\}$ converges to a stationary point of the problem (5.24) [3]. Meanwhile, for the proximal BCD algorithm (5.30) and (5.31), when $\mathcal{P}_\lambda$ and P_β are closed, proper, lower semi-continuous KL functions and $(\phi_k, \varphi_k) > 0$ for any $k > 1$, the generated sequence $\{(\mathcal{L}^k, \mathcal{S}^k)\}$ converges to a stationary point of the problem (5.25) [3]. Under these mild convergence conditions, it can be further shown that both algorithms satisfy a finite support identification property [53]. That is when $k > k^\bullet$ for some $k^\bullet$ large enough, the rank of the matrices $\bar{\mathbf{L}}_{(i)}^k$, $i = 1, \cdots, n_3$, and the support of $\mathcal{S}^k$ freeze. Then, the algorithms enter a regime with linear convergence rate, which is known as local linear convergence rate. When applying the ADMM framework, the ADMM algorithms for the formulations (5.24) and (5.25) can also be shown to converge to a stationary point under mild conditions.

Another approach to deal with large or even huge tensors is to adopt low-rank factorization, which represents a low-rank tensor $\mathcal{L} \in \mathbb{R}^{n_1 \times n_2 \times n_3}$ by the t-product of two (or more) smaller tensor as $\mathcal{A} = \mathcal{L} * \mathcal{R}$ with $\mathcal{L} \in \mathbb{R}^{n_1 \times r \times n_3}$ and $\mathcal{R} \in \mathbb{R}^{n_2 \times r \times n_3}$ for some $r \ll \min\{n_1, n_2\}$ [30,69]. The factorization facilitates the development of very efficient algorithms that only need to iteratively update two (or more) smaller factor tensors instead of a large tensor.

5.4 Generalized thresholding algorithms with learning

Recently, deep learning has achieved remarkable success in many applications, such as speech recognition, computer vision [46], and natural language processing [57]. Classical deep learning models are stacked by a series of linear calculation layers and nonlinear functions. Different models can be obtained by performing different calculation strategies and applying different connection strategies between layers. For example, convolutional neural networks (CNNs) are developed to process grid-like data, and recurrent neural networks aim at sequence-like data. However, these models do not have theoretical guarantees due to the black-box characteristic of deep learning [26].

Motivated by the success of deep learning, learnable algorithms for optimization have been developed. As explainable algorithms similar to classical ones, these learned algorithms enjoy the performance improvement from training data. There are mainly two deep learning-based strategies that can learn thresholding operators, namely deep unrolling and deep PnP. Deep unrolling maps the iterative thresholding algorithms onto deep neural networks, which are usually trained end-to-end. Deep PnP regards a specific subproblem of the model-based methods as a denoising problem and solves it using pretrained deep networks as thresholding functions. These two methods have the interpretability of the model-based methods while enjoying performance enhancement of deep networks.

5.4.1 Deep unrolling

As introduced in Section 5.2, a number of hand-crafted thresholding operators can be used for low-rank tensor recovery. However, their thresholding values are usually determined by some hyperparameters, whose appropriate values depend on specific applications. Deep unrolling models are designed to jointly learn thresholding values with other parameters. At present, methods of this kind mainly focus on the sparse coding [20] and CS problems [33].

Here we take CS as an example to briefly introduce a typical deep unrolling model which learns a soft-thresholding function, namely Learned ISTA (LISTA) [20]. Basically, CS aims to recover a sparse vector $\hat{\mathbf{x}}$ from its noisy linear measurements $\mathbf{b} = \mathbf{A}\hat{\mathbf{x}} + \boldsymbol{\varepsilon}$, where $\mathbf{b} \in \mathbb{R}^M$, $\hat{\mathbf{x}} \in \mathbb{R}^N$, $\mathbf{A} \in \mathbb{R}^{M \times N}$, $\boldsymbol{\varepsilon} \in \mathbb{R}^N$ is an additive white Gaussian noise, and $M \ll N$. A popular approach to recover $\hat{\mathbf{x}}$ is to solve the formulation as follows:

$$\min_{\mathbf{x}} \frac{1}{2} \|\mathbf{b} - \mathbf{A}\mathbf{x}\|_2^2 + P_\lambda(\mathbf{x}). \tag{5.32}$$

When $P_\lambda(\mathbf{x}) = \lambda \|\mathbf{x}\|_1$, (5.32) is usually called LASSO and it can be solved by the well-known ISTA:

$$\mathbf{x}^k = T_{P_{\lambda/L}} \left(\mathbf{x}^{k-1} + \frac{1}{L} \mathbf{A}^\mathsf{T} \left(\mathbf{b} - \mathbf{A}\mathbf{x}^{k-1} \right) \right), \tag{5.33}$$

where $T_{P_{\lambda/L}}(\cdot)$ is the soft-thresholding function in Table 5.1 and L is a proximal parameter no less than the largest eigenvalue of $\mathbf{A}^\mathsf{T}\mathbf{A}$ to guarantee convergence. It can be noticed that the thresholding value in (5.33) is determined by λ and $\mathbf{A}$.

Gregor et al. [20] unfolded ISTA into a neural network, which is composed of several phases with fixed numbers. The k-th phase of LISTA can be expressed as

$$\mathbf{x}^k = T_{P_{\theta^k}} \left(\mathbf{W}_\mathrm{e}^k \mathbf{b} + \mathbf{S}^k \mathbf{x}^{k-1} \right),$$

where $\mathbf{W}_\mathrm{e}^k$ is initialized as $1/L \cdot \mathbf{A}^\mathsf{T}$ and $\mathbf{S}^k$ is initialized as $\mathbf{I} - 1/L \cdot \mathbf{A}^\mathsf{T}\mathbf{A}$. In LISTA, $\mathbf{W}_\mathrm{e}^k$, $\mathbf{S}^k$, and θ^k are trained in an end-to-end manner, which makes θ^k fit to the training set. If the training and test sets are of the same distribution, the model can still work well in the test set. Fig. 5.2 shows the difference between ISTA and LISTA for the CS problem. It has been shown that LISTA can achieve satisfactory performance with only 10 to 20 phases [47,49]. Chen et al. [10] established the necessary condition for LISTA to converge, which shows the great potential of the learned soft-thresholding operator. Besides ISTA, the learned soft-thresholding function has been applied in other iterative algorithms [4,42].

Besides the soft-thresholding function, the works [10,48,50] considered the learning of some other threshold functions. For example, in [10], $p^k\%$ of entries are selected as the trust support in the k-th phase, and the soft-thresholding function

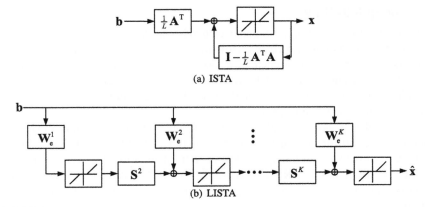

(a) ISTA

(b) LISTA

FIGURE 5.2

Typical penalty functions and the corresponding thresholding functions (with the same threshold).

with support selection is expressed as

$$
(T^{p^k}_{P_{\theta^k}}(\mathbf{x}))_i = \begin{cases}
\mathbf{x}_i, & \mathbf{x}_i > \theta^k, i \in \mathbb{S}^{p^k}(\mathbf{x}), \\
\mathbf{x}_i - \theta^k, & \mathbf{x}_i > \theta^k, i \notin \mathbb{S}^{p^k}(\mathbf{x}), \\
0, & \theta^k \leqslant \mathbf{x}_i \leqslant \theta^k, \\
\mathbf{x}_i + \theta^k, & \mathbf{x}_i \leqslant \theta^k, i \notin \mathbb{S}^{p^k}(\mathbf{x}), \\
\mathbf{x}_i, & \mathbf{x}_i \leqslant \theta^k, i \in \mathbb{S}^{p^k}(\mathbf{x}),
\end{cases}
$$

where $\mathbb{S}^{p^k}(\mathbf{x})$ is given by

$$
\mathbb{S}^{p^k}(\mathbf{x}) = \left\{ i_1, i_2, \cdots, i_{\lceil p^k\% \cdot N \rceil} \,\middle|\, |\mathbf{x}_{i_1}| \geqslant |\mathbf{x}_{i_2}| \geqslant \cdots |\mathbf{x}_{i_{\lceil p^k\% \cdot N \rceil}}| \cdots \geqslant |\mathbf{x}_{i_N}| \right\},
$$

where p^k is a hyperparameter. With support selection, elements trusted as "true support" are not passed through thresholding. In [61], a novel hard-thresholding function dubbed hard-thresholding linear unit has been proposed as

$$
(T_{P_{\theta^k}}(\mathbf{x}))_i = \theta^k T_1(\mathbf{x}_i / \theta^k), \tag{5.34}
$$

where T_1 is the soft-thresholding operator with a thresholding value of 1 and θ^k is a trainable parameter. Note that (5.34) is equivalent to the hard-thresholding function in Table 5.1 for easier training.

We demonstrate that the learned thresholding operators can also be used for singular value thresholding. For example, the generalized matrix singular value thresholding function in the k-th phase can be expressed as

$$\tilde{T}_{P_{\theta^k}}(\mathbf{M}^k) = \mathbf{U}^k \cdot \text{diag}\left\{T_{P_{\theta^k}}(\sigma_1^k, \cdots, \sigma_r^k)\right\} \cdot \mathbf{V}^{k\mathrm{T}}, \tag{5.35}$$

where $\{\sigma_1^k, \cdots, \sigma_r^k\}$ are the singular values of $\mathbf{M}^k$, $\mathbf{U} \in \mathbb{R}^{m \times r}$ and $\mathbf{V} \in \mathbb{R}^{r \times n}$ contain the corresponding singular vectors of $\mathbf{M}^k$, and θ^k's are the trainable parameters.

The generalized t-SVT operator can be expressed as

$$\mathcal{T}_{P_{\theta^k}}(\mathcal{Y}^k) = \mathcal{U}^k * \text{ifft}(T_{P_{\theta^k}}(\bar{\mathcal{D}}^k), [], 3) * \mathcal{V}^{k\mathrm{T}}, \tag{5.36}$$

where $\mathcal{Y}^k = \mathcal{U}^k * \mathcal{D}^k * \mathcal{V}^{k\mathrm{T}}$ is the t-SVD of $\mathcal{Y}^k$. Besides t-SVD, (5.36) can also be applied in other low-rank penalties like the Tucker rank. Furthermore, some existing Python frameworks for deep learning, such as Pytorch and Tensorflow, provide trainable SVD operation, which facilitates the implementation of (5.35) and (5.36).

Hand-crafted thresholding functions corresponding to hand-crafted penalties may ignore some semantic information in data recovery. In comparison, rather than learning thresholding values, deep neural networks have been used in generalized thresholding functions in deep unrolling models to better represent data priors for tensor recovery [13,21,37,61,67]. In this way, data priors including low-rankness can be learned by end-to-end training.

Here we give an example [37] which applies convolutional neural networks as thresholding functions for the video CS problem. In [37], the optimization problem is formulated as

$$\hat{\mathcal{X}} = \underset{\mathcal{X}}{\arg\min} \frac{1}{2} \|\mathbf{b} - \mathbf{A}\mathbf{x}\|_{\mathrm{F}}^2 + \sum_{f=1}^{F} w_f \|\mathcal{X}\|_{\Lambda_f,*}, \tag{5.37}$$

where $\mathbf{x} = \text{vec}(\mathcal{X})$, $\mathbf{b}$ is the vectorization form of the measurement, and $\mathbf{A}$ is the matrix form of the sampling tensor; $\|\cdot\|_{\Lambda_f,*}$ is the low-rank penalty under transformation Λ_f, and the nuclear norm $\|\cdot\|_*$ can be expressed as $\|\cdot\|_{\mathrm{DFT},*}$ in this way. Also, w_f's are hyperparameters. Inspired by the ADMM algorithm, the work [37] solves (5.37) by a deep unrolling model dubbed Tensor ADMM-Net with K phases like LISTA, and its k-th phase can be formulated as

$$\mathcal{X}^k = \underset{\mathcal{X}}{\arg\min} \sum_{f=1}^{F} \left\langle \mathcal{U}^{k-1}, \mathcal{X} - \mathcal{Z}_f^{k-1} \right\rangle + \frac{1}{2} \|\mathbf{b} - \mathbf{A}\mathbf{x}\|_{\mathrm{F}}^2 + \sum_{f=1}^{F} \frac{\rho_f}{2} \left\| \mathcal{X} - \mathcal{Z}_f^{k-1} \right\|_{\mathrm{F}}^2, \tag{5.38}$$

$$\mathcal{Z}_f^k = \underset{\mathcal{Z}}{\arg\min} \left\langle \mathcal{U}^{k-1}, \mathcal{X}^k - \mathcal{Z} \right\rangle + \frac{\rho_f}{2} \left\| \mathcal{X}^k - \mathcal{Z} \right\|_{\mathrm{F}}^2 + w_f \|\mathcal{Z}\|_{\Lambda_f,*}, \tag{5.39}$$

$$\mathcal{U}_f^k = \mathcal{U}_f^{k-1} + \eta_f(\mathcal{X}^k - \mathcal{Z}^k), \tag{5.40}$$

where $\mathcal{X}^k$ is the approximated tensor at the k-th iteration. Now (5.38) and (5.40) can be computed easily. Tensor ADMM-Net uses a learnable linear operation for transformation and applies CNNs to be the thresholding functions for low-rank penalties. The solution to (5.39) can be expressed as

$$\mathcal{Z}_f^k = T_{\text{L}f}^k(\mathcal{U}^k + D_f^k(\mathcal{X}^k)),$$

where $T_{\text{L}f}^k(\cdot)$ is the learned thresholding function and $D_f^k(\cdot)$ is the learned linear transformation. We emphasize that with minor modification, this strategy can be used to unfold other optimization problems for low-rank tensor approximation.

5.4.2 Deep plug-and-play

The PnP takes the strategy that replaces a suboptimization problem as follows with a better denoising process [58,63,68]:

$$\hat{\mathcal{X}} = \arg\min_{\mathcal{X}} \text{P}(\mathcal{X}) + \frac{1}{2\sigma^2}||\mathcal{X} - \mathcal{V}||_\text{F}^2, \tag{5.41}$$

where σ is related to the noise level and $\text{P}(\cdot)$ is the penalty. As introduced in Section 5.2, when $P(\cdot)$ is $\|\cdot\|_1$, (5.41) is the soft-thresholding function, and when $P(\cdot)$ is $\|\cdot\|_*$, it becomes the singular value soft-thresholding function. Different thresholding functions can be regarded as different denoisers which correspond to different data priors. In order to capture more details of data by learned priors, deep PnP uses pretrained deep neural networks as generalized thresholding functions to replace (5.41).

Here we give a deep PnP framework named DP3LRTC, which is designed for low-rank tensor completion. DP3LRTC extends (5.22) to

$$\min_{\mathcal{X}} \|\mathcal{X}\|_* + \lambda \text{P}(\mathcal{X}) \quad \text{subject to} \quad Q_\mathbb{O}(\mathcal{X}) = Q_\mathbb{O}(\mathcal{O}), \tag{5.42}$$

where $\mathcal{X}$ is the underlying low-rank tensor, $\mathcal{O}$ is the observed tensor, and $Q_\mathbb{O}(\mathcal{X})$ is used to denote the detail of observations. DP3LRTC uses ADMM to solve (5.42), and its k-th iteration can be expressed as

$$\mathcal{Y}^k = \arg\min_{\mathcal{Y}} \|\mathcal{Y}\|_\text{TNN} + \frac{\beta}{2}\left\|\mathcal{X}^{k-1} - \mathcal{Y} + \Lambda_1^{k-1}\Big/\beta\right\|_\text{F}^2, \tag{5.43}$$

$$\mathcal{Z}^k = \arg\min_{\mathcal{Z}} \lambda\, \text{P}(\mathcal{Z}) + \frac{\beta}{2}\left\|\mathcal{X}^{k-1} - \mathcal{Z} + \Lambda_2^{k-1}\Big/\beta\right\|_\text{F}^2, \tag{5.44}$$

$$\mathcal{X}^k = \arg\min_{\mathcal{X}} 1_\mathbb{S}(\mathcal{X}) + \frac{\beta}{2}\left\|\mathcal{X} - \mathcal{Y}^k + \Lambda_1^{k-1}\Big/\beta\right\|_\text{F}^2 + \frac{\beta}{2}\left\|\mathcal{X} - \mathcal{Z}^k + \Lambda_2^{k-1}\Big/\beta\right\|_\text{F}^2, \tag{5.45}$$

$$\Lambda_1^k = \Lambda_1^{k-1} + \beta(\mathcal{X}^k - \mathcal{Y}^k), \tag{5.46}$$

$$\Lambda_2^k = \Lambda_2^{k-1} + \beta(\mathcal{X}^k - \mathcal{Z}^k), \tag{5.47}$$

where β is a hyperparameter and $\mathcal{X}^k$ is the completed tensor at the k-th iteration; $\mathcal{Y}^k$, $\mathcal{Z}^k$, Λ_1^k, and Λ_2^k are intermediate dual variables, and $1_{\mathbb{S}}$ is defined as

$$1_{\mathbb{S}}(\mathcal{X}) = \begin{cases} 0, & \text{if } \mathcal{X} \in \mathbb{S}, \\ \infty, & \text{otherwise,} \end{cases}$$

where $\mathbb{S} := \{\mathcal{X} | Q_{\mathbb{O}}(\mathcal{X}) = Q_{\mathbb{O}}(\mathcal{O})\}$. The update steps (5.43), (5.45), (5.46), and (5.47) can be solved easily. DP3LRTC solves (5.44) using a pretrained deep neural network named FFDNet [62] as

$$\mathcal{Z}^{k+1} = T_{\text{FFD}}(\mathcal{X}^k + \Lambda_2^k \big/ \beta, \sigma),$$

where $T_{\text{FFD}}(\cdot, \sigma)$ is the FFDNet for denoising and $\sigma = \sqrt{\lambda/\beta}$ is related to the noise level.

Different from deep unrolling, deep PnP methods do not have a fixed iteration number and usually terminate until convergence. Furthermore, since (5.41) appears in many tensor recovery problems, this deep PnP method has a great application potential.

5.5 Numerical examples

Two examples are considered here to illustrate the generalized thresholding methods and unrolling methods for tensor completion and tensor RPCA. In these experiments, the PGD algorithm (5.26) and the BCD algorithm (5.30)–(5.31) are used to solve the tensor completion and RPCA problems, respectively. All the codes are online available at https://github.com/FWen/LRTT.

Example 5.1 (Tensor completion). This experiment considers the color image inpainting problem using the tensor completion formulation (5.24). The task is to restore a 318×500 color image from 50% of the pixels in the presence of entry noise. This is the case in many image inpainting and denoising applications, e.g., a large portion of the pixels are corrupted by salt-and-pepper noise. The ℓ_q penalty (i.e., $\mathcal{P}_\lambda$ being the tensor Schatten-q norm) is considered as it has a flexible parametric form that adapts to different penalty functions by varying the value of q. Two cases with different low-rankness are considered to illustrate the performance of the thresholding method in different low-rankness conditions. *Case 1 (Nonstrictly low-rank)*: The singular values of a natural image are not strictly low-rank but rather approximately following an exponential decay, as shown in Fig. 5.3 (left). *Case 2 (Synthetic strictly low-rank)*: To simulate a strictly low-rank case, the singular values of the original image are truncated and only the largest 30 singular values are retained, as shown in Fig. 5.3 (right), which results in a synthetic strictly low-rank image.

Fig. 5.4 presents the recovery peak signal-to-noise ratio (PSNR) of the PGD algorithm (5.26) for different values of $q \in [0, 1]$ and $\lambda \in [10^0, 10^5]$ in the two considered

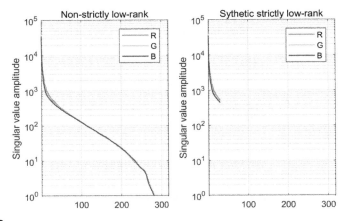

FIGURE 5.3

Sorted singular values of the three channels of the considered images in the two cases. *Left*: Nonstrictly low-rank case (the original image). *Right*: Synthetic strictly low-rank case (only the largest 30 singular values of the original image are retained).

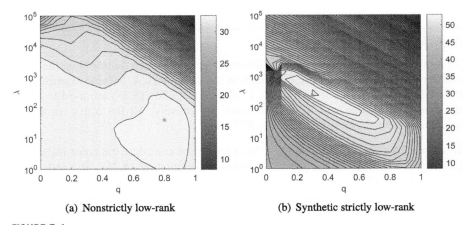

(a) Nonstrictly low-rank   (b) Synthetic strictly low-rank

FIGURE 5.4

Recovery PSNR of the PGD algorithm using ℓ_q penalty for different values of q and λ with SNR = 40 dB. (a) Nonstrictly low-rank (the original image). (b) Synthetic strictly low-rank.

cases. The entry-wise noise is Gaussian with an SNR of 40 dB. Fig. 5.5 compares the recovered images along with the PSNR and relative error of recovery (RelErr) by the hard-, soft-, and ℓ_q thresholding. Clearly, in the nonstrictly low-rank case, the non-convex ℓ_q regularization with the best choice of q (e.g., $q = 0.8$) only yields a slight improvement, e.g., about 0.3 dB improvement over the ℓ_1 regularization in terms of PSNR. In comparison, in the synthetic strictly low-rank case, ℓ_q regularization yields

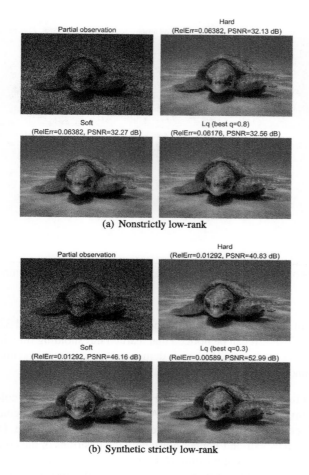

FIGURE 5.5

Recovered images of the PGD algorithm with SNR = 40 dB. (a) Nonstrictly low-rank (the original image). (b) Synthetic strictly low-rank.

a significant improvement over the ℓ_1 one, e.g., an improvement of more than 6 dB with the best choice of q.

There exist only a few learning-based thresholding algorithms for tensor recovery. Here we show the performance of a deep PnP method named DP3LRTC [63] as an example to illustrate the potential of learned thresholding functions. As shown in (5.43)–(5.47), DP3LRTC combines the TNN penalty and deep network-based thresholding functions for tensor completion. We compare DP3LRTC with the PGD algorithm (5.26) with the hard-, soft-, and ℓ_q thresholdings. The hyperparameters of DP3LRTC contain β and σ, and they are manually selected from a set $\{10^{-4}, 10^{-3}, 10^{-2}, 10^{-1}, 1, 10\}$ to obtain the highest PSNR. Fig. 5.6 shows the com-

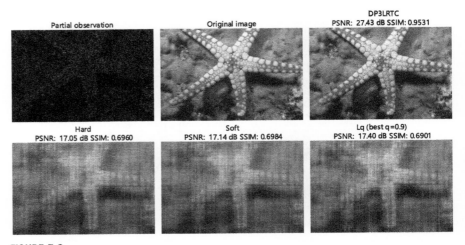

FIGURE 5.6

Recovery results of methods with different thresholding operators at the sampling ratio of 10%.

pletion results of different methods on a colorful image *starfish* sized 321×481 at a sampling ratio of 10%. It can be noticed that learned thresholding functions can yield significantly better performance, which demonstrates the great potential of learned thresholding functions.

Example 5.2 (Tensor RPCA). This experiment also considers the color image in-painting problem but using the tensor RPCA formulation (5.25). The goal is to restore the 318×500 color image in the presence of salt-and-pepper noise. Of the pixels, 30% are corrupted by salt-and-pepper noise with the positions of the corrupted pixels being unknown to the PCA algorithm. Note that when the positions of the corrupted pixels are assumed to be known as a prior, the problem degenerates to the completion problem. Similar to the first experiment, the ℓ_q penalty is considered due to its flexible parametric form, with $\mathcal{P}_\lambda$ being the tensor Schatten-q norm with parameter q_1, whilst R_β is the ℓ_q penalty with parameter q_2. The two cases in the first experiment, the original image (nonstrictly low-rank case) and singular value truncated synthetic image (synthetic strictly low-rank case), are considered.

Fig. 5.7 presents the recovery PSNR of the BCD algorithm (5.30)–(5.31) for different values of $q_1, q_2 \in [0, 1]$ (with one of q_1 and q_2 being fixed to 0.5) and $\lambda \in [10^{-5}, 10^0]$ in the two cases. The entry-wise noise is Gaussian with an SNR of 40 dB. Fig. 5.8 compares the recovered images along with the PSNR and RelErr by the hard-, soft-, and ℓ_q thresholding. It can be seen that using a more aggressive thresholding can yield better performance than soft-thresholding, especially in the strictly low-rank case. The best values of q_1 and q_2 depend on the low-rankness of $\mathcal{L}$ and the sparsity of the corruption $\mathcal{S}$. As the salt-and-pepper noise-like corruption is

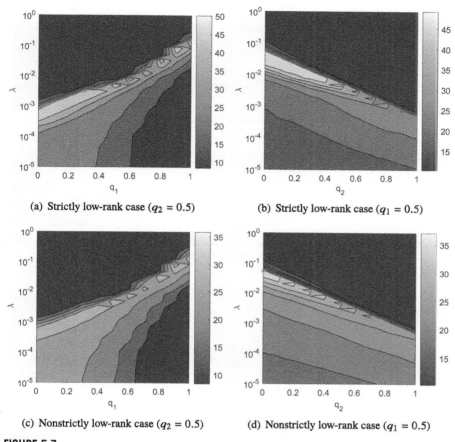

(a) Strictly low-rank case ($q_2 = 0.5$)   (b) Strictly low-rank case ($q_1 = 0.5$)

(c) Nonstrictly low-rank case ($q_2 = 0.5$)   (d) Nonstrictly low-rank case ($q_1 = 0.5$)

FIGURE 5.7

Recovery PSNR of the proximal BCD algorithm (5.30)–(5.31) using the ℓ_q penalty for different values of λ and (q_1, q_2) with SNR $= 40$ dB. (a) Varying q_1 with $q_2 = 0.5$ in case 1. (b) Varying q_2 with $q_1 = 0.5$ in case 1. (c) Varying q_1 with $q_2 = 0.5$ in case 2. (d) Varying q_2 with $q_1 = 0.5$ in case 2.

strictly sparse, a relatively small value of q_2 should be used to achieve the best performance. In the two low-rankness cases of $\mathcal{L}$, a relatively small value of q_1 should be used in the strictly low-rank case, while a relatively large value of q_1 should be used in the nonstrictly low-rank case.

5.6 Conclusion

This chapter has presented recent developments of thresholding-based low-rank tensor recovery in tensor completion and tensor RPCA, including various tensor low-

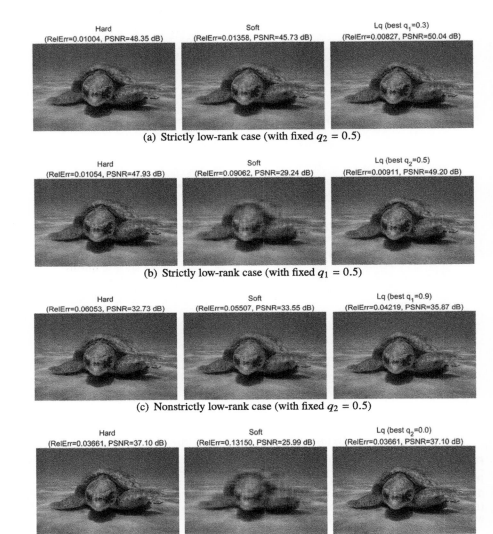

FIGURE 5.8

Recovered images of the PGD algorithm with SNR $= 40$ dB. (a) Varying q_1 with $q_2 = 0.5$ in case 1. (b) Varying q_2 with $q_1 = 0.5$ in case 1. (c) Varying q_1 with $q_2 = 0.5$ in case 2. (d) Varying q_2 with $q_1 = 0.5$ in case 2.

rank penalties, efficient first-order convex and nonconvex algorithms, and learning-based algorithms. Meanwhile, unified formulations and algorithms have been presented for the two problems with generalized tensor low-rank regularization. Moreover, experiments under different low-rankness conditions have been conducted to investigate the effect of penalty selection, which sheds some light on how to select a proper penalty. The results indicate that in some instances a nonconvex penalty can achieve significant performance improvement over a convex one. However, there exist certain instances where the use of nonconvex regularization will not significantly improve performance. It depends on the low-rankness of the intrinsic tensor. For example, the advantage of nonconvex regularization is prominent in the strictly low-rank case but is not prominent in the nonstrictly low-rank case. In the latter case, using nonconvex regularization may be unnecessary, since the involved nonconvex optimization problems are less tractable than convex problems. More specifically, the performance of a nonconvex regularized algorithm is closely related to initialization, and the convergence rate is usually lower than that of a convex regularized algorithm. Though it is difficult to theoretically select the best penalty for a specific instance, a proper penalty can be empirically selected in an application-dependent manner. For example, when the intrinsic tensor is strictly low-rank, a penalty with aggressive thresholding function (e.g., the ℓ_q-norm with a relatively small value of q) can be expected to yield satisfactory performance, whereas when the intrinsic tensor is nonstrictly low-rank, a penalty with less aggressive thresholding function (e.g., the ℓ_q-norm with a relatively large value of q) tends to yield better performance. The same philosophy applies to both the low-rank and sparse recovery problems, depending on the degree of the low-rankness or sparsity of the data to be recovered.

Moreover, the learning-based deep unrolling and deep PnP algorithms can also be viewed as generalized thresholding algorithms, which use learned thresholding functions rather than hand-crafted ones. A significant feature of such learning-based algorithms is that they have good interpretability like traditional model-based algorithms while enjoying performance enhancement of deep networks. Experimental results have shown great superiority of learning-based algorithms over model-based ones.

References

[1] A. Antoniadis, Wavelets in statistics: a review, Journal of the Italian Statistical Society 6 (2) (1997) 97–144.

[2] H. Attouch, J. Bolte, On the convergence of the proximal algorithm for nonsmooth functions involving analytic features, Mathematical Programming 116 (1–2) (2009) 5–16.

[3] H. Attouch, J. Bolte, P. Redont, A. Soubeyran, Proximal alternating minimization and projection methods for nonconvex problems: an approach based on the kurdyka-łojasiewicz inequality, Mathematics of Operations Research 35 (2) (2010) 438–457.

[4] M. Borgerding, P. Schniter, S. Rangan, Amp-inspired deep networks for sparse linear inverse problems, IEEE Transactions on Signal Processing 65 (16) (2017) 4293–4308.

[5] J.F. Cai, E.J. Candès, Z. Shen, A singular value thresholding algorithm for matrix completion, SIAM Journal on Optimization 20 (4) (2010) 1956–1982.

[6] E.J. Candès, X. Li, Y. Ma, J. Wright, Robust principal component analysis?, Journal of the ACM 58 (3) (2011) 1–37.

[7] R. Chartrand, Fast algorithms for nonconvex compressive sensing: mri reconstruction from very few data, in: 2009 IEEE International Symposium on Biomedical Imaging: from Nano to Macro, IEEE, 2009, pp. 262–265.

[8] L. Chen, X. Jiang, X. Liu, Z. Zhou, Robust low-rank tensor recovery via nonconvex singular value minimization, IEEE Transactions on Image Processing 29 (2020) 9044–9059.

[9] W. Chen, X. Gong, N. Song, Nonconvex robust low-rank tensor reconstruction via an empirical Bayes method, IEEE Transactions on Signal Processing 67 (22) (2019) 5785–5797.

[10] X. Chen, J. Liu, Z. Wang, W. Yin, Theoretical linear convergence of unfolded ISTA and its practical weights and thresholds, in: Advances in Neural Information Processing Systems, 2018, pp. 9061–9071.

[11] C. Croux, G. Haesbroeck, Principal component analysis based on robust estimators of the covariance or correlation matrix: influence functions and efficiencies, Biometrika 87 (3) (2000) 603–618.

[12] F. De La Torre, M.J. Black, A framework for robust subspace learning, International Journal of Computer Vision 54 (1–3) (2003) 117–142.

[13] S. Diamond, V. Sitzmann, F. Heide, G. Wetzstein, Unrolled optimization with deep priors, arXiv preprint, arXiv:1705.08041, 2017.

[14] D.L. Donoho, I.M. Johnstone, J.C. Hoch, A.S. Stern, Maximum entropy and the nearly black object, Journal of the Royal Statistical Society, Series B, Methodological 54 (1) (1992) 41–67.

[15] D.L. Donoho, J.M. Johnstone, Ideal spatial adaptation by wavelet shrinkage, Biometrika 81 (3) (1994) 425–455.

[16] J. Fan, R. Li, Variable selection via nonconcave penalized likelihood and its oracle properties, Journal of the American Statistical Association 96 (456) (2001) 1348–1360.

[17] M.A. Fischler, R.C. Bolles, Random sample consensus: a paradigm for model fitting with applications to image analysis and automated cartography, Communications of the ACM 24 (6) (1981) 381–395.

[18] S. Gandy, B. Recht, I. Yamada, Tensor completion and low-n-rank tensor recovery via convex optimization, Inverse Problems 27 (2) (2011) 025010.

[19] H.Y. Gao, A.G. Bruce, Waveshrink with firm shrinkage, Statistica Sinica (1997) 855–874.

[20] K. Gregor, Y. LeCun, Learning fast approximations of sparse coding, in: Proceedings of the 27th International Conference on International Conference on Machine Learning, 2010, pp. 399–406.

[21] X. Han, B. Wu, Z. Shou, X.Y. Liu, Y. Zhang, L. Kong, Tensor FISTA-Net for real-time snapshot compressive imaging, in: AAAI, 2020, pp. 10933–10940.

[22] T. Hastie, R. Tibshirani, M. Wainwright, Statistical Learning with Sparsity: The LASSO and Generalizations, CRC Press, 2015.

[23] B. Huang, C. Mu, D. Goldfarb, J. Wright, Provable models for robust low-rank tensor completion, Pacific Journal of Optimization 11 (2) (2015) 339–364.

[24] H. Huang, Y. Liu, Z. Long, C. Zhu, Robust low-rank tensor ring completion, IEEE Transactions on Computational Imaging 6 (2020) 1117–1126.

[25] Y. Huang, G. Liao, L. Zhang, Y. Xiang, J. Li, A. Nehorai, Efficient narrowband RFI mitigation algorithms for SAR systems with reweighted tensor structures, IEEE Transactions on Geoscience and Remote Sensing 57 (11) (2019) 9396–9409.

[26] Y. Huang, T. Würfl, K. Breininger, L. Liu, G. Lauritsch, A. Maier, Some investigations on robustness of deep learning in limited angle tomography, in: International Conference on Medical Image Computing and Computer-Assisted Intervention, Springer, 2018, pp. 145–153.

[27] M.E. Kilmer, K. Braman, N. Hao, R.C. Hoover, Third-order tensors as operators on matrices: a theoretical and computational framework with applications in imaging, SIAM Journal on Matrix Analysis and Applications 34 (1) (2013) 148–172.

[28] M.E. Kilmer, C.D. Martin, Factorization strategies for third-order tensors, Linear Algebra and Its Applications 435 (3) (2011) 641–658.

[29] T.G. Kolda, B.W. Bader, Tensor decompositions and applications, SIAM Review 51 (3) (2009) 455–500.

[30] H. Kong, X. Xie, Z. Lin, T-Schatten-p norm for low-rank tensor recovery, IEEE Journal of Selected Topics in Signal Processing 12 (6) (2018) 1405–1419.

[31] J. Liu, P. Musialski, P. Wonka, J. Ye, Tensor completion for estimating missing values in visual data, IEEE Transactions on Pattern Analysis and Machine Intelligence 35 (1) (2012) 208–220.

[32] Y. Liu, L. Chen, C. Zhu, Improved robust tensor principal component analysis via low rank core matrix, IEEE Journal of Selected Topics in Signal Processing 12 (2018) 1378–1389.

[33] Y. Liu, M. De Vos, I. Gligorijevic, V. Matic, Y. Li, S. Van Huffel, Multi-structural signal recovery for biomedical compressive sensing, IEEE Transactions on Biomedical Engineering 60 (10) (2013) 2794–2805.

[34] Y. Liu, Z. Long, H. Huang, C. Zhu, Low CP rank and Tucker rank tensor completion for estimating missing components in image data, IEEE Transactions on Circuits and Systems for Video Technology 30 (2020) 944–954.

[35] Y. Liu, Z. Long, C. Zhu, Image completion using low tensor tree rank and total variation minimization, IEEE Transactions on Multimedia 21 (2019) 338–350.

[36] C. Lu, J. Feng, Y. Chen, W. Liu, Z. Lin, S. Yan, Tensor robust principal component analysis with a new tensor nuclear norm, IEEE Transactions on Pattern Analysis and Machine Intelligence 42 (4) (2019) 925–938.

[37] J. Ma, X.Y. Liu, Z. Shou, X. Yuan, Deep tensor ADMM-Net for snapshot compressive imaging, in: Proceedings of the IEEE International Conference on Computer Vision, 2019, pp. 10223–10232.

[38] C. Mu, B. Huang, J. Wright, D. Goldfarb, Square deal: lower bounds and improved relaxations for tensor recovery, in: International Conference on Machine Learning, 2014, pp. 73–81.

[39] M.K.P. Ng, Q. Yuan, L. Yan, J. Sun, An adaptive weighted tensor completion method for the recovery of remote sensing images with missing data, IEEE Transactions on Geoscience and Remote Sensing 55 (6) (2017) 3367–3381.

[40] B. Romera-Paredes, M. Pontil, A new convex relaxation for tensor completion, Advances in Neural Information Processing Systems 26 (2013) 2967–2975.

[41] O. Semerci, N. Hao, M.E. Kilmer, E.L. Miller, Tensor-based formulation and nuclear norm regularization for multienergy computed tomography, IEEE Transactions on Image Processing 23 (4) (2014) 1678–1693.

[42] J. Sun, H. Li, Z. Xu, et al., Deep ADMM-Net for compressive sensing MRI, Advances in Neural Information Processing Systems 29 (2016) 10–18.

[43] R. Tibshirani, Regression shrinkage and selection via the lasso, Journal of the Royal Statistical Society, Series B, Methodological 58 (1) (1996) 267–288.

[44] R. Tomioka, K. Hayashi, H. Kashima, Estimation of low-rank tensors via convex optimization, arXiv preprint, arXiv:1010.0789, 2010.

[45] F. De la Torre, M.J. Black, Robust Principal Component Analysis for Computer Vision, in: Proceedings Eighth IEEE International Conference on Computer Vision, vol. 1, ICCV 2001, IEEE, 2001, pp. 362–369.

[46] A. Voulodimos, N. Doulamis, A. Doulamis, E. Protopapadakis, Deep learning for computer vision: a brief review, Computational Intelligence and Neuroscience 2018 (2018).

[47] Z. Wang, S. Chang, J. Zhou, M. Wang, T.S. Huang, Learning a task-specific deep architecture for clustering, in: Proceedings of the 2016 SIAM International Conference on Data Mining, SIAM, 2016, pp. 369–377.

[48] Z. Wang, Q. Ling, T. Huang, Learning deep ℓ_0 encoders, in: Proceedings of the AAAI Conference on Artificial Intelligence, vol. 30, 2016.

[49] Z. Wang, D. Liu, S. Chang, Q. Ling, Y. Yang, T.S. Huang, D3: Deep dual-domain based fast restoration of JPEG-compressed images, in: Proceedings of the IEEE Conference on Computer Vision and Pattern Recognition, 2016, pp. 2764–2772.

[50] Z. Wang, Y. Yang, S. Chang, Q. Ling, T. Huang, Learning a deep *ell_infty* encoder for hashing, arXiv preprint, arXiv:1604.01475, 2016.

[51] F. Wen, P. Liu, Y. Liu, R.C. Qiu, W. Yu, Robust sparse recovery in impulsive noise via *ell_p-ell_1* optimization, IEEE Transactions on Signal Processing 65 (1) (2016) 105–118.

[52] F. Wen, L. Pei, Y. Yang, W. Yu, P. Liu, Efficient and robust recovery of sparse signal and image using generalized nonconvex regularization, IEEE Transactions on Computational Imaging 3 (4) (2017) 566–579.

[53] F. Wen, R. Ying, P. Liu, T.K. Truong, Nonconvex regularized robust PCA using the proximal block coordinate descent algorithm, IEEE Transactions on Signal Processing 67 (20) (2019) 5402–5416.

[54] J. Wright, A. Ganesh, S. Rao, Y. Peng, Y. Ma, Robust principal component analysis: exact recovery of corrupted low-rank matrices via convex optimization, Advances in Neural Information Processing Systems 22 (2009) 2080–2088.

[55] Z. Xu, X. Chang, F. Xu, H. Zhang, $l_{\{1/2\}}$ regularization: a thresholding representation theory and a fast solver, IEEE Transactions on Neural Networks and Learning Systems 23 (7) (2012) 1013–1027.

[56] Q. Yao, J.T.Y. Kwok, B. Han, Efficient nonconvex regularized tensor completion with structure-aware proximal iterations, in: International Conference on Machine Learning, 2019, pp. 7035–7044.

[57] T. Young, D. Hazarika, S. Poria, E. Cambria, Recent trends in deep learning based natural language processing, IEEE Computational Intelligence Magazine 13 (3) (2018) 55–75.

[58] X. Yuan, Y. Liu, J. Suo, Q. Dai, Plug-and-play algorithms for large-scale snapshot compressive imaging, in: Proceedings of the IEEE/CVF Conference on Computer Vision and Pattern Recognition, 2020, pp. 1447–1457.

[59] C.H. Zhang, et al., Nearly unbiased variable selection under minimax concave penalty, The Annals of Statistics 38 (2) (2010) 894–942.

[60] F. Zhang, J. Wang, W. Wang, C. Xu, Low-tubal-rank plus sparse tensor recovery with prior subspace information, IEEE Transactions on Pattern Analysis and Machine Intelligence (2020).

[61] J. Zhang, B. Ghanem, ISTA-Net: interpretable optimization-inspired deep network for image compressive sensing, in: Proceedings of the IEEE Conference on Computer Vision and Pattern Recognition, 2018, pp. 1828–1837.

[62] K. Zhang, W. Zuo, L. Zhang, Ffdnet: toward a fast and flexible solution for CNN-based image denoising, IEEE Transactions on Image Processing 27 (9) (2018) 4608–4622.

[63] K. Zhang, W. Zuo, L. Zhang, Deep plug-and-play super-resolution for arbitrary blur kernels, in: Proceedings of the IEEE Conference on Computer Vision and Pattern Recognition, 2019, pp. 1671–1681.

[64] X. Zhang, D. Wang, Z. Zhou, Y. Ma, Robust low-rank tensor recovery with rectification and alignment, IEEE Transactions on Pattern Analysis and Machine Intelligence (2019).

[65] Z. Zhang, S. Aeron, Exact tensor completion using t-SVD, IEEE Transactions on Signal Processing 65 (6) (2016) 1511–1526.

[66] Z. Zhang, G. Ely, S. Aeron, N. Hao, M. Kilmer, Novel methods for multilinear data completion and de-noising based on tensor-SVD, in: Proceedings of the IEEE Conference on Computer Vision and Pattern Recognition, 2014, pp. 3842–3849.

[67] Z. Zhang, Y. Liu, J. Liu, F. Wen, C. Zhu, AMP-Net: denoising-based deep unfolding for compressive image sensing, IEEE Transactions on Image Processing 30 (2021) 1487–1500, https://doi.org/10.1109/TIP.2020.3044472.

[68] X.L. Zhao, W.H. Xu, T.X. Jiang, Y. Wang, M.K. Ng, Deep plug-and-play prior for low-rank tensor completion, Neurocomputing (2020).

[69] P. Zhou, C. Lu, Z. Lin, C. Zhang, Tensor factorization for low-rank tensor completion, IEEE Transactions on Image Processing 27 (3) (2017) 1152–1163.

Tensor principal component analysis

Pan Zhou[a], Canyi Lu[b], and Zhouchen Lin[c]
[a]*SEA AI Lab, Singapore, Singapore*
[b]*Carnegie Mellon University, Pittsburgh, PA, United States*
[c]*Key Lab. of Machine Perception, School of EECS, Peking University, Beijing, P.R. China*

CONTENTS

6.1 Introduction

Principal component analysis (PCA) [5] is a fundamental approach for data analysis. It exploits low-dimensional structures in high-dimensional data, which commonly exist in different types of data, e.g., images, texts, videos, and bioinformatics. It is computationally efficient and powerful for data which are mildly corrupted by small

Tensors for Data Processing. https://doi.org/10.1016/B978-0-12-824447-0.00012-1

Gaussian noise. Specifically, for two-way data (matrix) $X \in \mathbb{R}^{n_1 \times n_2}$ which can be decomposed into $L_0 + E_0$, where L_0 is low-rank and E_0 is Gaussian noise, PCA can recover the clean data L_0 by solving

$$\min_{\text{rank}(L) \leq k} \|L - X\|_F^2, \tag{6.1}$$

where $\text{rank}(L)$ denotes the matrix rank of L, $\|L\|_F$ denotes the Frobenius norm of matrix L, and k denotes how many principal factors are used to reconstruct the observed data X. It has been proved that problem (6.1) has a closed-form solution [5]. Assume that $X = USV^T$ is the singular value decomposition (SVD) of X. Then the optimal solution to problem (6.1) is $L_0 = \sum_{i=1}^{k} S_{ii} U_i V_i^T$, where U_i and V_i denote the i-th column in U and V, respectively, and S_{ii} is the (i, i)-th entry in S. Thanks to its simplicity and effectiveness, PCA has become a standard data analysis tool and has various applications across many domains, such as data denoising, data recovery, and data dimension reduction, to name a few.

One major issue of PCA is that it can only handle two-way (matrix) data. However, real data are usually multidimensional in nature and are stored in multiway arrays known as tensors [3,4,6,7]. For example, a color image is a three-way object with column, row, and color modes; a grayscale video is indexed by two spatial variables and one temporal variable. To use PCA, one has to first restructure the multiway data into a matrix. Such a preprocessing usually leads to information loss and could cause a performance degradation. To alleviate this issue, it is natural to consider extending PCA to manipulate the tensor data by taking advantage of its multidimensional structure.

In this chapter, we are particularly interested in tensor PCA (TPCA), which aims to exactly recover a low-rank tensor corrupted by noises or errors. More specifically, suppose that we are given a data tensor $\mathcal{X} \in \mathbb{R}^{n_1 \times n_2 \times n_3}$ and know that it can be decomposed as

$$\mathcal{X} = \mathcal{L}_0 + \mathcal{E}_0, \tag{6.2}$$

where $\mathcal{L}_0$ is low-rank and $\mathcal{E}_0$ is Gaussian noise. Note that we do not know the locations of the nonzero elements of $\mathcal{E}_0$, not even how many there are. Then we consider how to find a good approximation $\mathcal{L}_0$ to $\mathcal{X}$:

$$\min_{\text{rank}(\mathcal{L}) \leq k} \|\mathcal{L} - \mathcal{X}\|_F^2, \tag{6.3}$$

where $\text{rank}(\mathcal{L})$ denotes the tensor rank of $\mathcal{L}$, $\|\mathcal{L}\|_F$ denotes the Frobenius norm of tensor $\mathcal{L}$, and k also denotes how many principal factors are used to reconstruct the observed data $\mathcal{X}$. We will give the definitions of tensor rank and Frobenius norm in Section 6.2. Similar to PCA, this TPCA problem (6.3) also has many real applications, such as (medical) image denoising, video recovery, principal factor analysis, etc. For this TPCA for Gaussian noise, we will introduce it in Section 6.3.

Besides the above Gaussian noise setting,

(i)   the observed data $\mathcal{X}$ are corrupted by Gaussian noise, i.e., the noise $\mathcal{E}_0$ in Eq. (6.2) follows a Gaussian distribution,

we further consider another two more practical settings:

(ii)   the observed data $\mathcal{X}$ are sparsely and grossly corrupted, which means that the noise $\mathcal{E}_0$ in Eq. (6.2) is sparse but could have entries of arbitrary magnitude, and

(iii)   data $\mathcal{X}$ contain outliers (sample-specific corruptions), which means that large errors concentrate only on a number of samples or several parts of data.

Settings (ii) and (iii) are ubiquitous in real-world data, since sensor failures, malicious tampering, and other system errors can easily result in sparse noise or outliers [8–11]. However, TPCA is brittle to these two settings [8–11] and cannot handle such kinds of noisy data. One may consider the robust PCA methods in the two-way data, such as robust PCA [8] and outlier robust PCA [9,10], to handle the noises in settings (ii) and (iii). But, as mentioned, these methods require to vectorize tensor data into matrices first, which could destroy the intrinsic multiway structure in tensor data and could result in performance degradation. Fortunately, there are effective and efficient variants of TPCA that can exactly recover the clean tensor data in both settings (ii) and (iii) with provable performance guarantees. In Sections 6.4 and 6.5 we will introduce these methods for handling these kinds of noise, respectively.

This chapter is structured as follows. Section 6.2 introduces the commonly used notations, definitions, and preliminaries throughout the whole chapter. Then Section 6.3 presents the TPCA method [1,2] for recovering the clean data in setting (i). Next, Section 6.4 introduces two variants of TPCA, namely robust TPCA (R-TPCA) [2] and tensor low-rank representation (TLRR) [3], for handling the noise to recover the clean data in setting (ii). Section 6.5 introduces one variant of TPCA, i.e., outlier robust TPCA (OR-TPCA) [4], to detect the outlier position and recover the clean data in setting (iii). For all these TPCA methods, we will introduce them in detail, including their models, recovery theories, and optimization algorithms, and further provide their real applications. Next, Section 6.7 discusses the research directions that need to be further explored for tensor data analysis. Finally, Section 6.8 summarizes the whole chapter.

6.2 Notations and preliminaries

This section is structured as follows. Section 6.2.1 introduces the commonly used notations throughout the whole chapter. Then Section 6.2.2 presents the discrete Fourier transform (DFT) and its properties which will be commonly used later. Next, Section 6.2.3 elaborates on the tensor–tensor product, which is the basis to define the tensor SVD (t-SVD), the tensor rank, and the tensor nuclear norm in Section 6.3. Finally, Section 6.2.4 summarizes the whole section.

Table 6.1 Notational convention in this chapter.

$\mathcal{A}$	A tensor.	$\boldsymbol{a}$	A vector.
A	A matrix.	a	A scalar.
$\mathcal{I}$	The identity tensor.	$\mathcal{A}^*$	The conjugate transpose of $\mathcal{A}$.
$\mathcal{A}_{ijk}$	The (i, j, k)-th entry of $\mathcal{A}$.	$\bar{\mathcal{A}}$	The DFT of $\mathcal{A}$.
$\mathcal{A}(i,:,:)$	The i-th horizontal slice of $\mathcal{A}$	$\|\mathcal{A}\|_1$	$\|\mathcal{A}\|_1 = \sum_{ijk} |\mathcal{A}_{ijk}|$.
$\mathcal{A}(:,i,:)$	The i-th lateral slice of $\mathcal{A}$.	$\|\mathcal{A}\|_\infty$	$\|\mathcal{A}\|_\infty = \max_{ijk} |\mathcal{A}_{ijk}|$.
$\mathcal{A}(:,:,i)$	The i-th frontal slice of $\mathcal{A}$.	$\|\mathcal{A}(:,j,:)\|_F$	$\|\mathcal{A}(:,j,:)\|_F = \sqrt{\sum_{ik}|\mathcal{A}_{ijk}|^2}$.
$A^{(i)}$	$A^{(i)} = \mathcal{A}(:,:,i)$.	$\|\mathcal{A}\|_{2,1}$	$\|\mathcal{A}\|_{2,1} = \sum_j \|\mathcal{A}(:,j,:)\|_F$.
$\mathcal{A}(i,j,:)$	The (i, j)-th tube of $\mathcal{A}$.	$\|\mathcal{A}\|_F$	$\|\mathcal{A}\|_F = \sqrt{\sum_{ijk} |\mathcal{A}_{ijk}|^2}$.
rank(A)	The rank of matrix A.	$\|A\|_*$	Sum of the singular values of A.
$\|A\|_F$	$\|A\|_F = \sqrt{\sum_{ij} A_{ij}^2}$.	$\|A\|_1$	$\|A\|_1 = \sum_{ij} |A_{ij}|$.
Θ_0	The index of outliers in $\mathcal{E}$.	$\mathcal{P}_{\Theta_0}$	The projection onto Θ_0.
$\mathcal{P}_{\Theta_0^\perp}$	The projection onto $\Theta_0^\perp$.	$B(\mathcal{E})$	$\left\{ \widetilde{\mathcal{E}} : \widetilde{\mathcal{E}}(:,i,:) = \frac{\mathcal{E}(:,i,:)}{\|\mathcal{E}(:,i,:)\|_F} \ (i \in \Theta_0); \right.$
$\mathcal{P}_{\mathcal{U}}(\mathcal{A})$	$\mathcal{P}_{\mathcal{U}}(\mathcal{A}) = \mathcal{U} * \mathcal{U}^* * \mathcal{A}$.		$\left. \widetilde{\mathcal{E}}(:,i,:) = \mathbf{0} \ (i \notin \Theta_0) \right\}$.
$\mathring{e}_t^n$	\multicolumn{3}{l}{$\mathring{e}_t^n \in \mathbb{R}^{n \times 1 \times n_3}$ whose the $(t, 1, 1)$-th entry is 1 and the rest are $\mathbf{0}$.}
$\mathcal{U}_0 * \mathcal{S}_0 * \mathcal{V}_0^*$	\multicolumn{3}{l}{Skinny t-SVD of clean data $\mathcal{L}_0$. See Theorem 6.2.}
$\mathcal{U}_{\mathcal{A}} * \mathcal{S}_{\mathcal{A}} * \mathcal{V}_{\mathcal{A}}^*$	\multicolumn{3}{l}{Skinny t-SVD of clean data $\mathcal{A}$. See Theorem 6.2.}

6.2.1 Notations

Table 6.1 summarizes the notations used in this paper. We denote tensors by boldface Euler script letters, e.g., $\mathcal{A}$. Matrices are denoted by boldface uppercase letters, e.g., A. Vectors are denoted by boldface lowercase letters, e.g., $\boldsymbol{a}$, and scalars are denoted by lowercase letters, e.g., a. We denote $\boldsymbol{I}_n$ as the $n \times n$ identity matrix. The fields of real numbers and complex numbers are denoted as $\mathbb{R}$ and $\mathbb{C}$, respectively. For a three-way tensor $\mathcal{A} \in \mathbb{C}^{n_1 \times n_2 \times n_3}$, we denote its (i, j, k)-th entry as $\mathcal{A}_{ijk}$ or a_{ijk} and use the MATLAB® notation $\mathcal{A}(i,:,:)$, $\mathcal{A}(:,i,:)$, and $\mathcal{A}(:,:,i)$ to denote respectively the i-th horizontal, lateral, and frontal slice (see definitions in [6]). More often, the frontal slice $\mathcal{A}(:,:,i)$ is denoted compactly as $A^{(i)}$. The tube is denoted as $\mathcal{A}(i, j, :)$. The inner product between A and B in $\mathbb{C}^{n_1 \times n_2}$ is defined as $\langle A, B \rangle = \text{Tr}(A^*B)$, where A^* denotes the conjugate transpose of A and $\text{Tr}(\cdot)$ denotes the matrix trace. The inner product between $\mathcal{A}$ and $\mathcal{B}$ in $\mathbb{C}^{n_1 \times n_2 \times n_3}$ is defined as $\langle \mathcal{A}, \mathcal{B} \rangle = \sum_{i=1}^{n_3} \langle A^{(i)}, B^{(i)} \rangle$. For any $\mathcal{A} \in \mathbb{C}^{n_1 \times n_2 \times n_3}$, the complex conjugate of $\mathcal{A}$ is denoted as $\text{conj}(\mathcal{A})$, which takes the complex conjugate of each entry of $\mathcal{A}$. We denote $\lfloor t \rfloor$ as the nearest integer less than or equal to t and $\lceil t \rceil$ as the one greater than or equal to t.

Some norms of vector, matrix, and tensor are used. We denote the ℓ_1-norm as $\|\mathcal{A}\|_1 = \sum_{ijk} |a_{ijk}|$, the infinity norm as $\|\mathcal{A}\|_\infty = \max_{ijk} |a_{ijk}|$, and the Frobenius norm as $\|\mathcal{A}\|_F = \sqrt{\sum_{ijk} |a_{ijk}|^2}$. The above norms reduce to the vector or matrix norms if $\mathcal{A}$ is a vector or a matrix. For $\boldsymbol{v} \in \mathbb{C}^n$, the ℓ_2-norm is $\|\boldsymbol{v}\|_2 = \sqrt{\sum_i |v_i|^2}$.

The spectral norm of a matrix A is denoted as $\|A\| = \max_i \sigma_i(A)$, where $\sigma_i(A)$'s are the singular values of A. The matrix nuclear norm is $\|A\|_* = \sum_i \sigma_i(A)$.

6.2.2 Discrete Fourier transform

The DFT plays a core role in the tensor–tensor product introduced later. We give some related background knowledge and notations here. The DFT on $v \in \mathbb{R}^n$, denoted as $\bar{v}$, is given by

$$\bar{v} = F_n v \in \mathbb{C}^n, \tag{6.4}$$

where F_n is the DFT matrix defined as

$$F_n = [f_1, \cdots, f_i, \cdots, f_n] \in \mathbb{R}^{n \times n}, \tag{6.5}$$

where $f_i = [\omega^{0 \times (i-1)}; \omega^{1 \times (i-1)}; \cdots; \omega^{(n-1) \times (i-1)}] \in \mathbb{R}^n$. Here $\omega = e^{-\frac{2\pi i}{n}}$ is a primitive n-th root of unity in which $i = \sqrt{-1}$. Note that $F_n/\sqrt{n}$ is a unitary matrix, i.e.,

$$F_n^* F_n = F_n F_n^* = n I_n. \tag{6.6}$$

Thus $F_n^{-1} = F_n^*/n$. The above property will be frequently used in this chapter. Computing $\bar{v}$ by using (6.4) costs $O(n^2)$. A more widely used method is the fast Fourier transform (FFT), which costs $O(n \log n)$. By using the MATLAB command `fft`, we have $\bar{v} = \text{fft}(v)$. Denote the circulant matrix of v as

$$\text{circ}(v) = \begin{bmatrix} v_1 & v_n & \cdots & v_2 \\ v_2 & v_1 & \cdots & v_3 \\ \vdots & \vdots & \ddots & \vdots \\ v_n & v_{n-1} & \cdots & v_1 \end{bmatrix} \in \mathbb{R}^{n \times n}.$$

It is known that it can be diagonalized by the DFT matrix, i.e.,

$$F_n \cdot \text{circ}(v) \cdot F_n^{-1} = \text{Diag}(\bar{v}), \tag{6.7}$$

where $\text{Diag}(\bar{v})$ denotes a diagonal matrix with its i-th diagonal entry being $\bar{v}_i$. The above equation implies that the columns of F_n are the eigenvectors of $(\text{circ}(v))^\top$ and $\bar{v}_i$'s are the corresponding eigenvalues.

Lemma 6.1. *[12] Given any real vector $v \in \mathbb{R}^n$, the associated $\bar{v}$ satisfies*

$$\bar{v}_1 \in \mathbb{R} \text{ and } \text{conj}(\bar{v}_i) = \bar{v}_{n-i+2}, \ i = 2, \cdots, \left\lfloor \frac{n+1}{2} \right\rfloor. \tag{6.8}$$

Conversely, for any given complex $\bar{v} \in \mathbb{C}^n$ satisfying (6.8), there exists a real block-circulant matrix $\text{circ}(v)$ such that (6.7) holds.

As will be seen later, the above properties are useful for efficient computation and important for proofs. Now we consider the DFT on tensors. For $\mathcal{A} \in \mathbb{R}^{n_1 \times n_2 \times n_3}$, we denote $\bar{\mathcal{A}} \in \mathbb{C}^{n_1 \times n_2 \times n_3}$ as the result of DFT on $\mathcal{A}$ along the third dimension, i.e., performing the DFT on all the tubes of $\mathcal{A}$. By using the MATLAB command `fft`, we have $\bar{\mathcal{A}} = \text{fft}(\mathcal{A}, [\ ], 3)$. In a similar fashion, we can compute $\mathcal{A}$ from $\bar{\mathcal{A}}$ using the inverse FFT, i.e., $\mathcal{A} = \text{ifft}(\bar{\mathcal{A}}, [\ ], 3)$. In particular, we denote $\bar{A} \in \mathbb{C}^{n_1 n_3 \times n_2 n_3}$ as a block-diagonal matrix with its i-th block on the diagonal as the i-th frontal slice $\bar{A}^{(i)}$ of $\bar{\mathcal{A}}$, and we define the block-circulant matrix $\text{bcirc}(\mathcal{A}) \in \mathbb{R}^{n_1 n_3 \times n_2 n_3}$ of $\mathcal{A}$:

$$\bar{A} = \text{bdiag}(\bar{\mathcal{A}}) = \begin{bmatrix} \bar{A}^{(1)} & & & \\ & \bar{A}^{(2)} & & \\ & & \ddots & \\ & & & \bar{A}^{(n_3)} \end{bmatrix},$$

$$\text{bcirc}(\mathcal{A}) = \begin{bmatrix} A^{(1)} & A^{(n_3)} & \cdots & A^{(2)} \\ A^{(2)} & A^{(1)} & \cdots & A^{(3)} \\ \vdots & \vdots & \ddots & \vdots \\ A^{(n_3)} & A^{(n_3-1)} & \cdots & A^{(1)} \end{bmatrix}, \tag{6.9}$$

where `bdiag` is an operator which maps the tensor $\bar{\mathcal{A}}$ to the block-diagonal matrix $\bar{A}$. Just like the circulant matrix which can be diagonalized by DFT, the block-circulant matrix can be block-diagonalized, i.e.,

$$(F_{n_3} \otimes I_{n_1}) \cdot \text{bcirc}(\mathcal{A}) \cdot (F_{n_3}^{-1} \otimes I_{n_2}) = \bar{A}, \tag{6.10}$$

where $\otimes$ denotes the Kronecker product and $(F_{n_3} \otimes I_{n_1})/\sqrt{n_3}$ is unitary. By using Lemma 6.1, we have

$$\bar{A}^{(1)} \in \mathbb{R}^{n_1 \times n_2}, \quad \text{conj}(\bar{A}^{(i)}) = \bar{A}^{(n_3-i+2)}, \ i = 2, \cdots, \left\lfloor \frac{n_3 + 1}{2} \right\rfloor. \tag{6.11}$$

Conversely, for any given $\bar{\mathcal{A}} \in \mathbb{C}^{n_1 \times n_2 \times n_3}$ satisfying (6.11), there exists a real tensor $\mathcal{A} \in \mathbb{R}^{n_1 \times n_2 \times n_3}$ such that (6.10) holds. Also, by using (6.6), we have the following properties which will be used frequently:

$$\|\mathcal{A}\|_F = \frac{1}{\sqrt{n_3}} \|\bar{A}\|_F, \qquad \langle \mathcal{A}, \mathcal{B} \rangle = \frac{1}{n_3} \langle \bar{A}, \bar{B} \rangle. \tag{6.12}$$

6.2.3 T-product

For $\mathcal{A} \in \mathbb{R}^{n_1 \times n_2 \times n_3}$, we define

$$
\texttt{unfold}(\mathcal{A}) = \begin{bmatrix} A^{(1)} \\ A^{(2)} \\ \vdots \\ A^{(n_3)} \end{bmatrix}, \quad \texttt{fold}(\texttt{unfold}(\mathcal{A})) = \mathcal{A},
$$

where the unfold operator maps $\mathcal{A}$ to a matrix of size $n_1 n_3 \times n_2$ and fold is its inverse operator.

Definition 6.1. (T-product) [13] Let $\mathcal{A} \in \mathbb{R}^{n_1 \times n_2 \times n_3}$ and $\mathcal{B} \in \mathbb{R}^{n_2 \times l \times n_3}$. Then the t-product $\mathcal{A} * \mathcal{B}$ is defined to be a tensor of size $n_1 \times l \times n_3$,

$$
\mathcal{A} * \mathcal{B} = \texttt{fold}(\texttt{bcirc}(\mathcal{A}) \cdot \texttt{unfold}(\mathcal{B})). \tag{6.13}
$$

The t-product can be understood from two perspectives. First, in the original domain, a three-way tensor of size $n_1 \times n_2 \times n_3$ can be regarded as an $n_1 \times n_2$ matrix with each entry being a tube that lies in the third dimension. Thus, the t-product is analogous to the matrix multiplication except that the circular convolution replaces the multiplication operation between the elements. Note that the t-product reduces to the standard matrix multiplication when $n_3 = 1$. This is a key observation which makes the TPCA model shown later involve the matrix PCA as a special case. Second, the t-product is equivalent to the matrix multiplication in the Fourier domain; that is, $\mathcal{C} = \mathcal{A} * \mathcal{B}$ is equivalent to $\bar{C} = \bar{A}\bar{B}$ due to (6.10). Indeed, $\mathcal{C} = \mathcal{A} * \mathcal{B}$ implies

$$
\texttt{unfold}(\mathcal{C}) = \texttt{bcirc}(\mathcal{A}) \cdot \texttt{unfold}(\mathcal{B}) = (F_{n_3}^{-1} \otimes I_{n_1})
$$
$$
\cdot ((F_{n_3} \otimes I_{n_1}) \cdot \texttt{bcirc}(\mathcal{A}) \cdot (F_{n_3}^{-1} \otimes I_{n_2})) \cdot ((F_{n_3} \otimes I_{n_2}) \cdot \texttt{unfold}(\mathcal{B}))
$$
$$
= (F_{n_3}^{-1} \otimes I_{n_1}) \cdot \bar{A} \cdot \texttt{unfold}(\bar{\mathcal{B}}), \tag{6.14}
$$

where (6.14) uses (6.10). Left multiplying both sides with $(F_{n_3} \otimes I_{n_1})$ leads to $\texttt{unfold}(\bar{\mathcal{C}}) = \bar{A} \cdot \texttt{unfold}(\bar{\mathcal{B}})$. This is equivalent to $\bar{C} = \bar{A}\bar{B}$. This property suggests an efficient way based on FFT to compute the t-product instead of using (6.13). See Algorithm 1.

The t-product enjoys many similar properties to the matrix–matrix product. For example, the t-product is associative, i.e., $\mathcal{A} * (\mathcal{B} * \mathcal{C}) = (\mathcal{A} * \mathcal{B}) * \mathcal{C}$. We also need some other concepts on tensors extended from the matrix cases.

Definition 6.2. (Conjugate transpose) The conjugate transpose of a tensor $\mathcal{A} \in \mathbb{C}^{n_1 \times n_2 \times n_3}$ is the tensor $\mathcal{A}^* \in \mathbb{C}^{n_2 \times n_1 \times n_3}$ obtained by conjugate transposing each of the frontal slices and then reversing the order of transposed frontal slices 2 through n_3.

Algorithm 1 Tensor–tensor product.

Input: $\mathcal{A} \in \mathbb{R}^{n_1 \times n_2 \times n_3}$, $\mathcal{B} \in \mathbb{R}^{n_2 \times l \times n_3}$.
Output: $\mathcal{C} = \mathcal{A} * \mathcal{B} \in \mathbb{R}^{n_1 \times l \times n_3}$.

1. Compute $\bar{\mathcal{A}} = \texttt{fft}(\mathcal{A}, [\,], 3)$ and $\bar{\mathcal{B}} = \texttt{fft}(\mathcal{B}, [\,], 3)$.

2. Compute each frontal slice of $\bar{\mathcal{C}}$ by

$$\bar{C}^{(i)} = \begin{cases} \bar{A}^{(i)} \bar{B}^{(i)}, & i = 1, \cdots, \lceil \frac{n_3+1}{2} \rceil, \\ \texttt{conj}(\bar{C}^{(n_3-i+2)}), & i = \lceil \frac{n_3+1}{2} \rceil + 1, \cdots, n_3. \end{cases}$$

3. Compute $\mathcal{C} = \texttt{ifft}(\bar{\mathcal{C}}, [\,], 3)$.

The tensor conjugate transpose extends the tensor transpose [13] for complex tensors. As an example, let $\mathcal{A} \in \mathbb{C}^{n_1 \times n_2 \times 4}$ and let its frontal slices be A_1, A_2, A_3, and A_4. Then

$$\mathcal{A}^* = \texttt{fold}\left(\begin{bmatrix} A_1^* \\ A_4^* \\ A_3^* \\ A_2^* \end{bmatrix} \right).$$

Definition 6.3. (Identity tensor) [13] The identity tensor $\mathcal{I} \in \mathbb{R}^{n \times n \times n_3}$ is the tensor with its first frontal slice being the $n \times n$ identity matrix, other frontal slices being all zeros.

It is clear that $\mathcal{A} * \mathcal{I} = \mathcal{A}$ and $\mathcal{I} * \mathcal{A} = \mathcal{A}$ given the appropriate dimensions. The tensor $\bar{\mathcal{I}} = \texttt{fft}(\mathcal{I}, [\,], 3)$ is a tensor with each frontal slice being the identity matrix.

Definition 6.4. (Orthogonal tensor) [13] A tensor $\mathcal{Q} \in \mathbb{R}^{n \times n \times n_3}$ is orthogonal if it satisfies $\mathcal{Q}^* * \mathcal{Q} = \mathcal{Q} * \mathcal{Q}^* = \mathcal{I}$.

Definition 6.5. (f-Diagonal tensor) [13] A tensor is called f-diagonal if each of its frontal slices is a diagonal matrix.

These definitions are the basics to define t-SVD, the tensor rank, and the tensor nuclear norm in Section 6.3, which serve key roles in the TPCA formulations.

6.2.4 Summary

In this section, we mainly introduced the commonly used notations, definitions, and preliminaries used throughout the whole chapter. For example, the conjugate transpose of a tensor is obtained by conjugate transposing each of the frontal slices and then reversing the order of transposed frontal slices 2 through the third direction. An identity tensor is a tensor with its first frontal slice being an identity matrix, other frontal slices being all zeros. An orthogonal tensor is similar to an orthogonal matrix. In an f-diagonal tensor, each frontal slice is a diagonal matrix. Besides, we also introduce two key operations/transforms in detail, namely DFT and the t-product, which are the basics to define t-SVD, the tensor rank, and the tensor nuclear norm in Section 6.3.

6.3 Tensor PCA for Gaussian-noisy data

In this section, we consider the Gaussian-noisy data where the observed data $\mathcal{X} = \mathcal{L}_0 + \mathcal{E}_0 \in \mathbb{R}^{n_1 \times n_2 \times n_3}$ consist of a low-rank tensor $\mathcal{L}_0$ and Gaussian noise $\mathcal{E}_0$. In the following, we will ask the following question: how can we exactly recover $\mathcal{L}_0$ or find a good approximation to $\mathcal{L}_0$ by minimizing the TPCA problem $\min_{\text{rank}(\mathcal{L}) \leq k} \|\mathcal{L} - \mathcal{X}\|_F^2$, where rank $(\mathcal{L})$ denotes the tensor rank of $\mathcal{L}$, $\|\mathcal{L}\|_F$ denotes the Frobenius norm of tensor $\mathcal{L}$ defined in Section 6.2.1, and k denotes the estimated tensor rank of $\mathcal{L}_0$? To solve this problem, we will first introduce two important definitions, namely t-SVD and the tensor rank, in Section 6.3.1. Then we analyze the TPCA problem in Section 6.3.2. Finally, we summarize the whole section in Section 6.3.3.

6.3.1 Tensor rank and tensor nuclear norm

Based on the definition of tensor product, orthogonal tensor, and f-diagonal tensor, we can define the t-SVD of any tensor $\mathcal{A} \in \mathbb{R}^{n_1 \times n_2 \times n_3}$ as in Theorem 6.2.

Theorem 6.2. *(t-SVD) [2] Let $\mathcal{A} \in \mathbb{R}^{n_1 \times n_2 \times n_3}$. Then it can be factorized as*

$$\mathcal{A} = \mathcal{U} * \mathcal{S} * \mathcal{V}^*, \tag{6.15}$$

where $\mathcal{U} \in \mathbb{R}^{n_1 \times n_1 \times n_3}$, $\mathcal{V} \in \mathbb{R}^{n_2 \times n_2 \times n_3}$ are orthogonal and $\mathcal{S} \in \mathbb{R}^{n_1 \times n_2 \times n_3}$ is an f-diagonal tensor.

Proof. The proof is by construction. Recall that (6.10) holds and $\bar{A}^{(i)}$'s satisfy the property (6.11). Then we construct the SVD of each $\bar{A}^{(i)}$ in the following way. For $i = 1, \cdots, \lceil \frac{n_3+1}{2} \rceil$, let $\bar{A}^{(i)} = \bar{U}^{(i)} \bar{S}^{(i)} (\bar{V}^{(i)})^*$ be the full SVD of $\bar{A}^{(i)}$. Here the singular values in $\bar{S}^{(i)}$ are real. For $i = \lceil \frac{n_3+1}{2} \rceil + 1, \cdots, n_3$, let $\bar{U}^{(i)} = \text{conj}(\bar{U}^{(n_3-i+2)})$, $\bar{S}^{(i)} = \bar{S}^{(n_3-i+2)}$, and $\bar{V}^{(i)} = \text{conj}(\bar{V}^{(n_3-i+2)})$. Then, it is easy to verify that $\bar{A}^{(i)} = \bar{U}^{(i)} \bar{S}^{(i)} (\bar{V}^{(i)})^*$ gives the full SVD of $\bar{A}^{(i)}$ for $i = \lceil \frac{n_3+1}{2} \rceil + 1, \cdots, n_3$. Then,

$$\bar{A} = \bar{U} \bar{S} \bar{V}^*. \tag{6.16}$$

By the construction of $\bar{U}$, $\bar{S}$, and $\bar{V}$ and Lemma 6.1, $(F_{n_3}^{-1} \otimes I_{n_1}) \cdot \bar{U} \cdot (F_{n_3} \otimes I_{n_1})$, $(F_{n_3}^{-1} \otimes I_{n_1}) \cdot \bar{S} \cdot (F_{n_3} \otimes I_{n_2})$, and $(F_{n_3}^{-1} \otimes I_{n_2}) \cdot \bar{V} \cdot (F_{n_3} \otimes I_{n_2})$ are real block-circulant matrices. Then we can obtain an expression for $\text{bcirc}(\mathcal{A})$ by applying the appropriate matrix $(F_{n_3}^{-1} \otimes I_{n_1})$ to the left and the appropriate matrix $(F_{n_3} \otimes I_{n_2})$

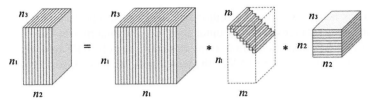

FIGURE 6.1

An illustration of the t-SVD of an $n_1 \times n_2 \times n_3$ tensor [14].

to the right of each of the matrices in (6.16) and folding up the result. This gives a decomposition of the form $\mathcal{U} * \mathcal{S} * \mathcal{V}^*$, where $\mathcal{U}$, $\mathcal{S}$, and $\mathcal{V}$ are real. $\qquad\square$

Theorem 6.2 shows that any three-way tensor can be factorized into three components, including two orthogonal tensors and an f-diagonal tensor. See Fig. 6.1 for an intuitive illustration of the t-SVD factorization. T-SVD reduces to the matrix SVD when $n_3 = 1$. This proof further leads to a more efficient way for computing t-SVD shown in Algorithm 2.

Algorithm 2 T-SVD.

Input: $\mathcal{A} \in \mathbb{R}^{n_1 \times n_2 \times n_3}$.
Output: T-SVD components $\mathcal{U}$, $\mathcal{S}$, and $\mathcal{V}$ of $\mathcal{A}$.

1. Compute $\bar{\mathcal{A}} = \mathtt{fft}(\mathcal{A}, [\ ], 3)$.

2. Compute each frontal slice of $\bar{\mathcal{U}}$, $\bar{\mathcal{S}}$, and $\bar{\mathcal{V}}$ from $\bar{\mathcal{A}}$ by

   for $i = 1, \cdots, \lceil \frac{n_3+1}{2} \rceil$ **do**

   $\qquad [\bar{U}^{(i)}, \bar{S}^{(i)}, \bar{V}^{(i)}] = \mathrm{SVD}(\bar{A}^{(i)});$

   end for

   for $i = \lceil \frac{n_3+1}{2} \rceil + 1, \cdots, n_3$ **do**

   $\qquad \bar{U}^{(i)} = \mathtt{conj}(\bar{U}^{(n_3-i+2)});$

   $\qquad \bar{S}^{(i)} = \bar{S}^{(n_3-i+2)};$

   $\qquad \bar{V}^{(i)} = \mathtt{conj}(\bar{V}^{(n_3-i+2)});$

   end for

3. Compute $\mathcal{U} = \mathtt{ifft}(\bar{\mathcal{U}}, [\ ], 3)$, $\mathcal{S} = \mathtt{ifft}(\bar{\mathcal{S}}, [\ ], 3)$, and $\mathcal{V} = \mathtt{ifft}(\bar{\mathcal{V}}, [\ ], 3)$.

It is a convention that the singular values of a matrix are arranged in decreasing order. Let $\mathcal{A} = \mathcal{U} * \mathcal{S} * \mathcal{V}^*$ be the t-SVD of $\mathcal{A} \in \mathbb{R}^{n_1 \times n_2 \times n_3}$. The entries on the diagonal of the first frontal slice $\mathcal{S}(:, :, 1)$ of $\mathcal{S}$ are also decreasing, i.e.,

$$\mathcal{S}(1, 1, 1) \geq \mathcal{S}(2, 2, 1) \geq \cdots \geq \mathcal{S}(n', n', 1) \geq 0, \qquad (6.17)$$

where $n' = \min(n_1, n_2)$. The above property holds since the inverse DFT gives

$$\mathcal{S}(i, i, 1) = \frac{1}{n_3} \sum_{j=1}^{n_3} \bar{\mathcal{S}}(i, i, j), \qquad (6.18)$$

and the entries on the diagonal of $\bar{\mathcal{S}}(:, :, j)$ are the singular values of $\bar{\mathcal{A}}(:, :, j)$. This actually means that the tensor nuclear norm depends only on the first frontal slice $\mathcal{S}(:, :, 1)$, which will be further analyzed later. Thus, we call the entries on the diagonal of $\mathcal{S}(:, :, 1)$ the singular values of $\mathcal{A}$.

Definition 6.6. (Tensor tubal rank) [1,15,16] For $\mathcal{A} \in \mathbb{R}^{n_1 \times n_2 \times n_3}$, the tensor tubal rank, denoted as $\mathrm{rank}_t(\mathcal{A})$, is defined as the number of nonzero singular tubes of $\mathcal{S}$, where $\mathcal{S}$ is from the t-SVD of $\mathcal{A} = \mathcal{U} * \mathcal{S} * \mathcal{V}^*$. We can write

$$\mathrm{rank}_t(\mathcal{A}) = \#\{i, \mathcal{S}(i, i, :) \neq \mathbf{0}\}.$$

By using property (6.18), the tensor tubal rank is determined by the first frontal slice $\mathcal{S}(:, :, 1)$ of $\mathcal{S}$, i.e.,

$$\mathrm{rank}_t(\mathcal{A}) = \#\{i, \mathcal{S}(i, i, 1) \neq 0\}.$$

Hence, the tensor tubal rank is equivalent to the number of nonzero singular values of $\mathcal{A}$. This property is the same as the matrix case.

Based on tubal rank, one can define the skinny t-SVD, which will be used subsequently.

Definition 6.7. (Skinny t-SVD) [3,4] For any $\mathcal{A} \in \mathbb{R}^{n_1 \times n_2 \times n_3}$, it can be factorized by t-SVD as $\mathcal{A} = \mathcal{U} * \mathcal{S} * \mathcal{V}^*$, where $\mathcal{U} \in \mathbb{R}^{n_1 \times n_1 \times n_3}$ and $\mathcal{V} \in \mathbb{R}^{n_2 \times n_2 \times n_3}$ are orthogonal and $\mathcal{S} \in \mathbb{R}^{n_1 \times n_2 \times n_3}$ is f-diagonal. Then the skinny t-SVD of $\mathcal{A}$ is $\mathcal{A} = \mathcal{U}_s * \mathcal{S}_s * \mathcal{V}_s^*$, where $\mathcal{U}_s = \mathcal{U}(:, 1 : r, :)$, $\mathcal{S}_s = \mathcal{S}(1 : r, 1 : r, :)$, and $\mathcal{V}_s = \mathcal{V}(:, 1 : r, :)$, in which r denotes the tensor tubal rank of $\mathcal{A}$.

Then we define tensor average rank as follows. This rank is closely related to the tensor tubal rank. Later, we will define a new tensor nuclear norm in Definition 6.9 which is the convex surrogate of the tensor average rank.

Definition 6.8. (Tensor average rank) [2] For $\mathcal{A} \in \mathbb{R}^{n_1 \times n_2 \times n_3}$, the tensor average rank, denoted as $\mathrm{rank}_a(\mathcal{A})$, is defined as

$$\mathrm{rank}_a(\mathcal{A}) = \frac{1}{n_3} \mathrm{rank}(\texttt{bcirc}(\mathcal{A})). \qquad (6.19)$$

The above definition has a factor $\frac{1}{n_3}$. Note that this factor is crucial as it guarantees that the convex envelope of the tensor average rank within a certain set is the tensor nuclear norm defined later. The underlying reason for this factor is the t-product definition. Each element of $\mathcal{A}$ is repeated n_3 times in the block-circulant matrix $\texttt{bcirc}(\mathcal{A})$ used in the t-product.

Then we define the tensor nuclear norm, denoted as $\|\mathcal{A}\|_*$, as the dual norm of the tensor spectral norm. For any $\mathcal{B} \in \mathbb{R}^{n_1 \times n_2 \times n_3}$ and $\tilde{B} \in \mathbb{C}^{n_1 n_3 \times n_2 n_3}$, we have

$$\|\mathcal{A}\|_* := \sup_{\|\mathcal{B}\| \leq 1} \langle \mathcal{A}, \mathcal{B} \rangle \overset{\text{\textcircled{1}}}{=} \sup_{\|\bar{B}\| \leq 1} \frac{1}{n_3} \langle \bar{A}, \bar{B} \rangle \overset{\text{\textcircled{2}}}{\leq} \frac{1}{n_3} \sup_{\|\tilde{B}\| \leq 1} |\langle \bar{A}, \tilde{B} \rangle| \overset{\text{\textcircled{3}}}{=} \frac{1}{n_3} \|\bar{A}\|_*$$

$$\overset{\text{\textcircled{4}}}{=} \frac{1}{n_3} \|\text{bcirc}(\mathcal{A})\|_* , \tag{6.20}$$

where ① is from (6.12), ② is due to the fact that $\bar{B}$ is a block-diagonal matrix in $\mathbb{C}^{n_1 n_3 \times n_2 n_3}$ while $\tilde{B}$ is an arbitrary matrix in $\mathbb{C}^{n_1 n_3 \times n_2 n_3}$, ③ uses the fact that the matrix nuclear norm is the dual norm of the matrix spectral norm, and ④ uses (6.10) and (6.6). Now we show that there exists $\mathcal{B} \in \mathbb{R}^{n_1 \times n_2 \times n_3}$ such that the equality ② holds and thus $\|\mathcal{A}\|_* = \frac{1}{n_3} \|\text{bcirc}(\mathcal{A})\|_*$. Let $\mathcal{A} = \mathcal{U} * \mathcal{S} * \mathcal{V}^*$ be the t-SVD of $\mathcal{A}$ and $\mathcal{B} = \mathcal{U} * \mathcal{V}^*$. We have

$$\langle \mathcal{A}, \mathcal{B} \rangle = \langle \mathcal{U} * \mathcal{S} * \mathcal{V}^*, \mathcal{U} * \mathcal{V}^* \rangle = \frac{1}{n_3} \left\langle \overline{\mathcal{U} * \mathcal{S} * \mathcal{V}^*}, \overline{\mathcal{U} * \mathcal{V}^*} \right\rangle$$

$$= \frac{1}{n_3} \left\langle \bar{U} \bar{S} \bar{V}^*, \bar{U} \bar{V}^* \right\rangle = \frac{1}{n_3} \text{Tr}(\bar{S}) = \frac{1}{n_3} \|\bar{A}\|_* = \frac{1}{n_3} \|\text{bcirc}(\mathcal{A})\|_* . \tag{6.21}$$

Therefore, we have $\|\mathcal{A}\|_* = \frac{1}{n_3} \|\text{bcirc}(\mathcal{A})\|_*$. On the other hand, by (6.21), we have

$$\|\mathcal{A}\|_* = \langle \mathcal{U} * \mathcal{S} * \mathcal{V}^*, \mathcal{U} * \mathcal{V}^* \rangle$$

$$= \langle \mathcal{U}^* * \mathcal{U} * \mathcal{S}, \mathcal{V}^* * \mathcal{V} \rangle = \langle \mathcal{S}, \mathcal{I} \rangle = \sum_{i=1}^{r} \mathcal{S}(i, i, 1), \tag{6.22}$$

where $r = \text{rank}_t(\mathcal{A})$ is the tubal rank. Thus, we define tensor nuclear norm as follows.

Definition 6.9. (Tensor nuclear norm)[2,17] Let $\mathcal{A} = \mathcal{U} * \mathcal{S} * \mathcal{V}^*$ be the t-SVD of $\mathcal{A} \in \mathbb{R}^{n_1 \times n_2 \times n_3}$ and $r = \text{rank}_t(\mathcal{A})$. The tensor nuclear norm of $\mathcal{A}$ is defined as

$$\|\mathcal{A}\|_* := \langle \mathcal{S}, \mathcal{I} \rangle = \sum_{i=1}^{r} \mathcal{S}(i, i, 1) = \frac{1}{n_3} \|\text{bcirc}(\mathcal{A})\|_* = \frac{1}{n_3} \|\bar{A}\|_* . \tag{6.23}$$

From (6.22), it can be seen that only the information in the first frontal slice of $\mathcal{S}$ is used when defining the tensor nuclear norm. Note that this is the first work which directly uses the singular values $\mathcal{S}(:,:,1)$ of a tensor to define the tensor nuclear norm. Such a definition makes it consistent with the matrix nuclear norm.

It is known that the matrix nuclear norm $\|A\|_*$ is the convex envelope of the matrix rank within the set $\{A \mid \|A\| \leq 1\}$ [18]. Now we show that the tensor average rank and tensor nuclear norm have the same relationship.

Theorem 6.3. [2] On the set $\{\mathcal{A} \in \mathbb{R}^{n_1 \times n_2 \times n_3} \mid \|\mathcal{A}\| \leq 1\}$, the convex envelope of the tensor average rank $\text{rank}_a(\mathcal{A})$ is the tensor nuclear norm $\|\mathcal{A}\|_*$.

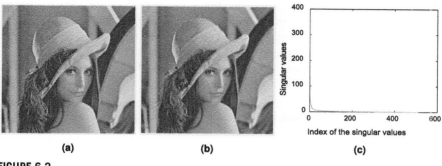

FIGURE 6.2

Color images can be approximated by low tubal rank tensors [2]. (a) A color image can be modeled as a tensor $\mathcal{M} \in \mathbb{R}^{512 \times 512 \times 3}$. (b) Approximation by a tensor with tubal rank $r = 50$. (c) Plot of the singular values of $\mathcal{M}$.

We would like to emphasize that the proposed tensor spectral norm, tensor nuclear norm, and tensor ranks are not arbitrarily defined. They are rigorously induced by the t-product and t-SVD. These concepts and their relationships are consistent with the matrix cases. This is important for the proofs, analysis, and computation in optimization.

6.3.2 Analysis of tensor PCA on Gaussian-noisy data

Based on the tensor tubal rank, we now define the TPCA problem in detail:

$$\min_{\mathrm{rank}_t(\mathcal{L}) \leq k} \|\mathcal{L} - \mathcal{X}\|_F^2, \tag{6.24}$$

where the observed data $\mathcal{X} = \mathcal{L}_0 + \mathcal{E}_0 \in \mathbb{R}^{n_1 \times n_2 \times n_3}$ consist of a low-rank tensor $\mathcal{L}_0$ and Gaussian noise $\mathcal{E}_0$. For this problem, we can prove that this problem has a closed-form solution stated in Theorem 6.4.

Theorem 6.4. *[1,2] Suppose $\mathcal{X} = \mathcal{U} * \mathcal{S} * \mathcal{V}^*$ is the t-SVD of $\mathcal{X}$. Then $\mathcal{L}_k = \sum_{i=1}^{k} \mathcal{U}(:, i, :) * \mathcal{S}(i, i, :) * \mathcal{V}(:, i, :)^*$ for some $k < \min(n_1, n_2)$ is the closed-form solution to problem (6.24).*

The proof can be found in [1,2]. Theorem 6.4 can be intuitively understood: since the singular values in $\mathcal{S}$ have the decreasing property as shown in (6.17), $\mathcal{L}_k$ contains the first top-k singular values and thus gives the smallest approximation error $\|\mathcal{L}_k - \mathcal{X}\|_F^2 = \sum_{i=k}^{r} \mathcal{S}(i, i, 1)$. For the details, please refer to [2]. This is very similar to PCA on matrix data. Fig. 6.2 gives an example to show that a color image can be well approximated by a low tubal rank tensor since most of the singular values of the corresponding tensor are relatively small.

Besides the tensor tubal rank proposed in [2,13,19], there are actually several different definitions of tensor rank because of the underlying multiway of tensor data and nonunified definitions of tensor ranks. For instance, the CP rank [20], defined as the smallest number of factors in rank-1 tensor decomposition. The Tucker rank [21] is defined on the unfolding matrices to depict the rank of a tensor. But there are some connections between different tensor ranks and these properties imply that the low tubal rank or low average rank assumptions are reasonable for their applications in real visual data. First, $\text{rank}_a(\mathcal{A}) \leq \text{rank}_t(\mathcal{A})$. Indeed,

$$\text{rank}_a(\mathcal{A}) = \frac{1}{n_3}\text{rank}\left(\bar{A}\right) \leq \max_{i=1,\cdots,n_3} \text{rank}\left(\bar{A}^{(i)}\right) = \text{rank}_t(\mathcal{A}),$$

where the first equality uses (6.10). This implies that a low tubal rank tensor always has low average rank. Second, let $\text{rank}_{tc}(\mathcal{A}) = \left(\text{rank}(A^{\{1\}}), \text{rank}(A^{\{2\}}), \text{rank}(A^{\{3\}})\right)$, where $A^{\{i\}}$ is the mode-i matricization of $\mathcal{A}$ which unfolds and reorganizes $\mathcal{A} \in \mathbb{R}^{n_1 \times n_2 \times \cdots \times n_i \times \cdots n_k}$ along the i-th direction as a matrix $A^{\{i\}} \in \mathbb{R}^{n_i \times \prod_{j \neq i} n_j}$, be the Tucker rank of $\mathcal{A}$. Then $\text{rank}_a(\mathcal{A}) \leq \text{rank}\left(A^{\{1\}}\right)$. This implies that a tensor with low Tucker rank has low average rank. The low Tucker rank assumption used in some applications, e.g., image completion [22], is applicable to the low average rank assumption. Third, if the CP rank of a three-way tensor $\mathcal{A}$ is r, then its tubal rank is at most r [10]. Let $\mathcal{A} = \sum_{i=1}^{r} a_i^{(1)} \circ a_i^{(2)} \circ a_i^{(3)}$, where $\circ$ denotes the outer product, be the CP decomposition of $\mathcal{A}$. Then $\bar{\mathcal{A}} = \sum_{i=1}^{r} a_i^{(1)} \circ a_i^{(2)} \circ \bar{a}_i^{(3)}$, where $\bar{a}_i^{(3)} = \text{fft}(a_i^{(3)})$. So $\bar{\mathcal{A}}$ has the CP rank at most r, and each frontal slice of $\bar{\mathcal{A}}$ is the sum of r rank-1 matrices. Thus, the tubal rank of $\mathcal{A}$ is at most r. In summary, the low tubal or average rank assumption in this section is often weaker than the low Tucker rank and low CP rank assumptions, and could better characterize the low-rank structure in data.

6.3.3 Summary

In this section, we introduced t-SVD and further define the tensor nuclear norm, tensor tubal rank, and tensor average rank. Based on these definitions, we analyze the solution to the TPCA problem. We also discuss the relations among the tensor rank in this section and other kinds of tensor rank, such as the CP rank and the Tucker rank.

6.4 Tensor PCA for sparsely corrupted data

The problem that we study in this section is to recover a low tubal rank tensor $\mathcal{L}_0$ from highly corrupted measurements $\mathcal{X} = \mathcal{L}_0 + \mathcal{E}_0$, where $\mathcal{L}_0$ is low-tubal rank clean data and $\mathcal{E}_0$ is sparse noise instead of the Gaussian noise in Section 6.3. We provide two methods to handle this problem. The first method is R-TPCA [2], which assumes that the clean data $\mathcal{L}_0$ only locate on a single tensor subspace. The second one is TLRR [3], which can handle the case that the data $\mathcal{L}_0$ are drawn from multiple tensor subspaces. Moreover, TLRR can also cluster tensor data while R-TPCA cannot. We will discuss these two methods and their differences in detail in the following sections.

This section is structured as follows. Section 6.4.1 introduces R-TPCA, including its model, recovery theory, and optimization algorithm. Then in Section 6.4.2, we elaborate on TLRR, including its model, clustering analysis, recovery theory, optimization algorithm, and dictionary construction methods. Next, in Section 6.4.3, we introduce real applications, such as image/video denoising and data clustering, of these TPCA methods. Finally, Section 6.4.4, we summarize the whole section.

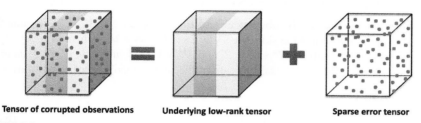

Tensor of corrupted observations   Underlying low-rank tensor   Sparse error tensor

FIGURE 6.3

Illustrations of R-TPCA: low-rank and sparse tensor decomposition from noisy tensor observations [2].

6.4.1 Robust tensor PCA

Equipped with these definitions in Sections 6.2 and 6.3, we study the following R-TPCA problem, which aims to recover the low-tubal rank component $\mathcal{L}_0$ and the sparse component $\mathcal{E}_0$ from noisy observations $\mathcal{X} = \mathcal{L}_0 + \mathcal{E}_0 \in \mathbb{R}^{n_1 \times n_2 \times n_3}$ by convex optimization:

$$\min_{\mathcal{L}, \mathcal{E}} \ \|\mathcal{L}\|_* + \lambda \|\mathcal{E}\|_1, \ \text{s.t.} \ \mathcal{X} = \mathcal{L} + \mathcal{E}, \tag{6.25}$$

where $\|\mathcal{L}\|_*$ is the tensor nuclear norm and λ is a constant. Such a model can be illustrated by Fig. 6.3. Lu et al. [2] proved that under certain incoherence conditions, the solution to (6.25) perfectly recovers the low-rank and sparse components, provided of course that the tubal rank of $\mathcal{L}_0$ is not too large and that $\mathcal{E}_0$ is reasonably sparse. A remarkable fact, like in R-PCA, is that (6.25) has no tuning parameter either. The analysis in [2] shows that $\lambda = 1/\sqrt{\max(n_1, n_2)n_3}$ guarantees the exact recovery when $\mathcal{L}_0$ and $\mathcal{E}_0$ satisfy certain assumptions. As a special case, if $\mathcal{X}$ reduces to a matrix ($n_3 = 1$ in this case), all the new tensor concepts reduce to the matrix cases: the R-TPCA model (6.25) reduces to R-PCA, and also the recovery guarantee in Theorem 6.5 reduces to Theorem 1.1 in [8]. Another advantage of (6.25) is that it can be solved by polynomial-time algorithms.

6.4.1.1 Tensor incoherence conditions

Recovering the low-rank and sparse components from their sum suffers from an identifiability issue. For example, the tensor $\mathcal{X}$, with $x_{ijk} = 1$ when $i = j = k = 1$ and zeros everywhere else, is both low-rank and sparse. One is not able to identify the

low-rank component and the sparse component in this case. To avoid such pathological situations, we need to assume that the low-rank component $\mathcal{L}_0$ is not sparse. To
this end, we assume $\mathcal{L}_0$ to satisfy some incoherence conditions. We denote $\mathring{\mathbf{e}}_i$ as the
tensor column basis, which is a tensor of size $n_1 \times 1 \times n_3$ with its $(i, 1, 1)$-th entry
equaling 1 and the rest equaling 0 [10]. We also define the tensor tube basis $\dot{\mathbf{e}}_k$, which
is a tensor of size $1 \times 1 \times n_3$ with its $(1, 1, k)$-th entry equaling 1 and all the rest
equaling 0. The following skinny t-SVD is defined in Definition 6.7 in Section 6.3.

Definition 6.10. (Tensor incoherence conditions) For $\mathcal{L}_0 \in \mathbb{R}^{n_1 \times n_2 \times n_3}$, assume that
$\text{rank}_t(\mathcal{L}_0) = r$ and it has the skinny t-SVD $\mathcal{L}_0 = \mathcal{U} * \mathcal{S} * \mathcal{V}^*$, where $\mathcal{U} \in \mathbb{R}^{n_1 \times r \times n_3}$
and $\mathcal{V} \in \mathbb{R}^{n_2 \times r \times n_3}$ satisfy $\mathcal{U}^* * \mathcal{U} = \mathcal{I}$ and $\mathcal{V}^* * \mathcal{V} = \mathcal{I}$ and $\mathcal{S} \in \mathbb{R}^{r \times r \times n_3}$ is an f-
diagonal tensor. Then $\mathcal{L}_0$ is said to satisfy the tensor incoherence conditions with
parameter μ if

$$\max_{i=1,\cdots,n_1} \left\| \mathcal{U}^* * \mathring{\mathbf{e}}_i \right\|_F \leq \sqrt{\frac{\mu r}{n_1 n_3}}, \tag{6.26}$$

$$\max_{j=1,\cdots,n_2} \left\| \mathcal{V}^* * \mathring{\mathbf{e}}_j \right\|_F \leq \sqrt{\frac{\mu r}{n_2 n_3}}, \tag{6.27}$$

$$\left\| \mathcal{U} * \mathcal{V}^* \right\|_\infty \leq \sqrt{\frac{\mu r}{n_1 n_2 n_3^2}}. \tag{6.28}$$

The exact recovery guarantee of R-PCA [8] also requires some incoherence conditions. Due to property (6.12), conditions (6.26)–(6.27) have equivalent matrix forms
in the Fourier domain, and they are intuitively similar to the matrix incoherence conditions (1.2) in [8]. But the joint incoherence condition (6.28) is somewhat different
from the matrix case (1.3) in [8], since it does not have an equivalent matrix form in
the Fourier domain. As observed in [23], the joint incoherence condition is not necessary for low-rank matrix completion. However, for R-PCA, it is unavoidable for
polynomial-time algorithms. Another identifiability issue arises if the sparse tensor
$\mathcal{E}_0$ has low tubal rank. This can be avoided by assuming that the support of $\mathcal{E}_0$ is
uniformly distributed.

6.4.1.2 Exact recovery guarantee of R-TPCA

Now we show that the convex program (6.25) is able to perfectly recover the low-rank
and sparse components. We define $n_{(1)} = \max(n_1, n_2)$ and $n_{(2)} = \min(n_1, n_2)$.

Theorem 6.5. *[2] Suppose that $\mathcal{L}_0 \in \mathbb{R}^{n \times n \times n_3}$ obeys (6.26)–(6.28). Fix any $n \times n \times$
n_3 tensor $\mathcal{M}$ of signs. Suppose that the support set $\mathbf{\Omega}$ of $\mathcal{E}_0$ is uniformly distributed
among all sets of cardinality m and that $\text{sgn}\left([\mathcal{E}_0]_{ijk}\right) = [\mathcal{M}]_{ijk}$ for all $(i, j, k) \in \mathbf{\Omega}$.
Then, there exist universal constants $c_1, c_2 > 0$ such that with probability at least
$1 - c_1(nn_3)^{-c_2}$ (over the choice of support of $\mathcal{S}_0$), $(\mathcal{L}_0, \mathcal{E}_0)$ is the unique minimizer
to (6.25) with $\lambda = 1/\sqrt{nn_3}$, provided that*

$$\text{rank}_t(\mathcal{L}_0) \leq \frac{\rho_r n n_3}{\mu (\log(nn_3))^2} \text{ and } m \leq \rho_s n^2 n_3, \tag{6.29}$$

where ρ_r and ρ_s are positive constants. If $\mathcal{L}_0 \in \mathbb{R}^{n_1 \times n_2 \times n_3}$ has rectangular frontal slices, R-TPCA with $\lambda = 1/\sqrt{n_{(1)}n_3}$ succeeds with probability at least $1 - c_1(n_{(1)}n_3)^{-c_2}$, provided that $\text{rank}_t(\mathcal{L}_0) \leq \frac{\rho_r n_{(2)} n_3}{\mu(\log(n_{(1)}n_3))^2}$ and $m \leq \rho_s n_1 n_2 n_3$.

Its proof can be found in [2]. The above result shows that for incoherent $\mathcal{L}_0$, the perfect recovery is guaranteed with high probability for $\text{rank}_t(\mathcal{L}_0)$ at the order of $nn_3/(\mu(\log nn_3)^2)$ and a number of nonzero entries in $\mathcal{E}_0$ at the order of $n^2 n_3$. For $\mathcal{E}_0$, we make only one assumption on the random location distribution, but no assumption about the magnitudes or signs of the nonzero entries. Also R-TPCA is parameter-free. The mathematical analysis implies that the parameter $\lambda = 1/\sqrt{nn_3}$ leads to the correct recovery. Moreover, since the t-product of three-way tensors reduces to the standard matrix–matrix product when $n_3 = 1$, the tensor nuclear norm reduces to the matrix nuclear norm. Thus, R-PCA is a special case of R-TPCA and the guarantee of R-PCA in Theorem 1.1 in [8] is a special case of Theorem 6.5. Both the R-TPCA model and its theoretical guarantee are consistent with R-PCA. Compared with SNN [24], the R-TPCA extension of R-PCA is much more simple and elegant.

When considering the application of R-TPCA, the way for constructing a three-way tensor from data is important. The reason is that the t-product is orientation-dependent, and so is the tensor nuclear norm. Thus, the value of the tensor nuclear norm may be different if the tensor is rotated. For example, a three-channel color image can be formatted as three different sizes of tensors under different rotations. Therefore, when using R-TPCA, which is based on the tensor nuclear norm, one has to format the data into tensors in a proper way by leveraging some prior knowledge, e.g., the low tubal rank property of the constructed tensor.

Later, Lu et al. [16] extended R-TPCA from the DFT to any linear transform. Specifically, the t-product in [2] is based on a convolution-like operation, which is implemented using the DFT. In order to properly motivate this transform-based approach, Lu et al. [16] proposed a more general t-product definition which is based on the invertible linear transforms, such as a transform based on a random orthogonal matrix. Moreover, a t-product based on the proposed invertible linear transform also owns a matrix-algebra-based interpretation in the spirit of [2]. In this way, Lu et al. [16] proposed a more general R-TPCA model based on a new tensor rank and tensor nuclear norm induced by invertible linear transforms, and also proved that the generalized R-TPCA can also exactly recover the clean low-rank tensor in the presence of sparse noise.

6.4.1.3 Optimization algorithm

Problem (6.25) can be solved by the standard alternating direction method of multipliers (ADMM) [25]. A key step is to compute the proximal operator of the tensor nuclear norm

$$\min_{\mathcal{X} \in \mathbb{R}^{n_1 \times n_2 \times n_3}} \tau \|\mathcal{X}\|_* + \frac{1}{2} \|\mathcal{X} - \mathcal{Y}\|_F^2. \qquad (6.30)$$

Algorithm 3 Tensor singular value thresholding (t-SVT).

Input: $\mathcal{Y} \in \mathbb{R}^{n_1 \times n_2 \times n_3}$, $\tau > 0$.
Output: $\mathcal{D}_\tau(\mathcal{Y})$ as defined in (6.31).

1. Compute $\bar{\mathcal{Y}} = \text{fft}(\mathcal{Y}, [\ ], 3)$.

2. Perform matrix SVT on each frontal slice of $\bar{\mathcal{Y}}$ by

   for $i = 1, \cdots, \lceil \frac{n_3+1}{2} \rceil$ **do**

   $[U, S, V] = \text{SVD}(\bar{Y}^{(i)})$;

   $\bar{W}^{(i)} = U \cdot (S - \tau)_+ \cdot V^*$;

   end for

   for $i = \lceil \frac{n_3+1}{2} \rceil + 1, \cdots, n_3$ **do**

   $\bar{W}^{(i)} = \text{conj}(\bar{W}^{(n_3-i+2)})$;

   end for

3. Compute $\mathcal{D}_\tau(\mathcal{Y}) = \text{ifft}(\bar{\mathcal{W}}, [\ ], 3)$.

We show that it also has a closed-form solution like that for the proximal operator of the matrix nuclear norm. Let $\mathcal{Y} = \mathcal{U} * \mathcal{S} * \mathcal{V}^*$ be the t-SVD of $\mathcal{Y} \in \mathbb{R}^{n_1 \times n_2 \times n_3}$. For each $\tau > 0$, we define the tensor singular value thresholding (t-SVT) operator as follows:

$$\mathcal{D}_\tau(\mathcal{Y}) = \mathcal{U} * \mathcal{S}_\tau * \mathcal{V}^*, \tag{6.31}$$

where

$$\mathcal{S}_\tau = \text{ifft}((\bar{\mathcal{S}} - \tau)_+, [\ ], 3). \tag{6.32}$$

Note that $\bar{\mathcal{S}}$ is a real tensor. Above t_+ denotes the positive part of t, i.e., $t_+ = \max(t, 0)$. That is, this operator simply applies a soft-thresholding rule to the singular values $\bar{\mathcal{S}}$ (not $\mathcal{S}$) of the frontal slices of $\bar{\mathcal{Y}}$, effectively shrinking these towards zero. The t-SVT operator is the proximity operator associated with the tensor nuclear norm.

Theorem 6.6. *[2] For any $\tau > 0$ and $\mathcal{Y} \in \mathbb{R}^{n_1 \times n_2 \times n_3}$, the t-SVT operator (6.31) obeys*

$$\mathcal{D}_\tau(\mathcal{Y}) = \arg \min_{\mathcal{X} \in \mathbb{R}^{n_1 \times n_2 \times n_3}} \tau \|\mathcal{X}\|_* + \frac{1}{2} \|\mathcal{X} - \mathcal{Y}\|_F^2. \tag{6.33}$$

Proof. The required solution to (6.33) is a real tensor and thus we first show that $\mathcal{D}_\tau(\mathcal{Y})$ in (6.31) is real. Let $\mathcal{Y} = \mathcal{U} * \mathcal{S} * \mathcal{V}^*$ be the t-SVD of $\mathcal{Y}$. We know that the frontal slices of $\bar{\mathcal{S}}$ satisfy the property (6.11) and so do the frontal slices of $(\bar{\mathcal{S}} - \tau)_+$.

Algorithm 4 Solve (6.25) by ADMM.

Initialize: $\mathcal{L}_0 = \mathcal{S}_0 = \mathcal{Y}_0 = 0$, $\rho = 1.1$, $\mu_0 = 1\mathrm{e}{-3}$, $\mu_{\max} = 1\mathrm{e}10$, $\epsilon = 1\mathrm{e}{-8}$.

while not converged **do**

1. Update $\mathcal{L}_{k+1}$ by

$$\mathcal{L}_{k+1} = \mathrm{argmin}_{\mathcal{L}} \ \|\mathcal{L}\|_* + \frac{\mu_k}{2}\|\mathcal{L} + \mathcal{E}_k - \mathcal{X} + \mathcal{Y}_k/\mu_k\|_F^2 \ ;$$

2. Update $\mathcal{E}_{k+1}$ by

$$\mathcal{E}_{k+1} = \mathrm{argmin}_{\mathcal{E}} \ \lambda\|\mathcal{E}\|_1 + \frac{\mu_k}{2}\|\mathcal{L}_{k+1} + \mathcal{E} - \mathcal{X} + \mathcal{Y}_k/\mu_k\|_F^2 \ ;$$

3. $\mathcal{Y}_{k+1} = \mathcal{Y}_k + \mu_k(\mathcal{L}_{k+1} + \mathcal{E}_{k+1} - \mathcal{X})$;

4. Update μ_{k+1} by $\mu_{k+1} = \min(\rho\mu_k, \mu_{\max})$;

5. Check the convergence conditions

$$\|\mathcal{L}_{k+1} - \mathcal{L}_k\|_\infty \le \epsilon, \ \ \|\mathcal{E}_{k+1} - \mathcal{E}_k\|_\infty \le \epsilon, \ \ \|\mathcal{L}_{k+1} + \mathcal{E}_{k+1} - \mathcal{X}\|_\infty \le \epsilon.$$

end while

By Lemma 6.1, $\mathcal{S}_\tau$ in (6.32) is real. Thus, $\mathcal{D}_\tau(\mathcal{Y})$ in (6.31) is real. Secondly, by using properties (6.23) and (6.12), problem (6.33) is equivalent to

$$\mathrm{argmin}_{\mathcal{X}} \frac{1}{n_3}\left(\tau\|\bar{X}\|_* + \frac{1}{2}\|\bar{X} - \bar{Y}\|_F^2\right)$$

$$= \mathrm{argmin}_{\mathcal{X}} \frac{1}{n_3}\sum_{i=1}^{n_3}\left(\tau\|\bar{X}^{(i)}\|_* + \frac{1}{2}\|\bar{X}^{(i)} - \bar{Y}^{(i)}\|_F^2\right). \qquad (6.34)$$

By Theorem 2.1 in [26], we know that the i-th frontal slice of $\overline{\mathcal{D}_\tau(\mathcal{Y})}$ solves the i-th subproblem of (6.34). Hence, $\mathcal{D}_\tau(\mathcal{Y})$ solves problem (6.33). $\qquad \square$

Theorem 6.6 gives the closed form of the t-SVT operator $\mathcal{D}_\tau(\mathcal{Y})$, which is a natural extension of the matrix SVT [26]. Note that $\mathcal{D}_\tau(\mathcal{Y})$ is real when $\mathcal{Y}$ is real. By using property (6.11), Algorithm 3 gives an efficient way for computing $\mathcal{D}_\tau(\mathcal{Y})$.

With t-SVT, we now give the details of ADMM to solve (6.25). The augmented Lagrangian function of (6.25) is

$$L(\mathcal{L}, \mathcal{E}, \mathcal{Y}, \mu) = \|\mathcal{L}\|_* + \lambda\|\mathcal{E}\|_1 + \langle\mathcal{Y}, \mathcal{L} + \mathcal{E} - \mathcal{X}\rangle + \frac{\mu}{2}\|\mathcal{L} + \mathcal{E} - \mathcal{X}\|_F^2.$$

Then $\mathcal{L}$ and $\mathcal{E}$ can be updated by minimizing the augmented Lagrangian function L alternately. Both subproblems have closed-form solutions. See Algorithm 4 for the whole procedure. The main per-iteration cost lies in the update of $\mathcal{L}_{k+1}$, which

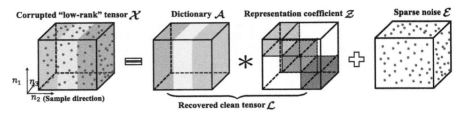

Corrupted "low-rank" tensor $\mathcal{X}$ Dictionary $\mathcal{A}$ Representation coefficient $\mathcal{Z}$ Sparse noise $\mathcal{E}$

n_1 n_3

n_2 **(Sample direction)**

Recovered clean tensor $\mathcal{L}$

FIGURE 6.4

Illustration of the TLRR method for tensor data recovery and clustering [3]. By exploiting the intrinsic low-rank structure of the input tensor data $\mathcal{X}$, TLRR can effectively recover the underlying low-rank tensor $\mathcal{L}$ in the presence of sparse noise $\mathcal{E}$ and cluster the samples in $\mathcal{X}$ (encoded by $\mathcal{Z}$ under dictionary $\mathcal{A}$).

requires computing FFT and $\lceil \frac{n_3+1}{2} \rceil$ SVDs of $n_1 \times n_2$ matrices. The per-iteration complexity is at the order of $O\left(n_1 n_2 n_3 \log n_3 + n_{(1)} n_{(2)}^2 n_3\right)$.

6.4.2 Tensor low-rank representation

This section continues to study the problem of how to recover a low-tubal rank tensor $\mathcal{L}_0 \in \mathbb{R}^{n_1 \times n_2 \times n_3}$ from a highly corrupted tensor $\mathcal{X} = \mathcal{L}_0 + \mathcal{E}_0 \in \mathbb{R}^{n_1 \times n_2 \times n_3}$, where $\mathcal{L}_0$ is low-tubal rank clean data and $\mathcal{E}_0 \in \mathbb{R}^{n_1 \times n_2 \times n_3}$ is sparse noise. This section introduces the TLRR method [3], which is the first approach that can exactly recover the clean data of intrinsic low-rank structure and accurately cluster them as well, with provable performance guarantees. Concretely, by assuming samples in $\mathcal{X}$ distribute along the third direction, TLRR proposes to seek the following low-rank representation on the raw tensor data (see illustration in Fig. 6.4):

$$\min_{\mathcal{Z},\mathcal{E}} \ \|\mathcal{Z}\|_* + \lambda \|\mathcal{E}\|_1, \ \text{s.t.} \ \mathcal{X} = \mathcal{A} * \mathcal{Z} + \mathcal{E}, \tag{6.35}$$

where $\|\mathcal{Z}\|_*$ is the tensor nuclear norm [27] of $\mathcal{Z} \in \mathbb{R}^{n_4 \times n_2 \times n_3}$ and is used to characterize the low-rank structure in the clean tensor $\mathcal{L}_0$ and $\|\mathcal{E}\|_1$ denotes the tensor ℓ_1-norm and aims to capture the sparsity property of the noise $\mathcal{E}_0$. See the definition of $\|\mathcal{E}\|_1$ in Table 6.1. Here $\mathcal{A} \in \mathbb{R}^{n_1 \times n_4 \times n_3}$ denotes a dictionary and each slice $\mathcal{A}(:, t, :)$ in $\mathcal{A}$ denotes a representation base. In this way, the feature $\mathcal{Z}(:, t, :)$ gives the corresponding representation of the t-th sample $\mathcal{X}(:, t, :)$.

Though both R-TPCA and TLRR can recover the clean data from sparsity-corrupted data, TLRR enjoys several advantages over R-TPCA. We will give a more rigorous theoretical comparison in Section 6.4.2.3. Here we only briefly discuss these advantages. Under certain conditions, R-TPCA can recover the clean data $\mathcal{L}_0$ from a noisy observation $\mathcal{X}$. Comparatively, TLRR can handle the real data sampled from a mixture of *multiple* tensor subspaces (see Theorem 6.9 given in the following section) spanned by the dictionary $\mathcal{A}$, and thus has wider applications for realistic data

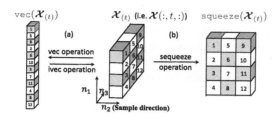

FIGURE 6.5

Illustration of the `vec`, `ivec`, and `squeeze` operations [3].

analysis than R-TPCA. Moreover, TLRR can also cluster tensor data since it learns the representations $\mathcal{Z}$, while R-TPCA cannot.

The following subsections are structured as follows. We will first introduce the tensor linear representation $\mathcal{X} = \mathcal{A} * \mathcal{Z} + \mathcal{E}$, including its meaningness and its advantages over the vector linear representation used in the two-way data. Then we present the clustering steps of TLRR and clustering performance, which is also an important basis for further analyzing the data recovery performance. Next, we show that TLRR can exactly recover the clean data $\mathcal{L}_0$ and enjoys a stronger recovery ability than R-TPCA. Finally we provide one effective optimization algorithm to solve problem (6.35).

6.4.2.1 Tensor linear representation

To understand our TLRR better, here we first explain the intuition behind the tensor linear representation $\mathcal{X} = \mathcal{A} * \mathcal{Z}$. This tensor linear representation actually extends the data linear representation from the vector space to the tensor space. Before that, we introduce two important operators: $\text{vec}(\cdot)$ and $\text{ivec}(\cdot)$. Define $\mathcal{X}_{(t)}$ by the t-th lateral slice $\mathcal{X}(:, t, :)$ (see Table 6.1 in Section 6.2). As illustrated in Fig. 6.5, vec vectorizes each sample $\mathcal{X}_{(t)}$ in $\mathcal{X}$ and ivec denotes its inverse operation.

We first look at vectorization vec. Given an arbitrary sample $\mathcal{X}_{(t)}$, if the bases in $A \in \mathbb{R}^{n_1 n_3 \times n_4}$ can linearly represent its vectorization $x_{(t)} = \text{vec}(\mathcal{X}_{(t)})$,

$$x_{(t)} = Az_{(t)}, \quad \forall t = 1, \cdots, n_2, \tag{6.36}$$

then there always exist two tensors $\mathcal{A}$ and $\mathcal{Z}$ such that the tensor linear representation $\mathcal{X} = \mathcal{A} * \mathcal{Z}$ holds. This can be formally stated in Theorem 6.7.

Theorem 6.7. *[3] If Eq. (6.36) holds, then there exist two tensors* $\mathcal{A} \in \mathbb{R}^{n_1 \times n_4 \times n_3}$ *and* $\mathcal{Z} \in \mathbb{C}^{n_4 \times n_2 \times n_3}$ *such that*

$$\mathcal{X}_{(t)} = \textit{ivec}(x_{(t)}) = \mathcal{A} * \mathcal{Z}_{(t)}, \quad (\forall t = 1, \cdots, n_2), \tag{6.37}$$

where $\mathcal{A}$ *can be found through* $\mathcal{A}_{(t)} = \textit{ivec}(A(:, t))$ *and* $\mathcal{Z}$ *can be computed as* $\mathcal{Z}_{(t)} = \textit{ifft}(\bar{\mathcal{Z}}_{(t)}, [\ ], 3)$ *in which* $\bar{\mathcal{Z}}_{(t)}(:, t, j) = z_{(t)}$ $(j = 1, \cdots, n_3)$. *However, if there exists a* $\mathcal{Z}_{(t)}$ *such that Eq. (6.37) holds, Eq. (6.36) may not hold.*

Algorithm 5 Data clustering.

Input: data $\mathcal{X}$, dictionary $\mathcal{A}$, and number k of clusters.
1. Obtain the minimizer $\mathcal{Z}_\star$ to problem (6.35).
2. Construct a similarity matrix $\widehat{\mathbf{Z}}$ by (6.38).
3. Perform Ncut on $\widehat{\mathbf{Z}}$ to cluster the samples into k clusters.
Output: clustering results.

The proof of Theorem 6.7 can be found in [3]. From Theorem 6.7, one can observe that if vectorized data samples can be linearly represented in the vector space, the tensor linear representation (6.37) for original tensor data also holds. One important advantage of the tensor linear representation over the vector linear representation is that the former one gets rid of vectorizing tensor data for describing and analyzing their relationship. Therefore, the tensor linear representation can effectively avoid destroying the multiway structure and losing information, which is also mentioned in [15,27,28]. Besides, Theorem 6.7 also indicates that compared with the vector linear representation, the tensor linear representation can capture more complex data relations that cannot be depicted by the vector linear representation. So in terms of tensor data analysis, the tensor linear representation is more general and advantageous over the vector linear representation.

6.4.2.2 TLRR for data clustering

In this section, we introduce how to apply TLRR formulated in Eq. (6.35) for tensor data clustering.

Algorithm for clustering. For clustering, we often view the datum $\mathcal{X}$ itself or the recovered data by other methods, e.g., R-TPCA [27], as the dictionary $\mathcal{A}$ in TLRR. As a result, each of the frontal slices $\mathbf{Z}_\star^{(i)} \in \mathbb{R}^{n_2 \times n_2}$ $(i = 1, \cdots, n_3)$ of the learned representation $\mathcal{Z}_\star$ denotes a similarity matrix of samples. To apply the existing clustering tools, e.g., Ncut [29], we combine all $\mathbf{Z}_\star^{(i)}$ into one affinity matrix $\widehat{\mathbf{Z}}$:

$$\widehat{\mathbf{Z}} = \frac{1}{2n_3} \sum_{i=1}^{n_3} \left(|\mathbf{Z}_\star^{(i)}| + |(\mathbf{Z}_\star^{(i)})^*| \right). \tag{6.38}$$

Then we can summarize the clustering framework in Algorithm 5 and will analyze its performance subsequently.

Tensor block-diagonal property. For analysis, here we consider a simple case. That is, the tensor data are noise-free. In this case, the TLRR problem (6.35) degenerates to

$$\min_{\mathcal{Z}} \|\mathcal{Z}\|_*, \text{ s.t. } \mathcal{X} = \mathcal{A} * \mathcal{Z}. \tag{6.39}$$

Note that if there are sparse corruptions, one can solve the original problem (6.35). In the following section, we analyze the structure of the minimizer to noiseless TLRR (6.39) for data clustering.

For analysis, we first extend some important subspace analysis tools to tensor data. A *tensor space* is a set of tensors that is closed under finite tensor addition and scalar multiplication. Here the *tensor space* specially refers to the set $\mathbb{S} = \{\forall \mathcal{S} \in \mathbb{R}^{n_1 \times 1 \times n_3}\}$. We say a set of tensors $\{\mathcal{D}_{(1)}, \cdots, \mathcal{D}_{(p)}\} \subseteq \mathbb{S}$ is *linearly independent* if there is no nonzero $\mathcal{C} \in \mathbb{R}^{p \times 1 \times n_3}$ satisfying $\mathcal{D} * \mathcal{C} = \mathbf{0}$, where $\mathcal{D}_{(i)}$ is the i-th lateral slice of $\mathcal{D} \in \mathbb{R}^{n_1 \times p \times n_3}$.

Definition 6.11. (Tensor subspace) [3] Given a set $\{\mathcal{D}_{(1)}, \cdots, \mathcal{D}_{(p)}\} \subseteq \mathbb{S}$ in which the elements $\mathcal{D}_{(i)}$ are linearly independent, the set $\mathcal{K} = \{\mathcal{Y} \mid \mathcal{Y} = \mathcal{D} * \mathcal{C}, \forall \mathcal{C} \in \mathbb{R}^{p \times 1 \times n_3}\}$ is called a tensor subspace of dimension $\dim(\mathcal{K}) = p$. Here $\mathcal{D}_{(1)}, \cdots, \mathcal{D}_{(p)}$ are the basis spanning $\mathcal{K}$.

This definition is in accordance with the vector subspace definition. Firstly, the defined tensor subspace includes the tensor $\mathbf{0}$ and is closed under tensor addition and scalar multiplication. Secondly, when $n_3 = 1$, the tensor subspace reduces to the subspace defined on vectors. Then we define another important concept, i.e., the tensor direct sum. This definition is also in accordance with the direct sum defined on the vector subspace when $n_3 = 1$.

Definition 6.12. (Tensor direct sum) [3] If for any $\mathcal{F} \in \mathbb{R}^{n_1 \times 1 \times n_3}$ in $\mathcal{K}$ there is a unique $\mathcal{F}_j \in \mathbb{R}^{n_1 \times 1 \times n_3}$ in $\mathcal{K}_j$ for $1 \leq j \leq k$ such that $\mathcal{F} = \sum_{j=1}^{k} \mathcal{F}_j$, then $\mathcal{K} = \bigoplus_{j=1}^{k} \mathcal{K}_j$ is called the direct sum of tensor subspaces $\{\mathcal{K}_1, \cdots, \mathcal{K}_k\}$.

We call the tensor subspaces $\{\mathcal{K}_1, \cdots, \mathcal{K}_k\}$ *independent* if they obey the condition $\sum_{j=1}^{k} \mathcal{K}_j = \bigoplus_{j=1}^{k} \mathcal{K}_j$. Based on these definitions, we summarize our main results in Theorem 6.8. It shows the tensor block-diagonal structure of the learned representation and indicates the clustering structure of tensors.

Theorem 6.8. *[3] Suppose $\mathcal{X} = [\mathcal{X}_1, \cdots, \mathcal{X}_k]$ and the samples $(\mathcal{X}_j(:, i, :))$ in $\mathcal{X}_j \in \mathbb{R}^{n_1 \times m_j \times n_3}$ are drawn from the j-th tensor subspace $\mathcal{K}_j$ whose p_j basis composes $\mathcal{A}_j \in \mathbb{R}^{n_1 \times p_j \times n_3}$. Then if $\{\mathcal{K}_1, \cdots, \mathcal{K}_k\}$ are independent, the minimizer $\mathcal{Z}_\star$ to problem (6.39) is tensor block-diagonal (see "$\mathcal{Z}$" in Fig. 6.4). Namely, each frontal slice $\mathbf{Z}_\star^{(i)}$ of $\mathcal{Z}_\star$ has the following block-diagonal structure:*

$$
\mathbf{Z}_\star^{(i)} = \begin{bmatrix} (\mathbf{Z}_\star^{(i)})_1 & \mathbf{0} & \cdots & \mathbf{0} \\ \mathbf{0} & (\mathbf{Z}_\star^{(i)})_2 & \cdots & \mathbf{0} \\ \vdots & \vdots & \ddots & \vdots \\ \mathbf{0} & \mathbf{0} & \cdots & (\mathbf{Z}_\star^{(i)})_k \end{bmatrix} \in \mathbb{R}^{(\sum_j p_j) \times (\sum_j m_j)},
$$

where $(\mathbf{Z}_\star^{(i)})_j \in \mathbb{R}^{p_j \times m_j}$ is a coefficient matrix. Then the DFT result $\bar{\mathcal{Z}}_\star$ of $\mathcal{Z}_\star$ has the same block-diagonal structure as $\mathcal{Z}_\star$.

Please find the proof of Theorem 6.8 in [3]. It should be mentioned that the subspace independence assumption is mild. Indeed, its vector version is a common assumption in sparse and low-rank data analysis [30–32]. Here we compare TLRR

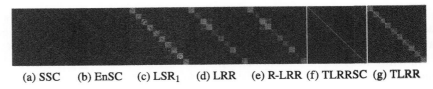

(a) SSC   (b) EnSC   (c) LSR$_1$ (d) LRR   (e) R-LRR (f) TLRRSC (g) TLRR

FIGURE 6.6

Comparison of block-diagonal structures learned by the compared methods [3]. **Best viewed in color pdf file.**

with other sparse and low-rank-based methods, including SSC [32], EnSC [33], LSR$_1$ [34], LRR [30], R-LRR [31], and TLRRSC [35], to investigate the subspace assumption. For TLRR, we use the datum $\mathcal{X}$ itself as the dictionary $\mathcal{A}$ and organize the images along the second dimension. Experimental results show that this organization can well capture the linear representation relations among samples. See more in the following discussion. Fig. 6.6 displays the block-diagonal structure learned by TLRR on FRGC 2.0 (the first 10 classes) [36]. One can observe the grouping effects of TLRR. It also helps explain the superiority of TLRR and reasonability of the tensor subspace assumption—the block-diagonal structures learned by TLRR coincide with Theorem 6.8.

For the clustering task, Theorem 6.8 is important and useful. This is because the block-diagonal structure of $\mathcal{Z}_\star$ directly indicates the tensor subspace membership of a specific sample, according to which one can easily predict its cluster membership. More specifically, given the t-th sample $\mathcal{X}_{(t)}$, we can rewrite its formulation as

$$\mathcal{X}_{(t)} = \mathcal{A} * \mathcal{Z}_{\star(t)} = \sum_{j=1}^{k} \mathcal{A}_j * \mathcal{Z}_{\star(t)}^{j}, \ \forall t = 1, \cdots, n_2, \tag{6.40}$$

where $\mathcal{Z}_{\star(t)}^{j} = \mathcal{Z}_\star(1 + \sum_{i=1}^{j-1} p_i : \sum_{i=1}^{j} p_i, t, :)$. From Theorem 6.8, one can observe that if $\mathcal{X}_{(t)}$ comes from the s-th subspace $\mathcal{K}_s$, $\mathcal{Z}_{\star(t)}^{s}$ will have nonzero entries while $\mathcal{Z}_{\star(t)}^{j}$ ($j \neq s$) will be $\mathbf{0}$. Then according to the position of the nonzero entries in $\mathcal{Z}_{\star(t)}$, we can cluster $\mathcal{X}_{(t)}$ precisely.

When the raw datum $\mathcal{X}$ itself is regarded as the dictionary, the learned representation $\mathcal{Z}_\star$ will be also block-diagonal, because the samples are drawn from independent tensor subspaces. Besides, by replacing $\mathcal{A}$ with $\mathcal{X}$ in Eq. (6.40), we have $\mathcal{X}_{(t)} = \sum_{j=1}^{n_2} \mathcal{X}_{(j)} * \mathcal{Z}_\star(j, t, :)$. So the coefficient $\mathcal{Z}_\star(j, t, :)$ can depict the similarity relationship between samples $\mathcal{X}_{(t)}$ and $\mathcal{X}_{(j)}$. Then to use the learned representation $\mathcal{Z}_\star$ for clustering, following Eq. (6.38) we combine the two vectors $\mathcal{Z}_\star(t, j, :)$ and $\mathcal{Z}_\star(j, t, :)$ into one entry as $\widehat{\mathbf{Z}}(t, j) = \frac{1}{n_3} \sum_{i=1}^{n_3} (|\mathcal{Z}_\star(t, j, i)| + |\mathcal{Z}_\star(j, t, i)|)$ that measures the similarity between the samples $\mathcal{X}_{(t)}$ and $\mathcal{X}_{(j)}$. Moreover, if $\mathcal{X}_{(t)}$ and $\mathcal{X}_{(j)}$ come from different tensor subspaces, one can expect that $\widehat{\mathbf{Z}}(t, j)$ would be zero. In this way, we can perform clustering on the similarity matrix $\widehat{\mathbf{Z}}$.

Now we discuss the corrupted data. Since Theorem 6.9 proves that TLRR can exactly recover the clean low-rank data under mild conditions, if the conditions in

Theorem 6.8 are satisfied, the minimizer $\mathcal{Z}_\star$ will be tensor block-diagonal. So this also guarantees the clustering performance as mentioned before. We will discuss this in the following section in more detail.

Multiview interpretation on TLRR. Here we give another explanation from the multiview aspect for improve our understanding of TLRR. According to the tensor nuclear norm definition $\|\mathcal{Z}\|_* = \frac{1}{n_3}\|\bar{Z}\|_*$ and the block-diagonal structure of $\bar{X}$, $\bar{A}$, and $\bar{Z}$ (see their definitions in (6.9)), we can rewrite (6.39) into its equivalent formulation as follows:

$$\min_{\bar{Z}^{(i)}} \|\bar{Z}^{(i)}\|_*, \text{ s.t. } \bar{X}^{(i)} = \bar{A}^{(i)}\bar{Z}^{(i)}, \ (i = 1, \cdots, n_3). \tag{6.41}$$

Meanwhile, when performing DFT on $\mathcal{X}$, the t-th column of $\bar{X}^{(i)}$ comes from the t-th sample $\mathcal{X}_{(i)}$. This is because we have

$$\bar{X}^{(i)} = \left[M^1 f_i, M^2 f_i, \cdots, M^t f_i, \cdots, M^p f_i \right],$$

where f_i denotes the i-th column of the DFT matrix F_{n_3} defined in (6.5) and $M^t = \text{squeeze}(\mathcal{X}_{(t)}) \in \mathbb{R}^{n_1 \times n_3}$, in which the operation squeeze transforms the t-th sample $\mathcal{X}_{(t)}$ into a matrix (see Fig. 6.5). Therefore, $\bar{X}^{(i)}$ can be regarded as the new features of samples in $\mathcal{X}$ under the i-th Fourier basis f_i. Similarly, $\bar{A}^{(i)}$ can be viewed as a new dictionary under the Fourier basis f_i. Thus, from a multiview aspect, the frontal slice $\bar{Z}^{(i)}$ $(i = 1, \cdots, n_3)$ learned by model (6.41) can be regarded as n_3 different representation matrices under n_3 different views and may better depict the relations among samples. Thus, the t-th lateral $\mathcal{Z}_{(t)}$ is the representation tensor of the t-th sample $\mathcal{X}_{(t)}$. Conducting inverse DFT on $\mathcal{Z}_{(t)}$ gives $\mathcal{Z}_{(t)} = \frac{1}{n_3} F_{n_3}^* \text{squeeze}(\mathcal{Z}_{(t)})$. This combines all the representation information under n_3 different views. This mechanism also makes the advantage of TLRR stand out, because matrix LRR [30,31] only learns the representation under a single view, while TLRR aims to seek n_3 representations under n_3 different views and may better capture the relations among samples.

6.4.2.3 TLRR for exact data recovery

In this section, we analyze the theoretical performance of TLRR in data recovery tasks. Zhou et al. [3] proved that under mild conditions TLRR in (6.35) can exactly recover the intrinsic low-rank data $\mathcal{L}_0$ lying in multiple tensor subspaces, even in the presence of gross noise $\mathcal{E}_0$. Assume that $\mathcal{U}_\mathcal{A} * \mathcal{S}_\mathcal{A} * \mathcal{V}_\mathcal{A}^*$ is the skinny t-SVD of $\mathcal{A}$. That is, the skinny t-SVD of $\mathcal{A}$ is $\mathcal{A} = \mathcal{U}_\mathcal{A} * \mathcal{S}_\mathcal{A} * \mathcal{V}_\mathcal{A}^*$, where $\mathcal{U}_\mathcal{A} = \mathcal{U}(:, 1 : r, :)$, $\mathcal{S}_\mathcal{A} = \mathcal{S}(1 : r, 1 : r, :)$, and $\mathcal{V}_\mathcal{A} = \mathcal{V}(:, 1 : r, :)$, in which r denotes the tensor tubal rank of $\mathcal{A}$. See Definition 6.7 in Section 6.3.

Incoherence condition for TLRR. Similar to matrix recovery [8,31], exactly separating $\mathcal{X}$ into the low-rank term $\mathcal{L}_0$ plus the sparse term $\mathcal{E}_0$ requires $\mathcal{L}_0$ to be not too sparse. Here we present the incoherence condition for low-rank tensors to characterize this condition. Let $r = \text{rank}_t(\mathcal{L}_0)$. We define the row incoherence parameter

μ_1, the column incoherence parameter μ_2, and the total incoherence parameter μ_3 as follows:

$$\mu_1(\mathcal{L}_0) = \frac{n_2 n_3}{r} \max_{j=1,\cdots,n_2} \left\| \mathcal{V}_0^* * \mathring{\mathfrak{e}}_j^{n_2} \right\|_F^2,$$

$$\mu_2(\mathcal{L}_0) = \frac{n_1 n_3}{r} \max_{i=1,\cdots,n_1} \left\| \mathcal{U}_0^* * \mathring{\mathfrak{e}}_i^{n_1} \right\|_F^2,$$

$$\mu_3(\mathcal{L}_0) = \frac{n_1 n_2 n_3^2}{r} \left(\| \mathcal{U}_0 * \mathcal{V}_0^* \|_\infty \right)^2,$$

where $\mathring{\mathfrak{e}}_j^{n_2}$ and $\mathring{\mathfrak{e}}_i^{n_1}$ denote the standard basis and are defined in Table 6.1. If $\mu(\mathcal{L}_0) = \max(\mu_1(\mathcal{L}_0), \mu_2(\mathcal{L}_0), \mu_3(\mathcal{L}_0))$ is small, then it means that the low-rank term $\mathcal{L}_0$ is not sparse. This condition is also critical for other tensor analysis methods, such as R-TPCA [27].

More importantly, because TLRR involves an extra dictionary $\mathcal{A}$, it requires a new necessary incoherence condition that cannot be straightforwardly generalized from the matrix case or the one used in R-TPCA [27]. Let $\mathrm{rank}_t(\mathcal{A}) = r_{\mathcal{A}}$. Then we define a new row incoherence parameter that is related to the dictionary $\mathcal{A}$:

$$\mu_1^{\mathcal{A}}(\mathcal{L}_0) = \mu_1(\mathcal{L}_0) \max_{i=1,\cdots,n_1} \left\| \mathcal{U}_{\mathcal{A}}^* * \mathring{\mathfrak{e}}_i^{n_1} \right\|_F^2 = \frac{r_{\mathcal{A}}}{n_1 n_3} \mu_1(\mathcal{L}_0) \mu_2(\mathcal{A}).$$

The *incoherence condition* of TLRR for exact recovery only requires $\max(\mu_2(\mathcal{L}_0)$ and $\mu_1^{\mathcal{A}}(\mathcal{L}_0))$ to be sufficiently small and does not rely on $\mu_3(\mathcal{L}_0)$. So it is a weaker condition compared with the exact recovery condition in R-TPCA [27].

Exact recovery performance guarantee. Theorem 6.9 summarizes the exact recovery performance guarantee of TLRR. Define $n_{(1)} = \max(n_1, n_2)$ and $n_{(2)} = \min(n_1, n_2)$. Recall $\mathcal{P}_{\mathcal{U}}(\cdot)$ is a projection operator which is defined in Table 6.1.

Theorem 6.9. *[3] Assume that the support set Ω of $\mathcal{E}_0$ is uniformly distributed, $\mathcal{P}_{\mathcal{U}_{\mathcal{A}}}(\mathcal{U}_0) = \mathcal{U}_0$, and $\mathcal{A}$ obeys that the ranks of $\bar{A}^{(i)}$ $(i = 1, \cdots, n_3)$ are equal. Let $\mu^{\mathcal{A}} = \max(\mu_2(\mathcal{L}_0), \mu_1^{\mathcal{A}}(\mathcal{L}_0))$. If*

$$rank_t(\mathcal{L}_0) \leq \frac{\rho_r n_{(2)}}{\mu^{\mathcal{A}} \log(n_{(1)} n_3)} \quad and \quad |\Omega| \leq \rho_s n_1 n_2 n_3,$$

where ρ_r and ρ_s are constants, then with probability at least $1 - n_{(1)}^{-10}$, $(\mathcal{Z}_\star, \mathcal{E}_\star)$, where $\mathcal{Z}_\star = \mathcal{A}^\dagger * \mathcal{L}_0$ and $\mathcal{E}_\star = \mathcal{E}_0$, is the unique optimal solution to problem (6.35) with $\lambda = 1/\sqrt{n_{(1)} n_3}$.

Please refer to the proof of Theorem 6.9 in [3]. The pseudo-inverse $\mathcal{A}^\dagger$ of a tensor $\mathcal{A}$ can be computed frontal-slice-wisely after DFT. See more details in [3]. Theorem 6.9 shows that TLRR can exactly recover the low-rank clean data $\mathcal{L}_0$ even when the amount of noise is at the same order as the entry number of the observed tensor and the tubal rank is as high as $\mathcal{O}(n_{(2)}/\log(n_{(1)} n_3))$. More importantly, the exact recovery does not require knowing a prior on the location of noise (the corrupted elements). This is very useful and important for data denoising tasks in practice, since noise is difficult to detect. Finally, this exact recovery performance guarantee also indicates that applying TLRR to recover clean data also benefits subsequent data clustering tasks. Superficially, if the clean data $\mathcal{L}_0$ are exactly recovered, by Theorem 6.8 the optimal solution $\mathcal{Z}_\star$ would be tensor block-diagonal, thus getting data clusters becomes straightforward.

Now we discuss the condition $\mathcal{P}_{\mathcal{U}_{\mathcal{A}}}(\mathcal{U}_0) = \mathcal{U}_0$ in Theorem 6.9. This condition is necessary and reasonable—each authentic sample in $\mathcal{L}_0$ drawn from a subspace should be linearly represented by the bases in $\mathcal{A}$. The condition on the ranks of $\bar{\mathcal{A}}^{(i)}$ $(i = 1, \cdots, n_3)$ is also indispensable for exact data recovery, because the equality $\mathcal{L}_0 = \mathcal{A} * \mathcal{Z}_\star = \mathcal{A} * \mathcal{A}^\dagger * \mathcal{L}_0$ implies $\mathcal{A} * \mathcal{A}^\dagger = \mathcal{I}$, which needs the ranks of $\bar{\mathcal{A}}^{(i)}$ $(i = 1, \cdots, n_3)$ to be equal. Note that such as condition is also required by R-TPCA, because R-TPCA can be viewed as a special case of TLRR by choosing the identity tensor $\mathcal{I}$ as the dictionary, naturally satisfying the condition. Moreover, if $\mathcal{A} = \mathcal{I}$, Theorem 6.9 still holds and ensures exact data recovery for R-TPCA. This means that Theorem 6.9 is also applicable when $n_3 = 1$. Thus performance guarantees for matrix LRR [31] can be derived as a special case of TLRR theory.

Comparison between TLRR and R-TPCA. Because TLRR and R-TPCA [27] are based on the recently proposed tensor tubal rank and t-SVD [13] and can be used for data recovery, it is natural to compare their recovery ability by analyzing their incoherence parameters.

Zhou et al. [3] found that along with the increasing number of tensor subspaces in data, the value of $\mu_1(\mathcal{L}_0)$ increases remarkably, but $\mu_2(\mathcal{L}_0)$ almost does not change. Such an observation is actually consistent with the matrix case in [31]. We explain this below. Assume that $\mathcal{L}_0$ obeys the assumptions on $\mathcal{X}$ in Theorem 6.8. Then $\mathcal{V}_0$ is tensor block-diagonal:

$$\mathcal{V}_0 = \begin{bmatrix} \mathcal{V}_1 & \mathbf{0} & \cdots & \mathbf{0} \\ \mathbf{0} & \mathcal{V}_2 & \cdots & \mathbf{0} \\ \vdots & \vdots & \ddots & \vdots \\ \mathbf{0} & \mathbf{0} & \cdots & \mathcal{V}_k \end{bmatrix},$$

where $\mathcal{V}_i$ $(i = 1, \cdots, k)$ is of size $p_i \times m_i \times n_3$. When the tensor subspace number k is large, $\mathcal{V}_0$ would be very sparse and $\|\mathcal{V}_0^* * \mathring{e}_j^{n_2}\|_F^2 = \|\mathcal{V}_0(:, j, :)\|_F^2$ would be close to 1, which leads to a large incoherence parameter $\mu_1(\mathcal{L}_0) \approx n_2 n_3 / r$. Differently, $\mathcal{U}_0$ is generally not block-diagonal and is indeed not sparse. Actually, when the rank of $\mathcal{L}_0$ is fixed, $\mathcal{U}_0$ is invariant to the number of tensor subspaces. This is because $\mathcal{U}_0$ just needs to span the tensor subspaces that samples lie in and only depends on the tensor rank of $\mathcal{L}_0$. So $\mu_2(\mathcal{L}_0)$ is nearly constant. This observation is also verified by empirical studies. Please refer to the results in Fig. 6.7. It also well explains why T-RPCA is less successful when dealing with multiple tensor subspaces. For exact

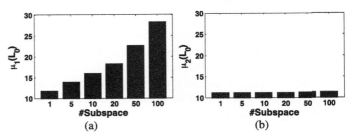

FIGURE 6.7

Illustration of effects of the tensor subspace number k on $\mu_1(\mathcal{L}_0)$ and $\mu_2(\mathcal{L}_0)$ [3]. We produce a random tensor $\mathcal{L}_0 \in \mathbb{R}^{1000 \times 1000 \times 10}$ with $\text{rank}_t(\mathcal{L}_0) = 100$. We increase the subspace number k and set the sample number as $100/k$ per subspace (see case (a) in synthetic data recovery of Section 6.4.3 for details of producing testing data).

recovery, R-TPCA requires

$$\text{rank}_t(\mathcal{L}_0) \leq \frac{\rho_r' n_{(2)}}{\mu(\mathcal{L}_0)(\log(n_{(1)}n_3))^2}.$$

Here ρ_r' is a constant, but $\mu(\mathcal{L}_0)$ ($\geq \mu_1(\mathcal{L}_0)$) is usually large.

In contrast, the incoherence parameter $\mu_1^{\mathcal{A}}(\mathcal{L}_0)$ can be small because of the dictionary $\mathcal{A}$. This is because although $\mu_1(\mathcal{L}_0)$ may become large when the tensor subspace number increases, $\mu_2(\mathcal{A})$ is constant and $r_{\mathcal{A}}/(n_1 n_3)$ remains small. As a result, Theorem 6.9 shows that TLRR has stronger data recovery power than R-TPCA. Moreover, R-TPCA requires an extra condition: $\mu_3(\mathcal{L}_0)$ should be sufficiently small. Such a restrictive condition is not necessary for TLRR. Finally, TLRR can not only exactly recover the clean data $\mathcal{L}_0$ but also learn the relationship among samples in $\mathcal{L}_0$, which benefit clustering and also other tasks, e.g., classification and metric learning.

6.4.2.4 Optimization technique

In this section, we first introduce an algorithm to optimize the TLRR model (6.35), and then analyze its convergence performance.

Optimization algorithms. For TLRR, many kinds of optimization algorithms, such as hard-thresholding algorithms [37–40] and Riemannian manifold algorithms [41,42], can be applied to solve it. Here we apply an ADMM algorithm [43] which is a straightforward optimization approach to solve problem (6.35). But if the sample number n_2 is large, directly applying ADMM is highly computationally expensive, because ADMM needs to compute n_3 SVD over $n_2 \times n_2$ matrices at each iteration. To reduce the computational cost, we provide a new and equivalent reformulation for (6.35). Assume that $\mathcal{U}_{\mathcal{A}} * \mathcal{S}_{\mathcal{A}} * \mathcal{V}_{\mathcal{A}}^*$ is the skinny t-SVD of $\mathcal{A}$. Please refer to Definition 6.7 in Section 6.3. Then, we respectively replace $\mathcal{A}$ and $\mathcal{Z}$ in (6.35) with $\mathcal{D} = \mathcal{U}_{\mathcal{A}} * \mathcal{S}_{\mathcal{A}} \in \mathbb{R}^{n_1 \times r_{\mathcal{A}} \times n_3}$ and $\mathcal{V}_{\mathcal{A}} * \mathcal{Z}'$, where $r_{\mathcal{A}} = \text{rank}_t(\mathcal{A})$ and $\mathcal{Z}' \in \mathbb{R}^{r_{\mathcal{A}} \times n_2 \times n_3}$ is a variable. In this way, we can obtain the following equivalent formulation:

$$\min_{\mathcal{Z}',\mathcal{E}} \|\mathcal{Z}'\|_* + \lambda\|\mathcal{E}\|_1, \text{ s.t. } \mathcal{X} = \mathcal{D} * \mathcal{Z}' + \mathcal{E}. \tag{6.42}$$

Thanks to such a reformulation, we only need to compute SVD for matrices whose size becomes $r_{\mathcal{A}} \times n_2$ and thus is much smaller at each iteration. In this way, we can first solve (6.42) to obtain its minimizer $(\mathcal{Z}'_\star, \mathcal{E}_\star)$ and then recover the minimizer $(\mathcal{V}_{\mathcal{A}} * \mathcal{Z}'_\star, \mathcal{E}_\star)$ to the vanilla problem (6.35). Theorem 6.10 guarantees the optimality of such a solution.

Theorem 6.10. *[3] Assume that the pair $(\mathcal{Z}'_\star, \mathcal{E}_\star)$ is an optimal solution to problem (6.42). Then, the pair $(\mathcal{V}_{\mathcal{A}} * \mathcal{Z}'_\star, \mathcal{E}_\star)$ is the minimizer to problem (6.35).*

The proof of Theorem 6.10 can be found in [3]. To apply ADMM for solving (6.42), one auxiliary variable $\mathcal{J}$ is introduced to decouple the variables from the objective and the constraint. In this way, we can easily update the variables. Accordingly, we rewrite the problem (6.42) as follows:

$$\min_{\mathcal{J},\mathcal{Z}',\mathcal{E}} \|\mathcal{Z}'\|_* + \lambda\|\mathcal{E}\|_1, \text{ s.t. } \mathcal{Z}' = \mathcal{J}, \mathcal{X} = \mathcal{D} * \mathcal{J} + \mathcal{E}. \tag{6.43}$$

Then we apply the augmented Lagrangian multiplier method and solve the following problem instead:

$$H(\mathcal{J}, \mathcal{Z}', \mathcal{E}, \mathcal{Y}^1, \mathcal{Y}^2) = \|\mathcal{Z}'\|_* + \lambda\|\mathcal{E}\|_1 + \langle \mathcal{Y}^1, \mathcal{Z}' - \mathcal{J}\rangle + \frac{\beta}{2}\|\mathcal{Z}' - \mathcal{J}\|_F^2$$
$$+ \langle \mathcal{Y}^2, \mathcal{X} - \mathcal{D} * \mathcal{J} - \mathcal{E}\rangle + \frac{\beta}{2}\|\mathcal{X} - \mathcal{D} * \mathcal{J} - \mathcal{E}\|_F^2,$$

where $\mathcal{Y}^1$ and $\mathcal{Y}^2$ denote the Lagrange multipliers introduced for the two constraints, respectively, and β is an auto-adjusted penalty parameter. Then we solve the problem through alternately updating two blocks, namely $\mathcal{J}$ and $(\mathcal{Z}', \mathcal{E})$, in each iteration to minimize $H(\mathcal{J}, \mathcal{Z}', \mathcal{E}, \mathcal{Y}_1, \mathcal{Y}_2)$ with other variables fixed. Algorithm 6 summarizes the whole optimization procedure. Both problems (6.44) for updating $\mathcal{J}_{k+1}$ and (6.45) for updating the block $(\mathcal{Z}'_{k+1}, \mathcal{E}_{k+1})$ have closed-form solutions. Details on the update of each variable are provided as follows.

Updating $\mathcal{J}$: We minimize the following problem:

$$\mathcal{J}_{k+1} = \operatorname{argmin}_{\mathcal{J}} \left\|\mathcal{Q}_k^1 - \mathcal{J}\right\|_F^2 + \left\|\mathcal{Q}_k^2 - \mathcal{D} * \mathcal{J}\right\|_F^2$$
$$= (\mathcal{D}^* * \mathcal{D} + \mathcal{I})^{-1} * \left(\mathcal{Q}_k^1 + \mathcal{D}^* * \mathcal{Q}_k^2\right), \tag{6.46}$$

where $\mathcal{Q}_k^1 = \mathcal{Z}'_k + \mathcal{Y}_k^1/\beta_k$ and $\mathcal{Q}_k^2 = \mathcal{X} - \mathcal{E}_k + \mathcal{Y}_k^2/\beta_k$. The pseudo-inverse $\mathcal{A}^\dagger$ of a tensor $\mathcal{A}$ can be computed frontal-slice-wisely after DFT and then transformed into a tensor via inverse DFT. See more details in [3]. The property $\|\mathcal{B}\|_F^2 = \frac{1}{n_3}\|\bar{\mathcal{B}}\|_F^2$

Algorithm 6 Tensor LRR (TLRR).

Input: Input $\mathcal{X} \in \mathbb{R}^{n_1 \times n_2 \times n_3}$, dictionary $\mathcal{A} \in \mathbb{R}^{n_1 \times n_4 \times n_3}$.

Initialize: $\mathcal{D} = \mathcal{U}_{\mathcal{A}} * \mathcal{S}_{\mathcal{A}}$ with skinny t-SVD $\mathcal{U}_{\mathcal{A}} * \mathcal{S}_{\mathcal{A}} * \mathcal{V}_{\mathcal{A}}^*$ of $\mathcal{A}$, $\mathcal{J}_0 = \mathcal{Z}_0' = \mathcal{Y}_0^1 = 0$, $\mathcal{E}_0 = \mathcal{Y}_0^2 = 0$, $\lambda = 1/\sqrt{n_3 \max(n_1, n_2)}$, $\gamma = 1.1$, $\beta_0 = 1e - 5$, $\beta_{\max} = 1e + 8$, $\epsilon = 1e - 8$, and $k = 0$.

While not converged **do**

1. Fix $\mathcal{Z}_k'$ and $\mathcal{E}_k$. Update $\mathcal{J}_{k+1}$ by solving

$$\mathcal{J}_{k+1} = \operatorname{argmin}_{\mathcal{J}} \left\| \mathcal{Z}_k' + \frac{\mathcal{Y}_k^1}{\beta_k} - \mathcal{J} \right\|_F^2 + \left\| \mathcal{X} - \mathcal{E}_k + \frac{\mathcal{Y}_k^2}{\beta_k} - \mathcal{D} * \mathcal{J} \right\|_F^2. \tag{6.44}$$

2. Fix $\mathcal{J}_{k+1}$. Update the block $(\mathcal{Z}', \mathcal{E})$ by solving

$$(\mathcal{Z}_{k+1}', \mathcal{E}_{k+1}) = \operatorname{argmin}_{\mathcal{Z}', \mathcal{E}} \|\mathcal{Z}'\|_* + \lambda \|\mathcal{E}\|_1 + \frac{\beta_k}{2} \left\| \mathcal{Z}' - \mathcal{J}_{k+1} + \frac{\mathcal{Y}_k^1}{\beta_k} \right\|_F^2$$
$$+ \frac{\beta_k}{2} \left\| \mathcal{E} - \mathcal{X} + \mathcal{D} * \mathcal{J}_{k+1} - \frac{\mathcal{Y}_k^2}{\beta_k} \right\|_F^2. \tag{6.45}$$

3. Update Lagrange multipliers with $\mathcal{G}_{k+1} = \mathcal{D} * \mathcal{J}_{k+1} + \mathcal{E}_{k+1}$:

$$\mathcal{Y}_{k+1}^1 = \mathcal{Y}_k^1 + \beta_k \left(\mathcal{Z}_{k+1}' - \mathcal{J}_{k+1} \right), \quad \mathcal{Y}_{k+1}^2 = \mathcal{Y}_k^2 + \beta_k \left(\mathcal{X} - \mathcal{G}_{k+1} \right).$$

4. $\beta_{k+1} = \min(\gamma \beta_k, \beta_{\max})$.

5. Check the convergence conditions:

$$\max(\|\mathcal{J}_{k+1} - \mathcal{J}_k\|_\infty, \|\mathcal{Z}_{k+1}' - \mathcal{Z}_k'\|_\infty, \|\mathcal{E}_{k+1} - \mathcal{E}_k\|_\infty) \le \epsilon,$$
$$\max(\|\mathcal{J}_{k+1} - \mathcal{Z}_{k+1}'\|_\infty, \|\mathcal{X} - \mathcal{D} * \mathcal{J}_{k+1} - \mathcal{E}_{k+1}\|_\infty) \le \epsilon.$$

6. $k = k + 1$.

end while

Output: $\mathcal{Z}_\star = \mathcal{V}_{\mathcal{A}} * \mathcal{Z}_{k+1}'$, $\mathcal{E}_\star = \mathcal{E}_{k+1}$, $\mathcal{L}_\star = \mathcal{X} - \mathcal{E}_\star$.

---

in (6.12) and the block-diagonal structure of $\bar{B}$ imply that solving problem (6.46) is equivalent to computing $\bar{\mathcal{J}}^{k+1}$ first:

$$\bar{J}_{k+1}^{(i)} = \bar{G}^{(i)} \left((\bar{Q}_k^1)^{(i)} + (\bar{D}^{(i)})^* (\bar{Q}_k^2)^{(i)} \right), \ \forall i = 1, \cdots, n_3, \tag{6.47}$$

where $\mathcal{G} = (\mathcal{D}^* * \mathcal{D} + \mathcal{I})^{-1}$. Then we can obtain $\mathcal{J}_{k+1} = \mathtt{ifft}(\bar{\mathcal{J}}_{k+1}, [], 3)$.

Updating the block $(\mathcal{Z}', \mathcal{E})$: For solving $\mathcal{Z}'$ and $\mathcal{E}$, we put $(\mathcal{Z}', \mathcal{E})$ into a large block of variables:

$$(\mathcal{Z}_{k+1}', \mathcal{E}_{k+1}) = \operatorname{argmin}_{\mathcal{Z}', \mathcal{E}} \|\mathcal{Z}'\|_* + \lambda \|\mathcal{E}\|_1 + \frac{\beta_k}{2} \left\| \mathcal{Z}' - \mathcal{R}_k^1 \right\|_F^2 + \frac{\beta_k}{2} \left\| \mathcal{R}_k^2 - \mathcal{E} \right\|_F^2, \tag{6.48}$$

where $\mathcal{R}_k^1 = \mathcal{J}_{k+1} - \mathcal{Y}_k^1/\beta_k$ and $\mathcal{R}_k^2 = \mathcal{X} - \mathcal{D} * \mathcal{J}_{k+1} + \mathcal{Y}_k^2/\beta_k$. Problem (6.48) can be split into subproblems for $\mathcal{Z}'$ and $\mathcal{E}$ as these two variables are independent in this minimization problem. Accordingly, we update the variable $\mathcal{Z}'$ as follows:

$$\mathcal{Z}'_{k+1} = \mathrm{argmin}_{\mathcal{Z}'} \|\mathcal{Z}'\|_* + \frac{\beta_k}{2} \left\| \mathcal{Z}' - \mathcal{R}_k^1 \right\|_F^2 .$$

Thus, by the properties $\|\mathcal{B}\|_F^2 = \frac{1}{n_3}\|\bar{B}\|_F^2$ and $\|\mathcal{B}\|_* = \frac{1}{n_3}\|\bar{B}\|_*$ in Eq. (6.12) in Section 6.2, we can optimize its equivalent problem:

$$\bar{Z}'_{k+1} = \mathrm{argmin}_{\bar{Z}'} \frac{1}{n_3} \left(\|\bar{Z}'\|_* + \frac{\beta_k}{2} \left\| \bar{R}_k^1 - \bar{Z}' \right\|_F^2 \right).$$

Since $\bar{Z}'$ is a block-diagonal matrix, we only need to update all the block matrices $(\bar{Z}')^{(i)}$ $(i = 1, \cdots, n_3)$ along the diagonal by following the closed-form solution:

$$(\bar{Z}'_{k+1})^{(i)} = \mathcal{S}_{\frac{1}{\beta_k}} \left((\bar{R}_k^1)^{(i)} \right), \; i = 1, \cdots, n_3. \tag{6.49}$$

Here $\mathcal{S}_{1/\beta_k}(\cdot)$ is the SVT operator [44]. Finally, we can compute $\mathcal{Z}'_{k+1} = \mathtt{ifft}(\bar{Z}'_{k+1}, [\,], 3)$. As for $\mathcal{E}$, we can update it by solving

$$\mathcal{E}_{k+1} = \mathrm{argmin}_{\mathcal{E}} \lambda\|\mathcal{E}\|_1 + \frac{\beta_k}{2} \left\| \mathcal{R}_k^2 - \mathcal{E} \right\|_F^2 .$$

Hence, we can obtain its closed-form solution:

$$\mathcal{E}_{k+1} = \Psi_{\lambda/\beta_k} \left(\mathcal{R}_k^2 \right), \tag{6.50}$$

where $\Psi_{\lambda/\beta_k}(\cdot)$ is the soft-thresholding in Theorem 6.6. The optimization details are summarized in Algorithm 6.

Convergence and complexity analysis. The convergence analysis in [43] can guarantee that Algorithm 6 would converge to the global optimum, because the problem (6.43) is a convex problem which only involves two blocks of variables, $\mathcal{J}$ and $(\mathcal{Z}', \mathcal{E})$, and only includes linear constraints. Then we consider the computational cost and use $\mathcal{O}$ to conceal the constant factors in the computational cost. At each iteration, when updating $\mathcal{J}_{k+1}$, computing the closed-form solution to problem (6.43) is of cost $\mathcal{O}\left(r_{\mathcal{A}}(n_1 + n_2)n_3 \log(n_3) + r_{\mathcal{A}}n_1n_2n_3\right)$. The major cost of computing the closed-form solution $(\mathcal{Z}'_{k+1}, \mathcal{E}_{k+1})$ to problem (6.49) includes n_3 SVD on $r_{\mathcal{A}} \times n_2$ matrices of cost order $\mathcal{O}(r_{\mathcal{A}}^2 n_2 n_3)$ and the tensor product of cost order $\mathcal{O}\left(r_{\mathcal{A}}n_1n_2n_3 + r_{\mathcal{A}}(n_1 + n_2)n_3 \log(n_3)\right)$. In this way, the total cost of Algorithm 6 is $\mathcal{O}\left(r_{\mathcal{A}}n_1n_2n_3 + r_{\mathcal{A}}(n_1 + n_2)n_3 \log(n_3)\right)$ for each iteration. Compared with directly solving problem (6.35), whose iteration cost is $\mathcal{O}\left((n_1 + n_2)n_2^2n_3\right)$, the reformulation (6.42) greatly reduces the computational cost.

6.4.2.5 Dictionary construction

In TLRR, one needs a qualified dictionary $\mathcal{A}$. This is because the bases in $\mathcal{A}$ should be able to linearly represent each authentic sample in the clean data $\mathcal{L}_0$. Accordingly, it is possible that the clean data can be recovered and the learned relationship among samples is accurate. To this end, two different approaches are introduced to construct a qualified dictionary $\mathcal{A}$ for TLRR.

Firstly, we can regard the raw tensor data $\mathcal{X}$ as the dictionary $\mathcal{A}$. This strategy is similar to that used in LRR [30]. In [3], this method is called *S-TLRR*, where "S" denotes "simple." As mentioned, in this case, the learned representation $\mathcal{Z}_\star$ can indicate the similarity relations between samples, and thus it can be used for clustering tasks.

But in practice, tensor data are usually corrupted. In this case, directly taking the contaminated data as the dictionary would reduce the performance. It can be understood as that the learned relationship among samples using a grossly corrupted dictionary would be far less accurate, and the performance for clustering or recovery can be greatly affected. Actually, Theorem 6.9 also reflects this limitation, since Theorem 6.9 proves that TLRR needs $\mathcal{P}_{\mathcal{U}_{\mathcal{A}}}(\mathcal{U}_0) = \mathcal{U}_0$ for recovery, which means that the dictionary $\mathcal{A}$ and the clean samples should share their tensor subspaces. In this challenging scenario, TLRR proposes to use the estimation $\mathcal{L}'$ for clean data $\mathcal{L}_0$ from R-TPCA as the dictionary. It also should be mentioned that although R-TPCA hardly exactly recovers $\mathcal{L}_0$ for a large number of subspaces, it can remove some noise from $\mathcal{X}$ to some extent and provide a less noisy dictionary $\mathcal{L}'$ than $\mathcal{X}$. Zhou et al. [3] call this method *Robust-TLRR* or *R-TLRR* in short.

Algorithm 7 Dictionary construction.

Input: Tensor data $\mathcal{X} \in \mathbb{R}^{n_1 \times n_2 \times n_3}$.
Initialize: $\lambda = 1/\sqrt{n_3 \max(n_1, n_2)}$.
1. Utilize R-TPCA to estimate $\mathcal{L}'$ with regularization parameter λ.
2. Estimate the tubal rank $r_{\mathcal{L}'}$ of $\mathcal{L}'$.
3. Truncate $\mathcal{L}'$ to obtain tensor $\mathcal{L}''$ obeying $\mathrm{rank}_t(\mathcal{L}'') \leq r_{\mathcal{L}'}$:

$$\mathcal{L}'' = \mathrm{argmin}_{\mathcal{L}} \|\mathcal{L} - \mathcal{L}'\|_F^2, \quad \text{s.t. } \mathrm{rank}_t(\mathcal{L}'') \leq r_{\mathcal{L}'}. \tag{6.51}$$

Output: dictionary $\mathcal{A} = \mathcal{L}''$.

The details to apply R-TPCA [27] for constructing the dictionary $\mathcal{A}$ are summarized in Algorithm 7. One can observe that Algorithm 7 first uses R-TPCA to denoise data $\mathcal{X}$ for obtaining an estimation $\mathcal{L}'$ to the clean data $\mathcal{L}_0$. Next, it regards a rank-truncated $\mathcal{L}'$ as the dictionary. The following two steps present the details in Steps 2 and 3.

Step 2. For each frontal slice $(\bar{L}')^{(i)}$ of $\bar{\mathcal{L}}'$, we first compute the nonzero singular values $\{\sigma_1^i, \cdots, \sigma_{n_i}^i\}$ (in descending order) of $(\bar{L}')^{(i)}$ and then let $c_j^i = \sigma_j^i/\sigma_{j+1}^i$ ($1 \leq j \leq n_i - 1$), $j_*^i = \mathrm{argmax}_j c_j^i$, and $c_*^i = c_{j_*^i}^i$. If $(n_i - 1)c_*^i / \sum_{j \neq j_*^i} c_j^i < 10$ (does not

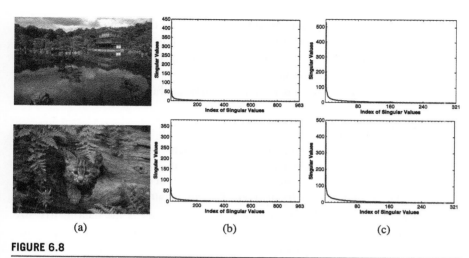

FIGURE 6.8

Illustration of the low tubal rank property of the images in the Berkeley Segmentation dataset [3]. (a) Two randomly selected images. (b) The singular values of $\bar{X}$ obtained by conducting linear transform on the DFT result $\mathcal{X}$ of image tensor $\mathcal{X}$. (c) $\sum_{i=1}^{n_3} s_i$, where s_i is the singular value vector (in descending order) of the i-th frontal slice $\bar{X}^{(i)}$ of $\bar{\mathcal{X}}$.

need truncation), then let $j_*^i = n_i$. Finally, we obtain the estimated tubal rank $r_{\mathcal{L}'} = \max(j_*^1, \cdots, j_*^{n_3})$.

Step 3. By Theorem 6.4 in Section 6.3, problem (6.51) in Algorithm 7 has a closed-form solution: $\mathcal{L}'' = \sum_{j=1}^{r_{\mathcal{L}'}} \mathcal{U}'(:, j, :) * \mathcal{S}'(j, j, :) * (\mathcal{V}'(:, j, :))^*$, where $\mathcal{U}' * \mathcal{S}' * (\mathcal{V}')^*$ is the t-SVD of $\mathcal{L}'$.

Thanks to Steps 2 and 3, the coherence parameter $\mu_1^{\mathcal{A}}(\mathcal{L}_0)$ would be reduced. This is because Step 2 may reduce the estimated tubal rank of $\mathcal{L}'$, together with (Step 3) the tubal rank $r_{\mathcal{A}}$ of the dictionary. As shown in Theorem 6.9, it can benefit R-TLRR in data recovery tasks.

More importantly, another appealing property is also found in the aforementioned dictionary construction method. Specifically, in applications, we find that the constructed dictionary $\mathcal{A} = \mathcal{L}''$ usually satisfies the exact recovery condition in Theorem 6.9—the ranks of $\bar{A}^{(i)}$ ($i = 1, \cdots, n_3$) are equal. The reason is that after Steps 2 and 3 in Algorithm 7, all frontal slices $(\bar{L}'')^{(i)}$ ($i = 1, \cdots, n_3$) of the estimated data $\mathcal{L}''$ have the same rank since the ranks of $(\bar{L}'')^{(i)}$ ($i = 1, \cdots, n_3$) are usually larger than the computed truncation rank $r_{\mathcal{L}'}$. To verify this, we randomly select two images (Fig. 6.8(a)) from the Berkeley Segmentation dataset [45] and plot the singular values of $\bar{X}$ in Fig. 6.8(b). We observe that most of these singular values are very close to 0 and much smaller than the leading singular values. Also, by definition, the tensor tubal rank $\text{rank}_t(\mathcal{X}) = \max(r_1, \cdots, r_{n_3})$, where r_i is the rank of $\bar{X}^{(i)}$. So we compute the singular value vector s_i (elements are in descending order) of $\bar{X}^{(i)}$ and plot $v = \sum_{i=1}^{n_3} s_i$ in Fig. 6.8(c). We find that the tubal rank of these images is indeed very low, since most values in v are almost zero. So by the truncation operation in Steps 2 and 3, the estimated tubal rank $r_{\mathcal{L}'}$ would be much smaller than the rank of all frontal slices $(\bar{L}'')^{(i)}$ $(i = 1, \cdots, n_3)$. Thus, the constructed dictionary $\mathcal{A} = \mathcal{L}''$ can obey the condition that the ranks of $\bar{A}^{(i)}$ $(i = 1, \cdots, n_3)$ are equal to each other. Accordingly, the exact recovery performance can be guaranteed.

6.4.3 Applications

In this section, we test TPCA on real applications, including data recovery/denoising and clustering. Actually, TPCA can also work well in many other tasks, e.g., recommendation systems. For experiments, we follow the theoretical parameter settings in [3,8,27,31]. Specifically, we fix the regularization parameters of R-PCA [8], LRR [30], and R-LRR [31] as $1/\sqrt{\max(n_1', n_2')}$, where $n_1' \times n_2'$ is the data matrix size processed by them. For R-TPCA [27], S-TLRR [3], and R-TLRR [3], the parameter takes $1/\sqrt{\max(n_1, n_2)n_3}$, where the data size is $n_1 \times n_2 \times n_3$. Here R-LRR uses the estimated data by R-PCA as its dictionary. In all experiments, S-TLRR regards the raw tensor data as its dictionary, and R-TLRR constructs its dictionary by using Algorithm 7 in Section 6.4.2. All the experimental results are adopted from [3].

6.4.3.1 Application to data recovery

Application to synthetic data recovery. In this subsection, we aim to investigate the data recovery performance of TLRR and further compare it with R-TPCA. Theorem 6.9 requires the dictionary $\mathcal{A}$ which (approximatively) meets the condition $\mathcal{P}_{\mathcal{U}_0}(\mathcal{U}_{\mathcal{A}}) = \mathcal{U}_{\mathcal{A}}$. So here we only test R-TLRR because it uses the recovered data by R-TPCA as the dictionary $\mathcal{A}$ which (approximatively) meets the condition $\mathcal{P}_{\mathcal{U}_0}(\mathcal{U}_{\mathcal{A}}) = \mathcal{U}_{\mathcal{A}}$ required for recovery, while S-TLRR does not. This help us verify Theorem 6.9.

To this end, we follow Zhou et al. [3] and generate $\mathcal{L}_0$ and $\mathcal{E}_0$ as follows. We first randomly generate $\mathcal{B}_i \in \mathbb{R}^{n_1 \times r_i \times n_3}$ and $\mathcal{C}_i \in \mathbb{R}^{r_i \times m_i \times n_3}$ whose entries are from independent identically distributed (i.i.d.) $\mathcal{N}(0, 1)$, and then produce six random low-rank tensors $\{\mathcal{L}_1, \cdots, \mathcal{L}_6\}$ with $\mathcal{L}_i = \mathcal{B}_i * \mathcal{C}_i$. In this way, one can easily know that the low-rank tensor $\mathcal{L}_i$ of m_i samples is of tubal rank r_i. Then let $\mathcal{L}_0 = [\mathcal{L}_1, \cdots, \mathcal{L}_6] \in \mathbb{R}^{n_1 \times n_2 \times n_3}$, where $n_2 = \sum_{i=1}^{6} m_i$ and $\text{rank}_t(\mathcal{L}_0) = \sum_{i=1}^{6} r_i$. Now we consider the noise tensor $\mathcal{E}_0$. For $\mathcal{E}$, its support set Ω is chosen uniformly at random. Then two kinds of noise are evaluated here. The first one is similar to [31]: (a) we normalize the values of entries in $\mathcal{L}_0$ such that $\|\mathcal{L}_0\|_\infty = 1$ and i.i.d. produce the noise in $\mathcal{E}_0$ as ± 1 with probability 0.5. For the second case, (b) $\mathcal{L}_0$ is not normalized and the noise in $\mathcal{E}_0$ is also drawn from i.i.d. $\mathcal{N}(0, 1)$. For simplicity, we set $n_1 = 240$, $n_3 = 20$, $m_i = 500$, and $r_i = r$, which varies from 1 to 24. The fraction $\rho = |\Omega|/(n_1 n_2 n_3)$ ranges from 2.5% to 65% with increment 2.5%. Similar to [31], for each pair (ρ, r), we simulate 20 test instances and declare a trial successful if the recovered $\mathcal{L}_\star$ obeys $\|\mathcal{L}_\star - \mathcal{L}_0\|_F / \|\mathcal{L}_0\|_F \leq 0.05$.

Fig. 6.9 reports the experimental results. From the results, one can observe that for both cases, for low tubal rank $\text{rank}_t(\mathcal{L}_0)$ and small noise ratio ρ, R-TLRR can exactly recover the clean data (gray and block areas). This observation is consistent with Theorem 6.9. More importantly, one can also find that R-TLRR achieves a better recovery performance than R-TPCA, because there are some cases (gray areas) where R-TLRR succeeds while R-TPCA fails. Such an observation is in accordance with the conclusion in Section 6.4.2: in most cases, R-TLRR enjoys a better recovery ability than R-TPCA. All these results also show validity of the dictionary built by T-RPCA.

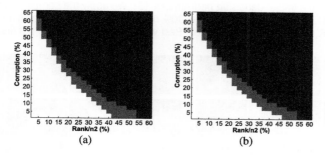

FIGURE 6.9

Comparison between R-TPCA and R-TLRR [3]. White region: Both R-TPCA and R-TLRR succeed. Gray regions: R-TLRR succeeds while R-TPCA fails. Black regions: Both R-TPCA and R-TLRR fail. (a) Normalize $\mathcal{L}_0$ such that $\|\mathcal{L}_0\|_\infty = 1$ and i.i.d. produce ± 1 noise in $\mathcal{E}_0$ with probability 0.5. (b) Produce i.i.d. $\mathcal{N}(0, 1)$ noise in $\mathcal{E}_0$.

Application to image denoising. In this section, we test the performance of R-TLRR, R-TPCA, and other baselines in a denoising task. As discussed above, since S-TLRR uses corrupted data as its dictionary, it cannot exactly recover the noisy data. For experiments, the Berkeley segmentation dataset [45] is used for testing. It includes 200 color images of various natural scenes and each image is of size $321 \times 481 \times 3$. In the experiments, we organize the color images along the channel direction to form a $w \times n \times h$ tensor with images size $w \times h$ and channel number n. We use the peak signal-to-noise ratio (PSNR) to evaluate the denoising performance:

$$PSNR = 10\log_{10}\left(n_1 n_2 n_3 \|\mathcal{L}_0\|_\infty^2 / \|\mathcal{L}_\star - \mathcal{L}_0\|_F^2\right),$$

where $\mathcal{L}_\star$ is the recovered tensor of $\mathcal{L}_0 \in \mathbb{R}^{n_1 \times n_2 \times n_3}$.

Because many previous works [3,4,7,8,27,31,46–49] empirically showed that image and video data can be well approximated by low-rank matrices/tensors, low rank-based methods can work for image/video denoising. This is also illustrated by Fig. 6.8.

To test the denoising performance, we first randomly set 5%–30% of pixels in each image to random values in $[0, 255]$ and then apply the compared methods to recover them. It should be mentioned that the corrupted locations are unknown for these compared methods. We summarize the experimental results in Fig. 6.10, i.e., the average PSNR values (on top of each bar) achieved by the compared methods. From the results, one can find that R-TLRR is always the best and performs about

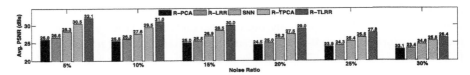

FIGURE 6.10

Comparison of the image denoising performance [3]. We apply the compared methods to recover the 200 images corrupted by 5%–30% noise in the Berkeley dataset and report the average PSNR values on the 200 images. Best viewed in ×2 sized color pdf file.

(a) Raw image (b) Corrupted (c) R-PCA (d) R-LRR (e) SNN (f) R-TPCA (g) R-TLRR

FIGURE 6.11

Examples of image denoising at a noise ratio of 20% [3]. (a) Raw image. (b) Corrupted image. (c)–(g) The recovered results by the compared methods. (h) PSNR values on the above six images. **Best viewed in ×2 sized color pdf file.**

1.5 dB better than the runner-up under different noise ratios in terms of the average PSNR values. Moreover, R-TLRR also performs better than others on every image. It can be illustrated by the test case where the noise ratio is 20%. In this case, R-TLRR makes at least 2.0, 1.5, 1.0, and 0.5 dB improvements compared with the second best on 41, 105, 174, and 194 images, respectively.

We show the visual denoising results when the noise ratio is 20% in Fig. 6.11. From the results, one also can observe that R-TLRR preserves more details in the images and achieves much better performance than others. For example, the contours of hydrophyte leaves and the spots of deers are well recovered. R-TLRR performs at least 2.4 dB better than the second best R-TPCA on the test images. Because both R-PCA and LRR recover the R, G, and B channels separately and do not fully use the structure information, they suffer from relatively poor performance compared with the tensor-based methods. By comparison, one can also see that matricization-based methods, e.g., SNN, may destroy the data structure and lose optimality of the low rank property [28,50]. Conversely, R-TLRR avoids the low-rank structure information loss [27,50], hence giving better performance. R-TLRR also outperforms

(a) Extended YaleB	(b) FRGC 2.0	(c) FRDUE

Dataset	#Class	#Per class	#Total image	Size	Difficulty
YaleB	28	30	840	80×60	ill.
FRGC 2.0	60	20	1200	32×36	ill. and exp.
FRDUE	153	≈ 20	3059	22×25	def. and pos.

(d) Descriptions of the three datasets. ("ill.", "exp.", "def." and "pos." are short for "illumination", "expression", "deformation" and "pose", respectively .

FIGURE 6.12

Experimental settings of the three test datasets [3].

R-TPCA, in accordance with Theorem 6.9: when given a qualified dictionary, R-TLRR has a stronger recovery guarantee than R-TPCA. This also demonstrates that the dictionary pursued by R-TPCA is qualified.

6.4.3.2 Application to data clustering

Now we evaluate the performance of S-TLRR and R-TLRR on a data clustering task. Here face data are used. This is because as shown in many works [51,52], most authentic face images approximately lie in a union of low-rank linear subspaces. We summarize the testing datasets in Fig. 6.12. Here we test Extended YaleB (uncropped) [53], FRGC 2.0 [36], and FRDUE.[1] For FRDUE, we respectively use its first 100 and all classes for testing. The test methods include the commonly used sparse and low rank-based ones, such as LSA [54], LSR$_1$ [34], LSR$_2$ [34], SSC [32], EnSC [33], R-PCA [8], LRR [30], R-LRR [31], TLRRSC [35], and R-TPCA [27]. For TLRR and T-RPCA, we organize the images along the second dimension. As we discussed above, this organization can well capture the linear representation relations among samples. Then after denoising, kmeans is used to cluster the estimated clean data by T-RPCA. To measure the performance, we use three metrics, i.e., accuracy (ACC) [32], normalized mutual information (NMI) [55], and purity (PUR) [56], to evaluate the clustering performance. We run all the experiments 20 times and report the average performance.

Table 6.2 reports the clustering results. In most cases, R-TLRR outperforms all other methods, and S-TLRR also achieves better performance than others. More specifically, in terms of the ACC metric, R-TLRR performs about 4.5%, 4.1%, 4.6%, and 3.9% better than the runner-up in the four test cases (top-down), respectively. These results clearly demonstrate that TLRR is very robust and superior. There are several reasons that lead to the advantages of TLRR. The first one is that S-TLRR and R-TLRR effectively exploit the multidimensional structure of the tensor data. In contrast, the matricization-based methods directly unfold the tensor data along a certain

---

[1] http://cswww.essex.ac.uk/mv/allfaces/.

Table 6.2 Clustering results (ACC, NMI, and PUR) and the algorithm running time (in seconds) on the three test databases [3].

Dataset	Metric	LSR$_1$	LSR$_2$	SSC	EnSC	R-PCA	LRR	R-LRR	TLRRSC	R-TPCA	S-TLRR	R-TLRR
YaleB	ACC	0.819	0.813	0.821	0.828	0.708	0.753	0.803	0.662	0.720	0.845	**0.873**
	NMI	0.882	0.876	0.885	0.890	0.820	0.871	0.888	0.787	0.832	0.897	**0.927**
	PUR	0.843	0.837	0.841	0.850	0.728	0.796	0.825	0.673	0.744	0.857	**0.877**
	Time	**0.22**	**0.26**	2027.4	42.3	1728.5	274.1	1813.6	728.2	200.7	555.3	697.6
FRGC 2.0	ACC	0.865	0.863	0.861	0.870	0.735	0.795	0.830	0.602	0.812	0.891	**0.911**
	NMI	0.927	0.921	0.924	0.933	0.873	0.901	0.922	0.841	0.906	0.947	**0.963**
	PUR	0.868	0.858	0.865	0.870	0.765	0.825	0.855	0.657	0.838	0.910	**0.929**
	Time	**0.24**	**0.25**	676.3	32.6	1611.4	304.7	1734.6	901.4	49.8	141.6	162.4
FRDUE (100 classes)	ACC	0.763	0.744	0.796	0.800	0.626	0.707	0.753	0.673	0.658	0.825	**0.846**
	NMI	0.918	0.911	0.921	0.920	0.821	0.884	0.920	0.858	0.837	0.927	**0.943**
	PUR	0.821	0.806	0.831	0.836	0.716	0.773	0.792	0.726	0.740	0.852	**0.874**
	Time	**0.96**	**0.88**	844.9	16.5	354.06	190.0	397.1	568.2	36.6	117.9	147.2
FRDUE (all classes)	ACC	0.740	0.712	0.773	0.779	0.632	0.702	0.721	0.635	0.695	**0.785**	**0.818**
	NMI	0.900	0.895	0.905	0.907	0.814	0.830	0.894	0.817	0.880	**0.914**	**0.932**
	PUR	0.801	0.781	0.816	**0.829**	0.725	0.770	0.775	0.704	0.752	0.821	**0.852**
	Time	**1.03**	**0.98**	1011.5	21.0	472.9	305.3	569.6	755.4	49.2	183.9	205.2

mode, which could destroy the multiway low-rank data structure and lead to degraded performance [27,50]. The second one is that unlike R-TPCA, which assumes data are from a single tensor subspace, both S-TLRR and R-TLRR consider the mixture structure in data (more consistent with reality) and learn more accurate relations among samples. Also, the results show that the robust versions, i.e., R-TLRR and R-LRR, usually outperform their counterparts, i.e., S-TLRR and LRR, since directly using the corrupted sample data as the dictionary could lead to an inaccurate representation. TLRRSC [35] does not perform well, for the following three reasons. (i) It reshapes the two-way face images into vectors and destroys the intrinsic multiway data structure. (ii) Randomly arranging the samples in the first $(k-1)$ modes may give a nonlow-rank tensor structure. (iii) The Frobenius norm in TLRRSC can deal with Gaussian noise but cannot handle the complex noise in face images well [8]. Table 6.2 also reports the algorithm running time. Note that the computational time of R-TLRR contains the time cost for dictionary construction and solving the TLRR problem (6.42). Besides, R-TLRR is always much faster than its counterpart R-LRR, and S-TLRR runs faster than LRR in most cases. Though LSR_1, LSR_2, and EnSC are also efficient, tuning their critical regularization parameters requires significant additional effort.

6.4.4 Summary

In this section, we introduce two effective tensor recovery methods, including R-TPCA [2] and TLRR [3], for recovering the clean low-tubal rank tensor $\mathcal{L}_0$ from a highly corrupted tensor $\mathcal{X} = \mathcal{L}_0 + \mathcal{E}_0$, where $\mathcal{E}_0$ is sparse noise. For both R-TPCA and TLRR, we introduce their model, their recovery theories, and optimization algorithms. For TLRR, we further introduce its clustering process and its two dictionary construction methods. Finally, we apply these methods to data denoising and clustering tasks, and compare them with other kinds of low-rank tensor recovery methods.

6.5 Tensor PCA for outlier-corrupted data

In this section, we introduce OR-TPCA [4]—a new method for tensor data analysis. As shown in Fig. 6.13, suppose we are given a three-way tensor datum $\mathcal{X} \in \mathbb{R}^{n_1 \times n_2 \times n_3}$ that is a mixture of a clean low-rank tensor $\mathcal{L}_0$ and sparse outlier noise $\mathcal{E}_0$: $\mathcal{X} = \mathcal{L}_0 + \mathcal{E}_0$. That is, as shown in Fig. 6.13, by assuming that samples distribute along the second direction in $\mathcal{X}$, outliers mean that large errors concentrate only on a number of samples or several parts of data. OR-TPCA aims to address such a problem, i.e., how to exactly recover the low-rank tensor $\mathcal{L}_0$ (or its column space) in the presence of outliers. It should be mentioned that such a problem is important in various kinds of applications, such as image/video denoising and inpainting [22,27], text analysis [59], data mining [57], and collaborative filtering [58]. There are two reasons that make the problem become more and more important. The first one is that high-dimensional tensor data, e.g., videos and image collections, are usually in-

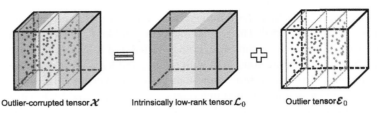

Outlier-corrupted tensor $\mathcal{X}$ Intrinsically low-rank tensor $\mathcal{L}_0$ Outlier tensor $\mathcal{E}_0$

FIGURE 6.13

The problem solved by this section: isolate the clean low-rank component from outliers for an outlier-corrupted tensor [4].

trinsically low-rank or approximately so [19]. Secondly, since in practice there are sensor failures, malicious tampering, or other system errors [9–11], the outliers or sample-specific corruptions are common in real data. In this way, recovering low-rank tensor data from outlier corruptions is important and necessary. However, as we discussed at the beginning of this chapter, most low-rank tensor analysis methods [8,24,27,60–62] assume the noise to be Gaussian or sparse and thus cannot handle outliers or sample-specific corruptions.

This section is structured as follows. Section 6.5.1 introduces OR-TPCA, including its model, recovery theory, and optimization algorithm. Then in Section 6.5.2, we elaborate on a fast algorithm to optimize the OR-TPCA model. Finally, in Section 6.5.3, we introduce real applications, such as data recovery, outlier detection, and semi-supervised and supervised classification tasks, of OR-TPCA.

6.5.1 Outlier robust tensor PCA

In this section, we introduce OR-TPCA [4] firstly, and then analyze its performance. Finally, we will introduce how to optimize its model. Define $n_{(1)} = \max(n_1, n_2)$ and $n_{(2)} = \min(n_1, n_2)$, which will be used in Section 6.5.

6.5.1.1 Formulation of OR-TPCA

In this section, we assume that outliers are distributed along the second dimension of a tensor $\mathcal{X}$. Possible outliers are denoted as $\mathcal{E}(:, i, :)$. Typically, compared with the sample number, the outlier number is actually small, which means that outliers are very sparse. To characterize this sparsity, we employ the tensor $\ell_{2,1}$-norm. Based on this, we can formulate the OR-TPCA model as follows:

$$\min_{\mathcal{L},\mathcal{E}} \|\mathcal{L}\|_* + \lambda \|\mathcal{E}\|_{2,1}, \text{ s.t. } \mathcal{X} = \mathcal{L} + \mathcal{E}, \tag{6.52}$$

where $\|\mathcal{L}\|_*$ denotes the tensor nuclear norm and $\|\mathcal{E}\|_{2,1} = \sum_i \|\mathcal{E}_{:,i,:}\|_F$ denotes the $\ell_{2,1}$-norm of tensor $\mathcal{E}$.

Now we discuss the tensor nuclear norm used in this section and the one used in other works. In this section, the tensor nuclear norm of $\mathcal{L}$ in Definition 6.9 in Section 6.3 is equivalent to the nuclear norm (with a factor $1/n_3$) of the block-circulant matrix $\texttt{bcirc}(\mathcal{L})$ in Eq. (6.9). Differently from other matricizations along a certain dimension, such as the Tucker rank [21], the block-circulant matricization may preserve more spatial relations among entries in the tensor and thus better depict the low-rank structure of the tensor [27]. Moreover, the tensor nuclear norm actually equals the sum of the nuclear norms of all frontal slices of $\bar{\mathcal{L}}$, which is the DFT of $\mathcal{L}$ along the third dimension. In this way, minimizing the tensor nuclear norm of $\mathcal{L}$ is equivalent to recovering the underlying low-rank structure of each frontal slice $\bar{L}^{(i)}$ ($i = 1, \cdots, n_3$). So it recovers the subspaces of data in the Fourier domain, i.e., the subspaces of all the frontal slices $\bar{L}^{(i)}$, while the noise is distributed in the original space. It should be mentioned that the t-product of three-way tensors becomes the standard matrix–matrix product and the tensor nuclear norm degenerates to the matrix nuclear norm when $n_3 = 1$. In this case, OR-TPCA becomes OR-PCA [9,10,63] and its theory also guarantees the performance of OR-PCA.

6.5.1.2 Exact subspace recovery guarantees

It is impossible to exactly separate $\mathcal{X}$ as the low-rank term $\mathcal{L}_0$ plus the outlier-sparse term $\mathcal{E}_0$, where $\mathcal{L}_0$ is the sparse true low-rank term and $\mathcal{E}_0$ are the low-rank true sparse outliers. This is similar to low-rank matrix recovery [9,10,63]. Therefore, we use two mild conditions (assumptions) to avoid these cases.

The tensor column-incoherence condition on clean low-rank data is widely used for evaluating the sparsity of a matrix, and we generalize it to tensors here. For a tensor $\mathcal{L} \in \mathbb{R}^{n_1 \times n_2 \times n_3}$, suppose $\text{rank}_t(\mathcal{L}) = r$ and its skinny t-SVD is $\mathcal{U} * \mathcal{S} * \mathcal{V}^*$ (see Definition 6.7 in Section 6.3). For $\mathcal{U} \in \mathbb{R}^{n_1 \times r \times n_3}$ and $\mathcal{V} \in \mathbb{R}^{n_2 \times r \times n_3}$, we have $\mathcal{U}^* * \mathcal{U} = \mathcal{I}$ and $\mathcal{V}^* * \mathcal{V} = \mathcal{I}$. Then the tensor column-incoherence condition with parameter μ_1 is defined as

$$\mu_1 \geq \frac{n_2 n_3}{r} \max_{i=1,\cdots,n_2} \left\| \mathcal{V}^* * \mathring{\mathfrak{e}}_i \right\|_F^2, \tag{6.53}$$

where $\mathring{\mathfrak{e}}_i$ is of size $n_2 \times 1 \times n_3$ with the $(i, 1, 1)$-th entry equal to 1 and the rest equal to $\mathbf{0}$s; μ_1 measures how far the tensor is from a column sparse one, and if μ_1 is small, the tensor $\mathcal{L}$ is not column sparse, hence avoiding the first case.

The unambiguity condition on outliers is used to distinguish low-rank terms from outliers. Here we also require that outliers are not in the subspace of the low-rank clean data and are not low-rank [10,63]. To avoid this case, similar to matrix OR-PCA [10], we introduce an unambiguity condition on outliers $\mathcal{E}$:

$$\|\mathsf{B}(\mathcal{E})\| \leq \sqrt{\log(n_2)}/4, \tag{6.54}$$

where $\mathsf{B}(\mathcal{E}) = \{\widetilde{\mathcal{E}} : \widetilde{\mathcal{E}}(:, i, :) = \frac{\mathcal{E}(:,i,:)}{\|\mathcal{E}(:,i,:)\|_F} \ (i \in \Theta_0); \widetilde{\mathcal{E}}(:, i, :) = \mathbf{0} \ (i \notin \Theta_0)\}$ in Table 6.1 and Θ_0 denotes the support set of outliers. Note that many noise models satisfy the above condition, including i.i.d. Gaussian noise. Indeed, (6.54) holds as long as the directions of the nonzero lateral slices of $\mathsf{B}(\mathcal{E})$ scatter sufficiently randomly. No matter how many outliers are present, (6.54) can guarantee the outliers to be not low-rank.

Main results: Before stating the main results, we first define the tensor column space which is related with the theoretical results.

Definition 6.13. (Tensor column space) [4] For an arbitrary tensor $\mathcal{A} \in \mathbb{R}^{n_1 \times n_2 \times n_3}$, assume that $r = (\text{rank}(\bar{A}^{(1)}); \cdots; \text{rank}(\bar{A}^{(n_3)})) \in \mathbb{R}^{n_3}$, $r = \max_i r_i$, and the t-SVD of $\mathcal{A}$ is $\mathcal{A} = \mathcal{U} * \mathcal{S} * \mathcal{V}^*$. Then its column space $\text{Range}(\mathcal{A})$ is spanned by $\mathcal{U}_{\mathcal{A}} \in \mathbb{R}^{n_1 \times r \times n_3}$, where the first r_i columns of each slice $\bar{\mathcal{U}}_{\mathcal{A}}(:, :, i)$ consist of the first r_i columns of $\bar{\mathcal{U}}(:, :, i)$ and the remaining columns are $\mathbf{0}$s.

Minimizing $\|\mathcal{A}\|_*$ means recovering the low-rank subspace of each frontal slice $\bar{A}^{(i)}$ $(i = 1, \cdots, n_3)$, because for a tensor $\mathcal{A}$, its tensor nuclear norm is equivalent to the sum of the nuclear norms of all frontal slices of $\bar{A}$. So it means that the union of the column spaces of all the frontal slices $\bar{A}^{(i)}$ is actually the column space of $\mathcal{A}$. Denote $\text{Range}(\mathcal{L}_0)$ by the column space of $\mathcal{L}_0$. Then Theorem 6.11 state the main results.

Theorem 6.11. *[4] Assume* $\text{Range}(\mathcal{L}_0) = \text{Range}(\mathcal{P}_{\Theta_0^\perp}(\mathcal{L}_0))$ *and* $\mathcal{E}_0 \notin \text{Range}(\mathcal{L}_0)$. *Then any optimal solution* $(\mathcal{L}_0 + \mathcal{H}, \mathcal{E}_0 - \mathcal{H})$ *to problem (6.52) with* $\lambda = 1/\sqrt{\log(n_2)}$ *exactly recovers the tensor column space* $\mathcal{U}_0$ *of* $\mathcal{L}_0$ *and the support set* Θ_0 *of* $\mathcal{E}_0$ *with a probability of at least* $1 - c_1 n_{(1)}^{-10}$, *where* c_1 *is a positive constant, if the support set* Θ_0 *is uniformly distributed among all sets of cardinality* $|\Theta_0|$ *and*

$$rank_t(\mathcal{L}_0) \leq \frac{\rho_r n_2}{\mu_1 \log(n_{(1)})} \quad and \quad |\Theta_0| \leq \rho_s n_2,$$

where ρ_r *and* ρ_s *are two constants,* $\mathcal{L}_0 + \mathcal{P}_{\Theta_0}\mathcal{P}_{\mathcal{U}_0}(\mathcal{H})$ *satisfies the column-incoherence condition (6.53), and* $\mathcal{E}_0 - \mathcal{P}_{\Theta_0}\mathcal{P}_{\mathcal{U}_0}(\mathcal{H})$ *satisfies the unambiguity condition (6.54).*

The proof of Theorem 6.11 can be found in [4]. From Theorem 6.11, one can observe that OR-TPCA can exactly recover $\mathcal{P}_{\Theta_0^\perp}(\mathcal{L}_0)$, i.e., the clean data in $\mathcal{X}$, and the support set Θ_0 of $\mathcal{E}_0$, with high probability. However, it does not mean that OR-TPCA can never recover the corrupted samples. Actually, the results in [10,64,65] and the experiments (see Fig. 6.16 in Section 6.5.3) show that OR-TPCA can well recover a sample that is not severely corrupted. Finally, when $n_3 = 1$, OR-TPCA becomes OR-PCA and Theorem 6.11 also provides the corresponding theoretical guarantee.

6.5.1.3 Optimization

In this section, similar to TLRR, ADMM [43] can be used to solve problem (6.52), since it is very efficient to solve this kind of problems where linear constraints and the nuclear and $\ell_{2,1}$-norms are involved. Moreover, the theoretical convergence analysis in [43] can guarantee the convergence of ADMM, because problem (6.52) is convex with two blocks of variables. To begin with, the corresponding augmented Lagrangian function is as follows:

$$H(\mathcal{L}, \mathcal{E}, \mathcal{J}, \beta) = \|\mathcal{L}\|_* + \lambda\|\mathcal{E}\|_1 + \langle \mathcal{J}, \mathcal{X} - \mathcal{L} - \mathcal{E} \rangle + \frac{\beta}{2}\|\mathcal{X} - \mathcal{L} - \mathcal{E}\|_F^2,$$

Algorithm 8 Outlier robust tensor PCA (OR-TPCA).

Input: Tensor data $\mathcal{X} \in \mathbb{R}^{n_1 \times n_2 \times n_3}$.

Initialize: $\mathcal{L}_0 = \mathcal{E}_0 = \mathcal{J}_0 = 0$, $\lambda = 1/\sqrt{\log(n_2)}$, $\gamma = 1.1$, $\beta_0 = 1e - 5$, $\beta_{\max} = 1e + 8$, $\epsilon = 1e - 8$, and $k = 0$.

While not converged **do**

1. Fix $\mathcal{E}_k$. Update $\mathcal{L}_{k+1}$ by $\mathcal{L}_{k+1} = \mathrm{argmin}_{\mathcal{L}} \|\mathcal{L}\|_* + \frac{\beta_k}{2} \|\mathcal{X} - \mathcal{L} - \mathcal{E}_k + \frac{\mathcal{J}_k}{\beta_k}\|_F^2$.

2. Fix $\mathcal{L}_{k+1}$. Update $\mathcal{E}_{k+1}$ by $\mathcal{E}_{k+1} = \mathrm{argmin}_{\mathcal{E}} \lambda \|\mathcal{E}\|_{2,1} + \frac{\beta_k}{2} \|\mathcal{X} - \mathcal{L}_{k+1} - \mathcal{E} + \frac{\mathcal{J}_k}{\beta_k}\|_F^2$.

3. $\mathcal{J}_{k+1} = \mathcal{J}_k + \beta_k(\mathcal{X} - \mathcal{L}_{k+1} - \mathcal{E}_{k+1})$.

4. $\beta_{k+1} = \min(\gamma \beta_k, \beta_{\max})$.

5. Check the convergence conditions: $\|\mathcal{E}_{k+1} - \mathcal{E}_k\|_\infty \le \varepsilon$, $\|\mathcal{L}_{k+1} - \mathcal{L}_k\|_\infty \le \varepsilon$, $\|\mathcal{X} - \mathcal{L}_{k+1} - \mathcal{E}_{k+1}\|_\infty \le \varepsilon$.

6. $k = k + 1$.

end while

Output: $\mathcal{L}_{k+1}$ and $\mathcal{E}_{k+1}$.

---

where $\mathcal{J}$ is a Lagrange multiplier and β is the penalty parameter. Then $\mathcal{L}$ and $\mathcal{E}$ are alternately updated in each iteration by minimizing $H(\mathcal{L}, \mathcal{E}, \mathcal{J}, \beta)$ with other variables fixed.

Updating $\mathcal{L}$: We only need to minimize the following optimization problem:

$$\mathcal{L}_{k+1} = \mathrm{argmin}_{\mathcal{L}} \|\mathcal{L}\|_* + \frac{\beta_k}{2} \left\| \mathcal{X} - \mathcal{L} - \mathcal{E}_k + \frac{\mathcal{J}_k}{\beta_k} \right\|_F^2.$$

In this way, we can minimize the equivalent problem:

$$\bar{L}_{k+1} = \mathrm{argmin}_{\bar{L}} \frac{1}{n_3} \left(\|\bar{L}\|_* + \frac{\beta_k}{2} \|\bar{R} - \bar{L}\|_F^2 \right),$$

where $\mathcal{R} = \mathcal{X} - \mathcal{E}_k + \mathcal{J}_k/\beta_k$, $\bar{\mathcal{R}} = \texttt{fft}(\mathcal{R}, [], 3)$, and $\bar{R} = \texttt{bdiag}(\bar{\mathcal{R}})$. Note that $\bar{L}$ is a block-diagonal matrix. Accordingly, we only need to update all the block-diagonal matrices $\bar{L}^{(i)}$ $(i = 1, \cdots, n_3)$ by

$$\bar{L}_{k+1}^{(i)} = \mathcal{S}_{\frac{1}{\beta_k}} \left(\bar{R}^{(i)} \right), \quad (i = 1, \cdots, n_3), \tag{6.55}$$

where $\mathcal{S}_v(\cdot)$ is the SVT operator [44]. Finally, we can compute $\mathcal{L}_{k+1} = \texttt{ifft}(\bar{\mathcal{L}}_{k+1}, [], 3)$.

Updating $\mathcal{E}$: We can update $\mathcal{E}$ by solving

$$\mathcal{E}_{k+1} = \mathrm{argmin}_{\mathcal{E}} \lambda \|\mathcal{E}\|_{2,1} + \frac{\beta_k}{2} \left\| \mathcal{X} - \mathcal{L}_{k+1} - \mathcal{E} + \frac{\mathcal{J}_k}{\beta_k} \right\|_F^2$$

and obtain its closed-form solution:

$$\mathcal{E}(:,i,:)_{k+1} = \begin{cases} \frac{\|\mathcal{Q}^i\|_F - \lambda/\beta_k}{\|\mathcal{Q}^i\|_F} \mathcal{Q}^i, & \text{if } \|\mathcal{Q}^i\|_F \geq \lambda/\beta_k, \\ \mathbf{0}, & \text{otherwise,} \end{cases} \tag{6.56}$$

where $\mathcal{Q} = \mathcal{X} - \mathcal{L}_{k+1} + \frac{\mathcal{I}_k}{\beta_k}$ and $\mathcal{Q}^i = \mathcal{Q}(:,i,:)$.

It should be mentioned that we can implement the above algorithm in a parallel manner. This is because all lateral slices $\bar{L}_{k+1}^{(i)}$ ($i = 1, \cdots, n_3$) of $\bar{L}$ in Eq. (6.55) can be parallelly updated when updating $\mathcal{L}_{k+1}$. From Eq. (6.56), one can also find that when updating $\mathcal{E}_{k+1}$, its frontal slices $\mathcal{E}_{k+1}(:,i,:)$ ($i = 1, \cdots, n_2$) can also be parallelly computed. For the computational complexity, at each iteration, $\mathcal{L}_{k+1}$ and $\mathcal{E}_{k+1}$ have closed-form solutions and their computational complexity at each iteration is $O\left(n_{(1)}n_{(2)}^2 n_3 + n_1 n_2 n_3 \log(n_3)\right)$. Note that the computation and memory costs of OR-TPCA are much lower than those of OR-PCA and R-PCA. This is because the main computation and memory costs lie in SVDs involved in these methods and OR-TPCA only requires n_3 SVDs of $n_1 \times n_2$ matrices (the lateral slices $\mathcal{L}_{k+1}^{(i)}$), while in OR-PCA and R-PCA, they have to compute the SVD of the whole data matrix, which is much larger and hence needs much more computational resources and memory.

6.5.2 The fast OR-TPCA algorithm

In practice, tensor data, such as long video sequences and collections of millions of images, are usually large-scale. To boost the efficiency, we introduced a fast OR-TPCA algorithm in [4]. This algorithm includes two steps which are introduced as follows.

6.5.2.1 Sketch of fast OR-TPCA

(1) Seed tensor recovery: When directly handling the whole data by adopting OR-TPCA, it has a very high computational cost when the data scale is very large. To solve this issue, we divide the whole tensor of interest into two tensors of smaller sizes. Among them, we call one small tensor "seed tensor," which is used for recovering the subspace of the whole tensor. Specifically, we first randomly sample a subtensor $\mathcal{X}_l \in \mathbb{R}^{n_1 \times k \times n_3}$ from $\mathcal{X}$, where k is much smaller than n_2. Accordingly, $\mathcal{X}, \mathcal{L}$, and $\mathcal{E}$ are respectively partitioned into

$$\mathcal{X} = [\mathcal{X}_l, \mathcal{X}_r], \quad \mathcal{L}_0 = [\mathcal{L}_l, \mathcal{L}_r], \quad \mathcal{E}_0 = [\mathcal{E}_l, \mathcal{E}_r].$$

In this way, we can use fast OR-TPCA to recover $\mathcal{L}_l$ from $\mathcal{X}_l$ by solving a small-sized OR-TPCA problem (6.52). Therefore, the computation of recovering $\mathcal{L}_l$ is much cheaper than that of recovering the whole $\mathcal{L}_0$, because compared with n_2, k is very small.

(2) Tensor $\ell_{2,1}$ filtering: Because we randomly select $\mathcal{X}_l$, with high probability $\mathcal{L}_l$ spans the same subspace as $\mathcal{L}_0$. Indeed, Theorem 6.12 (stated later) guarantees

---

Algorithm 9 Fast OR-TPCA.

Input: Tensor data $\mathcal{X} \in \mathbb{R}^{n_1 \times n_2 \times n_3}$ and parameter s/n_2.
1. Randomly sample each lateral slice of $\mathcal{X}$ by an i.i.d. Bernoulli distribution $\text{Ber}(s/n_2)$ to construct $\mathcal{X}_l$ and the remaining lateral slices are for constructing $\mathcal{X}_r$.
2. Compute the clean data $\mathcal{L}_l$ and outliers $\mathcal{E}_l$ by solving

$$(\mathcal{L}_l, \mathcal{E}_l) = \text{argmin}_{\mathcal{L}', \mathcal{E}'} \, \|\mathcal{L}'\|_* + \lambda \|\mathcal{E}'\|_{2,1}, \text{ s.t. } \mathcal{X}_l = \mathcal{L}' + \mathcal{E}'.$$

3. Compute $\mathcal{L}_r$ and $\mathcal{E}_r$ in $\mathcal{X}_r$ by the closed-form solution to problem (6.58).
Output: $\mathcal{L} = [\mathcal{L}_l, \mathcal{L}_r]$ and $\mathcal{E} = [\mathcal{E}_l, \mathcal{E}_r]$.

---

this. So there must exist a tensor $\mathcal{Q}$ such that

$$\mathcal{L}_r = \mathcal{L}_l * \mathcal{Q}.$$

On the other hand, because $\mathcal{E}_r$ sampled from outliers $\mathcal{E}$ is also sparse, we also use the $\ell_{2,1}$-norm to depict this sparse property. So we can find $\mathcal{Q}$ by solving

$$\min_{\mathcal{E}_r, \mathcal{Q}} \|\mathcal{E}_r\|_{2,1}, \quad \text{s.t. } \mathcal{X}_r = \mathcal{L}_l * \mathcal{Q} + \mathcal{E}_r. \tag{6.57}$$

Considering the DFT is conducted along the third dimension, the lateral slices are independent of each other. Then, with the definition $\|\mathcal{E}_r\|_{2,1} = \sum_{i=1}^{n_2} \|\mathcal{E}_r(:,i,:)\|_F$, we can further divide problem (6.57) into $(n_2 - k)$ subproblems along the second dimension and the i-th subproblem is written as

$$\min_{\mathcal{E}_r^i, \mathcal{Q}^i} \|\mathcal{E}_r^i\|_F, \quad \text{s.t. } \mathcal{X}_r^i = \mathcal{L}_l * \mathcal{Q}^i + \mathcal{E}_r^i, \tag{6.58}$$

where $\mathcal{X}_r^i$, $\mathcal{E}_r^i$, and $\mathcal{Q}^i$ denote $\mathcal{X}_r(:,i,:)$, $\mathcal{E}_r(:,i,:)$, and $\mathcal{Q}(:,i,:)$, respectively. As problem (6.58) is a least-squares problem, it admits a closed-form solution $\mathcal{E}_r^i = \mathcal{X}_r^i - \mathcal{P}_{\mathcal{U}_{\mathcal{L}_l}}(\mathcal{X}_r^i)$, where $\mathcal{U}_{\mathcal{L}_l}$ is the tensor column space of $\mathcal{L}_l$. We can further obtain $\mathcal{L}_r^i = \mathcal{P}_{\mathcal{U}_{\mathcal{L}_l}}(\mathcal{X}_r^i)$. We summarize the fast algorithm in Algorithm 9.

6.5.2.2 Guarantees for fast OR-TPCA

In this section, we analyze the data recovery performance of fast OR-TPCA. When the value of k is lower bounded by a positive constant, Step 1 in Algorithm 9 guarantees that $\mathcal{P}_{\Theta_0^\perp}(\mathcal{X}_l)$ of the randomly selected $\mathcal{X}_l \in \mathbb{R}^{n_1 \times k \times n_3}$ exactly spans the desired column space $\text{Range}(\mathcal{L}_0)$ with high probability. By Theorem 6.11, Step 2 can exactly recover the true low-rank structure of $\mathcal{L}_l$ and detect outliers $\mathcal{E}_l$ with high probability. So the remaining normal samples can be represented by $\mathcal{L}_l$ while outliers cannot be represented. Theorem 6.12 summarizes the main results.

Theorem 6.12. *[4] Assume that each lateral slice of $\mathcal{X}$ is sampled by an i.i.d. Bernoulli distribution $Ber(s/n_2)$ for constructing $\mathcal{X}_l$ and all the assumptions in Theorem 6.11 are fulfilled for the pair $(\mathcal{L}_l, \mathcal{E}_l)$. Then Algorithm 9 exactly recovers the tensor column space of $\mathcal{L}_0$ and the support set Θ_0 of $\mathcal{E}_0$ with a probability of at least $1 - \delta$, provided that*

$$s \geq \max\left(c_2\mu_1 r \log(n_{(1)}), 2\mu_1 r \log\left(\frac{r}{\delta}\right)\right), \tag{6.59}$$

where c_2 is a constant, $r = rank_t(\mathcal{L}_0)$, and μ_1 denotes the tensor column-incoherence parameter in Eq. (6.53).

The proof of Theorem 6.12 can be found in the Appendix or in [4]. Note that actually, this fast algorithm does not require stricter conditions than solving the original problem. This is because if $(\mathcal{L}_0, \mathcal{E}_0)$ obeys the assumptions in Theorem 6.11, the pair $(\mathcal{L}_l, \mathcal{E}_l)$ also meets them. More importantly, when dealing with large-scale tensor data, this fast algorithm is very useful. This is because generally the rank of large-scale data is much smaller than the size. Hence we can just set s/n_2 very small (e.g., 6%) and the randomly selected $\mathcal{X}_l$ obeys Eq. (6.59) with high probability, which is verified in Section 6.5.3. Indeed, by the Bernoulli trial property in [65], the sampled number k obeys $k \in [0.5s, 2s]$ with a probability of at least $1 - n_2^{-10}$ when sampling each lateral slice of $\mathcal{X}$ by $Ber(s/n_2)$. So this fast algorithm only needs a small fraction of samples and utilizes them to exactly recover the low-rank structure of the whole data, and then recovers the remaining samples one by one. Such a mechanism allows it to be applied to many tasks, such as supervised learning, video summary, etc.

6.5.3 Applications

In this section, we evaluate OR-TPCA [4] on real tasks, such as outlier detection, data clustering, and supervised and semi-supervised classification tasks. Moreover, we also compare it with other low-rank tensor data analysis techniques. All these experiments are adopted from [4].

6.5.3.1 Evaluation on synthetic data

We first investigate the implication of Theorem 6.11 via looking into the performance of OR-TPCA on recovering the low-rank tensor from synthetic data. We generate a tensor $\mathcal{X} = \mathcal{L}_0 + \mathcal{E}_0 \in \mathbb{R}^{n_1 \times n_2 \times n_3}$, where $\mathcal{L}_0$ is low-rank and $\mathcal{E}_0$ contains sparse outliers as follows. For $\mathcal{L}_0$, we produce $\mathcal{A} \in \mathbb{R}^{n_1 \times r \times n_3}$ and $\mathcal{B} \in \mathbb{R}^{r \times n_2 \times n_3}$ first whose entries of are from i.i.d. $\mathcal{N}(0, 1)$, and then generate a rank$_t$-r tensor as $\mathcal{L}_0 = \mathcal{A} * \mathcal{B}$. For $\mathcal{E}_0$, we uniformly select k lateral slices of $\mathcal{E}_0$ as outliers whose entries obey i.i.d. $\mathcal{N}(0, 1)$ and the support set of $\mathcal{E}_0$ is denoted by Θ_0. The remaining entries in $\mathcal{E}_0$ are 0s. We set $n_1 = n_2 = n_3 = n$ in this experiment just for simplicity.

Here we investigate the effects of tensor sizes, noise magnitudes, and different kinds of noise on the performance of OR-TPCA. To this end, we conduct two different experiments. The first one is that (i) we change the tensor dimension as $n =$

Table 6.3 Exact recovery on random problems of varying sizes [4].

$r = \text{rank}_t(\mathcal{L}_0) = 0.15n, \; k = 0.4n, \; \lambda = 1/\sqrt{\log(n)}, \; \Theta' = \Theta_0^\perp.$

n	r	k	$\text{rank}_t(\widetilde{\mathcal{L}})$	$\frac{\|\mathcal{P}_{\mathcal{U}_0} - \mathcal{P}_{\widetilde{\mathcal{U}}}\|_F}{\|\mathcal{P}_{\mathcal{U}_0}\|_F}$	$\frac{\|\mathcal{P}_{\Theta'}(\mathcal{L}_0) - \mathcal{P}_{\Theta'}(\widetilde{\mathcal{L}})\|_F}{\|\mathcal{P}_{\Theta'}(\mathcal{L}_0)\|_F}$	dist($\Theta_0, \widetilde{\Theta}$)
60	9	24	9	4.634e−15	5.518e−15	0
100	15	40	15	2.754e−15	3.322e−15	0
200	30	80	30	2.858e−15	2.870e−15	0

Table 6.4 Exact recovery on random problems of varying noise magnitudes and different kinds of noise [4].

$n = 80, \; r = \text{rank}_t(\mathcal{L}_0) = 0.15n, \; k = 0.4n, \; \lambda = 1/\sqrt{\log(n)}, \; \Theta' = \Theta_0^\perp.$

Outliers	$\text{rank}_t(\widetilde{\mathcal{L}})$	$\frac{\|\mathcal{P}_{\mathcal{U}_0} - \mathcal{P}_{\widetilde{\mathcal{U}}}\|_F}{\|\mathcal{P}_{\mathcal{U}_0}\|_F}$	$\frac{\|\mathcal{P}_{\Theta'}(\mathcal{L}_0) - \mathcal{P}_{\Theta'}(\widetilde{\mathcal{L}})\|_F}{\|\mathcal{P}_{\Theta'}(\mathcal{L}_0)\|_F}$	dist($\Theta_0, \widetilde{\Theta}$)
$\mathcal{N}(0, 0.01)$	12	5.007e−14	6.559e−14	0
$\mathcal{N}(0, 1)$	12	3.521e−15	3.753e−15	0
$\mathcal{N}(0, 100)$	12	2.306e−15	2.913e−15	0
Bin(1, −1)	12	3.980e−15	4.229e−15	0

60, 100, 200 and report the recovery error of OR-TPCA in Table 6.3. The second one is that (ii) we test the cases that the entries of $\mathcal{E}_0$ follow i.i.d. $\mathcal{N}(0, 0.01)$, $\mathcal{N}(0, 1)$, $\mathcal{N}(0, 100)$, and the distribution Bin(1, −1) which i.i.d. produces 1 or −1 with probability 0.5, and report the performance in Table 6.4. Each experiment is run 20 times and its corresponding average results are reported. In the tables, we use $\widetilde{\mathcal{L}}$ to denote the recovered tensor and adopt the support set $\widetilde{\Theta}$ of nonzero $\widetilde{\mathcal{E}}(:, i, :)$ to denote the recovered outlier support set. From the results in Table 6.3, one can clearly observe that the recovered tubal rank is exactly equal to r and the relative errors $\|\mathcal{P}_{\mathcal{U}_0} - \mathcal{P}_{\widetilde{\mathcal{U}}}\|_F / \|\mathcal{P}_{\mathcal{U}_0}\|_F$ and $\|\mathcal{P}_{\Theta_0^\perp}(\mathcal{L}_0) - \mathcal{P}_{\Theta_0^\perp}(\widetilde{\mathcal{L}})\|_F / \|\mathcal{P}_{\Theta_0^\perp}(\mathcal{L}_0)\|_F$ are very small, even less than 10^{-10}, where $\mathcal{P}_{\mathcal{U}} = \mathcal{U} * \mathcal{U}^*$. The Hamming distance dist(Θ_0, $\widetilde{\Theta}$) between Θ_0 and $\widetilde{\Theta}$ is always 0. All these results well demonstrate the strong performance of OR-TPCA in exactly recovering the tubal rank, column space $\mathcal{U}_0$, clean data $\mathcal{P}_{\Theta_0^\perp}(\mathcal{L}_0)$, and the support set Θ_0 of outliers. Moreover, from Table 6.4, one can also find that OR-TPCA is very robust to various noises and corresponding magnitudes.

6.5.3.2 Evaluation on real applications

In this section, we test OR-TPCA on four tensor analysis tasks, i.e., outlier detection, clustering, and semi-supervised and supervised classification. At the same time, we further compare OR-TPCA [4] with other state-of-the-art low-rank factorization methods, such as R-PCA [8], OR-PCA [10], LRR (with the $\ell_{2,1}$-norm) [30], SNN [24], and R-TPCA [27]. Our test datasets contain one handwriting dataset Mnist and

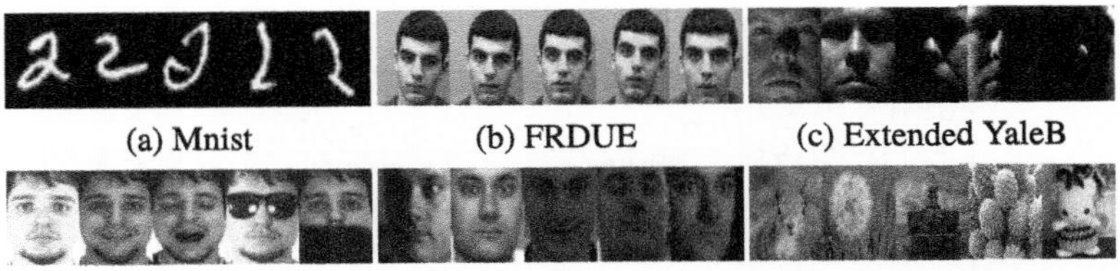

(a) Mnist   (b) FRDUE   (c) Extended YaleB

(d) AR   (e) PIE   (f) MIRFLICKR-25k

Database	#Class	Number of each class	Total number	Size	Difficulty
Mnist	10	100	1000	28×28	def.
FRDUE	153	≈ 20	3059	100×90	def. and pos.
YaleB	38	≈ 68	2414	96×84	ill.
AR	100	26	2600	165×120	ill., exp. and occ.
PIE	68	≈ 170	11554	96×96	ill., exp. and pos.

(g) Descriptions of the testing datasets. ("def.", "pos.", "ill.", "exp." and "occ." are short for "deformation", "pose", "illumination", "expression" and "occlusion", respectively.)

FIGURE 6.14

Examples and descriptions of the five test datasets and MIRFLICKR-25k [4].

Table 6.5 AUC of outlier detection and clustering results (ACC, NMI, and PUR) on FRDUE (averaged over 20 random runs) [4].

#Outlier	Metric	k-means	R-PCA	OR-PCA	LRR	SNN	R-TPCA	OR-TPCA
100	AUC	–	0.865	0.943	0.914	0.869	0.875	**0.951**
	ACC	0.407	0.436	0.520	0.492	0.491	0.499	**0.564**
	NMI	0.693	0.720	0.785	0.769	0.726	0.766	**0.818**
	PUR	0.427	0.482	0.552	0.499	0.522	0.527	**0.640**
200	AUC	–	0.823	0.886	0.892	0.827	0.835	**0.934**
	ACC	0.374	0.430	0.481	0.474	0.456	0.461	**0.531**
	NMI	0.650	0.694	0.750	0.716	0.724	0.728	**0.779**
	PUR	0.405	0.479	0.518	0.523	0.486	0.492	**0.566**

four face databases, i.e., the Face Recognition Data of University of Essex[2] (FRDUE), Extended YaleB [53], AR [66], and PIE [67]. All these datasets are introduced in Fig. 6.14. For fairness, all classification performance is evaluated by the following ridge regression (RR):

$$\min_{W} \|Y - WB\|_F^2 + v\|W\|_F^2, \tag{6.60}$$

where B is the recovered data by these compared methods and Y is the label matrix. To apply RR, we need to vectorize sample matrices for classification or clustering

---

[2] http://cswww.essex.ac.uk/mv/allfaces/.

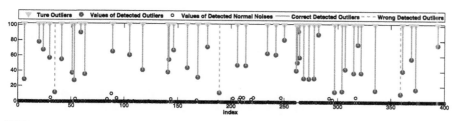

FIGURE 6.15

Outlier detection results of OR-TPCA on the first 400 samples in FRDUE with 100 outliers [4]. Best viewed in color pdf file.

Table 6.6 Clustering results (ACC, NMI, and PUR) and segmentation error (ERR, %) on Mnist (averaged over 20 random runs) [4].

Metric	k-means	R-PCA	OR-PCA	LRR	SNN	R-TPCA	OR-TPCA
ACC	0.490	0.512	0.520	0.538	0.559	0.781	**0.826**
NMI	0.468	0.500	0.495	0.513	0.535	0.803	**0.880**
PUR	0.532	0.563	0.574	0.568	0.586	0.823	**0.865**
ERR	0.575	0.491	0.479	0.461	0.452	0.258	**0.110**

for tensor-based methods (i.e., SNN, R-TPCA, and OR-TPCA). For OR-TPCA, we do not tune the parameter of RR for OR-TPCA and we set $\nu = 1$ in OR-TPCA and $\nu = 30$ in Fast OR-TPCA. For other compared methods, their parameters ν are tuned to be the best for different tasks on different datasets. For fairness, following the parameter setting in their corresponding works [8,10,27], we set the regularization parameters of R-PCA [8], OR-PCA [10], RT-PCA [27], and OR-TPCA as $1/\sqrt{\max(n'_1, n'_2)}$, $1/\sqrt{\log(n'_2)}$, $1/\sqrt{\max(n_1, n_2)n_3}$, and $1/\sqrt{\log(n_2)}$, respectively, where the data matrix size processed by R-PCA and OR-PCA is $n'_1 \times n'_2$ and outliers are column-wisely distributed, while in R-TPCA and OR-TPCA, the data size is $n_1 \times n_2 \times n_3$ and outliers are distributed along the second dimension. For LRR and SNN, we manually tune their parameters because there are no theoretical parameter settings for them.

6.5.3.3 Outlier detection

As suggested by Theorem 6.11, the computed noise solution $\mathcal{E}$ can help detect potential outliers in data. Specifically, when the data $\mathcal{P}_{\Theta_0^\perp}(\mathcal{X})$ are clean, the support set Θ of nonzero $\mathcal{E}(:, i, :)$ reveals the outlier location as in Section 6.5.3.1. But real data $\mathcal{P}_{\Theta_0^\perp}(\mathcal{X})$ are more often noisy, leading to more nonzero $\mathcal{E}(:, i, :)$. Moreover, the possible outliers in $\|\mathcal{E}(:, i, :)\|_F^2$ usually have a much larger norm than normal ones. This suggests us using k-means for clustering all $\|\mathcal{E}(:, i, :)\|_F^2$ into two classes (outliers vs. nonoutliers) for outlier detection.

Table 6.7 Classification accuracy (%) and average running time (in seconds) in a *semi-supervised learning* setting on the three face test databases [4]. The numbers, e.g., 1, 2, 3, denote the training numbers per person.

Method	Extended YaleB						FRDUE			
	3	6	9	12	15	time	1	2	3	time
RR	56.6±1.8	74.2±1.4	81.5±1.4	86.0±0.9	88.3±1.0	–	87.4±1.0	92.2±0.7	93.9±0.5	–
R-PCA	61.5±1.1	79.9±1.0	87.7±1.0	92.1±0.9	92.9±0.7	1.99	90.5±0.5	94.5±0.5	95.4±0.3	2.88
OR-PCA	61.8±1.3	80.5±1.1	88.3±0.8	92.9±0.7	93.4±0.5	1.26	90.6±0.7	95.0±0.5	96.0±0.4	1.85
LRR	58.9±1.5	72.9±1.3	79.3±1.0	86.0±0.8	88.3±0.7	2.04	90.3±0.6	95.1±0.4	96.6±0.4	3.16
SNN	63.1±1.2	81.7±0.9	89.8±0.5	93.6±0.3	94.1±0.3	2.67	92.2±0.7	95.9±0.5	96.9±0.4	4.01
R-TPCA	65.1±1.1	84.5±0.8	92.0±0.7	95.7±0.5	97.3±0.5	0.38	95.6±0.5	97.9±0.4	98.7±0.4	0.76
OR-TPCA	**71.4±1.1**	**90.3±0.9**	**95.9±0.6**	**98.2±0.4**	**98.6±0.3**	**0.24**	**97.3±0.6**	**98.6±0.4**	**99.2±0.2**	**0.69**

Method	AR					
	1	2	3	4	5	time
RR	39.6±1.9	64.8±1.3	77.5±1.2	84.9±0.8	87.8±0.5	–
R-PCA	43.8±1.2	73.0±1.0	84.5±0.8	89.8±0.6	92.4±0.5	6.23
OR-PCA	43.1±1.1	74.1±0.9	84.9±0.8	89.3±0.6	93.2±0.6	4.61
LRR	45.1±1.6	68.1±0.9	77.6±0.7	86.0±0.6	89.4±0.6	6.41
SNN	45.7±1.2	75.3±1.0	86.6±0.7	91.1±0.5	94.1±0.4	6.89
R-TPCA	49.3±1.2	78.9±0.8	89.7±0.7	93.6±0.6	96.0±0.6	1.43
OR-TPCA	**56.8±0.8**	**87.2±0.7**	**95.0±0.6**	**98.1±0.4**	**99.0±0.2**	**1.03**

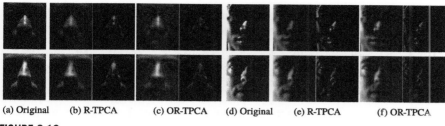

(a) Original   (b) R-TPCA   (c) OR-TPCA   (d) Original   (e) R-TPCA   (f) OR-TPCA

FIGURE 6.16

Examples of face image denoising results on Extended YaleB [4]. Best viewed in color pdf file.

For evaluation, we first construct a dataset by combining FRDUE with the MIRFLICKR-25k dataset [68]. We view the data in FRDUE as normal data, and regard the samples from MIRFLICKR-25k as the outliers. Specifically, we only use the first 40 subjects in FRDUE, resulting in 800 authentic samples from a low-rank subspace. For outliers, we randomly extract 100 and 200 images from MIRFLICKR-25k as outliers. See outlier examples in Fig. 6.12(f).

To measure the performance of outlier detection, the AUC metric is computed based on the detection results by conducting the k-means on $\mathcal{E}$. For clustering performance, we adopt the three commonly used metrics ACC, NMI, and PUR. For experiments, outliers detected by k-means (some normal samples may also be removed) are first moved. Then the remaining recovered data (possibly including undetected outliers) are clustered by k-means. We then report the clustering results of normal samples (the normal samples detected as outliers by k-means are given wrong labels). From the results in Table 6.5, one can observe that OR-TPCA outperforms all the compared algorithms in terms of both outlier detection and clustering performance. There are two reasons: (i) OR-TPCA takes advantage of the tensor multidimensional structure; and (ii) it uses the $\ell_{2,1}$-norm, which can better depict outliers than the ℓ_1-norm. Fig. 6.15 shows some outliers detected by OR-TPCA. Moreover, it can be observed that outlier detection can also help improve the clustering results.

6.5.3.4 Unsupervised and semi-supervised learning

In this section, we evaluate the performance of OR-TPCA in an image denoising task. Specifically, considering authentic handwriting and face images approximately lie on a union of low-rank subspaces [8,27,30,46,47,51,69–72], we apply OR-TPCA for removing noise and corruptions on face and handwritten digits via recovering their subspaces. Meanwhile, compared with the conventional ℓ_1-norm, the $\ell_{2,1}$-norm can characterize better the shadows, facial expressions, and occlusions on face images displayed in Fig. 6.12, because these noises are more like contiguous noise. In the experiments, we find that organizing the images along the third direction to form a $w \times h \times n$ tensor provides slightly better results. Interestingly, R-TPCA also performs better when its processed tensor is constructed in this way. More importantly, by using this construction method, one can expect higher efficiency. This is because the sample

Table 6.8 Subspace recovery performance of fast OR-TPCA on PIE [4]. ("#TSP" is short for "# of training samples per person.")

#TSP	6	10	14	18	22	26	30
$\frac{\|\mathcal{P}u_i - \mathcal{P}\tilde{u}\|_F}{\|\mathcal{P}\tilde{u}\|_F}$	5.1e−01	2.7e−15	2.7e−15	2.7e−15	2.7e−15	2.8e−15	2.7e−15

number n is usually much larger than its dimension w and h. Otherwise, we have to compute decompositions of w or h matrices of sizes $n \times h$ or $w \times n$.

Then three face datasets, including FRDUE, Extended YaleB, and AR, and one handwritten digits database, namely mnist, are used for testing the performance of OR-TPCA. Following conventional settings, four performance metrics, including ACC, NMI, PUR, and segmentation error (ERR), are employed to evaluate the clustering results on mnist, and the classification accuracy is regarded a performance metric on the three face datasets. Moreover, the average algorithm running time (total denoising time divided by the sample number) are also reported. For each classification experiment with a specific training size over 10 random train/test splits of the recovered data, its average results are reported.

From the clustering results in Table 6.6, one can observe that OR-TPCA achieves the best performance in terms of the four metrics. More specifically, it improves by 13.8% over the second best R-TPCA in terms of ERR. For the face datasets, we summarize the test results in Table 6.7. From it, we can observe that all methods achieve impressive good classification results on FRDUE, partially since it is easier than Extended YaleB and AR (see Fig. 6.12). On more challenging datasets, namely Extended YaleB and AR, one can observe that OR-TPCA still performs better than other methods across all settings, especially for insufficient cases of training samples (e.g., ≤ 6 and 3 training samples per person on Extended YaleB and AR, respectively). This clearly proves the superior robustness of OR-TPCA. Also, the results demonstrate that tensor-based methods, i.e., SNN, R-TPCA, and OR-TPCA, achieve higher classification accuracy, as they take advantage of the multidimensional structure of the tensor instead of directly vectorizing samples like the matrix-based baselines. We also observe that $\ell_{2,1}$-based methods, i.e., OR-TPCA and OR-PCA, usually outperform their ℓ_1 counterparts, i.e., R-TPCA and R-PCA. This is because the $\ell_{2,1}$-norm can better detect the contiguous noise. This is confirmed by results given in Fig. 6.16, where OR-TPCA deshadows and recovers faces much better than R-TPCA.

Another advantage is that OR-TPCA is much faster than others. This is because R-PCA, OR-PCA, and LRR need to perform SVD over a very large data matrix and SNN decomposes three large matrices (unfold the tensor along three modes), while OR-TPCA needs to do SVD on n matrices however each matrix is much smaller than those involved in the baselines.

6.5.3.5 Experiments on fast OR-TPCA

Finally, a large-scale face dataset, PIE, is used for testing. Similarly, we run each experiments for 10 times and compute the average results. Here we focus on the problem whether fast OR-TPCA can exactly recover the subspace of the whole data,

Table 6.9 Classification accuracy (%) and total running time (in hours) under the *semi-supervised learning* setting on PIE [4] ("#TSP" is short for "# of training samples per person").

#TSP	5	10	15	20	time
RR	63.1±1.7	76.0±1.1	83.4±1.2	85.8±0.9	–
R-PCA	66.1±1.2	79.5±0.9	85.8±0.7	88.1±0.3	>20
OR-PCA	63.2±1.4	78.3±1.0	86.5±0.8	88.9±0.4	>20
LRR	67.6±1.5	80.2±1.0	86.2±0.6	88.5±0.5	>20
SNN	69.0±1.3	82.0±0.6	87.3±0.5	89.9±0.3	>20
R-TPCA	70.1±1.1	83.1±0.8	88.5±0.6	90.9±0.3	1.74
Fast OR-TPCA (10)	73.3±1.2	85.0±0.7	89.5±0.4	**91.8±0.2**	**0.14**
Fast OR-TPCA (30)	**73.5±1.1**	84.5±0.7	89.6±0.6	91.6±0.3	0.22
OR-TPCA (all)	73.2±1.1	**85.3±0.6**	**89.7±0.5**	91.7±0.2	1.51

given a small fraction of the data. For this, we vary the sampled face numbers per subject from 6 to 30. We construct the corresponding tensor $h \times n \times w$ when given n images of size $h \times w$. We compute the relative error $\|\mathcal{P}_{\mathcal{U}_i} - \mathcal{P}_{\widetilde{\mathcal{U}}}\|_F / \|\mathcal{P}_{\widetilde{\mathcal{U}}}\|_F$ for performance measure, where $\mathcal{P}_{\mathcal{U}} = \mathcal{U} * \mathcal{U}^*$, $\mathcal{U}_i$ is the column space recovered by fast OR-TPCA using only i samples per person and $\widetilde{\mathcal{U}}$ is the column space obtained using all samples. From Table 6.8, one can observe that when given few samples ($i = 6$), there is a quality gap between $\mathcal{U}_i$ and $\widetilde{\mathcal{U}}$. But using more samples (larger i), the performance gap decreases rapidly. Even when the selected samples occupy less than 6% (about 10 samples per person), the relative error is already as low as 10^{-14}. This clearly demonstrates the ability and sample efficiency of fast OR-TPCA on recovering the subspace, consistent with the conclusions of Theorem 6.12.

Next, we evaluate fast OR-TPCA on a semi-supervised classification task. Specifically, for each person, we randomly select 10, 30, and all samples to construct the "seed tensor" used for fast OR-TPCA. In contrast, other compared methods utilize the whole data for recovery. Table 6.9 reports the average accuracy and total running time (total denoising time). One can observe that OR-PCA and fast OR-TPCA achieve similar accuracy with 10 and 30 samples per person. Using 10 samples per person as the "seed tensor," fast OR-TPCA is 10× faster than R-TPCA and the original OR-TPCA and 100× faster than other baselines, clearly demonstrating the high efficiency of fast OR-TPCA.

Now we apply fast OR-TPCA to large-scale real supervised classification. By robustly recovering the training/test shared subspace from noisy training data, fast OR-TPCA can boost supervised classification performance. In this experiment, we compare fast OR-TPCA with R-PCA, OR-PCA, and R-TPCA baselines. SNN and LRR are not applicable here. Note that for supervised classification, the baselines have to recover the "seed matrix (tensor)" constructed by training data first and use them to denoise and classify testing data, similar to fast OR-TPCA. This also gives their *accelerated version*. However, they do not enjoy performance guarantee as OR-

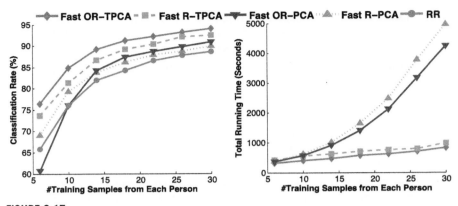

FIGURE 6.17

Classification accuracy (%) and total running time (denoising time on training and test samples, in seconds) of fast algorithms under the *supervised learning* setting on PIE [4].

TPCA. Note that a fast R-PCA is proposed in [73] though no guarantees are provided. We use this fast R-PCA as baseline. We evaluate all the methods on PIE by randomly selecting i (from 6 to 30) training images per person and testing on the remaining images.

From the results in Fig. 6.17, one can find that OR-TPCA achieves the highest classification accuracy in most cases. Besides, we can make the following observations. Along with more training samples, the performance of all the methods improves. Theorem 6.12 is also in accordance with this observation on OR-TPCA. When the training number is sufficiently large (e.g., 10 per person), the tensor subspace can be recovered correctly and higher classification accuracy is achieved. The total running time (denoising time on training and test samples) is also compared. It should be mentioned that RR has no denoising time. From the results, one can observe that fast OR-TPCA performs 2× faster than fast OR-PCA and R-PCA when the training number per person is 18. Moreover, the running time of fast OR-TPCA increases slowly when the training size increases. When processing k training samples of size $h \times w$, SVD consumes most computation time per iteration. The costs of fast OR-TPCA, R-PCA, and OR-PCA per iteration are respectively $O(kw^2h + kwh\log(w))$, $O(k^2wh)$, and $O(k^2wh)$. This is the main reason why fast OR-TPCA is much more efficient.

6.5.4 Summary

In this section, we introduced OR-TPCA [4] for recovering the clean low-rank tensor data and detecting the outlier positions. We first introduce the OR-TPCA model, its recovery theories, and an optimization algorithm. Finally, we apply OR-TPCA to data recovery tasks, outlier detection tasks, and supervised and semi-supervised classification tasks, and compare it with other kinds of low-rank tensor analysis methods.

6.6 **Other tensor PCA methods**

In this section, we briefly review other TPCA methods. Since sparse noise is much more common than Gaussian noise and outlier corruptions in practice, most TPCA methods study the problem of how to exactly recover the underlying low-rank clean tensor data in the presence of sparsely corrupted noise. So here we also focus on introducing the TPCA methods under the sparsely corrupted noise setting.

As mentioned in Section 6.3.1, besides the tensor rank definition used in this chapter, there are several different definitions of tensor rank, leading to different low-rank tensor analysis methods. For example, the CP rank [6], defined as the smallest number of rank-1 tensor decomposition, is generally NP-hard to compute. Also its convex relaxation is intractable. This makes the low-CP rank tensor recovery challenging. The tractable Tucker rank [6] and its convex relaxation are more widely used. For a k-way tensor $\mathcal{X}$, the Tucker rank is a vector defined as $\text{rank}_{\text{tc}}(\mathcal{X}) := \left(\text{rank}(X^{\{1\}}), \text{rank}(X^{\{2\}}), \cdots, \text{rank}(X^{\{k\}})\right)$, where $X^{\{i\}}$ is the mode-i matricization of $\mathcal{X}$ [6]. Motivated by the fact that the nuclear norm is the convex envelope of the matrix rank within the unit ball of the spectral norm, the sum of nuclear norms (SNN) [22], defined as $\sum_i \left\| X^{\{i\}} \right\|_*$, is used as a convex surrogate of $\sum_i \text{rank}(X^{\{i\}})$. Then the work [28] considers the low-rank tensor completion (LRTC) model based on SNN:

$$\min_{\mathcal{X}} \sum_{i=1}^{k} \lambda_i \left\| X^{\{i\}} \right\|_*, \text{ s.t. } \mathcal{P}_{\mathbf{\Omega}}(\mathcal{X}) = \mathcal{P}_{\mathbf{\Omega}}(\mathcal{M}), \tag{6.61}$$

where $\lambda_i > 0$ and $\mathcal{P}_{\mathbf{\Omega}}(\mathcal{X})$ denotes the projection of $\mathcal{X}$ on the observed set $\mathbf{\Omega}$. The effectiveness of this approach for image processing has been well studied in [22,74]. However, SNN is not the convex envelope of $\sum_i \text{rank}(X^{\{i\}})$ [75]. Actually, the above model can be substantially suboptimal [28]: reliably recovering a k-way tensor of length n and Tucker rank $(r, r, \cdots, r)$ from Gaussian measurements requires $O(rn^{k-1})$ observations. In contrast, a certain (intractable) nonconvex formulation needs only $O(rK + nrK)$ observations. A better (but still suboptimal) convexification based on a more balanced matricization is proposed in [28]. The work [24] presents the recovery guarantee for the SNN-based R-TPCA model

$$\min_{\mathcal{L}, \mathcal{E}} \sum_{i=1}^{k} \lambda_i \left\| L^{\{i\}} \right\|_* + \|\mathcal{E}\|_1, \text{ s.t. } \mathcal{X} = \mathcal{L} + \mathcal{E}. \tag{6.62}$$

A robust tensor CP decomposition problem is studied in [76]. Though the recovery is guaranteed, the algorithm is nonconvex. Song et al. [77] extended matrix CUR decomposition [78] to tensor CURT decomposition and proposed an algorithm to compute a low-rank CURT approximation to a tensor with performance guarantees. There are also many other related works that further explore tensor applications, e.g. [79,80].

There are also low-rank presentation-based recovery methods. For two-way tensor data, LRR [31,81] can cluster vector-valued samples X into corresponding subspaces through seeking low-rank linear representations Z w.r.t. a given dictionary A:

$$\min_{Z} \|Z\|_* + \lambda \|E\|_1, \text{ s.t. } X = AZ + E. \tag{6.63}$$

Here $\|\cdot\|_*$ and $\|\cdot\|_1$ respectively denote the matrix nuclear and ℓ_1-norms. Then to handle multiway tensor data, Fu et al. [35] proposed a TLRR and sparse coding-based method (TLRRSC) for data clustering. Specifically, they arranged n samples of feature dimension n_k into a tensor $\mathcal{X} \in \mathbb{R}^{n_1 \times n_2 \times \cdots \times n_k}$, where $n = n_1 n_2 \cdots n_{k-1}$. Then they adopted a low-rank Tucker decomposition on the spatial modes (modes 1 to $k-1$) to depict the low-rank spatial relations among samples, and used sparse coding [82] to capture the linear relations of samples in the feature space (mode k). However, TLRRSC still needs to reshape two-way data into vectors. Zhang et al. [83] proposed a low-rank tensor constrained multiview subspace clustering method (LT-MSC). LT-MSC first extracts several kinds of features to construct the multiview data, and then restrains the learned representation tensor constructed by the representation matrix for each view data to be of low Tucker rank. The issue for these two methods is that they have no theoretical guarantees for data recovery and clustering compared with TLRR [3].

6.7 Future work

Most works only consider one kind of three noise types, namely (i) Gaussian noise, (ii) sparse noise, and (iii) outliers. However, the observed data could be much more complex. For example, the observed tensor data can involve two types of noise or even all kinds of noise. In this case, the introduced method in this chapter cannot work well in the theoretical aspect. So it is important and necessary to develop more robust tensor methods and frameworks for handling those complex data that are corrupted by several kinds of noise. Moreover, it is also necessary to derive a new theory analysis framework, since current analysis frameworks can also be used to analyze one kind of noise instead of the mixture of two or even more kinds of noise.

6.8 Summary

In this chapter, we introduced TPCA for low-rank tensor data analysis. Specifically, we consider three kinds of data, including (i) Gaussian-noisy tensor data, (ii) sparsity-corrupted tensor data, and (iii) outlier-corrupted tensor data. To handle these data, we introduce TPCA [27] for setting (i), R-TPCA [1,27] and TLRR [3] for setting (ii), and OR-TPCA [4] for setting (iii). All these methods enjoy provable data recovery performance guarantees, and their models can be optimized via efficient convex programming with convergence guarantees. Finally, we also introduce the real applications of these methods, including data recovery/denoising, outlier detection, and supervised and semi-supervised classification tasks.

References

[1] Z. Zhang, G. Ely, S. Aeron, N. Hao, M. Kilmer, Novel methods for multilinear data completion and de-noising based on tensor-SVD, in: Proc. IEEE Conf. Computer Vision and Pattern Recognition, 2014.

[2] C. Lu, J. Feng, Y. Chen, W. Liu, Z. Lin, S. Yan, Tensor robust principal component analysis with a new tensor nuclear norm, IEEE Transactions on Pattern Analysis and Machine Intelligence (2018).

[3] P. Zhou, C. Lu, J. Feng, Z. Lin, S. Yan, Tensor low-rank representation for data recovery and clustering, IEEE Transactions on Pattern Analysis and Machine Intelligence (2019).

[4] P. Zhou, J. Feng, Outlier-robust tensor PCA, in: Proc. IEEE Conf. Computer Vision and Pattern Recognition, 2017.

[5] S. Wold, K. Esbensen, P. Geladi, Principal component analysis, Chemometrics and Intelligent Laboratory Systems 2 (1–3) (1987) 37–52.

[6] T.G. Kolda, B.W. Bader, Tensor decompositions and applications, SIAM Review 51 (3) (2009) 455–500.

[7] P. Zhou, C. Lu, Z. Lin, C. Zhang, Tensor factorization for low-rank tensor completion, IEEE Transactions on Image Processing (2017).

[8] E.J. Candès, X. Li, Y. Ma, J. Wright, Robust principal component analysis?, Journal of the ACM 58 (3) (2011) 11.

[9] H. Xu, C. Caramanis, S. Sanghavi, Robust PCA via outlier pursuit, in: Proc. Conf. Neural Information Processing Systems, 2010.

[10] H. Zhang, Z. Lin, C. Zhang, E. Chang, Exact recoverability of robust PCA via outlier pursuit with tight recovery bounds, in: AAAI Conf. Artificial Intelligence, 2015.

[11] M. Balcan, H. Zhang, Noise-tolerant life-long matrix completion via adaptive sampling, in: Proc. Conf. Neural Information Processing Systems, 2016, pp. 2955–2963.

[12] O. Rojo, H. Rojo, Some results on symmetric circulant matrices and on symmetric centrosymmetric matrices, Linear Algebra and Its Applications 392 (2004) 211–233.

[13] M.E. Kilmer, C.D. Martin, Factorization strategies for third-order tensors, Linear Algebra and Its Applications 435 (3) (2011) 641–658.

[14] N. Hao, M. Kilmer, K. Braman, R. Hoover, Facial recognition using tensor-tensor decompositions, SIAM Journal on Imaging Sciences 6 (1) (2013) 437–463.

[15] M. Kilmer, K. Braman, N. Hao, R. Hoover, Third-order tensors as operators on matrices: a theoretical and computational framework with applications in imaging, SIAM Journal on Matrix Analysis and Applications 34 (1) (2013) 148–172.

[16] C. Lu, P. Zhou, Exact recovery of tensor robust principal component analysis under linear transforms, arXiv preprint, arXiv:1907.08288, 2019.

[17] C. Lu, X. Peng, Y. Wei, Low-rank tensor completion with a new tensor nuclear norm induced by invertible linear transforms, in: Proc. IEEE Conf. Computer Vision and Pattern Recognition, 2019, pp. 5996–6004.

[18] M. Fazel, Matrix rank minimization with applications, PhD thesis, Stanford University, 2002.

[19] T. Kolda, B. Bader, Tensor decompositions and applications, SIAM Review 51 (3) (2009) 455–500.

[20] H. Kiers, Towards a standardized notation and terminology in multiway analysis, Journal of Chemometrics 14 (3) (2000) 105–122.

[21] L. Tucker, Some mathematical notes on three-mode factor analysis, Psychometrika 31 (3) (1966) 279–311.

[22] J. Liu, P. Musialski, P. Wonka, J. Ye, Tensor completion for estimating missing values in visual data, IEEE Transactions on Pattern Analysis and Machine Intelligence 35 (1) (2013) 208–220.

[23] Y. Chen, Incoherence-optimal matrix completion, IEEE Transactions on Information Theory 61 (5) (May 2015) 2909–2923.

[24] B. Huang, C. Mu, D. Goldfarb, J. Wright, Provable low-rank tensor recovery, Optimization Online 4252 (2) (2014).

[25] C. Lu, J. Feng, S. Yan, Z. Lin, A unified alternating direction method of multipliers by majorization minimization, IEEE Transactions on Pattern Analysis and Machine Intelligence 40 (3) (2018) 527–541.

[26] J. Cai, E. Candès, Z. Shen, A singular value thresholding algorithm for matrix completion, SIAM Journal on Optimization (2010).

[27] C. Lu, J. Feng, Y. Chen, W. Liu, Z. Lin, S. Yan, Tensor robust principal component analysis: exact recovery of corrupted low-rank tensors via convex optimization, in: Proc. IEEE Conf. Computer Vision and Pattern Recognition, 2016.

[28] C. Mu, B. Huang, J. Wright, D. Goldfarb, Square deal: lower bounds and improved relaxations for tensor recovery, in: Proc. Int'l Conf. Machine Learning, 2014, pp. 73–81.

[29] J. Shi, J. Malik, Normalized cuts and image segmentation, IEEE Transactions on Pattern Analysis and Machine Intelligence 22 (8) (2000) 888–905.

[30] G. Liu, Z. Lin, Y. Yu, Robust subspace segmentation by low-rank representation, in: Proc. Int'l Conf. Machine Learning, 2010.

[31] G. Liu, Q. Liu, P. Li, Blessing of dimensionality: recovering mixture data via dictionary pursuit, IEEE Transactions on Pattern Analysis and Machine Intelligence 35 (1) (2016) 171–184.

[32] E. Elhamifar, R. Vidal, Sparse subspace clustering: algorithm, theory, and applications, IEEE Transactions on Pattern Analysis and Machine Intelligence 35 (11) (2013) 2765–2781.

[33] C. You, C. Li, D. Robinson, R. Vidal, Oracle based active set algorithm for scalable elastic net subspace clustering, in: Proc. IEEE Conf. Computer Vision and Pattern Recognition, 2016, pp. 3928–3937.

[34] C. Lu, H. Min, Z. Zhao, L. Zhu, D. Huang, S. Yan, Robust and efficient subspace segmentation via least squares regression, in: Proc. European Conf. Computer Vision, 2012, pp. 347–360.

[35] Y. Fu, J. Gao, D. Tien, Z. Lin, H. Xia, Tensor LRR and sparse coding-based subspace clustering, IEEE Transactions on Neural Networks and Learning Systems 27 (10) (2016) 2120–2133.

[36] P.J. Phillips, P.J. Flynn, T. Scruggs, K.W. Bowyer, J. Chang, K. Hoffman, J. Marques, J. Min, W. Worek, Overview of the face recognition grand challenge, in: Proc. IEEE Conf. Computer Vision and Pattern Recognition, 2005, pp. 947–954.

[37] P. Zhou, X. Yuan, J. Feng, Efficient stochastic gradient hard thresholding, in: Proc. Conf. Neural Information Processing Systems, 2018.

[38] P. Zhou, X. Yuan, Hybrid stochastic-deterministic minibatch proximal gradient: less-than-single-pass optimization with nearly optimal generalization, in: Proc. Int'l Conf. Machine Learning, 2020.

[39] H. Zhang, P. Zhou, Y. Yang, J. Feng, Generalized majorization-minimization for non-convex optimization, in: Proc. Int'l Joint Conf. Artificial Intelligence, 2019.

[40] Z. Shen, P. Zhou, C. Fang, A. Ribeiro, A stochastic trust region method for non-convex minimization, arXiv preprint, arXiv:1903.01540, 2019.

[41] P. Zhou, X. Yuan, J. Feng, Faster first-order methods for stochastic non-convex optimization on Riemannian manifolds, in: Int'l Conf. Artificial Intelligence and Statistics, 2019.

[42] P. Zhou, X. Yuan, S. Yan, J. Feng, Faster first-order methods for stochastic non-convex optimization on Riemannian manifolds, IEEE Transactions on Pattern Analysis and Machine Intelligence (2019).

[43] Z. Lin, R. Liu, Z. Su, Linearized alternating direction method with adaptive penalty for low-rank representation, in: Proc. Conf. Neural Information Processing Systems, 2011.

[44] J. Cai, E. Candès, Z. Shen, A singular value thresholding algorithm for matrix completion, SIAM Journal on Optimization 20 (4) (2008) 1956–1982.

[45] D. Martin, C. Fowlkes, D. Tal, J. Malik, A database of human segmented natural images and its application to evaluating segmentation algorithms and measuring ecological statistics, in: IEEE International Conference on Computer Vision, 2001, pp. 416–423.

[46] P. Zhou, C. Zhang, Z. Lin, Bilevel model based discriminative dictionary learning for recognition, IEEE Transactions on Image Processing 26 (3) (2017) 1173–1187.

[47] P. Zhou, Z. Lin, C. Zhang, Integrated low-rank-based discriminative feature learning for recognition, IEEE Transactions on Neural Networks and Learning Systems 27 (5) (2016) 1080–1093.

[48] P. Zhou, C. Fang, Z. Lin, C. Zhang, E.Y. Chang, Dictionary learning with structured noise, Neurocomputing 273 (2017) 414–423.

[49] P. Zhou, Y. Hou, J. Feng, Deep adversarial subspace clustering, in: Proc. IEEE Conf. Computer Vision and Pattern Recognition, 2018.

[50] Z. Zhang, G. Ely, S. Aeron, N. Hao, M. Kilmer, Novel methods for multilinear data completion and de-noising based on tensor-SVD, in: Proc. IEEE Conf. Computer Vision and Pattern Recognition, 2014, pp. 3842–3849.

[51] J. Wright, A. Yang, A. Ganesh, S. Sastry, Y. Ma, Robust face recognition via sparse representation, IEEE Transactions on Pattern Analysis and Machine Intelligence 31 (2009) 210–227.

[52] Y. Wang, C. Xu, S. You, C. Xu, D. Tao, DCT regularized extreme visual recovery, IEEE Transactions on Image Processing 26 (7) (2017) 3360–3371.

[53] A. Georghiades, P. Belhumeur, D. Kriegman, From few to many: illumination cone models for face recognition under variable lighting and pose, IEEE Transactions on Pattern Analysis and Machine Intelligence 23 (6) (2001) 643–660.

[54] J. Yan, M. Pollefeys, A general framework for motion segmentation: independent, articulated, rigid, non-rigid, degenerate and non-degenerate, in: Proc. European Conf. Computer Vision, 2006, pp. 94–106.

[55] N. Vinh, J. Epps, J. Bailey, Information theoretic measures for clusterings comparison: variants, properties, normalization and correction for chance, Journal of Machine Learning Research 11 (2010) 2837–2854.

[56] C. Manning, P. Raghavan, H. Schutze, Introduction to Information Retrieval, Cambridge University Press, 2010.

[57] M. Mørup, Applications of tensor (multiway array) factorizations and decompositions in data mining, Wiley Interdisciplinary Reviews: Data Mining and Knowledge Discovery 1 (1) (2011) 24–40.

[58] A. Karatzoglou, X. Amatriain, L. Baltrunas, N. Oliver, Multiverse recommendation: n-dimensional tensor factorization for context-aware collaborative filtering, in: Proc. ACM Conf. Recommender Systems, 2010, pp. 79–86.

[59] M. Collins, S. Cohen, Tensor decomposition for fast parsing with latent-variable PCFGs, in: Proc. Conf. Neural Information Processing Systems, 2012, pp. 2519–2527.

[60] F. De La Torre, M.J. Black, A framework for robust subspace learning, International Journal of Computer Vision 54 (1–3) (2003) 117–142.

[61] P.J. Huber, Robust Statistics, Springer, 2011.

[62] A. Anandkumar, P. Jain, Y. Shi, U. Niranjan, Tensor vs matrix methods: robust tensor decomposition under block sparse perturbations, arXiv:1510.04747, 2015.

[63] H. Xu, C. Caramanis, S. Sanghavi, Robust PCA via outlier pursuit, IEEE Transactions on Information Theory 58 (5) (2012) 3047–3064.

[64] R. Liu, Z. Lin, F. De la Torre, Z. Su, Fixed-rank representation for unsupervised visual learning, in: Proc. IEEE Conf. Computer Vision and Pattern Recognition, 2012, pp. 598–605.

[65] H. Zhang, Z. Lin, C. Zhang, Completing low-rank matrices with corrupted samples from few coefficients in general basis, IEEE Transactions on Information Theory 62 (8) (2016) 4748–4768.

[66] A. Martinez, R. Benavente, The AR Face Database, CVC Tech. Rep. 24, Jun. 1998.

[67] T. Sim, S. Baker, M. Bsat, The CMU pose, illumination, and expression database, IEEE Transactions on Pattern Analysis and Machine Intelligence 25 (2003) 1615–1618.

[68] M.J. Huiskes, M.S. Lew, The MIR Flickr retrieval evaluation, in: Proc. ACM Int'l Conf. Multimedia Information Retrieval, 2008.

[69] E. Elhamifar, R. Vidal, Sparse subspace clustering, in: Proc. IEEE Conf. Computer Vision and Pattern Recognition, 2009.

[70] H. Zhang, Z. Lin, C. Zhang, J. Gao, Relations among some low rank subspace recovery models, Neural Computation 27 (9) (2015) 1915–1950.

[71] H. Zhang, Z. Lin, C. Zhang, J. Gao, Robust latent low rank representation for subspace clustering, Neurocomputing 145 (2014) 369–373.

[72] Y. Wang, C. Xu, C. Xu, D. Tao, Beyond RPCA: flattening complex noise in the frequency domain, in: AAAI Conf. Artificial Intelligence, 2017.

[73] R. Liu, Z. Lin, Z. Su, J. Gao, Linear time principal component pursuit and its extensions using ℓ_1 filtering, Neurocomputing 142 (2014) 529–541.

[74] R. Tomioka, K. Hayashi, H. Kashima, Estimation of low-rank tensors via convex optimization, arXiv preprint, arXiv:1010.0789, 2010.

[75] B. Romera-Paredes, M. Pontil, A new convex relaxation for tensor completion, in: Proc. Conf. Neural Information Processing Systems, 2013, pp. 2967–2975.

[76] A. Anandkumar, P. Jain, Y. Shi, U. Niranjan, Tensor vs. matrix methods: robust tensor decomposition under block sparse perturbations, in: Artificial Intelligence and Statistics, 2016, pp. 268–276.

[77] Z. Song, D.P. Woodruff, P. Zhong, Relative error tensor low rank approximation, arXiv: 1704.08246, 2017.

[78] M. Mahoney, P. Drineas, CUR matrix decompositions for improved data analysis, Proceedings of the National Academy of Sciences 106 (3) (2009) 697–702.

[79] L. Feng, Y. Liu, L. Chen, X. Zhang, C. Zhu, Robust block tensor principal component analysis, Signal Processing 166 (2020) 107271.

[80] J. Yang, X. Zhao, T. Ji, T. Ma, T. Huang, Low-rank tensor train for tensor robust principal component analysis, Applied Mathematics and Computation 367 (2020) 124783.

[81] G. Liu, Z. Lin, S. Yan, J. Sun, Y. Yu, Y. Ma, Robust recovery of subspace structures by low-rank representation, IEEE Transactions on Pattern Analysis and Machine Intelligence 35 (1) (2013) 171–184.

[82] H. Lee, A. Battle, R. Raina, A. Ng, Efficient sparse coding algorithms, in: Proc. Conf. Neutral Information Processing Systems, 2007, pp. 801–808.

[83] C. Zhang, H. Fu, S. Liu, G. Liu, X. Cao, Low-rank tensor constrained multiview subspace clustering, in: Proc. IEEE Conf. Computer Vision, 2016, pp. 1582–1590.

Tensors for deep learning theory

Analyzing deep learning architectures via tensorization

Yoav Levine, Noam Wies, Or Sharir, Nadav Cohen, and Amnon Shashua
School of Computer Science, Hebrew University of Jerusalem, Jerusalem, Israel

CONTENTS

7.1 Introduction

Over the past decade, deep learning has revolutionized a variety of artificial intelligence (AI)-related applications, such as computer vision, speech recognition, natural language processing, and more [43]. The simple operation at the core of deep learning architectures, of repeatedly applying a learned parametric block, has proved to yield powerful function families that are able to successfully describe complex real-world data.

Several prominent deep learning architecture classes, namely, convolutional, recurrent, and self-attention networks, have been widely employed across applications. These architectures extend the naive design of fully connected neural networks, shown in Fig. 7.1(a). The veteran class of *deep convolutional networks* (Fig. 7.1(b)), which has been around since the 1980s [42], was used in the seminal work of [40] that instigated the ensuing "deep learning era". Convolutional networks have since

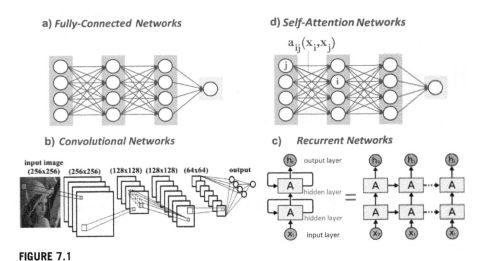

a) *Fully-Connected Networks*

d) *Self-Attention Networks*

$$a_{ij}(x_i, x_j)$$

b) *Convolutional Networks*

c) *Recurrent Networks*

FIGURE 7.1

Prominent deep learning architecture classes. At each layer, fully connected networks connect all outputs to all inputs via learned weights, while in self-attention networks these weights are input-dependent. See a thorough presentation and analysis of self-attention in Section 7.3.1. Convolutional and recurrent networks are discussed in Section 7.4.

led the field of computer vision, and were further widely deployed in various other domains. A second class of prominent architectures is *deep recurrent networks* [56] (Fig. 7.1(c)), which has been the architecture of choice when operating over sequential data in many domains [2,4,61].

Recently, *deep self-attention networks* [62] (Fig. 7.1(d)) have replaced recurrent networks as the main architecture used for natural language processing applications [20,52,53]. Self-attention networks demonstrated an impressive capability to process inherently sequential data such as text, though their core operation is nonsequential. Even more recently, as a result of their striking success in language, self-attention-based architectures have begun proliferating into other domains, setting the state-of-the-art performance on leading benchmarks in computer vision [10,23,39], audio [3,22], video [64], bioinformatics [55], and more [57,63].

The success of deep learning has given rise to theoretical questions that can be roughly divided into three high-level topics: (i) Expressivity: What architectural aspects of the abovementioned classes contribute to their ability to model elaborate functions required for challenging tasks? (ii) Optimization: Why does the gradient-based search in the architecture's nonconvex parameter space lead to convergence over the training data? (iii) Generalization: Given the large capacity of modern architectures, why do the optimized functions generalize also to unseen test examples?

The latter questions on optimization and generalization are widely studied (see, e.g., [9,30,38]). Naturally, the first question regarding network expressivity is tightly coupled to the specific architecture in question. For a given architecture class, there are a variety of hyperparameters that set the network's architectural configuration and resultant traits (to be presented per-class below). One can look for a theoretical framework that predicts the advantage of using one architectural configuration over another. Such explanations have potential to shed light on current heuristically established architecture design choices and, importantly, to provide theoretically motivated principles for better architecture selection.

This chapter describes a tensor analysis-based framework that progressed the theoretical understanding of expressivity aspects in each of the leading deep learning architectures depicted in Fig. 7.1. The grid tensor-based approach for analyzing deep learning architectures, presented below, was proposed in Cohen and Shashua [12], Cohen et al. [14] and employed by Cohen and Shashua [13], Cohen et al. [16], Levine et al. [44], Sharir and Shashua [59] for analyzing various architectural aspects of convolutional networks. Subsequently, it was used by Levine et al. [45] for analyzing recurrent networks and recently extended by Levine et al. [47], Wies et al. [65] to cover self-attention networks.

At the core of the approach lies a technique for discretizing the function realized by the deep learning architecture into a tensor. Specifically, the function is (conceptually) evaluated on an exponentially large grid in input space, and these values are stored as entries of a corresponding tensor, referred to as the function's *grid tensor*. In the following, we begin by introducing in Section 7.2 a proof methodology which uses the grid tensor of a function realized by a deep learning architecture in order to bound its ability to model input dependencies. After detailing the proof technique for general multivariate functions, we address in Section 7.3 the recent class of self-attention networks as a "full-details case study" for its application: we present open questions regarding the expressivity of these architectures and then show how the tensor analysis-based framework of this chapter provides insights into their current success, and we design guidelines for improvement of their expressive power. We expand on self-attention networks due to their growing relevance and present-day infiltration into many new domains, but in Section 7.4 we comment on similar findings that were established for the more veteran classes of convolutional and recurrent networks.

7.2 Bounding a function's expressivity via tensorization

In this section, we present the main proof methodology that was employed by Cohen and Shashua [12,13], Cohen et al. [14,17], Levine et al. [44,45,46,47], Sharir and Shashua [59], Wies et al. [65] in order to elucidate the operation of deep convolutional, recurrent, and self-attention networks. All of the analyzed deep learning architectures realize multivariate functions. We will analyze a setting in which a network computes a scalar function y over N input vectors $\{\mathbf{x}^j\}_{j=1}^N$ in dimension d_x, i.e., $y : (\mathbb{R}^{d_x})^N \rightarrow \mathbb{R}$. This setting is prominent in most deep learning applications, e.g., a function over an image of N pixel vectors in computer vision or a function over a sentence of N word embeddings in natural language processing.

In Section 7.2.1, we present the *separation rank* of such a multivariate function, as a measure that quantifies its ability to model dependencies between subsets of its variable set $\{\mathbf{x}^j\}_{j=1}^N$. The separation rank of the functions realized by the analyzed deep learning architectures is used (i) as a quantifier of their ability to model the elaborate input dependencies required for performing challenging tasks and (ii) as a technical tool for establishing the superiority of one architectural setting over another.

After presenting the separation rank as a quantity of interest, we present a tensor analysis-based method for bounding the separation ranks of general multivariate functions. Specifically, in Section 7.2.2 we present *grid tensors*, a form of function discretization into a tensor. We then show that the rank of an exponentially large matrix that stores the entries of a function's grid tensor, referred to as the matricization of the function's grid tensor, can be used for bounding the separation rank of the function. Subsequently, we present the leading methods for bounding the rank of a matricization of the analyzed deep learning architectures' grid tensors. This conceptual multistep proof structure is schematically illustrated in Fig. 7.2.

7.2.1 A measure of capacity for modeling input dependencies

Below, we present the separation rank of a multivariate function. The separation rank, introduced in [5] for high-dimensional numerical analysis, was employed for various applications, e.g., chemistry [31], particle engineering [28], and machine learning [6]. Cohen and Shashua [13] were the first to introduce the separation rank as a measure of the input dependencies modeled by deep learning architectures.

Let (A, B) be a partition of the input locations, i.e., A and B are disjoint subsets of $[N] := \{1, \ldots N\}$ whose union gives $[N]$. The separation rank of a function $y(\mathbf{x}^1, \ldots, \mathbf{x}^N)$ w.r.t. partition (A, B) is the minimal number of summands that together sum up to equal y, where each summand is *multiplicatively separable* w.r.t. (A, B), i.e., is equal to a product of two functions—one that takes in only inputs from one subset $\{\mathbf{x}^j : j \in A\}$ and another that takes in only inputs from the other subset $\{\mathbf{x}^j : j \in B\}$. Formally, the *separation rank* of $y : (\mathbb{R}^{d_x})^N \to \mathbb{R}$ w.r.t. the partition (A, B) is defined as follows:

$$\text{sep}_{(A,B)}(y) := \min \Big\{ R \in \mathbb{N} \cup \{0\} : \tag{7.1}$$

$$\exists g_1^A, \ldots, g_R^A, g_1^B, \ldots, g_R^B : \left(\mathbb{R}^{d_x}\right)^{N/2} \to \mathbb{R},$$

$$y\left(\mathbf{x}^1, \ldots, \mathbf{x}^N\right) =$$

$$\sum_{\nu=1}^R g_\nu^A\left(\{\mathbf{x}^i : i \in A\}\right) g_\nu^B\left(\{\mathbf{x}^i : i \in B\}\right) \Big\}.$$

If the separation rank of a function w.r.t. a partition of its input is equal to 1, the function is separable, meaning it cannot take into account consistency between the values of $\{\mathbf{x}^j\}_{j \in A}$ and those of $\{\mathbf{x}^j\}_{j \in B}$. In a statistical setting, if y is a probability density function, this would mean that $\{\mathbf{x}^j\}_{j \in A}$ and $\{\mathbf{x}^j\}_{j \in B}$ are statistically independent. The higher $\text{sep}_{(A,B)}(y)$ is, the further y is from this situation, i.e., the more it

$$y\left(\mathbf{x}^1,\ldots,\mathbf{x}^N\right) \overset{\text{eq. (1.2)}}{\longrightarrow} \mathcal{A}(y) \in \left(\mathbb{R}^M\right)^N \overset{\text{eq. (1.3)}}{\longrightarrow} [\![\mathcal{A}(y)]\!]_{A,B} \in \mathbb{R}^{M^{N/2}\times M^{N/2}}$$

$$\text{rank}\left([\![\mathcal{A}(y)]\!]_{A,B}\right) \overset{\text{claim 1}}{\leq} \text{sep}_{(A,B)}(y)$$

FIGURE 7.2

An overview of the proof structure for establishing a lower bound on the separation rank of a multivariate function, presented in Section 7.2.2. This proof scheme is used for bounding the ability of deep learning architectures for modeling input dependencies (see Section 7.3). First, given a set of template vectors, the function's grid tensor is computed (Eq. (7.2)). Then, for a given input partition $A \cup B = [N]$, the entries of the grid tensor are stored in its appropriate matricization (Eq. (7.3)). Claim 7.1 establishes that the rank of a function's grid tensor matricization w.r.t. (A, B) lower bounds its separation rank w.r.t. (A, B). Finally, Claim 7.2 allows to lower bound the matricization rank for grid tensors of the analyzed deep learning architectures, for all possible learned weight configurations but a set of zero measure.

models dependency between $\{\mathbf{x}^j\}_{j\in A}$ and $\{\mathbf{x}^j\}_{j\in B}$, or equivalently, the stronger the correlation it induces between the inputs indexed by A and those indexed by B.

The employed proof methodology bounds the separation rank of a function realized by an analyzed deep learning architecture: an upper bound limits its ability to model input dependencies and a lower bound guarantees that this ability is above a threshold. A superiority of one architectural configuration over another can be established via this approach; the separation rank can be upper bounded for a "weaker" architectural configuration and lower bounded for a "stronger" architectural configuration. This way, if the bounds do not intersect, a gap between architectural configurations is established, since by the definition in Eq. (7.1), two functions are different if their separation rank is not equal. For example, "depth efficiency" of a deep learning architecture is established by upper bounding the separation rank of stacking fewer layers (a "shallower" network), lower bounding the separation rank of stacking more layers (a "deeper" network), and showing that these bounds intersect only if the shallower network is much larger than the deeper network. As long as the bounds do not intersect, this analysis guarantees that the shallow network cannot replicate the operation of the deeper one.

Proving an upper bound on a function's separation rank may be technically challenging, but has a simple conceptual prescription. If one shows that the function can be written as a sum of R separable terms, then the minimal integer which defines the separation rank in Eq. (7.1) is upper bounded by R. In contrast, proving a lower bound on a function's separation rank is more elusive. Constructively finding a decomposition into a sum of separable functions is insufficient, since one must guarantee that a better decomposition does not exist. As a simple illustrative example, writing a function as $f(x, y) = 0.5xy + 0.5xy$ means that its separation rank is no more than 2, but it does not mean that its separation rank is lower bounded by 2 (clearly, in this example the separation rank w.r.t. (x, y) is equal to 1). In the following subsection, we provide a tensor analysis-based method for establishing a lower bound on the separation rank of the analyzed deep learning architectures, illustrated in Fig. 7.2.

7.2.2 Bounding correlations with tensor matricization ranks

We begin by laying out the basic concepts required for the upcoming analysis, and specifically we present tensors, grid tensors, and tensor matricization. The core concept of a *tensor* may be thought of as a multidimensional array. The *order* of a tensor is defined to be the number of indexing entries in the array, referred to as *modes*. The *dimension* of a tensor in a particular mode is defined as the number of values taken by the index in that mode. If $\mathcal{A}$ is a tensor of order N and dimension M_i in each mode $i \in [N]$, its entries are denoted $\mathcal{A}_{j_1 \ldots j_N}$, where the index in each mode takes values $j_i \in [M_i]$.

We will make use of the concept of grid tensors, which are a form of tensor-based multivariate function discretization [29]. Essentially, a multivariate function is evaluated for a set of points on an exponentially large grid in the input space and the outcomes are stored in a tensor. Formally, fixing a set of *template* vectors $\mathbf{x}^{(1)}, \ldots, \mathbf{x}^{(M)} \in \mathbb{R}^{d_x}$, the points on the grid are the set $\{(\mathbf{x}^{(j_1)}, \ldots, \mathbf{x}^{(j_N)})\}_{j_1, \ldots, j_N = 1}^{M}$. Given a function $y(\mathbf{x}^1, \ldots, \mathbf{x}^N)$, the set of its values on the grid arranged in the form of a tensor is called the grid tensor induced by y, denoted $\mathcal{A}(y) \in (\mathbb{R}^M)^N$. Its are entries given by

$$\mathcal{A}(y)_{j_1, \ldots, j_N} \equiv y\left(\mathbf{x}^1 = \mathbf{x}^{(j_1)}, \ldots, \mathbf{x}^N = \mathbf{x}^{(j_N)}\right). \tag{7.2}$$

We will make use of the concept of the *matricization of $\mathcal{A}$ w.r.t. the balanced partition (A, B)*, denoted $[\![\mathcal{A}]\!]_{A,B} \in \mathbb{R}^{M^{N/2} \times M^{N/2}}$, which is essentially the arrangement of the tensor elements as a matrix whose rows correspond to A and whose columns correspond to B. Suppose $\mathcal{A} \in \mathbb{R}^{M \times \cdots \times M}$ is a tensor of order N and let (A, B) be a balanced partition of $[N]$, i.e., A and B are disjoint size $N/2$ subsets of $[N]$ whose union gives $[N]$. We may write $A = \{a_1, \ldots, a_{N/2}\}$ where $a_1 < \cdots < a_{N/2}$, and similarly $B = \{b_1, \ldots, b_{N/2}\}$, where $b_1 < \cdots < b_{N/2}$. The *matricization of $\mathcal{A}$ w.r.t. the partition (A, B)*, denoted $[\![\mathcal{A}]\!]_{A,B}$, is the $M^{N/2}$-by-$M^{N/2}$ matrix holding the entries of $\mathcal{A}$, such that the entry $\mathcal{A}_{j_1 \ldots j_N}$ is stored in the following matrix entry:

$$\left([\![\mathcal{A}]\!]_{A,B}\right)_{row, col} = \mathcal{A}_{j_1 \ldots j_N}, \tag{7.3}$$

$$row = 1 + \sum_{t=1}^{N/2} (j_{a_t} - 1) M^{N/2 - t},$$

$$col = 1 + \sum_{t=1}^{N/2} (j_{b_t} - 1) M^{N/2 - t}.$$

A simple example of a matricization of an order-3 tensor is depicted in Fig. 7.3.

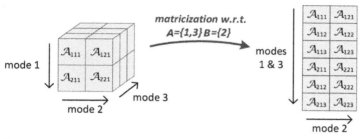

FIGURE 7.3

An illustrative example of a matricization of an order-3 tensor.

The following claim establishes a fundamental relation between a function's separation rank (see Section 7.2.1) and the rank of the matrix obtained by the corresponding grid tensor matricization, which lower bounds it.

Claim 7.1. *Let y be a scalar function over N inputs $\{\mathbf{x}^j \in \mathbb{R}^{d_x}\}_{j=1}^N$ and let (A, B) be any partition of N. For any integer M and any set of template vectors $\mathbf{x}^{(1)}, \ldots, \mathbf{x}^{(M)} \in \mathbb{R}^{d_x}$, we have*

$$\operatorname{sep}_{(A, B)}(y) \geq \operatorname{rank}\left(\llbracket \mathcal{A}(y) \rrbracket_{A, B}\right), \tag{7.4}$$

where $\mathcal{A}(y)$ is the grid tensor of y with respect to the above template vectors.

Proof. If $\operatorname{sep}_{(A, B)}(y) = \infty$, then the inequality is trivially satisfied. Otherwise, assume that $\operatorname{sep}_{(A, B)}(y) = R \in \mathbb{N}$ and let $\{g_\nu^A, g_\nu^B\}_{\nu=1}^R$ be the functions of the respective decomposition to a sum of separable functions in Eq. (7.1), i.e., the following holds:

$$y\left(\mathbf{x}^1, \ldots, \mathbf{x}^N\right) = \sum_{\nu=1}^R g_\nu^A\left(\mathbf{x}^i : i \in A\right) \cdot g_\nu^B\left(\mathbf{x}^i : i \in B\right).$$

Then, by definition of the grid tensor, for any template vectors $\mathbf{x}^{(1)}, \ldots, \mathbf{x}^{(M)} \in \mathbb{R}^{d_x}$ the following equality holds:

$$\mathcal{A}(y)_{j_1, \ldots, j_N} = \sum_{\nu=1}^R g_\nu^A\left(\mathbf{x}^{(j_i)} : i \in A\right) \cdot g_\nu^B\left(\mathbf{x}^{(j_i)} : i \in B\right)$$

$$\equiv \sum_{\nu=1}^R V_{j_i : i \in [A]}^\nu U_{j_i : i \in [B]}^\nu,$$

where V^ν and U^ν are the tensors holding the values of g_ν^A and g_ν^B, respectively, at the input points defined by the template vectors. Under the matricization according to the (A, B) partition, $\llbracket V^\nu \rrbracket_{A, B}$ and $\llbracket U^\nu \rrbracket_{A, B}$ are column and row vectors, respectively, which we denote by $\mathbf{v}_\nu$ and $\mathbf{u}_\nu^T$. It follows that the matricization of the grid tensor is given by

$$\big[\!\big[\mathcal{A}(y) \big]\!\big]_{A,B} = \sum_{\nu=1}^{R} \mathbf{v}_\nu \mathbf{u}_\nu^T,$$

which means that $\text{rank}(\big[\!\big[\mathcal{A}(y) \big]\!\big]_{A,B}) \leq R = \text{sep}_{(A,B)}(y)$. □

Claim 7.1 above shows that the rank of the matricization of a function's grid tensor, $\text{rank}(\big[\!\big[\mathcal{A}(y) \big]\!\big]_{A,B})$, lower bounds its separation rank, $\text{sep}_{(A,B)}(y)$. This means that if one can establish a lower bound on $\text{rank}(\big[\!\big[\mathcal{A}(y) \big]\!\big]_{A,B})$, then a lower bound guarantee is given regarding a function's ability to model dependencies among its inputs, as measured by the separation rank.

The analyzed classes of deep learning architectures are composed of sum and product operations, and specifically the entries of the analyzed functions' grid tensors vary polynomially with the architecture's learned weights Θ. In this case, we show that it suffices to find a single network weights assignment for which $\text{rank}(\big[\!\big[\mathcal{A}(y) \big]\!\big]_{A,B})$ is equal to a certain value, in order to prove that it does not fall below this value for almost all of the configurations of the network's learned weights. Stated alternatively, finding a single network weight configuration with the above property guarantees the bound for all configurations but a set of measure zero. We show this through the following claim that establishes a prevalence of the maximal matrix rank for matrices whose entries are polynomial functions.

Claim 7.2. *Let* $M, N, K \in \mathbb{N}$, $1 \leq R \leq \min\{M, N\}$, *and a polynomial mapping* $A : \mathbb{R}^K \to \mathbb{R}^{M \times N}$ *(i.e., for every* $i \in [M]$, $j \in [N]$, $A_{ij} : \mathbb{R}^K \to \mathbb{R}$ *is a polynomial function). If there exists a point* $\Theta \in \mathbb{R}^K$ *s.t.* $\text{rank}(A(\Theta)) \geq R$, *then the set* $\{\Theta \in \mathbb{R}^K \mid \text{rank}(A(\Theta)) < R\}$ *has zero measure.*

Proof. Recall that $\text{rank}(A(\Theta)) \geq R$ iff there exists a nonzero $R \times R$ minor of $A(\Theta)$, which is polynomial in the entries of $A(\Theta)$, and hence it is polynomial in Θ as well. Let $c = \binom{M}{R} \cdot \binom{N}{R}$ be the number of minors in A, denote the minors by $\{f_i(\Theta)\}_{i=1}^c$, and define the polynomial function $f(\Theta) = \sum_{i=1}^c f_i(\Theta)^2$. It thus holds that $f(\Theta) = 0$ iff for all $i \in [c]$ we have $f_i(\Theta) = 0$, i.e., $f(\Theta) = 0$ iff $\text{rank}(A(\Theta)) < R$. Now, $f(\Theta)$ is a polynomial in the entries of Θ, and so it either vanishes on a set of zero measure, or it is the zero polynomial (see Caron and Traynor [8] for proof). Since we assumed that there exists $\Theta \in \mathbb{R}^K$ s.t. $\text{rank}(A(\Theta)) \geq R$, the latter option is not possible. □

By relying on Claim 7.2 above, we establish lower bounds on $\text{rank}(\big[\!\big[\mathcal{A}(y) \big]\!\big]_{A,B})$ by choosing a simple-to-analyze assignment of the network's learned weights Θ and showing that for this value of the weights, there exist template vectors for which the rank of the grid tensor's matricization reaches a certain value. By relying on Claim 7.1 this in turn implies a lower bound on the separation rank of the analyzed architecture.

The following section includes an analysis of self-attention networks as a case study. After discussing the self-attention architecture, open theoretical questions regarding its operation, and insights provided by the framework of this chapter, we present in Section 7.3.4 an explicit derivation of upper and lower bounds on the separation of self-attention networks, via the proof technique outlined above.

7.3 A case study: self-attention networks

In this section, we present an analysis of the expressivity of self-attention-based deep learning architectures, which relies on the tensorial framework presented in the previous section. The prominent self-attention architecture, also referred to as the "Transformer," was introduced in Vaswani et al. [62]. Another important architecture is "BERT" [21], tightly related to the Transformer, which has demonstrated unprecedented performance across natural language understanding tasks. In the past couple of years, the self-attention architecture class has replaced more veteran architectures in several prominent AI applications, and is presently competing to do so in a variety of other domains. Therefore, the theoretical insights presented in this section exemplify the usefulness of the presented theoretical framework to a highly active contemporary empirical effort.

In this section, we show how fundamental questions regarding the operation of self-attention networks can be addressed via the tensorial framework of Section 7.2. We begin in Section 7.3.1 by describing the self-attention architecture operation, and then we present in Section 7.3.2 several riddles regarding the expressivity of this architecture class. In Section 7.3.3 we present the main insights into the operation of self-attention that were established in Levine et al. [47], Wies et al. [65] via the grid tensor framework. Finally, in Section 7.3.4 we present detailed derivations of the upper and lower bounds on the separation ranks of self-attention networks, for a comprehensive demonstration of the proof technique. In the next section, Section 7.4, we discuss the application of this theoretical framework to other prominent classes of deep learning architectures, namely, convolutional and recurrent networks.

7.3.1 The self-attention mechanism

7.3.1.1 The operation of a self-attention layer

The high-level operation of a self-attention network is similar to that of other deep learning architecture classes: a basic parametric operation is performed over the input and then recursively reapplied to the output of the previous computation. The application of the basic operation is called a *layer*, and the number of such concatenated layers is referred to as the network's *depth*, denoted by L. The N inputs to the network $\{\mathbf{x}^j \in \mathbb{R}^{d_x}\}_{j=1}^N$ are inserted into the first self-attention layer, which computes N outputs $\{\mathbf{y}^{1,j} \in \mathbb{R}^{d_x}\}_{j=1}^N$. The dimension of the above vectors, d_x, is referred to as the representation dimension, or synonymously, the network's *width*. Denoting the i-th output of layer $l \in [L]$ by $\mathbf{y}^{l,i} \in \mathbb{R}^{d_x}$, the operation of a simplified *single-headed* self-attention layer is

$$\mathbf{y}^{l+1,i}\left(\mathbf{y}^{l,1}, ..., \mathbf{y}^{l,N}\right) = \sum_{j=1}^{N} a_j^i \left(W^{V,l}\mathbf{y}^{l,j}\right), \tag{7.5}$$

$$a_j^i = \left\langle W^{Q,l}\mathbf{y}^{l,i}, W^{K,l}\mathbf{y}^{l,j}\right\rangle,$$

where the learned weight matrices $W^{K,l}$, $W^{Q,l}$, and $W^{V,l} \in \mathbb{R}^{d_x \times d_x}$ convert the layer's input into Key, Query, and Value representations, respectively. Observing the operation in Eq. (7.5), a self-attention output at position i is essentially a weighted sum of all inputs, where the weight of the input at position j in this summation, a_j^i, is given by an inner product between the inputs in positions i and j.

Practical self-attention networks use an enhancement that is referred to as *multi-headed* self-attention. The multiheaded self-attention layer that is analyzed in Levine et al. [47], Wies et al. [65] computes

$$\mathbf{y}^{l+1,i}\left(\mathbf{y}^{l,1}, ..., \mathbf{y}^{l,N}\right) = \sum_{h=1}^{H} W^{O,l,h} \sum_{j=1}^{N} a_{hj}^i \left(W^{V,l,h}\mathbf{y}^{l,j}\right), \tag{7.6}$$

$$a_{hj}^i = \left\langle W^{Q,l,h}\mathbf{y}^{l,i}, W^{K,l,h}\mathbf{y}^{l,j}\right\rangle,$$

where H is referred to as the number of attention heads and the learned weight matrices $W^{K,l,h}$, $W^{Q,l,h}$, and $W^{V,l,h} \in \mathbb{R}^{d_a \times d_x}$ convert the inputs from the representation dimension d_x into the attention dimension $d_a = d_x/H$,[1] creating per-attention-head Key, Query, and Value representations, respectively. The new learned weight matrix $W^{O,l,h} \in \mathbb{R}^{d_x \times d_a}$ converts the attention result from the attention dimension back into the representation dimension.

By recursively applying Eq. (7.6) L times we attain a depth-L self-attention network. In Section 7.3.4 we prove that the recursive relation in Eq. (7.6) implies that the function realized by a network with representation dimension d_x and H attention heads per layer at output location $i \in [N]$ can be written as (Corollary 7.1)

$$\mathbf{y}^{i,L,d_x,H,\Theta}\left(\mathbf{x}^1, ..., \mathbf{x}^N\right) := \sum_{j_1,...,j_C=1}^{N} \mathbf{g}^L\left(\mathbf{x}^i, \mathbf{x}^{j_1}, ..., \mathbf{x}^{j_C}\right), \tag{7.7}$$

where Θ stands for all $4LH$ learned weight matrices: $\forall (l,h) \in [L] \otimes [H]$: $W^{K,l,h}$, $W^{Q,l,h}$, $W^{V,l,h} \in \mathbb{R}^{d_a \times d_x}$, and $W^{O,l,h} \in \mathbb{R}^{d_x \times d_a}$, and the function $\mathbf{g}^L$ is a placeholder which integrates $C + 1 := \frac{3^L - 1}{2} + 1$ different network input vectors. Thus, comparing the form of Eq. (7.7) to the operation of a single layer in Eq. (7.6), it can be seen schematically that while a single layer mixes the output position i with every input

---

[1] Wies et al. [65] show a bottleneck related to attempted relaxations of this equality (detailed are given below in Section 7.3.3.2).

position j once and aggregates the result, depth brings forth an exponential enhancement to the amount of inputs mixed at once as well as to the amount of summed terms. In Section 7.3.3.1, we quantify this effect and analyze the limitations posed by the dimension of the internal representation (the width) on the network's ability to make use of this exponential growth with depth.

In the following subsection, we show that the capacity of the above defined self-attention architecture for modeling input dependencies, as measured by its separation rank (Section 7.2.1), does not depend on the identity of the examined input subsets.

7.3.1.2 Partition invariance of the self-attention separation rank

In contrast to self-attention, the layers of prior leading deep learning architectures are characterized by a predetermined connectivity with respect to their inputs (see Fig. 7.1 and the discussion in Section 7.4). For example, in convolutional networks, a layer's output at a certain location is affected only by a limited number of inputs to this layer that lie within a certain window (the "convolution window"). This fixed connectivity of convolutional networks has been shown to yield high separation ranks w.r.t. input partitions which separate neighboring inputs (e.g., as in Fig. 7.4(a)), while suffering from low separation ranks w.r.t. input partitions which separate distant inputs (e.g., as in Fig. 7.4(b)). The following proposition establishes a qualitatively different trait for self-attention networks, which are shown to treat all balanced partitions alike.

Proposition 7.1. *For $p \in [d_x]$, let $y_p^{i,L,d_x,H,\Theta}$ be the scalar function computing the p-th entry of an output vector at position $i \in [N]$ of the depth-L self-attention network with embedding dimension d_x and H attention heads per layer, defined in Eqs. (7.6) and (7.7). Then, its separation rank w.r.t. balanced partitions, which obey $A \cup B = [N]$, $|A|, |B| = N/2$, is invariant to the identity of the partition, i.e., $\forall A \cup B = [N]$, $\tilde{A} \cup \tilde{B} = [N]$, s.t. $|A|, |B|, |\tilde{A}|, |\tilde{B}| = N/2$:*

$$\mathrm{sep}_{(A,B)}\left(y_p^{i,L,d_x,H,\Theta}\right) = \mathrm{sep}_{(\tilde{A},\tilde{B})}\left(y_p^{i,L,d_x,H,\Theta}\right). \tag{7.8}$$

Accordingly, for the discussion on self-attention, we will omit the specification of the partition, denoting $\mathrm{sep}(y_p^{i,L,d_x,H,\Theta})$ as the separation rank of $y_p^{i,L,d_x,H,\Theta}$ w.r.t. any balanced partition of the inputs.

Proof. We will denote $A = (a_1, \ldots, a_{\frac{N}{2}})$, $B = (b_1, \ldots, b_{\frac{N}{2}})$, $\tilde{A} = (\tilde{a}_1, \ldots, \tilde{a}_{\frac{N}{2}})$, $\tilde{B} = (\tilde{b}_1, \ldots, \tilde{b}_{\frac{N}{2}})$ and by $\pi \in S_N$ the unique permutation that satisfies

$$\forall m \in \left[\frac{N}{2}\right] \quad \pi(a_m) = \tilde{a}_m \wedge \pi(b_m) = \tilde{b}_m.$$

Without loss of generality we will assume that $a_1 = \tilde{a}_1 = i$, where i is the output location specified in the definition of $y^{i,L,d_x,H,\Theta}$.

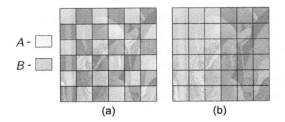

A - □
B - □

(a)   (b)

FIGURE 7.4

The separation rank of the function realized by self-attention networks is agnostic to the input partition. In contrast, the functions realized by convolutional and recurrent networks have exponentially higher separation ranks w.r.t. the interleaved partition (a) than w.r.t. the left-right partition (b).

Assuming that $\mathrm{sep}(y^{i,L,d_x,H,\Theta}; A, B) = R$, there exist $g_1^A, \ldots, g_R^A, g_1^B, \ldots, g_R^B$ s.t.

$$\forall \mathbf{x}^{(1)}, \ldots, \mathbf{x}^{(N)} \in \mathbb{R}^{d_x} :$$

$$y_p^{i,L,d_x,H,\Theta}\big(\mathbf{x}^{(1)}, \ldots, \mathbf{x}^{(N)}\big) = \sum_{v=1}^{R} g_v^A\big(\mathbf{x}^{(a_1)}, \ldots, \mathbf{x}^{(a_{\frac{N}{2}})}\big) g_v^B\big(\mathbf{x}^{(b_1)}, \ldots, \mathbf{x}^{(b_{\frac{N}{2}})}\big).$$

Since both a_1 and $\pi(a_1)$ are equal to i, the summations over $j_1, \ldots, j_C$ in Eq. (7.7) imply that for any $\mathbf{x}^{(1)}, \ldots, \mathbf{x}^{(N)} \in \mathbb{R}^{d_x}$ we have

$$y_p^{i,L,d_x,H,\Theta}\big(\mathbf{x}^{(1)}, \ldots, \mathbf{x}^{(N)}\big) = y_p^{i,L,d_x,H,\Theta}\big(\mathbf{x}^{(\pi(1))}, \ldots, \mathbf{x}^{(\pi(N))}\big),$$

and therefore

$$= \sum_{v=1}^{R} g_v\big(\mathbf{x}^{(\pi(a_1))}, \ldots, \mathbf{x}^{(\pi(a_{\frac{N}{2}}))}\big) g_v'\big(\mathbf{x}^{(\pi(b_1))}, \ldots, \mathbf{x}^{(\pi(b_{\frac{N}{2}}))}\big)$$

$$= \sum_{v=1}^{R} g_v\big(\mathbf{x}^{(\tilde{a}_1)}, \ldots, \mathbf{x}^{(\tilde{a}_{\frac{N}{2}})}\big) g_v'\big(\mathbf{x}^{(\tilde{b}_1)}, \ldots, \mathbf{x}^{(\tilde{b}_{\frac{N}{2}})}\big).$$

So we proved that

$$\mathrm{sep}\big(y_p^{i,L,d_x,H,\Theta}; \tilde{A}, \tilde{B}\big) \leq \mathrm{sep}\big(y_p^{i,L,d_x,H,\Theta}; A, B\big).$$

Finally, by switching the roles of $\tilde{A}, \tilde{B}$ and A, B, we can get the inverse inequality so we conclude that

$$\mathrm{sep}\big(y_p^{i,L,d_x,H,\Theta}; \tilde{A}, \tilde{B}\big) = \mathrm{sep}\big(y_p^{i,L,d_x,H,\Theta}; A, B\big). \qquad \square$$

This result is in accordance with the intuition regarding the flexibility of the self-attention mechanism—it does not integrate the input in a predefined pattern like convolutional networks, but rather computes the input integration in an input-dependent manner (the attention weights a_j^i in Eq. (7.6) depend on the input). Thus, self-attention can dynamically learn to correlate any inter-dependent subsets of the inputs. Natural text exhibits nonsmooth nonlocal dependency structures, as correlations between input segments can abruptly rise and decay with distance. The fact that self-attention facilitates all correlation patterns equally poses it as a more natural architecture for language modeling-related tasks. Convolutional networks, with their local connectivity, may have a good inductive bias for imagery data, but partitions unfavored by them may reflect more erratic correlations that are nonetheless relevant for natural language inputs.

However, the above property of indifference to the input partition is not enough for succeeding in tasks with elaborate input dependencies, since a function with equally low separation ranks for all input partitions has limited ability to model such dependencies. In the following sections, we show how the grid tensor framework presented in Section 7.2 allows bounding the separation rank of self-attention from below, and thus gaining insight into how different architectural parameters affect the network's ability to correlate its inputs.

7.3.2 Self-attention architecture expressivity questions

In this section, we examine open questions regarding the above self-attention architecture class that have been addressed by the tensor-based theoretical framework of this chapter.

7.3.2.1 The depth-to-width interplay in self-attention

The recent golden age of deep learning has popularized the depth efficiency notion: from an expressiveness standpoint, increasing a neural network's size by adding more layers (deepening) is advantageous relatively to other parameter increase alternatives, such as increasing the dimension of the internal representation (widening). Deep learning architectures that preceded self-attention have provided an overwhelming empirical signal for this notion [34,60], and depth efficiency was theoretically supported from a variety of angles on these architectures [18,24,54], including the one by Cohen et al. [15], which instigated the tensor analysis-based approach described in this chapter. Accordingly, diminishing returns in the case of very deep networks were mainly attributed to optimization issues, and indeed the alleviation of these issues has allowed network depths to mount from 10s to 100s and beyond [34], enabling deep convolutional networks to advance the state-of-the-art in computer vision applications.

However, in contrast to the depth "arms race" that took place in the case of convolutional networks, the leading self-attention networks are not much deeper than the original Transformer [62] and BERT [21] models. In fact, even the strongest self-attention models trained to date, which increased the 0.3B parameter count of BERT-large by factors of 100s to 11B [53] and 175B [7], have only increased its depth by factors of 2 and 4, respectively. The remaining size increase stems from an increase in layer widths, clearly countering the depth efficiency notion.

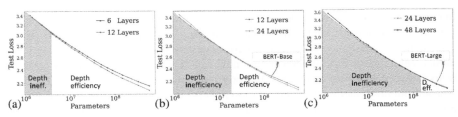

FIGURE 7.5

From [47], an experimental validation of the two depth efficiency/**in**efficiency regimes predicted by the tensorial framework of this chapter. [47] further showed that the transition between regimes occurs in exponentially larger network sizes as the networks gets deeper, in agreement with the theory in Section 7.3.3.1.

In Section 7.3.3, we address the above question of the depth-to-width interplay in self-attention networks and present fundamental subtleties in the above picture that are identified in Levine et al. [47] via the tensorial framework of Section 7.2. Their analysis predicts that self-attention will exhibit two qualitatively different depth efficiency and depth **in**efficiency behaviors, in two distinct parameter regimes. These theoretical predictions are clearly manifested in a corresponding empirical evaluation (Fig. 7.5), and have provided quantitative guidelines for optimal depth-to-width parameter allocation given a fixed parameter budget for a self-attention network. The current challenge in the natural language processing field, of reaching beyond-1-trillion-parameter language models, renders informed guidelines of how to optimally increase self-attention depth and width in tandem a mandatory ingredient. The results in Section 7.3.3 clearly show that the optimal path towards the 1T-parameter mark includes massive widening.

7.3.2.2 The input embedding rank bottleneck in self-attention

After their successful debut in natural language processing, self-attention architectures are gradually becoming the de facto standard in many domains. While the architecture's operation is mostly unchanged across different applications, the chosen ratio between the number of self-attention layers (depth) and the dimension of the internal representation (width) can vary greatly. For example, for a fixed size of 110 million parameters (matching the original BERT-Base network), popular architectures range from 12-layered networks to much "narrower" and deeper 128-layered networks.

In language applications, the depth-to-width ratio of self-attention models is relatively consistent: as mentioned above, an increase in model size is mainly achieved via widening [47], so that the largest self-attention architectures are very wide relative to their depths [7,53]. In other domains this aspect seems unresolved, even when comparing leading models within the same field. In computer vision, for example, the Vision Transformer (ViT) [23] sets the state-of-the-art on ImageNet in a transfer learning setup with depth-to-width ratios corresponding to common language models. Conversely, Image GPT [10] and Sparse Transformer [39] achieve state-of-the-art computer vision results in unsupervised learning and density estimation, respectively, by using significantly deeper and narrower models.

Recently, Henighan et al. [35] performed an ablation study which includes data from different domains and reported empirical evidence for the existence of different "ideal" depth-to-width ratios per data modality: the authors conclude that the depth-to-width ratio of image and math models should be 10 times larger than that of language models. A possible take-away can be that the representations of the different data types require different depth-to-width specifications from the architecture. However, in a contemporary study, described in the previous subsection, Levine et al. [47] quantified the optimal depth-to-width ratio per self-attention network size and justified the relative shallowness observed in current attention-based language models. Importantly, their tensor-based theoretical framework pertains to the self-attention architecture expressivity and is agnostic to the input modality.

The two different views above give rise to the following question: **does the optimal depth-to-width ratio depend on the data modality (i.e., text/images/other), or is it a consequence only of architecture expressivity considerations?** Wies et al. [65] established tensor-based architecture expressivity results that explain the observed variability in the architecture configurations across domains. By identifying expressivity bottlenecks that have manifested themselves mainly in nonlinguistic data modalities, they provide simple *domain-independent* practical guidelines for self-attention architecture selection.

Specifically, as detailed in Section 7.3.3, Wies et al. [65] identified an *input bottleneck* in self-attention, proving that when the dimensionality of the inputs is lower than the network width, the network width's contribution to expressivity is capped. Thus, they show that when the width exceeds the input rank, deepening is exponentially favorable over widening. Formally, this occurs when $\forall j$ the input $\mathbf{x}^j \in \mathbb{R}^{d_x}$ can be written as

$$\mathbf{x}^j = M\mathbf{w}^j \tag{7.9}$$

$$\text{for } M \in \mathbb{R}^{d_x \times r} \; ; \; \mathbf{w}^j \in R^r$$

$$\text{s.t. } r < d_x,$$

where r is referred to as the input embedding rank. For example, a naive representation of an image as a collection of N RGB vectors in $\mathbb{R}^3$ would imply that $r = 3$, and the identified bottleneck would come into play for $d_x > 3$.

The theoretically predicted input bottleneck and its implications on the depth-to-width interplay of self-attention architectures are empirically demonstrated. These findings directly link the depth-to-width ratio variability across domains to the often glossed-over usage of different input embedding ranks in different domains and counters the input modality-based interpretation.

7.3.2.3 Mid-architecture rank bottlenecks in self-attention

Modern self-attention-based language models have been recently scaled up to unprecedented sizes, giving rise to a rapid improvement of natural language understanding and generation abilities. This process promotes the question of how to increase model size in the most efficient manner. Given hardware constraints, there have been several works that diverge from the common architecture setup. For example, one of the largest models trained to date, which holds the state-of-the-art in many NLP benchmarks, T5-11B [53], has scaled up to its 11B-parameter count by keeping the representation dimension between layers relatively small, while investing most of the parameters in the self-attention operation itself. Specifically, the attention dimension (introduced after Eq. (7.6)) is commonly chosen such that $H \cdot d_a = d_x$. In contrast, T5-11B has held this dimension constant, while significantly increasing the number of attention heads, such that $H \cdot d_a >> d_x$.

Beyond the above discussed input embedding rank bottleneck, the tensor-based rank bottlenecking proof technique that was established by Wies et al. [65] applies to bottlenecks created mid-architecture. In Section 7.3.3 we show that a low representation dimension caps the ability to enjoy an excessive parameter increase in the self-attention operation. This prediction was validated empirically, projecting T5-11B to be $\sim 50\%$ redundant, i.e., it could achieve its language modeling performance with roughly half its size if trained with a regular architecture.

7.3.3 Results on the operation of self-attention

Below, we present the main insights regarding the operation of self-attention architectures, attained by tackling the architectural questions presented in Section 7.3.2. The full derivation of the bounds on the separation rank, which relies on the grid tensor technique that is detailed in Section 7.2, is presented in Section 7.3.4. In this section, we present the outcome of the analysis and its practical implications on self-attention network design.

7.3.3.1 The effect of depth in self-attention networks

We follow Levine et al. [47] and present bounds on the separation rank of self-attention networks that are tight with respect to the dependence on depth and width. The established bounds on the separation rank reveal two qualitatively different depth efficiency regimes. In the first regime of $L < \log_3(d_x)$, deepening is clearly preferable to widening (Theorem 7.1). In the second regime of $L > \log_3(d_x)$, deepening and widening play a similar role in enhancing the expressivity of self-attention networks (Theorem 7.2).

The recursive structure of deep self-attention, presented in the previous section, hints at an exponential increase of input mixing with depth: the output of each layer is introduced three times into the Key/Query/Value computation made by the subsequent layer. Below, this intuition for depth efficiency is formalized for self-attention networks of sufficient width: $d_x > 3^L$. Theorem 7.1 below bounds the separation rank of such networks, implying a requirement for a double exponential growth from a bounded depth network attempting to replicate a deeper one.

Theorem 7.1. *For $p \in [d_x]$, let $y_p^{i,L,d_x,H,\Theta}$ be the scalar function computing the p-th entry of an output vector at position $i \in [N]$ of the depth-L self-attention network* *with embedding dimension d_x and H attention heads per layer, defined in Eqs. (7.6) and (7.7). Let* $\text{sep}(y_p^{i,L,d_x,H,\Theta})$ *be its separation rank (Section 7.2). If L, d_x obey $L < \log_3(d_x)$, then the following holds almost everywhere in the network's learned parameter space, i.e., for all values of the weight matrices (represented by Θ) but a set of Lebesgue measure zero,*

$$3^{L-2}\left(\log_3(d_x - H) + a\right) \le \log_3\left(\text{sep}(y_p^{i,L,d_x,H,\Theta})\right) \le \frac{3^L - 1}{2}\log_3(d_x + H) \quad (7.10)$$

with $a = -L + [2 - \log_3 2]$ (note that $\log_3(d_x - H) + a > 0$ in this regime of $L < \log_3(d_x)$).

Proof. See Section 7.3.4.   □

Theorem 7.1 bounds the separation rank of a deep self-attention network of sufficient width $d_x > 3^L$ between two functions that grow double exponentially with depth and polynomially with width, tightly describing its behavior w.r.t. depth and width. Because equivalence cannot hold between two functions of different separation ranks, the above result implies a double exponential requirement from the width of a shallow network attempting to replicate the deep one, and clear depth efficiency holds.

Beyond establishing depth efficiency in early self-attention layers, the above analysis sheds light on the contribution of a self-attention network's depth to its ability to correlate input subsets. The separation rank (w.r.t. any partition) of a single layer, given by Eq. (7.6), is only linear in H and d_x, showcasing a limitation of the class of functions realized by single self-attention layers to model elaborate input dependencies. Theorem 7.1 quantifies the double exponential growth of this capacity measure with the number of stacked self-attention layers. The following theorem shows that this growth is capped in a practical case, when depth is larger than the logarithm of the dimension of the internal representation:

Theorem 7.2. *For $y_p^{i,L,d_x,H,\Theta}$ as defined in Theorem 7.1, if $L > \log_3(d_x)$, then the following holds almost everywhere in the network's learned parameter space, i.e., for all values of the weight matrices (represented by Θ) but a set of Lebesgue measure zero:*

$$\frac{1}{2}d_x \cdot L + b_1 + b_2 \le \log_3\left(\text{sep}(y_p^{i,L,d_x,H,\Theta})\right) \le 2d_x \cdot L + c_1 + c_2, \quad (7.11)$$

with corrections on the order of L: $b_1 = -L(\frac{H}{2} + 1)$, $c_1 = L$, and on the order of $d_x \log_3(d_x)$: $b_2 = -d_x(1 + \frac{1}{2}\log_3(\frac{d_x - H}{2}))$, $c_2 = -2d_x \cdot \log_3 d_x/2\sqrt{2e} + \log_3 d_x$.

Proof. See Section 7.3.4.   □

Theorem 7.2 states that when the network's depth passes a width-dependent threshold, the separation rank turns from increasing polynomially with width and double exponentially with depth, to increasing-exponentially with width and depth together. Thus, while an increase in network size increases its capacity to model input dependencies, our result shows that there is no longer a clear-cut advantage of depth in this respect.

Overall, this analysis predicts the existence of two different depth efficiency/ inefficiency regimes in self-attention networks and further quantifies the transition point between regimes to be exponential in network width. [47] demonstrated that these theoretical predictions are manifested in the performance of commonly employed self-attention networks. Fig. 7.5, taken from that study, shows that the predicted division into two depth efficiency/inefficiency regimes indeed takes place in common self-attention architectures. When comparing depths $(L^{shallow}, L^{deep}) = \{(6, 12), (12, 24), (24, 48)\}$, Fig. 7.5 shows a qualitatively different depth efficiency behavior as the network size varies. For smaller network sizes, deepening is not favorable over widening. The theoretical analysis predicts this, showing that when the width of the deeper network is not large enough it cannot use its excess layers efficiently. However, when the network's size is increased by widening, a transition into the depth efficiency regime is clearly demonstrated: for the same parameter budget the deeper network performs better. Once the deeper network becomes wide enough, such that the depth threshold for depth efficiency surpasses $L^{shallow}$, it is significantly more expressive.

Beyond a qualitative match to the two predicted depth efficiency/inefficiency behaviors, [47] corroborated the prediction for an exponential dependence of the "depth efficiency width"—the width for which a network becomes depth-efficient—on the network's depth. By quantifying this exponential behavior, predicted by the tensorial framework of this chapter, they attain practical guidelines for depth-to-width parameter allocation in a self-attention network of a given size.

7.3.3.2 The effect of bottlenecks in self-attention networks

In this section, we follow Wies et al. [65] and show how input and mid-architecture rank bottlenecks, discussed in Sections 7.3.2.2 and 7.3.2.3, respectively, affect self-attention architecture design. Theorem 7.3 below bounds the separation rank of the analyzed self-attention architecture by functions that grow exponentially with depth L times *the minimum* between the network width d_x and the input embedding rank r (presented in Eq. (7.9)).

Without considering the input rank bottleneck, Levine et al. [47] have shown that for $L > \log_3 d_x$, both depth and width contribute exponentially to the separation rank (Theorem 7.2 above), and have provided extensive empirical corroboration of this prediction for a "depth inefficiency" regime of self-attention. For the complementary regime of $L < \log_3 d_x$ they prove a "depth efficiency" result, by which deepening is favorable over widening (Theorem 7.1 above). The results below imply that when the input embedding rank is lower than the network width, the width-related parameters are underutilized and "depth efficiency" kicks in immediately, even within the more practical $L > \log_3 d_x$ regime. As part of the consequences of Theorem 7.3, discussed after its presentation, this explains the variability in optimal self-attention depth-to-width ratios that are observed across application and domains.

The following theorem states that the network's capacity to model dependencies is harmed by a low-rank input embedding.

Theorem 7.3. *Let $y_p^{i,L,d_x,H,r}$ be the scalar function computing the pth entry of an output vector at position $i \in [N]$ of the H-headed depth-L width-d_x self-attention network defined in Eq. (7.6), where the embedding rank r is defined by Eq. (7.9). Let $sep(y_p^{i,L,d_x,H,r})$ denote its separation rank (Section 7.2.1). Then the following holds (upper bound):*

$$\log\left(sep(y_p^{i,L,d_x,H,r})\right) = \tilde{O}\left(L \cdot \min\{r, d_x\}\right). \tag{7.12}$$

Further assume that $L > \log_3 d_x$, $H < r$. Then for all values of the network weights but a set of Lebesgue measure zero, the following holds (lower bound):

$$\log\left(sep(y_p^{i,L,d_x,H,r})\right) = \tilde{\Omega}\left(L \cdot \left(\min\{r, d_x\} - H\right)\right). \tag{7.13}$$

Proof. See [65]. □

Theorem 7.3 has direct implications on self-attention architecture design, detailed in the following.

1. **The input embedding rank bottleneck.** Since two functions can be equal only if they have the same separation rank, a network with a low-rank embedding $r < d_x$ cannot express the operation of a full-rank $r = d_x$ network. As Fig. 7.6(a) shows, this result translates into an empirical degradation in performance when $r < d_x$. A popular low-input rank method is ALBERT, of [41]; Fig. 7.6(a) shows that the low $r/d_x = 128/4096$ ratio implemented in their network yields a 25% redundancy in network size, i.e., a low-rank network is surpassed by a full-rank network with 75% of the parameters. The above input embedding bottleneck is even more common in nonlinguistic domains. For example, [55] trained a bioinformatics self-attention model with $r/d_x = 33/1280$. The result in Theorem 7.3 formalizes the suboptimality of these settings.

2. **Effect on the depth-to-width interplay.** Beyond establishing a degradation in performance for self-attention networks with low input embedding rank, Theorem 7.3 implies an advantage of deepening versus widening beyond the point of $d_x = r$, as deepening contributes exponentially more to the separation rank in this case. As Fig. 7.6(b) shows, when comparing two self-attention architectures of depths $L^{shallow} < L^{deep}$ with the same embedding rank r and the same number of parameters, the two networks perform comparably when $d_x^{shallow} \leq r$, and the deeper network is better when $d_x^{shallow} > r$. This implication directly explains the observed depth-to-width ratio differences between language models and vision models. The Sparse Transformer [39] over images, which is 128 layers deep at the same parameter count as the 12-layered BERT-Base in language, has a low pixel intensity input dimension which caps the contribution of the width. The same input dimension is used in the ablation of [35], who attribute the difference in optimal depth-to-width ratio to the

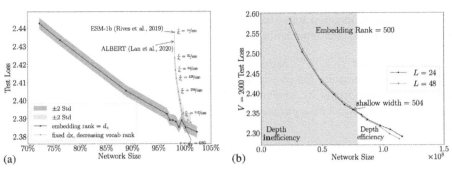

(a)   (b)

FIGURE 7.6

From [65]. **(a)** An experimental validation of the low-rank embedding bottleneck. The network size is reduced either by decreasing the width of all layers (green (gray in print version)) or by only decreasing the input embedding rank (orange (light gray in print version)). A rapid degradation is observed when the input embedding rank is decreased. This degradation affects leading models in NLP (ALBERT) and in other domains (ESM-1b). **(b)** An experimental validation of the effect of input embedding rank (Eq. (7.9)) on the depth-to-width trade-off in self-attention. A deeper network of the same parameter count becomes better after the width of the shallower network passes its rank-bottlenecking point $d_x^{\text{shallow}} = r$. [65] demonstrated that in the absence of a rank bottleneck, this transition into depth efficiency occurs for much larger networks.

difference in data modalities. The result in Theorem 7.3, along with the re-inforcing experiments in Fig. 7.6(a) and in Wies et al. [65], implies that this phenomenon is modality-independent and is in fact related to architecture expressivity.

3. **A mid-architecture bottleneck—width caps the internal attention dimension.** The above implications relate to the bottleneck caused by a low input embedding rank. By observing that the upper bound on the separation rank in Theorem 7.3 does not depend on the number of attention heads H, [65] established a mid-architecture bottleneck related to this architectural aspect, which affects leading self-attention architectures. Specifically, following the original implementation of [62], most common self-attention architectures set the number of heads to be $H = d_x/d_a$, i.e., the network width divided by the internal attention dimension (see text below Eq. (7.6)). However, in their effort to drastically increase network size under hardware restrictions, [53] trained their unprecedentedly sized 11B-parameter T5 model by decoupling the above: they trained a width $d_x = 1K$ network but increased the number of attention heads per layer to $H = 128$ while keeping the attention dimension fixed at $d_a = 128$. Thus, T5-11B achieves an internal attention embedding of $H \cdot d_a = 16K$ before projecting back down to the width value of 1K between layers. However, since the bounds in Theorem 7.3 are capped at d_x, the presented tensor-based theoretical framework predicts that this form of parameter increase is suboptimal, i.e., adding parameters to the internal attention

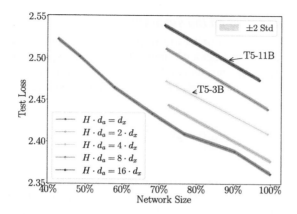

FIGURE 7.7

From [65], the $d_x < H \cdot d_a$ bottleneck of the T5 architecture degrades performance. As the bottleneck ratio increases, smaller baseline architectures outperform variants that invest parameters in the internal attention representation. T5-11B was trained with $H \cdot d_a = 16d_x$, implying a $\sim 50\%$ parameter redundancy.

representation beyond $H \cdot d_a = d_x$ is inferior to simply increasing the width d_x. This conclusion is verified in Fig. 7.7, which establishes that the configuration of T5-11B is indeed highly parameter redundant (around 45% redundancy).

7.3.4 Bounding the separation rank of self-attention

In this section, we explicitly derive some of the upper and lower bounds presented in Section 7.3.3. Though some of the technical details are omitted for the sake of clarity (full details can be found in Levine et al. [47]), the derivations in this section are quite technical: we include thorough derivations in order to provide a comprehensive example for how to establish tight bounds on the separation rank. The above presented practical insights into the operation of a successful deep learning architecture class can serve as motivation for following the methods shown below. The nontechnical reader can skip to Sections 7.4 and 7.5, where we comment on prior uses of this theoretical framework for the analyses of convolutional and recurrent networks, and then conclude this chapter.

We derive an upper bound on the separation rank of the function realized by a self-attention network in Section 7.3.4.1 by explicitly constructing a decomposition of this function into a sum of functions that are separable w.r.t. a given input partition. Per its definition (see Eq. (7.1)), a lower bound on the separation rank cannot be established via such an explicit decomposition, and we use the grid tensor-based methodology of Section 7.2.2 in order to derive in Section 7.3.4.2 a lower bound on the separation rank of the function realized by a self-attention network.

7.3.4.1 An upper bound on the separation rank

We begin by deriving the explicit form of $\mathbf{g}^L$ that is presented in Eq. (7.7), which would then allow us to construct a decomposition of the deep self-attention function into a sum of functions that are separable w.r.t. a given input partition. For a cleaner presentation, we will rewrite the operations of a self-attention layer, given in Eq. (7.6), in vectorized notation:

$$Y = \sum_{h=1}^{H} W^{O,h} W^{V,h} X X^T \left(W^{K,h}\right)^T W^{Q,h} X, \tag{7.14}$$

where $X, Y(X) \in \mathbb{R}^{d_x \times N}$ denote matrices respectively holding $\mathbf{x}^j, \mathbf{y}^j(\mathbf{x}^1, ..., \mathbf{x}^N)$ in their j-th column. Similarly treating Eq. (7.7), we will denote by $Y^{L,d_x,H,\Theta}(X) \in \mathbb{R}^{d_x \times N}$ the matrix holding $y^{j,L,d_x,H,\Theta}(x^1, ..., x^N)$ in its j-th column.

We prove the following lemma, to be used in the proof of the upper bound on the separation rank, and then present the structure of $\mathbf{g}^L$ as its corollary.

Lemma 7.1. *Defining $C(L) := \frac{3^L-1}{2}$, any depth-L composition of the self-attention layers defined in Eq. (7.6) can be written as*

$$Y^{L,d_x,H,\Theta} = \sum_{h \in [H]^{[C(L)]}} B^{(0,h)T} M^{(1,h)} \cdots M^{(C(L),h)} A^{(0,h)} X, \tag{7.15}$$

where $\forall h \in [H]^{[C]} 0 \le c \le C(L) : M^{(c,h)} = A^{(c,h)} X X^T B^{(c,h)T}$ and $A^{(c,h)}, B^{(c,h)} \in \mathbb{R}^{d_a \times d_x}$.

Proof. We provide a proof by induction on L. In the base case,

$$Y^{(1)}(X) = \sum_{h=1}^{H} \underbrace{W^{O,h}}_{B^T} \underbrace{W^{V,h} X X^T \left(W^{K,h}\right)^T}_{M} \underbrace{W^{Q,h}}_{A} X,$$

$$Y^{(L+1)}(X) = \sum_{h=1}^{H} W^{O,h} W^{V,h} Y^{(L)}(X) Y^{(L)}(X)^T \left(W^{K,h}\right)^T W^{Q,h} Y^{(L)}(X).$$

Now, substituting in the induction hypothesis on the structure of $Y^{(L)}(X)$ yields

$$= \sum_{h=1}^{H} W^{O,h} W^{V,h} \left(\sum_{h_1 \in [H]^{[C(L)]}} B^{(0,h_1)T} M^{(1,h_1)} \cdots M^{(C(L),h_1)} A^{(0,h_1)} X \right)$$

$$\left(\sum_{h_2 \in [H]^{[C(L)]}} X^T A^{(0,h_2)T} M^{(C(L),h_2)T} \cdots M^{(1,h_2)T} B^{(0,h_2)} \right) \left(W^{K,h}\right)^T W^{Q,h}$$

$$\left(\sum_{h_3 \in [H]^{[C(L)]}} B^{(0,h_3)T} M^{(1,h_3)} \cdots M^{(C(L),h_3)} A^{(0,h_3)} X \right).$$

Finally, unifying the summations over h, $h_1 h_2$, h_3 to a single sum over $[H]^{[C(L)\cdot 3+1=C(L+1)]}$ gives

$$
\sum_{h\in[H]^{[C(L+1)]}} \underbrace{W^{O,h} W^{V,h} B^{(0,h)T}}_{\in\mathbb{R}^{d_x\times d_a}} M^{(1,h)}\cdots M^{(C(L),h)}
$$

$$
\underbrace{A^{(0,h)} XX^T A^{(0,h)T}}_{\text{in the desired form of }M} M^{(C(L),h)T}\cdots M^{(2,h)T} \tag{7.16}
$$

$$
\underbrace{M^{(1,h)T} B^{(0,h)}\left(W^{K,h(0)}\right)^T W^{Q,h} B^{(0,h)T}}_{\text{in the desired form of }M} M^{(1,h)}\cdots M^{(C(L),h)} A^{(0,h)} X.
$$

Note that the number of M units, each with a summation on a different index $j\in[N]$, is $3C(L)+1 = C(L+1)$, implying $C(L) = \frac{3^L-1}{2}$, as needed. $\qquad\square$

Corollary 7.1. *Defining* $C(L) := \frac{3^L-1}{2}$, *any depth-L composition of L self-attention layers can be written as in Eq (7.7):*

$$
\mathbf{y}^{i,L,d_x,H,\Theta}\left(\mathbf{x}^1,...,\mathbf{x}^N\right) = \sum_{j_1,...,j_C=1}^{N} \mathbf{g}^L\left(\mathbf{x}^i,\mathbf{x}^{j_1},...,\mathbf{x}^{j_C}\right), \tag{7.17}
$$

where

$$
\mathbf{g}^L\left(\mathbf{x}^i,\mathbf{x}^{j_1},...,\mathbf{x}^{j_C}\right) :=
$$

$$
\sum_{h\in[H]^{[C(L)]}} \sum_{r_1,...,r_{C(L)+1}=1}^{d_a} \left[B^{(0,h)}\right]_{r_1,p} \left(\prod_{c=1}^{C(L)}\langle A_{r_c}^{(c,h)},\mathbf{x}^{(j_c)}\rangle\langle B_{r_{c+1}}^{(c,h)},\mathbf{x}^{(j_c)}\rangle\right)\langle A_{r_{C(L)+1}}^{(0,h)},\mathbf{x}^{(i)}\rangle,
$$

where $A_r^{(c,h)}$, $B_r^{(c,h)}\in\mathbb{R}^{d_x}$ *are the r-th row for* $r\in\mathbb{R}^{d_a}$ *of the A and B matrices introduced in Lemma 7.1 above.*

Proof. To get the required form, we will use Lemma 7.1 above and write the matrix multiplication in Eq. (7.15) explicitly:

$$
M_{r_1,r_2}^{(c,h)} = \sum_{j=1}^{N} \left[A^{(c,h)} X\right]_{r_1,j}\left[X^T B^{(c,h)T}\right]_{j,r_2} = \sum_{j=1}^{N}\langle A_{r_1}^{(c,h)},\mathbf{x}^{(j)}\rangle\langle B_{r_2}^{(c,h)},\mathbf{x}^{(j)}\rangle.
$$

Therefore,

$$
y_p^{i,L,d_x,H,\Theta}\left(\mathbf{x}^{(1)},...,\mathbf{x}^{(N)}\right) = \sum_{h\in[H]^{[C(L)]}} B_p^{(0,h)T} M^{(1,h)}\cdots M^{(C(L),h)} A^{(0,h)}\mathbf{x}^{(i)}
$$

$$= \sum_{j_1,\ldots,j_{C(L)}=1}^{N} \sum_{h\in[H]^{[C(L)]}} \sum_{r_1,\ldots,r_{C(L)+1}=1}^{d_a}$$

$$\left[B^{(0,h)}\right]_{r_1,p} \left(\prod_{c=1}^{C(L)} \langle A_{r_c}^{(c,h)}, \mathbf{x}^{(j_c)}\rangle \langle B_{r_{c+1}}^{(c,h)}, \mathbf{x}^{(j_c)}\rangle\right) \langle A_{r_{C(L)+1}}^{(0,h)}, \mathbf{x}^{(i)}\rangle. \qquad \square$$

In the following, we will use Lemma 7.1 above to prove the upper bound on the separation rank of self-attention networks presented in Theorem 7.1. The upper bounds of Theorems 7.2 and 7.3 are similarly a consequence of the above network form. Their derivations can be found in Levine et al. [47] and Wies et al. [65], respectively.

Proof of the upper bound in Theorem 7.2. In the following theorem, we show how an upper bound on the separation rank is implied by the form of Eq. (7.15) in the statement of Lemma 7.1. $\qquad \square$

Theorem 7.4. *Defining $C(L) := \frac{3^L-1}{2}$, for any depth $L \geq 1$, input size $N > 1$, partition $A \cup B = [N]$, and output locations $i \in [N]$, $p \in [d_x]$, the following holds:*

$$sep\left(y_p^{i,L,d_x,H,\Theta}, A, B\right) \leq \left(H(d_a+1)\right)^{C(L)}.$$

Note that the log of this dependence yields the upper bound in Theorem 7.1.

Proof. We begin by writing the matrix multiplication in the definition of M below Eq. (7.15) explicitly and dividing the sum over input locations to sums over inputs indexed by A and B:

$$M_{r_1,r_2}^{(c,h)} = \sum_{j=1}^{N} \left[A^{(c,h)}X\right]_{r_1,j} \left[X^T B^{(c,h)T}\right]_{j,r_2}$$

$$= \sum_{j\in A} \langle A_{r_1}^{(c,h)}, \mathbf{x}^{(j)}\rangle \langle B_{r_2}^{(c,h)}, \mathbf{x}^{(j)}\rangle + \sum_{j\in B} \langle A_{r_1}^{(c,h)}, \mathbf{x}^{(j)}\rangle \langle B_{r_2}^{(c,h)}, \mathbf{x}^{(j)}\rangle.$$

Therefore, inserting the above form of the M matrices and substituting summation to be over $\{P_c \in \{A, B\}\}_{c=1}^{C(L)}$ that correspond to the two partition segments A/B,

$$y_p^{i,L,d_x,H,\Theta}\left(\mathbf{x}^{(1)}, \ldots, \mathbf{x}^{(N)}\right) = \sum_{h\in[H]^{[C(L)]}} B_p^{(0,h)T} M^{(1,h)} \cdots M^{(C(L),h)} A^{(0,h)} \mathbf{x}^{(i)}$$

$$= \sum_{h\in[H]^{[C(L)]}} \sum_{r_1,\ldots,r_{C(L)+1}=1}^{d_a} \sum_{P_1,\ldots,P_{C(L)}\in\{A,B\}}$$

$$B_{r_1,p}^{(0,h)} \left(\prod_{c=1}^{C(L)} \sum_{j\in P_c} \langle A_{r_c}^{(c,h)}, \mathbf{x}^{(j)}\rangle \langle B_{r_{c+1}}^{(c,h)}, \mathbf{x}^{(j)}\rangle\right) \langle A_{r_{C(L)+1}}^{(0,h)}, \mathbf{x}^{(i)}\rangle.$$

Now we reorder the above sum by summing over indices of swaps between A and B, i.e., $\beta \in [C]$ such that $P_\beta \neq P_{\beta+1}$, and split the multiplication $\prod_{c=1}^{C(L)}$ according to the crossing indices:

$$
= \sum_{h \in [H]^{[C(L)]}} \sum_{r_1, \ldots, r_{C(L)+1}=1}^{d_a} \sum_{b=0}^{C(L)} \sum_{0=\beta_{b+1} < \beta_b \leq \beta_{b-1} \ldots \leq \beta_1 < \beta_0 = C(L)} B_{r_1, p}^{(0,h)}
$$

$$
\left(\left(\prod_{m=0}^{\lfloor \frac{b}{2} \rfloor} \prod_{c=\beta_{2m+1}+1}^{\beta_{2m}} \sum_{j \in A} \langle A_{r_c}^{(c,h)}, \mathbf{x}^{(j)} \rangle \langle B_{r_{c+1}}^{(c,h)}, \mathbf{x}^{(j)} \rangle \right) \langle A_{r_{C(L)+1}}^{(0,h)}, \mathbf{x}^{(i)} \rangle \right)
$$

$$
\left(\prod_{m=0}^{\lceil \frac{b}{2} \rceil - 1} \prod_{c=\beta_{2m+2}+1}^{\beta_{2m+1}} \sum_{j \in B} \langle A_{r_c}^{(c,h)}, \mathbf{x}^{(j)} \rangle \langle B_{r_{c+1}}^{(c,h)}, \mathbf{x}^{(j)} \rangle \right),
$$

where we assume without loss of generality that $i \in A$ and therefore $P_{\beta_1}, P_{\beta_1+1}, \ldots, P_{\beta_0-1}, P_{\beta_0} = A$. The above reordering allows pushing the summation of nonswapping r_c indices into the A, B parentheses:

$$
= \sum_{h \in [H]^{[C(L)]}} \sum_{b=0}^{C(L)} \sum_{0=\beta_{b+1} < \beta_b \leq \beta_{b-1} \ldots \leq \beta_1 \leq \beta_0 = C(L)} \sum_{r_{\beta_1+1}, \ldots, r_{\beta_b+1}=1}^{d_a} B_{r_1, p}^{(0,h)}
$$

$$
\left(\underbrace{\sum_{r_{C(L)+1}=1}^{d_a}}_{\substack{\text{just for } \beta_1 < C \\ \text{otherwise ignore}}} \underbrace{\sum_{r_1=1}^{d_a}}_{\substack{\text{used either} \\ \text{in } A \text{ or } B}} \left(\prod_{m=0}^{\lfloor \frac{b}{2} \rfloor} \underbrace{\sum_{r_{\beta_{2m+1}+2}}^{d_a} \vdots}_{\substack{\vdots \\ r_{\beta_{2m}}}} \overset{=1}{} \prod_{c=\beta_{2m+1}+1}^{\beta_{2m}} \sum_{j \in A} \langle A_{r_c}^{(c,h)}, \mathbf{x}^{(j)} \rangle \langle B_{r_{c+1}}^{(c,h)}, \mathbf{x}^{(j)} \rangle \right) \langle A_{r_{C(L)+1}}^{(0,h)}, \mathbf{x}^{(i)} \rangle \right)
$$

$$
\underbrace{}_{\text{function of } A}
$$

$$
\left(\underbrace{\sum_{r_1=1}^{d_a}}_{\substack{\text{used either} \\ \text{in } A \text{ or } B}} \prod_{m=0}^{\lceil \frac{b}{2} \rceil - 1} \sum_{r_{\beta_{2m+2}+2}, \ldots, r_{\beta_{2m+1}}=1}^{d_a} \prod_{c=\beta_{2m+2}+1}^{\beta_{2m+1}} \sum_{j \in B} \langle A_{r_c}^{(c,h)}, \mathbf{x}^{(j)} \rangle \langle B_{r_{c+1}}^{(c,h)}, \mathbf{x}^{(j)} \rangle \right).
$$

$$
\underbrace{}_{\text{function of } B}
$$

$$
(7.18)
$$

Since the separation rank of each term in the above summation is 1, we proved the following upper bound on the separation rank:

$$
sep\left(y_p^{i,L,d_x,H,\Theta}, A, B \right) \leq \sum_{h \in [H]^{[C(L)]}} \sum_{b=0}^{C(L)} \sum_{0=\beta_{b+1} < \beta_b \leq \beta_{b-1} \ldots \leq \beta_1 \leq \beta_0 = C(L)} \sum_{r_{\beta_1+1}, \ldots, r_{\beta_b+1}=1}^{d_a} 1
$$

$$
= H^{C(L)} \sum_{b=0}^{C(L)} \binom{C(L)}{b} (d_a)^b = H^{C(L)} (d_a + 1)^{C(L)} = \left(H(d_a + 1) \right)^{C(L)}.
$$

We note that unlike the d_a case, the same H index can affect nonconsecutive $M^{(c_1,h)}$, $M^{(c_2,h)}$; therefore, we cannot simply push the h indices as done for the r indices in Eq. (7.18). $\qquad\square$

From here, the upper bound in Theorem 7.1 follows by

$$\log_3\left(sep\left(y_p^{i,L,d_x,H,\Theta}, A, B\right)\right) \leq \log_3\left((H(d_a+1))^{C(L)}\right) = \frac{3^L-1}{2}\log_3(d_x+H).$$
(7.19)

7.3.4.2 A lower bound on the separation rank

In the following, we derive the lower bounds on the separation rank of a function realized by a self-attention network that are presented in Theorems 7.1 and 7.2. Following the grid tensor-based scheme of Section 7.2, depicted in Fig. 7.2, the proof strategy is to show that there exists an assignment for the weight matrices of a self-attention network, along with a specific choice of template vectors, for which rank($[\![\mathcal{A}(y_p^{i,L,d_x,H,\Theta})]\!]_{A,B}$) surpasses the lower bounds stated in Theorems 7.1 and 7.2 with the appropriate depth-to_width ratios.

Proof of the lower bounds in Theorems 7.1 and 7.2. Relying on Claim 7.1 we will bound the separation rank from below via the rank of the matricization w.r.t. a partition (A, B) of a grid tensor induced by $y_p^{i,L,d_x,H,\Theta}$, computed by any set of template vectors: $sep_{(A,B)}(y_p^{i,L,d_x,H,\Theta}) \geq$ rank($[\![\mathcal{A}(y_p^{i,L,d_x,H,\Theta})]\!]_{A,B}$). Relying on Claim 7.2, we ensure that the rank of $[\![\mathcal{A}(y_p^{i,L,d_x,H,\Theta})]\!]_{A,B}$ is above a certain value for all configurations of the self-attention network weights but a set of Lebesgue measure zero by finding an assignment of the network weights for which it achieves this value.

We will quote the result of Lemma 6 in Levine et al. [47], which via a specific weight assignment constructs the operation of a self-attention network to roughly resemble a sum of inner products raised to the power of the network depth. Specifically, this lemma assures us that for any matrix $V \in \mathbb{R}^{M/2 \times (d_x-H)/2}$ with l^2 normalized rows, there exists a choice of $M+1$ template vectors $\mathbf{x}^{(1)}, \ldots, \mathbf{x}^{(M+1)} \in \mathbb{R}^{d_x}$, as well as an assignment to the self-attention network weights Θ for which

$$\left[\!\left[\mathcal{A}\left(y_p^{i,L,d_x,H,\Theta}\right)\right]\!\right]_{\tilde{A},\tilde{B}} = \text{Const.} \cdot \left(VV^T\right)^{\odot(3^{L-2})},$$
(7.20)

where $[\![\mathcal{A}(y_p^{i,L,d_x,H,\Theta})]\!]_{\tilde{A},\tilde{B}}$ is a submatrix of the grid tensor matricization $[\![\mathcal{A}(y_p^{i,L,d_x,H,\Theta})]\!]_{A,B}$ of size $M/2 \times M/2$ and $\odot$ represents the Hadamard power operation, i.e., $(A^{\odot k})_{ij} = A_{ij}^k$. Since proving the existence of a submatrix of a certain rank lower bounds the rank of the full matrix by this rank, it suffices to find a matrix V such that rank($(VV^T)^{\odot(3^{L-2})}$) upholds the dependence stated in the lower bounds.

Noting that the operation of raising a rank-r matrix to the Hadamard power of p results in a matrix upper bounded by $\left(\!\!\binom{r}{p}\!\!\right)$ (see the proof in [1] for example) with the notation of the multiset coefficient $\left(\!\!\binom{n}{k}\!\!\right) := \binom{n+k-1}{k}$ and that the rank of VV^T is upper bounded by $(d_x-H)/2$ due to the dimensions of V, we choose the dimension of $[\![\mathcal{A}(y_p^{i,L,d_x,H,\Theta})]\!]_{\tilde{A},\tilde{B}}$ to be $M/2 = \binom{(d_x-H)/2}{3^{L-2}}$ to facilitate the rank increase. This is done by choosing the number of grid tensors M accordingly, as Lemma 6 in [47] allows.

For this choice, observe that it suffices to prove that the submatrix $[\![\mathcal{A}(y_p^{i,L,d_x,H,\Theta})]\!]_{\tilde{A},\tilde{B}} \in R^{M/2 \times M/2}$ is fully ranked in order to satisfy the lower bound dependence in both theorems. This follows by using the identity $\binom{n}{k} \geq (\frac{n}{k})^k$. We have $\binom{n}{k} = \binom{n+k-1}{k} = \binom{n+k-1}{n-1} \geq \max\{(\frac{n-1}{k}+1)^k, (\frac{k}{n-1}+1)^{n-1}\}$.

Accordingly,

$$
\binom{(d_x-H)/2}{3^{L-2}} \geq \max\left\{ \left(\frac{(d_x-H)/2-1}{3^{L-2}}+1\right)^{3^{L-2}}, \left(\frac{3^{L-2}}{(d_x-H)/2-1}+1\right)^{(d_x-H)/2-1} \right\},
$$

and the log of this bounds the expressions in the theorems' lower bounds, where for each regime, $L > \log_3 d_x$ or $L < \log_3 d_x$, the tighter lower bound is used.

Given the above, defining for brevity $d := (d_x-H)/2$ and $\lambda := 3^{L-2}$, it remains only to find a specific matrix $V \in \mathbb{R}^{(\binom{d}{\lambda}) \times d}$ with l^2 normalized rows such that the operation of raising the rank-d matrix $VV^\top$ to the Hadamard power of λ would result in a fully ranked $\binom{d}{\lambda} \times \binom{d}{\lambda}$ matrix. We will provide such a matrix V and prove for it that the following can be written:

$$
(VV^\top)^{\odot \lambda} = \sum_{k=1}^{\binom{d}{\lambda}} \mathbf{a}^{(k)} \otimes \mathbf{b}^{(k)} \tag{7.21}
$$

for $\{\mathbf{a}^{(k)}\}_{k=1}^{\binom{d}{\lambda}}$ and $\{\mathbf{b}^{(k)}\}_{k=1}^{\binom{d}{\lambda}}$, which are two sets of linearly independent vectors, thus proving that $(VV^\top)^{\odot \lambda}$ is indeed a fully ranked matrix, as required.

For $\alpha, \beta \in [\binom{d}{\lambda}]$, observing an entry of $(VV^\top)^{\odot \lambda}$,

$$
\left((VV^\top)^{\odot \lambda}\right)_{\alpha\beta} = (VV^\top)^\lambda_{\alpha\beta} = \left(\sum_{r=1}^d v_r^{(\alpha)} v_r^{(\beta)}\right)^\lambda = \tag{7.22}
$$

$$
\sum_{k_1+\cdots+k_d=\lambda} \binom{\lambda}{k_1,\ldots,k_d} \left[\prod_{r=1}^d (v_r^{(\alpha)})^{k_r}\right]\left[\prod_{r=1}^d (v_r^{(\beta)})^{k_r}\right], \tag{7.23}
$$

where the first equality follows from the definition of the Hadamard power, in the section we denoted $v_r^{(\alpha)}$, $v_r^{(\beta)}$ as the r-th entries in rows α and β of V, and in the second line we expanded the power with the basic multinomial identity.

Identifying the form of Eq. (7.23) with the schematic form of Eq. (7.21), it remains to find a specific matrix $V \in \mathbb{R}^{\binom{d}{\lambda} \times d}$ with l^2 normalized rows for which the size $\binom{d}{\lambda}$ set $\{\mathbf{a}^{(k_1,\ldots,k_d)}\}_{k_1+\cdots+k_d=\lambda}$ is linearly independent, where $a_\alpha^{(k_1,\ldots,k_d)} = \prod_{r=1}^{d}(v_r^{(\alpha)})^{k_r}$.

We show this is the case for V in which the rows are each associated with one of $\binom{d}{\lambda}$ configurations of distributing d integer numbers that sum up to λ, i.e., in which each row is associated with specific $\{q_1^\alpha,\ldots,q_d^\alpha \geq 0, \sum_{r=1}^{d}q_r^\alpha = \lambda\}$. Explicitly, we take the rows $\mathbf{v}_r^{(\alpha)}$ to be

$$\forall r \in [d]: v_r^{(\alpha)} = \Omega^{q_r^\alpha}/\sqrt{\sum_{r'=1}^{d}\Omega^{2q_{r'}^\alpha}}.$$

Given this V, the entry α of each vector in the above defined set $\{\mathbf{a}^{(k_1,\ldots,k_d)}\}_{k_1+\cdots+k_d=\lambda}$ is equal to

$$a_\alpha^{(k_1,\ldots,k_d)} = \prod_{r=1}^{d}(v_r^{(\alpha)})^{k_r} = \prod_{r=1}^{d}\left(\frac{\Omega^{q_r^\alpha}}{\sqrt{\sum_{r'=1}^{d}\Omega^{2q_{r'}^\alpha}}}\right)^{k_r} = \frac{\prod_{r=1}^{d}\Omega^{q_r^\alpha k_r}}{\prod_{r=1}^{d}(\sum_{r'=1}^{d}\Omega^{2q_{r'}^\alpha})^{\frac{k_r}{2}}}$$

$$= \left(\sum_{r'=1}^{d}\Omega^{2q_{r'}^\alpha}\right)^{-\frac{\lambda}{2}} \cdot \left[\Omega^{\sum_{r=1}^{d}q_r^\alpha k_r}\right].$$

Observing that the factor attained from the normalization depends only on the rows and does not vary with the different vectors labeled by $(k_1,\ldots,k_d)$, we note it does not affect their linear dependence (amounts to a multiplication by a diagonal matrix with nonzero entries on the diagonal—does not affect the rank). Therefore, if the set $\{\Omega^{\sum_{r=1}^{d}q_r^\alpha k_r}\}_{k_1+\cdots+k_d=\lambda}$ is linearly independent, then the set $\{\mathbf{a}^{(k_1,\ldots,k_d)}\}_{k_1+\cdots+k_d=\lambda}$ is linearly independent and the proof will follow.

We show the set $\{\Omega^{\sum_{r=1}^{d}q_r^\alpha k_r}\}_{k_1+\cdots+k_d=\lambda}$ to be linearly independent by arranging it as the columns of the matrix $A \in \mathbb{R}^{\binom{d}{\lambda}\times\binom{d}{\lambda}}$ and showing that A is fully ranked. Since the elements of A are polynomial in Ω, then as Lemma~7 in Levine et al. [47] shows, it is sufficient to show that there exists a single contributor to the determinant of A that has the highest degree of Ω in order to ensure that the matrix is fully ranked for all values of Ω but a finite set, so Ω should simply be chosen to be any number that is outside of this set. Observing the summands of the determinant, i.e., $\Omega^{\sum_{q_1+\cdots+q_d=\lambda}\langle\mathbf{q},\sigma(\mathbf{q})\rangle}$, where σ is a permutation on the columns of A, Lemma 8 in Levine et al. [47] assures us the existence of a strictly maximal contributor, satisfying the conditions of Lemma 7 in Levine et al. [47], thus the set $\{\mathbf{a}^{(k_1,\ldots,k_d)}\}_{k_1+\cdots+k_d=\lambda}$ is linearly independent, and the lower bounds in the theorems follow. □

7.4 Convolutional and recurrent networks

In the previous section, we presented in full detail an analysis of the expressivity of deep self-attention networks that was based on the grid tensor framework of Section 7.2. Below, we refer the reader to main results that were established by similar techniques regarding two more veteran classes of deep network architectures, still in wide usage across many domains: convolutional and recurrent networks.

7.4.1 The operation of convolutional and recurrent networks

For each layer of a convolutional network, a fixed-size convolution window is slid over its input computing a scalar per location. Thus, in contrast to naive fully connected and to the more sophisticated self-attention networks, each layer output is only affected by its neighboring locations, as opposed to having the entire layer input drive it. In the context of image processing (still the most common application of convolutional networks), this locality is believed to reflect the inherent dependency structure of the data—the closer pixels are in an image, the more likely they are to be correlated. In between layers, most convolutional networks will include a pooling operation, which essentially decimates the feature maps, i.e., the layer after the pooling operations will have fewer inputs than the preceding layer. This is done by replacing all outputs in a spatial window by a single value (e.g., their maximum or average). In the context of images, pooling is believed to create a hierarchy of abstraction in the patterns neurons respond to.

Recurrent networks are qualitatively different from convolutional or self-attention networks, which are both feed-forward networks, since they treat their input in a sequential manner. In every time step of the computation, a basic recurrent unit integrates a hidden memory state, which depends on inputs from previous time steps, with a new incoming input. An ongoing empirical effort to successfully apply recurrent networks to tasks of increasing complexity and temporal extent includes augmentations of the recurrent unit itself, such as in long short-term memory [37] and their variants (e.g., [11,25]). A parallel avenue for augmentation includes stacking of such recurrent layers to form deep recurrent networks [58]. Deep recurrent networks, which exhibit empirical superiority over shallow ones (see, e.g., [27]), implement hierarchical processing of information at every time step that accompanies their inherent time-advancing computation. These networks have been in wide use in domains that have inherently sequential data, such as speech recognition [2,27] and natural language processing [26,51,61].

7.4.2 Addressed architecture expressivity questions

7.4.2.1 Depth efficiency in convolutional and recurrent networks

As described in Section 7.3.2.1, empirical signals for the superiority of depth in neural networks are prevalent. However, theoretical treatment of depth efficiency mainly pertained to basic network architectures that did not resemble convolutional or recurrent networks (e.g., [19,32,33,48]). Cohen et al. [15], introducing a tensorial approach related to the one presented in this chapter, were the first to establish exponential depth efficiency in convolutional network architectures. Subsequently, Levine et al. [44] have tied their result to the tensor network framework that is widely used in the many-body quantum physics literature [50].

Deep recurrent networks have similarly enjoyed an empirical advantage over shallow ones. Moreover, evidence for a time scale-related effect has risen from experiment [36]—deep recurrent networks appear to model dependencies which correspond to longer time scales than shallow ones. These empirical findings, which imply that depth brings forth a considerable advantage both in complexity and in temporal capacity of recurrent networks, were explained in Levine et al. [45], via the tensorial framework of this chapter. There, the authors considered the separation rank with respect to the "Start-End" partition of the inputs, which segments the sequential input into its beginning and end, as a proxy for the network's long-term memory capacity. In this manner, a combinatorial advantage of depth to the network's long-term memory was established: deeper networks were shown to have combinatorially larger separation ranks than shallow ones with respect to the "Start-End" partition, via techniques resembling those detailed in Section 7.3.4.

7.4.2.2 *Further results on convolutional networks*

The pooling layer in convolutional networks, which performs decimation of the feature maps, commonly operates by grouping together neighboring inputs. Cohen and Shashua [13] analyzed the effect of this contiguous pooling versus other pooling types, such as mirror pooling, which groups together distant inputs, on the separation rank of convolutional networks. They concluded that the decimation is strongly correlated with the separation rank, and specifically that the common contiguous pooling favors local dependencies such as are prevalent in images and disfavors longer-ranged dependencies.

Sharir and Shashua [59] analyzed a different aspect of the convolution operation, namely, the overlapping between convolutional windows. In common convolutional networks, the convolution window is slid one input at a time, meaning that the windows "overlap" in their computation, or in other words that some of the inputs that affect spatially adjacent output computations are shared. Ref. [59] showed that these overlapping operations contribute exponentially to the expressivity of convolutional networks.

Finally, the tensor network-based analysis in [44,46] has generalized the above proof technique by showing an equivalence between convolutional networks and tree tensor networks [49]. This allowed a replication of the above results via the new technique and in addition provided insight into the importance of deeper layers in modeling longer-ranged correlations. This work made a conceptual interdisciplinary contribution by tying the separation rank to a family of quantum entanglement measures, which quantify the dependencies between quantum particles.

7.5 Conclusion

This chapter described a line of work that investigated the expressivity of prominent deep learning architectures by casting their computation in tensor analysis terms. The flexibility of this theoretical framework has allowed investigation of various relevant aspects of the examined architecture classes, oftentimes providing a unique theoretical ability to ask and answer subtle and complex questions regarding their operation. For example, for the above thoroughly discussed case study of self-attention networks, this chapter demonstrated that theoretically raised indications are clearly manifested in experiments (Figs. 7.5, 7.6, and 7.7). Thus, previously overlooked architectural design guidelines for increasing network expressivity were derived. The above flexibility of the theoretical framework, along with the consistent empirical reflection of its predictions, render it very attractive for future investigations in the rapidly advancing field of deep learning.

References

[1] A. Amini, A. Karbasi, F. Marvasti, Low-rank matrix approximation using point-wise operators, IEEE Transactions on Information Theory 58 (1) (2012) 302–310.

[2] D. Amodei, S. Ananthanarayanan, R. Anubhai, J. Bai, E. Battenberg, C. Case, J. Casper, B. Catanzaro, Q. Cheng, G. Chen, et al., Deep speech 2: end-to-end speech recognition in English and mandarin, in: International Conference on Machine Learning, 2016, pp. 173–182.

[3] A. Baevski, H. Zhou, A. Mohamed, M. Auli, wav2vec 2.0: a framework for self-supervised learning of speech representations, arXiv preprint, arXiv:2006.11477, 2020.

[4] D. Bahdanau, K. Cho, Y. Bengio, Neural machine translation by jointly learning to align and translate, arXiv preprint, arXiv:1409.0473, 2014.

[5] G. Beylkin, M.J. Mohlenkamp, Numerical operator calculus in higher dimensions, Proceedings of the National Academy of Sciences 99 (16) (2002) 10246–10251.

[6] G. Beylkin, J. Garcke, M.J. Mohlenkamp, Multivariate regression and machine learning with sums of separable functions, SIAM Journal on Scientific Computing 31 (3) (2009) 1840–1857.

[7] T.B. Brown, B. Mann, N. Ryder, M. Subbiah, J. Kaplan, P. Dhariwal, A. Neelakantan, P. Shyam, G. Sastry, A. Askell, et al., Language models are few-shot learners, arXiv preprint, arXiv:2005.14165, 2020.

[8] R. Caron, T. Traynor, The zero set of a polynomial, WSMR Report 05-02, 2005.

[9] S. Chatterjee, Coherent gradients: an approach to understanding generalization in gradient descent-based optimization, arXiv preprint, arXiv:2002.10657, 2020.

[10] M. Chen, A. Radford, R. Child, J. Wu, H. Jun, P. Dhariwal, D. Luan, I. Sutskever, Generative pretraining from pixels, 2020.

[11] K. Cho, B. Van Merriënboer, C. Gulcehre, D. Bahdanau, F. Bougares, H. Schwenk, Y. Bengio, Learning phrase representations using RNN encoder-decoder for statistical machine translation, arXiv preprint, arXiv:1406.1078, 2014.

[12] N. Cohen, A. Shashua, Convolutional rectifier networks as generalized tensor decompositions, in: International Conference on Machine Learning (ICML), 2016.

[13] N. Cohen, A. Shashua, Inductive bias of deep convolutional networks through pooling geometry, in: 5th International Conference on Learning Representations (ICLR), 2017.

[14] N. Cohen, O. Sharir, A. Shashua, Deep simnets, in: IEEE Conference on Computer Vision and Pattern Recognition (CVPR), 2016.

[15] N. Cohen, O. Sharir, A. Shashua, On the expressive power of deep learning: a tensor analysis, in: Conference on Learning Theory (COLT), 2016.

[16] N. Cohen, O. Sharir, Y. Levine, R. Tamari, D. Yakira, A. Shashua, Analysis and design of convolutional networks via hierarchical tensor decompositions, arXiv preprint, arXiv: 1705.02302, 2017.

[17] N. Cohen, R. Tamari, A. Shashua, Boosting dilated convolutional networks with mixed tensor decompositions, arXiv preprint, arXiv:1703.06846, 2017.

[18] A. Daniely, Depth separation for neural networks, arXiv preprint, arXiv:1702.08489, 2017.

[19] O. Delalleau, Y. Bengio, Shallow vs. deep sum-product networks, in: Advances in Neural Information Processing Systems, 2011, pp. 666–674.

[20] J. Devlin, M.-W. Chang, K. Lee, K. Toutanova Bert, Pre-training of deep bidirectional transformers for language understanding, arXiv preprint, arXiv:1810.04805, 2018.

[21] J. Devlin, M. Chang, K. Lee, K. Toutanova, BERT: pre-training of deep bidirectional transformers for language understanding, in: J. Burstein, C. Doran, T. Solorio (Eds.), Proceedings of the 2019 Conference of the North American Chapter of the Association for Computational Linguistics: Human Language Technologies, vol. 1 (Long and Short Papers), NAACL-HLT 2019, Minneapolis, MN, USA, June 2–7, 2019, Association for Computational Linguistics, 2019, pp. 4171–4186.

[22] P. Dhariwal, H. Jun, C. Payne, J.W. Kim, A. Radford, I. Sutskever, Jukebox: A generative model for music, arXiv preprint, arXiv:2005.00341, 2020.

[23] A. Dosovitskiy, L. Beyer, A. Kolesnikov, D. Weissenborn, X. Zhai, T. Unterthiner, M. Dehghani, M. Minderer, G. Heigold, S. Gelly, J. Uszkoreit, N. Houlsby, An image is worth 16x16 words: transformers for image recognition at scale, in: International Conference on Learning Representations, 2021, https://openreview.net/forum?id=YicbFdNTTy.

[24] R. Eldan, O. Shamir, The power of depth for feedforward neural networks, in: Conference on Learning Theory, 2016, pp. 907–940.

[25] F.A. Gers, J. Schmidhuber, Recurrent nets that time and count, in: Neural Networks, 2000. IJCNN 2000, Proceedings of the IEEE-INNS-ENNS International Joint Conference on, vol. 3, IEEE, 2000, pp. 189–194.

[26] A. Graves, Generating sequences with recurrent neural networks, arXiv preprint, arXiv: 1308.0850, 2013.

[27] A. Graves, A.-r. Mohamed, G. Hinton, Speech recognition with deep recurrent neural networks, in: IEEE International Conference on Acoustics, Speech and Signal Processing, IEEE, 2013, pp. 6645–6649.

[28] W. Hackbusch, On the efficient evaluation of coalescence integrals in population balance models, Computing 78 (2) (2006) 145–159.

[29] W. Hackbusch, Tensor Spaces and Numerical Tensor Calculus, vol. 42, Springer Science & Business Media, 2012.

[30] M. Hardt, B. Recht, Y. Singer, Train faster, generalize better: stability of stochastic gradient descent, in: International Conference on Machine Learning, PMLR, 2016, pp. 1225–1234.

[31] R.J. Harrison, G.I. Fann, T. Yanai, G. Beylkin, Multiresolution quantum chemistry in multiwavelet bases, in: Computational Science-ICCS 2003, Springer, 2003, pp. 103–110.

[32] J. Hastad, Almost optimal lower bounds for small depth circuits, in: Proceedings of the Eighteenth Annual ACM Symposium on Theory of Computing, ACM, 1986, pp. 6–20.

[33] J. Håstad, M. Goldmann, On the power of small-depth threshold circuits, Computational Complexity 1 (2) (1991) 113–129.

[34] K. He, X. Zhang, S. Ren, J. Sun, Deep residual learning for image recognition, in: Proceedings of the IEEE Conference on Computer Vision and Pattern Recognition, 2016, pp. 770–778.

[35] T. Henighan, J. Kaplan, M. Katz, M. Chen, C. Hesse, J. Jackson, H. Jun, T.B. Brown, P. Dhariwal, S. Gray, et al., Scaling laws for autoregressive generative modeling, arXiv preprint, arXiv:2010.14701, 2020.

[36] M. Hermans, B. Schrauwen, Training and analysing deep recurrent neural networks, in: Advances in Neural Information Processing Systems, 2013, pp. 190–198.

[37] S. Hochreiter, J. Schmidhuber, Long short-term memory, Neural Computation 9 (8) (1997) 1735–1780.

[38] Y. Jiang, B. Neyshabur, H. Mobahi, D. Krishnan, S. Bengio, Fantastic generalization measures and where to find them, arXiv preprint, arXiv:1912.02178, 2019.

[39] H. Jun, R. Child, M. Chen, J. Schulman, A. Ramesh, A. Radford, I. Sutskever, Distribution augmentation for generative modeling, in: H.D. III, A. Singh (Eds.), Proceedings of the 37th International Conference on Machine Learning, PMLR, 13–18 Jul 2020, in: Proceedings of Machine Learning Research, vol. 119, pp. 5006–5019, http://proceedings.mlr.press/v119/jun20a.html.

[40] A. Krizhevsky, I. Sutskever, G.E. Hinton, Imagenet classification with deep convolutional neural networks, in: Advances in Neural Information Processing Systems, 2012, pp. 1097–1105.

[41] Z. Lan, M. Chen, S. Goodman, K. Gimpel, P. Sharma, R. Soricut Albert, A lite bert for self-supervised learning of language representations, in: International Conference on Learning Representations, 2020, https://openreview.net/forum?id=H1eA7AEtvS.

[42] Y. LeCun, B. Boser, J.S. Denker, D. Henderson, R.E. Howard, W. Hubbard, L.D. Jackel, Backpropagation applied to handwritten zip code recognition, Neural Computation 1 (4) (1989) 541–551.

[43] Y. LeCun, Y. Bengio, G. Hinton, Deep learning, Nature 521 (7553) (2015) 436–444.

[44] Y. Levine, D. Yakira, N. Cohen, A. Shashua, Deep learning and quantum entanglement: fundamental connections with implications to network design, arXiv preprint, arXiv:1704.01552, 2017.

[45] Y. Levine, O. Sharir, A. Ziv, A. Shashua, Benefits of depth for long-term memory of recurrent networks, in: (ICLR 2018) International Conference on Learning Representations Workshop, 2018.

[46] Y. Levine, D. Yakira, N. Cohen, A. Shashua, Deep learning and quantum entanglement: fundamental connections with implications to network design, in: 6th International Conference on Learning Representations (ICLR), 2018.

[47] Y. Levine, N. Wies, O. Sharir, H. Bata, A. Shashua, The depth-to-width interplay in self-attention, in: Advances in Neural Information Processing Systems, 2020, https://papers.nips.cc/paper/2020/file/ff4dfdf5904e920ce52b48c1cef97829-Paper.pdf.

[48] J. Martens, V. Medabalimi, On the expressive efficiency of sum product networks, arXiv preprint, arXiv:1411.7717, 2014.

[49] V. Murg, F. Verstraete, Ö. Legeza, R.M. Noack, Simulating strongly correlated quantum systems with tree tensor networks, Physical Review B 82 (20) (2010) 205105.

[50] R. Orús, Tensor networks for complex quantum systems, Nature Reviews Physics 1 (9) (2019) 538–550.

[51] R. Pascanu, T. Mikolov, Y. Bengio, On the difficulty of training recurrent neural networks, in: International Conference on Machine Learning, 2013, pp. 1310–1318.

[52] A. Radford, J. Wu, R. Child, D. Luan, D. Amodei, I. Sutskever, Language models are unsupervised multitask learners.

[53] C. Raffel, N. Shazeer, A. Roberts, K. Lee, S. Narang, M. Matena, Y. Zhou, W. Li, P.J. Liu, Exploring the limits of transfer learning with a unified text-to-text transformer, arXiv preprint, arXiv:1910.10683, 2019.

[54] M. Raghu, B. Poole, J. Kleinberg, S. Ganguli, J.S. Dickstein, On the expressive power of deep neural networks, in: Proceedings of the 34th International Conference on Machine Learning-Volume 70, JMLR.org, 2017, pp. 2847–2854.

[55] A. Rives, J. Meier, T. Sercu, S. Goyal, Z. Lin, J. Liu, D. Guo, M. Ott, C.L. Zitnick, J. Ma, R. Fergus, Biological structure and function emerge from scaling unsupervised learning to 250 million protein sequences, bioRxiv, https://doi.org/10.1101/622803, https://www.biorxiv.org/content/10.1101/622803v4, 2019.

[56] D.E. Rumelhart, G.E. Hinton, R.J. Williams, Learning representations by back-propagating errors, Nature 323 (6088) (1986) 533–536.

[57] D. Saxton, E. Grefenstette, F. Hill, P. Kohli, Analysing mathematical reasoning abilities of neural models, in: International Conference on Learning Representations, 2019, https://openreview.net/forum?id=H1gR5iR5FX.

[58] J.H. Schmidhuber, Learning complex, extended sequences using the principle of history compression, Neural Computation (1992).

[59] O. Sharir, A. Shashua, On the expressive power of overlapping architectures of deep learning, in: 6th International Conference on Learning Representations (ICLR), 2018.

[60] K. Simonyan, A. Zisserman, Very deep convolutional networks for large-scale image recognition, arXiv preprint, arXiv:1409.1556, 2014.

[61] I. Sutskever, J. Martens, G.E. Hinton, Generating text with recurrent neural networks, in: Proceedings of the 28th International Conference on Machine Learning (ICML-11), 2011, pp. 1017–1024.

[62] A. Vaswani, N. Shazeer, N. Parmar, J. Uszkoreit, L. Jones, A.N. Gomez, Ł. Kaiser, I. Polosukhin, Attention is all you need, in: Advances in Neural Information Processing Systems, 2017, pp. 5998–6008.

[63] O. Vinyals, I. Babuschkin, W.M. Czarnecki, M. Mathieu, A. Dudzik, J. Chung, D.H. Choi, R. Powell, T. Ewalds, P. Georgiev, et al., Grandmaster level in starcraft II using multi-agent reinforcement learning, Nature 575 (7782) (2019) 350–354.

[64] D. Weissenborn, O. Täckström, J. Uszkoreit, Scaling autoregressive video models, in: International Conference on Learning Representations, 2020, https://openreview.net/forum?id=rJgsskrFwH.

[65] N. Wies, Y. Levine, D. Jannai, A. Shashua, Which transformer architecture fits my data? A vocabulary bottleneck in self-attention, in: Marina Meila, Tong Zhang (Eds.), Proceedings of the 38th International Conference on Machine Learning, in: Proceedings of Machine Learning Research, vol. 139, PMLR, 2021, pp. 11170–11181.

Tensor network algorithms for image classification

8

Cong Chen[a], Kim Batselier[b], and Ngai Wong[a]

[a]*Department of Electrical and Electronic Engineering, The University of Hong Kong, Pokfulam Road, Hong Kong*
[b]*Delft Center for Systems and Control, Delft University of Technology, Delft, the Netherlands*

CONTENTS

8.1 Introduction

Classification algorithm design has been an important topic in machine learning, pattern recognition, and computer vision for decades. Support vector machine (SVM) [1] and logistic regression (LR) [2] are two representative and popular classifiers, which achieve enormous success in pattern classification. However, standard SVM and LR models are based on vector inputs and cannot directly deal with matrices or higher-dimensional data structures (namely, tensors) which are very common in real-life applications. For example, a grayscale picture is stored as a matrix, which is a second-order tensor, while color pictures have a color axis and are naturally third-order

Tensors for Data Processing. **https://doi.org/10.1016/B978-0-12-824447-0.00014-5**

tensors. Therefore, tensorial data need to be vectorized before being fed into SVM or LR. However, this breaks the original data structure information and results in loss of the spatial relationship of nearby pixels [8], which may lead to poor classification performance. Moreover, this vectorization can easily result in a very high-dimensional vector, which results in the notorious curse of dimensionality problem. Consequently, when the number of training samples is relatively small compared to the feature vector dimension, the classifier may easily produce poor classification performance due to overfitting [5–7]. To alleviate overfitting, researchers have attempted to add sparseness constraints during the classifier training procedure. For example, [44] proposed a Bayesian LR approach to solve the overfitting problem. Specifically, this method assumes a prior probability distribution that favors sparseness in the trained classifier. However, the useful tensorial data structure is still disregarded. To solve the above two issues, researchers have focused on extending the traditional SVM and LR into their tensor-formatted counterparts. By doing so, the tensorial versions take the underlying data structural prior into account and at the same time reduce the number of model parameters. In fact, it can be observed that the tensor-based approaches generally outperform the traditional ones [4,29].

In terms of SVM, Ref. [4] proposes a supervised tensor learning (STL) scheme by replacing the vector inputs with tensor inputs and decomposing the corresponding weight vector into a rank-1 tensor, which is trained by the alternating projection optimization method. Based on this learning scheme, [4] extends the standard linear SVM to a general tensor form called the support tensor machine (STM). Although STM lifts the overfitting problem in traditional SVMs, the expressive power of a rank-1 weight tensor is limited, which may not be powerful enough to classify complicated data. In [15], the rank-1 weight tensor of STM is generalized to canonical polyadic (CP) forms for stronger model expressive power. However, the determination of a good CP rank is NP-complete [3]. In [29], an STM is generalized to a support Tucker machine (STuM), which replaces the rank-1 tensor in STM with a Tucker-decomposed tensor. Nevertheless, the number of parameters in the Tucker form is exponentially large, which still suffers from the curse of dimensionality. To alleviate the issue in STuM, [31] proposed to reformulate SVM with a more scalable tensor network called the tensor train (TT). The aforementioned tensorial extensions of SVM are all based on the assumption that the given tensorial data are linearly separable. However, this is not the case in most real-world data. Therefore, [37] further proposed the kernelized support TT machine (K-STTM), which employs the customized kernel functions for the TT structure in order to handle nonlinear tensorial classification problems.

As for LR, the tensorial extensions are similar to the cases in SVM. Ref. [38] replaces the weight vector into a rank-1 tensor, and the authors argue that this setting retains the structure of the spatial and spectral band information, which is a very important aspect for hyperspectral data classification. However, this method suffers from the same problems as in an STM. A more generalized tensor-based LR is proposed by [39], in which the weight vector in LR is replaced by a CP-decomposed tensor.

The rest of this chapter is organized as follows. Some background knowledge of this chapter is introduced in Section 8.2. In Section 8.3, the supervised learning scheme and different tensor-based SVM versions are demonstrated in detail. The tensor-based LR models are briefly introduced in Section 8.4, which are quite similar to the extension schemes in SVM. Lastly, the conclusion is drawn in Section 8.5.

8.2 Background

In this section, some basic tensor computation operations and decomposition methods are introduced. The ideas of traditional SVM and LR are also succinctly reviewed.

8.2.1 Tensor basics

Tensors are multidimensional arrays that are higher-order generalizations of vectors (first-order tensors) and matrices (second-order tensors). A d-th-order or d-way tensor is denoted as $\mathcal{A} \in \mathbb{R}^{I_1 \times I_2 \times \cdots \times I_d}$ and the element of $\mathcal{A}$ by $\mathcal{A}(i_1, i_2, \ldots, i_d)$, where $1 \leq i_k \leq I_k$, $k = 1, 2, \ldots, d$. The numbers $I_1, I_2, \ldots, I_d$ are called the dimensions of the tensor $\mathcal{A}$. We use boldface capital calligraphic letters $\mathcal{A}$, $\mathcal{B}$, ... to denote tensors, boldface capital letters A, B, ... to denote matrices, boldface letters a, b, ... to denote vectors, and roman letters a, b, ... to denote scalars. A^T and a^T are the transpose of a matrix A and a vector a, respectively. The unit matrix of order n is denoted I_n. An intuitive and useful graphical representation of scalars, vectors, matrices, and tensors is depicted in Fig. 8.1. The edges, also called free legs, are the indices of the array. Therefore scalars have no free edge, while matrices have two free edges. We will mainly employ these graphical representations to visualize the tensor networks and operations in the following sections whenever possible and refer to [18] for more details. We now briefly introduce some important tensor operations.

Definition 8.1. (Tensor k-mode product) The k-mode product of a d-way tensor $\mathcal{A} \in \mathbb{R}^{I_1 \times \cdots \times I_k \times \cdots \times I_d}$ with a matrix $U \in \mathbb{R}^{P_k \times I_k}$ is denoted as $\mathcal{B} = \mathcal{A} \times_k U$ and defined by

$$\mathcal{B}(i_1, \ldots, i_{k-1}, j, i_{k+1}, \ldots, i_d) = \sum_{i_k=1}^{I_k} U(j, i_k) \mathcal{A}(i_1, \ldots, i_k, \ldots, i_d),$$

where $\mathcal{B} \in \mathbb{R}^{I_1 \times \cdots \times I_{k-1} \times P_k \times I_{k+1} \times \cdots \times I_d}$.

The graphical representation of a three-mode product between a third-order tensor $\mathcal{A}$ and a matrix U is shown in Fig. 8.2, where the summation over the i_3 index is indicated by the connected edge.

Definition 8.2. (Matricization) The matricization (also known as unfolding or flattening of a tensor) is the reordering of the tensor elements into a matrix.

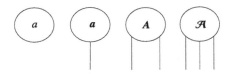

FIGURE 8.1

Graphical representation of a scalar a, vector $\boldsymbol{a}$, matrix $\boldsymbol{A}$, and third-order tensor $\boldsymbol{\mathcal{A}}$.

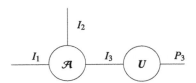

FIGURE 8.2

Three-mode product between a three-way tensor $\boldsymbol{\mathcal{A}}$ and matrix $\boldsymbol{U}$.

The k-th mode matricization of a tensor $\boldsymbol{\mathcal{A}} \in \mathbb{R}^{I_1 \times \cdots \times I_k \times \cdots \times I_d}$, denoted by $\boldsymbol{A}_{(k)} \in \mathbb{R}^{I_k \times (\prod_{k \neq i} I_i)}$, arranges the k-th mode fibers to become the columns of the final matrix. The element $(i_1, i_2, \ldots, i_d)$ in tensor $\boldsymbol{\mathcal{A}}$ is mapped to the matrix element (i_k, j), where

$$j = 1 + \sum_{t=1, t \neq k}^{d} (i_t - 1) J_t \ \ with \ \ J_t = \prod_{l=1, l \neq k}^{t-1} I_l.$$

Definition 8.3. (Reshaping) Employing MATLAB® notation, "reshape($\boldsymbol{\mathcal{A}}$, $[J_1, J_2, \ldots, J_d]$)" reshapes the tensor $\boldsymbol{\mathcal{A}}$ into another tensor with dimensions $J_1, J_2, \ldots, J_d$. The total number of elements of the tensor $\boldsymbol{\mathcal{A}}$ must be $\prod_{k=1}^{d} J_k$.

Definition 8.4. (Vectorization) Vectorization is a special reshaping operation that reshapes a tensor $\boldsymbol{\mathcal{A}}$ into a column vector, denoted as $vec(\boldsymbol{\mathcal{A}})$.

Definition 8.5. (Tensor inner product) For two tensors $\boldsymbol{\mathcal{A}}, \boldsymbol{\mathcal{B}} \in \mathbb{R}^{I_1 \times I_2 \times \cdots \times I_d}$, their inner product $\langle \boldsymbol{\mathcal{A}}, \boldsymbol{\mathcal{B}} \rangle$ is defined as

$$\langle \boldsymbol{\mathcal{A}}, \boldsymbol{\mathcal{B}} \rangle = \sum_{i_1=1}^{I_1} \sum_{i_2=1}^{I_2} \cdots \sum_{i_d=1}^{I_d} \boldsymbol{\mathcal{A}}(i_1, i_2, \cdots, i_d) \boldsymbol{\mathcal{B}}(i_1, i_2, \cdots, i_d).$$

Definition 8.6. (Frobenius norm) The Frobenius norm of a tensor $\boldsymbol{\mathcal{A}} \in \mathbb{R}^{I_1 \times I_2 \times \cdots \times I_d}$ is defined as $||\boldsymbol{\mathcal{A}}||_F = \sqrt{\langle \boldsymbol{\mathcal{A}}, \boldsymbol{\mathcal{A}} \rangle}$.

8.2.2 Tensor decompositions

Here we introduce four related tensor decomposition methods in this chapter, namely rank-1 tensor decomposition, CP decomposition, Tucker decomposition, and TT decomposition.

8.2.2.1 Rank-1 tensor decomposition

A d-way tensor $\mathcal{A} \in \mathbb{R}^{I_1 \times I_2 \times \cdots \times I_d}$ is rank-1 if it can be written as the outer product of d vectors

$$\mathcal{A} = u^{(1)} \circ u^{(2)} \circ \cdots \circ u^{(d)}, \tag{8.1}$$

where $\circ$ denotes the vector outer product and each element in $\mathcal{A}$ is the product of the corresponding vector elements:

$$\mathcal{A}(i_1, \ldots, i_d) = u^{(1)}(i_1) u^{(2)}(i_2) \cdots u^{(d)}(i_d).$$

Storing the component vectors $u^{(1)}, \ldots, u^{(d)}$ instead of the whole tensor $\mathcal{A}$ significantly reduces the required number of storage elements. However, a rank-1 tensor is rare in real-world applications, so that a rank-1 approximation to a general tensor usually results in unacceptably large approximation errors. This calls for a more general and powerful tensor approximation, for which the following CP decomposition serves as a more suitable choice.

8.2.2.2 Canonical polyadic decomposition

The CP decomposition factorizes a tensor into a sum of constituent rank-1 tensors. For example, a d-way tensor $\mathcal{A} \in \mathbb{R}^{I_1 \times I_2 \times \cdots \times I_d}$ can be written as

$$\mathcal{A} = \sum_{r=1}^{R} u_r^{(1)} \circ u_r^{(2)} \circ \cdots \circ u_r^{(d)}, \tag{8.2}$$

where R is a positive integer and $u_r^{(1)} \in \mathbb{R}^{I_1}$, $u_r^{(2)} \in \mathbb{R}^{I_2}$, ..., $u_r^{(d)} \in \mathbb{R}^{I_d}$, for $r = 1, \ldots, R$. If the mode j components $u_r^{(j)}$, $r = 1, \ldots, R$, are stacked together in a matrix $U^{(j)}$ as

$$U^{(j)} = \left[u_1^{(j)}, u_2^{(j)}, \ldots, u_R^{(j)} \right], \quad j = 1, \ldots, d, \tag{8.3}$$

then the j-th mode matricization of $\mathcal{A}$ can be computed as

$$A_{(j)} = U^{(j)} \left[U^{(d)} \odot \cdots \odot U^{(j+1)} \odot U^{(j-1)} \cdots \odot U^{(1)} \right]^T. \tag{8.4}$$

If we define

$$U^{(-j)} = U^{(d)} \odot \cdots \odot U^{(j+1)} \odot U^{(j-1)} \cdots \odot U^{(1)}, \tag{8.5}$$

Eq. (8.4) can be written as

$$A_{(j)} = U^{(j)} \left[U^{(-j)} \right]^T. \tag{8.6}$$

The inner product between $\mathcal{A}$ and itself can then be written as

$$\langle \mathcal{A}, \mathcal{A} \rangle = Tr\left[A_{(j)} A_{(j)}^T \right] = vec(A_{(j)})^T vec(A_{(j)}), \tag{8.7}$$

where $Tr[\cdot]$ denotes the trace of a matrix.

8.2.2.3 Tucker decomposition

The Tucker decomposition represents a tensor $\mathcal{A} \in \mathbb{R}^{I_1 \times I_2 \times \cdots \times I_d}$ as

$$\mathcal{A} = \mathcal{G} \times_1 P^{(1)} \times_2 P^{(2)} \cdots \times_d P^{(d)}, \tag{8.8}$$

where $\mathcal{G}$ is the Tucker core tensor and $P^{(1)}, \ldots, P^{(d)}$ are a set of (factor) matrices that are multiplied to the core tensor $\mathcal{G}$ along each tensor mode. The Kronecker product of all d matrices is defined as

$$P_{\otimes} = P^{(d)} \otimes \cdots \otimes P^{(1)}, \tag{8.9}$$

while the Kronecker product of $d - 1$ matrices is defined as

$$P_{\otimes}^{(-j)} = P^{(d)} \otimes \cdots \otimes P^{(j+1)} \otimes P^{(j-1)} \otimes \cdots \otimes P^{(1)}. \tag{8.10}$$

Therefore, the j-th mode matricization of $\mathcal{A}$ is

$$\begin{aligned} A_{(j)} &= P^{(j)} G_{(j)} \left(P^{(d)} \otimes \cdots \otimes P^{(j+1)} \otimes P^{(j-1)} \otimes \cdots \otimes P^{(1)} \right)^T \\ &= P^{(j)} G_{(j)} \left(P_{\otimes}^{(-j)} \right)^T. \end{aligned} \tag{8.11}$$

Eq. (8.11) can be further rewritten into the vectorized version when $j = 1$,

$$vec(A_{(1)}) = P_{\otimes} vec(G_{(1)}). \tag{8.12}$$

8.2.2.4 Tensor train decomposition

A TT decomposition [33] represents a d-way tensor $\mathcal{A}$ as d third-order tensors $\mathcal{A}^{(1)}$, $\mathcal{A}^{(2)}, \ldots, \mathcal{A}^{(d)}$ such that a particular entry of $\mathcal{A}$ is written as the following matrix product:

$$\mathcal{A}(i_1, \ldots, i_d) = \mathcal{A}^{(1)}(:, i_1, :) \cdots \mathcal{A}^{(d)}(:, i_d, :). \tag{8.13}$$

Each tensor $\mathcal{A}^{(k)}$, $k = 1, \ldots, d$, is called a TT core and has dimensions $R_k \times I_k \times R_{k+1}$. Storage of a tensor as a TT therefore reduces from $\prod_{i=1}^{d} I_i$ down to $\sum_{i=1}^{d} R_i I_i R_{i+1}$. In order for the left-hand side of (8.13) to be a scalar we require that $R_1 = R_{d+1} = 1$. The remaining R_k values are called the TT ranks. A simple illustration of utilizing TT decomposition to factorize a three-way tensor $\mathcal{A}$ is shown

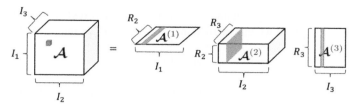

FIGURE 8.3

The TT cores of a three-way tensor $\mathcal{A}$ are two matrices $\mathcal{A}^{(1)}$, $\mathcal{A}^{(3)}$ and a three-way tensor $\mathcal{A}^{(2)}$.

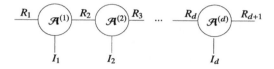

FIGURE 8.4

Tensor train decomposition of a d-way tensor $\mathcal{A}$ into d three-way tensors $\mathcal{A}^{(1)}, \mathcal{A}^{(2)} \ldots, \mathcal{A}^{(d)}$.

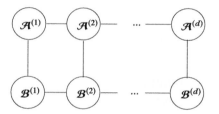

FIGURE 8.5

The inner product between two d-way tensor trains.

in Fig. 8.3. Note that the first and last TT cores are matrices since $R_1 = R_4 = 1$. A specific element in $\mathcal{A}$ is then computed as a vector–matrix–vector product. Fig. 8.4 demonstrates the general TT decomposition of a d-way tensor $\mathcal{A}$, where the edges connecting the different circles indicate the matrix–matrix products of (8.13). The simplifying notation $TT(\mathcal{A})$ denotes a TT decomposition of a d-way tensor $\mathcal{A}$ with user-specified TT ranks of (8.13).

Definition 8.7. (TT inner product) The inner product between two TTs $TT(\mathcal{A})$ and $TT(\mathcal{B})$ is denoted as $\langle TT(\mathcal{A}), TT(\mathcal{B}) \rangle$.

The tensor network diagram of the inner product of two TTs is shown in Fig. 8.5. The absence of free edges in Fig. 8.5 implies that $\langle TT(\mathcal{A}), TT(\mathcal{B}) \rangle$ is a scalar.

Definition 8.8. (Left orthogonal and right orthogonal TT cores) A TT core $\mathcal{A}^{(k)}$ ($1 \leq k \leq d$) is left orthogonal when reshaped into an $R_k I_k \times R_{k+1}$ matrix $\mathbf{A}$ we have

$$\mathbf{A}^T \mathbf{A} = \mathbf{I}_{R_{k+1}}.$$

Similarly, a TT core $\mathcal{A}^{(k)}$ is right orthogonal when reshaped into an $R_k \times I_k R_{k+1}$ matrix $\mathbf{A}$ we have

$$\mathbf{A} \mathbf{A}^T = \mathbf{I}_{R_k}.$$

Those two properties facilitate the computation of the Frobenius norm of a TT format tensor, as we will show later.

Definition 8.9. (Site-k-mixed-canonical tensor train) A TT is in site-k-mixed-canonical form [20] when all TT cores $\{\mathcal{A}^{(l)} \mid l = 1, \dots, k - 1\}$ are left orthogonal and $\{\mathcal{A}^{(l)} \mid l = k + 1, \dots, d\}$ are right orthogonal.

Turning a TT into its site-k-mixed-canonical form requires $d - 1$ QR decompositions of the reshaped TT cores. Changing k in a site-k-mixed-canonical form to either $k - 1$ or $k + 1$ requires one QR factorization of $\mathcal{A}^{(k)}$. It can be shown that the Frobenius norm of a tensor $\mathcal{A}$ in a site-k-mixed-canonical form is easily computed from

$$||\mathcal{A}||_F^2 = ||\mathcal{A}^{(k)}||_F^2 = vec\left(\mathcal{A}^{(k)}\right)^T vec\left(\mathcal{A}^{(k)}\right).$$

8.2.3 Support vector machines

We briefly introduce linear SVMs before discussing STMs. Assume we have a dataset $D = \{x_i, y_i\}_{i=1}^M$ of M labeled samples, where $x_i \in \mathbb{R}^n$ are the samples or feature vectors with labels $y_i \in \{-1, 1\}$. Learning a linear SVM is to find a discriminant hyperplane

$$f(x) = w^T x + b \tag{8.14}$$

that maximizes the margin between the two classes where w and b are the weight vector and bias, respectively. In practice, the data are seldom linearly separable due to measurement noise. A more robust classifier can then be found by introducing the slack variables $\xi_1, \dots, \xi_M$ and writing the learning problem as an optimization problem

$$\min_{w, b, \xi} \quad \frac{1}{2} ||w||_F^2 + C \sum_{i=1}^M \xi_i$$

$$\text{subject to} \quad y_i\left(w^T x_i + b\right) \geq 1 - \xi_i,$$

$$\xi_i \geq 0, \ i = 1, \dots, M. \tag{8.15}$$

The parameter C controls the trade-off between the size of the weight vector w and the size of the slack variables. It is common to solve the dual problem of (8.15) with quadratic programming, especially when the feature size n is larger than the sample size M. The dual problem of (8.15) is

$$\min_{\alpha_1,\alpha_2,\cdots,\alpha_M} \sum_{i=1}^{M} \alpha_i - \frac{1}{2} \sum_{i,j=1}^{M} \alpha_i \alpha_j y_i y_j \langle x_i, x_j \rangle$$

$$\text{subject to } \sum_{i=1}^{M} \alpha_i y_i = 0,$$

$$0 \le \alpha_i \le C, i = 1, \ldots, M, \tag{8.16}$$

where $\langle x_i, x_j \rangle$ represents the inner product between vectors x_i and x_j and α_i ($i = 1, \ldots, M$) are the Lagrange multipliers.

To solve a nonlinear classification problem with SVM, a nonlinear mapping function ϕ is introduced that projects the original vectorial data onto a much higher-dimensional feature space. In that feature space, the data generally become more (linearly) separable. Specifically, the optimization in (8.16) is transformed into

$$\min_{\alpha_1,\alpha_2,\cdots,\alpha_M} \sum_{i=1}^{M} \alpha_i - \frac{1}{2} \sum_{i,j=1}^{M} \alpha_i \alpha_j y_i y_j \langle \phi(x_i), \phi(x_j) \rangle \tag{8.17}$$

with the same constraints as in (8.16). The kernel trick allows us to compute the inner product term $\langle \phi(x_i), \phi(x_j) \rangle$ with a kernel function $k(x_i, x_j)$, thus avoiding the explicit construction of the possibly infinite-dimensional $\phi(x_i)$ vectors.

8.2.4 Logistic regression

LR [2] is a well-known binary classification approach. Given the same training dataset as in Section 8.2.3, the probability that a sample belongs to the positive class is of the form

$$p(y_i = +1 | w, b, x_i) = \frac{1}{1 + \exp(-w^T x_i - b)}. \tag{8.18}$$

The model parameter w and b are then estimated by solving the following maximum log-likelihood problem:

$$\min_{w,b} \sum_{i=1}^{M} \log\big(1 + \exp\big(-y_i\big(w^T x_i + b\big)\big)\big). \tag{8.19}$$

Based on this, some regularization norms are often applied to alleviate overfitting when implementing model training, e.g., the l_1-norm regularizer is a common choice to deal with high-dimensional features and obtain a robust and sparse classifier. As a result, the regularized LR optimization function can be written as

$$\min_{\boldsymbol{w},b} \; \sum_{i=1}^{M} \log\left(1 + \exp\left(-y_i\left(\boldsymbol{w}^T \boldsymbol{x}_i + b\right)\right)\right) + \lambda(\|\boldsymbol{w}\|_1 + |b|), \quad (8.20)$$

where $\lambda > 0$ is a tuning parameter used to control the sparsity.

8.3 Tensorial extensions of support vector machine

In this section, the STL [4] scheme is first described. Some typical tensorial extensions of SVM are then introduced.

8.3.1 Supervised tensor learning

In the STL scheme, a general formula for vector-based convex optimization problems is first assumed with a format of

$$\min_{\boldsymbol{w},b,\boldsymbol{\xi}} \quad f(\boldsymbol{w}, b, \boldsymbol{\xi})$$

$$\text{subject to} \quad y_i c_i\left(\boldsymbol{w}^T \boldsymbol{x}_i + b\right) \geq \xi_i,$$

$$i = 1, \ldots, M, \quad (8.21)$$

where $f : \mathbb{R}^{n+M+1} \to \mathbb{R}$ is a convex function for classification, $c_i : \mathbb{R}^{n+M+1} \to \mathbb{R}$, $1 \leq i \leq M$ are convex constraint function with inputs $\boldsymbol{w}, b, \boldsymbol{\xi}$, $\boldsymbol{x}_i \in \mathbb{R}^n$, $1 \leq i \leq M$, are training samples and the corresponding labels are represented by $y_i \in \{+1, -1\}$, $\boldsymbol{\xi} = [\xi_1, \xi_2, \ldots, \xi_M] \in \mathbb{R}^M$ are slack variables, and $\boldsymbol{w}$ and b are the classification hyperplane parameters, namely $y(\boldsymbol{x}) = \text{sign}(\boldsymbol{w}^T \boldsymbol{x} + b)$.

STL extends the above vector-based optimization problem into tensorial format, in which the training samples are tensors. Specifically, given M training samples $\boldsymbol{\mathcal{X}}_i \in \mathbb{R}^{I_1 \times I_2 \times \cdots \times I_d}$ and the corresponding labels $y_i \in \{+1, -1\}, 1 \leq i \leq M$, STL trains the classifier by solving the following optimization problem:

$$\min_{\boldsymbol{w}^{(k)}|_{k=1}^{d}, b, \boldsymbol{\xi}} \quad f\left(\boldsymbol{w}^{(k)}|_{k=1}^{d}, b, \boldsymbol{\xi}\right)$$

$$\text{subject to} \quad y_i c_i\left(\boldsymbol{\mathcal{X}}_i \prod_{k=1}^{d} \times_k \boldsymbol{w}^{(k)} + b\right) \geq \xi_i,$$

$$i = 1, \ldots, M. \quad (8.22)$$

Note that the input $\boldsymbol{x}_i$ in (8.21) is extended to $\boldsymbol{\mathcal{X}}_i$ in (8.22), while the model parameter $\boldsymbol{w}$ is replaced by $\boldsymbol{w}^{(k)}$, $1 \leq k \leq d$. The trained classification hyperplane function through (8.22) is formed as $y(\boldsymbol{\mathcal{X}}_i) = \text{sign}(\boldsymbol{\mathcal{X}}_i \prod_{k=1}^{d} \times_k \boldsymbol{w}^{(k)} + b)$. The Lagrangian for (8.22) can be written as

$$
L\left(\boldsymbol{w}^{(k)}|_{k=1}^{d}, b, \boldsymbol{\xi}, \boldsymbol{\alpha}\right)
$$

$$
= f\left(\boldsymbol{w}^{(k)}|_{k=1}^{d}, b, \boldsymbol{\xi}\right) - \sum_{i=1}^{M} \alpha_i \left(y_i c_i \left(\boldsymbol{\mathcal{X}}_i \prod_{k=1}^{d} \times_k \boldsymbol{w}^{(k)} + b \right) - \xi_i \right)
$$

$$
= f\left(\boldsymbol{w}^{(k)}|_{k=1}^{d}, b, \boldsymbol{\xi}\right) - \sum_{i=1}^{M} \alpha_i y_i c_i \left(\boldsymbol{\mathcal{X}}_i \prod_{k=1}^{d} \times_k \boldsymbol{w}^{(k)} + b \right) + \boldsymbol{\alpha}^T \boldsymbol{\xi} \qquad (8.23)
$$

with Lagrangian multipliers $\boldsymbol{\alpha} = [\alpha_1, \ldots, \alpha_M]^T$, $\alpha_i \geq 0$. The solution is determined by the saddle point of the Lagrangian, namely,

$$
\max_{\boldsymbol{\alpha}} \min_{\boldsymbol{w}^{(k)}|_{k=1}^{d}, b, \boldsymbol{\xi}} L\left(\boldsymbol{w}^{(k)}|_{k=1}^{d}, b, \boldsymbol{\xi}, \boldsymbol{\alpha}\right). \qquad (8.24)
$$

The derivatives of $L(\boldsymbol{w}^{(k)}|_{k=1}^{d}, b, \boldsymbol{\xi})$ with respect to $\boldsymbol{w}^{(j)}$ and b can then be derived as

$$
\partial_{\boldsymbol{w}^{(j)}} L = \partial_{\boldsymbol{w}^{(j)}} f - \sum_{i=1}^{M} \alpha_i y_i \partial_{\boldsymbol{w}^{(j)}} c_i \left(\boldsymbol{\mathcal{X}}_i \prod_{k=1}^{d} \times_k \boldsymbol{w}^{(k)} + b \right)
$$

$$
= \partial_{\boldsymbol{w}^{(j)}} f - \sum_{i=1}^{M} \alpha_i y_i \frac{dc_i}{dz} \partial_{\boldsymbol{w}^{(j)}} \left(\boldsymbol{\mathcal{X}}_i \prod_{k=1}^{d} \times_k \boldsymbol{w}^{(k)} + b \right)
$$

$$
= \partial_{\boldsymbol{w}^{(j)}} f - \sum_{i=1}^{M} \alpha_i y_i \frac{dc_i}{dz} \left(\boldsymbol{\mathcal{X}}_i \overline{\times}_j \boldsymbol{w}^{(j)} \right) \qquad (8.25)
$$

and

$$
\partial_b L = \partial_b f - \sum_{i=1}^{M} \alpha_i y_i \partial_{w_j} c_i \left(\boldsymbol{\mathcal{X}}_i \prod_{k=1}^{d} \times_k \boldsymbol{w}^{(k)} + b \right)
$$

$$
= \partial_b f - \sum_{i=1}^{M} \alpha_i y_i \frac{dc_i}{dz} \partial_b \left(\boldsymbol{\mathcal{X}}_i \prod_{k=1}^{d} \times_k \boldsymbol{w}^{(k)} + b \right)
$$

$$
= \partial_b f - \sum_{i=1}^{M} \alpha_i y_i \frac{dc_i}{dz}, \qquad (8.26)
$$

where $z = \boldsymbol{\mathcal{X}}_i \prod_{k=1}^{d} \times_k \boldsymbol{w}^{(k)} + b$. Setting $\partial_{\boldsymbol{w}^{(j)}} L = 0$ and $\partial_b L = 0$, we have

$$
\partial_{\boldsymbol{w}^{(j)}} L = 0 \Rightarrow \partial_{\boldsymbol{w}^{(j)}} f = \sum_{i=1}^{M} \alpha_i y_i \frac{dc_i}{dz} \left(\boldsymbol{\mathcal{X}}_i \overline{\times}_j \boldsymbol{w}^{(j)} \right), \qquad (8.27)
$$

Algorithm 1 STL algorithm.

Input: Training dataset $\{\mathcal{X}_i \in \mathbb{R}^{I_1 \times \cdots \times I_d}, y_i \in \{-1, 1\}\}_{i=1}^M$.
Output: The classification hyperplane parameters $\boldsymbol{w}^{(k)}|_{k=1}^d$; The bias b.

1: Initialize $\boldsymbol{w}^{(k)} \in \mathbb{R}^{I_k}$ as a random vector for $k = 1, 2, \ldots, d$.
2: Repeat steps 3–5 iteratively until convergence.
3: **for** $j = 1, \ldots, d$ **do**
4:   Derive $\boldsymbol{w}^{(j)}$ by optimizing (8.29).
5: **end for**

$$\partial_b L = 0 \Rightarrow \partial_b f = \sum_{i=1}^M \alpha_i y_i \frac{dc_i}{dz}. \tag{8.28}$$

From (8.27), we observe that the solution for $\boldsymbol{w}^{(j)}$ depends on $\boldsymbol{w}^{(k)}$, $1 \leq k \leq d, k \neq j$, and we cannot derive the solution directly. STL proposes to utilize an alternating projection optimization scheme to tackle this. Specifically, STL derives $\boldsymbol{w}^{(j)}$ by assuming $\boldsymbol{w}^{(k)}$, $1 \leq k \leq d, k \neq j$ are known. Therefore, the optimization problem is rewritten as

$$\min_{\boldsymbol{w}^{(j)}, b, \boldsymbol{\xi}} \quad f\left(\boldsymbol{w}^{(j)}, b, \boldsymbol{\xi}\right)$$

$$\text{subject to} \quad y_i c_i \left[\left(\boldsymbol{w}^{(j)}\right)^T \left(\mathcal{X}_i \overline{\times}_j \boldsymbol{w}^{(k)}\right) + b\right] \geq \xi_i,$$

$$i = 1, \ldots, M. \tag{8.29}$$

After updating $\boldsymbol{w}^{(j)}$, $\boldsymbol{w}^{(j+1)}$ is then updated in a similar way. The algorithm is summarized in Algorithm 1, whose convergence proof can be found in [4].

8.3.2 Support tensor machines

Base on the STL scheme, we now present the STM.

8.3.2.1 Methodology

Suppose the input samples in the dataset $D = \{\mathcal{X}_i, y_i\}_{i=1}^M$ are tensors $\mathcal{X}_i \in \mathbb{R}^{I_1 \times I_2 \times \cdots \times I_d}$. Following the STL scheme, a linear STM extends a linear SVM by defining d weight vectors $\boldsymbol{w}^{(k)} \in \mathbb{R}^{I_i}$ ($k = 1, \ldots, d$) and rewriting (8.14) as

$$f(\mathcal{X}) = \mathcal{X} \times_1 \boldsymbol{w}^{(1)} \times_2 \cdots \times_d \boldsymbol{w}^{(d)} + b. \tag{8.30}$$

The graphical representation of (8.30) is shown in Fig. 8.6. The tensor $\mathcal{X}$ is contracted along each of its modes with the weight vectors $\boldsymbol{w}^{(1)}, \ldots, \boldsymbol{w}^{(d)}$, resulting in a scalar that is added to the bias b. The weight vectors of the STM are computed by the alternating projection optimization procedure, which comprises d optimization problems. The main idea is to optimize each $\boldsymbol{w}^{(k)}$ in turn by fixing all weight vectors

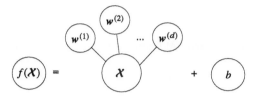

FIGURE 8.6

Graphical representation of an STM hyperplane function.

but $w^{(k)}$. The k-th optimization problem is

$$\min_{w^{(k)}, b, \xi} \quad \frac{1}{2} \beta \, ||w^{(k)}||_F^2 + C \sum_{i=1}^{M} \xi_i$$

$$\text{subject to} \quad y_i \left(\left(w^{(k)}\right)^T \hat{x}_i + b \right) \geq 1 - \xi_i,$$

$$\xi_i \geq 0, \ i = 1, \ldots, M, \tag{8.31}$$

where

$$\beta = \prod_{\substack{1 \leq l \leq d}}^{l \neq k} ||w^{(l)}||_F^2 \quad \text{and} \quad \hat{x}_i = \mathcal{X}_i \prod_{\substack{1 \leq l \leq d}}^{l \neq k} \times_l w^{(l)}.$$

The optimization problem (8.31) is equivalent to (8.15) for the linear SVM problem. This implies that any SVM learning algorithm can also be used for the linear STM. Each of the weight vectors of the linear STM is updated consecutively until the loss function of (8.31) converges. Each single optimization problem in learning an STM requires the estimation of only a few weight parameters, which alleviates the overfitting problem when M is relatively small. The weight tensor obtained from the outer product of the weight vectors

$$\mathcal{W} = w^{(1)} \circ w^{(2)} \circ \cdots \circ w^{(d)} \tag{8.32}$$

is per definition rank-1 and allows us to rewrite (8.30) as

$$f(\mathcal{X}) = \langle \mathcal{W}, \mathcal{X} \rangle + b. \tag{8.33}$$

8.3.2.2 Examples

Ref. [9] employs STM for text categorization. Different from traditional text categorization algorithms which consider a text document as a vector in $\mathbb{R}^n$ based on the vector space model, the work [9] considers a document as a second-order tensor in

Table 8.1 Performance comparison in Reuters-21578.

Train & test split	Method	micro F_1	macro F_1
5% Training	SVM	0.8490	0.3355
	STM	**0.8666**	**0.4818**

Table 8.2 Performance comparison in TDT2.

Train & test split	Method	micro F_1	macro F_1
5% Training	SVM	0.8881	0.6477
	STM	**0.9064**	**0.7507**

$\mathbb{R}^{I_1 \times I_2}$, where $I_1 \times I_2 = n$. Two standard document datasets are used in [9], namely Reuters-21578[1] and TDT2[2].

The classification performance is evaluated by comparing the predicted label of each test document with the true label. Specifically, F_1 measure is used here which combines recall (r) and precision (p) with an equal weight in the following form:

$$F_1(r, p) = \frac{2rp}{r + p}.$$

To measure the overall classification performance, Ref. [9] employs the following two metrics. The first is to simply average the F_1 scores of different categories and then derive a mean F_1 score, namely the macro-averaging F_1 score. In the second way, instead of calculating each category's F_1 score, the authors consider the global F_1 score over all the $n \times m$ binary decisions, where n is the total number of test documents and m is the number of categories under consideration, which is known as the micro-averaging score. Both scores are the larger the better.

5% documents are used as the training set for both Reuters-21578 and TDT2. Tables 8.1 and 8.2 show the classification results on two datasets. As can be seen from the results, STM outperforms SVM on both micro-averaged F_1 and macro-averaged F_1 with a large margin. The experimental results demonstrate the greater performance of STM on small training sample cases over SVM.

8.3.2.3 Conclusion

Based on the STL scheme, STM accepts tensors as input and therefore keeps the useful structural information in data. However, the constraint that the weight tensor $\mathcal{W}$ in STM is a rank-1 tensor has a significant impact on the expressive power of the STM, resulting in usually unsatisfactory classification accuracy for more complicated

---

[1] The Reuters-21578 corpus can be found at http://www.daviddlewis.com/resources/testcollections/reuters21578/.

[2] The Nist Topic Detection and Tracking corpus can be found at http://www.nist.gov/speech/tests/tdt/tdt98/index.html.

data. Therefore, it is necessary to generalize the rank-1 tensor in STM into a more general tensorial format.

8.3.3 Higher-rank support tensor machines

As mentioned, an STM assumes a simple rank-1 tensor as the classifier hyperplane parameter, which might not be powerful enough to model the hyperplane function. In [15], the authors propose a higher-rank STM wherein the classifier parameter is formulated as a sum of rank-1 tensors, namely the general CP tensor format. By doing so, the classification capability is significantly enhanced.

8.3.3.1 Methodology

Consider the following general higher-rank STM optimization problem:

$$\min_{\mathcal{W},b,\xi} \quad \frac{1}{2}\langle \mathcal{W}, \mathcal{W} \rangle + C\sum_{i=1}^{M}\xi_i$$

$$\text{subject to} \quad y_i\left(\langle \mathcal{W}, \mathcal{X}_i \rangle + b\right) \geq 1 - \xi_i,$$

$$\xi_i \geq 0, \ i = 1, \ldots, M, \tag{8.34}$$

where $\mathcal{W}$ is a general d-way parameter tensor with the same dimensions as the training sample $\mathcal{X}$. Adopting the alternating optimization scheme as in STL, each time only the parameters that are associated with the j-th tensor mode of $\mathcal{W}$ are updated, while fixing all other parameters. According to (8.7), (8.34) can be rewritten into the following format:

$$\min_{W_{(j)},b,\xi} \quad \frac{1}{2}Tr\left[W_{(j)}W_{(j)}^T\right] + C\sum_{i=1}^{M}\xi_i$$

$$\text{subject to} \quad y_i\left(Tr\left[W_{(j)}X_{(j)i}^T\right] + b\right) \geq 1 - \xi_i,$$

$$\xi_i \geq 0, \ i = 1, \ldots, M, \tag{8.35}$$

where $X_{(j)i}^T$ represents the j-th mode matricization of the i-th training sample. Under the assumption that the weight parameter tensor $\mathcal{W}$ can be decomposed into its CP tensor format as in (8.2), $W_{(j)}$ in (8.35) can be rewritten as $U^{(j)}(U^{(-j)})^T$ according to (8.6). Therefore, (8.35) can be rewritten as

$$\min_{U^{(j)},b,\xi} \quad \frac{1}{2}Tr\left[U^{(j)}(U^{(-j)})^T U^{(-j)}(U^{(j)})^T\right] + C\sum_{i=1}^{M}\xi_i$$

$$\text{subject to} \quad y_i\left(Tr\left[U^{(j)}(U^{(-j)})^T X_{(j)i}^T\right] + b\right) \geq 1 - \xi_i,$$

$$\xi_i \geq 0, \ i = 1, \ldots, M. \tag{8.36}$$

With the above optimization problem, we can iteratively update $U^{(j)}$, $j = 1, \ldots, d$, employing the idea of STL. To further facilitate the implementation of (8.36), we

---

Algorithm 2 Higher-rank STM algorithm.

Input: Training dataset $\{\mathcal{X}_i \in \mathbb{R}^{I_1 \times \cdots \times I_d}, y_i \in \{-1, 1\}\}_{i=1}^M$.
Output: The classification hyperplane parameters $\mathcal{W}$; The bias b.

1: Initialize $\mathcal{W}$ as a sum of random rank-1 tensors.
2: Repeat steps 3–6 iteratively until convergence.
3: **for** $j = 1, \ldots, d$ **do**
4:    Derive $\widetilde{U}^{(j)}$ by optimizing (8.39).
5:    Update $U^{(j)} = \widetilde{U}^{(j)} B^{-\frac{1}{2}}$
6: **end for**

---

transfer it into a classic vector-based SVM format. By doing so, any existing SVM solver can be employed to readily solve the higher-rank STM problem.

Let $B = (U^{(-j)})^T U^{(-j)}$ such that B is a positive-definite matrix. Defining $\widetilde{U}^{(j)} = U^{(j)} B^{\frac{1}{2}}$, we have

$$Tr\left[U^{(j)}(U^{(-j)})^T U^{(-j)}(U^{(j)})^T\right] = Tr\left[\widetilde{U}^{(j)}(\widetilde{U}^{(j)})^T\right] = vec(\widetilde{U}^{(j)})^T vec(\widetilde{U}^{(j)}).$$
(8.37)

Also, letting $\widetilde{X}_{(j)i} = X_{(j)i} U^{(-j)} B^{-\frac{1}{2}}$, we have

$$Tr\left[U^{(j)}(U^{(-j)})^T X_{(j)i}^T\right] = Tr\left[\widetilde{U}^{(j)} \widetilde{X}_{(j)i}^T\right] = vec(\widetilde{U}^{(j)})^T vec(\widetilde{X}_{(j)i}).$$
(8.38)

Therefore, (8.36) can be rewritten as

$$\min_{\widetilde{U}^{(j)}, b, \xi} \quad \frac{1}{2} vec(\widetilde{U}^{(j)})^T vec(\widetilde{U}^{(j)}) + C \sum_{i=1}^M \xi_i$$

$$\text{subject to} \quad y_i\left(vec(\widetilde{U}^{(j)})^T vec(\widetilde{X}_{(j)i}) + b\right) \geq 1 - \xi_i,$$

$$\xi_i \geq 0, \ i = 1, \ldots, M.$$
(8.39)

Eq. (8.39) is a classic vector-based SVM problem. After deriving the solution of $\widetilde{U}^{(j)}$ in each iteration, the model parameter $U^{(j)}$ is updated with $U^{(j)} = \widetilde{U}^{(j)} B^{-\frac{1}{2}}$. The overall procedure for implementing higher-rank STM is summarized in Algorithm 2.

8.3.3.2 Complexity analysis

Because the subproblem (8.39) of the higher-rank STM optimization problem is naturally an SVM problem, we analyze the computation complexity of SVM first. When there are M training samples and each sample is in $\mathbb{R}^n$, after constructing the linear kernel matrix, the worst case of the computation complexity of an SVM is $\mathcal{O}(M^3)$. When it comes to higher-rank STM, the overall optimization problem is separated into d subproblems, where d is the mode number of the training sample. Furthermore,

Table 8.3 Accuracies (%) achieved by various methods for the KTH action database.

Method	SVM	STM	Higher-rank STM
Accuracy	88.5	89.3	93.3

these subproblems would be solved for p iterations until convergence. Therefore, the complexity of solving a higher-rank STM problem is $\mathcal{O}(dpM^3)$.

8.3.3.3 Examples

Considering the fact that there is no known closed-form solution to determine the rank R of a tensor and that rank determination of a tensor is still an open problem [12,13], in higher-rank STM, the common way to determine the optimal weight tensor rank is by utilizing grid search.

Ref. [15] utilizes the higher-rank STM for human action recognition. Specifically, the KTH [27] dataset is employed to check the performance of higher-rank STM. The KTH Action Dataset depicts 25 subjects performing six different activities, namely, "boxing," "handclapping," "handwaving," "jogging," "running," and "walking." Each training sample is a three-way tensor with modes pixel–pixel–time. For a fair comparison, a linear kernel is applied in traditional SVM considering STM and higher-rank STM are all linear classifiers. The classification results are shown in Table 8.3. We note that the higher-rank STM achieves a 4% accuracy enhancement over STM, and they both perform better than traditional SVM.

Ref. [14] tests the performance of higher-rank STM on human face classification. Specifically, nine second-order face recognition datasets, namely Yale32×32, Yale64×64, ORL32×32, ORL64×64, C05, C07, C09, C27, and C29, from http://www.zjucadcg.cn/dengcai/Data/FaceData.html are employed. Moreover, since an SVM can naturally utilize the kernel trick and empower its classification capability, [14] compares the higher-rank STM with kernel SVM employing a Gaussian radial basis function (RBF) kernel. Table 8.4 shows the experimental results. We observe that in terms of test accuracy, STM outperforms SVM only in one dataset, while higher-rank STM outperforms SVM and STM in all nine datasets.

8.3.3.4 Conclusion

Higher-rank STM assumes the parameters defining the separating hyperplane form a tensor that can be written as a sum of rank-1 terms according to the CP decomposition. This generalizes STM and achieves better classification performance on several complicated tensorial data classification tasks.

8.3.4 Support Tucker machines

Apart from higher-rank STM, STuM [29] is another approach that generalizes STM by employing the Tucker tensor format to replace the rank-1 weight tensor.

Table 8.4 Comparison of the accuracies (%) of SVM, STM, and higher-rank STM on nine experimental datasets.

Dataset	SVM	STM	Higher-rank STM
Yale32 × 32	77.3	74.0	**79.0**
Yale64 × 64	84.3	82.3	**85.3**
ORL32 × 32	97.8	97.0	**98.0**
ORL64 × 64	97.8	76.5	**98.5**
C05	98.6	98.1	**98.8**
C07	96.5	95.4	**96.7**
C09	97.4	96.2	**97.5**
C27	**96.7**	95.1	**96.7**
C29	**96.6**	94.8	**96.6**

8.3.4.1 Methodology

Starting from (8.35), we now assume the weight tensor $\mathcal{W}$ is represented by a Tucker tensor decomposition. According to (8.11), (8.35) can be rewritten as

$$
\min_{P^{(j)},b,\xi} \quad \frac{1}{2} Tr\left[P^{(j)} G_{(j)} \left(P_{\otimes}^{(-j)} \right)^T P_{\otimes}^{(-j)} G_{(j)}^T \left(P^{(j)} \right)^T \right] + C \sum_{i=1}^{M} \xi_i
$$

$$
\text{subject to} \quad y_i \left(Tr\left[P^{(j)} G_{(j)} \left(P_{\otimes}^{(-j)} \right)^T X_{(j)i}^T \right] + b \right) \geq 1 - \xi_i,
$$

$$
\xi_i \geq 0, \ i = 1, \ldots, M. \tag{8.40}
$$

It is desirable to reformulate the above optimization problem such that the classic vector-based SVM implementation can be employed to solve it. We let $H^{(j)} = G_{(j)} \left(P_{\otimes}^{(-j)} \right)^T$. Now (8.40) can be rewritten as

$$
\min_{P^{(j)},b,\xi} \quad \frac{1}{2} Tr\left[P^{(j)} H^{(j)} \left(H^{(j)} \right)^T \left(P^{(j)} \right)^T \right] + C \sum_{i=1}^{M} \xi_i
$$

$$
\text{subject to} \quad y_i \left(Tr\left[P^{(j)} H^{(j)} X_{(j)i}^T \right] + b \right) \geq 1 - \xi_i,
$$

$$
\xi_i \geq 0, \ i = 1, \ldots, M. \tag{8.41}
$$

We further define $K = H^{(j)} (H^{(j)})^T$. Obviously, K is positive-definite. Also, letting $\widetilde{P}^{(j)} = P^{(j)} K^{\frac{1}{2}}$, we have

$$
Tr\left[P^{(j)} H^{(j)} \left(H^{(j)} \right)^T \left(P^{(j)} \right)^T \right] = Tr\left[\widetilde{P}^{(j)} \left(\widetilde{P}^{(j)} \right)^T \right] = vec\left(\widetilde{P}^{(j)} \right)^T vec\left(\widetilde{P}^{(j)} \right).
$$

$$
\tag{8.42}
$$

Algorithm 3 STuM algorithm.

Input: Training dataset $\{\mathcal{X}_i \in \mathbb{R}^{I_1 \times \cdots \times I_d}, y_i \in \{-1, 1\}\}_{i=1}^M$; the given Tucker ranks

Output: The classification hyperplane parameters $\mathcal{G}, \boldsymbol{P}^{(1)}, \boldsymbol{P}^{(2)}, \ldots, \boldsymbol{P}^{(d)}$; The bias b.

1: Initialize $\mathcal{G}, \boldsymbol{P}^{(1)}, \boldsymbol{P}^{(2)}, \ldots, \boldsymbol{P}^{(d)}$ randomly.
2: Repeat steps 3–8 iteratively until convergence.
3: **for** $j = 1, \ldots, d$ **do**
4:   Derive $\widetilde{\boldsymbol{P}}^{(j)}$ by optimizing (8.44).
5:   Update $\boldsymbol{P}^{(j)} = \widetilde{\boldsymbol{P}}^{(j)} \boldsymbol{K}^{-\frac{1}{2}}$
6: **end for**
7: Derive $\boldsymbol{G}_{(1)}$ by optimizing (8.45)
8: Reshape $\boldsymbol{G}_{(1)}$ back and derive $\mathcal{G}$

By defining $\widetilde{\boldsymbol{X}}_{(j)i} = \boldsymbol{X}_{(j)i}(\boldsymbol{H}^{(j)})^T \boldsymbol{K}^{-\frac{1}{2}}$, we have

$$Tr\left[\boldsymbol{P}^{(j)} \boldsymbol{H}^{(j)} \boldsymbol{X}_{(j)i}^T\right] = Tr\left[\widetilde{\boldsymbol{P}}^{(j)} \widetilde{\boldsymbol{X}}_{(j)i}^T\right] = vec\left(\widetilde{\boldsymbol{P}}^{(j)}\right)^T vec(\widetilde{\boldsymbol{X}}_{(j)i}). \qquad (8.43)$$

Therefore, (8.41) can be rewritten as

$$\min_{\widetilde{\boldsymbol{P}}^{(j)}, b, \xi} \quad \frac{1}{2} vec\left(\widetilde{\boldsymbol{P}}^{(j)}\right)^T vec\left(\widetilde{\boldsymbol{P}}^{(j)}\right) + C \sum_{i=1}^M \xi_i$$

$$\text{subject to} \quad y_i\left(vec\left(\widetilde{\boldsymbol{P}}^{(j)}\right)^T vec(\widetilde{\boldsymbol{X}}_{(j)i}) + b\right) \geq 1 - \xi_i,$$

$$\xi_i \geq 0, \ i = 1, \ldots, M. \qquad (8.44)$$

We note that (8.44) is a classic vector-based SVM problem. By solving it, we can derive $\widetilde{\boldsymbol{P}}^{(j)}$ and update $\boldsymbol{P}^{(j)} = \widetilde{\boldsymbol{P}}^{(j)} \boldsymbol{K}^{-\frac{1}{2}}$. After updating $\boldsymbol{P}^{(1)}, \boldsymbol{P}^{(2)}, \ldots, \boldsymbol{P}^{(d)}$, we then formulate the optimization problem for the Tucker core tensor $\mathcal{G}$. According to (8.7) and (8.12), the optimization problem (8.35) can be rewritten in terms of $\mathcal{G}$ as follows:

$$\min_{\boldsymbol{G}_{(1)}, b, \xi} \quad \frac{1}{2}\left(\boldsymbol{P}_\otimes vec(\boldsymbol{G}_{(1)})\right)^T \boldsymbol{P}_\otimes vec(\boldsymbol{G}_{(1)}) + C \sum_{i=1}^M \xi_i$$

$$\text{subject to} \quad y_i\left(\left(\boldsymbol{P}_\otimes vec(\boldsymbol{G}_{(1)})\right)^T vec(\boldsymbol{X}_{(j)i}) + b\right) \geq 1 - \xi_i,$$

$$\xi_i \geq 0, \ i = 1, \ldots, M. \qquad (8.45)$$

This problem can be solved by any classic vector-based SVM solver. The overall procedure for STuM is summarized in Algorithm 3.

Table 8.5 Comparison of proposed methods with state-of-the-art (CS-1/CS-5).

Test set	HMM [10]	LTN [25]	GEI [11]	ETG [23]	ETGLDA [23]	SVM	STM	STuM
A	99/**100**	94/99	**100/100**	92/96	99/**100**	80/97	92/**100**	99/**100**
B	**89/90**	83/85	85/85	85/90	88/**93**	79/**93**	81/90	85/**93**
C	78/90	78/83	80/88	76/81	**83/88**	68/85	73/88	79/90
D	35/65	33/65	30/55	39/55	36/**71**	30/54	47/67	**53/71**
E	29/65	24/67	33/55	29/52	29/60	23/46	48/79	**63/86**
F	18/60	17/58	21/41	21/58	21/59	24/49	29/49	**42/63**
G	24/50	21/48	29/48	21/50	21/60	12/37	31/71	**52/87**
Mean	53/74	50/72	54/67	52/69	54/76	45/62	57/68	**68/84**

Table 8.6 Accuracies (%) achieved by various methods for the KTH action database.

Method	[22]	[21]	[17]	[16]	SVM	STM	STuM
Accuracy	90.5	91.7	87.7	95.3	88.5	89.3	**92.3**

8.3.4.2 Examples

To prove the superiority of STuM, Ref. [29] implements experiments on gait and human action recognition.

For gait recognition, the USF HumanID Gait Challenge dataset [23] is used. The database consists of 452 sequences of 74 subjects walking in elliptical paths in front of the camera. Therefore, each sequence is a third-order tensor. The datasets are separated into one training set and seven test sets (A–G). The detailed experimental setting can be found in [24]. The results are shown in Table 8.5. Apart from SVM with linear kernel and STM, some common gait recognition methods are also included. The results are evaluated using the Cumulative Scores 1 and 5 (CS-1/CS-5, respectively) similarly to [23,25]. The results of STuM are reported by setting the Tucker core tensor with dimensions $18 \times 18 \times 18$ as in [29]. From Table 8.5, we observe that tensor-based methods largely outperform vector-based ones. We can also see that the STuMs outperform the classical STMs with a large margin.

For the human action recognition experiments, Ref. [29] employed the commonly used KTH dataset [27]. The KTH Action Dataset depicts 25 subjects performing six different activities, namely, "boxing," "handclapping," "handwaving," "jogging," "running," and "walking." The Tucker ranks are set to 6 for all modes in STuM, so that the Tucker core tensor is of size $6 \times 6 \times 6$. The comparison results are listed in Table 8.6. Again, STuMs perform significantly better than other methods.

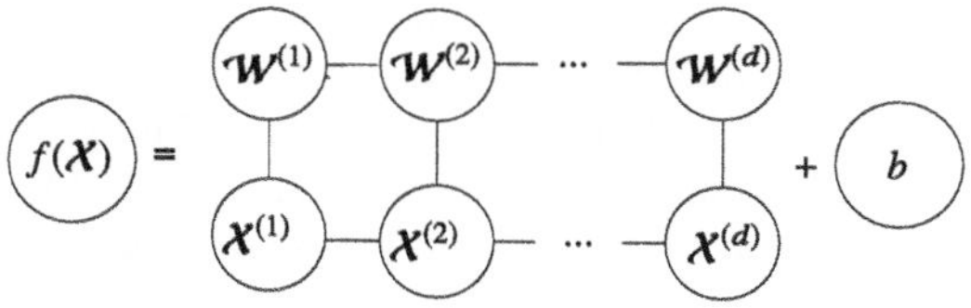

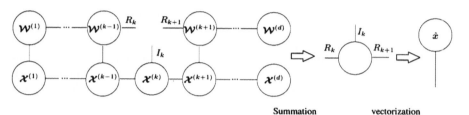

FIGURE 8.7

Tensor graphical representation of an STTM hyperplane function.

FIGURE 8.8

The computation diagram of $\hat{x}$.

8.3.5 Support tensor train machines

Although higher-rank STM and STuM generalize STM and achieve a better classification performance in high-dimensional data, they still suffer from various issues. First, determining the CP rank in higher-rank STM is NP-complete. Second, the number of model parameters in STuM is still exponentially large since the Tucker core tensor $\mathcal{G}$ has the same tensor modes as the original parameter tensor $\mathcal{W}$. To solve these issues, Ref. [31] proposes a support TT machine (STTM) wherein the rank-1 weight tensor of an STM is replaced by a TT that can approximate any tensor with a scalable number of parameters. Moreover, a TT mixed-canonical form has been exploited to speed up algorithmic convergence.

8.3.5.1 Methodology

As mentioned in Section 8.3.2, an STM suffers from its weak expressive power due to its rank-1 weight tensor $\mathcal{W}$. In [31], the proposed STTM replaces the rank-1 weight tensor by a TT with prescribed TT ranks. Moreover, most real-world data contain redundancies and uninformative parts. Based on this knowledge, STTM also utilizes a TT decomposition to approximate the original data tensor and further alleviates the overfitting problem. The conversion of the training samples into a TT can be done using the TT-SVD algorithm [33, p. 2301], which allows the user to determine the relative error of the approximation. A graphical representation of the STTM hyperplane equation is shown in Fig. 8.7. Both the data tensor $\mathcal{X}$ and the weight tensor $\mathcal{W}$ are represented by TTs, and the summations correspond to computing the inner product $\langle \mathcal{X}, \mathcal{W} \rangle$.

The TT cores $\mathcal{W}^{(1)}$, $\mathcal{W}^{(2)}$, ..., $\mathcal{W}^{(d)}$ are also computed using an alternating projection optimization procedure [4], namely, iteratively fixing $d - 1$ TT cores and updating the remaining cores until convergence. This updating occurs in a "sweeping" fashion, namely, first update $\mathcal{W}^{(1)}$ and proceed towards $\mathcal{W}^{(d)}$. Once the core $\mathcal{W}^{(d)}$ is updated, the algorithm sweeps back to $\mathcal{W}^{(1)}$ and repeats this procedure until the termination criterion is met.

Suppose we want to update $\mathcal{W}^{(k)}$. First, the TT of the weight tensor $\mathcal{W}$ is brought into site-k-mixed-canonical form (see Definition 8.9). From Section 8.2.2.4, the norm of the whole weight tensor is located in the $\mathcal{W}^{(k)}$ TT core. To reformulate the optimization problem (8.31) in terms of the unknown core $\mathcal{W}^{(k)}$, the inner product $\langle \mathcal{X}, \mathcal{W} \rangle$ is rewritten as $vec(\mathcal{W}^{(k)})^T \hat{x}$. The vector $\hat{x}$ is obtained by summing over the tensor network for $\langle \mathcal{W}, \mathcal{X} \rangle$ depicted in Fig. 8.7 with the TT core $\mathcal{W}^{(k)}$ removed and vectorizing the resulting three-way tensor. These two computational steps to compute $\hat{x}$ are graphically depicted in Fig. 8.8. The STTM hyperplane function can then be rewritten as $vec(\mathcal{W}^{(k)})^T \hat{x} + b$, so that $\mathcal{W}^{(k)}$ can be updated from the following optimization problem:

$$
\min_{\mathcal{W}^{(k)}, b, \xi} \quad \frac{1}{2} \| vec(\mathcal{W}^{(k)}) \|_F^2 + C \sum_{i=1}^{M} \xi_i
$$

$$
\text{subject to} \quad y_i \left(vec(\mathcal{W}^{(k)})^T \hat{x}_i + b \right) \geq 1 - \xi_i,
$$

$$
\xi_i \geq 0, \ i = 1, \ldots, M, \tag{8.46}
$$

using any computational method for standard SVMs. Suppose now that the next TT core to be updated is $\mathcal{W}^{(k+1)}$. The new TT for $\mathcal{W}$ then needs to be put into site-$(k + 1)$-mixed-canonical form, which can be achieved by reshaping the new $\mathcal{W}^{(k)}$ into an $R_k I_k \times R_{k+1}$ matrix $W^{(k)}$ and computing its thin QR decomposition

$$
W^{(k)} = QR,
$$

where Q is an $R_k I_k \times R_{k+1}$ matrix with orthogonal columns and R is an $R_{k+1} \times R_{k+1}$ upper triangular matrix. Updating the tensors $\mathcal{W}^{(k)}$ and $\mathcal{W}^{(k+1)}$ as

$$
\mathcal{W}^{(k)} := \text{reshape}\left(Q, [R_k, I_k, R_{k+1}] \right),
$$

$$
\mathcal{W}^{(k+1)} := \mathcal{W}^{(k+1)} \times_1 R
$$

results in a site-$(k + 1)$-mixed-canonical form for $\mathcal{W}$. An optimization problem similar to (8.46) can then be derived for $\mathcal{W}^{(k+1)}$.

The training algorithm of the STTM is summarized as pseudo-codes in Algorithm 4. The TT cores for the weight tensor $\mathcal{W}$ are initialized randomly. Bringing this TT into site-1-mixed-canonical form can then be done by applying the QR decomposition step starting from $\mathcal{W}^{(d)}$ and proceeding towards $\mathcal{W}^{(2)}$. The final R factor is absorbed into $\mathcal{W}^{(1)}$, which brings the TT into site-1-mixed-canonical form. The termination criterion in line 4 can be a maximum number of loops and/or when the training error falls below a prescribed threshold.

Algorithm 4 STTM algorithm.

Input: TT ranks $R_2, \ldots, R_d$ of $\mathcal{W}^{(1)}, \mathcal{W}^{(2)}, \ldots, \mathcal{W}^{(d)}$; Training dataset $\{\mathcal{X}_i \in \mathbb{R}^{I_1 \times \cdots \times I_d}, y_i \in \{-1, 1\}\}_{i=1}^M$; Relative error ϵ of TT approximation of $\mathcal{X}$.

Output: The TT cores $\mathcal{W}^{(1)}, \mathcal{W}^{(2)}, \ldots, \mathcal{W}^{(d)}$; The bias b.

1: Initialize $\mathcal{W}^{(k)} \in \mathbb{R}^{R_k \times I_k \times R_{k+1}}$ as a random/prescribed three-way tensor for $k = 1, 2, \ldots, d$.

2: Compute the TT approximation of training samples $\{\mathcal{X}_i\}_{i=1}^M$ with relative error ϵ using TT-SVD.

3: Cast $\mathcal{W}$ into the site-1-mixed-canonical TT form.

4: **while** termination criterion not satisfied **do**

5:     **for** $k = 1, \ldots, d - 1$ **do**

6:         $\mathcal{W}^{(k)}, b \leftarrow$ Solve optimization problem (8.46).

7:         $W^{(k)} \leftarrow$ reshape$(\mathcal{W}^{(k)}, [R_k I_k, R_{k+1}])$.

8:         Compute thin QR decomposition $W^{(k)} = QR$.

9:         $\mathcal{W}^{(k)} \leftarrow$ reshape$(Q, [R_k, I_k, R_{k+1}])$.

10:        $\mathcal{W}^{(k+1)} \leftarrow \mathcal{W}^{(k+1)} \times_1 R$.

11:     **end for**

12:     **for** $k = d, \ldots, 2$ **do**

13:         $\mathcal{W}^{(k)}, b \leftarrow$ Solve optimization problem (8.46).

14:         $W^{(k)} \leftarrow$ reshape$(\mathcal{W}^{(k)}, [R_k, I_k R_{k+1}])$.

15:         Compute thin QR decomposition $W^{(k)^T} = QR$.

16:         $\mathcal{W}^{(k)} \leftarrow$ reshape$(Q^T, [R_k, I_k, R_{k+1}])$.

17:        $\mathcal{W}^{(k-1)} \leftarrow \mathcal{W}^{(k-1)} \times_3 R^T$.

18:     **end for**

19: **end while**

8.3.5.2 Complexity analysis

Assume that the tensorial training data $D = \{\mathcal{X}_i \ y_i\}_{i=1}^M$ are given, where tensors $\mathcal{X}_i \in \mathbb{R}^{I_1 \times I_2 \times \cdots \times I_d}$ are in TT format and their ranks are $R_2, \ldots, R_d$. With $I := \max\{I_1, \ldots, I_d\}$ and $R := \max\{R_2, \ldots, R_d\}$, the computation complexity of forming the small-size SVM optimization problem (8.46) from the overall STTM optimization problem is $\mathcal{O}(MdIR^2)$. The complexity is linear to the tensorial data order d due to the TT structure. Moreover, real-world tensorial data often exhibit the low rank property, namely, R is often small, which indicates the overall complexity is also low. For data storage, the traditional SVM calls for $\mathcal{O}(MI^d)$ space, while that of the STTM is $\mathcal{O}(MIR^2)$. This again shows a great reduction especially when the data order d is large.

8.3.5.3 Effect of TT ranks on STTM classification

This section demonstrates the effect of TT ranks on tensor-based classification. Specifically, the CIFAR-10 database [26] is employed to evaluate the influence. The images of CIFAR-10 are of dimensions $32 \times 32 \times 3$. The TT ranks of the weight TT

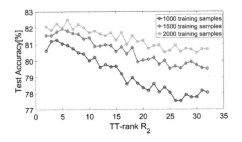

FIGURE 8.9

Test accuracy of STTM on different TT ranks R_2.

were fixed to $R_1 = R_4 = 1$, $R_3 = 3$ and different experiment runs were performed with R_2 varied from 2 to 32. The detailed experiment setting can be found in [31]. Fig. 8.9 shows the STTM test accuracy for different TT ranks when the training sample number is equal to $2k$, $3k$, and $4k$, respectively. The maximal test accuracy for these three sizes is achieved when R_2 is 4, 5, and 6, respectively. A downward trend of all three curves can be observed for TT ranks larger than the optimal value, indicating that higher TT ranks may lead to overfitting. On the other hand, decreasing the TT rank from its optimal value also decreases the test accuracy down to the rank-1 STM case.

8.3.5.4 Updating in site-k-mixed-canonical form

The authors of [31] investigated the effect of keeping the TT of $\mathcal{W}$ in a site-k-mixed-canonical form when updating $\mathcal{W}^{(k)}$. According to the setting of [31], two image classes of CIFAR-10 are chosen for this investigation, namely airplane and automobile. Three thousand samples of both classes were used for the STTM training. Fig. 8.10 shows the training accuracy for each TT core update iteration in Algorithm 4, with and without the site-k-mixed-canonical form. Updating without the site-k-mixed-canonical form implies that lines 3, 8–10, and 15–17 of Algorithm 4 are not executed, which results in an oscillatory training accuracy ranging between 50% and 89% without any overall convergence. Updating the TT cores $\mathcal{W}^{(k)}$ in a site-k-mixed-canonical form, however, displays a very fast convergence of the training accuracy to around 92%.

8.3.5.5 Examples

The performance of STTM is checked on several image datasets in [31]. Here we present the results on two of those datasets, namely MNIST [30] and ORL[3].

MNIST has a training set of 60k samples and a test set of 10k samples. Each sample is a 28×28 grayscale picture which is reshaped into a $7 \times 4 \times 7 \times 4$ tensor, as this provides more flexibility to choose TT ranks when applying Algorithm 4. For

---

[3] http://www.zjucadcg.cn/dengcai/Data/FaceData.html.

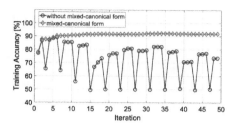

FIGURE 8.10

Comparison of training accuracy of STTMs trained with and without site-k-mixed-canonical form.

Table 8.7 Experiment settings for the four methods.

Method	Input structure	Tensor ranks
SVM	784×1 vector	NA
STM	28×28 matrix	1
STuM	$7 \times 4 \times 7 \times 4$ tensor	4, 4, 4, 4
STTM	$7 \times 4 \times 7 \times 4$ tensor	1, 5, 5, 4, 1

the STM initialization, the SVM weight vector is reshaped into a 28×28 matrix from which the best rank-1 approximation is used. For the STuM and STTM initialization, the SVM weight vector is reshaped into a $7 \times 4 \times 7 \times 4$ tensor and then converted into its Tucker and TT forms, respectively, with prescribed tensor ranks. Table 8.7 shows the experiment setting for those four methods. All classifiers were trained for training sample batch sizes of $10k$, $20k$, $30k$, and $60k$ in four different experiments. The test accuracy of the different methods for different batch sizes is listed in Table 8.8. STTM achieves the best classification performance for all sizes. The STM performs worse than the standard SVM due to the restrictive expressive power of the rank-1 weight matrix. The test accuracies of STuM are not posted when the training sample sizes are 30k and 60k since they cost much more time (more than 60 h) than the other three methods. This observation indicates that an STuM may not work well when the training sample size is large.

For the ORL database, it contains 400 grayscale face images, and the detailed information about ORL datasets is listed in Table 8.9. The dataset is separated into training and test sets. The detailed experiment settings and classification accuracies (average value of five repeated tests) for ORL32x32 and ORL64x64 when employing different methods are listed in Table 8.10 and Table 8.11. STTM achieves a similar classification performance compared with that of SVM, and they both perform better than STM and STuM.

Table 8.8 Test accuracy (%) under different training sample sizes.

Method	Training sample size			
	10k	**20k**	**30k**	**60k**
SVM	91.64	92.84	93.28	93.99
STM	88.36	89.96	89.82	90.54
STuM	90.45	92.28	–	–
STTM	**92.27**	**93.71**	**93.86**	**94.12**

Table 8.9 Detailed information of experimental datasets.

Datasets	Number of samples	Number of classes	Size
ORL 32x32	400	40	32x32
ORL 64x64	400	40	64x64

Table 8.10 Experimental settings and classification accuracy (%) of four methods for ORL32x32.

Method	Input structure	Tensor ranks	Test accuracy
SVM	1024x1 vector	NA	**96.25**
STM	32x32 matrix	1	93.75
STuM	8x4x8x4 tensor	4, 4, 4, 4	93.50
STTM	8x4x8x4 tensor	1, 4, 4, 4, 1	**96.25**

Table 8.11 Experimental settings and classification accuracy (%) of four methods for ORL64x64.

Method	Input structure	Tensor ranks	Test accuracy
SVM	4096x1 vector	NA	**96.25**
STM	64x64 matrix	1	92.71
STuM	8x8x8x8 tensor	4, 4, 4, 4	94.40
STTM	8x8x8x8 tensor	1, 4, 4, 4, 1	**96.25**

8.3.5.6 Conclusion

STTM employs a more general TT structure to largely escalate the model expressive power, which leads to a better classification accuracy than STM. Moreover, the tensor model in STTM is more scalable than that in STuM, which achieves faster training when the training sample size is large. The necessity of keeping the weight TT of STTM in a site-k-mixed-canonical form during model training is empirically confirmed through experiments, in which the algorithm convergence speed can be accelerated significantly.

8.3.6 Kernelized support tensor train machines

The aforementioned works are all based on the assumption that the given tensorial data are linearly separable. However, this is not the case in most real-world data. In [37], the authors proposed a K-STTM to deal with nonlinear tensorial classification problems. Firstly, the TT decomposition [33] is employed to decompose the given tensor data so that a more compact and informative representation of it can be derived. Secondly, the authors define a TT-based feature mapping strategy to derive a high-dimensional TT in the feature space. This strategy enables one to apply different feature mappings on different data modes, which naturally provides a way to leverage the multimode nature of tensorial data. Thirdly, the authors propose two ways to build the kernel matrix with the consideration of the consistency with the TT inner product and preservation of information. The constructed kernel matrix is then used by kernel machines to solve the image classification problems.

It is worth noting that though STTM sounds like the linear case of the proposed K-STTM, they are totally different when the linear kernel is applied on K-STTM. Specifically, K-STTM and STTM use two totally different schemes to train the corresponding model. For K-STTM, it first constructs the kernel matrix with the proposed TT-based kernel function, and then solves the standard SVM problem. However, in STTM, it assumes the parameter in the classification hyperplane can be modeled as a TT, and only updates one TT core at a time by reformulating the training data.

8.3.6.1 Methodology

Given M tensorial training data and their labels, i.e., dataset $D = \{\mathcal{X}_i, y_i\}_{i=1}^M$, where $\mathcal{X}_i \in \mathbb{R}^{I_1 \times I_2 \times \cdots \times I_d}$ and $y_i \in \{-1, 1\}$, the hyperplane can be defined as

$$f(\mathcal{X}) = \langle \mathcal{W}, \mathcal{X} \rangle + b \tag{8.47}$$

that separates the tensorial data into two classes. Here, $\mathcal{W}$ is the hyperplane weight tensor with the same dimensions as $\mathcal{X}_i$ and b is the bias. Similar to the primal problem in SVM, the corresponding primal optimization problem for (8.47) is derived as

$$\min_{\mathcal{W}, b, \xi} \quad \frac{1}{2}\|\mathcal{W}\|_F^2 + C\sum_{i=1}^M \xi_i$$
$$\text{subject to} \quad y_i\big(\langle \mathcal{W}, \mathcal{X}_i \rangle + b\big) \geq 1 - \xi_i,$$
$$\xi_i \geq 0, \ i = 1, \ldots, M. \tag{8.48}$$

Following the scheme of the kernel trick for conventional SVMs, it is necessary to define a nonlinear feature mapping function $\Phi(\cdot)$ for tensors. Specifically, given a tensor $\mathcal{X} \in \mathbb{R}^{I_1 \times I_2 \times \cdots \times I_d}$, it is mapped into the Hilbert space $\mathcal{H}$ by

$$\Phi(\cdot) : \mathbb{R}^{I_1 \times I_2 \times \cdots \times I_d} \to \mathbb{R}^{H_1 \times H_2 \times \cdots \times H_d}. \tag{8.49}$$

The dimension of the projected tensor $\Phi(\mathcal{X})$ can be infinite depending on the feature mapping function $\Phi(\cdot)$. The resulting Hilbert space is then called the *tensor feature space* and the following model is further developed:

$$
\min_{\mathcal{W},b,\xi} \quad \frac{1}{2}||\mathcal{W}||_F^2 + C\sum_{i=1}^{M}\xi_i
$$

$$
\text{subject to} \quad y_i\left(\langle \mathcal{W}, \Phi(\mathcal{X}_i)\rangle + b\right) \geq 1 - \xi_i,
$$

$$
\xi_i \geq 0, \; i = 1, \ldots, M, \tag{8.50}
$$

with parameter tensor $\mathcal{W} \in \mathbb{R}^{H_1 \times H_2 \times \cdots \times H_d}$. This model is naturally a linear classifier on the tensor feature space. However, when the classifier is mapped back to the original data space, it is a nonlinear classifier. To obtain the tensor-based kernel optimization model, the dual format of (8.50) is derived, namely

$$
\min_{\alpha_1,\alpha_2,\cdots,\alpha_M} \quad \sum_{i=1}^{M}\alpha_i - \frac{1}{2}\sum_{i,j=1}^{M}\alpha_i\alpha_j y_i y_j \langle \Phi(\mathcal{X}_i), \Phi(\mathcal{X}_j)\rangle
$$

$$
\text{subject to} \quad \sum_{i=1}^{M}\alpha_i y_i = 0,
$$

$$
0 \leq \alpha_i \leq C, i = 1, \ldots, M, \tag{8.51}
$$

where α_i are the Lagrange multipliers. The key task is to define a tensorial kernel function $\mathcal{K}(\mathcal{X}_i, \mathcal{X}_j)$ that computes the inner product $\langle \Phi(\mathcal{X}_i), \Phi(\mathcal{X}_j)\rangle$ in the original data space instead of the feature space.

Although tensor is a natural structure for representing real-world data, there is no guarantee that such a representation works well for kernel learning. Instead of the full tensor, K-STTM employs a TT for data representation due to the following reasons:

1. Real-life data often contain redundant information, which is not useful for kernel learning. The TT decomposition has proved to be efficient for removing the redundant information in the original data and provides a more compact data representation.
2. Compared to the Tucker decomposition whose storage scales exponentially with the core tensor, a TT is more scalable (parameter number grows linearly with the tensor order d), which reduces the computation during kernel learning.
3. Unlike the CP decomposition, determining the TT rank is easily achieved through a series of singular value decompositions (TT-SVD [33]). Moreover, instead of decomposing many tensorial data sample by sample, it is possible to stack them together and decompose the stacked tensor with TT-SVD in one shot. This naturally leads to a faster data transformation to the TT format.
4. It is convenient to implement different operations on different tensor modes when data are in the TT format. Since a TT decomposition decomposes the original data into many TT cores, it is possible to apply different kernel functions on different TT cores for better classification performance. Furthermore, it is possible to emphasize the importance of different tensor modes by putting different weights on

those TT cores during the kernel mapping. For example, a color image is a three-way (pixel–pixel–color) tensor. The color mode can be treated differently from the two pixel modes since they contain different kinds of information, as will be exemplified later.

To this end, a TT-based feature mapping approach is proposed in K-STTM. Specifically, all fibers in each TT core are mapped to the feature space through

$$\phi_i(\cdot) : \mathbb{R}^{I_i} \rightarrow \mathbb{R}^{H_i}, \quad i = 1, \ldots, d,$$

such that

$$\phi_i\left(\mathcal{X}^{(i)}(r_i, :, r_{i+1})\right) \in \mathbb{R}^{H_i}$$
$$1 \le r_i \le R_i, \quad 1 \le r_{i+1} \le R_{i+1}, \quad i = 1, \ldots, d, \tag{8.52}$$

where $\mathcal{X}^{(i)}$ and R_i are the i-th TT core and TT rank of $TT(\mathcal{X})$, respectively. The fibers of each TT core are vectors as the rank indices (r_i, r_{i+1}) are fixed to specific values, and hence the feature mapping works in the same way as for the conventional SVM. The resulting high-dimensional TT, which is in the tensor feature space, is then represented as $\Phi(TT(\mathcal{X})) \in \mathbb{R}^{H_1 \times H_2 \times \cdots \times H_d}$. Note that $\Phi(TT(\mathcal{X}))$ is still in a TT format with the same TT ranks as $TT(\mathcal{X})$. In this sense, the TT format data structure is preserved after the feature mapping.

After mapping the TT format data into the TT-based high-dimensional feature space, [37] proposes two approaches for computing the inner product between two mapped TT format data using kernel functions. The first method is called K-STTM-Prod since consecutive multiplication operations are implemented on d fiber inner products, which is consistent with the result of an inner product between two TTs. Assuming $\Phi(TT(\mathcal{X}))$ and $\Phi(TT(\mathcal{Y})) \in \mathbb{R}^{H_1 \times H_2 \times \cdots \times H_d}$ with TT ranks R_i and $\hat{R}_i$, $i = 1, 2, \ldots, d+1$, respectively, their inner product can be computed from

$$\left\langle \Phi(TT(\mathcal{X})), \Phi(TT(\mathcal{Y})) \right\rangle = \sum_{r_1=1}^{R_1} \cdots \sum_{r_{d+1}=1}^{R_{d+1}} \sum_{\hat{r}_1=1}^{\hat{R}_1} \cdots \sum_{\hat{r}_{d+1}=1}^{\hat{R}_{d+1}}$$
$$\left(\prod_{i=1}^{d} \left\langle \phi_i\left(\mathcal{X}^{(i)}(r_i, :, r_{i+1})\right), \phi_i\left(\mathcal{Y}^{(i)}(\hat{r}_i, :, \hat{r}_{i+1})\right) \right\rangle \right). \tag{8.53}$$

Note that (8.53) derives the exact same result as Fig. 8.5 (assuming $\mathcal{X} = \mathcal{A}$ and $\mathcal{Y} = \mathcal{B}$) when an identity feature mapping function $\Phi(\cdot)$ is used, namely $\Phi(TT(\mathcal{X})) = TT(\mathcal{X})$. Moreover, since each fiber of a mapped TT core is naturally a vector, the following equation is derived:

$$\left\langle \phi_i\left(\mathcal{X}^{(i)}(r_i, :, r_{i+1})\right), \phi_i\left(\mathcal{Y}^{(i)}(\hat{r}_i, :, \hat{r}_{i+1})\right) \right\rangle = k_i\left(\mathcal{X}^{(i)}(r_i, :, r_{i+1}), \mathcal{Y}^{(i)}(\hat{r}_i, :, \hat{r}_{i+1})\right),$$
$$\tag{8.54}$$

where $k_i(\cdot)$ can be any kernel function used for a standard SVM, such as a Gaussian RBF kernel, polynomial kernel, linear kernel, etc. Combining (8.53) and (8.54), the corresponding TT-based kernel function is obtained:

$$\mathcal{K}\big(TT(\mathcal{X}), TT(\mathcal{Y})\big) = \sum_{r_1=1}^{R_1} \cdots \sum_{r_{d+1}=1}^{R_{d+1}} \sum_{\hat{r}_1=1}^{\hat{R}_1} \cdots \sum_{\hat{r}_{d+1}=1}^{\hat{R}_{d+1}}$$
$$\left(\prod_{i=1}^{d} k_i \big(\mathcal{X}^{(i)}(r_i, :, r_{i+1}), \mathcal{Y}^{(i)}(\hat{r}_i, :, \hat{r}_{i+1}) \big) \right). \tag{8.55}$$

As mentioned before, in the K-STTM setting, different kernel functions k_i can be applied on different tensor modes i. One possible application is in color image classification, where one could apply Gaussian RBF kernels k_1 and k_2 on its two spatial modes, while choosing a linear or polynomial kernel k_3 for the color mode.

The second method proposed in [37] for constructing a TT kernel function is called the K-STTM-Sum. Instead of implementing continuous multiplication operations on d fiber inner products like in K-STTM-Prod, K-STTM-Sum performs consecutive addition operations on them. The authors mentioned that this idea is inspired by [32], which argues that the product of inner products can lead to the loss/misinterpretation of information. Take the linear kernel as an example. The inner product between two fibers of the same mode could be negative, which indicates a low similarity between those two fibers. However, by implementing consecutive multiplications of d fiber inner products, highly negative values could result in a large positive value. In that case, the overall similarity is high, which is clearly unwanted. This situation also appears when employing Gaussian RBF kernels. A nearly zero value would be assigned to two nonsimilar fibers, which could influence the final result significantly. To this end, the K-STTM-Sum is proposed. Similar to K-STTM-Prod, the corresponding kernel function is obtained as

$$\mathcal{K}\big(TT(\mathcal{X}), TT(\mathcal{Y})\big) = \sum_{r_1=1}^{R_1} \cdots \sum_{r_{d+1}=1}^{R_{d+1}} \sum_{\hat{r}_1=1}^{\hat{R}_1} \cdots \sum_{\hat{r}_{d+1}=1}^{\hat{R}_{d+1}}$$
$$\left(\sum_{i=1}^{d} k_i \big(\mathcal{X}^{(i)}(r_i, :, r_{i+1}), \mathcal{Y}^{(i)}(\hat{r}_i, :, \hat{r}_{i+1}) \big) \right). \tag{8.56}$$

After defining the TT-based kernel function, the term $\langle \Phi(\mathcal{X}_i), \Phi(\mathcal{X}_j) \rangle$ in (8.51) can be replaced with (8.55) or (8.56), and the final kernel optimization problem based on the TT structure can be derived as

$$\min_{\alpha_1, \alpha_2, \cdots, \alpha_M} \sum_{i=1}^{M} \alpha_i - \frac{1}{2} \sum_{i,j=1}^{M} \alpha_i \alpha_j y_i y_j \mathcal{K}\big(TT(\mathcal{X}_i), TT(\mathcal{X}_j)\big)$$

$$\text{subject to} \quad \sum_{i=1}^{M} \alpha_i y_i = 0,$$

$$0 \le \alpha_i \le C, i = 1, \dots, M. \tag{8.57}$$

After solving (8.57), the unknown model parameters $\alpha_1, \alpha_2, \dots, \alpha_M$ can be obtained and the resulting decision function is then represented as

$$f(\mathcal{X}) = \text{sign}\left(\sum_{i=1}^{M} \alpha_i y_i \mathcal{K}\big(TT(\mathcal{X}_i), TT(\mathcal{X})\big) + b \right). \tag{8.58}$$

The training algorithm of the K-STTM-Prod/Sum is described by pseudo-codes in Algorithm 5 using a Gaussian RBF kernel as an example. Hyperparameters can be tuned through a grid search or through cross-validation.

Algorithm 5 K-STTM-Prod/Sum algorithm.

Input: Training dataset $\{\mathcal{X}_i \in \mathbb{R}^{I_1 \times \cdots \times I_d}, \ y_i \in \{-1, 1\}\}_{i=1}^{M}$; Validation dataset $\{\mathcal{X}_j \in \mathbb{R}^{I_1 \times \cdots \times I_d}, y_j \in \{-1, 1\}\}_{j=1}^{N}$; The preset TT ranks $R_1, R_2, \dots, R_{d+1}$; The range of the performance trade-off parameter C and kernel width parameter σ, namely $[C_{min}, C_{max}]$, and $[\sigma_{min}, \sigma_{max}]$.

Output: The Lagrange multipliers $\alpha_1, \alpha_2, \dots, \alpha_M$; The bias b.

1: Stack the tensors in training dataset together as $\mathcal{X}_{\text{trainStack}}$; stack the tensors in validation dataset together as $\mathcal{X}_{\text{validStack}}$.
2: Compute the TT approximation $TT(\mathcal{X}_{\text{trainStack}})$ and $TT(\mathcal{X}_{\text{validStack}})$ with the given TT ranks using TT-SVD.
3: **for** C from C_{min} to C_{max} **do**
4:     **for** σ from σ_{min} to σ_{max} **do**
5:        Construct the K-STTM-Prod kernel matrix (8.55) or the K-STTM-Sum kernel matrix (8.56).
6:        Solve (8.57) using the resulting kernel matrix.
7:        Compute the classification accuracy on the validation set.
8:     **end for**
9: **end for**
10: Find the best C and σ according to the classification accuracy on the validation set.
11: Train the K-STTM with the best C and σ by implementing steps 6 and 7. Thus the Lagrange multipliers $\alpha_1, \alpha_2, \dots, \alpha_M$ and the bias b are obtained.

We note that the key task for kernelized tensor learning is to define a suitable tensor mapping scheme for the corresponding tensor decomposition. Apart from the demonstrated K-STTM, Ref. [35] proposed a customized kernel mapping scheme for CP decomposition, named DuSK. We therefore introduce it for comparison.

Let the CP decomposition of two tensorial samples $\mathcal{X}, \mathcal{Y} \in \mathbb{R}^{I_1 \times I_2 \times \cdots \times I_d}$ be $\mathcal{X} = \sum_{r=1}^{R} \prod_{i=1}^{d} \circ x_r^{(i)}$ and $\mathcal{Y} = \sum_{r=1}^{R} \prod_{i=1}^{d} \circ y_r^{(i)}$, respectively. Ref. [35] defines a kernel mapping scheme $\hat{\Phi}(\cdot)$ for CP format tensors, such that $\hat{\Phi}(CP(\mathcal{X})) \in \mathbb{R}^{H_1 \times H_2 \times \cdots \times H_d}$. Specifically, this is achieved by mapping all vectors $x_r^{(i)} \in \mathbb{R}^{I_i}$ into a high-dimensional feature space $\phi(x_r^{(i)}) \in \mathbb{R}^{H_i}$; therefore,

$$\hat{\Phi} : \sum_{r=1}^{R} \prod_{i=1}^{d} \circ x_r^{(i)} \rightarrow \sum_{r=1}^{R} \prod_{i=1}^{d} \circ \phi(x_r^{(i)}). \tag{8.59}$$

After mapping the CP factorization of the tensorial sample into the high-dimensional tensorial feature space, the kernel function is simply the standard inner product of tensors in that feature space, and it can be written as

$$\hat{\mathcal{K}}(CP(\mathcal{X}), CP(\mathcal{Y})) = \hat{\mathcal{K}} \left(\sum_{r=1}^{R} \prod_{i=1}^{d} \circ x_r^{(i)}, \sum_{r=1}^{R} \prod_{i=1}^{d} \circ y_r^{(i)} \right)$$

$$= \sum_{r_1} \sum_{r_2} \prod_{i=1}^{d} k\left(x_{r_1}^{(i)}, y_{r_2}^{(i)}\right), \tag{8.60}$$

where $k(\cdot)$ can be any vector-based kernel function. With (8.60), we can derive the kernel optimization problem based on CP decomposition as follows:

$$\min_{\alpha_1, \alpha_2, \cdots, \alpha_M} \sum_{i=1}^{M} \alpha_i - \frac{1}{2} \sum_{i,j=1}^{M} \alpha_i \alpha_j y_i y_j \hat{\mathcal{K}}(CP(\mathcal{X}_i), CP(\mathcal{X}_j))$$

$$\text{subject to} \quad \sum_{i=1}^{M} \alpha_i y_i = 0,$$

$$0 \le \alpha_i \le C, i = 1, \dots, M. \tag{8.61}$$

The comparison between DuSK and K-STTM is implemented in the K-STTM paper [37], and we also showcase the results in the example part of this section.

8.3.6.2 Kernel validity of K-STTM

According to Mercer's condition, a kernel function is valid when the constructed kernel matrix is symmetric and positive-semi-definite on the given training data. This guarantees that the mapped high-dimensional feature space is truly an inner product space. Therefore, it is necessary to show the validity of K-STTM-Prod and K-STTM-Sum. In this section, we provide Theorem 8.1 for this purpose. In the actual implementation of K-STTM-Prod and K-STTM-Sum, it is extremely inefficient to use TT decomposition to decompose each tensorial sample one by one. The way K-STTM does it is by first stacking all the d-way samples and then computing a TT decomposition on the resulting $(d + 1)$-way tensor directly. By doing so, all

TT-based training samples have the same TT ranks. That means R_i is equal to $\hat{R}_i$, $i = 1, \ldots, d + 1$, for all the TT-based training samples, which is also assumed in Theorem 8.1 and its proof.

Before proving Theorem 8.1, we first give the necessary lemma below.

Lemma 8.1. *The summation and Hadamard product between two symmetric and positive-semi-definite matrices A and $B \in \mathbb{R}^{n \times n}$ still result in a symmetric and positive-semi-definite matrix.*

Proof. According to the definition of symmetric and positive-semi-definite matrix, we have

$$\begin{cases} A = A^T, & u^T A u \geq 0, \\ B = B^T, & u^T B u \geq 0, \end{cases}$$

for every nonzero column vector $u \in \mathbb{R}^n$. For the summation case, obviously we can conclude that

$$(A + B)^T = A + B, \quad u^T (A + B) u \geq 0,$$

namely $A + B$ is still symmetric and positive-semi-definite. For the Hadamard product case, we refer to the Schur product theorem [28] and we can easily obtain

$$u^T (A \odot B) u \geq 0,$$

for every nonzero column vector $u \in \mathbb{R}^n$, where $\odot$ is the Hadamard product. It is obvious that $(A \odot B)^T = (A \odot B)$. Thus $A \odot B$ is still symmetric and positive-semi-definite. $\square$

We then depict Theorem 8.1 and its proof here.

Theorem 8.1. *Given a tensorial training dataset $\{\mathcal{X}_i\}_{i=1}^M$, where $\mathcal{X}_i \in \mathbb{R}^{I_1 \times I_2 \times \cdots \times I_d}$, and assumed TT ranks $R_1, \ldots, R_{d+1}$, the proposed kernel functions K-STTM-Prod and K-STTM-Sum are valid kernel functions, and they produce symmetric and positive-semi-definite kernel matrices.*

Proof. We first show the kernel function validity of K-STTM-Prod. For any tensor $\mathcal{X}, \mathcal{Y} \in \{\mathcal{X}_1, \mathcal{X}_2, \ldots, \mathcal{X}_M\}$, they are first decomposed into their TT formats, namely $TT(\mathcal{X})$ and $TT(\mathcal{Y})$, after which Eq. (8.55) is applied. Assuming all the indices over $\sum$ and $\prod$, namely $r_1, \ldots, r_{d+1}, \hat{r}_1, \ldots, \hat{r}_{d+1}$ and i, are fixed, (8.55) can be written as

$$\mathcal{K}\big(TT(\mathcal{X}), TT(\mathcal{Y})\big) = k_i \big(\mathcal{X}^{(i)}(r_i, :, r_{i+1}), \mathcal{Y}^{(i)}(\hat{r}_i, :, \hat{r}_{i+1})\big). \tag{8.62}$$

As mentioned before, $k_i(\cdot, \cdot)$ can be any valid kernel function used for a standard SVM. Therefore, the kernel matrix constructed by (8.62) is symmetric and positive-semi-definite. When only the indices over $\sum$, namely $r_1, \ldots, r_{d+1}, \hat{r}_1, \ldots, \hat{r}_{d+1}$, are fixed, (8.55) can be written as the following product kernel:

$$\mathcal{K}\big(TT(\mathcal{X}), TT(\mathcal{Y})\big) = \left(\prod_{i=1}^d k_i \big(\mathcal{X}^{(i)}(r_i, :, r_{i+1}), \mathcal{Y}^{(i)}(\hat{r}_i, :, \hat{r}_{i+1})\big) \right). \tag{8.63}$$

The kernel matrix constructed by (8.63) can be regarded as Hadamard products of the d valid kernel matrices constructed by (8.62) when $i = 1, \ldots, d$. Since the matrix constructed by (8.62) is symmetric and positive-semi-definite, according to Lemma 8.1, the matrix constructed by (8.63) is also symmetric and positive-semi-definite.

Similarly, we note that the kernel matrix constructed by (8.55) can be regarded as the summation of $R_1 \times \ldots \times R_{d+1} \times \hat{R}_1 \times \ldots \times \hat{R}_{d+1}$ kernel matrices constructed by (8.63) when $r_1, \ldots, r_{d+1}, \hat{r}_1, \ldots, \hat{r}_{d+1}$ are varied from 1 to their corresponding maximum values. According to Lemma 8.1, we conclude that the kernel matrix constructed by (8.55) is symmetric and positive-semi-definite, namely K-STTM-Prod is a valid kernel function.

The validity proof for K-STTM-Sum is similar to the proof for K-STTM-Prod. The kernel matrix constructed by (8.56) can be regarded as the summation of $R_1 \times \ldots \times R_{d+1} \times \hat{R}_1 \times \ldots \times \hat{R}_{d+1} \times d$ kernel matrices constructed by (8.62) when $r_1, \ldots, r_{d+1}, \hat{r}_1, \ldots, \hat{r}_{d+1}$ and i are varied from 1 to their corresponding maximum values. According to Lemma 8.1, the kernel matrix constructed by (8.56) is symmetric and positive-semi-definite. Therefore, K-STTM-Sum is a valid kernel function. $\qquad\square$

8.3.6.3 Complexity analysis

The original tensorial sample storage is $O(MI^d)$, where I is the maximum value of I_i, $i = 1, 2, \ldots, d$. After representing the original tensorial data as TTs, the data storage becomes $O(dIR^2 + MI_dR_d)$, where R is the maximum TT rank of R_i, $i = 1, \ldots, d-1$. This shows a great reduction especially when the data order d is large.

The computational complexity of constructing the kernel matrix in standard SVM is $O(M^2I^d)$, where n is the maximum dimension of I_i, $i = 1, 2, \ldots d$. As for the computational complexity of K-STTM-Prod and K-STTM-Sum, the overall results of them are similar if neglecting low-order terms. And their kernel matrix computation complexities are $O(dIR^4 + M^2I_dR_d^2)$ if we employ the accelerated computation approach as proposed in [37], where I and R are the maximum values of I_i and R_i, $i = 1, 2, \ldots, d-1$, respectively. Therefore, the K-STTM algorithm is more efficient than its vector counterpart as the computation complexity is reduced from exponential to polynomial.

8.3.6.4 Examples

Ref. [37] considers three high-dimensional fMRI datasets, namely, the StarPlus fMRI dataset[4], the CMU Science 2008 fMRI dataset (CMU2008) [34], and the ADNI fMRI dataset[5], to evaluate the classification performance of K-STTM. An fMRI image is essentially a three-way tensor. For the compared methods, apart from SVM, STM, STuM, and STTM, another kernelized STM method called DuSK [35] is further in-

---

[4] http://www.cs.cmu.edu/afs/cs.cmu.edu/project/theo-81/www/.
[5] http://adni.loni.usc.edu/.

Table 8.12 Classification accuracies (%) of different methods for different subjects in StarPlus fMRI datasets.

Subject	SVM	STM	STuM	STTM	DuSK	K-STTM-Prod	K-STTM-Sum
04799	50.00	36.67	35.83	39.61	47.50	**68.33**	66.67
04820	50.00	43.33	35.00	45.83	46.67	**70.00**	62.50
04847	50.00	38.33	17.50	47.50	53.33	**65.00**	**65.00**
05675	50.00	37.50	30.83	35.00	55.00	**60.00**	**60.00**
05680	50.00	38.33	39.17	40.00	64.17	73.33	**75.00**
05710	50.00	40.00	30.00	43.33	54.16	**59.17**	58.33

cluded. DuSK is a kernelized STM using the CP decomposition. Through introducing the kernel trick, it can deal with nonlinear classification tasks.

For the StarPlus dataset, each fMRI image is of dimensions $64 \times 64 \times 8$. The whole dataset contains the brain images of six human subjects, and each subject has 320 fMRI images: one half of them were collected when the subject was shown a picture, the other half were collected when the subject was shown a sentence. These fMRI images are randomly separated into training, validation, and test sets. The classification results are listed in Table 8.12. Due to the very high-dimensional and sparse data, SVM fails to find a good hyperparameter setting and classifies all test samples wrongly into one class. Since fMRI data are very complicated, those linear classifiers, namely STM, STuM, and STTM, cannot achieve acceptable performance, and the classification accuracies of them are all lower than 50%. The two K-STTM methods still achieve the highest classification accuracy on all human subjects.

The CMU2008 dataset shows the brain activities associated with the meanings of nouns. During the data collection period, the subjects were asked to view 60 different word-pictures from 12 semantic categories. There are five pictures in each category and each image is shown to the subject six times. Therefore, 30 fMRI images are collected for each semantic category, and each fMRI image is of dimensions $51 \times 61 \times 23$. Considering the extremely small number of samples in each category, [37] used the experimental settings in [36] which combine two similar categories into an integrated class. Specifically, [37] combines categories *animal* and *insect* as class **Animals** and categories *tool* and *furniture* as class **Tools**. By doing so, there are 60 samples in both **Animals** and **Tools** classes. Table 8.13 shows the binary classification results of different models. We note that the classification accuracies of SVM on four subjects are lower than 50%. The linear models, namely STM, STuM, STTM, and TT classifier, can only achieve acceptable performance on a few subjects. Because the dimensions of the data are very high, DuSK fails to find a good CP rank in an acceptable time and cannot achieve a good classification accuracy. The two K-STTM methods still achieve the best classification results in all subjects.

The ANDI fMRI dataset is collected from the Alzheimer's Disease Neuroimaging Initiative. It contains the resting-state fMRI images of 33 subjects. The subjects include patients (with mild cognitive impairment [MCI] or Alzheimer's disease [AD])

Table 8.13 Classification accuracies (%) of different methods for different subjects in CMU2008 fMRI datasets.

Subject	SVM	STM	STuM	STTM	DuSK	K-STTM-Prod	K-STTM-Sum
#1	68.00	66.00	68.00	66.00	48.00	**70.00**	**70.00**
#2	52.00	50.00	58.00	68.00	54.00	74.00	**84.00**
#3	50.00	60.00	58.00	64.00	58.00	66.00	**70.00**
#4	50.00	60.00	58.00	56.00	52.00	**76.00**	72.00
#5	56.00	58.00	64.00	66.00	44.00	**72.00**	**72.00**
#6	44.00	60.00	46.00	46.00	54.00	**70.00**	**70.00**
#7	50.00	52.00	48.00	52.00	52.00	68.00	**72.00**

Table 8.14 Classification accuracies (%) of different methods in the ADNI fMRI dataset.

	SVM	STM	STuM	STTM	DuSK	K-STTM-Prod	K-STTM-Sum
ADNI fMRI	49.33	50.00	38.00	53.67	54.94	**64.00**	62.33

and normal controls. Overall there are 33 fMRI images and each image has dimensions $61 \times 73 \times 61$. These fMRI images are separated into two classes. The positive class includes normal controls, while the negative class includes patients with MCI or AD. Table 8.14 lists the classification results of different methods. We can observe that the performance of SVM, STM, and STuM is still not good. STTM and DuSK achieve a slightly better performance than random classification. The two K-STTM methods achieve the best accuracy of all compared methods.

8.3.6.5 Conclusion

Ref. [37] has proposed a TT-based kernel trick for the first time and devised a K-STTM. Assuming a low-rank TT as the prior structure of multidimensional data, the authors first define a corresponding feature mapping scheme that keeps the TT structure in the feature space. Furthermore, two kernel function construction schemes are proposed with consideration of consistency with the TT inner product and the preservation of information, respectively. Moreover, it is possible to apply different kernel mappings on the tensor modes with different characteristics.

8.4 Tensorial extension of logistic regression

The idea for extending vector-based LR is similar to the case in SVM. In this section, we briefly introduce two tensorial extensions of LR, namely rank-1 LR [38] and logistic tensor regression [39]. Specifically, rank-1 LR replaces the weight vector in LR with a rank-1 tensor, while logistic tensor regression assumes a general CP format weight tensor.

Algorithm 6 Rank-1 LR algorithm.

Input: Training dataset $\{\mathcal{X}_i \in \mathbb{R}^{I_1 \times \cdots \times I_d}, y_i \in \{-1, 1\}\}_{i=1}^M$.
Output: LR model parameters $\boldsymbol{w}^{(j)}|_{l=1}^d$ and bias b.

1: Initialize $\boldsymbol{w}|_{l=1}^d$ randomly.
2: Repeat steps 3–5 iteratively until convergence.
3: **for** $j = 1, \ldots, d$ **do**
4:    Derive $\boldsymbol{w}^{(j)}$ by optimizing (8.67).
5: **end for**

8.4.1 Rank-1 logistic regression

Consider a training dataset $D = \{\mathcal{X}_i, y_i\}_{i=1}^M$, where tensors $\mathcal{X}_i \in \mathbb{R}^{I_1 \times I_2 \times \cdots \times I_d}$ and $y_i \in \{-1, +1\}$. The general tensorized LR model is based on the following expression for the conditional probabilities:

$$p(y_i = +1 | \mathcal{W}, b, \mathcal{X}_i) = \frac{1}{1 + \exp(-\langle \mathcal{W}, \mathcal{X}_i \rangle - b)}, \qquad (8.64)$$

where $\mathcal{W} \in \mathbb{R}^{I_1 \times I_2 \times \cdots \times I_d}$ and $b \in \mathbb{R}$ are the parameter tensor and the bias of the regression model. The corresponding maximum log-likelihood problem can be written as

$$\min_{\mathcal{W}, b} \sum_{i=1}^M \log\big(1 + \exp\big(-y_i(\langle \mathcal{W}, \mathcal{X}_i \rangle + b)\big)\big). \qquad (8.65)$$

In rank-1 LR models, the parameter tensor weight $\mathcal{W}$ is assumed to be a rank-1 tensor, namely, (8.65) can be rewritten as

$$\min_{\boldsymbol{w}^{(l)}|_{l=1}^d, b} \sum_{i=1}^M \log\left(1 + \exp\left(-y_i\left(\mathcal{X}_i \prod_{1 \leq l \leq d} \times_l \boldsymbol{w}^{(l)} + b\right)\right)\right), \qquad (8.66)$$

where $\mathcal{W} = \boldsymbol{w}^{(1)} \circ \boldsymbol{w}^{(2)} \circ \cdots \circ \boldsymbol{w}^{(d)}$. The optimization scheme is still an alternating optimization procedure. In particular, we solve for $\boldsymbol{w}^{(j)}$ at each iteration while keeping the parameters $\boldsymbol{w}^{(k)}|_{k=1, k \neq j}^d$ fixed. Therefore, each suboptimization problem is written as

$$\min_{\boldsymbol{w}^{(j)}, b} \sum_{i=1}^M \log\big(1 + \exp\big(-y_i\big((\boldsymbol{w}^{(j)})^T \hat{\boldsymbol{x}} + b\big)\big)\big), \qquad (8.67)$$

where $\hat{\boldsymbol{x}} = \mathcal{X}_i \prod_{1 \leq l \leq d}^{l \neq j} \times_l \boldsymbol{w}^{(l)}$. We note that (8.67) has the same optimization format as traditional vector-based LR. The overall optimization procedure is summarized in Algorithm 6.

Table 8.15 Test accuracy (%) under different training sample sizes of the Indian Pines dataset.

Method	Training sample size			
	50	100	150	200
Linear SVM	68.25	75.39	80.36	79.84
LR	63.44	67.64	72.64	73.52
Rank-1 LR	**75.22**	**80.41**	**82.65**	**83.76**

Table 8.16 Test accuracy (%) under different training sample sizes of the Pavia University dataset.

Method	Training sample size			
	50	100	150	200
Linear SVM	79.62	83.90	87.00	87.04
LR	71.82	77.89	82.19	82.27
Rank-1 LR	**84.16**	**86.69**	**88.04**	**88.76**

8.4.1.1 Examples

Ref. [38] employs rank-1 LR to classify hyperspectral data. A hyperspectral image is represented as a 3D tensor of dimensions $p_1 \times p_1 \times p_3$, where p_1 and p_2 correspond to the height and width of the image and p_3 to the spectral bands. Specifically, the North-western Indiana and Pavia University datasets are used [38]. To evaluate the performance of rank-1 LR under different number of training samples, 50, 100, 150, and 200 samples are randomly selected from each class, respectively, to train the model and the remaining data are used to test the performance. The rank-1 LR is compared with traditional vector-based LR and linear SVM.

Tables 8.15 and 8.16 list the classification accuracies on the two datasets. In both datasets and in all cases, the tensor-based model outperforms linear SVMs and vector-based LR, despite the fact that it employs the smallest number of parameters.

8.4.2 Logistic tensor regression

The issue in rank-1 LR is similar to the case in STM, namely the setting of rank-1 tensor weight is oversimplified such that the trained model is not powerful enough to classify some complicated data. Therefore, assuming a general tensor format for weight parameter is a better choice. Here we demonstrate logistic tensor regression (LTR) [39], which employs the CP tensor format to replace the rank-1 weight tensor setting in rank-1 LR.

Assume the weight tensor $\mathcal{W}$ can be represented as a CP tensor format, namely we have (8.2). Based on (8.65), we obtain the following equations according to the

---
Algorithm 7 LTR algorithm.

Input: Training dataset $\{\mathcal{X}_i \in \mathbb{R}^{I_1 \times \cdots \times I_d}, y_i \in \{-1, 1\}\}_{i=1}^{M}$, CP rank for weight tensor.

Output: LTR model parameters $U^{(j)}|_{l=1}^{d}$ and bias b.

1: Initialize $U^{(j)}|_{l=1}^{d}$ randomly.
2: Repeat steps 3–5 iteratively until convergence.
3: **for** $j = 1, \ldots, d$ **do**
4:     derive $U^{(j)}$ by optimizing (8.70)
5: **end for**

---

derivation from (8.34) to (8.36):

$$\langle \mathcal{W}, \mathcal{X}_i \rangle = Tr\left[W_{(j)}X_{(j)i}^T\right] = Tr\left[U^{(j)}(U^{(-j)})^T X_{(j)i}^T\right]. \tag{8.68}$$

Therefore, (8.65) can be rewritten as

$$\min_{U^{(j)},b} \sum_{i=1}^{M} \log\left(1 + \exp\left(-y_i\left(Tr\left[U^{(j)}(U^{(-j)})^T X_{(j)i}^T\right] + b\right)\right)\right). \tag{8.69}$$

Let $\widetilde{X}_{(j)i} = X_{(j)i}U^{(-j)}$. Since $Tr[U^{(j)}\widetilde{X}_{(j)i}^T] = (vec(U^{(j)}))^T vec(\widetilde{X}_{(j)i})$, we can rewrite (8.69) into its vector format as follows:

$$\min_{U^{(j)},b} \sum_{i=1}^{M} \log\left(1 + \exp\left(-y_i\left((vec(U^{(j)}))^T vec(\widetilde{X}_{(j)i}) + b\right)\right)\right). \tag{8.70}$$

By doing so, any optimization method applied to traditional LR can also be employed to train an LTR. The overall training scheme is still an alternating optimization procedure, as depicted in Algorithm 7. In each iteration, we solve for $U^{(j)}$ while keeping all other $U^{(j)}|_{k=1,k\neq j}^{d}$ fixed.

8.4.2.1 Examples

In [39], the performance of an LTR is evaluated through two public datasets, namely the FG-NET facial images dataset [40] and the Carnegie Mellon University's Graphics Lab human motion capture database [41]. Two metrics are employed to evaluate the LTR classification performance. The first one is the area under the ROC curve (AUC) [42]. More specifically, the MacroAUC (average on AUC of all the classes) and the MicroAUC (the global calculation of AUC regardless of classes) are used. The second one is the harmonic mean of precision and recall, called F_1 score [42]. The Macro F_1 (average on F_1 scores of all the classes) and the Micro F_1 (the global calculation of F_1 regardless of classes) are presented.

The rank of the weight tensor is determined by grid search. Tables 8.17 and 8.18 show the classification performance of LTR and other methods. It is observed that

Table 8.17 Comparison on facial images.

Method	MacroAUC	MicroAUC	Macro F_1	Micro F_1
LTR	**0.7482**	**0.8692**	**0.5697**	**0.5717**
SVR [45]	0.4956	0.6731	0.4073	0.3631
BLR [44]	0.5702	0.7984	0.4417	0.5231
hrTRR [43]	0.6153	0.8152	0.4568	0.4321
hrSTR [43]	0.6916	0.8250	0.5213	0.5037
orTRR [43]	0.5780	0.7756	0.3513	0.3231
orSTR [43]	0.5184	0.7555	0.3913	0.3114

Table 8.18 Comparison on motion data.

Method	MacroAUC	MicroAUC	Macro F_1	Micro F_1
LTR	**0.6976**	**0.9080**	**0.5218**	**0.5031**
SVR [45]	0.5413	0.7231	0.4006	0.4268
BLR [44]	0.5609	0.7527	0.4332	0.4367
hrTRR [43]	0.6708	0.8344	0.4359	0.4135
hrSTR [43]	0.6684	0.8686	0.4965	0.4631
orTRR [43]	0.6594	0.8894	0.5063	0.4792
orSTR [43]	0.5517	0.7932	0.3993	0.4010

all of the tensorial approaches outperform their vector-based counterparts in terms of the two kinds of evaluation metrics. Moreover, LTR outperforms the linear tensor regression methods in the task of classification.

8.5 Conclusion

Many real-world data appear in a matrix or tensor format. In such circumstances, extending the vector-based machine learning algorithms to their tensorial format has recently attracted significant interest in the machine learning and data mining communities since tensor algorithms can naturally utilize the multiway structure of the original tensor data, which is believed to be useful in many machine learning applications. In this chapter, we have reviewed some tensorial extensions of two traditional classifiers, namely SVM and LR. The classification performance enhancement is observed in various tensorial data classification tasks. These advantages would be more obvious in dealing with small-sample high-dimensional tensor classification problems due to the fact that collecting labeled data can be extremely expensive and time consuming in many practical scenarios.

There are still some open problems in this area. First, for the determination of tensor ranks, grid search is still the mainstream scheme for finding suitable tensor ranks, which is computationally demanding and does not guarantee optimality. Some works [46] have tried to explore the possibility of employing a probabilistic model to determine the tensor ranks automatically. Second, the training algorithms for tensor-based classifiers are mostly based on the alternating optimization procedure. Although the algorithmic convergence is guaranteed, it is still time consuming. A more efficient training scheme is still highly desired.

References

[1] Vladimir Vapnik, The Nature of Statistical Learning Theory, Springer Science & Business Media, 2013.

[2] Raymond E. Wright, Logistic regression, 1995.

[3] Johan Håstad, Tensor rank is NP-complete, in: International Colloquium on Automata, Languages, and Programming, Springer, Berlin, Heidelberg, 1989.

[4] Dacheng Tao, et al., Supervised tensor learning, in: Fifth IEEE International Conference on Data Mining (ICDM'05), IEEE, 2005.

[5] Shuicheng Yan, et al., Multilinear discriminant analysis for face recognition, IEEE Transactions on Image Processing 16 (1) (2006) 212–220.

[6] Dacheng Tao, et al., Asymmetric bagging and random subspace for support vector machines-based relevance feedback in image retrieval, IEEE Transactions on Pattern Analysis and Machine Intelligence 28 (7) (2006) 1088–1099.

[7] Jing Li, et al., Multitraining support vector machine for image retrieval, IEEE Transactions on Image Processing 15 (11) (2006) 3597–3601.

[8] Lior Wolf, Hueihan Jhuang, Tamir Hazan, Modeling appearances with low-rank SVM, in: 2007 IEEE Conference on Computer Vision and Pattern Recognition, IEEE, 2007.

[9] Deng Cai, et al., Support tensor machines for text categorization, 2006.

[10] A. Kale, A. Sundaresan, A.N. Rajagopalan, N.P. Cuntoor, A.K. Roy-Chowdhury, V. Kruger, R. Chellappa, Identification of humans using gait, IEEE Transactions on Image Processing 13 (9) (2004) 1163–1173.

[11] Jinguang Han, Bir Bhanu, Individual recognition using gait energy image, IEEE Transactions on Pattern Analysis and Machine Intelligence 28 (2) (2005) 316–322.

[12] Vin De Silva, Lek-Heng Lim, Tensor rank and the ill-posedness of the best low-rank approximation problem, SIAM Journal on Matrix Analysis and Applications 30 (3) (2008) 1084–1127.

[13] Carla D. Martin, The rank of a $2 \times 2 \times 2$ tensor, Linear and Multilinear Algebra 59 (8) (2011) 943–950.

[14] Zhifeng Hao, et al., A linear support higher-order tensor machine for classification, IEEE Transactions on Image Processing 22 (7) (2013) 2911–2920.

[15] Irene Kotsia, Weiwei Guo, Ioannis Patras, Higher rank support tensor machines for visual recognition, Pattern Recognition 45 (12) (2012) 4192–4203.

[16] Tae-Kyun Kim, Roberto Cipolla, Canonical correlation analysis of video volume tensors for action categorization and detection, IEEE Transactions on Pattern Analysis and Machine Intelligence 31 (8) (2008) 1415–1428.

[17] Saad Ali, Mubarak Shah, Human action recognition in videos using kinematic features and multiple instance learning, IEEE Transactions on Pattern Analysis and Machine Intelligence 32 (2) (2008) 288–303.

[18] Andrzej Cichocki, et al., Low-rank tensor networks for dimensionality reduction and large-scale optimization problems: perspectives and challenges part 1, arXiv preprint, arXiv:1609.00893, 2016.

[19] Yiming Yang, Xin Liu, A re-examination of text categorization methods, in: Proceedings of the 22nd Annual International ACM SIGIR Conference on Research and Development in Information Retrieval, 1999.

[20] Ulrich Schollwöck, The density-matrix renormalization group in the age of matrix product states, Annals of Physics 326 (1) (2011) 96–192.

[21] Konstantinos Rapantzikos, Yannis Avrithis, Stefanos Kollias, Dense saliency-based spatiotemporal feature points for action recognition, in: 2009 IEEE Conference on Computer Vision and Pattern Recognition, IEEE, 2009.

[22] Alireza Fathi, Greg Mori, Action Recognition by Learning Mid-Level Motion Features, 2008 IEEE Conference on Computer Vision and Pattern Recognition, IEEE, 2008.

[23] Haiping Lu, Konstantinos N. Plataniotis, Anastasios N. Venetsanopoulos, MPCA: Multilinear principal component analysis of tensor objects, IEEE Transactions on Neural Networks 19 (1) (2008) 18–39.

[24] Sudeep Sarkar, et al., The humanID gait challenge problem: data sets, performance, and analysis, IEEE Transactions on Pattern Analysis and Machine Intelligence 27 (2) (2005) 162–177.

[25] Nikolaos V. Boulgouris, Konstantinos N. Plataniotis, Dimitrios Hatzinakos, Gait recognition using linear time normalization, Pattern Recognition 39 (5) (2006) 969–979.

[26] Alex Krizhevsky, Geoffrey Hinton, Learning multiple layers of features from tiny images, 2009, p. 7.

[27] Christian Schuldt, Ivan Laptev, Barbara Caputo, Recognizing human actions: a local SVM approach, in: Proceedings of the 17th International Conference on Pattern Recognition, vol. 3, IEEE, 2004.

[28] Jssai Schur, Bemerkungen zur Theorie der beschränkten Bilinearformen mit unendlich vielen Veränderlichen, Journal für die reine und angewandte Mathematik (Crelles Journal) 1911 (140) (1911) 1–28.

[29] Irene Kotsia, Ioannis Patras, Support Tucker machines, in: CVPR 2011, IEEE, 2011.

[30] Yann LeCun, et al., Gradient-based learning applied to document recognition, Proceedings of the IEEE 86 (11) (1998) 2278–2324.

[31] Cong Chen, et al., A support tensor train machine, in: 2019 International Joint Conference on Neural Networks (IJCNN), IEEE, 2019.

[32] Lynn Houthuys, Johan AK Suykens, Tensor learning in multi-view kernel PCA, in: International Conference on Artificial Neural Networks, Springer, Cham, 2018.

[33] Ivan V. Oseledets , SIAM Journal on Scientific Computing 33 (5) (2011) 2295–2317.

[34] Tom M. Mitchell, et al., Predicting human brain activity associated with the meanings of nouns, Science 320 (5880) (2008) 1191–1195.

[35] Lifang He, et al., Dusk: a dual structure-preserving kernel for supervised tensor learning with applications to neuroimages, in: Proceedings of the 2014 SIAM International Conference on Data Mining, Society for Industrial and Applied Mathematics, 2014.

[36] Kittipat Kampa, et al., Sparse optimization in feature selection: application in neuroimaging, Journal of Global Optimization 59.2–3 (2014) 439–457.

[37] Cong Chen, et al., Kernelized support tensor train machines, arXiv preprint, arXiv:2001.00360, 2020.

[38] Konstantinos Makantasis, et al., Tensor-based classification models for hyperspectral data analysis, IEEE Transactions on Geoscience and Remote Sensing 56 (12) (2018) 6884–6898.

[39] Tan Xu, et al., Logistic tensor regression for classification, in: International Conference on Intelligent Science and Intelligent Data Engineering, Springer, Berlin, Heidelberg, 2012.

[40] A. Agarwal, B. Triggs, I. Rhone-Alpes, F. Montbonnot, The FG-NET aging database, http://www.fgnet.rsunit.com, 2010.

[41] Tommaso Piazza, et al., Predicting missing markers in real-time optical motion capture, in: 3D Physiological Human Workshop, Springer, Berlin, Heidelberg, 2009.

[42] Tom Fawcett, An introduction to ROC analysis, Pattern Recognition Letters 27 (8) (2006) 861–874.

[43] Weiwei Guo, Irene Kotsia, Ioannis Patras, Tensor learning for regression, IEEE Transactions on Image Processing 21 (2) (2011) 816–827.

[44] Sean M. O'brien, David B. Dunson, Bayesian multivariate logistic regression, Biometrics 60 (3) (2004) 739–746.

[45] Alex J. Smola, Bernhard Schölkopf, A tutorial on support vector regression, Statistics and Computing 14 (3) (2004) 199–222.

[46] Le Xu, et al., Learning tensor train representation with automatic rank determination from incomplete noisy data, arXiv preprint, arXiv:2010.06564, 2020.

References

High-performance tensor decompositions for compressing and accelerating deep neural networks

9

Xiao-Yang Liu[a,b], Yiming Fang[c], Liuqing Yang[c], Zechu Li[c], and Anwar Walid[d]

[a]*Department of Computer Science and Engineering, Shanghai Jiao Tong University, Shanghai, China*
[b]*Department of Electrical Engineering, Columbia University, New York, NY, United States*
[c]*Department of Computer Science, Columbia University, New York, NY, United States*
[d]*Nokia Bell Labs, Murray Hill, NJ, United States*

CONTENTS

Tensors for Data Processing. https://doi.org/10.1016/B978-0-12-824447-0.00015-7

293

9.1 Introduction and motivation

Deep neural networks (DNNs) yield state-of-the-art performance in numerous applications in the field of machine learning and artificial intelligence. Compared to traditional machine learning algorithms such as support vector machines, perceptrons, decision trees, and k-nearest neighbors, DNNs have significant advantages in extracting features at different levels of abstraction and thereby learning more complex patterns. DNNs compute their internal parameters in forward pass and then iteratively refine them during backpropagation to effectively extract input data features. These advantages give DNNs a greater learning capability, outperforming other methods in tasks such as computer vision, natural language processing, machine translation, speech recognition, genomics, quantitative trading, and self-driving cars. DNNs have become a powerful and valuable tool in many industrial and commercial applications. Recently, DNNs have achieved spectacular success across diverse fields: the AlphaGo and AlphaZero algorithms defeated human world champions in the game of Go [1], online entertainment platforms use DNNs to construct highly effective systems for personalized content recommendation [2], and medical professionals utilize deep learning tools to make diagnoses and discover new drugs [3,4].

However, as the complexities of the learning tasks and the size of the training data grow, wider utilization of DNNs is challenged by a prohibitively large number of parameters, long training and inference time, and extensive computational and memory resources. For example, the ResNet-50 model contains about 23 million trainable floating-point parameters, with a model size of roughly 100 MB [5]. Such models are not viable for some applications and implementations with strict resource constraints such as edge consumer and industrial devices [6].

The parameters of typical deep learning models often have a certain degree of redundancy (or sparsity in a transform domain), which can be exploited to reduce the model's computational cost and memory footprint. In traditional approaches, there is an efficiency–accuracy trade-off: using fewer parameters reduces the cost, but also compromises the model's accuracy. Prior works considered construction of compact models while maintaining performance accuracy, such as sparsity constraints [7], weight clustering and quantification [8], knowledge distillation [9], and structured projections [10]. There are many existing research works on addressing these challenges using tensor-based networks [11,12].

In this chapter, we focus on the utilization of tensor decompositions and tensor networks. To address the aforementioned challenges in deep learning, we utilize tensor networks for efficient representations of high-order tensors. This approach enables compression of the parameter tensors in DNNs while preserving the interactions between features (modes). Tensor operations enable us to conduct forward and backward update calculations efficiently in tensor format. Moreover, we exploit the power of parallelization on GPUs to accelerate neural network training and inference [13]. These techniques will enable DNNs to be used in a broader range of applications by lowering the hardware requirements and computational cost and enable deployment on portable smart devices and embedded systems.

The remainder of this chapter is organized as follows. In Section 9.2, we give a basic summary of key topics in DNNs: network architectures, convolutional and fully connected layers, backpropagation, loss functions, etc. In Section 9.3, we review the basics of tensor decomposition schemes such as CANDECOMP/PARAFAC, or canonical polyadic (CP), Tucker, tensor train (TT), hierarchical Tucker (HT), and transform-based decomposition and introduce the concept of tensor networks. In Section 9.4, we demonstrate applications of tensor decompositions to DNN layers, and we show how the layers are representable in the format of tensor networks. We also present ways in which we can accelerate the training and inference processes using parallelization on GPUs. Lastly, in Section 9.5, we showcase different methods of tensor-decomposed DNNs and compare their performance advantages with their undecomposed counterparts.

9.2 Deep neural networks

In this section, we introduce the components of DNNs [14]. Beginning with the mathematical expression of a linear layer, we describe the concepts of activation functions, loss functions, and gradient-based optimization. We then extend the simple model to more complex models, such as deep fully connected neural networks (FCNNs) and deep convolutional neural networks (CNNs).

9.2.1 Notations

We denote scalars, vectors, matrices, and tensors by lowercase letters, boldface lowercase letters, boldface uppercase letters, and calligraphic letters, respectively, for example, a scalar $x \in \mathbb{R}$, a vector $\boldsymbol{x} \in \mathbb{R}^n$, a matrix $\boldsymbol{X} \in \mathbb{R}^{m \times n}$, and a tensor $\mathcal{X} \in \mathbb{R}^{m \times n \times l}$.

We index the entries and slices of vectors, matrices, and tensors as follows: we index the i-th entry of a vector as $\boldsymbol{x}_i$, the i-th row of a matrix as $\boldsymbol{X}(i, :)$, the j-th column of a matrix as $\boldsymbol{X}(:, j)$ or $\boldsymbol{X}_j$, the (i, j)-th entry of a matrix as $\boldsymbol{X}(i, j)$, and the (i, j, k)-th entry of a tensor as $\mathcal{X}(i, j, k)$. We use the superscript notation to index elements in a set. For example, given a set of n matrices $\{\boldsymbol{A}^1, ..., \boldsymbol{A}^n\}$, we denote the k-th matrix in the set as $\boldsymbol{A}^k$. Table 9.1 summarizes the commonly used tensor operations.

9.2.2 Linear layer

Supervised learning

The central task underlying supervised learning schemes is selecting a model that fits the training data while achieving a certain degree of generalizability. Suppose the input data $\boldsymbol{X}$ is a set of m images, each of size $n \times n$. Each data point is reshaped to a vector $\boldsymbol{X}_i \in \mathbb{R}^{n^2}$ and an associated label $\boldsymbol{Y}_i \in \mathbb{R}^c$, where $i = [m]$ and c is the

Table 9.1 Tensor operations.

$\mathcal{C} = \mathcal{A} \times_n \boldsymbol{B}$	Mode-n contraction: $\mathcal{A} \in \mathbb{R}^{I_1 \times I_2 \times \cdots \times I_N}$, $\boldsymbol{B} \in \mathbb{R}^{J \times I_n}$, and $\mathcal{C} \in \mathbb{R}^{I_1 \times \cdots \times I_{n-1} \times J \times I_{n+1} \times \cdots \times I_N}$, where $\mathcal{C}_{i_1 \times \cdots \times i_{n-1} \times j \times i_{n+1} \times \cdots \times i_N} = \sum_{i_n=1}^{I_n} \mathcal{A}_{i_1, \ldots, i_N} \boldsymbol{B}_{j, i_n}$
$\mathcal{C} = \mathcal{A} \times^1 \mathcal{B}$	Mode-$(N, 1)$ contraction: $\mathcal{A} \in \mathbb{R}^{I_1 \times I_2 \times \cdots \times I_N}$, $\mathcal{B} \in \mathbb{R}^{J_1 \times J_2 \times \cdots \times J_M}$ and $\mathcal{C} \in \mathbb{R}^{I_1 \times \cdots \times I_{N-1} \times J_2 \times \cdots \times J_N}$, where $I_N = J_1$ and $\mathcal{C}_{i_1, \ldots, i_{N-1}, j_2, \ldots, j_M} = \sum_{i_N=1}^{I_N} \mathcal{A}_{i_1, \ldots, i_N} \mathcal{B}_{i_{N-1}, j_2, \ldots, j_M}$
$\mathcal{C} = \mathcal{A} \circ \mathcal{B}$	Outer product: $\mathcal{A} \in \mathbb{R}^{I_1 \times I_2 \times \cdots \times I_N}$, $\mathcal{B} \in \mathbb{R}^{J_1 \times J_2 \times \cdots \times J_M}$, and $\mathcal{C} \in \mathbb{R}^{I_1 \times \cdots \times I_N \times J_1 \times \cdots \times J_N}$, where $\mathcal{C}_{i_1, \ldots, i_N, j_1, \ldots, j_M} = \mathcal{A}_{i_1, \ldots, i_N} \mathcal{B}_{j_1, \ldots, j_M}$
$\mathcal{C} = \boldsymbol{A} \odot \boldsymbol{B}$	Khatri–Rao product: $\boldsymbol{A} = [\boldsymbol{a}_1, \ldots, \boldsymbol{a}_J] \in \mathbb{R}^{I \times J}$, $\boldsymbol{B} = [\boldsymbol{b}_1, \ldots, \boldsymbol{b}_J] \in \mathbb{R}^{K \times J}$, and $\mathcal{C} \in \mathbb{R}^{IK \times J}$, where $\boldsymbol{c}_j = \boldsymbol{a}_j \otimes \boldsymbol{b}_j$ for all columns.
$\mathcal{C} = [\![\mathcal{G}; \boldsymbol{B}^1, \boldsymbol{B}^2, \ldots, \boldsymbol{B}^N]\!]$	Multilinear (Tucker) product of a tensor $\mathcal{G}$ and factor matrices $\boldsymbol{B}^1, \ldots, \boldsymbol{B}^N$, where $\mathcal{C} = \mathcal{G} \times_1 \boldsymbol{B}^1 \times_2 \boldsymbol{B}^2 \times_3 \cdots \times_N \boldsymbol{B}^N$
$\mathcal{C} = \langle\!\langle \mathcal{G}^1, \mathcal{G}^2, \ldots, \mathcal{G}^N \rangle\!\rangle$	Multilinear product of core tensors $\mathcal{G}^1, \ldots, \mathcal{G}^N$, where $\mathcal{C} = \mathcal{G}^1 \times^1 \mathcal{G}^2 \times^1 \cdots \times^1 \mathcal{G}^N$

number of categories. We assume that there exists a true model, denoted by the function f^*, such that $f^*(\boldsymbol{X}_i) = \boldsymbol{Y}_i$ holds for the majority of the training data. Our goal is to estimate a model f that behaves similarly to f^*; that is, f maximizes the label agreement in the training set $(\boldsymbol{X}_i, \boldsymbol{Y}_i)$. This model is then applied to the unseen data, predicting a label $\widehat{\boldsymbol{Y}}_i = f(\boldsymbol{X}_i)$, and we always use the hat notation to denote a predicted value.

Linear layer

We start from a linear layer, which is generalized to high-dimensional cases and used to discuss DNNs and their tensorization. A linear layer maps a single data point $\boldsymbol{X}_i$ to an output $\widehat{\boldsymbol{Y}}_i$ as follows:

$$\widehat{\boldsymbol{Y}}_i = f(\boldsymbol{X}_i; \boldsymbol{W}, \boldsymbol{b}) = \boldsymbol{W}\boldsymbol{X}_i + \boldsymbol{b}, \tag{9.1}$$

where $\boldsymbol{W} \in \mathbb{R}^{c \times n^2}$ is the weight matrix and $\boldsymbol{b} \in \mathbb{R}^c$ is the offset, and both are the trainable parameters of the layer.

Activation functions

The linear model maps each data point $\boldsymbol{X}_i$ to its likelihood of belonging to a category. A linear layer is very precious at approximating linear functions, but in practice we need to approximate nonlinear functions to capture complex patterns in the data samples. An activation function is applied to the output, inducing nonlinearity to the model. The activation function is commonly denoted by $\sigma(\cdot)$, and popular choices include sigmoid, tanh, rectified linear unit (ReLU), leaky ReLU, etc. The sigmoid activation function is historically essential, where $\sigma(X_i; W) = \frac{1}{1+e^{-X_i}}$. However, most modern neural networks use the ReLU function $\sigma(X_i; W) = \max(0, WX_i)$, due to its efficient computation and superior performance.

Fully connected layer

Lastly, we group all the input data into a single batch (in practice, we often split the input data into smaller batches, and the typical batch size is 32, 64, or 128). Let $X = \{X_1, ..., X_m\} \in \mathbb{R}^{n^2 \times m}$, obtained by stacking the data points as columns. Let the overall offset matrix $B = \underbrace{\{b, ..., b\}}_{m \text{ times}} \in \mathbb{R}^{c \times m}$, so that the same offset is applied to each data point.

Putting the pieces together, we get

$$\widehat{Y} = \sigma(f(X; W, B)) = \sigma(WX + B), \tag{9.2}$$

where $\widehat{Y} \in \mathbb{R}^{c \times m}$ is the output of the function. This function serves as a linear layer: the inputs are passed into a single layer of neurons, which maps each data point from the input space $\mathbb{R}^{n^2}$ to the output space, $\mathbb{R}^c$. The layer's behavior can be interpreted as assigning each data point different likelihoods for each structural category.

Softmax

The softmax normalization function is typically applied to the model's output, $\widehat{Y}$. The function operates on each column $\widehat{Y}_i$, softmax$(\cdot) : \mathbb{R}^c \to \mathbb{R}^c$, as follows:

$$\text{softmax}(\widehat{Y})_i = \frac{e^{\widehat{Y}_i}}{\sum_{j \in [c]} e^{\widehat{Y}_j}}, \quad i \in [m]. \tag{9.3}$$

The softmax function maps the columns in an element-wise manner to range $[0, 1]$, making the resulting columns sum to 1. The output of the softmax function can be interpreted as a probability distribution, i.e., softmax$(\widehat{Y})_{j,i}$ is the probability that the i-th data point belongs to the j-th category.

Loss functions, cross-entropy, regularization

The loss function measures how well the network fits the training data. This function is evaluated for each data point in the training data, thus adding to the overall loss. The output of the network is passed into the loss function, which computes the fitting loss of the current iteration. The higher the loss, the worse the model's fitting performance. One of the most frequently used loss functions is the cross-entropy loss:

$$\mathcal{L}(A^N) = -\sum_i^N Y_i \log\left(\text{softmax}(\widehat{Y}_i)\right) = \sum_i^N \left(-\widehat{Y}_i + \log\sum_j^K e^{Y_j}\right). \tag{9.4}$$

Binary classification is frequently used, and many multicategory classification problems can be reduced to binary classification using techniques such as One-vs-All, so the binary form of the cross-entropy formula is very useful. The following

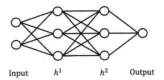

Input h^1 h^2 Output

FIGURE 9.1

Fully connected neural network.

formula is a special case of (9.4):

$$\mathcal{L}(\boldsymbol{A}^N) = -\sum_i^N \left(\boldsymbol{Y}_i \log \widehat{\boldsymbol{Y}}_i + (1 - \boldsymbol{Y}_i)\log(1 - \widehat{\boldsymbol{Y}}_i)\right). \tag{9.5}$$

It is often beneficial to include a regularization penalty because sometimes multiple sets of parameters fit the training data sufficiently well, but not all of them have the potential to generalize to unseen data. Suppose we want to make sure that we obtain a set of parameters that do not contain large parameters. We would add the regularization penalty $R(\boldsymbol{W}) = \sum_{j,k} \boldsymbol{W}_{i,j}^2$ to discourage large parameters. In practice, we often combine the loss function and the regularization penalty into a single cost function:

$$\mathcal{L}(\boldsymbol{A}^N) = \sum_i^N \left(-\widehat{\boldsymbol{Y}}_i + \log \sum_j^K e^{Y_j}\right) + \lambda R(\boldsymbol{W}), \tag{9.6}$$

where $\lambda \in \mathbb{R}^+$ is a hyperparameter that controls the amount of penalty we take into account. The regularization penalty prevents the network from overfitting, a common bottleneck in deep learning where the network performs well on the training data but poorly on unseen data.

9.2.3 Fully connected neural networks

Hidden units

We now lay out the architecture of the DNN. In Section 9.2.2, we obtain a mapping from the input space to the output space using a single linear layer. By including more intermediate layers in our model, we give it greater power to extract features at different levels of abstraction. This multilayered model consists of the input layer, the output layer, and the internal layers in between, commonly called the hidden units because their intermediate results do not show up in the final result.

Notations, importance

Fig. 9.1 demonstrates an example of an FCNN with three layers (by convention, we do not count the input layer). The input has two dimensions, the two hidden layers have three neurons (dimensions), and the output has a single dimension, i.e., it is a vector.

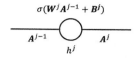

FIGURE 9.2

A neuron.

We denote the input layer as layer 0, the layer that follows it as layer 1, and so on. The weights and offsets of each layer are denoted by W^j and B^j, where j is the layer number. Each of the two hidden layers computes a linear mapping followed by a nonlinear activation function. We denote the result before the activation function is applied as Z^j and the layer's output as A^j.

This network is commonly known as an FCNN, because every neuron in a given layer receives inputs from all neurons in the previous layer. The term neural network comes from neuroscience, which served as an inspiration in the development of deep learning, though modern neural networks are far from accurate models of biological neural systems. The FCNN is of central importance for the field of deep learning, and many algorithms are built on top of this basic architecture.

Forward pass

Given the vectorized training dataset $X \in \mathbb{R}^{n^2 \times m}$, we calculate the output of the neural network by passing the data through the hidden units sequentially, i.e., from left to right. The computation done in an N-layer network is summarized by

$$
\begin{aligned}
Z^j &= W^j A^{j-1} + B^j, \\
A^j &= \sigma(Z^j), \quad j \in [N].
\end{aligned}
\tag{9.7}
$$

Note that for the input layer, A^0 is simply the training data X. We also compute the output for each neuron, following the formula $Z_i^j = W_i^j A_i^{j-1} + B_i^j$, where i is the index of the neuron of interest. The dimension of the weights and offsets in each layer depends on the number of neurons in the previous layer ℓ^{j-1} and subsequent layer ℓ^l, such that $W^j \in \mathbb{R}^{\ell_j \times \ell_{j-1}}$, $B^j = \underbrace{\{b^j, ..., b^j\}}_{m \text{ times}} \in \mathbb{R}^{\ell_j \times m}$. The last layer typically does not have an activation function, because its outputs represent the likelihood of the input data belonging to a certain category.

Fig. 9.2 provides a demonstration of each neuron's function, which conducts a linear transformation followed by an activation function on the input received from the previous layer.

Representational power

The end-to-end computation of the neural network is a function $f : \mathbb{R}^{n^2 \times m} \to \mathbb{R}^{c \times m}$, which has the exact same input/output behavior as the basic linear layer. The advantage of a DNN lies in its representational power: it has been proposed by the universal approximation theorem that a fully connected network is theoretically able

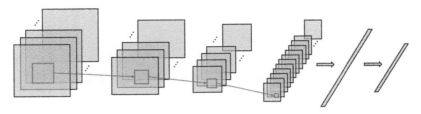

FIGURE 9.3

Convolutional neural network (LeNet).

to approximate any continuous function with an arbitrarily small error. Although in practice it is rarely possible to approximate the "ground truth" function perfectly, DNNs' greater representational power does make them more effective in tackling machine learning tasks, i.e., producing more accurate predictions.

9.2.4 Convolutional neural networks

Motivation, representational power

In many problems, especially in the field of computer vision, one often finds FC-NNs insufficient; that is, their representational power is not sufficient to learn the essential features from complex data such as images and videos. CNNs have been tailored to have more effective representations of images and multidimensional data. The advent of CNNs has enabled us to build more accurate models using fewer parameters.

Architecture

CNNs have architectures very similar to those of ordinary FCNNs: they have a sequential layout of layers followed by activation functions, the same input/output behavior, and a single differentiable loss function at the end. The only difference is that the convolutional layers in CNNs are often placed before the fully connected layers.

In a classic convolutional architecture, the LeNet [15], as shown in Fig. 9.3, the network takes 2D grayscale images as inputs. Four convolutional layers extract the input images' features, followed by two fully connected layers that classify the inputs. The network outputs a vector $\widehat{y} \in \mathbb{R}^{10}$, with each dimension corresponding to a category.

Another example of CNNs is the AlexNet [16], which takes 3D colored images as inputs, as shown in Fig. 9.4. Although this network is more complex and has one more dimension in its convolutional layers, the underlying architecture is the same.

Convolution operation

The convolutional operation, commonly denoted by $*$, is a feature map obtained by applying filters to the previous layer's output. In the simplest 1D case, given an input vector u and a kernel vector k, or the filter, we obtain the output vector v such

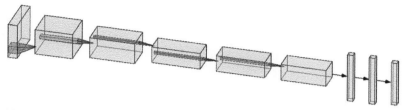

FIGURE 9.4

Convolutional neural network (AlexNet).

that

$$v(i) = (k * u)(i) = \sum_m k(n)u(i - m). \tag{9.8}$$

This operation is generalizable to higher dimensions. Suppose the input and kernel are no longer vectors, but matrices or tensors. Then the convolutional operation becomes

$$V(i, j) = (K * U)(i, j) = \sum_{m,n} K(m, n)U(i - m, j - n),$$

$$\mathcal{V}(i, j, k) = (\mathcal{K} * \mathcal{U})(i, j, k) = \sum_{l, m, n} \mathcal{K}(l, m, n)\mathcal{U}(i - l, j - m, k - n). \tag{9.9}$$

Convolutional layer

The convolutional layer conducts the convolutional operation between the inputs and the weights. The weights of the convolutional layer are commonly referred to as the kernel tensor, or the filters. Typically, the kernel tensor is composed of T square-shaped filters, each having a size of $d \times d$, and T is the number of output channels. This convolutional layer takes in an input tensor $\mathcal{U} \in \mathbb{R}^{X \times Y \times S}$, where X, Y are the spatial dimensions and S is the number of input channels. The output of the convolutional layer is a tensor $\mathcal{V} \in \mathbb{R}^{X' \times Y' \times T}$, where $X' = \frac{X - d + 2 \times \text{Padding}}{\text{stride}} + 1$, $Y' = \frac{Y - d + 2 \times \text{Padding}}{\text{stride}} + 1$. Padding and stride are two quantities that control how far the kernel moves after each dot product and how much it is allowed go out of the edge.

During a convolution operation, we fix the depth, or channel dimension, i.e., treat each tube across the depth as a whole. Then, we compute the dot product of the kernel and the input data on each position. This process is mathematically formulated as

$$\mathcal{V}(x, y, t) = (\mathcal{K} * \mathcal{U})(x, y, t) = \sum_{i=x-\delta}^{x+\delta} \sum_{j=y-\delta}^{y+\delta} \sum_{s=1}^{S} \mathcal{K}(i - x + \delta, j - y + \delta, s, t)\,\mathcal{U}(i, j, s), \tag{9.10}$$

where $\mathcal{K} \in \mathbb{R}^{d \times d \times S \times T}$ and $\delta = \frac{d-1}{2}$ is called the "half width" of the kernel.

To understand the convolution operation even further, let us consider a concrete example shown in Fig. 9.5. The kernel has size 3×3 and is convolving on a matrix of

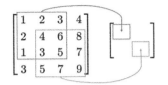

FIGURE 9.5

Matrix convolution.

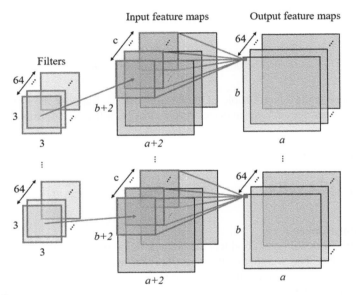

FIGURE 9.6

The convolution operation.

size 4×4. Assuming for simplicity that the stride is 1 and there is no added padding, we can calculate the size of the resulting matrix to be $(\frac{4-3+2\times0}{1} + 1) \times (\frac{4-3+2\times0}{1} + 1) = 2 \times 2$, where each index equals the dot product between the kernel tensor and the input matrix. After every dot product, we move the kernel to the next position and compute the following dot product.

Fig. 9.6 shows a full convolution operation in a convolutional layer. Suppose that the kernel tensor has 64 channels, i.e., it has 64 distinct filters. We convolve each filter on the input tensor by sliding it to cover the frontal slice and record the resulting dot product in the output tensor on the right.

Comparison with FCNNs, local connectivity

The advantage of convolutional layers over fully connected layers is that convolutional layers make the underlying assumption that the features on different spatial positions have commonalities. Learning a feature at a spatial position (x, y) is likely useful at another spatial position (x', y'). This use of kernel also introduces the concept of local connectivity; whereas in fully connected layers every neuron is connected to every entry of the data tensor, the kernels in the convolutional layer connect to only a selected portion of the data. This method allows us to drastically reduce the number of parameters needed to train the network and makes it feasible to train more extensive networks to solve complex problems.

9.2.5 Backpropagation

After defining the architecture of the network, we repeatedly conduct the forward pass and modify the network to improve its performance on the training data with a procedure called backpropagation. In this section, we will introduce backpropagation by gradient descent, show the calculation of gradients and Jacobians, and present the algorithm for training the neural network.

Backpropagation, Jacobian, autograd

Having obtained the loss value for a single forward pass, we use this value to improve the network by updating the trainable parameters to reduce the loss. We decide how much to modify each parameter by determining how much influence it has on the final output by calculating its gradient. This process is known as backpropagation, which is directly antithetical to the forward pass. Whereas during the forward pass we calculate the product of the weights and data sequentially from left to right, we now calculate the gradient of each parameter by first finding the derivative to the loss function and then calculating the derivative of the loss function with regard to each layer using the chain rule from the last layer to the first layer.

The first step is to take the derivative of the loss function with regard to the last layer's output, A^N. The derivation is somewhat involved, so we omit the intermediate steps. We have

$$\frac{\partial \mathcal{L}}{\partial A^N} = \text{softmax}(A^N) - Y. \tag{9.11}$$

It is also helpful to know the derivative for the activation functions:

$$\text{ReLU}'(x) = \begin{cases} 1 & \text{if } x > 0, \\ 0 & \text{otherwise,} \end{cases} \qquad \sigma'(x) = \sigma(x)(1 - \sigma(x)). \tag{9.12}$$

Then, after this step, we go backward layer-by-layer to calculate the gradient for each parameter. It is possible because the entire forward pass is completely sequential, and we trace the operation between operands for each of the operations. Therefore, for parameters in the j-th layer, we calculate $\partial \mathcal{L}/\partial A^j$, $\partial \mathcal{L}/\partial W^j$, and

$\partial \mathcal{L} / \partial \boldsymbol{b}^j$ as follows:

$$
\begin{aligned}
\frac{\partial \mathcal{L}}{\partial A_j} &= \frac{\partial \mathcal{L}}{\partial A^{j+1}} \frac{\partial A^{j+1}}{\partial A^j}, \\
\frac{\partial \mathcal{L}}{\partial W_j} &= \frac{\partial \mathcal{L}}{\partial A^j} \frac{\partial A^j}{\partial Z^j} \frac{\partial Z^j}{\partial W_j}, \\
\frac{\partial \mathcal{L}}{\partial b_j} &= \frac{\partial \mathcal{L}}{\partial b^j} \frac{\partial A^j}{\partial Z^j} \frac{\partial Z^j}{\partial b_j}.
\end{aligned}
\tag{9.13}
$$

In the backpropagation process, one often needs to compute the gradients of vectors, matrices, tensors, etc., and the Jacobian matrix is frequently used to represent such gradients. Suppose we want to find the gradient of $\boldsymbol{y} \in \mathbb{R}^{d_1}$ with regard to $\boldsymbol{x} \in \mathbb{R}^{d_2}$. We would obtain a $d_1 \times d_2$ matrix

$$
\frac{\partial \boldsymbol{y}}{\partial \boldsymbol{x}} =
\begin{bmatrix}
\frac{\partial y_1}{\partial x_1} & \cdots & \frac{\partial y_1}{\partial x_{d_2}} \\
\cdots & \cdots & \cdots \\
\frac{\partial y_{d_1}}{\partial x_1} & \cdots & \frac{\partial y_{d_1}}{\partial x_{d_2}}
\end{bmatrix}.
\tag{9.14}
$$

This representation extends to higher dimensions. As one may have noticed, backpropagation involves quite a bit of calculation and mathematical manipulation, which is tedious and error-prone, especially when the network becomes deep and complex. Luckily, numerous programming tools such as TensorFlow and PyTorch handle this entire process with their autograd packages. The user simply needs to define the network and the forward calculation, and backpropagation is carried out automatically. However, it is still important to clearly understand of the process, even though one almost never needs to do the computations manually in practice.

Gradient descent, stochastic gradient descent, momentum, learning rate

Having calculated the gradients for the trainable parameters, we update the parameters to reduce the loss. Intuitively, the larger the loss, the worse the model performs, and the further it is from the target function f^*; consequently we need to drastically modify the parameters to improve performance. Additionally, the more influence a parameter has on the overall loss value, the more it needs to be modified. Therefore, the following update rule is often used:

$$
\begin{aligned}
W^j &\leftarrow W^j - \alpha \frac{\partial \mathcal{L}}{\partial W^j}, \\
b^j &\leftarrow B^j - \alpha \frac{\partial \mathcal{L}}{\partial b^j}, \quad \alpha \in \mathbb{R}, \, j \in [N], \\
B^j &\leftarrow \underbrace{[b^j, \ldots, b^j]}_{m \text{ times}}.
\end{aligned}
\tag{9.15}
$$

This update rule is commonly known as gradient descent, and α is a hyperparameter called the learning rate, which controls the amount of change during one training cycle, or one epoch. In practice, the learning rate needs to be chosen carefully; if too large, the loss may diverge, and if too small, the network learns too slowly and incurs extra computational cost.

According to the gradient descent rule, we can decrease the loss in the most effective way by choosing to update the parameter along the direction that would result in the largest loss reduction, namely the direction of negative gradient. Geometrically, this approach would mean that we want to update the parameters in the "steepest" direction. We keep repeating this process until the loss value converges; in other words, we iteratively refine the parameters until the loss reaches the minimum.

There are a few caveats that need to be taken into account. First, as mentioned above, the choice of the learning rate is critical to the effectiveness of gradient descent. From the geometric perspective, if the learning rate is too high, it is possible to overstep the minimum. Second, although the algorithm always finds a relative minimum, it is not guaranteed that it always arrives at the global minimum when the objective function is nonconvex. Convex and nonconvex optimization is a sophisticated subject and is beyond the scope of this chapter, but there are numerous approaches that alleviate this drawback, including the usage of momentum. Third, it is often inefficient to train to calculate the gradient for the entire training set for a single parameter update; instead, we usually find it more effective to use a subset of the data, or mini-batch, for each epoch. This approach is called stochastic gradient descent and is widely used in practice.

There are many variations of the gradient descent algorithm, such as Adam, RMSprop, and Adagrad. One should have a basic idea of advantages of each and choose the most appropriate one to the application of interest.

Algorithm

To further discuss the FCNNs and CNNs, we now present the algorithm for training an N-layer network to yield the desired accuracy. The process is shown in Algorithm 1.

9.3 Tensor networks and their decompositions

9.3.1 Tensor networks

Curse of dimensionality

Machine learning relies heavily on efficient ways of processing and analyzing data. However, in recent years, as more powerful means of data collection have become available, the size and complexity of available data proliferate, and we begin to face the problem of the curse of dimensionality. In many industries and disciplines, effective analysis of multidimensional data with high volumes and great structural complexity is becoming crucial. Such data are very resource-expensive to analyze using traditional machine learning methods because the number of parameters in a dataset grows exponentially with regard to its order (or degrees of freedom). There has been growing interest in finding scalable machine learning algorithms that exploit

---

Algorithm 1: Training the neural network.

Input: data tensor $X \in \mathbb{R}^{n^2 \times m}$, $Y \in \mathbb{R}^{c \times m}$, N, and MaxEpoch.
Output: parameters $W^j \in \mathbb{R}^{\ell_j \times \ell_{j-1}}$, $B^j \in \mathbb{R}^{\ell_j \times m}$, $j \in [N]$.

1   Randomly initialize trainable parameters W^j, $B^j = \{\underbrace{b^j, ..., b^j}_{m \text{ times}}\}$, $j \in [N]$. Let

    $A^0 = X$ and set $t = 1$.

2   **while** *NOT converged or $t \leq$ MaxEpoch* **do**

3   **for** $j = 0, ..., N - 1$ **do**

4   Compute A^{j+1} via (9.7).

5   Compute $\mathcal{L}(A^N)$ via (9.4).

6   Compute $\partial \mathcal{L}/\partial A^N$ via (9.11).

7   **for** $j = N, ..., 1$ **do**

8   Compute $\partial \mathcal{L}/\partial A^j$, $\partial \mathcal{L}/\partial W^j$, and $\partial \mathcal{L}/\partial b^j$ via (9.13).

9   Update W^j and B^j via (9.15).

10      $t \leftarrow t + 1$.

11   **return** W^j, B^j, $j \in [N]$.

Algorithm 2: Inference using the neural network.

Input: unseen data $x \in \mathbb{R}^{n^2 \times 1}$ and trained parameters $W^j \in \mathbb{R}^{\ell_j \times \ell_{j-1}}$,
    $B^j = [\underbrace{b^j, ..., b^j}_{m \text{ times}}] \in \mathbb{R}^{\ell_j \times m}$, $j \in [N]$.
Output: predicted label $\widehat{y} \in \{1, ..., c\}$, where $c = \ell_N$.

1   Let $A^0 = x$.

2   **for** $j = 0, ..., N - 1$ **do**

3   Compute $A^{j+1} \leftarrow W^{j+1} A^j + b^j$.

4   Compute $\widehat{y} \leftarrow \text{softmax}(A^N)$.

5   Compute $\widehat{y} \leftarrow \arg\max \widehat{y}$.

6   **return** $\widehat{y}$.

---

the richness of big data while keeping computational and storage costs affordable. In the rest of this section, we will address this bottleneck of the curse of dimensionality using tensor networks.

Tensor network definitions and advantages

Tensor networks approximate high-order tensors via interconnected structures of low-rank core tensors (or tensors with small orders). Tensor networks have many major advantages that make them an attractive tool for tasks dealing with big data [17].

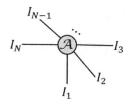

FIGURE 9.7

Graph representation of a tensor.

1. The ability to represent a high-volume tensor via a set of low-rank tensors makes the tasks of data processing and storage scalable enough for high-dimensional data, alleviating the curse of dimensionality.
2. The low-rank representation encapsulates the latent variables and interactions between modes in the original tensor, which helps achieve a sufficient rate of compression while maintaining the accuracy of the approximation.
3. Tensor networks allow mathematical operations to be carried out directly on the decomposed format, drastically reducing the computational cost.
4. The structures of tensor networks have intuitive graph representations, which increase the interpretability of mathematical operations and transformations.
5. The interconnection of the core tensors in the networks allows the extraction of information about correlations between different components.

Tensor network graphs

Fig. 9.7 represents an N-th-order tensor $\mathcal{X} \in \mathbb{R}^{I_1 \times I_2 \times \cdots \times I_N}$ in standard tensor graph notation, where each outgoing edge represents a mode, or a dimension, of the tensor.

Separation of variables, tensor decompositions

In order to obtain approximations of high-dimensional tensors in low-rank tensor format, we often utilize tensor decomposition algorithms, such as CP, Tucker, HT, and TT/TR. Before going into the technical details of each method, we need to introduce a general concept behind all decomposition algorithms: the separability of variables.

Assuming that the components of the high-dimensional tensor are to a certain extent independent, we approximate an N-variate function $f : \mathbb{R}^{I_1,...,I_N} \to \mathbb{R}^{I_1,...,I_N}$ with the sum of products of N one-variate functions f^n, for $n = 1, ..., N$:

$$f(x_1, ..., x_N) \approx f^1(x_1) f^2(x_2) \cdots f^N(x_N). \tag{9.16}$$

The function f is discretized to represent a multilinear transformation that describes an N-th-order tensor, and the one-variate functions f^n represent first-order tensors that collectively form the tensor network. In practice, the components of the data tensor are rarely independent, but this concept of approximation using the separation of variables underlies all decompositions.

9.3.2 CP tensor decomposition

CP format

The CP (CANDECOMP, PARAFAC, or Canonical Polyadic) decomposition [18] takes an order-N tensor $\mathcal{X} \in \mathbb{R}^{I_1 \times I_2 \times \cdots \times I_N}$, where I_n is the size of each mode, for $n \in [N]$. The CP format approximates the original with the sum of the outer products among a set of first-order tensors, $b_r^1, b_r^2, ..., b_r^N$.

The CP format is closely tied to the concept of the separation of variables. Using the terminologies in (9.16), we can express the CP format as

$$f(x_1, ..., x_N) \approx \sum_{r=1}^{R} g_r \times f_r^1(x_1) \circ \cdots \circ f_r^N(x_N). \tag{9.17}$$

Let $\mathcal{X} = f(x_1, ..., x_N)$ and $b^n = f^n(x_n)$ for $n = 1, ..., N$. We obtain the formal definition of the CP format:

$$\mathcal{X} \approx \sum_{r=1}^{R} g_r \times (b_r^1 \circ b_r^2 \circ \cdots \circ b_r^N), \tag{9.18}$$

where the quantity R is a parameter that controls how much the full tensor gets compressed; the larger the value R takes, the more accurate the approximation, and the smaller the compression ratio. Moreover, $g_r \in \mathbb{R}$ for $r = 1, ..., R$ is a set of scalar multipliers that control each outer product's weight.

Equivalently, the CP format is expressed in terms of tensor contractions:

$$\mathcal{X} \approx \mathcal{G} \times_1 B^1 \times_2 B^2 \times_3 \cdots \times_N B^N, \tag{9.19}$$

where $\mathcal{G} = \text{diag}(g_1, ..., g_R) \in \mathbb{R}^{R \times \cdots \times R}$ is the diagonal core tensor containing nonzero diagonal entries g_r for $r = 1, ..., R$, and each of the factor matrices has the shape $B^i \in \mathbb{R}^{I_i \times R}$. We write the CP format compactly using the multilinear product notation:

$$\mathcal{X} \approx [\![\mathcal{G}; B^1, B^2, ..., B^N]\!]. \tag{9.20}$$

Although this format yields simplicity and interpretability in decomposing the full tensor, its underlying assumption concludes that the modes are completely separable from the outer product, which is rarely applicable to real-world requirements. Therefore, this creates an error between the approximation and the original tensor larger than desired in certain applications.

Graphs

Fig. 9.8 demonstrates the two equivalent forms of the CP format of a third-order data tensor. On the top row, the full tensor is represented by the multilinear product between a diagonal core tensor and three factor matrices. On the bottom row, the data tensor is approximated by the sum of N order-1 tensors.

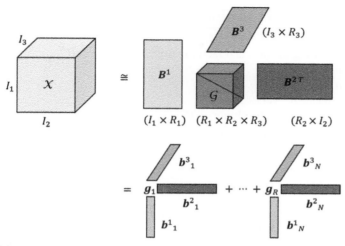

FIGURE 9.8

CP tensor decomposition.

Matricization and vectorization

The factor matrices in CP format also effectively compute the matricized format and vector format of the original full tensor $\mathcal{X}$ directly, using the Khatri–Rao product, $\odot$. Matricization and vectorization are commonly used operations that unfold or flatten the tensor into a matrix or a vector. We use $X_{(n)}$ and $X_{<n>}$ to represent the mode-n matricization and mode-n canonical matricization of $\mathcal{X}$, respectively. The ability to transform from factor matrices to different representations of the original tensor gives us more flexibility and control in manipulating the data.

The mode-n matricization of $\mathcal{X}$ is approximated by

$$
\begin{aligned}
X_{(n)} &\approx B^n \mathcal{G}(B^N \odot \cdots \odot B^{n+1} \odot B^{n-1} \odot \cdots \odot B^1)^T, \\
X_{<n>} &\approx (B^n \odot \cdots \odot B^1)\mathcal{G}(B^N \odot \cdots \odot B^{n+1})^T.
\end{aligned}
\tag{9.21}
$$

The vectorization of $\mathcal{X}$ is similarly approximated by

$$
\mathrm{vec}(\mathcal{X}) \approx (B^N \odot B^{N-1} \odot \cdots \odot B^1)g,
\tag{9.22}
$$

where $g = [g_1, ..., g_R]^T \in \mathbb{R}^R$.

Alternative least-squares algorithm

The CP format is iteratively approximated with the alternative least-squares (ALS) algorithms by updating each factor matrix regarding the loss function while keeping other factor matrices unchanged. To be precise, for each of the factor matrices, B^n, for $n = 1, ..., N$, we will update B^n with the formula

$$
B^n \leftarrow X^{(n)}[\odot_{k \neq n} B^k][\circledast_{k \neq n}(B^{(k)T} B^k)]^\dagger.
\tag{9.23}
$$

Algorithm 3: Basic ALS for CP decomposition.

Input: Tensor $\mathcal{X} \in \mathbb{R}^{I_1 \times I_2 \times \cdots \times I_N}$
Output: Scaling factor λ and factor matrices $\boldsymbol{B}^1, \boldsymbol{B}^2, ..., \boldsymbol{B}^N$

1 **while** *not converged* **do**
2   **for** *n = 1, ..., N* **do**
3   Update $\boldsymbol{B}^n$ via (9.23)
4   Normalize each column of $\boldsymbol{B}^n$
5   Store the norms in the scaling vector λ
6 **return** $\boldsymbol{B}^1, \boldsymbol{B}^2, ..., \boldsymbol{B}^N$ and λ.

This update is done for each factor matrix during each iteration and should be repeated until the loss function converges. Note that the speed of this algorithm is strongly influenced by the Khatri–Rao product and the pseudo-inverse operation.

Connection to tensor networks, complexity analysis

The CP format can be interpreted as a tensor network with a simple structure, where the high-dimensional input tensor is approximated by a set of second-order factor tensors. One important thing to note is the number of parameters required to describe the tensor network. Without loss of generality let us assume that the input tensor $\mathcal{X}$ has size I in each of its N components. Then the number of parameters in $\mathcal{X}$ is I^N. On the other hand, the tensor network parameters obtained by using CP decomposition have only $NRI < NI^2$, which scales linearly, rather than exponentially, with tensor order N.

9.3.3 Tucker decomposition

Tucker format, comparison with CP

The Tucker decomposition offers a more generalized representation of the high-dimensional tensor than the CP decomposition, and therefore its performance may be superior to that of CP. The Tucker format has factor matrices representing every mode in the original tensor, but the core tensor now has more representational power to capture the complexity of interactions between the factors [18].

Going back to the analogy with the separation of variables, we draw a parallel between Tucker decomposition and Eqs. (9.16) and (9.17):

$$f(x_1, ..., x_N) \approx \sum_{r_1=1}^{R_1} \cdots \sum_{r_N=1}^{R_N} g_{r_1, ..., r_N} \times f_{r_1}^1(x_1) \cdots f_{r_N}^N(x_N). \qquad (9.24)$$

Whereas the core tensor of the CP format is diagonal, the Tucker format has a full tensor, $\mathcal{G} \in \mathbb{R}^{R_1 \times R_2 \times \cdots \times R_N}$. Using the conventional notations, we have the following

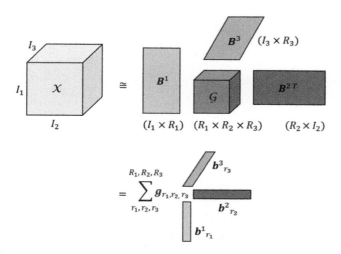

FIGURE 9.9

Tucker tensor decomposition.

decomposition formulas:

$$\mathcal{X} \approx \sum_{r_1=1}^{R_1} \cdots \sum_{r_N=1}^{R_N} g_{r_1,\dots,r_N} \times (b_{r_1}^1 \circ b_{r_2}^2 \circ \cdots \circ b_{r_N}^N)$$

$$= \mathcal{G} \times_1 B^1 \times_2 B^2 \times_3 \cdots \times_N B^N$$

$$= [\![\mathcal{G}; B^1, B^2, \dots, B^N]\!].$$

The CP format is a special case of the Tucker format, where all entries except the diagonal are zero in the core tensor.

Multilinear rank, independent/orthonormal Tucker format

The multilinear rank of the full tensor $\mathcal{X} \in \mathbb{R}^{I_1 \times I_2 \times \cdots \times I_N}$ is a set of N rank values $\{R_1, R_2, \dots, R_N\}$. Formally, the multilinear rank is expressed as

$$\text{rank}_{ML} = \{\text{rank}^{(1)}, \text{rank}^{(2)}, \dots, \text{rank}^{(n)}\}. \tag{9.25}$$

If the decomposed tensor has all its factor matrices in full column rank, it is called an independent Tucker format. Additionally, if a tensor is in independent format and has its factor matrices orthogonal to each other, it is in the orthonormal Tucker format. These special formats have many important properties with regard to the multilinear rank.

Graphs

Fig. 9.9 demonstrates the two equivalent forms of the Tucker format of a third-order data tensor. The full tensor is represented by the multilinear product between a

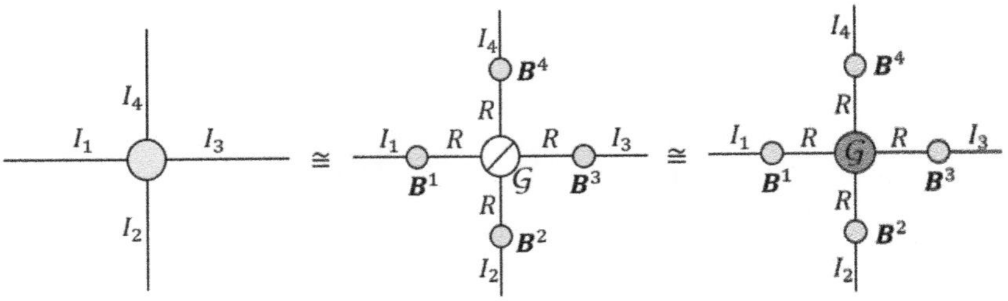

FIGURE 9.10

CP vs. Tucker tensor decompositions.

core tensor and three factor matrices, or equivalently by the scaled sum of N order-1 tensors. Unlike the CP format, the core tensor is nondiagonal.

Fig. 9.10 compares the CP and Tucker formats. On the leftmost is a fourth-order full tensor $\mathcal{X} \in \mathbb{R}^{I_1 \times I_2 \times I_3 \times I_4}$ in the standard tensor graph. In the middle and on the right are the CP- and the Tucker-decomposed $\mathcal{X}$, respectively.

Matricization and vectorization

The Tucker format also has direct operations that transform it into matrix and vector representations:

$$X_{(n)} \approx B^n \, G^{(n)} \, (B^N \otimes \cdots \otimes B^{n+1} \otimes B^{n-1} \otimes \cdots \otimes B^1)^T,$$
$$X_{<n>} \approx (B^n \otimes \cdots \otimes B^1) \, G_{<n>} \, (B^N \otimes \cdots \otimes B^{n+1})^T, \qquad (9.26)$$
$$\text{vec}(\mathcal{X}) \approx (B^N \odot B^{N-1} \odot \cdots \odot B^1) \, \text{vec}(\mathcal{G}).$$

The structures of the matricization and vectorization formulas for the Tucker format are very similar to the CP counterparts, except that the Khatri–Rao product is replaced by the Kronecker product and the core tensor is replaced by the matricization and vectorization in the mode of interest.

Singular value decomposition and higher-order singular value decomposition algorithms

The higher-order singular value decomposition (HOSVD) algorithm computes the Tucker format for a given tensor by iteratively applying the truncated SVD algorithm to each mode of the input tensor until the loss function converges.

The HOSVD algorithm does not always yield the optimal rank approximation, and it is often helpful to apply the higher-order orthogonal iteration (HOOI) algorithm to improve the accuracy of the approximation.

Higher-order orthogonal iteration algorithm.

Algorithm 4: Truncated HOSVD for Tucker decomposition.

Input: Tensor $\mathcal{X} \in \mathbb{R}^{I_1 \times I_2 \times \cdots \times I_N}$, approximation accuracy ϵ.
Output: Tucker format $\widehat{\mathcal{X}} = [\![\mathcal{G}; \boldsymbol{B}^1, \boldsymbol{B}^2, ..., \boldsymbol{B}^N]\!]$ such that $\|\mathcal{X} - \widehat{\mathcal{X}}\|_F \leq \epsilon$.

1 $\mathcal{S} \leftarrow \mathcal{X}$
2 **for** $n = 1, ..., N$ **do**
3 $\quad$ $[\boldsymbol{B}^n, \boldsymbol{S}, \boldsymbol{V}] = \text{truncated-SVD}(\boldsymbol{S}^{(n)}, \frac{\epsilon}{\sqrt{N}})$
4 $\quad$ $\mathcal{S} \leftarrow \boldsymbol{V}\boldsymbol{S}$
5 $\mathcal{S} \leftarrow \text{reshape}(\mathcal{S}, [R_1, ..., R_N])$
6 **return** core tensor $\mathcal{G}$ and orthogonal factor matrices $\boldsymbol{B}^n \in \mathbb{R}^{I_n \times R_N}$, for $n = 1, ..., N$.

Algorithm 5: Higher-order orthogonal iteration (HOOI).

Input: Tensor $\mathcal{X} \in \mathbb{R}^{I_1 \times I_2 \times \cdots \times I_N}$
Output: Improved approximation with ALS algorithm with factor matrices
$\quad\quad$ $\boldsymbol{B}^1, \boldsymbol{B}^2, ..., \boldsymbol{B}^N$

1 **while** *the cost function* $\|\mathcal{G}\|_F^2 - \|\mathcal{X}\|_F^2$ *is not converged* **do**
2 $\quad$ **for** $n = 1, ..., N$ **do**
3 $\quad\quad$ $\mathcal{Z} \leftarrow \mathcal{X} \times_{p \neq n} \boldsymbol{B}^{(p)T}$
4 $\quad\quad$ $\boldsymbol{C} \leftarrow \mathcal{Z}^{(n)} \mathcal{Z}^{(n)T} \in \mathbb{R}^{R \times R}$
5 $\quad\quad$ $\boldsymbol{B}^n \leftarrow$ leading R_n eigenvectors of $\boldsymbol{C}$
6 $\quad$ $\mathcal{G} \leftarrow \mathcal{Z} \times_N \boldsymbol{B}^{(n)T}$
7 **return** improved approximation with core tensor $\mathcal{G}$ and orthogonal factor matrices $\boldsymbol{B}^n \in \mathbb{R}^{I_n \times R_N}$, for $n = 1, ..., N$.

9.3.4 Hierarchical Tucker decomposition

Tree structure

HT decomposition, also known as hierarchical tensor decomposition, is a decomposition scheme that results in a tensor network with the structure of tree structures [19]. The HT has a flexible structure and has been found to be useful for compressing many network architectures such as CNNs and recurrent neural networks [20]. The tree topology is acyclic, meaning no path from any node goes back to itself, and each node has at most two children. Every mode of the full tensor is contained in the tree's leaf nodes, and each branch of the tree contains a subset of all modes. To be mathematically precise, we say that the topology of the HT decomposition is a binary dimension tree T that contains N nodes $\{t_1, ..., t_N\}$, regulated by the following principles.

1. For all nodes $t \in T_N$, the subtree T_t under t satisfies $T_t \subseteq \{1, ..., N\}$ and $T_t \neq \emptyset$.

2. The subtree under the root node of T satisfies $T_{root} = \{1, ..., N\}$.
3. Each nonleaf node t has two children $u, v \in T_N$ such that $T_u \cap T_v = \emptyset$ and $T_t = T_u \cup T_v$.

Implementation and algorithm

This decomposition is often implemented by recursively matricizng the core tensor and separating the modes with the truncated SVD algorithm.

First, the dimension tree is chosen before any decomposition is done so that the topology of the decomposition is decided based on prior knowledge. For example, we can choose the binary tree structure as discussed above. The dimension tree informs that certain groups of modes should be separated from another group of modes at a specific level in the tree structure.

Second, starting from the root node, the core tensor is matricized according to the dimension tree, such that its row and column contain the two disjoint sets of modes that are to be separated.

Then, the truncated SVD is applied to the matricized tensor, and the resulting matrices are reshaped into smaller core tensors that become the children of the current node.

This process is repeated recursively until the leaf nodes are reached:

$$\mathcal{X} = \sum_{r_{1234}=1}^{R_{1234}} \sum_{r_{5678}=1}^{R_{5678}} g_{r_{1234},r_{5678}}^{12...8} \mathcal{X}_{r_{1234}}^{1234} \circ \mathcal{X}_{r_{5678}}^{5678},$$

$$\mathcal{X}_{r_{1234}}^{1234} = \sum_{r_{12}=1}^{R_{12}} \sum_{r_{34}=1}^{R_{34}} g_{r_{12},r_{34},r_{1234}}^{1234} \mathcal{X}_{r_{12}}^{12} \circ \mathcal{X}_{r_{34}}^{34},$$

$$\mathcal{X}_{r_{5678}}^{5678} = \sum_{r_{56}=1}^{R_{56}} \sum_{r_{78}=1}^{R_{78}} g_{r_{56},r_{78},r_{5678}}^{5678} \mathcal{X}_{r_{56}}^{56} \circ \mathcal{X}_{r_{78}}^{78},$$

$$\mathcal{X}_{r_{12}}^{12} = \sum_{r_1=1}^{R_1} \sum_{r_2=1}^{R_2} g_{r_1,r_2,r_{12}}^{12} \boldsymbol{b}_{r_1}^1 \circ \boldsymbol{b}_{r_2}^2, \qquad (9.27)$$

$$\mathcal{X}_{r_{34}}^{34} = \sum_{r_3=1}^{R_3} \sum_{r_4=1}^{R_4} g_{r_3,r_4,r_{34}}^{34} \boldsymbol{b}_{r_3}^3 \circ \boldsymbol{b}_{r_4}^4,$$

$$\mathcal{X}_{r_{56}}^{56} = \sum_{r_5=1}^{R_5} \sum_{r_6=1}^{R_6} g_{r_5,r_6,r_{56}}^{56} \boldsymbol{b}_{r_5}^5 \circ \boldsymbol{b}_{r_6}^6,$$

$$\mathcal{X}_{r_{78}}^{78} = \sum_{r_7=1}^{R_7} \sum_{r_8=1}^{R_8} g_{r_7,r_8,r_{78}}^{78} \boldsymbol{b}_{r_7}^7 \circ \boldsymbol{b}_{r_8}^8.$$

Fig. 9.11 shows a concrete example of HT decomposition. An eighth-order data tensor $\mathcal{X} \in \mathbb{R}^{I_1 \times \cdots \times I_8}$ is approximated with a binary tree containing core tensors $\mathcal{G}^m$

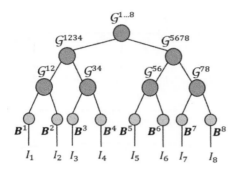

FIGURE 9.11

HT tensor decomposition.

and factor matrices $\boldsymbol{B}^n$. Each of these cores and factors is defined precisely with recursion.

Connection to Tucker, tree tensor network state

The HT decomposition can be viewed as a modification of the Tucker format, where the single core tensor in the Tucker format is replaced by a sparsely interconnected tensor network with the structure of a binary tree. In the Tucker format, the core tensor is connected to every factor matrix, whereas in the HT format, only a subset of core tensors are connected to the factors.

This concept of representing the core tensor with a tensor network leads to two generalizations: distributed tensor networks (DTNs) and tree tensor network state (TTNS). DTNs are tensor networks in which there are two types of cores: internal cores denote tensors whose edges are all connected to other tensors and external cores are tensors that have free edges representing the original modes of the full tensor. Another direct generalization of the HT format is TTNS, which are acyclic networks containing core tensors with orders of at least 3. These distributed models are in general not unique for any given high-dimensional tensor, allowing for diverse and context-specific representations of a data tensor in terms of a network of low-rank core tensors.

9.3.5 Tensor train and tensor ring decomposition

Tensor train definition

The TT format, which is also known as matrix product state (MPS), approximates a high-dimensional data tensor $\mathcal{X} \in \mathbb{R}^{I_1 \times \cdots \times I_N}$ with a set of third-order core tensors $\mathcal{G}^n$ for $n = 1, \ldots, N$, where $\mathcal{G}^n \in \mathbb{R}^{R_{n-1} \times I_n \times R_n}$ [21]. The tensor network constructed using TT decomposition has a cascade structure, such that the tensor cores are connected to their neighbors on the left and the right via a multilinear multiplication (tensor contraction). Here, I_n represents the physical modes in the data tensor and R_n regulates the rank of the internal modes that will be contracted to connect the core

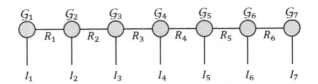

FIGURE 9.12

Tensor train decomposition.

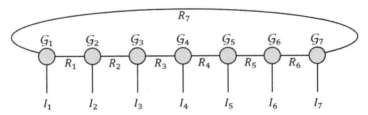

FIGURE 9.13

Tensor ring decomposition.

tensor to its neighbors. The leftmost and rightmost cores have only one neighbor, so $R_0 = R_N = 1$.

The TR format, also known as tensor chain format, is analogous to the TT format. The only difference is that there exists a nontrivial connection between the first and last cores, forming a cyclic network structure. In the case of TR decomposition, $R_0 = R_N = c \in \mathbb{N}$.

Figs. 9.12 and 9.13 show the topological structure of the decomposed seventh-order tensor in the TT and TR formats. In both cases, the original tensor is represented using a set of third-order cores, where one outgoing edge represents a physical dimension. The only difference between the TT and TR representations is the connectivity between the first and the last core.

Mathematical formulations

Formally, the TT decomposition takes the following form:

$$\mathcal{X} \approx \mathcal{G}^1 \times^1 \mathcal{G}^2 \times^1 \cdots \times^1 \mathcal{G}^N$$
$$= \langle\langle \mathcal{G}^1, \mathcal{G}^2, ..., \mathcal{G}^N \rangle\rangle, \tag{9.28}$$

where $\mathcal{G}^n \in \mathbb{R}^{R_{n-1} \times I_n \times R_n}$ for $n = 1, ..., N$ are the core tensors.

Fig. 9.14 shows how the TT format is expressed using a sequence of multilinear multiplications among sets of matrices. This interpretation of TT decomposition gives rise to convenient manipulation and computation of data.

It is also easy to obtain the approximation-specific entry in the data tensor using the slice representation:

$$\mathcal{X}(i_1, i_2, ..., i_N) \approx \mathcal{G}^1_{i_1} \times^1 \mathcal{G}^2_{i_2} \times^1 \cdots \times^1 \mathcal{G}^N_{i_N}. \tag{9.29}$$

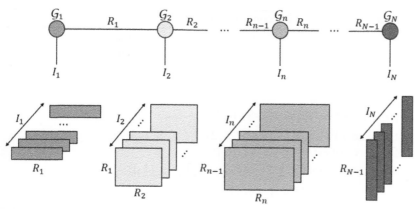

FIGURE 9.14

Matrix product state.

Equivalently, there is a representation using the sum of outer products between fiber vectors:

$$\mathcal{X} \approx \sum_{r_1=1}^{R_1} \cdots \sum_{r_N=1}^{R_N} g^1_{1,\, r_1} \circ g^2_{r_1,\, r_2} \circ \cdots \circ g^N_{r_{N-1},\, 1}, \tag{9.30}$$

where $g^n_{r_{n-1},r_n} \in \mathbb{R}^{I_n}$ are fiber vectors. This representation also gives rise to the entry-wise scalar form:

$$\mathcal{X}(i_1, i_2, ..., i_N) \approx \sum_{r_1=1}^{R_1} \cdots \sum_{r_N=1}^{R_N} g^1_{1,\, i_1,\, r_1} g^2_{r_1,\, i_2,\, r_2} \cdots g^N_{r_{N-1},\, i_n,\, 1}. \tag{9.31}$$

Algorithms for TT

The TT-SVD algorithm decomposes a data tensor into the TT format by matricizing the data tensor, applying the (truncated) SVD algorithm to this matrix to obtain factors U, S, V, extracting a core tensor from U, and reshaping SV^T to the next matrix to factor until all cores have been extracted.

Advantages of the TT format

The TT format is widely used in constructing tensor networks because it exhibits many significant advantages.

1. Basic mathematical operations are conveniently applied to tensors in the TT format.
2. Unlike the HT format, the topology of the tensor network does not need to be specified using prior knowledge about the data.
3. The TT format employs only core tensors and no factor matrices, achieving greater simplicity with fewer parameters.
4. The number of parameters scales linearly with the tensor order N.

Algorithm 6: Tensor train decomposition.

Input: Tensor $\mathcal{X} \in \mathbb{R}^{I_1 \times I_2 \times \cdots \times I_N}$, approximation accuracy ϵ.
Output: Tensor train format $\widehat{\mathcal{X}} = \langle\langle \mathcal{G}^1, \mathcal{G}^2, ..., \mathcal{G}^N \rangle\rangle$ such that $\| \mathcal{X} - \widehat{\mathcal{X}} \|_F \le \epsilon$.

1   $M_1 \leftarrow \mathcal{X}^{(1)}$
2   $R_0 \leftarrow 1$
3   **for** $n = 1, ..., N\text{-}1$ **do**
4     $[U^n, S^n, V^n] \leftarrow$ truncated-SVD$(M_n, \frac{\epsilon}{\sqrt{N-1}})$
5   Estimate TT rank $R_n \leftarrow$ size$(U^n, 2)$
6     $\mathcal{G}^n \leftarrow$ reshape$(U^n, [R_{n-1}, I_n, R_n])$
7     $M_{n+1} \leftarrow$ reshape$(S^n V^{(n)T}, [R_n I_{n+1}, \prod_{p=n+2}^{N} I_p])$
8   $\mathcal{G}^n \leftarrow$ reshape $(M_N, [R_{N-1}, I_N, 1])$
9   **return** tensor network $\widehat{\mathcal{X}} = \langle\langle \mathcal{G}^1, \mathcal{G}^2, ..., \mathcal{G}^N \rangle\rangle$.

9.3.6 Transform-based tensor decomposition

Motivation

So far, we have seen decomposition methods that are high-dimensional generalizations of the matrix SVD and QR algorithms and how these methods are used to construct tensor networks. However, these methods face many limitations, and most of them fail to preserve the original properties of the matrix SVD algorithm.

Now we introduce an alternative family of tensor decompositions that offers many attractive benefits. This family of decompositions uses the t-product as the core operation and decomposes third-order tensors in the transform domain [22]. Compared to other methods, the transform-based approach has greater potential of preserving matrix-like properties and enables greater utilization of parallelism, making it a useful and attractive choice for many applications.

Basic tensor operations

Here we introduce face-wise operations, tubal operations, and block-circulant structures.

First, let us define a few key notations commonly used in transform domain tensor operations. Note that the tubal structures are suitable to be computed on GPUs for high-performance tasks, as recent studies showed [23,24].

Given a third-order tensor $\mathcal{A} \in \mathbb{R}^{l \times m \times n}$, we define $a_{ij} \in \mathbb{R}^{1 \times 1 \times n}$, $i = 1, ..., l$, $j = 1, ..., m$, to be the tubal fibers of $\mathcal{A}$ taken along the third dimension (into the page). In MATLAB® notation, $a_{ij} = \mathcal{A}(i, j, :)$. We denote the frontal slices of $\mathcal{A}$ as $A^{(k)} \in \mathbb{R}^{l \times m \times 1}$, $k = 1, ..., n$. In MATLAB notation, $A^{(k)} = \mathcal{A}(:, :, k)$.

Fig. 9.15 shows the four different representations of a third-order tensor. From left to right are the full tenor, frontal slices, lateral slices, and tubal fibers.

The block-circulant (bcirc) matrix is a tensor representation that exhibits circulant structures, which is fundamental for the definition of the t-product. The block-

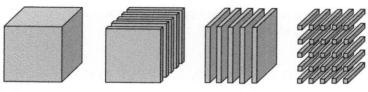

FIGURE 9.15

Slices and tubal fibers of a third-order tensor.

circulant matrix of the frontal slices of tensor $\mathcal{A}$ is defined to be

$$
\text{bcirc}(\mathcal{A}) = \begin{bmatrix} A^{(1)} & A^{(n)} & \dots & A^{(2)} \\ A^{(2)} & A^{(1)} & \dots & A^{(3)} \\ \vdots & \vdots & \ddots & \vdots \\ A^{(n)} & A^{(n-1)} & \dots & A^{(1)} \end{bmatrix} \in \mathbb{C}^{ln \times mn}. \tag{9.32}
$$

We also define the unfold($\mathcal{A}$) operation as the first column of bcirc($\mathcal{A}$), and fold(unfold($\mathcal{A}$)) = $\mathcal{A}$. Note that the fold($\cdot$) operation is well defined because one simply stacks the frontal slices along the third dimension.

One variation of the standard block-circulant matrix is the Toeplitz-plus-Hankel matrix which is relevant to our purposes:

$$
\text{mat}(\mathcal{A}) = \begin{bmatrix} A^{(1)} & A^{(2)} & \dots & A^{(n)} \\ A^{(2)} & A^{(1)} & \dots & A^{(n-1)} \\ \vdots & \vdots & \ddots & \vdots \\ A^{(n)} & A^{(n-1)} & \dots & A^{(1)} \end{bmatrix} + \begin{bmatrix} A^{(2)} & \dots & A^{(n)} & 0 \\ \vdots & \ddots & \ddots & A^{(n)} \\ A^{(n)} & 0 & \ddots & \vdots \\ 0 & A^{(n)} & \dots & A^{(2)} \end{bmatrix} \in \mathbb{C}^{ln \times mn}.
$$
$$\tag{9.33}$$

Similar to the fold($\cdot$) and unfold($\cdot$) operations, mat($\cdot$) also has a counterpart operation, ten($\cdot$), such that ten(mat($\mathcal{A}$)) = $\mathcal{A}$. It can be verified that this operation is also invertible and well defined.

Discrete Fourier transform, discrete cosine transform, t-product

The transform-based tensor decompositions are based upon the t-product, which is also known as the tensor–tensor product or the tensor product. Traditionally, the t-product is defined under the discrete Fourier transform (DFT) and the block-circulant matrix.

Given two third-order tensors $\mathcal{A} \in \mathbb{R}^{l \times m \times n}$ and $\mathcal{B} \in \mathbb{R}^{m \times p \times n}$, the t-product $\bullet$ with regard to the DFT is defined as follows:

$$
\mathcal{A} \bullet \mathcal{B} = \text{fold}(\text{bcirc}(\mathcal{A})\text{unfold}(\mathcal{B})). \tag{9.34}
$$

Let $\mathfrak{R} = \mathbb{R}^Q$, $Q = n$. We write the t-product between $\mathcal{A} \in \mathfrak{R}^{l \times m}$ and $\mathcal{B} \in \mathfrak{R}^{m \times p}$ as $\mathcal{C} = \mathcal{A} \bullet \mathcal{B} \in \mathfrak{R}^{l \times p}$, where

$$\mathcal{C}_{i,j} = \sum_{k=1}^{m} \mathcal{A}_{i,k} \cdot \mathcal{B}_{k,j}, \quad i \in [l], \; j \in [p]. \tag{9.35}$$

Let $\widetilde{\mathcal{A}}$ denote the representation of $\mathcal{A}$ in the transform domain, obtained after applying a certain transformation $\mathcal{F}$, such that $\widetilde{\mathcal{A}} = \mathcal{F}(\mathcal{A})$ and $\mathcal{A} = \mathcal{F}^{-1}(\widetilde{\mathcal{A}})$. In this context, let $\mathcal{F}(\cdot) = \mathrm{fft}(\cdot, [\;], 3)$ and $\mathcal{F}^{-1}(\cdot) = \mathrm{ifft}(\cdot, [\;], 3)$. We rewrite (9.35) using frontal slice operations, such that

$$\widetilde{\boldsymbol{C}}^{(q)} = \widetilde{\boldsymbol{A}}^{(q)} \cdot \widetilde{\boldsymbol{B}}^{(q)}, \quad q \in [Q]. \tag{9.36}$$

The usage of transform operations allows us to efficiently implement the t-product in the transform domain, without explicitly dealing with block-circulant matrices, which are often computationally expensive. Moreover, the t-product operation can be split into Q subroutines and thus enable the implementation of model parallelism using efficient distributed methods.

The t-product defined with regard to the DFT has a critical shortcoming: even for real-valued input tensors, the implementation involves using complex arithmetic in the intermediate steps, which is more computationally expensive than real arithmetic. Alternatively, the discrete cosine transform (DCT) variation of the t-product is defined using the Toeplitz-plus-Hankel matrix:

$$\mathcal{A} \bullet \mathcal{B} = \mathrm{ten}(\mathrm{mat}(\mathcal{A})\mathrm{mat}(\mathcal{B})). \tag{9.37}$$

Note that Eqs. (9.35) and (9.36) still hold under $\mathcal{F}(\cdot) = \mathrm{dct}(\cdot, [\;], 3)$ and $\mathcal{F}^{-1}(\cdot) = \mathrm{idct}(\cdot, [\;], 3)$. Due to the advantages of the DCT-based t-product, we use $\bullet$ to refer to the DCT-based t-product unless otherwise specified in the remainder of this chapter.

Parallel computing

To apply tensor decomposition algorithms to accelerate neural networks, the major advantage of transform-based tensor decomposition lies in its potential for parallelism. As demonstrated by Eq. (9.36), the implementation cosine transform product utilizes the face-wise operation, and the bulk of work is done between the frontal slices of the input tensors in the transform domain, which is highly parallelizable. Therefore, it is very natural to treat the frontal slices as separate entities, feed them into separate channels, and process them in parallel-computing devices, such as GPUs. This feature enables us to process the data using efficient computational techniques such as multiprocessing.

9.4 Compressing deep neural networks

9.4.1 Compressing fully connected layers

Compressing the weight matrix using SVD

The weights in fully connected layers are stored in a matrix instead of a tensor. Therefore, it is very natural and straightforward to approximate using the (truncated) SVD algorithm. As mentioned in Section 9.2.3, the operation in the j-th fully connected layer is described by a linear operation followed by an activation function.

Suppose $W \in \mathbb{R}^{S \times T}$. We can decompose $W = USV^T$ using the (truncated) SVD algorithm, where $U \in \mathbb{R}^{S \times R}$, $S \in \mathbb{R}^{R \times R}$, $V \in \mathbb{R}^{T \times R}$, $R \in \mathbb{Z}^+$. This decomposition allows us to conduct an approximated form of the original operation, such that

$$A^j = \sigma(U^j S^j (V^j)^T A^{j-1} + B^j), \quad j \in [N]. \tag{9.38}$$

This compression scheme allows us to reduce the number of parameters in the weight matrix, assuming that the choice of rank R makes R significantly smaller than both S and T.

High-order tensorization, TT decomposition

Although the SVD algorithm has the advantage of simplicity and the ease of implementation, it has limited potential in compressing large-scale weight matrices. Modern neural networks, especially CNNs, often use large weight matrices containing tens or hundreds of thousands of parameters, which motivates a higher rate of compression than that of SVD.

To the best of our knowledge, there is currently no research on decomposing the fully connected layers with CP or Tucker methods. Therefore, we first introduce the technique of decomposing the fully connected layer into the TT format proposed by Novikov et al. [25] and then extend the technique to other decomposition schemes. Novikov et al. [25] propose to first reshape the weight matrix $W \in \mathbb{R}^{S \times T}$ into a d-dimensional tensor $\mathcal{W} \in \mathbb{R}^{S_1 T_1 \times \cdots \times S_d T_d}$ and then reshape the offset matrix $B^T \in \mathbb{R}^T$ into a d-dimensional tensor $\mathcal{B} \in \mathbb{R}^{T_1 \times \cdots T_d}$, where $S = \Pi_{i=1}^d S_i$, $T = \Pi_{i=1}^d T_i$.

Given the matrix A obtained from (9.38) and its tensorized counterpart $\mathcal{A}$, we use $(\mu_k(\cdot), \nu_k(\cdot))$ as a compound index to establish a relationship between the matrix and tensor representations:

$$\begin{aligned} A(i, j) &= \mathcal{A}((\mu_1(i), \nu_1(j)), ..., (\mu_d(i), \nu_d(j))) \\ &\approx \mathcal{G}_1(\mu_1(i), \nu_1(j)), ..., \mathcal{G}(\mu_d(i), \nu_d(j)). \end{aligned} \tag{9.39}$$

Using the notation of compound index, we decompose $\mathcal{W}$ into the TT format and establish the following relationship:

$$\begin{aligned} W(t, l) &= \mathcal{W}((\mu_1(i), \nu_1(j)), ..., (\mu_d(i), \nu_d(j))) \\ &\approx \mathcal{G}_1(\mu_1(i), \nu_1(j)), ..., \mathcal{G}(\mu_d(i), \nu_d(j)). \end{aligned} \tag{9.40}$$

TT layer, forward pass

Using matrix decomposition, we express the entire layer in terms of tensor networks, specifically the TT format. The forward pass operation of a fully connected layer is done in tensor networks:

$$A(i_1, ..., i_d) = \sum_{j_1, ..., j_d} \mathcal{G}_1(i_1, j_1) \cdots \mathcal{G}_d(i_d, j_d) \mathcal{A}(j_1, ..., j_d) + \mathcal{B}(i_1, ..., i_d). \quad (9.41)$$

Compressing the weight matrix using CP and Tucker decompositions

Using the same technique of reshaping the weight matrix W, the offset matrix B, and the data matrix A into higher-order tensors $\mathcal{W}$, $\mathcal{B}$, and $\mathcal{A}$ respectively, we can apply CP and Tucker decompositions to compress the fully connected layers in a similar manner.

Using CP decomposition, with compound indexing, we can write the forward pass in a layer in the following way:

$$A^l(i_1, ..., i_d) = \sum_{j_1, ..., j_d} \left(\sum_{r=1}^R g_r \times \mathcal{G}_r^1(i_1, j_1) \circ \cdots \circ \mathcal{G}_r^d(i_d, j_d) \right) \mathcal{A}(j_1, ..., j_d)$$
$$+ \mathcal{B}(i_1, ..., i_d). \quad (9.42)$$

Similarly, the Tucker-decomposed fully connected layer is expressed as

$$A^l(i_1, ..., i_d) = \sum_{j_1, ..., j_d} \left(\sum_{r_1=1}^{R_1} \cdots \sum_{r_d=1}^{R_d} g_{r_1, ..., r_d} \times \mathcal{G}_{r_1}^1(i_1, j_1) \circ \cdots \circ \mathcal{G}_{r_d}^d(i_d, j_d) \right)$$
$$\mathcal{A}(j_1, ..., j_d) + \mathcal{B}(i_1, ..., i_d). \quad (9.43)$$

Having defined the explicit formula of forward pass with any of these schemes, the backward pass is done automatically with automatic differentiation.

9.4.2 Compressing the convolutional layer via CP decomposition

The typical CNN is comprised of a sequence of convolutional layers followed by a sequence of fully connected layers. Both the convolutional and fully connected layers contain weights that are stored in tensor or matrix format. The goal of all neural network decomposition methods is to approximate the weights using decomposed tensor formats and conduct the multiplication or convolution operations between the weights and data using tensor network operations. Using neural network compression, we reduce the required storage space while accelerating the training and inference process without significant sacrifice in performance. In this section, we are going to focus on the decomposition of convolutional layers.

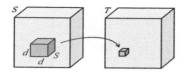

FIGURE 9.16

Full convolutional operation.

Convolution graphs

Fig. 9.16 represents the full convolution operation. The gray blocks represent the input and output data tensors in a convolutional layer, and the arrows represent linear mapping. The width and height dimensions represent the spatial dimensions, while the depth represents the channels. The yellow cube on the left represents the kernel tensor, and the smaller yellow cube on the right is the dot product of the kernel and the data tensors.

CP-decomposed kernel tensor

Lebedev et al. [26] propose applying CP decomposition to the kernel tensor and then fine-tune the resulting factor matrices as the weights of the decomposed network. Applying CP decomposition to the kernel tensor $\mathcal{K}$ in (9.10) gives the following expression:

$$\mathcal{K}(i, j, s, t) \approx \sum_{r=1}^{R} \boldsymbol{K}^x(i - x + \delta, r) \boldsymbol{K}^y(j - y + \delta, r) \boldsymbol{K}^s(s, r) \boldsymbol{K}^t(t, r), \qquad (9.44)$$

where $\boldsymbol{K}^x$, $\boldsymbol{K}^y$, $\boldsymbol{K}^s$, $\boldsymbol{K}^t$ are the factor matrices of $\mathcal{K}$, each representing a mode.

New convolutional operation

Using these factor matrices, we compute the forward pass by multiplying the data tensor along each dimension:

$$\mathcal{V}(x, y, t) \approx \sum_{r=1}^{R} \boldsymbol{K}^t(t, r)$$
$$\left[\sum_{i=x-\delta}^{x+\delta} \boldsymbol{K}^x(i', r) \left[\sum_{j=y-\delta}^{y+\delta} \boldsymbol{K}^y(j', r) \left[\sum_{s=1}^{S} \boldsymbol{K}^s(s, r) \mathcal{U}(i, j, s) \right] \right] \right],$$
$$(9.45)$$

where $i' = i - x + \delta$, $j' = j - y + \delta$. This calculation includes a sequence of convolutional operations between the data tensor and four smaller kernels. To be precise,

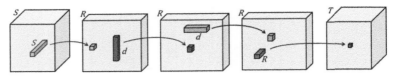

FIGURE 9.17

Convolutional operation with CP-decomposed kernel.

this sequence of operations is

$$\mathcal{U}^s(i,j,r) \leftarrow \sum_{s=1}^{S} \mathbf{K}^s(s,r)\,\mathcal{U}(i,j,s),$$

$$\mathcal{U}^{sy}(i,y,r) \leftarrow \sum_{j=y-\delta}^{y+\delta} \mathbf{K}^y(j',r)\,\mathcal{U}^s(i,j,r),$$

$$\mathcal{U}^{sxy}(x,y,r) \leftarrow \sum_{i=x-\delta}^{x+\delta} \mathbf{K}^x(i',r)\,\mathcal{U}^{sy}(i,y,r),$$

$$\mathcal{V}(x,y,t) \approx \sum_{r=1}^{R} \mathbf{K}^t(t,r)\,\mathcal{U}^{sxy}(x,y,r),$$

(9.46)

where $\mathcal{U}^s, \mathcal{U}^{sy}, \mathcal{U}^{sxy}$ are intermediate tensors.

Having defined the forward pass, we can calculate the gradients using autograd packages such as PyTorch and TensorFlow and perform optimization schemes such as gradient descent. This gives rise to the great ease of implementation for the compression of neural networks.

Convolution graphs

Fig. 9.17 represents the same convolutional operation, but with CP-decomposed kernel tensors. The intermediate steps represent the convolution operation between the data tensor and the CP-decomposed kernel tensor.

Fine-tuning and alternative approach

Lebedev et al. [26] propose applying CP decomposition after the network has already been trained and then applying fine-tuning to recover accuracy. This approach has good performance, but limited benefits. We found in our testing that it will be better to decompose the network first, and then train it from scratch. Using this method, we work with a smaller set of parameters, speeding up both the training and the inference process.

Complexity analysis

The original convolution operation has STd^2 trainable parameters and performs $STd^2(X-d+1)(Y-d+1)$ multiplication–addition operations in total. After the decomposition, the number of parameters is reduced to $R(S + 2d + T)$ and the number of multiplication–addition operations to $R(S + 2d + T)(X - d + 1)(Y - d + 1)$. Assuming that the selected rank R is much smaller than S and T ($R \approx \frac{ST}{S+T}$), the compression scheme has an order d^2 improvement in terms of complexity.

9.4.3 Compressing the convolutional layer via Tucker decomposition

Kernel, convolutional operation formula

Given the task of compressing the kernel tensor in order to speed up the training and inference process in a CNN, Kim et al. [27] propose using Tucker decomposition to compress the convolutional layer, and they have demonstrated a few advantages of Tucker over CP in this application.

The full Tucker format decomposes a fourth-order kernel tensor $\mathcal{K}$ into four factor matrices $\boldsymbol{K}^n$, for $n = 1, ..., 4$, and a core tensor $\mathcal{G} \in \mathbb{R}^{R_1 \times R_2 \times R_3 \times R_4}$ that represents the interactions between the modes:

$$\mathcal{K}(i, j, s, t) \approx \sum_{r_1=1}^{R_1} \sum_{r_2=1}^{R_2} \sum_{r_3=1}^{R_3} \sum_{r_4=1}^{R_4} \mathcal{G}(r_1, r_2, r_3, r_4) \boldsymbol{K}^1(i, r_1) \boldsymbol{K}^2(j, r_2) \boldsymbol{K}^3(s, r_3) \boldsymbol{K}^4(t, r_4).$$

$$(9.47)$$

However, it is not efficient to decompose every mode of the kernel tensor, because the spatial dimensions of the kernel tensor are usually very low (lower than 5). Therefore, we approximate $\mathcal{K}$ using a partial Tucker decomposition, meaning that performing decomposition is only in the channel dimensions while leaving the spatial dimensions fixed. This variant of Tucker decomposition is usually referred to as partial Tucker or Tucker-2 decomposition. Using this technique, we represent $\mathcal{K}$ as follows:

$$\mathcal{K}(i, j, s, t) \approx \sum_{r_3=1}^{R_3} \sum_{r_4=1}^{R_4} \mathcal{G}'(i, j, r_3, r_4) \boldsymbol{K}^s(s, r_3) \boldsymbol{K}^t(t, r_4). \qquad (9.48)$$

Here we represent the kernel tensor with a new core tensor $\mathcal{G}' \in \mathbb{R}^{d \times d \times R_3 \times R_4}$ and two factor matrices $\boldsymbol{K}^s \in \mathbb{R}^{S \times R_3}$ and $\boldsymbol{K}^t \in \mathbb{R}^{T \times R_4}$ that correspond to the two channel dimensions. Equivalently, one can interpret it as having its first two factor matrices in the full Tucker format "absorbed" into the core tensor $\mathcal{G}$ to form the new core tensor $\mathcal{G}'$.

New convolutional operation

Using the decomposed kernel tensor, we devise a new sequence of operations that approximate the original full convolutional operation:

$$\mathcal{U}^s(x, y, r_3) \leftarrow \sum_{s=1}^{S} \boldsymbol{K}^s(s, r_3) \, \mathcal{U}(x, y, s),$$

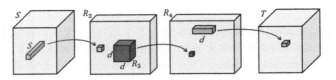

FIGURE 9.18

Convolutional operation with Tucker-decomposed kernel.

$$\mathcal{U}^{sxy}(x', y', r) \leftarrow \sum_{i=1}^{d} \sum_{j=1}^{d} \sum_{r_3=1}^{R_3} \mathcal{G}'(i, j, r_3, r_4)\, \mathcal{U}^s(x' + i - 1, y' + i - 1, r_3), \quad (9.49)$$

$$\mathcal{V}(x', y', t) \approx \sum_{r_4=1}^{R} K^t(t, r_4)\, \mathcal{U}^{sxy}(x', y', r_4),$$

where $\mathcal{U}^s \in \mathbb{R}^{X \times Y \times R_3}$ and $\mathcal{U}^{sxy} \in \mathbb{R}^{X' \times Y' \times R_4}$ are the intermediate tensors, with $X' = X - d + 1$, $Y' = Y - d + 1$. This sequence of operations takes the data tensor $\mathcal{U} \in \mathbb{R}^{X \times Y \times S}$ to the output tensor $\mathcal{V} \in \mathbb{R}^{X' \times Y' \times T}$. Note that this sequence of operations is very similar in structure to the CP compression scheme, except that now we are only compressing two out of the four modes in the original tensor.

Convolution graphs

Fig. 9.18 represents the sequence of operations required to approximate the full convolution using the Tucker-decomposed kernel tensor. Note that unlike what we do with CP decomposition, we leave the spatial dimensions unchanged and only partially decompose the kernel.

Comparison with CP

The Tucker-decomposed neural network has significant advantages over the CP counterpart. Experimentally, low-rank CP decomposition causes instability in training when applied to entire layers of larger neural networks. Tucker decomposition can sustain stability while achieving a greater ratio of compression because its structure is able to approximate richer interactions between modes.

Rank estimation

The rank of decomposition has a strong influence on the performance and compression ratio and controls the trade-off between these two metrics. It is also very inefficient and time consuming to obtain the optimal rank values using trial and error or cross-validation. Therefore it is useful to choose a stable and reproducible scheme to accomplish the optimal rank selection. Kim et al. [27] report that a variational Bayesian approach for matrix factorization yields outstanding performance in this task.

Complexity analysis

The original convolution operation has STd^2 trainable parameters and performs $STd^2 X'Y'$ multiplication–addition operations in total. According to [27], the Tucker-decomposed CNNs have a compression ratio M and a speedup ratio E of

$$M = \frac{STd^2}{SR_3 + TR_4 + R_3R_4d^2}, E = \frac{STd^2X'Y'}{SR_3XY + (R_3d^2 + T)R_4X'Y'}, \quad (9.50)$$

respectively. These quantities are both bounded by $\frac{ST}{R_3R_4}$.

9.4.4 Compressing the convolutional layer via TT/TR decompositions

Vanilla tensor train solution

We apply other formats of tensor decomposition, such as TT and TR, to the kernel tensor of the convolutional layer in order to reduce the number of parameters and speed up the neural network. A TT-decomposed network takes a structure similar to what we have seen previously in compression using CP and Tucker decompositions. Given a fourth-order kernel tensor $\mathcal{K} \in \mathbb{R}^{d \times d \times S \times T}$, we decompose it into four factor tensors and approximate each element of the tensor using a product of factor matrices:

$$\mathcal{K}(d_1, d_2, s, t) = \mathcal{G}^1(d_1)\,\mathcal{G}^2(d_2)\,\mathcal{G}^3(s)\,\mathcal{G}^4(t). \quad (9.51)$$

This format allows the forward pass to be done in a sequence of steps.

Garipov's paper, overview

Gavipov et al. [28] demonstrate that the vanilla application of TT to compressing the kernel tensor yields poor performance, and instead propose an alternative method that promises better results. This particular method they propose includes two steps. First, it reformulates the convolution operation between the kernel and the input into a matrix multiplication. Second, it reshapes the matricized kernel into another high-dimensional tensor and uses TT decomposition to factorize this tensor into a network of smaller, factor tensors.

Matricization, matrix multiplication

Garipov's paper proposes that the convolution could be represented by a single matrix multiplication. Given a data tensor $\mathcal{U} \in \mathbb{R}^{X \times Y \times S}$ and a kernel tensor $\mathcal{K} \in \mathbb{R}^{d \times d \times S \times T}$, we introduce two matrices U, K to hold the same data in matrix format:

$$\mathcal{U}(x + i - 1, y + j - 1, s) = U(x + X'(y - 1), i + d(j - 1) + d^2(s - 1)),$$
$$\mathcal{K}(i, j, s, t) = K(i + d(j - 1) + d^2(t - 1), s). \quad (9.52)$$

Using these two matrices, we compute the intermediate output matrix V with a matrix multiplication

$$V = UK. \quad (9.53)$$

Lastly, we recover the output tensor $\mathcal{V} \in \mathbb{R}^{X' \times Y' \times T}$ by reshaping the matrix V back into tensor format:

$$\mathcal{V}(x, y, t) = V(x, X'(y - 1), t). \quad (9.54)$$

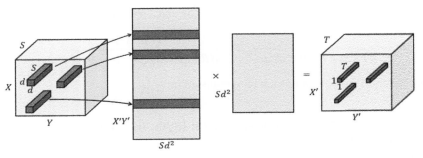

FIGURE 9.19

Convolutional operation with TT-decomposed kernel.

In Fig. 9.19, the leftmost block represents the data tensor $\mathcal{U}$, the next two rectangles represent the matrices U and K, and the last block represents the recovered output tensor $\mathcal{V}$.

High-order tensorization, TT decomposition

After the data tensor and the kernel tensor have been matricized, we reshape the kernel tensor into a high-dimensional tensor $\mathcal{K}' \in \mathbb{R}^{d^2 \times s_1 t_1 \times \cdots \times s_d t_d}$ where $S = \Pi_{i=1}^d S_i$, $T = \Pi_{i=1}^d T_i$, under the assumption that such a factorization exists (to make sure that it always exists, we add empty channels to make the factorization work). We essentially tensorize the kernel matrix K into a $(d+1)$-dimensional tensor, where the first dimension has size d^2 and other dimensions have size $S_i T_i$ for $i = 1, ..., d$.

We devise a method of compound indexing by defining bijective functions $\mu : \mathbb{R} \to \mathbb{R}^d$, $\nu : \mathbb{R} \to \mathbb{R}^d$, that map such that $\mu(t) = (\mu_1(t), ..., \mu_d(t))$ and $\nu(l) = (\nu_1(l), ..., \nu_d(l))$. Here, $\mu(\cdot)$ maps the row index of the matrix into a d-dimensional index $(\mu_k(\cdot))_{k=1}^d$ that ranges from 1 to S_k, while $\nu(\cdot)$ maps the column index of the matrix into a d-dimensional index $(\nu_k(\cdot))_{k=1}^d$ that ranges from 1 to T_k.

This tensorization process is mathematically formulated as

$$K(x + d(y-1) + d^2(s'-1), t') = \mathcal{K}'((x + d(y-1), 1, (s_1, t_1), ..., (s_d, t_d))$$
$$\approx \mathcal{G}^0(x + d(y-1), 1)\mathcal{G}^1(s_1, t_1) \cdots \mathcal{G}^d(s_d, t_d), \tag{9.55}$$

where $s' = s_1 + \sum_{i=2}^d (s_i - 1)\Pi_{j=1}^{i-1} S_j$, $t' = t_1 + \sum_{i=2}^d (t_i - 1)\Pi_{j=1}^{i-1} T_j$. Here we are utilizing a special notation where a tuple (s_k, t_k) denotes the compound index along the k-th dimension, using s_k as the row index and t_k as the column index.

Fig. 9.20 demonstrates the overall process of matricization, tensorization, and the decomposition of the kernel tensor. The third-order data tensor is first flattened into a matrix and then restructured into a high-dimensional tensor to be decomposed into a TT network.

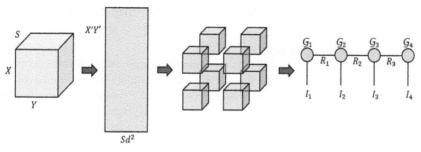

FIGURE 9.20

Matricization and tensorization pipeline.

Table 9.2 Comparison of complexities.

Method	Complexity
CP	$R(S + 2d + T)(X - d + 1)(Y - d + 1)$
Tucker	$ST/R_3 R_4$
TT/TR	$O(dr^2 s \max\{S, T\})$

Forward pass

Using the compound index defined in (9.39), we can formulate the forward pass. We reshape the data matrix U into a tensor $\mathcal{U}' \in \mathbb{R}^{X \times Y \times S_1 \times \cdots \times S_d}$ and compute $\mathcal{V}' \in \mathbb{R}^{X' \times Y' \times T_1 \times \cdots \times T_d}$ in the following way:

$$
\mathcal{V}' = \sum_{i,j}^{d} \sum_{s_1, \ldots, s_d} \mathcal{U}'(i + x - 1, j + y - 1, s_1, \ldots, s_d)
$$
$$
\times \mathcal{G}^0(x + d(y - 1), 1) \mathcal{G}^1(s_1, t_1) \cdots \mathcal{G}^d(s_d, t_d). \tag{9.56}
$$

We then reshape the intermediate output tensor $\mathcal{V}'$ into the final output tensor $\mathcal{V} \in \mathbb{R}^{X' \times Y' \times T}$. The tensor cores $\mathcal{G}$'s are trained as the parameters of the layer, and the optimization process can be accomplished using any autograd package.

Complexity

According to the calculation in [25], the complexity of the forward pass is reduced to $O(dr^2 s \max\{S, T\})$.

Table 9.2 summarizes the complexities of different compression schemes' forward passes. In practice, the difference in complexity leads to different capacities in speeding up the training and inference process, and one may choose the most appropriate compression scheme based on the network architecture, data structure, and properties of features in the data, so that the speedup ratio can be optimized.

9.4.5 Compressing neural networks via transform-based decomposition

T-product, fully connected layers

In Section 9.2.3 and Section 9.2.4, we defined the conventional fully connected layer and convolutional layer. In this section, we formulate a new framework for building the fully connected network and CNN using the cosine transform product, and we give the corresponding tensor operations for activation functions, softmax function, and cost functions. Recall that the forward pass in a single fully connected layer is defined as

$$A^j = \sigma(W^j A^{j-1} + B^j). \tag{9.57}$$

We use the t-product as a new form of representation for the weights and data. Suppose that we are given a set of m images having the size of $n \times n$. Let $\mathfrak{R} = \mathbb{R}^Q$, $Q = n$. We form a data tensor $\mathcal{X} \in \mathfrak{R}^{n \times m}$. We construct a network with N layers consisting of weight tensors $\mathcal{W}^j \in \mathfrak{R}^{\ell_j \times \ell_{j-1}}$ and offset tensors $\mathcal{B}^j = \underbrace{\{b^j, ..., b^j\}}_{m \text{ times}} \in$
$\mathfrak{R}^{\ell_j \times m}$, $j = [N]$ and $\ell_0 = n$. We formulate the forward pass in the transform domain as a sequence of (DCT-based) t-products,

$$\mathcal{A}^j = \varrho(\mathcal{W}^j \bullet \mathcal{A}^{j-1} + \mathcal{B}^j), \tag{9.58}$$

where $\mathcal{A}^j \in \mathfrak{R}^{\ell_j \times m}$ is the final output of layer j after applying the activation function, $\varrho(\cdot)$ is the tensor activation function defined under a transformation such that $\varrho(\alpha) = \mathcal{F}^{-1}(\sigma(\mathcal{F}(\alpha)))$, where $\alpha \in \mathfrak{R}$, and $\sigma(\cdot)$ is a conventional activation function. We have

$$\tilde{\mathcal{A}}^{j\ (q)} = \sigma(\tilde{\mathcal{W}}^{j\ (q)} \cdot \tilde{\mathcal{A}}^{j-1\ (q)} + \tilde{\mathcal{B}}^{j\ (q)}), \quad q \in [Q], \tag{9.59}$$

where $\tilde{\mathcal{A}}^{j\ (q)}$, $\tilde{\mathcal{W}}^{j\ (q)}$, and $\tilde{\mathcal{B}}^{j\ (q)}$ are the transform domain representation of $\mathcal{A}^{j\ (q)}$, $\mathcal{W}^{j\ (q)}$, and $\mathcal{B}^{j\ (q)}$ by taking the transform over $\mathfrak{R}$.

Tubal softmax, loss function

Recall the standard softmax function for 2D outputs in neural networks (9.3), where softmax : $\mathbb{R}^{c \times m} \to \mathbb{R}^{c \times m}$, where c is the number of categories and m is the size of the data.

For tensor outputs, we define a tensor softmax function $f : \mathfrak{R}^{\ell_N} \to \mathbb{R}^{\ell_N}$, composed of the tubal function $h : \mathfrak{R}^{\ell_N} \to \mathfrak{R}^{\ell_N}$ and scalar function $s : \mathfrak{R}^{\ell_N} \to \mathbb{R}^{\ell_N}$, as follows:

$$f(\mathcal{A}_j^N) = g(h(\mathcal{A}_j^N)), \quad j \in [m],$$

$$h(\mathcal{A}_j^N)_i = \exp\left(\mathcal{A}_j^N(i)\right) \left(\sum_i \exp\left(\mathcal{A}_j^N(i)\right)\right)^{-1}, \quad i \in [\ell_N], \tag{9.60}$$

$$s(\alpha) = \mathrm{sum}(\alpha), \quad \alpha \in \mathfrak{R},$$

where $\mathcal{A}_j^N$ is the j-th lateral slice of $\mathcal{A}^N$, $\mathcal{A}_j^N(i)$ is the tube fiber with index (i, j), $s(\cdot)$ is the sum along the third (tubal) dimension, and $\exp(\cdot)$ function is applied in an element-wise manner. The composite function $f(\cdot)$ calculates the softmax.

The training of a fully connected spectral tensor neural network will minimize a loss function

$$\mathcal{L} = \text{Loss}(f(\mathcal{A}^N), \boldsymbol{C}), \tag{9.61}$$

where $\text{Loss}(\cdot) : \mathbb{R}^{\ell_N \times m} \to \mathbb{R}$, $\boldsymbol{C} \in \mathbb{R}^{\ell_N \times m}$ is the true classification where $\boldsymbol{C}_{ij} = 1$ when the j-th image belongs to the i-th class, and the tensor softmax function $f : \mathfrak{R}^{\ell_N \times m} \to \mathbb{R}^{\ell_N \times m}$ in (9.60) maps the tensor representation to an estimate output $\widehat{\boldsymbol{C}}$, where each column is a probability distribution. The (i, j)-th entry of $f(\mathcal{A}^N) \in \mathbb{R}^{\ell_N \times m}$ denotes the probability that the j-th image belongs to the i-th category.

We allow different loss functions, such as least-squares loss and cross-entropy loss. Since the least-squares loss is straightforward, we will elaborate the cross-entropy loss under the newly defined tensor operations.

Tensor cross-entropy function

Cross-entropy loss is a measure of the distance between probability distributions, namely, the predicted distribution from the final layer compared to the "true" distributions from the classification. The tensor cross-entropy function is a negative-log-likelihood function

$$\text{Loss}(\boldsymbol{X}, \boldsymbol{C}) = -\sum_{j \in [m]} \log(\boldsymbol{X}_{c_j, j}), \tag{9.62}$$

where $\boldsymbol{X} = f(\mathcal{A}^N)$, c_j is the category to which the j-th image belongs, and $\boldsymbol{X}_{c_j, j}$ is the probability that the j-th image is successfully classified.

Convolutional layer

The operations in a convolutional layer can be equivalently conducted using the t-product and block-circulant structures. Recall that in a conventional convolutional layer, the weights are contained in a fourth-order kernel tensor $\mathcal{K} \in \mathbb{R}^{d \times d \times S \times T}$, where S and T are the input and the output channels and d is the size of the kernel. The data tensor $\mathcal{U}$ is passed through the layer by undergoing a 2D convolutional operation with $\mathcal{K}$ per (9.10).

Now we are going to make a structural assumption that the kernel tensor exhibits a circulant structure along the input and output channel dimensions. Fix the number of input and output channels to be the same by letting $S = T = pq$, $p, q \in \mathbb{Z}^+$. A hidden layer has input data $\mathcal{U}$ of size $n \times n \times m$, convolution kernel $\mathcal{K}$ size $d \times d \times pq \times pq$, and output $\mathcal{V}$ of size $n \times n \times m$ (here zero-padding is used on the boundaries of the image).

For our convolutional tensor layer, let the numbers of the input and output channels be the same n and $\mathfrak{R} = \mathbb{R}^n$. We represent the input, the convolution kernel, and the output as $\mathcal{U} \in \mathfrak{R}^{n \times n}$, $\mathcal{K} \in \mathfrak{R}^{d \times d}$, and $\mathcal{V} \in \mathfrak{R}^{n \times n}$, respectively. Let $\delta = (d - 1)/2$

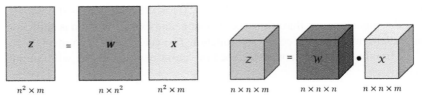

$n^2 \times m$ $n \times n^2$ $n^2 \times m$ $n \times n \times m$ $n \times n \times n$ $n \times n \times m$

FIGURE 9.21

Parameterization in real vs. transform domain for fully connected layers.

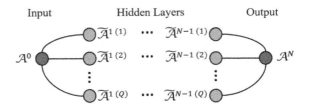

FIGURE 9.22

Parallel computation using transform-based networks.

denote the "half width" of the kernel. Then, we reshape the slice $K(i, j)$ to a third-order tensor $\mathcal{K}'(i, j) \in \mathbb{R}^{p \times p \times q}$, and we reshape $U(i, j)$ to $\mathcal{U}'(i, j) \in \mathbb{R}^{p \times 1 \times q}$. By the properties of circulant tensors, we represent a convolutional tensor layer as follows:

$$\mathcal{V}(x, y) = \sum_{i=x-\delta}^{x+\delta} \sum_{j=y-\delta}^{y+\delta} \mathcal{K}'(i - x + \delta + 1, j - y + \delta + 1) \bullet \mathcal{U}'(i, j). \qquad (9.63)$$

Better parameterization

This formulation is extremely useful for dealing with high-dimensional data (third-order or higher) because it has greater power of feature extraction using fewer parameters. For the sake of simplicity, let us suppose that we are given m data samples, each having shape $n \times n$. In a traditional fully connected network, we would have to vectorize each sample into a vector of length n^2, so the batch of data is represented as a matrix of shape $n^2 \times m$. In the transform-based network, we are able to represent the data as a tensor of shape $n \times n \times m$.

Fig. 9.21 demonstrates the superiority of the latter approach: while the fully connected network uses $O(n^4)$ weight parameters, the transform-based network only needs $O(n^3)$ to capture the same features. This computational advantage will become even more significant if the data have higher dimensions or larger sizes.

Advantage, model parallelism

Compared to other decomposition methods, the transform-based network has the advantage of parallelizability. Fig. 9.22 summarizes graphically how the forward pass

---

Algorithm 7: Training the transform-based neural network.

Input: $\mathcal{X} \in \mathfrak{R}^{\ell_0 \times m}$, $C \in \mathbb{R}^{\ell_N \times m}$, N, and MaxEpoch.

Output: trained parameters $\mathcal{W}^j \in \mathfrak{R}^{\ell_j \times \ell_{j-1}}$, $\mathcal{B}^j \in \mathfrak{R}^{\ell_j \times m}$, $j \in [N]$.

1 Randomly initialize trainable parameters $\widetilde{\mathcal{W}}^j$, $\widetilde{\mathcal{B}}^j$, $j \in [N]$. Let $\mathcal{A}^0 = \mathcal{X}$ and set $t = 1$.

2 **while** *NOT converged or $t \leq$ MaxEpoch* **do**

3   **for** $j = 0, ..., N - 1$ **do**

4          $\widetilde{\mathcal{A}}^j \leftarrow \mathrm{dct}(\mathcal{A}^j, [\,], 3)$.

5   **for** $q = 1, ..., Q$ **do**

6              $\widetilde{\mathcal{A}}^{j+1\,(q)} \leftarrow \sigma(\widetilde{\mathcal{W}}^{j+1\,(q)} \cdot \widetilde{\mathcal{A}}^{j\,(q)} + \widetilde{\mathcal{B}}^{j+1\,(q)})$.

7      $\mathcal{A}^N \leftarrow \mathrm{idct}(\widetilde{\mathcal{A}}^N, [\,], 3)$.

8   Compute $f(\mathcal{A}^N)$ via (9.60).

9   Compute $\mathcal{L}$ via (9.61).

10   Compute $\mathcal{Y} = \partial \mathcal{F} / \partial \mathcal{A}^N$ and obtain $\widetilde{\mathcal{Y}}$ by taking transform over $\mathfrak{R}$.

11   Compute $\delta \widetilde{\mathcal{A}}^N_{(q)}, q \in [Q]$.

12   **for** $j = N, ..., 1$ **do**

13   Compute $\delta \widetilde{\mathcal{A}}^{j\,(q)}, \delta \widetilde{\mathcal{W}}^{j\,(q)}, \delta \widetilde{\mathcal{B}}^{j\,(q)}, q \in [q]$.

14   **for** $q = 1, ..., Q$ **do**

15   Update $\mathcal{W}^{j\,(q)} \leftarrow \mathcal{W}^{j\,(q)} - \delta \widetilde{\mathcal{W}}^{j\,(q)}$.

16   Update $\mathcal{B}^{j\,(q)} \leftarrow \mathcal{B}^{j\,(q)} - \delta \widetilde{\mathcal{B}}^{j\,(q)}$.

17      $t \leftarrow t + 1$.

18 **return** $\mathcal{W}^j, \mathcal{B}^j, j \in [N]$.

---

is conducted in a transform-based network. Having processed the data and transformed into the transform domain, we use the frontal slices of $\widehat{\mathcal{Z}}$ independently: feed each frontal slice into a parallel channel and train the slice using a separate model. This process exhibits a high degree of model parallelism, which we exploit to accelerate the training process significantly. We can exploit this feature of transform-based networks by training them on GPUs, which are particularly designed for handling parallelisms. Much research has been done on the topic of accelerating tensor operations on GPUs [24], and transform-based networks are found to be applicable to other deep learning tasks [29].

Algorithm 7 and Algorithm 8 summarize the forward pass in the transform-based network.

9.5 Experiments and future directions

9.5.1 Performance evaluations using the MNIST dataset

MNIST dataset

Algorithm 8: Inference using the transform-based neural network.

Input: unseen data $x \in \Re^{\ell_0 \times 1}$ and trained parameters $\widetilde{\mathcal{W}}^j \in \Re^{\ell_j \times \ell_{j-1}}$,
$\quad \widetilde{\mathcal{B}}^j = \underbrace{[b^j, ..., b^j]}_{m \text{ times}} \in \Re^{\ell_j \times m}, \ j \in [N]$.

Output: predicted label $\widehat{y} \in \{1, ..., c\}$, where $c = \ell_N$.

1   **for** $j = 0, ..., N - 1$ **do**
2     $\widetilde{\mathcal{A}}^j \leftarrow \text{dct}(\mathcal{A}^j, [\ ], 3)$.
3   **for** $q = 1, ..., Q$ **do**
4       $\bigsqcup \ \widetilde{\mathcal{A}}^{j+1}\,(q) \leftarrow \sigma(\widetilde{\mathcal{W}}^{j+1}\,(q) \cdot \widetilde{\mathcal{A}}^j\,(q) + \widetilde{b}^{j+1}\,(q))$.

5   $\mathcal{A}^N \leftarrow \text{idct}(\widetilde{\mathcal{A}}^N, [\ ], 3)$.
6   Compute $\widehat{y} \leftarrow f(\mathcal{A}^N)$ via (9.60).
7   **return** $\widehat{y}$.

To test the performance of each decomposition scheme on CNNs, we apply each of the methods to the LeNet architecture to classify the MNIST handwritten digits dataset.

The MNIST dataset is commonly used in computer vision, in which each data point is a grayscale image of a handwritten digit with size $28 \times 28 \times 1$. The training dataset contains 60,000 images, and the test dataset contains 10,000 images. As of 2020, the state-of-the-art performance on the MNIST dataset is 99.84% accuracy.

LeNet overview

LeNet is a classic deep CNN architecture [15], and it is crafted specifically to work on the MNIST dataset. In a nutshell, it consists of two convolutional layers and two fully connected layers, with some max pooling layers and dropout layers in between. With the original, uncompressed LeNet architecture, we can arrive at 99.5% accuracy on the training set and 99.2% accuracy on the test set after 100 epochs.

Performance graphs

Fig. 9.23 shows the performance of the experiments on the MNIST dataset by decomposing the convolutional layer only. Note that after each training iteration, we run the newly trained model on the test data, and therefore we obtain an accuracy curve as the training process goes on.

Performance analysis

As shown in Fig. 9.23, there is no significant difference between the accuracy of the original neural network and the compressed networks. However, there are some minor issues worth discussing.

CP decomposition performs satisfactorily in classifying the MNIST dataset, as it compresses the network without significant loss in accuracy compared to the original, uncompressed network. Compared to other decomposition schemes, the CP-decomposed network learns at a slower rate and often suffers from overfitting. Therefore, it can perform well on the training data, but it performs poorly on the test

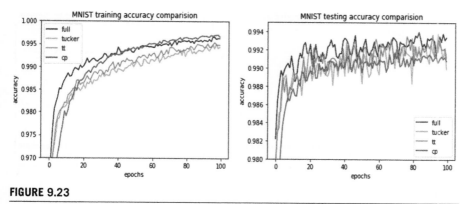

FIGURE 9.23

Training and testing accuracy on the MNIST dataset.

Table 9.3 Comparison of compression and speedup ratios.

	CP	Tucker	TT	TT (fully connected)
Compression ratio	8.5×	6×	9×	4×
Speedup		2×	1.5×	3×	1.2×

data. Moreover, the CP-decomposed network is highly sensitive to the choice of hyperparameters, such as the learning rate, and the network may fail to converge unless the hyperparameters are carefully chosen.

Tucker decomposition is superior to CP decomposition in compressing neural networks in all aspects. Tucker decomposition achieves better performance with a greater compression rate and a higher learning rate, resulting in higher accuracy and a shorter training time.

For compression with TT, we take the two dimensions in the convolutional layer corresponding to the input/output channels, matricize the tensor, decompose the result to a matrix product state, and reshape them back to fourth-order tensors. This gives us two decomposed convolutional layers for every convolutional layer in the original network. Experimentally, this method yields better results than Tucker and has a similar rate of compression and speedup as Tucker's.

We also test the performance of fully connected networks on the MNIST dataset and compare the results with the compressed network using TT-based techniques described in Section 9.4.1. As shown in Fig. 9.24, the compression scheme achieves a 4× compression ratio at the cost of 1% accuracy drop.

Table 9.3 summarizes the compression and speedup ratios of different compression methods. The best performing among the candidates is the TT-decomposed convolutional network. The compression ratios are calculated by dividing the total number of parameters in the undecomposed kernel tensors by the number of parameters in the decomposed tensors. The speedup ratios are calculated by dividing the time spent on forward pass of the original models by that of the compressed models.

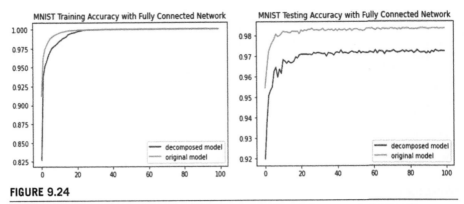

FIGURE 9.24

Training and testing accuracy on the MNIST dataset with a fully connected network.

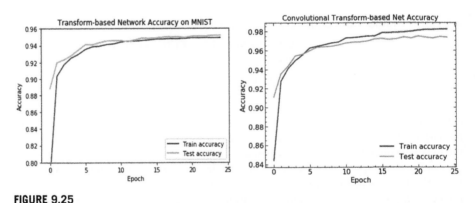

FIGURE 9.25

Transform-based networks' accuracies on the MNIST dataset.

Transform-based network performance

We also run the transform-based neural network on the MNIST dataset, with both a CNN and a traditional fully connected network, as shown in Fig. 9.25. Although the performance has a 1% accuracy drop on the LeNet dataset [15] with this method, parallelization and multiprocessing allow large ratios of speedup and compression.

9.5.2 Performance evaluations using the CIFAR10 dataset

CIFAR10 dataset

The CIFAR10 dataset is another popular computer vision dataset and a significantly more complex task than the MNIST dataset. Like MNIST, CIFAR10 also has 10 categories of images, 60,000 training data, and 10,000 test data. However, the images in the CIFAR10 dataset are colored, and the dimensions are larger: $32 \times 32 \times 3$. The shapes in each image are also more complex than handwritten digits, making the

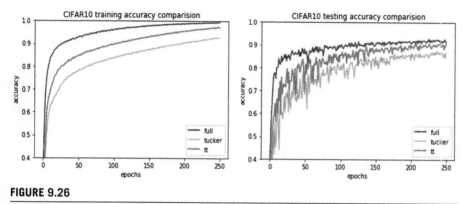

FIGURE 9.26

Training and testing accuracy on the CIFAR10 dataset.

classification much more challenging. As of 2020, the state-of-the-art performance of CNN on the CIFAR10 dataset is around 94% accuracy.

VGG16 overview

VGG16 [30] is a deep CNN architecture proposed in 2014 that won the Image-Net contest. This architecture consists of 13 convolutional layers followed by 3 fully connected layers, with a softmax layer at the output layer. Because this architecture is much deeper and more complex than LeNet, it requires much greater computational and storage resources, which makes the benefits of the decomposition approaches more significant.

Performance graphs

Fig. 9.26 shows the performance of the experiments on the CIFAR10 dataset by decomposing the convolutional layer only.

The CP format decomposition is not suitable for large networks, often suffering from instability, i.e., the training process is easily perturbed and may not always converge. In our experiments, the decomposition process not only takes a considerably long time, but also consumes a lot of RAM. For a convolutional layer with a size larger than 512×512, the memory requirement of the CP decomposition is prohibitive.

The Tucker works without any instability but suffers from limited accuracy: while the test accuracy of a full VGG16 network is around 91%, the Tucker-decomposed network has only 83% accuracy.

TT decomposition has the best overall performance among the decomposition schemes. It achieves a classification accuracy closely comparable to undecomposed networks while allowing a high compression ratio and a fast learning rate.

9.5.3 Future research directions

Even though the research on compressing DNNs with tensor networks is still in an early stage of development, the field attracts enormous interests from researchers and machine learning practitioners. This area has a few potential directions for future research, which are listed below.

Automatic rank selection

The quality of the approximation of the kernel tensors is highly influenced by the selection of the internal rank in the tensor network. However, the problem of selecting the optimal rank is known to be NP-hard, and there are many existing estimation algorithms based on heuristics, gradient descent, and other techniques. The development of more robust rank estimation algorithms will enable us to balance the number of required parameters and model accuracy.

Generalization to more complex tensor network structures

In this work, we have discussed the currently used tensor structures for compressing DNNs. However, there remain many tensor networks with great diversity and complexity, such as the multiscale entanglement renormalization ansatz (MERA) and projected entangled pair states (PEPS), which have not been considered for the task of network compression. The inclusion of structurally rich tensor networks will provide a more versatile toolbox for handling network compression problems.

AutoML with tensor network compression

Automated machine learning (AutoML) [31] is a fast growing area of research that studies how one can build successful DNNs without the aid of human expertise, but rather letting the model choose the favorable architectures and hyperparameters by itself. To the best of our knowledge, the compression of AutoML models using tensor networks has not been thoroughly explored.

Tensor networks with quantum computing

It has been shown theoretically that tensor networks can closely approximate quantum states [32], and quantum computing can be applied to data in tensor network structures naturally. This close relationship provides us with the potential of training and applying DNNs using quantum computing facilities.

References

[1] David Silver, et al., Mastering the game of go without human knowledge, Nature 550 (7676) (2017) 354–359.

[2] Carlos A. Gomez-Uribe, Neil Hunt, The Netflix recommender system: algorithms, business value, and innovation, ACM Transactions on Management Information Systems (TMIS) 6 (4) (2015) 1–19.

[3] Geert Litjens, et al., Deep learning as a tool for increased accuracy and efficiency of histopathological diagnosis, Scientific Reports 6 (2016) 26286.

[4] Hongming Chen, et al., The rise of deep learning in drug discovery, Drug Discovery Today 23 (6) (2018) 1241–1250.

[5] Kaiming He, et al., Deep residual learning for image recognition, in: Proceedings of the IEEE Conference on Computer Vision and Pattern Recognition, 2016, pp. 770–778.

[6] Mohammad Rastegari, et al., Enabling AI at the edge with XNOR-networks, Communications of the ACM 63 (12) (2020) 83–90.

[7] Wei Wen, et al., Learning structured sparsity in deep neural networks, arXiv:1608.03665, 2016.

[8] Yunchao Gong, et al., Compressing deep convolutional networks using vector quantization, arXiv preprint, arXiv:1412.6115, 2014.

[9] Geoffrey Hinton, Oriol Vinyals, Jeff Dean, Distilling the knowledge in a neural network, arXiv preprint, arXiv:1503.02531, 2015.

[10] Yu Cheng, et al., An exploration of parameter redundancy in deep networks with circulant projections, in: Proceedings of the IEEE International Conference on Computer Vision, 2015, pp. 2857–2865.

[11] J. Ma, et al., Deep tensor ADMM-net for snapshot compressive imaging, in: ICCV, 2019.

[12] X. Han, et al., Tensor FISTA-net for real-time snapshot compressive imaging, in: AAAI, 2020.

[13] X.-Y. Liu, et al., High performance computing primitives for tensor networks learning operations on GPUs, in: Quantum Tensor Networks in Machine Learning Workshop at NeurIPS, 2020.

[14] Ian Goodfellow, et al., Deep Learning, vol. 1, 2, MIT Press, Cambridge, 2016.

[15] Yann LeCun, et al., Gradient-based learning applied to document recognition, Proceedings of the IEEE 86 (11) (1998) 2278–2324.

[16] Alex Krizhevsky, Ilya Sutskever, Geoffrey E. Hinton, Imagenet classification with deep convolutional neural networks, Communications of the ACM 60 (6) (2017) 84–90.

[17] Andrzej Cichocki, et al., Tensor decompositions for signal processing applications: from two-way to multiway component analysis, IEEE Signal Processing Magazine 32 (2) (2015) 145–163.

[18] Tamara G. Kolda, Brett W. Bader, Tensor decompositions and applications, SIAM Review 51 (3) (2009) 455–500.

[19] Lars Grasedyck, Hierarchical singular value decomposition of tensors, SIAM Journal on Matrix Analysis and Applications 31 (4) (2010) 2029–2054.

[20] Miao Yin, et al., Towards extremely compact recurrent neural networks: enabling few thousand parameters-only RNN models for video recognition with fully decomposed hierarchical Tucker structure, in: CVPR, 2021.

[21] Ivan V. Oseledets, Tensor-train decomposition, SIAM Journal on Scientific Computing 33 (5) (2011) 2295–2317.

[22] Elizabeth Newman, et al., Stable tensor neural networks for rapid deep learning, arXiv: 1811.06569, 2018.

[23] T. Zhang, X.-Y. Liu, X. Wang, High performance GPU tensor completion with tubal-sampling pattern, in: IEEE Transactions on Parallel and Distributed Systems, 2020.

[24] T. Zhang, et al., CuTensor-tubal: efficient primitives for tubal-rank tensor operations on GPUs, in: IEEE Transactions on Parallel and Distributed Systems, 2019.

[25] Alexander Novikov, et al., Tensorizing neural networks, in: Advances in Neural Information Processing Systems, 2015, pp. 442–450.

[26] V. Lebedev, et al., Speeding-up convolutional neural networks using fine-tuned CP-decomposition, in: 3rd International Conference on Learning Representations, ICLR 2015-Conference Track Proceedings, 2015.

[27] Yong-Deok Kim, et al., Compression of deep convolutional neural networks for fast and low power mobile applications, arXiv:1511.06530, 2015.

[28] Timur Garipov, et al., Ultimate tensorization: compressing convolutional and fc layers alike, arXiv preprint, arXiv:1611.03214, 2016.

[29] Y. Zhang, et al., Video synthesis via transform-based tensor neural networks, in: ACM Multimedia, 2020.

[30] Karen Simonyan, Andrew Zisserman, Very deep convolutional networks for large-scale image recognition, arXiv preprint, arXiv:1409.1556, 2014.

[31] Xin He, Kaiyong Zhao, Xiaowen Chu, AutoML: a survey of the state-of-the-art, Knowledge-Based Systems 212 (2019) 106622.

[32] Jacob Biamonte, Ville Bergholm, Tensor networks in a nutshell, arXiv preprint, arXiv: 1708.00006, 2017.

Coupled tensor decompositions for data fusion

10

Christos Chatzichristos[a], Simon Van Eyndhoven[a,b], Eleftherios Kofidis[c], and Sabine Van Huffel[a]

[a]*KU Leuven, Department of Electrical Engineering (ESAT), STADIUS Center for Dynamical Systems, Signal Processing and Data Analytics, Leuven, Belgium*
[b]*icometrix, Leuven, Belgium*
[c]*Dept. of Statistics and Insurance Science, University of Piraeus, Piraeus, Greece*

CONTENTS

10.1 Introduction

Data fusion, defined as the analysis of several datasets such that they can interact with and inform each other, is well established as one of the most promising analysis approaches in an increasing number of diverse application areas involving inter-related datasets. The motivation for data fusion is manifold. Data fusion models can be used for better understanding a natural phenomenon, for improving the performance of classification tasks, or for providing a unified picture of a system under examination

Tensors for Data Processing. https://doi.org/10.1016/B978-0-12-824447-0.00016-9

and in general extracting knowledge from diverse inter-related datasets. The purpose of this chapter is to introduce the reader to the problem of data fusion and motivate for its adoption in practice. From a methodological point of view, the added value of the use of tensor decompositions in this context is given special emphasis.

In Section 10.2 we introduce different ways with which data fusion can be realized. We also point out the main challenges that need to be taken into consideration and propose ways to alleviate them.

The datasets to be fused are very often heterogeneous in nature and of a high (explicit or intrinsic), mutually possibly different, dimensionality. For example, in the fusion of the electroencephalography (EEG) and functional magnetic resonance imaging (fMRI) modalities of brain imaging, the EEG dataset is most commonly represented by a 3D or 4D array (tensor) while a matrix representation is adopted for the fMRI signal. It is thus of no surprise that various tensor decomposition models have been considered in their coupled configuration to fully exploit the complementary information "hidden" in the diverse datasets. Coupled tensor decomposition models and methods most frequently used in data fusion are the subject of Section 10.3.

The fusion in multimodal data analysis is a quite old concept and practice (and also ubiquitous in species and crucial to their survival), which has been gaining increasing attention over the past three decades, in an increasing number of applications involving diverse sets of inter-related data. These include several biomedical engineering applications [1–4], fusion of different kinds of images in order to improve their quality [5,6], metabolomics [7,8], array processing [9–11], sentiment analysis [12], thermodynamics [13], forecasting chronic diseases [14], and prediction of missing data [15,16], to only mention a few.

The range of data fusion applications is so wide that we will have to limit ourselves here to only a nonexhaustive subset of them. In Section 10.4 we will briefly discuss fusion applications in the areas of biomedical engineering and remote sensing (with a focus on the pan-sharpening problem). Section 10.5 briefly describes the different tensor-based approaches that have been employed in a specific application of biomedical engineering, namely the fusion of EEG and fMRI. Section 10.6 reviews toolboxes that can be used in data fusion problems along with related demos. Section 10.7 summarizes the main conclusions of the chapter and points to the most challenging open directions for future research.

10.2 What is data fusion?
10.2.1 Context and definition

Although the concept of data fusion is not new, the recent technological advances in computing power and storage capabilities along with the emergence of new sensor and advanced processing methods have increased the availability of multiple datasets that describe the same phenomenon and have made the fusion of big data viable. The origin of data fusion as a research subject dates back to the early 1990s. The impact and growth of the area over the last 30 years is reflected in the explosive

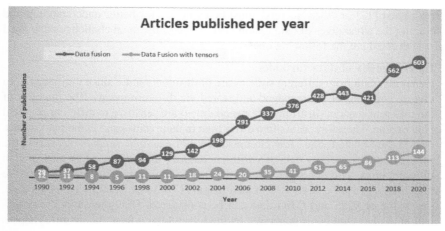

FIGURE 10.1

Number of publications on data fusion and on data fusion with tensors per year, for the last 30 years (results of searching in Scopus).

increase of the number of papers on the subject (Fig. 10.1). Data fusion techniques combine data from multiple sensors and relevant external information (if available) to achieve more accurate inferences compared to the use of a single sensor, or multiple sensors the outputs of which are separately treated. Crucial for the success of data fusion is the complementary nature of different sources, which allows the retrieval of latent knowledge not possible otherwise. Based on the characteristics of the problem at hand, a distinctive selection of the degree of generalization and formalization of the model that will be used is necessary. Proper selection of the model and the way of linking (coupling) the datasets can reveal new forms of diversity which is the cornerstone of data fusion [17].

Since the number of parameters that characterize a given dataset or a combination of datasets as in data fusion can be enormous, it is very important to learn a factorization (decomposition) of the data and how to reduce that number to a workable size. Put differently, a compact low-dimensional encoding of the high-dimensional data must be learned and subsequently used for performing the given analysis in a more efficient way [18]. For example, in fMRI, most of the voxel activations are close to zero and can be neglected, while the stronger (nonzero) ones have a low-rank structure, which can be exploited to provide a more compact representation of the dataset through an appropriate decomposition. In data fusion, the datasets are coupled along one or more of their modes implying equality or, more generally, similarity of some of their factors. Hence, coupled (linked) decompositions are pertinent.

10.2.2 Challenges of data fusion

Working with datasets from different sources can be beneficial in several applications. However, it is not an easy task, in general, and multiple challenges need to be addressed [17] or "dirty secrets" must be exploited for better understanding and leveraging the advantages of data fusion [19]. Some of the main challenges that need to be addressed are the following ones:

- **Heterogeneity of data variables**
  Generally, data from different sources are of different nature since they stem from diverse activities or are managed and stored via different means. The majority of the different sensors (instruments or modalities) are sensitive to different physical phenomena. Therefore, data often differ both in their values and in their structures, even if they relate to the same circumstance. For example, sensors measuring the same event may produce data of a different nature which are therefore measured in different units. This condition is known as noncommensurability and is one of the first challenges to be addressed in data fusion [17]. As an example of such a case, the fusion of EEG and fMRI data can be considered. EEG measures the propagation of electrical fields generated by the ions released from the neural synapses when neurons are activated [20] while fMRI measures induced changes in magnetization between oxygenated and nonoxygenated blood [21]. Thus, the same event, namely the activation of a brain area, is measured through different physical phenomena (electrical activity and magnetic properties of the blood) and hence the two datasets are not homogeneous. Furthermore, the majority of imaging modalities are nonquantitative and need complementary information from other sources of data [22]. For example, the fMRI signal is a measure of neuronal activity that induces hemodynamic changes and the amplitude of the brain activation can only be considered relatively to other areas of the same image. In different subjects, the same level of neuronal activity can evoke fMRI signals of different amplitudes (inter-subject variability of the hemodynamic response of the brain [23]). As a direct consequence, fMRI images of different subjects cannot be directly compared, since fMRI signals can only be considered as being proportional to the activity of neurons, and hence a nonquantitative measure. On the contrary, for example, EEG is a quantitative modality since the activation (on every subject) is measured in Volts, a unit that is quantitatively defined and allows comparisons among different subjects.

- **Registration**
  A standard process in signal and image processing is the registration of multimodal signals or images to standardized templates and to the same coordinate system. The registration process aims to improve the quality of data fusion by minimizing distortions and differences among the fused datasets induced by artifacts, noise, or even the nature of the different modalities. Image registration is usually based on the assumption that image intensities are linearly correlated [24], an assumption that can be far from being valid, especially in the registration of multimodal medical images. The inherent difference in the nature of the medical imaging modalities minimizes the correlation among the intensities. Furthermore, some neuroimaging modalities are prone to geometric distortions. Echo-planar imaging (EPI), for example, offers very high acquisition speed but at the expense of possible distortion and intensity loss mainly caused by rapidly changing field

inhomogeneities [25]. Furthermore, differences (delays) in time might be induced by the human body itself, such as the delays induced by the hemodynamic response function (HRF) of the brain in fMRI. The HRF is the blood oxygenation level-dependent (BOLD) signal corresponding to a transient neural activity and is a rather slow signal. It can be thought of as the impulse response of a filter (brain) and introduces a delay to the stimulus [21].

- **Variability in resolution and dimensions**
  Even in the case that the datasets share the same coordinate system (or the same units), their resolution might be very disparate. Regarding again the previous example with the fusion of EEG and fMRI, EEG has very good temporal resolution (in the scale of milliseconds) but low spatial resolution (limited, mainly, by the number of electrodes used). In contrast, fMRI has very good spatial resolution (thousands of voxels, each of which is limited to a few cubic millimeters in size) but a very low time resolution (a new image is acquired every 2–3 seconds). Based on the nature of the different modalities (sensors) or based on the coupling assumptions, datasets of unequal dimensions might result. For example, a fourth-order tensor in EEG (time × electrodes × frequency × subjects) might be coupled with a third-order tensor in fMRI (time × space × subjects) [26]. Analogous challenges are faced in many other applications such as multiresolution image sharpening [27], the fusion of positron emission tomography (PET) images with computed tomography (CT) [22] scans, and the fusion of satellite images [28].

All previous challenges must be addressed in the preprocessing phase of the datasets and scaling and normalization can be used as the main tools in this phase. The normalization and scaling process is not trivial and the specific nature of the data and problem at hand must be carefully considered for that purpose. This is the reason that a large volume of the literature has been devoted to relative approaches [29,30]. As an alternative to scaling and normalization, the use of different weights per dataset (modality/sensor) in the course of the fusion process has been proposed [31–35].

- **Different types of noise and artifacts**
  With the heterogeneity in the data comes, unavoidably, heterogeneity in the type of noise. Depending on the task at hand and the type of the modalities, different types of noise and artifacts can be expected. Thermal noise, extraterrestrial noise (for space applications), shot noise, and generally noise sources of different frequency content and statistical properties might be present in our data. Furthermore, calibration errors, quantization, movement (either of the sensor or of the object monitored), thermal drift of the machine, and power line interference are some of the artifacts, which may also affect the quality of the data [17,36]. In general, the imperfection of equipment and nonoptimal experimental conditions may result in information loss, noise amplification, and artifacts, resulting in distortion of the signal. How to jointly balance different sources of noise and artifacts and alleviate their influence is one of the main challenges in data fusion. However, in most of the studies, the differences in the types of noise are not taken into consideration or oversimplified assumptions (e.g., white noise in both modalities) are made [37].

- **Data uncertainties**

  Data uncertainties can in general be categorized into missing data and data conflict. The missing data are due to various causes, with the failure of the equipment being the most common of them. Nevertheless, the nature of the modalities and of the problem at hand may also cause data uncertainties. For example, having to convert the data to common formats for the purposes of joint analysis (e.g., complex values to real values or coping with different sampling frequencies among modalities, etc.) can also result in missing data and it is even possible that a modality can only partially report a phenomenon (such as, for example, the spatial information of EEG and fMRI). In general, when the correspondence among multimodal data cannot be established, the result of the fusion might present missing data (for some of the modalities). Data conflict, instead, is a contradiction between two nonnull values for the same property and the same entity among the data points of the different modalities. The way to handle data uncertainties is a fundamental challenge in data fusion and the first step to solving this is to correctly identify the mechanisms (and reasons) behind them. Different approaches can be employed, which fall under three main categories: ignoring, avoiding, and resolving. For a detailed analysis and examples of such strategies the interested reader is referred to [27,38].

- **Validation**

  Another fundamental challenge is related to the validation of the results. It is a quite common problem in data fusion tasks where no ground truth exists. We need to take into consideration that a "perfect" sensor does not exist; hence, if something cannot be actually observed or inferred from the events (and hence theoretically from a perfect sensor), then fusion of data from multiple sensors in whatever form is not able to overcome this problem. Since the validation of the results (usually) cannot be performed directly due to a lack of ground truth, different metrics can be employed to evaluate the performance of each sensor and select which sensors are more trustworthy [17]. For example, the selection of the model can be performed via the comparison of each possible fusion setting to theoretical lower bounds (e.g., posterior Cramér–Rao bounds [39,40]). The model whose performance is closest to the theoretical lower bound is considered being the best and is adopted. However, such methods, which use an exhaustive comparison of possible candidate models, are expensive in terms of computation. Failure to accurately assess the accuracy of a sensor or of the quality of a dataset may lead to addition of bias or deterioration in the results, since the value of extra sources in data fusion is difficult to be quantified and the addition of extra modalities (that bear no relevant information) may result in deterioration of the overall result. A validation process is therefore essential to decide whether all sources of data (modalities) are relevant and necessary or whether any of those are redundant or may even deteriorate the quality of the analysis [15].

- **Types of coupling**

  As explained, considering data that are not relevant for the application could even harm the analysis. The same holds for links or connections among different modalities that are not accurate. The use of extra links will result in a further increase of the computational complexity of the data fusion architecture employed. Furthermore, if phantom connections are imposed, the performance will deteriorate. Hence, a key point is choosing the way that the data will be fused in order to capture the actual relationships among modalities and be able to fully exploit their complementary nature. The underlying idea of data fusion is that an ensemble of datasets is "more than the sum of its parts" in the sense that it contains latent information that will not be exploited if those connections are ignored [17]. The different types of fusion architectures and levels of fusion will be further analyzed in the following subsection.

The heterogeneity (in all the aspects defined above) of the data available for fusion greatly influences the selection of the appropriate model to be employed. It is highly unlikely that general-purpose data fusion strategies will be able to deal with the different characteristics of all fusion tasks. All the steps (from the preprocessing to the actual analysis of the data) must be tailored to the specific needs of the problem at hand. Moreover, no model is ideal under all settings. Generally, in order to achieve the best performance, a priori information about the application and knowledge of the characteristics of the different modalities and data should be considered in advance. Choosing sophisticated data fusion methods will not be a substitute, by any means, for the accurate and thorough preprocessing: the "downstream processing cannot absolve upstream sins" [19]. Every link of the data fusion chain, from data refinement to knowledge discovery, must be properly designed for a given problem and a given scenario.

10.2.3 Types of fusion and data fusion strategies

Different types of fusion can be realized [17,41,42] but generally the definition may differ with regard to the degree of generality and also depending on the specific research areas [27]. Data fusion techniques can be categorized in various ways. The main categorizations are based on (i) the level where and (ii) the way in which the fusion is performed (Fig. 10.2). Two main levels and two sublevels have been defined and become a reference classification [42,43], namely, "early"/low-level fusion and "late" fusion, which is in turn subdivided into mid-level and high-level fusion. In "early"/low-level (or observational level) fusion, raw datasets (or blocks of data) are used. Mid-level (feature level or state-vector level) fusion is considered when the data fusion methods operate on features extracted from each dataset separately, so, instead of using raw data for modeling the task at hand, features of the data are used. The high-level (decision/information level) fusion methods model each dataset separately and only decisions (model outcome) from processing each data block are fused. The latter is also referred to as data integration, implying that the parallel processing of the various modalities is performed followed by a decision making step at the end.[1]

---

[1] For some authors (e.g., [17]), data integration is considered as a third way of fusing the data instead of a different level of fusion.

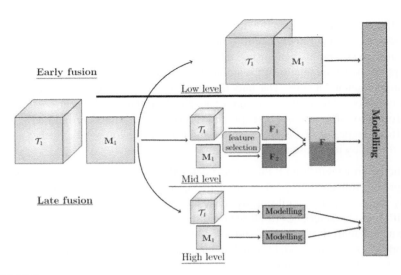

FIGURE 10.2

Categorization of fusion methods [26].

Late fusion approaches are more commonly used in order to more easily overcome any difficulties that may arise from the heterogeneity of the data.

In terms of the way the fusion is performed, the categorization is two-way. The earliest approaches for fusion (and a large number of recent ones, e.g., [44]) are essentially "integrative" in nature. The rationale behind these methods is to employ objective functions for decomposition of a specific modality with constraints based on information from another. Recently, the emphasis has been turned to "true" fusion (e.g., [45–50]), where the decomposition of the data from each modality can influence the other using all the common latent information that may exist. When optimizing the objective function, the factors that have been identified as shared are appropriately "coupled" and thus a bridge between the two modalities is established.

10.3 Decompositions in data fusion

The factorization or decomposition of datasets is a versatile instrument for data fusion, which consists of factorizing all involved datasets so that one or more factors are shared (fully or partially and in a hard or smooth sense) among them. Fusing data is only meaningful in the presence of a common representation that allows to exploit a relationship among the different datasets. Decomposing the data can precisely offer such a common representation or *latent space* [17].

Consider a use case in which two sets of sensors measure different physical properties of a time-varying process. For example, consider the scenario of an airplane that is tracked by several radars and a forward looking infrared (FLIR) imaging sensor [36]. The resulting data arrays *share* a temporal mode, since they simultaneously capture fluctuations of the route of the aircraft, and thus any two measured time courses can in principle be mutually compared, in order to understand correlations among any physical parameters being measured. The use of multiple radars yields a more accurate estimation of the velocity and position of the aircraft by combining the different observations. The use of the FLIR sensor provides complementary information, since we can estimate with it the angular direction of the aircraft, which is not possible with the use of pulsed radars. On the other hand, the FLIR sensor is not able to provide accurate information for the airplane range [36].

Even for a moderate number of such sensors, the assessment of all pair-wise correlations quickly becomes intractable, as the number of pairs of data samples grows quadratically with the number of sensors. This is the main reason that a low-rank decomposition of the data can be sought for, namely in order to offer improved interpretability with the reduced number of parameters which need to be estimated and interpreted, of course in a complexity–accuracy trade-off. The goal of different types of decompositions is to estimate the different components ("causes," sources, original signals) that underlie and/or generate the data, based only on the observations, that is, "blindly." This is why such techniques are considered as methods of blind source separation (BSS) [18]. BSS can be considered as a type of unsupervised learning. We can couple (indirectly) those different decompositions by adding extra constraints on the data, for example, that the temporal components of all radars are equal (expressing that they all measure similar fluctuations).

In the example above, we have silently ignored issues of identifiability. If all datasets exist in a matrix form, then a two-way decomposition of each, even when constrained to share a factor with others, suffers from rotational ambiguity, which precludes interpretation of the components (if there are more than one). Without additional constraints that can narrow down the solution space so that the decomposition is unique, this unidentifiability problem is inherent to the matrix form of the data.

There is thus the need to move to representations that do not suffer from such an ambiguity. Tensor decompositions are useful for data fusion for several reasons. The representations that are possible with such models facilitate the ability of extracting interpretable modes of interest, which may be unique (modulo scaling and permutation ambiguities) under mild conditions [51] and hence there is no need for structural constraints or assumptions such as statistical independence, nonnegativity, sparsity, or smoothness in order to achieve a unique decomposition. Moreover, tensorial methods are able to make predictions more robustly in the presence of noise, compared to their two-way counterparts [52–54]. The uniqueness conditions mentioned can be relaxed even more in the case of coupled tensor decompositions, as compared to their single-tensor counterparts. Furthermore, in the joint analysis of tensors, the arbitrary permutation of the components that arises if each decomposition is done separately becomes common to all decompositions, thus resolving the permutation ambiguity. It has been demonstrated that coupling through one or more common factors that are shared among tensors can ensure uniqueness beyond what is possible when considering separate decompositions [55–57].

The aforementioned properties of tensor decompositions, along with the increase of the available computing power and availability of methods for handling big tensors [58], resulted in a significantly increased rate of adoption of such methods in the context of data fusion. This is also reflected in the number of related publications over the last 10 years (cf. Fig. 10.1, orange line (light gray in print version)).

10.3.1 Matrix decompositions and statistical models

Despite the fact that they suffer in general from the ambiguities previously described, matrix methods are currently the state-of-the-art in data fusion, relying one way or another on the idea of independent component analysis (ICA). ICA is a powerful tool for separating a multivariate signal into additive components based on the assumption that they are statistically independent. In other words, the assumption of uncorrelated components of the well-known principal component analysis (PCA) is strengthened to that of statistically independent components. ICA has been successfully employed in numerous applications [59,60].

ICA alternatives can be used in different ways and at different levels of fusion. Parallel ICA (pICA) [61,62] and linked ICA (LICA) [60] are late fusion approaches (data integration). In pICA, each modality is first processed separately using ICA and in a later phase the sources are matched across the modalities through the maximization of the correlation of a fixed, preselected, number of sources. This is performed iteratively by optimizing an augmented cost that takes both intra-modality independence and inter-modality correlation into account. The resulting components are not, in general, as independent as in a single-dataset ICA. LICA uses a Bayesian framework which determines automatically the optimal weighting of each modality, and can also detect nonshared components, in case they exist.

Low- and mid-level fusion models exploiting ICA have also been proposed, both for true and integrative fusion. The main assumption in most of their applications is the fact that a common dimension exists across the different datasets with which they can be linked. Joint ICA (jICA) [3,61,63–66] is the most common of the true fusion approaches. It processes the modalities simultaneously, allowing a bidirectional flow of information, and hence each dataset may influence the decomposition of the others. It is applied in different (usually imaging) modalities and extracts the independent components for each of them. Usually these components are linked (coupled) together with a shared loading parameter. For example, often the fusion of EEG and fMRI [67] relies on the assumption that the electrical activity and the BOLD response are generated by the same population of neurons. Hence, their amplitudes will increase and decrease synchronously: a stronger peak activation in EEG will yield a stronger BOLD response in this particular brain region, and vice versa. Following this assumption, the fMRI activation maps can be concatenated with the average EEG response corresponding to the same stimulus and linked with a common mixing matrix (representing the activation of the time courses). An alternative approach (of true fusion also) is the transposed independent vector analysis (tIVA), which uses the principle of IVA in a transposed dataset. IVA maximizes the independence among component vectors (i.e., sets of sources from different datasets) and the dependence among different source signals within each vector [68]. For a single dataset, ICA results as a special case.

Other matrix-based methods that are also used in data fusion include the family of partial least-squares (PLS) [49,69,70] methods that maximize the cross-covariance among the datasets and canonical correlation analysis (CCA) which aims to maximize the correlation among datasets [71,72]. Combinations are also common of either of the two types of methods or with ICA [59,73,74]. Detailed reviews of such matrix-based methods using statistical models for data fusion problems can be found, for example, in [3,75].

10.3.2 Tensor decompositions

Tensors, i.e., multidimensional arrays, are a natural way of representing systems and data involving (explicitly or implicitly) multiple dimensions (or "ways"/ "modes"). Besides their being a natural representation model, able to capture multiple dependencies and relations, tensors are useful for their richness of decomposition models and methods, which allow to unveil latent information in the data not recoverable otherwise. If the tensor is expressed as the sum of R rank-1 tensors and R is minimal (= tensor rank), the so-called canonical polyadic decomposition (CPD) [76] results. CPD (less frequently referred to as CANDECOMP/PARAFAC or Kruskal decomposition) is the most widely known and used tensor decomposition model, due to its conceptual simplicity and its uniqueness guaranteed under only mild conditions. Each of the R rank-1 terms can be seen as representing one of the R components that form the tensor (Fig. 10.3(a)).

It is important, however, to note that imposing a rank-1 structure for all terms of the sum can be too restrictive or even unrealistic in some applications [54,77]. Under conditions that are of course stronger than those for CPD, a decomposition into terms of rank higher than 1 (namely of multilinear rank higher than $(1, 1, \ldots, 1)$) can still be (essentially) unique while enjoying a higher representation ability. We denote such generalized decompositions as block term decompositions (BTDs) [78–80]. The most popular example is schematically depicted in Fig. 10.3(b) and is referred to as BTD in multilinear rank-$(L, L, 1)$ terms.

The Tucker decomposition is a form of higher-order PCA [81]. It decomposes a tensor into a core tensor multiplied by a matrix along each mode. CPD can be considered a special case of Tucker decomposition where the core tensor is superdiagonal. Moreover, BTD can in fact be seen as a Tucker decomposition with block-diagonal core. Obviously, uniqueness for a Tucker decomposition is much more difficult to be guaranteed, unless strong constraints are imposed on its core and/or factors. This is why this decomposition model is only adopted when information about the mode subspaces of the tensor is sufficient for the problem at hand. PARAFAC2 [82,83] is another generalization of CPD and is not a tensor model in the strict sense as it can

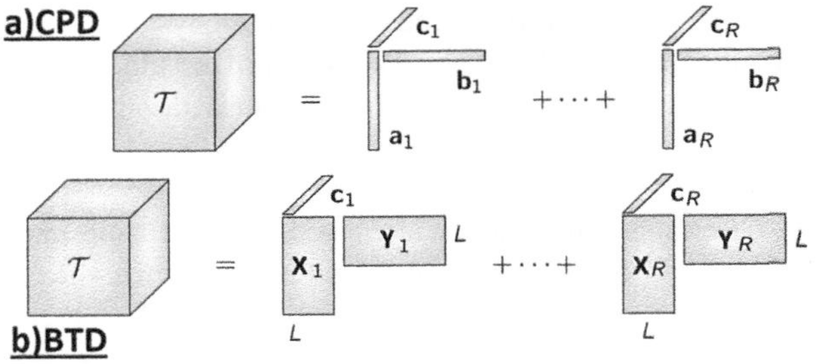

FIGURE 10.3

Schematic representation of (a) CPD and (b) BTD.

represent both regular tensors as well as irregular tensors (collections of matrices of different dimensions) with size variations along one of the modes.

For more details on these tensor decomposition models, the reader is referred to the corresponding chapters of this book and in the related references.

10.3.3 Coupled tensor decompositions

While several approaches to data fusion have been proposed in the form of decompositions of two (or more) matrices, as briefly reviewed in Section 10.3.1, a drawback is that they are only unique under certain constraints. Indeed, all such purely matrix-based methods require the user to formulate one or more constraints and a certain objective to be maximized. For example, methods based on IVA maximize a measure of statistical independence intra-dataset and simultaneously maximize dependence of sources inter-dataset. Alternatively, methods such as CCA and PLS maximize cross-correlation or cross-covariance in the process of extracting sources from the data. Whether these constraints or objective functions are sensible depends on the application at hand, and hence an informed choice must be made by the user, disqualifying these methods somewhat from bearing the label "unsupervised." Tensors can fill this gap to some extent. As highlighted above, the decomposition of tensors of order three and higher into low-rank components is easily unique, without additional constraints. For data fusion, they can hence be employed as a powerful tool to force identifiability of the sources, even in a more unsupervised fashion (i.e., without the need for constraints or optimization criteria beyond maximizing a measure of fit). The simplest imaginable model which benefits from this property is the joint decomposition of two datasets, of which one is represented as a matrix, while the other comes as a tensor of order three or higher. Such a coupled matrix tensor factorization (CMTF) inherits the uniqueness property of a simple tensor decomposition, which carries over to the matrix part of the decomposition, since the components of the matrix part are tied to the components of the tensor part, fixing any rotational ambiguity that would otherwise exist [55].

CMTF was first proposed in [84] and later extended in [15,85]. For a third-order tensor $\mathcal{T}$ and a matrix $\mathbf{M}$ it can be written as

$$\mathcal{T} \approx \sum_{r=1}^{R} \mathbf{c}_r \otimes \mathbf{a}_r^{(2)} \otimes \mathbf{a}_r^{(3)} = \left[\!\!\left[\mathbf{C}, \mathbf{A}^{(2)}, \mathbf{A}^{(3)} \right]\!\!\right], \tag{10.1}$$

$$\mathbf{M} \approx \sum_{r=1}^{R} \mathbf{c}_r \otimes \mathbf{b}_r^{(2)} = \left[\!\!\left[\mathbf{C}, \mathbf{B}^{(2)} \right]\!\!\right], \tag{10.2}$$

where $\otimes$ denotes the vector outer product and $\mathbf{A}^{(2)} = [\mathbf{a}_1^{(2)}, \mathbf{a}_2^{(2)}, \ldots, \mathbf{a}_R^{(2)}]$ and similarly for the other factors. We use the notation $[\![\cdot]\!]$ to denote the CPD model. The optimization function of the CMTF can be formulated as

$$\min_{\mathbf{C}, \mathbf{A}^{(2)}, \mathbf{A}^{(3)}, \mathbf{B}^{(2)}} \left\| \mathcal{T} - \left[\!\!\left[\mathbf{C}, \mathbf{A}^{(2)}, \mathbf{A}^{(3)} \right]\!\!\right] \right\|_F^2 + \left\| \mathbf{M} - \left[\!\!\left[\mathbf{C}, \mathbf{B}^{(2)} \right]\!\!\right] \right\|_F^2. \tag{10.3}$$

The factor $\mathbf{C}$, with columns $\mathbf{c}_r$ ($r = 1, 2 \ldots R$), is shared between the decomposition of the third-order tensor, $\mathcal{T}$, and the decomposition of the matrix, $\mathbf{M}$. The matrices $\mathbf{A}^{(2)}$ and $\mathbf{A}^{(3)}$ correspond to the nonshared second and third mode of $\mathcal{T}$, respectively. Similarly, $\mathbf{B}^{(2)}$ corresponds to the second mode of $\mathbf{M}$; $\|\cdot\|_F$ denotes the Frobenius norm for higher-order tensors/matrices and $\|\cdot\|_2$ the 2-norm for vectors.

The decomposition of $\mathcal{T}$ into low-rank factors "transfers" its uniqueness properties via the factor matrix $\mathbf{C}$ to the matrix decomposition, removing any ambiguities in $\mathbf{B}^{(2)}$ (provided that $\mathbf{C}$ is of full column rank) [55,57].

In a more generic setting, the datasets share some common components, but possess individual variability as well. In such a case, a model in which also unshared factors are presented, is more suited. Hence, the decompositions of both $\mathcal{T}$ and $\mathbf{M}$ would receive additional low-rank terms which are not coupled. Fig. 10.4 depicts an example of such a CMTF, in which two of the components are shared and an additional unshared rank-1 term exists (partially shared factors).

An advanced CMTF (ACMTF) [46,47] model has also been proposed in order to allow the presence of both shared and unshared components in the coupled factor(s) and provides a way to automatically determine them. ACMTF identifies the shared and unshared components by revealing the corresponding weights as follows:

$$\min_{\boldsymbol{\lambda}, \boldsymbol{\sigma}, \mathbf{C}, \mathbf{A}^{(2)}, \mathbf{A}^{(3)}, \mathbf{B}^{(2)}} = \left\| \mathcal{T} - \left[\!\!\left[\boldsymbol{\lambda}; \mathbf{C}, \mathbf{A}^{(2)}, \mathbf{A}^{(3)} \right]\!\!\right] \right\|_F^2 + \left\| \mathbf{M} - \left[\!\!\left[\boldsymbol{\sigma}; \mathbf{C}, \mathbf{B}^{(2)} \right]\!\!\right] \right\|_F^2$$
$$+ \beta \|\boldsymbol{\lambda}\|_1 + \beta \|\boldsymbol{\sigma}\|_1 \tag{10.4}$$
$$\text{s.t.} \quad \|\mathbf{c}_r\|_2 = \|\mathbf{a}_r^{(2)}\|_2 = \|\mathbf{a}_r^{(3)}\|_2 = \|\mathbf{b}_r^{(2)}\|_2 = 1, \qquad r = 1, 2, \ldots, R,$$

where $\boldsymbol{\lambda}$ and $\boldsymbol{\sigma}$ correspond to the weights of the rank-1 components in the third-order tensor and the matrix, respectively; $\|.\|_1$ denotes the 1-norm of a vector and β is a positive penalty parameter. The goal of ACMTF is the sparsification of the weights $\boldsymbol{\lambda}$

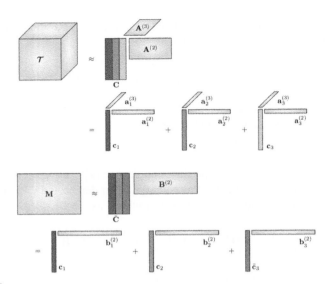

FIGURE 10.4

Data fusion can offer a holistic view on a certain phenomenon when complementary data are available. Coupled tensor decompositions reveal sources that underlie the data which are fully or partially shared among the involved tensors. An example is shown of a partially coupled matrix tensor factorization (CMTF) of a tensor $\mathcal{T}$ and a matrix $\mathbf{M}$, which are measured along a shared first mode. Both $\mathcal{T} \approx [\![\mathbf{C}, \mathbf{A}^{(2)}, \mathbf{A}^{(3)}]\!]$ and $\mathbf{M} \approx [\![\check{\mathbf{C}}, \mathbf{B}^{(2)}]\!]$ are decomposed into a sum of rank-1 terms, two of which share their factor in the coupled mode. A third source (with green (light gray in print version) mode-1 signature) is not shared and is specific to the decomposition of $\mathcal{T}$, whereas another source (with brown (gray in print version) mode-1 signature) is specific to the decomposition of $\mathbf{M}$. Figure adapted from [86].

and $\boldsymbol{\sigma}$ via the use of the 1-norm penalties. The weights of the unshared components will result in values equal or close to zero (at least in one of the datasets).

The uniqueness of such partially coupled decompositions is in practice verified only experimentally, via cross-validation [87]. It is only recently that such decompositions with partial sharing of the factors in the coupled mode(s) are theoretically studied in their generality [57,88].

One of the weaknesses of ACMTF is that it forces equality of the coupled components, which may influence the result of the decomposition in the presence of a model inaccuracy. In an attempt to smear such effects, relaxed ACMTF (RACMTF) properly modifies the ACMTF model, with the adoption of soft coupling [89]. Following the same rationale in order to remove the strict assumption of identical shared components of ACMTF, another alternative approach is to maximize the correlation between the shared components of the tensor and the matrix in the common mode. This method is called correlated CMTF (CCMTF) [90].

A wide variety of constraints, loss functions, and different linear couplings (couplings with linear transformations) can be added in the CMTF rationale. Recently, a

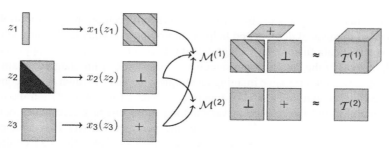

FIGURE 10.5

Schematic of an example of SDF. The vector z_1, the triangular matrix z_2, and the full matrix z_3 are transformed into a Toeplitz, orthogonal, and nonnegative matrix, respectively. The resulting factors are then used to jointly factorize two coupled datasets with the use of SDF [100].

flexible optimization framework that facilitates the use of such couplings and constraints has been proposed [91], while also allowing the incorporation of nonhard couplings as in [92].

More general (than CMTF) coupled tensor decomposition models, involving an arbitrary number of tensors and/or matrices, can be conceived and have been extensively studied [55,56] and applied in diverse application areas as outlined in the following. Coupled CPDs [1,93], BTDs [55,94], and Tucker decompositions [95] have been successfully employed in diverse applications, while also double coupled CPDs have been recently proposed [26,96,97].

In addition to these models, the so-called structured data fusion (SDF) framework [98] deserves to be mentioned here as it offers an extremely flexible and modular way of rapid prototyping coupled decompositions, with a wealth of constraints on the factors and/or the coupling mechanisms. To develop a constrained coupled decomposition in SDF one needs to define its (shared and unshared) factors as chains of transformations for which the derivative with respect to the input can be computed. An example of such a constrained coupled decomposition with SDF can be viewed in Fig. 10.5, where a Toeplitz, an orthogonal, and a nonnegative matrix are involved as factors in a constrained CMTF. The (transformed) factors can be computed by means of simple, first-order methods based on gradient descent [98], but also via second-order methods that enjoy both faster convergence and computational efficiency [99]. Additional information and guidelines for the use of the SDF framework can be found in [100].

10.4 Applications of tensor-based data fusion

10.4.1 Biomedical applications

In an attempt to better understand a system as complex as the human body, multimodal measurements can be beneficial in view of their ability to provide information on complementary aspects of the same system. More accurate prognostic tools can be provided to medical doctors and help in improving everyday healthcare, which is the reason that data fusion plays a significant role in lots of biomedical applications.

A large part of the data fusion research has focused on brain imaging. Brain studies largely rely on noninvasive imaging techniques, the aim of which is to reconstruct a high-resolution anatomical and/or functional image of the brain. Often the underlying principles and the resolution vary among those imaging techniques but they may also be complementary. For instance, the neuronal activity is conducted via the release of ions, which induce electric and magnetic fields that can be directly recorded by EEG and magnetoencephalography (MEG), respectively. Furthermore, the activation of the brain regions require extra oxygen, which induces changes in magnetization between oxygen-rich and oxygen-poor blood, giving rise to the BOLD signal that can be detected by fMRI. These imaging techniques vary greatly in their spatiotemporal resolution and their fusion can be beneficial, given the fact that they all aim at capturing the same brain activations, each in its own manner. The fusion of EEG and fMRI using tensors will be presented in detail in the last section of this chapter. It should be noted that the fusion of MEG and fMRI has also been studied with similar tools [4,41].

Furthermore, the fusion of EEG and MEG via coupled CP decompositions has been explored for several applications such as the study of the photic driving effect [101] or for the estimation of the lead-field matrices and preprocessing [102] and for improving classification tasks [103]. Despite the fact that EEG and MEG have similar temporal and spatial resolution and they measure similar natural events, their fusion helps to significantly improve the performance in all of the abovementioned applications. This argument may seem to be contradicting to what we stated earlier, but it is a nice example of the fact that the complementarity of different datasets might lie in different aspects. The fusion of EEG and MEG allows an indirect improvement of the spatial resolution by increasing the number of recording channels (EEG electrodes plus MEG sensors, since they are not placed at exactly the same location) and the overall head surface coverage. Furthermore, it has been shown that the two modalities are sensitive to sources of different depth [104].

Functional imaging techniques can be complemented also by modalities that convey structural information. In particular, MRI is based on nuclear magnetic resonance of water molecules and provides anatomical information of the brain (distribution of gray matter, white matter, and cerebrospinal fluid in the brain). Diffusion tensor imaging (DTI) measures the diffusion process of water molecules along the fiber tracts of the brain and plays a significant role in modeling the structural (and effective) connectivity of the human brain. The combination of structural and functional information (MRI, DTI, fMRI) can result in an enhanced visualization and mapping of the human brain [4,27,47,105,106]. PET and single-photon emission CT (SPECT) are nuclear medicine imaging techniques which provide metabolic and functional information. They can be combined with MRI to provide anatomical information with strong soft-tissue contrast for accurately detecting areas with physiological abnormalities. MRI provides images in grayscale and at high resolution while PET and SPECT images are colorful and have rather low spatial resolution. Therefore the fusion of PET/SPECT and MRI images to a single fused image that contains both spatially and spectrally useful information is really beneficial, since it has been shown to lead to a more precise evaluation and treatment of several pathologies, such as brain and neck cancer. CMTF and linked decompositions have been employed for the fusion of MRI and PET/SPECT [107,108].

The fusion of biomedical modalities with behavioral scores or psychological scores is an emerging research area. A new model for estimating classical developmental diagnostic scores by exploiting data fusion in a joint tensor matrix decomposition of the EEG and phenotypic scores of child development has been proposed in [109]. An extension of this work incorporates also MRI data to further improve the estimation of the development of children while maintaining a high degree of similarity at a population level [110].

Although a brain–computer interface (BCI) is not (strictly speaking) a biomedical application, one relies on medical imaging data (mainly EEG) in order to analyze and translate it into commands that are connected to an output device to carry out a desired action. BCI applications can also benefit from the fusion approaches with tensor decompositions. Although fMRI is not commonly used for BCI applications, due to its immobility because of the size of the magnet, recently fusion of EEG-fMRI via tensor decompositions has been used in the training phase of a BCI [111]. The training phase of the BCI is performed in a hospital environment with the aid of fMRI, while the actual use of the BCI was performed (in a mobile context) only with EEG. The increased accuracy of the training (due to the fMRI) improves the general use of the BCI. Furthermore, the standard CCA method has been extended in a tensor counterpart in a steady-state visual evoked potential (SSVEP) BCI application [112], by jointly analyzing a three-way EEG tensor (channel × time × trial) and a reference dataset of sine-cosine (harmonic × time). Similarly, the multiway counterpart of PLS, multiway PLS (MPLS) [113], has also been used for predicting scalp-recorded EEG signals from invasively recorded EEG signals in an oddball experiment in a BCI [114].

10.4.2 Image fusion

Pan-sharpening is one of the most prominent problems of data fusion in remote sensing and consists of the integration of a hyperspectral image (HSI) and a multispectral image (MSI), both of which cover the same object or area. MSI has a high spatial resolution but limited spectral bands (panchromatic, black and white), whereas HSI is multispectral with low spatial resolution. In an attempt to circumvent the physical limitations of imaging sensors, the aim of the fusion is to obtain a superresolution image (SRI), with high resolution in both the spatial and spectral domains, which can help in the precise identification of the materials present in a scene and also enhance performance in many applications other than remote sensing like object detection for military purposes and tracking.

The existing pan-sharpening fusion methods are mostly based on the matrix factorizations, which by definition fall short in fully making use of the inherent 3D structure of HSI and MSI. Assuming that HSI and MSI admit low-rank CPDs, the pan-sharpening problem can be cast as a coupled CPD approximation. In [5] for example, recovery of the HRI was shown to be guaranteed provided that the CPD of the MSI is identifiable.

Recently this approach was extended by assuming that the high-resolution images follow a BTD model [78–80]. This facilitates the addition of prior knowledge to the spectral images since the latent factors have clear physical meaning [94]. A Tucker decomposition has also been considered [95] under the assumption that the superresolution image has approximately (and not exactly) low multilinear rank.

The success of those approaches significantly increased the number of publications that aim to fully exploit the advantages of tensor decompositions in this problem. Alternatives of the aforementioned methods have been proposed in an attempt to combine the advantages of the tensor decomposition models with prior knowledge. This includes approaches which employ sparsity constraints [115,116] or try to exploit a combination of the nonlocal HSI spatial similarities with the tensor formulations [117,118].

More challenging scenarios are now being examined, for example, with inter-image spectral variability [119]. Similar approaches have been followed also for the fusion of MSI with other modalities such as light detection and ranging (LiDAR) imaging [120] or have been generalized for the fusion of general images for different applications such as image compression [121].

10.5 Fusion of EEG and fMRI: a case study

Two of the most commonly used modalities for monitoring the brain activity are EEG and fMRI. fMRI is a noninvasive brain imaging technique, which indirectly studies brain activity by measuring fluctuations of the BOLD signal [21]. The first BOLD fluctuation occurs roughly 2–3 seconds after the onset of the neural activity, when the oxygen-rich (oxygenated) blood starts displacing the oxygen-depleted (deoxygenated) blood. This rises to a peak after 4–6 seconds, before falling back to the baseline (and typically undershooting slightly). The time course of the BOLD signal corresponding to transient neural activity is called the HRF. Although fMRI has a high spatial resolution, often at the millimeter scale, it is a "delayed" measure of the brain activity, with its temporal resolution being limited by the repetition time of the scanner (TR), usually of the order of seconds [21].

EEG provides information with respect to the neural electrical activity in the brain as a function of time. This is done via the use of multiple electrodes that are placed at certain locations over the scalp or (in more rare cases) over the cortex under the skull. The EEG signal results from the electrical measurement of the neuronal activation, realized through the movement of charged ions at the junction between the synapses of (the dendrites of) the neurons. This provides a more direct measure of the neuronal activity compared to fMRI (sensitive to millisecond changes in neural processing) and hence a better temporal resolution. However, EEG has poor spatial resolution, limited by the number of electrodes employed and the resistive properties of the extra-cerebral tissues. Furthermore, due to the fact that electrodes are more sensitive to neural activations that occur closer to the scalp, the determination of the exact location of activations that take place in deeper areas is more challenging [20]. The complementary nature of their spatiotemporal resolution motivates the fusion of EEG and fMRI towards a better localization of the brain activity, both in time and space [50,122], which can help in mapping the human brain more accurately.

Multivariate bilinear (i.e., matrix-based) methods, mainly based on ICA [61,63–65] and relying on the concatenation of different modes, have been, up to recently, the state-of-the-art for jointly analyzing EEG and fMRI. However, by definition such methods fall short in exploiting the inherently multiway nature of these data. fMRI and EEG datasets are inherently multidimensional, comprising information in time and along different voxels or channels, subjects, trials, etc. For EEG, in order to unveil more of the latent information, the signal can be expanded in additional dimensions, e.g., through incorporating spectral features by computing a wavelet transform of the EEG data or using the segment/event-related potential (ERP) mode (ERP is the response to a specific sensory, cognitive, or motor stimulus) [123]. This multidimensional nature of the EEG and fMRI datasets points to the adoption of tensor models instead of the matrix ones. The localization of the activated brain areas is a challenging BSS problem, in which the sources consist of a combination of the activated areas (spatial maps in fMRI and topoplots in EEG) and time courses. Several tensor decomposition methods have been applied in fMRI and EEG BSS, including CPD [52,124] and generalizations as PARAFAC2 [44,54] and BTD [78–80].

Various ways to realize the coupling have been considered, depending on the coupled mode: (i) coupling in the spatial domain with the use of the so-called lead-field matrix, which summarizes the volume conduction effects in the head (by transforming the 2D spatial information of the EEG to the 3D spatial information of the fMRI) [50], (ii) coupling in the subject domain, using the assumption that the same neural processes are reflected in both modalities with the same covariation [45,64,67], and, most commonly, (iii) coupling in the time domain using the convolution of the EEG time course with an HRF [49].

One of the first attempts for true fusion of EEG and fMRI was presented in [49], where the MPLS has been employed. The EEG dataset therein is modeled as channels × time × frequency, and fMRI as a time × space (voxels) matrix. The fMRI matrix and the EEG tensor are then coupled in the time domain. After up-sampling and convolving the time courses of the fMRI matrix with an a priori known HRF, the covariance with the EEG time courses is maximized.

In order to achieve coupling in the spatial domain, similarly to the a priori known HRF, an a priori known lead-field matrix must be assumed [41]. Extra constraints such as nonnegativity, sparsity, orthogonality, and smoothness are imposed on the spatial factors in order to ensure uniqueness of the coupled decomposition.

Heterogeneity in the datasets is also manifested in the models used to represent them. In the EEG-fMRI fusion example, classical approaches adopt a space (channels) × time × frequency/ERP tensor model for EEG (for the single-subject case)

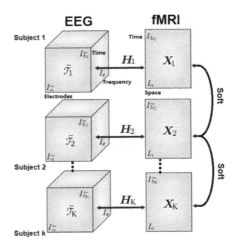

FIGURE 10.6

Schematic representation of DCMTF for *K* subjects.

whereas the fMRI signal is commonly represented as a matrix with its dimensions corresponding to space (voxels) × time. Their fusion relies on the coupling of the EEG tensor and the fMRI matrix along their common mode (which can be any of the above in different applications). There are only two very recent approaches that handle both modalities as tensors [1,93] while also lately a double coupled [97] approach has also been proposed and studied [26]. In a multisubject scenario, in order to analyze subjects with different time courses, a double CMTF (DCMTF) architecture has been adopted. Other than the coupling between the subjects in the time domain (via CMTF), an extra soft coupling among the spatial domains of the different subjects is enforced. The coupling among the spatial components retains the multiway nature of the multisubject fMRI case (keep in mind that a three-way tensor can also be seen as a set of matrices hard coupled in both of their modes), so that the multiway nature of the data is still exploited (Fig. 10.6).

Most of the existing methods rely on preprocessing of the fMRI data within the general linear model (GLM) framework. A spatial map of interest (areas of activation) per subject is extracted and all the spatial maps are stacked in a matrix (space × subjects), hence discarding the extra dimension of time and relying on CMTF to solve the joint BSS problem (Section 10.3.2). The use of the spatial maps of GLM categorizes such CMTF-based methods as late fusion [42].

In all of the previously described approaches, the coupling across the corresponding modes is "hard," meaning that the shared factors are constrained to be equal in the fused datasets (after any transformation applied, e.g., convolution with an HRF). Such an assumption might be very restrictive, since it implies that the used transformation is valid for every area of the brain and any subject. In order to avoid problems caused in the modeling by this constraint, a "soft" assumption of similarity (or with similar properties), that is, less stringent than imposing equality, can be made instead [1,92]. Furthermore, different methods can be used to account for a possible misspecification of the HRF. Constraining the HRF to a class of "plausible" waveforms and estimating the optimal one from the data themselves has been proposed in [2,48] for the single-subject case. Such approaches can be called "flexible."

PARAFAC2 has been used in an integrative fusion approach [44]. Therein, fMRI is modeled with a PARAFAC2 model with its modes representing time × voxels-per-slice × slice amplitude. This model splits the spatial domain of the fMRI dataset into two modes. The free mode of PARAFAC2 is the spatial domain per slice (since the size of each slice of the human brain is different in size) and the time course of electrode C2 (motor cortex) is used as a regressor of interest.

10.6 Data fusion demos

There exist several toolboxes and packages that can be used to develop and apply data fusion models. Structured data fusion [98], implemented in Tensorlab, and the Flexible Optimization Framework proposed in [91] offer great flexibility to the user to employ different transformations and linear couplings.

A number of the studies reviewed in Section 10.5 have used Tensorlab for implementing the proposed fusion methods. Tensorlab [100] is a Matlab$^{®}$[2] toolbox that can be used for rapid prototyping of (coupled) tensor models including various tools for tensor computations, (coupled) tensor decompositions with structured factors and complex optimization.

We will provide links, where the interested reader can find the Matlab code to reproduce (part of) the results reported in those studies. EEG-fMRI data from 10 temporal lobe epilepsy patients are used in [45]. The CMTF code along with the features from the real data used to explore epileptic network activity are available in: https://github.com/borbala-hunyadi/CMTF_hunyadi. Simulated data of EEG and fMRI along with the code to reproduce the soft coupled tensor decomposition model used in [1] and the DCMTF used in [26] can be found in: https://github.com/chrichat/Fusion. The pipeline for structured CMTF (sCMTF) of simultaneously recorded EEG and fMRI data and the collection of all Matlab functions that are needed to perform the computations described in [2] along with some simulated data are available in: https://github.com/svaneynd/structured-cmtf.

10.6.1 SDF demo – approximate coupling

As explained in previous sections, the coupling between two or more tensors does not need to be exact, that is, the shared factors can only be approximately eqal [26]. In this subsection, we will reproduce a demo from the Tensorlab [100] user guide that

---

[2] Matlab is a trademark of MathWorks, Inc. https://nl.mathworks.com/products/matlab.html.

employs the SDF framework [98] in an example of approximate coupling between two tensors. Let the 3-way tensors $\mathcal{T}$ and $\mathcal{S}$ be coupled in their first mode. To model an inexact coupling, the mode-1 CPD factor of $\mathcal{T}$ is perturbed by an additive 'noise' term, N, to give the corresponding factor for $\mathcal{S}$, D = A + N. When the noise term is large compared to A, the coupling is weak, while as the noise strength decreases, the coupling becomes stronger and approaches hard coupling.

To model the approximate coupling in SDF, two transformations are needed: `struct_select` and `struct_plus`. The former selects one entry from a cell variable. The latter can be used to sum all entries in a cell variable. The noise term N should be small enough, otherwise the tensors would be practically uncoupled. This is effected via L_2 regularization (line 28 in the code below). The relative error of the computed decomposition can be viewed in the `relerr` field of the output (`output.relerr`).

```
1   %% Build 10x11x12 tensor T of rank 3
2   % Randomly generated factors A,B,C in cell array U1
3   U1 = cpd_rnd([10,11,12],3);
4   % Generate tensor T from factors in U1
5   T = cpdgen(U1);
6
7   %% Build 10x13x14 tensor S of rank 3
8   % Randomly generate factors D,E,F in cell array U2
9   U2 = cpd_rnd([10,13,14],3);
10  U2{1} = U1{1}+1e-3*randn(10,3); % D = A + N;
11  % Generate tensor S from factors in U2
12  S = cpdgen(U2);
13
14  %% Build SDF model
15  model = struct;
16  % Define and initialize model variables; same dimensions
         with factors
17  model.variables.an = {randn(10,3),1e-2*randn(10,3)};
18  model.variables.b = randn(11,3);
19  model.variables.c = randn(12,3);
20  model.variables.e = randn(13,3);
21  model.variables.f = randn(14,3);
22
23  % Define model factors as (transformed) variables
24  % Select first entry in the cell, A
25  model.factors.A = {'an',@(z,task)struct_select(z,task,1)
         };
26  model.factors.B = 'b'; % B factor
27  model.factors.C = 'c'; % C factor
28  model.factors.D = {'an',@struct_plus}; % A+N
29  model.factors.E = 'e'; % E factor
30  model.factors.F = 'f'; % F factor
```

```
31  % Select first entry in the cell, N
32  model.factors.N = {'an',@(z,task)struct_select(z,task,2)
       };
33
34  % Define the model factorizations
35  % Tensor to be factorized
36  model.factorizations.T1.data = T;
37  % Choose CPD model with factors A,B,C
38  model.factorizations.T1.cpd = {'A','B','C'};
39  % Tensor to be factorized
40  model.factorizations.S1.data = S;
41  % Choose CPD model with factors D,E,F
42  model.factorizations.S1.cpd = {'D','E','F'};
43  % L2 regularization for N
44  model.factorizations.N.regL2 = {'N'};
45
46  % Compute coupled CPD, using nonlinear least squares
47  [sol,output] = sdf_nls(model,'Display',10,'CGMaxIter'
       ,100,'MaxIter',200);
```

More demos and examples of the use of Tensorlab and data fusion sith SDF can be found in https://www.tensorlab.net/doc/sdf-examples.html.

10.7 Conclusion and prospects

In light of the rapid evolution of technology, diverse data sources have become ubiquitous and it has been practically impossible to ignore the abundance of such inter-related datasets in our everyday lives. The common latent information in these datasets is discovered and exploited through data fusion.

The motivating assumption in data fusion is that its result will be more informative than any result obtained by the separate analysis of each single dataset. In other words, it is assumed that the combined analysis of different datasets will highlight their complementarity or synergy and will enable an enhanced view of the phenomenon under study. Of course this is not an easy task. Several challenges must be addressed and different modeling choices need to be considered, as explained in this chapter. In order to fully exploit the added value of data fusion, the proper understanding of the nature of the problem and the identification of the particularities of the inter-linked data are necessary. Furthermore, the accurate joint analysis of multiple datasets is adhered to the understanding of the individual datasets, which (along with accurate preprocessing) will lead to proper selection of the type of coupling of the datasets and superior performance.

Coupled tensor decomposition models and methods in data fusion can properly account for the links among datasets and have the potential to achieve gains and benefits that go far beyond those possible when each dataset is processed individually. In particular, they allow to reduce the degrees of freedom, thereby enhancing uniqueness and interpretability (among others). The potential impact of tensor decompositions in data fusion is high and spans the whole spectrum of applications.

All coupled tensor decompositions are burdened with the selection of hyperparameters. Notably, the selection of the number of sources is a recurring and often hard problem in BSS. Some prior efforts have been directed to this rank estimation problem. A large number of such methods are based on information theory or automatic relevance determination with Bayesian principles. A similar burden exists in the selection of the weights of regularizers that are being added for either selecting the coupled components [87] or forcing soft coupling [26] or even for ensuring uniqueness in some cases. We therefore expect that further innovation in a priori rank estimation, but especially in post hoc rank selection methods, may improve the performance of tensor-based methods in the context of data fusion. Furthermore, future research in data fusion should focus on devising ways of automatically selecting the weights of the different constraints.

Acknowledgments

We would like to thank Prof. Borbala Hunyadi, Delft Univ. for making her code used in [45] available as a demo and Prof. Lieven De Lathauwer, KUL and the Tensorlab [100] team for giving us the permission to reproduce one of their examples as a demo and generally for providing support when needed with tensor problems. Research funded by Bijzonder Onderzoeksfonds KU Leuven (BOF): Prevalentie van epilepsie en slaapstoornissen in de ziekte van Alzheimer: C24/18/097; EIT: 19263 – SeizeIT2: Discreet Personalized Epileptic Seizure Detection Device. This research received funding from the Flemish Government (AI Research Program). Sabine Van Huffel and Christos Chatzichristos are affiliated to Leuven, AI – KU Leuven institute for AI, B-3000, Leuven, Belgium.

References

[1] C. Chatzichristos, et al., Fusion of EEG and fMRI via soft coupled tensor decompositions, in: Eur. Signal Process. Conf. (EUSIPCO), Rome, Italy, Sep. 2018.

[2] S. Van Eyndhoven, et al., Augmenting interictal mapping with neurovascular coupling biomarkers by structured factorization of epileptic EEG and fMRI data, NeuroImage 228 (2021) 117652.

[3] T. Adalı, et al., Multimodal data fusion using source separation: two effective models based on ICA and IVA and their properties, Proceedings of the IEEE 103 (9) (Sep. 2015) 1478–1493.

[4] X. Fu, et al., Brainzoom: high resolution reconstruction from multi-modal brain signals, in: SIAM Int'l Conf. Data Mining (SDM), Houston, TX, USA, Apr. 2017.

[5] C.I. Kanatsoulis, et al., Hyperspectral super-resolution: a coupled tensor factorization approach, IEEE Transactions on Signal Processing 66 (24) (2018) 6503–6517.

[6] Y. Bu, et al., Hyperspectral and multispectral image fusion via graph Laplacian-guided coupled tensor decomposition, IEEE Transactions on Geoscience and Remote Sensing 59 (1) (Jan. 2020) 648–662.

[7] E. Acar, et al., Data fusion in metabolomics using coupled matrix and tensor factorizations, Proceedings of the IEEE 103 (9) (Sep. 2015) 1602–1620.

[8] E. Acar, et al., Structure-revealing data fusion model with applications in metabolomics, in: Int'l Conf. Eng. Med. Biol. Soc. (EMBC), 2013.

[9] M. Sørensen, L. De Lathauwer, Coupled tensor decompositions for applications in array signal processing, in: Int'l Workshop on Comput. Adv. in Multi-Sensor Adapt. Process (CAMSAP), St. Martin, France, Dec. 2013.

[10] M. Sørensen, L. De Lathauwer, Multidimensional harmonic retrieval via coupled canonical polyadic decomposition – part I: model and identifiability, IEEE Transactions on Signal Processing 65 (2) (Jan. 2017) 517–527.

[11] M. Sørensen, L. De Lathauwer, Multidimensional harmonic retrieval via coupled canonical polyadic decomposition – part II: algorithm and multirate sampling, IEEE Transactions on Signal Processing 65 (2) (Jan. 2017) 528–539.

[12] A. Zadeh, et al., Tensor fusion network for multimodal sentiment analysis, in: Conf. on Empirical Methods in Natural Language Processing, Copenhagen, Denmark, Sep. 2017.

[13] Y. Coutinho, et al., Combining thermodynamics with tensor completion techniques to enable multicomponent microstructure prediction, NPJ Computational Materials 6 (2) (Jan. 2020).

[14] E. Acar, et al., Forecasting chronic diseases using data fusion, Journal of Proteome Research 16 (7) (2017) 2435–2444.

[15] E. Acar, et al., Understanding data fusion within the framework of coupled matrix and tensor factorizations, Chemometrics and Intelligent Laboratory Systems (Nov. 2013) 53–64.

[16] Y. Wu, et al., A fused CP factorization method for incomplete tensors, IEEE Transactions on Neural Networks and Learning Systems 30 (3) (Mar. 2019) 751–764.

[17] D. Lahat, et al., Multimodal data fusion: an overview of methods, challenges, and prospects, Proceedings of the IEEE 103 (9) (Sep. 2015) 1449–1477.

[18] S. Theodoridis, Machine Learning: A Bayesian and Optimization Perspective, 2nd edition, Academic Press, 2020.

[19] D.L. Hall, A. Steinberg, Dirty secrets in multisensor data fusion, in: Nat. Symp. Sensor Data Fusion (NSSDF), San Antonio, TX, Jun. 2010.

[20] S. Sanei, J.A. Chambers, EEG Signal Processing, John Wiley & Sons Ltd, 2007.

[21] M.A. Lindquist, The statistical analysis of fMRI data, Statistical Science 23 (4) (Jun. 2008) 439–464.

[22] Y.-D. Zhang, et al., Advances in multimodal data fusion in neuroimaging: overview, challenges, and novel orientation, Information Fusion 64 (2020) 149–187.

[23] D.A. Handweker, et al., Variation of BOLD hemodynamic responses across subjects and brain regions and their effects on statistical analyses, NeuroImage 21 (4) (Apr. 2004) 1639–1651.

[24] F. Maes, et al., Multimodality image registration by maximization of mutual information, IEEE Transactions on Medical Imaging 16 (2) (Apr. 1997) 187–198.

[25] X. Hong, et al., Evaluation of EPI distortion correction methods for quantitative MRI of the brain at high magnetic field, Magnetic Resonance Imaging 33 (9) (Nov. 2015) 1098–1105.

[26] C. Chatzichristos, et al., Early soft and flexible fusion of EEG and fMRI via tensor decompositions, arXiv preprint, arXiv:2005.07134, May 2020.

[27] M. Cocchi, in: Data Fusion Methodology and Applications, Elsevier, May 2019.

[28] L. Wald, et al., Fusion of satellite images of different spatial resolutions: assessing the quality of resulting images, Photogrammetric Engineering and Remote Sensing 63 (6) (Jun. 1997) 691–699.

[29] S. Wu, et al., Evaluating Score Normalization Methods in Data Fusion, AIRS2006: Information Retrieval Technology, vol. 123, Springer, 2006, pp. 642–648.

[30] M. Singh, et al., A comprehensive overview of biometric fusion, Information Fusion 52 (Dec. 2019) 187–205.

[31] Q. Xue, et al., AWDF: an adaptive weighted deep fusion architecture for multi-modality learning, in: IEEE Int'l Conf. Big Data (Big Data), Los Angeles, CA, Dec. 2019.

[32] T. Wilderjans, et al., Simultaneous analysis of coupled data blocks differing in size: a comparison of two weighting schemes, Computational Statistics & Data Analysis 4 (2009) 1086–1098.

[33] M. Vervloet, et al., On the selection of the weighting parameter value in principal covariates regression, Chemometrics and Intelligent Laboratory Systems 123 (2013) 36–43.

[34] A. Kendall, et al., Multi-task learning using uncertainty to weigh losses for scene geometry and semantics, in: EEE/CVF Conf. Computer Vision and Pattern Recognition, Salt Lake City, Ut, Jun. 2018.

[35] T.F. Wilderjans, E. Ceulemans, Clusterwise PARAFAC to identify heterogeneity in three-way data, Chemometrics and Intelligent Laboratory Systems 129 (2013) 87–97.

[36] M.E. Liggins, et al., Handbook of Multisensor Data Fusion, CRC Press, 2008.

[37] C. Chatzichristos, et al., Tensor-based blind fMRI source separation without the Gaussian noise assumption – a β-divergence approach, in: IEE Global Conf. Signal Inf. Proc. (GlobalSIP), Ottawa, Canada, Nov. 2019.

[38] G. Saporta, Data fusion and data grafting, Computational Statistics & Data Analysis 38 (4) (2002) 465–473.

[39] P. Wang, et al., The estimation fusion and Cramér-Rao bounds for nonlinear systems with uncertain observations, in: 20th Int'l Conf. Information Fusion (Fusion), Xian, China, Jul. 2017.

[40] S. Subedi, et al., Cramér–Rao type bounds for sparsity-aware multi-sensor multi-target tracking, Signal Processing 145 (2018) 68–77.

[41] E. Karahan, et al., Tensor analysis and fusion of multimodal brain images, Proceedings of the IEEE 103 (9) (Sep. 2015) 1531–1559.

[42] D. Ramachandram, G.W. Taylor, Deep multimodal learning, IEEE Signal Processing Magazine 69 (Nov. 2017) 96–108.

[43] J. Llinas, D.L. Hall, An introduction to multisensor data fusion, in: Int'l Symp. Circuits and Systems (ISCAS), Monterrey, Mexico, Nov. 1998.

[44] S. Ferdowsi, et al., A new informed tensor factorization approach to EEG–fMRI fusion, Journal of Neuroscience Methods 254 (1) (Oct. 2015) 27–35.

[45] B. Hunyadi, et al., Fusion of electroencephalography and functional magnetic resonance imaging to explore epileptic network activity, in: Eur. Signal Process. Conf, (EUSIPCO), Budapest, Hungary, Aug.–Sep, 2016.

[46] E. Acar, et al., Tensor based fusion of EEG and fMRI to understand neurological change in schizophrenia, in: Int'l Symp. Circuits and Systems (ISCAS), Baltimore, MD, May 2017.

[47] E. Acar, et al., ACMTF for fusion of multi-modal neuroimaging data and identification of biomarkers, in: Eur. Signal Process. Conf. (EUSIPCO), Kos, Greece, Aug.–Sep, 2017.

[48] S.V. Eyndhoven, et al., Flexible fusion of electroencephalography and functional magnetic resonance imaging: revealing neural-hemodynamic coupling through structured matrix-tensor factorization, in: Eur. Signal Process. Conf. (EUSIPCO), Kos, Greece, Aug.–Sep, 2017.

[49] E. Martínez-Montes, et al., Concurrent EEG/fMRI analysis by partial least squares, NeuroImage 22 (Sep. 2004) 1023–1034.

[50] E. Karahan, et al., Tensor analysis and fusion of multimodal brain images, Proceedings of the IEEE 103 (9) (Sep. 2015) 1531–1559.

[51] N. Sidiropoulos, R. Bro, On the uniqueness of multilinear decomposition of n-way arrays, Journal of Chemometrics 14 (3) (May 2000) 229–239.

[52] A.H. Andersen, W.S. Rayens, Structure-seeking multilinear methods for the analysis of fMRI data, NeuroImage 22 (2) (Jun. 2004) 728–739.

[53] N. Sidiropoulos, et al., Tensor decomposition for signal processing and machine learning, IEEE Transactions on Signal Processing 65 (13) (Jul. 2017) 3551–3582.

[54] C. Chatzichristos, et al., Blind fMRI source unmixing via higher-order tensor decompositions, Journal of Neuroscience Methods 315 (Mar. 2019) 17–47.

[55] M. Sørensen, L. De Lathauwer, Coupled canonical polyadic decompositions and (coupled) decompositions in multilinear rank-$(L_{r,n}, L_{r,n}, 1)$ terms—part I: uniqueness, SIAM Journal on Matrix Analysis and Applications 36 (3) (Jul. 2015) 496–522.

[56] M. Sørensen, et al., Coupled canonical polyadic decompositions and (coupled) decompositions in multilinear rank-$(L_{r,n}, L_{r,n}, 1)$ terms — part II: algorithm and multirate sampling, SIAM Journal on Matrix Analysis and Applications 36 (3) (Jul. 2015) 528–539.

[57] L. De Lathauwer, E. Kofidis, Coupled matrix-tensor factorizations–the case of partially shared factors, in: Asilomar Conf. Signals, Systems and Computers, Pacific Grove, CA, USA, Nov. 2017.

[58] N. Vervliet, Compressed sensing approaches to large-scale tensor decompositions, PhD thesis, KU Leuven, Belgium, May 2018.

[59] T. Adalı, et al., ICA and IVA for data fusion: an overview and a new approach based on disjoint subspaces, IEEE Sensors Letters 3 (1) (Jan. 2019).

[60] A.R. Groves, et al., Linked independent component analysis for multimodal data fusion, NeuroImage 54 (3) (Feb. 2011) 2198–2217.

[61] B. Hunyadi, et al., Exploring the epileptic network with parallel ICA of interictal EEG-fMRI, in: Eur. Signal Process. Conf. (EUSIPCO), Nice, France, Aug. 2015.

[62] X. Lei, et al., A parallel framework for simultaneous EEG/fMRI analysis: methodology and simulation, NeuroImage 52 (3) (Sep. 2010) 1123–1134.

[63] V.D. Calhoun, et al., A review of group ICA for fMRI data and ICA for joint inference of imaging, genetic, and ERP data, NeuroImage 45 (Mar. 2009) 163–172.

[64] W. Swinnen, et al., Incorporating higher dimensionality in joint decomposition of EEG and fMRI, in: Eur. Signal Process. Conf, (EUSIPCO), Lisbon, Portugal, Sep. 2014.

[65] B. Mijovic, et al., The "why" and "how" of JointICA: results from a visual detection task, NeuroImage 60 (2) (Apr. 2012).

[66] T. Adalı, et al., Multimodal data fusion using source separation: application to medical imaging, Proceedings of the IEEE 103 (9) (Sep. 2015) 1494–1505.

[67] V.D. Calhoun, et al., Neuronal chronometry of target detection: fusion of hemodynamic and event–related potential data, NeuroImage 30 (2) (Apr. 2006) 544–553.

[68] T. Adali, et al., Diversity in independent component and vector analyses: identifiability, algorithms, and applications in medical imaging, IEEE Signal Processing Magazine 31 (3) (2014) 18–33.

[69] H. Men, et al., Data fusion of electronic nose and electronic tongue for detection of mixed edible-oil, Sensors 2014 (2014) 1–7.

[70] E. Borràs, et al., Olive oil sensory defects classification with data fusion of instrumental techniques and multivariate analysis (PLS-DA), Food Chemistry 203 (2016) 314–322.

[71] G. Zhou, et al., Group component analysis for multiblock data: common and individual feature extraction, IEEE Transactions on Neural Networks and Learning Systems 27 (11) (Nov. 2016) 2426–2439.

[72] N.M. Correa, et al., Canonical correlation analysis for data fusion and group inferences, IEEE Signal Processing Magazine 27 (4) (2010) 39–50.

[73] J. Sui, et al., A CCA+ICA based model for multi-task brain imaging data fusion and its application to schizophrenia, NeuroImage 51 (1) (May 2010) 123–134.

[74] M.A.B.S. Akhonda, et al., Consecutive independence and correlation transform for multimodal fusion: application to EEG and fMRI data, in: Int'l. Conf. Acoustics, Speech Signal Proc. (ICASSP), Calgary, Alberta, Apr. 2018.

[75] V.D. Calhoun, J. Sui, Multimodal fusion of brain imaging data: a key to finding the missing link(s) in complex mental illness, Biological Psychiatry: Cognitive Neuroscience and Neuroimaging 1 (3) (2016) 230–244.

[76] R.A. Harshman, Foundations of the PARAFAC procedure: models and conditions for an "explanatory" multi-modal factor analysis, in: UCLA Work. Papers in Phonetics, 1970, pp. 1–84.

[77] B. Hunyadi, et al., Block term decomposition for modelling epileptic seizures, EURASIP Journal on Advances in Signal Processing (2014).

[78] L. De Lathauwer, Decompositions of a higher-order tensor in block terms–part I: lemmas for partitioned matrices, SIAM Journal on Matrix Analysis and Applications 30 (3) (Sep. 2008) 1022–1032.

[79] L. De Lathauwer, Decompositions of a higher-order tensor in block terms–part II: definitions and uniqueness, SIAM Journal on Matrix Analysis and Applications 30 (3) (Sep. 2008) 1033–1066.

[80] L. De Lathauwer, D. Nion, Decompositions of a higher-order tensor in block terms–part III: alternating least squares algorithms, SIAM Journal on Matrix Analysis and Applications 30 (3) (Sep. 2008) 1067–1083.

[81] R.A. Harshman, M. Lundy, Uniqueness proof for a family of models sharing features of Tucker's three-mode factor analysis and PARAFAC/CANDECOMP, Psychometrika 61 (1) (Mar. 1996) 133–154.

[82] H.A. Kiers, et al., PARAFAC2 part I: a direct fitting algorithm for the PARAFAC2 model, Journal of Chemometrics 13 (3) (May 1999) 275–294.

[83] R. Bro, et al., PARAFAC2 part II: modeling chromatographic data with retention time shifts, Journal of Chemometrics 13 (3) (May 1999) 295–309.

[84] E. Acar, et al., All-at-once optimization for coupled matrix and tensor factorizations, in: Workshop on Mining and Learning with Graphs (MLG), San Diego, CA, Aug. 2011.

[85] E. Acar, et al., Structure-revealing data fusion, BMC Bioinformatics 15 (1) (2014) 239.

[86] S. Van Eyndhoven, Tensor-based blind source separation for structured EEG-fMRI data fusion, Ph.D. dissertation, KU Leuven, 2020.

[87] E. Acar, et al., Unraveling diagnostic biomarkers of schizophrenia through structure-revealing fusion of multi-modal neuroimaging data, Frontiers in Neuroscience 13 (May 2019).

[88] M. Sørensen, N. Sidiropoulos, Multi-set low-rank factorizations with shared and unshared components, IEEE Transactions on Signal Processing 68 (Aug. 2020) 5122–5137.

[89] B. Rivet, et al., Multimodal approach to estimate the ocular movements during EEG recordings: a coupled tensor factorization method, in: 37th Annual Int'l Conf. IEEE Eng. Med. Biology Society (EMBC), Milan, Italy, Aug. 2015.

[90] R. Mosayebi, G.-A. Hossein-Zadeh, Correlated coupled matrix tensor factorization method for simultaneous EEG-fMRI data fusion, Biomedical Signal Processing and Control 62 (Sep. 2020).

[91] C. Schenker, et al., A flexible optimization framework for regularized matrix-tensor factorizations with linear couplings, IEEE Journal of Selected Topics in Signal Processing 15 (3) (Apr. 2021).

[92] N. Seichepine, et al., Soft nonnegative matrix co-factorization, IEEE Transactions on Signal Processing 62 (22) (Nov. 2014) 5940–5949.

[93] Y. Jonmohamadi, et al., Extraction of common task features in EEG-fMRI data using coupled tensor-tensor decomposition, Brain Topography 33 (5) (Sep. 2020) 636–650.

[94] G. Zhang, et al., Hyperspectral super-resolution: a coupled nonnegative block-term tensor decomposition approach, in: Int'l Workshop on Comput. Adv. in Multi-Sensor Adapt. Process. (CAMSAP), Guadeloupe, West Indies, Dec. 2019.

[95] C. Prévost, et al., Hyperspectral super-resolution with coupled Tucker approximation: recoverability and SVD-based algorithms, IEEE Transactions on Signal Processing 68 (2020) 931–946.

[96] X.-F. Gong, et al., Coupled rank-$(l_m, l_n, \cdot)$ block term decomposition by coupled block simultaneous generalized Schur decomposition, in: Int'l. Conf. Acoustics, Speech Signal Proc. (ICASSP), Shanghai, China, Mar. 2016.

[97] X.-F. Gong, et al., Double coupled canonical polyadic decomposition for joint blind source separation, IEEE Transactions on Signal Processing 66 (13) (Jul. 2018) 3475–3490.

[98] L. Sorber, et al., Structured data fusion, IEEE Journal of Selected Topics in Signal Processing 9 (4) (Jun. 2015) 586–600.

[99] N. Vervliet, L. De Lathauwer, Numerical optimization-based algorithms for data fusion, Data Handling in Science and Technology 31 (2019) 81–128.

[100] N. Vervliet, et al., Tensorlab 3.0, [Online]. Available http://www.tensorlab.net, Mar. 2016.

[101] K. Naskovska, et al., Analysis of the photic driving effect via joint EEG and MEG data processing based on the coupled CP decomposition, in: Eur. Signal Process. Conf. (EUSIPCO), Kos, Greece, Aug. 2017.

[102] H. Becker, et al., Tensor-based preprocessing of combined EEG/MEG data, in: Eur. Signal Process. Conf. (EUSIPCO), Bucharest, Romania, Aug. 2012.

[103] K. Fonał, et al., Feature-fusion HALS-based algorithm for linked CP decomposition model in application to joint EMG/MMG signal classification, in: Int'l Conf. Patt. Recogn. (ICPR), Beijing, China, Aug. 2018.

[104] R. Chowdhury, et al., MEG–EEG information fusion and electromagnetic source imaging: from theory to clinical application in epilepsy, Brain Topography 28 (6) (Nov. 2015) 785–812.

[105] E. Acar, et al., ACMTF for fusion of multi-modal neuroimaging data and identification of biomarkers, in: Eur. Signal Process. Conf. (EUSIPCO), Kos, Greece, Aug. 2017.

[106] J. Muraskin, et al., Fusing multiple neuroimaging modalities to assess group differences in perception action coupling, Proceedings of the IEEE 105 (1) (Jan. 2017) 83–100.

[107] J. Du, et al., Three-layer medical image fusion with tensor-based features, Information Sciences 525 (2020) 93–108.

[108] J. Sui, et al., A review of multivariate methods for multimodal fusion of brain imaging data, Journal of Neuroscience Methods 204 (1) (Feb. 2012) 68–81.

[109] E. Kinney-Lang, et al., Introducing the joint EEG-development inference (JEDI) model: a multi-way, data fusion approach for estimating paediatric developmental scores via EEG, IEEE Transactions on Neural Systems and Rehabilitation Engineering 27 (3) (Mar. 2019) 348–357.

[110] N. Dron, et al., Preliminary fusion of EEG and MRI with phenotypic scores in children with epilepsy based on the canonical polyadic decomposition, in: Int'l Conf. Eng. Med Biol. Soc. (EMBC), Berlin, Germany, Aug. 2019.

[111] G. Deshpande, et al., A new generation of brain-computer interfaces driven by discovery of latent EEG-fMRI linkages using tensor decomposition, Frontiers in Neuroscience 11 (Jun. 2017).

[112] Y. Zhang, et al., L1-regularized multiway canonical correlation analysis for SSVEP-based BCI, IEEE Transactions on Neural Systems and Rehabilitation Engineering 21 (6) (2013) 887–896.

[113] R. Bro, Multi-way analysis in the food industry, PhD thesis, University of Amsterdamn and Royal Veterinary University of Denmark, Feb. 1998.

[114] F. Camarrone, M.M. Van Hulle, Fast multiway partial least squares regression, IEEE Transactions on Biomedical Engineering 66 (2) (Feb. 2019) 433–443.

[115] Z. Xue, et al., Coupled higher-order tensor factorization for hyperspectral and LiDAR data fusion and classification, Remote Sensing 11 (17) (1959, Aug. 2019).

[116] S. Li, et al., Fusing hyperspectral and multispectral images via coupled sparse tensor factorization, IEEE Transactions on Image Processing 27 (8) (Aug. 2018) 4118–4130.

[117] R. Dian, et al., Nonlocal sparse tensor factorization for semiblind hyperspectral and multispectral image fusion, IEEE Transactions on Cybernetics 50 (10) (Oct. 2020) 4469–4480.

[118] Y. Xu, et al., Nonlocal coupled tensor CP decomposition for hyperspectral and multispectral image fusion, IEEE Transactions on Geoscience and Remote Sensing 58 (1) (Jan. 2020) 348–362.

[119] R.A. Borsoi, et al., Coupled tensor decomposition for hyperspectral and multispectral image fusion with variability, arXiv preprint, arXiv:2028.16968, Dec. 2020.

[120] J. Xue, et al., Hyperspectral and multispectral image fusion via tensor sparsity regularization, in: IEEE Int'l Geosci. Remote Sens. Symp. (IGARSS), Yokohama, Japan, Aug. 2019.

[121] J. Du, et al., Exploring coupled images fusion based on joint tensor decomposition, Human-Centric Computing and Information Sciences 10 (2020) 93–108.

[122] Y. Levin-Schwartz, Blind source separation for multimodal fusion of medical imaging data, PhD thesis, University of Maryland, USA, May 2017.

[123] F. Cong, et al., Tensor decomposition of EEG signals: a brief review, Journal of Neuroscience Methods 248 (Jun. 2015) 59–69.

[124] E. Acar, et al., Multiway analysis of epilepsy tensors, Bioinformatics 23 (13) (Sep. 2007).

Tensor methods for low-level vision

11

Tatsuya Yokota[a,b], **Cesar F. Caiafa**[c,b], **and Qibin Zhao**[b,d]

[a]*Nagoya Institute of Technology, Aichi, Japan*
[b]*RIKEN Center for Advanced Intelligence Project, Tokyo, Japan*
[c]*Instituto Argentino de Radioastronomía – CCT La Plata, CONICET / CIC-PBA / UNLP, Villa Elisa, Argentina*
[d]*Guangdong University of Technology, Guangzhou, China*

CONTENTS

11.1 Low-level vision and signal reconstruction

Low-level vision [58] is a processing system that plays an important role in human as well as in machine visual pattern recognition. It is often used to refer to information processing based on local visual features such as edges, corners, colors, and self-similarity. Typical examples in the research fields of computer vision and image/signal processing are compression, noise removal, deblurring, superresolution, image inpainting, computed tomography, and compressed sensing. In this chapter, we introduce the tensor representations, mathematical models, and optimization algorithms and illustrate their application to selected low-level vision tasks.

Please note that we explain the technical details of tensor methods by focusing on the image inpainting task in order to compose this chapter concisely. However, Sections 11.2.1.6 and 11.2.2.2 provide the instructions to apply those methods to other low-level vision tasks. Moreover, in Section 11.4, we illustrate the methods for application, not only to the image inpainting problem but also to denoising, deblurring, and superresolution.

11.1.1 Observation models

Here, we characterize some low-level vision tasks as a general tensor/signal reconstruction problem. The objective of these tasks is to reconstruct an N-th-order tensor $\widehat{\mathcal{X}} \in \mathbb{R}^{I_1 \times I_2 \times \cdots \times I_N}$ from an observed data $\mathbf{b} \in \mathbb{R}^M$. The observation model is assumed as follows:

$$\mathbf{b} = \mathcal{A}(\mathcal{X}_0) + \mathbf{n}, \tag{11.1}$$

where $\mathcal{X}_0 \in \mathbb{R}^{I_1 \times I_2 \times \cdots \times I_N}$ is the ground-truth tensor, $\mathcal{A} : \mathbb{R}^{I_1 \times I_2 \times \cdots \times I_N} \to \mathbb{R}^M$ is a linear mapping representing observation model, and $\mathbf{n} \in \mathbb{R}^M$ represents some observation noise. Since the observation model $\mathcal{A}(\cdot)$ is a linear operator, the m-th entry of $\mathbf{b}$ can be represented by

$$b_m = \langle \mathcal{W}_m, \mathcal{X}_0 \rangle + n_m, \tag{11.2}$$

where $\langle \cdot, \cdot \rangle$ is the inner product and $\mathcal{W}_m \in \mathbb{R}^{I_1 \times I_2 \times \cdots \times I_N}$ is a tensor of the same size as $\mathcal{X}_0$. It is assumed that the m-th entry of observed data is obtained by the inner product between its corresponding m-th tensor $\mathcal{W}_m$ and the ground truth tensor $\mathcal{X}_0$ with additive noise. Since the observation model $\mathcal{A}$ is determined by combinations of the tensors $\{\mathcal{W}_1, \mathcal{W}_2, ..., \mathcal{W}_M\}$, the observation model $\mathcal{A}$ can be seen as an $(N+1)$-th-order tensor of size $(M, I_1, I_2, ..., I_N)$. At the same time, since $\langle \mathcal{Y}, \mathcal{X} \rangle = \langle \text{vec}(\mathcal{Y}), \text{vec}(\mathcal{X}) \rangle$, the observation model $\mathcal{A}$ can also be seen as a matrix of size $(M, \prod_{n=1}^N I_n)$ which is given by

$$\mathbf{A} := \begin{pmatrix} \text{vec}(\mathcal{W}_1)^{\mathrm{T}} \\ \vdots \\ \text{vec}(\mathcal{W}_M)^{\mathrm{T}} \end{pmatrix} \in \mathbb{R}^{M \times \prod_{n=1}^N I_n}. \tag{11.3}$$

Let us put $\mathbf{x}_0 := \text{vec}(\mathcal{X}_0)$. The observation model can be seen as a matrix–vector product as $\mathcal{A}(\mathcal{X}_0) = \mathbf{A}\mathbf{x}_0$. Subsequently, its adjoint (transposed) operation $\mathcal{A}^* : \mathbb{R}^M \to \mathbb{R}^{I_1 \times I_2 \times \cdots \times I_N}$ ($\mathbf{A}^{\mathrm{T}} : \mathbb{R}^M \to \mathbb{R}^{\prod_{n=1}^N I_n}$) of $\mathbf{b} \in \mathbb{R}^M$ is given by

$$\mathcal{A}^*(\mathbf{b}) = \sum_{m=1}^M b_m \mathcal{W}_m \quad \text{or} \quad \mathbf{A}^{\mathrm{T}}\mathbf{b} = \sum_{m=1}^M b_m \text{vec}(\mathcal{W}_m). \tag{11.4}$$

Note that $\text{vec}(\mathcal{A}^*(\mathbf{b})) = \mathbf{A}^{\mathrm{T}}\mathbf{b}$. Finally, the composite mapping $\mathcal{A}\mathcal{A}^*$ (or $\mathbf{A}\mathbf{A}^{\mathrm{T}}$) : $\mathbb{R}^M \to \mathbb{R}^M$ can be represented by a matrix of size (M, M) as follows:

$$[\mathcal{A}\mathcal{A}^*](m, k) = [\mathbf{A}\mathbf{A}^{\mathrm{T}}](m, k) = \langle \mathcal{W}_m, \mathcal{W}_k \rangle. \tag{11.5}$$

In this way, the observation model $\mathcal{A}(\mathcal{X}_0)$ considered in this chapter can be written more generally using the matrix vector representation $\mathbf{A}\mathbf{x}_0$. It is useful for understanding the low-level vision problems from a numerical calculation or linear algebraic perspective. On the other hand, one of the features of this chapter is to define the original signal as a tensor instead of a vector and consider modeling unique to the tensor. Therefore, note that in this chapter, even linear operations that can be described as matrix products such as pseudo-inverse, linear projection, and binary masks are often represented by tensor-aware formulations.

In general, different low-level vision tasks have associated different observation models $\mathcal{A}$. Table 11.1 shows variants of observation models $\mathcal{A}$ and what the observed data $\mathbf{b}$ represents. Below, we describe possible operations involved in the observation model $\mathcal{A}$.

In practice, the observed data is also often a tensor, but here it is defined as a vector $\mathbf{b}$ to emphasize that it is not necessarily a tensor. Therefore, in most cases in Table 11.1, $\mathcal{A}$ contains vectorization $\mathrm{vec}(\cdot)$, but it should be noted that this vectorization operation is less important because it is just a reordering of tensor entries as a vector. For example, for the noise removal task, we assume that $\mathcal{A}$ is the essentially identity mapping.

A function $\mathrm{conv}(\cdot, \mathcal{K})$ represents a convolution with some kernel $\mathcal{K} \in \mathbb{R}^{\tau_1 \times \tau_2 \times \cdots \times \tau_N}$, which is defined as follows:

$$[\mathrm{conv}(\mathcal{X}, \mathcal{K})](i_1, ..., i_N) := \sum_{t_1=1}^{\tau_1} \cdots \sum_{t_N=1}^{\tau_N} \mathcal{X}(i_1 - t_1, ..., i_N - t_N) \mathcal{K}(t_1, ..., t_N). \quad (11.6)$$

Note that when $i_n - t_n < 1$, $\mathcal{X}$ does not have entries. There are two types of convolution: circular convolution, which considers $\mathcal{X}$ as a periodic function, and linear convolution, which considers the value of $\mathcal{X}$ outside the entries to be 0. The blur kernel is also called as point spread function (PSF) and can be of different types such as Gaussian blur and motion blur [15]. In this chapter, we assume that the blur kernel is known in advance: only the blur kernel is known but the additive noise $\mathbf{n}$ is unknown.[1] When the blur kernel is unknown, the task is called blind deblurring/deconvolution [15], and it is much more difficult than normal deblurring/deconvolution. A more difficult case is when the kernel is not space-invariant so each part of the input signal is affected by a different kernel operation. In fact, in the latter case the observation model cannot be represented by a convolution but it can still be represented as a linear mapping.

In the superresolution task [32], it is assumed that the observation model performs a straight down-sampling (DS) after a convolution operation with some kernel, $\mathrm{conv}(\cdot, \mathcal{K})$. The convolution here is not arbitrary and basically means a low-pass filter. This is because direct sampling without a low-pass filter causes aliasing. As a low-pass filter, bilinear, bicubic, Gaussian, and Lanczos kernels can be used [6]. Although each has its advantages, the Lanczos kernel is often used in superresolution

---

[1] Only its main properties can be assumed: noise type, covariance structure, etc.

Table 11.1 Variants of problem settings for individual tasks.

Task	$\mathcal{A}(\cdot)$	b
Noise removal [68]	$vec(\cdot)$	Noisy image
Deblurring [15]	$vec(conv(\cdot, \mathcal{K}))$	Blurred image
Superresolution [32]	$vec(DS(conv(\cdot, \mathcal{K})))$	Low-resolution image
Inpainting [35]	$vec(\mathcal{P}_\Omega(\cdot))$	Incomplete image
Computed tomography [44]	Radon transform	Sinogram
Compressed sensing [11,29]	Random projection	Compressed measurements

because it is superior in terms of maintaining local contrast. A DS operation simply means getting entries at the same intervals and discarding intermediate entries.

The observation model considered in the inpainting task [35] is, in a sense, a generalization of the DS operation. In other words, it is an operation that keeps the value of only the entries included in the set Ω and discards the other entries. In this chapter, for the sake of simplification, the operation of discarding entries of a tensor is defined by the entry-wise product of the original tensor by a tensor mask, which has 0's at positions of discard entries and 1's otherwise. In other words, the operation $\mathcal{P}_\Omega$ does not change the number of entries of both input and output tensors. More specifically, considering a binary tensor (mask) $\mathcal{Q} \in \{0, 1\}^{I_1 \times I_2 \times \cdots \times I_N}$ that can be expressed as $\mathcal{P}_\Omega(\mathcal{X}) = \mathcal{Q} * \mathcal{X}$, where $*$ is the Hadamard product.

The problem setting of computed tomography (CT) [44] is a little different from the previous ones. The observed data is not an image of the original space, but a projection of it. This projection is an operation that integrates the pixel values along the line segment passing through the image. Although a detailed definition is avoided here and explained roughly, it can be mathematically assumed to be the Radon transform $\mathcal{R}(\cdot)$. The observed data is called a sinogram.

Compressed sensing (CS) [11,29] can be considered as a more generalized version of the conventional observation models described before. Alternatively, CS considers mapping the original signal to smaller space by applying typically a random projection. CS has been successfully applied in CT in order to reduce the number of used projections. It should be noted that it is assumed that the reconstruction in the CS is performed with prior knowledge such as the existence of sparse or low-rank representations of images. The CS framework is useful for simplifying measuring equipment or reducing the time required for measurement.

11.1.2 Inverse problems

Obtaining $\widehat{\mathcal{X}}$ from b can be regarded as operating the inverse transformation of observation model $\mathcal{A}$. If $\mathbf{n} = \mathbf{0}$ and there is an inverse transformation $\mathcal{A}^{-1}$ that satisfies $\mathcal{A}^{-1}\mathcal{A} = \mathcal{A}\mathcal{A}^{-1} = \mathcal{I}$, the solution of $\widehat{\mathcal{X}}$ is uniquely given as $\widehat{\mathcal{X}} = \mathcal{A}^{-1}\mathbf{b} = \mathcal{A}^{-1}(\mathcal{A}(\mathcal{X}_0) + \mathbf{n}) = \mathcal{X}_0$. However, in most low-level vision tasks, $\mathbf{n} \neq \mathbf{0}$ and/or there is no inverse transformation of $\mathcal{A}$. For example, in the case of noise removal, $\mathcal{A}$ is an operation of vectorization which is essentially an identity map $\mathcal{I}$. In this case, the problem is whether to separate the noise component and the signal component. If $\mathbf{x} = \mathrm{vec}(\mathcal{X})$, it should satisfy $\mathbf{b} = \mathbf{x} + \mathbf{n}$. Both $\mathbf{x}$ and $\mathbf{n}$ are unknown, and there is no mathematical distinction between $\mathbf{x}$ and $\mathbf{n}$. Here, the solution of $\mathbf{x}$ and $\mathbf{n}$ that satisfies $\mathbf{b} = \mathbf{x} + \mathbf{n}$ is not unique, because there exists $\widehat{\mathbf{n}} = \mathbf{b} - \widehat{\mathbf{x}}$ for any $\widehat{\mathbf{x}}$.

Even if $\mathbf{n} = \mathbf{0}$, there is no unique solution of $\widehat{\mathcal{X}}$ when there is no inverse transform of $\mathcal{A}$. For example in image inpainting, it is assumed that the value of the observed entry of the tensor is the same as the true value of $\mathcal{X}_0$ and the value of the missing entry is unknown. A trivial solution $\widehat{\mathcal{X}} = \mathcal{P}_\Omega(\mathcal{X}_0)$ satisfies $\mathbf{b} = \mathrm{vec}(\mathcal{P}_\Omega(\widehat{\mathcal{X}}))$. Since the missing entries do not affect this equation, $\mathcal{P}_{\bar{\Omega}}(\mathcal{Z})$ for any $\mathcal{Z} \in \mathbb{R}^{I_1 \times I_2 \times \cdots \times I_N}$ can be added to $\widehat{\mathcal{X}}' = \mathcal{P}_\Omega(\mathcal{X}_0) + \mathcal{P}_{\bar{\Omega}}(\mathcal{Z})$, and it still satisfies $\mathbf{b} = \mathrm{vec}(\mathcal{P}_\Omega(\widehat{\mathcal{X}}'))$, where $\bar{\Omega}$ is a complement set of Ω. Therefore, there is no unique solution for $\widehat{\mathcal{X}}$ in this case as well. More generally, for some $\mathcal{A}$ whose null space[2] is not the empty set, a solution can be given by $\widehat{\mathcal{X}} = \mathcal{A}^\dagger \mathbf{b}$, where $\mathcal{A}^\dagger := \mathcal{A}^*(\mathcal{A}\mathcal{A}^*)^{-1}$ is a Moore–Penrose pseudo-inverse of $\mathcal{A}$. Note that $\widehat{\mathcal{X}} = \mathcal{A}^\dagger \mathbf{b}$ is not a unique solution of the equation $\mathbf{b} = \mathcal{A}(\mathcal{X})$. Let us consider any nonzero $\mathcal{Z}$ such that $\mathcal{A}(\mathcal{Z}) = \mathbf{0}$. Then it satisfies

$$\mathcal{A}(\widehat{\mathcal{X}} + \mathcal{Z}) = \mathcal{A}(\widehat{\mathcal{X}}) + \mathcal{A}(\mathcal{Z}) = \mathcal{A}(\widehat{\mathcal{X}}). \tag{11.7}$$

Thus, any $\widehat{\mathcal{X}} + \mathcal{Z}$ can be a solution, and it is not unique. In this way, the ill-posedness of a low-level vision task largely depends on the noise properties and the observation model $\mathcal{A}$.

In order to separate noise and signal and/or to select an appropriate $\mathcal{Z}$ from a set of $\{\mathcal{Z} \mid \mathcal{A}(\mathcal{Z}) = \mathbf{0}\}$, it is necessary to incorporate useful information from something other than observed data. For example, it is useful to assume the difference in statistical properties between the noise distribution and the signal distribution or to assume the structural constraints that the original tensor may have. Such models/assumptions are often called constraints, priors, and regularization. A unified formulation of the tensor reconstruction for low-level vision tasks that incorporate structural constraints can be given by

$$\underset{\boldsymbol{\theta}}{\mathrm{minimize}} \; d(\mathbf{b}, \mathcal{A}(\mathcal{X}_{\boldsymbol{\theta}})) + p(\boldsymbol{\theta}), \tag{11.8}$$

where

- $\mathbf{b} \in \mathbb{R}^M$ is an observed (input) M-dimensional array of data,
- $\mathcal{X}_{\boldsymbol{\theta}} \in \mathbb{R}^{I_1 \times I_2 \times \cdots \times I_N}$ is a target (output) N-th-order tensor parameterized by $\boldsymbol{\theta} \in \mathbb{R}^D$,
- $\mathcal{A} : \mathbb{R}^{I_1 \times I_2 \times \cdots \times I_N} \to \mathbb{R}^M$ is a linear mapping representing the observation model,
- $d(\cdot, \cdot)$ is a scalar function representing dissimilarity of two inputs, and
- $p(\cdot)$ is a scalar function of penalty with respect to $\boldsymbol{\theta}$ whose minimization imposes some constraints in the space of all possible parameter vectors.

---

[2] The null space of $\mathcal{A}$ is defined as $\mathrm{Ker}(\mathcal{A}) := \{\mathcal{X} \in \mathbb{R}^{I_1 \times I_2 \times \cdots \times I_N} ; \mathcal{A}(\mathcal{X}) = \mathbf{0}\}$.

Many tensor reconstruction methods (models) can be interpreted as special cases of this optimization problem.

For example, a naive Tucker tensor decomposition of an N-th-order tensor $\mathcal{Y} \in \mathbb{R}^{I_1 \times I_2 \times \cdots \times I_N}$ is given by the following equation:

$$\underset{\mathcal{G}, \mathbf{U}^{(1)}, \ldots, \mathbf{U}^{(N)}}{\text{minimize}} \quad ||\mathcal{Y} - \mathcal{X}||_F^2$$

$$\text{subject to} \quad \mathcal{X} = \mathcal{G} \times_1 \mathbf{U}^{(1)} \cdots \times_N \mathbf{U}^{(N)}, \tag{11.9}$$

$$\mathbf{U}^{(n)\mathrm{T}} \mathbf{U}^{(n)} = \mathbf{I}_{R_n} \text{ (for all } n\text{)},$$

where $\mathcal{X} \in \mathbb{R}^{I_1 \times I_2 \times \cdots \times I_N}$ is a reconstructed tensor by Tucker decomposition, $\mathcal{G} \in \mathbb{R}^{R_1 \times R_2 \times \cdots \times R_N}$ is a core tensor, and its factor matrices are $\mathbf{U}^{(n)} \in \mathbb{R}^{I_n \times R_n}$. The optimization problem (11.8) reduces to the Tucker decomposition (11.9) by the following settings:

$$\boldsymbol{\theta} = \{\mathcal{G}, \mathbf{U}^{(1)}, \ldots, \mathbf{U}^{(N)}\}, \tag{11.10}$$

$$\mathcal{X}_{\boldsymbol{\theta}} = \mathcal{G} \times_1 \mathbf{U}^{(1)} \cdots \times_N \mathbf{U}^{(N)}, \tag{11.11}$$

$$\mathbf{b} = \text{vec}(\mathcal{Y}), \tag{11.12}$$

$$\mathcal{A}(\cdot) = \text{vec}(\cdot), \tag{11.13}$$

$$d(\mathbf{b}, \mathcal{A}(\mathcal{X}_{\boldsymbol{\theta}})) = ||\mathcal{Y} - \mathcal{G} \times_1 \mathbf{U}^{(1)} \cdots \times_N \mathbf{U}^{(N)}||_F^2, \tag{11.14}$$

$$p(\boldsymbol{\theta}) = \sum_{n=1}^{N} i_{\text{orth}}(\mathbf{U}^{(n)}), \tag{11.15}$$

$$i_{\text{orth}}(\mathbf{U}) := \begin{cases} 0 & \mathbf{U}^{\mathrm{T}}\mathbf{U} = \mathbf{I}, \\ \infty & \text{otherwise.} \end{cases} \tag{11.16}$$

Note that the orthogonality constraints of $\mathbf{U}^{(n)}$ are equivalently represented by the sum of indicator functions of orthogonality. It can be generalized for the various parametric mathematical models that reconstruct $\mathcal{X}$. In addition, the function of dissimilarity $d(\cdot, \cdot)$ can be modified to various functions such as Kullback–Leibler divergence and absolute errors. Furthermore, for the penalty function, various structures such as sparseness, nonnegativity, and smoothness can be assumed as prior information in the core tensor and factor matrices.

For another example, a problem of low-rank tensor completion with noise can be formulated by

$$\underset{\mathcal{X}}{\text{minimize}} \sum_{n=1}^{N} \alpha_n ||\mathbf{X}_{(n)}||_* \tag{11.17}$$

$$\text{subject to} \quad ||\mathcal{P}_{\Omega}(\mathcal{Y} - \mathcal{X})||_F^2 \leq \delta,$$

where $||\cdot||_*$ denotes the nuclear norm which is defined as a sum of all singular values of an input matrix, $\mathbf{X}_{(n)} \in \mathbb{R}^{I_n \times \prod_{k \neq n} I_k}$ is a mode-n unfolding matrix of tensor $\mathcal{X}$, $\alpha_n \geq$

0 are weight parameters, and $\delta \geq 0$ is a noise variance parameter. The optimization problem (11.8) reduces to the low-rank tensor completion with noise (11.17) by the following settings:

$$\theta = \{\mathcal{X}\}, \tag{11.18}$$

$$\mathcal{X}_\theta = \mathcal{X}, \tag{11.19}$$

$$\mathbf{b} = \mathrm{vec}(\mathcal{P}_\Omega(\mathcal{Y})), \tag{11.20}$$

$$\mathcal{A}(\cdot) = \mathrm{vec}(\mathcal{P}_\Omega(\cdot)), \tag{11.21}$$

$$d(\mathbf{b}, \mathcal{A}(\mathcal{X}_\theta)) = \begin{cases} 0 & ||\mathcal{P}_\Omega(\mathcal{Y} - \mathcal{X})||_F^2 \leq \delta, \\ \infty & \text{otherwise,} \end{cases} \tag{11.22}$$

$$p(\theta) = \sum_{n=1}^{N} \alpha_n ||\mathbf{X}_{(n)}||_*. \tag{11.23}$$

Note that the dissimilarity function $d(\cdot, \cdot)$ is represented by an indicator function in this case. In this way, the evaluation of dissimilarity can be set as a hard constraint, and conversely, the penalty function can be set as continuous functions.

Most of the tensor reconstruction methods introduced in this chapter can be interpreted as a tug of war between the two terms in Eq. (11.8). The first term is the criterion for quantifying the goodness of fit with the observed data, and the other term is the criterion for the goodness of fit with prior knowledge. From the Bayesian point of view, this approach can also be interpreted as maximum a posteriori (MAP) estimation: $\mathrm{maximize}_\theta \ \mathrm{Prob}(\theta|\mathbf{b})$, where $\mathrm{Prob}(\theta|\mathbf{b})$ denotes a conditional probability of parameters θ given observed data $\mathbf{b}$. Based on Bayes' theorem, we have $\mathrm{Prob}(\theta|\mathbf{b}) = \frac{\mathrm{Prob}(\mathbf{b}|\theta)\mathrm{Prob}(\theta)}{\mathrm{Prob}(\mathbf{b})}$. Since the logarithm does not change the magnitude relation of the function, the MAP estimation can be given by

$$\underset{\theta}{\mathrm{minimize}} - \log \mathrm{Prob}(\mathbf{b}|\theta) - \log \mathrm{Prob}(\theta). \tag{11.24}$$

The first and second terms correspond to $d(\mathbf{b}, \mathcal{A}(\mathcal{X}_\theta))$ and $p(\theta)$ in Eq. (11.8), respectively.

Let us consider these two terms separately. The first term largely depends on the data observation model and the type of noise. Several observation models were briefly introduced in Section 11.1.1. This will lead to a wide range of research areas related to measuring instruments and physical quantities. On the other hand, the second term gives a mathematical model to the target tensor data. This plays a more essential role in tensor data analysis. In other words, the prior knowledge of the tensor data given by the second term plays an essential role in improving the tensor reconstruction, which converts ill-posed problems to well-posed problems and improves the robustness to noise. Therefore, in the following sections, we will introduce various tensor reconstruction methods using priors, mainly focusing on the design of the second term $p(\theta)$. For the first term, we basically assume some simple setting so that there is Gaussian noise or no noise, and $\mathcal{A}$ is identity mapping or sampling $\mathcal{P}_\Omega$ for simple explanation. Note that we also discuss a perspective to generalize it for arbitrary observation models $\mathcal{A}$ in Sections 11.2.1.6 and 11.2.2.2, and we show examples of applications to denoising, deblurring, and superresolution in Section 11.4.3.

11.2 Methods using raw tensor structure

Here, we mainly focus on the problem of tensor completion without noise because of its simplicity. Note that the important concept in this chapter is understanding how to consider the priors for the tensor data.

Tensor completion is a technique for estimating (restoring) the values of the missing entries of tensor data. In general, the only information used for tensor completion are the observed entries and the structural assumptions that we have as prior knowledge. If the observed entries and the missing entries are independent and there is no relationship between them, tensor completion is impossible. However, in real-world applications, the tensor data often has a redundant structure such as correlation, latent factor, symmetry, continuity, and periodicity. Thus, the tensor completion is possible in many cases. For example, if we assume that the tensor is obtained by discretizing a continuous multivariate function with missing entries, simple linear interpolation, spline interpolation, and polynomial interpolation are effective. Also, if the tensor is assumed to be low-rank, the value of the missing entries can be estimated by fitting the low-rank tensor model to the observed incomplete tensor.

Fig. 11.1 shows examples of tensor completion applied for 2D and 3D grayscale image inpainting. Entries of the images are randomly sampled from original images with ratios of 20% and 5%, respectively. The figure shows that these incomplete images are completed by using the technique of tensor completion. The reason why this is possible is that there is a dependency between the observed and missing entries in natural images. This dependency can be considered as the priors in natural images. This section introduces tensor completion methods that uses priors of low rank and smooth properties which are typical for natural images.

From the viewpoint of optimization and mathematical modeling, the methods for tensor completion or reconstruction can be roughly divided into two approaches. One is an approach that expresses the tensor as it is and indirectly controls its structure by minimizing the penalty functions such as the nuclear [10] or total variation (TV) norm [68]. Since this approach expresses the full tensor and all entries are considered in the penalization, increasing the size of the tensor directly affects the problem of the associated computational cost. On the other hand, it can often be formulated as a convex optimization problem, and the algorithm can be derived relatively easily by applying it to a unified framework such as alternating direction method of multipliers (ADMM) [4], primal-dual hybrid gradient (PDHG) [102], and primal-dual splitting (PDS) [31].

The second approach that directly controls the structure of the tensor is representing it with a mathematical model such as CP decomposition [12,40,46], Tucker de-

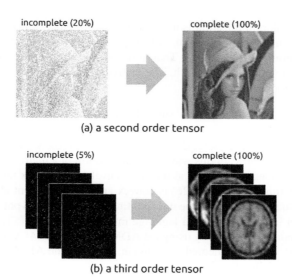

(a) a second order tensor

(b) a third order tensor

FIGURE 11.1

Examples of tensor completion.

composition [25,76], sparse Tucker representation [8,9,82], non-negative matrix/tensor factorization (NMF/NTF) [19], and linear sum of basis functions [84,92,96,97]. This approach represents the tensor with a small number of parameters by a mathematical model, so it is often superior in terms of computational cost. On the other hand, optimization problems are often complicated and difficult to apply to a unified framework. In other words, when adopting this approach, it is necessary to derive the algorithm individually to solve the optimization problems. In this section, we try to explain that a relatively wide range of problems in this approach can be solved by using the majorization-minimization (MM) algorithm [43,51,62,64].

11.2.1 Penalty-based tensor reconstruction

11.2.1.1 Low-rank matrix completion

First, we introduce low-rank matrix completion [10]. When we consider to control the rank of the matrix to be minimized directly, the optimization problem is given as follows:

$$\underset{\mathbf{X}}{\text{minimize}} \quad \text{rank}(\mathbf{X}) \quad \text{subject to } \mathcal{P}_\Omega(\mathbf{X}) = \mathcal{P}_\Omega(\mathbf{T}), \tag{11.25}$$

where $\mathbf{X} \in \mathbb{R}^{I \times J}$ is the matrix as a result of completion, $\mathbf{T} \in \mathbb{R}^{I \times J}$ is the incomplete input matrix, and Ω is the set of the indices (i, j) of the observed entries. The sampling rate (%) can be defined by $100\frac{|\Omega|}{IJ}$. Constraint $\mathcal{P}_\Omega(\mathbf{X}) = \mathcal{P}_\Omega(\mathbf{T})$ means that the observed entries of $\mathbf{X}$ and $\mathbf{T}$ are equal: $\mathbf{X}(i, j) = \mathbf{T}(i, j)$, for all $(i, j) \in \Omega$. Matrix completion by rank minimization is useful when the true matrix is low-rank, but the matrix rank is a nonconvex function with respect to $\mathbf{X}$, and the rank minimization problem is generally NP-hard [36]. Therefore, nuclear norm minimization is often adopted as a more practical approach. The matrix completion problem with nuclear norm minimization is shown as

$$\underset{\mathbf{X}}{\text{minimize}} \ ||\mathbf{X}||_* \ \text{subject to } \mathcal{P}_\Omega(\mathbf{X}) = \mathcal{P}_\Omega(\mathbf{T}), \tag{11.26}$$

where $||\mathbf{X}||_* := \sum_i \sigma_i(\mathbf{X})$ denotes the nuclear norm of matrix $\mathbf{X}$ and $\sigma_i(\mathbf{X})$ is the i-th largest singular value of $\mathbf{X}$. In this way, the nuclear norm of a matrix is defined by the sum of singular values. It is known as a convex envelope of matrix rank [67].

The optimization problem (11.26) is convex and many efficient algorithms have been proposed such as singular value thresholding (SVT) [7], fixed point continuation (FPC) [56], and inexact augmented lagrange multiplier (IALM) [53]. Nowadays, it has become standard to solve it by using the ADMM algorithm [4], which is a method in the framework of the augmented Lagrangian. To apply the ADMM algorithm, we convert (11.26) as follows:

$$\underset{\mathbf{X}}{\text{minimize}} \ i_{\mathbf{T}_\Omega}(\mathbf{X}) + ||\mathbf{Y}||_* \ \text{subject to } \mathbf{Y} = \mathbf{X}, \tag{11.27}$$

where $\mathbf{Y} \in \mathbb{R}^{I \times J}$ is a slack variable matrix of the same size as $\mathbf{X} \in \mathbb{R}^{I \times J}$ and

$$i_{\mathbf{T}_\Omega}(\mathbf{X}) := \begin{cases} 0 & \mathcal{P}_\Omega(\mathbf{X}) = \mathcal{P}_\Omega(\mathbf{T}), \\ \infty & \text{otherwise} \end{cases} \tag{11.28}$$

is an indicator function which represents a hard constraint of $\mathcal{P}_\Omega(\mathbf{X}) = \mathcal{P}_\Omega(\mathbf{T})$. Note that the optimization problems (11.26) and (11.27) are equivalent because we have a hard constraint of $\mathbf{Y} = \mathbf{X}$. Next, we put the augmented Lagrangian function as follows:

$$L_A(\mathbf{X}, \mathbf{Y}, \mathbf{Z}) = i_{\mathbf{T}_\Omega}(\mathbf{X}) + ||\mathbf{Y}||_* + \langle \mathbf{Z}, \mathbf{Y} - \mathbf{X} \rangle + \frac{\beta}{2}||\mathbf{Y} - \mathbf{X}||_F^2, \tag{11.29}$$

where $\mathbf{Z} \in \mathbb{R}^{I \times J}$ is a Lagrange multiplier and $\beta > 0$ is a parameter of the augmented term. Then the algorithm of ADMM for low-rank matrix completion [16,34,53,54] is given as the iteration of the following steps:

$$\mathbf{X} \leftarrow \underset{\mathbf{X}}{\text{argmin}} \ L_A(\mathbf{X}, \mathbf{Y}, \mathbf{Z}), \tag{11.30}$$

$$\mathbf{Y} \leftarrow \underset{\mathbf{Y}}{\text{argmin}} \ L_A(\mathbf{X}, \mathbf{Y}, \mathbf{Z}), \tag{11.31}$$

$$\mathbf{Z} \leftarrow \mathbf{Z} + \beta(\mathbf{Y} - \mathbf{X}). \tag{11.32}$$

Each update can be calculated analytically.

For the update of $\mathbf{X}$, we solve the following problem:

$$\underset{\mathbf{X}}{\text{minimize}} \ i_{\mathbf{T}_\Omega}(\mathbf{X}) + \langle \mathbf{Z}, \mathbf{Y} - \mathbf{X} \rangle + \frac{\beta}{2}||\mathbf{Y} - \mathbf{X}||_F^2. \tag{11.33}$$

Since terms without $\mathbf{X}$ can be summarized into a constant, the second and third terms can be transformed as follows:

$$
\langle \mathbf{Z}, \mathbf{Y} - \mathbf{X} \rangle + \frac{\beta}{2} ||\mathbf{Y} - \mathbf{X}||_F^2
$$

$$
= -\langle \mathbf{X}, \mathbf{Z} \rangle + \frac{\beta}{2} \langle \mathbf{X}, \mathbf{X} \rangle - \beta \langle \mathbf{X}, \mathbf{Y} \rangle + \text{const}
$$

$$
= \frac{\beta}{2} \left(\langle \mathbf{X}, \mathbf{X} \rangle - 2\langle \mathbf{X}, \mathbf{Y} + \frac{1}{\beta}\mathbf{Z} \rangle \right) + \text{const}
$$

$$
= \frac{\beta}{2} \left|\left| \mathbf{X} - \left(\mathbf{Y} + \frac{1}{\beta}\mathbf{Z} \right) \right|\right|_F^2 + \text{const}. \tag{11.34}
$$

Optimization problem (11.33) can be transformed as

$$
\underset{\mathbf{X}}{\text{minimize}} \ \left|\left| \mathbf{X} - \left(\mathbf{Y} + \frac{1}{\beta}\mathbf{Z} \right) \right|\right|_F^2 \ \text{subject to } \mathcal{P}_\Omega(\mathbf{X}) = \mathcal{P}_\Omega(\mathbf{T}). \tag{11.35}
$$

Solution of the above problem is given by a projection from a point $\mathbf{Y} + \frac{1}{\beta}\mathbf{Z}$ onto a convex set $\{ \mathbf{X} \mid \mathcal{P}_\Omega(\mathbf{X}) = \mathcal{P}_\Omega(\mathbf{T})\}$. Thus, it can be given by

$$
\mathbf{X} \leftarrow \mathcal{P}_\Omega(\mathbf{T}) + \mathcal{P}_{\bar{\Omega}} \left(\mathbf{Y} + \frac{1}{\beta}\mathbf{Z} \right), \tag{11.36}
$$

where $\mathcal{P}_{\bar{\Omega}}(\mathbf{X}) = (\mathbf{1} - \mathbf{Q}) * \mathbf{X}$ is an operation to discard the values of entries in the set Ω and keep the rest. Since $\mathcal{P}_\Omega$ and $\mathcal{P}_{\bar{\Omega}}$ are orthogonal to each other, any input of $\mathcal{P}_{\bar{\Omega}}(\cdot)$ satisfies the constraint. Under that condition, the update Eq. (11.36) is obtained as a result of the closest point to $\mathbf{Y} + \frac{1}{\beta}\mathbf{Z}$.

For the update of $\mathbf{Y}$, we solve the following problem:

$$
\underset{\mathbf{Y}}{\text{minimize}} \ ||\mathbf{Y}||_* + \langle \mathbf{Z}, \mathbf{Y} - \mathbf{X} \rangle + \frac{\beta}{2}||\mathbf{Y} - \mathbf{X}||_F^2. \tag{11.37}
$$

Since terms without $\mathbf{Y}$ can be summarized into a constant, the second and third terms can be transformed as follows:

$$
\langle \mathbf{Z}, \mathbf{Y} - \mathbf{X} \rangle + \frac{\beta}{2} ||\mathbf{Y} - \mathbf{X}||_F^2
$$

$$
= \langle \mathbf{Y}, \mathbf{Z} \rangle + \frac{\beta}{2} \langle \mathbf{Y}, \mathbf{Y} \rangle - \beta \langle \mathbf{Y}, \mathbf{X} \rangle + \text{const}
$$

$$
= \frac{\beta}{2} \left(\langle \mathbf{Y}, \mathbf{Y} \rangle - 2\langle \mathbf{Y}, \mathbf{X} - \frac{1}{\beta}\mathbf{Z} \rangle \right) + \text{const}
$$

$$
= \frac{\beta}{2} \left|\left| \mathbf{Y} - \left(\mathbf{X} - \frac{1}{\beta}\mathbf{Z} \right) \right|\right|_F^2 + \text{const}. \tag{11.38}
$$

Algorithm 1 ADMM for low-rank matrix completion.

1: **Input:** $\mathbf{T} \in \mathbb{R}^{I \times J}$, Ω
2: **Initialize:** $\mathbf{X}, \mathbf{Y}, \mathbf{Z} \in \mathbb{R}^{I \times J}$, $\beta \geq 0$
3: **repeat**
4:    $\mathbf{X} \leftarrow \mathcal{P}_{\Omega}(\mathbf{T}) + \mathcal{P}_{\bar{\Omega}}(\mathbf{Y} + \frac{1}{\beta}\mathbf{Z})$;
5:    $\mathbf{Y} \leftarrow \operatorname{prox}_{\frac{1}{\beta}||\cdot||_*}(\mathbf{X} - \frac{1}{\beta}\mathbf{Z})$;
6:    $\mathbf{Z} \leftarrow \mathbf{Z} + \beta(\mathbf{Y} - \mathbf{X})$;
7:    update β; (if necessary)
8: **until** convergence
9: **output:** $\mathbf{X}$

Optimization problem (11.37) can be transformed as

$$\underset{\mathbf{Y}}{\text{minimize}} \quad \frac{1}{\beta}||\mathbf{Y}||_* + \frac{1}{2}\left\|\mathbf{Y} - \left(\mathbf{X} - \frac{1}{\beta}\mathbf{Z}\right)\right\|_F^2. \tag{11.39}$$

Solution of the above problem is given by a proximal mapping of $\frac{1}{\beta}||\cdot||_*$ from a point $\mathbf{X} - \frac{1}{\beta}\mathbf{Z}$ as follows:

$$\mathbf{Y} \leftarrow \operatorname{prox}_{\frac{1}{\beta}||\cdot||_*}\left(\mathbf{X} - \frac{1}{\beta}\mathbf{Z}\right). \tag{11.40}$$

The proximal mapping of the nuclear norm is generally given by

$$\operatorname{prox}_{\gamma||\cdot||_*}(\mathbf{B}) = \mathbf{U}\max(\mathbf{\Sigma} - \gamma, 0)\mathbf{V}^{\mathsf{T}}, \tag{11.41}$$

where we consider the singular value decomposition, $\mathbf{B} = \mathbf{U}\mathbf{\Sigma}\mathbf{V}^{\mathsf{T}}$.

Finally, we summarize the algorithm of low-rank matrix completion in Algorithm 1. All optimization parameters $\mathbf{X}$, $\mathbf{Y}$, and $\mathbf{Z}$ can be initialized randomly. The positive parameter β usually remains fixed, but a scheduling method has been proposed in which β is gradually increased for early convergence [34,39,53].

11.2.1.2 Low-rank tensor completion

Here, we consider how to extend the method of low-rank matrix completion to tensors. One of the important viewpoints for that is how to extend the nuclear norm of the matrix to the tensor. Assuming that the nuclear norm extended to the tensor is $\mathcal{R}(\cdot)$, the optimization problem is given as follows:

$$\underset{\mathcal{X}}{\text{minimize}} \quad \mathcal{R}(\mathcal{X}) \quad \text{subject to} \quad \mathcal{P}_{\Omega}(\mathcal{X}) = \mathcal{P}_{\Omega}(\mathcal{T}), \tag{11.42}$$

where $\mathcal{X} \in \mathbb{R}^{I_1 \times I_2 \times \cdots \times I_N}$ is the tensor as a result of completion and $\mathcal{T} \in \mathbb{R}^{I_1 \times I_2 \times \cdots \times I_N}$ is the incomplete input tensor. Since the only difference between the optimization

---

Algorithm 2 ADMM for low-rank tensor completion with $\mathcal{R}(\cdot)$.

1: **Input:** $\mathcal{T} \in \mathbb{R}^{I_1 \times I_2 \times \cdots \times I_N}$, Ω
2: **Initialize:** $\mathcal{X}, \mathcal{Y}, \mathcal{Z} \in \mathbb{R}^{I_1 \times I_2 \times \cdots \times I_N}$, $\beta \geq 0$
3: **repeat**
4:   $\mathcal{X} \leftarrow \mathcal{P}_\Omega(\mathcal{T}) + \mathcal{P}_{\bar{\Omega}}(\mathcal{Y} + \frac{1}{\beta}\mathcal{Z})$;
5:   $\mathcal{Y} \leftarrow \text{prox}_{\frac{1}{\beta}\mathcal{R}(\cdot)}(\mathcal{X} - \frac{1}{\beta}\mathcal{Z})$;
6:   $\mathcal{Z} \leftarrow \mathcal{Z} + \beta(\mathcal{Y} - \mathcal{X})$;
7:   update β; (if necessary)
8: **until** convergence
9: **output:** $\mathcal{X}$

---

problems (11.42) and (11.26) is the function of the nuclear norm, a similar ADMM-based algorithm can be derived when an efficiently computable proximal mapping of $\mathcal{R}(\cdot)$ exists. Algorithm 2 shows the ADMM for low-rank tensor completion with $\mathcal{R}(\cdot)$. A typical example of $\mathcal{R}(\cdot)$ is a tubal-nuclear norm (based on t-SVD) [99] defined for third-order tensors and has an efficiently computable proximal mapping.

Another example of $\mathcal{R}(\cdot)$ is given by the linear sum of the nuclear norm of matrices unfolded along all modes of a tensor as follows:

$$\mathcal{R}(\mathcal{X}) := \sum_{n=1}^{N} \alpha_n ||\mathbf{X}_{(n)}||_*, \tag{11.43}$$

where $\alpha_n \geq 0$ are weight parameters. It is called overlapped nuclear/trace/Schatten norm [54,75]. In this case, the optimization problem can be given by

$$\underset{\mathcal{X}}{\text{minimize}} \sum_{n=1}^{N} \alpha_n ||\mathbf{X}_{(n)}||_* \quad \text{subject to } \mathcal{P}_\Omega(\mathcal{X}) = \mathcal{P}_\Omega(\mathcal{T}). \tag{11.44}$$

In [54], it is called high-accuracy low-rank tensor completion (HaLRTC). The ADMM algorithm can be derived by transforming this optimization problem into an equivalent optimization problem with variable splitting as follows:

$$\underset{\mathcal{X}}{\text{minimize}} \ i_{\mathcal{T}_\Omega}(\mathcal{X}) + \sum_{n=1}^{N} \alpha_n ||\mathbf{Y}_n||_*$$
$$\text{subject to } \mathbf{Y}_n = \mathbf{X}_{(n)} \text{ for all } n, \tag{11.45}$$

where $\mathbf{Y}_n \in \mathbb{R}^{I_n \times \prod_{k \neq n} I_k}$ are slack variable matrices. Next, we put the augmented Lagrangian function as follows:

$$L_A(\mathcal{X}, \mathbf{Y}_1, ..., \mathbf{Y}_N, \mathbf{Z}_1, ..., \mathbf{Z}_N)$$

$$= i_{\mathcal{T}_\Omega}(\mathcal{X}) + \sum_{n=1}^{N} \left\{ \alpha_n \|\mathbf{Y}_n\|_* + \langle \mathbf{Z}_n, \mathbf{Y}_n - \mathbf{X}_{(n)} \rangle + \frac{\beta}{2} \|\mathbf{Y}_n - \mathbf{X}_{(n)}\|_F^2 \right\}, \quad (11.46)$$

where $\mathbf{Z}_n \in \mathbb{R}^{I_n \times \prod_{k \neq n} I_k}$ are Lagrange multipliers and $\beta > 0$ is a parameter of augmented term. Then the algorithm of ADMM for HaLRTC [54] is given as the iteration of the following steps:

$$\mathcal{X} \leftarrow \operatorname*{argmin}_{\mathcal{X}} L_A(\mathcal{X}, \mathbf{Y}_1, ..., \mathbf{Y}_N, \mathbf{Z}_1, ..., \mathbf{Z}_N), \quad (11.47)$$

$$\mathbf{Y}_n \leftarrow \operatorname*{argmin}_{\mathbf{Y}_n} L_A(\mathcal{X}, \mathbf{Y}_1, ..., \mathbf{Y}_N, \mathbf{Z}_1, ..., \mathbf{Z}_N) \text{ for all } n, \quad (11.48)$$

$$\mathbf{Z}_n \leftarrow \mathbf{Z}_n + \beta(\mathbf{Y}_n - \mathbf{X}_{(n)}) \text{ for all } n. \quad (11.49)$$

Each update can be calculated analytically.

For the update of $\mathcal{X}$, we solve the following problem:

$$\operatorname*{minimize}_{\mathcal{X}} \ i_{\mathcal{T}_\Omega}(\mathcal{X}) + \sum_{n=1}^{N} \left\{ \langle \mathbf{Z}_n, \mathbf{Y}_n - \mathbf{X}_{(n)} \rangle + \frac{\beta}{2} \|\mathbf{Y}_n - \mathbf{X}_{(n)}\|_F^2 \right\}. \quad (11.50)$$

Since terms without $\mathcal{X}$ can be summarized into a constant, others than the first term can be transformed as follows:

$$\sum_{n=1}^{N} \left\{ \langle \mathbf{Z}_n, \mathbf{Y}_n - \mathbf{X}_{(n)} \rangle + \frac{\beta}{2} \|\mathbf{Y}_n - \mathbf{X}_{(n)}\|_F^2 \right\}$$

$$= -N\langle \mathcal{X}, \bar{\mathcal{Z}} \rangle + \frac{\beta N}{2} \langle \mathcal{X}, \mathcal{X} \rangle - \beta N \langle \mathcal{X}, \bar{\mathcal{Y}} \rangle + \text{const}$$

$$= \frac{\beta N}{2} \left(\langle \mathcal{X}, \mathcal{X} \rangle - 2\langle \mathcal{X}, \bar{\mathcal{Y}} + \frac{1}{\beta} \bar{\mathcal{Z}} \rangle \right) + \text{const}$$

$$= \frac{\beta N}{2} \left\| \mathcal{X} - \left(\bar{\mathcal{Y}} + \frac{1}{\beta} \bar{\mathcal{Z}} \right) \right\|_F^2 + \text{const}, \quad (11.51)$$

where $\bar{\mathcal{Y}} = \frac{1}{N} \sum_{n=1}^{N} \text{fold}(\mathbf{Y}_n)$ and $\bar{\mathcal{Z}} = \frac{1}{N} \sum_{n=1}^{N} \text{fold}(\mathbf{Z}_n)$. Optimization problem (11.50) can be transformed as

$$\operatorname*{minimize}_{\mathcal{X}} \ \left\| \mathcal{X} - \left(\bar{\mathcal{Y}} + \frac{1}{\beta} \bar{\mathcal{Z}} \right) \right\|_F^2 \text{ subject to } \mathcal{P}_\Omega(\mathcal{X}) = \mathcal{P}_\Omega(\mathcal{T}). \quad (11.52)$$

Solution of the above problem is given by a projection from a point $\bar{\mathcal{Y}} + \frac{1}{\beta} \bar{\mathcal{Z}}$ onto a convex set $\{\mathcal{X} | \mathcal{P}_\Omega(\mathcal{X}) = \mathcal{P}_\Omega(\mathcal{T})\}$. Thus, it can be given by

$$\mathcal{X} \leftarrow \mathcal{P}_\Omega(\mathcal{T}) + \mathcal{P}_{\bar{\Omega}} \left(\bar{\mathcal{Y}} + \frac{1}{\beta} \bar{\mathcal{Z}} \right), \quad (11.53)$$

Algorithm 3 ADMM for low-rank tensor completion with $\sum_{n=1}^{N} \alpha_n ||\mathbf{X}_{(n)}||_*$ (HaL-RTC [54]).

1: **Input:** $\mathcal{T} \in \mathbb{R}^{I_1 \times I_2 \times \cdots \times I_N}$, Ω, $\{\alpha_n \geq 0\}_{n=1}^{N}$
2: **Initialize:** $\mathcal{X} \in \mathbb{R}^{I_1 \times I_2 \times \cdots \times I_N}$, $\{\mathbf{Y}_n, \mathbf{Z}_n \in \mathbb{R}^{I_n \times \prod_{k \neq n} I_k}\}_{n=1}^{N}$, $\beta \geq 0$
3: **repeat**
4:   $\bar{\mathcal{Y}} \leftarrow \frac{1}{N} \sum_{n=1}^{N} \text{fold}(\mathbf{Y}_n)$;
5:   $\bar{\mathcal{Z}} \leftarrow \frac{1}{N} \sum_{n=1}^{N} \text{fold}(\mathbf{Z}_n)$;
6:   $\mathcal{X} \leftarrow \mathcal{P}_\Omega(\mathcal{T}) + \mathcal{P}_{\bar{\Omega}}(\bar{\mathcal{Y}} + \frac{1}{\beta}\bar{\mathcal{Z}})$;
7:   **for** $n = 1, ..., N$ **do**
8:     $\mathbf{Y}_n \leftarrow \text{prox}_{\frac{\alpha_n}{\beta} ||\cdot||_*}(\mathbf{X}_{(n)} - \frac{1}{\beta}\mathbf{Z}_n)$;
9:     $\mathbf{Z}_n \leftarrow \mathbf{Z}_n + \beta(\mathbf{Y}_n - \mathbf{X}_{(n)})$;
10:   **end for**
11:   update β; (if necessary)
12: **until** convergence
13: **output:** $\mathcal{X}$

---

where $\mathcal{P}_{\bar{\Omega}}(\mathcal{X}) = (\mathbf{1} - \mathcal{Q}) * \mathcal{X}$ is an operation to discard the value of only the entries included in the set Ω and retain the other entries.

For the update of each $\mathbf{Y}_n$, we solve the following problem:

$$\underset{\mathbf{Y}_n}{\text{minimize}} \quad \alpha_n ||\mathbf{Y}_n||_* + \langle \mathbf{Z}_n, \mathbf{Y}_n - \mathbf{X}_{(n)} \rangle + \frac{\beta}{2} ||\mathbf{Y}_n - \mathbf{X}_{(n)}||_F^2. \tag{11.54}$$

Note that the optimization problems (11.37) and (11.54) are equivalent. In analogy to the low-rank matrix completion, solution of above problem is given by a proximal mapping of $\frac{\alpha_n}{\beta} ||\cdot||_*$ from a point $\mathbf{X}_{(n)} - \frac{1}{\beta}\mathbf{Z}_n$ as follows:

$$\mathbf{Y}_n \leftarrow \text{prox}_{\frac{\alpha_n}{\beta} ||\cdot||_*} \left(\mathbf{X}_{(n)} - \frac{1}{\beta}\mathbf{Z}_n \right). \tag{11.55}$$

Finally, we summarize the algorithm of low-rank tensor completion in Algorithm 3. All optimization parameters can be initialized randomly.

11.2.1.3 Smooth tensor completion

Smoothness is another important prior for tensor reconstruction. There are close relationships between adjacent entries of tensors representing images. In this case, it is important to regard the tensor as a scalar value function with multiple inputs such like $x_{i,j,k} = \mathcal{X}(i, j, k)$. In the penalty-based approach, we define the non-smoothness of the tensors and minimize it. To do so, here, we introduce TV of a vector $\mathbf{x} \in \mathbb{R}^I$ as follows:

$$||\mathbf{x}||_{\text{TV}} := \sum_{i=1}^{I-1} |\mathbf{x}(i+1) - \mathbf{x}(i)|. \tag{11.56}$$

TV is a sum of absolute values of differences between adjacent entries. In addition, its extension [68] to a matrix $\mathbf{X} \in \mathbb{R}^{I \times J}$ is given by

$$\|\mathbf{X}\|_{\text{TV}} := \sum_{i,j} \sqrt{\mathbf{X}_v(i,j)^2 + \mathbf{X}_h(i,j)^2} = \sum_{i,j} \left\| \begin{pmatrix} \mathbf{X}_v(i,j) \\ \mathbf{X}_h(i,j) \end{pmatrix} \right\|_2, \quad (11.57)$$

where $\mathbf{X}_v(i,j) := \mathbf{X}(i+1,j) - \mathbf{X}(i,j)$ and $\mathbf{X}_h(i,j) := \mathbf{X}(i,j+1) - \mathbf{X}(i,j)$. The matrix TV is given by the sum of the lengths of the difference vectors (i.e., l_2-norm) in individual entries. Finally, we extend it to tensor $\mathcal{X} \in \mathbb{R}^{I_1 \times I_2 \times \cdots \times I_N}$ as follows:

$$\|\mathcal{X}\|_{\text{TV}} := \sum_{\mathbf{i}=(i_1,\ldots,i_N) \in \mathbb{S}} \|\mathbf{V}_{\mathbf{i}}(\mathcal{X})\|_2, \quad (11.58)$$

where $\mathbb{S}$ is a set of indices of a tensor, $\mathbf{V}_{\mathbf{i}}(\mathcal{X}) \in \mathbb{R}^N$ is an N-dimensional vector whose entries are respectively the adjacent differences along N modes at the $(i_1, \ldots, i_N)$-th entries of the tensor. Note that TV is a convex function since $\mathbf{V}_{\mathbf{i}}$ is a linear operator and the l_2-norm is convex.

We consider the following smooth tensor completion problem:

$$\underset{\mathcal{X}}{\text{minimize}} \ \|\mathcal{X}\|_{\text{TV}} \ \text{ subject to } \mathcal{P}_\Omega(\mathcal{X}) = \mathcal{P}_\Omega(\mathcal{T}). \quad (11.59)$$

Note that TV is a convex function, but it is not always differentiable. There are a subgradient method [24] and the MM algorithm [62,70] for optimization. Recently, ADMM or PDHG is often used for the TV minimization problem [14,39,87,102].

11.2.1.4 Smooth tensor completion: an ADMM algorithm

First, we derive an ADMM-based algorithm for TV minimization. The optimization problem with variable splitting is given by

$$\underset{\mathcal{X}}{\text{minimize}} \ i_{\mathcal{T}_\Omega}(\mathcal{V}) + \sum_{\mathbf{i} \in \mathbb{S}} \|\mathbf{y}_{\mathbf{i}}\|_2$$

$$\text{subject to } \mathcal{V} = \mathcal{X}, \mathbf{y}_{\mathbf{i}} = \mathbf{V}_{\mathbf{i}}(\mathcal{X}) \text{ for all } \mathbf{i} \in \mathbb{S}, \quad (11.60)$$

where $\mathcal{V} \in \mathbb{R}^{I_1 \times \cdots \times I_N}$ and $\mathbf{y}_{\mathbf{i}} \in \mathbb{R}^N$ are slack variables. When we put $\mathbf{Y} = [\mathbf{y}_{(1,\ldots,1)}, \ldots, \mathbf{y}_{(I_1,\ldots,I_N)}] \in \mathbb{R}^{N \times \prod_n I_n}$, we have $\|\mathbf{Y}\|_{2,1} = \sum_{\mathbf{i} \in \mathbb{S}} \|\mathbf{y}_{\mathbf{i}}\|_2$, and the optimization problem can be simplified as

$$\underset{\mathcal{X}}{\text{minimize}} \ i_{\mathcal{T}_\Omega}(\mathcal{V}) + \|\mathbf{Y}\|_{2,1} \text{ subject to } \mathcal{V} = \mathcal{X}, \mathbf{Y} = \mathcal{L}(\mathcal{X}), \quad (11.61)$$

where $\mathcal{L}(\mathcal{X}) = [\mathbf{V}_{(1,\ldots,1)}(\mathcal{X}), \ldots, \mathbf{V}_{(I_1,\ldots,I_N)}(\mathcal{X})]$. The augmented Lagrangian function is given by

$$L_A(\mathcal{X}, \mathcal{V}, \mathcal{W}, \mathbf{Y}, \mathbf{Z}) = i_{\mathcal{T}_\Omega}(\mathcal{V}) + \langle \mathcal{W}, \mathcal{V} - \mathcal{X} \rangle + \frac{\beta}{2} \|\mathcal{V} - \mathcal{X}\|_F^2$$

$$+ \|\mathbf{Y}\|_{2,1} + \langle \mathbf{Z}, \mathbf{Y} - \mathcal{L}(\mathcal{X}) \rangle + \frac{\beta}{2} \|\mathbf{Y} - \mathcal{L}(\mathcal{X})\|_F^2. \quad (11.62)$$

The algorithm of ADMM is given by

$$\mathcal{X} \leftarrow \underset{\mathcal{X}}{\operatorname{argmin}} \, L_A(\mathcal{X}, \mathcal{V}, \mathcal{W}, \mathbf{Y}, \mathbf{Z}), \tag{11.63}$$

$$\mathcal{V} \leftarrow \underset{\mathcal{V}}{\operatorname{argmin}} \, L_A(\mathcal{X}, \mathcal{V}, \mathcal{W}, \mathbf{Y}, \mathbf{Z}), \tag{11.64}$$

$$\mathbf{Y} \leftarrow \underset{\mathbf{Y}}{\operatorname{argmin}} \, L_A(\mathcal{X}, \mathcal{V}, \mathcal{W}, \mathbf{Y}, \mathbf{Z}), \tag{11.65}$$

$$\mathcal{W} \leftarrow \mathcal{W} + \beta(\mathcal{V} - \mathcal{X}), \tag{11.66}$$

$$\mathbf{Z} \leftarrow \mathbf{Z} + \beta(\mathbf{Y} - \mathcal{L}(\mathcal{X})). \tag{11.67}$$

For updating $\mathcal{X}$, we solve the following optimization problem:

$$\underset{\mathcal{X}}{\text{minimize}} \; -\langle \mathcal{W}, \mathcal{X} \rangle + \frac{\beta}{2} \|\mathcal{V} - \mathcal{X}\|_F^2 - \langle \mathbf{Z}, -\mathcal{L}(\mathcal{X}) \rangle + \frac{\beta}{2} \|\mathbf{Y} - \mathcal{L}(\mathcal{X})\|_F^2. \tag{11.68}$$

Note that it is a quadratic function with respect to $\mathcal{X}$. A solution is obtained by seeking the point where the partial derivative of $\mathcal{X}$ is 0, which is given as the solution of the following linear equation:

$$(\mathcal{L}^*\mathcal{L} + \mathcal{I})(\mathcal{X}) = \mathcal{L}^* \left(\mathbf{Y} + \frac{1}{\beta}\mathbf{Z} \right) + \mathcal{V} + \frac{1}{\beta}\mathcal{W}. \tag{11.69}$$

Inversion of $(\mathcal{L}^*\mathcal{L} + \mathcal{I})$ is generally expensive for high-order tensors. The conjugate gradient method [42] is useful to solve linear equations with low memory requirements. In a very particular case where $\mathcal{X}$ is a periodic signal, defining $\mathcal{L}$ as a cyclic linear operator, there is a convolutional kernel $\mathcal{K}$ such that $(\mathcal{L}^*\mathcal{L} + \mathcal{I})(\mathcal{X}) = \text{conv}(\mathcal{X}, \mathcal{K})$. In this case, the solution of Eq. (11.69) can be obtained using the N-dimensional Fourier transform $\mathcal{F}(\cdot)$ as follows:

$$\mathcal{X} \leftarrow \mathcal{F}^{-1}(\mathcal{F}(\mathcal{B}) \oslash \mathcal{F}(\mathcal{K})), \tag{11.70}$$

where $\mathcal{B} := \mathcal{L}^*(\mathbf{Y} + \frac{1}{\beta}\mathbf{Z}) + \mathcal{V} + \frac{1}{\beta}\mathcal{W}$ and $\oslash$ denotes entry-wise division.

For updating $\mathcal{V}$ and $\mathbf{Y}$, we solve the following subproblems:

$$\underset{\mathcal{V}}{\text{minimize}} \; i_{\mathcal{T}_\Omega}(\mathcal{V}) + \langle \mathcal{W}, \mathcal{V} - \mathcal{X} \rangle + \frac{\beta}{2} \|\mathcal{V} - \mathcal{X}\|_F^2, \tag{11.71}$$

$$\underset{\mathbf{Y}}{\text{minimize}} \; \|\mathbf{Y}\|_{2,1} + \langle \mathbf{Z}, \mathbf{Y} - \mathcal{L}(\mathcal{X}) \rangle + \frac{\beta}{2} \|\mathbf{Y} - \mathcal{L}(\mathcal{X})\|_F^2. \tag{11.72}$$

Due to the analogy, the update rules are as follows:

$$\mathcal{V} \leftarrow \mathcal{P}_\Omega(\mathcal{T}) + \mathcal{P}_{\bar{\Omega}} \left(\mathcal{X} - \frac{1}{\beta}\mathcal{W} \right), \tag{11.73}$$

$$\mathbf{Y} \leftarrow \text{prox}_{\frac{1}{\beta}\|\cdot\|_{2,1}} \left(\mathcal{L}(\mathcal{X}) - \frac{1}{\beta}\mathbf{Z} \right), \tag{11.74}$$

Algorithm 4 ADMM for low TV tensor completion (a special case of [14]).

1: **Input:** $\mathcal{T} \in \mathbb{R}^{I_1 \times I_2 \times \cdots \times I_N}$, Ω
2: **Initialize:** $\mathcal{X}, \mathcal{V}, \mathcal{W} \in \mathbb{R}^{I_1 \times I_2 \times \cdots \times I_N}$, $\mathbf{Y}, \mathbf{Z} \in \mathbb{R}^{N \times \prod_n I_n}$, $\beta \geq 0$
3: **repeat**
4:     $\mathcal{X} \leftarrow$ solution of the linear equation (11.69);
5:     $\mathcal{V} \leftarrow \mathcal{P}_\Omega(\mathcal{T}) + \mathcal{P}_{\bar{\Omega}} \left(\mathcal{X} - \frac{1}{\beta}\mathcal{W} \right)$;
6:     $\mathbf{Y} \leftarrow \text{prox}_{\frac{1}{\beta}||\cdot||_{2,1}} \left(\mathcal{L}(\mathcal{X}) - \frac{1}{\beta}\mathbf{Z} \right)$;
7:     $\mathcal{W} \leftarrow \mathcal{W} + \beta(\mathcal{V} - \mathcal{X})$;
8:     $\mathbf{Z} \leftarrow \mathbf{Z} + \beta(\mathbf{Y} - \mathcal{L}(\mathcal{X}))$;
9:     update β; (if necessary)
10: **until** convergence
11: **output:** $\mathcal{X}$

---

where the proximal mapping of $\lambda || \cdot ||_{21}$ is

$$\text{prox}_{\lambda||\cdot||_{2,1}}([\mathbf{u}_1, ..., \mathbf{u}_J]) = [\text{prox}_{\lambda||\cdot||_2}(\mathbf{u}_1), ..., \text{prox}_{\lambda||\cdot||_2}(\mathbf{u}_J)], \tag{11.75}$$

$$\text{prox}_{\lambda||\cdot||_2}(\mathbf{u}) = \max(||\mathbf{u}||_2 - \lambda, 0)\frac{\mathbf{u}}{||\mathbf{u}||_2}. \tag{11.76}$$

Finally, the optimization algorithm based on ADMM for TV minimization is summarized as Algorithm 4. All optimization parameters can be initialized randomly. Unlike the case of the nuclear norm, the algorithm for TV minimization requires to solve the linear equation iteratively. When this is solved by inverse matrix calculation, the size of the matrix is $(\prod_{n=1}^N I_n, \prod_{n=1}^N I_n)$, and this is serious with large N. Since the computational cost of $(\mathcal{L}^*\mathcal{L} + \mathcal{I})(\mathcal{X})$ itself is relatively small, it is efficient to solve it using the conjugate gradient method. Note that it becomes a double loop algorithm because the conjugate gradient is a sequential algorithm. It requires some adjustment of the convergence conditions (or numbers of iterations) of the inner and outer loops [28].

11.2.1.5 Smooth tensor completion: a PDHG/PDS algorithm

It is known that the PDHG/PDS can efficiently solve the TV minimization problem [13,102]. The main difference between ADMM and PDHG/PDS is that TV minimization can involve large matrix inversions/linear equations in ADMM, while PDHG/PDS can avoid this. Therefore, PDHG/PDS is used in many TV minimization techniques such as TV denoising/deconvolution [102], vector TV regularization [63], and generalized variation of diffusion tensor imaging [78]. We rewrite the TV minimization problem as

$$\underset{\mathcal{X}}{\text{minimize}} \; i_{\mathcal{T}_\Omega}(\mathcal{X}) + \sum_{i \in \mathbb{S}} ||\nabla_i(\mathcal{X})||_2 \tag{11.77}$$

and consider the convex conjugate as

$$||\mathbf{V}_\mathbf{i}(\mathcal{X})||_2 = \max_{||\mathbf{y}_\mathbf{i}||_2 \leq 1} \langle \mathbf{V}_\mathbf{i}(\mathcal{X}), \mathbf{y}_\mathbf{i} \rangle, \tag{11.78}$$

where $\mathbf{y}_\mathbf{i} \in \mathbb{R}^N$ is a dual parameter. Substituting (11.78) into (11.77) and considering the convexity of the original problem, the min-max problem can be obtained as

$$\min_{\mathcal{X}} \max_{\mathbf{Y}} f(\mathcal{X}, \mathbf{Y}) = i_{\mathcal{T}_\Omega}(\mathcal{X}) + \langle \mathcal{L}(\mathcal{X}), \mathbf{Y} \rangle - \sum_{i \in \mathbb{S}} i_{||\cdot||_2 \leq 1}(\mathbf{y}_\mathbf{i}), \tag{11.79}$$

where we summarize dual parameters into a matrix $\mathbf{Y} = [\mathbf{y}_{(1,...,1)}, ..., \mathbf{y}_{(I_1,...,I_N)}]$ and a linear operator $\mathcal{L}(\mathcal{X}) = [\mathbf{V}_{(1,...,1)}(\mathcal{X}), ..., \mathbf{V}_{(I_1,...,I_N)}(\mathcal{X})]$, and the convex conjugate of the l_2-norm is an indicator function as follows:

$$i_{||\cdot||_2 \leq 1}(\mathbf{u}) = \begin{cases} 0 & ||\mathbf{u}||_2 \leq 1, \\ \infty & \text{otherwise.} \end{cases} \tag{11.80}$$

To solve (11.79), we use the following two steps:

$$\mathcal{X}^{k+1} \leftarrow \operatorname*{argmin}_{\mathcal{X}} \, f(\mathcal{X}, \mathbf{Y}^k) + \frac{1}{2\gamma_1}||\mathcal{X}^k - \mathcal{X}||_F^2, \tag{11.81}$$

$$\mathbf{Y}^{k+1} \leftarrow \operatorname*{argmin}_{\mathbf{Y}} \, -f(\mathcal{X}^{k+1}, \mathbf{Y}) + \frac{1}{2\gamma_2}||\mathbf{Y}^k - \mathbf{Y}||_F^2, \tag{11.82}$$

where $\gamma_1 > 0$ and $\gamma_2 > 0$ are step size parameters for primal and dual steps, respectively. This is called the PDHG or PDS algorithm.

To update $\mathcal{X}$, we consider the following optimization problem:

$$\min_{\mathcal{X}} i_{\mathcal{T}_\Omega}(\mathcal{X}) + \langle \mathcal{L}(\mathcal{X}), \mathbf{Y}^k \rangle + \frac{1}{2\gamma_1}||\mathcal{X}^k - \mathcal{X}||_F^2. \tag{11.83}$$

Regarding terms without $\mathcal{X}$ as constant, the cost function can be summarized as follows:

$$i_{\mathcal{T}_\Omega}(\mathcal{X}) + \langle \mathcal{L}(\mathcal{X}), \mathbf{Y}^k \rangle + \frac{1}{2\gamma_1}||\mathcal{X}^k - \mathcal{X}||_F^2$$

$$= i_{\mathcal{T}_\Omega}(\mathcal{X}) + \frac{1}{2\gamma_1}(\langle \mathcal{X}, \mathcal{X} \rangle - 2\langle \mathcal{X}, \mathcal{X}^k - \gamma_1 \mathcal{L}^*(\mathbf{Y}^k) \rangle) + \text{const}$$

$$= i_{\mathcal{T}_\Omega}(\mathcal{X}) + \frac{1}{2\gamma_1}||\mathcal{X} - (\mathcal{X}^k - \gamma_1 \mathcal{L}^*(\mathbf{Y}^k))||_F^2 + \text{const}. \tag{11.84}$$

Solution of the above problem is given by a projection onto a convex set as follows:

$$\mathcal{X}^{k+1} \leftarrow \mathcal{P}_\Omega(\mathcal{T}) + \mathcal{P}_{\bar{\Omega}}(\mathcal{X}^k - \gamma_1 \mathcal{L}^*(\mathbf{Y}^k)). \tag{11.85}$$

To update $\mathbf{Y}$, we consider the following optimization problem:

$$\min_{\{\mathbf{y_i}\}_{i \in \mathbb{S}}} \sum_{i \in \mathbb{S}} \left\{ i_{\|\cdot\|_2 \le 1}(\mathbf{y_i}) - \langle \mathbf{V_i}(\mathcal{X}^{k+1}), \mathbf{y_i} \rangle + \frac{1}{2\gamma_2} \|\mathbf{y_i^k} - \mathbf{y_i}\|_2^2 \right\}. \tag{11.86}$$

Note that the optimization problem for each column of $\mathbf{Y}$ is completely independent. Thus, we consider the optimization problem for each $\mathbf{y_i}$. Regarding terms without $\mathbf{y_i}$ as constant, the cost function can be summarized as follows:

$$i_{\|\cdot\|_2 \le 1}(\mathbf{y_i}) - \langle \mathbf{V_i}(\mathcal{X}^{k+1}), \mathbf{y_i} \rangle + \frac{1}{2\gamma_2} \|\mathbf{y_i^k} - \mathbf{y_i}\|_2^2$$

$$= i_{\|\cdot\|_2 \le 1}(\mathbf{y_i}) + \frac{1}{2\gamma_2} (\langle \mathbf{y_i}, \mathbf{y_i} \rangle - 2 \langle \mathbf{y_i}, \mathbf{y_i^k} + \gamma_2 \mathbf{V_i}(\mathcal{X}^{k+1}) \rangle) + \text{const}$$

$$= i_{\|\cdot\|_2 \le 1}(\mathbf{y_i}) + \frac{1}{2\gamma_2} \|\mathbf{y_i} - (\mathbf{y_i^k} + \gamma_2 \mathbf{V_i}(\mathcal{X}^{k+1}))\|_2^2 + \text{const}. \tag{11.87}$$

Solution of the above problem is given by a projection onto a convex set as follows:

$$\mathbf{y_i^{k+1}} \leftarrow \text{proj}_{\|\cdot\|_2 \le 1}(\mathbf{y_i^k} + \gamma_2 \mathbf{V_i}(\mathcal{X}^{k+1})), \tag{11.88}$$

where the projection into the unit sphere is given by

$$\text{proj}_{\|\cdot\|_2 \le 1}(\mathbf{u}) = \frac{\mathbf{u}}{\max(1, \|\mathbf{u}\|_2)}. \tag{11.89}$$

Finally, the PDHG/PDS algorithm for TV minimization can be summarized as Algorithm 5. All optimization parameters can be initialized randomly. We can see both primal and dual steps are given by the projection onto a convex set, and these are computationally easy. The theory of fixed-point algorithms has proved the global convergence of the PDS method at sufficiently small step sizes [13,31,41]. However, smaller step sizes usually slow down convergence. In addition, the optimal step size may not be constant during the optimization process. It is not easy to obtain the best setting of γ_1 and γ_2 for the optimization problem. There are studies to automatically adapt the step size parameters by considering the balance between primal and dual residuals [37,86,89].

11.2.1.6 *Tensor reconstruction via minimization of convex penalties*

Finally, we generalize the tensor reconstruction problem using convex optimization. It includes the optimization problems introduced above and combinations of multiple penalties such as the nuclear norm and TV. In addition, it can include other low-level vision tasks such as tensor completion with noisy observation (denoising), deblurring, and superresolution.

We consider the following generalized tensor reconstruction problem:

$$\underset{\mathcal{X}}{\text{minimize}} \; d(\mathbf{b}, \mathcal{A}(\mathcal{X})) + \sum_{r=1}^{R} h_r(\mathcal{L}_r(\mathcal{X})), \tag{11.90}$$

Algorithm 5 PDHG/PDS for low TV tensor completion (a special case of [87,89]).

1: **Input:** $\mathcal{T} \in \mathbb{R}^{I_1 \times I_2 \times \cdots \times I_N}$, Ω
2: **Initialize:** $\mathcal{X}^0 \in \mathbb{R}^{I_1 \times I_2 \times \cdots \times I_N}$, $\mathbf{y}_{\mathbf{i}}^0 \in \mathbb{R}^N$ for all $\mathbf{i} \in \mathbb{S}$, $\gamma_1, \gamma_2 \geq 0$, $k = 0$
3: **repeat**
4:     $\mathbf{Y}^k \leftarrow [\mathbf{y}_{(1,\ldots,1)}^k, \ldots, \mathbf{y}_{(I_1,\ldots,I_N)}^k]$;
5:     $\mathcal{X}^{k+1} \leftarrow \mathcal{P}_\Omega(\mathcal{T}) + \mathcal{P}_{\bar{\Omega}}(\mathcal{X}^k - \gamma_1 \mathcal{L}^*(\mathbf{Y}^k))$;
6:     $\mathbf{y}_{\mathbf{i}}^{k+1} \leftarrow \text{proj}_{||\cdot||_2 \leq 1}(\mathbf{y}_{\mathbf{i}}^k + \gamma_2 \mathbf{V}_{\mathbf{i}}(\mathcal{X}^{k+1}))$ for all $\mathbf{i} \in \mathbb{S}$;
7:     update γ_1, γ_2; (if necessary)
8:     $k \leftarrow k + 1$;
9: **until** convergence
10: **output:** $\mathcal{X}^k$

---

where $d(\mathbf{b}, \mathcal{A}(\mathcal{X}))$ is a measure of dissimilarity between observed data $\mathbf{b}$ and the reconstructed tensor $\mathcal{X}$ and $\sum_{r=1}^R h_r(\mathcal{L}_r(\mathcal{X}))$ are penalty terms to impose some a priori structure of the reconstructed tensor. For simplicity, we restrict ourselves to use the notations with $\mathbf{x} = \text{vec}(\mathcal{X})$, $\mathbf{Ax} = \mathcal{A}(\mathcal{X})$, and $\mathbf{L}_r\mathbf{x} = \mathcal{L}_r(\mathcal{X})$. Furthermore, $d(\cdot)$ can be integrated to penalties as $h_0(\mathbf{L}_0\mathbf{x}) := d(\mathbf{b}, \mathbf{Ax})$ with $\mathbf{L}_0 := \mathbf{A}$. Thus, we have the following optimization problem:

$$\underset{\mathbf{x}}{\text{minimize}} \sum_{r=0}^R h_r(\mathbf{L}_r\mathbf{x}). \tag{11.91}$$

Note that we assume all $h_r(\cdot)$ are convex functions that have efficiently computable proximal mappings. Using the relationship of convex conjugate $h^*(\cdot)$ as

$$h(\mathbf{Lx}) = \max_{\mathbf{y}} \langle \mathbf{y}, \mathbf{Lx} \rangle - h^*(\mathbf{y}), \tag{11.92}$$

a min-max problem is then obtained by

$$\min_{\mathbf{x}} \max_{\mathbf{y}_0,\ldots,\mathbf{y}_R} f(\mathbf{x}, \mathbf{y}_0, \ldots, \mathbf{y}_R) = \sum_{r=0}^R \left\{ \langle \mathbf{y}_r, \mathbf{L}_r\mathbf{x} \rangle - h_r^*(\mathbf{y}_r) \right\}. \tag{11.93}$$

Primal and dual steps can be given by the solution of the following optimization problems:

$$\mathbf{x}^{k+1} \leftarrow \underset{\mathbf{x}}{\text{argmin}} \, f(\mathbf{x}, \mathbf{y}_0^k, \ldots, \mathbf{y}_R^k) + \frac{1}{2\gamma_1} ||\mathbf{x}^k - \mathbf{x}||_2^2, \tag{11.94}$$

$$\mathbf{y}_r^{k+1} \leftarrow \underset{\mathbf{y}_r}{\text{argmin}} -f(\mathbf{x}^{k+1}, \mathbf{y}_r) + \frac{1}{2\gamma_2} ||\mathbf{y}_r^k - \mathbf{y}_r||_2^2 \text{ for all } r. \tag{11.95}$$

Note that each dual step of $\mathbf{y}_r$ does not depend on other dual variables $\mathbf{y}_s (s \neq r)$.

The objective function of (11.94) is just a quadratic form of $\mathbf{x}$ as follows:

$$\sum_{r=0}^{R} \langle \mathbf{y}_r^k, \mathbf{L}_r \mathbf{x} \rangle + \frac{1}{2\gamma_1} \|\mathbf{x}^k - \mathbf{x}\|_2^2$$

$$= \frac{1}{2\gamma_1} \left(\langle \mathbf{x}, \mathbf{x} \rangle - 2 \left\langle \mathbf{x}, \mathbf{x}^k - \gamma_1 \sum_{r=0}^{R} \mathbf{L}_r^T \mathbf{y}_r^k \right\rangle \right) + \text{const}$$

$$= \frac{1}{2\gamma_1} \left\| \mathbf{x} - \left(\mathbf{x}^k - \gamma_1 \sum_{r=0}^{R} \mathbf{L}_r^T \mathbf{y}_r^k \right) \right\|_2^2 + \text{const}. \tag{11.96}$$

Then $\mathbf{x}$ is updated by

$$\mathbf{x}^{k+1} \leftarrow \mathbf{x}^k - \gamma_1 \sum_{r=0}^{R} \mathbf{L}_r^T \mathbf{y}_r^k. \tag{11.97}$$

To update each $\mathbf{y}_r$, the optimization problem can be given by

$$\underset{\mathbf{y}_r}{\text{minimize}} \ h_r^*(\mathbf{y}) - \langle \mathbf{y}_r, \mathbf{L}_r \mathbf{x}^{k+1} \rangle + \frac{1}{2\gamma_2} \|\mathbf{y}_r^k - \mathbf{y}_r\|_2^2. \tag{11.98}$$

Note that the problems (11.86) and (11.98) have analogy. It can be transformed as

$$\underset{\mathbf{y}_r}{\text{minimize}} \ \gamma_2 h_r^*(\mathbf{y}) + \frac{1}{2} \|\mathbf{y}_r - (\mathbf{y}_r^k + \gamma_2 \mathbf{L}_r \mathbf{x}^{k+1})\|_2^2. \tag{11.99}$$

Then the update rule can be given by

$$\mathbf{y}_r^{k+1} \leftarrow \text{prox}_{\gamma_2 h_r^*} \left(\mathbf{y}_r^k + \gamma_2 \mathbf{L}_r \mathbf{x}^{k+1} \right). \tag{11.100}$$

In addition, putting $\mathbf{z}_r = \mathbf{y}_r^k + \gamma_2 \mathbf{L}_r \mathbf{x}^{k+1}$ and considering Moreau decomposition [20, 60],

$$\mathbf{z} = \text{prox}_{\gamma h^*}(\mathbf{z}) + \gamma \text{prox}_{\frac{1}{\gamma} h} \left(\frac{1}{\gamma} \mathbf{z} \right), \tag{11.101}$$

the update rule can be transformed as

$$\mathbf{y}_r^{k+1} \leftarrow \mathbf{z}_r - \gamma_2 \text{prox}_{\frac{1}{\gamma_2} h_r} \left(\frac{1}{\gamma_2} \mathbf{z}_r \right). \tag{11.102}$$

We can properly use (11.100) or (11.102) depending on the ease of obtaining a proximal mapping.

The PDHG/PDS for general tensor reconstruction is summarized as Algorithm 6. All optimization parameters can be initialized randomly. The list of solutions for various proximal mapping is available in [20]. Especially for low-level vision tasks, noise inequality and box constraints are useful [89].

Algorithm 6 PDHG/PDS for general tensor reconstruction (a generalized formulation of [102]).

1: **Input**: A problem defined by penalty functions $\{h_r(\cdot), \mathbf{L}_r\}_{r=0}^R$
2: **Initialize**: $\mathbf{x}^0$, $\mathbf{y}_r^0$ for all $r \in \{0, 1, ..., R\}$, $\gamma_1, \gamma_2 \geq 0$, $k = 0$
3: **repeat**
4:     $\mathbf{x}^{k+1} \leftarrow \mathbf{x}^k - \gamma_1 \sum_{r=0}^R \mathbf{L}_r^{\mathsf{T}} \mathbf{y}_r^k$;
5:     $\mathbf{y}_r^{k+1} \leftarrow \mathrm{prox}_{\gamma_2 h^*} \left(\mathbf{y}_r^k + \gamma_2 \mathbf{L}_r \mathbf{x}^{k+1} \right)$ for all r;
6:     update γ_1, γ_2; (if necessary)
7:     $k \leftarrow k + 1$;
8: **until** convergence
9: **output**: $\mathcal{X}^k = \mathrm{fold}(\mathbf{x}^k)$

11.2.2 Tensor decomposition and reconstruction

In this section, we introduce the tensor reconstruction method using tensor decomposition. The strength of this approach is that the structure of the tensor can be controlled more finely and directly, but in general, the optimization problem becomes nonconvex and it is difficult to find a global solution. In addition, since the nature of the optimization problem changes depending on the mathematical model, individual optimization algorithms are often applied according to the problems. On the other hand, we show that the optimization problems of tensor completion based on several mathematical models can be solved by the framework of the majorization-minimization/maximization (MM) algorithm [43,64]. We also discuss the generalization for applying the MM algorithm to tasks other than tensor completion (i.e., various types of $\mathcal{A}$). According to this framework, various tensor completion models can be easily applied to other low-level vision tasks such as superresolution, deblurring, and compressed sensing by changing only one step. However, it should be noted that some implementation issues may remain.

11.2.2.1 Majorization-minimization algorithm for tensor decomposition with missing entries

In this section, we consider the following optimization problem:

$$\underset{\boldsymbol{\theta}}{\text{minimize}} \;\; ||\mathcal{P}_\Omega(\mathcal{T} - \mathcal{X}_{\boldsymbol{\theta}})||_F^2, \qquad (11.103)$$

where $\mathcal{X}_{\boldsymbol{\theta}} \in \mathbb{R}^{I_1 \times I_2 \times \cdots \times I_N}$ is the tensor as a result of completion and $\mathcal{T} \in \mathbb{R}^{I_1 \times I_2 \times \cdots \times I_N}$ is the incomplete input tensor. A resultant tensor is reconstructed by low-rank tensor decomposition with parameters $\boldsymbol{\theta}$. In this section, we do not assume a specific model for $\mathcal{X}_{\boldsymbol{\theta}}$. For example, $\mathcal{X}_{\boldsymbol{\theta}}$ can be a CP decomposition or a Tucker decomposition. In the case of CP decomposition, $\boldsymbol{\theta}$ is a collective representation of N factor matrices, and in the case of Tucker decomposition, $\boldsymbol{\theta}$ is a collective representation of the core tensor and its factor matrices.

It should be noted that problem (11.103) is generally nonconvex, its solution is not unique, and it is not easy to obtain its global solution [47]. In the case of Tucker decomposition without missing entries, it is known that the alternating least-squares (ALS) algorithms [25] can efficiently converge to a stationary point. In the case with missing entries, algorithms for obtaining solutions have been proposed that use the gradient descent method [33] and manifold optimization [45,49] in recent years. Gradient descent is usually slow to converge and manifold optimization can accelerate it by correcting its update direction on the manifold. However, a common issue with both methods is step size parameter selection because the convergence time is sensitive to the step size parameter.

Here, we introduce MM algorithms [43,64] to perform tensor decomposition with missing entries. First, we define the original cost function and auxiliary function by

$$f(\boldsymbol{\theta}) := ||\mathcal{P}_{\Omega}(\mathcal{T} - \mathcal{X}_{\boldsymbol{\theta}})||_F^2, \tag{11.104}$$

$$h(\boldsymbol{\theta}|\boldsymbol{\theta}') := ||\mathcal{P}_{\Omega}(\mathcal{T} - \mathcal{X}_{\boldsymbol{\theta}})||_F^2 + ||\mathcal{P}_{\bar{\Omega}}(\mathcal{X}_{\boldsymbol{\theta}'} - \mathcal{X}_{\boldsymbol{\theta}})||_F^2, \tag{11.105}$$

where $f(\boldsymbol{\theta})$ is the original cost function and $h(\boldsymbol{\theta}|\boldsymbol{\theta}')$ is an auxiliary function. Note that the first term of the auxiliary function is the same as the original cost function $h(\boldsymbol{\theta}|\boldsymbol{\theta}') = f(\boldsymbol{\theta}) + ||\mathcal{P}_{\bar{\Omega}}(\mathcal{X}_{\boldsymbol{\theta}'} - \mathcal{X}_{\boldsymbol{\theta}})||_F^2$. Thus, clearly we have the relation

$$h(\boldsymbol{\theta}|\boldsymbol{\theta}) = f(\boldsymbol{\theta}), \text{ and } h(\boldsymbol{\theta}|\boldsymbol{\theta}') \geq f(\boldsymbol{\theta}) \ (\boldsymbol{\theta} \neq \boldsymbol{\theta}'). \tag{11.106}$$

Let us consider the following algorithm:

$$\boldsymbol{\theta}^{k+1} = \underset{\boldsymbol{\theta}}{\text{argmin}}\, h(\boldsymbol{\theta}|\boldsymbol{\theta}^k), \tag{11.107}$$

where the cost function is monotonically nonincreasing since we have

$$f(\boldsymbol{\theta}^k) = h(\boldsymbol{\theta}^k|\boldsymbol{\theta}^k) \geq h(\boldsymbol{\theta}^{k+1}|\boldsymbol{\theta}^k) \geq f(\boldsymbol{\theta}^{k+1}). \tag{11.108}$$

It should be noted that $\boldsymbol{\theta}^{k+1}$ only has to satisfy $h(\boldsymbol{\theta}^k|\boldsymbol{\theta}^k) \geq h(\boldsymbol{\theta}^{k+1}|\boldsymbol{\theta}^k)$ to have a nonincreasing property. Furthermore, the auxiliary function can be transformed as

$$\begin{aligned} h(\boldsymbol{\theta}|\boldsymbol{\theta}^k) &= ||\mathcal{P}_{\Omega}(\mathcal{T} - \mathcal{X}_{\boldsymbol{\theta}})||_F^2 + ||\mathcal{P}_{\bar{\Omega}}(\mathcal{X}_{\boldsymbol{\theta}^k} - \mathcal{X}_{\boldsymbol{\theta}})||_F^2 \\ &= ||(\mathcal{P}_{\Omega}(\mathcal{T}) + \mathcal{P}_{\bar{\Omega}}(\mathcal{X}_{\boldsymbol{\theta}^k})) - (\mathcal{P}_{\Omega}(\mathcal{X}_{\boldsymbol{\theta}}) + \mathcal{P}_{\bar{\Omega}}(\mathcal{X}_{\boldsymbol{\theta}}))||_F^2 \\ &= ||\widetilde{\mathcal{X}}^k - \mathcal{X}_{\boldsymbol{\theta}}||_F^2, \end{aligned} \tag{11.109}$$

where $\widetilde{\mathcal{X}}^k = \mathcal{P}_{\Omega}(\mathcal{T}) + \mathcal{P}_{\bar{\Omega}}(\mathcal{X}_{\boldsymbol{\theta}^k})$. Note that $\mathcal{X}_{\boldsymbol{\theta}} = \mathcal{P}_{\Omega}(\mathcal{X}_{\boldsymbol{\theta}}) + \mathcal{P}_{\bar{\Omega}}(\mathcal{X}_{\boldsymbol{\theta}})$ since the entries that are discarded by $\mathcal{P}_{\Omega}$ are not discarded by $\mathcal{P}_{\bar{\Omega}}$ and the entries that are not discarded by $\mathcal{P}_{\Omega}$ are discarded by $\mathcal{P}_{\bar{\Omega}}$. Thus, the minimization of the auxiliary function itself can be regarded as the standard tensor decomposition without missing entries.

In practice, the MM algorithm comprises the following two-step algorithm:

$$\widetilde{\mathcal{X}}^k \leftarrow \mathcal{P}_{\Omega}(\mathcal{T}) + \mathcal{P}_{\bar{\Omega}}(\mathcal{X}_{\boldsymbol{\theta}^k}), \tag{11.110}$$

$$\boldsymbol{\theta}^{k+1} \leftarrow \underset{\boldsymbol{\theta}}{\text{argmin}}\, ||\widetilde{\mathcal{X}}^k - \mathcal{X}_{\boldsymbol{\theta}}||_F^2. \tag{11.111}$$

Note that the first step (11.110) can be interpreted as a solution of the optimization problem minimize$_{\mathcal{X}}$ $i_{\mathcal{T}_\Omega}(\mathcal{X}) + ||\mathcal{X}_{\theta^k} - \mathcal{X}||_F^2$, and it is a projection from a point $\mathcal{X}_{\theta^k}$ onto a convex set $\{\mathcal{X}|\mathcal{P}_\Omega(\mathcal{T}) = \mathcal{P}_\Omega(\mathcal{X})\}$. In addition, $\mathcal{X}_{\theta^{k+1}}$ obtained by the second step (11.111) is also a projection from a point $\widetilde{\mathcal{X}}^k$ onto a set $\{\mathcal{X}|\mathcal{X} = \mathcal{X}_\theta$ for all $\theta\}$.

In other words, the MM algorithm introduced here can be interpreted as an algorithm that alternately projects a convex set that satisfies the condition of the observed entries and a nonconvex set that represents a low-rank tensor for a certain initial tensor. In addition, we showed that this alternating projection algorithm monotonically nonincreases the cost function.

This property of the MM algorithm holds even in the more general case of adding a penalty term to the cost function as follows:

$$f_{\mathrm{p}}(\theta) := ||\mathcal{P}_\Omega(\mathcal{T} - \mathcal{X}_\theta)||_F^2 + p(\theta), \tag{11.112}$$

$$h_{\mathrm{p}}(\theta|\theta') := ||\mathcal{P}_\Omega(\mathcal{T} - \mathcal{X}_\theta)||_F^2 + p(\theta) + ||\mathcal{P}_{\bar{\Omega}}(\mathcal{X}_{\theta'} - \mathcal{X}_\theta)||_F^2. \tag{11.113}$$

We have

$$h_{\mathrm{p}}(\theta|\theta) = f_{\mathrm{p}}(\theta), \; h_{\mathrm{p}}(\theta|\theta') \geq f_{\mathrm{p}}(\theta) \; (\theta \neq \theta'), \tag{11.114}$$

and

$$h_{\mathrm{p}}(\theta|\theta^k) = h(\theta|\theta^k) + p(\theta)$$
$$= ||\widetilde{\mathcal{X}}^k - \mathcal{X}_\theta||_F^2 + p(\theta). \tag{11.115}$$

The minimization of $h_{\mathrm{p}}(\theta|\theta^k)$ is just a penalized tensor decomposition of $\widetilde{\mathcal{X}}^k$. Note that $p(\theta)$ could be an indicator function. The important point is that the MM algorithm can be used for tensor completion by any tensor decomposition model with a monotonous nonincreasing algorithm (e.g., ALS) such as matrix decomposition [83], CP decomposition [84,93], Tucker decomposition [85,88], and tensor train (TT) decomposition [69], regardless of penalties or constraints.

Finally, we summarize the MM algorithm for tensor completion in Algorithm 7. Note that θ may be initialized randomly, but some specific initialization techniques may be required to obtain a better local solution. Step 5 in Algorithm 7 is not necessary to achieve a strict minimization of the auxiliary function, and it still has the monotonic nonincreasing property.

11.2.2.2 MM algorithm for other low-level vision tasks

We discuss applying the MM algorithm introduced in the previous section to low-level vision tasks other than tensor completion. In other words, we consider the following optimization problem:

$$\underset{\theta}{\text{minimize}} \; f_0(\theta) := ||\mathbf{b} - \mathcal{A}(\mathcal{X}_\theta)||_2^2. \tag{11.116}$$

When we apply the MM algorithm to the above problem, it should be noted that the following approach may be limited depending on the noise property in $\mathbf{b}$ and the

---

Algorithm 7 An MM algorithm for tensor completion.

1: **input:** $\mathcal{T} \in \mathbb{R}^{I_1 \times \cdots \times I_N}$, Ω, and the tensor decomposition model $\mathcal{X}_\theta$
2: **initialize:** θ
3: **repeat**
4: $\quad \mathcal{Z} \leftarrow \mathcal{P}_\Omega(\mathcal{T}) + \mathcal{P}_{\bar{\Omega}}(\mathcal{X}_\theta)$;
5: $\quad \theta \leftarrow \mathrm{argmin}_\theta \|\mathcal{Z} - \mathcal{X}_\theta\|_F^2 + p(\theta)$;
6: **until** convergence
7: **output:** θ

---

uniformity of singular values of $\mathcal{A}$. Because the MM approach below modifies the metric space depending on the positive singular values of $\mathcal{A}$, noise characteristics could be largely changed when the distribution of singular values is not uniform. In other words, we should be careful when both strong noise and nonuniform singular values are present at the same time.

In many cases of low-level-vision tasks, the null space of $\mathcal{A}$ is not empty. Thus, we assume the following two sets:

$$\{ \mathcal{X} \mid \mathbf{b} = \mathcal{A}(\mathcal{X}) \}, \tag{11.117}$$

$$\{ \mathcal{X} \mid \mathcal{X} = \mathcal{X}_\theta \text{ for all } \boldsymbol{\theta} \}. \tag{11.118}$$

Recall from the previous section that the MM algorithm can be interpreted as an alternating projection onto two sets. Thus, here we consider two steps as follows:

$$\widetilde{\mathcal{X}}^k \leftarrow \underset{\mathbf{b}=\mathcal{A}(\mathcal{X})}{\mathrm{argmin}} \|\mathcal{X}_{\theta^k} - \mathcal{X}\|_F^2, \tag{11.119}$$

$$\theta^{k+1} \leftarrow \underset{\theta}{\mathrm{argmin}} \|\widetilde{\mathcal{X}}^k - \mathcal{X}_\theta\|_F^2. \tag{11.120}$$

To obtain a solution of (11.119), we introduce the following projection operators:

$$\mathcal{P}_{\mathrm{A}} := \mathcal{A}^*(\mathcal{A}\mathcal{A}^*)^{-1}\mathcal{A}, \tag{11.121}$$

$$\mathcal{P}_{\bar{\mathrm{A}}} := \mathcal{I} - \mathcal{P}_{\mathrm{A}}. \tag{11.122}$$

Note that the projection operators satisfy

$$\mathcal{P}_{\mathrm{A}}\mathcal{P}_{\mathrm{A}} = \mathcal{A}^*(\mathcal{A}\mathcal{A}^*)^{-1}\mathcal{A}\mathcal{A}^*(\mathcal{A}\mathcal{A}^*)^{-1}\mathcal{A} = \mathcal{P}_{\mathrm{A}}, \tag{11.123}$$

$$\mathcal{A}\mathcal{P}_{\bar{\mathrm{A}}} = \mathcal{A}(\mathcal{I} - \mathcal{P}_{\mathrm{A}}) = \mathcal{A} - \mathcal{A}\mathcal{A}^*(\mathcal{A}\mathcal{A}^*)^{-1}\mathcal{A} = \mathbf{0}, \tag{11.124}$$

$$\mathcal{P}_{\mathrm{A}}\mathcal{P}_{\bar{\mathrm{A}}} = \mathcal{P}_{\mathrm{A}}(\mathcal{I} - \mathcal{P}_{\mathrm{A}}) = \mathcal{P}_{\mathrm{A}} - \mathcal{P}_{\mathrm{A}}\mathcal{P}_{\mathrm{A}} = \mathbf{0}. \tag{11.125}$$

For any $\mathcal{Y} \in \mathbb{R}^{I_1 \times \cdots \times I_N}$,

$$\mathcal{X} = \mathcal{A}^*(\mathcal{A}\mathcal{A}^*)^{-1}\mathbf{b} + \mathcal{P}_{\bar{\mathrm{A}}}(\mathcal{Y}) \tag{11.126}$$

satisfies $\mathbf{b} = \mathcal{A}(\mathcal{X})$. Let us put $\mathcal{T} = \mathcal{A}^*(\mathcal{A}\mathcal{A}^*)^{-1}\mathbf{b}$. We have

$$\mathcal{P}_{\mathrm{A}}(\mathcal{T}) = \mathcal{A}^*(\mathcal{A}\mathcal{A}^*)^{-1}\mathcal{A}\mathcal{A}^*(\mathcal{A}\mathcal{A}^*)^{-1}\mathbf{b} = \mathcal{T}. \tag{11.127}$$

Let $\mathcal{Y}$ be the optimization parameter. The problem (11.119) can be converted as

$$\underset{\mathcal{Y}}{\text{minimize}} \, ||\mathcal{X}_{\theta^k} - (\mathcal{P}_{\mathrm{A}}(\mathcal{T}) + \mathcal{P}_{\bar{\mathrm{A}}}(\mathcal{Y}))||_F^2. \tag{11.128}$$

Note that $\mathcal{X}_{\theta^k} = \mathcal{P}_{\mathrm{A}}(\mathcal{X}_{\theta^k}) + \mathcal{P}_{\bar{\mathrm{A}}}(\mathcal{X}_{\theta^k})$, and the cost function can be simplified as

$$\begin{aligned}
||\mathcal{P}_{\mathrm{A}}(\mathcal{X}_{\theta^k}) &+ \mathcal{P}_{\bar{\mathrm{A}}}(\mathcal{X}_{\theta^k}) - (\mathcal{P}_{\mathrm{A}}(\mathcal{T}) + \mathcal{P}_{\bar{\mathrm{A}}}(\mathcal{Y}))||_F^2 \\
&= ||\mathcal{P}_{\mathrm{A}}(\mathcal{X}_{\theta^k} - \mathcal{T}) + \mathcal{P}_{\bar{\mathrm{A}}}(\mathcal{X}_{\theta^k} - \mathcal{Y})||_F^2 \\
&= ||\mathcal{P}_{\mathrm{A}}(\mathcal{X}_{\theta^k} - \mathcal{T})||_F^2 + ||\mathcal{P}_{\bar{\mathrm{A}}}(\mathcal{X}_{\theta^k} - \mathcal{Y})||_F^2,
\end{aligned} \tag{11.129}$$

where we used $\mathcal{P}_{\mathrm{A}}\mathcal{P}_{\bar{\mathrm{A}}} = \mathbf{0}$. Since $\mathcal{Y} = \mathcal{X}_{\theta^k}$ can be a solution, (11.119) can be analytically obtained as

$$\tilde{\mathcal{X}}^k \leftarrow \mathcal{P}_{\mathrm{A}}(\mathcal{T}) + \mathcal{P}_{\bar{\mathrm{A}}}(\mathcal{X}_{\theta^k}). \tag{11.130}$$

Note that there is analogy to a case of $\mathcal{P}_\Omega$ in (11.110).

Due to the analogy between $\mathcal{P}_{\mathrm{A}}$ and $\mathcal{P}_\Omega$, we can consider the following objective and auxiliary functions:

$$f(\boldsymbol{\theta}) := ||\mathcal{P}_{\mathrm{A}}(\mathcal{T} - \mathcal{X}_{\boldsymbol{\theta}})||_F^2, \tag{11.131}$$

$$h(\boldsymbol{\theta}|\boldsymbol{\theta}') := ||\mathcal{P}_{\mathrm{A}}(\mathcal{T} - \mathcal{X}_{\boldsymbol{\theta}})||_F^2 + ||\mathcal{P}_{\bar{\mathrm{A}}}(\mathcal{X}_{\boldsymbol{\theta}'} - \mathcal{X}_{\boldsymbol{\theta}})||_F^2. \tag{11.132}$$

Note that the MM algorithm with the above functions guarantees the monotonically nonincreasing property of the function $f(\boldsymbol{\theta})$, but it is slightly different from the original objective function $f_0(\boldsymbol{\theta})$ in (11.116). Note that we have

$$f(\boldsymbol{\theta}) = ||\mathcal{P}_{\mathrm{A}}(\mathcal{T} - \mathcal{X}_{\boldsymbol{\theta}})||_F^2 = ||\mathcal{A}^\dagger(\mathbf{b} - \mathcal{A}(\mathcal{X}_{\boldsymbol{\theta}}))||_F^2, \tag{11.133}$$

where $\mathcal{A}^\dagger = \mathcal{A}^*(\mathcal{A}\mathcal{A}^*)^{-1}$ is a Moore–Penrose pseudo-inverse of $\mathcal{A}$. We can see that both objective functions $f_0(\boldsymbol{\theta})$ and $f(\boldsymbol{\theta})$ are the same in the sense that the values of the objective functions change depending only on the difference between $\mathbf{b}$ and $\mathcal{A}(\mathcal{X}_{\boldsymbol{\theta}})$. However, optimal solutions are generally different because metric spaces are different. When we assume $\mathbf{n} \approx \mathbf{0}$ and some good estimator $\widehat{\boldsymbol{\theta}}$ with $||\mathbf{b} - \mathcal{A}(\mathcal{X}_{\widehat{\boldsymbol{\theta}}})||_2^2 \approx 0$ can be found, the above MM algorithm may work. In addition, it is preferable that the positive singular values of $\mathcal{A}$ are uniform like the inpainting task.

Finally, we summarize the MM algorithm for general tensor reconstruction in Algorithm 8. Step 5 in Algorithm 8 is not necessary to achieve a strict minimization of the auxiliary function, and it still has the monotonic nonincreasing property.

Algorithm 8 MM algorithm for general tensor reconstruction.

1: **input:** $\mathbf{b} \in \mathbb{R}^M$, $\mathcal{A}$, and the tensor decomposition model $\mathcal{X}_\theta$
2: **initialize:** $\mathcal{T} = \mathcal{A}^\dagger \mathbf{b}$, θ
3: **repeat**
4:    $\mathcal{Z} \leftarrow \mathcal{P}_A(\mathcal{T}) + \mathcal{P}_{\tilde{A}}(\mathcal{X}_\theta)$;
5:    $\theta \leftarrow \arg\min_\theta ||\mathcal{Z} - \mathcal{X}_\theta||_F^2 + p(\theta)$;
6: **until** convergence
7: **output:** θ

11.2.2.3 Low-rank CP decomposition for tensor completion

In this section, we consider CP decomposition in the tensor completion problem as follows:

$$\min_{\mathbf{U}^{(1)},...,\mathbf{U}^{(N)}} ||\mathcal{P}_\Omega(\mathcal{T} - \mathcal{X})||_F^2,$$
$$\text{subject to} \quad \mathcal{X} = \mathcal{I}_{SP} \times_1 \mathbf{U}^{(1)} \cdots \times_N \mathbf{U}^{(N)}, \quad (11.134)$$

where $\mathcal{X} \in \mathbb{R}^{I_1 \times I_2 \times \cdots \times I_N}$ is a tensor reconstructed by CP decomposition, $\mathcal{I}_{SP} \in \mathbb{R}^{R \times R \times \cdots \times R}$ is a superdiagonal core tensor whose superdiagonal entries are 1, and its factor matrices are $\mathbf{U}^{(n)} \in \mathbb{R}^{I_n \times R}$.

Following the MM algorithm, we only consider to solve the standard CP decomposition of an arbitrary tensor $\mathcal{Z} \in \mathbb{R}^{I_1 \times I_2 \times \cdots \times I_N}$ as follows:

$$\min_{\mathbf{U}^{(1)},...,\mathbf{U}^{(N)}} ||\mathcal{Z} - \mathcal{I}_{SP} \times_1 \mathbf{U}^{(1)} \cdots \times_N \mathbf{U}^{(N)}||_F^2. \quad (11.135)$$

Following the ALS algorithm, we consider to solve the following suboptimization problem for each $\mathbf{U}^{(n)}$:

$$\min_{\mathbf{U}^{(n)}} ||\mathbf{Z}_{(n)} - \mathbf{U}^{(n)}\mathbf{V}_n^T||_F^2, \quad (11.136)$$

where $\mathbf{V}_n = \mathbf{U}^{(N)} \odot \cdots \odot \mathbf{U}^{(n+1)} \odot \mathbf{U}^{(n-1)} \odot \cdots \odot \mathbf{U}^{(1)} \in \mathbb{R}^{\prod_{k \neq n} I_k \times R}$. The n-th factor matrix can be updated by

$$\mathbf{U}^{(n)} \leftarrow \mathbf{Z}_{(n)}\mathbf{V}_n(\mathbf{V}_n^T\mathbf{V}_n)^{-1}. \quad (11.137)$$

Note that $\mathbf{V}_n^T\mathbf{V}_n = \mathbf{U}^{(N)T}\mathbf{U}^{(N)} * \cdots * \mathbf{U}^{(n+1)T}\mathbf{U}^{(n+1)} * \mathbf{U}^{(n-1)T}\mathbf{U}^{(n-1)} * \cdots * \mathbf{U}^{(1)T}\mathbf{U}^{(1)}$.

Finally, CP-based tensor completion can be summarized in Algorithm 9. Algorithm 9 updates $\mathbf{U}^{(n)}$ for only one cycle of the ALS, and it does not achieve a strict minimization of the auxiliary function. However, it is guaranteed to decrease the auxiliary function because each update obtains the global minimum of the suboptimization problem of (11.136) with respect to the corresponding parameter. Thus, Algorithm 9 still has the monotonically nonincreasing property.

Algorithm 9 CP decomposition for tensor completion.

1: **input:** $\mathcal{T} \in \mathbb{R}^{I_1 \times \cdots \times I_N}$, Ω, and R.
2: **initialize:** $\{\mathbf{U}^{(n)} \in \mathbb{R}^{I_n \times R}\}_{n=1}^{N}$
3: **repeat**
4:     $\mathcal{X} \leftarrow \mathcal{I} \times_1 \mathbf{U}^{(1)} \cdots \times_N \mathbf{U}^{(N)}$;
5:     $\mathcal{Z} \leftarrow \mathcal{P}_\Omega(\mathcal{T}) + \mathcal{P}_{\bar{\Omega}}(\mathcal{X})$;
6:     **for** $n = 1, ..., N$ **do**
7:         $\mathbf{V}_n \leftarrow \mathbf{U}^{(N)} \odot \cdots \odot \mathbf{U}^{(n+1)} \odot \mathbf{U}^{(n-1)} \odot \cdots \odot \mathbf{U}^{(1)}$;
8:         $\mathbf{U}^{(n)} \leftarrow \mathbf{Z}_{(n)} \mathbf{V}_n (\mathbf{V}_n^{\mathrm{T}} \mathbf{V}_n)^{-1}$;
9:     **end for**
10: **until** convergence
11: **output:** $\mathbf{U}^{(1)}, ..., \mathbf{U}^{(N)}$;

11.2.2.4 Low-rank Tucker decomposition for tensor completion

In this section, we consider Tucker decomposition in the tensor completion problem as follows:

$$\begin{aligned}
&\underset{\mathcal{G}, \mathbf{U}^{(1)}, ..., \mathbf{U}^{(N)}}{\text{minimize}} \quad ||\mathcal{P}_\Omega(\mathcal{T} - \mathcal{X})||_F^2 \\
&\text{subject to} \quad \mathcal{X} = \mathcal{G} \times_1 \mathbf{U}^{(1)} \cdots \times_N \mathbf{U}^{(N)}, \\
&\qquad\qquad \mathbf{U}^{(n)\mathrm{T}} \mathbf{U}^{(n)} = \mathbf{I}_{R_n} (\text{ for all } n),
\end{aligned} \tag{11.138}$$

where $\mathcal{X} \in \mathbb{R}^{I_1 \times I_2 \times \cdots \times I_N}$ is a tensor reconstructed by Tucker decomposition, $\mathcal{G} \in \mathbb{R}^{R_1 \times R_2 \times \cdots \times R_N}$ is a core tensor, and its factor matrices are $\mathbf{U}^{(n)} \in \mathbb{R}^{I_n \times R_n}$.

Following the MM algorithm, we only solve the standard Tucker decomposition of an arbitrary tensor $\mathcal{Z} \in \mathbb{R}^{I_1 \times I_2 \times \cdots \times I_N}$ as follows:

$$\underset{\mathcal{G}, \mathbf{U}^{(1)}, ..., \mathbf{U}^{(N)}}{\text{minimize}} \quad ||\mathcal{Z} - \mathcal{G} \times_1 \mathbf{U}^{(1)} \cdots \times_N \mathbf{U}^{(N)}||_F^2 + \sum_{n=1}^{N} i_{\text{orth}}(\mathbf{U}^{(n)}). \tag{11.139}$$

Because of the orthogonal constraints for factor matrices, analytical solution of a core tensor can be obtained as $\mathcal{G} = \mathcal{Z} \times_1 \mathbf{U}^{(1)\mathrm{T}} \cdots \times_N \mathbf{U}^{(N)\mathrm{T}}$. Then, the objective function can be simplified as

$$\underset{\mathbf{U}^{(1)}, ..., \mathbf{U}^{(N)}}{\text{minimize}} \quad -||\mathcal{Z} \times_1 \mathbf{U}^{(1)\mathrm{T}} \cdots \times_N \mathbf{U}^{(N)\mathrm{T}}||_F^2 + \sum_{n=1}^{N} i_{\text{orth}}(\mathbf{U}^{(n)}). \tag{11.140}$$

Note that a parameter $\mathcal{G}$ is eliminated in this optimization problem. Following the ALS algorithm, we solve the following suboptimization problem for each $\mathbf{U}^{(n)}$:

$$\underset{\mathbf{U}^{(n)}}{\text{maximize}} \quad ||\mathbf{U}^{(n)\mathrm{T}} \mathbf{Y}_n||_F^2 \quad \text{subject to} \quad \mathbf{U}^{(n)\mathrm{T}} \mathbf{U}^{(n)} = \mathbf{I}_{R_n}, \tag{11.141}$$

Algorithm 10 Tucker decomposition for tensor completion.

1: **input:** $\mathcal{T} \in \mathbb{R}^{I_1 \times \cdots \times I_N}$, Ω, and $(R_1, ..., R_N)$.
2: **initialize:** $\mathcal{G} \in \mathbb{R}^{R_1 \times \cdots \times R_N}$, and $\{\mathbf{U}^{(n)} \in \mathbb{R}^{I_n \times R_n}\}_{n=1}^{N}$
3: **repeat**
4:      $\mathcal{X} \leftarrow \mathcal{G} \times_1 \mathbf{U}^{(1)} \cdots \times_N \mathbf{U}^{(N)}$;
5:      $\mathcal{Z} \leftarrow \mathcal{P}_\Omega(\mathcal{T}) + \mathcal{P}_{\bar{\Omega}}(\mathcal{X})$;
6:      **for** $n = 1, ..., N$ **do**
7:          $\mathbf{Y}_n \leftarrow \mathbf{Z}_{(n)}(\mathbf{U}^{(N)} \otimes \cdots \otimes \mathbf{U}^{(n+1)} \otimes \mathbf{U}^{(n-1)} \otimes \cdots \otimes \mathbf{U}^{(1)})$;
8:          $\mathbf{U}^{(n)} \leftarrow R_n$ leading singular vectors of $\mathbf{Y}_n$;
9:      **end for**
10:     $\mathcal{G} \leftarrow \mathcal{Z} \times_1 \mathbf{U}^{(1)\mathrm{T}} \cdots \times_N \mathbf{U}^{(N)\mathrm{T}}$;
11: **until** convergence
12: **output:** $\mathcal{G}, \mathbf{U}^{(1)}, ..., \mathbf{U}^{(N)}$;

---

where $\mathbf{Y}_n = \mathbf{Z}_{(n)}(\mathbf{U}^{(N)} \otimes \cdots \otimes \mathbf{U}^{(n+1)} \otimes \mathbf{U}^{(n-1)} \otimes \cdots \otimes \mathbf{U}^{(1)}) \in \mathbb{R}^{I_n \times \prod_{k \neq n} R_k}$. The solution of this suboptimization problem can be given as the R_n leading singular vectors of $\mathbf{Y}_n$.

Finally, Tucker-based tensor completion can be summarized in Algorithm 10. Algorithm 10 updates $\mathbf{U}^{(n)}$ and $\mathcal{G}$ for only one cycle of the ALS, and it does not achieve a strict minimization of the auxiliary function. However, it is guaranteed to decrease the auxiliary function because each update obtains the global minimum of the suboptimization problem of (11.141) with respect to the corresponding parameter. Thus, Algorithm 10 still has the monotonically nonincreasing property.

11.2.2.5 Parallel matrix factorization for tensor completion

Here, we introduce a low-rank tensor completion algorithm named tensor completion by parallel matrix factorization (TMac) [81], and we show that TMac can be interpreted as an MM algorithm. TMac aims to solve the following optimization problem:

$$\underset{\mathcal{Z}, \{\mathbf{A}_n, \mathbf{B}_n\}_{n=1}^{N}}{\text{minimize}} \sum_{n=1}^{N} \alpha_n ||\mathbf{Z}_{(n)} - \mathbf{A}_n \mathbf{B}_n||_F^2 \quad \text{subject to } \mathcal{P}_\Omega(\mathcal{Z}) = \mathcal{P}_\Omega(\mathcal{T}), \quad (11.142)$$

where $\alpha_n \geq 0$, $\sum_{n=1}^{N} \alpha_n = 1$, $\mathbf{A}_n \in \mathbb{R}^{I_n \times R_n}$, and $\mathbf{B}_n \in \mathbb{R}^{R_n \times \prod_{k \neq n} I_k}$. Putting $\boldsymbol{\theta}_\mathbf{A} = \{\mathbf{A}_1, ..., \mathbf{A}_N\}$ and $\boldsymbol{\theta}_\mathbf{B} = \{\mathbf{B}_1, ..., \mathbf{B}_N\}$, we define the cost function as follows:

$$f(\mathcal{Z}, \boldsymbol{\theta}_\mathbf{A}, \boldsymbol{\theta}_\mathbf{B}) := \sum_{n=1}^{N} \alpha_n ||\mathbf{Z}_{(n)} - \mathbf{A}_n \mathbf{B}_n||_F^2. \quad (11.143)$$

Then, the following alternating optimization is proposed:

$$\boldsymbol{\theta}_\mathbf{A} \leftarrow \underset{\boldsymbol{\theta}_\mathbf{A}}{\operatorname{argmin}} f(\mathcal{Z}, \boldsymbol{\theta}_\mathbf{A}, \boldsymbol{\theta}_\mathbf{B}), \quad (11.144)$$

$$\boldsymbol{\theta}_B \leftarrow \operatorname*{argmin}_{\boldsymbol{\theta}_B} f(\mathcal{Z}, \boldsymbol{\theta}_A, \boldsymbol{\theta}_B), \tag{11.145}$$

$$\mathcal{Z} \leftarrow \operatorname*{argmin}_{\mathcal{Z}} f(\mathcal{Z}, \boldsymbol{\theta}_A, \boldsymbol{\theta}_B) + i_{\mathcal{T}_\Omega}(\mathcal{Z}). \tag{11.146}$$

Note that the updates of $\mathbf{A}_n$ or $\mathbf{B}_n$ for all n are independent of each other, and parallel processing is possible.

For updating each $\mathbf{A}_n$ or $\mathbf{B}_n$, we consider to minimize $||\mathbf{Z}_{(n)} - \mathbf{A}_n\mathbf{B}_n||_F^2$ with respect to $\mathbf{A}_n$ or $\mathbf{B}_n$. Thus, the update rule can be given by a simple least-squares solution as

$$\mathbf{A}_n \leftarrow \mathbf{Z}_{(n)}\mathbf{B}_n^{\mathsf{T}}(\mathbf{B}_n\mathbf{B}_n^{\mathsf{T}})^{-1}, \tag{11.147}$$

$$\mathbf{B}_n \leftarrow (\mathbf{A}_n^{\mathsf{T}}\mathbf{A}_n)^{-1}\mathbf{A}_n^{\mathsf{T}}\mathbf{Z}_{(n)}. \tag{11.148}$$

For updating $\mathcal{Z}$, we solve the following optimization problem:

$$\underset{\mathcal{Z}}{\text{minimize}} \ \sum_{n=1}^{N} \alpha_n ||\mathbf{Z}_{(n)} - \mathbf{A}_n\mathbf{B}_n||_F^2 \quad \text{subject to } \mathcal{P}_\Omega(\mathcal{Z}) = \mathcal{P}_\Omega(\mathcal{T}). \tag{11.149}$$

For simplicity, we put $\mathcal{X}_n := \text{fold}(\mathbf{A}_n\mathbf{B}_n) \in \mathbb{R}^{I_1 \times I_2 \times \cdots \times I_N}$ and $\mathcal{X} := \sum_{n=1}^{N} \alpha_n \mathcal{X}_n$. Then the objective function can be summarized as follows:

$$
\begin{aligned}
f(\mathcal{Z}, \boldsymbol{\theta}_A, \boldsymbol{\theta}_B) &= \sum_{n=1}^{N} \alpha_n ||\mathcal{Z} - \mathcal{X}_n||_F^2 \\
&= \sum_{n=1}^{N} \{\alpha_n \langle \mathcal{Z}, \mathcal{Z} \rangle - 2\alpha_n \langle \mathcal{Z}, \mathcal{X}_n \rangle + \alpha_n \langle \mathcal{X}_n, \mathcal{X}_n \rangle\} \\
&= \langle \mathcal{Z}, \mathcal{Z} \rangle - 2\langle \mathcal{Z}, \mathcal{X} \rangle + \sum_{n=1}^{N} \alpha_n \langle \mathcal{X}_n, \mathcal{X}_n \rangle + \langle \mathcal{X}, \mathcal{X} \rangle - \langle \mathcal{X}, \mathcal{X} \rangle \\
&= \langle \mathcal{Z}, \mathcal{Z} \rangle - 2\langle \mathcal{Z}, \mathcal{X} \rangle + \langle \mathcal{X}, \mathcal{X} \rangle + \sum_{n=1}^{N} \alpha_n \langle \mathcal{X}_n, \mathcal{X}_n \rangle - \langle \mathcal{X}, \mathcal{X} \rangle \\
&= ||\mathcal{X} - \mathcal{Z}||_F^2 + \sum_{n=1}^{N} \alpha_n ||\mathcal{X}_n - \mathcal{X}||_F^2. \tag{11.150}
\end{aligned}
$$

For the above formulation, we used

$$
\begin{aligned}
\sum_{n=1}^{N} \alpha_n ||\mathcal{X}_n - \mathcal{X}||_F^2 &= \sum_{n=1}^{N} \{\alpha_n \langle \mathcal{X}_n, \mathcal{X}_n \rangle - 2\alpha_n \langle \mathcal{X}_n, \mathcal{X} \rangle + \alpha_n \langle \mathcal{X}, \mathcal{X} \rangle\} \\
&= \sum_{n=1}^{N} \alpha_n \langle \mathcal{X}_n, \mathcal{X}_n \rangle - 2\langle \mathcal{X}, \mathcal{X} \rangle + \langle \mathcal{X}, \mathcal{X} \rangle
\end{aligned}
$$

Algorithm 11 TMac: Parallel matrix factorization for tensor completion.

1: **input:** $\mathcal{T} \in \mathbb{R}^{I_1 \times \cdots \times I_N}$, Ω, and $(R_1, ..., R_N)$.
2: **initialize:** $\{\mathbf{A}_n \in \mathbb{R}^{I_n \times R_n}, \mathbf{B}_n \in \mathbb{R}^{R_n \times \prod_{k \neq n} I_k}\}_{n=1}^N$
3: **repeat**
4:      $\mathcal{X} \leftarrow \sum_{n=1}^N \alpha_n \text{fold}(\mathbf{A}_n \mathbf{B}_n)$;
5:      $\mathcal{Z} \leftarrow \mathcal{P}_\Omega(\mathcal{T}) + \mathcal{P}_{\bar{\Omega}}(\mathcal{X})$;
6:      $\mathbf{A}_n \leftarrow \mathbf{Z}_{(n)} \mathbf{B}_n^{\mathsf{T}} (\mathbf{B}_n \mathbf{B}_n^{\mathsf{T}})^{-1}$ for all n;
7:      $\mathbf{B}_n \leftarrow (\mathbf{A}_n^{\mathsf{T}} \mathbf{A}_n)^{-1} \mathbf{A}_n^{\mathsf{T}} \mathbf{Z}_{(n)}$ for all n;
8: **until** convergence
9: **output:** $\mathbf{A}_n$ and $\mathbf{B}_n$ for all n;

$$= \sum_{n=1}^N \alpha_n \langle \mathcal{X}_n, \mathcal{X}_n \rangle - \langle \mathcal{X}, \mathcal{X} \rangle. \tag{11.151}$$

Note that the second term in (11.150) does not depend on $\mathcal{Z}$, and the update of $\mathcal{Z}$ can be obtained by a projection onto a convex set as

$$\mathcal{Z} \leftarrow \mathcal{P}_\Omega(\mathcal{T}) + \mathcal{P}_{\bar{\Omega}}(\mathcal{X}). \tag{11.152}$$

Finally, the TMac algorithm is summarized in Algorithm 11. From the formulation of the objective function (11.150), TMac can be interpreted as a tensor reconstruction model with parallel matrix factorization $\mathcal{X}_\theta = \sum_{n=1}^N \alpha_n \text{fold}(\mathbf{A}_n \mathbf{B}_n)$ with penalty $p(\boldsymbol{\theta}) = \sum_{n=1}^N \alpha_n \|\mathcal{X}_n - \mathcal{X}\|_F^2$. In other words, the perspective of the MM algorithm supports the monotonically nonincreasing property of TMac.

11.2.2.6 Tucker decomposition with rank increment

A difficult and important issue with the simultaneous tensor decomposition and completion method is determining an appropriate rank setting such as $(R_1, ..., R_N)$ for Tucker rank. This section introduces a typical greedy algorithm for rank determination in the tensor decomposition and completion. This algorithm has been employed for matrix recovery [59,74,77,83], TMac [81], CP decomposition [84,93], Tucker decomposition [85,88], and TT decomposition [69]. Here, Tucker decomposition is considered as an example.

If we aim to obtain the lowest rank setting for sufficient approximation, the rank estimation problem can be considered as

$$\underset{(R_1, ..., R_N)}{\text{minimize}} \sum_{n=1}^N R_n$$
$$\text{s.t. } \|\mathcal{P}_\Omega(\mathcal{T} - \mathcal{X}_\theta)\|_F^2 \leq \delta, \tag{11.153}$$

where δ is a noise threshold parameter. However, we do not know the existence of the unique solution $(R_1^*, ..., R_N^*)$ for problem (11.153) and it will be dependent on δ.

Furthermore, even if the best rank setting is unique, the resultant low-rank tensor $\mathcal{X}_{\theta^*}$ is not unique.

To address this issue, we introduce an important strategy called the "rank increment" method. The main reason for using the rank increment method is the nonuniqueness of the solution for the tensor $\mathcal{X}$. Thus, the resultant tensor depends on its initialization. The main feature of the rank increment method is that the tensor should be initialized by a lower rank approximation than its target rank. Based on this strategy, the proposed algorithm can be described as follows.

- Step 1: Set initial $R_n = 1$ for all n.
- Step 2: Obtain $\mathcal{G}$ and $\{\mathbf{U}^{(n)}\}_{n=1}^N$ with $(R_1, ..., R_N)$ using Algorithm 10 and obtain $\mathcal{X} = \mathcal{G} \times_1 \mathbf{U}^{(1)} \cdots \times_N \mathbf{U}^{(N)}$.
- Step 3: Check the noise condition $||\mathcal{P}_\Omega(\mathcal{T} - \mathcal{X})||_F^2 \le \delta$, where the algorithm is terminated if it is satisfied; otherwise, go to the next step.
- Step 4: Choose the incremental mode n' and increment $R_{n'}$, and then go back to step 2.

The problems are how to choose n' and how to increase the rank $R_{n'}$. We consider choosing n' using the "n-th mode residual" of the cost function, which is defined as a residual on the multilinear subspace spanned by all the factor matrices excluding the n-th mode factor [69,85]. This is mathematically formulated as

$$n' = \underset{n}{\operatorname{argmax}} ||\mathcal{E}_n||_F^2, \tag{11.154}$$

where $\mathcal{E}_n = (\mathcal{P}_\Omega(\mathcal{T} - \mathcal{X})) \times_1 \mathbf{U}^{(1)\mathrm{T}} \cdots \times_{n-1} \mathbf{U}^{(n-1)\mathrm{T}} \times_{n+1} \mathbf{U}^{(n+1)\mathrm{T}} \cdots \times_N \mathbf{U}^{(N)\mathrm{T}}$. We can interpret this as that the selected n'-th mode has a high expectation of cost reduction when $R_{n'}$ increases while the other mode ranks remain fixed.

The proposed method for Tucker-based tensor completion with rank increment is summarized in Algorithm 12.

11.2.2.7 Smooth CP decomposition for tensor completion

Here, we briefly introduce a method of tensor completion using both low CP rank and smoothness priors. It is named the smooth PARAFAC decomposition for tensor completion (SPC) [93]. The SPC is a CP-based tensor reconstruction model with smoothness penalty applied to factor vectors. In addition, the algorithm of SPC is based on the MM algorithm with rank increment.

At first, the optimization problem of fixed-rank SPC (FR-SPC) is given by

$$\underset{\mathbf{g}, \mathbf{U}^{(1)}, ..., \mathbf{U}^{(N)}}{\operatorname{minimize}} \frac{1}{2}||\mathcal{P}_\Omega(\mathcal{T} - \mathcal{X})||_F^2 + \sum_{r=1}^R \frac{g_r^2}{2} \sum_{n=1}^N \rho^{(n)} ||\mathbf{L}^{(n)} \mathbf{u}_r^{(n)}||_2^2 \tag{11.155}$$

$$\text{s.t. } \mathcal{X} = \sum_{r=1}^R g_r \mathbf{u}_r^{(1)} \circ \mathbf{u}_r^{(2)} \circ \cdots \circ \mathbf{u}_r^{(N)}, ||\mathbf{u}_r^{(n)}||_2 = 1,$$

Algorithm 12 Tucker-based tensor completion with rank increment.

1: **input:** $\mathcal{T} \in \mathbb{R}^{I_1 \times \cdots \times I_N}$, Ω, δ, tol
2: **initialize:** R_n (e.g., $R_1 = \ldots = R_N = 1$), $\mathcal{G} \in \mathbb{R}^{R_1 \times \cdots \times R_N}$, and $\{\mathbf{U}^{(n)} \in \mathbb{R}^{I_n \times R_n}\}_{n=1}^N$;
3: $\quad \mathcal{X} \leftarrow \mathcal{G} \times_1 \mathbf{U}^{(1)} \cdots \times_N \mathbf{U}^{(N)}$;
4: $\quad f_1 \leftarrow \|\mathcal{P}_\Omega(\mathcal{T} - \mathcal{X})\|_F^2$;
5: **repeat**
6: $\quad\quad \mathcal{Z} \leftarrow \mathcal{P}_\Omega(\mathcal{T}) + \mathcal{P}_{\bar{\Omega}}(\mathcal{X})$;
7: $\quad\quad$ **for** $n = 1, \ldots, N$ **do**
8: $\quad\quad\quad \mathbf{Y}_n \leftarrow \mathbf{Z}_{(n)}(\mathbf{U}^{(N)} \otimes \cdots \otimes \mathbf{U}^{(n+1)} \otimes \mathbf{U}^{(n-1)} \otimes \cdots \otimes \mathbf{U}^{(1)})$;
9: $\quad\quad\quad \mathbf{U}^{(n)} \leftarrow R_n$ leading singular vectors of $\mathbf{Y}_n$;
10: $\quad\quad$ **end for**
11: $\quad\quad \mathcal{G} \leftarrow \mathcal{Z} \times_1 \mathbf{U}^{(1)\mathrm{T}} \cdots \times_N \mathbf{U}^{(N)\mathrm{T}}$;
12: $\quad\quad \mathcal{X} \leftarrow \mathcal{G} \times_1 \mathbf{U}^{(1)} \cdots \times_N \mathbf{U}^{(N)}$;
13: $\quad\quad f_2 \leftarrow \|\mathcal{P}_\Omega(\mathcal{T} - \mathcal{X})\|_F^2$;
14: $\quad\quad$ **if** $|f_2 - f_1| \leq$ tol **then**
15: $\quad\quad\quad \hat{\mathcal{X}} \leftarrow \mathcal{P}_\Omega(\mathcal{T} - \mathcal{X})$;
16: $\quad\quad\quad$ **for** $n = 1, \ldots, N$ **do**
17: $\quad\quad\quad\quad \mathcal{E}_n \leftarrow \hat{\mathcal{X}} \times_1 \mathbf{U}^{(1)\mathrm{T}} \cdots \times_{n-1} \mathbf{U}^{(n-1)\mathrm{T}} \times_{n+1} \mathbf{U}^{(n+1)\mathrm{T}} \cdots \times_N \mathbf{U}^{(N)\mathrm{T}}$;
18: $\quad\quad\quad$ **end for**
19: $\quad\quad\quad n' \leftarrow \mathrm{argmax}_n \|\mathcal{E}_n\|_F^2$;
20: $\quad\quad\quad$ Update $R_{n'}$ to be increased; (e.g., $R_{n'} \leftarrow R_{n'} + 1$)
21: $\quad\quad$ **else**
22: $\quad\quad\quad f_1 \leftarrow f_2$;
23: $\quad\quad$ **end if**
24: **until** $f_2 \leq \delta$
25: **output:** $\mathcal{G}, \mathbf{U}^{(1)}, \ldots, \mathbf{U}^{(N)}$;

---

where $\mathbf{g} = [g_1, \ldots, g_R]^\mathrm{T} \in \mathbb{R}^R$ represents superdiagonal entries of the core tensor, $\mathbf{U}^{(n)} = [\mathbf{u}_1^{(n)}, \ldots, \mathbf{u}_R^{(n)}] \in \mathbb{R}^{I_n \times R}$ are factor matrices, $\mathbf{L}^{(n)} \in \mathbb{R}^{(I_n-1) \times I_n}$ is a linear differential operator defined as

$$\mathbf{L}^{(n)} := \begin{pmatrix} 1 & -1 & & & \\ & 1 & -1 & & \\ & & \ddots & \ddots & \\ & & & 1 & -1 \end{pmatrix}, \tag{11.156}$$

and $\rho^{(n)} \geq 0$ are hyperparameters to adjust the weight of penalty for smoothness. The first term evaluates the consistency between the observed data and the reconstructed tensor by smooth CP decomposition, and the second term constrains each column vector of the factor matrices by a quadratic variation penalty[3]; $\rho^{(n)}$ is for adjusting the smoothness of each mode. For example, since the color axis of an RGB image does not need to be smooth, we reduce the corresponding value of $\rho^{(n)}$.

Note that the length of each factor vector is normalized to 1 and the adaptive factors g_r^2 depend on penalty levels of the smoothness constraint terms in (11.155). This allows us to adaptively enforce the different levels of smoothness for different components. For image completion, the proposed method decomposes an image adaptively into a strong smooth background and a weaker smooth foreground. In other words, considering the Fourier domain of image data, low-frequency components are generally stronger than high-frequency components. Therefore, we propose to use different penalty levels of individual rank-1 components depending on their scales g_r.

We solve the optimization problem (11.155) using the hierarchical ALS (HALS) approach [18,19]. The HALS algorithm, included in a block coordinate descent scheme, considers rank-1 component-wise updates which allows us to treat each unit-norm constraint separately. According to the HALS approach, we consider the minimization of the following local cost functions for each r-th rank-1 component:

$$\underset{\boldsymbol{\theta}_r = \{g_r, \mathbf{u}_r^{(1)}, ..., \mathbf{u}_r^{(N)}\}}{\text{minimize}} \quad \frac{1}{2}||\mathcal{P}_\Omega(\mathcal{Y}_r - \mathcal{X}_r)||_F^2 + \frac{g_r^2}{2} \sum_{n=1}^N \rho^{(n)} ||\mathbf{L}^{(n)} \mathbf{u}_r^{(n)}||_2^2$$

$$\text{subject to} \quad \mathcal{X}_r = g_r \mathbf{u}_r^{(1)} \circ \mathbf{u}_r^{(2)} \circ \cdots \circ \mathbf{u}_r^{(N)} \tag{11.157}$$

$$||\mathbf{u}_r^{(n)}||_2 = 1, \forall n \in \{1, ..., N\},$$

where $\mathcal{Y}_r = \mathcal{T} - \sum_{k \neq r} g_k \mathbf{u}_k^{(1)} \circ \mathbf{u}_k^{(2)} \circ \cdots \circ \mathbf{u}_k^{(N)}$. The local problem (11.157) only involves the r-th rank-1 component of CP decomposition. Note that $\mathcal{X} = \sum_{r=1}^R \mathcal{X}_r$, and it is analogous to an interpretation of parallel matrix factorization in the sense that a tensor is reconstructed by the sum of low-rank tensors.

With a tensor $\mathcal{Z}_r$, we define the following auxiliary function:

$$f_r(\boldsymbol{\theta}_r | \mathcal{Z}_r) := \frac{1}{2}||\mathcal{Z}_r - \mathcal{X}_r||_F^2 + \frac{g_r^2}{2} \sum_{n=1}^N \rho^{(n)} ||\mathbf{L}^{(n)} \mathbf{u}_r^{(n)}||_2^2 + i_{\mathbb{U}^{I_n}}(\mathbf{u}_r^{(n)}), \tag{11.158}$$

where $\mathbb{U}^{I_n} = \{\mathbf{u} \in \mathbb{R}^{I_n} \mid ||\mathbf{u}||_2 = 1\}$ is a set of unit vectors. We update $\boldsymbol{\theta}_r$ by the following steps:

$$\mathcal{Z}_r \leftarrow \mathcal{P}_\Omega(\mathcal{Y}_r) + \mathcal{P}_{\bar{\Omega}}(\mathcal{X}_r), \tag{11.159}$$

$$\mathbf{u}_r^{(n)} \leftarrow \underset{\mathbf{u}_r^{(n)}}{\arg\min} \, f_r(\boldsymbol{\theta}_r | \mathcal{Z}_r) \text{ for all } n, \tag{11.160}$$

$$g_r \leftarrow \underset{g_r}{\arg\min} \, f_r(\boldsymbol{\theta}_r | \mathcal{Z}_r). \tag{11.161}$$

---

[3] The version of total variation has also been proposed in [93]. Here, we introduce only the quadratic version for simplicity.

The problem (11.160) can be considered as a unit-norm constrained optimization. Since the objective function without indicator functions is a quadratic function with respect to $\mathbf{u}_r^{(n)}$, it can be formulated as spherical constrained quadratic optimization [72]. Here, we consider the gradient-based coefficient normalization update method [30,65]. Although it does not guarantee global convergence generally, sticking into local minima of the suboptimization problem is not a critical issue because the objective of suboptimization is to decrease the global cost function rather than to obtain a strict solution of itself. As other options, several alternative optimization schemes can be also applied such as the Lagrange multiplier method [21], the tangent gradient [48], and an optimization method on manifolds [1]. Thus, the update of $\mathbf{u}_r^{(n)}$ is given by

$$\mathbf{u}_r^{(n)} \leftarrow \frac{\mathbf{u}_r^{(n)} - \alpha \partial f_r^{(n)}}{\sqrt{1 - 2\alpha \mathbf{u}_r^{(n)\mathrm{T}} \partial f_r^{(n)} + \alpha^2 \partial f_r^{(n)\mathrm{T}} \partial f_r^{(n)}}}, \tag{11.162}$$

where $\partial f_r^{(n)} = \frac{\partial f_r}{\partial \mathbf{u}_r^{(n)}}$ is the partial differential of f_r with $\mathbf{u}_r^{(n)}$ and α is a step size parameter which should be tuned so that the objective function f_r decreases. The partial differential of f_r can be given by

$$\partial f_r^{(n)} = g_r^2 (\mathbf{I} + \rho^{(n)} \mathbf{L}^{(n)\mathrm{T}} \mathbf{L}^{(n)}) \mathbf{u}_r^{(n)} - g_r \mathbf{Z}_{r(n)} \mathbf{v}_r, \tag{11.163}$$

where $\mathbf{v}_r^{(n)} = \mathbf{u}_r^{(N)} \otimes \cdots \otimes \mathbf{u}_r^{(n+1)} \otimes \mathbf{u}_r^{(n-1)} \otimes \cdots \otimes \mathbf{u}_r^{(1)} \in \mathbb{R}^{\prod_{k \neq n} I_k}$. We iterate (11.162) until convergence.

Because the problem in (11.161) is an unconstrained quadratic optimization, the unique solution can be obtained analytically. The objective function can be simplified as

$$\frac{1}{2} g_r^2 - g_r \langle \mathcal{Z}_r, \mathbf{u}_r^{(1)} \circ \cdots \circ \mathbf{u}_r^{(N)} \rangle + \frac{1}{2} g_r^2 \sum_{n=1}^{N} \rho^{(n)} \|\mathbf{L}^{(n)} \mathbf{u}_r^{(n)}\|_2^2 + \text{const.} \tag{11.164}$$

Therefore, the update rule is given by

$$g_r \leftarrow \frac{\langle \mathcal{Z}_r, \mathbf{u}_r^{(1)} \circ \cdots \circ \mathbf{u}_r^{(N)} \rangle}{(1 + \sum_{n=1}^{N} \rho^{(n)} \|\mathbf{L}^{(n)} \mathbf{u}_r^{(n)}\|_2^2)}. \tag{11.165}$$

Finally, the optimization scheme named FR-SPC is summarized in Algorithm 13. Note that the seventh line is essentially the same as (11.159) because

$$\begin{aligned} \mathcal{P}_\Omega(\mathcal{Y}_r) + \mathcal{P}_{\bar{\Omega}}(\mathcal{X}_r) &= \mathcal{P}_\Omega(\mathcal{T} - \mathcal{X} + \mathcal{X}_r) + \mathcal{P}_{\bar{\Omega}}(\mathcal{X}_r) \\ &= \mathcal{P}_\Omega(\mathcal{T} - \mathcal{X}) + \mathcal{P}_\Omega(\mathcal{X}_r) + \mathcal{P}_{\bar{\Omega}}(\mathcal{X}_r) \\ &= \mathcal{E} + \mathcal{X}_r. \end{aligned} \tag{11.166}$$

Algorithm 13 FR-SPC: smooth CP decomposition for tensor completion.

1: **input:** $\mathcal{T}$, Ω, R and $\rho^{(n)}$.
2: **initialize:** $\{g_r, \{\mathbf{u}_r^{(n)} \in \mathbb{U}^{I_n}\}_{n=1}^N\}_{r=1}^R$, randomly;
3: $\mathcal{X} \leftarrow \sum_{r=1}^R g_r \mathbf{u}_r^{(1)} \circ \cdots \circ \mathbf{u}_r^{(N)}$;
4: $\mathcal{E} \leftarrow \mathcal{P}_\Omega(\mathcal{T} - \mathcal{X})$;
5: **repeat**
6:    **for** $r = 1, ..., R$ **do**
7:       $\mathcal{Z}_r \leftarrow \mathcal{E} + g_r \mathbf{u}_r^{(1)} \circ \cdots \circ \mathbf{u}_r^{(N)}$;
8:       $\mathbf{u}_r^{(n)} \leftarrow \operatorname{argmin}_{\mathbf{u}_r^{(n)}} f_r(\boldsymbol{\theta}_r | \mathcal{Z}_r)$ for all n;
9:       $g_r \leftarrow \dfrac{\langle \mathcal{Z}_r, \mathbf{u}_r^{(1)} \circ \cdots \circ \mathbf{u}_r^{(N)} \rangle}{(1 + \sum_{n=1}^N \rho^{(n)} \|\mathbf{L}^{(n)} \mathbf{u}_r^{(n)}\|_2^2)}$;
10:      $\mathcal{E} \leftarrow \mathcal{P}_\Omega(\mathcal{Z}_r - g_r \mathbf{u}_r^{(1)} \circ \cdots \circ \mathbf{u}_r^{(N)})$;
11:   **end for**
12: **until** convergence
13: **output:** $\{g_r, \{\mathbf{u}_r^{(n)}\}_{n=1}^N\}_{r=1}^R$

The tenth line is also essentially same as the fourth line with a new reconstructed tensor $\mathcal{X}^{\text{new}} = \mathcal{X}^{\text{old}} - \mathcal{X}_r^{\text{old}} + \mathcal{X}_r^{\text{new}}$ because

$$
\begin{aligned}
\mathcal{P}_\Omega(\mathcal{T} - \mathcal{X}^{\text{new}}) &= \mathcal{P}_\Omega(\mathcal{T} - (\mathcal{X}^{\text{old}} - \mathcal{X}_r^{\text{old}} + \mathcal{X}_r^{\text{new}})) \\
&= \mathcal{P}_\Omega((\mathcal{T} - \mathcal{X}^{\text{old}} + \mathcal{X}_r^{\text{old}}) - \mathcal{X}_r^{\text{new}}) \\
&= \mathcal{P}_\Omega(\mathcal{Z}_r - \mathcal{X}_r^{\text{new}}).
\end{aligned} \tag{11.167}
$$

11.2.2.8 FR-SPC with rank increment

The key problem of FR-SPC is choosing the optimal number of components R. CP models with too low values for R are not able to fit the data, and CP models with too high values for R may suffer from overfitting problems. In addition, initialization is important to obtain a good local solution. Especially in the problem of image restoration, the low-frequency component is dominant, and the high-frequency component is often reconstructed little by little as the rank increases. Especially when the missing rate is high, it can be expected that the low-frequency component mainly contributes to the restoration.

In order to estimate an optimal value of R, we gradually increase R until we achieve the desired fit by formulating the following optimization problem:

$$
\underset{R}{\text{minimize}} \quad R \tag{11.168}
$$

$$
\text{subject to} \quad \|\mathcal{P}_\Omega(\mathcal{T} - \mathcal{X}_{\boldsymbol{\theta}}(R))\|_F^2 \le \delta,
$$

where $\mathcal{X}_{\boldsymbol{\theta}}(R)$ is a solution of FR-SPC with R for given $\mathcal{T}$ and Ω. The criterion (11.168) allows us to finds a tensor $\mathcal{X}_{\boldsymbol{\theta}}$ represented by the smooth CP model, with

---

Algorithm 14 SPC: Smooth CP decomposition for tensor completion with rank increment.

1: **input:** $\mathcal{T}$, Ω, $\rho^{(n)}$, and δ.
2: **initialize:** $R = 0$;
3: **repeat**
4:     $R \leftarrow R + 1$;
5:     initialize $\{g_R, \{\mathbf{u}_R^{(n)} \in \mathbb{U}^{I_n}\}_{n=1}^N\}$, randomly;
6:     $\mathcal{X} \leftarrow \sum_{r=1}^{R} g_r \mathbf{u}_r^{(1)} \circ \cdots \circ \mathbf{u}_r^{(N)}$;
7:     $\mathcal{E} \leftarrow \mathcal{P}_\Omega(\mathcal{T} - \mathcal{X})$;
8:     **repeat**
9:         **for** $r = 1, ..., R$ **do**
10:           $\mathcal{Z}_r \leftarrow \mathcal{E} + g_r \mathbf{u}_r^{(1)} \circ \cdots \circ \mathbf{u}_r^{(N)}$;
11:           $\mathbf{u}_r^{(n)} \leftarrow \text{argmin}_{\mathbf{u}_r^{(n)}} f_r(\boldsymbol{\theta}_r | \mathcal{Z}_r)$ for all n;
12:           $g_r \leftarrow \dfrac{\langle \mathcal{Z}_r, \mathbf{u}_r^{(1)} \circ \cdots \circ \mathbf{u}_r^{(N)} \rangle}{(1 + \sum_{n=1}^{N} \rho^{(n)} ||\mathbf{L}^{(n)} \mathbf{u}_r^{(n)}||_2^2)}$;
13:           $\mathcal{E} \leftarrow \mathcal{P}_\Omega(\mathcal{Z}_r - g_r \mathbf{u}_r^{(1)} \circ \cdots \circ \mathbf{u}_r^{(N)})$;
14:         **end for**
15:     **until** convergence
16: **until** $||\mathcal{E}||_F^2 \leq \delta$
17: **output:** $\{g_r, \{\mathbf{u}_r^{(n)}\}_{n=1}^N\}_{r=1}^R$

---

the minimum number of smooth components that guarantees a sufficient accuracy to fit the input tensor $\mathcal{T}$. Note that $||\mathcal{T} - \mathcal{X}_\theta(R)||_F^2$ is a monotonically nonincreasing function with respect to R. Algorithm 14 is an implementation to solve (11.168), and it allows us to obtain a good estimation for R. We simply refer to it as SPC.

Here, we discuss the benefits of the rank increasing approach rather than the rank decreasing approach for the smooth CP decomposition model. If there is no smoothness constraint, then the weak upper bound of the tensor rank is $\min_k(\prod_{n \neq k} I_n)$ for a general N-th-order tensor $\mathcal{X} \in \mathbb{R}^{I_1 \times I_2 \times \cdots \times I_N}$, because any $\mathcal{X}$ can be factorized by only one dense matrix $\mathbf{U}^{(k)} = \mathbf{X}_{(k)}$ and an identity matrix constructed as $\mathbf{I} = \mathbf{U}^{(1)} \odot \mathbf{U}^{(2)} \odot ... \odot \mathbf{U}^{(k-1)} \odot \mathbf{U}^{k+1} \odot ... \odot \mathbf{U}^{(N)} \in \mathbb{R}^{\prod_{n \neq k} I_n \times \prod_{n \neq k} I_n}$. However, such an identity matrix is not suitable for a smooth constraint, and it is difficult to estimate the upper bound of the tensor rank, because it depends on the imposed level of smoothness. In contrast, the rank increasing approach can easily be applied to various problems in practice since it does not require prior information for the tensor rank.

In addition, the rank increasing scheme is useful for the initialization. In general, even if we know the exact minimum (canonical) tensor rank of the smooth PARAFAC/Tucker decomposition for a completion problem, many local minima may exist for the optimization problem. Considering several local optimal solutions for the problem, the results of optimization methods will depend on the initialization. The algorithm starts from a rank-1 tensor ($R = 1$), the initialization of which has no critical meaning at this moment. The initialization of the rank-R tensor factorization is given by the rank-$(R-1)$ tensor factorization, which gives a better initialization for the completion problem, because this initialization arises from the lower-rank tensor space. When the algorithm is finally stopped, the SPC algorithm is able to find a good solution that is close to the lower-rank tensor space.

In recent years, the rank increasing approach is a relatively hot topic in matrix and tensor factorization models [27,59,69,74,77,83,85]. The main statement in these papers is that the rank increasing (greedy) approach is more efficient for large-scale and ill-posed settings than nuclear norm-based schemes. There are other methods for determining the rank of tensors using automatic relevance determination (ARD) [61,100], sparse models [82], and information criteria [91].

11.3 Methods using tensorization

In the previous section, we introduced the processing methods for the data represented by tensors. The discussion so far has assumed a direct tensor representation of images such as third-order tensors of x, y, and colors. On the other hand, recent studies have proposed approaches in which the image is represented as other higher-order tensors rather than a direct tensor representation [17,66,69,71,73,80,85,88,90,94,95, 101]. From this point of view, it can be seen that the study of tensor methods has two aspects: representation and processing. In this section, we discuss tensor methods including both representation and processing methods.

Since this chapter focuses on the problem of low-level vision, we consider the tensor representation of image data. Here, images include 2D data such as grayscale images, 3D data such as MRI, and sequences of images (videos). For example, the simplest way to represent a grayscale image would be a matrix. The columns and rows represent the vertical and horizontal axes of the 2D coordinates, respectively, and the adjacent entries of the matrix represent spatial adjacencies as they are. The low-rank matrix completion and TV minimization introduced so far are also effective for such direct representation. However, it is unclear whether such a direct representation is the best.

Nonlocal similar patch grouping is considered to be a very promising method for representing images, focusing on the nonlocal similarity of images. Image processing methods that utilize nonlocal similarity of images are sometimes collectively referred to as nonlocal filtering [5,22,23,38,98]. For example, BM3D [23] is one of the most famous noise removal methods. In addition, many methods used for image completion, deblurring, and compressed sensing have been proposed [98]. There are two main flows of nonlocal filtering. First, one local rectangular area (called a patch) of an image is extracted, and multiple similar patches are extracted from the peripheral area. When all patches are vectorized, the group of patches is represented as a matrix. It can be said that this is one of the image representation methods obtained from the data. Then, some processing methods such as averaging, low-rank approximation, and sparse coding are applied to the matrix. Nonlocal filtering is quite powerful in

---

Algorithm 15 Tensor completion with higher-order tensorization.

1: **input:** $\mathcal{T}, \Omega$
2: $\mathcal{T}_H \leftarrow$ tensorization of $\mathcal{T}$;
3: $\mathcal{X}_H \leftarrow$ tensor completion of $\mathcal{T}_H$ with Ω;
4: $\mathcal{X} \leftarrow$ inverse transform of $\mathcal{X}_H$;
5: **output:** $\mathcal{X}$

---

low-level vision problems, but since there is a lot of literature, we will not introduce its details in this chapter.

Instead, here we will discuss two image representation methods using tensors. One is the tensorization of images by folding [17,66,73,80,94,95,101], and the other is the tensorization of images by delay embedding [69,71,85,88,90]. Both have in common that a higher-order tensor is constructed from the direct representation of the image, and processing such as low-rank approximation is performed on the higher-order tensor. The meaning of representing an image with a higher-order tensor is that the number of axes literally increases. In other words, when focusing on a certain pixel, the number of adjacent pixels increases. For example, in the case of a 2D grayscale image, there are four adjacent pixels on the left, right, top, and bottom. In the same way, when it is represented as an N-th-order tensor, there are $2N$ adjacent pixels because the adjacent pixels are before and after each axis. In other words, increasing the order of the tensors means reorganizing the relationships between pixels. Since the increase of adjacent pixels means that the connection between pixels becomes stronger at the same time, the tensor processing based on the higher-order tensorization is considered to be more restrictive than the conventional direct representation.

In order to interpret the methods using tensorization in a unified manner, we consider the following three steps: (1) tensorization, i.e., conversion from a direct representation of images to a higher-order tensor representation, (2) tensor processing, i.e., the application of tensor processing methods to the higher-order tensor, and (3) inverse transform, i.e., the conversion from the higher-order tensor to an image. Algorithm 15 shows the algorithm of tensor completion using tensorization. Step 2 was discussed in Section 11.2 (methods using a raw tensor structure). This section mainly introduces steps 1 and 3. Since steps 1 and 3 are respectively the transformation to representation in higher-order tensor space and its (pseudo-)inverse transformation, they must exist as a pair. The representation methods in steps 1 and 3 and the tensor processing methods in step 2 are independent and can be freely combined. For example, if we combine three representation methods and five tensor processing methods, the number of combinations is simply 15. In other words, 15 types of image processing methods can be considered. In this way, the study of tensor representations has the possibility to widely extend the tensor-based image processing.

11.3.1 **Higher-order tensorization**
11.3.1.1 *Vector-to-tensor*

Here, we introduce a method of simple tensorization, that is, folding. First, vector-to-matrix folding is given by

$$\mathbf{X} = \text{fold}_{(I,J)}(\mathbf{x}) \in \mathbb{R}^{I \times J}, \tag{11.169}$$

where $\mathbf{x} \in \mathbb{R}^{IJ}$ is an input vector. The entries of both matrix $\mathbf{X}$ and vector $\mathbf{x}$ are related as

$$\mathbf{X}(i, j) = \mathbf{x}((j - 1)I + i). \tag{11.170}$$

From another perspective, let us put $\mathbf{X} = [\mathbf{x}_1, ..., \mathbf{x}_J]$. Then we have

$$\mathbf{x} = \text{vec}(\mathbf{X}) = \begin{pmatrix} \mathbf{x}_1 \\ \vdots \\ \mathbf{x}_J \end{pmatrix}. \tag{11.171}$$

Next, vector-to-third-order tensor folding is given by

$$\mathcal{Y} = \text{fold}_{(I,J,K)}(\mathbf{y}) \in \mathbb{R}^{I \times J \times K}, \tag{11.172}$$

where $\mathbf{y} \in \mathbb{R}^{IJK}$ is an input vector. The entries of both tensor $\mathcal{Y}$ and vector $\mathbf{y}$ are related as

$$\mathcal{Y}(i, j, k) = \mathbf{y}((k - 1)IJ + (j - 1)I + i). \tag{11.173}$$

From another perspective, let us put $\mathbf{Y}_{(1)} = [\mathbf{Y}_1, ..., \mathbf{Y}_K]$ and $\mathbf{Y}_k = [\mathbf{y}_{1k}, ..., \mathbf{y}_{Jk}]$. Then we have

$$\mathbf{y} = \text{vec}(\mathcal{Y}) = \text{vec}(\mathbf{Y}_{(1)}) = \begin{pmatrix} \text{vec}(\mathbf{Y}_1) \\ \vdots \\ \text{vec}(\mathbf{Y}_K) \end{pmatrix} = \begin{pmatrix} \mathbf{y}_{11} \\ \vdots \\ \mathbf{y}_{JK} \end{pmatrix}. \tag{11.174}$$

Finally, we generalize it as vector-to-tensor folding represented by

$$\mathcal{Z} = \text{fold}_{(I_1, I_2, ..., I_N)}(\mathbf{z}) \in \mathbb{R}^{I_1 \times I_2 \times \cdots \times I_N}, \tag{11.175}$$

where $\mathbf{z} \in \mathbb{R}^{\prod_{n=1}^{N} I_n}$ is an input vector, and we have $\mathbf{z} = \text{vec}(\mathcal{Z})$.

11.3.1.2 *Benefits of the folding operation*

Vector–tensor folding can be useful in capturing the periodic or exponential properties of signals. As an extreme example, suppose the vector $\mathbf{x} \in \mathbb{R}^{IJ}$ is a time series signal with period I. In this case, the matrix $\mathbf{X} \in \mathbb{R}^{I \times J}$ can be decomposed as

$$\mathbf{X} = [\mathbf{x}_1, ..., \mathbf{x}_1] = \mathbf{x}_1 \mathbf{1}^{\text{T}}. \tag{11.176}$$

It is a rank-1 matrix. As another example, suppose that the entries of the vector $\mathbf{y} \in \mathbb{R}^{I^N J}$ can be expressed as an exponential function $\mathbf{y}(t) = e^t$. In this case as well, the matrix $\mathbf{Y} \in \mathbb{R}^{I^N \times J}$ becomes a rank-1 matrix as

$$
\mathbf{Y} =
\begin{pmatrix}
e^1 & e^{I^N+1} & \cdots & e^{(J-1)I^N+1} \\
e^2 & e^{I^N+2} & \cdots & e^{(J-1)I^N+2} \\
\vdots & \vdots & \ddots & \vdots \\
e^{I^N} & e^{2I^N} & \cdots & e^{JI^N}
\end{pmatrix}
=
\begin{pmatrix}
e^1 \\
e^2 \\
\vdots \\
e^{I^N}
\end{pmatrix}
\begin{pmatrix}
e^0 & e^{I^N} & \cdots & e^{(J-1)I^N}
\end{pmatrix}.
$$

(11.177)

Its tensorization $\mathcal{Y} = \mathrm{fold}_{(I^{N-1}, I, J)}(\mathbf{y})$ can be also rank-1 because the left-hand vector can be also folded into a rank-1 matrix as

$$
\begin{pmatrix}
e^1 & e^{I^{N-1}+1} & \cdots & e^{(I-1)I^{N-1}+1} \\
e^2 & e^{I^{N-1}+2} & \cdots & e^{(I-1)I^{N-1}+2} \\
\vdots & \vdots & \ddots & \vdots \\
e^{I^{N-1}} & e^{2I^{N-1}} & \cdots & e^{I^N}
\end{pmatrix}
$$

$$
=
\begin{pmatrix}
e^1 \\
e^2 \\
\vdots \\
e^{I^{N-1}}
\end{pmatrix}
\begin{pmatrix}
e^0 & e^{I^{N-1}} & \cdots & e^{(I-1)I^{N-1}}
\end{pmatrix}.
$$

(11.178)

Finally, $(N+1)$-th-order tensorization $\mathcal{Y} \in \mathbb{R}^{I \times \cdots \times I \times J}$ can be rank-1 as follows:

$$
\mathrm{fold}_{(I,\dots,I,J)}(\mathbf{y}) =
\begin{pmatrix}
e^1 \\
e^2 \\
\vdots \\
e^I
\end{pmatrix}
\circ
\begin{pmatrix}
e^0 \\
e^I \\
\vdots \\
e^{(I-1)I}
\end{pmatrix}
\circ \cdots \circ
\begin{pmatrix}
e^0 \\
e^{I^{N-1}} \\
\vdots \\
e^{(I-1)I^{N-1}}
\end{pmatrix}
\circ
\begin{pmatrix}
e^0 \\
e^{I^N} \\
\vdots \\
e^{(J-1)I^N}
\end{pmatrix}.
$$

(11.179)

Let us consider the number of parameters required to represent this signal. In the case of a vector it is simply the number of entries $I^N J$, in the case of a matrix it is $I^N + J$, and in the case of an $(N+1)$-th-order tensor it is $NI + J$. Clearly, we have $I^N J > I^N + J \gg NI + J$. In other words, it can be seen that a more compact representation can be obtained by converting to a tensor and performing low-rank tensor decomposition. This does not hold for all time series, but it is a powerful tool when we apply it to natural signals having a sparse Fourier expansion, for example.

11.3.1.3 Tensor representation of images: TS type I

First, we introduce one of the tensor representations of images. It just applies folding for each mode. Let us consider the third-order tensor $\mathcal{X} \in \mathbb{R}^{(I_1^{N_1}, I_2^{N_2}, I_3^{N_3})}$. Then we fold each mode as follows:

$$\mathcal{Y} = \text{fold}_{(I_1,...,I_1,I_2,...,I_2,I_3,...,I_3)}(\text{vec}(\mathcal{X})), \tag{11.180}$$

where $\mathcal{Y}$ is a $(N_1 + N_2 + N_3)$-th-order tensor. We refer to this as "TS type I." TS type I has been employed and discussed in [17,80,94,95,101]. For example, an RGB image of size $(4^4, 4^4, 3)$ is folded into $(4, 4, 4, 4, 4, 4, 4, 4, 3)$.

11.3.1.4 Tensor representation of images: TS type II

Next, we introduce another tensor representation of images. It applies both folding and unfolding. Let us consider a tensor $\mathcal{X} \in \mathbb{R}^{(\prod_{n=1}^{N} I_n) \times (\prod_{n=1}^{N} J_n) \times (\prod_{n=1}^{N} K_n)}$. Note that N is the same for all modes. Then, we tensorize this as follows:

$$\mathcal{Y} = \text{tens}^{\text{II}}_{(I_1 J_1 K_1, I_2 J_2 K_2,...,I_N J_N K_N)}(\mathcal{X}), \tag{11.181}$$

where $\mathcal{Y} \in \mathbb{R}^{I_1 J_1 K_1 \times I_2 J_2 K_2 \times \cdots \times I_N J_N K_N}$ is an N-th-order tensor. The concept of TS type II was firstly discussed in [50], and it has been employed for tensor completion in [2,3,66,73]. In [2,3], it has been referred to as ket augmentation. For example, an RGB image of size $(4^4, 5^4, 3)$ is folded into $(20, 20, 20, 20, 3)$.

11.3.2 Delay embedding/Hankelization

11.3.2.1 Delay embedding/Hankelization of time series signals

In this section, we explain the delay embedding operation. For simplicity, we first define a standard delay embedding transform for a vector, which can be interpreted as a time series signal. Let us consider a vector $\mathbf{v} = [v_1, v_2, ..., v_L]^{\text{T}} \in \mathbb{R}^L$, a standard delay embedding transform of $\mathbf{v}$ with τ given by

$$\mathcal{H}_\tau(\mathbf{v}) := \begin{pmatrix} v_1 & v_2 & \cdots & v_{L-\tau+1} \\ v_2 & v_3 & \cdots & v_{L-\tau+2} \\ \vdots & \vdots & \ddots & \vdots \\ v_\tau & v_{\tau+1} & \cdots & v_L \end{pmatrix} \in \mathbb{R}^{\tau \times (L-\tau+1)}. \tag{11.182}$$

Thus, a standard delay embedding transform produces a duplicated matrix from a vector, which is also referred to as "Hankelization" since $\mathcal{H}_\tau(\mathbf{v})$ is a Hankel matrix. If $\mathbf{S} \in \{0, 1\}^{\tau(L-\tau+1) \times L}$ is a duplication matrix that satisfies

$$\text{vec}(\mathcal{H}_\tau(\mathbf{v})) = \mathbf{S}\mathbf{v}, \tag{11.183}$$

then the standard delay embedding transform can be obtained by

$$\mathcal{H}_\tau(\mathbf{v}) = \text{fold}_{(\tau, L-\tau+1)}(\mathbf{S}\mathbf{v}), \tag{11.184}$$

where $\text{fold}_{(I,J)} : \mathbb{R}^{IJ} \to \mathbb{R}^{I \times J}$ is a folding operator from a vector to a matrix.

Next, we consider an inverse transform of standard delay embedding. The forward transform can be decomposed into duplication and folding, so the inverse transform can also be decomposed into the individual corresponding inverse transforms: a vectorization operation and the Moore–Penrose pseudo-inverse $\mathbf{S}^\dagger := (\mathbf{S}^T\mathbf{S})^{-1}\mathbf{S}^T$. Thus, the inverse delay embedding transform for a Hankel matrix $\mathbf{V}_H$ can be given by

$$\mathcal{H}_\tau^{-1}(\mathbf{V}_H) = \mathbf{S}^\dagger \text{vec}(\mathbf{V}_H). \tag{11.185}$$

Note that the diagonal entries of $(\mathbf{S}^T\mathbf{S})$ comprise the numbers of duplication for individual entries, which are usually τ, but low for marginal entries.

11.3.2.2 Benefits of delay embedding/Hankelization

Delay embedding can be considered as an overlapped version of vector-to-matrix folding. Then it has properties similar to folding. For example, a Hankel matrix of exponential time series is rank-1 as follows:

$$\begin{pmatrix} e^1 & e^2 & \cdots & e^{L-\tau+1} \\ e^2 & e^3 & \cdots & e^{L-\tau+2} \\ \vdots & \vdots & \ddots & \vdots \\ e^\tau & e^{\tau+1} & \cdots & e^L \end{pmatrix} = \begin{pmatrix} e^1 \\ e^2 \\ \vdots \\ e^\tau \end{pmatrix} \begin{pmatrix} e^0 & e^1 & \cdots & e^{L-\tau} \end{pmatrix}. \tag{11.186}$$

In addition, a Hankel matrix of a single $\sin(\cdot)$ function can be represented by rank-2 decomposition as follows:

$$\begin{pmatrix} \sin(1) & \sin(2) & \cdots & \sin(L-\tau+1) \\ \sin(2) & \sin(3) & \cdots & \sin(L-\tau+2) \\ \vdots & \vdots & \ddots & \vdots \\ \sin(\tau) & \sin(\tau+1) & \cdots & \sin(L) \end{pmatrix}$$

$$= \begin{pmatrix} \sin(1) & \cos(1) \\ \sin(2) & \cos(2) \\ \vdots & \vdots \\ \sin(\tau) & \cos(\tau) \end{pmatrix} \begin{pmatrix} \cos(0) & \cos(1) & \cdots & \cos(L-\tau) \\ \sin(0) & \sin(1) & \cdots & \sin(L-\tau) \end{pmatrix}. \tag{11.187}$$

Note that $\sin(\alpha + \beta) = \sin(\alpha)\cos(\beta) + \cos(\alpha)\sin(\beta)$.

Delay embedding provides a good representation for signals whose Hankel matrix has a low rank [26,55,57,79]. For example, Li et al. [52] proposed a method for modeling damped sinusoidal signals based on a low-rank Hankel approximation. Ding et al. [26] proposed the use of rank minimization of a Hankel matrix for the video inpainting problem by assuming an auto-regressive moving average model.

11.3.2.3 Multiway delay embedding/Hankelization of tensors

In this section we consider the tensor extension of delay embedding. We call it multiway delay embedding transform (MDT) [85]. The MDT of $\mathcal{X} \in \mathbb{R}^{I_1 \times \cdots \times I_N}$ with $\boldsymbol{\tau} = [\tau_1, ..., \tau_N] \in \mathbb{N}^N$ is defined by

$$\mathcal{H}_{\boldsymbol{\tau}}(\mathcal{X}) = \text{fold}_{(\tau_1, I_1 - \tau_1 + 1, ..., \tau_N, I_N - \tau_N + 1)}(\mathcal{X} \times_1 \mathbf{S}_1 \cdots \times_N \mathbf{S}_N), \qquad (11.188)$$

where $\text{fold}_{(\tau_1, I_1 - \tau_1 + 1, ..., \tau_N, I_N - \tau_N + 1)}$: $\mathbb{R}^{\tau_1(I_1 - \tau_1 + 1) \times \tau_2(I_2 - \tau_2 + 1) \times \cdots \times \tau_N(I_N - \tau_N + 1)} \rightarrow$ $\mathbb{R}^{\tau_1 \times (I_1 - \tau_1 + 1) \times \tau_2 \times (I_2 - \tau_2 + 1) \times \cdots \times \tau_N \times (I_N - \tau_N + 1)}$ constructs a $2N$-th-order tensor from the input N-th-order tensor. In a similar manner to how the vector delay embedding is a combination of linear duplication and folding operations, the MDT is also a combination of multilinear duplication and multiway folding operations. Finally, the inverse MDT for a block Hankel tensor $\mathcal{X}_{\text{H}}$ is given by

$$\mathcal{H}_{\boldsymbol{\tau}}^{-1}(\mathcal{X}_{\text{H}}) = \text{unfold}_{(\tau_1(I_1 - \tau_1 + 1), ..., \tau_N(I_N - \tau_N + 1))}(\mathcal{X}_{\text{H}}) \times_1 \mathbf{S}_1^{\dagger} \cdots \times_N \mathbf{S}_N^{\dagger}, \qquad (11.189)$$

where $\text{unfold}_{(\tau_1(I_1 - \tau_1 + 1), ..., \tau_N(I_N - \tau_N + 1))} = \text{fold}_{(\tau_1, I_1 - \tau_1 + 1, ..., \tau_N, I_N - \tau_N + 1)}^{-1}$. The MDT is employed and discussed in [69,71,85,88,90]. For example, an image of size $(256, 256, 3)$ is represented as a fifth-order tensor of size $(32, 225, 32, 225, 3)$ by using MDT with $\boldsymbol{\tau} = [32, 32, 1]$.

11.4 Examples of low-level vision applications

11.4.1 Image inpainting with raw tensor structure

In this section, various tensor reconstruction methods are applied to an actual low-level vision task of image inpainting. HaLRTC [54], t-SVD [99], and LRTV [87,89] are used as approaches using the corresponding penalty functions. In the approach using the tensor decomposition model, CP decomposition (part of [93]), TMac [81], Tucker decomposition (part of [85]), and SPC [93] are employed. In all four tensor decomposition methods, the ranks are determined by the (greedy) rank increment algorithm.

Experiments were conducted using three RGB images: "house," "facade," and "peppers." The size of all three images is $(256, 256, 3)$ which is directly represented as a third-order tensor. We set the sampling rate to 50%, 10%, and 5% and assume that the entries of the third-order tensor are randomly observed. The given incomplete tensors are restored by using various methods.

Fig. 11.2 shows the results of reconstructed images. For the "house" image with a sampling rate of 50%, highly accurate reconstruction was obtained with all methods. For the "facade" image with a sampling rate of 10%, the method of only rank minimization achieved highly accurate reconstruction. This is because the "facade" image has a remarkable low-rank structure. On the other hand, since the TV minimization penalty forces a direct smoothness between adjacent pixels, the LRTV has removed the edge components of the "facade" image. In SPC, since the smoothness

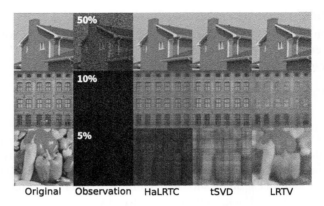

FIGURE 11.2

Examples of image inpainting with raw tensor structure: three RGB images with randomly missing pixels are reconstructed by various methods. Sampling rates are set as 50%, 10%, and 5%.

constraint is applied to the factor vectors and the low-rank structure itself is not disturbed, it is considered that the side effects of smooth constraints such like LRTV are reduced. Finally, for the "peppers" image with a sampling rate of 5%, on the contrary, the methods of only rank minimization failed to restore, and LRTV and SPC including smoothness constraints achieved highly accurate reconstruction. This is because the "peppers" image has both a low rank and a smooth structure. However, LRTV has a problem that the edge component of the image is removed. On the other hand, SPC was the only method that achieved highly accurate reconstruction for all three images.

11.4.2 Image inpainting using tensorization

In this section, several combinations of higher-order tensor representation and reconstruction methods are applied to an actual low-level vision task of image inpainting.

First, we consider four tensor representation methods for images: raw representation, TS type I, TS type II, and MDT. Furthermore, we consider three methods of tensor reconstruction: TMac, CP decomposition, and Tucker decomposition. Since the four representations are combined with the three reconstruction methods, a total of 12 results are obtained. In all three tensor decomposition methods, the ranks are determined by the (greedy) rank increment algorithm. The reconstruction methods using the penalty function were not applied this time because these often require large-scale singular value decomposition and the calculation cost is high. Note that the key point of this section is to demonstrate the differences between the four tensor representations rather than the reconstruction methods.

Experiments were conducted using two RGB images: "facade" and "baboon." The size of both images is (256, 256, 3). The "facade" image has randomly missing slices and the "baboon" image has randomly missing entries (sampling rate is only 1%). We consider a raw third-order tensor representation (256,256,3), a seventh-order tensor representation by TS type I (8,8,4,8,8,4,3), a fifth-order tensor representation by TS type II (16,16,16,16,3), and a fifth-order tensor representation by MDT (32,225,32,225,3).

Fig. 11.3 shows the results of reconstructed images. First, in a "facade" images with slice missing, it can be seen that rank minimization under raw representation totally failed. This is because missing slices directly deflate the tensor rank in the raw representation. In this case, low-rank approximation does not provide any information to restore the missing slice part. On the other hand, under the higher-order tensor representations, highly accurate reconstruction is achieved. By performing operations such as folding, the slice missing under the raw representation is no longer the slice missing in the higher-order tensor. Next, the "baboon" image with a very low sampling rate of only 1% is very difficult to reconstruct because there is too little information. It seems that the reconstruction is getting better little by little in the order of raw representation, TS type I, TS type II, and MDT. It also seems that the reconstruction is improving little by little in the order of TMac, CP decomposition, and Tucker decomposition. The exact reason is unclear; however, it is interesting to see these differences. In particular, the combination of MDT and Tucker decomposition has achieved significantly better reconstruction than the other combinations.

11.4.3 Denoising, deblurring, and superresolution

In this section, penalty function- and tensor decomposition-based general tensor reconstruction methods which are discussed in Sections 11.2.1.6 and 11.2.2.2 are applied to three low-level vision tasks: denoising, deblurring, and superresolution. An original RGB image $\mathcal{X}_0 \in \mathbb{R}^{256 \times 256 \times 3}$ is corrupted by additive Gaussian noise, blur, or down-sampling. Three different observation models were considered with different $\mathcal{A}$, but all tasks can be treated by the general tensor reconstruction methods. For denoising, we considered $\mathbf{b} = \text{vec}(\mathcal{X}_0) + \mathbf{n}$ as observation model with identity mapping and additive Gaussian noise $\mathbf{n}$ of standard deviation $\sigma = 40$. For deblurring,

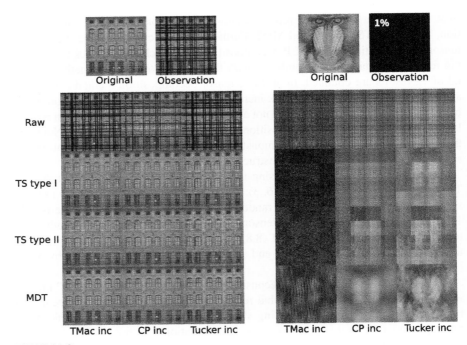

FIGURE 11.3

Examples of image inpainting using tensorization: one RGB image has randomly missing slices and the another RGB image has randomly missing pixels (sampling rate is only 1%). These incomplete tensors are tensorized by using TS type I, TS type II, and MDT and reconstructed by using low-rank tensor decomposition methods.

we considered $\mathbf{b} = \mathrm{vec}(2\mathrm{Dconv}(\mathcal{X}_0, \mathbf{K}))$ as observation model, where a linear operator $2\mathrm{Dconv}(\cdot, \mathbf{K})$ provides 2D convolution with a same kernel $\mathbf{K} \in \mathbb{R}^{21 \times 21}$ for each channel slice. For superresolution, we considered $\mathbf{b} = \mathrm{vec}(\mathrm{DS}(2\mathrm{Dconv}(\mathcal{X}_0, \mathbf{F})))$ as observation model which is 2D down-sampling with a factor of 4 ($\mathbb{R}^{256 \times 256 \times 3} \rightarrow \mathbb{R}^{64 \times 64 \times 3}$) after 2D convolution with Lanczos kernel $\mathbf{F} \in \mathbb{R}^{16 \times 16}$. Note that we assume no noise for deblurring and superresolution. Original and three observed images with noise, blur, and low resolution are shown in Fig. 11.4.

We reconstruct three observed images by using two methods: (i) convex optimization with low-rank and smooth penalty functions and (ii) Tucker decomposition with rank increment. Convex optimization can be formulated by

$$\underset{\mathcal{X} \in \mathbb{R}^{256 \times 256 \times 3}}{\mathrm{minimize}} \frac{1}{2} ||\mathbf{b} - \mathcal{A}(\mathcal{X})||_2^2 + \sum_{n=1}^{3} \lambda_n ||\mathbf{X}_{(n)}||_* + \sum_{n=1}^{2} \frac{\alpha_n}{2} ||\mathbf{L}^{(n)} \mathbf{X}_{(n)}||_F^2. \quad (11.190)$$

This is a low-rank and smooth tensor reconstruction model with nuclear norm and quadratic variation penalties. The PDHG/PDS algorithm can be derived by following

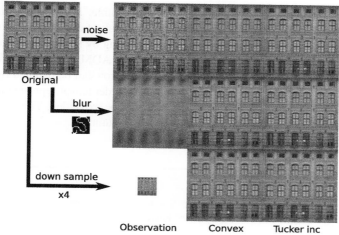

FIGURE 11.4

Examples of image denoising, deblurring, and superresolution: three corrupted observed RGB images with random Gaussian noise ($\sigma = 40$), motion blur, and low resolution (down-sampled by factor 4) are considered. No noise was added to blurred and down-sampled images. A convex penalty-based method (with low rank and smooth regularizers) and a Tucker decomposition-based method reconstructed these images with different observation models with different $\mathcal{A}$. We assumed that $\mathcal{A}$ is the identity mapping for the denoising task, $\mathcal{A}$ is the convolution for the deblurring task, and $\mathcal{A}$ is the down-sampling operator for the superresolution task.

Section 11.2.1.6. Tucker decomposition with rank increment can be formulated by

$$\underset{(R_1,\ldots,R_N)}{\text{minimize}} \sum_{n=1}^{N} R_n, \quad \text{s.t.} \ \ ||\mathcal{P}_\mathcal{A}(\mathcal{T} - \mathcal{X}_\theta)||_F^2 \leq \delta, \tag{11.191}$$

where $\mathcal{T} = \mathcal{A}^\dagger \mathbf{b}$. The MM algorithm can be derived by following Sections 11.2.2.2 and 11.2.2.6. Fig. 11.4 shows the results of reconstructed images. In this way, different low-level vision tasks can be solved by the general tensor reconstruction methods. For denoising, low-rank and smooth constraints helped to separate noise and signal components. For deblurring in this case, very weak constraints were necessary because $\mathcal{A}$ was almost full-rank. For superresolution, low-rank and smooth constraints helped to select more natural solution points from innumerable solution candidates that satisfy $\mathbf{b} = \mathcal{A}(\mathcal{X})$.

11.5 Remarks

In this chapter, we aimed to organize the knowledge to solve various low-level vision tasks such as inpainting, noise removal, deblurring, and superresolution in a unified tensor reconstruction framework as much as possible. The tensor reconstruction method was discussed in two parts: modeling by penalty functions and modeling by tensor decompositions. It was shown that the modeling by the penalty functions can be handled by proximal splitting algorithms such as ADMM and PDHG/PDS. It is also showed that the modeling by tensor decomposition can be handled by the MM algorithms. Furthermore, by incorporating a higher-order tensor representation of the images, the possibility of tensor reconstruction can be expanded. This is one of the hot topics that can be discussed more actively in the future.

Acknowledgments

This work was supported in part by Japan Science and Technology Agency (JST) ACT-I under Grant JPMJPR18UU, in part by JSPS KAKENHI under Grant 20H04249 and Grant 20H04208.

References

[1] P.-A. Absil, R. Mahony, R. Sepulchre, Optimization Algorithms on Matrix Manifolds, Princeton University Press, 2009.

[2] J.A. Bengua, H.D. Tuan, H.N. Phien, M.N. Do, Concatenated image completion via tensor augmentation and completion, in: Proceedings of 10th International Conference on Signal Processing and Communication Systems (ICSPCS), 2016, pp. 1–7.

[3] J.A. Bengua, H.N. Phien, H.D. Tuan, M.N. Do, Efficient tensor completion for color image and video recovery: low-rank tensor train, IEEE Transactions on Image Processing 26 (5) (2017) 2466–2479.

[4] D.P. Bertsekas, J.N. Tsitsiklis, Parallel and Distributed Computation: Numerical Methods, Prentice-Hall, Inc., Upper Saddle River, NJ, USA, 1989.

[5] A. Buades, B. Coll, J.-M. Morel, A non-local algorithm for image denoising, in: Proceedings of CVPR, vol. 2, 2005, pp. 60–65.

[6] W. Burger, M.J. Burge, Principles of Digital Image Processing: Core Algorithms, Springer Science & Business Media, 2010.

[7] J.F. Cai, E.J. Candes, Z. Shen, A singular value thresholding algorithm for matrix completion, SIAM Journal on Optimization 20 (4) (2010) 1956–1982.

[8] C.F. Caiafa, A. Cichocki, Computing sparse representations of multidimensional signals using Kronecker bases, Neural Computation 25 (1) (2013) 186–220.

[9] C.F. Caiafa, A. Cichocki, Multidimensional compressed sensing and their applications, Wiley Interdisciplinary Reviews: Data Mining and Knowledge Discovery 3 (6) (2013) 355–380.

[10] E.J. Candes, B. Recht, Exact matrix completion via convex optimization, Foundations of Computational Mathematics 9 (6) (2009) 717–772.

[11] E.J. Candes, J.K. Romberg, Signal recovery from random projections, Proceedings of Computational Imaging III, vol. 5674, International Society for Optics and Photonics, 2005, pp. 76–86.

[12] J. Carroll, J.-J. Chang, Analysis of individual differences in multidimensional scaling via an n-way generalization of "Eckart-Young" decomposition, Psychometrika 35 (1970) 283–319.

[13] A. Chambolle, T. Pock, A first-order primal-dual algorithm for convex problems with applications to imaging, Journal of Mathematical Imaging and Vision 40 (1) (2011) 120–145.

[14] S.H. Chan, R. Khoshabeh, K.B. Gibson, P.E. Gill, T.Q. Nguyen, An augmented Lagrangian method for total variation video restoration, IEEE Transactions on Image Processing 20 (11) (2011) 3097–3111.

[15] T.F. Chan, C.-K. Wong, Total variation blind deconvolution, IEEE Transactions on Image Processing 7 (3) (1998) 370–375.

[16] C. Chen, B. He, X. Yuan, Matrix completion via an alternating direction method, IMA Journal of Numerical Analysis 32 (1) (2012) 227–245.

[17] A. Cichocki, Tensor networks for big data analytics and large-scale optimization problems, arXiv preprint, arXiv:1407.3124, 2014.

[18] A. Cichocki, R. Zdunek, S. Amari, Hierarchical ALS algorithms for nonnegative matrix and 3D tensor factorization, in: Proceedings of International Conference on Independent Component Analysis and Signal Separation, in: LNCS, vol. 4666, Springer, 2007, pp. 169–176.

[19] A. Cichocki, R. Zdunek, A.H. Phan, S. Amari, Nonnegative Matrix and Tensor Factorizations: Applications to Exploratory Multi-Way Data Analysis and Blind Source Separation, John Wiley & Sons, 2009.

[20] P.L. Combettes, J.-C. Pesquet, Proximal splitting methods in signal processing, in: Fixed-Point Algorithms for Inverse Problems in Science and Engineering, Springer, 2011, pp. 185–212.

[21] R. Courant, D. Hilbert, Methods of Mathematical Physics 1 (1966), CUP Archive.

[22] K. Dabov, A. Foi, V. Katkovnik, K. Egiazarian, Color image denoising via sparse 3D collaborative filtering with grouping constraint in luminance-chrominance space, in: Proceedings of ICIP, vol. 1, 2007, I–313.

[23] K. Dabov, A. Foi, V. Katkovnik, K. Egiazarian, Image denoising by sparse 3-D transform-domain collaborative filtering, IEEE Transactions on Image Processing 16 (8) (2007).

[24] Q. Dai, W. Sha, The physics of compressive sensing and the gradient-based recovery algorithms, arXiv preprint, arXiv:0906.1487, 2009.

[25] L. De Lathauwer, B. De Moor, J. Vandewalle, On the best rank-1 and rank-$(r_1, r_2,..., r_n)$ approximation of higher-order tensors, SIAM Journal on Matrix Analysis and Applications 21 (4) (2000) 1324–1342.

[26] T. Ding, M. Sznaier, O.I. Camps, A rank minimization approach to video inpainting, in: Proceedings of ICCV, 2007, pp. 1–8.

[27] S.V. Dolgov, D.V. Savostyanov, Alternating minimal energy methods for linear systems in higher dimensions. Part I: SPD systems, arXiv preprint, arXiv:1301.6068, 2013.

[28] L. Donati, M. Nilchian, C.O.S. Sorzano, M. Unser, Fast multiscale reconstruction for cryo-EM, Journal of Structural Biology 204 (3) (2018) 543–554.

[29] D.L. Donoho, Compressed sensing, IEEE Transactions on Information Theory 52 (4) (2006) 1289–1306.

[30] S.C. Douglas, S. Amari, S.-Y. Kung, On gradient adaptation with unit-norm constraints, IEEE Transactions on Signal Processing 48 (6) (2000) 1843–1847.

[31] E. Esser, X. Zhang, T. Chan, A general framework for a class of first order primal-dual algorithms for convex optimization in imaging science, SIAM Journal on Imaging Sciences 3 (4) (2010) 1015–1046.

[32] S. Farsiu, D. Robinson, M. Elad, P. Milanfar, Advances and challenges in super-resolution, International Journal of Imaging Systems and Technology 14 (2) (2004) 47–57.

[33] M. Filipovic, A. Jukic, Tucker factorization with missing data with application to low-n-rank tensor completion, Multidimensional Systems and Signal Processing 26 (3) (2015) 677–692.

[34] S. Gandy, B. Recht, I. Yamada, Tensor completion and low-n-rank tensor recovery via convex optimization, Inverse Problems 27 (2) (2011).

[35] P. Getreuer, Total variation inpainting using split Bregman, in: Image Processing on Line, vol. 2, 2012, pp. 147–157.

[36] N. Gillis, F. Glineur, Low-rank matrix approximation with weights or missing data is NP-hard, SIAM Journal on Matrix Analysis and Applications 32 (4) (2011) 1149–1165.

[37] T. Goldstein, M. Li, X. Yuan, Adaptive primal-dual splitting methods for statistical learning and image processing, in: Proceedings of NeurIPS, 2015, pp. 2089–2097.

[38] S. Gu, L. Zhang, W. Zuo, X. Feng, Weighted nuclear norm minimization with application to image denoising, in: Proceedings of CVPR, 2014, pp. 2862–2869.

[39] X. Guo, Y. Ma, Generalized tensor total variation minimization for visual data recovery, in: Proceedings of CVPR, 2015, pp. 3603–3611.

[40] R. Harshman, Foundations of the PARAFAC procedure: model and conditions for an 'explanatory' multi-mode factor analysis, UCLA Working Papers in Phonetics 16 (1970) 1–84.

[41] B. He, X. Yuan, Convergence analysis of primal-dual algorithms for a saddle-point problem: from contraction perspective, SIAM Journal on Imaging Sciences 5 (1) (2012) 119–149.

[42] M.R. Hestenes, E. Stiefel, Methods of Conjugate Gradients for Solving Linear Systems, vol. 49, NBS, 1952.

[43] D.R. Hunter, K. Lange, A tutorial on MM algorithms, American Statistician 58 (1) (2004) 30–37.

[44] E. Jonsson, S.-c. Huang, T. Chan, Total variation regularization in positron emission tomography, CAM Report 9848 (1998).

[45] H. Kasai, B. Mishra, Low-rank tensor completion: a Riemannian manifold preconditioning approach, in: Proceedings of ICML, 2016, pp. 1012–1021.

[46] H.A. Kiers, Towards a standardized notation and terminology in multiway analysis, Journal of Chemometrics 14 (3) (2000) 105–122.

[47] T.G. Kolda, B.W. Bader, Tensor decompositions and applications, SIAM Review 51 (3) (2009) 455–500.

[48] T. Krasulina, Method of stochastic approximation in the determination of the largest eigenvalue of the mathematical expectation of random matrices, Automation and Remote Control (1970) 50–56.

[49] D. Kressner, M. Steinlechner, B. Vandereycken, Low-rank tensor completion by Riemannian optimization, BIT Numerical Mathematics 54 (2) (2014) 447–468.

[50] J.I. Latorre, Image compression and entanglement, arXiv:quant-ph/0510031, 2005.

[51] D.D. Lee, H.S. Seung, Algorithms for non-negative matrix factorization, in: Proceedings of NeurIPS, 2001, pp. 556–562.

[52] Y. Li, K.R. Liu, J. Razavilar, A parameter estimation scheme for damped sinusoidal signals based on low-rank Hankel approximation, IEEE Transactions on Signal Processing 45 (2) (1997) 481–486.

[53] Z. Lin, M. Chen, Y. Ma, The augmented Lagrange multiplier method for exact recovery of corrupted low-rank matrices, arXiv preprint, arXiv:1009.5055, 2010.

[54] J. Liu, P. Musialski, P. Wonka, J. Ye, Tensor completion for estimating missing values in visual data, IEEE Transactions on Pattern Analysis and Machine Intelligence 35 (1) (2013) 208–220.

[55] E.N. Lorenz, Deterministic nonperiodic flow, Journal of the Atmospheric Sciences 20 (2) (1963) 130–141.

[56] S. Ma, D. Goldfarb, L. Chen, Fixed point and Bregman iterative methods for matrix rank minimization, Mathematical Programming 128 (1–2) (2011) 321–353.

[57] I. Markovsky, Structured low-rank approximation and its applications, Automatica 44 (4) (2008) 891–909.

[58] D. Marr, Vision, W. H. Freeman, 1982.

[59] B. Mishra, G. Meyer, F. Bach, R. Sepulchre, Low-rank optimization with trace norm penalty, SIAM Journal on Optimization 23 (4) (2013) 2124–2149.

[60] J.J. Moreau, Fonctions convexes duales et points proximaux dans un espace Hilbertien, Reports of the Paris Academy of Sciences, Series A 255 (1962) 2897–2899.

[61] M. Morup, L.K. Hansen, Automatic relevance determination for multi-way models, Journal of Chemometrics: A Journal of the Chemometrics Society 23 (7–8) (2009) 352–363.

[62] J.P. Oliveira, J.M. Bioucas-Dias, M.A. Figueiredo, Adaptive total variation image deblurring: a majorization–minimization approach, Signal Processing 89 (9) (2009) 1683–1693.

[63] S. Ono, I. Yamada, Decorrelated vectorial total variation, in: Proceedings of CVPR, IEEE, 2014, pp. 4090–4097.

[64] J. Ortega, W. Rheinboldt, Iterative Solution of Nonlinear Equations in Several Variables, Vol. 30, SIAM, 1970.

[65] N.L. Owsley, Adaptive data orthogonalization, in: Proceedings of ICASSP, vol. 3, 1978, pp. 109–112.

[66] A.-H. Phan, A. Cichocki, P. Tichavský, G. Luta, A. Brockmeier, Tensor completion through multiple Kronecker product decomposition, in: Proceedings of ICASSP, IEEE, 2013, pp. 3233–3237.

[67] B. Recht, M. Fazel, P.A. Parrilo, Guaranteed minimum-rank solutions of linear matrix equations via nuclear norm minimization, SIAM Review 52 (3) (2010) 471–501.

[68] L.I. Rudin, S. Osher, E. Fatemi, Nonlinear total variation based noise removal algorithms, Physica D: Nonlinear Phenomena 60 (1) (1992) 259–268.

[69] F. Sedighin, A. Cichocki, T. Yokota, Q. Shi, Matrix and tensor completion in multiway delay embedded space using tensor train, with application to signal reconstruction, IEEE Signal Processing Letters 27 (2020) 810–814.

[70] I. Selesnick, Total variation denoising (an MM algorithm), NYU Polytechnic School of Engineering Lecture Notes, 2012.

[71] Q. Shi, J. Yin, J. Cai, A. Cichocki, T. Yokota, L. Chen, M. Yuan, J. Zeng, Block Hankel tensor ARIMA for multiple short time series forecasting, in: Proceedings of AAAI, 2020, pp. 5758–5766.

[72] D. Sorensen, Minimization of a large-scale quadratic function subject to a spherical constraint, SIAM Journal on Optimization 7 (1) (1997) 141–161.

[73] W. Sun, Y. Chen, H.C. So, Tensor completion using Kronecker rank-1 tensor train with application to visual data inpainting, IEEE Access 6 (2018) 47804–47814.

[74] M. Tan, I.W. Tsang, L. Wang, B. Vandereycken, S.J. Pan, Riemannian pursuit for big matrix recovery, in: Proceedings of ICML, 2014, pp. 1539–1547.

[75] R. Tomioka, T. Suzuki, Convex tensor decomposition via structured Schatten norm regularization, in: Proceedings of NeurIPS, 2013, pp. 1331–1339.

[76] L.R. Tucker, Implications of factor analysis of three-way matrices for measurement of change, in: Problems in Measuring Change, University of Wisconsin Press, 1963, pp. 122–137.

[77] A. Uschmajew, B. Vandereycken, Greedy rank updates combined with Riemannian descent methods for low-rank optimization, in: Proceedings of International Conference on Sampling Theory and Applications, 2015, pp. 420–424.

[78] T. Valkonen, K. Bredies, F. Knoll, Total generalized variation in diffusion tensor imaging, SIAM Journal on Imaging Sciences 6 (1) (2013) 487–525.

[79] P. Van Overschee, B. De Moor, Subspace algorithms for the stochastic identification problem, in: Proceedings of IEEE Conference on Decision and Control, 1991, pp. 1321–1326.

[80] W. Wang, V. Aggarwal, S. Aeron, Efficient low rank tensor ring completion, in: Proceedings of ICCV, 2017, pp. 5697–5705.

[81] Y. Xu, R. Hao, W. Yin, Z. Su, Parallel matrix factorization for low-rank tensor completion, Inverse Problems and Imaging 9 (2) (2015).

[82] T. Yokota, A. Cichocki, Multilinear tensor rank estimation via sparse Tucker decomposition, in: Proceedings of the Joint 7th International Conference on Soft Computing and Intelligent Systems (SCIS) and 15th International Symposium on Advanced Intelligent Systems (ISIS), IEEE, 2014, pp. 478–483.

[83] T. Yokota, A. Cichocki, A fast automatic rank determination algorithm for noisy low-rank matrix completion, in: Proceedings of APSIPA ASC, 2015, pp. 43–46.

[84] T. Yokota, A. Cichocki, Tensor completion via functional smooth component deflation, in: Proceedings of ICASSP, IEEE, 2016, pp. 2514–2518.

[85] T. Yokota, B. Erem, S. Guler, S.K. Warfield, H. Hontani, Missing slice recovery for tensors using a low-rank model in embedded space, in: Proceedings of CVPR, 2018, pp. 8251–8259.

[86] T. Yokota, H. Hontani, An efficient method for adapting step-size parameters of primal-dual hybrid gradient method in application to total variation regularization, in: Proceedings of APSIPA ASC, 2017, pp. 973–979.

[87] T. Yokota, H. Hontani, Simultaneous visual data completion and denoising based on tensor rank and total variation minimization and its primal-dual splitting algorithm, in: Proceedings of CVPR, 2017, pp. 3732–3740.

[88] T. Yokota, H. Hontani, Tensor completion with shift-invariant cosine bases, in: Proceedings of APSIPA ASC, IEEE, 2018, pp. 1325–1333.

[89] T. Yokota, H. Hontani, Simultaneous tensor completion and denoising by noise inequality constrained convex optimization, IEEE Access 7 (2019) 15669–15682.

[90] T. Yokota, H. Hontani, Q. Zhao, A. Cichocki, Manifold modeling in embedded space: an interpretable alternative to deep image prior, IEEE Transactions on Neural Networks and Learning Systems (2020), https://doi.org/10.1109/TNNLS.2020.3037923, pre-printed.

[91] T. Yokota, N. Lee, A. Cichocki, Robust multilinear tensor rank estimation using higher order singular value decomposition and information criteria, IEEE Transactions on Signal Processing 65 (5) (2017) 1196–1206.

[92] T. Yokota, R. Zdunek, A. Cichocki, Y. Yamashita, Smooth nonnegative matrix and tensor factorizations for robust multi-way data analysis, Signal Processing 113 (2015) 234–249.

[93] T. Yokota, Q. Zhao, A. Cichocki, Smooth PARAFAC decomposition for tensor completion, IEEE Transactions on Signal Processing 64 (20) (2016) 5423–5436.

[94] L. Yuan, J. Cao, X. Zhao, Q. Wu, Q. Zhao, Higher-dimension tensor completion via low-rank tensor ring decomposition, in: Proceedings of APSIPA ASC, IEEE, 2018, pp. 1071–1076.

[95] L. Yuan, C. Li, D. Mandic, J. Cao, Q. Zhao, Tensor ring decomposition with rank minimization on latent space: an efficient approach for tensor completion, in: Proceedings of AAAI, vol. 33, 2019, pp. 9151–9158.

[96] R. Zdunek, Approximation of feature vectors in nonnegative matrix factorization with Gaussian radial basis functions, in: Neural Information Processing, in: LNCS, vol. 7663, Springer, 2012, pp. 616–623.

[97] R. Zdunek, A. Cichocki, T. Yokota, B-spline smoothing of feature vectors in nonnegative matrix factorization, in: Artificial Intelligence and Soft Computing, in: LNCS, vol. 8468, Springer, 2014, pp. 72–81.

[98] J. Zhang, D. Zhao, W. Gao, Group-based sparse representation for image restoration, IEEE Transactions on Image Processing 23 (8) (2014) 3336–3351.

[99] Z. Zhang, G. Ely, S. Aeron, N. Hao, M. Kilmer, Novel methods for multilinear data completion and de-noising based on tensor-SVD, in: Proceedings of CVPR, 2014, pp. 3842–3849.

[100] Q. Zhao, L. Zhang, A. Cichocki, Bayesian CP factorization of incomplete tensors with automatic rank determination, IEEE Transactions on Pattern Analysis and Machine Intelligence 37 (9) (2015) 1751–1763.

[101] Q. Zhao, G. Zhou, S. Xie, L. Zhang, A. Cichocki, Tensor ring decomposition, arXiv preprint, arXiv:1606.05535, 2016.

[102] M. Zhu, T. Chan, An Efficient Primal-Dual Hybrid Gradient Algorithm for Total Variation Image Restoration, UCLA CAM Report 2008, pp. 08–34.

Tensors for neuroimaging

12

A review on applications of tensors to unravel the mysteries of the brain

Aybüke Erol and Borbála Hunyadi

*Circuits and Systems, Department of Microelectronics, Delft University of Technology, Delft,
The Netherlands*

CONTENTS

12.1 Introduction

Understanding how the brain works has always been a challenge for humankind, for both cognitive and clinical purposes. Neurosurgery is believed to be the oldest medical specialty, dating back to ancient times [1]. Today, neuroscience combines the advances in neuroimaging technology and signal processing, and while the mystery of the brain keeps being unraveled, we have achieved many breakthroughs in diagnostic tools and treatments of neurological or psychosomatic diseases.

In fact, the relationship between neuroscience and engineering technologies is two-sided. Certainly, engineering is involved in every aspect of neuroimaging, and in the development of diagnostic tools and medical care systems. However, understanding of the brain's anatomy and functioning has also inspired the making of such engineering tools, and even more. The most straightforward, yet powerful example of this phenomenon is given by artificial neural networks, which mimic the human nervous system for artificial intelligence tasks. Artificial neural networks are used in various fields, including medicine, nanotechnology, telecommunications, autonomous vehicles, art, and finance [2].

Overall, modeling of the structure and function of the brain gains more and more attention every day. In this review, we look into where tensors stand on the way to understanding the mechanisms behind brain function. The main motivation for the use of tensors to model brain signals follows from the fact that brain signals are inherently large-scale and can hold various modes such as time, space, frequency, channel, experimental condition, modality, trial, and subject. The interactions across different modes can only be fully captured by expanding the order of simple space-time representations, and as such call for tensor-based (multiway) methods instead of matrix-based (two-way) methods. Tensors are increasingly used in a broad range of neuroimaging applications, from filling in missing or noisy recordings to feature extraction and classification for brain–computer interfaces (BCIs).

The rest of this chapter is organized as follows. First, fundamentals of the most common neuroimaging modalities are provided. Each neuroimaging modality grasps the brain data based on different biophysical principles (such as electrical or magnetic outcomes of neuronal transmission) and presents them in different fashions for different objectives (such as temporal evolution of brain images in order to reveal the functioning of neural circuits, unlike structural neuroimaging, which focuses on the brain anatomy). These fundamentals are necessary to understand the nature of the input data for accurate modeling and further processing.

Next, the convenience of using tensor-based modeling of neural signals and images is discussed. This section focuses on the multiway nature and the complex organization of the brain and explains how tensors essentially fit brain data representations.

This is followed by a section highlighting the most common tensor decomposition structures, which will be referred to in the upcoming sections. These structures include canonical polyadic (CP) decomposition, Tucker decomposition, and block term decomposition (BTD), together with their commonly used variants.

Subsequently, various applications of tensors in the neuroimaging literature are presented. This section is organized in parallel with an intuitive ordering of the main steps in data analysis pipelines, ranging from preprocessing strategies (such as denoising and dimensionality reduction) to classification of brain data for the purpose of BCIs. In the end, a summary of the considered tensor-based methods is provided, along with the most common practical challenges that are encountered while using these methods. Several strategies that can be used to tackle the presented challenges are also mentioned.

Last but not least, we point out future challenges that await medical technology and the widespread adoption of tensor tools to address these challenges.

12.2 Neuroimaging modalities

A diagram of main neuroimaging modalities is provided in Fig. 12.1. This review will investigate these modalities from the perspective of how tensors can be useful to capture the multiway nature of acquired brain signals for various applications.

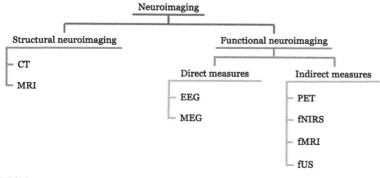

FIGURE 12.1

Categorization of neuroimaging modalities.

The area of neuroimaging can be divided into two main fields, namely structural and functional neuroimaging [3]. Structural imaging deals with the analysis of anatomical properties of the brain and is useful for diagnosing intracranial lesions such as tumors. The earliest technique used for imaging the brain structure is computed tomography (CT), which utilizes X-rays to visualize brain slices [4]. Later, magnetic resonance imaging (MRI), which uses powerful magnets instead of ionizing radiation, has replaced CT, offering greater contrast between normal and abnormal brain tissue [5]. There exist several variants of MRI such as magnetic resonance spectroscopic imaging (MRSI), which includes an extra dimension for spectroscopic information besides the MRI data. Other variants include T1- (and T2-)weighted MRI, perfusion-weighted imaging (PWI), diffusion-weighted imaging (DWI), and diffusion tensor imaging (DTI), which further enhance the contrast in MR images by incorporating the effect of tissue relaxation times, the hemodynamic status of tissues, tissue water diffusion rates, and tissue water anisotropies, respectively [6,7].

On the other hand, functional imaging is used to identify brain areas and processes that are associated with performing a particular cognitive or behavioral task. Information flow in the brain while processing a task is controlled by the firing of neurons via both electrical and chemical signals [8]. Provided in Fig. 12.2 is an illustration showing the effects of neuronal activity together with the modalities that make use of those effects for neuroimaging.

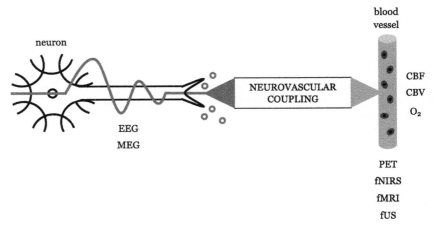

FIGURE 12.2

Functional neuroimaging modalities, which are discussed in this review in detail, are shown in relation to neurovascular coupling. Neurovascular coupling describes the relationship between neuronal activity (which takes place using both electrical and chemical signals) and the resulting changes in blood flow. EEG and MEG directly measure neuronal activity whereas PET, fNIRS, fMRI, and fUS provide an indirect measure through neurovascular coupling.

The neuronal activity of the brain can be recorded directly by electroencephalography (EEG) and magnetoencephalography (MEG) in the form of aggregated postsynaptic potentials of larger neuronal populations. EEG is the oldest functional brain imaging technique, with the first reported human EEG dating back to 1929. In EEG, the electrical activity of neurons is detected via electrodes placed along or below (intracranial EEG or electrocorticography [ECoG]) the scalp [9]. On the other hand, MEG records the magnetic field produced by this electrical activity using magnetometers, which are most commonly selected as superconducting quantum unit interference devices [10].

The indirect measures of neuronal activity rely on a phenomenon known as neurovascular coupling. When a brain region becomes active, it starts to consume more glucose and oxygen. These changes are met by an increasing blood flow to the region, known as the hemodynamic response. Neurovascular coupling describes this interaction between local neuronal activity and cerebral blood flow (CBF) [11] and forms the basis of many functional neuroimaging techniques including positron emission tomography (PET), functional near-infrared spectroscopy (fNIRS), functional magnetic resonance imaging (fMRI), and functional ultrasound (fUS) (Fig. 12.2).

PET measures the alterations in glucose levels in response to metabolic activity by injection of radioactive tracers to the brain which are attached to glucose

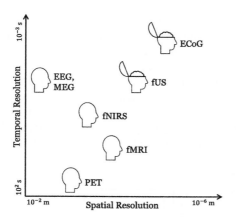

FIGURE 12.3

Functional neuroimaging modalities with their temporal and spatial resolutions, where an opened skull refers to invasive imaging [16].

and absorbed by the bloodstream [12]. Meanwhile, the changes in oxygenation of hemoglobin in red blood cells can be detected by fNIRS and fMRI. In fNIRS, near-infrared light is used to track hemodynamic changes based on the differential optical properties of hemoglobin states [13]. The magnetic properties of hemoglobin are affected as well by the amount of oxygen that the cells carry, resulting in the blood oxygen level-dependent (BOLD) signal detected by fMRI via electromagnets. Since the early 1990s, fMRI has come to dominate brain mapping research due to its non-invasive nature (requiring no injections or surgery) and high spatial resolution [14]. Nevertheless, fUS, a recently developed neuroimaging technique, is able to image the brain with higher spatiotemporal resolution than fMRI, yet at lower cost. In fUS imaging, ultrasound waves are transmitted to the brain through a cranial window and the strength of the reflected waves is directly proportional to the number of moving red blood cells in the local region, i.e., the local CBF or cerebral blood volume (CBV) [15]. The temporal and spatial resolutions of the aforementioned functional neuroimaging modalities are compared in Fig. 12.3.

12.3 **Multidimensionality of the brain**

Brain activity exists and spreads in time and space. Hence, temporal and/or spatial modes follow straightforwardly while describing brain data [17]. In structural neuroimaging, the objective is to only visualize brain anatomy; therefore, the collected brain data have only spatial information. These visualizations can be brought in pixels of 2D slices or voxels of 3D volumes. On the other hand, in functional neuroimaging, the functioning of the brain is to be monitored, which means that temporal information is involved as well as spatial information. In the case of EEG and MEG, spatial information is depicted by channel locations instead of pixels or voxels.

Many studies have also considered the frequency mode and worked on space-time-frequency models of neural signals [89]. Furthermore, the increasing use of multiple subjects, experimental conditions, modalities, or trials have naturally introduced other modes in brain data representations. Such multiway models are naturally fit to multidimensional arrays, named as tensors. Fig. 12.4 shows several examples of third-order tensor models (although higher orders are also possible, only third-order tensors are given for visualization) used in the neuroimaging literature.

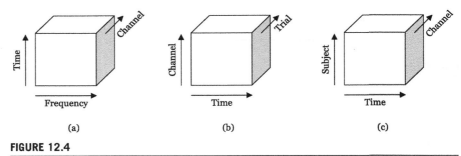

FIGURE 12.4

Examples of third-order tensor representations used in neuroimaging literature. The models provided in (a), (b), and (c) are utilized in [89], [43], and [18], respectively.

It is possible and quite common to unfold such modes of a tensor to obtain a matrix, so that well-established decomposition methods that are set in the 2D framework such as principal component analysis (PCA) or independent component analysis (ICA) can be utilized. PCA is a technique to identify modes of variation in a data matrix by defining orthogonal subspaces of the data. The most common tool to perform PCA is singular value decomposition (SVD). SVD uniquely decomposes an input matrix to its orthogonal singular (i.e., basis) vectors, which are ordered from most to least significant in terms of how much variance in the data matrix they account for. Hence, PCA can be obtained by truncation of the less important singular vectors from the original SVD subspaces. On the other hand, the goal of ICA is to find a set of statistically independent basis vectors whose linear combination (i.e., the mixing matrix) returns the data matrix.

However, both methods require any extra mode, such as subjects, to be represented in the input data matrix by concatenation in time or space. Such matricization of a tensor causes underestimation of existing interactions between the folded modes [19] and neglects variations over the unfolded mode, i.e., time courses or spatial maps that are common across the new modes (e.g., subjects) are obtained. Group ICA methods can partially address this problem by later predicting the individual maps or courses using back-projection, but the multidimensional structure of data is not reflected in the estimation stage itself [20]. In addition, the assumptions made by PCA and ICA, i.e., orthogonality and independence, respectively, may be physically irrelevant [90].

On the contrary, there is a trend to tensorize data that were originally in matrix form. For instance, fusing cumulant information with the covariance of the measurement matrix and stacking several time-lagged covariance matrices have been shown to improve ICA results [21]. Such tensorization, or imposing a priori information on neural data [103], leads to decompositions that exhibit certain structures, such as in the form of Hankel [103] or Toeplitz [81] blocks. These structures often change across modes and/or factors, which is much easier to incorporate using tensor models.

Last but not least, many conventional approaches require an a priori selection of a region of interest along one or more modes, such as a time window [22], an anatomical area [23], or a frequency band [24], to be examined. On the other hand, tensors can handle the whole dimensionality of the brain and can be applied in a completely data-driven manner.

To summarize, tensors are the natural representations of neural signals, considering both the way they are acquired and the complexity of brain activity itself. As such, tensors also facilitate drawing neurophysiologically meaningful conclusions [25]. Accompanied by the escalating development of mathematical tools to perform tensor-based analyses, the ability of tensors to fairly model and process the large-scale and multidimensional neural data favors the utilization of tensors in neuroimaging applications.

12.4 **Tensor decomposition structures**

As one of the most important tools in 2D analysis, SVD (along with PCA) has been at the core of data analysis since more than a century ago. Using SVD, any matrix $\mathbf{X}$ can be factorized as follows [26]:

$$\mathbf{X} = \mathbf{U}\boldsymbol{\Sigma}\mathbf{V}^{\mathrm{H}}, \tag{12.1}$$

where $\mathbf{U}$ and $\mathbf{V}$ are unitary matrices whose columns stand for the left and right singular vectors of $\mathbf{X}$, respectively, and $\boldsymbol{\Sigma}$ is a diagonal matrix. The diagonal elements of $\boldsymbol{\Sigma}$, denoted by $\sigma_i \geq 0$, appear in decreasing order and are called the singular values of $\mathbf{X}$. If $\mathbf{X}$ is real, $\mathbf{U}$ and $\mathbf{V}$ are real orthogonal matrices. Eq. (12.1) can also be expressed using the outer product as follows:

$$\mathbf{X} = \sum_i \sigma_i \mathbf{u}_i \circ \mathbf{v}_i, \tag{12.2}$$

where $\mathbf{u}_i$ and $\mathbf{v}_i$ show the i-th column of $\mathbf{U}$ and $\mathbf{V}$, respectively.

SVD is used in all areas of science, engineering, and statistics [27]. However, as mentioned in the previous section, reducing the dimensionality of a multiway array by unfolding causes a loss of information and variance over the unfolded mode(s). Therefore, tensor decomposition methods are necessary for analyzing multiway data.

The goal of tensor decomposition is to approximate an original input tensor using a smaller number of parameters by expressing it in terms of lower-dimensional subspaces. This section provides a short introduction to the main tensor decomposition structures that are different generalizations of matrix SVD to tensors and which will also be referred to in the later parts of this chapter. These structures are CP decomposition (CPD), also known as CANDECOMP/PARAFAC analysis, Tucker decomposition, BTD, and their commonly used variants. In order to be able to formulate these decompositions, various product operations defined on tensors are also presented.

12.4.1 Product operations for tensors

There are four product operations defined on tensors which are essential to fully acknowledge the tensor decompositions, as well as many other computations in the tensor framework that are used in various applications, as will be seen in the later sections.

- The outer product of N vectors $\mathbf{u}^{(1)}, \mathbf{u}^{(2)}, ..., \mathbf{u}^{(N)}$ produces a rank-1 tensor $\mathcal{X} \in \mathbb{R}^{I_1 \times I_2 \times ... \times I_N}$ denoted as $\mathcal{X} = \mathbf{u}^{(1)} \circ \mathbf{u}^{(2)} \circ ... \circ \mathbf{u}^{(N)}$. The elements of $\mathcal{X}$ are given by

$$x_{i_1 i_2 ... i_N} = u_{i_1}^{(1)} u_{i_2}^{(2)} ... u_{i_N}^{(N)}. \tag{12.3}$$

- The n-mode (matrix) product of a tensor $\mathcal{X} \in \mathbb{R}^{I_1 \times I_2 \times ... \times I_N}$ and a matrix $\mathbf{U} \in \mathbb{R}^{J \times I_n}$ is given by a tensor $\mathcal{Z} = \mathcal{X} \times_n \mathbf{U}$, whose elements satisfy the following [28]:

$$z_{i_1 ... i_{n-1} j \, i_{n+1} ... i_N} = \sum_{i_n=1}^{I_n} x_{i_1 i_2 ... i_N} u_{j i_n}. \tag{12.4}$$

- The generalization of the n-mode product to two tensors is called a tensor contraction. While an n-mode product is computed along one common dimension (I_n) of a given matrix and tensor, two tensors may share multiple common dimensions, along which contraction is defined. Formally, if two tensors carry common dimension(s) $J_1, J_2, ..., J_M$ such that $\mathcal{X} \in \mathbb{R}^{I_1 \times I_2 \times ... \times I_N \times J_1 \times J_2 \times ... \times J_M}$ and $\mathcal{Y} \in \mathbb{R}^{J_1 \times J_2 \times ... \times J_M \times K_1 \times K_2 \times ... \times K_P}$, then their tensor contraction over the common dimensions $\mathcal{Z} = \mathcal{X} \bullet_{\{J_1, J_2, ..., J_M\}} \mathcal{Y}$ gives

$$z_{i_1 ... i_N k_1 ... k_p} = \sum_{j_1 ... j_M=1}^{J_1 ... J_M} x_{i_1 ... i_N j_1 ... j_M} y_{j_1 ... j_M k_1 ... k_p}. \tag{12.5}$$

- The tensor–tensor product (or t-product) $\mathcal{Z} = \mathcal{X} \star \mathcal{Y}$, $\mathcal{Z} \in \mathbb{R}^{I \times L \times K}$ of two 3D tensors $\mathcal{X} \in \mathbb{R}^{I \times J \times K}$ and $\mathcal{Y} \in \mathbb{R}^{J \times L \times K}$ is defined using convolution as follows [124]:

$$\mathbf{Z}_k = \sum_{k'=1}^{K} \mathbf{X}_{k'} \bullet_{\{J\}} \mathbf{Y}_{k-k'}, \tag{12.6}$$

where $(.)_k = (.)_{::k}$ denotes the k-th frontal slice of the corresponding tensor.

12.4.2 Canonical polyadic decomposition

CPD expresses an input tensor $\mathcal{X}$ of size $I_1 \times I_2 \times \ldots \times I_N$ as a sum of R rank-1 terms (Fig. 12.5):

$$\mathcal{X} \approx \sum_{r=1}^{R} \mathbf{u}_r^{(1)} \circ \mathbf{u}_r^{(2)} \circ \ldots \circ \mathbf{u}_r^{(N)}, \tag{12.7}$$

where R gives the rank of the tensor and each term $\mathbf{u}_r^{(n)}$, $n = 1, 2 \ldots N$, is a column vector of length I_n and gives rise to the factor matrices $\mathbf{U}^{(n)} = [\mathbf{u}_1^{(n)} \ldots \mathbf{u}_R^{(n)}]$.

CPD can be viewed as an extension of SVD (Eq. (12.2)) to higher orders, with the difference that factor matrices are not necessarily orthogonal [29]. CPD is unique under mild constraints [30].

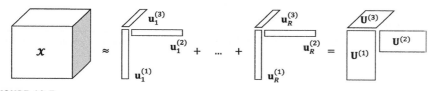

FIGURE 12.5

CPD of a 3D tensor.

For 3D arrays, CPD can also be expressed in matrix notation at each slice $\mathbf{X}_k$ of $\mathcal{X}$ as follows:

$$\mathbf{X}_k \approx \mathbf{U}^{(1)} \mathbf{D}_k (\mathbf{U}^{(2)})^{\mathrm{T}}, \tag{12.8}$$

where $\mathbf{D}_k$ is a diagonal matrix whose diagonal is composed of k-th row elements of $\mathbf{U}^{(3)}$ (Fig. 12.6(a)).

PARAFAC2 is an extension of CPD that is able to represent both regular and irregular tensors which are collections of matrices with changing size along one of the modes (Fig. 12.6(b)). CPD assumes one factor matrix along each mode, meaning that the same set of factor matrices is valid across all slices of a tensor, whereas PARAFAC2 relaxes this constraint by allowing variation across one mode [78]. PARAFAC2 factorizes the input tensor $\mathcal{X}$ at each slice k as $\mathbf{X}_k \approx \mathbf{U}_k^{(1)} \mathbf{D}_k (\mathbf{U}^{(2)})^{\mathrm{T}}$, which is unique under mild constraints [31].

12.4.3 Tucker decomposition

Tucker decomposition (Fig. 12.7) approximates $\mathcal{X}$ as

$$\mathcal{X} \approx \mathcal{S} \times_1 \mathbf{U}^{(1)} \times_2 \mathbf{U}^{(2)} \times_3 \cdots \times_N \mathbf{U}^{(N)}, \tag{12.9}$$

where $\mathcal{S}$ is a core tensor of size $R_1 \times R_2 \times \cdots \times R_N$ ($R_n \leq I_n$, $\forall n$) and each factor $\mathbf{U}^{(n)}$ is a matrix of size $I_n \times R_n$. Note that Tucker decomposition becomes equivalent to CPD when the core tensor $\mathcal{S}$ is diagonal.

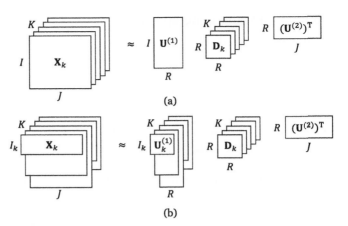

(a)

(b)

FIGURE 12.6

(a) CPD of a regular 3D tensor and (b) PARAFAC2 decomposition of an irregular 3D tensor, both shown in matrix notation over frontal tensor slices [32].

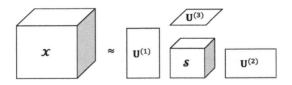

FIGURE 12.7

Tucker decomposition of a 3D tensor.

Referring back to Eq. (12.1), Tucker decomposition with orthogonal factor matrices and an all-orthogonal core tensor corresponds to a multilinear SVD (MLSVD), also known as higher-order SVD (HOSVD) [33]. Owing to the orthogonality conditions, MLSVD is essentially unique [34].

Furthermore, if an input tensor admits to an MLSVD with a diagonal core (i.e., when $\mathcal{S}$ is a diagonal core tensor and factor matrices $\mathbf{U}^{(n)}$ are orthogonal), a decomposition known as tensor SVD is obtained. In the case of 3D tensors, tensor SVD shares the same form as matrix SVD with tensor factors such that

$$\mathcal{X} = \mathcal{U} \star \mathcal{S} \star \mathcal{V}^{\mathrm{T}}, \tag{12.10}$$

where $\mathcal{U}$ and $\mathcal{V}$ are orthogonal tensors and $\mathcal{S}$ is diagonal at each frontal slice (Fig. 12.8) [35].

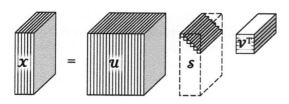

FIGURE 12.8

Tensor SVD of a 3D tensor [36].

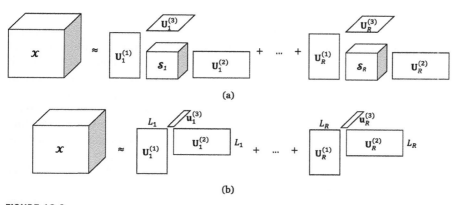

FIGURE 12.9

(a) BTD and (b) rank-$(L_r, L_r, 1)$ BTD of a 3D tensor.

12.4.4 Block term decomposition

BTD can be interpreted as a generalization of CPD where factors can be higher-order tensors (Fig. 12.9(a)) as follows:

$$\mathcal{X} \approx \sum_{r=1}^{R} \mathcal{S}_r \times_1 \mathbf{U}_r^{(1)} \times_2 \mathbf{U}_r^{(2)} \times_3 \cdots \times_N \mathbf{U}_r^{(N)}. \tag{12.11}$$

A special case of BTD, known as rank-$(L_r, L_r, 1)$ BTD, decomposes a 3D input tensor into multilinear rank-$(L_r, L_r, 1)$ terms (Fig. 12.9(b)). The rank-$(L_r, L_r, 1)$ BTD achieves a more general low-rank structure compared to CPD while preserving uniqueness under relatively mild conditions [37].

12.5 Applications of tensors in neuroimaging

This section gives an overview of successful tensor-based analysis techniques in neuroimaging studies. It will become evident that tensor structures and decompositions can be useful at any given stage of the data processing pipeline. First, various preprocessing problems are discussed. Images may be corrupted; therefore, filling in missing data (Section 12.5.1), denoising, and artifact removal may be necessary. Furthermore, dimensionality reduction may be applied in order to reduce the computational complexity of subsequent processing steps (Section 12.5.2). Once the images are conditioned, image segmentation (Section 12.5.3) may be applied in order to select areas of interest (e.g., a tumor) or reject areas of no interest (e.g., skull or ventricles). When multiple images need to be compared or processed together – such as in a longitudinal study, tracking the evolution of a patient using repeated images over time—these need to be coregistered first (Section 12.5.4).

While the preprocessing steps mentioned above are important both in structural and functional imaging, certain data processing problems are specific for functional imaging. Functional neuroimaging techniques record a time series at different spatial locations, and they typically capture various sources of brain and other physiological activity, as well as noise. Source separation (Section 12.5.5) techniques are crucial to disentangle the activity of these sources. In many applications the ultimate goal is to recognize a specific activity of interest (e.g., the occurrence of an epileptic seizure) and to localize it, as discussed in Section 12.5.6. In other contexts, understanding the global behavior of the brain can be of interest. Structural connectivity analysis aims to establish how the anatomically distinct brain regions are physically interconnected. Functional connectivity analysis, on the other hand, explores the statistical interdependence between the activity time courses of different anatomical regions (Section 12.5.7). These interdependencies may provide insight into the intrinsic organization of the brain activity and how distinct brain regions cooperate. Functional connectivity may be studied in the resting state or examined during task execution. In the latter case—in a well-controlled experiment—the known time course of the task paradigm can be used as a model for the expected brain activity. Then, regression analysis (Section 12.5.8) can reveal if the model explains the observed brain activity, to what extent, and in which brain regions exactly. The ultimate goal of (clinical) neuroimaging is assisting diagnosis: distinguishing between healthy and pathological images or activity. To this end, Section 12.5.9 introduces tensor techniques for feature extraction and classification.

Besides the listed applications, tensors are excessively used in data fusion to handle large-scale data acquired from different modalities. Particularly, fusion of EEG and fMRI has been very prevalent in neuroscience due to the high temporal resolution of the first and high spatial resolution of the latter. Therefore, tensor-based fusion methods of EEG and fMRI are investigated in detail separately in Chapter 11 (Coupled tensor decompositions for data fusion).

12.5.1 Filling in missing data

Estimation of missing data is essential in many signal and image processing applications arising from any kind of information loss or errors in data collection. For instance, in the concept of neural signals, a sensing component such as an electrode might become loose, the signal may become saturated due to large movements, or data may be lost during transfer. These problems may lead to missing fibers or random missing entries throughout the tensor, respectively (Fig. 12.10). Tensor completion methods aim at filling such missing entries of incomplete tensors.

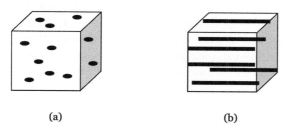

(a)   (b)

FIGURE 12.10

An example tensor with (a) random missing entries and (b) missing channels [43].

The first application of tensor completion on neuroimaging data is proposed in [38]. The authors reformulate the CANDECOMP/PARAFAC (CP) model for EEG data as a weighted least-squares problem where only the known entries are modeled. The developed algorithm, named CP-weighted optimization (CP-WOPT), expresses the weighted CP formulation as

$$f_{\mathcal{W}}(\mathbf{U}^{(1)}, \mathbf{U}^{(2)}, \mathbf{U}^{(3)}) = \sum_{i=1}^{I}\sum_{j=1}^{J}\sum_{k=1}^{K}\left\{w_{ijk}\left(x_{ijk} - \sum_{r=1}^{R} u_{ir}^{(1)} u_{jr}^{(2)} u_{kr}^{(3)}\right)\right\}^2, \quad (12.12)$$

where $\mathcal{X}$ shows the EEG tensor with factor matrices $\mathbf{U}^{(1)}, \mathbf{U}^{(2)}$, and $\mathbf{U}^{(3)}$, i, j, and k denote the indices in the first, second, and third mode, respectively, of the corresponding tensor, and $\mathcal{W}$ is the weight tensor defined as

$$w_{ijk} = \begin{cases} 1 & \text{if } x_{ijk} \text{ is known,} \\ 0 & \text{if } x_{ijk} \text{ is missing.} \end{cases} \quad (12.13)$$

Finally, Eq. (12.12) is directly solved using first-order nonlinear optimization.

The authors test CP-WOPT on EEG data recorded during proprioceptive stimuli of the left and right hands of 14 subjects, making 28 measurement conditions in total. The constructed EEG tensor has three modes: *measurement condition*, *channel*, and *time-frequency*, which is obtained using continuous wavelet transform. Their results show that CP-WOPT can capture the underlying brain activity even when almost half of the electrodes are missing. Last but not least, CP-WOPT is noted to be much faster than its matrix- and tensor-based alternatives due to the fact that the missing entries are neglected in the cost function.

In CP-WOPT, the rank of the input tensor is assumed to be known, i.e., it has to be entered manually. In return, [39] states that a rising number of missing entries increases the chance of incorrect specification of the tensor rank, which results in deterioration of the performance of such tensor factorization schemes. Instead, the authors propose to model the input tensor as a combination of the true latent tensor (generated by tensor factorization with a low CP rank), sparse outliers, and isotropic Gaussian noise (Fig. 12.11) and determine the rank of the latent tensor automatically by minimizing the dimensionality of the latent space. This minimization corresponds to column-wise sparsity of factor matrices in each mode. Thus, sparsity inducing priors are employed over all unknown parameters. This way, all parameters, including the CP rank, are determined automatically under a Bayesian framework. This method is known as Bayesian CP factorization (BCPF). BCPF is used to recover EEG data with missing entries and denoise noisy MRI data in [40].

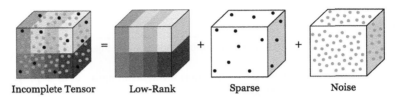

Incomplete Tensor   Low-Rank   Sparse   Noise

FIGURE 12.11

An incomplete tensor can be approximated as the summation of a low-rank tensor, sparse outliers, and isotropic noise [39].

In [41], the CP-WOPT is extended with rank regularization such that the proposed cost function becomes as follows:

$$\tilde{\mathcal{X}} = \arg\min_{\mathcal{Y}} \frac{1}{2}||(\mathcal{X} - \mathcal{Y}) * \mathcal{W}||_F^2 + \lambda||\mathcal{Y}||_*, \qquad (12.14)$$

where $\mathcal{W}$ is the binary weight tensor (Eq. (12.13)) that accounts for the missing entries, $||.||_*$ shows the nuclear norm operator, and $\lambda \geq 0$ is the rank controlling parameter. Simply put, Eq. (12.14) searches for a low-rank tensor $\tilde{\mathcal{X}}$ that has minimal distance to the original input tensor $\mathcal{X}$ over the available entries while achieving a low-rank structure via nuclear norm regularization.

The nuclear norm is used widely in optimization problems to search for low-rank solutions. In the case of a matrix, the nuclear norm becomes equivalent to the sum of its singular values, whereas the tensor nuclear norm is dependent on the choice of base field [42]. In [41], the authors define the nuclear norm of a third-order tensor $\mathcal{Y}$ based on CPD as

$$||\mathcal{Y}||_* = \min_{\{\mathbf{U}^{(1)}, \mathbf{U}^{(2)}, \mathbf{U}^{(3)}\}} \frac{1}{2}(||\mathbf{U}^{(1)}||_F^2 + ||\mathbf{U}^{(2)}||_F^2 + ||\mathbf{U}^{(3)}||_F^2) \qquad (12.15)$$

$$\text{subject to } \mathcal{Y} = \sum_{r=1}^{R} \mathbf{u}_r^{(1)} \circ \mathbf{u}_r^{(2)} \circ \mathbf{u}_r^{(3)}.$$

Expressing the CPD of $\mathcal{Y}$ with unit norm terms such that $\mathbf{a}_r = \mathbf{u}_r^{(1)}/||\mathbf{u}_r^{(1)}||$, $\mathbf{b}_r = \mathbf{u}_r^{(2)}/||\mathbf{u}_r^{(2)}||$, and $\mathbf{c}_r = \mathbf{u}_r^{(3)}/||\mathbf{u}_r^{(3)}||$ gives

$$\mathcal{Y} = \sum_{r=1}^{R} \gamma_r (\mathbf{a}_r \circ \mathbf{b}_r \circ \mathbf{c}_r) \qquad (12.16)$$

with weights $\gamma_r = ||\mathbf{a}_r|| \, ||\mathbf{b}_r|| \, ||\mathbf{c}_r||$, $r = 1 \ldots R$.

Finally, the completion problem can be reformulated as follows:

$$\tilde{\mathcal{X}} = \underset{\{\mathcal{Y}, \gamma, \mathbf{a}_r, \mathbf{b}_r, \mathbf{c}_r\}}{\arg\min} \frac{1}{2}||(\mathcal{X} - \mathcal{Y}) * \mathcal{W}||_F^2 + \frac{\lambda}{2}||\gamma||_{2/3}^{2/3} \qquad (12.17)$$

$$\text{subject to } \mathcal{Y} = \sum_{r=1}^{R} \gamma_r (\mathbf{a}_r \circ \mathbf{b}_r \circ \mathbf{c}_r).$$

The cost function provided above controls the tensor rank by inducing sparsity on the amplitudes of its rank-1 components. These priors are introduced on the tensor factors via a Bayesian framework. The proposed method is observed to outperform CP-WOPT when tested on corrupted 3D MR images.

In [43], the authors utilize tensor completion to fill in corrupted EEG data, which might originate from a high impedance between electrodes and scalp, motion, eye blinks, and so on. In other words, noisy measurements are treated as missing samples or unknowns, which are later inferred using a tensor approach. They model the EEG data as a tensor with modes *channel*, *time*, and *trial* and apply the following tensor completion algorithms: CP-WOPT, BCPF, 3D patch-based tensor completion [44], and high-accuracy low-rank tensor completion [45]. They evaluate the performance of the aforementioned completion methods by testing the classification accuracy of imagined movement in a BCI experiment with corruptions and missing channels. All four algorithms are reported to increase the classification accuracy when compared to the conventional approach of average interpolation across trials.

12.5.2 Denoising, artifact removal, and dimensionality reduction

Denoising, artifact removal, and dimensionality reduction algorithms are prerequisites to a majority of signal processing applications. An omnipresent tool in this context for matrix data is SVD, as it can capture signals and noise in different subspaces. Recognizing and rejecting the noise subspace achieves all above objectives. Therefore, multilinear extensions of SVD—MLSVD and CPD—are natural methods of choice in the case of tensor data. Indeed, many methods covered in this review intrinsically denoise or reduce the volume of input data by low-rank approximating them or by separating its components of interest from background data via various tensor decomposition techniques. Nevertheless, this section will be dedicated to algorithms that solely aim at denoising, artifact removal, or dimensionality reduction.

To begin with, different imaging modalities are prone to different types of artifacts. For instance, MRSI data are often corrupted by residual water, EEG signals may be corrupted with ocular artifacts, while functional images are seriously distorted by head motion. These phenomena call for custom solutions, especially when it comes to identifying the noise subspace. Some examples are outlined below.

Residual water in MRSI accounts for a large variance in the data and should be suppressed to accurately assign brain metabolite signals [46]. In [47], the purification of MRS images from residual water is regarded as a source separation problem. To this end, first the MRSI input tensor $\mathcal{X}$ is compressed via truncated MLSVD, leading to a core tensor $\mathcal{S}$ and factor matrices $\mathbf{U}^{(n)}$ as given in Eq. (12.9). Truncated MLSVD is used to approximate $\mathcal{X}$ as a smaller tensor $\mathcal{S}$, whose size R_n is smaller than the actual column rank of $\mathcal{X}_{(n)}$ along one or more modes (n) [28]. Next, CPD is applied on the compressed core tensor $\mathcal{S}$. Finally, the components whose resonance frequencies (as given by MRSI) are outside the region of interest are marked as water components. As expected, such a twofold procedure with MLSVD and CPD is observed to be particularly beneficial when the input tensor is large.

EEG signals can be seriously distorted by ocular artifacts, i.e., large changes in the electric field caused by the movement of the eyeball which acts as a dipole [48]. Assuming that the ocular artifacts and brain activity are independent, [49] proposes a tensor decomposition scheme to automatically remove these artifacts. As the cumulants of such independent sources lead to a superdiagonal tensor [50], [49] diagonalizes the fourth-order EEG cumulant tensor through CPD. The extracted components are thresholded in terms of their kurtosis values in order to automatically identify the ocular artifacts to be removed.

Like many neuroimaging modalities, fNIRS data are prone to artifacts caused by relative motion between the scalp and fNIRS optical fibers [51]. For removal of motion artifacts, [52,53] apply CPD to 3D fNIRS tensors with modes *space*, *time*, and *wavelength* (accounting for the different wavelengths used in fNIRS for absorption of both oxygenated and deoxygenated hemoglobin). Similarly, [54] uses CPD on 3D water diffusion maps of DT images in order to extract only the components of interest that correspond to major fiber orientations.

The approaches described above consider the existence of undesired artifact components in data, which can be even more powerful than the activities of interest [46]. Therefore, after decomposing the input tensor into its components, some of these components (that point to artifacts) are removed either manually or automatically. However, tensor decomposition techniques can also be used to denoise an input tensor by finding a low-rank approximation of it, without explicitly rejecting a portion of the extracted components. For example, [55] proposes a method to jointly reconstruct and denoise PET images via low-rank approximating a PET feature tensor $\mathcal{X}$ using tensor nuclear norm regularization:

$$\tilde{\mathcal{X}} = \underset{\mathcal{Y}}{\arg\min} \frac{1}{2} ||(\mathcal{X} - \mathcal{Y})||_{\mathrm{F}}^2 + \lambda ||\mathcal{Y}||_*, \tag{12.18}$$

where $\mathcal{Y}$ can be decomposed using tensor SVD (Eq. (12.10)) and λ controls the nuclear norm regularization. The authors use an intuitive approach [56] based on tensor SVD to define the tensor nuclear norm:

$$||\mathcal{Y}||_* = \sum_{r=1}^{R} s_{rr1}, \tag{12.19}$$

where R defines the rank. This way, a closed-form solution is obtained for reconstruction. The proposed scheme is observed to accomplish more than mere denoising of PET data, providing enhancement to the reconstructed images by intensifying structural information.

Moreover, tensor decomposition methods can be used to reduce the dimensionality of input data without losing valuable information. Considering the remarkable performances achieved by deep learning methods in various signal processing applications over the past decade, dimensionality reduction becomes even more critical due to the curse of dimensionality of input training data. The curse of dimensionality refers to the fact that an increase in the dimensionality of input data will demand an exponentially growing storage space.

Particularly in medical image processing, convolutional neural networks (CNNs) have gained significant attention, which have the advantage of combining feature extraction and classification steps. To reduce the dimensionality of CNN inputs, [57] proposes a CPD-based framework for an input EEG tensor $\mathcal{X}$ with modes *time*, *frequency*, and *channel*.

First, CPD is applied on the input tensor producing the factor matrices $\mathbf{U}^{(1)}$, $\mathbf{U}^{(2)}$, and $\mathbf{U}^{(3)}$ along the modes *time*, *frequency*, and *channel*, respectively. In order to reduce the number of channels by only selecting the ones that are of interest, a projection matrix is defined as $\mathbf{P} = ((\mathbf{U}^{(3)})^{\mathsf{T}}\mathbf{U}^{(3)})^{-1}(\mathbf{U}^{(3)})^{\mathsf{T}}$. The new low-rank representation $\tilde{\mathcal{X}}$ of $\mathcal{X}$ is found by $\tilde{\mathcal{X}} = \mathcal{X} \times_3 \mathbf{P}$, which converts the original channel slices into superslices. The number of superslices is equal to the rank of CPD. Employing superslices does not only reduce the dimension of CNN training inputs, but also handles the artifacts and redundancies of the EEG signals. The proposed method is tested with various time-frequency transformations and CNN parameters. Compared to 1D and 2D state-of-the-art dimensionality reduction techniques including PCA, the proposed tensor-based framework is observed to perform better in terms of classification accuracy for seizure detection.

In parallel to the increasing interest towards dimensionality reduction methods that keep out the redundant parts of acquired data, a theory known as compressed sensing (CS) has emerged. Most neural signals exhibit a sparse representation naturally or in another domain. Using such sparse representations, CS techniques aim at directly sensing data in a compressed form. Conventionally, 1D or 2D sparsity bases are utilized to solve even higher-order problems. To make use of and preserve the high-dimensional structure in CS applications, [58] proposes MLSVD as a tensor sparsifying transform for 3D MRI data. More specifically, the authors directly apply MLSVD to the inverse Fourier transform of the zero-filled undersampled k-space measurements ($\mathcal{X}$) as in Eq. (12.9). The factor matrices $\mathbf{U}^{(n)}, n = 1, 2, ...N$, give the sparsity bases and are obtained by applying matrix SVD to the mode-n unfolding matrices $\mathbf{X}_{(n)}, n = 1, 2, ...N$. MLSVD leads to a sparse core tensor $\mathcal{S}$ due to the all-orthogonality and ordering conditions applied to it, which guarantee that most of the energy of the core tensor lies around one vertex. The proposed approach is reported to improve image reconstruction quality when compared to 1D/2D sparsifying transforms.

12.5.3 Segmentation

Segmentation, as opposed to the preprocessing steps discussed so far, is specific for images rather than signals. The purpose of segmentation may be to discard nonbrain tissue from the image (skull, ventricles, etc.) or to partition the image of the brain into smaller meaningful regions. This can be achieved in a supervised or an unsupervised manner, i.e., with or without known labels. We will begin our overview with the latter.

For differentiation of tumor, necrotic, and normal brain tissue types, a nonnegative CPD (NCPD)-based segmentation from MRSI and multiparametric MRI (MP-MRI) data is proposed in [59] and [60] respectively. For MRSI data, a feature vector $\mathbf{x}$ is calculated for each voxel based on their spectra. For MP-MRI data, $\mathbf{x}$ at each voxel is constructed in a way that highlights different information brought from different modalities, namely MRI, PWI, DWI, and MRSI. By stacking the matrices $\mathbf{x}\mathbf{x}^T$ for all voxels, a tensor $\mathcal{X}$ is obtained. Next, $\mathcal{X}$ is decomposed into R sources using NCPD. It should be mentioned that imposing constraints on factor matrices, such as the nonnegativity constraint here, can help to relax the uniqueness condition, reduce the computational cost, enhance robustness against noise, and increase the interpretability of the results [61]. In MP-MRI data, R is set manually whereas in MRSI data, R is automatically determined as follows. First, a data matrix is constructed by concatenating the spectra of each voxel and the covariance of the data matrix is estimated. Then, the eigenvalues of the spectra covariance matrix are calculated. Finally, R is estimated as the minimum number of eigenvalues whose cumulative sum is greater than 99% of the sum of all eigenvalues. The results on both imaging types show that NCPD is better at separating tumor tissue compared to matrix-based decompositions.

Although the approaches described above can successfully segment the images, the found segments still lack a label, for which a supervised classification approach is required. To this end, [62] proposes a two-stage fully automated superpixel-wise tumor tissue segmentation algorithm for MP-MRI data. The algorithm employs a random forest classifier with truncated MLSVD-based feature extraction, which first identifies the whole tumor and then divides it into its subregions. In [63], a CNN architecture with MLSVD-based low-rank regularization on the convolutional layers is proposed to label MRSI voxels as "tumor," "bad quality," or "normal." MLSVD is observed to give faster results (as the number of computations is lowered) without causing a significant change in the performance of CNN.

Medical images are volumetric, and hence many neural network models have also embraced 3D CNN architectures for their segmentation. These models include the 3D extension of the U-Net, which is one of the most prominent medical image segmentation networks so far [64]. U-Net takes its name from its architecture, which indeed looks similar to the letter U. The first half of the network is the contracting part, where the input image is encoded into feature maps at various levels for classification. The second half is the expanding part which up-samples the feature maps to be localized at the input pixel space [65]. The 3D U-Net model replaces the 2D operations in the original model with their 3D versions. In [66], the authors propose adding volumetric feature recalibration (VFR) layers to the 3D U-Net architecture as shown in Fig. 12.12. A VFR layer takes an input feature tensor and low-rank regularizes it to a rank-1 tensor using CPD. Such regularization forces only the most critical patterns within the feature tensor to be captured and leads to smooth spatial changes in the segmented tissues across adjacent slices, which is in line with the anatomical organization of the brain. The proposed model is used for segmentation of major brain tissues—namely the white matter, gray matter, and cerebrospinal fluid—from MRI data, and currently ranks first in the MRBrainS13 Challenge [67].

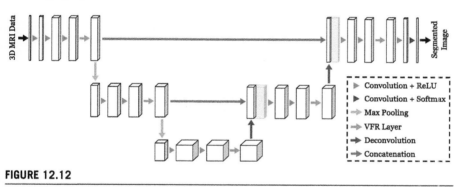

FIGURE 12.12

The 3D U-net architecture with VFR layers proposed in [66].

12.5.4 Registration and longitudinal analysis

Image registration is defined as the process of geometrically aligning two or more images and allows comparison of datasets across subjects, conditions, modalities, or time. Thus, it is a prerequisite to numerous neuroimaging applications [68]. For instance, registration of a subject and a control brain helps revealing abnormal regions in the subject brain. As a particular case of neurological image registration, longitudinal studies explore the changes in a subject's brain across his/her life span and show the evolution of the structure or function of progressive diseases [69].

Tensor-based morphometry (TBM) is a tensor solution to track differences in two brain images by constructing a Jacobian change map at the voxel level that is computed by nonlinearly registering a scan of interest to a baseline scan. Mathematically, for each voxel (x, y, z), a displacement vector $\mathbf{d} = (d_x, d_y, d_z)$ is found between a 3D study scan $\mathcal{S}$ and a 3D template scan $\mathcal{T}$ such that $t_{(x-d_x)(y-d_y)(z-d_z)} = s_{xyz}$. Then, the Jacobian matrix of the deformation field at (x, y, z) is calculated as [70]

$$\mathbf{J}(x, y, z) = \begin{pmatrix} \partial(x - d_x)/\partial x & \partial(x - d_x)/\partial y & \partial(x - d_x)/\partial z \\ \partial(y - d_y)/\partial x & \partial(y - d_y)/\partial y & \partial(y - d_y)/\partial z \\ \partial(z - d_z)/\partial x & \partial(z - d_z)/\partial y & \partial(z - d_z)/\partial z \end{pmatrix}. \quad (12.20)$$

The determinant of Eq. (12.20) gives the Jacobian at (x, y, z). For instance, a Jacobian value of 0.9 or 1.1 corresponds to a 10% tissue loss or a 10% tissue gain, respectively, in the local volume [71]. The 3D Jacobian change map is obtained by calculating the Jacobian for all voxels. An illustration of longitudinal analysis by TBM is given in Fig. 12.13.

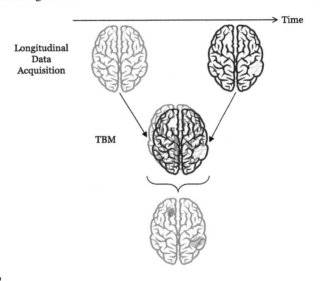

FIGURE 12.13

Illustration of TBM for longitudinal analysis. The template brain is a prior scan of the same subject to quantify the voxel-level differences that have occurred in time. These differences are marked by TBM based on the Jacobian of the deformation field.

In [72], the authors apply TBM to 3D MR images acquired 1 year apart from three groups of subjects: patients with Alzheimer's disease (AD), patients with mild cognitive impairment (MCI), and a control group of healthy patients. Consistent with prior studies, the authors report a widespread cerebral atrophy in patients with AD and a more restricted atrophic pattern in patients with MCI.

In [71], it is argued that using logarithmic transformation on the Jacobian values is crucial while evaluating the volumetric differences as it symmetrizes the Jacobian distribution by assigning equal probabilities to tissue gains and losses that are recip-rocals of each other. The authors validate their claim on sequential MRI scans of a patient diagnosed with semantic dementia.

TBM is used to demonstrate HIV-induced brain damage from T1-weighted MR images in [73]. A 3D profile of brain tissue reduction is constructed by calculating the ratio of the mean Jacobian in HIV patients to the mean Jacobian in control subjects at each voxel. In addition, using the Mann–Whitney U test, which evaluates the randomness of the voxel-wise difference between the mean log-Jacobian in HIV patients and the control group, a significance map is constructed (high significance corresponds to the differences being true, i.e., not random). Their results show that the greatest tissue loss occurs in primary and association sensorimotor areas.

Anatomical differences in the brains of HIV patients are also examined in [70] from their MRI scans. The authors also compare using multivariate statistics of the Jacobian matrix to the conventional approach of using its univariate statistics (such as its determinant). The proposed multivariate method (based on manifold testing) is observed to more extensively reveal the atrophy of gray and white matter caused by HIV.

TBM analysis with log-transformed Jacobian maps is used to identify regional differences in brain volume based on prenatal alcohol exposure in [74]. To this end, the T1-weighted MR scan acquired from each subject is compared to an average anatomical template obtained from the control group. Furthermore, ICA is applied on the log-Jacobian maps to better identify brain tissue deformations. The deformations obtained after ICA are observed to be useful indicators of the presence and extent of prenatal alcohol exposure.

Finally, it is also possible to reflect on longitudinal analysis from a tensor decomposition point of view. In [75], a DTI tensor with modes *fiber*, *longitudinal features*, and *cross-section* is constructed and factorized using CPD. In the end, pathological longitudinal changes appearing along white matter fibers caused by multiple sclerosis are detected.

12.5.5 Source separation

Blind source separation (BSS) is the unmixing of original source signals from their intermixed observations. In general, tensor decomposition methods aim at factorizing a data tensor into several components. However, in many cases, the defined objective requires focusing on only one of those components, such as the seizure component, whereas the others are simply regarded as background noise [90]. We discuss the use of tensor decompositions for denoising in Section 12.5.2. Similarly, even when the objective is to compare the content of data along various modes across different experimental conditions, such as during the resting state and during a mental task, the data belonging to these conditions can be collected at different times and analyzed individually [89], without the need for source separation. This section will be dedicated to algorithms which consider *multiple* sources of interest that are active during the experiment time.

BSS is divided into the following two main groups: instantaneous (Eq. (12.21)) and convolutive (Eq. (12.22)), i.e.,

$$x_i(t) = \sum_{r=1}^{R} a_{ir} s_r(t) + e_i(t), \tag{12.21}$$

$$x_i(t) = \sum_{r=1}^{R} \sum_{l=0}^{L} h_{ir}(l) s_r(t-l) + e_i(t), \tag{12.22}$$

where $x_i(t)$, $s_r(t)$, and $e_i(t)$ are measurement, source, and noise signals, respectively, and R is the number of sources. The linear mixing coefficients a_{ir} of the instantaneous case are generalized by incorporating memory to the system in the form of convolutive mixing filters $h_{ir}(l)$ of length L in the convolutive case.

Tensor decompositions are common and intuitive tools for solving the BSS problem [76]. Indeed, note that Eq. (12.21) can be written in the form of

$$\mathbf{X} = \sum_{r=1}^{R} \mathbf{a}_r \circ \mathbf{s}_r + \mathbf{E}, \tag{12.23}$$

where the measurement matrix $\mathbf{X}$ holds all measurement vectors along its rows and the mixing vector $\mathbf{a}_r$ holds all a_{ir} coefficients. As described in Section 12.3, neuroimaging data often take the form of a tensor, either when a number of measurements are made in multiple domains, such as at multiple locations (channels), in multiple patients, in multiple conditions, etc., or via the tensorization of a measurement matrix. Then, the above equation becomes

$$\mathcal{X} = \sum_{r=1}^{R} \mathbf{a}_r \circ \mathbf{b}_r \circ \dots \circ \mathbf{s}_r + \mathcal{E}, \tag{12.24}$$

which is analogous to the definition of CPD in Eq. (12.7). Then, the result of CPD can be interpreted as follows. Each of the R components $\mathbf{a}_r \circ \mathbf{b}_r \circ \dots \circ \mathbf{s}_r$ corresponds to an individual source, each of the signatures $\mathbf{a}_r$, $\mathbf{b}_r$, ... describes a certain property of the source, such as its variability in space, among patients, etc., and the temporal signature $\mathbf{s}_r$ describes the time course of the source.

For example, [77] uses CPD to localize several epileptogenic sources from EEG measurements, where these sources are simultaneously active at different brain regions. The EEG data are tensorized as a 3D *space*, *time*, and *wave* vector (STWV), regarding which more details will follow in Section 12.5.6.1. The spatial signatures of the extracted CPD components are observed to be pointing to the epileptogenic sites as confirmed directly by intracerebral stereotactic EEG recordings. An illustration of the presented methodology is provided in Fig. 12.14.

Despite the fact that neuroimaging data are often inherently multidimensional, matrix-based methods are well established and widely used. ICA, for example, is widely used for matricized fMRI data where the spatial modes are unfolded into a single long voxel mode. As a result, the spatial structure of the data is lost. In order to retain the spatial structure, [78] represents the fMRI data as a 4D tensor with modes

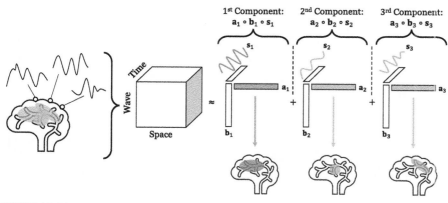

FIGURE 12.14

An illustration of CPD-based source separation with three sources. This approach is utilized in [77], where the collected EEG data consisting of mixed observations of the underlying sources are tensorized according to the STWV format (the spatial and temporal signals of this illustration are arbitrary and provided only for visualization). Each extracted component is defined by the outer product of its signatures and stands for one site of epileptic activity.

depth-length $\times$ *width* $\times$ *time* $\times$ *subject*. Then, various tensor-based instantaneous BSS techniques are applied, which are explained below.

The standard CPD modeling assumes the same (up to a scaling) underlying signal sources (spatial maps and time courses) for all subjects. However, empirical studies show that the impulse responses, known as the hemodynamic response functions (HRFs), leading to the blood signals acquired with fMRI change across subjects and brain regions. PARAFAC2 relaxes the strict multilinear assumption of CPD by allowing variation along one mode, i.e., subjects, as shown in Fig. 12.15.

Nevertheless, similar to CPD, PARAFAC2 still holds the rank-1 assumption, which is unrealistic for the spatial signatures of true brain sources. Consequently, the authors propose a PARAFAC2-like BTD model to achieve nonstrict multilinear modeling while incorporating higher-order components. When applying BTD/BTD2, the spatial signature of each source is assumed to be low-rank and the temporal signature is assumed to be rank-1. Different from BTD, BTD2 offers different time courses for each subject. Both in simulations and augmented datasets, nonmultilinear methods (BTD2 and PARAFAC2) are shown to be more suitable for BSS of fMRI data. Furthermore, BTD2 is observed to be significantly more robust to noise compared to PARAFAC2 at the cost of increasing computational complexity. Note that the assumption of independent sources—which has proved to be powerful in the fMRI literature—was not made in this study.

A second-order tensor-based convolutive ICA method is utilized to jointly address convolutive source separation and blind deconvolution of fUS data in [81]. In the proposed signal model (Eq. (12.22)), the hemodynamic response signals acquired with fUS correspond to the measurement signals $x_i(t)$, whereas the source signals $s_r(t)$

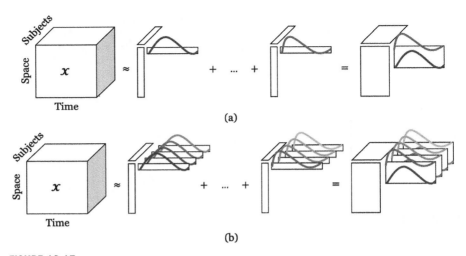

FIGURE 12.15

(a) CPD and (b) PARAFAC2 over an example space-time-subject tensor [79]. CPD can accommodate different temporal and spatial signature pairs for different neural components, but these are assumed to be the same for each subject up to a scaling factor. On the other hand, PARAFAC2 offers flexible temporal representations (which is necessary to model the HRF variability) across subjects.

represent the events that trigger these responses in the brain. Finally, the convolutive mixing filters $h_{ir}(l)$ stand for the HRFs. It is shown that if the sources are assumed to be uncorrelated, the tensor consisting of lagged measurement autocorrelation matrices can be factorized with a block-diagonal core tensor with inner Toeplitz blocks, which in the end leads to a BTD with constant rank terms [80].

The proposed approach has three main advantages. The first one is that the HRFs can be estimated differently based on the measurement and source index, which accounts for the HRF variability across brain regions and events, respectively. The second one is that the model offers a multiple input–multiple output solution, which is suitable for representing the complex interactions leading to hemodynamic activity of brain voxels. Last but not least, the unknown HRFs and neural stimuli can be identified simultaneously via BTD.

The convenience of tensor-based solutions to BSS problems is investigated in a wide range of neural signal processing applications in [82]. Several methods including tensor-based singular spectrum analysis and complex PARAFAC2 are employed for analysis of both single and multichannel signals. For more information on the topic, we refer the reader to the abovementioned paper.

In the following section, we discuss an important application of tensor-based BSS in neuroimaging. More specifically, careful interpretation of the signatures resulting from appropriate tensor decompositions can lead to successful activity recognition and source localization.

12.5.6 **Activity recognition and source localization**

Functional neuroimaging tools collect signals (directly or indirectly) from millions of neurons, which communicate in time and space through short bursts of oscillations. The goal of activity recognition is to establish if and when a certain neural process takes place, such as a particular stage of cognitive processing or a pathological event (e.g., an epileptic spike). Subsequently, one may aim to localize those neuronal populations which are involved in the activity of interest.

Brain data have conventionally been described by a matrix, with time courses or spectral information along one mode and information from different channels organized along the other mode. The data are later decomposed using a matrix factorization technique, such as PCA [83] or ICA [84]. Finally, each component is represented by two vectors (time *or* frequency and space) which are often called signatures. The assumption of orthogonality (PCA) or independence (ICA) ensures a unique solution. If the assumption is plausible, one can be confident that the components correspond to the actual sources and the signatures describe the true physical properties of the sources. In turn, these signatures allow to recognize the activity of interest. As described in the previous section, this idea can be extended to multilinear analysis using CPD, with the advantage that it can describe the data in more than two domains (i.e., time *and* frequency and space), and leads to a unique solution without hard constraints as in the matrix case [85].

CPD has been developed in 1970 in psychometrics by two independent studies that extend factor analysis to multiway signals, one of which has defined the process as parallel factor analysis, whereas the other defined it as canonical decomposition [86]. Approximately a decade later, [87] has practiced, to the best of our knowledge, one of the very first uses of CPD (and multidimensional analysis) on brain signals. In this study, the authors report differential hemispheric activity with positive emotional tasks being associated to right temporal activity after applying CPD on an EEG tensor with *channel* × *time* × *subject* modes. CPD was later used by [88] under the name of topographic component analysis for processing of event-related potentials (ERPs) described by the same modes and supported with biophysical considerations.

Another common three-way representation of EEG data combining *spatial*, *spectral*, and *temporal* modes is proposed initially in [89]. The spectral information is obtained using wavelet transform, which is often chosen for its optimal time-frequency resolution by resolving high-frequency components within small time windows and low-frequency components in larger time windows [90]. After applying CPD on the 3D EEG tensors with space-time-frequency (STF) modes, in line with previous findings, frontal theta components and occipital alpha components were identified during separate analysis of a mental arithmetic task and the resting condition, respectively.

This work was extended by addition of *condition* and *subject* modes [91]. This way, the differences in STF modes can be identified based on subjects and conditions (object or nonobject drawings are presented to subjects) through a single CPD computation. For instance, the "object condition" is observed to be more active in the occipital region at the lower gamma band than the "nonobject" condition. In [92], the same 5D tensorization (except with Hanning windowed fast Fourier transform for construction of the spectral mode) is used to analyze transcranial magnetic simulation (TMS)-induced EEG responses, known as TMS-evoked potentials (TEPs). Using CPD, TEPs are analyzed under four conditions as predrug and postdrug status of two different drug types. The results unveil three unique signatures along the space and frequency modes as frontal-sensorimotor beta, posterior alpha, and theta (whose location is observed to depend on the site of stimulation) components. Furthermore, the inter-subject variability is characterized by the fourth mode, whereas on the fifth mode drug effects are revealed, such as an observed reduction in postconditions of both drugs for all components.

CPD of evoked EEG signals acquired from healthy subjects and patients with chronic pain, each condition represented by an STF tensor, was also used to highlight differences across modes based on the subject's health condition [93]. More specifically, the active neural response of chronic pain patients was spotted around the frontal region with lower frequency values compared to the control group, whose active location is detected around the central region.

On fNIRS data, CPD is applied to identify the temporal and spatial characteristics of a verbal task in [52]. For this purpose, a 3D tensor with modes *space*, *time*, and *wavelength* was constructed. The wavelength mode entails two bands in the near-infrared spectrum for extraction of the hemodynamic response based on oxygenation of hemoglobin. The results show that CPD is capable of both motion-artifact removal and identification of task-related activity, which is confirmed with commonly used approaches in the fNIRS literature such as the general linear model. CPD of fNIRS data (*time* × *channel* × *frequency* × *subject*) is also used to investigate differences in spatial, temporal, and spectral patterns of infant brain reactions to human and mechanical hands [94].

Detection and localization algorithms focusing on epileptic seizures will be investigated separately considering the significance of and the large amount of work dedicated to epilepsy, which is one of the most common neurological disorders, influencing around 70 million people worldwide [95]. Epilepsy is characterized by recurrent seizures which take place due to excessive electrical discharges in a group of brain cells which are observed as rhythmic patterns in brain recordings. Seizures can start in one part of the brain and continue to spread throughout the brain, affecting more parts of the body unless prevented, as shown in Fig. 12.16. These seizures can potentially be cured by surgically removing the seizure focus, if it is accurately localized, or by blocking the spread of the seizures using medication or stimulation if the onset of the seizure is detected early on [97]. Neuroimaging tools combined with signal processing techniques can be helpful in both treatment approaches.

12.5.6.1 Seizure localization

Seizure localization aims to identify the seizure onset zone in the brain. In other words, the main interest is on the spatial content of seizure component(s).

Applying CPD on EEG data for seizure localization is proposed in [90] by constructing a 3D STF tensor with wavelet transform defining the spectrum array. The optimal rank value for CPD is determined as two by applying the core consistency

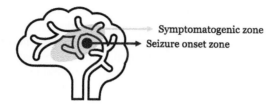

Symptomatogenic zone
Seizure onset zone

FIGURE 12.16

Epileptic activity zones. The seizures start in the seizure onset zone and might spread to adjacent areas (symptomatogenic zone) [96].

diagnostic [98]. In order to identify which of the two components arises from epileptic activity, both components are ordered according to their contribution in the spatial mode in terms of their variance, and the component with the highest contribution is classified as the epileptic component. The authors claim the following for this selection. Seizure activity has more stable spectral and spatial signatures compared to background EEG, which is expected to be more random. Therefore, CPD will be relatively insensitive to background EEG, and model the dominant, i.e., epileptic, activity. Although the spatial signature of the epileptic component is assumed to correspond to the spatial distribution of epileptic activity, only the electrodes showing a potential above a predefined threshold are used to define the exact focus of the seizure. Furthermore, it is observed that the maximum frequency in the spectral content of the epileptic component corresponds to the frequency of the rhythmic seizure.

A Tucker decomposition approach for seizure localization on EEG data is proposed in [99]. Tucker decomposition on STF tensors is compared to two-way decomposition methods such as SVD and PCA constructed with either *space × time* or *space × frequency* modes. The results obtained show that multiway analysis achieves more precise localization compared to two-way analyses. Nevertheless, the authors state that it is much more difficult to interpret the resulting components from Tucker decomposition compared to those from CPD. This is due to the fact that CPD extracts multilinear components, where each component is described by the interactions of exactly one signature from each mode, which directly match the properties of the given component. However, Tucker decomposition employs a core tensor that allows the interaction of multiple signatures from each mode (Section 12.4). Therefore, the individual signatures cannot be interpreted alone.

Overall, CPD provides a more restricted and simpler model compared to Tucker decomposition for seizure localization [100]. However, EEG data recorded during a seizure are often contaminated with eye blinks, eye movements, and muscle artifacts, which might interfere with the expected dominance of epileptic activity over background EEG in the case artifacts account for most of the variation. Therefore, [100] proposes combining CPD of STF tensors of EEG data with an artifact removal stage through multilinear subspace analysis. The optimal rank value for CPD is determined via the core consistency diagnostic. Although the decomposed terms are labeled as artifact or seizure using clinical feedback from neurologists, when the spectral signatures of components were compared, the authors noticed that most artifacts lie in a low-frequency band whereas high-frequency content is present for epileptic activity, which can be a potential lead for automating the component selection process. For artifact removal, the authors suggest using Tucker decomposition which returns factor matrices along STF modes. Based on visual inspection of the components in the spatial mode, the artifact components are determined. The original tensor is then projected onto the null space determined by the artifact components. The resulting artifact-free tensor is then provided as input to CPD.

Seizure localization on neonatal EEG data is investigated under two different seizure types in [101], namely oscillatory and spike-train type seizures. For oscillatory seizures, CPD is applied to the STF tensor using the core consistency diagnostic as in [90] whereas for spike-train type seizures, the 3D EEG tensor is constructed differently. More specifically, spikes are detected [102] and segmented from each channel and placed into a tensor. In other words, the constructed tensor at each slice has the segmented data from all channels where the segments are constructed whenever a spike is detected. This tensor is decomposed into its signatures using a rank-1 CPD as the proposed tensorization method only captures seizure data (Fig. 12.17). Consequently, the resulting spatial signature corresponds to the spatial distribution of the seizure.

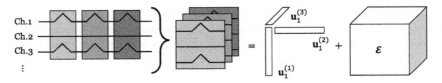

FIGURE 12.17

CPD-based approach for spike-train seizure localization proposed in [101] where $\mathcal{E}$ shows the residual tensor. As the input tensor is constructed using only seizure segments, a rank-1 CPD is applied to obtain the seizure component.

CPD expresses the STF EEG tensor into a sum of rank-1 tensors, which means every extracted term is defined by the combination of exactly one spatial, temporal, and spectral signature. Therefore, stating that in cases where the seizure pattern is nonstationary such a trilinear signal model will be insufficient, [103] proposes to use BTD for seizure localization with EEG. Decomposition into rank-$(L_r, L_r, 1)$ terms facilitates the extraction of sources that are rather fixed along one mode but vary in others, such as sources with a constant spectral structure that spatially spread over time or sources which evolve in frequency but are spatially constrained. BTD is also useful in combination with a Hankel expansion (instead of time-frequency expansion) of the data, based on the assumption that EEG signals can be modeled as a sum of exponentially damped sinusoids. The Hankel matrix of a time series has a low rank depending on the number of underlying sinusoids. Assuming that the multichannel EEG records the linear mixture of such sources, the data admits a rank-$(L_r, L_r, 1)$

model indeed. The authors show three scenarios in which BTD is more successful than CPD in localizing the seizure according to clinical assessment: a seizure with severe eye artifacts, with evolving frequency, and with varying locations. Nevertheless, the performance of BTD is observed to depend heavily on the appropriate selection of the number of extracted components (R) and the rank of the factor matrices (L_r).

CPD is applied to STWV tensors for seizure localization on EEG data in [77]. A wave vector corresponds to a local spatial Fourier transform within a certain region on the scalp defined by a spherical window function. The STWV modeling is shown to yield better results compared to STF, especially with correlated sources, i.e., when similar epileptic spikes spread in multiple regions with short time delays in between. In addition, the authors provide a theoretical explanation on the conditions explaining the functioning and performance of trilinear STF and STWV analyses such as the source strengths and source correlations in time and space.

12.5.6.2 Seizure recognition

Seizure recognition refers to determining the time intervals in which a seizure takes place (detection) or there are indications that a seizure might be approaching (prediction). While the former can replace a manual seizure diary, the latter especially can allow triggering of warning devices beforehand and prevent serious injury.

One way for seizure detection is dividing the brain data into time segments (epochs), extract features from each epoch, and classify the features as "seizure" or "nonseizure." In [104], an EEG tensor for each epoch is constructed using wavelet or Hilbert–Huang transform with STF modes. Features from each epoch are extracted from the signatures obtained with CPD and BTD of the corresponding tensor. In order to determine the optimal rank value for decomposition, MLSVD is utilized. The MLSVD core is truncated until the singular values represent more than 95% of the data variance. Low-multilinear rank approximation is initialized with the truncated MLSVD core, which finds the multilinear rank that best approximates the tensor in the least-squares sense. Several classifiers are used to label the epoch features, namely K-nearest neighbor, radial basis support vector machine (SVMRB) and linear discriminant analysis. The classifiers are trained with one seizure segment while the remaining data are used for testing. The block diagram of the proposed method is provided in Fig. 12.18. The best results are obtained when spatial signatures are used as features and the SVMRB as classifier.

Alternatively, features can be included inside the tensor. One such feature tensor is proposed in [105] with modes *time epoch*, *feature*, and *channel*, where the features are created in time and frequency modes in a way to create distinction between seizure and nonseizure periods of EEG data. The tensor is regressed to seizure and nonseizure classes using multilinear partial least-squares.

A deep learning solution to seizure detection has been proposed in [57] and discussed in detail in Section 12.5.2. In summary, the authors introduce a CPD-based dimensionality reduction stage to obtain a low-rank approximation of the original EEG tensor to be given as input to a CNN.

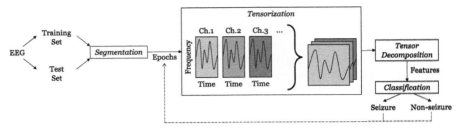

FIGURE 12.18

The block diagram of the proposed algorithm in [104] for seizure detection using tensor decomposition-based feature extraction.

In [106], EEG signals are recorded from multiple patients in 3-hour sessions that include the preictal period (before seizures take place) as well as the seizure. After applying fast Fourier transform, an STF tensor is obtained from each patient. The STF tensors are decomposed using CPD. In order to assess if any of the extracted components are related to the preictal period, a binary target vector showing the time instants of the preictal period is constructed. The correlation between the temporal signatures of all extracted components and the target is computed. Almost in all cases, a component that is significantly correlated to the preictal period is found. The spatial and spectral signatures of the preictal components suggest that a common structure might be involved in seizure generation, which can be useful in prediction of a seizure.

12.5.7 Connectivity analysis

Brain connectivity can be investigated in three subcategories, i.e., structural, functional, and effective connectivity (Fig. 12.19). Structural connectivity defines the existence of white matter tracts physically interconnecting brain regions whereas functional connectivity describes the statistical dependencies between neural signals acquired from different brain areas using measures such as correlation and coherence [107]. Effective connectivity can be considered as the combination of the two, as it attempts to extract networks quantifying the directional effects of one neural population on another one, characterized by axonal pathways [108].

12.5.7.1 Structural connectivity

In [109], a tensor network is proposed which shows the strength of white matter tracts between each pair of brain regions that are of interest. To start with, a tensor of size $M \times M \times S$ is constructed from DWI and MRI scans of S subjects covering M brain regions. For quantifying the relation between two regions, different features are tried, such as the fiber counts in-between or the water diffusivity along the fibers. Next, a semi-symmetric CPD is applied whose factors along the first two modes are equal $(\mathbf{u}_r^{(1)} = \mathbf{u}_r^{(2)})$ due to the symmetry of structural connectivity between two regions.

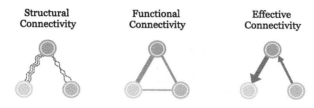

Structural Connectivity   Functional Connectivity   Effective Connectivity

FIGURE 12.19

Types of brain connectivity [108]. Three brain regions are shown to be connected structurally (via fiber pathways), functionally (via statistical relations), and effectively (via information flow).

The number of components R is selected based on cumulative proportion of variation explained [110].

In order to discover a connectivity network that captures the most variation in the structural connectomes across all subjects, a weighted sum of $\mathbf{u}_r^{(1)}(\mathbf{u}_r^{(1)})^{\mathrm{T}}$ for $r = 1, 2, ..., R$ is calculated. Finally, the connectivity networks from different subject groups are compared. The obtained results reveal that stronger interconnections exist in the cortical area in people with positive traits, such as high language learning and motion ability, whereas weaker interactions exist in people with negative traits, such as use of alcohol.

12.5.7.2 Functional connectivity

Functional connectivity of the brain was assumed to be constant with respect to time until recently. As a consequence, functional connectivity networks (FCNs) were commonly represented with nodes that correspond to brain regions and edges that describe their pair-wise associations. After experimental studies that unveiled the time dependency of functional connectivity, dynamic FCNs have gained significant attention [111]. For dynamic FCNs where temporal information is incorporated as a third mode besides pairs of brain regions, tensors become the intrinsic representations.

In [112], the authors propose a tensor decomposition scheme for dynamic functional connectivity analysis on resting-state fMRI data. For this purpose, a tensor $\mathcal{X}$ of dimensions $M \times M \times W$ is constructed as shown in Fig. 12.20, where M is the number of brain regions and W is the number of time windows. The time windows are obtained by overlapping sliding windows over the time courses of investigated brain regions. For each time window w ($w = 1, 2, ..., W$), a matrix of size $M \times M$ showing the pair-wise connectivity values (computed using Pearson correlation or mutual information [113]) is constructed and placed into the w-th slice of $\mathcal{X}$.

Next, CPD is applied on $\mathcal{X}$, leading to factor matrices $\mathbf{U}^{(1)}$, $\mathbf{U}^{(2)}$, and $\mathbf{U}^{(3)}$ of dimensions $(M \times R)$, $(M \times R)$, and $(W \times R)$, respectively. Note that due to the assumed symmetry of functional connectivity between two regions, $\mathbf{U}^{(1)} = \mathbf{U}^{(2)}$. The columns of $\mathbf{U}^{(1)} = \mathbf{U}^{(2)}$ correspond to spatial signatures that are interpreted as connectivities. Both the input tensor and the approximated tensor obtained with CPD are denoised using binarization via thresholding.

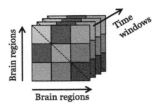

FIGURE 12.20

A 3D tensor model for dynamic functional connectivity [112]. The matrices at each slice showing pair-wise connectivity between brain regions are symmetric.

In order to find spatial maps that are common across subjects, K-means clustering is applied to the set of all spatial signatures extracted from all subjects. Finally, the cluster centers are assigned as prototype brain networks, which are found to be similar to several known resting state networks.

The model in Fig. 12.20 is extended with the *subject* mode in [114] for classification of multisubject fMRI data using MLSVD under two sets of conditions: (i) low vs. high walking speed in the elderly and (ii) resting vs. stress state in moderate-heavy alcohol consumers. The proposed approach is observed to provide a better classification accuracy than conventional SVD, which is applied after matricization of the original 4D tensor. MLSVD is also employed in [115] to analyze functional connectivity from fMRI data, but this time on a 3D tensor model with modes *connectivity*, *time*, and *subject*. In other words, unlike previous approaches, here the connectivity is not represented in a symmetric matrix form; instead, it is vectorized. The authors also propose a general linear model using the extracted temporal signatures to determine which connectivity maps are related to the experimental paradigm.

In [116], CPD is compared to Tucker decomposition for dynamic FCNs on resting-state multisubject fMRI data using sliding window correlation analysis. The authors conclude that although interpreting the components of CPD is more straightforward than interpreting those of Tucker decomposition, the Tucker model is often more effective for group differentiation.

Instead of using fixed-sized sliding windows, [117] proposes an approach to automatically determine different FCN states. The authors utilize a twofold algorithm to define the FCNs from a cognitive EEG study with multiple subjects. The first step is to identify the change points in time where the FCNs indicate a significant alteration. For this purpose, a low-rank approximation of the third-order tensor containing the pair-wise connectivities of a random subset of subjects at each time point is calculated via convex hull optimization [118], which selects an optimal value for the tensor rank. Tucker decomposition is applied to the tensors with the calculated rank value. Note that the factors along the first and second mode are equal ($\mathbf{U}^{(1)}(t) = \mathbf{U}^{(2)}(t)$) due to the symmetry of matrices at each slice. Finally, the subspace distance between consecutive (in time) basis elements of the decomposed matrices along the first mode is calculated as explained in [119]. The change points are detected by thresholding the distance (Fig. 12.21).

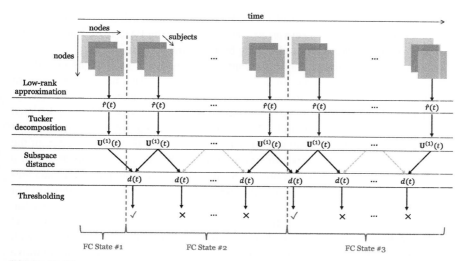

FIGURE 12.21

Steps of change detection in FCNs over an example [117]. Low-rank approximation is applied on the 3D tensors with a randomly selected subset of subjects at each time point to estimate their rank ($\hat{r}(t)$). Tucker decomposition is applied based on the rank values. The subspace distance $d(t)$ between the column subspaces obtained via Tucker decomposition ($\mathbf{U}^{(1)}(t)$) is calculated. Every distance value above a threshold yields a new functional connectivity state.

The change points define the time boundaries for functional connectivity states. The second task is to summarize the functional connectivity states inside these boundaries across subjects. Assuming that the functional connectivity states should remain stationary and common across subjects, the summarized states are obtained via tensor-matrix projections across time and space using another Tucker decomposition stage. The results demonstrate the formation of transient frontal networks during error processing.

In [120], PARAFAC2 is applied in the complex domain to compute functional connectivity by relating the extracted components to one another. For this purpose, received EEG signals are expressed as a linear mixture of multiple sources, which are modeled as auto-regressive (AR) processes. The EEG data are tensorized using short-time Fourier transform with Hanning windows, yielding three modes as *channel*, *complex frequency*, and *complex trial*. The connectivity metric is computed via a phase-lag index which estimates phase differences between trials that are extracted using PARAFAC2. PARAFAC2 adds the flexibility of expressing the trials in terms of frequency, and thus producing different connectivity maps for different frequency bands. On the other hand, [121] uses PARAFAC2 to obtain subject-specific network scaling as follows. First, functional connectivity is formulated as the covariance matrix of an fMRI data matrix (*voxels* × *time*). However, in order to obtain networks that are generalizable (among subjects) and interpretable, the data matrices from each subject are first stacked into a 3D tensor and later decomposed into their low-rank components prior to covariance estimation. Using PARAFAC2, the strength of underlying networks is allowed to vary based on the subject.

Functional connectivity is an important field of research as changes in connectivity may serve as a biomarker in neurological disorders. This has been shown, for example, in [129] for autism spectrum disorder (ASD). The authors work on a third-order tensor of fractional amplitude of low-frequency fluctuations (fALFF) calculated for each voxel in an fMRI dataset. The metric fALFF characterizes the intensity of spontaneous brain activities and provides a measure of functional architecture of the brain. A linear tensor regression model is proposed by the authors, about which a more detailed explanation will follow in Section 12.5.8. Simply put, the image tensor serves as the observation whereas the subject's diagnosis status (as 0 [healthy] or 1 [having ASD]) and other variables such as age and sex form the covariate vector. The estimated coefficient tensors from healthy subjects and subjects who have ASD show clear distinctions in regions that are consistent with the autism literature such as the cerebellum, which is responsible for motor learning, coordination, cognitive functions, and effective regulation.

12.5.7.3 Effective connectivity

Functional connectivity explores the statistical similarities between the nodes in a physiological network, whereas effective connectivity searches for the direct (causal) interactions between them. Consequently, while describing effective connectivity, it is quite common to use multivariate AR modeling which expresses the dependency of the value of a node at a given time to the past values of all the nodes employed in the network.

For instance, [122] uses time-variant partial directed coherence (tvPDC) based on the Fourier transform of time-variant multivariate AR models on EEG data. The general form of a time-variant multivariate AR process of order P and with M nodes is expressed as [123]

$$\mathbf{x}(t) = \sum_{q=1}^{P} \mathbf{A}^{(q)}(t)\mathbf{x}(t-q) + \mathbf{e}(t), \qquad (12.25)$$

where $\mathbf{x}(t) \in \mathbb{R}^M$ is the data vector at time t, $\mathbf{A}^{(q)}(t) \in \mathbb{R}^{M \times M}$ contains the q-th-order AR coefficients at time t, $\mathbf{e}(t) \in \mathbb{R}^M$ is the innovation noise, and the order P determines the total number of time lags included in the model.

The Fourier transform of the time-variant AR coefficients is defined as

$$\mathbf{A}(t, f) = \mathbf{I} - \sum_{q=1}^{P} \mathbf{A}^{(q)}(t)e^{-2\pi \mathrm{i} fr}, \qquad (12.26)$$

where $\mathbf{I}$ is the identity matrix.

The degree of causal influence from node j to node i at time t and frequency f can then be quantified by tvPDC as follows:

$$\text{tvPDC}_{i \leftarrow j}(t, f) = \frac{|\mathbf{A}_{ij}(t, f)|}{\sqrt{\sum_{m=1}^{M} |\mathbf{A}_{mj}(t, f)|^2}} \in [0, 1], i \neq j. \tag{12.27}$$

Hence, the tvPDC analysis of a single subject results in a 3D tensor containing the modes *space* (expressed for each node pair), *time*, and *frequency*. In order to enhance the interpretability of tvPDC analysis while incorporating an extra mode for different *subjects*, [122] proposes to apply CPD after obtaining the 4D tvPDC tensor from EEG data. The results show that the relation between the stimulus onset and signatures in temporal mode becomes more prominent in multisubject decomposition than in single-subject decomposition, meaning that the addition of the *subject* mode can provide critical input. In general, applying CPD on the tvPDC tensor is observed to reduce the amount of results to be investigated to a smaller but more informative subset, and this reduction can be taken even further by displaying the computed networks only if their associated content satisfies certain constraints. These constraints can be temporal resemblance to the onsets of a stimulus or be linked to a spectral window of interest.

Effective connectivity of the brain is studied on fMRI signals using Granger causality (GC) in [124]. GC is used to investigate the direction and magnitude of information flow between two simultaneously recorded time series [125].

Let the fMRI data matrix $\mathbf{X}$ be of size $M \times T$, where M is the total number of voxels and T is the number of time samples. Based on the multivariate AR model given in Eq. (12.25), [124] expresses the BOLD signal $\mathbf{x}_t = \mathbf{X}_{:t}$ for P time lags, only $\mathbf{A}^{(q)}(t)$ is replaced by $\mathbf{A}^{(q)}$, i.e., AR coefficients are not time-varying (referred to as spatial multivariate AR model). Any nonzero coefficient $\mathbf{A}_{ij}^{(q)}$ refers to the time series j (Granger) influencing time series i after q lags.

GC can be written as a tensor regression by extending Eq. (12.25) to multiple time samples $t = P + 1, ..., T + P$:

$$\mathbf{X}_{t-q} = [\mathbf{x}_{P+1-q}, ..., \mathbf{x}_{T+P-q}]^{\mathsf{T}}. \tag{12.28}$$

Then, by stacking all time lags ($q = 1, ..., P$) together, the data tensor $\mathcal{X} \in \mathbb{R}^{P \times M \times T}$ and the AR coefficient tensor (i.e., the connectivity tensor) $\mathcal{A} \in \mathbb{R}^{M \times M \times P}$ is obtained. Finally, the tensor regression based on the multivariate AR model is expressed as

$$\mathbf{X}_t = \mathcal{A} \bullet_{\{M,P\}} \mathcal{X} + \mathbf{E}_t, \tag{12.29}$$

where $\bullet_{M,P}$ shows tensor contraction over common dimensions M and P and $\mathbf{E}_t$ is the innovation noise. The connectivity tensor can be estimated as

$$\hat{\mathcal{A}} = \arg\min_{\mathcal{A}} \left\{ ||\mathbf{X}_t - \mathcal{A} \bullet_{\{M,P\}} \mathcal{X}||_2^2 + \pi(\mathcal{A}) \right\}, \tag{12.30}$$

where $\pi(.)$ shows the penalty function.

Effective connectivity suggests structured sparsity on the connectivity tensor to avoid any forced connections. Therefore the authors posit a CPD structure for the connectivity tensor. The factors along the first, second, and third modes correspond to the spatial signature for receiving nodes, the spatial signature for sender nodes, and the temporal signature for causal lags, respectively.

12.5.8 Regression

Regression analysis aims to estimate the relationship between a set of dependent variables (i.e., the observations, responses, or outcomes) and independent variables (i.e., covariates, predictors, or explanatory variables). Particularly, the generalized linear model (GLM), which is a generalization of ordinary linear regression through a link function, is used for modeling in many areas of neuroimaging due to its flexible framework.

GLM is used to explain the expected value μ of the observation vector $\mathbf{y}$ given the matrix of covariates $\mathbf{X}$ with the help of regression coefficients ($\boldsymbol{\beta}$) and a link function $g(.)$ as follows [126]:

$$g(\mu) = g(\mathrm{E}(\mathbf{y}|\mathbf{X})) = \mathbf{X}\boldsymbol{\beta}. \tag{12.31}$$

Note that the ordinary linear regression model can be obtained by exploiting an identity link function. As observed from Eq. (12.31), classical regression methods treat each covariate as a vector (which are later concatenated in the matrix $\mathbf{X}$) while estimating the corresponding regression coefficients. However, new advances in neuroimaging require covariates of higher dimensions.

To adapt the GLM framework for higher-order data models, [127] proposes a generalized linear tensor regression model for a scalar observation y, a conventional covariate vector $\mathbf{z} \in \mathbb{R}^{I_0}$, and a general covariate tensor $\mathcal{X} \in \mathbb{R}^{I_1 \times I_2 \times \dots \times I_N}$:

$$g(\mu) = \alpha + \boldsymbol{\gamma}^{\mathsf{T}}\mathbf{z} + <\mathcal{B}, \mathcal{X}>, \tag{12.32}$$

where α is the intercept value, $\boldsymbol{\gamma} \in \mathbb{R}^{I_0}$ is the conventional regression coefficient vector, and $\mathcal{B} \in \mathbb{R}^{I_1 \times I_2 \times \dots \times I_N}$ is the coefficient tensor that captures the strength of the entries of the covariate tensor. In this model, clinical outcome (a binary value indicating the diagnosis status) is treated as the observation, multidimensional neuroimaging data (from 3D MR or 4D fMR images) correspond to the covariate tensor, and other predictors such as age and gender are included in the conventional covariate vector.

The challenge that comes with regressing such a model is its ultrahigh dimensionality. Therefore, the authors assume a low-rank structure of $\mathcal{B}$ by expressing it with a rank-R CPD. This significantly reduces the dimensionality from $(I_0 + \prod_{n=1}^{N} I_n)$ to $(I_0 + R \times \sum_{n=1}^{N} I_n)$. Maximum likelihood estimation is performed for parameter prediction by introducing sparsity regularization that is used to identify subregions that are associated with the response traits.

This approach is adopted in [128] by representing the coefficient tensor $\mathcal{B}$ with Tucker decomposition which provides a more flexible and practical model especially in brain images with skewed dimensions as it allows a different number of factors along each mode, unlike CPD. The authors test their method on an attention deficit hyperactivity disorder dataset with T1-weighted MR images by first estimating the coefficient tensor from the training subjects and then predicting the clinical outcome for the rest of the subjects. Their results show that Tucker decomposition outperforms CPD in terms of classification accuracy.

Alternatively, [129] proposes to treat the observation as a tensor variable ($\mathcal{Y} \in \mathbb{R}^{I_1 \times I_2 \times \ldots \times I_N}$) instead of a scalar and expresses the linear tensor regression model as follows:

$$\mathcal{Y} = \mathcal{B} \times_{N+1} \mathbf{x} + \mathcal{E}, \tag{12.33}$$

where $\mathbf{x} \in \mathbb{R}^d$ is the covariate vector, $\mathcal{B} \in \mathbb{R}^{I_1 \times I_2 \times \ldots \times I_N \times d}$ is the $(N+1)$-th-order coefficient tensor, and $\mathcal{E} \in \mathbb{R}^{I_1 \times I_2 \times \ldots \times I_N}$ is the independent error tensor. Here, the brain image serves as the observation tensor, and the diagnosis status, age, gender, etc., form the covariate vector. The proposed method embeds two key sparse structures on $\mathcal{B}$, element-wise sparsity and low-rankness, through a weighted CPD. The prediction of weights and regression coefficients constitutes a nonconvex optimization problem, for which an alternating updating algorithm is developed. The authors use the proposed model on fMRI data to demonstrate the differences in functional brain connectivity caused by ASD (Section 12.5.7.2).

For regression of tensor observations on tensor predictors, a tensor subspace regression model, called higher-order partial least-squares (HOPLS), is proposed in [130]. To achieve this goal, a tensor subspace for both covariates and observations is constructed via Tucker decomposition. The authors test their method on simultaneously recorded EEG (scalp EEG, measured noninvasively) and ECoG (intracranial EEG, measured invasively) data, which are both represented as 4D arrays with modes *trial*, *channel*, *frequency*, and *time*. Their results show that HOPLS performs superior over ordinary PLS approaches for decoding of the ECoG data using EEG signals.

12.5.9 Feature extraction and classification

Feature extraction aims at summarizing the initial raw data using a smaller amount of entries which still capture their essence such that meaningful models can be learned from them in a more computationally efficient manner. From this perspective, it is not surprising that tensor decompositions, which can well approximate low-rank data using fewer parameters, are well suited for this task. Extracted features can later be used for classification purposes. Some topics related to feature extraction and classification (e.g., segmentation and seizure detection) or classification (e.g., binary regression algorithms) have been described in Section 12.5.3, Section 12.5.6.2, and Section 12.5.8; therefore, they will not be elaborated here. For details about the related works, aforementioned sections should be (re)visited.

CPD and Tucker decomposition are used to extract features for EEG-based classification of patients with Alzheimer's disease in [131]. To achieve this, an EEG tensor is constructed with modes *space*, *frequency*, and *subject* for both training and test sets. First, *subject*-mode unfolding of the training tensor $\mathcal{X}$ is approximated via a tensor decomposition. Using the factor matrices extracted from the rank-R CPD of $\mathcal{X}$, mode-n unfolding matrix of $\mathcal{X}$ can be expressed as

$$\mathbf{X}_{(n)} \approx \mathbf{U}^{(n)}[\mathbf{U}^{(N)} \odot ... \odot \mathbf{U}^{(n+1)} \odot \mathbf{U}^{(n-1)} \odot ... \odot \mathbf{U}^{(1)}]^{\mathrm{T}}, \tag{12.34}$$

$$\mathbf{X}_{(n)} \approx \mathbf{U}^{(n)}\mathbf{E}, \tag{12.35}$$

where $\odot$ shows the Khatri–Rao product. Here, $\mathbf{U}^{(n)}$ is a matrix of size $I_n \times R$ and holds R signatures of the unfolded mode n, each of which can be regarded as a feature vector. Therefore, $\mathbf{U}^{(n)}$ can be denoted as a feature matrix $\mathbf{F}$. For the given case $\mathbf{X}_{(\text{subject})}$ is computed, thus $\mathbf{F}$ holds the subject features. On the other hand, the encoding matrix $\mathbf{E}$ holds the information from *space* and *frequency* modes. The equivalent of encoding matrix in Tucker decomposition is given as the product of the core tensor with the factor matrices along *space* and *frequency*.

When unseen test data are received, a *subject*-mode unfolding matrix of the new tensor $\mathcal{Y}$ is calculated by directly unfolding the tensor, denoted as $\mathbf{Y}_{(\text{subject})}$. The least-squares projection of the encoding matrix $\mathbf{E}$ on any $\mathbf{Y}_{(\text{subject})}$ returns the feature matrix $\mathbf{F}'$ of $\mathcal{Y}$:

$$\mathbf{F}' = \mathbf{Y}_{(\text{subject})}\mathbf{E}^{\dagger}. \tag{12.36}$$

Finally, a feed-forward multilayer perceptron is used for classifying the feature matrices. Note that the proposed method reduces overall complexity by applying tensor decomposition to only the training data from which a dictionary is obtained and used for projecting on any unseen test data. The steps of this method are illustrated in Fig. 12.22.

A similar approach is utilized for drowsiness detection with EEG using a support vector machine classifier [132]. Furthermore, the authors propose a nonparametric Bayesian model to automatically determine the underlying CP rank by involving prior gamma distributions of factor matrices.

In [133], PARAFAC2 and CPD are used to extract refined composite multiscale entropy features from MEG data which are shown to differ between patients with Alzheimer's disease and healthy subjects. Another CPD-based feature extraction describing the mismatch negativity in EEG ERPs is defined in [134] to classify children with reading disability and attention deficit.

A multivariate TBM method is proposed in [135] for group-based classification of patients with Williams syndrome based on 3D MR images. First, individual surface deformation tensors are obtained by registering brain images to a common template. Since the resulting 3D maps provide many more features than the number of subjects included, a feature reduction step is found to be necessary. Consequently, a linear classifier is utilized to learn the feature weights with l_1-norm regularization which enforces sparsity on the surface features.

Another promising use of neural signal classification (besides for diagnostic purposes) is BCIs. A BCI receives brain signals from a subject and translates these signals to an external device that will take the subject's commands into action

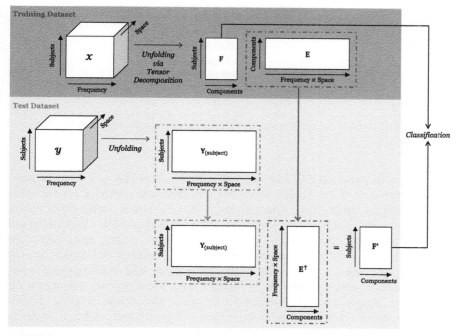

FIGURE 12.22

Feature extraction using an encoding matrix [131]. The encoding matrix $\mathbf{E}$ is calculated from the training dataset using CPD or Tucker decomposition (top row). The least-squares projection of the encoding matrix on the *subject*-mode unfolding matrix of any test dataset returns the new feature matrix $\mathbf{F}'$.

(Fig. 12.23). For instance, if a subject imagines to move his left arm, even if he does not actually move it, his neural activation will still point out that he wishes to do so. This way, by establishing a connection with the recording device, a robot arm can realize the desired movement for the subject. BCIs can be driven by mental imagination of an activity (such as motor imagery) or by responses to external stimuli (such as P300 and steady-state visually evoked potentials [SSVEPs]).

The main paradigms used by the vast majority of BCIs are motor imagery, P300, and SSVEP. In motor imagery, subjects imagine themselves moving their body parts, which creates event-related (de)synchronizations in sensorimotor areas. P300-based BCI takes its name from the P300 wave, which is a type of ERP that occurs in the human brain as a positive deflection with a time delay of around 300 ms after a specific auditory, visual, or somatosensory event has taken place. SSVEPs are evoked in the occipital cortex when the user concentrates on flickering visual stimuli [136].

For classifying left and right hand imagery movement, CPD and Tucker decomposition of 4D EEG tensors with modes *frequency* (based on Morlet wavelets), *time*, *channel*, and *trial* is proposed in [137]. Both techniques are reported to outperform

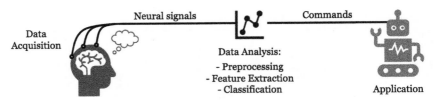

FIGURE 12.23

Illustration of BCIs. BCIs convert the subject's neural signals to commands that control external devices.

common spatial pattern (CSP) filtering. CSP filtering finds spatial filters that maximize the variance of the filtered signal for one class and minimize for the other using training set labels [138]. Alternatively, a 4D EEG tensor consisting of modes *frequency* (based on Morlet wavelets), *time*, *channel*, and *condition* is decomposed using CPD and Tucker decomposition in [139] for the same imagery movement problem. To extract the most discriminative components for different classes (left hand or right hand), sparseness is imposed on the condition mode. The resulting components unveil differences across conditions in channel, time, and frequency signatures; for example, the components that correspond to imagined motor tasks covering sensorimotor areas reveal symmetrical behavior in their topography and condition modes as expected, i.e., the left class shows a higher amplitude (than the right class) when the left hemisphere is active, and vice versa. The authors however note that the proposed offline method should be extended for dynamic and window-based time analysis in order to capture the changing neural streams over time.

An online BCI system for predicting left and right hand imagery movement is combined with several tensor completion algorithms (Section 12.5.1) to analyze a rather flawed EEG dataset along modes *time*, *channel*, and *trial* that includes corrupted entries and channels in [43]. Feature vectors are extracted from the completed tensors using CSP filtering. To evaluate the improvement achieved by each algorithm, linear discriminant analysis and linear support vector machine classification is utilized. For each subject, the first run is recorded where a cue (left or right arrow) is shown to the subject and used to train the classifier. The system also gives an online feedback by showing the result of classification.

Single-trial EEG classification remains a challenging but important task in BCI applications, considering that it offers a more convenient and faster framework for the subjects. Taking into the account the low number of training samples and high dimensionality of the data in such a case, [140] proposes spectral regularization using the nuclear norm due to the fact that it conveys a priori structural information. To construct the tensorial EEG model, first each channel is segmented into time windows. For each channel, the Hankel matrix of a feature vector containing mean signal amplitudes of each time window is calculated. Channel Hankel matrices are stacked to obtain the EEG tensor. Compared to linear discriminant analysis with shrinkage applied to the feature vector, nuclear norm regularization on tensorial EEG is observed to perform significantly better in classifying P300 ERPs in an auditory oddball paradigm.

In [141], multilinear discriminant analysis of an EEG feature tensor is proposed to classify ERPs from a visual P300-based BCI experiment, in which a matrix of letters is presented to the subjects who silently count how many times the indicated target letter is intensified. The feature tensor is constructed by appending degrees of polynomial fittings for each channel and time segment.

In order to carry BCIs to a practical real-life use, there are two main challenges: subject mobility and subject-specific calibrations (such as in [43] mentioned above). A subject-specific calibration-free method for mobile BCI is proposed based on CPD and BTD of EEG data in [142] with P300 auditory oddball paradigm. For this purpose, the average ERP of all subjects except one is calculated during baseline and target stimuli. This way, two template matrices (one for the baseline and one for target stimuli) are constructed with modes *channel* and *time*. Each trial pair (with the same modes as the templates) of the unknown subject are stacked into a tensor and appended with the baseline and target template obtained from all other subjects to construct the final 3D tensor. The addition of these templates to the trial pair data tensor enhances the likelihood of extracting a task-related signature. After decomposition, the value in the trial-mode signature cues the presence of the target. The classification results are observed to be similar to subject-specific trained models.

Another subject-specific calibration-free classification for an SSVEP-based BCI experiment is proposed in [143] using CPD on a 4D EEG tensor with modes *trial*, *space*, *frequency*, and *subject*. The experiment involves a left and right button flashing with different frequencies and the objective is to identify which button the subject is focused on at a given time. Nonnegativity is enforced in the *trial*, *space*, and *subject* modes which facilitates their interpretation while orthogonality is imposed on the *frequency* mode which guarantees linear independence between factors representing the distinct frequency SSVEP peaks. The rank of CPD is kept constant at 3 so that distinct factors for the two SSVEP signals of interest could be uniquely described whereas the third factor can account for background activity. The factor matrices obtained by decomposing the training tensor along the *space* and *frequency* modes ($U^{(2)}$ and $U^{(3)}$, respectively) are used to define the encoding matrix $E = [U^{(2)} \odot U^{(3)}]^T$, which is projected on data tensors from new subjects and trials as described above ([131]).

A method based on l_1-regularized multiway canonical correlation analysis (multiway CCA [MCCA]) for an SSVEP-based BCI with frequencies $f_1, ..., f_M$ is proposed in [144]. CCA attempts to find a pair of linear transforms for two random variables that maximize the correlation coefficient between them. In the training stage, 3D EEG tensors $\mathcal{X}^{(m)}$ (*channel* × *time* × *trial*) whose trials belong to a specific frequency f_m and matrices $Y^{(m)}$ (*harmonic* × *time*) which store the harmonics of f_m are constructed. The l_1-regularized MCCA searches for the optimum linear transforms in *channel* and *trial* modes for $\mathcal{X}^{(m)}$ and in *harmonic* mode for $Y^{(m)}$ as follows:

$$\mathbf{w}_1^{(m)}, \mathbf{w}_3^{(m)}, \mathbf{v}^{(m)} = \arg\min_{\mathbf{w}_1, \mathbf{w}_3, \mathbf{v}} \frac{1}{2} ||\boldsymbol{\mathcal{X}}^{(m)} \times_1 \mathbf{w}_1^{\mathsf{T}} \times_3 \mathbf{w}_3^{\mathsf{T}} - \mathbf{v}^{\mathsf{T}} \mathbf{Y}^{(m)}||_2^2 \tag{12.37}$$

$$+ \lambda_1 ||\mathbf{w}_1||_1 + \lambda_2 ||\mathbf{v}||_1 + \lambda_3 ||\mathbf{w}_3||_1 \tag{12.38}$$

$$\text{s.t. } ||\mathbf{w}_1||_2 = ||\mathbf{v}||_2 = ||\mathbf{w}_3||_2 = 1, \tag{12.39}$$

where λ_1, λ_2, and λ_3 are regularization parameters to control the sparsity of the linear transforms $\mathbf{w}_1$, $\mathbf{v}$, and $\mathbf{w}_3$ respectively. The results produce one optimized reference vector for each frequency as $\mathbf{z}^{(m)} = \boldsymbol{\mathcal{X}}^{(m)} \times_1 (\mathbf{w}_1^{(m)})^{\mathsf{T}} \times_3 (\mathbf{w}_3^{(m)})^{\mathsf{T}}$. When a single-trial data ($\mathbf{X}$: *channel × time*) is received, the CCA coefficient ρ_m between $\mathbf{X}$ and $\mathbf{z}^{(m)}$, $m = 1, ..., M$, is calculated. Finally, the frequency of the trial is estimated by $\hat{m} = \arg\max_m \rho_m$, and thus $\hat{f} = f_{\hat{m}}$. The block diagram of the proposed method is demonstrated in Fig. 12.24.

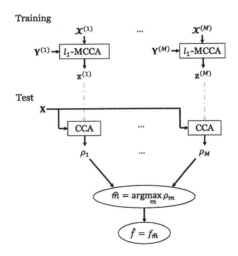

FIGURE 12.24

Steps of l_1-MCCA for SSVEP-based BCI [144]. During training, optimal reference signals $\mathbf{z}^{(m)}$ are learned by applying l_1-MCCA between $\boldsymbol{\mathcal{X}}^{(m)}$ (from multiple trials) and $\mathbf{Y}^{(m)}$ for each frequency index m. For new single-trial data $\mathbf{X}$, the CCA between $\mathbf{X}$ and each $\mathbf{z}^{(m)}$ is calculated. The frequency of the new SSVEP trial is estimated as the one leading to the highest CCA coefficient.

12.5.10 Summary and practical considerations

The multiway structure of the brain, including various modes that are introduced by the experimental designs (such as multiple subjects, conditions, trials, etc.) or by the imaging modality (such as the use of different wavelengths in fNIRS) or incorporated during analysis for a more comprehensive capture of the underlying dynamics (such as frequency expansion via wavelet transform), designates the use of tensors as the intuitive approach for modeling and processing of neuroimaging data. Moreover, comparative studies that evaluate the performance of tensors with respect to their 1D or 2D alternatives show that tensors reveal better results in numerous applications ranging from dimensionality reduction [57] and seizure localization [99] to segmentation [59] and analysis of brain connectivity [114]. Tensor-based solutions for neuroimaging applications reviewed in this chapter are listed in Table 12.1 according to the imaging modality.

In terms of practicality of tensor decompositions, there exist several challenges that can be categorized under the correct choice of rank, components of interest, and initial parameters.

Various approaches have been utilized so far for automatic determination of rank. These include the core consistency diagnostic [90], cumulative proportion of variation explained [109], minimization of the dimensionality of the latent space as described in a Bayesian framework [39], and truncation based on the MLSVD core [104] or based on eigenvalues of the measurement covariances [59].

In addition, some applications require selecting a subset of extracted components, such as for removal of artifact terms, dimensionality reduction, seizure localization, or connectivity analysis. For instance, [90] orders components according to their variance to automatically determine the dominant (epileptic) component, whereas [47] defines an a priori frequency band separating the noise and signal subspaces for automatic removal of residual water in MRS images. Alternatively, [122] proposes to extract only the FCNs that are related to the experimental paradigm, i.e., whose temporal signatures follow the stimulus onsets. Even when component selections are made based on external clinical input, significant differences are observed between signatures belonging to different activity components [100]. The more field expertise or previous empirical findings about the activities of interest are embraced as prior knowledge, the more informed and stable decisions can be made while automating component selection.

Last but not least, as with any optimization problem, good initialization is required to ensure convergence to global optima. Optimization-based tensor decomposition algorithms require any factor matrices and core tensors involved to be initialized. Tensorlab [145] offers internally integrated initialization method(s) for CPD, MLSVD, and $(L_r, L_r, 1)$-BTD based on randomized SVD with randomized subspace iterations to approximate the SVDs of tensor unfoldings. The same method can be used in structured data fusion to reduce the computation time. Another general option is to initialize all values randomly (most likely multiple times, among which the best-cost solution should be determined). For example, [47] uses a quality metric to evaluate the decomposition result based on the variance of component subspaces, which, if found poorly, sends a feedback for reinitialization. Alternatively, the results from a previous decomposition run can be used to initialize a new run [124].

In summary, tensors can be very powerful tools for analyzing multidimensional neuroimaging data, but their success depends on well-informed and appropriate choices for the critical steps explained above.

Table 12.1 A summary of the tensor-based algorithms reviewed in this work with their corresponding applications to neuroimaging data.

Neuroimaging modality	Tensor-based analysis	Application
EEG	CPD, PARAFAC2	Filling in missing data [38,40,43], denoising, artifact removal, and dimensionality reduction [57], source separation [77,82], activity recognition and source localization [87–93,100,101,104,106], connectivity analysis [120,122], feature extraction and classification [43,131,132,134,137,139,142,143]
	Tucker, MLSVD	Denoising, artifact removal, and dimensionality reduction [100], activity recognition and source localization [99,104], connectivity analysis [117], regression [130], feature extraction and classification [131,137,139]
	BTD	Activity recognition and source localization [103,104], feature extraction and classification [142]
	MCCA	Feature extraction and classification [144]
	TBM	Registration and longitudinal analysis [70–74], feature extraction and classification [135]
MRI (and variants)	CPD	Filling in missing data [41], denoising, artifact removal, and dimensionality reduction [40, 54], segmentation [59,60,63,66], registration and longitudinal analysis [75], connectivity analysis [109], regression [127]
	Tucker, MLSVD	Denoising, artifact removal, and dimensionality reduction [47,58,63], segmentation [62, 63], regression [128]
fMRI	CPD, PARAFAC2	Source separation [78], connectivity analysis [112,116,121,124,129], regression [127, 129]
	Tucker, MLSVD	Connectivity analysis [114–116]
	BTD, BTD2	Source separation [78]
fNIRS	CPD	Denoising, artifact removal, and dimensionality reduction [52,53], activity recognition and source localization [52,94]
PET	Tensor SVD	Denoising, artifact removal, and dimensionality reduction [55]
fUS	BTD	Source separation [81]
MEG	CPD, PARAFAC2	Feature extraction and classification [133]

12.6 **Future challenges**

Evolution of medical technology, as well as the ever-increasing demand for it, has led to escalating data sizes with higher spatiotemporal resolution, longer recordings, and a rising number of patients. By 2020, the amount of health care data worldwide has reached 25,000 petabytes, whereas it amounted to approximately 500 petabytes in 2012 [146]. The availability of data at such a large quantity encourages the development of data-driven approaches for medical care purposes. These include patient diagnoses, treatments, and continuous monitoring of patients' health status. Inevitably, the future of medical care relies on Big Data solutions.

Indeed, during the last decade we witnessed the power and effectiveness of deep learning methods in solving very complex tasks using vast amounts of available training data [147]. This is true in particular for image processing, including medical imaging. However, deep learning falls short in transparency: its decision structure is highly complex and nonlinear, and therefore not interpretable. Understanding how and why a certain decision is made, however, is crucial in medical decision support systems in order to maintain trust and avoid unexpected behavior [148]. We believe that tensors can play a role in making deep learning solutions more transparent. Indeed, a series of theoretical research studies has shown links between (deep) neural networks and tensor decompositions. Their results suggest that, by analyzing and modeling certain classes of deep neural networks (DNNs) using tensor tools, we obtain simpler network structures of enhanced expressive power and reduced complexity [149].

Reduced complexity is not only important for transparency; it is also crucial for computational efficiency. When the input data are high-dimensional, the number of entries and hence the number of DNN parameters become intractable. This problem is referred to as the curse of dimensionality: the number of entries in a tensor grows exponentially with its order. Dimensionality reduction using MLSVD (as described in Section 12.5.2) may not be helpful: the core tensor, having the same order as the original tensor, still has a large number of entries even in the case of low multilinear rank [150]. Tensor trains overcome this problem by expressing a high-order tensor as a series of tensor contractions between consecutive low (typically second and third)-order tensors [151]. Tensor trains are still scarcely used in biomedical signal processing. A remarkable application for whole-brain fMRI pattern recognition is presented in [152], where the weight matrix of the fully connected layer of a neural network is compressed via a tensor train.

In many applications it is easy to collect large amounts of normal and healthy data, but abnormal examples, such as rare diseases or epileptic seizures, are scarce. This results in unbalanced training data, which is a challenging machine learning problem. In order to be able to learn and generalize from a few examples in the target class, the machine learning model can benefit from prior knowledge based on expert input. In practice, the prior knowledge can be incorporated in the form of constraints in the optimization problem. The constraint reduces the solution search space and therefore helps to converge to the global minimum. As real-life data are often low-rank, a simple regularization using the trace norm (i.e., the convex relaxation of the rank function) or its tensorial extensions can already be helpful [153,154]. When more specific knowledge is available (e.g., sparsity, nonnegativity, or a parametric generating function), these can be conveyed via explicit constraints such as sparsity, nonnegativity, or a parametric generating function [155]. As tensors can admit different constraints along each of their modes simultaneously [21], they are especially fit for this task.

Many studies that have been performed on multiple subjects highlight the necessity to deliver personalized health care and medicine, taking into consideration each patient's medical history and even their genetics [156]. In this context, multimodal fusion will gain importance. We believe that tensor techniques will play an important role here as well, as they allow to handle heterogeneous data (e.g., EEG, structural images, and phenotypic scores [157]) simultaneously and—again—to impose constraints that ensure interpretability.

Tensors were formulated in 1900 [158], but it was only in the last few decades that they have been extensively recognized by the signal processing and machine learning community. In our opinion, the use of tensor tools at their full potential, especially in applied and clinical contexts, depends on two crucial factors. Good software tools are needed and the users of such tools have to be appropriately educated about their use.

There are various software toolboxes available that allow novice users to apply standard tensor decomposition structures. For an overview, see [150]. These allow quick prototyping and testing of new tensor models, and some offer heuristics for practical choices. However, as the complexity of the model increases (e.g., coupled factorizations and constraints) the computational time needed to solve the optimization problems becomes excessive. Before such tensor tools can be used in practice, custom-made efficient optimization algorithms are needed. The practical challenges outlined in Section 12.5.10 also become more pronounced. Therefore, young researchers should be provided with in-depth training material about the correct use and interpretation of tensor models. Tensor overview articles such as [28], [150], and [159] contribute well to this objective. We believe that tensors will become an increasingly tackled topic in the near future at workshops, tutorials, and summer schools and as elective courses in electrical, computer, and mathematical engineering curricula.

12.7 Conclusion

This chapter provides a general overview on the use of tensors for a wide range of neuroimaging applications. When experimental data are inherently multidimensional, 1D or 2D methods that require unfolding of the original tensor are not fully capable of representing all variations and interplay of the data in each mode. Meanwhile, multidimensionality is an indispensable property of neural data, especially if one wishes to obtain results that are generalizable, such as over multiple subjects, trials, or conditions. Furthermore, keeping the natural formation of the data makes individual structuring of its modes and interpretation of the modeling and results simpler.

Tensor-based solutions exist in all stages of the neural signal processing pipeline, ranging from denoising and dimensionality reduction to BCIs. As with any mathematical algorithm, one might face several challenges when using a tensor-based method, such as parameter selection. However, with a correct understanding of the nature of input neural data and, accordingly, an appropriate choice of the tensor tool, it has been possible to build completely data-driven end-to-end systems. In this chapter, we aimed to list existing employments of tensors in neuroimaging, along with several reasons why we expect to see more of tensors while addressing the needs of future medical technology regarding Big Data applications in diagnosis and monitoring of patients, providing them with the right personalized medical care.

References

[1] R. Marino Jr., M. Gonzales-Portillo, Preconquest Peruvian neurosurgeons: a study of inca and pre-Columbian trephination and the art of medicine in ancient Peru, Neurosurgery 47 (4) (2000) 940–950.

[2] O.I. Abiodun, A. Jantan, O.E. Omolara, K. Dada, N. Mohamed, H. Arshad, State-of-the-art in artificial neural network applications: a survey, Heliyon 4 (11) (2018) e00938.

[3] G.V. Hirsch, C.M. Bauer, L.B. Merabet, Using structural and functional brain imaging to uncover how the brain adapts to blindness, Annals of Neuroscience and Psychology 2 (5) (2015).

[4] S.A. Bunge, I. Kahn, Cognition: An overview of neuroimaging techniques, Encyclopedia of Neuroscience (2009) 1063–1067.

[5] A.M. Aisen, W. Martel, E.M. Braunstein, K.I. McMillin, W.A. Phillips, T.F. Kling, MRI and CT evaluation of primary bone and soft-tissue tumors, American Journal of Roentgenology 146 (4) (1986) 749–756.

[6] J.M. Soares, P. Marques, V. Alves, N. Sousa, A Hitchhiker's guide to diffusion tensor imaging, Frontiers in Neuroscience 7 (2013) 31.

[7] T. Neumann-Haefelin, H.J. Wittsack, F. Wenserski, M. Siebler, R.J. Seitz, U. Mödder, H.J. Freund, Diffusion- and perfusion-weighted MRI. The DWI/PWI mismatch region in acute stroke, Stroke 30 (8) (1999) 1591–1597.

[8] A.E. Pereda, Electrical synapses and their functional interactions with chemical synapses, Nature Reviews. Neuroscience 15 (2014) 260–263.

[9] H. Berger, Über das Elektrenkephalogramm des Menschen, Archiv für Psychiatrie und Nervenkrankheiten 87 (1929) 527–570.

[10] S.P. Sanjay, Magnetoencephalography: basic principles, Annals of Indian Academy of Neurology 17 (1) (2014) 107–112.

[11] C. Huneau, H. Benali, Hugues Chabriat, Investigating human neurovascular coupling using functional neuroimaging: a critical review of dynamic models, Frontiers in Neuroscience 9 (2015) 467.

[12] H.T. Chugani, M.E. Phelps, J.C. Mazziotta, Positron emission tomography study of human brain functional development, Annals of Neurology 22 (4) (1987) 487–497.

[13] J.B. Balardin, G.A. Zimeo Morais, R.A. Furucho, L. Trambaiolli, P. Vanzella, C. Biazoli Jr, J.R. Sato, Imaging brain function with functional near-infrared spectroscopy in unconstrained environments, Frontiers in Human Neuroscience 11 (2017) 258.

[14] G.H. Glover, Overview of functional magnetic resonance imaging, Neurosurgery Clinics of North America 22 (2) (2011) 133–139.

[15] E. Macé, G. Montaldo, I. Cohen, M. Baulac, M. Fink, M. Tanter, Functional ultrasound imaging of the brain, Nature Methods 8 (2011) 662–664.

[16] T. Deffieux, C. Demené, M. Pernot, M. Tanter, Functional ultrasound neuroimaging: a review of the preclinical and clinical state of the art, Current Opinion in Neurobiology 50 (2018) 128–135.

[17] G. Northoff, Z. Huang, How do the brain's time and space mediate consciousness and its different dimensions? Temporo-spatial theory of consciousness (TTC), Neuroscience & Biobehavioral Reviews 80 (2017) 630–645.

[18] E. Acar, Y. Levin-Schwartz, V.D. Calhoun, T. Adali, ACMTF for fusion of multi-modal neuroimaging data and identification of biomarkers, in: 2017 25th European Signal Processing Conference (EUSIPCO), 2017, pp. 643–647.

[19] F. Cong, Q. Lin, L. Kuang, X. Gong, P. Astikainen, T. Ristaniemi, Tensor decomposition of EEG signals: a brief review, Journal of Neuroscience Methods 248 (2015) 59–69.

[20] C.F. Beckmann, S.M. Smith, Tensorial extensions of independent component analysis for multisubject FMRI analysis, NeuroImage 25 (1) (2005) 294–311.

[21] L. Sorber, M. Van Barel, L. De Lathauwer, Structured data fusion, IEEE Journal of Selected Topics in Signal Processing 9 (4) (2015) 586–600.

[22] Y. Murin, J. Kim, J. Parvizi, A. Goldsmith, SozRank: A new approach for localizing the epileptic seizure onset zone, PLoS Computational Biology 14 (1) (2018) e1005953.

[23] W.S. Sohn, K. Yoo, Y.B. Lee, S.W. Seo, D.L. Na, Y. Jeong, Influence of ROI selection on resting state functional connectivity: an individualized approach for resting state fMRI analysis, Frontiers in Neuroscience 9 (2018) 280.

[24] D. Gajic, Z. Djurovic, J. Gligorijevic, S. Di Gennaro, I.M.S. Gajic, Detection of epileptiform activity in EEG signals based on time-frequency and non-linear analysis, Frontiers in Computational Neuroscience 9 (2015) 38.

[25] C. Chatzichristos, K. Eleftherios, Y. Kopsinis, M. Morante, S. Theodoridis, Higher-order block term decomposition for spatially folded fMRI data, Lecture Notes in Computer Science (2017) 3–15.

[26] D. Kalman, A singularly valuable decomposition: the SVD of a matrix, The College Mathematics Journal 27 (1) (1996) 2–23.

[27] A. Zhang, D. Xia, Tensor SVD: statistical and computational limits, IEEE Transactions on Information Theory 64 (11) (2018) 7311–7338.

[28] T.G. Kolda, B.W. Wader, Tensor decompositions and applications, SIAM Review 51 (3) (2009) 455–500.

[29] J.H.de M. Goulart, M. Boizard, R. Boyer, G. Favier, P. Comon, Tensor CP decomposition with structured factor matrices: algorithms and performance, IEEE Journal of Selected Topics in Signal Processing 10 (4) (2016) 757–769.

[30] A. Cichocki, D.P. Mandic, A. Phan, C.F. Caiafa, G. Zhou, Q. Zhao, L. De Lathauwer, Tensor decompositions for signal processing applications from two-way to multiway component analysis, IEEE Signal Processing Magazine 32 (2) (2014) 145–163.

[31] H.A.L. Kiers, J.M.F. ten Berge, R. Bro, PARAFAC2—Part I. A direct fitting algorithm for the PARAFAC2 model, Journal of Chemometrics 13 (3) (1998) 275–294.

[32] I. Perros, E.E. Papalexakis, F. Wang, R. Vuduc, E. Searles, M. Thompson, J. Sun, SPAR-Tan: Scalable PARAFAC2 for large & sparse data, in: Proceedings of the 23rd ACM SIGKDD International Conference on Knowledge Discovery and Data Mining, 2017, pp. 375–384.

[33] L. De Lathauwer, B. De Moor, J. Vandewalle, A multilinear singular value decomposition, SIAM Journal on Matrix Analysis and Applications 21 (4) (2000) 1253–1278.

[34] G. Bergqvist, E.G. Larsson, The higher-order singular value decomposition: theory and an application [lecture notes], IEEE Signal Processing Magazine 27 (3) (2010) 151–154.

[35] J. Chen, Y. Saad, On the tensor SVD and the optimal low rank orthogonal approximation of tensors, SIAM Journal on Matrix Analysis and Applications 30 (4) (2008) 1709–1734.

[36] N. Hao, M. Kilmer, K. Braman, R. Hoover, Facial recognition using tensor-tensor decompositions, SIAM Journal on Imaging Sciences 6 (1) (2013) 437–463.

[37] L. Sorber, M. Van Barel, L. De Lathauwer, Optimization-based algorithms for tensor decompositions: canonical polyadic decomposition, decomposition in rank-(lr, lr, 1) terms, and a new generalization, SIAM Journal on Optimization 23 (2) (2013) 695–720.

[38] E. Acar, D.M. Dunlavy, T.G. Kolda, M. Mørup, Scalable tensor factorizations with missing data, in: Proceedings of the SIAM International Conference on Data Mining, 2010, pp. 701–712.

[39] Q. Zhao, G. Zhou, L. Zhang, A. Cichocki, S. Amari, Bayesian robust tensor factorization for incomplete multiway data, IEEE Transactions on Neural Networks and Learning Systems 27 (4) (2010) 736–748.

[40] G. Cui, L. Zhu, L. Gui, Q. Zhao, J. Zhang, J. Cao, Multidimensional clinical data denoising via Bayesian CP factorization, Science China. Technological Sciences 63 (2019) 249–254.

[41] J.A. Bazerque, G. Mateos, G.B. Giannakis, Rank regularization and Bayesian inference for tensor completion and extrapolation, IEEE Transactions on Signal Processing 61 (22) (2013) 5689–5703.

[42] S. Friedland, L. Lim, Nuclear norm of higher-order tensors, Mathematics of Computation 87 (311) (2017) 1255–1281.

[43] J. Solé-Casals, C.F. Caiafa, Q. Zhao, A. Cichocki, Brain-computer interface with corrupted EEG data: a tensor completion approach, Cognitive Computation 10 (2018) 1062–1074.

[44] C. Caiafa, A. Cichocki, Multidimensional compressed sensing and their applications, Data Mining and Knowledge Discovery 3 (6) (2013) 355–380.

[45] J. Liu, P. Musialski, P. Wonka, J. Ye, Tensor completion for estimating missing values in visual data, IEEE Transactions on Pattern Analysis and Machine Intelligence 35 (1) (2013) 208–220.

[46] H. Zhu, R. Ouwerkerk, P.B. Barker, Dual-band water and lipid suppression for MR spectroscopic imaging at 3 tesla, Magnetic Resonance in Medicine 63 (6) (2010) 1486–1492.

[47] H.N. Bharath, O. Debals, D.M. Sima, U. Himmelreich, L. De Lathauwer, S. Van Huffel, Tensor-based method for residual water suppression in ^{1}h magnetic resonance spectroscopic imaging, IEEE Transactions on Biomedical Engineering 66 (2) (2019) 584–594.

[48] R.J. Croft, R.J. Barry, Removal of ocular artifact from the EEG: a review, Clinical Neurophysiology 30 (1) (2000) 5–19.

[49] S. Ge, M. Han, X. Hong, A fully automatic ocular artifact removal from EEG based on fourth-order tensor method, Biomedical Engineering Letters 4 (2014) 55–63.

[50] L. De Lathauwer, J. Castaing, J. Cardoso, Fourth-order cumulant-based blind identification of underdetermined mixtures, IEEE Transactions on Signal Processing 55 (6) (2007) 2965–2973.

[51] R.J. Cooper, J. Selb, L. Gagnon, D. Phillip, H.W. Schytz, H.K. Iversen, M. Ashina, D.A. Boas, A systematic comparison of motion artifact correction techniques for functional near-infrared spectroscopy, Frontiers in Neuroscience 6 (2012) 147.

[52] A. Hüsser, L. Caron-Desrochers, J. Tremblay, P. Vannasing, E. Martínez-Montes, A. Gallagher, Parallel Factor Analysis (PARAFAC) for Multidimensional Decomposition of FNIRS Data – a Validation Study, bioRxiv, 806778, 2019.

[53] J. Tremblay, E. Martínez-Montes, A. Hüsser, L. Caron-Desrochers, P. Pouliot, P. Vannasing, A. Gallagher, LIONirs: Flexible Matlab Toolbox for fNIRS Data Analysis, bioRxiv, 2020.09.11.257634, 2020.

[54] L. Ying, Y.M. Zou, D.P. Klemer, J. Wang, Determination of fiber orientation in MRI diffusion tensor imaging based on higher-order tensor decomposition, in: 2007 29th Annual International Conference of the IEEE Engineering in Medicine and Biology Society, 2007, pp. 2065–2068.

[55] N. Xie, Y. Chen, H. Liu, 3D tensor based nonlocal low rank approximation in dynamic PET reconstruction, Sensors 19 (23) (2019) 1–20.

[56] C. Lu, J. Feng, W. Liu, Z. Lin, S. Yan, Tensor robust principal component analysis with a new tensor nuclear norm, IEEE Transactions on Pattern Analysis and Machine Intelligence 42 (4) (2020) 925–938.

[57] M. Taherisadr, M. Joneidi, N. Rahnavard, EEG signal dimensionality reduction and classification using tensor decomposition and deep convolutional neural networks, in: 2019 IEEE 29th International Workshop on Machine Learning for Signal Processing (MLSP), 2019, pp. 1–6.

[58] Y. Yu, J. Jin, F. Liu, S. Crozier, Multidimensional compressed sensing MRI using tensor decomposition-based sparsifying transform, PLoS ONE 9 (6) (2014) e98441.

[59] H.N. Bharath, D.M. Sima, N. Sauwen, U. Himmelreich, L. De Lathauwer, S. Van Huffel, Nonnegative canonical polyadic decomposition for tissue-type differentiation in gliomas, IEEE Journal of Biomedical and Health Informatics 21 (4) (2017) 1124–1132.

[60] H.N. Bharath, N. Sauwen, D.M. Sima, U. Himmelreich, L. De Lathauwer, S. Van Huffel, Canonical polyadic decomposition for tissue type differentiation using multiparametric MRI in high-grade gliomas, in: 2016 24th European Signal Processing Conference (EUSIPCO), 2017, pp. 547–551.

[61] M. Sørensen, L. De Lathauwer, Blind signal separation via tensor decomposition with Vandermonde factor: canonical polyadic decomposition, IEEE Transactions on Signal Processing 61 (22) (2013) 5507–5519.

[62] H.N. Bharath, S. Colleman, D.M. Sima, S. Van, Huffel Tumor, Segmentation from multimodal MRI using random forest with superpixel and tensor based feature extraction, in: BrainLes 2017: Brainlesion: Glioma, Multiple Sclerosis, Stroke and Traumatic Brain Injuries, 2018, pp. 463–473.

[63] H.N. Bharath, Tensor Based Approaches in Magnetic Resonance Spectroscopic Imaging and Multi-parametric MRI Data Analysis, 2018.

[64] Ö. Çiçek, A. Abdulkadir, S.S. Lienkamp, T. Brox, O. Ronneberger, 3D u-net: learning dense volumetric segmentation from sparse annotation, Medical Image Computing and Computer-Assisted Intervention 9901 (2016) 424–432.

[65] O. Ronneberger, P. Fischer, T. Brox, U-Net: Convolutional networks for biomedical image segmentation, Medical Image Computing and Computer-Assisted Intervention 9351 (2015) 234–241.

[66] L. Sun, W. Ma, X. Ding, Y. Huang, D. Liang, J. Paisley, A 3D spatially weighted network for segmentation of brain tissue from MRI, IEEE Transactions on Medical Imaging 39 (4) (2020) 898–909.

[67] A.M. Mendrik, K.L. Vincken, H.J. Kuijf, M. Breeuwer, W.H. Bouvy, J. de Bresser, A. Alansary, M. de Bruijne, A. Carass, A. El-Baz, A. Jogh, R. Katyal, A.R. Khan, F. van der Lijn, Q. Mahmood, R. Mukherjee, A. van Opbroek, S. Paneri, S. Pereira, M. Persson, M. Rajchl, D. Sarikayan, O. Smedby, C.A. Silva, H.A. Vrooman, S. Vyas, C. Wang, L. Zhaon, G.J. Biessels, M.A. Viergever, MRBrainS challenge: online evaluation framework for brain image segmentation in 3T MRI scans, Computational Intelligence and Neuroscience (2015) 1–16.

[68] A.W. Toga, P.M. Thompson, The role of image registration in brain mapping, Image and Vision Computing 19 (1–2) (2001) 3–24.

[69] K. Mills, C. Tamnes, Methods and considerations for longitudinal structural brain imaging analysis across development, Developmental Cognitive Neuroscience 9 (2014) 172–190.

[70] N. Lepore, C. Brun, Y. Chou, M. Chiang, R.A. Dutton, K.M. Hayashi, E. Luders, O.L. Lupez, H.J. Aizenstein, A.W. Toga, J.T. Becker, P.M. Thompson, Generalized tensor-based morphometry of HIV/AIDS using multivariate statistics on deformation tensors, IEEE Transactions on Medical Imaging 27 (1) (2008) 129–141.

[71] A.D. Leow, I. Yanovsky, M. Chiang, A.D. Lee, A.D. Klunder, A. Lu, J.T. Becker, S.W. Davis, A.W. Toga, P.M. Thompson, Statistical properties of Jacobian maps and the realization of unbiased large-deformation nonlinear image registration, IEEE Transactions on Medical Imaging 26 (6) (2007) 822–832.

[72] A. Leow, I. Yanovsky, N. Parikshak, X. Hua, S. Lee, A. Toga, C. Jack, M. Bernstein, P. Britson, J. Gunter, C. Ward, B. Borowski, L. Shaw, J. Trojanowski, A. Fleisher, D. Harvey, J. Kornak, N. Schuff, G. Alexander, M. Weiner, P.M. Thompson, Alzheimer's disease neuroimaging initiative: a one-year follow up study using tensor-based morphometry correlating degenerative rates, biomarkers and cognition, NeuroImage 45 (3) (2009) 645–655.

[73] M. Chiang, R. Dutton, K.M. Hayashi, O. Lopez, H. Aizenstein, A. Toga, J. Becker, P. Thompson, 3D pattern of brain atrophy in HIV/AIDS visualized using tensor-based morphometry, NeuroImage 34 (1) (2007) 44–60.

[74] E.M. Meintjes, K.L. Narr, A.J.W. Van Der Kouwe, C.D. Molteno, T. Pirnia, B. Gutman, R.P. Woods, P.M. Thompson, J.L. Jacobson, S.W. Jacobson, A tensor-based morphometry analysis of regional differences in brain volume in relation to prenatal alcohol exposure, NeuroImage: Clinical 5 (2014) 152–160.

[75] C. Stamile, F. Cotton, D. Sappey-Marinier, S. Van Huffel, Constrained tensor decomposition for longitudinal analysis of diffusion imaging data, IEEE Journal of Biomedical and Health Informatics 24 (4) (2020) 1137–1148.

[76] M. Boussé, O. Debals, L. De Lathauwer, A tensor-based method for large-scale blind source separation using segmentation, IEEE Transactions on Signal Processing 65 (2) (2017) 346–358.

[77] H. Becker, L. Albera, P. Comon, M. Haardt, G. Birot, F. Wendling, M. Gavaret, C.G. Bénar, I. Merlet, EEG extended source localization: tensor-based vs. conventional methods, NeuroImage 96 (2014) 143–157.

[78] C. Chatzichristos, E. Kofidis, M. Morante, S. Theodoridis, Blind fMRI source unmixing via higher-order tensor decompositions, Journal of Neuroscience Methods 315 (2019) 17–47.

[79] J. Pérez Outeiral, S. Elcoroaristizabal, J.M. Amigo, M. Vidal, Development and validation of a method for the determination of regulated fragrance allergens by high-performance liquid chromatography and parallel factor analysis 2, Journal of Chromatography A 1526 (2017) 82–92.

[80] F. Van Eeghem, L. De Lathauwer, Second-order tensor-based convolutive ICA: deconvolution versus tensorization, in: 2017 IEEE International Conference on Acoustics, Speech and Signal Processing (ICASSP), 2017, pp. 2252–2256.

[81] A. Erol, S. Van Eyndhoven, S. Koekkoek, P. Kruizinga, B. Hunyadi, Joint estimation of hemodynamic response and stimulus function in functional ultrasound using convolutive mixtures, in: 2020 54th Asilomar Conference on Signals, Systems and Computers, 2020, pp. 246–250.

[82] S. Kouchaki, Tensor based source separation for single and multichannel signals, 2015.

[83] A.C.K. Soong, Z.J. Koles, Principal-component localization of the sources of the background EEG, IEEE Transactions on Biomedical Engineering 42 (1) (2001) 59–67.

[84] E. Urrestarazu, J. Iriarte, M. Alegre, M. Valencia, C. Viteri, J. Artieda, Independent component analysis removing artifacts in ictal recordings, Epilepsia 45 (9) (2004) 1071–1078.

[85] B. Hunyadi, P. Dupont, W. Van Paesschen, S. Van Huffel, Tensor decompositions and data fusion in epileptic electroencephalography and functional magnetic resonance imaging data, Wiley Interdisciplinary Reviews: Data Mining and Knowledge Discovery 7 (1) (2017) e1197.

[86] R. Bro, PARAFAC. Tutorial and applications, Chemometrics and Intelligent Laboratory Systems 38 (2) (1997) 149–171.

[87] H. Cole, W. Ray, EEG correlates of emotional tasks related to attentional demands, International Journal of Psychophysiology 3 (1) (1985) 33–41.

[88] J. Möcks, Decomposing event-related potentials: a new topographic components model, Biological Psychology 26 (1–3) (1988) 199–215.

[89] F. Miwakeichi, E. Martínez-Montes, P. Valdés-Sosa, N. Nobuaki, H. Mizuhara, Y. Yamaguchi, Decomposing EEG data into space-time-frequency components using parallel factor analysis, NeuroImage 22 (3) (2004) 1035–1045.

[90] M. De Vos, A. Vergult, L. De Lathauwer, W. De Clercq, S. Van Huffel, P. Dupont, A. Palmini, W. Van Paesschen, Canonical decomposition of ictal scalp EEG reliably detects the seizure onset zone, NeuroImage 37 (3) (2007) 844–854.

[91] M. Mørup, L. Hansen, C. Herrmann, J. Parnas, S.M. Arnfred, Parallel factor analysis as an exploratory tool for wavelet transformed event-related EEG, NeuroImage 29 (3) (2006) 938–947.

[92] C. Tangwiriyasakul, I. Premoli, L. Spyrou, R.F.M. Chin, J. Escudero, M.P. Richardson, Tensor decomposition of TMS-induced EEG oscillations reveals data-driven profiles of antiepileptic drug effects, Scientific Reports 9 (1) (2019) 17057.

[93] W. Juan, X. Li, C. Lu, L. Voss, J. Barnard, J. Sleigh, Characteristics of evoked potential multiple EEG recordings in patients with chronic pain by means of parallel factor analysis, Computational & Mathematical Methods in Medicine (2012) 279560.

[94] M. Hssayeni, T. Wilcox, B. Ghoraani, Tensor decomposition of functional near-infrared spectroscopy (fNIRS) signals for pattern discovery of cognitive response in infants, in: 2020 42nd Annual International Conference of the IEEE Engineering in Medicine and Biology Society (EMBC), 2020, pp. 394–397.

[95] A. Singh, S. Trevick, The epidemiology of global epilepsy, Neurologic Clinics 34 (4) (2016) 837–847.

[96] C. Nagesh, S. Kumar, R. Menon, B. Thomas, A. Radhakrishnan, C. Kesavadas, The imaging of localization related symptomatic epilepsies: the value of arterial spin labelling based magnetic resonance perfusion, Korean Journal of Radiology 19 (5) (2018) 965–977.

[97] B. Litt, R. Esteller, J. Echauz, M. D'Alessandro, R. Shor, T. Henry, P. Pennell, C. Epstein, R. Bakay, M. Dichter, G. Vachtsevanos, Epileptic seizures may begin hours in advance of clinical onset: a report of five patients, Neuron 30 (1) (2001) 51–64.

[98] R. Bro, H. Kiers, A new efficient method for determining the number of components in PARAFAC models, Journal of Chemometrics 17 (5) (2003) 274–286.

[99] E. Acar, C. Bingol, H. Bingol, B. Yener, Computational analysis of epileptic focus localization, in: Proceedings of the Fourth IASTED International Conference on Biomedical Engineering, 2006.

[100] E. Acar, C. Bingol, H. Bingol, R. Bro, B. Yener, Multiway analysis of epilepsy tensors, Bioinformatics 23 (13) (2007), I10–I18.

[101] W. Deburchgraeve, P.J. Cherian, M. De Vos, R.M. Swarte, J.H. Blok, G.H. Visser, P. Govaert, S. Van Huffel, Neonatal seizure localization using PARAFAC decomposition, Clinical Neurophysiology Official Journal of the International Federation of Clinical Neurophysiology 120 (10) (2009) 1787–1796.

[102] W. Deburchgraeve, P.J. Cherian, M. De Vos, R.M. Swarte, J.H. Blok, G.H. Visser, P. Govaert, S. Van Huffel, Automated neonatal seizure detection mimicking a human observer reading EEG, Clinical Neurophysiology 119 (11) (2008) 2447–2454.

[103] B. Hunyadi, D. Camps, L. Sorber, W. Van Paesschen, M. de Vos, S. Van Huffel, L. De Lathauwer, Block term decomposition for modelling epileptic seizures, EURASIP Journal on Advances in Signal Processing (2014) 1–19.

[104] Y.R. Aldana, B. Hunyadi, E.J.M. Reyes, V.R. Rodríguez, S. Van Huffel, Nonconvulsive epileptic seizure detection in scalp EEG using multiway data analysis, IEEE Journal of Biomedical and Health Informatics (2019) 660–671.

[105] E. Acar, C. Bingol, H. Bingol, R. Bro, B. Yener, Seizure recognition on epilepsy feature tensor, in: Annual International Conference of the IEEE Engineering in Medicine and Biology Society, 2007, pp. 4273–4276.

[106] B. Direito, C. Teixeira, B. Ribeiro, M. Castelo-Branco, A. Dourado, Space time frequency (STF) code tensor for the characterization of the epileptic preictal stage, in: 2012 Annual International Conference of the IEEE Engineering in Medicine and Biology Society, 2012, pp. 621–624.

[107] L.Q. Uddin, Complex relationships between structural and functional brain connectivity, Trends in Cognitive Sciences 17 (12) (2013) 600–602.

[108] G. Leismanm, A. Moustafa, T. Shafir, Thinking, walking, talking: The development of integratory brain function, Frontiers in Public Health 4 (2016) 94.

[109] Z. Zhang, G.I. Allen, H. Zhu, D. Dunson, Tensor network factorizations: relationships between brain structural connectomes and traits, NeuroImage 197 (2019) 330–343.

[110] G.I. Allen, Sparse higher-order principal components analysis, in: Proceedings of the Fifteenth International Conference on Artificial Intelligence and Statistics, vol. 22, 2012, pp. 27–36.

[111] R. Prabhakaran, S.E. Blumstein, E.B. Myers, E. Hutchison, B. Britton, An event-related fMRI investigation of phonological-lexical competition, Neuropsychologia 44 (12) (2006) 2209–2221.

[112] K. Glomb, A. Ponce-Alvarez, M. Gilson, P. Ritter, G. Deco, Resting state networks in empirical and simulated dynamic functional connectivity, NeuroImage 159 (2017) 388–402.

[113] A. Kraskov, H. Stögbauer, P. Grassberger, Estimating mutual information, Physical Review E 69 (2004) 066138.

[114] F. Mokhtari, R.E. Mayhugh, C.E. Hugenschmidt, W.J. Rejeski, P.J. Laurienti, Tensor-based vs. matrix-based rank reduction in dynamic brain connectivity, in: Proceedings of the SPIE Medical Imaging Conference, 2018, p. 10574.

[115] N. Leonardi, D. Van de Ville, Identifying network correlates of brain states using tensor decompositions of whole-brain dynamic functional connectivity, 2013 International Workshop on Pattern Recognition in Neuroimaging (2013) 74–77.

[116] F. Mokhtari, P.J. Laurienti, W.J. Rejeski, G. Ballard, Dynamic functional magnetic resonance imaging connectivity tensor decomposition: a new approach to analyze and interpret dynamic brain connectivity, Brain Connectivity 9 (1) (2019) 95–112.

[117] A.G. Mahyari, D.M. Zoltowski, E.M. Bernat, S. Aviyente, A tensor decomposition-based approach for detecting dynamic network states from EEG, IEEE Transactions on Biomedical Engineering 64 (1) (2017) 225–237.

[118] E. Ceulemans, H.A. Kiers, Selecting among three-mode principal component models of different types and complexities: a numerical convex hull based method, British Journal of Mathematical and Statistical Psychology 59 (1) (2006) 133–150.

[119] K. Ye, L. Lim, Schubert varieties and distances between subspaces of different dimensions, SIAM Journal on Matrix Analysis and Applications 37 (3) (2016) 1176–1197.

[120] L. Spyrou, M. Parra, J. Escudero, Complex tensor factorization with PARAFAC2 for the estimation of brain connectivity from the EEG, IEEE Transactions on Neural Systems and Rehabilitation Engineering 27 (1) (2018) 1–12.

[121] K.H. Madsen, N.W. Churchill, M. Mørup, Quantifying functional connectivity in multi-subject fMRI data using component models, Human Brain Mapping 38 (2) (2016) 882–899.

[122] B. Pester, C. Ligges, L. Leistritz, H. Witte, K. Schiecke, Advanced insights into functional brain connectivity by combining tensor decomposition and partial directed coherence, PLoS ONE 10 (6) (2015) e0129293.

[123] M.F. Pagnotta, G. Plomp, Time-varying MVAR algorithms for directed connectivity analysis: critical comparison in simulations and benchmark EEG data, PLoS ONE 13 (6) (2018) e0198846.

[124] E. Karahan, P.A. Rojas-López, M.L. Bringas-Vega, P.A. Valdés-Hernández, P.A. Valdes-Sosa, Tensor analysis and fusion of multimodal brain images, Proceedings of the IEEE 103 (9) (2015) 1531–1559.

[125] S. Bressler, A. Seth, Wiener–granger causality: a well established methodology, NeuroImage 58 (2) (2010) 323–329.

[126] P. McCullagh, J.A. Nelder, Generalized Linear Models (Mono-Graphs on Statistics and Applied Probability), Chapman & Hall, London, 1983.

[127] H. Zhou, L. Li, H. Zhu, Tensor regression with applications in neuroimaging data analysis, Journal of the American Statistical Association 108 (502) (2013) 540–552.

[128] X. Li, D. Xu, H. Zhou, L. Li. Tucker, Tensor regression and neuroimaging analysis, Statistics in Biosciences 10 (2018) 520–545.

[129] W.W. Sun, L. Li, STORE: sparse tensor response regression and neuroimaging analysis, Journal of Machine Learning Research 18 (2017) 1–37.

[130] Q. Zhao, C.F. Caiafa, D. Mandic, L. Zhang, T. Ball, A. Schulze-Bonhage, A. Cichocki, Multilinear subspace regression: an orthogonal tensor decomposition approach, in: Advances in Neural Information Processing Systems (NIPS), 2011, pp. 1269–1277.

[131] C.F.V. Latchoumane, F. Vialatte, J. Solé-Casals, M. Maurice, S. Wimalaratna, N. Hudson, J. Jeong, A. Cichocki, Multiway array decomposition analysis of EEGs in Alzheimer's disease, Journal of Neuroscience Methods 207 (1) (2012) 41–50.

[132] D. Qian, B. Wang, X. Qing, T. Zhang, Y. Zhang, X. Wang, M. Nakamura, Bayesian nonnegative CP decomposition-based feature extraction algorithm for drowsiness detection, IEEE Transactions on Neural Systems and Rehabilitation Engineering 25 (8) (2017) 1297–1308.

[133] J. Escudero, E. Acar, A. Fernández, R. Bro, Multiscale entropy analysis of resting-state magnetoencephalogram with tensor factorisations in Alzheimer's disease, Brain Research Bulletin 119 (2015) 136–144.

[134] F. Song, A.H. Phan, Q. Zhao, T. Huttunen-Scott, J. Kaartinen, T. Ristaniemi, H. Lyytinen, A. Cichocki, Benefits of multi-domain feature of mismatch negativity extracted by non-negative tensor factorization from EEG collected by low-density array, International Journal of Neural Systems 22 (6) (2012) 1250025.

[135] Y. Wang, L. Yuan, J. Shi, A. Greve, J. Ye, A. Toga, P. Thompson, Applying tensor-based morphometry to parametric surfaces can improve MRI-based disease diagnosis, NeuroImage 74 (2013) 209–230.

[136] A. Rezeika, M. Benda, P. Stawicki, F. Gembler, A. Saboor, I. Volosyak, Brain-computer interface spellers: a review, Brain Sciences 8 (4) (2018) 57.

[137] A.H. Phan, A. Cichocki, Tensor decompositions for feature extraction and classification of high dimensional datasets, Nonlinear Theory and Its Applications, IEICE 1 (1) (2010) 37–68.

[138] H. Ramoser, J. Muller-Gerking, G. Pfurtscheller, Optimal spatial filtering of single trial EEG during imagined hand movement, IEEE Transactions on Rehabilitation Engineering 8 (4) (2000) 441–446.

[139] A. Cichocki, Y. Washizawa, T. Rutkowski, H. Bakardjian, A.H. Phan, S. Choi, H. Lee, Q. Zhao, L. Zhang, Y. Li, Noninvasive BCIs: multiway signal-processing array decompositions, Computer 41 (10) (2008) 34–42.

[140] B. Hunyadi, M. Signoretto, S. Debener, S. Van Huffel, M. de Vos, Classification of structured EEG tensors using nuclear norm regularization: improving P300 classification, in: 2013 International Workshop on Pattern Recognition in Neuroimaging, Philadelphia, 2013, pp. 98–101.

[141] A. Onishi, A.H. Phan, K. Matsuoka, A. Cichocki, Tensor classification for P300-based brain computer interface, in: 2012 IEEE International Conference on Acoustics, Speech and Signal Processing (ICASSP), 2012, pp. 581–584.

[142] R. Zink, B. Hunyadi, S. Van Huffel, M. de Vos, Tensor-based classification of an auditory mobile BCI without a subject-specific calibration phase, Journal of Neural Engineering 13 (2) (2016) 026005.

[143] E. Kinney-Lang, A. Ebied, J. Escudero, Building a tensor framework for the analysis and classification of steady-state visual evoked potentials in children, in: 2018 26th European Signal Processing Conference (EUSIPCO), vol. 21(6), 2018, pp. 296–300.

[144] Y. Zhang, G. Zhou, J. Jin, M. Wang, X. Wang, A. Cichocki, L1-regularized multiway canonical correlation analysis for SSVEP-based BCI, IEEE Transactions on Neural Systems and Rehabilitation Engineering 21 (6) (2013) 887–896.

[145] N. Vervliet, O. Debals, L. Sorber, M. Van Barel, L. De Lathauwer, Tensorlab 3.0, Available online https://www.tensorlab.net, Mar. 2016.

[146] C. Orphanidou, A review of big data applications of physiological signal data, Biophysical Reviews 11 (1) (2019) 83–87.

[147] J. Schmidhuber, Deep learning in neural networks: an overview, Neural Networks 61 (2015) 85–117.

[148] W. Samek, G. Montavon, A. Vedaldi, L.K. Hansen, K.-R. Müller, Explainable AI: Interpreting, Explaining and Visualizing Deep Learning, Springer, 2019, p. 11700.

[149] A. Cichocki, A.H. Phan, Q. Zhao, N. Lee, I.V. Oseledets, M. Sugiyama, D. Mandic, Tensor networks for dimensionality reduction and large-scale optimizations: part 2 applications and future perspectives, arXiv preprint, arXiv:1708.09165, 2017.

[150] N.D. Sidiropoulos, L. De Lathauwer, X. Fu, K. Huang, E.E. Papalexakis, C. Faloutsos, Tensor decomposition for signal processing and machine learning, IEEE Transactions on Signal Processing 65 (13) (2017) 3551–3582.

[151] I. Oseledets, Tensor-train decomposition, SIAM Journal on Scientific and Statistical Computing 33 (5) (2011) 2295–2317.

[152] X. Xu, Q. Wu, S. Wang, J. Liu, J. Sun, A. Cichocki, Whole brain fMRI pattern analysis based on tensor neural network, IEEE Access 6 (2018) 29297–29305.

[153] B. Hunyadi, M. Signoretto, W. Van Paesschen, J.A.K. Suykens, S. Van Huffel, M. De Vos, Incorporating structural information from the multichannel EEG improves patient-specific seizure detection, Clinical Neurophysiology 123 (12) (2012) 2352–2361.

[154] M. Signoretto, Q.T. Dinh, L. De Lathauwer, J.A.K. Suykens, Learning with tensors: a framework based on convex optimization and spectral regularization, Machine Learning 94 (3) (2014) 303–351.

[155] S. Van Eyndhoven, P. Dupont, S. Tousseyn, N. Vervliet, W. Van Paesschen, S. Van Huffel, B. Hunyadi, Augmenting interictal mapping with neurovascular coupling biomarkers by structured factorization of epileptic EEG and fMRI data, arXiv preprint, arXiv:2004.14185, 2020.

[156] E.A. Ashley, Towards precision medicine, Nature Reviews. Genetics 17 (9) (2016) 507–522.

[157] N. Dron, R.F.M. Chin, J. Escudero, Canonical polyadic and block term decompositions to fuse EEG, phenotypic scores, and structural MRI of children with early-onset epilepsy, in: 2020 28th European Signal Processing Conference (EUSIPCO), 2020, pp. 1145–1149.

[158] M.M.G. Ricci, T. Levi-Civita, Méthodes de calcul différentiel absolu et leurs applications, Mathematische Annalen 54 (1900) 125–201.

[159] A. Cichocki, D. Mandic, L. De Lathauwer, G. Zhou, Q. Zhao, C.F. Caiafa, A. Phan, Tensor decompositions for signal processing applications: from two-way to multiway component analysis, IEEE Signal Processing Magazine 32 (2) (2015) 145–163.

Tensor representation for remote sensing images

13

Yang Xu[a], Fei Ye[a], Bo Ren[b], Liangfu Lu[c], Xudong Cui[c], Jocelyn Chanussot[d], and Zebin Wu[a]

[a]*School of Computer Science and Engineering, Nanjing University of Science and Technology, Nanjing, China*
[b]*Key Laboratory of Intelligent Perception and Image Understanding of Ministry of Education of China, Xidian University, Xi'an, China*
[c]*School of Mathematics, Tianjin University, Tianjin, China*
[d]*LJK, CNRS, Grenoble INP, Inria, Université Grenoble, Alpes, Grenoble, France*

CONTENTS

13.1 Introduction

Remote sensing is the science and art of obtaining information about an object, area, or phenomenon through the analysis of data acquired by a device that is not in contact with the target under investigation [29]. Modern remote sensing technology has advanced significantly in the past several decades. Current sensors equipped on airborne or spaceborne platforms cover large areas of the Earth's surface with unprecedented spatial, spectral, radiometric, and temporal resolutions. These characteristics enable a myriad of applications requiring fine identification of materials or estimation of physical parameters [6,63].

One of the most commonly applied remote sensing technologies is optical remote sensing. Optical remote sensing with visible and near-infrared electromagnetic waves takes advantage of natural radiation of the sun that is reflected from the Earth's surface [3,36]. The sum of the reflected radiation, emission from the ground, and the path

Tensors for Data Processing. https://doi.org/10.1016/B978-0-12-824447-0.00019-4

FIGURE 13.1

The tensor structure of a hyperspectral image.

radiance is sensed through the optical sensors and converted into electrical signals by detectors. However, restricted by the amount of incident energy, there is always a trade-off between spatial and spectral resolution [31]. Thus, it is of interest to make use of information from several distinct data sources to synthesize images with high resolution in the spatial, spectral, radiometric, and temporal domains simultaneously. Remote sensing image fusion provides a proper framework to deal with the diversity of data and ensures an optimum information outcome. The most extensively studied related research is pan-sharpening [4,16,42,47], which fuses the low-resolution (LR) multispectral image (MSI) with a corresponding high-resolution (HR) panchromatic image (PAN). By means of pan-sharpening, the spectral characteristics of MSI can be retained, whilst the spatial structures of PAN can be incorporated, which can represent the detected scene in more detail.

Hyperspectral imaging simultaneously acquires images of the same scene in many continuous narrow spectral bands. In the resulting hyperspectral image (HSI), each pixel shows abundant details of object surface reflectance across a number of bands ranging from the visible band to the near-infrared one, which means HSI can be regarded as a three-way tensor as displayed in Fig. 13.1. Thus, an HSI often contains more faithful knowledge of real scenes compared with conventional images (e.g., color images or grayscale images). However, the abundant spectral information of HSIs comes at the cost of greatly reducing spatial resolution, which hinders the widespread applications of HSIs. Compared with HSI, MSI has much fewer spectral bands, while the MSI contains more spatial information. Thus, it is of interest to synthesize HR-HSI by fusing LR-HSI with corresponding MSI. The hyperspectral superresolution task, illustrated in Fig. 13.2, is well motivated since both spectral and spatial information are rich and valuable to analytics and can benefit a number of applications.

Based on the latest achievements in pan-sharpening, more sophisticated attempts have been made to adapt pan-sharpening techniques to the field of the HSI and MSI (HSI-MSI) fusion problem [31,63]. Representative techniques can be roughly divided into four categories: matrix factorization-based [1,13,40,46,50,64,67], Bayesian-based [2,52,53], deep learning-based [12,28,65], and tensor representation-based methods [10,11,27,55,68].

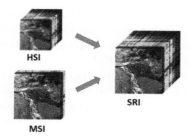

FIGURE 13.2

Illustration of the hyperspectral superresolution task.

Matrix factorization is a common HSI-MSI fusion approach, which unfolds the multiband image into a matrix with specific methods. Coupled nonnegative matrix factorization (CNMF) [64] is a classic matrix factorization-based HSI-MSI fusion method. The latent HR-HSI is reconstructed from an endmember spectra matrix and an abundance matrix estimated from the LR-HSI and HR-MSI, respectively. Based on the linear mixing model [6,23,35], Simões et al. [40] introduced the vector-total-variation (VTV) regularization in the spatial domain to a fusion variational problem that incorporates the LR-HSI fidelity and the HR-MSI fidelity. Considering the spatial correlation of the HSI, Veganzones et al. [46] decomposed the HSI with the locally low-rank prior, conducted on each HSI patch. These methods can serve the purpose of generating acceptable fusion results. Meanwhile, these methods unfold the HR-HSI into a matrix, which will destroy the intrinsic structure of the HSI.

Bayesian method is an alternative approach to matrix factorization. In Bayesian methods, the fusion problems are regularized by the maximum a posteriori (MAP) framework. The Bayesian approach made a subspace assumption [66] of the HSI data and introduced appropriate prior distribution of the HR-HSI, such as naive Gaussian [51] and sparsity promoting prior [50]. Akhtar et al. [2] first introduced a nonparametric Bayesian dictionary learning with corresponding Bayesian sparse coding to construct an HR-HSI. Furthermore, the fast fusion based on Sylvester equation (FUSE) [52] is introduced to solve the Sylvester equation derived from the HSI-MSI fusion issue. The performances of Bayesian-related methods are highly dependent on the prior information, which is often hard to be determined.

Different from the abovementioned traditional methods, deep learning-based methods aim at learning a nonlinear mapping between the observed and desired samples. Dian et al. [12] proposed to learn the spectral prior of HSI via deep residual convolutional neural networks. In [62], a fusion method is proposed which uses two branches to learn the spatial and spectral information from the HR-MSI and LR-HSI, respectively. Most deep learning-based models have achieved the state-of-the-art performance; however, in these methods, large amounts of training samples are necessary to estimate the parameters in the network.

Apart from the three aforementioned classes, tensor representation-based methods regard HSI as a third-order (3D) tensor rather than a matrix. For a 3D HSI tensor, the underlying data structure can be preserved and uncovered with tensor decomposition methods. In [10], Tucker decomposition was used to model the nonlocal patches with two spatial dictionaries and a spectral dictionary simultaneously. Based on [10], Li et al. considered the entire HSI as a 3D tensor and proposed a coupled sparse tensor factorization (CSTF) model [27] to reconstruct the HR-HSI. A low-rank tensor decomposition model that is regularized by the spatial-spectral graph for HSI-MSI fusion is proposed in [68]. Kanatsoulis et al. [22] proposed a coupled canonical polyadic (CP) tensor decomposition method and proved the identifiability of the solution. Zhang et al. [69] introduced a spatial manifold regularization in the nonlocal tensor extracted from the latent HR-HSI.

Synthetic aperture radar (SAR) imaging is another most widely used remote sensing technology. Different from optical remote sensing systems, SAR is an active microwave remote sensing system for providing large-scale 2D images of the land covering Earth. The active operating mode makes it working in the day and night time independent of the influence of the solar illumination. Polarimetric SAR (PolSAR) as a typical multichannel radar system can obtain refined geometrical and geophysical information by transmitting and receiving the radar electromagnetic wave. The principle of PolSAR is depicted in Fig. 13.3. PolSAR can acquire quad-polarization information to measure the targets in four receiving/transmitting models, including HH, HV, VH, and VV, and records more complete backscattering information than traditional SAR. The obtained polarization information can describe the geometrical structure and the geophysical properties of the targets. On the one hand, it provides more information for remote sensing image understanding and interpretation. With the development of imaging radar systems, more and more advanced airborne and spaceborne polarimetric SAR systems have launched, i.e., ALOS2, RADARSAT2, and TerraSAR. On the other hand, it also contributes to the advancement of PolSAR techniques and expands the application fields, which include military and civilian application domains, such as natural resource exploration, environmental monitoring, agriculture control, forest vegetation change detection, and recognition and monitoring of military objects.

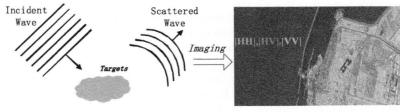

FIGURE 13.3

Principle of PolSAR.

Land cover classification is a prevalent application of PolSAR technology, which aims at assigning each pixel to a land cover type. There is no conclusion whether it is better to employ one view of features or multiview features in image processing techniques for PolSAR land cover classification. Some researchers employ the manifold techniques to exploit the intrinsic distances of data points and obtain the similarity matrix, such as applying Laplacian eigenmaps (LEs) and supervised graph embedding methods to reduce the dimensionality [39,43]. The abovementioned manifold-related algorithms all initially construct a local structure between pixels in manifold space and then utilize those local structures to embed pixels into a low-dimensional space. Those manifold algorithms, such as locally linear embedding (LLE) [38], LE [5], and local tangent space alignment (LTSA) [70], can accurately learn the nonlinear structures of real data, but they have the drawback that the computation complexity is high and they are sensitive to outliers and noise.

Furthermore, linear reduction algorithms are developed for obtaining projection matrices to solve the out-of-sample problem. Multidimensional scaling (MDS), neighbor preserving embedding (NPE) [18], locality preserving projection (LPP) [17], and linear LTSA (LLTSA) [70] are the linear versions of ISOMAP, LLE, LE, and LTSA, respectively. At the same time, principal component analysis (PCA), linear discriminant analysis (LDA), and local discriminant embedding (LDE) are all linear algorithms employed to reduce the data dimensions under unsupervised and supervised conditions for some land cover classification tasks. It is noteworthy that the linear embedding methods can be easily extended to a tensor embedding form, because each pixel can be represented by a feature cube that is constructed by groups of polarimetric scattering signals and target decomposition features in a fixed-size patch.

Tensors, as the high order of vectors and matrices, can preserve the intrinsic data structure and offer a better explanation for the data processing. In particular, for PolSAR classification, the features of each pixel are always extracted from a patch around the pixel. Those features can be represented by a 3D cube similar to other remote sensing image processing methods [45,56,57], on which multilinear-algebraic techniques can then be applied. Recently, many DR techniques were modified into a high-order tensorial form to analyze the data structure. Those tensor-based DR algorithms include tensor linear discriminant analysis (TLDA) [41,60], tensor locality preserving projection (TLPP) [9], tensor local discriminant embedding (TLDE) [9,20], tensor neighborhood preserving embedding (TNPE) [17,49], tensor PCA (TPCA) [33,61], and other modified versions of those tensorial DR algorithms [34].

In this chapter, some tensorial methods are investigated and several advanced models for HSI-MSI fusion and PolSAR feature extraction are presented. More specifically, we will discover more structural information in the HSI with tensorial models and discuss three tensor representation-based HSI-MSI fusion methods in detail. Furthermore, a case study of a tensorial method will be given, which extracts the intrinsic features by incorporating the spectral-spatial information of multimodal space properties of PolSAR data.

13.2 Optical remote sensing: HSI and MSI fusion

In the existing conventional HSI-MSI fusion approaches, the spatial and spectral data are always unfolded in vector or matrix form and processed separately. However, techniques belonging to this class tend to break the intrinsic structures when reconstructing the HR-HSI. Since the raw HSIs are organized in 3D data cubes, representativeness and informativeness play a vital role in real applications. For this reason, several tensor-based methods have been proposed to fuse HR-MSI and LR-HSI efficiently. Although these tensor-based models can well preserve the spectral and spatial structures of the HR-HSI, some deeper structural information, such as nonlocal similarities and multiscale relations, are not taken into consideration. In this section, three state-of-the-art tensor-based HSI-MSI fusion methods are proposed to further explore the intrinsic structures of HSIs. More specifically, the first case constructs a nonlocal patch tensor and seeks the spectral and spatial correlations of the nonlocal patch with tensor sparse representation. To make full use of the infrastructural information of HSI, a high-order coupled tensor ring (TR) representation-based HSI-MSI fusion model is introduced in Case 2, which can facilitate the exploration of multiscale information and high-order correlations. Most off-the-shelf algorithms assume the degeneration operators of HR-MSI and LR-HSI to be available, which is practically absent. For the sake of model robustness, the third case introduces a joint tensor factorization-based blind HSI-MSI fusion technique by taking advantage of the multidimensional correlations. Furthermore, the proposed blind fusion model can rigorously guarantee the identifiability of the outcome under mild and realistic conditions.

13.2.1 Tensor notations and preliminaries

Throughout this section, a tensor, also known as multidimensional data array, is denoted by Euler script letters, e.g., $\mathcal{X}$. A slice of a tensor is a 2D section defined by all but two indices. A fiber of tensor is a 1D section defined by fixing all indices but one. For a third-order tensor $\mathcal{X} \in \mathbb{R}^{I_1 \times I_2 \times I_3}$, we use $\mathcal{X}(k, :, :)$, $\mathcal{X}(:, k, :)$, and $\mathcal{X}(:, :, k)$ to denote the horizontal, lateral, and frontal slices; $\mathcal{X}(:, i, j)$, $\mathcal{X}(i, :, j)$, and $\mathcal{X}(i, j, :)$ denote the (i, j)-th mode-1, mode-2, and mode-3 fiber. Particularly, $\mathbf{X}^{(k)}$ represents $\mathcal{X}(:, :, k)$. The Frobenius norm of a tensor is defined as $\|\mathcal{X}\|_F = \sqrt{\sum_{ijk} |\mathcal{X}(i, j, k)|^2}$. The mode-$i$ *unfolding* (matricization) of the tensor $\mathcal{X}$ is the matrix denoted by $\mathbf{X}_{(i)}$ that is obtained by arranging (lexicographically in the indices other than the i-th index) the mode-i fibers as the columns of the matrix and denoted by $unfold_i(\mathcal{X}) = \mathbf{X}_{(i)}$, $\mathcal{X} = fold_i(\mathbf{X}_{(i)})$.

13.2.2 Nonlocal patch tensor sparse representation for HSI-MSI fusion

Inspired by the tensor–tensor product (t-product) [24,32,72], this work proposed a nonlocal patch tensor sparse representation (NPTSR) [57] for the HSI-MSI fusion problem. This model exploits the tensor sparse representation (TSR) to characterize the nonlocal patch tensor which is formed by the similar 3D patches in the HSI. The t-product-based TSR is based on the circular convolution operator which can generate the data by shifted versions of dictionary atoms. Thus, through this well-designed nonlocal patch tensor and the novel TSR, both spatial and spectral similarities of nonlocal patches in HSI are considered. Further, by discovering the relationship between HR-MSI and LR-HSI using the t-product, this case combines TSR and the reconstruction problem in one objective function with the nonlocal constraint. The tensor dictionary learning and sparse coding problems are solved in the optimization of the proposed model simultaneously.

13.2.2.1 Problem formulation

In the NPTSR, the two complementary HR-MSI and LR-HSI are assumed to be available to reconstruct the target HR-HSI. As Eq. (13.1), the acquired LR-HSI $\mathcal{X} \in \mathbb{R}^{w \times h \times L}$ can be regarded as the spatially down-sampled version of the latent $\mathcal{Z} \in \mathbb{R}^{W \times H \times L}$,

$$X_{(3)} = Z_{(3)}BH + E_{h(3)}, \tag{13.1}$$

where $H \in \mathbb{R}^{WH \times wh}$ represents the spatial down-sampling operator, $B \in \mathbb{R}^{WH \times WH}$ denotes the spatial blurring operator, $X_{(3)}$ and $Z_{(3)}$ are the mode-3 unfolding matrices of tensor $\mathcal{X}$ and $\mathcal{Z}$, respectively, and $E_{h(3)}$ is the independent and identically distributed (i.i.d.) Gaussian noise of LR-HSI. Similarly, the HR-MSI can be expressed as the degraded $\mathcal{Z}$ in the spectral domain,

$$Y_{(3)} = RZ_{(3)} + E_{m(3)}, \tag{13.2}$$

where $R \in \mathbb{R}^{l \times L}$ is the spectral responses of the multispectral sensor and $E_{m(3)}$ is the i.i.d. noise of HR-MSI.

According to the degradation model, the HSI-MSI fusion problem can be formulated as

$$Z_{(3)} = \arg\min\left\{ \frac{1}{2}\|X_{(3)} - Z_{(3)}BH\|_F^2 + \frac{\beta}{2}\|Y_{(3)} - RZ_{(3)}\|_F^2 \right\}, \tag{13.3}$$

where β is a nonnegative trade-off parameter that controls the relative importance of the two terms. Model (13.3) can be rewritten in tensor form as

$$\min_{\mathcal{Z}}\left\{ \frac{1}{2}\|\mathcal{X} - \mathcal{Z}\mathcal{B}\mathcal{H}\|_F^2 + \frac{\beta}{2}\|\mathcal{Y} - \mathcal{R}\mathcal{Z}\|_F^2 \right\}. \tag{13.4}$$

The symbols $\mathcal{H}$ and $\mathcal{B}$ represent the down-sampling and spatial blurring operators on the tensor, which have the same effect as H and B on $Z_{(3)}$.

13.2.2.2 Nonlocal patch extraction

Nonlocal similarity is a common property of images, which has been widely applied in the image processing community. The nonlocal similarity means that a patch may have several patches with similar structure within the same image. According to recent work, nonlocal similarity can be extended to the 3D case [15,54,59].

For HSI-MSI fusion, the desired HR-HSI $\mathcal{Z}$ is spatially partitioned into a group of overlapping 3D cubes $\{\mathcal{P}_{ij}\}_{\substack{1 \leq i \leq W-d_w \\ 1 \leq j \leq H-d_h}} \subset \mathbb{R}^{d_w \times d_h \times L}$, where d_w and d_h represent the width and height of a 3D cube, respectively. Conventionally, similar cubes are clustered into the same group with some unsupervised clustering methods, such as K-means and K-means ++ [7,54]. In this case, an alternative method [37] is used to obtain the clustering result. Compared with the abovementioned methods, the adopted one reorders the extracted patches such that they are chained in the "shortest possible path" [37], and the reordered 3D cubes are supposed to induce a smooth ordering. Thus, by setting a given number of consecutive cubes in a cluster, the partitioned cubes can be divided into several nonlocal similar groups, and the k-th cluster is denoted as $\{\mathcal{P}_i^k\}_{1 \leq i \leq N_k} \subset \mathbb{R}^{d_W \times d_H \times L}$, where N_k is the number of nonlocal cubes in the cluster.

In the HSI case, the similarity between nonlocal patches indicates that these patches are correlative in the spatial and spectral domains simultaneously, which means that the spectral vectors in the same spatial location belonging to different patches may represent similar material. To make full use of the spectral and spatial relevance of similar patches, all the 3D cubes are unfolded in the mode-3 manner, and the unfolded matrices belonging to the same cluster are stacked along the third dimension. Thus, a new nonlocal patch tensor (NPT), denoted as $\mathcal{Z}^k \in \mathbb{R}^{L \times d_W d_H \times N_k}$, is constructed. In the subsequent portion, the operator that constructs the k-th NPT of HR-HSI is denoted as $\mathcal{G}_k$, i.e., $\mathcal{G}_k \mathcal{Z} = \mathcal{Z}^k$. Then the corresponding original $\mathcal{Z}$ can be expressed as

$$\mathcal{Z} = \left(\sum_k \mathcal{G}_k^T \mathcal{G}_k \right)^{-1} \sum_k \mathcal{G}_k^T \mathcal{Z}^k, \tag{13.5}$$

which indicates that $\mathcal{Z}$ is acquired by summing all NPTs followed by an averaging operation.

Analogously, the LR-HSI and HR-MSI are represented as

$$\mathcal{X} = \left(\sum_k \mathcal{G}_k^T \mathcal{G}_k \right)^{-1} \sum_k \mathcal{G}_k^T \mathcal{X}^k, \tag{13.6}$$

$$\mathcal{Y} = \left(\sum_k \mathcal{G}_k^T \mathcal{G}_k \right)^{-1} \sum_k \mathcal{G}_k^T \mathcal{Y}^k. \tag{13.7}$$

Given the lack of HR-HSI, the optimal $\mathcal{G}$ is unavailable, whereas the spatial structures of the latent HR-HSI mainly exist in the HR-MSI, which suggests that the patches of HR-MSI share the same correlation as those of HR-HSI. In the NPTSR, HR-MSI is employed in place of HR-HSI to determine the nonlocal patches and corresponding clustering order. By means of this method, the operator $\mathcal{G}$ can be acquired, leading to a more reliable clustering result.

13.2.2.3 Tensor sparse representation for nonlocal patch tensors

In the constructed NPT $\mathcal{Z}^k$, each lateral slice is a sample formed by the similar spectral vectors in the same spatial location of the patches. Therefore, the lateral slice can be represented as the linear combination of tensor atom $\mathcal{D}^k$ with corresponding coefficients $\mathcal{S}^k$, which can be regarded as the extension of matrix-based sparse representation

$$
\begin{aligned}
\mathcal{Z}^k(:,i,:) &= \mathcal{D}^k * \mathcal{S}^k(:,i,:) \\
&= \mathcal{D}^k(:,1,:) * \mathcal{S}^k(1,i,:) + \cdots + \mathcal{D}^k(:,r,:) * \mathcal{S}^k(r,i,:),
\end{aligned}
\tag{13.8}
$$

where r is the number of tensor atoms in the dictionary. As an extension of the matrix-based sparse representation, the NPT can be represented as the t-product of $\mathcal{D}^k$ and $\mathcal{S}^k$:

$$
\mathcal{Z}^k = \mathcal{D}^k * \mathcal{S}^k.
\tag{13.9}
$$

According to the definition of t-product, Eq. (13.9) can be rewritten in matrix form:

$$
\begin{bmatrix}
Z^{k(1)} \\
Z^{k(2)} \\
\vdots \\
Z^{k(N_k)}
\end{bmatrix}
=
\begin{bmatrix}
D^{k(1)} & D^{k(N_k)} & \cdots & D^{k(2)} \\
D^{k(2)} & D^{k(1)} & \cdots & D^{k(3)} \\
\vdots & \vdots & \vdots & \vdots \\
D^{k(N_k)} & D^{k(N_k-1)} & \cdots & D^{k(1)}
\end{bmatrix}
\begin{bmatrix}
S^{k(1)} \\
S^{k(2)} \\
\vdots \\
S^{k(N_k)}
\end{bmatrix}.
\tag{13.10}
$$

It can be observed that each sample can be represented by not only the linear combination of the tensor atoms, but also the shifted versions of the original tensor atoms.

Compared with other sparse representation methods [2,19], the NPTSR is superior in three ways:

- The circular convolution between the atom and sparse coefficient indicates that the shift versions of the atom are used to represent the sample. Therefore, the spectra are represented by the same basis, while the conventional sparse representation represents the spectra with different basis in the same sample.
- In the tensor sparse representation, every atom in the dictionary has multiple spectra, thus the NPTSR can characterize the spectral variability [14] efficiently, which is not a common advantage of conventional sparse representation.
- The size of the dictionary in the tensor sparse representation is N_k times smaller than that of the conventional sparse representation [21].

The pixel intensity in HR-MSI equals the spectral response times the corresponding pixel intensity, i.e., $Y^{k(i)} = RZ^{k(i)}$. Stacking the frontal slices of HR-MSI along the second dimension, the unfolded matrix can be expressed as

$$
\begin{bmatrix} Y^{k\,(1)} \\ Y^{k\,(2)} \\ \vdots \\ Y^{k\,(N_k)} \end{bmatrix} = \begin{bmatrix} R & 0 & \cdots & 0 \\ 0 & R & \cdots & 0 \\ \vdots & \vdots & \vdots & \vdots \\ 0 & 0 & \cdots & R \end{bmatrix} \begin{bmatrix} Z^{k\,(1)} \\ Z^{k\,(2)} \\ \vdots \\ Z^{k\,(N_k)} \end{bmatrix}.
\tag{13.11}
$$

Thus, the NPT Y^k in HR-MSI can be rewritten in t-product form as follows:

$$
Y^k = R * Z^k + \mathcal{E}_m^k = R * D^k * S^k + \mathcal{E}_m^k,
\tag{13.12}
$$

where $R = fold_V([R; 0; \ldots; 0]) \in \mathbb{R}^{l \times L \times N_k}$ and $\mathcal{E}_m^k \in \mathbb{R}^{l \times d_w d_h \times N_k}$ is the i.i.d. Gaussian noise. Therefore, the fidelity term of HR-MSI can be expressed as $\sum_{k=1}^{K} \| Y^k - R * D^k * S^k \|_F^2$. Denoting $D_{msi}^k = R * D^k$, it represents the dictionary of NPT in HR-MSI. As all the latent NPTs Y^k are unavailable, D_{msi}^k and S^k can be obtained by solving the following tensor sparse representation manner:

$$
\min_{D_{msi}^k, S^k} \left\{ \frac{1}{2} \| Y^k - D_{msi}^k * S^k \|_F^2 + \lambda \| S^k \|_1 \right\}.
\tag{13.13}
$$

Combing Eq. (13.4), Eq. (13.5), Eq. (13.9), and Eq. (13.13), the NPTSR can be modeled as

$$
\min_{Z, D^k, S^k} \left\{ \frac{1}{2} \| \mathcal{X} - ZBH \|_F^2 + \sum_{k=1}^{K} \left(\frac{\beta}{2} \| Y^k - R * D^k * S^k \|_F^2 + \lambda \| S^k \|_1 \right) \right\}
$$

$$
\text{s.t.} \quad Z = \left(\sum_{k=1}^{K} \mathcal{G}_k^T \mathcal{G}_k \right)^{-1} \sum_{k=1}^{K} \mathcal{G}_k^T (D^k * S^k).
\tag{13.14}
$$

13.2.2.4 Experiments and results

In this subsection, experiments on both synthetic and real datasets are conducted to demonstrate the performance of the NPTSR. The synthetic dataset and quality measures used in the experiments are described subsequently. Furthermore, the experimental results of the NPTSR and compared methods are given.

In the experiment, a synthetic dataset and a real dataset are employed to evaluate the performance of the NPTSR and comparing methods. The synthetic dataset is from the University of the Pavia, and was collected using the Reflective Optics System Imaging Spectrometer (ROSIS) sensor over Pavia, Italy, in 2003. After the removal of the water vapor absorption and noisy bands, from the original 224 spectral bands between 0.43 and 0.84 μm, 103 bands remained. Thus, the final size of the reference image is $610 \times 340 \times 103$. The real dataset consists of an LR-HSI collected by a Hyperion HSI sensor and an HR-MSI collected by a WorldView-3 MSI sensor. The raw data are taken over the Cuprite district, Nevada, US. The original size of the HR-MSI and LR-HSI are $3708 \times 1516 \times 8$ and $927 \times 379 \times 167$, respectively.

In the experiments, the NPTSR is compared with other state-of-the-art methods mentioned in [31,63] including CNMF [64], HSI superresolution (HySure) [40], naive Bayes, sparse Bayes [50], nonnegative structured sparse representation (NSSR) [13], and CSTF [27]. The spatial degeneration operators used in the CSTF method are rewritten according to the Gaussian kernel.

For the quantitative assessment, the research community has come up with a variety of established quantitative criteria that can be applied for result assessment [63]. In this section, a selection of commonly used indices and assessment methods including the peak signal-to-noise ratio (PSNR), the average spectral angle mapper (SAM), the relative dimensionless global error in synthesis (ERGAS) as well as cross-correlation (CC) are employed for the quality measures.

Fig. 13.4 shows the results of the various methods for the University of Pavia dataset. The pseudo-color images of HSI which are produced by the 40th, 30th, and 5th band are displayed for visual inspection. Specifically, the pseudo-images of LR-HSI, HR-HSI, and HR-MSI are displayed in Figs. 13.4(a)–13.4(c), respectively. The results of all the compared results are shown in Figs. 13.4(d)–13.4(j). Visually, all the comparison methods can recover most of the spatial details by fusing the HR-MSI, whereas there are some areas that are not recovered well. For example, in the result of CNMF, the grass is not well preserved in the middle bottom of the image. On the contrary, the NPTSR gives better spatial structural images than the other methods.

To compare the performance of the methods in terms of spectral preservation, Fig. 13.5 shows the spectral curves of a specific pixel located in the reconstructed HSIs. It can be seen that some methods cannot approximate the reference spectral curves after the 70th band. Compared with other methods, the NPTSR fits the reference curve before the 70th band accurately. For the bands after 70, the NPTSR has the best accuracy, which also indicates the superiority of the spectral preservation of the NPTSR. Furthermore, the quantitative results are shown in Table 13.1. The results reported in Table 13.1 are consistent with the conclusion that NPTSR outperforms the other methods in all the quality measures.

Table 13.1 Performances of the HSI superresolution methods on University of Pavia: PSNR, ERAGS, SAM, CC.

Algorithm	PSNR	ERGAS	SAM	CC
CNMF	31.98	3.78	5.82	0.91
HySure	36.8	3.08	5.17	0.93
Naïve Bayes	37.17	3.4	6.64	0.92
Sparse Bayes	37.22	3.36	6.58	0.93
NSSR	36.9	2.25	4.36	0.96
CSTF	36.68	2.97	6.08	0.94
NPTSR	**39.09**	**2.16**	**4.05**	**0.96**

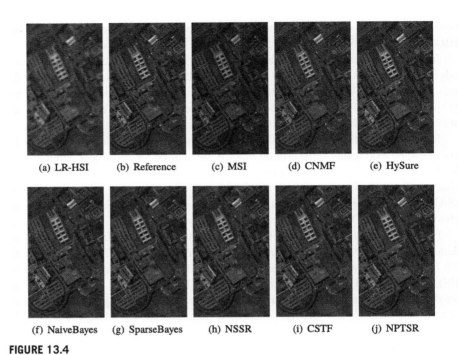

FIGURE 13.4

HSI superresolution results (University of Pavia dataset).

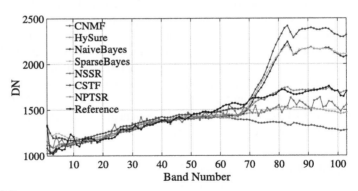

FIGURE 13.5

Spectral curve of the [200, 200]-th pixel in the reconstructed University of Pavia HSI.

In the real dataset fusion experiment, the Cuprite district dataset is employed to demonstrate the fusion performances of the methods when applied to a real scenario. Given the absence of the reference HR-HSI, the spectral response, the blurring kernel, and the down-sampling operator, HSI-MSI fusion cannot be achieved in the real scenario. In this experiment, the spectral response and blurring kernel are estimated by using the method in HySure [40]. In addition, CSTF requires a separable blurring kernel, and therefore, the two separated blurrings in the spatial domain are estimated respectively.

Figs. 13.6(c)–13.6(i) display the pseudo-color images composed of the reconstructed HR-HSIs by different methods. Some artificial effects in the boundary of the CSTF result can be observed, which can be induced by the two separated blurring responses in the spatial modes. The Bayesian-based methods tend to produce oversmooth results. The other methods can well reconstruct the spatial structure of the captured scene.

The spectral curve of pixel [160, 160] in the reconstructed HR-HSIs and pixel [40, 40] in the LR-HSI are plotted in Fig. 13.7. As one can observe from the curves, the spectral structures are well preserved by these methods and the spectral curve of NPTSR is the closest to that of the LR-HSI. This result demonstrates the superiority of the NPTSR when applied for real HSI-MSI data.

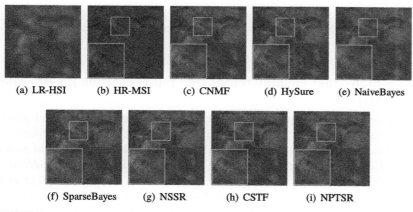

(a) LR-HSI   (b) HR-MSI   (c) CNMF   (d) HySure   (e) NaiveBayes

(f) SparseBayes   (g) NSSR   (h) CSTF   (i) NPTSR

FIGURE 13.6

Pseudo-color images of a real dataset and the reconstructed pseudo-color images using the compared methods.

13.2.2.5 Conclusion

In this case, a new NPTSR HSI superresolution method is proposed. The advanced t-product-based tensor sparse representation model is used to characterize the nonlocal patch tensor which can preserve both the spatial and the spectral similarities between similar nonlocal patches in HSI. Instead of solving the dictionary learning, sparse representation, and fusion problems separately, this work designed an objective function with nonlocal constraints that integrates all the information. The alternating direction method of multipliers (ADMM) is used to solve the proposed optimization problem. The updates for the tensor dictionary and sparse code are completed in the Fourier domain which is not computationally intensive. Numerical experiments showed that

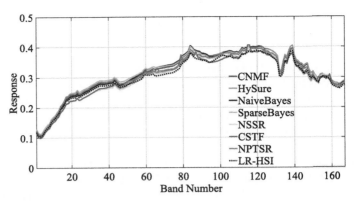

FIGURE 13.7

Spectral curves of pixel [160, 160] in the reconstructed HSIs and pixel [40, 40] in the LR-HSI of a real dataset.

the proposed NPTSR achieved the best results compared with the state-of-the-art methods.

13.2.3 High-order coupled tensor ring representation for HSI-MSI fusion

To preserve the intrinsic structures of the HSI, the existing tensor-based methods usually regard the HSI as a 3D tensor or extract 3D patches from the HSI directly [55, 57]. However, these methods cannot make full use of the infrastructural information of the HSI, especially in the spatial domain. Actually, the HSI can be represented by a higher-order tensor though tensorization, which represents the original data in a more structural manner without any information loss. In this case, the HR-HSI is tensorized to a high-order tensor by reshaping and permuting the spatial domain data. To fuse the tensorized LR-HSI and HR-MSI effectively, a high-order coupled TR (HCTR) [58] representation-based method is illustrated in this subsection.

13.2.3.1 Multiscale high-order tensorization

Most tensor-based methods regard HSI as a 3D tensor directly or construct a 4D NPT [11] to preserve the intrinsic structure of the HSI. Although these tensor-based models can well keep the spectral and spatial structures of the HR-HSI, the high-order correlations, such as nonlocal similarities and multiscale relations, contained in the HSI are not fully exploited by the 3D or 4D tensor. It has been demonstrated that a 2D image can be converted to a high-order tensor without any loss of information [71]. In the converted tensor, each mode shows the patch structure at a specific scale resolution. Thus, the tensorization method can capture multiscale information and provide high-order correlations in the image.

In the HCTR, the tensorization technique is generalized to the HSI and the degradation expressions of LR-HSI and HR-MSI in this tensorization are explored. The

HR-HSI to be estimated is $\mathcal{Z} \in \mathbb{R}^{W \times H \times L}$, and the sizes of rows and columns are assumed to be the multiplication of d integers, i.e., $W = W_1 \times W_2 \times \cdots \times W_d$, $H = H_1 \times H_2 \times \cdots \times H_d$. Firstly, $\mathcal{Z}$ is tensorized in the spatial domain with the spectral structure fixed; therefore, a tensor of size $W_1 \times \cdots \times W_d \times H_1 \times \cdots \times H_d \times L$ is obtained. Subsequently, a permutation operator is processed to obtain a tensor of size $W_1 \times H_1 \times W_2 \times H_2 \times \cdots \times W_d \times H_d \times L$. In the last step, the high-order tensor is reshaped in every two modes and we obtain a $(d+1)$-th order of size $W_1 H_1 \times W_2 H_2 \times \cdots \times W_d H_d \times L$. In the tensorized high-order tensor, the first and last modes correspond to the smallest- and largest-scale spatial patches, respectively.

In the tensorization, the spectral mode remains unchanged in every step, and the tensorization operator is denoted as $\mathcal{T}\{\cdot\}$, so the final high-order tensor is $\mathcal{T}\{\mathcal{Z}\} \in \mathbb{R}^{W_1 H_1 \times W_2 H_2 \times \cdots \times W_d H_d \times L}$. Similarly, the tensorization can be applied to LR-HSI and HR-MSI; then we obtain $\mathcal{T}\{\mathcal{X}\} \in \mathbb{R}^{w_1 h_1 \times W_2 H_2 \times \cdots \times W_d H_d \times L}$, $\mathcal{T}\{\mathcal{Y}\} \in \mathbb{R}^{W_1 H_1 \times W_2 H_2 \times \cdots \times W_d H_d \times l}$, respectively. Since the spectral mode remains unchanged, the degradation from the HR-HSI to the HR-MSI can be transferred to the high-order tensorized data as follows:

$$\mathcal{T}\{\mathcal{Y}\} = \mathcal{T}\{\mathcal{Z}\} \times_{d+1} \boldsymbol{R} \in \mathbb{R}^{W_1 H_1 \times W_2 H_2 \times \cdots \times W_d H_d \times l}. \tag{13.15}$$

The down-sampling operator is processed in every $w \times h$ patch and produces a $w/p \times h/p$ patch, where p is the down-sampling ratio. In the high-order tensorized LR-HSI, the degradation process can be formulated as

$$\mathcal{T}\{\mathcal{X}\} = \mathcal{T}\{\mathcal{Z}\} \times_1 \boldsymbol{S} \in \mathbb{R}^{w_1 h_1 \times W_2 H_2 \times \cdots \times W_d H_d \times L}, \tag{13.16}$$

where $\boldsymbol{S} \in \mathbb{R}^{w_1 h_1 \times W_1 H_1}$ is the spatial down-sampling matrix.

13.2.3.2 High-order tensor ring representation for HSI-MSI fusion
In the HCTR, the tensorized $(d+1)$-th tensor $\mathcal{T}\{\mathcal{Z}\}$ is represented as

$$\mathcal{T}\{\mathcal{Z}\} = \mathcal{R}(\mathcal{U}_1, \mathcal{U}_2, \ldots, \mathcal{U}_{d+1}) + \mathcal{E}_{\mathcal{Z}}, \tag{13.17}$$

where $\mathcal{R}$ represents the TR representation operator, $\mathcal{E}_{\mathcal{Z}}$ stands for the i.i.d. Gaussian noise, $\mathcal{U}_k \in \mathbb{R}^{r_k \times W_k H_k \times r_{k+1}}$, $k = 1, \cdots, d$, $\mathcal{U}_{d+1} \in \mathbb{R}^{r_{d+1} \times L \times r_1}$ are the core tensors of $\mathcal{Z}$, and $[r_1, r_2, \ldots, r_{d+1}]$ is the TR rank of $\mathcal{Z}$. According to Eq. (13.15), Eq. (13.16), and Eq. (13.17), the tensorized $\mathcal{T}\{\mathcal{X}\}$, $\mathcal{T}\{\mathcal{Y}\}$ can be represented as

$$\mathcal{T}\{\mathcal{X}\} = \mathcal{R}((\mathcal{U}_1 \times_2 \boldsymbol{S}), \mathcal{U}_2, \ldots, \mathcal{U}_{d+1}) + \mathcal{E}_{\mathcal{X}}, \tag{13.18}$$

$$\mathcal{T}\{\mathcal{Y}\} = \mathcal{R}(\mathcal{U}_1, \mathcal{U}_2, \ldots, (\mathcal{U}_{d+1} \times_2 \boldsymbol{R})) + \mathcal{E}_{\mathcal{Y}}, \tag{13.19}$$

where $\mathcal{E}_{\mathcal{X}} \in \mathbb{R}^{w_1 h_1 \times W_2 H_2 \times \cdots \times W_d H_d \times L}$ and $\mathcal{E}_{\mathcal{Y}} \in \mathbb{R}^{W_1 H_1 \times W_2 H_2 \times \cdots \times W_d H_d \times l}$ are the i.i.d. Gaussian noise of tensorized LR-HSI and HR-MSI, respectively.

The reconstruction of $\mathcal{T}\{\mathcal{Z}\}$ is related to the core tensors $\mathcal{U}_k$, which means the superresolution problem can be formulated as

$$
\min_{\mathcal{U}_{k,k=1,\ldots,d+1}} \frac{1}{2}\|\mathcal{T}\{\mathcal{Y}\} - \mathscr{R}(\mathcal{U}_1,\mathcal{U}_2,\ldots,(\mathcal{U}_{d+1}\times_2 R))\|_F^2
$$
$$
+\frac{\lambda}{2}\|\mathcal{T}\{\mathcal{X}\} - \mathscr{R}((\mathcal{U}_1\times_2 S),\mathcal{U}_2,\ldots,\mathcal{U}_{d+1})\|_F^2,
$$

(13.20)

where λ is the trade-off parameter that controls the balance of the two terms.

However, in the real scenario, the spatial down-sampling matrix S can be hard to estimate. To make the fusion model more reliable, a new variable $\mathcal{V}$ satisfying $\mathcal{V} = \mathcal{U}_1\times_2 S \in \mathbb{R}^{r_1\times w_1 h_1\times r_2}$ is introduced; therefore, the new objective function can be reformulated as

$$
\min_{\mathcal{U}_{k,k=1,\ldots,d+1},\mathcal{V}} \frac{1}{2}\|\mathcal{T}\{\mathcal{Y}\} - \mathscr{R}(\mathcal{U}_1,\mathcal{U}_2,\ldots,(\mathcal{U}_{d+1}\times_2 R))\|_F^2
$$
$$
+\frac{\lambda}{2}\|\mathcal{T}\{\mathcal{X}\} - \mathscr{R}(\mathcal{V},\mathcal{U}_2,\ldots,\mathcal{U}_{d+1})\|_F^2.
$$

(13.21)

In (13.21), the spatial down-sampling matrix is eliminated by introducing a new variable. The objective function is composed of two parts: the HR-MSI fidelity term and the LR-HSI fidelity term. Each part is a TR representation problem, and the two terms are connected by sharing same latent core tensors. Thus, this HSI-MSI fusion model is denoted as high-order coupled TR representation model.

13.2.3.3 Spectral manifold regularization

The TR representation gives a compact and efficient representation for high-order tensors. However, it fails to take the spectral manifold structure into consideration. Given the correlation between the adjacent bands, many manifold-based techniques have been applied to the HSI analysis [48]. In the HCTR, the graph Laplacian manifold is adopted to preserve the spectral manifold. As the LR-HSI contains the full spectral information of HR-HSI, which is not known a priori, the graph Laplacian is built based on the LR-HSI. Firstly, a graph $G = (\mathcal{V},\mathcal{E})$ is built, where $\mathcal{E}$ is the set of edges and $\mathcal{V}$ is the set of vertices standing for the bands the LR-HSI. Denoting $W = \{W_{ij}\} \in \mathbb{R}^{L\times L}$ as the weight matrix, each entry can be computed as

$$
W_{ij} = \begin{cases} \exp(-\frac{\|\mathcal{Y}(:,:,i)-\mathcal{Y}(:,:,j)\|_F^2}{\sigma^2}), & j \in N_{(i)}, \\ 0, & \text{otherwise}, \end{cases}
$$

(13.22)

where σ is a parameter that controls the smoothness of the graph and $j \in N_{(i)}$ means that band j is adjacent to band i.

In the TR representation of HR-HSI, the last 3D core tensor $\mathcal{U}_{d+1}$ determines the spectral structure of the reconstructed HR-HSI, which means $\mathcal{U}_{d+1}$ can be regarded as the low-dimensional representation of the HR-HSI in the spectral mode. Therefore, the spectral graph Laplacian matrix G learned from the LR-HSI is incorporated into $\mathcal{U}_{d+1}$. In mathematics, the manifold preservation can be formulated as

$$\min_{\mathcal{U}_{d+1}} \frac{1}{2} \sum_{ij} \|\mathcal{U}_{d+1}(:,i,:) - \mathcal{U}_{d+1}(:,j,:)\|_F^2 W_{ij}$$
$$= \mathrm{Tr}\left(U_{d+1\,(2)}^T L_S U_{d+1\,(2)}\right), \tag{13.23}$$

where $U_{d+1\,(2)}$ is the mode-2 unfolding of $\mathcal{U}_{d+1}$, $L_S = D - W$ is the graph Laplacian matrix, $D = diag(d_1, d_2, \ldots, d_B)$, and $d_i = \sum_j W_{ij}$. In fact, W_{ij} can be seen as the probability of band i and band j to be correlated. To keep the intrinsic spectral structure, the i-th and j-th front slices of $\mathcal{U}_{d+1}$ should be close when W_{ij} is relatively large. Incorporating the spectral graph Laplacian regularization into Eq. (13.21), the final fusion model can be obtained:

$$\min_{\mathcal{U}_{k,k=1,\ldots,d+1},\mathcal{V}} \frac{1}{2} \|\mathcal{T}\{\mathcal{Y}\} - \mathcal{R}(\mathcal{U}_1, \mathcal{U}_2, \ldots, (\mathcal{U}_{d+1} \times_2 R))\|_F^2$$
$$+ \frac{\lambda}{2} \|\mathcal{T}\{\mathcal{X}\} - \mathcal{R}(\mathcal{V}, \mathcal{U}_2, \ldots, \mathcal{U}_{d+1})\|_F^2 \tag{13.24}$$
$$+ \frac{\beta}{2} \mathrm{Tr}\left(U_{d+1\,(2)}^T L_S U_{d+1\,(2)}\right) + \frac{\eta}{2}\left(\sum_{i=1}^d \|\mathcal{U}_i\|_F^2 + \|\mathcal{V}\|_F^2\right),$$

where β and η are trade-off parameters that control the importance of the spectral manifold regularization and Frobenius norm regularization, respectively.

13.2.3.4 Results on synthetic datasets

In this subsection, experiments are conducted on the same datasets as in the previous subsection to demonstrate the superiority of the HCTR in terms of fusion performance. In these experiments, the HCTR is compared with other state-of-the-art methods including CNMF [64], HySure [40], NSSR [13], CSTF [27], FUSE [52], and low tensor-train rank (LTTR) representation [11]. For the quantitative assessment, PSNR, ERGAS, SAM, and Q2^n are employed for the quality measures.

The HCTR fusion model and the other compared methods are evaluated using different spatial degeneration methods. To verify the robustness of all the methods, the San Diego dataset is further adopted for experiments. Note that the LTTR is implemented using a different spatial degeneration method as that in the source code.

- Average down-sampling: The first degeneration method is to generate the LR-HSI by sampling the reference images by average 8×8 disjoint spatial blocks. Numerical results of the superresolution results for the University of Pavia dataset are shown in Table 13.2. The HCTR achieves the best results in most of the quantitative metrics. The CSTF is a competitive method, which achieves remarkable performance. For better comparison of all the compared methods, the 40th band images in the reconstructed HR-HSIs are displayed in Fig. 13.8. The residual images between the reconstructed and the reference images are shown in the

Table 13.2 Performances of the HSI superresolution methods on the University of Pavia dataset with average down-sampling: PSNR, ERAGS, SAM, and $Q2^n$.

Algorithm	PSNR	ERGAS	SAM	$Q2^n$
FUSE	33.32	1.64	6.19	0.72
CNMF	35.14	1.30	4.58	0.80
HySure	33.49	1.63	6.00	0.74
NSSR	31.66	2.04	4.04	0.65
CSTF	36.77	1.09	4.04	**0.85**
LTTR	32.98	1.71	6.56	0.69
HCTR	**37.18**	**1.04**	**3.72**	0.84

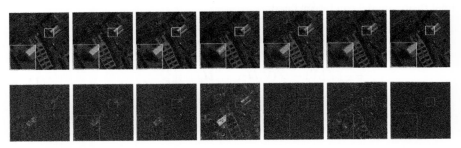

FIGURE 13.8

Visual quality comparison for reconstructed images of the synthetic datasets using average down-sampling. Pictures in rows 1, 3, and 5 are reconstructed single-band images in band 40. Pictures in rows 2, 4, and 6 are the residual images between the reference and the reconstructed images in band 40.

following row. A region of size 40×40 is enlarged and shown in the bottom-left corner. From Fig. 13.8, it can be found that the HCTR method can reconstruct the HR-HSI with fewer errors.

- Gaussian blurs: In the abovementioned experiments, the LR-HSI is generated by averaging over disjoint 8×8 blocks as the spatial degeneration. However, the optics blurring occurs during the down-sampling process. In this experiment, this situation is simulated by blurring the reference image with a Gaussian kernel before down-sampling. The size of the Gaussian blur kernel is 9×9 with a standard deviation (std) of 3. Therefore, the spatial degeneration operators are also changed in the compared methods, while in the HCTR, the spatial degeneration operators are not required. Fig. 13.9 displays the reconstructed and residual images in band 40, and Table 13.3 shows the quantitative metrics of all the compared methods. Still, one can find that the HCTR achieves the best results in most of the quantitative metrics. It can be observed that the CSTF and HCTR produce the smallest errors, whereas the HCTR does not require the spatial degeneration operator as an

Table 13.3 Performances of the HSI superresolution methods on the University of Pavia dataset with optic blurs in spatial degeneration: PSNR, ERAGS, SAM, and $Q2^n$.

Algorithm	PSNR	ERGAS	SAM	$Q2^n$
FUSE	33.40	1.66	6.38	0.80
CNMF	36.43	1.13	4.02	0.80
HySure	34.29	1.53	5.81	0.82
NSSR	30.81	2.28	8.54	0.59
CSTF	36.99	1.06	3.86	**0.85**
HCTR	**37.14**	**1.04**	**3.76**	0.81

Table 13.4 Performances of the HSI superresolution methods on different down-sampling methods.

Down-sampling method	PSNR	ERGAS	SAM	$Q2^n$
Kernel 1, Down-sample1	34.20	0.79	2.87	0.84
Kernel 2, Down-sample1	33.05	0.91	3.21	0.78
Kernel 1, Down-sample2	34.35	0.82	3.04	0.87
Kernel 2, Down-sample2	32.33	0.98	3.41	0.72

input. This demonstrates the effectiveness of the introduced multiscale high-order TR representation model for HSI-MSI fusion.

- Robustness to spatial degeneration: One advantage of the HCTR method is that the spatial degeneration information is not required. Usually, the spatial degeneration operator is composed of two parts: spatial blurring and down-sampling. In this experiment, two different Gaussian blurring kernels are used to compare the robustness of the HCTR and other methods. The first kernel is of size 7×7 with std 3, denoted as Kernel 1, and the second kernel is of size 11×11 with std 5, denoted as Kernel 2. In addition, two different down-sampling methods are considered in this experiment. The first is taking one pixel in every $p \times p$ block denoted as Down-sample1. The second is the bicubic down-sampling method denoted as Down-sample2. Results on the San Diego dataset are shown in Table 13.4. From Table 13.4, one can see that the overall performance of HCTR is rather robust. More specifically, the numerical results are stable with different down-sampling operators and the results using Kernel 1 are better than with Kernel 2. Thus, it can be concluded that the HCTR is robust to the down-sampling method and performs better with weak blurring.

13.2.3.5 Results on a real dataset

In the real data fusion experiment, the two datasets are part of the original Cuprite dataset. Given the absence of the spectral response function (SRF) and the blurring kernel, in this experiment, the SRF and the blurring kernel are estimated with the

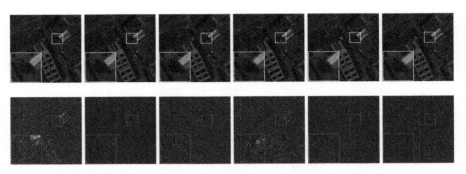

FIGURE 13.9

Visual quality comparison for reconstructed images of the synthetic datasets using the optic blurs in the spatial degeneration. Pictures in rows 1, 3, and 5 are reconstructed single-band images in band 40. Pictures in rows 2, 4, and 6 are the residual images between the reference and the reconstructed images in band 40.

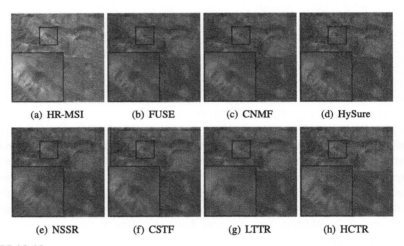

| (a) HR-MSI | (b) FUSE | (c) CNMF | (d) HySure |
| (e) NSSR | (f) CSTF | (g) LTTR | (h) HCTR |

FIGURE 13.10

False color images of HR-MSI in real dataset 1 and the reconstructed false color images using the compared methods.

method proposed in HySure [40]. The original size of the real data 1 and data 2 is $200 \times 200 \times 167$.

Fig. 13.10 and Fig. 13.11 show the obtained pseudo-color images using all the compared methods. It can be observed that the HCTR recovers the spatial structures of the captured scene accurately, and the CSTF performs the worst among all the methods. This can be caused by the separated blurring kernels. In addition, the spectral curves of pixel [180, 180] in the reconstructed HR-HSIs are presented in Fig. 13.12, and the reference curve in LR-HSI of pixel [45, 45] is drawn for compari-

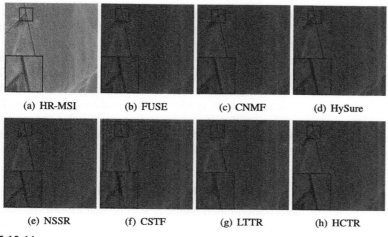

(a) HR-MSI   (b) FUSE   (c) CNMF   (d) HySure

(e) NSSR   (f) CSTF   (g) LTTR   (h) HCTR

FIGURE 13.11

False color images of HR-MSI in real dataset 2 and the reconstructed false color images using the compared methods.

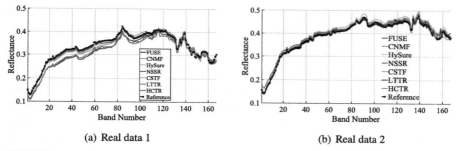

(a) Real data 1   (b) Real data 2

FIGURE 13.12

Spectral curves of pixel [180, 180] in the reconstructed HR-HSIs for the two real datasets. The reference curves are extracted from the LR-HSIs in pixel [45, 45].

son. It can be found that all the methods can well preserve the spectral structures, and the spectral curves obtained by the HCTR are close to the reference spectral curves in both datasets. According to the abovementioned results, it can be concluded that the HCTR can well preserve the spatial and spectral structures in real HSI-MSI fusion.

13.2.3.6 Conclusion

In this chapter, an HCTR representation method is introduced for HSI superresolution. First of all, the HSI is tensorized into a high-order tensor, in which the multiscale spatial information and spectral structure are included. Then, a coupled TR representation model is learned to fuse the LR-HSI and the HR-MSI. The core idea in HCTR model is that the latent core tensors in the TR representation of the LR-HSI and the

HR-MSI can be shared and the relationship between the latent spectral core tensors can be used. In addition, a spectral manifold regularization is introduced to the core tensor representing spectral structure. The spectral manifold is learned from the input LR-HSI which reveals the real spectral structure. To make the HCTR more robust, the authors introduce the Frobenius norm regularization to the other core tensors in the TR representation. An efficient algorithm based on an alternating optimization framework is designed. Experiments on both synthetic and real datasets corresponding to different sensors and platforms, with different spectral characteristics and resolutions, and with different contexts demonstrate that the HCTR achieves promising results among state-of-the-art HSI superresolution methods.

13.2.4 Joint tensor factorization for HSI-MSI fusion

Most existing tensor factorization-based methods assume that known (or easily estimated) degenerate operators are applied to superresolution images (SRIs) to form the corresponding HSIs and MSIs, which are practically absent. In this case, the superresolution problem is solved under the condition that the degenerate operators are seldom known and contain noise. A joint tensor factorization (JTF) model is proposed by taking advantage of the multidimensional tensor structure of the HSI and MSI. Furthermore, most methods cannot ensure a unique outcome; in this case, the proposed model guarantees the identifiability of SRI under mild and realistic conditions.

13.2.4.1 Problem formulation

Matrix-based methods usually assume that degradation operators are known or easily estimated, but in practice, they are difficult to be determined. By comparing the spectral properties of hyperspectral and multispectral sensors, the degradation operator $\mathbf{D_M}$ can be modeled and estimated relatively easily. However, the spatial operator becomes a bit difficult. A common model assumption from SRI to HSI conversion is a combination of the blurring by a Gaussian kernel and a down-sampling process. Of course, this is a rough approximation and may be far from accurate. Even if this assumption is approximately correct, there are still many uncertainties.

In order to solve the nonuniqueness of matrix decomposition and under the condition of little knowledge of degenerate operators and noise, we propose a method based on joint tensor decomposition to fuse the HSI and MSI in this section. Tensor-based models have many advantages. For example, it is a very efficient strategy to abstract image data into tensor representation and then input them in the image fusion model. For the output data, we can choose the desired format to save them conveniently. Formally, we represent the SRI as the following equation via CP decomposition:

$$\mathcal{S} = [\![\mathbf{A}, \mathbf{B}, \mathbf{C}]\!], \tag{13.25}$$

where $\mathcal{S} \in \mathbb{R}^{I \times J \times K}$, $\mathbf{A} \in \mathbb{R}^{I \times R}$, $\mathbf{B} \in \mathbb{R}^{J \times R}$, $\mathbf{C} \in \mathbb{R}^{K \times R}$, and R is the number of components.

The HSI is the spatial down-sampling version of the SRI. Assuming that the point spread function (PSF) of the hyperspectral sensor is separable from the down-sampling matrix of the wide mode and the high mode, we can have

$$\mathcal{H} = \mathcal{S} \times_1 \mathbf{D}_1 \times_2 \mathbf{D}_2, \tag{13.26}$$

where $\mathbf{D}_1 \in \mathbb{R}^{I \times i}$, $\mathbf{D}_2 \in \mathbb{R}^{J \times j}$ are the spatial degradation along the width and height modes, respectively. For subsampling, the separability hypothesis implies that the function of the spatial subsampling matrix $\mathbf{D_H}$ is decoupled from the two spatial patterns of $\mathcal{S}$, and thus, the degenerate operator $\mathbf{D_H} = \mathbf{D}_2 \otimes \mathbf{D}_1$ in the matricized form. Under the separability assumption, the HSI ($\mathcal{H}$) can be represented as

$$\mathcal{H} = [\![\mathbf{A}', \mathbf{B}', \mathbf{C}]\!], \tag{13.27}$$

where $\mathbf{A}' = \mathbf{D}_1\mathbf{A} \in \mathbb{R}^{I \times R}$, $\mathbf{B}' = \mathbf{D}_2\mathbf{B} \in \mathbb{R}^{J \times R}$, and $\mathbf{C} \in \mathbb{R}^{k \times R}$. In this section, we assume that the spectral response $\mathbf{D_M}$ has noise, i.e., rough sampling in the process of conversion from the SRI to the MSI. Formally, we represent it as

$$\mathbf{D}'_\mathbf{M} = \mathbf{D_M} + \Gamma, \tag{13.28}$$

where Γ is Gaussian random noise. Analogously, the MSI ($\mathcal{M}$) can be represented as

$$\mathcal{M} = \mathcal{S} \times_3 \mathbf{D}'_\mathbf{M}, \tag{13.29}$$

where $\mathbf{D}'_\mathbf{M} \in \mathbb{R}^{K \times k}$ is the down-sampling matrix of the spectral mode. We substitute Eq. (13.25) into Eq. (13.29) to obtain

$$\mathcal{M} = [\![\mathbf{A}, \mathbf{B}, \mathbf{C}']\!], \tag{13.30}$$

where $\mathbf{A} \in \mathbb{R}^{i \times R}$, $\mathbf{B} \in \mathbb{R}^{j \times R}$, and $\mathbf{C}' = \mathbf{D}'_\mathbf{M}\mathbf{C} \in \mathbb{R}^{K \times R}$. In order to reconstruct the SRI, we need to estimate the factor matrices $\mathbf{A}, \mathbf{B}, \mathbf{C}$.

Theorem 13.1. *Correspondingly, we consider how many rank-one tensors (components) of the decomposition of the CP model are added to minimize the error. The usual practice is to start with $R = 1$ until you encounter a "good" result. Of course, if you have a strong application background and prior information, you can also specify it in advance. For a given number of components, there is still no universal solution for CP decomposition. Specifically, the alternating least squares (ALS) algorithm is a more popular method in the case that the number of components is pre-given [25]. For the CP decomposition of tensors, even if R is much larger than max$\{i, j, k\}$, the CP decomposition model is essentially unique. The lower order decomposition of matrices and Tucker decomposition of tensors are generally not unique, which is a significant difference between them. The most famous result about the uniqueness of tensor decomposition is due to Kruskal [8]. One result of the Kruskal criteria is the following statement, which applies to general tensors, which provides the uniqueness proof of the CP decomposition model.*

Suppose $\mathcal{X} = [\![\mathbf{A}, \mathbf{B}, \mathbf{C}]\!]$ and tensor $\mathcal{X} \in \mathbb{R}^{I \times J \times K}$ of rank R has a unique decomposition if:

$$R \leq \frac{1}{2}[min(I, R) + min(J, R) + min(K, R) - 2].$$

where $\mathbf{A} \in \mathbb{R}^{I \times R}$, $\mathbf{B} \in \mathbb{R}^{J \times R}$, and $\mathbf{C} \in \mathbb{R}^{K \times R}$.

13.2.4.2 The joint tensor decomposition method

In this section, we consider that when $\mathbf{D_M}$ contains noise and the spatial degradation operator $\mathbf{D_H} = \mathbf{D_2} \otimes \mathbf{D_1}$ is completely unknown, even though this type of operation is called a combination of blurring and down-sampling, in practice, hyperparameters such as the blurring kernel type, kernel size, and down-sampling offset are barely known. Therefore, the joint tensor decomposition model can be generalized to the following model:

$$\min_{\mathbf{A},\mathbf{B},\mathbf{C}} \| \mathcal{H} - [\![\mathbf{A}', \mathbf{B}', \mathbf{C}]\!] \|_F^2 + \| \mathcal{M} - [\![\mathbf{A}, \mathbf{B}, \mathbf{C}']\!] \|_F^2 + \beta \| \mathbf{C}' - \mathbf{D}'_\mathbf{M}\mathbf{C} \|_F^2. \quad (13.31)$$

We use the following optimization models to obtain factor matrices $\mathbf{A}, \mathbf{B}$, and $\mathbf{C}$, where β is the regularization parameter. The above optimization problem is nonconvex, and the solutions of the factor matrices $\mathbf{A}, \mathbf{B}$, and $\mathbf{C}$ are not unique. However, the objective function in Eq. (13.31) is convex for each variable block, remaining unchanged with other variables. Therefore, we choose the proximal alternate optimization (PAO) scheme to solve the above optimization problem, which guarantees that the optimization problem converges to the critical point under certain conditions. Then, each step of the iterative update of the factor matrix is reduced to solving an easy-to-handle Sylvester equation by matricization of tensor HSI and MSI. Specifically, the $\mathbf{A}, \mathbf{B}$, and $\mathbf{C}$ iterations are updated as follows:

- Optimization with respect to $\mathbf{C}$:

When $\mathbf{A}, \mathbf{B}, \mathbf{A}', \mathbf{B}'$, and $\mathbf{C}'$ are fixed, the optimization w.r.t. $\mathbf{C}$ in (13.31) can be written as

$$\min_{\mathbf{C}} \| \mathcal{H} - [\![\mathbf{A}', \mathbf{B}', \mathbf{C}]\!] \|_F^2 + \| \mathcal{M} - [\![\mathbf{A}, \mathbf{B}, \mathbf{C}']\!] \|_F^2 + \beta \| \mathbf{C}' - \mathbf{D}'_\mathbf{M}\mathbf{C} \|_F^2 .$$

The above optimization problem can be transformed into the following one by using the properties of n-mode matrix unfolding:

$$\min_{\mathbf{C}} \| \| \mathbf{H}_{(3)} - \mathbf{C}(\mathbf{B}' \odot \mathbf{A}')^{\mathrm{T}}) \|_F^2 + \beta \| \mathbf{C}' - \mathbf{D}'_\mathbf{M}\mathbf{C} \|_F^2, \quad (13.32)$$

where $\mathbf{H}_{(3)}$ is the three-mode unfolding matrix of tensors $\mathcal{H}$. The optimization problem Eq. (13.32) is quadratic, and its unique solution is equal to the calculation of the general Sylvester matrix equation,

$$\beta \mathbf{D}'^{\mathrm{T}}_\mathbf{M}\mathbf{D}'_\mathbf{M}\mathbf{C} + \mathbf{CE} - \beta \mathbf{D}'^{\mathrm{T}}_\mathbf{M}\mathbf{C}' = \mathbf{H}_{(3)}\mathbf{E}, \quad (13.33)$$

where $\mathbf{E} = (\mathbf{B'}^T \mathbf{B'}) * (\mathbf{A'}^T \mathbf{A'})$.

We use the Sylvester function in the MATLAB® toolbox to solve the above equation.

- Optimization with respect to $\mathbf{A'}$:

When $\mathbf{A}, \mathbf{B}, \mathbf{C}, \mathbf{B'}$, and $\mathbf{C'}$ are fixed, the optimization w.r.t. $\mathbf{A'}$ in (13.31) can be written as

$$\min_{\mathbf{A'}} \| \mathcal{H} - [\![\mathbf{A'}, \mathbf{B'}, \mathbf{C}]\!] \|_F^2 . \tag{13.34}$$

The above optimization problem can be transformed into the following one by using the properties of n-mode matrix unfolding:

$$\min_{\mathbf{A'}} \| \mathbf{H}_{(1)} - \mathbf{A'}(\mathbf{C} \odot \mathbf{B'})^T) \|_F^2, \tag{13.35}$$

where $\mathbf{H}_{(1)}$ is the one-mode unfolding matrix of tensors $\mathcal{H}$. The optimization problem Eq. (13.35) is convex, and the optimal solution is then given by

$$\mathbf{A'} = \mathbf{H}_{(1)} \big[(\mathbf{C} \odot \mathbf{B'})^T \big]^\dagger . \tag{13.36}$$

According to the property of the Khatri–Rao product pseudo-inverse, we can rewrite the solution as

$$\mathbf{A'} = \mathbf{H}_{(1)}(\mathbf{C} \odot \mathbf{B'})(\mathbf{C}^T \mathbf{C} * \mathbf{B'}^T \mathbf{B'})^\dagger . \tag{13.37}$$

The advantage of solving the above equation is that we only need to compute the pseudo-inverse matrix of the $R \times R$ matrix, but not the $jK \times R$ matrix. The solution process of factor matrix $\mathbf{B'}$ is similar to that of $\mathbf{A'}$, and we can rewrite the solution as

$$\mathbf{B'} = \mathbf{H}_{(2)}(\mathbf{C} \odot \mathbf{A'})(\mathbf{C}^T \mathbf{C} * \mathbf{A'}^T \mathbf{A'})^\dagger . \tag{13.38}$$

- Optimization with respect to $\mathbf{C'}$:

When $\mathbf{A}, \mathbf{B}, \mathbf{C}, \mathbf{A'}$, and $\mathbf{B'}$ are fixed, the optimization w.r.t. $\mathbf{C'}$ in (13.31) can be written as the following one by using the properties of n-mode matrix unfolding:

$$\min_{\mathbf{C'}} \| \mathbf{M}_{(3)} - \mathbf{C'}(\mathbf{B} \odot \mathbf{A})^T) \|_F^2 + \beta \| \mathbf{C'} - \mathbf{D'_M} \mathbf{C} \|_F^2, \tag{13.39}$$

where $\mathbf{M}_{(3)}$ is the three-mode unfolding matrix of tensors $\mathcal{M}$. The optimization problem Eq. (13.39) is quadratic, and its unique solution is equal to the calculation of the general Sylvester matrix equation,

$$\beta \mathbf{I}^T \mathbf{I} \mathbf{C'} + \mathbf{C'} \mathbf{F} - \beta \mathbf{D'_M} \mathbf{C} = \mathbf{H}_{(3)} \mathbf{F}, \tag{13.40}$$

where $\mathbf{F} = (\mathbf{B}^T \mathbf{B}) * (\mathbf{A}^T \mathbf{A})$ and $\mathbf{I}$ is the unit matrix of 4×4.

We use the Sylvester function in the MATLAB toolbox to solve the above equation.

- Optimization with respect to $\mathbf{A}$:

When $\mathbf{B}$, $\mathbf{C}$, $\mathbf{A}'$, $\mathbf{B}'$, and $\mathbf{C}'$ are fixed, the optimization w.r.t. $\mathbf{A}$ in (13.31) can be written as

$$\min_{\mathbf{A}} \| \mathcal{M} - [\![\mathbf{A}, \mathbf{B}, \mathbf{C}']\!] \|_F^2 . \qquad (13.41)$$

The above optimization problem can be transformed into the following one by using the properties of n-mode matrix unfolding:

$$\min_{\mathbf{A}} \| \mathbf{M}_{(1)} - \mathbf{A}(\mathbf{C}' \odot \mathbf{B})^T \|_F^2, \qquad (13.42)$$

where $\mathbf{M}_{(1)}$ is the one-mode unfolding matrix of tensors $\mathcal{M}$. The optimization problem Eq. (13.42) is convex, and the optimal solution is then given by

$$\mathbf{A} = \mathbf{M}_{(1)}\left[(\mathbf{C}' \odot \mathbf{B})^T\right]^\dagger . \qquad (13.43)$$

According to the property of the Khatri–Rao product pseudo-inverse, we can rewrite the solution as

$$\mathbf{A} = \mathbf{M}_{(1)}(\mathbf{C}' \odot \mathbf{B})(\mathbf{C}'^T\mathbf{C} * \mathbf{B}'^T\mathbf{B})^\dagger . \qquad (13.44)$$

Similarly, we only need to compute the pseudo-inverse matrix of the $R \times R$ matrix, but not the $Jk \times R$ matrix. The solution process of factor matrix $\mathbf{B}$ is similar to that of $\mathbf{A}$, and we can rewrite the solution as

$$\mathbf{B} = \mathbf{M}_{(2)}(\mathbf{C}' \odot \mathbf{A})(\mathbf{C}'^T\mathbf{C}' * \mathbf{A}^T\mathbf{A})^\dagger . \qquad (13.45)$$

We discuss each iteration update in detail. The specific algorithm is shown in Algorithm 1. After obtaining the estimated values of $\mathbf{A}$, $\mathbf{B}$, and $\mathbf{C}$, the superresolution tensor reconstruction is obtained from the following formula:

$$\mathcal{S} \approx [\![\mathbf{A}, \mathbf{B}, \mathbf{C}]\!] . \qquad (13.46)$$

The detailed steps of the proposed method are given in Algorithm 1.

13.2.4.3 Selection of parameters

In this section, we select different iterations and the number of components of CP decomposition and experimented under these conditions to obtain the best parameter values, so as to evaluate the sensitivity of the **JTF** algorithm to important parameters in the model. Because the algorithm in this section is based on the unknown $\mathbf{D_H}$, we first consider experimenting under the condition that the algorithm incorrectly assumes a 7×7 Gaussian blur kernel instead of using the correct 9×9 Gaussian kernel. Certainly, we have also made experimental comparisons under the correct Gaussian kernels.

Considering the **JTF** algorithm under different signal-to-noise ratios (SNRs) and assuming that the SNR ratio of the HSI and MSI is the same, where the SNR here

---

Algorithm 1 Algorithm for coupled images.

Initialization: $\beta, R, \mathbf{A}_0, \mathbf{B}_0, \mathbf{C}_0, \mathbf{A}'_0, \mathbf{B}'_0, \mathbf{C}'_0$

  Apply Blind Stereo with random

  Initializations to obtain $\mathbf{A}, \mathbf{B}, \mathbf{C}, \mathbf{A}', \mathbf{B}', \mathbf{C}'$

While not converged, do

  $\mathbf{C} \leftarrow \arg\min_{\mathbf{C}} \| \mathbf{H}_{(3)} - \mathbf{C}(\mathbf{B}' \odot \mathbf{A}')^{\mathsf{T}}) \|_{\mathrm{F}}^2 + \beta \| \mathbf{C}' - \mathbf{D}'_{\mathbf{M}}\mathbf{C} \|_{\mathrm{F}}^2,$

  $\mathbf{A}' \leftarrow \arg\min_{\mathbf{A}'} \| \mathbf{H}_{(1)} - \mathbf{A}'(\mathbf{C} \odot \mathbf{B}')^{\mathsf{T}}) \|_{\mathrm{F}}^2,$

  $\mathbf{B}' \leftarrow \arg\min_{\mathbf{B}'} \| \mathbf{H}_{(2)} - \mathbf{B}'(\mathbf{C} \odot \mathbf{A}')^{\mathsf{T}}) \|_{\mathrm{F}}^2,$

  $\mathbf{C}' \leftarrow \arg\min_{\mathbf{C}'} \| \mathbf{M}_{(3)} - \mathbf{C}'(\mathbf{B} \odot \mathbf{A})^{\mathsf{T}}) \|_{\mathrm{F}}^2 + \beta \| \mathbf{C}' - \mathbf{D}'_{\mathbf{M}}\mathbf{C} \|_{\mathrm{F}}^2,$

  $\mathbf{A} \leftarrow \arg\min_{\mathbf{A}} \| \mathbf{M}_{(1)} - \mathbf{A}(\mathbf{C}' \odot \mathbf{B})^{\mathsf{T}}) \|_{\mathrm{F}}^2,$

  $\mathbf{B} \leftarrow \arg\min_{\mathbf{B}} \| \mathbf{M}_{(2)} - \mathbf{B}(\mathbf{C}' \odot \mathbf{A})^{\mathsf{T}}) \|_{\mathrm{F}}^2.$

end while

---

is set at 20 dB, to evaluate the effect of the number of iterations **Iter** on the image fusion in the algorithm, we run the **JTF** algorithm based on the number of iterations **Iter**. Because the **JTF** algorithm is based on the modification of the **Blind Stereo** algorithm [22], we compare the performance of the algorithms with or without noise of the degenerate operator. Fig. 13.13 shows the evaluation metrics of SRI after the reconstruction of the Pavia University dataset with the change of iteration number **Iter**. In order to reduce the running time of the algorithm, without loss of generality, here $R = 100$, $\beta = 1$, where the black line represents the **Blind Stereo** algorithm performance in matrix $\mathbf{D_M}$ with noise, the red line (light gray in print version) shows the reconstruction results of the **JTF** algorithm under the same condition, and the blue (dark gray in print version) trend line indicates the fusion performance by the **Blind Stereo** algorithm when $\mathbf{D_M}$ does not contain noise.

As can be seen from Fig. 13.13, when **Iter** changes from 1 to 20, the reconstruction SNR (R-SNR) of the Pavia University dataset decreases, while the values of NMSE, ERGAS, and SAM increase. Among them, R-SNR declines sharply and then rises, while the other evaluation metrics show the opposite trend. When the number of iterations is less than five, the reconstruction effect is better. Therefore, the maximum number of iterations of the **JTF** algorithm is set between one and five. In addition, the reconstruction effect of this algorithm is always superior to the Blind Stereo fusion algorithm with noise.

Then, we change the number of components from $R = 50$ to $R = 600$ to observe the effect of the number of tensor decomposition components on the image fusion, which depicts different evaluation metrics of the recovered HSIs for the Pavia University dataset (Fig. 13.14).

Fig. 13.14 shows the effect of image fusion in three cases with a different number of components. When $\mathbf{D_H}$ is unknown and $\mathbf{D_M}$ contains noise, we compare the above three cases. From the six evaluation metrics, it can be seen that when the number of components is less than 100, the performance of the proposed algorithm is almost the same as the case that $\mathbf{D_M}$ is clean. It completely achieves the denoising effect and is always better than the **Blind Stereo** algorithm in the same situation. With the

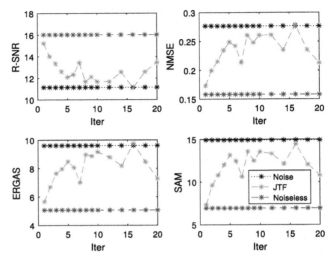

FIGURE 13.13

The results of the evaluation criterion as functions of the number of iterations **Iter** for the proposed joint tensor decomposition (JTF) method. SAM, spectral angle mapper; ERGAS, relative dimensionless global error in synthesis; R-SNR, reconstruction signal-to-noise ratio.

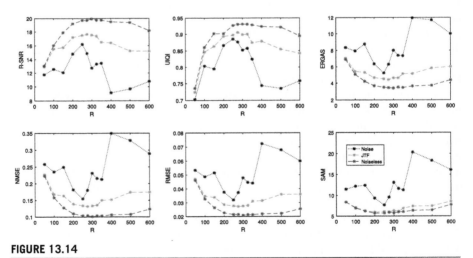

FIGURE 13.14

The results of evaluation metrics as functions of the number of components *R* for the proposed JTF method. UIQI, universal image quality index.

increase of the number of components, all three cases show good performance. However, when the number of components increases to more than 300, the reconstruction effect has a downward trend. According to the above theorem [8], this is because when the number of components does not satisfy Theorem 13.1, the algorithm cannot guarantee the uniqueness of CP decomposition, which affects the initialization of the initial factor matrix in the algorithm, resulting in poor performance of the algorithm.

Then, consider the selection range of the number of components under the condition of the uniqueness of tensor decomposition. As the **JTF** algorithm only decomposes MSI by CP, we set $I = 608$, $J = 336$, $K = 4$ in Theorem 13.1. According to the dimension of MSI, we can divide the selection of parameter R into the following four cases:

1. When $R < K = 4$, bring R into Theorem 13.1, i.e.,

$$R \leq \frac{1}{2}(R + R + R - 2) \Rightarrow R \geq 1. \tag{13.47}$$

By synthesizing the formulas and conditions, we can get the range of R in the first case, which is $1 \leq R < 4$.

2. When $4 = K \leq R < J = 336$, bring R into Theorem 13.1, i.e.,

$$R \leq \frac{1}{2}(R + R + 4 - 2) \Rightarrow R \leq R + 1. \tag{13.48}$$

The above derivation is obviously valid, so we only consider the conditions, and we can get the range of R in the second case, which is $4 \leq R < 336$.

3. When $J = 336 \leq R < I = 608$, bring R into Theorem 13.1, i.e.,

$$R \leq \frac{1}{2}(R + 336 + 4R - 2) \Rightarrow R \geq 338. \tag{13.49}$$

By synthesizing the formulas and conditions, we can get the range of R in the third case, which is $336 \leq R < 338$.

4. When $R \geq 608 = I$, bring R into Theorem 13.1, i.e.,

$$R \leq \frac{1}{2}(608 + 336 + 4R - 2) \Rightarrow R \geq 475. \tag{13.50}$$

As such, we can get the range of R in the fourth case, which is $R < 475$ and $R \geq 608$, by synthesizing the formulas and conditions. Therefore, we can conclude that there is a contradiction between the deduced range of R and the range of conditions, so this situation does not exist.

To sum up, combining the above four cases, in order to guarantee the uniqueness of CP decomposition, the range of the number of components is $1 \leq R \leq 338$. In this section, according to the fusion effect of the algorithm while ensuring the uniqueness of CP decomposition, we fixed $R = 275$.

13.2.4.4 Experimental results

To further investigate the performance of the method, we conduct experiments under the incorrect Gaussian kernel (3×3, 5×5, 7×7) and correct Gaussian kernel

(9×9) and show the fusion effect of the six test methods on the Pavia University dataset. Table 13.5 shows the R-SNR, NMSE, RMSE, ERGAS, SAM, and universal image quality index (UIQI) of the HSI recovered from the Pavia University dataset, and we present the best of the six algorithms in bold. As can be seen from the table, in the case of incorrect estimation of the Gaussian kernel, the fusion effect of other algorithms excluding **JTF** is worse than that of the correct Gaussian kernel. The closer these five algorithms are to the correct Gaussian kernel, the better the results will be. Nevertheless, the **JTF** method performs best in the comparison of the methods in terms of reconstruction accuracy whether the Gaussian kernel is correctly estimated or not. Overall, the **JTF** and **CNMF** methods are very effective in the reconstruction of the Pavia University dataset. On the contrary, proposed the **JTF** algorithm does not degrade the image reconstruction effect due to the incorrect estimation of the Gaussian kernel. More specifically, the property of the proposed algorithm is greater under the hypothetical Gaussian kernel, which also proves that the **JTF** algorithm has more generalization significance and application prospects.

Fig. 13.15 reveals the fusion experimental results for the Pavia University dataset under the incorrect Gaussian kernel (7×7), which contains the 50th and 100th bands' fused images and the corresponding error images reconstructed by the six algorithms, where line 1 and line 2 in Fig. 13.15 denote the fused HSIs of the 50th band and the corresponding error HSIs of each method, respectively. Moreover, Fig. 13.15(g) shows the reference HSIs, while the third and forth rows show the reconstructed images for the 100th band and corresponding error images, respectively. Except for the last column, each column in Fig. 13.15 shows the experimental results corresponding to each method. The error image reflects the difference between the fusion result and the ground truth. As depicted in Fig. 13.15, this section uses the red (light gray in print version) box to show the more obvious areas in order to compare the difference of error images of different algorithms clearly. By visualized comparison of the fused HSIs with the reference HSIs, the fusion result of the **Blind Stereo** method shows slight spectral distortion on the top of the building, while the MAP estimation with a stochastic mixing model (**MAPSMM**) method generates fuzzy spatial details in some areas, and the spatial information of the fused image is well enhanced by the **CNMF** method. A closer inspection reveals that the spectral and spatial differences of fused HSIs obtained by the six methods are not obvious. Therefore, in order to further compare the performance of each fusion method, the second and fourth lines of Fig. 13.15 show the error images of the six methods under two spectral bands. The error image is the difference (absolute value) between the fused HSI and the reference HSI pixel value. We magnify the data element value in the error image by 10 times, so that we can inspect it more carefully. It can be seen that the **Blind Stereo**, smoothing filter-based intensity modulation (**SFIM**), modulation transfer function-based generalized Laplacian pyramid (**MTF-GLP**), and **MAPSMM** methods have large differences, while the **CNMF** method generates relatively smaller differences and the **JTF** method has the smallest differences in most regions, indicating that this method has good fusion ability and provides clearer spatial details than the other five algorithms.

Table 13.5 Quantitative results of the test methods on the Pavia University dataset under the different Gaussian kernels. CNMF, coupled nonnegative matrix factorization; SFIM, smoothing filter-based intensity modulation; MTF-GLP, modulation transfer function-based generalized Laplacian pyramid; MAPSMM, maximum a posteriori estimation with a stochastic mixing model.

Gaussian kernel	Method	R-SNR	NMSE	RMSE	ERGAS	SAM	UIQI
3 × 3	JTF	**17.8267**	**0.1284**	**0.0266**	**4.3495**	**5.95**	**0.9031**
	Blind Stereo	11.0252	0.281	0.0581	9.9924	15.841	0.7777
	CNMF	15.8798	0.1607	0.0332	5.684	7.8655	0.8922
	SFIM	10.7811	0.289	0.0598	10.3849	11.2828	0.7374
	MTF-GLP	12.8459	0.2279	0.0471	7.608	10.4577	0.7845
	MAPSMM	11.8642	0.2551	0.0528	8.3346	10.4203	0.7449
5 × 5	JTF	**17.6357**	**0.1313**	**0.0272**	**4.4351**	**5.9266**	**0.8983**
	Blind Stereo	11.163	0.2766	0.0572	9.6563	15.6988	0.7938
	CNMF	15.5546	0.1668	0.0345	5.7987	7.9809	0.8623
	SFIM	12.6416	0.2333	0.0483	7.9097	10.2705	0.7725
	MTF-GLP	13.6742	0.2072	0.0428	6.9561	9.7086	0.8038
	MAPSMM	12.8407	0.228	0.0472	7.4954	9.5283	0.7733
7 × 7	JTF	**17.7156**	**0.1301**	**0.0269**	**4.4008**	**5.8517**	**0.9001**
	Blind Stereo	13.4084	0.2136	0.0442	7.421	11.9428	0.8584
	CNMF	16.0028	0.1584	0.0328	5.5489	7.2096	0.8747
	SFIM	13.1113	0.221	0.0457	7.493	9.9524	0.7804
	MTF-GLP	13.9393	0.2009	0.0416	6.7583	9.461	0.8057
	MAPSMM	13.1616	0.2197	0.0454	7.2442	9.3344	0.7777
9 × 9	JTF	**17.603**	**0.1318**	**0.0273**	**4.4091**	**5.7811**	**0.8991**
	Blind Stereo	13.7402	0.2056	0.0425	7.0851	11.3721	0.8621
	CNMF	16.3576	0.1521	0.0315	5.3307	7.1092	0.8792
	SFIM	13.3654	0.2147	0.0444	7.2704	9.7603	0.7875
	MTF-GLP	14.1333	0.1965	0.0406	6.6077	9.3225	0.8109
	MAPSMM	13.2983	0.2163	0.0447	7.1304	9.1704	0.7813

Similar to the previous experiments, Fig. 13.16 shows the fusion experimental results for the Pavia University dataset under the correct Gaussian kernel (9 × 9), which contain the 50th and 100th bands' fused images and the corresponding error images reconstructed by the six algorithms. Fig. 13.16 shows the fused HSIs of the 50th band and the corresponding error HSIs of each method, which are displayed in lines 1 and 2. Moreover, Fig. 13.16(g) shows the reference HSIs, while the third and fourth rows show the reconstructed images for the 100th band and corresponding error images, respectively. Similarly, in order to compare the differ-

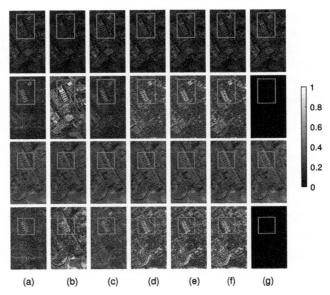

FIGURE 13.15

Reconstructed images and corresponding error images of the Pavia University dataset for the 50th and 100th bands with unknown D_H and noisy D_M. (a) JTF. (b) Blind Stereo. (c) CNMF. (d) SFIM. (e) MTF-GLP. (f) MAPSMM. (g) Ground truth.

ence of the error images of different algorithms clearly, the data element values in the error image are magnified 10 times, and the red (light gray in print version) box is applied to display the region with obvious errors. The spectral distortion caused by the **Blind Stereo** method is very obvious and is affected by the Gaussian kernel changes, as shown in Fig. 13.16(b). Compared with the **Blind Stereo** method, other methods can effectively improve the spatial performance while maintaining the spectral information, and the difference between the fused images is not significant. Therefore, in order to further verify the fusion performance of the proposed method, the second and fourth lines of Fig. 13.16 show the error images corresponding to different methods, respectively. It can be seen that the error image obtained by the **JTF** method is the lowest in most regions, and the fusion effect is not affected by the Gaussian kernel, which indicates that the **JTF** method has a superior image reconstruction effect and is more robust. Overall, the **JTF** method has better reconstruction performance and clearer fusion effects than the other five algorithms.

13.2.4.5 Experimental results of the noise

In practice, there exists additive noise in the hyperspectral and multispectral imaging processes. Therefore, to test the robustness of the proposed **JTF** method to noise, we firstly simulate the tensor images $\mathcal{M}$ and $\mathcal{H}$ in the same way as the previous

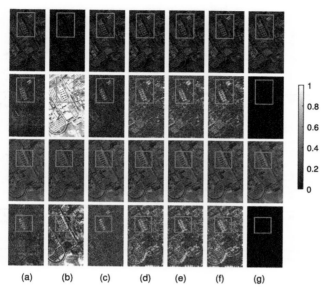

FIGURE 13.16

Reconstructed images and corresponding error images of the Pavia University dataset for the 20th and 60th bands with unknown $\mathbf{D_H}$ and noisy $\mathbf{D_M}$. (**a**) JTF. (**b**) Blind Stereo. (**c**) CNMF. (**d**) SFIM. (**e**) MTF-GLP. (**f**) MAPSMM. (**g**) Ground truth.

experiments for the Pavia University dataset and then add Gaussian noise to the HSI and MSI. Because the noise level in the HSI is often higher than that of the MSI, we fix the SNR added to the HSI to be 20 dB and compare the evaluation indicators with the traditional five classical models with the change of noise added to MSI.

Fig. 13.17 presents the quality metric values of the noisy cases for the Pavia University dataset. It can be seen that from the reconstruction performance of the six fusion algorithms a trend emerges of enhancement with the increase of MSI image noise. Although the fusion effect of **CNMF** is closer to that of the **JTF** algorithm when the noise is high, the **JTF** method is still better than other test methods in the case of noise as a whole.

13.2.4.6 Analysis of computational costs

In this section, experiments are carried out on six classical methods to demonstrate the computational efficiency of the proposed method, which are accomplished with MATLAB R2016b on a PC with Intel Core i7-7500 CPU and 8 GB RAM. The mean time (in terms of seconds) of all comparison methods is shown in Table 13.6.

As can be seen from Table 13.6, the method based on the filter fusion (**SFIM**) does not need to calculate the optimal factor matrix of each mode, and its running time is shorter than that of the method based on tensor samples. For tensor-based methods, since the iterative strategy is used to obtain the optimal solution of each unknown

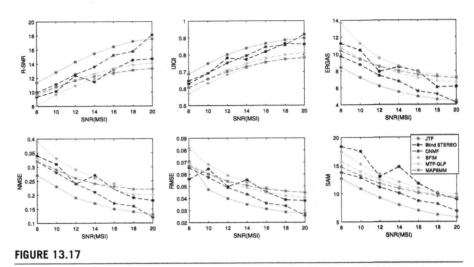

FIGURE 13.17

The results of evaluation metrics under different noises. MSI, multispectral image.

Table 13.6 Time (s) of the test methods on the Pavia University dataset under different conditions.

Method	Gaussian kernel (7 × 7) (SNR 10 dB)	Gaussian kernel(9 × 9) (SNR 10 dB)	Gaussian kernel (7 × 7) (SNR 20 dB)	Gaussian kernel (9 × 9) (SNR 20 dB)
JTF	17.266912	15.883985	15.303149	15.035694
Blind Stereo	15.179482	13.761605	13.057704	12.79495
CNMF	91.838425	89.438305	82.124058	82.466387
SFIM	1.421629	0.821533	0.836197	0.829191
MTF-GLP	24.859017	25.753572	24.809271	31.731484
MAPSMM	301.682105	283.545812	266.800409	299.233003

factor, the time of the two methods (**JTF** and **Blind Stereo**) is almost the same. **MTF-GLP** runs between the first two classes of methods, while **CNMF** and **MAPSMM** have long running times. Compared with the excellent performance, the running time of **JTF** is acceptable. Analyses were conducted based on various noises under different Gaussian kernels to further observe the performance of different algorithms. The results indicate that the running time of most algorithms is shorter under the premise of correct estimation of Gaussian kernels. However, there is little difference with the running time of the **JTF** algorithm under unknown Gaussian kernels, and the running time has little relation with the magnitude of additive noise, which indirectly proves that our algorithm is more robust.

13.3 **Polarimetric synthetic aperture radar: feature extraction**

Polarimetric SAR (PolSAR), a typical multichannel radar system, can obtain refined geometrical and geophysical information by transmitting and receiving radar electromagnetic waves. From different perspectives, there are lots of ways to describe the original PolSAR data, such as physical scattering, the target decomposition mechanism, and image information. So the PolSAR data can be naturally represented by multimodal space, but how to effectively combine those multimodal features and extract discriminant information for the following tasks is still an urgent problem. In order to accurately reflect the similarities between data points and extract the features for data interpretation, the graph embedding techniques, an efficient method to capture the relationship between samples, are taken to compute the sample space properties and develop dimensionality reduction (DR) techniques. In the land cover classification task, it aims at assigning each pixel to a land cover type. It is reasonable to extend the linear embedding methods to a tensor embedding form, because each pixel can be represented by a feature cube that is constructed by groups of polarimetric scattering signals and target decomposition features in a fixed-size patch. This section will introduce some tensor-based feature extraction methods for PolSAR land cover classification.

In image segmentation, target recognition, land cover/use classification, and other remote sensing data interpretation tasks, the study of machine learning-based methods is one of the most significant research directions in PolSAR data processing. And for machine learning-based methods, feature extraction/fusion/selection and classifier design are two significant steps [30]. In this section, the polarimetric properties and spatial information are explored by tensorial embedding methods for achieving a group of distinctive features for land cover classification.

There is no conclusion whether it is better to employ one view of features or multiview features in image processing techniques for PolSAR land cover classification. Some researchers employ the manifold techniques to exploit the intrinsic distances of data points and obtain the similarity matrix such as applying LEs and a supervised graph embedding method to reduce the dimensionality [39,43]. Those manifold-related algorithms all initially construct a local structure between pixels in manifold space and then utilize those local structures to embed pixels into a low-dimensional space. Those manifold algorithms, such as LLE [38], LE [5], and LTSA [70], can accurately learn the nonlinear structures of real data, but they have the drawback that the computation complexity is high and they are sensitive to outliers and noise. They are very difficult to apply in large-scale image classification and target recognition tasks.

Furthermore, linear reduction algorithms are developed for obtaining projection matrices to solve the out-of-sample problem. MDS, NPE [18], LPP [17], and LLTSA [70] are the linear versions of ISOMAP, LLE, LE, and LTSA, respectively. At the same time, PCA, LDA, and LDE are all linear algorithms employed to reduce the data dimensions under unsupervised and supervised conditions for some land cover classification tasks.

Tensors, as the high order of vectors and matrices, can preserve the intrinsic data structure and offer a better explanation for the data processing. In particular, for PolSAR classification, the features of each pixel are always extracted from a patch around the pixel. Those features can be represented by a 3D cube similar to other remote sensing image processing methods [45,56,57], on which multilinear-algebraic techniques can then be applied. Recently, many DR techniques were modified to a high-order tensorial form to analyze the data structure. Those tensor-based DR algorithms include TLDA [41,60], TLPP [9], TLDE [9,20], TNPE [17,49], TPCA [33,61], and other modified versions of those tensorial DR algorithms [34].

In this section, some tensorial methods are investigated and several advanced models for PolSAR feature extraction are presented. More specifically, a case study of tensorial methods will be given, which extract the intrinsic features by incorporating the spectral-spatial information of multimodal space properties of PolSAR data. In PolSAR land cover classification, each pixel can be represented by a 3D feature cube, in which the length and width of the cube are the same as the size of the patch covering the pixel and the height of the cube is the dimensionality of the feature vector. A tensor embedding framework extracts the discriminative features from the feature cubes constructed by redundant features.

13.3.1 Brief description of PolSAR data

PolSAR is a multiple-channel radar system. It can acquire quad-polarization information to measure the targets in four receiving/transmitting models, including HH, HV, VH, and VV, and records more complete backscattering information than traditional single-polarization SAR. The obtained polarization information can describe the geometrical structure and the geophysical properties of the targets. On the one hand, it provides more information for remote sensing image understanding and interpretation. With the development of imaging radar systems, more and more advanced airborne and spaceborne PolSAR systems have launched, i.e., ALOS2, RADARSAT2, and TerraSAR. On the other hand, it also contributes to the advancement of PolSAR techniques and expands the application fields, which include military and civilian application domains, such as natural resource exploration, environmental monitoring, agriculture control, forest vegetation change detection, and recognition and monitoring of military objects.

The radar equation, which can generate the different forms of polarimetirc data, always describe the interaction of an electromagnetic wave with a given target for reflecting the relationship between the power intercepting by the incident electromagnetic wave and the power reradiated by the same target. The scattering matrix $\mathbf{S}$ is defined to characterize a given target from the radar equation, and can be expressed as the following formulation: $\mathbf{S} = \begin{bmatrix} S_{HH} & S_{HV} \\ S_{VH} & S_{VV} \end{bmatrix}$.

In the monostatic backscattering case, the Sinclair scattering matrix is symmetrical, and then $S_{HV} = S_{VH}$. Then the 3×3 polarimetric Pauli coherency matrix $\mathbf{T}_3$

and the 3×3 lexicographic covariance matrix $\mathbf{C}_3$ are computed by the outer product of the corresponding target vector with its conjugate transpose as $\mathbf{T}_3 = \langle \mathbf{k} \cdot \mathbf{k}^{*T} \rangle$ and $\mathbf{C}_3 = \langle \mathbf{\Omega} \cdot \mathbf{\Omega}^{*T} \rangle$. In those two equations, the "3D lexicographic feature vector" and the "3D Pauli feature vector" are as follows:

$$\mathbf{\Omega} = [S_{HH}, \sqrt{2} S_{HV}, S_{VV}]^T,$$

$$\mathbf{k} = \frac{1}{\sqrt{2}} [S_{HH} + S_{VV}, S_{HH} + S_{VV}, 2S_{HV}]^T. \tag{13.51}$$

Those target vectors (Pauli target vector and lexicographic target vector) are all first-order statistical vectors. Meanwhile, those matrices (Sinclair matrix $\mathbf{S}$, coherency matrix $\mathbf{T}$, and covariance matrix $\mathbf{C}$) are the second-order statistical matrices. The averaging of matrices $\mathbf{T}$ and $\mathbf{C}$ can sufficiently reduce the speckle noise, but it leads to the "distributed target" and opposes the stationary target (always represented by a Sinclair matrix and single look coherency $\mathbf{T}$ and covariance matrix $\mathbf{C}$).

Target decomposition theorems aiming at providing a physical interpretation to describe the original data properties can also provide another kind of data form. It includes coherency and incoherency decomposition according to whether the target is pure or distributed. Furthermore, it can be divided into four main types: based on dichotomy of the Kennaugh matrix $\mathbf{K}$, modal-based decomposition of a coherency matrix and a covariance matrix, eigenvector and eigenvalues analysis of a coherency matrix and a covariance matrix, and the composition of a Sinclair matrix. Those different data forms provide sufficient content to describe the targets and land covers. The feature extraction methods can be mainly divided into three categories, including image features, data features, and target decomposition features, summarized in Fig. 13.18 [26,44].

13.3.2 The tensorial embedding framework

Consider a set of tensors $\{\mathcal{X}_i\}_{i=1}^N \in \mathbb{R}^{I_1 \times I_2 \times \cdots \times I_M}$, in which I_m is the dimension in m-mode and M is the order of the tensor. The tensor embedding framework seeks to find M projection matrices $\mathbf{U}_m \in \mathbb{R}^{P_m \times I_m}$, $m = 1, 2, ..., M$, for transforming the dimension in each mode. Then it obtains the tensor $\{\mathcal{Z}_i\}_{i=1}^N \in \mathbb{R}^{P_1 \times P_2 \times \cdots \times P_M}$. The tensor can be projected by the following equation:

$$\mathcal{Z}_i = \mathcal{X}_i \times_1 \mathbf{U}_1 \times_2 \mathbf{U}_2 \times_3 \cdots \times_M \mathbf{U}_M. \tag{13.52}$$

The projection matrices map the data from the original dimension and keep the intrinsic topological structure in the low dimension. Then we can extend the linear embedding methods into a high-order DR framework, and the LPP objective function is as follows:

$$
\begin{aligned}
\mathbf{P}^* &= \underset{\text{s.t.tr}(\mathbf{P}^T \mathbf{XBX}^T \mathbf{P})=c}{\arg \min} \sum_{i,j=1}^N \left\| \mathbf{P}^T x_i - \mathbf{P}^T x_j \right\|^2 S_{i,j} \\
&= \underset{\text{s.t.tr}(\mathbf{P}^T \mathbf{XBX}^T \mathbf{P})=c}{\arg \min} \operatorname{tr}(\mathbf{P}^T \mathbf{XLX}^T \mathbf{P})
\end{aligned}
\tag{13.53}
$$

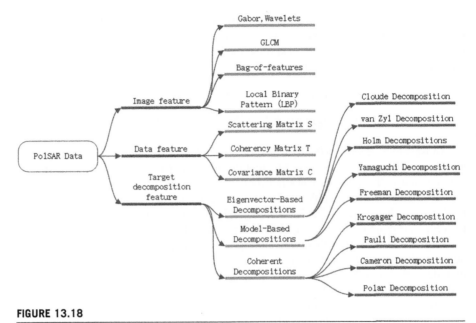

FIGURE 13.18

Feature extraction methods.

can be extended into a tensor form, in which the projection matrix $\mathbf{P}$ extends to a series of projection matrices $\{\mathbf{U}_m\}_{m=1}^M$; $\mathbf{S}$ is the similarity matrix, which is computed by pair-wise vertexes and is a constraint matrix that can be defined under the relationship between the samples from a penalty matrix or simply be a diagonal matrix for scale normalization. The similarity matrix $\mathbf{S}$ and the constraint matrix $\mathbf{B}$ keep the similar information in TLPP to form the objective function as follows:

$$\mathbf{U}_m^*|_{m=1}^M = \arg\min F(\mathbf{U}_1, \mathbf{U}_2, ..., \mathbf{U}_M)$$
$$= \arg\min \sum_{i,j=1}^N \left\| (\boldsymbol{\mathcal{X}}_i - \boldsymbol{\mathcal{X}}_j) \times_1 \mathbf{U}_1 \times_2 \mathbf{U}_2 \times \cdots \times_m \mathbf{U}_M \right\|_F^2 S_{i,j} \qquad (13.54)$$
$$\text{s.t.} \sum_{i=1}^N \left\| \boldsymbol{\mathcal{X}}_i \times_1 \mathbf{U}_1 \times_2 \mathbf{U}_2 \times \cdots \times_M \mathbf{U}_M \right\|_F^2 B_{i,j} = c.$$

For optimizing the objective function, one needs to change the high-order programming problem into a matrix form, i.e., according to alternative iteration of each transform matrix $\mathbf{U}_f$ and mode-f flattening of this high-order tensor into a matrix form. Then one tensor sample can be projected in all modes except the f-th:

$$\boldsymbol{\mathcal{Y}}_i = \boldsymbol{\mathcal{X}}_i \times_1 \mathbf{U}_1 \times \cdots \times_{f-1} \mathbf{U}_{f-1} \times_{f+1} \mathbf{U}_{f+1} \cdots \times_M \mathbf{U}_M. \qquad (13.55)$$

Due to the tensor mode-f flattening, the indices changed from m to f and the above objective function can be converted to

$$\mathbf{U}_f^*|_{f=1}^M = \arg\min F(\mathbf{U}_1, \mathbf{U}_2, \cdots, \mathbf{U}_M)$$
$$= \arg\min \sum_{i,j=1}^N \|\mathcal{Y}_i \times_f \mathbf{U}_f - \mathcal{Y}_j \times_f \mathbf{U}_f\|_F^2 S_{i,j} \tag{13.56}$$
$$\text{s.t.} \sum_{i=1}^N \|\mathcal{Y}_i \times_f \mathbf{U}_f\|_F^2 B_{i,j} = c.$$

It will be transformed by mode-f unfolding $\mathcal{Y} \times_f \mathbf{U}_f \Leftrightarrow \mathbf{U}_f \mathbf{Y}^{(f)}$, and we get the matrix form. Then Eq. (13.56) can be reformulated as

$$\mathbf{U}_f^*|_{f=1}^M = \arg\min F(\mathbf{U}_1, \mathbf{U}_2, ..., \mathbf{U}_M)$$
$$= \arg\min \sum_{i,j=1}^N \|\mathbf{U}_f \mathbf{Y}_i^{(f)} - \mathbf{U}_f \mathbf{Y}_j^{(f)}\|_F^2 S_{i,j} \tag{13.57}$$
$$\text{s.t.} \sum_{i=1}^N \|\mathbf{U}_f \mathbf{Y}_i^{(f)}\|_F^2 B_{i,j} = c.$$

We obtain the trace form of the function as follows:

$$\mathbf{U}_f^*|_{f=1}^M = \arg\min F(\mathbf{U}_1, \mathbf{U}_2, ..., \mathbf{U}_M)$$
$$= \arg\min \operatorname{tr}\left(\mathbf{U}_f \sum_{i,j=1}^N ((\mathbf{Y}_i^{(f)} - \mathbf{Y}_j^{(f)})(\mathbf{Y}_i^{(f)} - \mathbf{Y}_j^{(f)})^\mathsf{T} S_{ij})\mathbf{U}_f^\mathsf{T}\right) \tag{13.58}$$
$$\text{s.t.} \operatorname{tr}\left(\mathbf{U}_f \sum_{i,j=1}^N (\mathbf{Y}_i^{(f)}(\mathbf{Y}_i^{(f)})^\mathsf{T} B_{ij})\mathbf{U}_f^\mathsf{T}\right) = c.$$

After obtaining this reformulated function, we can utilize a pair of matrices $\mathbf{H}_1$ and $\mathbf{H}_2$ to unify the objective function into a unified framework. The first matrix $\mathbf{H}_1$ can be computed from the intrinsic graph and some statistical property. It is also called intrinsic matrix. The second matrix $\mathbf{H}_2$ is constructed under the constraint of statistical or geometrical properties and is defined as a penalty matrix. In Eq. (13.58), we have $\mathbf{H}_1 = \sum_{i,j=1}^N ((\mathbf{Y}_i^{(f)} - \mathbf{Y}_j^{(f)})(\mathbf{Y}_i^{(f)} - \mathbf{Y}_j^{(f)})^\mathsf{T} S_{ij})$ and $\mathbf{H}_2 = \sum_{i,j=1}^N (\mathbf{Y}_i^{(f)}(\mathbf{Y}_i^{(f)})^\mathsf{T} B_{ij})$. When $B_{ij} = D_{ii} = \sum_{j=1}^N S_{ij}$, Eq. (13.58) defines the objective function of TLPP. The construction of those two matrices is not only limited to a fixed unsupervised construction method, but they can also formed under supervised constraints and data distribution or other prior information. TLPP, TPCA, TNPE, TLDE, and TLDA obtain the corresponding intrinsic and penalty matrices from Table 13.7.

After obtaining two matrices $\mathbf{H}_1$ and $\mathbf{H}_2$ by the corresponding constraints, the objective function has a unified model:

$$\mathbf{U}_f^*|_{f=1}^M = \arg\min \operatorname{tr}(\mathbf{U}_f \mathbf{H}_1 \mathbf{U}_f^\mathsf{T})$$
$$\text{s.t.} \operatorname{tr}(\mathbf{U}_f \mathbf{H}_2 \mathbf{U}_f^\mathsf{T}) = c. \tag{13.59}$$

Table 13.7 Matrices $\mathbf{H_1}$ and $\mathbf{H_2}$ in a tensor embedding framework.

Matrix	H1	H2
TLPP	$\sum\limits_{i,j=1}^{N} \left((\mathbf{Y}_i^{(f)} - \mathbf{Y}_j^{(f)}) \right.$ $\left. \cdot (\mathbf{Y}_i^{(f)} - \mathbf{Y}_j^{(f)})^{\mathrm{T}}(S_{i,j}) \right)$	$\sum\limits_{i=1}^{N} (\mathbf{Y}_i^{(f)}(\mathbf{Y}_i^{(f)})^{\mathrm{T}} D_{ij})$
TNPE	$\sum\limits_{i=1}^{N} \left((\mathbf{Y}_i^{(f)} - \sum_{j=1}^{N} S_{i,j} \mathbf{Y}_i^{(f)}) \right.$ $\left. \cdot (\mathbf{Y}_i^{(f)} - \sum_{j=1}^{N} S_{i,j} \mathbf{Y}_i^{(f)})^{\mathrm{T}} \right)$	$\sum\limits_{i=1}^{N} (\mathbf{Y}_i^{(f)}(\mathbf{Y}_i^{(f)})^{\mathrm{T}})$
TLDE	$\sum\limits_{i,j=1}^{N} \left((\mathbf{Y}_i^{(f)} - \mathbf{Y}_j^{(f)}) \right.$ $\left. \cdot (\mathbf{Y}_i^{(f)} - \mathbf{Y}_j^{(f)})^{\mathrm{T}} S_{i,j} \right)$	$\sum\limits_{i,j=1}^{N} (\mathbf{Y}_i^{(f)} - \mathbf{Y}_j^{(f)})$ $\cdot (\mathbf{Y}_i^{(f)} - \mathbf{Y}_j^{(f)})^{\mathrm{T}} S'_{i,j}$
TLDA	$\sum\limits_{c=1}^{C} \sum\limits_{i=1}^{N_c} \left((\mathbf{Y}_{c_i}^{(f)} - \bar{\mathbf{Y}}_c^{(f)}) \cdot (\mathbf{Y}_{c_i}^{(f)} - \bar{\mathbf{Y}}_c^{(f)})^{\mathrm{T}} \right)$	$\sum\limits_{c=1}^{C} \left((\bar{\mathbf{Y}}_c^{(f)} - \bar{\mathbf{Y}}^{(f)}) \right.$ $\left. \cdot (\bar{\mathbf{Y}}_c^{(f)} - \bar{\mathbf{Y}}^{(f)})^{\mathrm{T}} \right)$
TPCA	$\mathbf{I}$	$\sum\limits_{i=1}^{N} (\mathbf{Y}_i^{(f)}(\mathbf{Y}_i^{(f)})^{\mathrm{T}})$

This equation shows that the objective function has one closed-form solution. The optimization process needs alternative iteration, in other words, updating one parameter while fixing the others. The projection matrix $\mathbf{U}_f$ obtains the optimal solution after initialization and the iterative process. In each iteration, one suboptimization can be solved by a generalized eigenvalue decomposition $\mathbf{H_1}\alpha = \lambda\mathbf{H_2}\alpha$, and the projection matrix $\mathbf{U}_f$ will be constructed by permutating the eigenvectors according to the values of eigenvalues. Finally, the optimal projection matrix will be employed in feature extraction to project the high-dimensional feature vectors into an intrinsic space. With this tensorial framework, we can extract intrinsic PolSAR features. This framework is summarized in Algorithm 2.

13.3.3 Experiment and analysis

13.3.3.1 Experiment preparation

In this section, three PolSAR datasets will be employed to demonstrate the superiority of tensor-based embedding techniques. The results will be compared with several state-of-the-art methods. Support vector machine (SVM) and K-nearest neighbor (KNN) are regarded as impartial classifiers to estimate the efficiency of the features extracted from those DR techniques.

- Xi'an-3 dataset. It covers three typical land covers, including buildings, grass, and water. Its size and spatial resolution are 512×512 pixels and 10×5 m.

Algorithm 2 Tensor embedding framework utilized in PolSAR land cover classification.

---

1. Extract features and construct the feature cube: Extract the polarimetric backscattering data and polarimetric target decomposition parameters as features to represent data points. Each pixel is described by a patch (the pixel is in the center of the patch). And construct a feature cube $\mathcal{X}_j \in \mathbb{R}^{I_1 \times I_2 \times I_3}$ to represent each pixel, in which $I_1 \times I_2$ denotes the patch size and I_3 denotes the number of original features.

2. Construct the intrinsic and penalty matrices: Choose some pixels from the dataset as training samples (unsupervised without labels and supervised with labels) according to the geometrical and statistical properties of training samples to construct the intrinsic matrix and constraints and some prior information to construct the penalty matrix.

3. Obtain the projection matrix for each order of tensors: Utilize the pairs of matrices $\mathbf{H}_1$ and $\mathbf{H}_2$, update the projection matrix according to alternative iterations, and obtain the optimal matrices $\{\mathbf{U}_f^*\}_{f=1}^3 \in \mathbb{R}^{P_f \times I_f}$.

4. Reduce the feature dimension and classification: Employ the optimal matrices $\{\mathbf{U}_f^*\}_{f=1}^3$ to reduce the dimensionality of samples. With those low-dimensional features, utilize KNN and SVM classifiers to achieve the final classification result.

- Flevoland-4 dataset. It covers four terrains, including woodland, urban, cropland, and water. The data describes the region of Flevoland, the Netherlands, produced by RADARSAT-2. Its size and spatial resolution are 796×769 pixels and 10×5 m.
- SanFrancisco-4 dataset. It covers four terrains, including high-density urban, water, vegetation, and low-density urban. The data cover the region of the Golden Gate Bridge in San Francisco. Its size and spatial resolution are 814×781 pixels and 10×5 m.

The contrast methods include several state-of-the-art algorithms, such as unsupervised PCA and ICA and linearization of manifold learning methods (NPE, LPP). Meanwhile, five tensor-based method in this framework, including supervised methods (TLDA, TLDE) and unsupervised methods (TLPP, TNPE, TPCA), are selected for comparison. The window size for the feature cube is 9×9. The original feature dimension is 22. So each pixel is represented by a $9 \times 9 \times 22$ cube. They are constructed by the original nine freedom parameters from the coherency matrix and the coefficients of different components from four selected target decomposition mechanisms, including Freeman, VanZyl, Yamaguchi, and Krogager decomposition.

Two typical tensor-based algorithms are carried out many times to test the number of learning the projection matrix and the patch size for feature extraction. General tensor discriminant analysis (GTDA) as a typical variant of tensor-based LDA algorithm is employed to represent the supervised tensorial algorithms, and TPCA is selected to represent unsupervised algorithms.

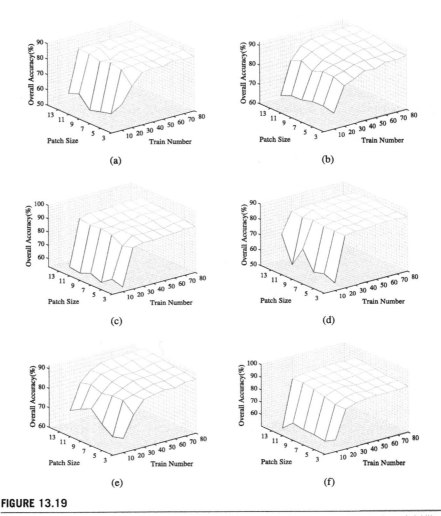

FIGURE 13.19

Overall accuracy of a KNN classifier with variation of patch size and train number. (a) Xi'an dataset with GTDA. (b) Flevoland dataset with GTDA. (c) San Francisco dataset with GTDA. (d) Xi'an dataset with TPCA. (e) Flevoland dataset with TPCA. (f) San Francisco dataset with TPCA.

Because the three datasets are all produced by RADARSAT-2 with the same spatial resolution, the patch size is 3×3, 5×5, 7×7, 9×9, 11×11, or 13×13. The samples for learning the projection matrix are defined as training samples in this section, and the number of training samples varies in the range [10, 20, 30, 40, 50, 60, 70, 80].

We can see the performance variation with the two parameters increasing in Fig. 13.19. Overall accuracy (OA) increases with increasing training sample number.

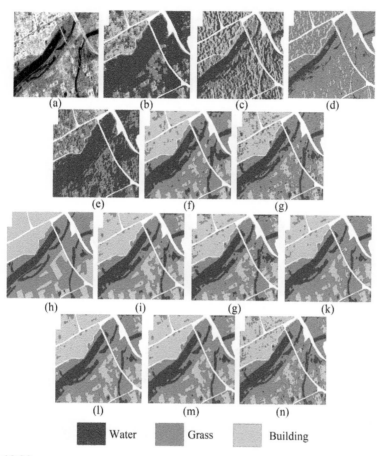

FIGURE 13.20

Classification results with the KNN classifier of different methods on the RADARSAT2 Xi'an dataset. (a) Pauli image. (b) ICA. (c) LDA. (d) LPP. (e) NPE. (f) PCA. (g) Original data. (h) Ground truth. (i) GTDA. (g) TLDE. (k) TLPP. (l) TNPE. (m) TPCA. (n) Wishart classifier.

As the training sample number is greater than 10, the OA growth will keep steady and remain at a high level. Therefore some following experiments are conducted with the training number greater than or equal to 20. With increasing patch size, OA improves slowly and shows a balanced growth after the 9 × 9 size. The bigger the feature patch is, the more geographic and spatial information will be captured. Thus, a reasonably large patch can achieve a better classification result. For the three kinds of RADARSAT2 datasets, the patch size are all set as 9 × 9. This size can get a good enough performance without large calculation and has lower RAM requirements.

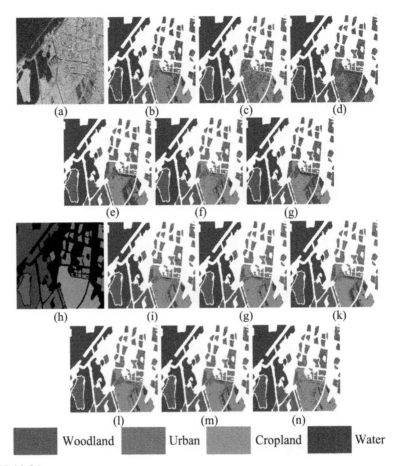

FIGURE 13.21

Classification results with the KNN classifier of different methods on the RADARSAT2 Flevoland dataset. (a) Pauli image. (b) ICA. (c) LDA. (d) LPP. (e) NPE. (f) PCA. (g) Original data. (h) Ground truth. (i) GTDA. (g) TLDE. (k) TLPP. (l) TNPE. (m) TPCA. (n) Wishart classifier.

13.3.3.2 Experiment and analysis

For a fair comparison, five linear and another five tensorial DR methods are utilized to process 22D high-dimensional features. This target decomposition information for constructing the high-dimensional vectors are redundant enough, and sensitive to different terrains and land covers. The constructed feature vectors can be combined to extract discriminant features. For tensorial algorithms, a pixel is represented by a 3D feature cube $\mathcal{X}_i \in \mathbb{R}^{I_1 \times I_2 \times I_3}$. The length of the feature vector is 22. Then the same size features are input into linear DR techniques. Because one pixel can be represented by a coherent/covariance matrix, an original 9D feature vector constructed by

Table 13.8 OA (%), AA (%), class-specific accuracy (%), and Kappa coefficient for the RADARSAT2 Xi'an dataset with 9D.

	Result	Original data	ICA	LDA	LPP	NPE	PCA	GTDA	TLDE	TLPP	TNPE	TPCA	Wishart
1	KNN	95.36	93.04	91.82	92.87	**95.68**	92.60	90.31	89.99	90.17	91.25	91.29	
	SVM	94.42	88.35	0.03	91.52	89.70	**91.74**	89.85	83.48	88.47	87.70	87.78	94.25
2	KNN	75.88	53.41	76.77	68.95	54.57	82.92	88.14	85.66	87.26	**88.15**	86.36	
	SVM	80.89	89.70	0.14	78.70	3.39	80.60	87.69	81.81	**89.19**	88.37	88.47	82.16
3	KNN	84.22	90.34	83.24	84.32	75.47	85.05	84.88	79.16	**85.56**	83.60	84.27	
	SVM	79.82	74.26	99.99	82.60	26.87	**80.11**	71.69	69.92	74.26	73.94	75.70	83.49
OA	KNN	83.85	77.69	82.24	80.17	71.12	85.43	**86.85**	83.09	86.85	86.36	86.06	
	SVM	82.39	81.84	49.62	82.56	28.01	82.03	80.08	76.16	81.68	81.11	**83.03**	84.64
AA	KNN	85.15	78.93	83.94	82.05	75.24	86.86	**87.78**	84.94	87.66	87.67	87.31	
	SVM	85.04	84.10	33.35	84.27	39.99	84.15	83.08	78.40	83.97	83.33	**84.26**	86.64
Kappa	KNN	0.7228	0.6248	0.7153	0.6777	0.5380	0.7624	**0.7856**	0.7270	0.7855	0.7787	0.7732	
	SVM	0.7158	0.7095	0.3267	0.7160	0.2428	0.7101	0.6842	0.6211	0.7076	0.6975	**0.7732**	0.7503

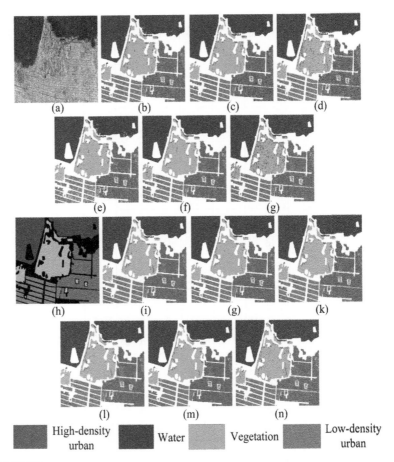

FIGURE 13.22

Classification results with the KNN classifier of different methods on the RADARSAT2 San Francisco dataset. (a) Pauli image. (b) ICA. (c) LDA. (d) LPP. (e) NPE. (f) PCA. (g) Original data. (h) Ground truth. (i) GTDA. (g) TLDE. (k) TLPP. (l) TNPE. (m) TPCA. (n) Wishart classifier.

nine freedom parameters is also input into SVM and KNN classifiers. All methods should reduce the high-dimensional vector into a same size feature. The Wishart classifier is significant in PolSAR data classification, and hence regarded as a benchmark.

As discussed above, the patch size is 9×9. The experiments for each algorithm are carried out 10 times to obtain the mean value for comparison. OA, average accuracy (AA), class-specific accuracy, and Kappa coefficients are employed to show the experimental results. The quantification and visualization results are shown in Figs. 13.20–13.22 and Tables 13.8–13.10. For learning the projection matrices $\mathbf{U}_f$, the classification maps are randomly selected from one of the repeated experiments.

Table 13.9 OA (%), AA (%), class-specific accuracy (%), and Kappa coefficient for the RADARSAT2 Flevoland dataset with 9D.

	Result	Original	ICA	LDA	LPP	NPE	PCA	GTDA	TLDE	TLPP	TNPE	TPCA	Wishart
1	KNN	85.86	70.25	88.51	53.10	77.56	93.32	94.51	94.76	94.81	**94.87**	94.18	
	SVM	66.07	80.03	81.64	6.82	90.96	**94.25**	88.99	89.48	86.21	85.96	87.71	89.47
2	KNN	68.01	73.64	65.47	28.70	61.32	73.06	**77.74**	75.91	73.11	75.25	76.93	
	SVM	22.69	79.65	60.97	9.46	67.18	71.22	**85.39**	82.78	83.68	84.74	84.11	81.95
3	KNN	99.43	99.19	97.75	96.68	99.64	99.05	98.88	99.02	**99.07**	98.78	98.90	
	SVM	99.92	97.18	96.68	90.26	99.19	**99.44**	95.55	96.42	96.62	96.00	95.85	99.00
4	KNN	49.48	44.47	27.34	41.22	55.46	65.35	78.27	77.17	79.51	**79.81**	79.38	
	SVM	4.27	68.12	51.23	13.39	73.69	62.10	**84.67**	81.69	79.51	84.45	82.27	54.30
OA	KNN	79.81	77.79	74.72	61.98	78.02	85.12	**88.88**	88.29	88.04	88.55	88.84	
	SVM	56.75	84.52	76.59	42.03	84.87	84.33	**89.87**	89.06	88.45	89.37	89.01	84.69
AA	KNN	82.70	71.89	69.77	54.93	73.49	75.69	**87.35**	86.72	86.62	87.18	87.35	
	SVM	81.75	81.24	72.64	29.98	82.75	48.24	88.65	87.59	86.50	**87.79**	87.49	81.18
Kappa	KNN	0.7147	0.6790	0.6437	0.4544	0.6847	0.7914	**0.8443**	0.8360	0.8326	0.8398	0.8437	
	SVM	0.3716	0.7837	0.6743	0.1026	0.7872	0.7793	**0.8589**	0.8476	0.8387	0.8518	0.8468	0.7859

Table 13.10 OA (%), AA (%), class-specific accuracy (%), and Kappa coefficient for the RADARSAT2 San Francisco dataset with 9D.

	Result	Original	ICA	LDA	LPP	NPE	PCA	GTDA	TLDE	TLPP	TNPE	TPCA	Wishart
1	KNN	99.51	99.44	99.98	99.54	99.06	99.85	**99.99**	99.99	99.97	99.99	100.00	99.90
	SVM	86.18	99.91	99.94	99.58	97.41	99.99	99.98	99.98	99.99	**99.99**	99.99	
2	KNN	86.19	90.82	91.90	85.52	91.65	90.99	91.90	**92.30**	92.27	91.95	91.99	90.88
	SVM	63.48	93.57	91.90	74.93	94.06	88.57	94.16	**94.65**	94.24	94.40	94.17	
3	KNN	70.97	84.74	85.79	86.86	63.88	81.53	84.32	88.33	**89.11**	86.33	88.54	78.70
	SVM	7.36	86.07	79.81	65.02	44.00	84.81	92.76	93.13	94.21	**94.52**	93.53	
4	KNN	54.34	56.84	71.46	48.49	60.29	70.48	75.83	76.67	77.50	**79.42**	78.03	55.82
	SVM	2.83	78.40	76.63	5.08	58.06	64.10	85.17	86.92	86.32	**87.03**	86.34	
OA	KNN	79.01	82.85	87.87	80.90	81.82	86.33	89.44	**90.76**	90.33	90.35	90.21	82.54
	SVM	85.30	90.53	88.83	62.53	78.52	87.07	93.48	94.14	94.02	**94.30**	93.92	
AA	KNN	77.14	82.70	87.16	80.59	78.09	77.01	88.15	**89.80**	89.42	89.42	89.51	81.32
	SVM	82.91	89.49	87.07	61.15	73.38	86.58	93.02	93.67	93.69	**93.99**	93.51	
Kappa	KNN	0.7145	0.7687	0.8345	0.7426	0.7513	0.8141	0.8556	**0.8736**	0.8679	0.8681	0.8663	0.7637
	SVM	0.7986	0.8703	0.8469	0.4899	0.7057	0.7984	0.9106	0.9196	0.9179	**0.9217**	0.9166	

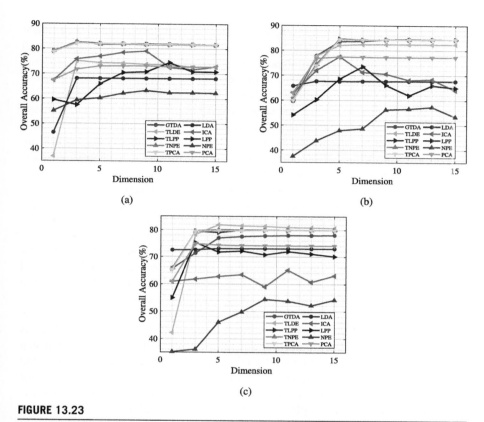

FIGURE 13.23

Overall accuracy with dimension variation in three PolSAR datasets by the KNN classifier. (a) Xi'an dataset. (b) Flevoland dataset. (c) San Francisco dataset.

Fifty samples per class are randomly selected for learning the projection matrix $\mathbf{P}$ of linear DR techniques and the set of projection matrices $\mathbf{U}_f \in \mathbb{R}^{P_f \times I_f}$, $f = 1, 2, 3$. SVM and KNN are also trained by 50 samples per class. The nearest neighbor k in KNN is set as 21. The radial basis function (RBF) is employed, and a three cross-validation is used to seek the optimal parameters. Because the parameter variation in SVM is too high, those classification maps are chosen from the KNN classification result.

Based on the quantitative indices in Tables 13.8–13.10, the tensorial embedding methods all achieve the best performance, such as TLDA, which yields the highest OA value of 86.85% and is better than the best linear method (PCA) by 1.5%. In these tables, we assign a number to each category of land cover. In Table 13.8, 1, 2, and 3 denote the grass, building, and water, respectively. In Table 13.9, 1, 2, 3, and 4 denote water, cropland, woodland, and urban areas, respectively. In Table 13.10, 1, 2, 3, and 4 represent water, vegetation, and low-density and high-density urban areas, respectively. It can be seen from Fig. 13.20 that in the Xi'an-3 dataset, the tensor embedding framework achieves a better region uniformity compared to other linear embedding methods. Especially in Fig. 13.20(i) and (m), the tensor-based methods all get a good performance in discriminating grass and building areas. It can be seen from the results of the Wishart classifier and the original 9D vector that the homogeneous area cannot obtain good classification results.

For the Flevoland-4 dataset, the urban area (red (gray in print version)), always mixed with some woodland in the Pauli image, is hard to distinguish in Fig. 13.21. Most of the algorithms cannot classify this region well, and many urban pixels are recognized as woodland. By comparing the first row (linear embedding techniques) with the second row (tensor embedding methods), the tensorial methods provide a better spatial consistency and get a good urban region classification result.

For the SanFrancisco-4 dataset, although the linear embedding techniques, original 9D feature, and Wishart classifier methods perform a good homogeneous result in the regions of water and vegetation, the visualization results for low-density and high-density urban areas are not good. OA values of those techniques are almost all lower than 80% due to the high similarities in urban regions. However, it can be observed from Fig. 13.22 that those tensor-based methods can achieve the best visualization performance with KNN classifier, especially in the urban areas.

The dimensionality analysis is conducted by changing the dimension of those series of the projection matrix $\mathbf{U}_f$. The KNN classification results of three datasets are shown in Fig. 13.23, with the dimensionality changing from 1 to 15 with a step length of 2. All tensor embedding DR methods have a higher OA performance than linear techniques. In particular, the dimensionality is higher than 5 and all the tensor embedding techniques can reach the best OA. This means the tensor method has low sensitivity to the training sample. After the methods retained a stable performance, all the proposed methods can get a better OA.

References

[1] Naveed Akhtar, Faisal Shafait, Ajmal Mian, Sparse spatio-spectral representation for hyperspectral image super-resolution, in: European Conference on Computer Vision, Springer, 2014, pp. 63–78.

[2] Naveed Akhtar, Faisal Shafait, Ajmal Mian, Bayesian sparse representation for hyperspectral image super resolution, in: Proceedings of the IEEE Conference on Computer Vision and Pattern Recognition, 2015, pp. 3631–3640.

[3] Luciano Alparone, Bruno Aiazzi, Stefano Baronti, Andrea Garzelli, Remote Sensing Image Fusion, CRC Press, 2015.

[4] Luciano Alparone, Lucien Wald, Jocelyn Chanussot, Claire Thomas, Paolo Gamba, Lori Mann Bruce, Comparison of pansharpening algorithms: outcome of the 2006 GRS-S data-fusion contest, IEEE Transactions on Geoscience and Remote Sensing 45 (10) (2007) 3012–3021.

[5] Mikhail Belkin, Partha Niyogi, Laplacian eigenmaps and spectral techniques for embedding and clustering, in: Adv. Neur. In, 2002, pp. 585–591.

[6] José M. Bioucas-Dias, Antonio Plaza, Gustavo Camps-Valls, Paul Scheunders, Nasser Nasrabadi, Jocelyn Chanussot, Hyperspectral remote sensing data analysis and future challenges, IEEE Geoscience and Remote Sensing Magazine 1 (2) (2013) 6–36.

[7] Wenfei Cao, Yao Wang, Jian Sun, Deyu Meng Can Yang, Andrzej Cichocki, Zongben Xu, Total variation regularized tensor rpca for background subtraction from compressive measurements, IEEE Transactions on Image Processing 25 (9) (2016) 4075–4090.

[8] Luca Chiantini, Giorgio Ottaviani, On generic identifiability of 3-tensors of small rank, SIAM Journal on Matrix Analysis and Applications 33 (3) (2012) 1018–1037.

[9] Guang Dai, Dit-Yan Yeung, Tensor embedding methods, in: AAAI, vol. 6, 2006, pp. 330–335.

[10] Dian Renwei, Leyuan Fang, Shutao Li, Hyperspectral image super-resolution via nonlocal sparse tensor factorization, in: Proceedings of the IEEE Conference on Computer Vision and Pattern Recognition, 2017, pp. 5344–5353.

[11] Dian Renwei, Shutao Li, Leyuan Fang, Learning a low tensor-train rank representation for hyperspectral image super-resolution, IEEE Transactions on Neural Networks and Learning Systems 30 (9) (2019) 2672–2683.

[12] Renwei Dian, Shutao Li, Anjing Guo, Leyuan Fang, Deep hyperspectral image sharpening, IEEE Transactions on Neural Networks and Learning Systems (99) (2018) 1–11.

[13] Weisheng Dong, Fazuo Fu, Guangming Shi, Xun Cao, Jinjian Wu, Guangyu Li, Xin Li, Hyperspectral image super-resolution via non-negative structured sparse representation, IEEE Transactions on Image Processing 25 (5) (2016) 2337–2352.

[14] Lucas Drumetz, Miguel-Angel Veganzones, Simon Henrot, Ronald Phlypo, Jocelyn Chanussot, Christian Jutten, Blind hyperspectral unmixing using an extended linear mixing model to address spectral variability, IEEE Transactions on Image Processing 25 (8) (2016) 3890–3905.

[15] Bo Du, Mengfei Zhang, Lefei Zhang, Ruimin Hu, Dacheng Tao Pltd, Patch-based low-rank tensor decomposition for hyperspectral images, IEEE Transactions on Multimedia 19 (1) (2016) 67–79.

[16] Du Qian, Nicholas H. Younan, Roger King, Vijay P. Shah, On the performance evaluation of pan-sharpening techniques, IEEE Geoscience and Remote Sensing Letters 4 (4) (2007) 518–522.

[17] Xiaofei He, Deng Cai, Partha Niyogi, Tensor subspace analysis, in: Adv. Neur. In, 2006, pp. 499–506.

[18] Xiaofei He, Deng Cai, Shuicheng Yan, Hong-Jiang Zhang, Neighborhood preserving embedding, in: Proc. IEEE Int. Conf. Comput. Vis, vol. 2, Dec. 2005, pp. 1208–1213.

[19] Bo Huang, Huihui Song, Hengbin Cui, Jigen Peng, Zongben Xu, Spatial and spectral image fusion using sparse matrix factorization, IEEE Transactions on Geoscience and Remote Sensing 52 (3) (2013) 1693–1704.

[20] Xiayuan Huang, Hong Qiao, Bo Zhang, Xiangli Nie, Supervised polarimetric sar image classification using tensor local discriminant embedding, IEEE Transactions on Image Processing (2018).

[21] Fei Jiang, Xiao-Yang Liu, Hongtao Lu, Ruimin Shen, Efficient multi-dimensional tensor sparse coding using t-linear combination, in: Thirty-Second AAAI Conference on Artificial Intelligence, 2018.

[22] Charilaos I. Kanatsoulis, Xiao Fu, Nicholas D. Sidiropoulos, Wing-Kin Ma, Hyperspectral super-resolution: a coupled tensor factorization approach, IEEE Transactions on Signal Processing 66 (24) (2018) 6503–6517.

[23] Nirmal Keshava, John F. Mustard, Spectral unmixing, IEEE Signal Processing Magazine 19 (1) (2002) 44–57.

[24] Misha E. Kilmer, Carla D. Martin, Factorization strategies for third-order tensors, Linear Algebra and Its Applications 435 (3) (2011) 641–658.

[25] T.G. Kolda, B.W. Bader, Tensor decompositions and applications, SIAM Review 51 (2009) 455–500.

[26] Jong-Sen Lee, Eric Pottier, Polarimetric Radar Imaging: From Basics to Applications, CRC Press, 2017.

[27] Shutao Li, Renwei Dian, Leyuan Fang, José M. Bioucas-Dias, Fusing hyperspectral and multispectral images via coupled sparse tensor factorization, IEEE Transactions on Image Processing 27 (8) (2018) 4118–4130.

[28] Yunsong Li, Jing Hu, Xi Zhao, Weiying Xie, JiaoJiao Li, Hyperspectral image super-resolution using deep convolutional neural network, Neurocomputing 266 (2017) 29–41.

[29] Thomas Lillesand, Ralph W. Kiefer, Jonathan Chipman, Remote Sensing and Image Interpretation, John Wiley & Sons, 2015.

[30] Xun Liu, Chenwei Deng, Jocelyn Chanussot, Danfeng Hong, Baojun Zhao Stfnet, A two-stream convolutional neural network for spatiotemporal image fusion, IEEE Transactions on Geoscience and Remote Sensing (2019).

[31] Laetitia Loncan, Luis B. De Almeida, José M. Bioucas-Dias, Xavier Briottet, Jocelyn Chanussot, Nicolas Dobigeon, Sophie Fabre, Wenzhi Liao, Giorgio A. Licciardi, Miguel Simoes, et al., Hyperspectral pansharpening: a review, IEEE Geoscience and Remote Sensing Magazine 3 (3) (2015) 27–46.

[32] Canyi Lu, Jiashi Feng, Yudong Chen, Wei Liu, Zhouchen Lin, Shuicheng Yan, Tensor robust principal component analysis with a new tensor nuclear norm, IEEE Transactions on Pattern Analysis and Machine Intelligence 42 (4) (2019) 925–938.

[33] Haiping Lu, Konstantinos N. Plataniotis, Anastasios N. Venetsanopoulos, Mpca: multilinear principal component analysis of tensor objects, IEEE Transactions on Neural Networks 19 (1) (2008) 18–39.

[34] Haiping Lu, Konstantinos N. Plataniotis, Anastasios N. Venetsanopoulos, Uncorrelated multilinear principal component analysis for unsupervised multilinear subspace learning, IEEE Transactions on Neural Networks 20 (11) (2009) 1820–1836.

[35] Wing-Kin Ma, José M. Bioucas-Dias, Tsung-Han Chan, Nicolas Gillis, Paul Gader, Antonio J. Plaza, ArulMurugan Ambikapathi, Chong-Yung Chi, A signal processing perspective on hyperspectral unmixing: insights from remote sensing, IEEE Signal Processing Magazine 31 (1) (2013) 67–81.

[36] Christine Pohl, John Van Genderen, Remote Sensing Image Fusion: A Practical Guide, CRC Press, 2016.

[37] Idan Ram, Michael Elad, Israel Cohen, Image processing using smooth ordering of its patches, IEEE Transactions on Image Processing 22 (7) (2013) 2764–2774.

[38] Sam T. Roweis, Lawrence K. Saul, Nonlinear dimensionality reduction by locally linear embedding, Science 290 (5500) (2000) 2323–2326.

[39] Lei Shi, Lefei Zhang, Jie Yang, Liangpei Zhang, Pingxiang Li, Supervised graph embedding for polarimetric SAR image classification, IEEE Geoscience and Remote Sensing Letters 10 (2) (2013) 216–220.

[40] Miguel Simoes, José Bioucas-Dias, Luis B. Almeida, Jocelyn Chanussot, A convex formulation for hyperspectral image superresolution via subspace-based regularization, IEEE Transactions on Geoscience and Remote Sensing 53 (6) (2014) 3373–3388.

[41] Dacheng Tao, Xuelong Li, Xindong Wu, Stephen J. Maybank, General tensor discriminant analysis and Gabor features for gait recognition, IEEE Transactions on Pattern Analysis and Machine Intelligence 29 (10) (2007) 1700–1715.

[42] Claire Thomas, Thierry Ranchin, Lucien Wald, Jocelyn Chanussot, Synthesis of multi-spectral images to high spatial resolution: a critical review of fusion methods based on remote sensing physics, IEEE Transactions on Geoscience and Remote Sensing 46 (5) (2008) 1301–1312.

[43] Shang Tan Tu, Jia Yu Chen, Wen Yang, Hong Sun, Laplacian eigenmaps-based polari-metric dimensionality reduction for SAR image classification, IEEE Transactions on Geoscience and Remote Sensing 50 (1) (2012) 170–179.

[44] Stefan Uhlmann, Serkan Kiranyaz, Integrating color features in polarimetric sar image classification, IEEE Transactions on Geoscience and Remote Sensing 52 (4) (2014) 2197–2216.

[45] Miguel A. Veganzones, Jeremy E. Cohen, Rodrigo Cabral Farias, Jocelyn Chanussot, Pierre Comon, Nonnegative tensor cp decomposition of hyperspectral data, IEEE Transactions on Geoscience and Remote Sensing 54 (5) (2015) 2577–2588.

[46] Miguel A. Veganzones, Miguel Simoes, Giorgio Licciardi, Naoto Yokoya, José M. Bioucas-Dias, Jocelyn Chanussot, Hyperspectral super-resolution of locally low rank images from complementary multisource data, IEEE Transactions on Image Processing 25 (1) (2015) 274–288.

[47] Gemine Vivone, Luciano Alparone, Jocelyn Chanussot, Mauro Dalla Mura, Andrea Garzelli, Giorgio A. Licciardi, Rocco Restaino, Lucien Wald, A critical comparison among pansharpening algorithms, IEEE Transactions on Geoscience and Remote Sensing 53 (5) (2014) 2565–2586.

[48] Qi Wang, Jianzhe Lin, Yuan Yuan, Salient band selection for hyperspectral image clas-sification via manifold ranking, IEEE Transactions on Neural Networks and Learning Systems 27 (6) (2016) 1279–1289.

[49] Wenqi Wang, Vaneet Aggarwal, Shuchin Aeron, Tensor train neighborhood preserving embedding, IEEE Transactions on Signal Processing 66 (10) (2018) 2724–2732.

[50] Qi Wei, José Bioucas-Dias, Nicolas Dobigeon, Jean-Yves Tourneret, Hyperspectral and multispectral image fusion based on a sparse representation, IEEE Transactions on Geo-science and Remote Sensing 53 (7) (2015) 3658–3668.

[51] Qi Wei, Nicolas Dobigeon, Jean-Yves Tourneret, Bayesian fusion of multi-band images, IEEE Journal of Selected Topics in Signal Processing 9 (6) (2015) 1117–1127.

[52] Qi Wei, Nicolas Dobigeon, Jean-Yves Tourneret, Fast fusion of multi-band images based on solving a Sylvester equation, IEEE Transactions on Image Processing 24 (11) (2015) 4109–4121.

[53] Qi Wei, Nicolas Dobigeon, Jean-Yves Tourneret, José Bioucas-Dias, Simon Godsill, R-fuse: Robust fast fusion of multiband images based on solving a Sylvester equation, IEEE Signal Processing Letters 23 (11) (2016) 1632–1636.

[54] Qi Xie, Qian Zhao, Deyu Meng, Zongben Xu, Shuhang Gu, Wangmeng Zuo, Lei Zhang, Multispectral images denoising by intrinsic tensor sparsity regularization, in: Pro-ceedings of the IEEE Conference on Computer Vision and Pattern Recognition, 2016, pp. 1692–1700.

[55] Yang Xu, Zebin Wu, Jocelyn Chanussot, Pierre Comon, Zhihui Wei, Nonlocal coupled tensor CP decomposition for hyperspectral and multispectral image fusion, IEEE Trans-actions on Geoscience and Remote Sensing 58 (1) (2019) 348–362.

[56] Yang Xu, Zebin Wu, Jocelyn Chanussot, Zhihui Wei, Joint reconstruction and anomaly detection from compressive hyperspectral images using Mahalanobis distance-regularized tensor rpca, IEEE Transactions on Geoscience and Remote Sensing 56 (5) (2018) 2919–2930.

[57] Yang Xu, Zebin Wu, Jocelyn Chanussot, Zhihui Wei, Nonlocal patch tensor sparse representation for hyperspectral image super-resolution, IEEE Transactions on Image Processing (2019).

[58] Yang Xu, Zebin Wu, Jocelyn Chanussot, Zhihui Wei, Hyperspectral images super-resolution via learning high-order coupled tensor ring representation, IEEE Transactions on Neural Networks and Learning Systems (2020).

[59] Jize Xue, Yongqiang Zhao, Rank-1 tensor decomposition for hyperspectral image denoising with nonlocal low-rank regularization, in: 2017 International Conference on Machine Vision and Information Technology (CMVIT), IEEE, 2017, pp. 40–45.

[60] Shuicheng Yan, Dong Xu, Qiang Yang, Lei Zhang, Xiaoou Tang, Hong-Jiang Zhang, Multilinear discriminant analysis for face recognition, IEEE Transactions on Image Processing 16 (1) (2007) 212–220.

[61] Jian Yang, David D. Zhang, Alejandro F. Frangi, Jing-yu Yang, Two-dimensional pca: a new approach to appearance-based face representation and recognition, IEEE Transactions on Pattern Analysis and Machine Intelligence (2004).

[62] Jingxiang Yang, Yong-Qiang Zhao, Jonathan Cheung-Wai Chan, Hyperspectral and multispectral image fusion via deep two-branches convolutional neural network, Remote Sensing 10 (5) (2018) 800.

[63] Naoto Yokoya, Claas Grohnfeldt, Jocelyn Chanussot, Hyperspectral and multispectral data fusion: a comparative review of the recent literature, IEEE Geoscience and Remote Sensing Magazine 5 (2) (2017) 29–56.

[64] Naoto Yokoya, Takehisa Yairi, Akira Iwasaki, Coupled nonnegative matrix factorization unmixing for hyperspectral and multispectral data fusion, IEEE Transactions on Geoscience and Remote Sensing 50 (2) (2011) 528–537.

[65] Yuan Yuan, Xiangtao Zheng, Xiaoqiang Lu, Hyperspectral image superresolution by transfer learning, IEEE Journal of Selected Topics in Applied Earth Observations and Remote Sensing 10 (5) (2017) 1963–1974.

[66] Changqing Zhang, Huazhu Fu, Qinghua Hu, Xiaochun Cao, Yuan Xie, Dacheng Tao, Dong Xu, Generalized latent multi-view subspace clustering, IEEE Transactions on Pattern Analysis and Machine Intelligence 42 (1) (2018) 86–99.

[67] Kai Zhang, Min Wang, Shuyuan Yang, Multispectral and hyperspectral image fusion based on group spectral embedding and low-rank factorization, IEEE Transactions on Geoscience and Remote Sensing 55 (3) (2016) 1363–1371.

[68] Kai Zhang, Min Wang, Shuyuan Yang, Licheng Jiao, Spatial–spectral-graph-regularized low-rank tensor decomposition for multispectral and hyperspectral image fusion, IEEE Journal of Selected Topics in Applied Earth Observations and Remote Sensing 11 (4) (2018) 1030–1040.

[69] Lei Zhang, Wei Wei, Chengcheng Bai, Yifan Gao, Yanning Zhang, Exploiting clustering manifold structure for hyperspectral imagery super-resolution, IEEE Transactions on Image Processing 27 (12) (2018) 5969–5982.

[70] Zhenyue Zhang, Hongyuan Zha, Nonlinear dimension reduction via local tangent space alignment, in: International Conference on Intelligent Data Engineering and Automated Learning, Springer, 2003, pp. 477–481.

[71] Qibin Zhao, Masashi Sugiyama, Longhao Yuan, Andrzej Cichocki, Learning efficient tensor representations with ring-structured networks, in: ICASSP 2019-2019 IEEE International Conference on Acoustics, Speech and Signal Processing (ICASSP), IEEE, 2019, pp. 8608–8612.

[72] Pan Zhou, Canyi Lu, Zhouchen Lin, Chao Zhang, Tensor factorization for low-rank tensor completion, IEEE Transactions on Image Processing 27 (3) (2017) 1152–1163.

Structured tensor train decomposition for speeding up kernel-based learning

Yassine Zniyed[a], **Ouafae Karmouda**[b], **Rémy Boyer**[b], **Jérémie Boulanger**[b], **André L.F. de Almeida**[c], and **Gérard Favier**[d]

[a]*Université de Toulon, Aix-Marseille Université, CNRS, LIS, Toulon, France*
[b]*CRIStAL, Université de Lille, Villeneuve d'Ascq, France*
[c]*Department of Teleinformatics Engineering, Federal University of Fortaleza, Fortaleza, Brazil*
[d]*Laboratoire I3S, Université Côte d'Azur, CNRS, Sophia Antipolis, France*

CONTENTS

Tensors for Data Processing. https://doi.org/10.1016/B978-0-12-824447-0.00020-0

14.1 **Introduction**

High-order tensors are multidimensional data arrays that allow to efficiently exploit multiple "modalities" present in the data. In these last two decades, the interest in tensor decompositions has been expanded to different fields, e.g., machine learning, signal processing, communication systems, numerical linear algebra, and graph analysis. This interest is justified by the fact that high-order tensor methods yield physically interpretable and meaningful models for multidimensional data in terms of lower-order factors. One of the main advantages of certain tensor decompositions, like PARAFAC, over matrix ones is their essential uniqueness property under mild conditions, i.e., the identifiability of the parameters to be estimated, as well as the availability of powerful tools and algorithms to perform tensor decompositions.

In several application fields, the goal of using tensor models is to find low-rank approximations to multidimensional data, usually in the presence of noise or model errors. Low-rank tensor approximation is one of the major challenges in the information scientific community; see for instance [12,38]. It is useful to extract relevant information confined into a small-dimensional subspace from a massive volume of data. In the matrix case, the approximation of a full rank matrix by a (fixed) low-rank matrix is a well-posed problem. The famous Eckart–Young theorem [17] provides both theoretical guarantees on the existence of a solution and a convenient way to compute it. Specifically, the set of low-rank matrices is closed and the best low-rank approximation (in the sense of the Frobenius norm) is obtained via the truncated singular value decomposition (SVD). This fundamental result is at the origin of principal component analysis (PCA) [20]. When the measurements are naturally modeled according to more than two axes of variations, i.e., in the case of high-order tensors, the problem of obtaining a low-rank approximation faces a number of practical and fundamental difficulties. Indeed, even if some aspects of tensor algebra can be considered as mature, several algebraic concepts such as decomposition uniqueness, rank determination, and the notion of singular values and eigenvalues remain challenging research topics [3,15].

Tucker decomposition (TD) and high-order SVD (HOSVD) [14,51] are two popular decompositions being an alternative to the canonical polyadic decomposition (CPD) [8,25,28]. The HOSVD of a tensor is based on the notion of multilinear rank, which is defined as the set of Q positive integers $\{T_1, \ldots, T_Q\}$, where each T_q is the usual (in the matrix sense) rank of the q-th mode unfolding of the tensor. TD of a tensor is composed of a core tensor of the same order multiplied by a factor matrix along each mode. Although TD and HOSVD became popular and different computationally efficient algorithms exist [6], they have a poor compactness property compared to CPD. For a multilinear rank $\{T, \ldots, T\}$, the number of free parameters is about $QNT + T^Q$ for a Q-order tensor of size $N \times \ldots \times N$, and therefore grows exponentially with the order Q. In the context of massive data processing, i.e., when $Q >> 1$, this decomposition is irrelevant and cannot break the curse of dimensionality [40], since the core tensor is generally not sparse, and therefore leads to a storage cost that grows exponentially with the order Q.

Recently, a new tensor decomposition concept has been proposed, usually referred to as *tensor networks* [10], with the aim to break the curse of dimensionality [40] by decomposing high-order tensors into distributed sparsely interconnected cores of lower order. This principle allows to develop more sophisticated tensor models with the ability of performing distributed computing while capturing multiple interactions and couplings, as opposed to standard tensor decompositions. These tools found applications in very large-scale problems in scientific computing, such as supercompression, tensor completion, blind source separation, and machine learning, to mention a few. Multiple tensor networks exist, such as the so-called hierarchical Tucker (HT) [24], which is an alternative to TD where the core tensor is replaced by lower-order tensors resulting in a network where some cores are directly connected with factor matrices. Different configurations of networks may exist for a given high-order tensor.

One of the simplest tensor networks is tensor train decomposition (TTD) [39]. It can be considered as a special case of HT decomposition, where all the tensors of the underlying networks are aligned (i.e., no cycles exist in the representation) and where the leaf matrices are all equal to the identity. The two main advantages of this decomposition are its compactness, i.e., its storage cost scales linearly with the order, and its computation, since it relies on a stable (i.e., noniterative) and hierarchical SVD-based algorithm called the tensor train hierarchical SVD (TT-HSVD) algorithm [55], which is a generalization of the state-of-the-art TT-SVD algorithm [39].

In this chapter, we present equivalence relations between TTD and TD for an estimation purpose. We show that a high-order TD is equivalent to a train of third-order TDs with known structure. This equivalence allows to mitigate the curse of dimensionality problem when dealing with high-order data tensors, for which the storage cost and the computation complexity grow exponentially with the tensor order. Breaking the dimensionality of TD tensors, using TTD, allows to accomplish a fast computation of TD with orthonormal factors.

In the context of supervised classification, support vector machines (SVMs) [9,48] have been widely used due to their solid theoretical foundations, good performance, and ease of implementation. Despite dealing with linear classification only, they can be modified to treat nonlinear problems via kernel methods. The main idea is to map data that are initially not linearly separable into a reproducing kernel Hilbert space (RKHS), where it becomes linearly separable using a mapping ϕ. In practice (thanks to the kernel trick), the explicit computation of ϕ is not required as long as an expression for the kernel $k(.,.) = <\phi(.), \phi(.)>$ exists. The exploitation of the HOSVD and SVMs to tensorial data has been introduced in [46]. This method relies on the computation of the HOSVD factors, without the need of the core tensor, to classify multidimensional data. In this chapter, we rely on the equivalence between TTD and TD to speed up the computation of TD with orthonormal factors, which implies speeding up the classification task. The proposed method, denoted Fast Kernel Subspace Estimation based on Tensor Train decomposition (FAKSETT), shows good classification performance with a lower computational complexity compared to the state-of-the-art method. The main idea of the FAKSETT method is to decrease this complexity using the proposed framework.

In Section 14.2, we introduce notations and the algebraic background used throughout the chapter. Section 14.3 recalls the standard tensor decompositions. The equivalence results between TTD and TD are given in Section 14.4. Section 14.5 presents and compares the sequential and the hierarchical TTD algorithms, which allow to accomplish the dimensionality reduction step. In Section 14.6, we recall the principle of the SVM algorithm for tensors and detail the proposed FAKSETT algorithm. Numerical simulations are given in Section 14.7, while Section 14.8 concludes this chapter.

14.2 Notations and algebraic background

The notations used throughout this chapter are now defined. Scalars, vectors, matrices, and tensors are represented by x, $\mathbf{x}$, $\mathbf{X}$, and $\mathcal{X}$, respectively.

The symbols $(\cdot)^T$, $(\cdot)^\dagger$, and $\mathrm{rank}(\cdot)$ denote, respectively, the transpose, the Moore–Penrose pseudo-inverse, and the rank. We denote by $\times_n$ the n-mode product. The symbols $\langle \cdot \rangle$ and $\overset{\triangle}{=}$ denote spanned subspace and an equality by definition. We denote by $\mathbf{A}(:, i)$ (resp. $\mathbf{A}(i, :)$) the i-th column (resp. row) of the matrix $\mathbf{A}$; $\mathcal{X}(i, :, :)$, $\mathcal{X}(:, j, :)$, and $\mathcal{X}(:, :, k)$ are the i-th horizontal, j-th lateral, and k-th frontal slices of sizes $N_2 \times N_3$, $N_1 \times N_3$, and $N_1 \times N_2$, respectively, of the tensor $\mathcal{X}$ of size $N_1 \times N_2 \times N_3$. The unfold$_q$ $\mathcal{X}$ of size $N_q \times (N_1 \cdots N_{q-1} N_{q+1} \cdots N_Q)$ refers to the mode-q unfolding of tensor $\mathcal{X}$; $\mathcal{I}_{q,R}$ denotes the q-order identity tensor of size $R \times \cdots \times R$. It is a hypercubic tensor of order q, with ones on its diagonal and zeros otherwise, and we have $\mathcal{I}_{2,R} = \mathbf{I}_R$. The contraction product $\times_q^p$ between two tensors $\mathcal{A}$ and $\mathcal{B}$ of size $N_1 \times \cdots \times N_Q$ and $M_1 \times \cdots \times M_P$, where $N_q = M_p$, is a tensor of order $Q + P - 2$ such as [10]

$$[\mathcal{A} \times_q^p \mathcal{B}]_{n_1, \ldots, n_{q-1}, n_{q+1}, \ldots, n_Q, m_1, \ldots, m_{p-1}, m_{p+1}, \ldots, m_P}$$

$$= \sum_{k=1}^{N_q} [\mathcal{A}]_{n_1, \ldots, n_{q-1}, k, n_{q+1}, \ldots, n_Q} [\mathcal{B}]_{m_1, \ldots, m_{p-1}, k, m_{p+1}, \ldots, m_P}.$$

In tensor-based data processing, it is standard to unfold a tensor into matrices. We refer to eq. (5) in [18] for a general matrix unfolding formula, also called tensor reshaping. The q-th generalized unfolding $\mathbf{X}_{(q)}$ of size $(\prod_{s=1}^{q} N_s) \times (\prod_{s=q+1}^{Q} N_s)$ of the tensor $\mathcal{X} \in \mathbb{R}^{N_1 \times N_2 \times \cdots \times N_Q}$ using the native reshape function of the MATLAB® software program (for instance) is defined by

$$\mathbf{X}_{(q)} = \mathrm{reshape}\left(\mathcal{X}; \prod_{s=1}^{q} N_s, \prod_{s=q+1}^{Q} N_s\right).$$

Another type of reshaping is tensor unfolding, which transforms the tensor $\mathcal{X} \in \mathbb{R}^{N_1 \times N_2 \times \cdots \times N_Q}$ into a third-order tensor $\mathcal{X}_q$ of size $(N_1 \cdots N_{q-1}) \times N_q \times (N_{q+1} \cdots N_Q)$ where

$$\mathcal{X}_q = \text{reshape}\left(\mathcal{X}; \prod_{s=1}^{q-1} N_s, N_q, \prod_{s=q+1}^{Q} N_s\right).$$

The last transformation is square matrix tensorization, which transforms a square matrix $\mathbf{I} \in \mathbb{R}^{N \times N}$, with $N = N_1 N_2$, to a third-order tensor according to

$$\mathcal{T} = \text{reshape}\,(\mathbf{I}; N_1, N_2, N) \tag{14.1}$$

or

$$\bar{\mathcal{T}} = \text{reshape}\,(\mathbf{I}; N, N_1, N_2), \tag{14.2}$$

where $\mathcal{T} \in \mathbb{R}^{N_1 \times N_2 \times N}$ and $\bar{\mathcal{T}} \in \mathbb{R}^{N \times N_1 \times N_2}$. These two last reshapings will be used in Theorem 14.1 to define a one-to-one mapping between an identity matrix and a sparse tensor filled with binary values.

In this chapter, factor graph representations will be intensively used. In a factor graph, a node can be a vector, a matrix, or a tensor as illustrated in Fig. 14.1(a), (b), and (c). The edges encode the dimensions of the node. The order of the node is given by the number of edges. In Fig. 14.1(d), the $\times_3^1$ product of two third-order tensors with a common dimension is illustrated.

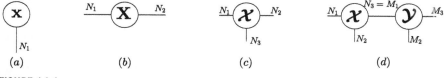

(a)   (b)   (c)   (d)

FIGURE 14.1

(a) Vector $\mathbf{x}$ of size $N_1 \times 1$. (b) Matrix $\mathbf{X}$ of size $N_1 \times N_2$. (c) Third-order tensor $\mathcal{X}$ of size $N_1 \times N_2 \times N_3$. (d) $\times_3^1$ product of two third-order tensors.

14.3 Standard tensor decompositions

A natural generalization to high-order tensors of the usual concept of matrix rank leads to canonical polyadic decomposition (CPD) [8,16,25,28,50]. The canonical rank of a Q-order tensor is equal to the minimal number, say R, of rank-1 tensors that must be linearly combined to reach a perfect recovery of the initial tensor. A rank-1 tensor of order Q is given by the outer product of Q vectors. In the context of massive data processing and analysis, this decomposition and its variants [10,11] are attractive in terms of compactness thanks to the minimality constraint on R. In addition, the CPD has remarkable uniqueness properties [50] and involves only QNR free parameters for a Q-order rank-R tensor of size $N \times \ldots \times N$. Unfortunately, unlike the matrix case, the set of tensors with low (tensorial) rank is not closed [27]. This singularity implies that the problem of computing the CPD is mathematically ill-posed. The consequence is that its numerical computation remains nontrivial and is usually done using suboptimal iterative algorithms [37]. Note that this problem can sometimes be avoided by exploiting some natural hidden structures in the physical model [49] or by considering some constraints such as the coherence constraint as in [44].

TD and HOSVD [14,51] are two popular decompositions that are very useful alternatives to the CPD. In this case, the notion of canonical rank is no longer relevant and a new rank definition has to be introduced. Specifically, the multilinear rank of a tensor is defined as the set of Q positive integers $\{T_1, \ldots, T_Q\}$, where each T_q is the usual (in the matrix sense) rank of the q-th mode unfolding of this tensor. Its practical construction is algebraic, noniterative, and optimal in the sense of the Eckart–Young theorem, applied to each matrix unfolding.

In this section, we will recall two of the standard tensor decompositions, namely TD and the HOSVD algorithm, and discuss some of their drawbacks regarding the computation and the storage cost before presenting the tensor network paradigm.

14.3.1 Tucker decomposition

TD was proposed in [51]. It decomposes a tensor into a core tensor of the same order, multiplied by a factor matrix along each mode. It can be seen as a generalization of CPD [8,25,28].

Definition 14.1. A Q-order tensor of size $N_1 \times \ldots \times N_Q$ that follows a TD can be written as

$$\mathcal{X} = \mathcal{C} \times_1 \mathbf{F}_1 \times_2 \mathbf{F}_2 \times_3 \ldots \times_Q \mathbf{F}_Q, \tag{14.3}$$

where $\mathbf{F}_q$ is of size $N_q \times T_q$, $1 \leq q \leq Q$, and $\mathcal{C}$ is the core tensor of size $T_1 \times \ldots \times T_Q$. The multilinear rank [14] of the tensor $\mathcal{X}$ is defined as the Q-uplet $\{T_1, \cdots, T_Q\}$, such that $T_1 \times \cdots \times T_Q$ is the minimal possible size of the core tensor $\mathcal{C}$. The storage cost of TD is $O(QNT + T^Q)$, where $N = \max\{N_1, \cdots, N_Q\}$ and $T = \max\{T_1, \cdots, T_Q\}$.

14.3.2 HOSVD

HOSVD [1,14] is the second approach for decomposing a high-order tensor. In the case of HOSVD, the Q factor matrices are obtained from a low-rank approximation of the unfolding matrices of the tensor, which is possible by means of the SVD, under an orthonormality constraint on the factor matrices. Unfortunately, this orthonormality constraint implies that the core tensor $\mathcal{C}$ is generally not diagonal. Two remarks can be made at this point. First, as SVD is a rank revealing decomposition of a matrix [20], HOSVD is a rank revealing decomposition for a high-order tensor [4] but does not reveal the *canonical* rank. Second, the storage cost associated with the computation of the core tensor grows exponentially with the order Q of the data tensor.

Definition 14.2. The HOSVD is a special case of the TD defined in Eq. (14.3), where the factors $\mathbf{F}_q$ are column-orthonormal. Generally, HOSVD is not optimal in terms of low-rank approximation, but it relies on the stable (i.e., noniterative) SVD-based algorithm. In the real case, the core tensor can be expressed as

$$\mathcal{C} = \mathcal{X} \times_1 \mathbf{F}_1^T \times_2 \mathbf{F}_2^T \times_3 \ldots \times_Q \mathbf{F}_Q^T.$$

14.3.3 Tensor networks and TT decomposition

14.3.3.1 Tensor networks and their graph-based illustrations

Recently, a new paradigm for dimensionality reduction has been proposed [10], therein referred to as tensor networks. The main idea of tensor networks [2,11] is to split a high-order ($Q > 3$) tensor into a product set of lower-order tensors represented as a factor graph. Factor graphs allow visualizing the factorization of multivariate or multilinear functions (the nodes) and their dependencies (the edges) [35]. The graph formalism is useful in the Big Data context [45].

In this context, higher-order tensor networks give us the opportunity to develop more sophisticated models performing distributed computing and capturing multiple interactions and couplings, instead of standard pair-wise interactions. In other words, to discover hidden components within multiway data the analysis tools should account for intrinsic multidimensional distributed patterns present in the data. Tensor network diagrams are very useful not only for visualizing tensor decompositions, but also for their different transformations/reshapings and graphical illustrations of mathematical (multilinear) operations. In general, tensor networks can be considered as a generalization and extension of standard tensor decompositions and are promising tools for the analysis of Big Data due to their very good compression performance and distributed and parallel processing.

Particularly, tensor train (TT) decomposition [23,39,41] is one of the simplest tensor networks. It represents a Q-order tensor by a product of Q third-order tensors. Each third-order tensor is associated to a node of the graph and is connected to its left and right "neighbors" encoded in a one-to-one directional edge [43]. The storage cost with respect to the order Q has the same linear behavior [39] for CPD and TT decomposition. Moreover, TTD has a stable (noniterative) SVD-based algorithm [39], even for large tensors. Therefore, TTD helps to break the *curse of dimensionality* [40], as it can be seen as a special case of HT decomposition [22,23,40,47,52]. Note that the HT and TT decompositions allow to represent a Q-order tensor of size $N \times \cdots \times N$ with a storage cost of $O(QNR + QR^3)$ and $O(QNR^2)$, respectively [10,21], where R is the rank of the considered decomposition. The use of TTD is motivated by its applicability in a number of interesting problems, such as supercompression [32], tensor completion [34], blind source separation [5], and fast SVD of large-scale matrices [36], for linear diffusion operators [31], and in machine learning [38], to mention a few. Fig. 14.2(a) gives a graph-based representation of TD of a sixth-order tensor. Its graph-based decompositions are given in Fig. 14.2(b). The decomposition of the initial tensor is not unique since we have several possible graph-based configurations

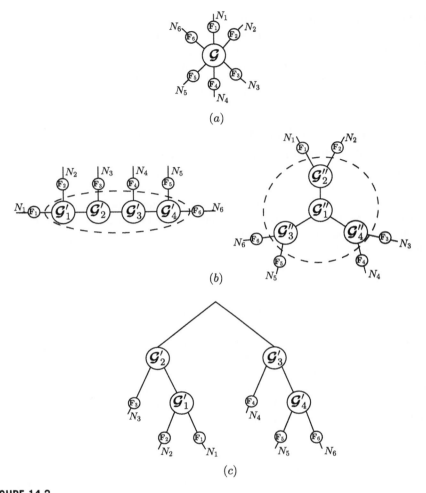

FIGURE 14.2

(a) Graph-based Tucker decomposition of a sixth-order tensor. (b) TT-based (*left*) and tensor network-based (*right*) decompositions. (c) HT decomposition.

depending on the tensor order and the number of connected nodes. In the literature, the graph on the right of Fig. 14.2(b) is viewed as a tensor network, also called HT decomposition [24]. This is due to the property that a tensor network can be alternatively represented as a tree (Fig. 14.2(c)) where the nodes are called leaves. The graph-based representation on the left of Fig. 14.2(b) is viewed as a train of tensors with nonidentity leaves. We use the name *tensor train* decomposition [39,40] if all the leaves are associated with an identity matrix except the first and last ones. TTD is one of the compact tensor networks, and it is a special case of HT decomposition [22,23,52].

14.3.3.2 TT decomposition

TTD was proposed in [39,41]. It transforms a high-order tensor into a set of third-order core tensors. It is one of the simplest tensor networks that allows to break the "curse of dimensionality." Indeed, it has a low storage cost, and the number of its parameters is linear in Q.

Definition 14.3. Let $\{R_1, \ldots, R_{Q-1}\}$ be the TT ranks with bounding conditions $R_0 = R_Q = 1$. A Q-order tensor of size $N_1 \times \ldots \times N_Q$ admits a decomposition into a train of tensors written as

$$\mathcal{X} = \mathbf{G}_1 \times_2^1 \mathcal{G}_2 \times_3^1 \mathcal{G}_3 \times_4^1 \ldots \times_{Q-1}^1 \mathcal{G}_{Q-1} \times_Q^1 \mathbf{G}_Q, \qquad (14.4)$$

with the TT cores of dimensions

$$\mathbf{G}_1 : N_1 \times R_1,$$
$$\mathbf{G}_Q^T : N_Q \times R_{Q-1},$$
$$\mathcal{G}_q : R_{q-1} \times N_q \times R_q, \text{ for } 2 \leq q \leq Q-1,$$

where $\mathrm{rank}(\mathbf{G}_1) = R_1$, $\mathrm{rank}(\mathbf{G}_Q) = R_{Q-1}$ and for $2 \leq q \leq Q-1$,

$$\mathrm{rank}(\mathrm{unfold}_1 \mathcal{G}_q) = R_{q-1},$$
$$\mathrm{rank}(\mathrm{unfold}_2 \mathcal{G}_q) = R_q.$$

A graph-based representation of the TTD of a Q-order tensor is given in Fig. 14.3.

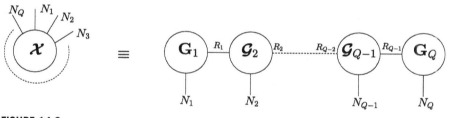

FIGURE 14.3

TT decomposition of a Q-order tensor.

14.4 Dimensionality reduction based on a train of low-order tensors

In this section, equivalence relations between TTD [39] and TD [8,51] are investigated. It is shown that a Q-order tensor following TD with $Q > 3$ can be written using the graph-based formalism as a train of Q tensors of order at most 3. This means that for any practical problem of interest involving a TD, an equivalent TT-based formulation exists. As a consequence, TTD deserves to become a fundamental and a more useful representation than the standard and popular TD. In addition, this equivalence allows us to overcome the curse of dimensionality [40], which is one of the main goals in the context of Big Data processing. Indeed, our methodology has two main advantages. First, we show that the native difficult optimization problem in a Q-dimensional space can be efficiently solved according to flexible strategies involving $Q - 2$ optimization problems in (low) 3D spaces. In the curse of dimensionality, the number of free parameters grows exponentially with Q. On the contrary, our methodology involves a number of free parameters linear with Q and thus allows to mitigate this problem. Another contribution consists in the proposition of an algorithm based on TTD to accomplish a fast computation of TD with orthonormal factors. In particular, based on the TT-SVD and TT-HSVD algorithms, we show how to exploit coupling properties existing between two successive TT cores in the graph-based formalism. The advantages of the proposed approach in terms of storage cost, computational complexity, and factor estimation accuracy are pointed out.

14.4.1 TD-train model: equivalence between a high-order TD and a train of low-order TDs

In Theorem 14.1, we present an algebraic equivalence between TD and TTD. We show how the matrix factors and the core tensor of a TD can be recast into the TT format.

Theorem 14.1. *Assume that tensor $\mathcal{X}$ follows a Q-order Tucker model of multilinear rank $(T_1, \cdots, T_Q)$, given by Eq. (14.3). The TTD (14.4) of $\mathcal{X}$ is then given by*

$$\mathbf{G}_1 = \mathbf{F}_1,$$
$$\mathcal{G}_q = \mathcal{T}_q \times_2 \mathbf{F}_q, (1 < q < \bar{q})$$
$$\text{with } \mathcal{T}_q = \text{reshape}(\mathbf{I}_{R_q}; T_1 \cdots T_{q-1}, T_q, T_1 \cdots T_q),$$
$$\mathcal{G}_{\bar{q}} = \mathcal{C}_{\bar{q}} \times_2 \mathbf{F}_{\bar{q}}$$
$$\text{with } \mathcal{C}_{\bar{q}} = \text{reshape}(\mathcal{C}; R_{\bar{q}-1}, T_{\bar{q}}, R_{\bar{q}}),$$
$$\mathcal{G}_q = \bar{\mathcal{T}}_q \times_2 \mathbf{F}_q, (\bar{q} < q < Q)$$
$$\text{with } \bar{\mathcal{T}}_q = \text{reshape}(\mathbf{I}_{R_{q-1}}; T_q \cdots T_Q, T_q, T_{q+1} \cdots T_Q),$$
$$\mathbf{G}_Q = \mathbf{F}_Q^T,$$

where $\mathcal{T}_q$ and $\bar{\mathcal{T}}_q$ result from the tensorization as defined in (14.1) and (14.2), respectively, and:

- $\bar{q}$ *is the smallest q that verifies $\prod_{i=1}^{q} T_i \geq \prod_{i=q+1}^{Q} T_i$, corresponding to the smallest q such that $\mathbf{C}_{(q)}$ has at least as many rows as columns;*

- *the TT ranks verify*

$$R_q = \min(\prod_{i=1}^{q} T_i, \ \prod_{i=q+1}^{Q} T_i). \tag{14.5}$$

Proof. It is straightforward to verify that the TTD of the Q-order Tucker core $\mathcal{C}$ takes the following expression:

$$\mathcal{C} = \mathbf{I}_{R_1} \times_2^1 \mathcal{T}_2 \times_3^1 \cdots \times_{\bar{q}-1}^1 \mathcal{T}_{\bar{q}-1} \times_{\bar{q}}^1 \mathcal{C}_{\bar{q}} \times_{\bar{q}+1}^1 \mathcal{T}_{\bar{q}+1} \times_{\bar{q}+2}^1 \cdots$$
$$\times_{Q-1}^1 \mathcal{T}_{Q-1} \times_Q^1 \mathbf{I}_{R_{Q-1}}, \tag{14.6}$$

where tensors $\mathcal{T}_q$ and $\bar{\mathcal{T}}_q$ have been defined in the theorem thanks to the reshaping of Eq. (14.1) and Eq. (14.2), respectively. Replacing the TTD of $\mathcal{C}$ in Eq. (14.3), the q-th third-order tensor in Eq. (14.6) is multiplied in its second mode by its corresponding factor $\mathbf{F}_q$. By identifying the final TT cores, the theorem is proved. $\square$

Note that all the TT cores follow a third-order Tucker1 model, whose second factor is the q-th factor of the original TD, hence the name TD-Train. More specifically, for $q < \bar{q}$ and $q > \bar{q}$, the corresponding TT cores have Tucker1 structures whose core tensors have fixed 1 and 0 patterns. We recall that a Tucker1 model is a third-order TD with two factor matrices equal to identity matrices. For $q = \bar{q}$, the associated TT core has a Tucker1 structure with a core tensor $\mathcal{C}_{\bar{q}}$ obtained from the core tensor of the original TD. To illustrate this result, consider the TTD of the core tensor $\mathcal{C}$ in Eq. (14.3). Note that $\bar{q}$ corresponds to the smallest q such that $\mathbf{C}_{(q)}$ has at least as many rows as columns. For example, if $\mathcal{C}$ is a fifth-order tensor of size $2 \times 3 \times 2 \times 4 \times 2$, then $\bar{q} = 3$, since $2 \times 3 \times 2 > 4 \times 2$. Another example where $\mathcal{C}$ is of size $2 \times 2 \times 3 \times 4 \times 4$ corresponds to $\bar{q} = 4$.

The cores of the TD-Train can be recovered by using the TT-SVD algorithm [39] in practice. However, the application of this algorithm will recover the cores up to nonsingular transformation matrices [55]. In the following theorem, the structure of the TT cores associated with a TD-Train are given.

Theorem 14.2. *Applying the TT-SVD algorithm on the tensor* (14.3) *under the assumptions that*

- $\mathbf{F}_q$ *is a full column rank matrix of size* $N_q \times T_q$ *and*
- $\mathbf{C}_{(q)} = \text{reshape}(\mathcal{C}; \prod_{i=1}^{q} T_i, \prod_{i=q+1}^{Q} T_i)$ *has full rank*

allows to recover the TT cores according to

$$\mathbf{G}_1 = \mathbf{F}_1 \mathbf{M}_1^{-1},$$
$$\mathcal{G}_q = \mathcal{T}_q \times_1 \mathbf{M}_{q-1} \times_2 \mathbf{F}_q \times_3 \mathbf{M}_q^{-T} \quad (1 < q < \bar{q}),$$
$$\mathcal{G}_{\bar{q}} = \mathcal{C}_{\bar{q}} \times_1 \mathbf{M}_{\bar{q}-1} \times_2 \mathbf{F}_{\bar{q}} \times_3 \mathbf{M}_{\bar{q}}^{-T},$$

$$\mathcal{G}_q = \bar{\mathcal{T}}_q \times_1 \mathbf{M}_{q-1} \times_2 \mathbf{F}_q \times_3 \mathbf{M}_q^{-T} \quad (\bar{q} < q < Q),$$

$$\mathbf{G}_Q = \mathbf{M}_{Q-1} \mathbf{F}_Q^T,$$

where $\mathbf{M}_q$ is an $R_q \times R_q$ *nonsingular* change-of-basis *matrix and the quantities* $\mathcal{T}_q$, $\bar{\mathcal{T}}_q$, $\mathcal{C}_{\bar{q}}$, *and* R_q *are defined in Theorem 14.1.*

Note that the TT cores follow Tucker models with nonsingular transformation matrices along their first and third modes. These matrices compensate each other due to the train format. The proof relies on the TT-SVD algorithm applied to a Q-order TD. It can be found in [54].

Remark 14.1. One may note that in Theorem 14.1, no assumption on the rank of the Tucker core nor the factors is made, thus there is no guarantee that the considered TT ranks are minimal, i.e., applying a decomposition algorithm such as TT-SVD may estimate different (lower) TT ranks and provide different TT core structures. In Theorem 14.2, additional rank assumptions are made, especially on the Tucker core $\mathcal{C}$, allowing to guarantee the minimality of the given TT ranks and to provide constructive/exploitable results from an estimation point of view.

14.5 Tensor train algorithm

The first proposed algorithm to compute a TTD is the TT-SVD algorithm [39]. This algorithm minimizes the following least-squares criterion:

$$\psi(\mathcal{X}) = \left\| \mathcal{X} - \mathbf{G}_1 \times_2^1 \mathcal{G}_2 \times_3^1 \cdots \times_{Q-1}^1 \mathcal{G}_{Q-1} \times_Q^1 \mathbf{G}_Q \right\|^2. \tag{14.7}$$

Unfortunately, the TT-SVD, as described in [39], is a sequential algorithm, i.e., the TT cores are computed one after the other, which is not the appropriate strategy when we deal with high-order Big Data tensors. To tackle the computational complexity problem associated with the decomposition of high-order tensors, a new algorithm called TT-HSVD was proposed in [55]. This algorithm minimizes the same criterion (14.7) and it adopts a new unfolding and reshaping strategy that, on the one hand, enables to parallelize the decomposition using several processors and, on the other hand, results in a less expensive computational cost compared to TT-SVD.

14.5.1 Description of the TT-HSVD algorithm

In this section, we recall the recently proposed TT-HSVD algorithm [55]. This algorithm allows to decompose tensors in the TT format, in a parallel/hierarchical manner. As opposed to the TT-SVD algorithm, the TT-HSVD algorithm suggests to use a different reshaping strategy, i.e., the way to reshape the SVD factors ($\mathbf{U}_q$, $\mathbf{V}_q$), at each step. Fig. 14.4 illustrates the proposed strategy by means of the graph-based representation of the TTD of a fourth-order tensor. Using TT-HSVD, we first choose an index $\bar{Q} \in \{1, \ldots, Q\}$, and the first matrix unfolding $\mathbf{X}_{(\bar{Q})}$ is of size

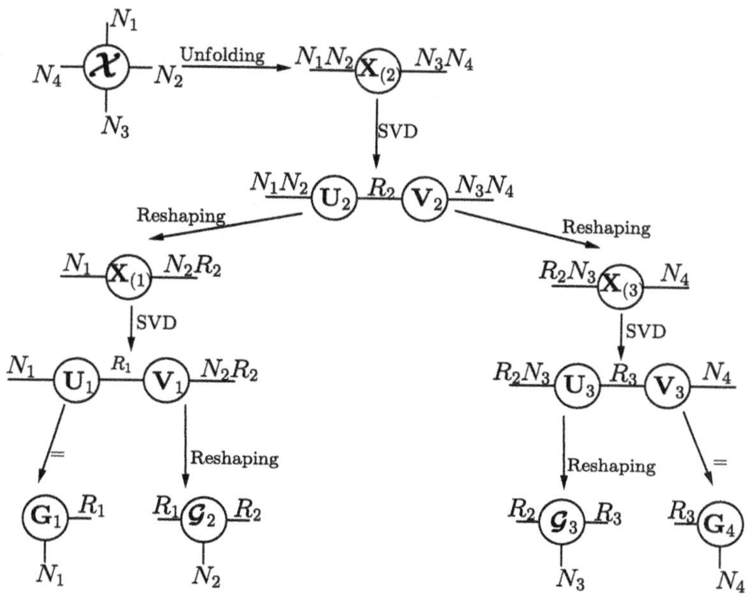

FIGURE 14.4

TT-HSVD applied to a 4-order tensor.

$(N_1 \cdots N_{\bar{Q}}) \times (N_{\bar{Q}+1} \cdots N_Q)$ instead of $N_1 \times (N_2 \cdots N_Q)$ as for the TT-SVD algorithm, which leads to a more square matrix. The $(R_{\bar{Q}})$-truncated SVD of $\mathbf{X}_{(\bar{Q})}$ provides two factors $\mathbf{U}_{\bar{Q}}$ and $\mathbf{V}_{\bar{Q}}$ of size $(N_1 \cdots N_{\bar{Q}}) \times R_{\bar{Q}}$ and $R_{\bar{Q}} \times (N_{\bar{Q}+1} \cdots N_Q)$, respectively. These two factors are now reshaped in parallel, which constitutes the main difference with the TT-SVD algorithm for which only a single reshaping operation is applied to $\mathbf{V}_1$. This processing is repeated after each SVD computation, as illustrated in Fig. 14.4. Generally speaking, the choice of the best reshaping strategy, i.e., the choice of the index $\bar{Q}$, depends on an a priori physical knowledge related to each application [7,33], as for instance in biomedical signal analysis or in wireless communications [13,18,53]. In [55], this best choice is discussed in terms of algorithmic complexity. It was noted that choosing the most "square" unfolding matrix (i.e., the one with more balanced row and column dimensions) results in a lower overall computational complexity. From this simple example, one can conclude that the TT-SVD algorithm can be seen as a special case of the TT-HSVD algorithm, where only one and the same reshaping strategy is considered at each step and where the TT cores are calculated one by one.

14.5.2 Comparison of the sequential and the hierarchical schemes

It is proved in [55] that, from an algebraic perspective, TT-SVD and TT-HSVD estimate the same TT core up to different change-of-basis matrices up to different change-of-basis matrices $\mathbf{P}_q$ and $\mathbf{Q}_q$, respectively. This result is illustrated in Figs. 14.5 and 14.6, where $\hat{\boldsymbol{\mathcal{G}}}_q^{hrl}$ and $\hat{\boldsymbol{\mathcal{G}}}_q^{sql}$ refer to the q-th estimated TT-cores, using the hierarchical TT-HSVD algorithm and the sequential TT-SVD algorithm, respectively. Based on the expressions of the structure of the TT cores, the following result can be stated.

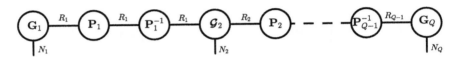

FIGURE 14.5

Structure of the sequentially estimated TT cores.

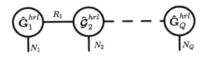

FIGURE 14.6

Structure of the hierarchically estimated TT cores.

Lemma 14.1. *Let* $\{\mathbf{H}_1, \ldots, \mathbf{H}_{Q-1}\}$ *be the set of matrices defined as* $\mathbf{H}_q = \mathbf{P}_q^{-1}\mathbf{Q}_q$. *The relation between the TT cores obtained by the TT-SVD and TT-HSVD algorithms is given by*

$$\hat{\mathbf{G}}_1^{hrl} = \hat{\mathbf{G}}_1^{seq}\mathbf{H}_1, \tag{14.8}$$

$$\hat{\boldsymbol{\mathcal{G}}}_q^{hrl} = \mathbf{H}_{q-1}^{-1} \times_2^1 \hat{\boldsymbol{\mathcal{G}}}_q^{seq} \times_3^1 \mathbf{H}_q \qquad \text{for } 2 \leq q \leq Q-1, \tag{14.9}$$

$$\hat{\mathbf{G}}_Q^{hrl} = \mathbf{H}_{Q-1}^{-1}\hat{\mathbf{G}}_Q^{seq}. \tag{14.10}$$

Proof. Using the identity $\mathbf{A} \times_2^1 \mathbf{B} = \mathbf{AB}$, based on the result in Figs. 14.5 and 14.6, we can deduce

$$\mathcal{G}q = \mathbf{P}_{q-1} \times_2^1 \hat{\mathcal{G}}_q^{seq} \times_3^1 \mathbf{P}_q^{-1}.$$

Substituting this last equation into

$$\hat{\mathcal{G}}_q^{hrl} = \mathbf{Q}_{q-1}^{-1} \times_2^1 \mathcal{G}_q \times_3^1 \mathbf{Q}_q,$$

we have

$$\hat{\mathcal{G}}_q^{hrl} = (\mathbf{P}_{q-1}^{-1}\mathbf{Q}_{q-1})^{-1} \times_2^1 \hat{\mathcal{G}}_q^{seq} \times_3^1 (\mathbf{P}_q^{-1}\mathbf{Q}_q) \qquad \text{for } 2 \leq q \leq Q - 1. \qquad \square$$

The above lemma allows us to formulate the following theorem.

Theorem 14.3. *The TT ranks are equal for the TT-SVD and the TT-HSVD algorithms.*

Proof. From Eqs. (14.8) and (14.10) in Lemma 14.1, the proof of the theorem is straightforward for $q = 1$ and $q = Q$. For $2 \leq q \leq Q - 1$, two alternative Tucker-based formulations of (14.9) are

$$\hat{\mathcal{G}}_q^{hrl} = \hat{\mathcal{G}}_q^{seq} \times_1 \mathbf{H}_{q-1}^{-1} \times_2 \mathbf{I}_{N_q} \times_3 \mathbf{H}_q^T,$$
$$\hat{\mathcal{G}}_q^{seq} = \hat{\mathcal{G}}_q^{hrl} \times_1 \mathbf{H}_{q-1} \times_2 \mathbf{I}_{N_q} \times_3 \mathbf{H}_q^{-T}.$$

Based on the two above relations, tensors $\hat{\mathcal{G}}_q^{hrl}$ and $\hat{\mathcal{G}}_q^{seq}$ have a multilinear (R_{q-1}, N_q, R_q)-rank. Since the TT ranks correspond to the dimensions of the first and third modes of $\hat{\mathcal{G}}_q^{hrl}$ or $\hat{\mathcal{G}}_q^{seq}$, the proof is completed. $\qquad \square$

Intuitively, the above theorem seems natural since the TT ranks are essentially related to the TT model, and in particular to the unfolding matrices, and not to the choice of the algorithm.

14.6 Kernel-based classification of high-order tensors

In the rest of this chapter, we will be interested in the algorithms of SVMs for tensors. We will first present the formulation of SVMs, next we will recall some existing work in this field, and finally we will show how the proposed method FAKSETT allows to decrease the complexity of the state-of-the-art method. The idea of the FAKSETT method is to use the structured TT model described in Theorem 14.2 to compute the orthonormal factors used in the SVM, instead of using the classical HOSVD algorithm. This accelerates the calculation of the factors.

14.6.1 Formulation of SVMs

Let us consider a binary classification problem where the dataset is composed of M Q-order tensors $\mathcal{X}_i \in \mathbb{R}^{N_1 \times \cdots \times N_Q}$ labeled with $y_i \in \{-1, 1\}$. This classification problem is said to be linearly separable if its decision function has the following form:

$$f(\mathcal{X}) = \langle \mathcal{W}, \mathcal{X} \rangle + b, \tag{14.11}$$

where $\mathcal{W} \in \mathbb{R}^{N_1 \times \cdots \times N_Q}$ is a Q-order tensor of weights and b is the bias.

In order to estimate $\mathcal{W}$ and b, a generalization of the SVM formulation problem was introduced in several works such as [26] as follows:

$$\begin{cases} \min_{\mathcal{W}, b, \xi} \; \frac{1}{2} \|\mathcal{W}\|_F^2 + C \sum_{i=1}^{M} \xi_i \\ \text{subject to } y_i(\langle \mathcal{W}, \mathcal{X}_i \rangle + b) \geq 1 - \xi_i, \\ \xi_i \geq 0, \, 1 \leq i \leq M, \end{cases} \tag{14.12}$$

where ξ_i is the error of the i-th training example of the dataset and C is the regularization parameter chosen for ensuring a trade-off between the misclassification error and the classification margin.

When the dataset is not linearly separable, the previous formulation of SVM is no longer adapted, and hence the idea of kernel methods is to represent the dataset in a high-dimensional pre-Hilbert space usually named the *feature space* in which the dataset is linearly separable. The projection of data in the feature space is done via an implicit feature map $\Phi(\cdot)$. The constraints in Eq. (14.12) expressed in the feature space can be written as [26]

$$y_i(\langle \mathcal{W}, \Phi(\mathcal{X}_i) \rangle + b) \geq 1 - \xi_i. \tag{14.13}$$

After solving the dual problem of Eq. (14.12) in the feature space taking account the constraints in Eq. (14.13), the decision function (14.11) can be expressed as follows [26]:

$$f(\mathcal{X}) = \text{sgn}\left(\sum_{i=1}^{M} \alpha_i y_i \langle \Phi(\mathcal{X}_i), \Phi(\mathcal{X}) \rangle + b \right), \tag{14.14}$$

where "sgn" denotes the sign function and α_i is the i-th Lagrangian variable.

In general, the feature map Φ is unknown, only the inner product of the projection of the couple $(\mathcal{X}_i, \mathcal{X}_j)$ is required which is given by a symmetric positive-definite function k named kernel function. Therefore, the decision function Eq. (14.14) can be expressed using the kernel function as

$$f(\mathcal{X}) = \text{sgn}\left(\sum_{i=1}^{M} \alpha_i y_i k(\mathcal{X}_i, \mathcal{X}) + b \right). \tag{14.15}$$

14.6.2 Polynomial and Euclidean tensor-based kernel

Let us consider two Q-order tensors $\mathcal{X}, \mathcal{Y} \in \mathbb{R}^{N_1 \times \cdots \times N_Q}$. In order to take account of the multidimensional structure of input data tensors, an idea presented in [46] consists in decomposing $\mathcal{X}$ and $\mathcal{Y}$ into their HOSVD:

$$
\begin{aligned}
\mathcal{X} &= \mathcal{G} \times_1 \mathbf{U}_1 \times_2 \ldots \times_Q \mathbf{U}_Q, \\
\mathcal{Y} &= \mathcal{H} \times_1 \mathbf{V}_1 \times_2 \ldots \times_Q \mathbf{V}_Q.
\end{aligned}
\tag{14.16}
$$

The kernel-based part of the proposed method is

$$
k(\mathcal{X}, \mathcal{X}) = \prod_{q=1}^{Q} k_q \left(\mathbf{U}_q, \mathbf{V}_q \right),
\tag{14.17}
$$

where $k_q(., .)$ is a positive-definite kernel defined on the matrices $\mathbf{U}_q \in \mathbb{R}^{N_q \times T_q}$ and $\mathbf{V}_q \in \mathbb{R}^{N_q \times T_{q'}}$. One can also use the expression of the kernel used in [26]. The kernel between two CPD tensors was defined in [26] in terms of Gaussian–Euclidean kernels between respective columns of CP factors. We propose to use this kernel for a different model of data tensors i.e., between respective columns of HOSVD and FAKSETT factors. More formally, given the decompositions in Eq. (14.16), the kernel is defined as

$$
k(\mathcal{X}, \mathcal{Y}) = \sum_{r_1=1}^{T_1} \cdots \sum_{r_Q=1}^{T_Q} \sum_{r_1'=1}^{T_{1'}} \cdots \sum_{r_Q'=1}^{T_{Q'}} \prod_{q=1}^{Q} k_{poly}(\mathbf{x}_{r_q}, \mathbf{y}_{r_q'}),
\tag{14.18}
$$

where $\mathbf{x}_{r_q}$ and $\mathbf{y}_{r_q}$ are respectively the columns of $\mathbf{U}_q$ and $\mathbf{V}_q$ defined in Eq. (14.16), T_q and T_q' are respectively the multilinear ranks of $\mathcal{X}$ and $\mathcal{Y}$, and k_{poly} is the standard polynomial kernel defined as

$$
k_{poly}(\mathbf{x}_{r_q}, \mathbf{y}_{r_q'}) = (\gamma \mathbf{x}_{r_q}^T \mathbf{y}_{r_q'} + 1)^d,
\tag{14.19}
$$

where γ is a hyperparameter and d is the degree of the polynomial kernel.

We can use the Gaussian–Euclidean kernel k_{gauss} instead of k_{poly} in Eq. (14.18) defined as

$$
k_{gauss}(\mathbf{x}_{r_q}, \mathbf{y}_{r_q'}) = \exp\left(-\gamma \|\mathbf{x}_{r_q} - \mathbf{y}_{r_q}\|^2\right).
\tag{14.20}
$$

14.6.3 Kernel on a Grassmann manifold

It shall be noted that the decompositions (14.16) are not unique [33]. The output class will be affected by this lack of nonuniqueness. To mitigate this issue in the learning context, one can consider the subspaces spanned by the factors $\{\mathbf{U}_1, ..., \mathbf{U}_Q\}$ and $\{\mathbf{V}_1, ..., \mathbf{V}_Q\}$. Indeed, the subspaces spanned by the factor $\mathbf{U}_Q, q \le N$ (respectively

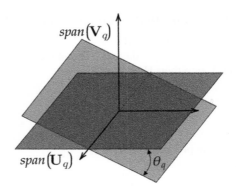

FIGURE 14.7

Illustration of the angle θ_q from Eq. (14.21).

$\mathbf{V}_Q$) are invariant to any right multiplication by a nonsingular matrix. Therefore, let us consider the subkernels k_q in the form

$$k_q\left(\mathbf{U}_q, \mathbf{V}_q\right) = \tilde{k}_q\left(\text{span}(\mathbf{U}_q), \text{span}(\mathbf{V}_q)\right),$$

where $\tilde{k}_q$ is a kernel defined on the Grassmann manifold $\mathbb{G}(T_q, N_q)$, i.e., the subspaces from $\mathbb{R}^{N_q}$ with dimension T_q.

A popular choice for $\tilde{k}_q$ that gives rise to a positive-definite kernel and is used in [46] is given by

$$k_q\left(\mathbf{U}_q, \mathbf{V}_q\right) = \exp\left(-\gamma \sin^2\left(\theta_q\right)\right), \tag{14.21}$$

where θ_q is the principal angle between span$(\mathbf{U}_q)$ and span$(\mathbf{V}_q)$. It should be noted that despite θ_q being the geodesic distance in the Grassmann manifold between the two subspaces, the expression $\sin(\theta_q)$ is considered instead, making the kernel k_q definite positive [29]. Readers can refer to [29] for explicit ways of computing the principal angles. In our case, it is possible to directly use the projectors:

$$\sin^2\left(\theta_q\right) = 2\left\|\mathbf{U}_Q\mathbf{U}_Q^T - \mathbf{V}_Q\mathbf{V}_Q^T\right\|_F^2.$$

The principal angle θ_q is illustrated in Fig. 14.7.

14.6.4 The fast kernel subspace estimation based on tensor train decomposition (FAKSETT) method

In order to decrease the complexity of the HOSVD-based methods [46] described in Sections 14.6.2 and 14.6.3, we propose to use the FAKSETT method. FAKSETT first computes the orthonormal factors using the fast multilinear projection (FMP)

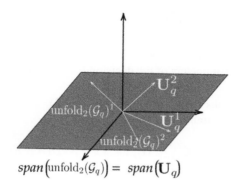

$$span\left(\text{unfold}_2(\mathcal{G}_q)\right) = span\left(\mathbf{U}_q\right)$$

FIGURE 14.8

Illustration of the subspaces spanned by HOSVD factors (U_q^1, U_q^2) and FAKSETT factors $(\text{unfold}_2\mathcal{G}_q^1, \text{unfold}_2\mathcal{G}_q^2)$ in the case $T_q = 2$.

method. FMP suggests to compute the orthonormal factors by applying a truncated SVD on the second unfoldings of the structured TT cores given in Theorem 14.2 and illustrated in Fig. 14.8. Compared to the HOSVD algorithm, FMP does not give guarantees on the all-orthogonality property of the core tensor, but allows to compute orthonormal factors faster than HOSVD. The orthonormal factors provided by the FMP and HOSVD algorithms span the same subspaces, which is necessary and sufficient for the SVM method. It is worth noting that the computational cost to have orthonormal factors from a hypercubic Q-order tensor of dimension N, with multi-linear ranks all equal to T, is $2QTN^Q$ flops using HOSVD and $2TN^Q$ flops using FMP [54]. This shows that FMP allows to compute the orthonormal factors faster than the HOSVD algorithm.

Afterwards, FAKSETT computes the kernel based on these factors using either the polynomial or the Euclidean kernels defined in Eq. (14.19) and Eq. (14.20), or the Grassmannian kernel defined in Eq. (14.17) and Eq. (14.21). A pseudo-code of the FAKSETT method is given in Algorithm 1.

14.7 Experiments

For the following datasets, a classification task is realized via SVM [9]. This relies on the similarity matrix obtained using the kernel defined previously. The kernel is computed with FAKSETT and is compared to the native method of [46].

14.7.1 Datasets

- **UCF11 dataset**: This dataset [30] contains 1600 video clips belonging to 11 human actions such as *diving*, *trampoline jumping*, *walking*, and *shooting*. Two hu-

---

Algorithm 1 FAKSETT algorithm.

Input: Training dataset $\{\mathcal{X}_i \in \mathbb{R}^{N_1 \times \cdots N_Q}, y_i \in \{-1, 1\}\}_{i=1}^M$, multilinear rank $\{T_1, \cdots, T_Q\}$, performance trade-off C, width parameter γ.
Output: The learning parameters of the decision function in Eq. (14.15).

  1: Compute the TT ranks $R_1, \cdots, R_Q$ using Eq. (14.5).
  2: Compute the TTD of training samples $\{\mathcal{X}_i\}_{i=1}^M$:

$$[\mathbf{G}_1^{(i)}, \mathcal{G}_2^{(i)}, \cdots, \mathcal{G}_{Q-1}^{(i)}, \mathbf{G}_Q^{(i)}] = \text{TT} - \text{SVD}(\mathcal{X}_i; R_1, \cdots, R_Q).$$

  3: Compute the orthonormal factors for each training sample $\mathcal{X}_i$:
  4: **for** $q = 2, \cdots, Q - 1$ **do**
  5:    $\mathbf{U}_q^{(i)} \leftarrow$ Matrix of the left singular vectors of $\text{unfold}_2 \mathcal{G}_q^{(i)}$. {This step can be executed in a parallel way.}
  6: **end for**
  7: Construct the kernel matrix $\mathbf{K}_{i,j} = k(\mathcal{X}_i, \mathcal{X}_j)$ using Eq. (14.17).
  8: Determine the decision function f from Eq. (14.15) by solving the dual of the optimization problem in Eq. (14.12) using the kernel matrix $\mathbf{K}$.

FIGURE 14.9

Three classes from the Extended Yale dataset B.

FIGURE 14.10

Two classes from the UCF11 dataset.

man actions are chosen: *trampoline jumping* and *walking*, presented in Fig. 14.10. They represent two classes for the classification. A sequence that contains the first 240 frames from each clip video where the resolution of each RGB frame equal to 320×240 is considered. These clip videos can be viewed as tensors of order four with dimensions $240 \times 240 \times 320 \times 3$. Each class contains a total of 109 tensors. Randomly selecting 60% of them generates the training set. The rest is left for the test.

- **Extended Yale dataset B**: This dataset [19] contains 28 human subjects. For each subject, there are 576 images of size 480×640 taken in nine poses. Each pose is taken under 64 different illuminations. Hence, we can organize data of each subject into a tensor of size $pose \times dim1 \times dim2 \times illumination$, where $dim1 \times dim2$ is the size of the images. This corresponds to the size $9 \times 480 \times 640 \times 64$. We consider three subjects in our work that correspond to three classes represented in Fig. 14.9. In order to construct the training and test sets, we break the tensor of each subject in 16 tensors by considering four illuminations for each subject which gives a tensor of size $9 \times 480 \times 640 \times 4$.

14.7.2 Classification performance

In this section, we report on numerical experiments where we use classification accuracy as a performance measure defined as the ratio of correctly predicted observation over the total observations.

Both the SVM regularization parameter and the kernel bandwidth γ from Eq. (14.21) are selected from the grid of values $\{2^{-9}, 2^{-8}, ..., 2^8, 2^9\}$ by a fivefold cross-validation. Recall that when we use a k-fold cross-validation, the training set is randomly partitioned into k equal-sized subsamples. Of the k subsamples, a single subsample is retained as the validation data for testing the model, and the remaining subsamples are used as training data. The cross-validation process is then repeated k times, with each of the k subsamples used exactly once as the validation data. The k results can then be averaged to produce a single estimation. All the experiments are conducted on a computer with Intel Core i7 9th generation 2.6 GHz processor and 32 Go RAM memory running Windows 10. Computations of SVDs are done using the optimized TensorLy (Tensor Learning in Python) library [42].

- Table 14.2 and Table 14.1 show very close accuracy scores between FAKSETT and the method of [46] for classification tasks on both real datasets. This indicates that the FAKSETT method operates as efficiently as the state-of-the-art method. Reducing the size of the training dataset (i.e., training with less data) does not significantly impact the performances.
- However, it is noticeable from Table 14.3 that FAKSETT significantly reduces the running time for the computation of the factors, despite working with only fourth-order tensors. Higher orders would lead to an even higher running time gain between the two methods. It shall be noted that on the Extended Yale dataset (resp. the UCF11 dataset), the computational time required by SVMs for a couple of hyperparameters (C, γ) is around 5 s (resp. 18 s) when multilinear ranks are equal to [1, 2, 2, 1] (resp. [2,2,2,2]).
- Tables 14.4 and 14.5 show accuracy scores using Gaussian–Euclidean kernels defined in Eq. (14.18). We can remark that the Gaussian–Euclidean kernel is highly impacted by the nonuniqueness of the decomposition defined in Eq. (14.16) since

Table 14.1 Accuracy scores (mean accuracy [standard deviation]) using the kernel defined in Eq. (14.17) on FAK-SETT factors and HOSVD factors for different multilinear ranks varying the size of the training set. These numerical results are obtained on the Extended Yale dataset.

s%	m-ranks	TT ranks	FAKSETT	HOSVD [46]
%50	[1,1,1,1]	[1,1,1,1,1]	1(0)	1(0)
	[1,2,2,1]	[1,1,2,1,1]	0.97(0.05)	1(0)
	[1,3,2,1]	[1,1,2,1,1]	0.98(0.05)	**0.99(0.01)**
%60	[1,1,1,1]	[1,1,1,1,1]	1(0)	1(0)
	[1,2,2,1]	[1,1,2,1,1]	**0.99(0.02)**	**0.99(0.01)**
	[1,2,3,1]	[1,1,2,1,1]	0.95(0.1)	**0.96(0.01)**

Table 14.2 Accuracy scores (mean accuracy [standard deviation]) using the kernel defined in Eq. (14.17) on FAK-SETT factors and HOSVD factors for different multilinear ranks varying the size of the training set. These numerical results are obtained on the UCF11 dataset.

s%	m-ranks	TT ranks	FAKSETT	HOSVD
%50	[1,1,1,1]	[1,1,1,1,1]	$0.82(10^{-2})$	$\mathbf{0.86(10^{-2})}$
	[2,2,2,2]	[1,2,4,2,1]	$0.72(10^{-2})$	$\mathbf{0.73(10^{-2})}$
	[3,3,3,3]	[1,3,9,3,1]	$0.68(10^{-2})$	$\mathbf{0.71(10^{-2})}$
%60	[1,1,1,1]	[1,1,1,1,1]	$0.8(10^{-2})$	$\mathbf{0.84(10^{-2})}$
	[2,2,2,2]	[1,2,4,2,1]	$0.71(10^{-2})$	$\mathbf{0.74(10^{-2})}$
	[3,3,3,3]	[1,3,9,3,1]	$\mathbf{0.7(10^{-2})}$	$\mathbf{0.7(10^{-2})}$
%80	[1,1,1,1]	[1,1,1,1,1]	$0.82(10^{-2})$	$\mathbf{0.82(10^{-1})}$
	[2,2,2,2]	[1,2,4,2,1]	$0.7(10^{-2})$	$\mathbf{0.74(10^{-2})}$
	[3,3,3,3]	[1,3,9,3,1]	$0.76(10^{-2})$	$\mathbf{0.77(10^{-2})}$

the maximum score of classification is around 62% compared to the score 85% obtained with a polynomial kernel of degree 3.

14.8 Conclusion

In many important applications, it is crucial to extract the dominant singular subspaces associated to the factors of a TD, while the computation of the core tensor is not a primary goal. This scenario is usually known as a multilinear projection. One of these applications, that is considered in this chapter, is the kernel-based learning for a classification purpose of multidimensional datasets. In this chapter, we propose a TTD-based method for breaking the dimensionality and speeding up the computation

Table 14.3 Computational time in seconds for computing the factors using the FAKSETT method and the state-of-the-art method presented in [46]. These numerical experiments concern the UCF11 and Extended Yale datasets.

Database	m-ranks	TT ranks	FAKSETT	HOSVD [46,46]
UCF11	[1,1,1,1]	[1,1,1,1,1]	**24**	63
	[2,2,2,2]	[1,2,4,2,1]	**14**	69
	[3,3,3,3]	[1,3,9,3,1]	**15**	104
Extended Yale	[1,1,1,1]	[1,1,1,1,1]	**3**	9
	[1,2,2,1]	[1,2,4,2,1]	**2.56**	9.47
	[1,2,3,1]	[1,3,9,3,1]	**2.58**	9.34

Table 14.4 Accuracy scores (mean accuracy [standard deviation]) on test data for UCF11 and Extended Yale datasets using kernel SVMs with the kernel formula given in Eq. (14.18) with degrees $1 \le d \le 4$ for different values of multilinear ranks.

Polynomial kernel's degree	Database	m-ranks	FAKSETT	HOSVD
$d = 1$	UCF11	$[2, 2, 2, 2]$	$0.52(10^{-2})$	$\mathbf{0.54(10^{-2})}$
	UCF11	$[3, 3, 3, 2]$	$0.54(10^{-2})$	$\mathbf{0.57(10^{-2})}$
	Extended	$[1, 2, 2, 1]$	$0.41(10^{-2})$	$0.6(10^{-2})$
$d = 2$	UCF11	$[2, 2, 2, 2]$	$0.71(10^{-2})$	$\mathbf{0.83(10^{-2})}$
	UCF11	$[3, 3, 3, 3]$	$0.77(10^{-2})$	$\mathbf{0.84(10^{-2})}$
	Extended	$[1, 2, 2, 1]$	$0.97(10^{-2})$	$\mathbf{1(0)}$
$d = 3$	UCF11	$[2, 2, 2, 2]$	$0.71(10^{-2})$	$\mathbf{0.85(10^{-2})}$
	UCF11	$[3, 3, 3, 3]$	$0.74(10^{-2})$	$\mathbf{0.83(10^{-2})}$
	Extended	$[1, 2, 2, 1]$	$0.99(10^{-2})$	$\mathbf{1(0)}$
$d = 4$	UCF11	$[2, 2, 2, 2]$	$0.68(10^{-2})$	$\mathbf{0.83(10^{-2})}$
	UCF11	$[3, 3, 3, 3]$	$0.67(10^{-2})$	$\mathbf{0.84(10^{-2})}$
	Extended	$[1, 2, 2, 1]$	$0.98(10^{-2})$	$\mathbf{1(0)}$

Table 14.5 Accuracy scores (mean accuracy [standard deviation]) on test data for the UCF11 dataset using the Gaussian–Euclidean kernel given in Eq. (14.20).

m-ranks	FAKSETT	HOSVD
$[1, 1, 1, 1]$	$0.62(10^{-2})$	$\mathbf{0.63(10^{-2})}$
$[2, 2, 2, 2]$	$0.56(10^{-2})$	$\mathbf{0.62(10^{-2})}$
$[3, 3, 3, 3]$	$0.57(10^{-2})$	$\mathbf{0.61(10^{-2})}$

of TD with orthonormal factors. This is a two-step approach that, firstly, breaks the dimensionality of a high-order TD based on the TT-SVD/TT-HSVD algorithm, transforming it into a train of third-order TDs with known structure. Secondly, it applies a truncated SVD on the second unfoldings of the TT cores to recover the corresponding projector matrix. We show theoretically and numerically that this method is faster than the HOSVD algorithm. This approach is then applied to a more general learning method. The proposed supervised leaning scheme is called FAKSETT, for Fast Kernel Subspace Estimation based on Tensor Train decomposition. By capitalizing on TTD, the FAKSETT approach allows us to classify multidimensional datasets with a lower complexity compared to the state-of-the-art method. Numerical simulations on real datasets show the effectiveness of the proposed FAKSETT scheme in terms of classification accuracy and computational time compared to the state-of-the-art method.

References

[1] R. Badeau, R. Boyer, Fast multilinear singular value decomposition for structured tensors, SIAM Journal on Matrix Analysis and Applications 30 (2008) 1008–1021.

[2] J. Ballani, L. Grasedyck, M. Kluge, Black box approximation of tensors in hierarchical Tucker format, Linear Algebra and Its Applications 438 (2) (2013) 639–657.

[3] J. Berge, the k-rank of a Khatri-Rao product, Unpublished Note, Heijmans Institute of Psychological Research, University of Groningen, the Netherlands, 2000.

[4] G. Bergqvist, E. Larsson, The higher-order singular value decomposition: theory and an application [lecture notes], IEEE Signal Processing Magazine 27 (3) (2010) 151–154.

[5] M. Boussé, O. Debals, L.D. Lathauwer, A tensor-based method for large-scale blind source separation using segmentation, IEEE Transactions on Signal Processing 65 (2016) 346–358.

[6] R. Boyer, R. Badeau, Adaptive multilinear SVD for structured tensors, in: IEEE International Conference on Acoustics, Speech and Signal Processing (ICASSP), 2006.

[7] R. Boyer, R. Badeau, G. Favier, Fast orthogonal decomposition of Volterra cubic kernels using oblique unfolding, in: 36th IEEE International Conference on Acoustics, Speech and Signal Processing, 2011.

[8] J. Carroll, J.-J. Chang, Analysis of individual differences in multidimensional scaling via an n-way generalization of 'Eckart-Young' decomposition, Psychometrika 35 (3) (1970) 283–319.

[9] J.-C.B. Christopher, A tutorial on support vector machines for pattern recognition, Data Mining and Knowledge Discovery 2 (2) (1998) 121–167.

[10] A. Cichocki, Era of Big Data Processing: A New Approach via Tensor Networks and Tensor Decompositions, CoRR, 2014.

[11] A. Cichocki, Tensor networks for big data analytics and large-scale optimization problems, arXiv preprint, arXiv:1407.3124, 2014.

[12] A. Cichocki, D. Mandic, L. De Lathauwer, G. Zhou, Q. Zhao, C. Caiafa, A. Huy, Tensor decompositions for signal processing applications, IEEE Signal Processing Magazine 32 (2015) 145–163.

[13] A. de Almeida, G. Favier, J. Mota, A constrained factor decomposition with application to MIMO antenna systems, IEEE Transactions on Signal Processing 56 (2008) 2429–2442.

[14] L. De Lathauwer, B. De Moor, J. Vandewalle, A multilinear singular value decomposition, SIAM Journal on Matrix Analysis and Applications 21 (2000) 1253–1278.

[15] L. De Lathauwer, B. De Moor, J. Vandewalle, On the best rank-1 and rank-$(r_1, r_2, ..., r_n)$ approximation of higher-order tensors, SIAM Journal on Matrix Analysis and Applications 21 (4) (2006) 1324–1342.

[16] I. Domanov, L. De Lathauwer, Canonical polyadic decomposition of third-order tensors: relaxed uniqueness conditions and algebraic algorithm, Linear Algebra and Its Applications 513 (Supplement C) (2017) 342–375.

[17] C. Eckart, G. Young, The approximation of one matrix by another of lower rank, Psychometrika (1936) 211–218.

[18] G. Favier, A. de Almeida, Tensor space-time-frequency coding with semi-blind receivers for MIMO wireless communication systems, IEEE Transactions on Signal Processing 62 (2014) 5987–6002.

[19] A. Georghiades, P. Belhumeur, J. Kriegman, From few to many: illumination cone models for face recognition under variable lighting and pose, IEEE Transactions on Pattern Analysis and Machine Intelligence 23 (6) (2001) 643–660.

[20] G.H. Golub, C.F. van Loan, Matrix Computations, 4th edition, The Johns Hopkins University Press, Baltimore, 2013.

[21] L. Grasedyck, Hierarchical singular value decomposition of tensors, SIAM Journal on Matrix Analysis and Applications 31 (2010) 2029–2054.

[22] L. Grasedyck, W. Hackbusch, An introduction to hierarchical (h-) rank and TT-rank of tensors with examples, Computational Methods in Applied Mathematics 11 (3) (2011) 291–304.

[23] L. Grasedyck, D. Kressner, C. Tobler, A literature survey of low-rank tensor approximation techniques, CGAMM-Mitteilungen 36 (3) (2013) 53–78.

[24] W. Hackbusch, S. Kühn, A new scheme for the tensor representation, The Journal of Fourier Analysis and Applications 15 (2009) 706.

[25] R.A. Harshman, Foundations of the PARAFAC procedure: models and conditions for an explanatory multimodal factor analysis, UCLA Working Papers in Phonetics 16 (1970) 1–84.

[26] L. He, X. Kong, S.Y. Philip, B.A. Ragin, Z. Hao, X. Yang Dusk, A dual structure-preserving kernel for supervised tensor learning with applications to neuroimages, CoRR, arXiv:1407.8289 [abs], 2014.

[27] C.J. Hillar, L.-H. Lim, Most tensor problems are NP-hard, Journal of the ACM 60 (6) (Nov. 2013) 45:1–45:39.

[28] F.L. Hitchcock, Multiple invariants and generalized rank of a p-way matrix or tensor, Journal of Mathematics and Physics 7 (1927) 39–79.

[29] S. Jayasumana, R. Hartley, M. Salzmann, H. Li, M. Harandi, Kernel methods on Riemannian manifolds with Gaussian RBF kernels, IEEE Transactions on Pattern Analysis and Machine Intelligence 37 (12) (2015) 2464–2477.

[30] L. Jingen, L. Jiebo, S. Mubarak, Recognizing realistic actions from videos "in the wild.", in: 2009 IEEE Conference on Computer Vision and Pattern Recognition, 2009, pp. 1996–2003.

[31] V. Kazeev, O. Reichmann, C. Schwab, Low-rank tensor structure of linear diffusion operators in the TT and QTT formats, Linear Algebra and Its Applications 438 (11) (2013) 4204–4221.

[32] B. Khoromskij, O($d \log N$)-quantics approximation of n-d tensors in high-dimensional numerical modeling, Constructive Approximation 34 (2) (2011) 257–280.

[33] T.G. Kolda, B.W. Bader, Tensor decompositions and applications, SIAM Review 51 (2009) 455–500.

[34] D. Kressner, M. Steinlechner, B. Vandereycken, Low-rank tensor completion by Riemannian optimization, BIT Numerical Mathematics 54 (2014) 447–468.

[35] S. Lauritzen, Graphical Models, vol. 17, Clarendon Press, 1996.

[36] N. Lee, A. Cichocki, Very large-scale singular value decomposition using tensor train networks, arXiv:1410.6895v2, 2014.

[37] N. Li, S. Kindermann, C. Navasca, Some convergence results on the regularized alternating least-squares method for tensor decomposition, Linear Algebra and Its Applications 438 (2) (2013) 796–812.

[38] N. Sidiropoulos, L.D. Lathauwer, X. Fu, K. Huang, E. Papalexakis, C. Faloutsos, Tensor decomposition for signal processing and machine learning, IEEE Transactions on Signal Processing 65 (2017) 3551–3582.

[39] I. Oseledets, Tensor-train decomposition, SIAM Journal on Scientific Computing 33 (5) (2011) 2295–2317.

[40] I. Oseledets, E. Tyrtyshnikov, Breaking the curse of dimensionality, or how to use SVD in many dimensions, SIAM Journal on Scientific Computing 31 (2009) 3744–3759.

[41] I. Oseledets, E. Tyrtyshnikov, TT-cross approximation for multidimensional arrays, Linear Algebra and Its Applications 432 (1) (2010) 70–88.

[42] J.K.Y. Panagakis, A. Anandkumar, M. Pantic, Tensorly: tensor learning in python, Journal of Machine Learning Research 20 (1) (Jan. 2019) 925–930.

[43] R. Orus, A practical introduction to tensor networks: matrix product states and projected entangled pair states, Annals of Physics 349 (2014) 117–158.

[44] S. Sahnoun, K. Usevich, P. Comon, Joint source estimation and localization, IEEE Transactions on Signal Processing 63 (10) (2015) 2485–2495.

[45] A. Sandryhaila, J. Moura, Big data analysis with signal processing on graphs: representation and processing of massive data sets with irregular structure, IEEE Signal Processing Magazine 31 (5) (2014) 80–90.

[46] M. Signoretto, L.D. Lathauwer, A.K. Suykens, A.K. Johan, A kernel-based framework to tensorial data analysis, Neural Networks: the Official Journal the International Neural Network Society 24 (8) (2011) 861–874.

[47] C.D. Silva, F. Herrmann, Optimization on the hierarchical Tucker manifold – applications to tensor completion, Linear Algebra and Its Applications 481 (Supplement C) (2015) 131–173.

[48] A.J. Smola, S. Bernhard, A tutorial on support vector regression, Statistics and Computing 14 (3) (2004) 199–222.

[49] M. Sørensen, L. De Lathauwer, Multidimensional harmonic retrieval via coupled canonical polyadic decomposition – part I: model and identifiability, IEEE Transactions on Signal Processing 65 (2016) 517–527.

[50] A. Stegeman, N. Sidiropoulos, On Kruskal's uniqueness condition for the candecomp/parafac decomposition, Linear Algebra and Its Applications 420 (2) (2007) 540–552.

[51] L. Tucker, Some mathematical notes on three-mode factor analysis, Psychometrika 31 (3) (1966) 279–311.

[52] A. Uschmajew, B. Vandereycken, The geometry of algorithms using hierarchical tensors, Linear Algebra and Its Applications 439 (1) (2013) 133–166.

[53] L. Ximenes, G. Favier, A. de Almeida, Y. Silva, PARAFAC-PARATUCK semi-blind receivers for two-hop cooperative MIMO relay systems, IEEE Transactions on Signal Processing 62 (2014) 3604–3615.

[54] Y. Zniyed, R. Boyer, A. de Almedia, G. Favier, High-order tensor factorization via trains of coupled third-order cp and Tucker decompositions, Linear Algebra and Its Applications (LAA) 588 (2020) 304–337.

[55] Y. Zniyed, R. Boyer, A. de Almedia, G. Favier, A tt-based hierarchical framework for decomposing high-order tensors, SIAM Journal on Scientific Computing (SISC) 42 (2020) 822–848.

Index

CPI Antony Rowe
Eastbourne, UK
April 22, 2024

new york in store

valérie weill & philippe chancel

new york in store

preface by harry mathews

 Thames & Hudson

First published in the United Kingdom in 2007 by
Thames & Hudson Ltd, 181A High Holborn, London WC1V 7QX

www.thamesandhudson.com

Photographs © 2007 Philippe Chancel
New York in Store © 2007 Thames & Hudson Ltd, London
Preface © 2007 Harry Mathews

British Library Cataloguing-in-Publication Data
A catalogue record for this book is available from
the British Library

ISBN-13: 978-0-500-51339-2
ISBN-10: 0-500-51339-2

Printed and bound in China by Midas Printing

preface

by harry mathews

A Unicyclist's Periscope

This is perfectly crazy. The city was laid out to be a grid, something simple, easy to get around in, with a handful of balloons stuck here and there to make it interesting—one might on reflection even say that Broadway takes off like a balloon. But the present point is that something so simple makes you see different places as the same. There's no denying it: a depressing unity of perspective has got me totally lost.

Where is she? For the moment the perspective is nil, I think I'm looking at a snake fight like Laocoön's, 115 on a mean close-up grid where moments of domestic felicity are proposed as the outcome. Really? So I go into a store I see elsewhere. (It's an imposed itinerary, shopwindow to shopwindow—to find her, my own her, the one with the balloons.) This is a family place at least, judging by the photographs on the wall, which 117 are reflections of public and private successes—but does anyone care? They're all askew, except for the crowning high altar with its reflection of sunlight:

this is the shrine of pasta, green and yellow, in six thicknesses—a perspective that makes me hungry. You were on your way to a vacation in Touraine, where *ballons* are other things—you couldn't know.

Bring me wines in correct order, bring me a proper grid instead of these slant-legged housewives, 113 not desperate, mind you, but delicious, even—see for yourself—"deliciously devious," meaning a bracelet on each rubber glove and a see-through dance into passing-taxi-land, and golden bottled shelves that are no reflection of these other, no-nonsense racks for useful metal machines, too packed together maybe, 119 but the grid orders the mess by means of ten governing chairs overhead, whether truly suspended or a trick of perspective we'll never know; whereas if we look at this nicely framed window, we clearly have three cakes like 111 balloons, three like cigar boxes, three like castles, not to mention red hearts like smaller balloons—obviously tempting, although I feel I might prefer the deli two or so doors down that you see reflected in the door; or a can of soup—notice the minestrone item missing in this [121] perspective-free (and also balloon-free) exemplary orderliness, although it's hard to tell one from another —a reflection of the urban problem referred to above.

I'm far from home. But at least there's a glimpse of sky in the grid of vertical blinds at the kindly dentist's [109] where petunias play balloons. But what of the grid of barbells, weights, tough metal rack and posts, black [123] frames and bobbled tin ceiling? Words cannot justify the deep space squashed flat and the gang of Marvell Comics numbers painted on the wall but bulging to the front of the room. It's a slightly numbing but exuberant relief to go into a Chinese restaurant where the bal- [107] loons *are* the grid, and I wish Alice were here to kiss amidst this pink perfection—no, there's a chair out of [125] line. Nuts. I'll still take that kiss while I gaze at a tree against a pale sky above a man's suit, also pink—as for the grid, forget it (thank God for the divided glass and

the names to keep us from going happily to pieces). At least the multitudinous orchids are acting too proper [105] for words; perhaps their train-conductor guardians keep them in line. Decimal-free numbers price meat hunks shrouded by more sky, more traffic, but prosciut- tos in a jolly chorus line do their numbers precisely, like [127] true infra-cultural signs. I subsequently know better than to kiss an Amazonian parrot or two, even if they're both called Alice. Ouch! Grouch!—words they may well [103] utter. (Despite riotous appearances, their setting is assured not by a grid so much as an unfinished menorah—see below—crowned with feeders.)

And now, friends, for our ballooning intestinal [129] health, we go to an all-too-well documented if clean and orderly massage parlor. Out! Go on: and remem- ber these lovely suspended bodies, imprisoned like Bluebeard's wives; numbers, neither of bars, nor of [101] pilasters or hangers can define the massiveness of the grid that encloses them, them and the utopian illusions above and below—a horizon behind Spring Street! I kiss fifteen white and two black babies in medically correct toques to celebrate all mysteries beyond words (but why is one baby missing?) What vanishing point for this perspective? Probably the same as for the words and numbers of the fruit, and the fruit itself, oranges tumbling upwards backed with berried ranks straining to go against a fortification of cans.

It's too early to think of babies and oranges. Let's sit in a laundry cart and kiss, beloved Sandra, while the soap center gets its labels straightened, while we dream of inexhaustible numbers of groupers and bonefish waiting in the painted Caribbean, in the exquisite grid of the ocean's horizon and forty-eight fishing rods hanging straight up-and-down. And elsewhere are mild white perspective lines pointing to invisible glass panels reflecting another whiteness that sweetly clouds the kissing, fading paper colors; and more whiteness, lumpish this time, struggling (beneath jerseys with names many know) to achieve verticality and justify their on-sale price. Then a table empty of food and bowlers but so level and happy already with real and painted balloons (but I have to pass on the pot of gold, if not the rainbow). Rainbow colors in the glasses I pass (frames, lenses towering and teetering)—green, blue, red, white, yellow, pink, maroon—but no perspective to mitigate their glistening blindness.

So far to go, and no sign of food, only two blue cool chicks and one uptown type, bent legs entrancing perfect horizontalities. I'd rather kiss you, uncool Elaine. These calling cards are cute—they won't cooperate and be a decent grid. The names don't matter. But in the rumpus of jerseys and caps (with a white off-center post for stability) names certainly do matter (even I know Jeter) and numbers, too. And lo! at last an eatery comes to pass, seeming perfect, as if waiting for inspection. But there are blinds that slouch, and the jukebox says "Out of order." I kiss the place goodbye and move on to Abe Lebewohl's foursquare glass-and-silver kosher perspective; but can you believe the pictures (except for the sweet muddled side ones)? And there's no food at the Cake Shop! Unless you count "Cream Corn," an exactly aligned square in three rows of LP's on the wall, and there's food for the soul underneath ("Beautiful Savior") in the more lackadaisical racks. And such lovely faded colors and names!

Another chance for food: a dainty, sweet-toned alignment—the jumbled pastoral perspective of the wall tapestry is like Central Park in mid grid. An exit sign jarringly passes the rectangularity test; but who left that rumpled napkin on the table? A religious emporium makes me want to kiss you, Margot—saints, crèche, patriotic wreath, stabilizing strip of flag stuff— but how can I kiss you with that TV off, empty, and blue as the back wall?

Straight shelves of soft store-roasted food disgust me now (junk underneath, hypnotic rows of frosted bulbs). (I guess I should pass by the Agreement Department.) The grand supermarket parade is indifferent to names, with frozen foods for stragglers, containers and cans for troops, and a three-deep marching band of toilet paper—a perspective natural but less than appetizing. Shades are less manageable—no reflection on their usefulness, but can you neatly stack truncated cones in numbers?

Floor tiles point to a bend in (perhaps) the Rio Grande. Indifferent to the vista, pink chairs converse pleasantly and ignore the bicycle wheel. A blue, blue room: Heraklion gymnast on bull that I remember, here as if submerged; gridded beds, but ballooning pillows, and one bed has *slumped*. And to complete our dreams, vast shelves of white movies, and two racks of blue ones—are these blue movies? Are we completely prepared for Hanukkah? One shelf of plastic-wrapped silver menorahs, like a gauzy reflection of robed priests marching; two shelves like crowded square-rigged ships. Remember that there may be a python in the fitting closet of a magically vertical room, with its vintage numbers including Monument boots; and that an illusion of perspective may produce its converse—that leftmost mirror is in truth out of sight across the way.

"We're ready, come feast and converse with your neighbor!" Checkerboard tiles and counter clean, plates stacked, complete with an attendant at attention. Level old furniture, an upright skeleton, and babies in checkered numbers—the span of a lifetime— encourage the use of house-made lotions. And if you prefer action to reflection, one plunging crowded room before your eyes transforms rumpled and soiled to smooth and clean. I suggest you remember that the cat is real, unlike the dog bones, and is running the place. I myself do not remember having had a laundry bag as clean and bright as these, like rumps of Muslims in converse with their deity; or perhaps, balloons.

More like deflating balloons are rolls of fabric, but there is a reflection of their quality in their round tasseled seals, each a little phylactery crying "Unroll me!" And there are balloonlets that promise complete satisfaction, forty-four mozzarellas sweet as shmoos, no doubt in even greater numbers hanging on their unended horizontal bars. Under four square-framed makers and five grand pianos, numberless swirls confuse the floor's diagonal parquetry: castors' doing.

There is nothing I can remember about golf (at age six); but I salute the erect row of bags, like soldiers, like vases complete with clubhead flowers, and the very flat putting square. Also soldierlike but of converse sex, a squad of modish mannequins (from the army of alterable law) march against a reflection of eternal forms.

Straightness of spine and lampshade are not eternal forms. We see, however, pleasant ephemeral forms—wrinkled flag, round brass clock, that allow us to go on to the comforting details. Another consolation is a perfect shrinelike grid of thirty-five Nikes: we can virtually kiss, Madeleine, the feet of heroes and jerks. A lower disorder weakens the grid of shirts I next pass. A hazy, bluish, Dolomitic landscape manages to include a Brooklyn bakery at its pondside, complete with classic waitress; and classic Americans, heads or childhood figures, smile at us, completely bluebound except for Messrs. Ali and Columbus. At a newsstand (like Europe's, plus cigarettes, candy, and aspirin) we see our quintessential New York display-and-sale space, with a necessary alert genius presiding. I pass to another perfection: immaculate order with balloons, gumdrops, and floral lollipops added, before I go look at further utilitarian neatness: round clocks, fat curved arrows, square price cards showing how you can kiss the folks back at foreign homes.

The kid in the toy store's less lucky: where is *anything*? Go kiss the lad, sweetie pie! The masters of masquerade are an unscary, unfunny mess, I guess they're striving for completeness (Darth Vader and Superman, twice each). Information and admission at MoMA restore a perfect order—but where did the people go? And now behold a painted city, Chrysler Building included, and a furnished earth, and we see that heaven is visually ours, with a special offer in centered neon, we needn't care what is where but pass into real human space, the two conversely dressed men making strict alignments passable via their lively backs. Maybe the two boys reading menus will complete the pattern (one has a finger up his nose, the other's balloonish head is like those of the kindly oriental stars above him).

Bright brass stiff-standing posts are gentled by deferential plush dividers, all spic and span—see the sweepers resting behind?—waiting for a human surge. Siblings and relatives in the even stricter array of skateboards kiss and call one another across its riotous grid. When you go into the Barclay, you look past, not at, the big ball of lilies and roses; for the bar, 183 I suspect you go right at the back. But don't blame drink if you're confused by reflectors swamped by reflection passing the Flash Clinic. (A man is standing 47 near the delivery van.)

A second-hand store may be a complete second-hand mess, but soft-colored shirts are demurely 185 dancing in line for you.

It's hard to think of kissing this mannequin— perhaps she was beheaded by the crashed chandelier, 45 although fox and raised stitches are intact. I'll see you at the bookstore, Zoe, and we'll kiss in the back among slack quiet titles under their straight bars of light. 187 Remember Bluebeard's wives? They're back again, gazing across the reflected street at the shoes they can 43 no longer escape in. Completely naked mannequins are ranged in order here: the army of unalterable law, 189 even by halves or seated, like the immortals they are.

Back to mortality and the aching feet on which we move—their outlines on glass and floormat lead us 41 into this pristine and explicit place. Globes sprouting lilium, globed fruit, and two young heads are 191 welcome to another and no less rectangular place (a splinter of doorlight and the view of a tousled bed also reassure us).

Gravely framed family scenes (remember the pasta shrine!) surmount Spanish-speaking pillboxes 39 that seem to move in sprightly dance, with no strings attached; whereas the Rx jars at serious CVS complete 193 a stricter if benign decorum.

We come to a scene, duly framed but quite unlike 37 what we've witnessed: "A Morning Fit for a Queen"— but the queen may well be dead, her space is like the netherworld, an unearthly form (her spirit? her underworld guide?) gazes through a melting place of reflections and misty gauze, with Park Avenue's real flowers in the oval on the wall to complete our con-

fusion. But "We The People" can withstand all mis- 195
leading reflections: here we remember our obligations
(issues in blue, prices in red, on white, over patriotic
stars). The consolations of wine move in massive per- 35
spective away from us; but I remember when you were
driving towards the "little town of Vouvray, on the road
to Amboise"—most unlike us here!—"where you can
drink a delicious sparkling wine." And not only that, as I
remember. Here a well-watered puppy looks out at
you, posing with knowledgeable sweetness: one who 197
will know his place.

　　With neither toe- nor fingernails for the puglike
driers, roundbacked chairs contemplate the waters of 33
Niagara, complete with their imaginary roar. A black
customer and one of many empty silvery chairs gaze 199
at a wall completely inset with TVs (five on, thirteen
blazing white). Sheets of ice cubes discourage water- 31
and juice-bottles on the move. A ceiling fan aligns its
fifth blade with the strip bisecting a case where are 201

placed square cakes lighted in mauve and crimson.
Macy's straight shelves lift bubble-like wine glasses, 29
packed, unpacked, and then topped with round slices
of lemon. These *ballons* don't make me remember
Thanksgiving balloons, not at all.

　　A man in front of a van pushes a stroller out of a 203
monstrous blender, part of a grid of similar machines
redly boxed in with others—simple enough compared
to the space in which seventeen spotlit fans and venti- 27
lators float with ambiguous brightness in the green
revision of what's behind us, including the store
truck. A coincidence of art echoes the starfish fan in
an outsize sunflower, from which a seabird carries 205
(one surmises) pharmaceutical promise towards
two unenviable musclemen. Misted glass invests nine
shelves of cakes with the promise not of food but of 25
Monet-like visual rapture. How stark in comparison,
and how useful, the informative grid (functions, dimensions, prices) of cartons, demos set up, buyables flat. 207

13

Elsewhere art resumes its spatial magic: all seems a grid of varied rectangles (boxes also) that we thor- 23 oughly ignore to discover the space beyond, a sumptuous hall with blue glass ceiling and walls and marble flooring, and even one contemplative couple bright at its edge. Not, however, among the disciplined sausages looped or stiff, as bright as the red *1* in "*one* 209 dollar and ninety-nine cents."

Ten TV monitors and a ceiling *under* them 21 promise calculated mistrust and a mind-boggling mix of plunging, near, and attractively disordered space. Beers shine bright above ranked tables where poppa 211 ketchups and momma napkins wait under the grid of smiling patrons of yore. Bound in a perfect frame, mundane sundries by the sublimation of art are confounded with the traffic outside: one shelf has turned 19 to asphalt.

What is art if not the preservation of asymmetry in an illusion of order? You may notice the varying brightness of the poker-shaded lamps, and the black 213 white-collar worker in the Philatelic window. The grid is clear and irrelevant, except to show us such things. I wish that Owney, mutt of promise and love, was trotting in his jingling jacket through this serene, obliging space.

We had begun with an inside view of the outside 17 city, three views in one little space, not credible or beautiful in their ethereal verticality, more inaccurate as memorials than art allows; while four blue apples don't pretend to remind us of apples: their promise is of crystal itself, even if on special sale…. The simple made complex, the complex clear, and a bunch of bright balloons saying farewell to your pleasures, 215 Valérie, dismissing the irrelevant grid.

the stores

TELEPHONE 212-245 5566
FAX   212-977 5424
TOLL FREE 877-88 JEWEL

LOUIS MARTIN JEWELERS
30 ROCKEFELLER PLAZA
54 WEST 50th ST
NEW YORK N.Y. 10112-1507

X _____   FINE JEWELRY

VISIT US ON OUR WEBSITE WWW.LMJEWEL.COM

GENUINE CRYSTAL
SMALL APPLE
YOUR CHOICE
SPECIAL SALE
$16 EA

GENUINE CRYSTAL
TRAIN SET
5PC SET
SPECIAL SALE
$49 90 SET

99¢ DISCOUNT CENTER 99C
440 EAST 14ST
NEW YORK NY 10009
212 533 1683

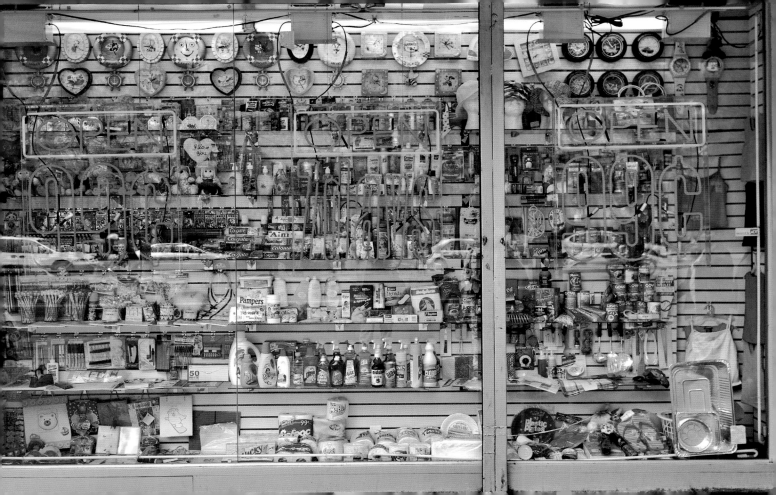

ZABARS®

2245 Broadway (at 80th Street)

New York, NY 10024 • (212) 787-2000

www.zabars.com

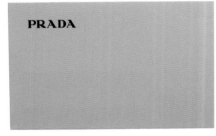

Purifying Toner/Face
Purifying Milk/Face
Hydrating Serum/Face
Hydrating Gel Cream/Face
Soothing Cream/Face
Purifying Gel/Face
Hydrating Cream/Face
Hydrating Serum/Body

EST. 1912

Egidio Pastry Shop Inc.

ITALIAN & FRENCH PASTRY
CAPPUCCINO AND ESPRESSO
WEDDING & BIRTHDAY CAKES
(718) 295-6077
FAX: (718) 295-1468

CARMELA LUCCIOLA

622 EAST 187TH ST.
BRONX, N.Y. 10458

GRACIOUS HOME®

Please Tell Macy*s How My Service Was Today @www.fds.com

Information
Service Ambassador
macy$

151 West 34th Street
New York, N.Y. 10001
(212) 494-2098 / 7373
Fax (212) 494-1057

OPEN 24 HOURS   **TEL:(212) 721-0285**

2383 BROADWAY FRUIT & VEGETABLE
Deli, Cold Cut, Fruit, Veg., Flower
Imported Grocery, Cold Beer, Cigarette, Soda

2383 BROADWAY
(87TH-88TH ST.)
FREE DELIVERY   NEW YORK, NY 10024

Mon. - Sat.: 9:30am-10:00pm
Sun.: 10:00am- 8:00pm

NAIL & MORE

Tel : (212) 595-6500

2113 Broadway
(Bet. 73 & 74St.)
New York, NY 10023

crush
WINE CO.

info@crushwineco.com

153 East 57th Street
New York, NY 10022
T: 212.980.WINE
F: 212.980.9468

The Waldorf-Astoria

301 PARK AVENUE, NEW YORK, NY 10022-6897
TELEPHONE 212.355.3000 FAX 212.872.7272
FOR RESERVATIONS PLEASE CALL 1 800 HILTONS
OR CALL US DIRECTLY AT 1 800 WALDORF
WEB SITE: WWW.WALDORF.COM

A MORNING FIT FOR A QUEEN

Dr. Rico Pérez

SALUD
EN
CUERPO Y ALMA®

ORLANDO
154 SOUTH SEMORAN BLVD.
ORLANDO, FL 32807
(407) 249-0088

HIALEAH
6500 W. 4 AVE., SUITE 45
HIALEAH, FL 33012
(305) 827-6556

ORDENES:
1-800-633-6799
www.dr-ricoperez.com

MIAMI
2295 CORAL WAY
MIAMI, FL 33145
1 (800) 633-6799 (305) 854-6200

OPEN

VISA

BODYWORK-FOOT RUB

PRICE LIST FOR BODYWORK
15 MINUTES.....................$15
30 MINUTES.....................$25
45 MINUTES.....................$35
60 MINUTES.....................$45
40 MINUTES(FOOT RUB)...$38
AFTER 10 VISITS, GET ONE FREE (EQUAL VALUE)

THANK YOU

YVES SAINT LAURENT
■ *rive gauche* ■

855 Madison Avenue New York, NY 10021
TEL +212.988.3821 FAX +212.517.4814
ysl.com

(212) 872-2840

BERGDORF GOODMAN
754 FIFTH AVENUE · NEW YORK, NY 10019-2581
·ON THE PLAZA·

DIEGO ERAZO-VILLAO
ON 5IVE SPORTSWEAR

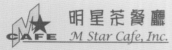

明星茶餐廳
M Star Cafe, Inc.

七 天 營 業
Free Delivery
免 費 送 餐

地藏臣街19號
（孔子大廈對面）
19 DIVISION STREET
NEW YORK, NY 10002
TEL 212-966-8988
　　212-966-4882

PCC
90$ Manhattan Ave
BROOKLYN NY 11222

150 Fulton St
News Stand Subway
212 227-0976 4,5 Train
platform

60

atmos

RICHARD S. WEINBERG, D.C.

GREENPOINT CHIROPRACTIC CENTER
Mon. to Fri. 10 -7 Sat. 10 - 1

880 Manhattan Ave.
Brooklyn, NY 11222   (718) 389-1159

Gil Boggs
Academy Director

GOLF CLUB CHELSEA PIERS

Golf Academy

The Golf Club
Chelsea Piers - Pier 59
New York, New York 10011

212.336.6444
Fax 212.336.6410
boggsg@chelseapiers.com

Pepato
$4.99 lb

Aged
Cacciocavallo
On Sale 8.99 per lb

Lic #0926784

8171

WASH · DRY · FOLD

ABC
DryCleaners & Laundromat
619 HUDSON ST. • NEW YORK, NY 10014
(212) 620-0899

DATE	4/25		$28.00 ¢
NAME	Lacher		

ADDRESS/
PHONE   APT.

Ready	MON	TUE	WED	THU	FRI	SAT	AM	PM
		3 lbs						
		Green						
		Soft 1.25						

Not responsible for shrinkage, fading, trimmings, pads, buckles, beads, belts, buttons, or goods left over 30 days. Curtains, silks and dye work done at customer's risk. No goods returned without ticket. **NOT RESPONSIBLE FOR FIRE OR BURGLARY.**

70

J & J HARMONY CLEANERS

71 UNIVERSITY PLACE   212-420-9574
NEW YORK, N.Y. 10003

THANK YOU

HECTOR'S CAFE RESTAURANT
44 LITTLE WEST 12TH ST.
NEW YORK, NY 10014
212-206-7592

FOR BEING PART OF OUR SUCCESS

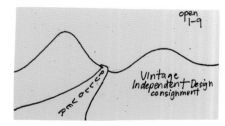

open
1-9

Vintage
Independent Design
consignment

212-691-1281   Fax 212-627-1095
                      Linda Samuels

**World
Video**

New York's Best Selection of Videos
51 Greenwich Ave. New York NY 10014

Yummy Taco

The Fresh Tortillas As
Taco Tex-Mexican Food

**941 MANHATTAN AVE.
BROOKLYN, NY 11222**

TEL: (718) 349-7731
(718) 349-7632

**FAST FREE
DELIVERY**
(Min. $5.00)

- We Are Open Public Holidays.
- We Use Natural Ingredients Only.
- We Do Catering of Small or Large Parties.
- We Are Open Seven Days a Week
- We Use Olive Oil Only

STORE HOURS
Mon. - Thurs.: 11:30 am - 11:30 pm
Fri. & Sat.: 11:30 am - 12:00 mid.
Sunday: 12:00 noon - 11:30 pm

SAN PABLO
LIBRERIA
CATOLICA

VotiyeCandles

Baking Done
on Premises

Phone: 718-392-1222
Fax 718-392-1380
www.courtdiner.com

Catering for
All Occasions

Free
Delivery
24 Hours

COURT SQUARE
DINER

45-30 23rd Street • Long Island City, NY 11101

MONDAY - FRIDAY
9AM - 7PM

THE OFFICIAL PRESS

Complete Printing Service

159 WEST 26TH STREET • NEW YORK, N.Y. 10001
TEL: (212) 244-5320/675-2529 • FAX: (212) 691-9264
E-MAIL: OFFICIALPRESS@EARTHLINK.NET

A.R. TRAPP OPTICIANS

488 MADISON AVENUE
BET. 51st & 52nd STREET
NEW YORK, N.Y. 10022

ANDREW JANEDIS
PRESIDENT

(212) 752-6890
FAX (212) 752-6891

OPEN 7 DAYS   TEL/FAX (718) 389-9670

DREAM FISHING TACKLE
(IMPORTERS OF FINEST EUROPEAN FISHING TACKLE)

ATTN: 673 MANHATTAN AVENUE
ROBERT PISKORSKI   BROOKLYN, N.Y. 11222

Community Store
Soho

ny4store@americanapparel.net

American Apparel
121 Spring St.
New York, NY 10012
Phone: (212) 226-4880
Fax: (212) 226-4887

www.americanapparel.net

American Apparel™ aa

NO
PEDDLERS

PETLAND DISCOUNTS #93
846 MANHATTAN AVE.
GREEN POINT, NY 11222
(718) 349-6370

FOLIAGE PARADISE INC.

112 W. 28TH ST.(BET. 6 & 7 AVE.), N.Y., N.Y. 10001
PHONE (212) 675-9696 • FAX (212) 675-0501

Design Specialists
Interior • Exterior
Landscaping • Maintenance
Home • Office

永順海鮮酒樓
Wing Shoon Seafood Restaurant

紐約華埠東百老匯165號
165 East Broadway, New York, NY 10002
Tel: (212) 780-0238 • (212) 780-0217

Neil R. Mate, DDS
Terry D. Liebman, DDS

947 Manhattan Avenue
Brooklyn, NY 11222
718-389-4266 • 718-389-7259(Fax)
www.ManhattanAvenueDental.com

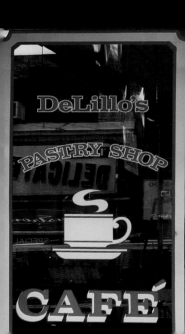

DeLillo's

PASTRY SHOP

CAFÉ

HENRI BENDEL
NEW YORK

712 FIFTH AVENUE NEW YORK NY 10019
212 904 7976

GRACIOUS HOME

Gamal Sarour
Assistant Manager
Housewares

1220 Third Avenue, New York, NY 10021
Tel: (212) 517-6300   Fax: 212-249-1534

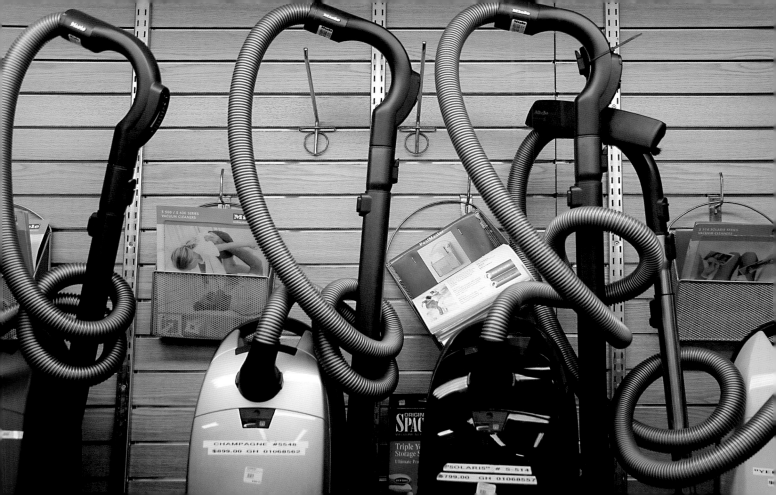

(718) 367-3799

Borgatti's
Ravioli & Egg Noodles

Tues. - Sat. 9 am - 6 pm
Sunday 8 am - 1 pm
Closed Mondays

632 East 187th Street
Bronx, NY 10458

廚 CHEF 都

Restaurant Supplies

294-298 BOWERY (COR. E. HOUSTON ST.) N.Y., N.Y, 10012

(N.Y.) (212) 254-6644   USA-1-800-228-6141

GRISTEDE'S FOODS, INC.
SUPERMARKETS

Serving New York
For 100 Years

Cell: 646-235-9758
Fax: 212-496-3941
NGreer@gristedes.com

823 Eleventh Avenue
New York, NY 10019

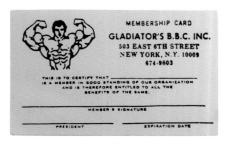

MEMBERSHIP CARD

GLADIATOR'S B.B.C. INC.
503 EAST 6TH STREET
NEW YORK, N.Y. 10009
674-9803

THIS IS TO CERTIFY THAT _____
IS A MEMBER IN GOOD STANDING OF OUR ORGANIZATION
AND IS THEREFORE ENTITLED TO ALL THE
BENEFITS OF THE SAME.

_____
MEMBER'S SIGNATURE

_____   _____
PRESIDENT   EXPIRATION DATE

243 West 125th Street, New York, N.Y. 10027

www.portabellastores.com   (212) 663-6375

PLEASE TURN OVER FOR OTHER LOCATIONS

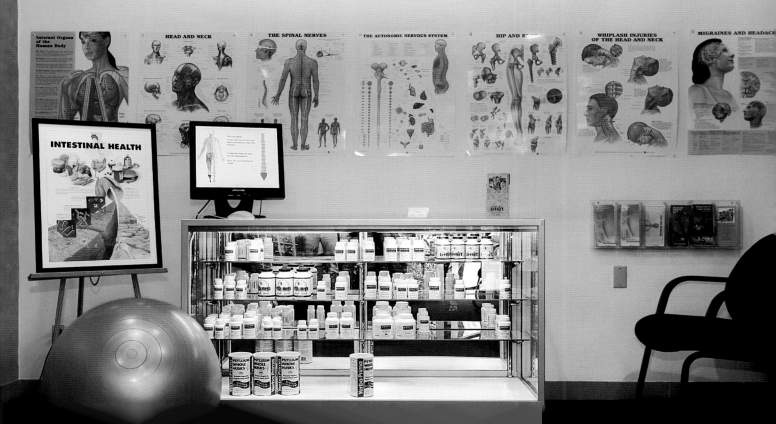

F·A·O·SCHWARZ

767 Fifth Avenue, New York, NY 10153
(212) 644-9400 FAX (212) 239–7211
www.fao.com

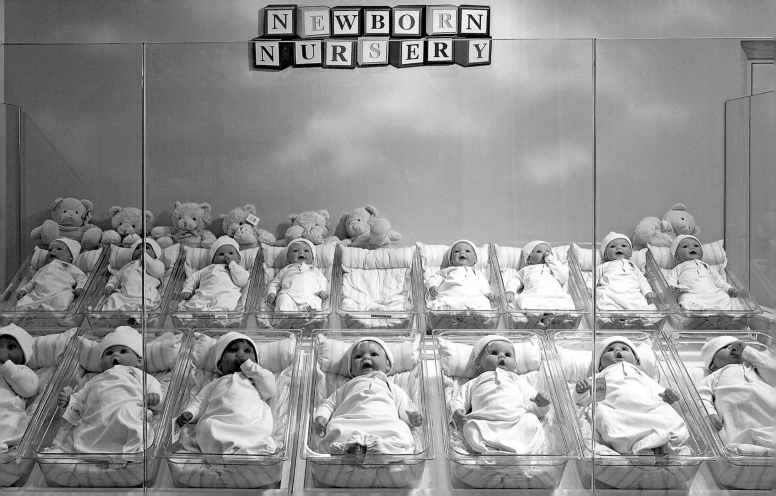

```
        CLEAN HOUSE
   2429  ARTHUR AVENUE
   BRONX NEW YORK 10458




   07/16/05 11:05AM      02
   123456 #0769

   NO SALE


        CLEAN HOUSE
   2429  ARTHUR AVENUE
   BRONX NEW YORK 10458




   07/16/05 11:20AM      02
   123456 #0770

   NO SALE
```

SOAP CENTER

SOAP
BLEACH
SOFTENERS
LAUNDRY BAGS

OUT OF PRODUCT

1. INSERT CARD
2. PUSH BUTTON BELOW
   FOR SELECTION
3. REMOVE CARD

.50¢ EACH.

VENDMASTER BY VEND-RITE CHICAGO, IL 60647

Catherine Deas
Party Coordinator

AMF *Always Means Fun!* ™

AMF Chelsea Piers Lanes
Pier 60   (212) 835-2695 Telephone
23rd St. & West Side Hwy.   (212) 337-9984 Facsimile
New York, NY 10011

ST. JOHN

BOUTIQUE
Wardrobe Consultant

DON KLEIN
665 Fifth Avenue • New York, NY 10022 • Tel. (212) 755-5252 • Fax (212) 755-1829
www.stjohnknits.com

(212) 244-4544   Fax: (212) 594-1696

MODELL'S
SPORTING GOODS®
Gotta Go To Mo's SINCE 1889

1293 Broadway, New York , N.Y . 10001

2ND AVE DELI

KOSHER RESTAURANT AND CATERERS

156 Second Avenue
(Corner 10th Street)
New York, NY 10003

Tel. (212) 677-0606
Fax (212) 477-5327

Angel's Grill

SPANISH & AMERICAN FOOD

720 E. 187ST.
(cor. Crotona Ave.)
Bronx, NY   Tel.(718) 329-8828

TEL: 212/966-2757   9:30 – 5:00
FAX: 212/334-6129   CLOSED SUN. & MON.

Just Shades
SILK • PARCHMENT • PAPER
LAMP SHADES

                            21 SPRING STREET
                            NEW YORK, NY 10012
CONNIE RAKOWER   E-mail: justshadesny@verizon.net
STEVE RAKOWER   Website: www.justshadesny.com

abc home
888 broadway
new york, ny 10003
212 473 3000
fax 212 777 5341

B. RUBIN   ANTIQUE REPRODUCTIONS

Grand Sterling Co.

"The most trusted name in silver"

4921 13th AVENUE	345 GRAND ST.
BROOKLYN, NY 11219	NEW YORK, NY 10002
(718) 854-0623	(212) 674-6450
FAX: 854-1243	FAX: 979-0578

Kiehl's

SINCE 1851

NEW YORK FLAGSHIP STORE

109 THIRD AVENUE, NEW YORK, NY 10003
PHONE (212) 677-3171 FAX (212) 674-3544
www.kiehls.com

(212) 477-3235   fax (212) 477-6769

Mikey's Pet Shop, Inc.

130 East 7th Street NYC 10009 (open 7 days 9-9 Sun. 12-8)

STEINWAY & SONS

Steinway Hall

212 246-1100
Fax 212 397-4621
Service 718 204-3131

109 West 57th Street
New York, NY 10019-2202

PRADA

575 Broadway
10012 New York USA
phone +1.212.334 8888
fax +1.212.274 1043

•Marché Madison•

931 MADISON AVENUE   TEL: 212/794-3360
NEW YORK, NY 10021   FAX: 212/772-3412

(718) 855-1921
Modell's
360 Fulton
St.

BARNES&NOBLE

BOOKSELLERS

396 Avenue of the Americas
New York, NY 10011

(212) 674-8780   Fax (212) 475-9082

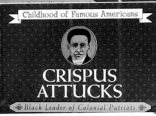
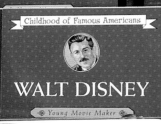

DYLAN'S CANDY BAR
315 East 62nd Street
New York, New York 10021

www.dylanscandybar.com

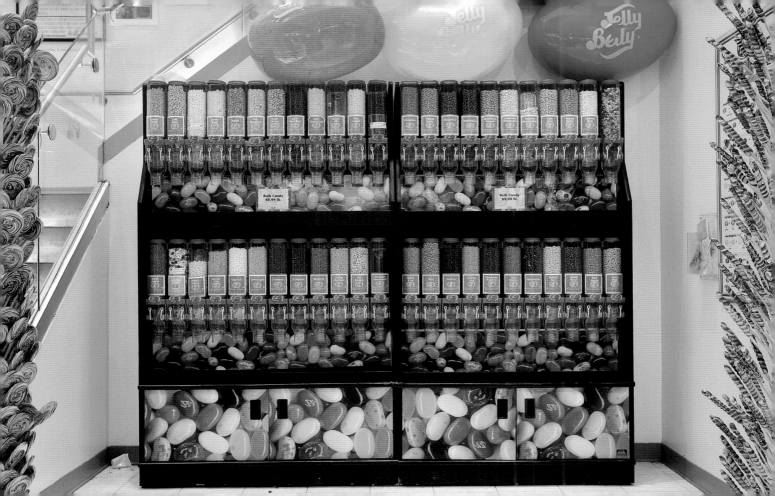

270 Seventh Avenue • New York, New York 10001
(917) 344-1555 • Fax (917) 344-1566
Website: www.buybuybaby.com

General Admission
$20.00

Adult
Sun   10:36 AM
4/24/05

VIRGINIA
TICKETS
2161994

The Museum of Modern Art

Information

Ford Family Programs
A Closer Look
for Kids
(5-10 year-olds only)

Gallery Talks

Will Call
Pick-up

Will Call
Pick-up

Will Call
Pick-up
Only

EMPIRE STATE BUILDING OBSERVATORY

Observatory Only

With this ticket, all New York as far
as you can see, and New Jersey too!

Adult (18—61)	$14
Youth (12—17)	$13
Child (6—11)	$9
Senior (62+)	$13
Military (with ID)	$12

Observatory+AudioView

Upgrade your experience

With this ticket, you'll love seeing the view and
hearing Tony the cab driver give you the scoop.

Adult (18—61)	$20
Youth (12—17)	$19
Child (6—11)	$17
Senior (62+)	$19
Military (with ID)	$18

What's an AudioView?

A recorded program in seven 3-minute segments,
one for each part of the view, numbered on the fence.
Listen in any order. Stop and start when you want.

CitiPass Discount Book

(Observatory+AudioView plus 5 NY attractions)
Best tourist deal in the city!

Adult (18—61)	$53
Youth (12—17)	$41
Child (6—11)	$41
Senior (62+)	$52

Just tell the cashier which ticket you want.

INTERCONTINENTAL.
THE BARCLAY
NEW YORK

111 East 48th Street, New York, NY 10017
Tel:(212)755-5900   Fax:(212)644-0079
www.new-york.intercontinental.com • barclay@interconti.com

Miracle Trading Corp.

SHIMON ZLOTNIKOV
EXECUTIVE VICE PRESIDENT

1. 12 WARREN STR.

PHONE: (212) 791-3119
FAX: (212) 962-4557
PHONE 2: (212) 962-4556
EMAIL: SHIMZLOT@AOL.COM

2. 28 WARREN STREET
   NEW YORK, NY 10007

shirts

BERNSTEIN
d i s p l a y

DOREEN MANZI
SALES

151 WEST 25TH STREET
NEW YORK, NY 10001
T 212 337 9578
T 212 683 2406
F 212 337 9579

HOTEL ON RIVINGTON
107 RIVINGTON STREET, NEW YORK NY 10002
T. 212 475 2600 F. 212 475 5959
WWW.HOTELONRIVINGTON.COM

CVS/pharmacy®

750 6th Avenue
New York, NY 10010
646-336-8484

SAMUEL STOWERS
Store Manager

Mario Melendez
Manager

We The People®
Forms and Service Center of Belmont

2349 Arthur Avenue, Bronx, NY 10458
tel 718.295.5700 • fax 718.295.5887
Established 1985 - Offices Nationwide

JOHN MORALES
General Manager

Cell: 973-202-0730
Tel: 212-244-1730
Fax: 212-244-2082

Return this card and receive

$1.00 OFF ANY
VALUE MEAL

Valid at Manhattan Mall Only
100 West 33rd Street
New York, New York 10001

One offer per card. Not to be
combined with any other offer.
Expires 12/31/05.

Manhattan Mall
100 West 33rd Street
New York, New York 10001

Open 7 Days   Tel: (718) 388-4486

LA MODERNA BAKERY INC.
Cakes For All Ocassions

Maria J. Chaviano   279 Broadway
President   Brooklyn, NY, 11211

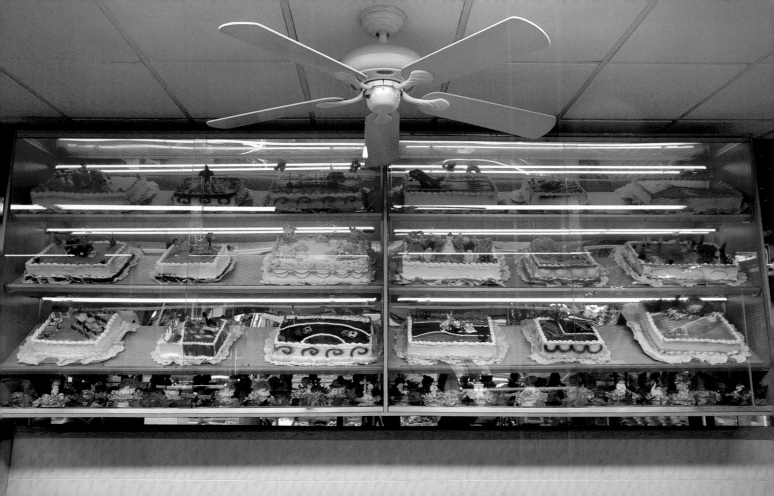

Christine Prieto, R.Ph.
Pharmacist

PHARMACARE
specialty pharmacy

138 2nd Avenue
New York, NY 10003

www.pharmacare.com

212-254-7760
Toll Free 800-317-0187
Fax 212-982-3275
Toll Free Fax 800-507-0477

ELECTRONIC BOX

FOR: VCR'S, KEYBOARDS, TUNERS, AMPLIFIERS, ETC.

Electronic Box
20x20x12
$5.50 each

Double wall

Mirror/Picture
40 x 33 x 4
$ 5.25 each

OUTER

Lamp Box
12 x 12 x 40
$ 5.25 each

SB12
12 x 12 x 12
$ 2.60 each

SB10
10 x 10 x 10
$ 1.75 each

SB8
8 x 8 x 8
$ 1.25 each

SB6
6 x 6 x 6
$ 1.00 each

WSB38
16 x 12 x 10
$ 2.25 each

WSB36
16 x 12 x 8
$ 2.00 each

WSB26
12 x 8 x 6
$ 1.70 each

WSB24
10 x 8 x 6
$ 1.50 each

WSB21
9 x 7 x 5
$ 1.40 each

WSB34
14 x 12 x 8
$ 1.90 each

WSB30
12 x 10 x 8
$ 1.80 each

Large Wardrobe
(With Bar)
24 x 21 x 47
$ 9.95 each

1 99

SIBERIA

- SIBERIAN DU
- PIROGI WITH
- PIROGI WITH
- PIROGI WITH
- PIROGI WITH
- PIROGI WITH
- KHINKALI
- MANTY

TEL: (212) 254-2246
FAX: (212) 674-3270
1-800-4-HOTDOG

WEBSITE: www.katzdeli.com
ESTABLISHED 1888

"OUR ONLY STORE"

Katz's Delicatessen® of Houston Street, Inc.

OPEN 365 DAYS A YEAR
"A DELICATESSEN FOR 117 YEARS"

- HIGH GRADE PROVISIONS
- DELICATESSEN
- CATERING

205 EAST HOUSTON STREET
(CORNER OF LUDLOW STREET)
NEW YORK N.Y. 10002

***** WELCOME TO *****
JAMES A FARLEY APC#2
421 8TH AVENUE
NEW YORK, NY 10199-9998
07/18/05 04:38PM

Transaction Number   86
USPS #   359628-9551

1. Express Mail service
   with $100.00 insurance   15.40
   Destination: 11980
   Weight: 0 lb 1.90 oz
   Total Cost: 15.40
   Base Rate: 13.65
        SERVICES
   Return Receipt   1.75

UNITED STATES POSTAL SERVICE®

Amount (Written Out)

Purpose

Is any Portion of this Sale a Ch

☐ Ye

If "Yes," the fair market value c
First-Class postage rate.

By (Signature and Title)

PS Form 1096, April 1998

212

Hallmark

PARTY BASKET ENTERPRISES, INC.
DIAMOND'S HALLMARK

Häagen-Dazs
Ice Cream Cakes
Friendly Cakes

464 Madison Avenue
New York, NY 10022
212-838-0880
FAX 212-750-3035

the directory

acknowledgments

All my thanks to Harry Mathews,
for his "New York story," through the winding streets of the unseen city,
to all the team at Thames & Hudson France,
to Marion Angebault and Marie Chaix for their collaboration,
to my friend Nadia Legendre,
and to Philippe always.